I AM THE GREAT HORSE

KATHERINE ROBERTS

Chicken House

2 Palmer Street, Frome, Somerset BA11 1DS

For Barry

Text © Katherine Roberts 2007
Cover illustration © Angelo Rinaldi

First published in Great Britain in 2007
The Chicken House
2 Palmer Street
Frome, Somerset BA11 1DS
United Kingdom
www.doublecluck.com

Cover design by Ian Butterworth
Typeset by Dorchester Typesetting Group Ltd
Printed in the UK by CPI Bookmarque, Croydon, CR0 4TD

3 5 7 9 10 8 6 4

British Library Cataloguing in Publication data available.

ISBN 978 1 905294 27 5

CONTENTS

Have you given the horse strength?
Have you clothed his neck with thunder?
Can you make him leap like a grasshopper?
The glory of his nostrils is terrible.
He paws in the valley and rejoices in his strength.
He goes to meet the armed men,
He mocks at fear and is not afraid,
Neither does he turn back from the sword.
The quiver rattles against him,
The glittering spear and the shield.
He swallows the ground with fierceness and rage,
He is trained to charge at the sound of the trumpet –
He says among the trumpets, 'Ha! Ha!'
And he smells the battle from afar,
The thunder of the captains, and the shouting.

The Bible (Book of Job, 39:19–25)

FROM THE HORSE'S MOUTH

My name is Bucephalas, and you should know right away that I'm no Black Beauty.

My coat is the colour of oil-from-the-ground, but that's where the resemblance stops. I have a big head, a white splodge between my eyes, battle scars, and a brand the shape of two horns burnt into my backside. I am, however, very strong and worth my (considerable) weight in gold as a warhorse. At least, I used to be, until I did the most shameful thing a horse can ever do. I killed my own rider.

I didn't mean to trample the poor man to death. All I remember is the enemy's pike, five times longer than a normal spear, hitting me in the eye. My rider fell off. The rest was a confusion of ghosts and screams. For half a year I lived in darkness. Once I could see again, the ghosts had not vanished like they usually do, but lurked in the shadows of my damaged eye.

An inferior horse would have panicked. But I am a stallion trained for war, so I tried to fight them. Ha! It took me a while to realize no one can dominate a ghost, by which time I had gained my reputation for being unrideable. No one dared sit on me – until the day our trader took us north, to the land of my enemy, where I met two remarkable humans who were not afraid of me:

Alexander, Crown Prince of Macedonia.

Charmeia, the only other person who could ride me.

For ever after, our lives were joined by the invisible bond that links human to horse and can be escaped only by death. People may tell you some of this story isn't true. But Alexander's royal historian was paid to write lies, and he never ventured down to the horse lines anyway, so what could he know?

Climb on my back, if you dare, and let ME carry you into the battles that changed the world.

8

First Hoofprint
Pella, Macedonia, 344 bc

Dominating dung

When we reach the river landing, I can't get off the ship fast enough. A storm hit us during our voyage up the coast, which is no fun if you're tethered in a dung-spattered hold with a hundred terrified horses slipping and neighing around you.

I gallop down the ramp, dragging with me the two strongest man-colts employed by our trader Philonicus. The little curved spikes of the rough bit I'm wearing dig into the corners of my mouth as I fight against it, and they've attached a rein to each side of my bridle so I can't bite them. They haven't a hope of controlling me, of course. The only reason I'm going in the direction they want me to go is because I NEVER abandon my herd.

The sand steams under our hooves as we are led on to the riding ground. It smells of strange horses, and I need to stop several times to dominate dung, lifting my tail over the stranger's pile and dropping my own dung on top to show I'm boss. My grooms jerk my bit, so I rear up and fight them. By the time we catch up with the others at the far side of the ground, I am covered in white foam and the corners of my mouth are bleeding.

Philonicus squeals at my grooms, who mumble that I'm mad-fresh after being on the ship and that the state I'm in ain't their fault. Nothing ever is with man-colts, I've found. The Macedonians who have come to try us out give me wary looks.

'He's a bit excitable after the voyage,' Philonicus tells them. 'He's high-spirited, like all the best warhorses. He'll calm down in a moment.'

Ha! Not unless he finds me a groom who knows what he's doing, I won't.

Philonicus gives the man-colts a glower that is the human form of flat ears, then hisses, 'Take him over there and walk him round until he's cooled off. And for Zeus' sake, wipe that blood off his mouth before King Philip gets here! If you let this horse get worked up like that again, I'll take my whip to the pair of you when we get back to the ship.'

The two grooms drag me away, complaining in low voices. All that kicking and neighing on the ship has taken more out of me than I thought, and I take a breather to listen. They assume, just because we horses don't speak in words, that we can't understand human language. But we're not as stupid as you think, and while they lead me around, I learn a few things about this Macedonian king.

The battle that killed my rider and gave me my bad reputation wasn't the only one the Macedonian king has made.

Soon, he's going to make a big battle in another world across the sea to the east, where the sun rises, because the king of that world stole some cities from our world. Many squealing threats have been issued by both kings, which is what stallions do before a battle. But humans make these threats by sending one another rolls of flattened grass with marks on them. Dominating dung would be easier, but you don't understand smells like we do.

That's why the Macedonian king wants to buy so many of us, because he needs horses to train as cavalry mounts for his battle in the other world. He's also looking for a horse to carry his son Alexander into his first battle. The king wants a quiet, well-trained mare. But the prince has his own ideas, because he is a man-colt and wants to be a hero. Ha! Sounds to me as if the king will soon have more than one battle to fight.

It is quiet at this end of the ground, and I've dominated all the dung within smelling distance. As my grooms talk, I relax a bit and my stride lengthens.

'I think he's cooling off at last,' says one of them. 'Get your mitten on and give him a bit of a polish. I'll hold him so he don't bite you.'

The other groom eyes me warily. 'Why bother? No one's goin' to buy him once they've tried to mount him.'

'The Macedonian royal horsemaster is supposed to be a good rider.'

'Ha! That's what they said about the horsemaster back in the last place, and look what happened to him!'

What happened was a ghost moved in the corner of my bad eye, and I panicked. The man fell off and rolled under my feet where I couldn't see him. I accidentally stamped on his arm and broke it.

'C'mon! If he looks the part, the Macedonians might buy him untried. Then at least we'll be rid of the brute.'

'*You* polish him, then!' says the other groom, still eyeing me nervously. 'I'll hold his head.'

They take turns to run their grooming mittens down my neck and over my back, while the other one stands in front of me and hangs on to my reins tightly as if I am acting wild, which I'm not because it's quite nice being groomed in those places. But they can't decide who is going to do my belly, which is where I sweat most. I give them flat ears to warn them not to try, and they jump clear. I have my second wind now, so I take advantage of my slack reins to drag them back across the ground. I want to see what the Macedonians are doing to my herd.

Alexander

By the time we reach the other horses, the king's family and friends have arrived from the palace along with a pack of dogs that run around our heels, barking loudly. They have enough brains to keep away from *me*, though. My herd are being trotted up and down, while the king's horsemaster checks their legs and teeth. Bridles are brought, and riding-cloths fastened on burnished backs. The men vault on, and try out battle manoeuvres. I keep a close eye on the horsemaster, because I don't like his smell.

The young Prince Alexander watches the others eagerly. I can't see him very well, because most of his friends are taller than him. But I can see his energy, bathing everyone around him in its light. This fascinates me so much, I prick my ears and stand still. My grooms breathe a sigh of relief, and even pluck up enough courage to wipe the blood off my mouth.

One of the king's eyes is a mess of scar tissue, but his good eye watches the horses with interest. Finally, he calls a dappled grey mare across and orders her rider to dismount so the prince can try her. She has big brown eyes, and is gentle and kind. Her name's Aura, and I'd like to have her in my pasture. I give her a nicker, and she nickers back.

But Alexander tilts up his chin and says he wants to ride a stallion, not some soft mare. His friends laugh. The one-eyed king smiles and shakes his head. The king's horsemaster scowls. He says that since none of the other horses are suitable for the prince, he will have to wait for the next shipload.

Bags of gold change hands. Horses are led away towards unseen stables.

My companions from the voyage, all going!

I neigh to them. Heads shoot up, and there are some whinnies in reply. I try to follow Aura. My grooms stop me with a jerk on my spiked bit, and get another telling-off from Philonicus. He brushes aside their boasts of how they polished me, grabs my rein and leads me towards the one-eyed king.

'Here's the perfect horse for Prince Alexander, Your Majesty!' he says. 'He's called Bucephalas – after his brand. See? It's an ox-head – very valuable type. He's as strong as an ox too, extremely fast, and sound as a trumpet. Look at those high hooves! He's experienced, too. Twelve years old, the same age as your son. He'd make a fine warhorse to keep Prince Alexander out of trouble in his first few battles. Not *cheap*, of course . . . but I'm sure a man of Your Majesty's experience understands that quality comes at a price.'

The king's gaze runs over me. He looks interested. So does his horsemaster, who runs his hands down my legs and looks at my teeth – though he doesn't get a very good look because he prods my sore mouth and I nearly bite off his finger.

The horsemaster's eyes narrow. 'Put a riding-cloth on him,' he orders. 'I'll try him out.'

My grooms glance at each other, and Philonicus goes a bit quiet. But the cloth is brought, and the girth and breast strap are tightened, making me shiver and sweat. For my last rider, I used to settle down, bending my knees to lower my withers, so my rider could get on more easily when he was tired, wounded or wearing armour. But I don't want this man on my back, so he is forced to vault on to me.

Like most humans who spend a lot of time around horses, he mounts from the left. It's my blind side, but he doesn't realize. When he reaches for a cavalry spear, it's all shadows, and my head whirls in panic.

I act WILD.

His weight is soon gone. I gallop off, scattering the crowd and leaving the ghosts behind me.

There is an outcry as everyone gives chase. The king's grooms vault on to the horses they were leading away and gallop round the far side of the ground to head me off. Philonicus' grooms race after me on foot, shouting for them to watch out and not to get too close in case I attack their horses.

As I wheel back towards the royal party, I hear the queen laughing.

'A fine warhorse, eh? He'll certainly be able to run away from a battle! Horsemaster, aren't you always telling the boys to hold on to their reins if they fall off?'

Philonicus tries to explain that the storm has upset me, that I'm highly strung and I've been trained to leap like that in battle. But the royal horsemaster does not appreciate being

14

laughed at by the queen. He's like a stallion who wants to be boss of the herd but isn't, so is quick to take out his frustration on those who are weaker than him. He picks himself up, clouts a groom who is giggling at the queen's comment, and makes himself huge. He says I'm obviously unrideable, Philonicus is asking a crazy price for a rogue like me, and that I'm too old to retrain.

The king nods.

But the prince ducks under his arm and stares at me, his eyes shining with admiration. 'He's the best of the lot, Father!' he says fiercely. 'I bet *I* can ride him.'

'That's a man's horse, Alexander,' says the king. 'We're looking for an experienced mount for you so you can concentrate on your weapons training, not one you'll have to fight every step of the way. He's evil, you can see it in his eye.'

'I want that horse.'

The king sighs. 'The last thing you want is a half-broken stallion you can't trust in battle! Besides, the price is a joke, ox-head brand or not. I wouldn't be surprised if old Philonicus didn't brand the horse himself – I see the brute has a fresh whip scar on his nose. What happened, Horse-trader? He try to bite you?'

Philonicus flushes, because that is exactly what happened when he tried to stop me kicking a hole in the ship during the storm.

But the prince hasn't given up. 'If I prove I can ride him, Father, can I have him?'

The king looks angry. 'I'm not shelling out good Macedonian gold for a rogue.'

'If he throws me, I'll pay for him myself out of my allowance. Let the price of the horse be the bet.' He gives the one-eyed king a calculating look. 'That means if I stay on, you'll have to buy him for me, Father.'

There is an uncomfortable pause. Everyone watches as the king and his young son glare at each other like challengers for the herd. The queen says Alexander is a better rider than most trained cavalrymen and should be allowed to try. The horse-master whispers something in the king's ear, while giving me a dark look.

The king grimaces and gives a reluctant nod. '*If* you stay on,' he mutters, 'I'll buy him. My horsemaster tells me there's a thing the Scythian tribes do to their colts to make them more manageable. We could always try it with this horse, though he's a bit old so it won't be easy on him.'

The prince's friends whisper excitedly, betting on the out-come. The horsemaster, smirking at this mention of the unpleasant thing, seizes a rope from one of them and gives me another dark look. He starts to organize the grooms to drive me into a corner. But the prince ignores his warning shout and sprints across the riding ground towards me.

I flatten my ears and gallop straight at him. This usually frightens man-colts into jumping out of the way. But Prince Alexander does not move. He stands in front of me, his stocky legs planted firmly in the sand and his arms spread wide as if to catch me. An untidy pale mane flops into his eyes, which are fixed on mine. His chin tilts up to one side.

'Steady, Bucephalas!' he calls in a shrill voice. 'Time to stop running now.'

'Get out of the way, you fool!' yells one of Philonicus' grooms, not realizing it is the king's son he's shouting at. 'That horse is a maniac! He'll kill you!'

But Alexander does not move a muscle. He keeps his odd

eyes on mine. One is brown, the other flecked with blue. I've never seen a human with eyes like that. Nor have I seen a man-colt so determined and with such bright energy inside him.

Something shifts in my head. I forget the grooms chasing me, dig in my hooves, and come to a snorting stop, a whisker's length away from the prince.

One of Philonicus' grooms puffs up behind me. 'Slowly,' he says. 'Grab his lead rein. Then we'll come and get him. He knows we won't stand for no nonsense.'

Alexander grins. 'Don't worry, I know how to handle horses. I could ride before I could walk.' In one smooth movement, he steps forward and lifts the reins over my ears.

I can feel the blood pounding through his body, so I know I scared him. But he does not tremble like most man-colts do when they hold my rein. While I am deciding whether to let him lead me back to the others without a fight, he squints up at the sun and turns me so that the light shines into my eyes and makes the ghosts disappear. Before I know what is happening, he has moved to my shoulder, gripped my withers and vaulted softly on to my back.

Philonicus' groom takes an anxious step towards us, but stops, not wanting to startle me. The king's horsemaster stops, too. He stands well back with his rope coiled and an expectant smile, giving me space to act wild, as I did with him.

I just stand there, I am so surprised. Alexander's legs reach only halfway down my flanks. I have no idea how he got up there on his own. His hand is still gripping my withers, and his other hand holds my reins loosely. He doesn't dig his knees in like the horsemaster did, nor pull on the bit to hurt my sore mouth. He simply sits on my cloth, his heart still pounding, talking to me in his high voice as the whole Macedonian crowd comes running towards us.

The one-eyed king watches me closely, while the prince's friends call out advice.

'Be careful, Alex!' 'Keep his head up!' 'Mind he doesn't bolt!'

Philonicus puffs after them, quick to take advantage of my apparent calmness. 'See, Your Majesty? What did I tell you? He just needs the right handling, that's all.'

The king's horsemaster scowls. He clears his throat and gives orders as to how I am to be tried out properly as a warhorse, including having blunt javelins thrown at me to test my reflexes.

Alexander gives the horsemaster a mischievous look. I feel his hands tighten on my reins as if he is going to ride me through the crowd to the gate. Then he changes his mind, clamps his heels into my sides and heads me for the fence. 'Come on, Bucephalas!' he says. 'Let's get away from these idiots, shall we?'

I need no urging. I take three strides, clear the fence with a huge bound, and gallop across the plain towards the river. I throw a couple of bucks to let the man-colt on my back know I am boss. But he makes no attempt to stop me. He has the most amazing balance, and somehow he stays seated on my cloth.

Behind us, the king yells for someone to accompany the prince. I suppose I must look out of control. The horsemaster vaults on to a bay stallion and gives chase, but we soon leave him far behind.

It is a wild freedom to gallop so fast. I've done it before, sometimes with my rider's permission, sometimes not, but never with so young a man-colt perched on my back. Yet Alexander's hand is strong on my withers, and now his fear has gone he holds my bit firmly enough with the reins so that I know he'll never let me fall if I stumble. It feels good.

On my back, Alexander must be feeling good, too. He shakes his mane out of his eyes and laughs. 'Oh, my crazy, beautiful Bucephalas!' he shouts as he turns me along the riverbank, the wind whipping his words to pieces. 'That showed them, didn't it? My fine, strong warhorse! You wouldn't throw me, would you? I was right. You're like Father. You can't see much out of your left eye, can you? Don't worry, it'll be our secret. I bet you're not afraid of anything. I'll ride you in my first battle, then together we'll conquer the world!'

I toss my head and gallop even faster, because his excitement infects me and he looks so happy.

You may think I was acting like some crazed youngster given the run of my first pasture, but it had been a long time since I'd galloped so fast with such a brave man-colt on my back. With some riders, you just know you will give your life for them, if they ask you to.

A plot against the prince

Instead of bucking Alexander off when we returned to the riding ground, I arched my neck to accept the bit. Then I made myself huge so everyone stared at us.

The king's horsemaster scowled at me as if I were doing this deliberately to show him up, which I was. He tried to snatch my reins as we passed. I gave him flat ears and carried Alexander to safety. The queen clapped her hands in delight, smiling at her son as she called him clever and brave and all sorts of other things guaranteed to make his head swell.

The one-eyed king's fearful expression melted into one of pride. He gave me a wary look, then helped the prince down from my back and embraced him with tears in his eyes. 'Alexander, you scared us!' he exclaimed. 'If you're going to carry on like this, you'd better find yourself a larger kingdom because Macedonia won't be big enough for you.'

Alexander, his cheeks still flushed from our gallop, gave him that upward tilt of his chin and grinned cheekily. 'How about leaving Persia for me, Father? You've conquered just about everywhere else, and as you've just seen, my new horse Bucephalas likes to run east.'

This set them all off laughing again. As they returned to the palace, the prince's friends crowded round to hear his account of how he'd 'tamed' me. Some of them wanted to know if he was serious about Persia. The queen followed, still praising her son's bravery and skill.

But the one-eyed king remained on the riding ground, frowning after Alexander.

When the others were out of earshot, he took the horse-master's arm and said, 'I don't want to see my son riding that horse again. Put him in a back stable away from the others, and if he doesn't calm down in a few weeks find a Scythian who can do the deed. Before I leave on my next campaign, I'm going to make arrangements for Prince Alexander to go away to finish his schooling. He'll soon forget the horse, don't worry. In the meantime, find him another stallion more suited to his size and experience, and train it well so I don't have to be looking out for him when the time comes for him to join me on the battlefield.'

The king's horsemaster smiled his dark smile and ordered his grooms to take me to the stables. I didn't make trouble, because I'd had a good gallop and was looking forward to my barley. But as we passed the crowd of onlookers at the edge of the ground, I caught a smell that reminded me of the time before the ghosts came, and saw a girl-filly clutching what looked like a mule's hoof. She was glaring at the one-eyed king with as much hatred as a colt that had just been driven out of the herd.

This was rather strange. But the horsemaster's grooms did not see her, because human eyes can't see all round like horses' eyes can, so I lowered my head and walked on.

Whatever the Scythian thing is, it can't be as bad as a spiked bit.

SECOND HOOFPRINT
ROYAL STABLES, PELLA, 344–340 BC

Living with mules

I made an enemy that day on the riding ground, and the one-eyed king had delivered me into his hands.

Straight away, the king's horsemaster set out to break my spirit. The stall he'd ordered the grooms to put me in was dark and airless, tucked away in a back corner where I couldn't see what was going on. It had thick iron bars that reached to the rafters, and my only stable companions were mules. MULES, I ask you! (To make a mule, shave off a mare's mane when she is in foal-season and put her with a male donkey. Her foal will turn out to be a mule, which has long donkey-ears and a sticking-up mane, and is the lowest form of life. Mules cannot even sire more mules, because they are sterile. They are useful, though, for pulling heavy carts and carrying baggage.)

Even the mules have better stalls than mine, set in rows

down each side of the stable block with windows in the back walls. Their doors do not have bars, so they can put their heads over and take a drink from the marble water trough in the passage whenever they want.

The muleteers who look after them are almost as bad. Rough, loud and dirty, these men lurk like outcast stallions at the edge of the herd, causing trouble. They like to run their sticks along the bars of my stable, which makes me mad enough to kick the walls. Then they laugh at me, which makes me even madder. They say Alexander should have been made to stay here in Pella and ride me every day instead of being sent off to school. They say he'd learn a lot more by having me knock the stuffing out of him, than he ever will from useless scrolls. Then they go off to drink magic made from our barley and snigger about the royal family. They say any fool can see Alexander looks nothing like King Philip, and that he's only heir to Macedonia because his older brother is a halfwit. They reckon King Philip would be better off staying at home to sire a legitimate son, and if he ever does get around to crossing the Hellespont the Persian king will thrash him like a mule and send him home with his tail between his legs.

Muleteers are even too stupid to know that kings don't have tails.

As well as muleteers, the royal stable employs horsemen to train the cavalry mounts, and hundreds of scruffy man-colt slaves as grooms. The grooms are too afraid of me to come in and take out my dung, so I am forced to stand in a squelchy mess for days at a time. It's a miracle I haven't got hoof-rot, I can tell you. A muzzle of bronze wire hangs outside my stall for them to use when they lead me out for exercise. But they often leave it on me because they are so scared of me biting them. Then they forget to take it off, and I can't eat my hay.

Enough said. You've probably worked out by now that those first few months in the Macedonian king's stables were not much fun for me. The only good part was that the Scythian thing the horsemaster had threatened for me didn't happen. When he and a flat-faced stranger crept into the mule stables one night and opened my door, the flat-faced man took one look at me, threw down his knife and fled. I acted wild, of course. But wouldn't you if your enemy and a knife-wielding stranger roused you from your bed in the middle of the night?

Apart from this, nothing happened to me in the royal stables of Macedonia that has not happened in all my previous stables. I am starting to think the routine is the same everywhere in the world:

Breakfast.

Mucking out (in theory).

Exercise (lead-outs only – after the Scythian thing failed, the horsemaster forbade anyone to ride me until he got a chance to 'sort me out').

Roll in the sand (if the grooms are feeling brave enough).

Lunch.

Afternoon snooze.

Mucking out.

Grooming (Ha! I'd be lucky!).

Sleep.

I got frustrated because I was not allowed to work off my energy with a good gallop. But I was still the boss, even if no one saw me. I could hear the others clopping past on the cobbles on their way to the riding ground, and every morning I whinnied loudly to remind them I was still around. Aura always whinnied back.

I was starting to think everyone had forgotten me, when something different happened.

Charmides

I have finished my morning feed, kicked the wall to let the mule in the next stall know I'm boss, and whinnied to Aura and the others as they go out to exercise. It doesn't look as if anyone is coming to lead me out today. I am about to settle down to my usual morning entertainment of chewing the wood off the top of my door, when there's laughter and a lot of noise outside.

Some of the grooms come into the stable block, hustling a small groom between them. I think they're going to throw the small one into the water trough, which is something they often do to new grooms. I think it's a human form of dominating dung. But they push the small one past the water trough, right up to my stall. They're still making a lot of noise. So I give them flat ears, rear up and smash my hooves against the door.

The older grooms grin at one another. One of them grabs a pitchfork and unlocks my door. Another one grabs the small groom. The mulemaster, who is working nearby, spits on the floor and wanders up to see what's going on.

'New slave, ain't he?' explains one of the grooms, jerking his head at the new one. 'Says he's worked in stables before, though no one seems to know where he's come from. Horsemaster says we're to give him a test on some horse that don't matter.' They put the pitchfork into the small groom's hand and open my door a crack. 'Here's your test, new boy! This horse's stall's not been cleaned out properly in ages. He needs a good currying, too. Make a good job of it!' Laughing, they push the small one through the gap and slam the door.

The new groom stumbles, and the pitchfork clatters to the floor on my blind side, bringing ghosts. I panic, forget I'm in my stall, and crash into the opposite wall. The mulemaster and the grooms push eager faces against the bars to see what's happening.

'Watch him, new boy!' one calls. 'He's a bit wild. He killed the man who rode him in his last battle!'

'Killed hundreds!' says another. 'He likes the taste of human flesh. We throw all the king's criminals in here so he can eat 'em!'

'He tried to trample the master to death, first day he was here, and no one's been on his back since!'

'Yeah, and he *ate* that Scythian the master brought in here to take away his spirit. Every last bone! The king paid thirteen whole talents for him, but he's less use than a mule.'

Which is all lies, of course. And the groom they've thrown into my stall knows this as well as I do.

Once I realize the pitchfork is lying safely by the wall, my head calms and I recognize her smell. You, with your human nose, might be surprised, but we horses only have to smell someone once and we remember them for life. I know this girl-filly from the time before the battle that gave me my bad reputation, when she used to creep into my stable and feed me pastries stolen from the kitchens. It was her I saw watching from the edge of the riding ground on my first day, when the king told the horsemaster to put me in here. She's cut her long mane, and like the man-colts she's wearing a baggy brown tunic with a belt for grooming tools. But underneath she still smells like spring grass.

'Oh, poor Bucephalas!' she whispers, getting to her feet and moving close to my shoulder. Her fingers go to the base of my mane, find the itchy spot on my withers, and do mutual grooming: gently scratch teeth along another horse's mane and spine, concentrating on the withers, which get itchy because we can't reach them with our own teeth. She uses her finger-nails for this, of course, not her teeth. But it is VERY nice, and a long time since I've been allowed near enough to another horse to do it. I can't enjoy it with all those faces jammed up against my stall, though. I squeal and lunge at the bars, scraping the metal with my teeth to make them go away.

They leap clear, laughing. 'Good luck, new boy!' they shout as they run off. 'We'll be back for your corpse later!'

The mulemaster stays, chewing a stalk of hay and watch-ing us with his wily eyes. 'Not much point wasting time on that horse, lad,' he says, when the girl-filly makes a chirrup-ing sound with her tongue to soothe me. 'He's a rogue, through and through, and I've seen a few in my time. Best get out of there, before he 'urts you.'

'Why's he in here with the mules?' asks the girl-filly, still mutual grooming me.

The mulemaster spits. 'Best place for him. He'd only sav-age the other horses. Mules keep him in his place, at least. Old Philonicus pulled a fast one on the king with him, all right. Experienced warhorse, my foot! Only young Prince Alexander could ever sit on him, and he and his friends have been sent away to study philosophy and other useless stuff with that ponce Aristotle. King Philip's off fightin' again, and the royal horsemaster's far too busy to deal with him because he's trainin' up cavalry for the Persian campaign.'

'He been out lately?'

'Are you jokin'? Grooms are all too scared of him, ain't

27

they? Last time he went out, he got loose, and we had a devil of a time catchin' him. Took ten of us in the end. We had to drive him back into his stall with sticks. Makes a change to find someone who can quiet him, truth to tell. I wouldn't push your luck, though. Want me to let you out? Them cowards have shut the bottom latch on you.'

'You can pass me a wet sponge,' the girl-filly says softly, still scratching my withers. 'And his halter, too.'

'I suppose a good groomin' wouldn't hurt him.' The mule-master lifts down my muzzle. 'Better put this on him, though, or he'll 'ave your arm off.'

'I won't need that till I'm ready to take him out,' the girl-filly says. 'He'll be fine.'

'Take him *out*?' The mulemaster shakes his head and shrugs. 'Up to you, I suppose.' He watches a bit longer as the girl-filly sets to work on my matted and dusty coat.

'What's your name, lad?' he asks.

She pauses, just slightly, then says, 'Charmides.'

'Charmides, huh? One of them fancy Greek names. What you doin' workin' here, then? King Philip capture your family on one of his raids down south?'

'Most people call me Charm,' she says quickly, and I notice her accent has become rougher, more like the mulemaster's. 'And I don't have a family any more.' She takes the wooden comb, scrapes it down my neck, and spits a mouthful of my dust on the floor.

The mulemaster regards her with narrow eyes, as if he thinks she might be doing this to make fun of him. Then he laughs.

'If you can keep that horse from upsettin' my mules, young Charmides, we'll be yer family and look after you. Them young grooms are useless, most of 'em. And the ones that are any good race about on their fine horses like they're in the royal cavalry, or somethin'. Too stuck-up to talk to the likes of us.' He spits again, watching her clean my head carefully with the sponge.

'You ever thought of becomin' a muleteer? We could do with more sensible lads like you.'

A secret

That was how I got the girl-filly as my personal groom, and life improved. Although I still had my dark stall at the back of the mule stables, it was now cleaned properly every day so that I could feel the cobbles massaging my hooves again. I got proper grooming and exercise – long walks through the streets of Pella and along the riverbank with Charm at my head. I learnt all the smells, until I knew I could find my way back to the stables from any part of my new home in Macedonia.

Now that I had an outlet for my energy, I grew much calmer in my stall. After a sharp talking-to by their mule-master, the muleteers stopped banging their sticks on the bars to tease me, and the other grooms were relieved they didn't have to come near me any more. They were so impressed when Charm led me out of the stable the first time and held on to me grimly while I plunged about in excitement, they never suspected she wasn't a man-colt like them. Most man-colts think girl-fillies can't do things like that. And Charm was clever. She smeared my dung on her face to hide her smooth girl-filly skin, which made her look a bit strange. But since she smelt so strongly of me, I didn't need to dominate her.

The royal horsemaster narrowed his eyes when he saw Charm leading me out, but he didn't bother us. Charm said he couldn't decide whether to be glad I was behaving myself, or be angry he didn't have an excuse to try the Scythian thing on me again.

Summer turned to winter and back to summer again, and still Alexander did not return from his Aristotle school. I was starting to think he had forgotten me. But the horsemaster had not forgotten the one-eyed king's last order before he went away to fight – that his son was not to ride me again.

One day, when Charm leads me out to exercise, I see a strange horse being put through his paces on the riding ground with the rest. He is bright red like the rising sun and very full of himself, although only half my age and size. When he sees me, he gives a cheeky squeal. So I squeal back to put him in his place. The red stallion loses concentration, and the horsemaster scowls at me.

'Quiet, Bucephalas!' Charm says, frowning. 'We'd better go down to the river. That's a special horse the royal horse-master is training, for when Prince Alexander gets home.'

This is bad news. Alexander is going to ride *me* when he returns, not some half-trained youngster who won't know the first thing about looking after such a headstrong man-colt.

There's only one thing to do. I go up on my hind legs, rip-ping the lead rein out of Charm's hand. I leap the fence from a standstill, find some of the red stallion's dung, and dominate it. Then I make myself huge and gallop straight for him, ears flat.

The red stallion isn't stupid. He spins out of range quicker than most, leaving the horsemaster sitting on air.

Charm catches up, breathless, and grabs my trailing lead rein. 'Oh, I'm sorry, Sir! I couldn't hold him—'

The horsemaster gets to his feet, yells for someone to catch the red stallion, and glares at her. 'Take that brute out of here, and don't bring him back until he's too tired to lift his head! You're lucky he didn't injure Petasios. The king paid a whole talent for this horse. If Bucephalas gets loose on the riding ground again, you'll feel my whip. The sooner King Philip gets back and we can get rid of the animal, the better.'

Charm bows her head in submission and leads me away. The boys training the other horses straighten their faces as the horsemaster remounts. I find another of Petasios' dung piles and dominate it on our way to the gate. Then I dominate one of Aura's, too, to remind her she's part of my herd.

This makes me feel better. But Charm is strangely quiet as she leads me to the river.

'Oh, Bucephalas!' she says crossly. 'What did you have to go and do that for? The horsemaster had almost forgotten about us, and now he'll be watching us again. That's the second time you've made him fall off in front of everyone. Another stupid walk's not going to calm you down, is it? What you need is a decent gallop to take the tickle out of your hooves.'

As she talks, her fingers loosen my muzzle, which is unusual but nice. She hangs it carefully from a branch and checks there are no boats in sight. Then she leads me to a rock, climbs up on it and throws herself at my back. She chooses my left side, which startles me. I jump sideways, and she falls into the river. She gets up, wipes the fringe out of her eyes, and climbs back up on to the rock.

When I wouldn't settle down to be mounted by my previous riders, they used to get on me by vaulting from the ground or off their spear. So I don't know quite what she is up to, and it upsets me. Once, she gets herself lying across my back, but

31

before she can swing her leg over I break into a gallop and she falls off again. This time, she stays sitting in the shallows and starts to cry.

I can't work it out. Charm never cries, even when I nip her.

I nibble the reeds around her for a bit, thinking she will get up out of the river and take me for my walk soon. But she sobs even louder.

'Oh, Bucephalas! You stupid great lump of a horse! Don't you see, you've got to behave, or the king will sell you for horsemeat when he gets back! I'm sure you'd like a gallop along this nice, soft riverbank, wouldn't you? But first you've got to let me get on you, because if I let you loose out here, the horsemaster will beat me for sure. Then he'll find out I'm a girl, and I won't be able to look after you any more.'

When she finishes crying, she spends some time stroking me and talking to me. The next time she leads me to the boulder I am calmer, and she manages to slither on to my back. As soon as I feel she is balanced, I arch my neck and jump out of the water. Both her hands are twisted tightly in my mane. She laughs nervously. I prance, testing her seat. Then I give a small buck and break into a gallop.

Oh, the joy! Oh, it is wonderful! You have no idea how good it feels to stretch your legs after so long being restrained to human pace. I throw several huge bucks in a row, forgetting it is Charm on my back and not a trained horseman.

And suddenly, I realize she isn't on my back any more.

I pull up, a bit out of breath. There's nothing like standing in a stall all day to take the fitness off a horse. Charm is some way back along the riverbank, a crumpled heap of muddy brown tunic and dung-smeared flesh.

I trot back and sniff her to check she isn't dead. She groans, rolls over and blinks up at me. 'Bucephalas? You came back for me!'

Well, of course. We warhorses are trained to do so, aren't we? Wouldn't do to go galloping off in the middle of a battle and leave your rider lying injured on the ground at the mercy of the enemy. I snort at her. Then I settle to my knees, as I have been taught to do.

She stares at me, surprised. 'And you've been trained to settle down, as well! Oh, Bucephalas, you clever, clever horse!'

She climbs on my back (a lot more easily than last time), and laughs as I lurch to my feet. I dance sideways, champing impatiently on my bit.

'All right, once more! But if I get caught riding you like this, I'm *really* going to be in for it with the horsemaster!'

This is a perfect example of what you humans do all the time. You pretend to submit, then you do what you want when the boss isn't looking.

After that, Charm rode me bareback whenever we were out of sight of the stables. But I didn't mind, because she never tried to dominate me. I knew I could throw her off whenever I liked, and she knew it too. Sometimes I wished she would ride me more like Alexander did, because she didn't hold the reins very tightly, which meant I couldn't trust her not to let me stumble when I galloped fast. It was nice to have her on my bare back, though. She was always gentle, and she often mutual groomed me as she rode.

With proper exercise I grew fit again and my coat regained its black gleam. Charm grew taller, and had to bind her teats tightly under her tunic so the other grooms wouldn't notice them. She learnt the muleteers' rough language, how to spit, and how to drink magic without getting sick, so they would think her one of them.

Aura went in and out of foal-season several times without mating. Petasios never squealed at me again. The youngsters who came with me on the ship were trained to gallop and turn quickly, not to startle at trumpets, and to carry a rider armed with javelins and a curved cavalry sword. The mules stayed as stupid as ever, though some went away to carry bags for the king's army, and others replaced them. I remained the boss, and Charm remained my special groom, sleeping in my stall so no one would discover her big secret.

Then Alexander returned from school, and all our lives got turned upside down.

Third Hoofprint
THRACIAN BORDER, 340 BC

Prince Regent

I am eating my breakfast in nervous mouthfuls when Charm comes rushing into the stable. Her cheeks are flushed, and she is carrying an exercise cloth with a bridle lying over the top. I start to sweat and shiver at the sight of it.

There has been much shouting and running around already this morning. Hooves clatter on the cobbles as horses are taken to the riding ground in greater numbers than usual. Men's excited voices ring out. They must be dressed for battle – I can smell the oil they put on the leather straps of their armour. I hear Aura whinny, and send her a ringing reply. I am so worked up by now I abandon my breakfast and press impatiently against the door. Charm has to dig her elbow into my chest before she can get in.

'You know as well as I do the horsemaster said he's got to be kept in today,' says the old mulemaster, who has been looking out for Charm since her first day. 'You'll be in for a beatin', if you're not careful.'

Charm sets her jaw and doesn't reply. She's having trouble fastening my girths. The last time I wore a cloth was when Alexander rode me, four years ago at my trial. She gets it on eventually, pulls out her mitten and rubs it over my neck. It's soon soaked with my sweat.

'Be sensible for once, Bucephalas!' she says. 'If you don't behave yourself, Prince Alexander will ride Petasios into the battle instead of you.'

This is not what I want to hear.

The mulemaster shakes his head. 'So that's what you're up to, is it? Well, it's your funeral.'

He opens my door and I barge out, knocking him against the trough and dragging Charm after me. The mules withdraw their heads quick. They've learnt to keep out of the way whenever they see me coming. My neigh rings out as I emerge into the sunshine, and replies come from several horses I recognize. I prance beside Charm as she leads me to the riding ground.

Petasios is there already, wearing a quilted battle-cloth with a purple trim. I have to admit he looks magnificent, his red coat polished to perfection. He arches his neck and paws the sand while the horsemaster holds his lead rein. Other horses trot in circles, already mounted, their riders carrying spears and javelins.

Standing in the middle of the ground, frowning at the horsemaster, is Prince Alexander. I'd know his smell anywhere. It's slightly sweet, like sherbet.

He's not much taller than when I last saw him. But he's more muscular, has the same bright energy, and carries himself like a young boss-stallion who has just taken over the herd. The one-eyed king is not here, so maybe he has. His helmet is under one arm, so his untidy mane blows across his eyes. He is wearing a gleaming new breastplate bearing a design of a human head with snakes instead of hair. It glints and flashes as he moves. A purple cloak billows from his shoulders.

'Where's *my* horse?' he demands, his shrill voice carrying across the ground. 'I'm not riding this one.'

The horsemaster explains how wonderful Petasios is and how well-trained.

Alexander cuts him off with a flick of his hand. 'Put that little horse away and bring me Bucephalas. The Maedi tribe need a lesson in manners. If I'm going to give them one, I must be properly mounted.'

An older man, standing at Alexander's shoulder, whispers something to the prince.

Alexander scowls at him. 'No, Antipater, I'm *not* going to wait. My father's in Byzantium. If nothing's done about the Maedi, they and the other Thracian tribes will have overrun Macedonia by the time he gets home. We have to drive them back behind the border and show the others we mean business before it's too late. Father left me the royal seal, which means I'm in charge until he gets home, so it's my decision. Horsemaster, if you want to keep your job, have my horse Bucephalas brought out at once!'

At this point, Petasios spots me coming and whinnies nervously. I squeal at him and make myself huge. Charm clings grimly to my lead rein as she wrestles with the gate. The horsemaster sees us and curses under his breath.

Alexander has seen me, too. He narrows his eyes, taking in

my sweaty neck and the old exercise cloth. He frowns a little. 'I suppose he looks fit enough. Bring him over here, boy!'

Charm dips her head as she does so, hiding her face under her fringe. I give Petasios flat ears to warn him to keep his distance.

Alexander hardly looks at Charm. He runs his hands down my legs and steps back to look me over again. He gives the horsemaster a strong glare. 'Who's been riding him?'

The royal horsemaster bites his lip. 'No one, Sir.'

'Someone has. There's a chunk missing from his mane where they've been holding on. You, boy, what's your name?'

Charm swallows, staring at her feet. 'Charm. . .ides, Sir Prince.'

'You're Bucephalas' groom?'

'Yes, Sir.'

'Do you ride him?'

Charm glances at the horsemaster. Her cheeks flush under the smears of dung.

But the horsemaster laughs. 'Do you really think this slip of a groom could manage him, Sir? The idiot boy can't even hang on to the horse when he's leading him out! This is quite ridiculous. Bucephalas has been standing in a stall for four years! He's nowhere near battle-fit. Take the chestnut, Sir, and you'll win your battle against the Maedi. Take this horse, and he'll dump you in the middle of the fight and probably expire from the strain. He must be sixteen, at least, by now, which is no small age for a horse. And his temper hasn't improved one bit since you went away to school.'

Alexander's eyes narrow again. 'Sixteen's a good age to be,' he says. 'Or are you trying to suggest your Prince Regent is past it, too?'

Some of his friends laugh.

The prince turns his back on the horsemaster's spluttered reply and questions Charm closely about where I've been stabled, and my care and feeding. He says nothing more about her riding me, so she answers truthfully enough, and tells him all about the mule stable.

Alexander frowns.

His friends – who are nearly grown like him, and full of themselves like colts on the verge of becoming stallions – stop making jokes about the horsemaster and gather round to listen. Their horses champ their bits and paw the ground. Aura has a rider, but Petasios is still riderless. Ha! That'll teach him not to get above himself! Then Charm taps my shoulder, and I settle to my knees for Alexander to mount.

There is a collective intake of breath. The horsemaster stares at me in amazement.

'Temper not improved, huh?' Alexander says with a sudden laugh, and springs on to my lowered back. 'It looks good enough to me.'

When Charm takes off the lead rein and steps clear I immediately prance to my feet. Feeling how firm Alexander is on my cloth, I give a little leap of celebration and flick my tail in Petasios' face.

Alexander laughs again, gathers up my reins, and looks down at the horsemaster. 'I'll soon tell you if Bucephalas is fit for battle, when we thrash the Maedi! In the meantime, you'd better find yourself another position. As from today, you're no longer the royal horsemaster. I don't take kindly to people who keep my valuable warhorse in a mule stable, try a barbarian operation to ruin him for life, leave his feeding up to the grooms, and saddle him for battle with the oldest of cloths. I don't expect to see you here when I return.'

The horsemaster's mouth drops open. He gives Charm an evil look and pushes back his shoulders in an attempt to make himself huge. 'You've no right to do this to me! When King Philip gets back, he'll hear about this. I've trained Petasios personally, and got him ready for you to ride in battle just as your father ordered. You're making a big mistake, Sir— Antipater, tell him!'

The older man sighs and shakes his head. 'As Prince Regent, I'm afraid it is Prince Alexander's right to hire and dismiss staff in his father's absence. I'm very sorry. I'll make sure you are given a good reference.'

Alexander has already forgotten the horsemaster. He puts on his helmet and tests my reflexes, making me gallop down the ground, turn, and charge the other way. It calms me to practise the old battle manoeuvres I learned when I was young. I soon stop shivering and start to enjoy myself. It works Petasios up, though, since he still hasn't got a rider. The horsemaster is dragged unceremoniously about the ground as he tries to keep hold of him.

'Can I ride the chestnut stallion, Alex?' asks one of the man-colts who is not yet mounted. 'He looks spirited. He might have a chance of keeping up with Bucephalas, so I can watch your back.'

Alexander grins and strokes my damp neck. 'You do that, Hephaestion, my friend! He's yours. I make you a present of him. Oh, and Horsemaster . . . don't even think about dismissing my horse's groom before you leave, or when I get back from Thrace I swear by Zeus I'll hunt you down and have you executed for treason. You, boy . . . Charmides . . . while I'm gone, prepare the best stable for Bucephalas so it's

40

ready for him when we get back.' His grip on my reins tightens, and he looks suddenly serious and determined.

'Now, gentlemen, we've wasted enough time! Hand me my spear! We ride for Thrace!'

Alexander's Guard

In the space of half a day, I was a warhorse again. But not just any old warhorse, oh no! I was the Prince Regent of Macedonia's mount, trotting at the head of his army with Petasios beside me and everyone else trotting along behind in a great jangling of shields and weapons. Also, my enemy the horsemaster had been dominated. Oh, it was a great day!

We travelled north into the mountains. We were nearly two hundred cavalry, with no hoplites (that's human for foot-soldiers) to slow us down. The Thracian border, where the battle would be, was not far enough for Alexander to bother with baggage carts, so we took a few mules to carry the food and spare weapons, and went as fast as we could.

There were eight horses in Alexander's Guard, all ridden by his friends. Alexander had obviously dominated Hephaestion and the other man-colts a long time ago, but it was the first time we had all been together in a herd, so there was a bit of tail-lashing, nipping and squealing until we settled down. Here are their names and colours, because it's far too complicated to tell you their smells:

Petasios – red stallion, carrying Hephaestion.
Aura – dapple-grey mare, *very* beautiful, carrying Demetrius.
Psylla – bay mare, quite sweet, carrying Hector.
Harpinna – speckled red mare, carrying Ptolemy.
Apollo – palomino stallion, carrying Perdiccas.

Borealis – strong brown stallion, carrying Leonnatus.

Zephyr – yellow mare, carrying Philotas.

Hades – small dark bay stallion, carrying Iolaus.

As we go on they will all no doubt impress you with their bravery, so there's one thing I should add: they are all smaller than me, even Borealis with his massive crest, and leggy Harpinna, and only Aura is as well-bred as me. That is why I am the boss.

Alexandropolis

We find the enemy in the foothills near their scruffy little city. They are clearly surprised to see Alexander riding at the head of an army, and their scouts run back from the rocks, shouting the alarm. Alexander immediately puts his heels to my sides and urges me after them, and the whole cavalry breaks into a gallop. The enemy are on foot, so they cannot outrun us. But they scramble up the steep slope where we cannot follow, take cover behind boulders, and hurl their javelins at us.

Alexander gallops me out of range and throws up his hand to stop the others. The Guard closes about me, dancing and snorting. I am trembling so much, it takes me a moment to realize Alexander is trembling too.

'Steady, Bucephalas,' he whispers, pulling my ear. 'I am Achilles of the *Iliad*, and you're my immortal horse, gifted to me by the gods. We're not going to die today. Don't let me down. I've *got* to win this battle.'

That is when I realize his only experience of battle comes from stories like the *Iliad*, where the heroes never die. This is his first time in a real battle, ever.

Judging by their expressions, it is the first time for most of

42

his friends too. Only Philotas, who is a bit older than the others, seems to know what he's doing – but he is too busy looking down his nose at Alexander to be of much help.

My young rider's nerves remind me it is my job to look after him, and the panic leaves me. I nicker to Aura to tell her I'll look after her, too. Then I give the others flat ears to warn them to pay attention because the man-colts will need our experience today.

Perhaps I should explain here how important we horses are in a battle. At this stage of the fight, our riders are each armed with:

2 javelins for throwing at the enemy as we charge, or
1 spear for stabbing the enemy when we get close enough.
1 curved sword, for when the spear breaks or gets stuck in a dead body.
1 shield, for emergencies.

But humans have only two hands. So you tell me how many hands they have to spare for holding our reins?

In the end, it was a small battle. When human squealing matches become a fight, the army with the most men and horses usually wins. The Maedi had about the same number of men as us, but fewer horses. We were obviously much better trained, and they were not prepared for us.

Alexander didn't waste time squealing. He sent some men to flush out the enemy hiding in the rocks, while we led a cavalry charge on those defending the city. One of them threw a javelin on my blind side, but Petasios whinnied to warn me and I leapt to avoid it. Alexander barely moved on my cloth as it scratched my flank. I expected him to gallop me out of range, but instead he gave a shout of anger that one of the enemy had dared injure me, cast aside his spear and drew his curved sword. With a wild war cry, 'ALALALAI!', he dug his heels into my sides. His sword flashed down, again and again, sending Maedi ghosts rippling into the air. The rest of the enemy fled.

I felt so powerful with Alexander on my back, I would gladly have carried him until I collapsed. But just as I am starting to feel my lack of fitness, the Maedi city surrenders.

The gates open, and a man mounted on the scruffiest horse I have ever seen trots out to meet us. Alexander pulls off his helmet to free his mane, which is plastered to his forehead with sweat. He is shining with victory, and his breastplate reflects a shaft of sunlight breaking through the mountain mists. It has a spatter of enemy blood across it, and there's more blood on his face. None of it is his. I did my job well today.

The Maedi boss has an old scar across his forehead. He looks about three times Alexander's age, and the ghosts of his people cling to him as they are sucked away. Although he can't see them, I think he must feel something, because he shivers.

For a moment, Alexander seems unsure what to say. Then he sets his jaw, tilts up his chin and says in a tough voice, 'You broke your agreement with my father King Philip of Macedon. As Prince Regent, I have his full authority to execute every last man, woman and child in your city and wipe the Maedi from the face of the earth.' He pauses to let this sink in, and there is a horrified hush among the enemy. 'On the other hand,' Alexander continues smoothly, 'my father is not here, so if you surrender you can negotiate terms with me.'

He holds his breath. Behind us, Philotas shakes his head.

But the Maedi boss knows a good deal when he hears one. He looks at his dead tribesmen strewn about the plateau, eyes the grim-faced Macedonians and their frightened prisoners, and gives Alexander's breastplate a sideways look. He bows his head. 'Prince Alexander, please spare our families. The Maedi will serve you for the rest of your life. We'll do anything you ask.'

Alexander's hand relaxes on my rein. He thinks a moment. Then he says, 'You'll bring a hundred of your best javelin-throwers to Pella when I send for you. In the meantime, I'll leave a hundred of my father's men here to keep an eye on things in your city, which will from now on be called . . .'

'Philippopolis?' suggests the Maedi boss, relieved to have escaped the legendary Macedonian wrath, and keen to co-operate.

Alexander looks up at the walls and gives a boyish grin. 'Alexandropolis!'

That's typical human arrogance for you. Really, it should be *my* city. Who was it that kept Prince Alexander out of trouble in his first battle, carried him to victory, and intimidated the enemy into the bargain?

I bite the scruffy Maedi horse on the neck, and he drops dung in terror. As he carries his master back into the city that is now a Macedonian garrison, I lift my tail and dominate his pile.

A new stall

We trotted home with two dead cavalrymen, each one tied across his horse's back. A few others were wounded, but they would live to fight again. That's not bad for a human battle. We horses were all fine. Alexander's friends were in high

45

spirits, laughing and telling stories of their own bravery. While Alexander discussed the battle with Hephaestion, planning how next time he would do better to avoid unnecessary Macedonian deaths, I blew gently at Petasios to tell him I forgave him for squealing at me the first time we met. His whinnied warning quite possibly saved me and Alexander from injury today.

Charm was waiting for us at the stable gates, sitting on a rock with her head in her hands. When she saw us coming, she jumped up and ran into the road to take my rein. She smelt of strange dung, which I did not like. Her groom's tunic was torn, and one of her eyes had a big purple bruise around it. I snorted at her, while she tried to see if I was sound.

Hephaestion chuckled. 'Looks like your groom found a battle of his own while we were off conquering the Maedi, Alex!'

Alexander frowned, but said nothing about Charm's eye. He ordered her to tend my wound, and said he'd be down to check on me later.

My new stall was big and airy, right next to the door, with a grand view of the yard and the palace gates. There were marble pillars around the water trough. Borealis was solid and comforting in the stall next to mine. My new friend Petasios was across the passage, and – joy, oh joy – I could see Aura's grey head looking out of her window at me from the mares' stable! A pile of sweet-smelling hay was waiting for me in the corner, and Charm tipped a warm barley mash smelling of herbs into my manger. Best of all, there were no mules.

I was so hungry that at first I did not notice Alexander come into the passage. He watched Charm tending my javelin scratch with warm water and salve. She obviously hadn't noticed him either, because she nearly jumped out of her skin when he asked, 'Who did that to your eye?'

'N-no one, Sir Prince!' she stammered, letting her fringe flop over her face. 'I fell off a horse at exercise.'

Alexander's eyes narrowed. 'If you're going to be Bucephalas' groom, you're going to have to start telling me the truth. I know you're a good rider. You must be, if you've been riding my horse.'

Charm stopped sponging my wound and stood frozen.

'How many times has he thrown you?' Alexander insisted, opening my door.

'Hundreds,' she whispered. 'But he always comes back for me. I ride him bareback by the river. No one else knows. Please, Sir Prince, don't send me away! I only did it to calm him down. He was going crazy in his stall, and the horse-master said—'

Alexander held up a hand to silence her. 'I'm not angry. I was starting to wonder who I'd find to exercise him when I can't do it. My father's old horsemaster has gone as I ordered, hasn't he?'

'Yes, Sir Prince.'

'And your eye?'

Charm dipped her head and mumbled, 'The horsemaster said he'd teach me a lesson. But the mulemaster called some of his muleteers to stop it. They were a bit rough. I think they broke his knee. They chased him off.'

Alexander grimaced. 'Good. Some people only understand roughness. I shouldn't think he'll bother you again now I'm back, but if there's any more trouble you let me know right away.' He considered me while I ate. 'Bucephalas is to rest for a few days, slow lead-outs only, and then I'll be exercising him myself. So there'll be no more falling off him for a while,

47

Charmides. Understood?'

Charm gave him a flash of her eye, fighting a smile. 'Yes, Sir Prince!'

He studied her in much the same way he had studied me earlier. He frowned. 'Bucephalas can't have a groom who looks like a muleteer. Clean yourself up a bit, then go and ask the new horsemaster for a spare tunic so you can wash that one. Tell him I sent you. I think you're hiding quite a handsome face under all that muck, and you've got brains, which some haven't. But next time I ride into battle, I expect you to saddle my horse with a proper cloth. I won't have him injured again through that sort of carelessness.'

'But it wasn't my fau—' Remembering who she was talking to, Charm broke off and looked at the floor.

Alexander gave her a curious look with his odd eyes. He waited a moment to see if she would say anything else. Then he patted my neck and hurried up to the palace, where his friends were busy celebrating their victory the way you humans like to do, with a lot of noise and magic drink.

With the one-eyed king away, there were many such parties up at the palace. Alexander exercised me whenever he could, battle training with the others on the riding ground, and on longer rides to inspect his father's kingdom. We nine of the Guard got to know one another and became an excellent herd.

If you ask me, that was a good winter. I had the best stall in the royal stables, the best groom, and the best rider. But we often saw the prince's adviser Antipater striding across the yard red-faced, muttering under his breath about Alexander's crazy ideas of running a kingdom. He and Alexander had lots of public squealing matches, and our grooms made bets on who would become the new boss of Macedonia if the one-eyed king got killed on campaign:

Alexander – favourite.
Antipater – second favourite.
Philotas – long-odds outsider, but he's the son of the general of the Macedonian army, so would make a stronger king than Alexander's drooling half-brother who can't even ride Aura without a lead rein.

Ha! Antipater and Philotas don't stand a chance.

Fourth Hoofprint
GREECE, 339–338 BC

Squealing at the Greek border

The one-eyed king did not die on campaign. He brought his army back from Byzantium and ordered Alexander and his friends to arm themselves ready to accompany him to Greece. He was in a rotten temper because the Athenian and Persian herds had joined forces against Macedonia, then on top of that a rebel tribe had ambushed his troops on the way home through the hills and thrown a javelin through his thigh.

Charm was in a strange mood the whole time the royal physician was treating the king's leg. While she rubbed me over with long slow strokes of her grooming glove, she kept glancing at the palace. 'Doesn't look like he's going to die of it,' she muttered in the end. 'Maybe I shouldn't have got rid of that mule's hoof? But if I'd used its contents on the king as I'd planned to when I first came here, I'd have been arrested and wouldn't have been able to look after you – oh,

Bucephalas, what shall I do? He's going to take Prince Alexander into battle, I know he is! It was bad enough when Alexander went off to fight the Maedi, but they were only a disorganized tribe. The Greeks have trained armies! I can't bear the thought of you in a real battle. You're all I have. If you get hurt, I'll never forgive myself.'

But she was just a groom, and had no choice but to obey when Alexander ordered her to get me ready for the march south.

When she led me out, resplendent in my new purple-tasselled battle-cloth, there was a short squealing match between the one-eyed king and Alexander. The king did not want his son to ride me in the battle against the Greeks. He said I was too big for him and couldn't be trusted. Charm stroked my nose, holding her breath in sudden hope. But when Alexander pointed out I'd already carried him to victory against the Maedi, he got his own way.

This time we took lots of mules and baggage carts, because we would camp many times en route to the battle. This meant no dry stall, and having to eat our barley from a leather nosebag. The good thing was that Charm got to come too, riding in a cart at the back of the army with the other grooms. There was quite a lot of kicking and squealing in the horse lines, because the excitement infected us all. We knew the battle would be a big one, since the one-eyed king and the Athenian boss did their version of dominating dung, sending marks to each other on rolls of flattened grass for a very long time. But we couldn't attack the enemy yet, because they had blocked the passes through the mountains. Our grooms complained it would take forever to lure the cowardly Greeks out to fight a proper battle, and they were right, because we ended up camping all winter.

This was not as boring as it sounds. There were plenty of little battles in the hills to keep us occupied, like the one when we dominated the Maedi. Every time we returned flushed and triumphant from one of these skirmishes, we found Charm waiting for us at the edge of the camp. Alexander laughed at her anxiety as he handed her my reins so she could take me for my roll.

Alexander was excited about fighting in his first major battle, of course. But he was frustrated that we were stuck in Greece, rather than driving the Persians out of Anatolia. 'Father got it wrong,' he told Charm during one of his visits to the horse lines. 'So now we've got to fight Greeks before we even *think* about crossing the Hellespont! I could have told him the Athenians would make trouble if he went marching off to Byzantium without first taking care of things properly over here. People are saying he's losing his touch, getting old.' He gave my neck an affectionate slap and eyed Charm over my withers. 'What do you say, Charmides? Do *you* think my father should be retired and put out to pasture to make way for a younger horse?'

Charm pretended to groom my other side, but that was only so she could keep me between her and Alexander. 'I think you should retire Bucephalas, Sir, before he gets hurt.'

He chuckled. 'Don't worry so! I won't let anything happen to Bucephalas, I give you my word as future King of Macedonia. After he's carried me in a few more battles, I'll let him breed with the best mares in the royal stable. That grey, Aura, for a start. And maybe the little bay, Psylla. Then I'll raise his foals to carry me to Persia. Bucephalas is far too valuable to let some barbarian kill him on the battlefield. Aren't you, my beautiful brave warhorse?'

He gave my ear a fond tug, and I gave him an equally fond nip, just to remind him who was boss around here. I wonder when he decided I was not his immortal horse, after all? Or maybe he was lying to Charm? (To tell a lie – say human words that mean one thing while holding your body very still so no one can tell what you *really* think. Very confusing.)

Alexander rubbed my teeth marks from his arm with a tolerant smile. As he left, he pointed to my shoulder. 'You missed a bit. I can see I'll have to stand on the other side next time, or my horse's coat will soon look as odd as his eyes.'

This made Charm blush. She started to polish the place on my shoulder Alexander had told her she'd missed, then closed her eyes and clutched my mane. 'Oh, Zeus,' she whispered. 'Why does he keep coming down here and teasing me like that? He's the *prince*. He's going to be King of Macedonia one day. Worse, he still thinks I'm a boy!'

When summer came, the one-eyed king got fed up with squealing, and told a lie on flattened grass to make the enemy think we were going back home to deal with a rebel uprising in the North. This did the trick. The Greeks ventured out of their hills, thinking we were retreating. By the time they realized we were not leaving, but coming after them instead, it was too late for them to run and hide.

A test of killing

We have our big battle at dawn outside a little town called Chaeronea, between the mountains and the river. Mist hangs over the plain, making everyone look like ghosts. I can't stop trembling, and Alexander's hand is tense on my rein. The horses of the Guard chew their bits and snort. Apollo keeps rearing, which is very annoying.

The enemy form up to face us with their backs to the mountains – a solid line of men and spears, stretching across the plain from the walls of the town to the river. Their cavalry is behind them, which is a pretty useless place to be, if you ask me. They can't gallop to engage us without trampling their own men. Our hoplites are angled down the slope to our right, the whole line bristling with long Macedonian pikes. The one-eyed king and his officers are out of sight at the far end of our line.

The final squealing matches and pre-battle sacrifices take *ages*. While we wait, Alexander's friends nervously tell one another stories about the enemy band directly opposite us – a grim and battle-scarred herd of foot-soldiers from a city called Thebes. They were supposed to be on our side but joined the Greeks at the last moment. The one-eyed king is very angry about this and has ordered Alexander to dominate them thoroughly. Too right. With the Thebans on the enemy side, our two armies – Greek and Macedonian – are more or less the same size. This, as I explained before, is NOT GOOD.

The remains of a sacrificed goat are carried away behind our line, and a hush falls over the two armies. My heart is pounding so hard I think it might burst. A trumpet blast echoes in the mountains, and a great roar goes up from our men.

With much rattling and creaking of armour, our hoplites form into a phalanx: a solid mass of men, eight rows deep, longest pikes at the back so the points are like a wall of spears when they charge the enemy. Last time I was in a battle like this, I was facing that lethal wall of spikes. The memory makes me shiver. I toss my head, looking for ghosts, and

Alexander runs a calming hand down my neck.

'Remember, I am Achilles and you are immortal,' he whispers.

Looks like he's decided we're heroes again.

Our phalanx advances at a steady pace, and the whole enemy line ripples. Finally, the Greeks can stand it no longer, and their line breaks with blood-curdling yells as they charge towards us. The horses of the Guard leap and plunge around me, fighting their reins.

'Wait for my order!' Alexander shouts. 'Wait!'

The Greeks run at an angle to meet our phalanx. Only the battle-scarred Thebans opposite us stay put on their mound. They look nervous. They should be: a gap has opened up between them and the rest of their army, and now our phalanx is retreating under the one-eyed king's order, luring the rest of their herd even further away from them.

Alexander shifts his javelins under his arm so he can pull my ear. 'This is it, Bucephalas, my brave horse,' he says. 'Our first real battle. Let's show Father what we can do!'

I snort and shake my head. He laughs, digs his heels into my sides, and waves his javelins in the air with a great shout:

'ALALALALAI! ALALALALAI!'

The bit slackens in my mouth, and I leap forward in a thunder of hooves. I feel Alexander take a firm hold to keep me from stumbling over the plain, but my head is so full of the excitement of galloping at the head of such a huge herd, I've forgotten we are racing into danger. On my back, Alexander yells encouragement to the others in his shrill voice. He sounds confident and he is shining with excitement, but I can feel his terror. The horses of the Guard are flat out, trying to keep up with me as we stream through the gap in the

Greek lines and gallop in an arc to trap the Thebans on their hill. The rest of our cavalry thunder in a cloud of dust behind us.

They must be very brave humans, to stand and face us galloping horses. Alexander throws one of his javelins and scores a direct hit. The enemy soldier falls under my hooves, and his ghost ripples past my nose. I check my mad gallop to jump over his body, and swerve before I impale my rider on a spear. Hephaestion cheers. 'First blood to Alex! Hurrah!'

From then on, it is a confusion of flying javelins, flashing swords, blood, shouts, neighs, and the ghosts of men and horses vanishing through the dust to wherever they go when they leave this world. Alexander fights with wild energy, like he did in the hills, and the others of our herd see this and fight furiously, too. But the Thebans are a wiser enemy than the Maedi, and it takes us a lot longer to dominate them. Soon the mound is thick with enemy dead. I tread on their bodies, rolling my eyes.

There is a pause when no enemy is near enough to fight us. Alexander allows me to catch my breath while he takes a look at what's happening to everyone else. The Greek line is breaking up as they flee into the mountains. Petasios joins me, black with sweat. Alexander mutters to Hephaestion, 'This is awful! How many more of them do we have to kill before they give in? Father's routed the rest of the Greek army. Surely they must see they can't hope to win now?'

'They're the Theban Sacred Band,' Hephaestion says. 'It's said they never abandon their post— look out!' He kills another of the enemy, who has just run up the hill and tried to spear Alexander.

Alexander curses, and urges me back into the fight. Several

times, he calls for the Thebans to surrender, but either they don't hear him or they refuse to listen. Finally, someone kills their boss, and the few Thebans still on their feet throw down their swords. Alexander flops forward on to my neck, his arms hanging limply. 'Thank Zeus,' he breathes.

Our cavalry forms a circle around the prisoners. Alexander's friends pull off their helmets, still panting, and silently survey the piles of dead. Most of our men and horses have minor injuries, and I realize I'm bleeding, too, as a hot trickle runs down my left foreleg. It's odd, but in the midst of a battle you never notice it happen. I am trembling again, this time with exhaustion.

Alexander dismounts to check my leg. Clinging to my mane, he stares at the dead Thebans.

'They fought bravely,' he says. Then he bends over and is violently sick.

No one says anything.

He wipes his mouth on his sleeve. In a very controlled voice, he tells our cavalrymen they have fought well, and orders Hephaestion to take charge the prisoners. Then he leads me slowly back to camp across the blood-soaked plain, past all the bodies and the loose horses. He hands me over to Charm without a word, ignores an order to report to his father's tent, and walks off alone.

Charm fusses over my injured leg, so I snap at her. Petasios lifts a hoof at me, so I snap at him, too. Psylla and Zephyr both nicker softly, but I am not in the mood to talk to mares, so they get snaps from me as well. I am in a snappy mood like my rider. Although we dominated the Thebans, the one-eyed king won the battle because he was boss. Some colts are content to be second in the herd – but not me, and not Alexander!

Another plot against Alexander

You humans are weird about your dead. It's as if you think the departed members of your herd will be pleased if you do special things to their bodies. Any horse could tell you that's a load of dung. Once a ghost is gone from the world, it never returns. On a battlefield, the bodies of dead horses are left to feed the crows.

There would have been a lot less trouble if the one-eyed king had left the dead Greeks for the crows, too. But no, he had to burn their bodies on a huge pyre that darkened the sky, and send their ashes home to the Athenians. Another form of human squealing, I suppose.

Since my cut leg wasn't bad enough to make me lame, but the one-eyed king's leg had suffered in the battle, Alexander volunteered to lead the victory procession. This sparked off another squealing match. The one-eyed king said his son was too young. Alexander said if he was old enough to dominate the Theban Sacred Band, then he was old enough to dominate a few soft-handed Athenians whose only weapons were words. In the end, Alexander got his own way, though we had to take Antipater along to keep an eye on us. Charm rode in a cart with the ashes, very quiet.

This was better, because we got to lead the herd again. The men cheered Alexander and called him their 'young king', praising his bravery in the battle, which soon had him shining with his old energy again.

Athens is a fortress built on a hill by the sea. As we arrive, the setting sun stains its walls violet, which makes the city look very fine. We trot through the gates in a clatter of armour and hooves. I forget about my injured leg and make myself huge. Crowds fill the streets to see us. As soon as he dismounts, Alexander springs up the steps to the citadel to meet the Athenian bosses, his Guard following.

Frowning after the prince, Antipater comes with us to the stables. When Charm goes to fetch my barley, a man with a familiar smell limps out of the shadows, making me break into a sweat. He looks different. He's clipped off his beard and is wearing the dirty tunic of a groom. But I *never* forget a smell. It's the disgraced horsemaster who was dismissed by Alexander in Pella.

I kick the wall and squeal a challenge.

'Well?' Antipater whispers to the man, ignoring me. 'What are the Athenians going to do now? King Philip's just thrashed the Greek army, and young Alexander's a hero. Listen to the fools cheering him out there! The boy's uncontrollable, and Philip just refuses to get himself killed in battle. Persian gold obviously isn't going to buy us victory. We'll have to think of something else.'

The horsemaster glances round, checking none of the grooms are close enough to overhear. He doesn't seem worried about nine sharp-eared horses. 'I've persuaded the Athenians that the sooner you take over the throne of Macedonia, the better it'll be for Greece. They'll help us. Perhaps an unfortunate accident at the victory games?' He glances up at the citadel.

Antipater shakes his head. 'We daren't touch Alexander yet. Philip would bring the entire Macedonian army after us. He must be made to reject the boy himself. There are already rumours about Prince Alexander's legitimacy. All we need is someone who will 'confess' to sleeping with the queen while King Philip was away on campaign, then we can remove Philip, and with public opinion turning against Alexander I'll be the obvious choice for the throne.' He gives the horse-master a sly look. 'You can have your old job back once I'm king, of course. And compensation. Philip might not believe us, and the queen will deny it, naturally. But Alexander did dismiss you while his father was away in Byzantium. I think that should seed enough doubt in the king's mind for our purposes.'

The horsemaster scowls. 'Are you suggesting I pretend Alexander could be *my* son? I'll be in a lot of trouble if something goes wrong!'

Antipater puts a finger to his lips and takes the horsemaster's arm, steering him away from me. 'You've nothing to lose and everything to gain. You certainly had the opportunity, so King Philip will believe it once I've had time to work on him. It might take some of the wind out of Alexander's sails if he thinks his father could be a commoner, rather than a king. Even if his mother insists on bringing the boy back to court, things will be different once Philip is dead. If the worst comes to the worst, and Alexander is still the popular choice for the throne, I'll simply present him to the army as their new commander and pack him off to Anatolia with General Parmenio. Let him amuse himself fighting the Persians, while I keep the throne warm for him over here. The boy's such a hot-head, he's bound to get himself killed eventually. I can't think how he's survived this long, though the men say no spear can touch him while he's riding his horse. They're saying the animal came from the gods, like Achilles' horses did in the *Iliad*.'

The horsemaster looks at me, and a darkness flickers behind his eyes. 'I'll have my old job back, you say?'

Antipater nods.

'And you'll give me a free hand to deal with Bucephalas

however I see fit?'

Antipater nods again. 'Of course. I'll head back to Pella and work on Philip as soon as I can get away, but we must make sure young Alexander isn't around to interfere. Perhaps you can arrange a small insurance to make sure our heroic prince stays in Athens long enough for me to convince the king of the queen's unfaithfulness?'

The horsemaster smiles coldly. He gives me the same dark look as when he brought the Scythian and his knife into my stall that night in the mule stable. 'I understand his horse picked up a minor wound in the battle? A cut like that can swell up badly if it's not properly looked after. Alexander loves the brute. He's unlikely to leave him behind in enemy territory, no matter what rumours come from Pella. Don't worry! This is the last time you'll hear anyone call Prince Alexander *"King"*.'

FIFTH HOOFPRINT
MACEDONIA, 338–336 BC

Running with mares

If the horsemaster had tried to come into my stall, I would have killed him. But he was too clever for that. Instead, he sent one of the Athenian grooms to Charm with a paste to put on my leg. Believing it to be special Greek medicine, she thanked the groom. And because I know Charm would never hurt me I stood still for her, even though the paste smelt funny and stung a bit.

Overnight, my leg swelled as fat as a temple column. Charm fell to her knees, begging Alexander to forgive her. She promised she'd sleep in my stall every night until I was cured, which wasn't really a hard promise to make because she sleeps in my stall anyway. Alexander ordered a citywide search for the treacherous Athenian groom. Then he took Charm aside and told her that in future if she didn't know what medicine to use on a horse she should ask him or one of his Guard, and

KATHERINE ROBERTS

that she deserved to be beaten for crippling me. Charm burst into tears.

The groom, of course, was nowhere to be found. Neither was the disgraced royal horsemaster, but Alexander didn't know he was supposed to be looking for him, anyway. Antipater took advantage of my lameness to head home early and 'report the successful surrender of Athens'. But I expect you know what he was *really* up to.

By the time we reached Pella, the damage was done. I was still lame, so Alexander had to ride some other stallion who didn't even know enough to make himself huge when we entered the city. No one cheered their prince, as they should have done after he'd helped to dominate the Greeks so well. There were even some boos and hisses, and someone threw an egg, which smelt bad when it broke.

When Alexander heard there were rumours about him not being King Philip's son but the son of a commoner, and that the queen had been deceiving the court for years because she wanted him to inherit the throne, he went pale. He told Charm to look after me. Then he took a deep breath, made himself huge, and strode off to the palace.

I knew he couldn't ride me because I was lame, but something must have been very wrong because Alexander did not come to see me for AGES. Charm said he'd gone off with his mother to visit his grandparents in a place called Epirus, which is beyond Macedonia's southwest border. She said they'd gone because he and his father had fought at a party over the king's marriage to another woman, and the one-eyed king had drunk too much magic and nearly killed Alexander. I don't know how much of this is true, but when you humans drink magic, things do tend to get out of hand.

63

I didn't really understand what all the fuss was about. It's natural for a strong boss like the one-eyed king to breed with as many mares as possible so he can have lots of strong foals like Alexander. Then, if something happens to one of the foals before it is grown, the herd will still have a strong leader when the old boss dies. But I suppose you humans take a different view of things.

With the king taking a new wife, and the rumours started by Antipater flying around, that Alexander had dismissed the royal horsemaster so the king wouldn't find out the truth about him and the queen, groom-gossip was all about who Alexander's father REALLY was. The main suspects were:

The one-eyed king – still possible, though it's true Alexander does not look much like him.

Antipater – unlikely after what I heard in Athens. Besides, he is the father of Iolaus, one of Alexander's Guard, and those two man-colts look nothing alike.

King Darius of Persia – ridiculous, because we have just declared war on Persia.

One of the queen's pet snakes, which is a demon in disguise – I have never seen a snake change into a demon. Have you?

The horsemaster – ha, he couldn't sire a mule!

A god – this is what the queen claims. I do worry about you humans sometimes.

Meanwhile, with Charm's excellent care, my leg healed. And in the spring – joy, oh joy! – the one-eyed king ordered me turned out in the mare pasture. I couldn't run with Aura, since she had gone away with Alexander to carry the queen. But since Alexander's friends had been sent away from court in disgrace and told to leave their horses behind, I got to run with Psylla.

Oh, it was a fine time out in that pasture with the sun on my back, the soft summer rains to bathe me, and the river to cool my legs. But you're going to have to use your imagination here, because the next bit is strictly CENSORED!

Dominating the one-eyed king

There were lots of new horses around that year, so I had my work cut out squealing challenges over the fence at them all. The new horsemaster was buying from every ship. The riding ground was permanently full of youngsters, bucking and rearing and playing at being in battles. Meanwhile, foot-soldiers drilled on the parade ground, with their battle-scarred bosses shouting at them in loud voices until my heart started to pound.

Charm said there would be another campaign soon. She said the one-eyed king was going to rejoin his general in Anatolia to fight the Persians, and Alexander would come back to ride me. Then people would forget about the quarrel, and everything would be all right again.

But the one-eyed king never got to lead his herd to Anatolia.

One night in the spring, there is a lot of commotion over at the palace. People have been drinking magic to celebrate the wedding of one of Alexander's sisters, so at first I don't realize what has happened. I am far more interested in Psylla, who chooses that night to drop her foal.

She is a beautiful, long-legged filly, black like me but with no white on her head. I make myself huge and prance up to introduce myself, full of fatherly pride. But Psylla squeals and gives me flat ears, so I leave them alone. It's the one time I let a mare get away with this sort of behaviour, because all mares are willing to fight to the death to protect their foals.

Charm does not visit me in the pasture that night. But in the morning, before it is properly light, I see a lone figure standing on the riverbank, staring at me.

He's downwind, so I can't smell him from here. But something about the way he stands with his chin tilted upward and his pale curls blowing around his head makes me shiver all over. He's wearing a purple cloak, and there's a dagger in his belt. Apart from that, he is unarmed. He walks slowly towards me, and the mares' heads shoot up nervously as they catch his smell.

Another shiver goes through me. At first, remembering all the ghosts we made in Greece, I want to turn and gallop away. But he calls, 'Bucephalas! My beautiful one, what are you doing out here in the mare pasture? Is that your foal?' His voice sends ripples down my legs, and I can almost feel his hand firm on my rein.

I whinny a greeting, make myself huge and trot towards him.

His eyes narrow as he watches me approach. They are red around the edges, and he looks very serious and grown-up.

'Well, Charmides is right. You look sound enough.' As his hands rub my forehead, pull my ears, and tease the burrs out of my mane, he relaxes a bit. 'Have you missed me as much as everyone else seems to have done?'

I give him flat ears, and he laughs.

'Oh, horse . . . at least *you* don't change! But your holiday is over, I'm afraid. They've killed my father. From now on, you'll be ridden into battle by a king . . .' His voice falters.

He clutches my withers, and in a fierce whisper tells me everything that happened in the night.

During the wedding party, the one-eyed king was assassinated. That's a Persian word which means to dominate a herd in a sneaky way by killing its boss. I use it here because most people claimed the Persians were behind the assassination plot. Even though the man who stabbed the king was caught and tortured, he wouldn't say who had told him to do it.

'Antipater says the King's Guard were bribed with Persian gold to plot against my father,' Alexander tells me in the same fierce tone. 'But I'm sure he knows more than he lets on. Mother says I shouldn't trust Antipater to look after Macedonia for me. But I'm not staying here to let someone put a knife between *my* ribs! As soon as I can, I'm going to take the army down the coast and deal with the Persians in Anatolia – finish what Father started. And while I'm over there, I'll visit the famous Siwa Oracle in Egypt, ask it who my father was, to settle that for once and all.' He pauses to stare at the palace, and his voice quietens. 'I don't believe for a moment I'm the son of that vile old horsemaster! He's obviously still angry with me for dismissing him. But there's been plenty of gossip about other men, and the worst of it is, Mother won't tell me the truth. All she says is that she prayed to Zeus for a son who would have the power of a god, and he answered her prayer by making her pregnant with me, but I think she's just making that up. Some people are even saying I planned the king's assassination myself so I could lead them into Persia on some sort of crusade, which is just ridiculous. I know we argued a lot about the campaign, but I'd never hurt my father, *never!*'

Sounds about right to me. That's what happens when a

strong young colt grows up and the boss-stallion gets old. It's perfectly natural and good for the herd. But Alexander smells very upset, so I expect it's like the mare thing – different for humans.

I push him with my nose, searching his pockets for apples, and he sighs. 'Oh, horse! What if it's true, and I'm not really a prince? People threw eggs at me – *eggs!*'

That was before Psylla's foal, though. If he's the king now, they won't dare throw eggs any more. Besides, he'll be riding *me* next time we enter a city, and I won't let him get hit by an egg, or anything else.

Alexander stays a bit longer, telling me his plans and sniffing into my mane every time he mentions his father. A lot of it is boring, so don't ask me to tell you everything he said. His Guard eventually work out where he is, and run across the mare pasture calling for him to hurry up and get ready, because Antipater wants to present him to the army.

He gives a shudder, wipes an arm across his face, and takes a deep breath. Then he pushes me away, and turns to meet his friends with a bright smile. None of them realize he has been crying.

I think he is going to make a very good king.

THE NORTH WEST FRONTIER, 335 BC

A prophetic dream

When an old boss dies, it is natural for all the neighbouring herds to test the strength of the new boss to see if they can steal any mares or pasture land. So the first thing Alexander did was take the army south to make sure the Greeks knew he was strong enough to lead the Macedonian herd. Charm had orders to get me fit while he was away.

Having spent so long in the pasture, my muscles were flabby and my dung had become liquid grass. It was embarrassing, to say the least, leaving such a mess on top of other horses' piles in the riding ground. But after my long rest, I was as sound as ever. By the time Alexander and his friends returned, laughing and joking about how much they'd scared everyone down in Greece, I felt great. After all Charm's polishing and oiling, my coat gleamed like ebony as she proudly led me out for inspection.

Alexander looked nearly as good as I did. He was relaxed and smiling, his cheeks ruddy with southern sun. He wore a circlet of golden leaves in his mane, which made him look very handsome. Groom-gossip claimed he'd made all the Greek states sign a treaty that named him boss of something called the Hellenic League. He did this without a single blow being struck, which makes sense to me. Often flat ears or a loud squeal are enough to dominate the enemy, provided you are big enough.

We spent that winter on training exercises in the mountains. The Macedonian hoplites with their long pikes were joined by ragged bands of mercenaries with slings and bows, so we were a very fierce herd. In the spring, we collected the Maedi javelin-throwers from Alexandropolis and went north to try out our mountain skills by dominating some more rebel herds.

At first, it was easy. The enemy either ran away when they saw us coming, or surrendered immediately. But one tribe tried to trap us in a narrow pass through the mountains. They lined up their carts at the top and hid behind them like foals hide behind the mares when something threatens the herd.

We horses were so fit by then, we could have galloped up the steep slope and jumped the blockade, no trouble. But Alexander halted the army at the bottom and squinted up the hill, muttering to himself. He ran a hand down my tense neck. 'What are they up to, Bucephalas? They haven't got archers. They fight with swords, normally. Are they planning to throw rocks at us?'

Philotas thought Alexander was scared, and rode Zephyr so close to me I had to lash my tail to stop her treading on my heels. 'Anyone can see they haven't a hope of holding us off!' he said in his haughty voice. 'We've got far more men than they have. What are you waiting for? We should just charge them.'

'Shut up and let me think!' Alexander snapped.

Philotas did the typical human trick of bowing his head and pretending to be dominated, while scowling at his boss's back. We horses pawed the ground nervously. Despite all our mountain training, we don't like steep-sided passes. Our hoof-beats echo in them. And if we whinny, it sounds as if strange horses are hiding behind the rocks and whinnying back. The hoplites with their long pikes were not very happy, either. The track was so narrow, they couldn't form their phalanx.

As Alexander hesitated, there was a commotion behind us, and Charm ran up. I whinnied to my groom, and Alexander looked round. He didn't seem very pleased to see Charm at such a critical moment, but he told the Guard to let her approach. She hurried to my shoulder and lowered her eyes. She was very out of breath. On a mountain road, it is a long trot from the baggage wagons to the front of our herd.

'What is it?' Alexander snapped. 'Make it quick.'

'Those carts up there, Sir . . . you mustn't get below them!'

Alexander frowned and leant down beside my neck to hear her frightened whisper. '*Please* don't ride Bucephalas up there, Sir! I had a dream last night. Carts were lined up just like those along the top of a ridge and they came rolling down the slope right into the army! The horses' legs broke, and our men were crushed to death.'

'Rubbish,' Philotas muttered.

Alexander gave Philotas a strong glare. He waited until Charm was safely out of the way, then turned to his officers and gave his orders in a calm tone. 'It's a trick, but we can beat them at their own game. Send the phalanx up first. Tell the men at the front on the steepest part of the track to watch the carts carefully. When they see them start to move, they're to crouch down all together and put their shields over their heads. The ones behind must be ready to open ranks and let the carts through. No one is to panic. The carts will bounce over the men's heads if they lie low and don't run. All cavalry to stay well back until the last carts have come down. We can't risk the horses.'

It turns out this is exactly what happens. Our men have been well trained, and because Alexander has warned them what to expect, they don't panic. We horses are *very* brave. We simply snort and dance back a bit as the whole crashing, snapping mass of wood and iron-rimmed wheels bounces down from the top of the pass towards us. As the echoes die away, I stand like a rock so Alexander can watch everything with his narrowed eyes.

When the carts have all come down, the stupid enemy have nothing left to hide behind. Our hoplites rush the top of the pass, and we horses of the Guard leap up the ridge and easily dominate them.

Not bad for a kitchen boy

We camp that night on the plain north of the pass, next to a noisy river. Charm is very quiet as she rubs me down and gives me my nosebag. I know Alexander has been watching her for some time from the trees, because I can smell him. But humans can't smell as well as horses, so Charm jumps when he steps out of the shadows.

At first he doesn't say anything, just runs his hands down

72

my legs to check for heat. I am hungry and tired after all the steep mountain roads, so I give him flat ears to let him know I want to be left alone.

He pushes my nose away and frowns at Charm. 'So, you have prophetic dreams, do you?'

Charm whispers, 'Sometimes, Sir. Please don't tell anyone.'

'Don't call me "Sir", Charmides. It makes me feel old. How long has this been going on?'

'Since I came to Pella, Your Majesty—'

'*Alexander*. That's an order.'

She flushes. 'But I can't call you that. You're the king now!'

Alexander smiles at her. 'Sometimes I don't feel very much like a king, Charmides. Sometimes I wish I was more like you. Just a groom, with nothing to worry about except the horses you look after. But I want to know more about these dreams of yours. I want to know how you came to be looking after Bucephalas. I never seem to have enough time to thank you for what you've done for the horse. He's a credit to you.'

She relaxes a little. 'Thank you, Sir— Alexander. I ran away from home when my mother died. I was too upset to think straight. I didn't know what I was going to do, but I ended up in Pella, and . . . er . . . thought I might find work in the palace kitchens. Then I saw Bucephalas on your riding ground and recognized him as a horse I used to know when I was small. He's older now, of course, and he never used to be so wild, but he's so big and proud, there's no mistaking him. When I saw you ride him, I knew for sure he was the same horse. I still meant to go to the kitchens, but that night I dreamt Bucephalas was in danger, so I asked for work at the stables instead.'

'Interesting.' Alexander is watching her closely. 'So where's home? By law, as a runaway slave you can be executed, you know.'

She shudders. 'Methone. I used to work with my mother in the kitchens there, but I was always sneaking down to the stables to see the horses. My old master wouldn't let me groom them because I was a g—' She breaks off, flushing. 'I mean, I'd rather clean horses than clean pots, Sir.'

Alexander laughs. 'Methone, huh? A spirited people. You might be too young to remember, but that's where my father lost his eye in battle, subduing the town. I was only a baby at the time, of course, but so many people have told me the story I feel as if I was there. And here you are, grooming the king's horse! Not bad for a kitchen boy.' He grows serious again. 'As soon as we get back, I'll see to it the garrison commander at Methone is compensated for losing you. In the meantime, if you have any other dreams like that one, be sure to tell me, won't you? *Before* we meet the enemy would be good, next time.'

She flushes again. 'Of course, Sir. Er . . . are we going home now we've beaten the rebels?'

He gives me a pat and gazes at the river with a gleam in his eye. 'Not yet, Charmides. In three days, we should reach the Danube. I've ordered General Parmenio to send ships from Byzantium to meet us there with some rather interesting siege engines my father was working on. We'll take them upriver and let all the tribes round these parts know I'm not going to stand for any nonsense while I'm away chasing the Persians out of Anatolia. We can head back through the mountains and check the western frontier on our way home. Should be easy enough. Then we'll call on those ships Athens

74

promised me, and take the army to the Hellespont to meet old Parmenio.' He stares across the plain at the campfires and dark tents. 'I'm finally going to see Troy, Charmides! The very city the great Achilles conquered in the *Iliad!*' His eyes glitter as he speaks, and I can feel his excitement running down his arm.

I stop eating. Charm bites her lip. She doesn't look nearly as excited as the king about seeing this city called Troy.

Alexander doesn't notice. He grins and gives me a slap on the rump that makes me snort into my barley. 'We'll soon take care of these mountain tribes, don't worry! Then when I cross the Hellespont and liberate Anatolia from the Persian yoke, no one will be able to say I'm not the son of a king.'

At the Danube, the tribe across the river tried to join forces with the one we were dominating on our side and make a fight of it. But Alexander ordered the men to stuff their tent covers with our hay and make rafts. Then he used the rafts and the ships from Byzantium to ferry his entire herd across the Danube during the night, and chased them away.

After that, the northern tribes couldn't surrender fast enough. They said we'd crossed the river by magic, and the story spread like fire. Lots of other bosses came to submit to Alexander as well; he didn't even have to use the siege engines to frighten them. He ordered his men to transfer the engines to our mule carts, reloaded the ships with the plunder we took from the enemy and sent them home, then marched us west to secure his final border.

Tydeos

Groom-gossip on our way through the mountains was all about the siege engines the mules were pulling along in pieces at the back of the army. Whenever we stopped for the night, an excited group of man-colts formed to discuss how they might work. Charm hovered at the edge of the group, pretending to be interested, but glancing round nervously as if she expected Alexander to appear at any moment. But the young king stayed in his tent talking to his officers. Our grooms said they were probably trying to work out how to use the siege engines, too.

'They throw stones,' one groom claimed. 'Like the slingers.'

'I 'eard they throw boulders as big as 'ouses!'

'Don't be stupid. How are boulders goin' to get in the engine in the first place, if they're that big? Even King Alexander couldn't lift one.'

'Mules drag 'em, of course. Then they sit down on the engine, and the boulder rolls off their back into the throwing cup.'

'Sit down! Don't be an idiot. How are you supposed to make a mule do that?'

'Maybe they throw mules!'

The grooms laughed, so I gave them flat ears. Mules are stupid, yes, but that's just bad taste.

'I bet Bucephalas could lift the rocks with his teeth,' one of the quieter grooms said, eyeing me. 'Eh, Charm?'

Charm gave him a tense smile. His name was Tydeos, and he had been helping her with the Guard's horses, so he was part of our special herd.

'I don't see why we need the siege engines at all,' she said. 'The king told me there isn't going to be any more fighting – at least, not until he goes to Anatolia,' she added, frowning.

'Ha!' One of the older grooms gave her a sly look. 'You

haven't heard the latest, have you?'

'What's that?'

'The Illyrians are rebelling now. Apparently, they've taken over a big fortress up in the mountains. We'll need our siege engines there, all right! I can't wait to see them in action.'

Charm went pale. 'But Alexander said we were just checking the border, then going home—'

'Oh,' Tydeos said, teasing her. '*Alexander* now, is it? Other duties come with looking after his horse, do they?'

Charm blushed. 'No!'

'I've seen him down here, sweet-talking you.'

'Just talking.'

By this time, they were all laughing at her. 'Ha! Charm's soft on the king!' 'Better not tell anyone, or you'll make Hephaestion jealous!'

Tydeos smiled and said gently, 'Don't waste your feelings on him, Charm. It's well known kings and princes don't bother with grooms. They don't even see us most of the time. We're like mule bags to them, or . . . pairs of boots! Just something useful to keep them from getting dirty. Then, when we're all old and used up with hard work, they throw us away and get new ones.'

'Alexander's not like that,' Charm said, defensive now. 'He *does* care. He gave me gold before he went away with his mother.'

'For his horse!' This set them all off laughing again. 'I hope you didn't spend any on yourself?'

She shook her head. She didn't, knowing Charm. Both her tunics are patched, her grooming-belt is stitched together where it broke, and her sandals have holes in them from the mountain roads. I, however, have a nice new battle-cloth.

The grooms went back to arguing about the siege engines, and Tydeos went off with Charm to talk about something else. I don't think it will be very long before he works out she's a girl-filly.

A trap

Alexander must have been as eager to try out his new siege engines as our grooms were to see them in action, because he made the army march extremely fast to reach the Illyrian fortress. It was an eerie place. Steep, wooded mountainsides loomed over our camp like shadowy walls. With the fortress perched at the top of the valley, the only way in or out was across a fast-flowing river and through a narrow pass. The cliffs were impossible for horses, and to climb them our riders would have been forced to leave their weapons behind. We horses knew a trap when we saw one, and laid back our ears. But Alexander stroked my neck and told me not to fret because this would only be a small battle. Then he led our entire herd straight in.

While our men hammered the siege engines together, winched back the arms, and sent rocks clattering against the fortress walls to frighten the Illyrians inside, the rest of the Illyrian herd was creeping up behind us. After squealing a few threats at Alexander, they left us to spend a miserable night without any food on the plain under their fortress. Our grooms huddled under their cloaks nibbling hard cheese and talking in whispers. They were very scared. Alexander must have been worried, too, because a lamp burned all night in his tent, flickering through the leather. At dawn, he came down to the horse lines to ask Charm if she'd had any dreams.

Charm shook her head. 'Your Majesty, I'm sorry. I haven't

had a dream about this place.'

Alexander sighed. 'At least that means we're not going to die here – or is it just Bucephalas who survives? Of course the Illyrians will probably take the horses as spoils of war, so I expect he'll be all right.'

Charm went still. 'They won't *win*, will they?'

Alexander passed a hand across his eyes. 'They have us in a bad place. The phalanx can't fight them effectively in the pass – it's too narrow. We'll thrash them if we meet them on the plain, of course, but they're too wily to face us in battle. Know-it-all Philotas says we should wait till they get bored and come out to fight. That's all very well, but we *can't* wait. We're running out of food. The Illyrians know that. And we can't continue our attack on the fortress with them at our backs. What do you think we should do, Charmides?'

Charm thought for a moment. 'Maybe you need a bucket and some barley, Sir?' she said.

He gave her a distracted frown, as if he thought she was complaining about our lack of fodder. Then he looked thoughtful. 'Something to lure them out, you mean? Yes, I've thought of that. But we haven't got anything they can't wait for. We certainly haven't got any spare barley. The poor horses are half starved.'

Charm looked at the mud under her feet and said slowly, 'When Bucephalas was in the mare pasture he didn't want to be caught, not even for a bucket of barley. So I gave up trying to catch him and sat down in the middle of the field. He got curious and came to see what I was doing. That's how I got him in.'

Alexander gave her an amused look. 'You sat down in the middle of the field? That's probably what the Illyrians are hoping we'll do! But it's an interesting idea. Maybe something else might do it, something they *don't* understand?' He looked at the damp tents and the gloomy men stirring in their bedrolls. The light returned to his face, and he grinned.

What Alexander did was order us all to form up for a parade.

The men polished their weapons and helmets and put on full armour. We horses wore our best cloths and bridles with all our trappings. The hoplites formed up the first pattern of their phalanx, and the cavalry made neat squares. I stood at the front and made myself huge so that Alexander could watch, and the eight horses of the Guard stood in a neat line behind me, champing on their bits. Petasios, Borealis, Aura, Apollo, Zephyr, Hades, Harpinna . . . even Psylla's replacement, a dark grey stallion called Arion, knew he was in superior company and arched his neck proudly. The cavalry practised battle manoeuvres in close formation at the trot, while the men did slow pike-lowering and raising, changing the shape of their phalanx in response to signals from their officers. Usually, these are trumpet blasts, but that morning they were silent signals given with hands.

Our parade was perfect. The only noise was the snorting of horses and the soft rhythm of our hooves in the dawn air. Meanwhile, the mules had been harnessed up with the siege engines balanced on the baggage carts, and the grooms and muleteers waited with them near the river. They couldn't go anywhere with the Illyrians blocking the pass, of course. But as our parade continued, more and more Illyrians ventured out to watch. Soon they were sitting on the rocks with their spears over their knees, fascinated.

I am starting to get bored, when Alexander's weight

suddenly shifts. He draws his sword and stabs the sky.

'ALALALALALAI!' he screams, startling me into a rear.

As if they have been waiting for this, the entire army breaks into the same cry.

'ALALALALAI! ALALALALALAI! ALALALALAI!'

The men beat their pikes on their shields, the cavalry turn as a herd, and the phalanx charges the unprepared enemy at the mouth of the pass. Half of them are still sitting down when we burst through their ranks.

The Illyrian boss is furious we tricked him. He yells after our retreating army, 'That's right, Macedonian pup! Run back home with your tail between your legs! Best wait until you've grown a bit before you take on the men of Illyria again!'

Alexander flings him a vicious glare and hauls on my mouth to turn me back. But Hephaestion rides Petasios close to me and grabs my rein. 'No, Alex!' he shouts. 'He's angry we got past his men, that's all – don't let him provoke you into doing something stupid, after you got us out of that trap so cleverly.'

Something flickers across Alexander's face, and his blade lowers. He urges me down the hillside beside Petasios, and we gallop to safety.

When we finally pull up, the Guard are quiet. Philotas mutters something about us being lucky to have escaped with our lives, and this time Alexander doesn't argue. But it could have been worse. We didn't dominate the Illyrians that day – but they didn't dominate us, either.

A wonderful roll

Alexander did not take us home, of course. But it seemed he had learnt a valuable lesson about dominating. We retreated a short way and made camp in a wide valley with lots of exits, every route carefully watched by sentries.

After a few days, barley and other supplies arrived from a friendly garrison, and so did a roll of flattened grass with marks on it. This must have been some kind of squealing challenge, because it put Alexander into a wild rage. We heard him from the horse lines as he threw things around in his tent and yelled at his friends. The dogs began to bark, and the men jumped up and seized their weapons, looking for an enemy.

'Oh, what's up *now*?' Tydeos mutters. 'I'm getting sick of these mountains. Look at this poor mare's foot.' He lifts one of Aura's hooves. 'Bruised half to death. Where's that paste we've been using?'

'All gone,' Charm says, her voice tight. 'I used the last of it on Bucephalas last night.'

They go quiet, because they are still a bit scared of the Illyrians. Groom-gossip over the past few days has been about how close we all came to being killed on the plain under their fortress.

'Well, I hope it's done the trick,' Tydeos says, nodding to the tent where Alexander is still raging. 'Because it sounds like the king's in a bad enough mood already, without his horse going lame as well.'

Charm makes a face at the king's tent, and – strangely for this time of day – decides to take me for a roll.

Usually we roll in sand, but there's no sand here so we're using a muddy patch by the river, and it's WONDERFUL. Why you humans don't try it more often, I don't know. Inferior horses can't flip over when they roll, and have to get up and then down again to do the other side. But I can keep going, over and back again, for as long as I feel like it. Charm

82

holds the end of my lead rein and smiles. 'Get as dirty as you like, Bucephalas,' she murmurs. Which is strange, because usually she tells me off for getting too muddy.

I could have rolled in that mud for ages. But then I catch Alexander's sweet sherbet smell. I scramble to my feet and nudge Charm. She's standing in the mud, looking at me, when she ought to take me back to the lines and groom me.

Alexander strides towards us, buckling on his armour, a furious look on his face. 'What are you doing down here?' he snaps. 'I need my horse! I'm going to finish off those Illyrians, once and for all. We've been messing around in these mountains far too long.'

Charm lowers her eyes. 'I'm sorry, but he's just had a roll, Your Majesty.'

Alexander sees the wet mud on me and swears under his breath. 'Then get him clean. You can't put a battle-cloth on that. Give him a bath. Come on, get going, I haven't got all day.'

Charm doesn't move. 'And he's footsore.'

'So are half the horses in the cavalry! I need Bucephalas ready for battle, *now!*'

'You could ride another horse today, Sir.' Charm's voice is barely a whisper.

Alexander has turned to rejoin his men. But when she says this, he whirls back. He clenches a fist and says in a danger-ous voice, '*Get him clean!* Zeus, I've enough to worry about, without grooms who can't do as they're told! You're going the right way about losing your job and getting sent back to the kitchens.'

Charm's hand trembles on my rein. I get anxious and whinny, and some of the Guard come down to the rolling place to see what's wrong.

Hephaestion eyes the mud on me, and Charm's determined mud-spattered face. He fights a smile and puts a hand on the king's arm. 'Alex . . . why don't you give the old horse a rest? If the scouts are correct, it won't be much of a fight. The Illyrians haven't even dug any defences. Their camp's wide open, and they're the ones in the trap this time. Give the lad a break. He wasn't to know.'

Alexander looks hard at Charm. He sends Hephaestion and the others to mount up and takes a deep breath. When he next speaks, his voice is calmer. 'All right, Charmides, you win this time. But while I'm gone, make sure you treat Bucephalas' feet. We've a long way to go once I've finished with these Illyrians, and we're going to have to travel fast.'

She starts to lead me away in relief, but he puts out an arm to stop her. His eyes narrow. 'Why did you do it? Did you have another dream?'

Charm shakes her head, unable to meet his gaze.

Alexander frowns at her. Then he sighs. 'Just as well. I wouldn't want to die twice in the same day.'

This didn't make much sense to me at the time. But when Alexander had galloped off to deal with the Illyrians, the gossip filtered down to the horse lines: a letter had come from his mother the queen, saying that someone (no prizes for guessing who!) had started a rumour that Alexander and his entire army had been killed fighting the border tribes. As a result, Thebes had thrown out their Macedonian garrison and declared themselves a free city again. Athens and the rest of Greece were ready to follow. Antipater was about to recall General Parmenio and the rest of the advance Macedonian troops from Anatolia.

This news made Alexander so angry that when the Illyrians saw him coming they burnt down their own fortress and fled. When he returned, he was in a much better mood. He should have been. With only a few hundred dead Macedonians and no dead horses, he and I have so far dominated:

the Maedi
the Theban Sacred Band
several Celtic herds
the Illyrians.

Our grooms quickly forgot how afraid they'd been, and said King Alexander would soon scare the Greeks back into submission. But dominating is a dangerous game, and it's never a good idea to turn your back on sly stallions like Antipater and the horsemaster.

SEVENTH HOOFPRINT
THEBES, SUMMER 335 BC

A message

You should have seen their faces when the Thebans realized Alexander was still alive! We reached their big, proud city just two weeks after leaving Illyria, and camped outside their thick walls to remind them who was boss. They took one look at Alexander, mounted on me at the front of the army with his head bare and his untidy mane blowing around his face, and slammed their gates shut in terror.

Alexander sent a message to the city before he'd even dismounted. He told the messenger to say four things:

As they could see, the rumours of his death were greatly exaggerated.

They were breaking their promise to him, made under the terms of the Hellenic League.

They must open their gates at once and let him reinstate

the Macedonian garrison.

If they did as he asked, he would pardon them – since their mistake had been easy enough to make – and take his army home.

Then he handed my rein to Charm, stretched the kinks out of his shoulders, and strode off to his tent. His friends followed, congratulating one another on having marched out of the mountains so fast that the Thebans never knew they were coming. No one else, they said, could have made it from Illyria to Thebes in just thirteen days.

Trouble in the horse lines

That night Petasios, and the others who have been to Thebes before, munch their hay as happily as they would have at home. I am more alert. I've already dominated several piles of enemy dung, but I still need to keep throwing up my head to check for ghosts.

Our grooms sit on a pile of our cloths, rubbing oil into our bridles, while Tydeos tells Charm this is exactly how King Alexander frightened the citizens of Thebes into surrendering to him the last time he came here. He says not to worry, because the same thing will happen now, and we'll soon be home. Charm does not look convinced.

Our campfires burn lower. The grooms finish their work and curl up in their cloaks. The sentry at the end of the horse lines dozes off, exhausted from the march. I am about to relax, too, when I smell the disgraced horsemaster, whom I last saw in Athens, before my leg went bad.

I break into a sweat and give a loud whinny to wake Charm. The sentry jerks awake, reaches for his spear – and gasps as a shadowy figure puts a thong around his neck and pulls him over backwards. His ghost struggles to stay, then floats quietly away into the night. There are shouts of alarm as shadowy figures run through the camp, swords in their hands. Sleepy Macedonians stagger out of their tents half dressed, and pairs of men stumble into the horse lines, fighting furiously.

From the darkness, a mule brays in fear. I whinny again, pulling at my halter. Petasios tries to rear up, gets a leg over the line, and falls over, causing the other horses to panic. The grooms come running to sort us out. But Charm cannot come to me, because the horsemaster has her trapped next to our fodder wagon. He's blackened his face with soot, and Charm is trying to fend him off with my metal grooming-comb.

He catches her wrist and twists it until she lets go.

'Well, well,' he says. 'So, you're still looking after Alexander's old horse? I'm surprised the brute hasn't collapsed on the battlefield by now.'

'Let me go!' Charm yells, kicking him. 'If I shout for help, thirty thousand men will come to arrest you.'

'Not quite thirty thousand by now, I suspect,' says the horsemaster, gripping her tightly. 'I don't think young Alexander will find Thebes as easily frightened as those barbarian tribes up north. I want you to help me put the bridle on his horse. I'm taking the animal back to Thebes with me. Then we'll see how eager Alexander is to make demands.'

'You're not taking Bucephalas anywhere!' Charm struggles furiously, yelling for help. Tydeos and some of the other grooms leave the horses and come running. But the horsemaster pulls out his dagger, puts it across Charm's throat, and glares at them.

'Keep out of it,' he threatens. 'You remember me, don't you? Remember the beatings I gave you all, back in Pella?'

Some of them obviously do, and back off warily.

'I'll fetch the sentries,' Tydeos says. 'Don't panic, Charm! He won't dare harm you. He'll never get out of the camp alive.'

The horsemaster chuckles. 'What sentries?'

Our grooms finally notice the dead sentry lying at the end of the horse lines. Charm goes limp with fear. It's just as well you humans don't have a horse's vision; it would only scare you if you could see as much as we can.

I rear up as the horsemaster limps closer, dragging Charm. But I've forgotten I'm still tethered to the stupid line, and almost fall over like Petasios did earlier. I swing round and try to kick the horsemaster, but he is holding Charm in front of him, and he is too good a horseman to get behind me. He grabs a freshly-oiled bridle and growls, 'Put it on him!'

Charm drops it in the dust. 'You do it. I'm not helping you steal Bucephalas!'

The horsemaster hisses in rage. He throws Charm to the ground, grabs the bridle and a whip, and approaches me with a determined scowl.

I act wild. He strikes me on the nose with his whip, so I rear up again. This time my tether breaks. One of my hooves catches him on the shoulder. He stumbles, suddenly pale, his bad knee giving way.

Charm picks herself up, blood pouring from her nose, and flings herself on top of the horsemaster with a cry of rage. This is stupid of her, because I can't dominate him properly with her in the way.

They roll on the ground like ferocious man-colts. Charm is

strong and lean after the mountains, and acting very fierce tonight. But the horsemaster is stronger. He pins her down and is just about to punch her in the face, when his eyes go wide.

'You're a *girl!*' he gasps, lowering the fist in confusion.

Finally someone's noticed.

Charm takes advantage of his hesitation to squirm out from under him. Tugging her tunic straight, she runs to me and scrambles up on my back. I don't need any encouragement. We wheel round and gallop through the dark lines of tents, dodging ropes and jumping the glowing embers of fires, until my enemy is left far behind us.

When I feel Charm begin to slip, I slow to a walk. She flops over my neck, sobbing, and buries her bloody nose in my mane. I stop and turn my head to nibble her sandal. By this time, the alarm has been raised, and the Macedonians are busy chasing off the Thebans. Dark figures race back towards the high walls of the city and vanish inside its gates.

I am too far away to smell if the horsemaster is among them. If he's got any sense, though, he'll be running as fast as he can. I mean to say, trying to kidnap the king's warhorse! Whatever next?

Dominating Thebes

In the morning, Alexander orders the men to break camp. We stand outside the closed gate of Thebes with the breeze blowing our tails sideways and our banners snapping like whips. Alexander watches the walls with a calculating expression, his chin tilted up and his eyes narrow. There's a trumpeter standing beside us, keeping a safe distance away from my teeth, but Alexander doesn't tell him to blow the trumpet yet. He simply waits. Except to give orders, he hasn't spoken since Charm told him how the Thebans tried to kidnap me in the night. Behind us, the Guard and the rest of the army also wait.

At last, some Thebans appear on the tower above the gate. As soon as he sees them, Alexander makes himself huge and calls, 'I've come to give you this message myself, since you seem to have ignored my previous one. Last night's raid on my camp will not go unpunished. But first, I'd like to extend the hand of friendship to any who still wish to keep the peace as agreed by the Hellenic League. Hand over the ringleaders of the rebellion and the man who tried to kidnap my horse last night, open your gates to me, and I'll deal with you lightly.'

His voice is shrill and echoes slightly under the garrison rock. The other horses fidget and champ on their bits, but I do not move a muscle as Alexander makes squealing threats at the Thebans. This is a very important time. We might not need an actual battle at all, if Alexander squeals loudly enough.

But this enemy squeals back just as loudly.

'How about you hand over your regent Antipater, and General Parmenio's son Philotas, whom we see sitting behind you on the yellow mare? Since it seems you are not King Philip's son, both of them have more of a claim than you to the throne of Macedonia. *Then* we might consider negotiating with you, Alexander, as a very distant third. May we also make it known to your men that if any of them wish to join us in overthrowing the tyrant who dares sit before the historic Electra Gate of Thebes on a broken-down old nag groomed by a *girl*, they are welcome to enter our city as friends.'

There is a deathly silence as this insult sinks in. Some of the Guard whisper in consternation. Alexander's hand tightens on my rein. His face reddens. The tendons of his neck stand out, and he begins to breathe very fast. Out of the corner of my good eye, I see Hephaestion go pale and nudge Petasios forward with his knees, but it is too late.

With a terrible cry, Alexander whips out his sword and yells for his men to bring up the siege engines. 'Destroy the city!' he cries. 'Break down the walls! Give no quarter! Find the traitor who tried to kidnap my horse! Do not stop until every last man, woman and child in Thebes is either dead or begging for mercy at my feet!'

It is a VERY fierce battle.

Alexander digs in his spurs and wrenches at my mouth until it bleeds as much as Charm's nose did the night before. The Thebans send out their army to meet ours on the plain, and Alexander lays about him with his sword, galloping with his Guard here, there, and everywhere in the thick of the fighting, until we horses are all foaming with sweat and as weary of the fighting as our riders.

Alexander is the only one who doesn't seem to get tired. Fuelled by rage, he keeps on hacking at the enemy with his sword, grunting things like: 'That'll show you who's the rightful King of Macedonia!' 'That'll teach you to call me a tyrant!' 'King Philip *was* my father, he *was!*'

All the while, stones are whistling overhead from our siege engines. But although they frighten the enemy, they don't make much impression on the thick walls of Thebes. Alexander eventually realizes this and pulls me up, squinting thoughtfully into the shadows beneath the wall. The others pull up around us, panting, their swords drooping from their hands, and their horses' heads low. My legs are trembling with exhaustion from leaping out of the way of spear thrusts and arrows, and a hundred little places on my body sting where the enemy's weapons have scratched me. But I am still ready to fight.

Alexander's voice has an icy edge to it. 'Do you see any guards watching the side gate?' he asks.

Hephaestion shakes his head. 'No, Alex . . . they must have joined the struggle in the garrison.'

My rider smiles for the first time since the squealing match outside the Electra Gate, and his brightness returns. 'I need a volunteer to take a strike force through that gate. Organize whatever men you can find, go in through the garrison and get the main gates open. We'll strike them where they least expect it, from the inside. It's dangerous, but whoever does it will be a hero.'

Hephaestion frowns at the little gate and strokes Petasios' sweaty neck. He opens his mouth to volunteer, but Philotas hauls Zephyr's head up and coughs. 'I'm rather embarrassed about what they said earlier, Alexander. Maybe I'd better—'

'I'll do it,' Perdiccas says, raising his chin and wiping the blood off his breastplate. 'Apollo's not as tired as Zephyr.' He claps Philotas on the shoulder. 'You're third in line to the throne, Philo. We've got to look after you in case anything happens to Alex. Your father would never forgive us if we got you killed over here in Greece before you even set foot in Anatolia.'

Now the others are all quick to say they will do it, ashamed they didn't volunteer first. But there isn't time to argue. Apollo makes himself huge and gallops off, his pale tail rippling.

While we wait for Perdiccas and Apollo, Alexander rides me up a slope so he can survey the battle. He notices for the first time that my mouth is bleeding, leans forward and wipes the bloody foam with his finger.

'Oh, I'm sorry, my brave horse! Sometimes they make me so angry I don't know what I'm doing. Charmides will soon make you better—' He breaks off and curses under his breath. 'Though I don't suppose that's her real name. A *girl*? No, it can't be true. Surely they were just trying to provoke me? Oh, Zeus! I haven't time to think about grooms now! I've got Thebes to worry about.'

He looks round at Hephaestion. 'Any sign of Perdiccas yet?'

Hephaestion shakes his head. 'Not yet, but it looks like the Thebans are retreating.'

Alexander watches the struggling crush of men near the wall, then grins. 'Look, they're opening the Electra Gate! Perdiccas must have done it! Come on, gentlemen, one last effort. We'll get through after them, if we're quick.'

That was how we got into Thebes. Another typical human trick. All night, the city was a confusion of screams and flames and horses galloping through the streets. Our army poured in through the gates, dragged out the Theban women and children, killed anyone who tried to stop them, and ransacked their houses. The mercenaries were the fiercest, taking revenge for something the Thebans had once done to their herds. I've no idea what, but it must have been bad because they dominated the Theban herd with more violence than I have seen in all my years of battle. Men died, and kept on dying, until the air was thick with ghosts. Alexander gave up trying to control them, and led his Guard up to the garrison.

We found Perdiccas covered in blood, lying on a bench in the yard with an army physician treating his wound. Apollo stood nearby, still wearing his battle-cloth and caked in dried sweat. His proud head hung almost to the ground and his reins were broken. A sword cut had severed his breast girth and sliced into his chest. When he smelt us coming, he gave a forlorn little whinny.

Alexander flung himself off my back, raced to his friend's side and clasped his hand. 'Don't die,' he said fiercely. 'That's an order. You're not allowed to die, Perdiccas, do you hear?'

Perdiccas gave him a wan smile and croaked, 'No chance. What's happening? I can hear screaming . . . are we winning?'

'Yes,' Alexander said, his voice tight. 'Don't worry about it. The city's ours.'

While the Guard gathered round Perdiccas, I nipped Apollo to show him what I thought of him for letting his rider get hurt. But not too hard, because we were all pleased to find the vain little horse, with his funny coloured mane and tail, alive.

A ruin with no name

We spent the remaining few hours of darkness in the garrison stables without our grooms, and in the morning Alexander bridled me and led his Guard through the smouldering streets. Two men from the garrison carried Perdiccas behind us on a stretcher, while Demetrius led Apollo with Aura at the back.

We went slowly because there were many bodies and much wreckage to avoid, stopping often so that Alexander could give orders to the officers. Our hooves echoed in the hush, and ash drifted around us, making us toss our heads and snort. I dominated a few piles of strange dung, but my heart wasn't in it. I badly needed a roll.

Outside the gates, we found men of both sides burying their dead. Flies buzzed around the piles of corpses, and smoke from the huge funeral pyres darkened the sun, masking all other smells. If you've never been in a battle, you should believe me when I tell you this was just as well.

Alexander ordered a tent to be set up outside the city, and disappeared inside it with some important-looking men who had just turned up from Athens. Hephaestion took Perdiccas to the blood tent, and Iolaus was left outside to look after us horses. As he tied our reins to the line he'd set up, he grumbled about having to do a common groom's job and gave poor Hades a completely unnecessary whack on the nose. When he came near me, I bit him to let him know how it felt.

The talking in the king's tent went on for ages. Some of the other grooms came to tend their horses, and I started to wonder where Charm was. It's sometimes difficult to find people in an army the size of Alexander's, but she's usually the first to rush up and check me for injuries. When Alexander finally came out of the tent and sent off his Guard to convey his orders to the men, there was still no sign of her.

He frowned at Iolaus. 'Where's my groom?'

'How do I know?' Iolaus said, still grumpy. 'Maybe the lad got fed up with your horse biting him?' He seemed to have forgotten the squealing on the walls before the battle, but he hadn't forgotten the nip I gave him. Too right.

Alexander gave the smoking city and the lines of prisoners being escorted out of the Electra Gate a bleak look. 'The Hellenic League says Thebes must be punished for rebelling. They want me to deport all the citizens as slaves and raze the city to the ground.'

Iolaus' eyes widened slightly. 'But we've already won.

They're not going to give us any more trouble, not after last night. It'll only make the rest of Greece hate you.'

'I know!' Alexander seized my reins, jerking my sore mouth as he untied me. 'But what choice do I have? If I show any weakness now, we might as well forget the Anatolian campaign. I've tried peace talks, and they didn't work. The Greeks will follow me because they fear me. It's their own fault. Besides, Thebes insulted me before my men. Go and help the others. I need a moment alone.'

He led me through the camp, one hand pressed to his forehead. No one bothered us. I don't think many of the men even recognized their king, because both he and I were so dirty. Alexander was not acting much like the boss, either, walking with his head down and his shoulders slumped.

As soon as we reached the horse lines, he started calling for Charm. The grooms jumped at the sound of his voice and called for her too. But I couldn't smell her anywhere. At last, we reached the place where Petasios was picketed with the other horses of the Guard. I whinnied to my friends in relief, and there were quite a few whinnies back. But Charm still didn't appear, which was MOST strange.

Tydeos was sponging Apollo's chest wound, while the silly horse flinched and made little snorting noises. But when Tydeos saw me with Alexander, he rushed out to meet us, looking concerned.

'Where's Charmides?' Alexander demanded.

Tydeos paled. 'No one's seen him since yesterday, Your Majesty. We thought he was with you.'

Alexander gave him the same bleak look he'd given Thebes. He said quietly, 'Did *you* realize Charmides was a girl?'

Tydeos gave him a startled look. His lips moved a little, as if he couldn't work out if the king was making a joke. 'A girl, Your Majesty? Of course not—' Then he broke off, frowned, and whispered, 'Oh, Zeus, you're serious.'

'Just tell me the truth!' Alexander shouted. 'Is my groom Charmides a girl?'

By this time, all the grooms were staring. They whispered and muttered among themselves. 'I always knew there was something strange about that boy.' 'Always kept to himself, didn't he?' 'But he used to *ride* Bucephalas! How could a *girl* ever manage a horse like that?' They eyed me uncertainly, and I gave them flat ears to warn them to keep their distance.

Alexander took a final look around and shook his head. 'So, she's gone, has she? Couldn't face me, I suppose. It's not the first time she's run away, if she was telling the truth about that – which I very much doubt.' His hand tightened again on my rein. He picked out two unfortunate grooms at the front. 'You and you! Take this horse and get him cleaned up! I can't waste any more of my time down here.'

The grooms eyed my flat ears. One of them approached me from my blind side, and I struck out at him in reflex. He jumped back, whimpering and clutching his knee where my hoof had got him. Usually, the others would laugh if one of them had been careless enough to get kicked like that. But they didn't dare, not with the king standing among them.

Alexander gave my reins a jerk and the grooms an exasperated look. 'Get a muzzle on him if you're frightened. The horse is twenty years old, for Zeus' sake! Come on, there must be someone who can handle him.'

Tydeos ventured forward. Alexander threw my reins at him and stood on tiptoe to fasten the muzzle himself. The others watched, embarrassed but too afraid to help.

Alexander turned and eyed his audience. 'See? All he needs is a firm hand. But if I hear any of you has taken a whip to Bucephalas, or is not giving him the very best of care as befits a king's horse, you'll join the citizens of Thebes in chains. Understand?'

His voice was icy. Tydeos swallowed. The other grooms shuddered and stared at their feet. Even the muleteers who had gathered round to watch went pale, and it takes a lot to frighten them. Tydeos put a tentative hand on my neck. I tolerated this, because I knew his smell and I was very tired. He relaxed slightly and muttered something about taking me for a roll.

Alexander had already gone striding back through the camp. He was acting like the boss again, shouting orders as he went. I snorted at Tydeos and gave him a nudge with my nose to get him moving, because he was just standing there, looking round for Charm.

Eventually, Tydeos got me clean after a fashion, and settled me in the horse lines in my usual spot between Petasios and Borealis. He gave me too much barley in my nosebag, but it was better than too little. I tucked in, listening to groom-gossip and hoping Charm would come back soon and groom me properly.

But all I discovered were the details of the domination of Thebes, which upset some of our grooms so much they shed tears.

Theban prisoners: 30,000
Theban dead: 6,000
Macedonian dead: 500

Horses dead: 8 (sad, sad, sad, sad, sad, sad, sad, sad)

Thebans spared: 3 poets, 24 priests, and the wife of the Theban boss

We didn't even get to rename the city. Instead of another Alexandropolis, Thebes became a ruin with no name.

EIGHTH HOOFPRINT
TROY, SPRING 334 BC

Charm's scent

When we got home to Pella, Charm's scent was everywhere. It was in the corners of my stall where she used to sleep. It was on my grooming tools. And it was on the rakes and shovels she used to clean out my bedding.

I spent the first few days after we got back walking round and round my stable, licking all these places. I kept expecting her to open the door, chirrup to me, and do mutual grooming on my withers. But always it was one of the other grooms who came, usually Tydeos, who had got the job of looking after me after we'd dominated Thebes. I tolerated him because he was quiet around me. He didn't trust me enough to turn his back on me, though, and he was careful to put my muzzle on whenever he groomed me or took me out for my roll. Needless to say, I wouldn't let him anywhere NEAR my back.

The only person who rode me during that winter was Alexander. I know the grooms thought this strange, because they gave Tydeos sideways looks and teased him about not being able to ride as well as a girl, but I noticed they kept well away from me themselves. Tydeos breathed a sigh of relief that he wasn't expected to exercise me, and told me not to worry – Charm loved me too much to abandon me, and would come back once things had settled down.

While he fed me apples, Alexander pulled my ears and poured out all his worries about the Anatolian campaign. Don't ask me to tell you everything he said, because most of it was very complicated. The things I understood were:

Alexander desperately wants to prove it was King Philip who sired him. This is understandable, because it's good to know what herd you belong to. That's why he wants to get to Siwa in Egypt as soon as possible, so he can visit the oracle, a place where gods answer your questions.

Antipater is eager for Alexander to go (you know why!), and General Parmenio is waiting for him at the Hellespont with the rest of the one-eyed king's herd. But, despite all the treasure and slaves he took from Thebes, Alexander has a definite lack of gold coins, which all humans, including the soldiers of the Macedonian army, seem to want before they will do anything. (In my opinion, you humans should get rid of those silly coins. It would make your lives a lot simpler.)

My life that winter was just as complicated. Psylla came back to the stables, having weaned our beautiful black filly, which the grooms named Electra in memory of the gate where we had squealed at Thebes. So I had four mares – Aura, Psylla, Harpinna and Zephyr – to whinny at every morning and protect from the other stallions. Also, many youngsters were being broken on the riding ground. There were foolish displays of acting wild and squeal-challenges from the colts, which meant I had my work cut out, squealing and dominating dung, until the new generation learnt I was boss.

Things did not settle down – far from it! Spring brought lots of strangers, who unloaded strange-shaped packs from their mule carts. They talked in excited voices about all the things they were going to discover on their way to Egypt, and hung about the stables admiring us horses, until our grooms got fed up with them. Tydeos called them 'stupid scientists', and they must have been stupid because they were going with us into enemy territory without so much as a dagger to defend themselves.

The army started to parade again in the mornings, and Alexander rode me down to watch them. A HUGE white tent arrived for the king, which the men set up on the riverbank. It held a hundred couches, and they filled it with fancy rugs and lamps, then carried in tables groaning with food. Alexander held a party inside it, which went on all night and kept us horses awake.

After the party, the tent was taken down and packed carefully, along with all its furniture and fittings, into carts. Then one bright dawn, with the smell of new grass in the air, Alexander came to the stables dressed in his armour and travelling cloak, and we all formed up and clattered out of Pella, going east towards the rising sun.

Nothing in the world compares to leading an army! I pranced like a four-year-old and made myself huge. On my back, Alexander sat equally proud, his mane freshly washed and shining in the sun, a huge grin on his face.

This was our complete herd, in marching order:

ME, Bucephalas, carrying Alexander, King of Macedonia, Captain of the Hellenic League, the reborn Achilles!
Petasios, carrying Hephaestion.
Aura, carrying Demetrius.
Zephyr, carrying Philotas.
Apollo, carrying the battle-scarred Perdiccas.
Borealis, carrying Leonnatus.
Harpinna, carrying Ptolemy.
Psylla, carrying Hector.
Hades, carrying Iolaus.
1,800 Macedonian cavalry.
1,000 Thessalian cavalry.
100 mounted scouts on scruffy ponies.
600 Hellenic League cavalry on inferior Greek horses.
12,000 Macedonians with their long pikes.
2,000 Hellenic League hoplites.
1,000 archers and slingers.
2,000 troops from tribes we'd dominated in the mountains.
5,000 mercenaries (the only ones who have been paid, but don't tell the men or there'll be grumbling in the ranks).
Baggage train and mules at the back, where they belong.

We didn't take many supplies, since General Parmenio had organized food for the first part of our march. But all the scientists came with us, bringing their equipment, and we also had Alexander's big white pavilion and our siege engines. So we had more baggage than last time, for half the number of men. The only bad part was leaving Charm's scent behind.

At the queen's urging, Alexander left the other half of the army to guard the borders while we were gone. I expect he knows what he is doing. The Persians probably don't have a very big herd.

General Parmenio

When we reach the water that separates our world from the Anatolian world, we find the ships Athens promised us, ready and waiting to take us across. This proves that the Greeks have been well and truly dominated. We also find the one-eyed king's general and a herd of 12,000 battle-scarred Macedonians camped on the shore, along with many horses I have never smelt before. While I squeal a challenge to the strange stallions, Alexander orders the army to make camp and tells his Guard to follow him to General Parmenio's tent.

'You made good time, Alexander,' the General says, coming out with his breakfast in his hand and making a rough count of our herd. He takes another bite of his bread and honey. Still chewing, he walks round Alexander and his Guard, giving them the kind of calculating stare you humans give us horses when you're thinking about buying us. He pauses to adjust Zephyr's breast girth and greets his son Philotas with a slap on the thigh. Finally, he returns to Alexander, spits, and says, 'Bit old to ride into battle, that nag of yours, isn't he?'

I don't like the way this old general smells, so I give him flat ears. He has almost as many battle scars as me, and he is not very clean. A dark beard, currently full of crumbs, has been allowed to sprout on his chin, and his unlaced tunic shows hair on his chest. But he has big muscles, and he is quick. When his hand shoots out to grab my rein, it comes on my blind side. I rear up, striking out at him with my hooves. He lets go in surprise and steps back out of range.

Alexander's smile vanishes. His weight hardly shifted when I reared, and he runs a soothing hand down my neck.

'It's *King* Alexander in front of my men,' he says. 'And as you can see, there's nothing wrong with Bucephalas' battle sense. Take care, General, in case he thinks you're the enemy. He's not yet accustomed to your smell.'

General Parmenio grunts. 'I suppose he's the one all the grooms are scared of, the famous man-eater? Looks to me like he needs a man's firm hand. Better get him down to the horse lines and slap a muzzle on him. Then you can help me get these ships loaded, before King Darius sends his fleet up here to sink us all like stones in the Hellespont before we even get started.'

The Guard give the water worried looks.

I feel Alexander stiffen a little on my back. But he shakes his head and laughs.

'I don't see any Persian ships, do you, General? And I'm quite sure a commander of your years and experience doesn't need my help to supervise the crossing. I'm going to visit Troy, so I'll need some horse transports sent down to ferry my men across the Hellespont from Elaeum. See to it, will you?'

He feels the bit and nudges me with his knees so that I make myself huge, then deliberately rides me past the general so close that the older man has to step out of the way. From the corner of my good eye, I see him glare after Alexander. Philotas hesitates. But the rest of the Guard exchange grins as they follow us.

'That told him!' Leonnatus says, bringing Borealis up beside me. 'Good for you, Alex.'

'Are we still going to Troy?' Philotas asks. 'Father knows what he's talking about. Maybe it would be as well to stay with the rest of the troops, in case the Persian fleet does turn up?'

But Alexander laughs again and waves a hand at the shimmering water and the hazy shoreline beyond. 'He was trying to scare us, that's all. The Persian ships aren't here, even I can see that. Look! Over there lies Troy, the city of the *Iliad*! Don't you want to see the ancient ruins, Philo? Don't you want to stand where Achilles himself stood, and gaze over the hills at the land of legend?'

'All the same, it might be worth taking some of the cavalry with us, Alex,' Hephaestion says. 'Just in case.'

Alexander pulls me up, leans a hand on my quarters and turns to look at their anxious faces. 'Where's your sense of adventure, gentlemen? You're not turning weak-kneed on me before we've even set foot across the Hellespont, are you? Remember how we dealt with the Illyrians and the Thebans? We didn't need old Parmenio for that, did we? But I'm not stupid. I'll take 3,000 . . . no, make that 6,000 of the men with us. That make you feel better?'

Their faces relax, and they grin back at him. Even Philotas seems happier.

'Troy!' Iolaus breathes. 'Are we really going there, Alex? I can't believe it's a real place.'

Alexander gives the water a faraway look. 'It's real, all right. Don't worry so, gentlemen! Troy is friendly these days. General Parmenio knows that, or he wouldn't let us go. This might be the last time we have to ourselves until we get to Egypt. We're allowed a little fun before the fighting starts.'

Sacrifices at Troy

It was an easy march to Elaeum, with the members of the Guard laughing and joking as they used to do before Thebes.

While we waited for the ships to arrive, Alexander made a sacrifice to Zeus on the shore and prayed for victory over the Persians. Then our grooms loaded us up, and we set sail for another world.

We horses of the Guard were tethered on the deck of Alexander's ship, so we saw the bull he sacrificed halfway across. Its dying bellow made Psylla and Aura tremble, and we all flared our nostrils. Bulls are not horses, so we weren't sad, but to see an animal as big as a horse killed like that is not nice. Over the hot tang of the bull's blood was the salt smell of the sea, and with the stiff wind blowing up the Hellespont the ship rolled under our hooves and spray hit us in the face.

Charm would have understood my fear. But she still hadn't turned up.

By the time we landed at Troy, I was sweating and trembling like a two-year-old. Alexander didn't notice. He was too busy putting on all his armour and throwing his spear into the sand. What for, I don't know. Maybe he thought he saw an enemy lurking there. I've suspected for some time that his eyesight is even worse than mine. But his friends cheered, anyway, and we were finally led off the ships on to the beach, while Alexander performed yet another sacrifice to the gods.

I've worked out that there are three reasons why you humans do this barbaric thing to animals. You spill their blood and send their ghosts to the other world because you are:

a priest, and it is your job;
scared of something, and want the gods on your side;
relieved to be alive after a battle, and want to say 'thank you'.

108

Alexander was not a priest, and we had not been in a battle since Thebes. So, you tell me why Alexander made so many sacrifices at Troy!

A mouthful of curls

For a legendary city, Troy was rather disappointing. After everything Alexander had told me about it, while he pulled my ears and fed me apples back in Pella, I was expecting something more like Thebes (before we dominated it, that is). But the little town with its crumbling walls wasn't even as big as Alexander's first city Alexandropolis in the mountains of Thrace.

All the same, Alexander and his friends told our grooms to take us to the stables, then they rushed off to see the sights while the men posted sentries on the hills and made camp outside the walls. The men didn't seem too impressed with Troy, either. They grumbled about the detour and seemed worried someone might try to attack the king.

The stables were cramped and dark. There were no cobbles to massage our hooves, and the stall Tydeos put me in was filthy. I had to dominate several piles of stale dung before I could bear to take a single mouthful of my barley. The other horses were uneasy, too. They kept shooting up their heads and pricking their ears at the door, listening to the music and laughter coming from the town.

Tydeos and the other grooms settled us as best they could, then went off to find food for themselves. As it grew dark, there was still no sign of Alexander and his friends. Clearly we were going to be here all night.

I used the doorpost to scratch my sweaty neck where Tydeos had not groomed me properly, and resigned myself to sleeping standing up. I was missing Charm again, when two men crept into the passage and stopped outside my stall. At once, I recognized the disgraced horsemaster's smell coming from under the first one's dusty cloak. The other man had perfume in his beard and was holding his fancy robe up out of the dirt.

I gave them both flat ears to warn them not to touch me.

'That's the king's horse,' whispered the horsemaster, keeping a wary distance from me. 'An ugly brute, as you can see. Alexander rides him in every battle.'

'I'll get a description off to the Persians,' muttered the other. 'General Memnon's in charge of the Greek mercenary forces here in Anatolia – he'll pass it on. Then, even if your King Alexander refuses our gift of the Achilles armour, they'll still be able to target him on the battlefield.'

The horsemaster chuckled. 'Alexander will accept your gift, Priest, don't you worry. It'll appeal to his vanity.'

The priest smiled. 'Is it true he sleeps with a copy of the *Iliad* under his pillow?'

'That, and his dagger!' said the horsemaster with a frustrated look. 'Seems our young Alexander isn't quite so confident of his invincibility as he likes us all to think. I'd take the horse with me now, but I haven't a hope of getting away with the animal if it plays me up like it did at Thebes. Alexander's brought a small army with him to Troy!'

'Yes, that's a shame. Without them, we might try sending an assassin to cut his throat in the night. But you've got to be careful when dealing with Persian honour. King Darius has heard of your young king's exploits and wants to defeat him in the field, which is probably just as well. I certainly wouldn't want to be the one caught creeping into King Alexander's tent with a knife.'

The horsemaster drew his cloak closer and peered at the shadows. 'Where's Alexander now?'

'Still playing at being Achilles conquering Troy!' the priest said with a look of contempt. 'He'll soon find out real life isn't quite as easy as it seems in stories.'

'The Achilles armour was supposed to be magic, though, wasn't it?'

The priest laughed. 'All that stuff about it being made by the gods, you mean? It's been hanging in the temple of Troy for a thousand years, and it's as brittle as any other old armour, believe me. If your King Alexander is foolish enough to wear it in battle, the Persian spears will go through it as if it were papyrus. Does the horse have any markings on its legs?'

As the priest peered over my door I lunged at him and grabbed a mouthful of oiled curls before he stumbled back in alarm. 'Athene's flashing spear!' he exclaimed. 'The beast is mad!'

The horsemaster pulled a face. 'I warned you. That horse half killed me at Thebes, and it was responsible for me losing my job in Pella. When Alexander's no longer around, I'm going to teach the brute a lesson it won't forget. I've a score to settle with its little groom, too, if she ever turns up again.'

They left quickly after that. They knew better than to try to touch me again.

I chewed the mouthful of curls to see if they were edible. But they tasted disgusting, so I spat them out. Then I lifted my tail and dropped dung to get rid of my enemy's smell.

The Achilles armour

I am so glad to leave the Trojan stables the next morning, I drag Tydeos out into the street. He stumbles over a fork in

111

the narrow passage and lets go of me. The other grooms snigger, but the king and his Guard are coming, so they don't have time to tease him. Tydeos regains his feet, red-faced, brushes himself off and hurries to catch me. He sorts out my reins just in time – and gapes at Alexander in amazement.

All the grooms are staring. So are the people of Troy, who have lined the streets to see the young King of Macedonia who has come to drive the Persians out of their world. Our men hold them back with their pikes, but no one can stop them cheering and waving and throwing flowers. I prick my ears and stare at Alexander, too; I have never seen him look quite so fine.

He is wearing new armour. It glitters and flashes in the morning sunshine, surrounding him with a golden glow. At his shoulder, Demetrius carries a huge shield decorated with a gold and silver rim, the leather with its snake pattern dark and scarred where ancient blades have scratched it. Alexander's shins and thighs are covered with glittering greaves, and his breastplate is beautifully polished. On his head, he wears a helmet with two huge horsehair plumes bouncing on top. They are the colour of Apollo's mane and tail, a faded gold that shimmers white in the sun.

I look round to check Apollo still has his mane and tail. Then I snort at Alexander, extending my nose to sniff the unfamiliar armour.

He laughs as he takes my rein from Tydeos. 'See, gentlemen! Even Bucephalas thinks I look like Achilles!' As he taps my shoulder to let me know he wants to get on my back, ghosts flicker in the shadows behind me. I give his new armour flat ears and dance backwards.

He frowns at me and looks for Tydeos. 'What's wrong

with my horse this morning? You did stay with him last night as I ordered, didn't you?'

Tydeos goes red. 'Of course, Your Majesty. He's probably upset by the strange stable. Er . . . do you want me to boost you up, Your Majesty?'

Alexander scowls. 'Since when have I needed anyone to leg me up on my horse? Stand clear!'

He runs a hand down my neck and talks to me in a soothing voice, like he did the first time he rode me, until I lower my head and forget the ghosts. Then he holds out his hand for a spear, walks round to my other side, and uses it to vault on to me in a gleam of gold and white. With the plumes of his helmet flaring behind him like wings, he flies.

The crowd gives a great cheer as he lands lightly astride my cloth. Alexander gathers up my reins, then takes the big shield from Demetrius and settles it on his knee. He punches the air as I prance forwards. His friends laugh, take their horses from the grooms, and mount up. The people of Troy throw more flowers. The petals fall into our manes like snow. I toss my head and make myself huge.

It makes no difference to me if Alexander wants to wear the Achilles armour. I am strong enough to carry him, whatever he's wearing. I just hope Achilles' ghost has gone.

Ninth Hoofprint
RIVER GRANICUS, SPRING 334 BC

Liberating or dominating?

Not even a strong young human like Alexander can wear armour and carry a shield all the time. He would soon begin to smell bad, and shields get in the way. They're supposed to, of course – that's the whole point of shields. But what is useful in a battle can be a real pain on a march, believe me.

As soon as we were out of sight of Troy, Alexander appointed Demetrius his official shield-bearer, and stopped to take off the glittering Achilles armour and plumed helmet. He had them packed into the baggage cart with the spare weapons and put on his cloak and hat instead. Then we rejoined the rest of the army.

For a while, it was rather dull, just a long trek with no galloping. We dominated all the towns and cities on our route without a blow being struck. Alexander and General Parmenio claimed we were 'liberating' them, but I can't see there was

114

much difference, except that we didn't get to rename any of them, which was a pity, if you ask me.

Percote – already dominated by the one-eyed king, like Troy.

Lampsacus – refused to let us in, but paid us to leave them alone.

Colonae – refused to let us in, didn't even pay.

Priapus – opened the gates to let us in, no fighting.

Zeleia – refused to let us in.

I'm not entirely sure that marching past the ones who wouldn't let us in without a fight counts as dominating them. But you humans have your own ideas, and Alexander was anxious to get on. After every town, he leapt on to my back and urged his Guard and the cavalry on the road again, leaving General Parmenio to follow with the rest of the army, and the baggage train trailing far behind.

'This is easy!' he said as we left Zeleia. 'I can't think why my father had so much trouble.'

Hephaestion smiled. 'Maybe they've all heard what you did to Thebes.'

But Philotas muttered, 'Father says the Persians will try to stop us soon. They're probably waiting for us around the next bend.'

The others laughed and said the Persians were obviously too scared to face us.

But Philotas was right this time.

When the phalanx did not follow

We find the Persian army on the other side of a deep river called the Granicus. Like most rivers at this time of the year, it is in full flood. The shadows under the bank are long in the afternoon sun. I can hear strange horses whinnying nearby. Sounds like a big herd.

Alexander's heart beats faster. Though it is late in the day, he orders his men to prepare for battle and rides me forward for a closer look. I arch my neck and play with my bit while he squints at the fast-flowing river, the steep bank and the line of enemy spears dark against the sky.

'Oh Zeus, Bucephalas,' he whispers, running a sweaty hand down my neck. 'This isn't going to be easy.' Then he shakes himself and smiles. 'You'll just have to swim for me like you did at the Danube. Remember, I'm Achilles and you're my immortal horse. We're not going to die today.'

General Parmenio, however, has a different view. When Alexander rides me back to the arms wagon and starts strapping on the glittering armour he took from Troy, the general strides across and seizes his wrist.

'What do you think you're doing, Alexander?' he growls. 'What's with the fancy helmet? You're not seriously thinking of wearing that armour into battle, are you? It must be a thousand years old! It'll shatter at the first spear thrust.'

Alexander snatches his wrist free, and glowers at the general. 'It's *Achilles*' armour. It was made by the gods, so it will never shatter. I must look my best when we meet the Persians.'

'So, you're going to wear it all night, are you?' Parmenio snorts down his nose like a horse. 'Up to you.'

'I am not going to wear it all night,' Alexander says with dangerous calm, 'because we'll have beaten the Persians by then. We're going to attack across the river as soon as the men are ready.'

General Parmenio gives him a disbelieving stare. 'Are you crazy? It'll be dark soon! That river's a deathtrap. They'll massacre us before we even get up the bank. The phalanx is crippled in such situations, you know that. We have to meet the Persians on open ground. We need to wait for the baggage train to catch up, make camp and decide on the best plan of attack for the morning. They won't come across here, don't you worry. And I can tell you right now what we should do. We should send out scouts to find another crossing place. Then when it's dark enough, we can leave our campfires burning and take the men quietly across the river out of sight of the Persians, get behind them and engage them in battle tomorrow on the plain on the other side. *Then* we might have a chance of beating them.'

'No,' Alexander says, putting on his plumed helmet. 'I'm going to finish the Persians now.'

The general's face hardens, and he says in a low tone, 'If you don't listen to me, Alexander, you're not going to be king for long. I've been commanding armies longer than you've been alive, and most of these men have been fighting at my side just as long. I'm warning you now, if you try to lead the army across that river tonight, they won't follow you.'

Alexander's hands pause on the fastening of the helmet. He says, very quietly, 'Is that a threat, General?'

The general shakes his head, impatient. 'No, it's not a threat! It's the truth, and you know it as well as I do. Think for a moment! We all know how brave you are. But the Persians will still be there in the morning, and so will their treasure. Across the river on the plain, where we'll win the day with minimum losses.'

Tydeos, who is holding me nearby and looking as if he

would rather be somewhere else, shuffles his feet. But generals and kings ignore grooms the way horses ignore mules. The argument continues, with Alexander's voice getting shriller and General Parmenio's face becoming redder and redder.

Finally, Alexander marches across to me and snatches my rein from Tydeos. 'Enough! I've already told the men we're going to attack. I can't suddenly change my mind now. While we stand here arguing, the light's going. Get the phalanx ready, General. Since you seem so scared of the enemy, I'll take the cavalry across first. They'll follow me.'

General Parmenio looks alarmed. 'Cavalry against an infantry blockade? That's just *stupid*—'

But Alexander is already on my back, and we're galloping to join the others, his helmet plumes pale against the darkening sky. He mutters under his breath as we go. 'Thinks he commands the army . . . I'll show him . . . can't let the men think I'm scared – oh curses, Bucephalas, why does he have to be so *right?*' But no one hears this except me, and he is shining with energy as he always is before a battle.

The Guard cheer as he joins them, and the rest of the cavalry form up behind in a jangle of bits and spears. Alexander doesn't wait to see if General Parmenio is obeying his order, but cries, 'Follow me, gentlemen! King Darius is waiting!' and we lead our cheering herd at a gallop into the river.

The water isn't as cold as the Danube. But the current is worse. *Much* worse. I am struggling to keep straight, and some of the smaller horses get washed downstream. I see Aura swimming valiantly behind me, at an angle to the current, her dappled neck twisted with effort. Psylla's in trouble, and little Hades is in danger of whirling away into the shadows with Iolaus clinging pale-faced to his mane. Borealis sees this and swims beside him, pushing him back upstream with his bulk. Zephyr is all right, and so are Apollo and Harpinna. Petasios stays next to me all the way, his nostrils flaring and his eyes rolling. We nine are still together when we reach the shallows on the other side and splash out of the water in a huge spray, yelling the Macedonian war cry.

'ALALALAI! ALALALALAI! ALALALALAI!'

The enemy boss gives a shout, too, and javelins rain down on our heads from the overhanging bank, many finding their mark. Several men fall off their horses and splash into the water. Hephaestion gives an anguished cry.

'Hector's hit!'

I see Psylla struggling in the mud behind me, riderless. Hector floats in the river, face-down, blood swirling around him and a javelin stuck in his back. Iolaus urges Hades across, screaming for his friend to get up. But Psylla's rider will never sit on her back again. His ghost has already gone, and the current is carrying his body downstream. Poor Psylla! Frightened to be alone, she rolls her eyes and whinnies at us not to leave her behind.

'Keep together!' Philotas yells. 'Iolaus! Get back here! Alex, we have to go back. *Now*! Father's right. This is a deathtrap. *The phalanx isn't following us!*'

Only one line of foot-soldiers has ventured into the river, struggling to swim against the current. The rest of the army are still formed up in neat squares on the far bank, watching the fight from a safe distance. This is NOT GOOD. We are vastly outnumbered. We can't get up the bank because of the enemy's spears and the overhang, and our backs are to the river. That's the only way to go. Sometimes you have to run from a battle if you want to fight another day.

But Alexander is now close enough to see the designs on the enemy's shields, and his hand tightens on my rein. 'Those are *Greeks* up there!' he hisses. 'Greek mercenaries, fighting for the Persians against me! I'm not running from them!'

Philotas shakes his head. 'If you want to get yourself killed, that's up to you. I'm taking the men back before we get massacred.'

Alexander glares at him. But this is no time to divide our herd, and he knows it. I whinny to Psylla, warning her to stay close. As we begin the retreat, another volley of javelins comes down from the bank, but I leap to avoid them.

Then I smell strange horses coming out of the shadows.

I squeal a challenge as they charge us from both sides. They are small and dainty, their bridles are decorated with silly tassels, and they carry their tails stupidly high. But they are fast and light-footed in the mud. One of the yellow-turbaned riders gallops straight at us, and a javelin flies out of his hand towards Alexander's throat. I whirl out of the way, but my hooves slip on the steep bank. Demetrius raises the Achilles shield. The point goes right through it and pierces Alexander's glittering armour.

He gasps in shock and goes white. A wave of shame comes over me as I regain my balance. If he falls off me like Hector did off Psylla . . . but he plucks out the javelin, pushes Demetrius aside, and turns me to face the Persian who threw it. We horses squeal and snap at one another, while Alexander thrusts his spear into the enemy's chest with a cry of rage.

Hephaestion and Petasios are fighting at my side. I see Harpinna biting and kicking with the same fury she showed in Illyria, and another Persian taking a swipe at Aura's beautiful head with his spear as Demetrius struggles with the shield. She rears and knocks the weapon out of his hand with her neat hooves. Ha! That's my mare!

Our Persian is not yet dominated, though. The spear snapped on his breastplate, so he is only bruised. He draws his curved sword and bares his teeth. 'You are going to die today, King Iskander,' he calls with a strange accent that makes Alexander's name sound different. 'Your armour looks very splendid, but it seems remarkably old for a battle.'

'This is Achilles' own armour, made by the gods!' Alexander shouts back. 'It'll protect me even if it's broken. Where's your King Darius? Is he a coward, to hide behind his Greek mercenaries? Why doesn't he come down here and fight me himself?'

The Persian smiles. 'The Great King sent us to finish you off. He's got more important things to do than cross spears with a half-grown boy playing at leading his father's army.'

Alexander's face flushes, and his whole body trembles with anger. He ducks the long sword, and jabs his broken spear shaft into the Persian's mocking smile. The silly Persian horse rears, and its rider falls off backwards over its tail. I grab one of its stupid tassels in my teeth and it gallops away, snorting in fear.

Ha! Dominated!

But another Persian has sneaked up on my blind side; I don't see him until he brings his sword down on top of Alexander's plumed helmet. The shock goes right through me, and half the helmet splashes into the river behind us. I feel Alexander's weight sway dangerously, and have to stand still until he regains his balance. He has his sword out now. There is a ringing of blades before Alexander scores a cut to the Persian's throat and sends him thudding into the mud at our feet.

I don't even have time to dominate the enemy horse.

Hephaestion yells, 'Alex, *look out!*' And behind us, yet another Persian sabre flashes down.

I leap forward, my hooves sliding in the mud. The blade misses Alexander's exposed head by a hair's breadth. One of the older cavalrymen, Commander Cleitus, bravely gets between us and chops off the Persian's arm.

Petasios gallops up beside us with flat ears. Hephaestion has lots of little cuts, and his sword drips with Persian blood. 'We've got to get out of here, Alex!' he shouts above the noise of the battle. 'Philo's right, this is crazy. It's getting dark. I can't see a thing under this bank. Alex – what's wrong? Oh, Zeus, you're wounded! Your head's bleeding—'

Alexander's hand loosens on my rein. I feel his weight slide again, but this time there is nothing I can do to keep him on my back. He slips over my shoulder and crumples, groaning, into the mud.

Philotas mutters a curse and yells for the surviving members of the Guard. They crowd round to keep the Persians away, while Hephaestion jumps off Petasios and tries to make the king get up. I immediately settle to my knees in the mud so my wounded rider can get on my back again. But there is such a fight going on around him, I can't even see him any more. And while I am on my knees, two Persians ride their horses straight at me and drop a noose around my neck. Before I can get to my feet, one of them has the cheek to leap on to my back and grab my reins!

I surge to my feet with an outraged squeal, but the noose tightens around my neck, half choking me. The man on my back clings tightly, and a third Persian rides his horse up behind me and brings the flat of his sword down across my quarters. It stings like crazy. I squeal again in anger and go up on my hind legs, striking out at their horses with my hooves and trying to bite their riders. Soon we are struggling as furiously as Alexander's Guard is around the groaning king. But whatever I do, the Persians keep forcing me further away from Alexander.

We are struggling on the riverbank. It is so dark I can't see the edge. The rope tangles around my legs, and suddenly I am in the water, upside down. The Persian on my back slides off me with a curse and splashes towards the bank. But my legs are still tangled up in rope and leather, and though I fight like mad, the current takes me.

I whinny desperately to my herd. I hear Petasios whinny faintly in reply. But he has to keep Hephaestion alive, so he can't help me. It is all I can do to keep my head above the water. My heart bursts with shame when I think of Alexander lying in the mud.

My rider, hurt and helpless, without me.

At some stage, my cloth comes off. But I am too exhausted to break the ropes, and the river is very strong. As my struggles weaken, its current carries me further and further downstream, away from the battle into the night of a strange world.

Groom in a dress

In the end, the noose saves me. The rope snags around a tree root and holds me fast against the bank, where the river forms a pool. As I lie there with my nostrils just above the water and my breath wheezing against the tight rope, I smell our Macedonian army. The whole phalanx is moving downriver, a dark mass of men without lights, just as General Parmenio planned. I struggle afresh and whinny hopefully to my herd, but the only horses with them are Greek ones of the Hellenic

League. They are too stupid to know it is me.

The last of them pass, and I lie half in and half out of the water, giving little hopeful whinnies into the night. Even a mule would be welcome, but there is no sign of the baggage train. I keep hoping Alexander will come and find me. Then the smell of the river reminds me of how I let him get wounded, and I feel ashamed all over again.

I grow shivery and cold. I think I hear more horses on the other side of the river, a huge herd of them going down the Persian side. But I am too exhausted to whinny very loudly, and they don't hear me. Everything fades away, and I drift in black clouds of ghosts.

I am about to go with them when a familiar smell tugs me back. It makes me remember being warm and clean and well fed. I can almost feel Charm's fingers mutual grooming my withers. At first, I can't work out where I am. Then I feel the cold water around me, and start to struggle again.

'Steady, Bucephalas, steady, it's me.'

Gentle hands loosen the noose.

It sounds so much like her voice whispering in my ear, a little nicker of greeting escapes me.

'Oh, Bucephalas.' Charm's voice chokes. 'Oh, horse . . . please wake up! I couldn't bear to lose you!'

I open my eyes. It is her. It IS!

Her hair has grown longer and is twisted in a scarf. She wears a cloak of patterned wool over a woman's dress with a muddy, torn hem. But she smells just the same. Sweet, like spring grass. She pulls a dagger from her girdle and cuts the tangle of rope and leather that is keeping me prisoner. I scramble up the bank, and she runs her hands all over me, laughing in relief.

'Oh, Bucephalas! If you knew how frightened I was for you! I came as fast as I could. But what have you done with Alexander? Did they kill him, like in my dream? Though you're still alive, so maybe Alexander is, too. In my dream, I saw you both fall together . . . I promise I won't leave you again, no matter what the king does to me.'

We find the baggage train camped near to where Alexander squealed at General Parmenio before we crossed the river to meet the enemy. The scientists look up from their breakfast and stare at us. It's Charm they are staring at, sitting astride me in her dress. I am so bedraggled from my night in the river, they obviously don't recognize me.

She takes me to the horse lines, and my heart lifts as I recognize Aura's smell. Though my mare is not around, her dung is quite fresh. I trot about with my nose to the ground, sniffing other piles. Petasios, Borealis, Zephyr, Apollo . . . Harpinna . . . Hades . . . Psylla. I stop sniffing and snort in relief, which brings Tydeos rushing out to meet us.

'Bucephalas!' he gasps, so busy examining me for injuries that he doesn't recognize Charm. 'Wherever did you find him? Hey, how come you're riding him? He never usually lets anyone but King Alexander or his groom on his back—' As he looks properly at Charm for the first time, his mouth drops open.

Charm smiles. 'Don't you recognize me, Tydeos?'

Tydeos' face goes slack with astonishment. '*Charmides!* So Alexander wasn't joking – you *are* a girl! And you're . . . you're beautiful.'

'Don't be stupid,' Charm says, flushing as she slides off me. 'I'm just the same as I always was. Help me see to Bucephalas. He's had a bad time of it in the river. I think he's all right, but that cut on his quarters needs treating, and he'll want a warm barley mash and a good rub down.' She works on me as she speaks.

'B-but where have you *been* all this time? How did you get here? And how did you find Bucephalas? The king was so upset last night, you wouldn't believe! And he was so sick from that blow to his head, he could hardly walk straight, but he still rode off into battle this morning. He'll be pleased you're back.'

Charm mumbles something about helping the cooks in General Parmenio's camp and following the army in the baggage train. Then she frowns at the river. 'You said he's fighting again?'

Tydeos finally stops staring at her and grins. 'No one could stop him! Took the cavalry across as soon as it got light enough to see the water. The Persians decamped in the night, leaving their Greek mercenaries to hold us up here. They must have thought King Alexander was finished. When they realized he wasn't dead, they sent a herald across to beg for mercy, but King Alexander was so angry about them fighting on the Persian side, he wouldn't give them any. Did you see General Parmenio on your way upriver? He took the rest of the army off in the night.'

Charm shakes her head. 'Maybe he's found the Persians.'

By now, the other grooms have noticed I am back. They crowd round, all talking at once.

'Hey, Charmides! Is that really you?'

'Nice dress!'

'Where've you bin all winter?'

'The king wasn't half furious with you at Thebes!'

'You'll be for it when he gets back, all right!'

And a lot more rubbish of the same sort. Grooms do so like to gossip.

Charm ignores them and carries on tending my cut. She glances up at Tydeos, and he gives her a quick smile. 'I'll get his mash ready,' he says, and hurries off to boil water.

With Charm's gentle care I soon start to feel better, and give the other grooms flat ears until they drift back to their work. They keep glancing at Charm, though, and whispering about her being a girl.

I don't see what the problem is. Mares go into battle and still have healthy foals. But you humans seem to think your females are good for nothing but breeding, and won't even let them be grooms. This is clearly stupid, because Charm is a good groom, and anyway she's not in foal.

Charm's dream comes true

I am digesting my mash and flicking flies away with my tail, when Charm comes rushing back to the horse lines. She has changed her dress for a groom's tunic, and in the daylight I see that her scarf, which she's used to tie back her mane, is red.

I nicker to her, hoping for some mutual grooming. But she pushes my nose away and starts to put on my bridle. Her hands are trembling. I throw up my head and begin to shiver. The sounds of the battle across the river are faint, but Charm's tension upsets me.

'Oh, Bucephalas! Stop it. You know I can't reach when you do that.' Charm makes another attempt to get the bit in, and this time I lower my head and open my mouth for her. 'I'm sorry, horse,' she whispers, doing up the straps. 'But in my dream – when I saw the horse killed under Alexander, and he got killed too – it wasn't dark, like the grooms say it was when Alexander fell off you last night. It was daylight! Oh, I hope we're not too late!'

She struggles up on to my back. She's lost a bit of fitness, but she is desperate enough to make it. Then she heads me out of the camp towards the river. A sentry calls after her. But she calls back, 'Spare horse for the king!' and urges me into a gallop before he can send anyone after her.

She wants me to swim the River Granicus AGAIN.

I hesitate as I remember what happened last time. But Charm whispers to me and strokes my neck until I jump in. It is not so bad this time. Charm is lighter than Alexander, and there are no Greek spears coming down at us from the top of the far bank.

The screams and Macedonian war cries ahead of us fill me with nervous energy. I bound up a steep path and emerge in the sun on the enemy's side of the river, where the noise hits us.

The Greek mercenaries are trapped on a small hill in a defensive circle with their spears pointing outwards, while our cavalry gallop around them. Alexander is leading a charge barely twenty strides away from us, and doesn't see me. He is riding Psylla. She looks very tired. But the little mare carries him valiantly into the hedge of spears, and the others close around her, fighting furiously. A lot of the Greeks seem to be dead, but the survivors are not giving up.

Charm tightens her hands on my reins. 'Someone warn the king!' she shouts. 'They're going to kill his horse!'

I prance and shake my head, impatient to join the herd. That should be *me* at the front carrying Alexander, not little Psylla.

Charm holds me back, still shouting warnings. But her voice is small in the noise of the battle. Everyone is fighting so hard, no one notices us. 'We'll have to get closer,' she mutters, and loosens my rein.

It is what I have been waiting for. My legs fly over the ground to catch up with the others. Charm clings to my mane. She's dropped the reins, so there is nothing to support me, and I stumble slightly. But I soon find my feet again and gallop on. Oh, the joy! Oh, the excitement! I can see Aura up at the front of the herd, just behind Psylla, her rider Demetrius carrying the big shield of Achilles, which has been patched where it got pierced by the Persian spear. I flatten my ears as I pass the stragglers at the back, and one of the older cavalry-men finally notices Charm.

'What the—?'

'It's a crazy *girl*! Get back to camp, you idiot! Do you want to die?'

Charm is very pale. She hasn't a hope of stopping me now, and she knows it. I have the bit between my teeth, metal discs and all. I barge past more horses, and now it is just the Guard ahead of me. Zephyr's yellow tail whips my face as I whinny loudly to tell them I'm back.

Charm shouts at Philotas, 'You have to tell the king to retreat! They're going to— *no!*'

A horse falls in front of us. It's Psylla. She's going so fast that she rolls right over, kicks once and lies still. Her ghost ripples past my nose. I neigh at it, but it doesn't come back. Two spears are sticking out of her chest.

The others pull up in a confusion of shouts and flashing swords. We horses snort over poor Psylla, while our riders battle the Greeks. Alexander shakes his head, dazed, and gets to his feet. He was thrown clear, several paces behind where Psylla lies dead. But he's wearing a good helmet today, not the plumed one the Persians cracked last night. He looks more angry than hurt.

'Alex!' Hephaestion yells, springing off Petasios. 'Take my horse. I'll find another.'

With a huge whinny, I barge through the others, nipping them and giving them flat ears until I reach my rider. I settle down to my knees, forgetting Charm is still on my back, and whinny to him again.

The Greeks are fighting for their lives, but Alexander has eyes only for me and Charm. She has caught her balance and is leaning backwards, her feet almost on the ground. She seems frozen with terror.

Then she steps off me, throws my reins to Alexander and gasps, 'I've brought your horse, Your Majesty!'

Hephaestion recovers first. 'Don't just stand there, Alex!' he yells. Grabbing Charm's wrist, he throws her up on Petasios' back and leaps up behind her. 'I'll see your groom to safety.' Petasios gallops off towards the river, carrying his double burden easily.

Alexander does not hesitate. He springs on to my back and gathers up my reins with a firm hand. 'Bucephalas . . .' he whispers in a choked voice as I rise to my feet. 'Bucephalas, old horse, don't ever, *ever* scare me like that again.' He gives my neck a quick, trembling stroke. Then he punches the air with his spear and shouts for his Guard.

We are together again. Alexander's energy flows into me, and mine into him, until we shine. I make myself huge with pride. But the battle is already over.

While Charm and Alexander were staring at each other,

the boss of the Greeks broke out of the trap and fled with some of his men. It doesn't take the others long to throw down their weapons and surrender. Alexander gives poor Psylla a regretful look, and leads the Guard back to the river.

We find Charm sitting on the bank, hugging her knees and shivering. When she sees us coming, she leaps to her feet, fists clenched. Alexander dismounts, pulls off his helmet and leads me across to her. The others hang back tactfully, keeping a good look out for Persians. I nicker to Charm, and her lips tremble. But she doesn't move.

'Another dream, Charmides?' Alexander asks in a weary tone.

She bites her lip. 'Yes, Your Majesty.'

'I told you back in Thrace, you really should try to tell me *before* we meet the enemy. It would make things a lot easier for both of us.'

She gives him an uncertain look and lowers her eyes. 'I . . . yes, Your Majesty. I'm sorry. I came as fast as I could. But I was in the baggage train, and you were already fighting before we got here.'

'You were in my baggage train all this time? What were you doing?'

'Helping General Parmenio's cooks, Your Majesty.' Her voice is a whisper.

'Did he know you used to be my groom?'

She shakes her head.

'All right, I'll sort it out.' He frowns, and asks in a softer tone, 'What's your real name, Charmides?'

She goes rigid and whispers, 'Charmeia.'

'Charmeia, of course.' He shakes his head and smiles. 'It's no good, I just can't see you as a girl. I'll have to keep calling you Charmides. So you ran away at Thebes, but you came back to save my horse's life?'

'Yes, Your Majesty.' Even with my sharp ears, I can barely hear her.

He nods. 'Good enough. But I've told you before – if you're going to be Bucephalas' groom you'll have to learn to be less formal. I can't put up with "Your Majesty" all the way to Egypt.'

Charm looks up, her eyes bright. 'I can still be your groom? You're not angry with me?'

Alexander glances at the Guard, who are watching him and Charm with little wondering smiles, and sighs. 'No one else looks after Bucephalas as well as you do, and my official seer doesn't have dreams half as useful as yours. You're wasted as a cook. I need you. We can talk about this later. I've a lot to do. I've got to find old Parmenio, for one.'

Charm fights a grin. She straightens her face and says, 'The other grooms think he is downriver fighting the Persians, Alexander Sir!'

'Well then, I expect he is.' He looks at the line of Greek prisoners being escorted from the hillside littered with their dead, and smiles again. 'You grooms always seem to know more about what's going on than I do.'

A splendid victory

Charm was sent back to the camp with an escort, while the foot-soldiers who had stayed with Alexander remained behind to burn the Greek dead. We cavalry trotted down the Persian side of the river and found their camp guarded only by old men and boys. Persians travel with even more baggage than we do! Alexander paused to load up their carts with golden cups, fancy carpets and glittering shields from the tents. Then we went to find the rest of our army.

Before long, we horses caught the unmistakable battle-smell of sweat and blood. Small herds of Persians came galloping towards us, looking over their shoulders. They panicked when they saw us and scattered into the trees. Alexander smiled grimly and pressed on, not bothering to chase them.

We found General Parmenio striding through flattened, blood-spattered corn, barking out orders. But he was merely telling his men to collect up the dead and catch the loose horses. I squealed a challenge, and finally some of the men noticed us. They stared in amazement at our triumphant cavalry, the treasure piled in the Persian carts, and the line of Greek prisoners stumbling along behind us. Alexander took off his helmet to let his sweaty mane dry in the sun, and sat up straighter. A hasty trumpet blared out, and someone called in a loud voice:

'The *king*! The king is back!'

The others dropped what they were doing and rushed to see if it was true. At once, they began cheering and calling to Alexander. Although I was getting a bit tired, I arched my neck and made myself huge.

General Parmenio looked round to see what all the fuss was about. He went quite still when he saw us. Alexander rode me right up to him, the Guard following – except Psylla and Hector, of course. Their absence was like a hole in my cloth, not that I was wearing any kind of cloth that day, because Charm had not stopped to put one on me before she rode me into the battle.

Alexander halted me, and I champed at my bit while my

rider looked down at the general. The men fell silent to hear what he would say.

'I see you've dealt admirably well with the Persians as I ordered, General,' Alexander called out in a clear voice. 'As you can see, we have dealt with the Greek mercenaries. These prisoners are to be put in chains and sent back to Macedonia to work the mines, as an example to all Greeks who think it's clever to join with the enemy and fight against me.'

He looked at the Hellenic League troops, who were the only ones who didn't cheer when they saw us, and stared at General Parmenio in a very challenging way. If they were stallions, they would have been making squealing threats by now.

But the general was wise and said nothing.

Alexander nudged me with his knees until I took another step forward. He then leant down and hissed so quietly that only General Parmenio and I could hear, 'And if you *ever* leave me to face the enemy alone like that again, old man, you and all your officers will be joining them. Understand?'

The general went pale. He nodded, glanced at his son Philotas, and said in his loud voice, 'I'm glad you approved of my battle plan, King Alexander. Your brave charge across the river last night won us time to cross and get behind them. Congratulations on your splendid victory over the Persians!'

Alexander nodded and smiled, and the army broke into wild cheering. They thought the king and the general had been working together all along. But before we left, I gave General Parmenio flat ears to remind him he had been dominated.

Mourning Psylla

There were several changes after our first battle with the Persians in the other world. Charm being my personal groom again was by far the best, of course. But here's what else happened.

Zephyr and Philotas left the Guard to command another part of the army. Alexander said it was a promotion, but he told me he had sent Philotas away because he'd defied him at the Granicus. It is often better to let a troublesome rival lead his own little band; then he will be too busy to challenge for leadership of the herd.

Two new horses joined us to replace Psylla and Zephyr: Arion, the grey stallion who had fought with us in Illyria, carrying Attalus; and Xanthus, a big stallion the colour of ripe corn with dark legs. Xanthus dared to give me flat ears and a squeal, so I had to bite his nose to put him in his place. He might be big, but he's a very inferior breed. His rider is called Craterus.

All the cities that had closed their gates to us very quickly opened them and sent us treasure in apology, so we left the Hellenic League troops behind to look after them.

The men got paid out of the Persian gold. This meant another all-night party in the king's pavilion, much singing and drinking of magic in the camp, and no sleep for us horses.

Before we broke camp, Alexander ordered that all the horses of the Guard should have their manes cut off in mourning for Psylla and Hector. Silky hair fell to the ground in waves: white from Aura, pale gold from Apollo, red from Petasios and Harpinna, yellow from Zephyr, brown from Borealis, black from Hades. Apollo kicked up a bit of a fuss, but when I nipped him, he snorted and stood still.

Not even Charm dared touch *my* mane.

I don't know about General Parmenio's battle with the Persians, because I wasn't there. But our battle against the

Greek mercenaries went like this:

> *Greek dead*: 3,000.
> *Greek prisoners in chains for the mines*: 2,000.
> *Macedonian dead from Alexander's command*: 70, including Hector of the Guard.
> *Horses dead*: 3, including poor Psylla. (SAD!!!)

It might have taken us two days and three battles, but in the end the Persians and the Greek mercenaries who fought against us at the River Granicus were well and truly dominated. Ha!

TENTH HOOFPRINT
HALICARNASSUS, 334 BC

Honey cakes at Alinda

No one tried to stop us on our way south from the River Granicus, and the weather was good so we marched fast. Alexander wanted to dominate the boss of the Greek mercenaries, who had run away from the battle and taken refuge in a big city further down the coast. Alexander knew very well the Greek boss was called General Memnon, but he called him a traitor, a Persian-slipper-licking slave, and a lot of less polite things besides. On the way, we dominated two smaller cities with no trouble:

> Ephesus – no fighting, since the Greek mercenaries defending the garrison ran away when they saw us coming. A pretty place, so Alexander and I had our portrait painted there, while General Parmenio went to liberate the surrounding towns.

Miletus – squealed a bit, but not strong enough to keep us out. Its Greek mercenaries changed sides and joined our herd when Alexander gave them the choice between death and dishonour. (That's mercenaries for you.)

Hephaestion laughed and said at this rate we'd liberate Anatolia before winter. But Alexander pulled a face. 'We haven't achieved anything yet. Memnon's holed up in Halicarnassus with the Persian fleet, and King Darius won't come out and face me. By all reports, he's hiding in Persia. He pays Greeks to fight his battles, while he directs the war from the luxury of his own palace! And they call *him* "Great King"? Yet I, who have fought in the front line of battle since I was sixteen years old, must struggle every single day to prove I'm good enough to lead my own army!'

His fist clenched on my rein, and Hephaestion laid a gentle hand over it. 'Alex, of course you're good enough. The men love you – they'll follow you anywhere. What happened back at the Granicus was just old Parmenio trying to hang on to his power. His troops hadn't seen you in battle, remember? They probably thought the news of your conquests in Greece was exaggerated. But they know now how brave and strong you are, and that you'll always be the first into the fight, no matter what the odds. That makes a difference to soldiers. You should have seen their faces when you cheated death at the Granicus, then rode on to the battlefield with your prisoners in chains and all that Persian treasure! They'll follow you against Memnon next time, don't you worry!'

'I did see their faces,' Alexander said with a smile. 'I was there, remember? But I've got an idea how we might capture Halicarnassus without another messy battle. Come on, my friend, we're going to visit a queen!'

Alexander's idea was to visit Queen Ada, who used to be boss of Halicarnassus before the Persians dominated her, and persuade her to give him detailed plans of the city together with all the weak points in its walls. He sent General Parmenio on ahead to start the siege, while we Guard and the rest of the cavalry took a detour into the mountains to visit her stronghold of Alinda.

He was clever enough to send Queen Ada some friendly nickers and whinnies on rolls of flattened grass, so by the time we arrived she was waiting eagerly to meet us at the gates of her fortress. Alexander's energy and smile did the rest.

The queen kissed Alexander on the cheek, called him her darling boy, and promised he would inherit her throne after her death if he chased Memnon and the Persians out of Halicarnassus for her. Meanwhile, Charm and Tydeos led us horses into the stables. They were rather cramped and dark, and I resigned myself to another uncomfortable night. But later, a girl-filly came down from the kitchens with a basket smelling of warm honey. We pricked our ears in interest as she lugged it up to our grooms and pulled back the cloth.

'Queen Ada sent these cakes for you,' she said. 'King Alexander said to be sure to give one to his horse.' She looked sideways at me and giggled. 'I wouldn't, though, if I were you. They're much too good to waste on horses!' She snatched one from the top and crammed it into her mouth as she ran off.

Fortunately, Charm took no notice of the silly girl-filly and brought me a whole handful of honey cakes. They tasted as good as they smelt. As Charm fed them to me, she whispered, 'I like Queen Ada already, but Alexander's sure to rush off to Halicarnassus just as soon as he's got all the information he needs . . . oh, Bucephalas! How much further? He says that after we've finished liberating all the cities here in Anatolia, we're going to Egypt. That's such a long way, I can't even *imagine* it. And the Persian army is still around somewhere. I couldn't bear it if he rode you into another big battle like the one at the river Granicus, I just couldn't.'

I nudged her to give me the last cake, and she laughed as I licked her hand clean of sticky crumbs. 'You silly brute! All you think of is your stomach. That, and fighting over mares! It must be nice to be a horse. You've no worries at all, have you?'

Which only goes to show how little you humans know about us.

Squealing at Halicarnassus

From the start, I suspect Halicarnassus will be no fun. As we draw rein at the top of the hill and look down on the city and its harbour, the wind blows hot and dry through my coat. A few yellow stalks under my hooves are all I can see to eat. The city has plenty of gardens inside, but out here is just white rock, sun-shrivelled grass, and turquoise sea.

'Queen Ada wasn't joking about that ditch, Hephaestion,' Alexander whispers, pointing to a deep, wide trench encircling the high walls. 'It's going to be difficult to get our siege machines close enough. The men will have to fill it in, I suppose, and that'll take ages. Look at all those guard towers! Just as well she gave us the plans, or I wouldn't know where to start. And the Persian fleet's still in the harbour. I just hope old Parmenio's managed to get the transports through.'

'I don't see any of our siege equipment, Alex.' Hephaestion leans on Petasios' withers and studies General Parmenio's herd, which is camped outside the east gate of the city.

Alexander squints at the camp, too. He is in a good mood after Queen Ada's honey cakes, so he doesn't get angry. 'Maybe he hasn't unloaded it yet. He's probably waiting for me to tell him what to do. Come on, gentlemen! Let's get a closer look at those walls. I want to know the worst!'

The Greek mercenaries defending Halicarnassus are not scared of us like the ones we dominated at Ephesus and Miletus. When they spot us trotting down the hill on the other side of their ditch, they throw spears at us from the walls. Then the city gate opens a crack, and a whole herd of them runs out, squealing threats and brandishing their swords.

Alexander tightens my rein in surprise. He's not even wearing his armour; his shield, javelins and spear are still in the wagon, along with most of the Guard's weapons. Hephaestion draws his sword, drags Petasios round to face the Greeks, and yells, 'Look out! Someone sound the alarm!'

A trumpet blares three times to call the rest of the cavalry. One of the Greeks rushes us, and I leap at him, teeth bared. Alexander's sword is in his hand now. He cuts the Greek mercenary across the neck. Although his ghost does not leave his body our enemy falls to his knees, choking. Ha! All the Guard are fighting as the cavalry gallop across to join us, brandishing their spears.

'Quick!' Alexander yells at them, shining with energy. 'That gate's open! Charge!'

But even as he turns me towards it and digs his heels into my ribs, the Greeks swarm back across the bridge and slam the gate shut. We pull up at a safe distance, surrounded by the cavalry, snorting from the sudden exertion.

'King Alexander!' shouts a herald from the wall. 'General

Memnon says that's just a taste of what you can expect if you attack Halicarnassus! Leave now and take your army with you, before we have to kill you.'

Alexander whirls me back to face the city. He leans forward and shivers all over. I think for a moment he's going to make me gallop across the bridge and attack the gate anyway, even though it's shut. I make myself huge in anticipation. But Hephaestion says softly, 'Alex, remember the Granicus . . .' and my rider's weight shifts back again.

'Tell the *traitor* Memnon,' Alexander calls, 'that I will not go away until he is chained in my mines with the rest of his men, chipping gold out of Macedonian rocks!'

After giving them that good squeal, he wheels me round and we gallop back to the camp, where General Parmenio strides out to meet us.

Alexander doesn't even have time to dismount, before the general starts another squealing match. 'What did you think you were doing over there, Alexander?' he says. 'Are you trying to get yourself killed?'

'They opened the gate! I saw an opportunity. It might have worked. Where's my siege equipment? Why haven't you started attacking the walls?'

That's when we learn the worst.

Our siege equipment and most of our supplies are stuck out at sea, prevented from landing by the Persian ships. Persian-slipper-licking Memnon has at least three thousand enemy troops inside Halicarnassus. He has stores enough for a long siege, and he has anti-siege machines ready to destroy our towers if we do ever manage to land them.

General Parmenio says it's Alexander's fault for sending the Athenian fleet home instead of having them protect the transports, and Alexander says it's General Parmenio's fault for transporting the equipment and stores by sea, rather than by land under a decent guard.

Then Alexander squeals that he wants to move the camp north of the city, where Queen Ada's plans show the weakest defences. But General Parmenio squeals back that his men have only just finished setting up their tents on hard rock, and won't be very happy about being ordered to move so soon.

The Guard glance at one another. We horses fidget, picking up the tension of our riders. Zephyr tosses her head, while Philotas stares from his father to Alexander as if he can't decide which herd he belongs to. That could be awkward if it comes to a battle.

But in the end, Alexander works out a cunning way to dominate General Parmenio without fighting him. He sends Philotas off with his band to secure a landing place for the transport ships and orders General Parmenio's men to start filling in the ditch on the side of the city where they are camped, ready for when the siege equipment gets through. Then he leads our half of the army back up the hill to make camp where he wanted to in the first place.

Petasios and I walk side by side, our necks stretched out in relief. Out of the corner of my good eye, I see Alexander run a hand through his hair. 'Why can nothing ever be easy?' he grumbles to Hephaestion. 'Could I really have a demon for a father, and that's why the gods hate me?'

Hephaestion is too sensible to answer. 'I don't know, Alex. But if liberating the Anatolian cities were easy, King Philip would already have done it. You're the only one who has ever managed to get this far. You must be giving King Darius nightmares in his luxurious Persian bed.'

Alexander smiles. 'Good! Then when we've finished off Memnon, maybe he'll come out and fight me! I'm fed up with fighting Greeks. Bucephalas is as eager as I am to get his teeth into some Persian flesh. Aren't you, my brave horse?'

I toss my head and snort, because he knows very well I don't eat meat. I'd much rather have another basket of Queen Ada's honey cakes.

Our siege equipment eventually arrived, but it didn't do us much good. As fast as our men filled in the ditch and dragged the towers up to the wall, the Persian-slipper-licking Greeks drove them back again and undid all our hard work. Whenever our siege engines made a hole in the wall big enough for our phalanx to climb through, the enemy fought so hard our men couldn't get in. Then, during the night when the fighting stopped, they built another wall across the gap to keep us out.

We horses got very bored and irritable, and our feeds began to get smaller again. The only good thing was that Harpinna came into foal-season, and I managed to break my halter and visit her in the night before Charm caught me. *That* showed Xanthus who was boss all right.

Alexander spent a lot of time in his big white pavilion with his friends, poring over the plans Queen Ada had given him. But he still didn't lead an attack on the city, and the grooms grumbled that at this rate we'd be here ten years, like Achilles sitting outside the walls of Troy.

We might have been, too, if it hadn't been for Charm's dream.

A dream of flames

Charm is curled up in her cloak near me. I think she's asleep like the other grooms, but she suddenly sits up with a gasp.

She stares at Alexander's pavilion, which is lit up as usual with some sort of party, then at the sleeping city, and pulls her cloak closer.

'Fire, Bucephalas,' she whispers. 'I saw Halicarnassus burning – oh, no, he can't do that again!'

Because she is so agitated, I check my blind side, but I can't see any ghosts. I nicker to her. She gives me a distracted look, scrambles to her feet, and rushes off towards the king's pavilion.

She's gone quite a long time, and I start to worry she's left me again. Then she comes back with Alexander and some of his Guard. Alexander has his hand on her elbow, and his friends are laughing and staggering a little. As they come closer, I smell magic drink on their breath. They stop near our lines, and Alexander points at the city, silver and quiet in the starlight.

'Look, Charmides! Do you see any flames?'

Charm is breathing hard. She tries to free her elbow, but he won't let go.

'It hasn't happened yet,' she says. 'But it's going to happen. I dreamt it. Please, Alexander Sir . . . *please* don't burn the city, like you did to Thebes. Think of all those women and children who lost their homes and were sold as slaves! It wasn't fair.'

His face hardens. 'That wasn't my decision. The League wanted it done.'

'But *your* men did it.'

He frowns, and lets her go so suddenly she stumbles. 'And what will you do if Halicarnassus burns, Charmides? Run away again? Abandon me and poor old Bucephalas here, because you can't stomach the sight of a few children in chains? This is war. Better their children than ours.'

'I didn't run away because of that! You don't understand!' Charm starts to cry. Alexander's friends go quiet, watching the king and his groom.

'How can I understand, if you refuse to talk about it?' His voice has risen. He takes a deep breath, and shakes his head as Charm looks at her feet. 'Oh, for Zeus' sake, you're only a groom. Why is it you disturb me so much? So! You saw the city burning, did you? Then let's see if we can't make your dream come true.'

He turns to his friends and tilts up his chin. 'Right, you've all seen Ada's plans. The wall has been breached at its weakest point. I want two volunteers to creep inside and open the north gate. I'll get the men ready.'

'*Now*, Alex?' Hephaestion stares at him. 'Tonight?'

'Yes, tonight!' Alexander gives Charm a thoughtful glance. 'My groom's been right before, and they won't be expecting a night attack. If we don't do something soon, General Parmenio's going to say "I told you so". We have to lure Memnon out to fight.' He grins a challenge, shining with the energy that infects people and horses alike. 'It's dangerous.'

His friends' eyes glitter with excitement.

'I'll go, Alex!' Demetrius offers, with a hiccup.

'And me,' Leonnatus says. 'We'll get our weapons!'

They rush off, and Alexander raises his eyebrows at Charm. 'Well, girl? What are you waiting for? Get Bucephalas ready for me. Wake the other grooms. Quietly, though. We don't want to spoil the surprise.'

Charm is agitated. She wakes Tydeos and some of the others, and puts my battle-cloth on me with trembling hands. It's the middle of the night, which is a VERY strange time for a battle, but my heart starts to pound. Action, at last!

Alexander returns, wearing his armour and carrying a pair of javelins and his spear. He vaults on to me, and the reduced Guard form up behind. Borealis and Aura whinny from the horse lines, confused as to why their riders have gone into the city without them. Men stream out of our camp, armed and eager for action. Whispered orders pass along the ranks, and we set off for the gate at a trot.

At first, the city seems just as quiet as it was before Demetrius and Leonnatus crept inside. Then a shout goes up from the guard tower, and a whole section of the wall flares with torches, showing the dark silhouettes of running men. Alexander looks at the closed gate and curses. 'Over the wall!' he cries, and rides me at the ditch towards the breach.

Our men have filled the ditch with rubble to get the siege engines close enough, but it is not easy ground. I gather myself for a jump, but at the last moment decide not to try it: it's a lot wider than I thought. Instead, I drop on to the rubble, stumble as my hooves hit the uneven surface, and feel something wrench in my left foreleg.

I'm so excited, there is no pain. I canter across and jump the remains of the wall on the other side. Petasios and Xanthus are still with me, but the other horses are floundering on the bridge of rubble. Alexander calls for Demetrius and Leonnatus, and their frightened shouts come back to him out of the night. I see them fighting a whole herd of Persian-slipper-licking Greeks with their backs to a wall the enemy have built inside the damaged one.

Alexander kills one of the Greeks with his first javelin, gives a great cry of 'ALALALAI!' and shouts for the others to follow. My blood is up. I gallop through the enemy, scattering them with flat ears and snapping teeth, and Alexander's second javelin sends another Greek ghost rippling into the night.

Petasios and Hephaestion are fighting in the shadows nearby. Xanthus is kicking, leaping and biting almost as brilliantly as me, while his rider Craterus hacks about him with his sword. The rest of the Guard have made it across the rubble, and most of the men. But we are trapped between the old wall and the new one, with no way through. With triumphant cries, more enemy Greeks stream out of the guard towers at either side of us.

'Get the boy who thinks he's king!' calls one, and Alexander hauls me round to see who has insulted him.

'*Memnon!*' he hisses. He casts aside his spear, which is useless in our tight spot, and drags out his sword. He urges me into a gallop, straight at the Greek boss.

Several Greeks try to stop us, and fall beneath my hooves. Their ghosts rise from their bodies and are lost. Hephaestion calls something after us, but Alexander is deaf and blind to all except Persian-slipper-licking Memnon, who watches me come with a smile that turns to panic as he realizes we are not going to stop. He starts to run for cover, but I am VERY fast. Alexander's sword slashes down and catches him on the shoulder. The night ripples as Memnon's ghost leaks out of the wound. But it clings on stubbornly, and does not leave him. Memnon gives a cry of pain and stumbles behind his men, who close up around him. Even Alexander and I cannot get through.

That is when I smell smoke.

'Alex!' Hephaestion yells, pointing back the way we came. 'The devils have sneaked out of the gate and are burning our siege towers!'

Alexander says some very bad words, gives the wounded Memnon a final glare, and leads the Guard back over the rubble to the ditch.

The Greeks outside the city are already running back inside with their flaming torches. The dark siege engine we passed on our way across the ditch is now a great tower of flame crackling fiercely ahead of us, flares of it falling through the darkness. They destroy my night sight, so I can't see the bridge. I stop dead, throw up my head and blow at it in alarm.

Alexander hits me on the backside with the shaft of his spear, which hurts. 'Get on, Bucephalas! It's only fire. This is no time to be scared!'

As I hesitate, something sharp comes flying out of my blind spot and bites me beside my tail. Shocked, I leap forward through the wall of flame and the others follow me, neighing in terror as the sparks singe their manes.

The whole of our camp is awake by now, and men are running up the hill from General Parmenio's camp. But the Greeks have retreated back behind their walls, and there is no one left to fight outside the city.

General Parmenio gallops up to us on a strange horse. I try to make myself huge. But now the excitement of the battle is over, my foreleg hurts where I wrenched it on the rubble, and my wound stings. I settle for giving the general's horse flat ears. Alexander plucks the spear out of me and snaps it over his knee, making the general's horse shy.

'What on earth's going on?' General Parmenio yells. 'Did you try a night attack? Why wasn't I consulted?'

Alexander glares at him. 'It's better than sitting out here all winter, as you seem happy to do! I wounded Memnon. Maybe they'll surrender now.'

The general looks at the burning siege towers. Four of them are on fire. 'Oh, well done, Alexander! And what are we going to use to get through their walls if they decide to stay inside until General Memnon recovers? At this rate, we're not only going to be here all winter, but all next summer, too!'

'The men can easily build more towers!' Alexander snaps. 'We'll talk about this later. I have to see to my horse. He's hurt.' He jumps off me, turns his back on the furious general, and leads me back to the horse lines.

Charm races out to meet us, sees I am limping, and angrily grabs my rein from the king. Then she notices my spear wound and lets out a choked cry. 'You let him get wounded!'

Alexander opens his mouth to squeal at her. Then he remembers she's not the enemy, and the anger runs out of him. He walks behind me (only Alexander would ever dare do that) and peers at my injury. 'It's quite shallow – the cloth stopped it going in too deep. Find the horse doctor. Takes more than a scratch like that to put Bucephalas out of action.'

Charm feels my sore leg and frowns. 'His leg's very hot. Did you gallop over any rough ground?'

Alexander gives her a distracted look. 'Get the horse doctor to take a look at that as well. Charmides, I need to know. Did you . . . I mean, was your dream . . .?'

She glances up.

Alexander clears his throat and crouches beside her. His voice softens. 'I didn't mean to make fun of you, earlier this evening. You caught me at a bad time. Is this what you saw in your dream? The siege towers burning?'

Charm looks at the fires and bites her lip. 'Maybe. I don't know. I thought it was the whole city, but I might have been remembering Thebes. That was a bad time for me.'

150

Alexander nods and watches her examine my leg. Finally, he gives a sheepish smile. 'Well, that wasn't much of a success, was it? I didn't kill Memnon, and Queen Ada's maps didn't allow for his men building emergency walls. I'd better go and see if I can get General Parmenio to calm down. We're obviously going to have to think of something else.'

A bucket of sea water

I didn't see much of the fighting after that. I had to stand with my foot in a bucket of sea water, while Alexander rode Xanthus to supervise the siege. Then one morning, a messenger galloped back to camp, yelling that the Greeks had finally come out to face us. The cavalry mounted up and galloped off after Alexander with the phalanx racing after them. General Parmenio's veterans shook their heads, muttered something about showing the king they still knew how to fight, and followed. With all the excitement, I kicked over my bucket and squashed it, so Charm had to fetch me another.

In the afternoon, the men began to stagger back to camp, tired and bleeding, but boasting about how they'd dominated the enemy. Xanthus came back to the horse lines with a small spear wound in his chest. It wasn't nearly as deep as mine, though you'd have thought he was dying from all the fuss he made when Tydeos bathed it.

Groom-gossip that evening was all about a monstrous tower the enemy had brought out of Halicarnassus, stuffed full of Greeks to throw spears at our men. They said it was as big as a mountain and could hold the whole Persian army (which was rubbish, because everyone knew their herd was still hiding in Persia with King Darius). The grooms also said Alexander deliberately led some of the Macedonians into a trap so that Memnon would give the order to open the main gates and send out the rest of his troops. I don't know if that's true, either.

But one thing did come true. Charm's dream. That night, Halicarnassus burned.

Alexander didn't start the fire this time, though. Persian-slipper-licking Memnon set the armouries alight before fleeing on his ships with the Persians who had been living in Queen Ada's palace, leaving our men to put out the fires and save as much of the city as we could.

It took us nearly two months, but in the end, we dominated Halicarnassus from all sides:

East – General Parmenio was stupid and tried to attack the city without any siege equipment.

North – Alexander was stupid and tried to attack at night, after drinking too much magic at a party.

West – Persian-slipper-licking Memnon was stupid and tried to frighten us with a big tower stuffed full of Greeks.

South – the Persian fleet did the only sensible thing by running away.

ELEVENTH HOOFPRINT
GORDIUM, SPRING 333 BC

Winter leave

As soon as the fires were out, Queen Ada moved back into her palace, and our herd split up again. As a reward for fighting so well, Alexander let the married men go home to Pella for the winter so they could see their families. He sent General Parmenio and his veterans north with the baggage train to a place called Sardis, where we all planned to meet up again ready for the spring campaign. Then he mounted Xanthus, and took his archers and slingers and what remained of the cavalry on a winter campaign to secure the rest of the Anatolian harbours so that the Persians would not be able to use them. I was stiff from my wound and too lame to travel, which meant Charm and I had to stay behind.

Once I'd got over the misery of neighing goodbye to my friends, it was not too bad. Alexander had left a garrison in Halicarnassus to help Queen Ada dominate the remaining

Greek mercenaries who had holed up in the city's fortresses, and the queen's stables housed some nice Persian mares, so I wasn't lonely. We ate honey cakes every single day, and Charm devised an exercise programme to get me fit. Soon, I could manage gentle trots through the streets.

A huge marble tomb stood at the crossroads in the centre of the city. Our scientists called it the Mausoleum and were measuring it for their list of the wonders of the world. I didn't like it. The place was haunted by the ghost of the king who was buried there, and I never knew when it might ripple out and chase me. I always pranced and snorted as we passed it, making Charm laugh and call me a big baby.

But towards the end of the winter, it is not just the ghost that scares me. As we trot past the outer wall, I smell an enemy among the crowd around the gate.

I leap sideways in alarm. Charm, who was admiring the marble statues instead of paying attention to her riding, falls off over my shoulder.

The disgraced horsemaster limps across, and sneers down at her. 'So, you're still looking after the old horse? I must say I'm surprised at King Alexander, trusting his precious Bucephalas to a girl. But it seems young Alexander's full of surprises. He's survived a lot longer than anyone expected him to, but he won't get much further. I happen to know King Darius has sent General Memnon an army to get rid of him.'

Charm recovers her wits and pulls out her dagger, which she wears all the time since Alexander left her here to look after me. 'Leave us alone, or I'll have you arrested!'

The horsemaster laughs at her wavering blade. 'Oh! You've got yourself a little knife, have you? Be careful not to cut your-self – be a shame to spoil that pretty face of yours. When King

Darius kills Alexander, you'll be spending the rest of your days in a Persian harem, and the old horse will be mine.'

Charm shouts for help.

The horsemaster casts a frustrated glance at the Macedonian sentries running towards us, and hisses, 'You might think you're safe here under King Alexander's protection, but I want you to know I'll get my revenge eventually, if I have to follow you to the ends of the earth. In war, things can change as easily as *that*.' He snaps his fingers in Charm's face.

He's not watching me, and I catch his hand in my teeth. Small bones crunch. He yells in pain, gives me an evil look, and hurries off clutching his broken hand.

Ha, dominated!

The sentries gave chase, but the horsemaster had already vanished into the crowd. Grave-faced, they escorted Charm and me back to the palace, where they reported the incident to Queen Ada. She hurried down to the stables to find out what had happened.

'I hear a man attacked you up at the Mausoleum,' the queen said, as I sniffed her to see if she had brought any honey cakes. 'Who was he?'

Charm burst into tears and told her all about the horsemaster. 'It's my fault,' she sniffed. 'I told King Alexander how his father's old horsemaster had mistreated Bucephalas back in Pella, and now the man hates us. I think he's following us. He said King Darius has sent General Memnon an army to stop Alexander— That's not true, is it?'

Queen Ada looked thoughtful. 'I expect Darius is worried that Alexander has got this far, so it's certainly possible. But an army marching all the way from Persia is unlikely to get here before next summer, and by all reports Alexander's winter campaign is going very well, so I don't think we need worry too much.'

'The Persians wouldn't come if King Alexander didn't keep fighting,' Charm said in a small voice.

'I know, my dear. But Alexander's young, and he's been hurt. His father publicly rejected him, and then there was the assassination. It must have been terribly upsetting for the poor boy. He needs to prove to the world that he's good enough to be king. He thinks he can do that by making war and winning battles. Maybe he can – he certainly has a gift for making men follow him. He's already a stronger king than Philip ever was.'

'I hate war!' Charm sniffed. 'I hate all the killing and burning and slave-taking. Alexander almost got Bucephalas killed at the Granicus. That's why I came back. I thought he'd be furious I'd pretended to be a boy, when he found out at Thebes. But all he said was he couldn't see me as a girl.'

Queen Ada was silent for a moment. Then she said, 'I think that's a compliment, my dear. What he probably means is you're too good a groom to be a girl in his eyes.'

Charm looked at her feet. 'I'm not good. There's something I haven't told you. I didn't end up in Pella by chance. I went there to avenge my mother. I never knew my father – I thought he'd been killed in the fighting at Methone before I was born. But when she was dying, Mother told me she was raped when the Macedonians captured the city after the siege. That's how she got pregnant with me, and why she was never very well when I was growing up. I came to Pella with some poison in a mule's hoof. I meant to get work in the kitchens and put it in King Philip's food. But I recognized Bucephalas, fighting his grooms on the riding ground, and knew I had to help him. Then King Philip went away and I met Alexander, and things . . . changed. I never managed to get the poison into the kitchens, and poisoning the king wouldn't have been that simple anyway. In the end, one of his own Guard stabbed him.'

Queen Ada studied Charm's face over my door. She sighed. 'Ah, I begin to see. Perhaps the horse saved you, as much as you saving him. Does Alexander know all this?'

'No! I told him I ran away from Methone, but I didn't dare tell him about the poison, especially not after what happened to King Philip.'

'Then don't tell him. You're not the first child to have a conquering soldier as a father, and you won't be the last.' Queen Ada frowned at Charm. 'You're going to have to stop torturing yourself like this, my dear. Follow Alexander, if you must, but don't expect any sympathy from him. Men like him, who have been touched by the gods, don't understand the concerns of us lesser mortals. Take the advice of an old woman, and make a life for yourself before it's too late.'

'I can't leave Bucephalas, Your Majesty,' Charm said, giving me a desperate look. 'Not if there's going to be another battle.'

'I know *that*, dear. I'm quite certain the horse wouldn't have got this far without your care, and I suspect Alexander wouldn't have got this far without the horse. There's something between the three of you. Some *power*. A bond, I don't know what, but I can sense it. It's like a light surrounding you – which is why we must get you reunited with the king as soon as possible, certainly before he reaches Gordium.'

Charm looked up with renewed fear. 'Why? Where's that? Is it in Egypt?'

The queen smiled. 'It's near Sardis. Knowing Alexander, Gordium is where he plans to start his spring campaign – you'll find out why when you get there. And don't worry about your old horsemaster. He won't get into the palace, these stables are too well guarded. But Bucephalas is sound enough to travel now, so to be on the safe side I'm going to send you north to General Parmenio. Meanwhile, I'll order a search of the city, though if your horsemaster's got any sense he'll already have cleared out.'

Charm managed a small smile. 'Thank you, Your Majesty.'

The queen smiled back. 'The first step in becoming free, Charmeia my dear, is to stop thinking of yourself as a slave. Promise me you'll take that step when you rejoin Alexander?'

Charm straightened a tangle in my mane. This time, her smile was real. 'I promise, Your Majesty!'

I remember Charm telling Alexander some of this, but I don't think it was quite the same story she told Queen Ada. This means one of three things:

Charm lied to Alexander.

Charm lied to Queen Ada.

Charm lied to them both.

As long as she stays to look after me, I don't mind if she lies to everyone.

A huge filly

We travelled to Sardis with the scientists who had stayed behind to measure the Mausoleum. Queen Ada sent honey cakes for Alexander, and also some mares from the palace stables. It was tremendously exciting to be back with my herd again. I carried Charm with my head high and my neck arched, swivelling my ears to catch the sounds of the moun-

158

tains, and flaring my nostrils. The air smelt of melting snow, which still lay in the shade of rocks beside the road.

We found General Parmenio's part of the army camped outside the town, together with the men back from their winter leave and new recruits from Macedonia. They had brought fresh horses with them, so there was a lot of excited whinnying going on in the horse lines.

I made myself huge, and filled my lungs to let out one of my loudest neighs. Charm grabbed my mane as my whole body shuddered. The sound echoed across the rocks, and several of the horses threw up their heads and pricked their ears at me in admiration. One of the fillies whinnied back. I recognized her at once. It was Psylla's filly, from my winter in the mare pasture.

I neighed in delight and gathered myself to gallop down the hill, but Charm hauled on my reins. 'No, Bucephalas, don't show me up, please! General Parmenio's coming. Behave yourself. You'll be seeing your friends soon enough.'

I still wanted to gallop to the horse lines and say hello to little Electra. But the general's hand grabbed my rein, heavy and commanding. I restrained myself and sent Electra a whinny instead. Then I gave the general flat ears. His smell had not improved over the winter.

'I see the old horse is sound again,' General Parmenio said, pulling a wry face at me. 'I hope that'll cheer the king up, because he hasn't got much else to be cheerful about.'

'Sir?' Charm said, still holding me tightly. 'King Alexander's all right, isn't he?'

The General must have heard the fear in her voice, for he laughed. 'Oh yes, young Alexander's fine! By all accounts he's waiting for us in Gordium, having trekked halfway round the

snowbound mountains of Anatolia chasing robbers and capturing fortresses. Apparently, Gordium surrendered without a
fight as soon as the defenders saw him coming. I didn't think
he had it in him, but he's done what he said he would do, and
secured all the harbours as far as Phoenicia. Makes my efforts
here in Sardis seem dull by comparison. But it might all be for
nothing. That meddlesome Greek Memnon is undoing all our
good work behind us, despite hardly being able to hold his
sword after getting himself wounded at Halicarnassus.
Alexander doesn't know it yet, but the men coming off leave
say General Memnon's men have already captured several of
the Aegean islands, and now he's preparing to invade
Macedonia! There's nothing else for it, we'll have to go back.'

Charm's hands tightened in my mane. 'Back home?' she
breathed.

The officers around us nodded grimly. Some of them
looked rather relieved.

'Back to deal with Memnon, anyway. Though it's King
Alexander's decision, of course.' The general coughed, as if he
had just remembered he was talking to a mere groom. 'Can
you control this horse? I can't be looking out for you all the
time.'

Charm stiffened and took a better grip on my mane. 'Of
course, Sir. I've already ridden him all the way here from
Halicarnassus.'

He grunted and let go of my rein.

I threw up my head and leapt forwards, carrying Charm
with me. She pretended she had given me the signal to do this,
and called back over her shoulder, 'I'll just settle him in the
horse lines, Sir!' Then we were going where I wanted to go
and she gave up trying to stop me, though she kept my reins

tight so I couldn't break out of a canter. She was still on my back when we reached the other horses, which shows how much she'd learnt. When she first started riding me back in Pella, she'd not have stayed on nearly so long. I headed straight for Electra's familiar whinny and stopped dead in amazement, nearly throwing Charm over my shoulder.

Where had this huge black filly come from? She was almost as big as me, but she had Psylla's eyes and pretty head. Her tail was like smoke and looked as if it had been recently combed out by her groom. She was beautiful, and I nickered to tell her so. She stretched out her nose and nickered back, warm and soft.

'Careful!' said her groom, jumping up to separate us. 'This is a filly, you know!'

But Charm had recognized Electra too. She slipped off me on trembling legs to take my head. 'Is that really Bucephalas' filly?' she said in wonder. 'She's only a two-year-old. Look at the size of her!'

'Yeah, ain't she great?' Her groom puffed up with pride. 'We backed her early, she grew so big and strong. The new horsemaster said it would be easier than leavin' her another year. But she's sweet and kind, not like her brute of a sire.' When I snapped at him, he jumped backwards, and gave Charm a closer look. 'You really are a girl, ain't you? I thought the other grooms were havin' me on.'

Charm smiled and gave me a pat. 'Well, they weren't. What's wrong? Don't you think a girl can do a groom's job?'

'Um ...' The young groom flushed. 'I s'pose it must be all right if King Alexander lets you look after Bucephalas. Look at them sniffing each other! Do you think he recognizes her?'

'Of course he does! Bucephalas isn't stupid. Are you, old

161

horse? Don't look so worried. Stallions don't mate with their own fillies.' Charm pulled one of my ears and looked round. 'I don't suppose Tydeos is here?'

The groom shook his head. 'Afraid not. I think he's with the king.'

Charm's face fell a bit. 'I'll have to wait until we get to Gordium, then.'

Dominating the Gordian Knot

We leave the next day. General Parmenio is anxious to tell Alexander the news about Memnon, and strides about the camp shouting at the men to hurry. But most of them have been here all winter and have to dismantle the huts they built, which takes AGES. By the time we reach Gordium, Alexander's part of the army is already camped outside the town.

I whinny in delight when I smell the horses, but only one familiar whinny comes back from the lines. It's Harpinna. Her belly is big with foal, which is obviously why she is here on her own. Confused, I prick my ears at the camp as the dogs jump about, barking excitedly to welcome us. Where is the rest of my herd?

Before the echoes of our trumpet have died away, a breathless soldier runs up to General Parmenio. 'You're just in time!' he gasps out. 'King Alexander's gone up to the Temple of Zeus to try his luck with the Gordian Knot! If he manages to untie it, he'll be Lord of all Anatolia.'

The men around us smile. 'He already thinks he is,' someone says.

General Parmenio frowns at the city, which is glowing in a burst of evening sunshine. On the Acropolis hill, the Temple of Zeus stands against fiery clouds. Charm tenses, which makes me tense too. Is there going to be a battle?

'Impetuous young fool,' General Parmenio mutters under his breath. 'I might have known Alexander wouldn't be able to resist it. Undoing some old knot is hardly going to drive Memnon out of Anatolia for us! But people are superstitious around these parts. If he's not careful, he'll undo everything we've achieved so far. I bet he never stopped to think what might happen if he fails.'

I don't know what this Gordian Knot is, but it seems we are going to find out: General Parmenio orders his men to make camp, and seems about to order Charm to go with them. Then he sets his jaw and says, 'Bring the king's horse up to the temple. Maybe it'll distract Alexander from this stupid test of kingship.'

So Charm and I enter Gordium at the front of our herd where we belong, with General Parmenio beside us. We pass under a massive archway, its crumbling stone carved with bearded men dressed in long robes rather like Queen Ada's. Charm stares up at it and shivers. My hooves echo and I feel a bit nervous, too: ghosts lurk under this arch. Once through, however, we find the usual streets, houses and temples. People line our route to catch a glimpse of us, exactly as they did in all the other cities we dominated on the way here.

We head up the hill to the temple courtyard. I smell all my friends, and give General Parmenio's horse flat ears until he lets me put my head in front. First, I see Petasios and Xanthus at the edge of the courtyard, being held by Iolaus. They both have new battle scars. When I whinny, they throw up their heads. Petasios whinnies back, but Xanthus has the cheek to give me a loud squeal. Carrying Alexander all winter has

obviously gone to his head. I squeal back to remind him I'm
boss, but this is not the place for a battle. Behind them, tethered in a line, are Arion, Hades, Apollo, Borealis, Zephyr, and
last but far from least . . . AURA! I give my favourite mare
a special nicker. She shoots up her white ears, whirls around
on her tether and nickers back at me.

'Keep a good hold of him,' General Parmenio mutters to
Charm, urging his horse into a trot. 'I only hope we're not too
late.'

As we cross the courtyard, I catch Alexander's sherbet
smell and let out another whinny. I can't see him yet, though.
There are too many people crowded around what appears to
be an old cart, with the king somewhere in the middle.
Charm's fingers tighten on my mane, and she pushes one of
her escaped curls back under her scarf.

The crowds part when they see us coming. General
Parmenio dismounts and jerks his head at Charm. She slides
off me and takes hold of my bit. At last, I see Alexander; he
has his back to us, and is examining the yoke of the cart. He's
wearing the glittering armour he took from Troy and the
helmet with the white plumes, which has been mended and
reinforced since being fished out of the River Granicus.
Nearby, Demetrius holds the big shield of Achilles.

I give Alexander my special nicker. He swings round, and
his whole face lights up. 'Bucephalas!' My heart pounds as he
strides towards me, with Hephaestion following as usual.
There's a fresh scar on Alexander's cheek, but he's flushed
with health and he walks with a bigger stride than he did at
Halicarnassus.

As he approaches General Parmenio, he makes himself
huge and says with a little smile, 'I'm glad you finally made

164

it, General. I was about to untie the Gordian Knot without you.'

General Parmenio looks hard at Alexander. He shades his eyes against the sun reflecting off the Achilles armour and says carefully, 'There isn't time for you to try the Gordian Knot now, King Alexander. We must talk about General Memnon. It's bad news, I'm afraid.'

Alexander's chin tilts up. He considers the general with his odd eyes and says quietly, 'I've already announced I'm going to undo it.'

'In the morning, then. Memnon is much more important.'

A lot of people are listening. Not just Alexander's Guard and Parmenio's officers, but also the people of Gordium and the priests of the temple in their long robes. Charm grips my bit as tightly as she held my mane earlier. Alexander's eyes narrow, but he is in a very good mood and doesn't lose his temper. 'I gave Memnon a fatal wound at Halicarnassus, remember? I've secured all the harbours and taken care of everything here. He won't bother us for much longer.'

He turns his back on the seething general and smiles at me.

'Bucephalas,' he murmurs, stroking my nose. 'My beautiful horse! I've missed you. Xanthus tries hard, but he's not as good as you are at avoiding enemy spears. He looks well, Charmides. Bring him across so he can watch me untie this knot.'

He is already walking back to the temple, one hand on my rein. Charm has no option but to come, too. General Parmenio hurries after us, dragging his horse and scowling.

When we reach the cart, I finally see what all the fuss is about. A big tangle of ancient rope is wound about the yoke. It looks like a groom's first efforts to tie a proper knot in a halter, except it's massive – more like a whole stable of novice grooms have tied halters around it and couldn't get them untied again. There are not even any ends sticking out to chew. I stretch out my nose, curious. The Gordian Knot smells FOUL. I curl my upper lip in disgust.

Alexander laughs. 'See! That's what Bucephalas thinks of your famous knot, priest! And you say that Zeus will bless whoever manages to untie it and make him Lord of Anatolia?'

The priest smiles. 'No one has ever managed it, not even King Darius.'

Alexander walks around the cart, considering the knot. 'Did Memnon fail, too?'

'General Memnon hasn't tried. I hear he is very sick.'

Alexander turns to General Parmenio. 'See, General? I've prayed to Zeus to help me. If I undo this knot, we won't have to worry about Memnon any more.'

The general's face tightens. He mutters something about being realistic and says quietly, 'And what'll happen if you fail to untie it, King Alexander? Have you thought of that?'

There is a hush as the crowd realizes this is turning into a squealing match. Some of them push closer to hear better, but I give them flat ears, and they jump back again.

Alexander frowns slightly. Then he raises his chin and says in a strong voice, 'I'm not going to fail, General. I've already conquered all the Anatolian cities, haven't I? Zeus will aid me in ending Memnon's life, you'll see.'

General Parmenio rolls his eyes. 'If you think Zeus is going to—'

He gets no further. A rumble of thunder on the horizon makes my mane stand on end. General Parmenio's horse throws up its head. Across the courtyard, Petasios and the others give little whinnies of unease. People glance round and pull their cloaks closer.

The priest looks up at the storm clouds and says, 'King Alexander, the light's going and it looks like rain. It might be a good idea to hurry?'

Alexander nods. He walks slowly around the knot, rubbing his chin and frowning. He whispers to Charm, 'Any dreams about this?' but she shakes her head. He scowls and mutters, 'Oh, what difference does it make how I undo it?'

He moves so fast, the priest doesn't realize what he intends.

I jump in alarm as Alexander whips out his sword and slices through the Gordian Knot with as much force as if it were Persian-slipper-licking Memnon's head. Lightning zigzags across the sky, reflecting off the blade. The tangle of rope falls apart in a blinding flash. There's a crack of thunder, and the earth under my hooves ripples like the sea.

Startled, I drag Charm back a few paces. A coldness goes through me as Memnon's ghost, which I last saw clinging to his body during the fighting at Halicarnassus, screams past my blind side and vanishes.

This is too much for General Parmenio's horse. It rips the reins from the general's hand and takes off across the courtyard. I want to follow it. But Charm clings desperately to my bridle, and eventually the sound of her voice calms me down. Still shivering, I check my blind side, but Memnon's ghost has gone. The ground is solid again. Big drops of rain start to fall, making cold spots on my back.

Alexander laughs. He lifts his sword to the storm, his armour glittering and the lightning flashing around him. The crowd – who went quiet when he cut the famous knot – lets out a great roar.

'Alex-an-der!' they chant. 'Alexander, the reborn Achilles, King of Macedonia, Lord of Anatolia! HURRAH FOR KING ALEXANDER!'

The news travels fast. Those who were unable to get into the courtyard to watch take up the shout in the streets. Even with the rain hissing down and thunder rumbling overhead, people come out of their houses to cheer Alexander. When he puts his sword away and vaults on to me, my heart swells with pride, and although I hate thunder and lightning, and the rain is getting in my ears, I make myself huge.

Petasios, carrying Hephaestion, soon joins me, and the other horses of the Guard fall in behind. General Parmenio, who couldn't catch his horse, has to ride Xanthus at the back. Ha, that'll teach Xanthus to get above himself!

People are still cheering as we splash through the puddles and out of the city. They climb on walls and cling to statues to catch a glimpse of Alexander. They throw handfuls of tiny, wet spring flowers into our manes. Their clothes are soaked, but they don't seem to care. Alexander's legs grip my sides. Without my cloth, they feel hot and shivery against my coat. His excitement infects me in the same way it did back in Pella the first time he rode me, though he feels a lot more confident now.

'That showed old Parmenio, didn't it?' he shouts to Hephaestion between the rumbles of thunder. 'Congratulations, gentlemen! We've successfully liberated Anatolia from Persian rule. Next, we ride for Egypt!'

TWELFTH HOOFPRINT
TARSUS, SUMMER 333 BC

Favoured by the gods

The first part of our journey to Egypt lay through friendly territory, with plenty to eat, and people who cheered us for liberating their land. The king was in such a confident mood, it made our whole herd happy from the officers down to our grooms. The Persian army didn't appear, and the men joked that King Darius was too scared to challenge us now Alexander had proved he was favoured by the gods.

Needless to say, General Parmenio wasn't convinced by Alexander's claim that Memnon would be no further threat to us. But I knew better, because I'd seen his ghost. And not long after Alexander dominated the Gordian Knot, news came that Memnon had died of his sickness, leaving his herd leaderless and frightened. Groom-gossip was full of it for a while. They could not decide whether Memnon had got sick and died from the wound Alexander gave him during our night attack on Halicarnassus, or Zeus had killed Memnon in answer to Alexander's prayers.

I don't see that it makes much difference. Dead is dead, horse or human. Besides, a much stranger thing happened the day Alexander cut the Gordian Knot.

He shook the world so powerfully, the veil between the living and the dead tore. Before the hole closed, a herd of female warriors rode through it and joined our army. The Greeks call them Amazons, and there are a lot of silly stories about them, such as that they live without men and are immortal. Though, if the first is true, it's just as well they never die, because without men they might have a hard time making more Amazon girl-fillies to replace the dead ones. Think about it!

Our grooms said, with little sniggers, that the Amazon queen had come to lie with King Alexander to make a strong girl-filly to lead their herd when she retired. I don't know if this was true. But when Charm saw the Amazons setting up their strange round tents at the edge of our camp, she went very quiet.

'Do you think the Amazons really fight their own battles?' she asked Tydeos. 'Alexander says they came to help Troy at the end of the *Iliad*, and they're supposed to be immortal. That can't be true, can it?'

Tydeos grunted. 'Who knows? I never believed the Gordian Knot was magic, until King Alexander cut it and made the world shake.'

'That was just an earthquake, you dolt,' Charm said. But she bit her lip and looked at the Amazon camp again. 'Their horses look tough. People say they've got horns—'

'Forget them, Charm!' Tydeos said with a laugh. 'We've got enough horses of our own to worry about. That roan mare's about to foal any day now, and we'll have to keep an eye on Bucephalas and Xanthus when the other mares come into season. The last thing we want is both of King Alexander's mounts getting injured in a stallion battle. When they get going, they're like Alexander and General Parmenio fighting over the command.'

Charm was not really listening. 'I wish Alexander wasn't the king,' she said suddenly.

Tydeos gave her a startled look and began to laugh. 'Oh, so *that's* it! And we all thought you came back for the horse!' He sobered. 'It's not just you, Charm. King Alexander doesn't look at any woman, does he? I suppose he has other things to think about. That Amazon queen hasn't got a hope either, if he's what she came for. Besides, it'd only end in tears, you know that. Alexander is King of Macedonia and Lord of Anatolia, and you're . . . a groom.'

I don't know what he had been about to say, but Charm gave him a fierce look. 'I did come back for Bucephalas,' she said. 'Of course I did. But Alexander's . . . oh, never mind.'

Tydeos pushed one of her curls behind her ear. 'I know,' he said quietly. 'King Alexander's like that, isn't he? He's not handsome like Hephaestion, and he's got a fierce temper on him. But no matter what he does, everyone seems to want to be near him. Maybe he really is the reborn Achilles. After what happened with the Gordian Knot, I wouldn't be surprised if he turned out to be the son of Zeus! If I were the Persian king, I'd take my army back home quick and keep running. All right now?'

Charm sniffed and smiled at him. 'Yes, I expect you're right . . . that horsemaster was probably just trying to scare me, back in Halicarnassus. How could he know what the

Persians are planning, anyway?'

Harpinna's colt was born black with white specks in its coat. It was healthy and strong, and undoubtably MINE. (Remember when I broke my halter at Halicarnassus?) Charm named him Hoplite – after the foot-soldiers – because he had been born in the army.

She promised me that once we reached Egypt we'd be able to sail all the way back to Pella and give my poor legs a rest. She said I wouldn't have to fight in any more battles, because the Persians had obviously heard about Alexander cutting the Gordian Knot and gone home.

This only goes to show how little grooms know about dominating.

Still human

General Parmenio thought the Persians might be planning to ambush us at the Cilician Gates, a pass through the mountains which was supposed to be so narrow only four men could walk through it abreast. Alexander told him not to worry, because Zeus would look after us just as he had finished off General Memnon. General Parmenio rolled his eyes and ordered the men to arm themselves and carry their shields.

Strangely, Alexander did not squeal at this. He felt a bit unsteady on my back. He kept wiping his forehead and running his hand down my neck, whispering, 'Not far now, Bucephalas, I promise. When we get to Egypt, we can both have a rest.'

The road got worse. Sharp stones lay in wait to bruise our hooves. The sun shimmered over the rocks. Mosquitoes bit us. There was not enough water. And it was HOT. We horses were dark with sweat the whole time. The men marched grimly, eyeing the high cliffs on both sides of us.

Something was definitely wrong with my rider: beads of sweat glistened on his forehead, his cheeks were an unhealthy yellow, and he swayed over my shoulder. But when Hephaestion suggested he should lie down in one of the baggage carts, he gripped my mane with sweaty hands and sat up straighter. 'I'm not going to enter Tarsus in a mule cart! I'd never live it down. I'm the *king*, Hephaestion. I'm the reborn Achilles! I conquered the Gordian Knot. I can't be *ill*.'

Since I carried him with extra care, Alexander managed to stay on my cloth until we reached the Cilician Gates. To keep General Parmenio quiet, he sent some men to check there were no Persians hiding in the pass and asked Charm if she'd had any dreams about the place. When she said she hadn't, he wiped his brow and turned to General Parmenio with a smile.

'See, General? What did I tell you? There's nothing to fear. Zeus has made the pass safe for us.'

The general muttered that we weren't through it yet, and the Persians were probably waiting for us on the other side. Alexander gave him a withering look. He said since the general seemed to be so scared, he himself would go first. Ignoring Hephaestion's whispered query after his health, he gathered up my reins and headed me into the pass.

He urged me into a trot, and as if to prove he wasn't ill, kept up the pace right through the Cilician Gates and all the way across the plain beyond with barely a pause to rest or eat. This was just as well, because someone had burnt the crops on the other side. Our hooves raised a smoky cloud of ash that made our riders cough almost as much as Alexander.

The men defending Tarsus ran away when they saw us coming, and I made myself huge as we trotted through the city gates. But instead of parading through the streets as he usually did, to show the citizens he was boss, Alexander galloped me straight for the river that flowed through the middle of the city. He leapt down from my back without waiting for me to stop, staggered a little, stripped off his armour and threw himself headfirst into the water.

I snorted at him in surprise. But he must have been as hot and thirsty as I was. I plunged my muzzle into the water and gulped without pausing for breath. The river was freezing. It chilled my stomach, but I didn't care. I could have drunk it dry.

'Alex!' Hephaestion cried, as Petasios caught up. 'What are you doing? That water's deep – *Alex!*'

The other horses saw me drinking and lunged towards the river as well, but their riders hauled up their heads. There was a lot of shouting and confusion as more of our men caught up. A curious crowd formed on the bank as Hephaestion dismounted and plunged into the river after Alexander. I didn't realize what all the fuss was about, until I paused in my glorious drink and raised my head.

Then I saw Alexander in mid-stream, white and shivering violently. He was thrashing and moaning like Harpinna when she gave birth to her foal.

By now, several of the Guard were in the water, swimming towards him. Hephaestion reached Alexander first and put an arm around his neck, lifting his face to the surface. The rest splashed across to help, and between them they dragged the unconscious king out on to the bank. Iolaus and some of the phalanx held their horses for them. No one dared try to catch me, though, and I got several more gulps of icy water before Charm finally rushed up and seized my reins.

'No, Bucephalas!' she scolded. 'You're much too hot. You'll get a chill – *oh!*' She had seen Alexander, lying motionless on the bank surrounded by his friends. Hephaestion wrapped his cloak around him, and they lifted him on to the Achilles shield and carried him away. Charm gave a funny little gasp and started to drag me after them. But Iolaus threw the tangle of reins at her and called as he ran after them, 'Stay here, Groom, and look after the horses! I have to be with the king!'

I gave Xanthus flat ears, but I had bellyache from the water, so my heart wasn't in it. Charm sorted out our reins, muttering to herself. 'I *knew* he was ill! Oh, I hope he's all right! That water's so cold. He's such an idiot. Did he think Zeus was going to stop him from drowning? What are we all going to do if he dies?' She bit her lip and stared after Alexander.

Tydeos ran up, breathless, closely followed by our other grooms. Everyone was asking questions at once. They seemed to have forgotten we were hungry and thirsty and badly in need of a roll.

'Can't the king swim?'

'Is he sick?'

'Is he going to die?'

I could have told them the answers to all those questions:

No.

Yes.

Yes, of course, one day. (You humans never ask the more helpful question: '*When?*')

But they didn't think to ask me. They were too busy arguing about why the gods had let the king get ill. Some said perhaps Zeus was angry with King Alexander for cutting the

Gordian Knot instead of untying it. Others said the Persians had tried to kill him by poisoning the river in Tarsus (which was silly, because no one else got sick from drinking the water). The only thing they could agree on was that King Darius' army must be nearby, because General Parmenio said the Persians had burnt all the crops around Tarsus to stop our herd from using them for food.

Charm went very quiet when she heard this.

'Cheer up,' Tydeos whispered. 'At least if King Alexander dies, General Parmenio will take us all home.'

Charm's hand clenched on my rein, and she shot him a fierce look. 'You don't understand, do you? You don't understand *at all!*'

Later, Hephaestion emerged from the city and announced that since Alexander was favoured by the gods we needn't worry, because Zeus would make him better. But I knew my rider was suffering, because that night my bellyache got so bad, I lay down and rolled in the horse lines.

Tydeos rushed across to help Charm untangle me and get me to my feet. I was mad with pain for a while, so I don't remember how it happened, but in the morning she had a big, hoof-shaped bruise on her cheek. The horse doctor came and forced foul-tasting medicine down my throat. Then Charm led me round for the rest of the night, while the pain in my belly gradually eased.

Charm visits the Amazons

By the time the sun comes up, we are at the edge of the camp where the Amazons have pitched their round tents. The Amazons' horses are small and strong. They have blue circles painted on their necks and quarters and – yes, it's true! – little stubby horns in the middle of their foreheads. They throw up their heads as I get closer, and one or two squeal challenges at me. I am feeling a bit better, so I squeal back. A woman with braided hair, and wearing leather, is washing the circles off them. She has a deep scar across her cheek. When she sees me coming, she picks up an axe that was lying nearby.

Charm wrenches her gaze from the horses and halts me out of range, very tense. 'You're the Amazon leader, aren't you?' she says.

The woman inclines her head. She isn't as young as Charm, but she is quite a bit taller than Alexander and as muscular as a man. 'I am Queen Penthesilea, yes.'

Charm bites her lip, eyeing the woman's scar. 'I want to join you!' she blurts out. 'I have a horse and a weapon. When are you going home?'

The Amazon queen frowns and says slowly, as if speaking Greek is difficult for her, 'This is the first time we have been called from our land since the long war at Troy. When King Alexander cut the Gordian Knot, he opened the way. We must stay and fight for him until he opens the hole in the world again to release us.' Her gaze sweeps over Charm, taking in her tangled curls, her dagger and her grubby tunic. 'You are one of King Alexander's grooms?'

Charm nods, still biting her lip. 'My name's Charmeia. Please let me join you. I'm a woman, and I'm willing to fight.'

Queen Penthesilea lowers the axe and gives her an amused look. 'A woman, yes, just about. A fighter, I think not. You have never been in a battle, young Charmeia, I can tell.'

Charm's lip trembles. 'I have! I rode Bucephalas into battle at the river Granicus to save the king's life, when the mare he was riding got killed under him!'

Queen Penthesilea's frown returns. 'This is King Alexander's famous horse?' She puts down her axe and rubs my forehead thoughtfully with her callused hand.

That is when I see her ghost is outside her body, rather than inside it like other people's. I give her flat ears and scrabble back in terror, but she takes my rein in her strong hand, unafraid. I try to bite her, but she laughs and knocks my muzzle away with her fist. Even in my weak state I could have dominated her easily, of course, but her ghost confuses me.

'Hmm, he certainly has spirit. And you ride him? Maybe you are more of a fighter than you look, young Charmeia. But I think we will be in a lot of trouble if we take King Alexander's horse and groom away from him. He might try to follow us home.'

'He won't invade your land,' Charm says softly, glancing round to make sure none of the Macedonian sentries are close enough to hear. 'He doesn't even know where it is, and he hasn't got time. He's taking the army to Egypt so he can ask the oracle about his father. General Parmenio says we've done most of what we came to do, liberating Anatolia, and there won't be another battle unless the Persians try to stop us. So, you see, King Alexander won't need you, and he won't need his horse, either.'

Penthesilea gives Charm a narrow-eyed look. 'Maybe. And maybe King Alexander sent you here to test us? Should I tell him we passed the test?'

'No! Don't tell him what I said, *please!*'

Charm sounds so frightened that the Amazon queen's expression softens. She lets go of my rein and steps out of range of my teeth.

'Take the king's horse back, Charmeia. I shall not tell. The

Persians are going to try to stop Alexander, as I think you know very well. You have yet to see us in battle. You might change your mind about joining us, once you do. But when we go home, I will ask if you still want to come with us. It may not be possible to bring the horse. We do not harbour thieves.' She looks at me pointedly.

Charm bows her head. 'It doesn't matter about me. I only want Bucephalas to be safe, but I daren't run away with him on my own. Alexander would be furious and send his Guard after us. Also, there's a man hunting us – oh, you don't want to hear this! You're right, I could never join you. I'm too much of a coward! I'm sorry. I shouldn't have come.' She vaults on to me and turns me back towards the horse lines, tears glistening in her eyes.

Queen Penthesilea puts a hand on Charm's knee and looks up into her face. 'I do not think you are a coward, young Charmeia. Bravery is doing what scares you, and often fighting is not the most frightening thing. That is the first lesson an Amazon learns. I meant what I said. I will come to you before we leave. In the meantime, be very careful of King Alexander. The Gordian Knot is a test of kingship in more ways than one. Unravelling it would have required imagination, skill, and patience – three of the qualities a man needs to rule wisely. Alexander cut it with his sword. I do not know what that means for us, but men like Alexander do not have easy lives nor easy deaths, and neither do those who get too close to them.'

Which pass?

Alexander and his Guard remained in the city for three whole days, while General Parmenio took part of the army south to find out what the Persians were up to. The camp was gloomily quiet. Then, on the fourth morning, the gates opened, and a chariot rumbled out drawn by two captured Persian horses.

The men at the edge of the camp started cheering, and everyone rushed out of their tent to see what was happening. Charm, who had been sitting on a pile of cloths oiling my bridle, jumped up on to the nearest cart to get a better view. She didn't seem to know whether to laugh or cry, and ended up doing both at once, which was a bit confusing.

'It's *him!*' someone shouted. 'It's the *king!*'

By now the camp was so noisy you'd think we had just won a battle. Alexander's chariot drove slowly up and down the lines of tents to let everyone see him, and stopped at the end of our horse line. The grooms hastily brushed off their tunics and tidied up our buckets. Charm fiddled with her mane and retied her scarf. I shivered all over as Alexander walked slowly towards me.

He smiled and opened his hand to reveal a honey cake. I licked his palm clean of crumbs and nudged him for more. Unusually, he staggered.

Hephaestion caught his elbow with a concerned look. 'You shouldn't overdo it, Alex,' he whispered.

Alexander shrugged his friend off and looked round for Charm. 'How is the old horse, Charmides? I heard he had colic while I was sick.'

Charm ducked her head to hide her bruise. 'Yes, Sir, but he's fine now.' She chewed her lip. 'Sir, is it true we're going to have to fight the Persian army before we get to Egypt? Maybe we could stay here and wait for them to go home? You shouldn't fight them until you're stronger, Sir. Everyone thought you were going to die . . .' Her voice trailed off.

Alexander gave Hephaestion an amused look. 'What rumours have you been spreading about me?' He spread his arms and turned in a circle. 'As you can see, Charmides, I've never felt better! Do you think Zeus would let me die of a little chill, after making me Lord of all Anatolia? As for the Persians, General Parmenio's scouts say they're already on their way to meet us. So, you see, there's no question of anyone going home.'

Charm glanced around in alarm, as if she expected the Persian army to appear there and then, and Alexander noticed the bruise on her cheek.

He lifted her curls away from her face and frowned. 'Who did that to you? My father's old horsemaster hasn't been creeping around here, has he? Because if he has, I'll have him hunted down and punished. I'm getting very tired of him.' His tone had turned cold and dangerous. Hephaestion shook his head and tried to steer him back to the chariot, but Alexander stood his ground.

'Charmides! I order you to tell me the truth.'

She flushed. 'Bucephalas kicked me, Sir, when he was ill.'

Alexander gave a sharp laugh and patted me again. 'Oh, horse! Don't you dare kick my groom again, all right? It was careless of her to let you get sick, but I'm the one who gives out the punishments around here, and since she's made you well again I've decided to forgive her.'

There was a big party that night to celebrate the king's recovery. The men feasted and ran races, while Alexander made sacrifices to Asclepius, the god of healing. His pavilion glimmered with torches, and the laughter and drinking continued all night, keeping us horses awake.

Our grooms got hold of some of the muleteers' magic

drink, and spent the night laying bets on which pass the Persian army would come through to meet us. There were only two choices, which ended up equal favourites because no one could agree:

The Syrian Gates.
The Amanic Gates.

Charm put her money on the Amanic Gates, then changed her mind and put it on the Syrian Gates instead. No prizes for guessing what sort of dream she had the night before.

General Parmenio said the best thing we could do was wait for King Darius between the mountains and the sea, near a town called Issus which we had already dominated. He said the Persian army was bigger than ours, and at Issus we'd have less chance of being outflanked. If we went through one of the passes to meet them, we'd have to fight with the mountains at our back and enemy territory ahead. This would be bad for us, since the towns and villages in the south still supported the Persians and might send King Darius reinforcements.

For the first time ever, it looked as if Alexander was going to take General Parmenio's advice. But then Charm slipped away from the horse lines and ran off towards the king's pavilion. When she returned, she wore a determined little smile. Shortly afterwards, Alexander announced that only the sick and the baggage train would stay camped at Issus. He then marched the rest of us fast down the coast to the Syrian Gates to lie in wait for the Persian army.

The plan is to attack them as they come through. They won't be able to make battle formation in the narrow pass, so we'll have the advantage and King Darius will be history. Alexander seems very confident again. Even General

Parmenio didn't squeal too much, since the latest reports from his scouts say that the Persians are indeed camped on the other side.

You should realize that this information is already half a day out of date, though. Only three of us know we came here on the strength of a dream: Charm, Alexander, and me. (And now you, of course.)

Thirteenth Hoofprint
ISSUS, NOVEMBER 333 BC

Charm's mistake

We made camp near the Syrian Gates, but remained on full alert. The night had a prickly feel that made me tremble, and my nerves were not helped by the fact I was wearing my battle-cloth with the purple trim. Charm had my bridle ready to put on at short notice, and Alexander's javelins and spear waited beside it for her to pass up to him. The big shield of Achilles was propped nearby. Demetrius was going to carry it into battle to show that Alexander had the power of Achilles.

Alexander had sent scouts into the pass to keep watch for the Persians, and an expectant hush lay over the camp. Everyone listened out for the trumpets that would signal the attack. While we waited, Charm combed my mane. It didn't need combing, but her fingers felt nice so I didn't complain. Beside us, Tydeos fiddled with Petasios's girth. Petasios didn't think much of this, and gave him flat ears and a little squeal.

Suddenly, Charm's comb stopped moving, and her fingers gripped my crest. 'Do you think it's wrong to lie to save someone's life?' she said.

Tydeos gave her a puzzled look. 'What do you mean?'

'Alexander wanted to know which pass the Persians will come through. It wasn't really a lie. I might have dreamt it wrong. These passes all look the same to me, it's hard to tell sometimes.'

He saw her glance towards the Syrian Gates, and his eyes went wide. 'Are you saying what I think you're saying? Have you done something extremely stupid?'

She bit her lip and rested her forehead against my neck. 'I only wanted to stop the battle,' she said in a whisper. 'If the Persian army goes through the other pass, then they'll miss us. We can carry on through the Syrian Gates and get to Egypt without having to fight them.'

There was a silence – not even the sound of horses munching hay, because we hadn't been fed in case we had to gallop after the Persians. Charm lifted her face from my neck and looked at Tydeos with pleading eyes.

'Oh, Zeus,' Tydeos whispered, glancing round to check no one else had heard. 'Do you mean you dreamt of them going through the *Amanic* Gates?'

Charm nodded miserably, and Tydeos paled.

'You little *idiot*! What do you think King Darius is going to do when he discovers he's got behind us? Do you think he'll just lead the Persians north on through the Cilician Gates and into Anatolia, leaving his enemies in the mountains? Do you really think King Alexander is just going to ride on to Egypt without a fight? He's been looking forward to meeting the Persian king in battle for years! Probably ever since the day he jumped on to Bucephalas' back when he was twelve years old!'

His voice rose. Some of the grooms glanced our way. Tydeos put an arm around Charm and steered her away from the horse lines, whispering fiercely.

Thunder rumbled over the mountains, and our grooms glanced up nervously. I wanted Charm to come back and continue combing my mane. Xanthus shifted his big golden quarters sideways into Arion, and the two of them started a kicking match. I squealed at Xanthus to tell him to behave, but it made no difference. We were all far too tense.

A message from King Darius

The storm hits us in the night, and rain comes down so hard and violently that rivers of mud flow through the camp. Several tents are washed away; the men splash after their belongings, shouting and swearing. Charm, Tydeos and the other grooms have their work cut out rescuing our tack and fodder and our riders' weapons from the flood. We horses hate every moment of it. My quilted battle-cloth soon becomes sodden and clings to me as heavily as the horsemaster did on my first day in Pella. It makes my back so cold, I start to shiver. Thankfully, Charm notices this and takes off my cloth to wring it out.

The other grooms are following her example when urgent shouts and trumpet blasts come from the side of the camp furthest from the pass. The dogs go crazy, barking and whining in a horrible way that makes my hair stand on end. The men look up from their rescue work in alarm.

They are right to be worried: the sky is paling behind the

clouds, and dawn is a favourite time to attack an enemy camp.

The officers yell orders. The men strap on their armour and grab their weapons, while the grooms hastily put our wet cloths back on us and tighten our girths. Charm gives Tydeos a wild-eyed look.

'Don't just stand there, then!' says Tydeos. 'Your dream about the Amanic Gates must have come true. The Persians are going to attack us from behind, just like I said they would! I wouldn't want to be in your sandals when the king gets down here.'

Charm shakes her head, very pale. 'They can't have had time to go through the Amanic Gates and bring their army all the way up here after us. It can't be them . . . it *can't!*' But she is breathing hard, and I can feel the fear coming off her in waves. She tries to put my cloth back on me, but it's still wet, and even colder than before. Her hands are trembling, which makes me nervous too. I give her flat ears and rear up to tell her I don't want it on my back yet. She ducks to avoid my hooves, and my cloth drops into the muddy stream running past the horse lines. Charm picks it up and says a bad word she learnt from the muleteers.

Into this chaos strides Alexander, followed by an alarmed Hephaestion. The king's face is flushed with anger. He is dragging a man with him by the elbow.

I come down to earth and snort as I recognize the man's smell. It brings memories of the mule stable back in Pella, for it is the old mulemaster who helped Charm on her first day. We left him with the baggage train and the mares and foals at the camp in Issus. Blood is running from a cut on his head, and his face is blank with shock. There is something wrong with his hands. His arms end too early, and the stumps of his wrists are covered in a sticky black mess that smells horrible. One of the younger grooms gives a strangled gasp and is sick in the mud.

Alexander lifts the mulemaster's arm and waves the blackened stump at Charm. 'See this?' he shouts in his shrill voice. 'See? This poor man has just ridden all the way from Issus without his *hands*. King Darius took his army through the Amanic Gates in the night and attacked our base camp. He cut the hands off anyone strong enough to sit on a mule, and sent them up here as a warning to me. He murdered the ones who couldn't ride. All my sick and wounded, butchered by the Persians! Now tell me again, Charmides, which pass the Persians were going to come through in the night?'

All the blood has drained from Charm's face. My cloth slips from her hands. She stares at the mulemaster's blackened stumps in horror. 'I'm sorry,' she whispers. 'Oh . . . I'm sorry.'

It's not clear whether she's apologising to the king or to the mulemaster. But Alexander assumes her words are for him and in an icy voice he says, 'You will be!'

'Alex, for Zeus' sake!' Hephaestion hisses, glancing at Charm's white face. 'It was only a *dream*! Your official seer gets it wrong all the time. How was your groom to know? I thought we came up here because of General Parmenio's intelligence reports, not because of some silly dream. Let the poor man go to the blood tent with the others. Maybe the doctors can do something for him.'

'Stick his hands back on, maybe?' Alexander shoves the mulemaster roughly away from him. 'This man's useless to me now! How can he look after mules with no hands? I should have left my groom in the base camp instead.'

Charm shudders, but says nothing. I can see Tydeos out of

the corner of my eye, standing nearby with his fists clenched. The other grooms are too afraid to say anything. We horses are upset by the king's anger, and tug at our halters as we dance round in our lines.

'General Parmenio's coming,' Hephaestion warns in a low voice, and Alexander shakes himself like a wet horse.

'Get out of my sight!' he yells at Charm. 'Report to the garrison kitchen in Tarsus, and don't let me see you near my horses again. Think yourself lucky I haven't time now to deal with you as you deserve. You, Tydeos, or whatever your name is! Get that cloth back on my horse and get him ready for battle.'

Charm sucks in her breath and flings herself at Alexander's feet. 'Please, Your Majesty!' she gasps. '*Please* don't send me away! Punish me, whip me, anything! But let me stay and look after Bucephalas! He needs me.'

Alexander's face twists as he looks down at her. 'If you're here when I get back, being a girl won't save you. For the last time, *go!*'

'No . . .' Charm is sobbing now. 'You don't understand, you can't send me away . . . *please.*' Alexander gives her tears a peculiar look, orders Hephaestion to make sure she leaves, and strides off to meet General Parmenio.

As the general and the young king approach each other, they both make themselves huge. This is a certain sign there will be a battle for the herd. But when General Parmenio says, 'If we had waited at Issus as I advised, this wouldn't have happened—' Alexander shoulders him aside. 'Assemble the men, General!' he orders as he strides past. 'I want to talk to them. We can't change what's happened, but King Darius is going to pay for what he did to my people. Tomorrow, Persian blood will run as deep as the flood water Zeus sent down on our camp last night.' His tone is chilling. His fists clench, and energy flickers around him. When he glares back down the slope, he looks twice as frightening as the day we dominated Thebes. 'I swear it on my father's name.'

Charm went, as ordered. I don't know where. Tydeos stayed long enough to put my cloth back on, then followed her. Meanwhile, the damp tents were packed and the men assembled on the mountainside. Alexander stood on a rock above them, wearing his reinforced Troy helmet with the white plumes, and talked. He said a lot of things about glory and honour in his loud, shrill voice. We horses soon got bored and nosed about in the mud for something to eat. But the men, who had been badly frightened by the mutilated captives King Darius had sent them, stopped muttering, stood up straighter, and gripped their weapons with fresh determination. When the king finally finished, they cheered wildly.

When Alexander came to mount me, there was still no sign of Tydeos or Charm, so he had to bridle me himself. He vaulted on to my back without a word, and we took our usual place at the front of the army.

At midnight, we saw the Persian fires glittering like stars below us. They filled the whole valley where we'd left Harpinna with little Hoplite and the baggage train. I flared my nostrils, but we were too far away to smell my mare.

Alexander rode on ahead with Hephaestion, halted me at the edge of the cliff and squinted at the Persian camp. He was silent for a long while. Then he said, 'Those poor men they sent back to us weren't exaggerating, my friend. I think they outnumber us, but not by much. It could be worse, but I must make the proper sacrifices tonight. We're going to need Zeus on our side tomorrow.'

Hephaestion reined in Petasios beside me. He said softly, 'Are you sure it was wise to dismiss your groom back there, Alex? The other grooms are all scared of Bucephalas, you know that.'

Alexander frowned. 'The last thing I need to worry about right now is who's going to look after my horse! Ask me again after we've beaten the Persians. Won't do the stupid girl any harm to spend a night in the hills. She'll soon come running back to us for protection when she sees King Darius' army down there.'

When we rejoined the others, Tydeos still hadn't turned up, so Alexander removed my cloth and settled me himself. Then he vanished into the night with Hephaestion to make his sacrifices. No one noticed that the king didn't know the proper order for the horse lines and had tethered me next to Xanthus, instead of in my usual spot between Petasios and Borealis.

Spies and assassins

Our grooms are all curled up in their cloaks, asleep. The men sit in groups, talking quietly as they sharpen their swords and spearheads. There is the sound of happy munching in the horse lines. All the other horses have hay soaked in honeyed water, our usual last meal before a battle. But Petasios and I are hungry, because no one has thought to give us any.

I reach my nose across to take some of Xanthus' hay. He gives me flat ears and a cheeky squeal. I give him flat ears and a squeal back, then snatch a mouthful anyway. I'm the boss, and he ought to let me have it. But the big fool goes up in the air, breaks his tether and comes at me with bared teeth. So I break my tether, too, and fasten my teeth in his neck.

Xanthus shrieks. The grooms wake up, but dare not come near my hooves and teeth. Some of the men run across and try to separate us by swinging their long pikes at our heads. It's like being back in the battle that half-blinded me, and I wheel away in panic. I have no rider to guide me, and no one around me smells familiar. Some of the grooms, arms outstretched, make a half-hearted attempt to block my way. But when I bare my teeth and gallop at them, they jump aside. Their shouts fade as I flee into the night.

By the time the ghosts stop chasing me, I am surrounded by black rocks. I slow to a trot, and snort to clear my nose. One of my forelegs has a little nick from a sharp stone. I am high in the mountains, and the sky is paling over the mountaintops. I suck in the cool air and send a ringing whinny to my friends.

Very faintly, off to my right, a strange horse replies.

I sniff the ground, searching for familiar smells. But our army has not come this way. The strange horses have left dung, which I pause to dominate, and mixed with the smell of their herd is a familiar scent . . . CHARM! I whinny again, this time with joy, and set off at a trot with my nose to the ground and my broken halter lead trailing, following her spring-grass scent.

I find the herd of strangers hiding in a canyon. There must be a hundred of them, small with dainty hooves, like the ones we dominated at the Granicus. They are carrying riders dressed in trousers with yellow scarves wrapped around spiked helmets. Tassels dangle from their bridles and cloths. Some of the men in the centre of the herd have dismounted. One of them is holding a small human by the arm; I can't see her, but I catch another whiff of Charm's spring-grass smell. It's sharp with fear.

I whinny in delight and canter towards them.

The men look round in alarm and draw their long, curved swords. They smile when they see I am alone, and call out to their boss in a strange tongue. One of them rides up to me and tries to catch my halter lead. I squeal at his horse, give its rider flat ears, and barge through the herd to reach my groom.

Her face lights up. '*Bucephalas!*'

I open my mouth and charge the man holding her. His horse spins round, dragging the reins from his arm. I fasten my teeth in his wrist. He lets go of Charm with a startled yell, and she runs to me, grabs my mane and makes a leap for my back.

She doesn't make it. I am still acting wild, because the strangers have surrounded us. They laugh at their boss and call to one another to catch me. Charm cowers by my shoulder and points her wavering dagger at the men.

'Stay away from me!' she says in a shrill, scared voice. 'Or King Alexander will come up here and kill you all!'

The Persians laugh. Their boss calms his horse and says in good Greek, 'I don't think so. We have your young Alexander exactly where we want him, trapped between our army and the mountains. Now be sensible, girl. Tell us his plans, and maybe we'll let you go back to him alive.'

Charm shakes her head. 'I wouldn't tell you anything, even if I knew! But I know he's going to make your horrid King Darius pay for chopping off our men's hands.'

The Persian boss eyes her dagger and my snapping teeth. He says something to his herd in his own language, and smiles at Charm. 'We don't anticipate much trouble chasing your men back home. But if King Alexander has more women and horses in his army who fight like you two, maybe Great King

Darius ought to be more worried!'

'King Darius should be *very* worried,' calls a strong voice behind us. 'Let the girl go. She is King Alexander's personal groom. If you harm a hair of her head, he will pursue you to the ends of the earth.'

The Persians stop laughing at Charm and me, and whirl in alarm to face this new threat. Charm gives a cry of relief.

'Queen Penthesilea!'

I smell the Amazon horses and whinny to them. They remember me, and whinny back. In the dawn light, ghostly blue circles show on their coats, and their little horns glint. The Amazons have daubed their own cheeks with blood. Their hair is braided tightly, and their war axes rest across their knees. Bows and quivers full of arrows are slung over their shoulders.

While the Persians stare in amazement at the Amazon herd, the Persian boss smiles. 'So, there *are* more of you! The Macedonian army is led by a boy, lets girls groom its horses, and sends women to fight its battles . . . on second thoughts, Great King Darius doesn't have much to worry about, after all. But thank you for telling us who this girl is, warrior woman. We'd hoped simply for information. Now perhaps, your king will negotiate a ransom for his pretty groom?'

With a wild warbling cry, Penthesilea sets her horse into a gallop, whirling her axe over her head. The other Amazons charge, too, and there are thuds and cries as they battle with the Persian herd. A spray of blood hits me on my blind side, and a ghost ripples into the dawn. The men who were still on foot leap on to their horses. One of them tries to grab Charm and pull her up in front of him. She grips her dagger in a tight fist and stabs him in the leg. I bite his horse on the neck, and it wheels away in terror.

A space opens around us. Charm finally struggles up on to my back, grabs my trailing halter lead and drags my head round.

'Go with the others, Charmeia!' Queen Penthesilea shouts, axing another Persian.

Amazon horses surround me, and we are galloping again. It is very exciting. I charge through them, giving them flat ears. By the time we reach the rocks the queen indicated, Charm and I are in the lead, where we belong.

We pull up, dancing and snorting. There is still a lot of yelling behind us; most of the Amazon herd stayed with their queen to fight the Persians. The ones who came with us stand guard around me, alert. Charm slides off my back and collapses in a little heap at my feet. I lower my head and snort into her mane. She is shaking all over. I graze a few stalks around her legs, and gradually she becomes calmer.

The sun rises, bringing colour to the mountains, before the rest of the Amazon herd joins us. Persian ghosts are still whirling away. But none of the Amazon ghosts have left their bodies, because they are already on the outside. The scar on Queen Penthesilea's cheek pulses purple, and her face is spattered with blood. Her axe drips.

'Spies and assassins!' She spits on the rocks. 'King Darius sent them to raid the Macedonian camp for the king's horse, and ordered them to block the Syrian Gates in case King Alexander tried to retreat through them. I think they do not know King Alexander very well. They certainly did not expect to meet us!'

She hands the reins of her horse to one of her herd and

kneels beside Charm. She's within reach of my teeth but I back away, disturbed by her inside-out ghost. She puts her arms around Charm and holds her tightly. 'They have gone,' she murmurs. 'You are safe now.'

Charm bursts into tears.

Queen Penthesilea holds her until she stops crying. She pushes a curl out of Charm's eye, sighs, and says, 'You have bloodied your weapon. You must wear the Amazon mark now.' She wipes her finger through the wet blood on the blade of her axe and draws a red circle on Charm's cheek. 'There! You are now a warrior!'

The other Amazons smile and give a cheer.

But Charm struggles to her feet and smudges the mark with her palm. She shakes her head. 'I'm not a warrior! I could never kill anyone like you did just now. I felt sick when I stabbed that Persian . . . but I didn't have any choice. Oh, Queen Penthesilea, I was so *scared*. I thought they were going to chop off my hands, like they did to the poor mulemaster! But then Bucephalas came.' She looks at me in wonder and whispers, 'He came to find me.'

The Amazon queen gives her a steady look. 'You didn't steal him, then? You weren't running away?'

'No!' Charm's eyes widen. 'King Alexander *sent* me away. I was following the army, hiding in the rocks. That's when the Persians found me, and then Bucephalas . . .' She stares up at the sky. 'It's morning! I have to get him back to the king before the battle! But he said he never wants to see me near his horse again. Queen Penthesilea, what am I going to do?'

The queen looks at my broken halter rope. She nods. 'I believe you, and I think King Alexander will have to reconsider. I think you share the horse bond with Bucephalas as strongly as your king does, though I have never seen it work between a horse and two humans before – no wonder there is such power when the three of you are together! Those Persian spies could have done a lot of damage if they had captured you both. But it is too late. King Alexander has already begun his battle formation. He sent us up here because the scouts reported seeing Persian troops behind his line.'

Charm stares at her in horror. 'But he has to be properly mounted when he meets King Darius! He told me so himself.' Then she looks at me, and her face relaxes as she realizes I am going to miss the battle, after all. 'Who's he riding?'

Queen Penthesilea smiles. 'Let us go and see, shall we, young Charmeia?'

Ghosts and rumours

Charm rides me at the front of the Amazon herd next to Queen Penthesilea's horse with its blue circles. As we descend through the clouds into the valley where the Persian fires burned last night, a great noise rises to meet us – war cries, shouts, screams, and frightened neighs. We flick our ears back and forth and flare our nostrils: we can smell the blood. Then a trumpet echoes from the mountainsides, and the sound makes me shiver all over. Charm winds her fingers into my mane and tightens my halter lead.

'Steady, Bucephalas,' she whispers. 'Steady.'

Queen Penthesilea gives me a sideways look. 'I think this is close enough. We shall wait here.'

'No,' Charm says, gripping my mane tighter. 'I can manage him. I have to see Alexander. I have to see if he's . . . winning.'

The Amazon queen looks hard at her, then dismounts with

a sigh and takes the bridle off her own horse. 'Swap!' she orders, handing it to Charm. 'I am not going to be responsible for losing you on the battlefield because I let you ride Bucephalas in a halter.'

I don't like the Amazon bit because it tastes of strange horse. But Queen Penthesilea pulls my ear, and between them they get the bridle on me. Charm remounts, and we follow a gully with a stream running down it. The rocks block our view of the battle, but I can smell that my herd went this way, and take hold of the strange bit impatiently. I should be at the front, not the back. I wish Charm would let me gallop.

Finally, we emerge on to a plateau near the coast and see the battle below us. It looks like the usual chaos. In the centre, our phalanx is struggling against the Persian line. Our cavalry seems to be mixed in with the enemy, and there is a thick knot of fighting around the Persian chariots. Dead and dying men and horses lie everywhere, their ghosts escaping through the dust. Down by the beach, there is more fierce fighting.

'Where's Alexander?' says Charm, frantically searching the field. 'Can anyone see the king? Are we winning?'

Penthesilea smiles. 'Looks like it. The Persians are running away. See?' She points to the mountains, where small groups of men in yellow scarves are fleeing for their lives.

'But where's the *king*?' Charm looks at the knot of men and horses round the chariots. 'I can't see him. He might have been killed!'

'Not a chance!' Penthesilea says, giving her a frown. 'If King Alexander were dead, the Macedonians would have stopped fighting. Come. I think we can risk going down now.'

As we get closer to the valley floor, a herd of blood-spattered Persians run up the slope towards us, looking over their shoulders. They don't notice us until we are upon them. The Amazons cut them down with their axes, and their ghosts ripple past us. Charm grips my mane and watches with a sick expression. Further down, bodies fill the gullies, and I have to tread carefully to avoid stepping on them. Loose horses join us. I give them flat ears and send them to the back so they are not in the way. None of them put up a fight – they have all lost their riders, so they are ashamed.

At the river, we find a detachment of Macedonians with their long pikes, weary but grinning, standing on a makeshift bridge. In the dusk, it takes me a moment to realize the bridge is made of Persian dead. Nearby, a horse lies in the water, spears sticking out of it. We snort sadly as we pass it.

Queen Penthesilea questions the men about Alexander's whereabouts, but they don't seem to know much more than we do. 'Last I saw, he was leadin' the charge on King Darius' Royal Guard,' says one. 'He's probably still up by the chariots.'

'Nah, he went to help General Parmenio down by the beach.'

'Don't be stupid! He was right here in the centre, didn't you see? Cut down a hundred Persians before my very eyes!'

'Zeus was looking after him, all right. I saw lightnin' flashing around his head.'

'That was when *you* got hit on the head, you fool! Look sharp! Here come more Persian deserters!'

Without seeing us, the Persians jump down a little cliff on the far side of the river, only to find themselves trapped. Our men's long pikes soon release their ghosts, and the Amazons catch those who try to flee. I dance impatiently, trying to reach the enemy with my teeth and hooves as I have been trained to do. But the Amazon horses are in the way, and Charm holds me on a tight rein, flinching whenever another Persian dies.

'I reckon King Alexander must've killed King Darius,' another Macedonian says, once they have finished off the Persians. 'That's why they're all runnin' away, ain't it?'

'Yeah, I heard they had a duel, just like Achilles and Prince Hector did in the *Iliad*. King Darius wounded King Alexander, but King Alexander struggled up again and killed him.'

Charm gives a little gasp.

'Nonsense!' says their officer, arriving on a mare covered in grime from the river. He gives me and Charm a frown, as if he thinks he should know us. I know who *he* is at once, because it's Zephyr under all that mud, who – if you remember – carries General Parmenio's son, Philotas. The little mare whinnies a weary greeting. I nicker to her in sympathy, because I can see she's had a hard battle.

'Alexander's gone chasing after King Darius,' Philotas says. 'The Persian coward left his chariot behind, jumped on a fresh horse and fled into the hills. He abandoned his men, that's why they're running. We're to mop up here, and meet the king at the Persian camp when he decides to return. Watch out in the dark for more deserters. They're sneaky fellows.'

Queen Penthesilea nods and turns her horse, but Charm drags my head round and urges me after Zephyr. 'Which horse is the king riding?'

Philotas gives her an irritated look. 'How would I know? That big gold horse with a scar on its head, I think. Stupid grooms let his precious Bucephalas run off into the hills last night. The king wasn't too happy, I can tell you, especially after that business with the severed hands. Never seen him in such a mood as when he marched us all down here. I swear we could all feel his fury rippling right along the line. I wouldn't want to be in King Darius' slippers when Alexander catches up with him, that's for sure!' He drags Zephyr's head round and shouts at his men, who are leaning on their pikes discussing the battle. 'Get moving, you lot! The sooner we finish up here, the sooner you can all get your hands on some Persian loot and start celebrating.'

He still doesn't recognize me, but then I suppose I'm not looking my best. No one's groomed me since the Syrian Gates, and I'm wearing a scruffy Amazon bridle. Charm looks a bit like an Amazon, too, since the queen painted blood on her cheeks.

'Xanthus!' she whispers to the queen, relieved. 'He'll be all right on Xanthus – he's almost as big as Bucephalas.'

Sometimes, I think my groom understands nothing at all.

Zoroaster

The Persian camp was almost as chaotic as the battlefield. Blood-spattered Macedonians were raiding the tents, piling gold and jewels into great heaps that glittered in the firelight. They also found some Persian women, who screamed as our men invaded their tents. Some ran across our path, their dresses torn and their long manes flying. The Amazons gave them grim looks, but did nothing to help. 'Do not think about it,' Queen Penthesilea advised Charm, when she opened her mouth to protest. 'It is war. At least they will stay alive. King Alexander is sensible not to bring women with his army.'

'What about us?' Charm whispered.

We passed an enormous pavilion, even fancier than King

Alexander's. Macedonian guards stood with crossed pikes at the entrance, and soft weeping came from inside. More guards stood round a huge chariot of gold, its shaft and footplate carved with pictures of monsters. Its wheel hubs glittered with huge red jewels. Queen Penthesilea rode across for a closer look, but a Macedonian pike blocked her way.

'Keep away!' the man shouted. 'This is King Darius' tent. No one's to touch anything of his until King Alexander gets here!'

We found our grooms setting up the horse lines. I smelt Harpinna, and whinnied in delight. Little Hoplite bounded out, tail flicking, to greet us. The lines were not yet full. The horses who had been in the battle were tired and sweaty, and some had wounds that their grooms were sponging clean. I couldn't smell any of the horses of the Guard, and started to worry. But as we neared the lines, Tydeos came running towards us, grinning.

'You found Bucephalas!'

Queen Penthesilea smiled and tactfully led her herd away to find a space for the Amazon camp, while Charm slid down from my back and threw herself into Tydeos' arms.

'Where were you?' he said, embarrassed but smiling in a funny way. 'I looked all over for you! We thought the Persians had captured you.'

'They nearly did! But Bucephalas saved me, and then the Amazons came and killed the Persians who'd grabbed me . . . I know Alexander will be furious when he finds me here, but I had to bring Bucephalas back. Is he in the camp?' She stared round nervously.

But Tydeos shook his head. 'Not yet. He's still off chasing King Darius. Come and have something to eat. The Persians have left enough food and treasure to feed and clothe all Macedonia and half of Greece for a hundred years!' He pushed Charm's mane behind her ear and touched the smudged circle of blood on her cheek. 'Don't worry, we'll hide you when he comes back. No one will tell on you. It weren't fair, what he said to you, even if you did lie to him about your dream. He's the king. It was his decision to take the army to the Syrian Gates, not yours. Come on, cheer up! We've found the most incredible horse . . .'

I have already smelt him. He is tethered at the end of our horse line near my usual spot. He is white all over and nearly as big as me, though he is fat and soft, not hard and muscular like us warhorses. His mane has been braided with silver threads, and his tail has little bells in it that tinkle whenever he flicks away a fly.

He smells of flowers, and he looks ridiculous.

I make myself huge and squeal at him. Charm gives a little gasp and tugs on my rein. 'No, Bucephalas – not another battle, please!' But the white horse doesn't squeal back. He simply turns his big dark eyes on us, pricks his ears and stares at me. Then he gives a big sigh and goes back to his hay.

This is MOST confusing! It is a male horse, but it acts more like a mare.

'He's supposed to be sacred to the sun,' Tydeos whispers. 'Part of King Darius' divine power, or something. The Persian captives say he's never carried anyone on his back. But he'll have to learn. He's King Alexander's now!'

Charm strokes my nose. 'Don't worry, Bucephalas. Alexander still loves you the most.' But she is interested in the white horse, I can tell. All the time, as she settles and rubs me down, she's looking at it. 'So gentle,' she murmurs eventually.

'I wonder why Bucephalas didn't fight? It's not like him.'

Tydeos laughs. 'You don't want to know the details. The Persians have taken his spirit away and given it to their god. It means he'll never be able to get a mare in foal. They do the same thing to their male slaves, apparently – and they call *us* barbarians!'

Charm stares at the white horse. 'Oh, poor horse . . . I thought that was just a Scythian thing? And to think the old horsemaster tried to make Bucephalas fat and soft like that! What's his name?'

'We've called him Zoroaster, after the Persians' holy prophet.'

So THAT is what happens to a horse after the Scythian thing? You get to wear ridiculous silver bells, go fat and soft, and lose interest in fighting?

It must be worse than a spiked bit, after all.

Forgiveness

Alexander did not catch the Persian king that night.

The horses of the Guard came back around midnight, their heads low and their coats caked in dried sweat and grime. Too tired to whinny, Petasios and Borealis blew at me as Tydeos tethered them beside me. Aura lay down immediately her cloth was removed. Arion, Hades and Apollo walked past the new horse without even noticing it, and drank noisily from the buckets of water the grooms brought them from the river.

Xanthus, who had been carrying Alexander, was in the worst state of all. He limped to the horse lines, snorting with pain, and barely looked at me as he passed my swishing tail. He had a deep spear wound in his neck and dried blood all down his shoulder. I gave him a little squeal to let him know what I thought of him for challenging me in the hills earlier. But afterwards, I sent him a low whinny of sympathy to show I had forgiven him. I know what it is like after a big battle, when the excitement has worn off and you start to feel the pain of your wounds. Alexander would have caught King Darius easily if he had been riding ME, of course. But you can't blame Xanthus for being a bit slow.

Charm and Tydeos worked in silence until all the horses were watered, doctored, clean, fed and settled. This took them the rest of the night, so Charm was dirty and tired by the time Alexander came to see us.

This time, he didn't come unannounced. Trumpets sounded, and the big golden chariot we had seen the previous night rumbled through the piles of Persian treasure, glittering in the sunrise. Alexander stood in it, wearing a long purple cloak trimmed with gold. His mane had been freshly washed and was caught in a golden crown. Hephaestion drove the two Persian horses at a slow trot so all the men could cheer their king. Sitting in the chariot behind Alexander was a small man-colt with a long black mane, holding a wriggling puppy in his arms.

Charm wiped her hands on her filthy tunic and stood stiffly beside me. Tydeos squeezed her arm and stood between her and the chariot.

Alexander called for Hephaestion to stop. He took a good look at me, then turned his attention to Charm. 'I see you caught Bucephalas,' he called. 'Come here.'

Tydeos stiffened, but Charm took a deep breath and walked bravely up to the chariot, where she bowed her head.

Alexander looked down at her matted curls and her ragged scarf. He sighed and jumped down – rather stiffly – from the platform. His cloak billowed, and I saw he had a bandage around his thigh. Charm saw it too, and her eyes flickered from the bandage to his face.

'It's nothing.' Alexander waved a hand. 'King Darius pricked me with his dagger, that's all. Here, Ochus!' He pulled the man-colt to the side of the chariot and pointed to me. 'See that horse? He's not as friendly as my dog. You can play with Perita, but you're not to go near Bucephalas. Understand? Dangerous horse. Dangerous!'

He bared his teeth and mimed flat ears with his hands. The man-colt smiled. His eyes were black and curious. Alexander ruffled the man-colt's mane and sighed. 'The boy doesn't understand a word, of course, but he'll soon learn Greek. Look out for him, Charmides. Don't let Bucephalas hurt him. He's a valuable hostage.'

I didn't know what a hostage was, but it couldn't have been anything too bad because Ochus was happily playing with the puppy Perita in the chariot. They were having a tug-of-war with one of the silly tassels the Persian horses wear on their bridles. Perita was winning. Alexander smelt faintly of flowers, but it didn't hide his familiar sherbet sweetness when he ran his hand down my nose. He had a stale honey cake in his pocket. I licked the crumbs greedily from his palm, and he smiled again.

'Ah, Bucephalas, I missed you yesterday! Why did you have to run off like that? I wouldn't *really* dismiss your groom, you know.'

Charm, who was hovering near me, sucked in her breath and gave the king a flash of her eye. 'Aren't you angry with me for coming back, Sir?'

Alexander laughed. 'Angry? When you brought my

Bucephalas back to me? How could anyone possibly be angry today? We won, didn't we?' His eyes shone. He patted my neck with a firm hand and spun round, arms spread wide, purple cloak flying. 'Look at all this treasure! I bathed in King Darius' golden tub last night, and ate off a golden plate. And this isn't even half of it. The main Persian baggage train is still in Damascus – I've sent General Parmenio on ahead to collect it. King Darius has fled back to Persia. There's no one to stop me marching straight down the coast to Egypt. But I can't have my horse undressed and my groom looking like a muleteer when we get there. This is for Bucephalas to wear on the march.'

He lifted a tasselled cloth out of the chariot and dumped it in Charm's arms. He hesitated, glanced at Hephaestion, then pulled from his pocket a length of purple silk embroidered with gold thread, and draped it round her neck with a man-coltish grin. 'And this scarf is for your hair! When you've cleaned yourself up, get Bucephalas ready for parade – we've a military funeral to take care of before we leave.'

Charm's cheeks flared red. Before she could speak, Alexander climbed back into his chariot and ordered Hephaestion to drive him around the rest of the camp.

That was how we dominated the Persians at Issus:

Persian dead: 2,000

Macedonian dead: 450

Horses dead: 150 (VERY sad, but pulling a chariot is like being tethered in a battle, so the poor Persian horses didn't stand a chance.)

Hostages: King Darius' mother, wife, two daughters, his son Ochus, and Persian-slipper-licking Memnon's wife Lady Barsine

Before we left, Alexander renamed a little harbour town at the mouth of the river 'Alexandretta'. I assume that means we have stopped liberating and started dominating again. Ha!

Fourteenth Hoofprint
PHOENICIA, 333–332 BC

Squealing at Tyre

With me prancing at the front of the battle-hardened army, wearing my new tasselled cloth and carrying Alexander in his white-plumed Troy helmet, we made a fine sight as we marched down the Phoenician coast. More mercenaries joined us, attracted (as you humans are) by the gold Alexander had captured from the Persians, so we were a big herd. News of our victory at Issus travelled ahead of us, and we dominated lots of towns without a fight:

Gabala, Paltos, Aradus, Marathus, Mariamne, Tripolis, Byblos, Sidon.

Since they all submitted quickly and brought gifts of golden crowns to Alexander, he let them keep their silly names. But he left a Macedonian garrison on the coast in case any of them changed their minds later. He called this new town

Alexandria, which I'm sure you'll agree is a better name than Alexandropolis or Alexandretta. I didn't fight in the battle at Issus so I'm not *too* upset he didn't name it after me. At least he didn't name it after Xanthus.

We ignored King Darius' squeals that we go home (which he sent on flattened grass because he was still licking his wounds after the battle), and everything went well until we reached a place called Tyre, which made the mistake of closing its gates against us.

Tyre stands on an island off the Phoenician shore. It has high, rocky walls and several harbours crammed with warships. No one can get into the city without swimming or going on a ship. If this city were a horse, it would be Borealis – strong and steady, but not big enough to challenge the boss. If only someone had told them.

We horses stop on the beach and snort at the sea. The channel between the mainland and the island looks deep, and crests of white foam dance along it. The wind smells of salt.

At first, everything seems fine. Men row a boat across from the city, bringing the usual gold crown. Alexander smiles as he leans down from my back to accept the gift. I give the fat man who hands it up to him flat ears to warn him not to touch the king, and he retreats hurriedly.

'The city of Tyre congratulates King Alexander on his victory at Issus,' announces the fat man in an important-sounding voice. 'And begs that he accept an additional gift of provisions for his army, so that his men will not go hungry as they pass through our lands on their way to Egypt. Tyre will not oppose you. You may continue your march.'

Alexander looks up from examining the glittering stars on the crown, and frowns. 'I may continue my march? That's generous of you.'

His words are very quiet. The Tyrian envoys do not realize what a dangerous sign this is, and smile in relief.

'We'll send them over to you at once so you won't need to linger here,' says the fat man, still smiling. 'Fresh supplies just in from Carthage, plenty of grain for your horses.' He eyes me. 'Your royal charger looks as if he has a good appetite.'

I give a little squeal and shake my head at him. Alexander steadies me and passes the crown to Hephaestion. He narrows his eyes at the fat Tyrian and says in the same dangerously quiet voice, 'And why do you assume we want to continue our march so soon? My men are weary, my horses need rest, and I would like to make a sacrifice in your city's temple.'

The envoys glance at one another. The fat man clears his throat. 'Of course, Your Majesty! A sacrifice of thanks for your victory at Issus, of course! Please feel free to camp for as long as you want, and use the temple in our old city on the shore.'

'I want to sacrifice inside your city walls,' Alexander says. 'I'd like to take a look around. With some of my men, of course.'

There is a longer pause. The envoys shuffle their feet in the sand. The fat man clears his throat again. 'I assure you, Your Majesty, our god will hear you at the temple in the old city just as loudly as he will inside Tyre. We mean no offence, but I'm sure you understand that until this war is over we must preserve our neutrality. We can't afford to show favour to either side, Persian or Macedonian. We said the same to King Darius, and he in his royal wisdom respected our wishes.' He gives Alexander a sly look. 'Or is Darius, perhaps, more of a king than Alexander?'

WRONG thing to say.

Alexander's fist tightens on my rein. His entire body goes rigid. The blood rises to his cheeks, and his breathing quickens. Hephaestion urges Petasios forward, bringing the gold crown to remind Alexander of the gift. But it is too late.

Alexander snatches the crown, digs his heels into my sides and rides me straight at the fat man. The envoy throws himself into the sand in terror. Alexander hurls the crown at him like a javelin, hitting him on the cheek. The other envoys scatter and stare in terror at the king.

Alexander has drawn his sword. It flashes in the winter sunlight as he holds it over his head. He looks as if he intends to cut the fat man in two, like he did the Gordian Knot. Sensing his fury, I make myself huge.

'Get out of my sight!' Alexander yells. 'Go back and hide behind your walls! If you won't welcome me into your city as a king, then I'll force my way in. But you'll be sorry when I do. Yours won't be the first city my army has destroyed.'

The fat man cowers with the other envoys, one palm pressed to his cheek, which is bleeding where the gold stars on the crown cut him. The crown dangles from his other hand. He doesn't seem to know what to do with it. Then one of the others nudges him, and he holds it out again with trembling fingers.

'Please, King Alexander . . . look at our defences! You have no ships, and our city has never submitted to a siege. Please take the crown and reconsider? We merely ask to be allowed to remain neutral. I promise we won't oppose you if you leave us alone.'

But Alexander is past listening. He wheels me round and jerks his head at his Guard. 'Escort these men back to their boat,' he orders in an icy voice. 'And if any of them say another word about me being less of a king than Darius, kill them.'

The envoys flee, taking the crown with them. They are not that stupid.

As their boat rows back through the choppy waves, there is silence on the shore. The Guard glance at one another with stricken faces. We horses stamp and snort, impatient for battle. But it doesn't look as if there will be one just yet.

Alexander puts his sword away, and Hephaestion rides Petasios up beside me. He says softly, 'Was that wise, Alex? They're right. We don't have ships with us any more, so we can't attack them from the sea. And aren't you anxious to reach Egypt to talk to the oracle? That island's too far from shore to use our catapults, and not even Zeus could roll siege towers through that channel!' He smiles ruefully and adds, 'Though no doubt if you could find a way, you'd do it.'

Alexander's breathing slows. The fierce light around him fades. He closes his eyes and presses his palm to his forehead. Then with a sigh he runs a hand down my neck. 'Ah, horse, fools like that make me so angry. They shouldn't have suggested I wasn't a proper king. Why does everyone call Darius "Great King", anyway? He ran away from the battle and left his whole family behind in enemy hands! I'd never leave *my* mother in such danger.'

'Which is why the queen mother is safe back in Pella,' Hephaestion says smoothly. 'And why you're a better king than Darius.' He looks thoughtfully at Tyre. 'What do you think? Shall we send them a formal demand for surrender, now you've scared them? See what they say? If they've got any sense, they'll let us in this time. You were terrifying! I thought

Bucephalas was going to eat that fat man alive.'

Alexander chuckles. 'Bucephalas has got more sense. He'd have choked on the Tyrian arrogance.' He squints across the channel at the city. 'Yes, I suppose that would be easiest. The last thing we need is another long siege like Halicarnassus. Maybe they realize who they're dealing with now. Find me some heralds.'

You might think this was amazingly calm and sensible of Alexander. Not many who dared suggest he wasn't a proper king got a second chance. They were lucky his good mood from Issus hadn't quite worn off. But the Tyrians did something extremely stupid. Our heralds did not return with the answer Alexander wanted. Instead, their headless bodies came back over the walls of Tyre and splashed into the sea. Needless to say, their ghosts had already gone.

This time, not even Hephaestion could persuade Alexander to march past Tyre without a fight.

The Persian god's curse

Alexander assembled the army and announced they would build a land bridge across the channel to Tyre, strong enough for the siege engines and wide enough for the phalanx to attack. The men stared at him in horror. Some muttered that it was impossible. Alexander assured them it was not, and claimed he'd had a prophetic dream in which the Greek hero Hercules had beckoned to him from the walls of Tyre. He ordered them to demolish the ruins of the old city for foundation stones, and sent troops inland to secure a supply of timber and to conscript men from the local towns and villages to help. Then he put the scientists to work designing the great bridge.

While the men and mules sweated at Tyre, the rest of us made camp on the banks of the nearest river, where we older horses had a holiday and the youngsters learnt battle manoeuvres. My huge filly Electra became quite fierce when Ptolemy charged the hay-stuffed targets with his spear. Although my colt Hoplite was still too young to carry a rider, Charm led him around the camp to get him used to the noise and smells. Most of the horses who had fought in the battle needed the rest, though Apollo used the tiniest scratch on his leg as an excuse to limp.

Then there was ridiculous Zoroaster.

After we had been camped at Tyre for a month, and everyone had realized the bridge wouldn't be finished for ages, Alexander ordered that the white horse be backed so he would be of some use. He gave the job to Charm and Tydeos, saying he wanted to prove Darius' 'divine power' was so small it could be taken away by mere grooms. The truth was, no one wanted to waste their time training a horse who would be useless in battle, and none of the men could be spared from the building work.

Our grooms choose a cool bright morning before the breeze gets up. Charm puts Zoroaster's bridle on him and fastens an old exercise cloth over his back. He must have worn such things before on parades, because he doesn't mind. He turns his head to chew a corner of the cloth, which is not exactly the Persian finery he is used to. Charm fastens a lead rein to his noseband, and spends ages fiddling with the straps to get the bit at the right height in his mouth.

Tydeos calls out for her to hurry up because he still has four horses to exercise that morning. So does Charm, and one of them is me. But before they can lead Zoroaster out of the lines, Prince Ochus darts up to the white horse and starts tugging at his breast strap. Alexander's puppy Perita, who is much bigger now, bounds about his feet yapping. She thinks it is a game.

'Stop that, Ochus!' Charm says. 'He has to be ridden today, do you understand? The king ordered it.'

Ochus shakes his head and gabbles something in his own tongue. Zoroaster blows into the prince's dark mane, curious.

Tydeos shrugs at Charm. 'Can you understand a word he's saying?'

She shakes her head. But I'd say it's obvious: the prince does not want them to ride Zoroaster. Meanwhile, an excited Perita yaps around Zoroaster's hooves. It's a good job the Persians took his spirit away, I can tell you. If those were the hooves of any other horse, she'd have got kicked halfway back to Anatolia by now.

Before our grooms can decide what to do with the prince, a breathless Lady Barsine arrives. She, if you remember, is Persian-slipper-licking Memnon's widow, the woman General Parmenio sent to Alexander from Damascus after he'd captured the Persian baggage train. She smells of barley mash when she gets warm, which she is at the moment because she's just run from the centre of our camp chasing Ochus and Perita.

'I'm sorry,' Lady Barsine says, drawing the man-colt away from us. 'I tried to keep him in the tent with his mother, but he's as slippery as an eel.'

Charm bites her lip. 'What's he saying?'

Lady Barsine smiles. 'He says you mustn't ride the sacred horse – it would bring bad luck on his family, and you'd die from the curse. The Persians believe the sacred sun-horse is a bond between the royal family and their god.'

216

Tydeos and Charm glance at each other.

'King Alexander thinks backing him will take King Darius' power away,' Charm says. 'Is that true?'

Lady Barsine smiles again as she straightens Ochus' tunic. 'Who knows? Stranger things happen in this world. Who would have believed young Alexander would ever defeat Great King Darius in battle? The last time I saw Alexander, he was Ochus' age and playing with a wooden sword.'

'You knew the king when he was small?' Charm says, a bit too sharply. 'What was he like?'

'Like all small boys,' Lady Barsine says. 'He thought the world was his to conquer. Most of them soon realize they have to share it. Alexander still believes it's his, that's the difference. Boys like him don't come along very often, thank the gods.' She sighs and stares across the camp. 'General Parmenio didn't send me to Alexander by chance, you know. He hopes I will take the place of his mother, maybe calm his temper and take his mind off this burning desire he has to prove he is better than every other king in the world. But I think the damage has already been done. I heard how he cut the Gordian Knot and the sky cracked open. Maybe those rumours about him being fathered by a demon are truer than we think.'

She gives Charm a steady look. 'You know the Amazon queen thinks there's a bond between you and Alexander, through Bucephalas? If that's true, then anything that happens to you will affect the king and his horse. I don't know if the Persian curse exists, but only a fool invites that kind of trouble.'

Out of the corner of my eye, I see Tydeos shaking his head. But Charm stiffens. 'Maybe we shouldn't back the sacred horse?' she whispers to Tydeos. 'We could just pretend to have done it.'

Tydeos frowns. 'No, we couldn't! What'll happen when King Alexander tells one of his men to mount the horse, expecting him to be broken? Zoroaster might look quiet now, but he's big. If he decided to throw someone off, he could do it, no trouble! What if the king himself got on him?'

'Zoroaster couldn't throw Alexander,' Charm says. 'Perhaps I could tell him I had another prophetic dream.'

'He won't fall for that again.'

'*He* lied, about his dream of Hercules standing on the walls of Tyre.'

'How do you know?'

'Because if Alexander really did have prophetic dreams, he wouldn't need to keep asking me and his official seer, would he? And he'd have known about the Amanic Gates . . .'

Lady Barsine is listening carefully. Ochus asks her something, but she shakes her head. 'Speak Greek, Ochus,' she says. 'Ask them yourself.'

Ochus straightens his shoulders and clenches his small fists. 'Me – ride – horse.'

Charm looks surprised and her expression softens. 'He wants to go for a ride? Is that allowed? Maybe we could put him up on Aura.'

But Ochus shakes his head fiercely and points to Zoroaster.

Tydeos laughs. 'Oh no, little prince, not that horse! He's not broken yet. You don't understand, do you? Can't you explain to him, Lady? I don't think he's allowed to go riding, anyway. Isn't he supposed to be King Alexander's hostage?'

Lady Barsine's lips tighten. She glances at the sentries, who are watching but don't interfere. She often brings Prince Ochus down to the horse lines to teach him the Greek words for things.

Ochus gabbles something to her. Another question in Persian, though he uses the same word 'hostage' that Tydeos used.

Lady Barsine smooths Ochus' mane and says softly, 'The guards won't let his grandmother, mother, or his sisters out of their pavilion. He'll hardly run away on his own. He's only seven.'

'We'll get into trouble if we let him go riding,' Tydeos says with a stubborn look. 'I'm sorry, Lady, but we can't take orders from you. You're a prisoner, too. You'll have to ask King Alexander.'

Lady Barsine's eyes cloud in anger. Ochus is still asking her about 'hostage', tugging at her sleeve. She snaps something in Persian at the boy, and his face goes still. He frowns at Zoroaster, then calls Perita and heads back towards King Darius' pavilion. His head is high and his back stiff, exactly like Alexander's when he strides away from someone who has just said something he doesn't like. Lady Barsine gives Tydeos a look that is the human equivalent of flat ears, and hurries after the man-colt.

'What did I say?' Tydeos mutters to Charm as he unties Zoroaster from the horse lines. 'Why's she so upset? Who does she think she is, anyway? Coming down here with the boy, expecting us to give him a ride on one of King Alexander's horses! What a cheek.'

'I don't think Prince Ochus knows he's supposed to be a hostage. He calls Alexander "Uncle", doesn't he? And Alexander's always nice to him.'

'So? He'll still kill him if King Darius tries to fight us again.'

Charm bites her lip. 'Do you think it's true? That whoever rides Zoroaster will die?'

'Of course it's not true! Zoroaster's not Bucephalas. The worst he can do is buck us off, and it won't be the first time a horse has done that to me. Don't worry, I'll sit on him. You can lead him round. Here, hold him still so I can lean over his back to get him used to my weight.'

'No, Tydeos!' Charm sounds more scared for Tydeos than she is for herself.

'I'll do it,' says a rough voice on my blind side.

At first, I think it is a ghost standing there. I leap in alarm, nearly breaking my tether. Then I recognize his smell. It is the mulemaster whose hands were chopped off by the Persians at Issus. He had refused to stay with the other crippled men Alexander left behind.

'If that horse is cursed, there's no point two youngsters like you fallin' foul of it. What would Bucephalas do without you? Me, I'm no use to anyone now. What's the Persian god goin' to do to me that's worse than what Darius' men have already done? Let me sit on 'im.'

Charm stares at his ruined wrists. 'No, you shouldn't have to—' she starts to say.

But Tydeos says with some relief, 'Good idea! You won't need to hold the reins the first time. We should have thought of it before. We'll lead him round while you sit on his back and teach him to obey your legs and weight. Er . . . you do know how to ride a horse, don't you?'

The mulemaster spits. 'I was backin' mules before you two were born! Horses are a piece of cake after them, believe me.'

They lead Zoroaster away to a quiet spot, and bring him back at a trot soon afterwards, with Charm running beside his head and Tydeos flicking a whip behind his tail to keep him moving. Zoroaster seems perfectly happy, though he is sweating and breathless. Bouncing on his cloth is the old mulemaster, his ruined arms spread wide for balance, and an even bigger grin on his face than when he used to tease me back in Pella.

'No problem!' he announces as he slithers off the white horse. 'King Darius' divine power ain't worth nothin' now. Next time they meet, King Alexander will be able to kill him.'

Dominating Tyre

By summer, Alexander's 'impossible' bridge had reached the walls of Tyre. This is how he did it:

Our herd: throw stones into the sea.

Tyrian herd: laugh.

Our herd: throw more stones into the sea and fix tree trunks on top.

Tyrian herd: get worried and start making anti-siege equipment.

Our herd: throw more stones into the sea.

Tyrian herd: send out ships to kill the men working on the bridge.

Our herd: call on dominated towns to send us some ships so we can fight back.

Tyrian herd: panic!

We horses didn't get to fight in the battle, though. Alexander told the grooms to keep us bridled in case we were needed in a hurry. Then he led his entire army to Tyre, even those injured during the building work, who were so furious with the Tyrians they didn't want to miss the final fight.

With all the men except a handful of sentries gone off to Tyre, it is eerily quiet in the camp. Wearing our quilted battle-cloths, we horses sweat in the Phoenician heat. We have been given hay, but none of us has much appetite because Charm and Tydeos are weaning Hoplite, and Harpinna's distressed neighs upset us.

Charm tethers Hoplite securely to the other end of our horse line, while Tydeos and two other strong grooms take Harpinna along the riverbank out of sight. Their whinnies get louder and more frantic. Hoplite is still only a yearling, but he's definitely *my* yearling: he fights very fiercely, and Charm calls for help. The remaining grooms and our sentries go to watch the fun.

None of them notice Zoroaster is loose, until a white flash passes behind our tails and disappears on my blind side. I whinny to warn the silly horse not to run off without his groom. But Zoroaster is not loose. Crouched on his back, clinging to his long white mane, is Prince Ochus. He's pounding Zoroaster's sides with his small heels to make him go faster.

The sentries sound the alarm. Charm leaves Hoplite in the care of the other grooms, drags off my cloth and scrambles on to my back. I flatten my ears and gallop after Zoroaster. More hooves pound after us, and I see Harpinna out of the corner of my eye with Tydeos crouched over her neck, urging her on with a whip.

Zoroaster has a good start, and he's quite fit now he's had some training. We chase him for a surprising distance before I manage to get my head in front. I give Zoroaster flat ears and a squeal. But he doesn't slow down to fight me, like a normal stallion would, nor does he swerve like a mare. He merely sticks out his white neck and gallops on.

'Turn him, Charm!' Tydeos yells behind us. 'Head him back to camp. Don't let him get to Tyre, whatever you do!'

We reach the beach where Alexander's bridge crosses over to Tyre, and the noise of the battle makes me shiver all over. The air is full of shouts, screams, war cries, the crack of our siege engines, and the splash of missiles falling into the sea. Our ships surround Tyre, bristling with men and siege equipment. A phalanx of Macedonian pikemen blocks the end of the bridge to catch those trying to escape from the city.

This must frighten Ochus, because he stops kicking Zoroaster. As the white horse slows, Charm leans across to grab the reins. Harpinna catches up, covered in foam and breathing hard. Tydeos takes hold of Ochus' ankle and tips him off into the sand. Charm leads Zoroaster clear so he doesn't tread on the man-colt, and I bite the white horse on the nose to tell him what I think of him. He lowers his head and looks ashamed.

'You little idiot!' Tydeos yells, throwing himself off Harpinna and grabbing Ochus by the arm. 'What did you think you were doing? You could have got yourself killed!' He shakes Ochus until tears glisten in the prince's eyes, turns him round and points to the island with its massive land bridge. 'See that? That's what King Alexander will do to your home when we get there, if you don't behave so your father will surrender to him.'

'Don't, Tydeos. It's not his fault. If I were a hostage, I'd try to run away too.' Charm is panting nearly as much as Harpinna. 'Ochus, you have to come back with us. Understand? Your mother and Lady Barsine will be worried about you, and you have to look after Perita for King Alexander.'

Ochus glances quickly at her, and turns his dark eyes on

Tydeos. His chin juts out stubbornly. 'My home not in sea,' he says. 'My father rescue me soon!'

'Ha! You'll be lucky. I heard that in his last letter, King Darius offered to leave you with King Alexander permanently if he'd take his army home.' Tydeos misses the anguished look on the man-colt's face, and stares at the walls of Tyre. 'Charm, see there! Isn't that the king?'

She stiffens. I prick my ears at the city. It is too far away to catch individual smells in the confusion of sweat and smoke mingling with the sea breeze, but I see Alexander's Troy helmet flash on the highest platform of one of the siege ships as he leaps across the gap to the walls. The white plumes flare in the Phoenician sunshine, like the wings of a seabird. With his golden energy shining around him, he flies.

Charm puts her knuckles to her mouth.

A great roar goes up from the Macedonians as Alexander lands safely on the battlements and raises his sword to the sky. He shouts something, pushes three Tyrian soldiers off the wall, and disappears into the city. There are more screams, and a great coil of smoke rises from within the walls.

'Oh, Zeus,' Charm whispers. 'I can't watch this! It'll be just like Thebes, I know it will!' But she keeps staring at the battlements where the king disappeared.

Ochus watches with big eyes. He says nothing.

Finally, Tydeos shudders and says in a sick voice, 'This is no place for us. Come on, let's go.' He lifts the prince on to Zoroaster's back, and I nip the white horse until he puts his muzzle behind Charm's knee, in the easiest place for her to lead him from my back. Tydeos vaults on to Harpinna and rides her on Zoroaster's other side so he can't get away. But Ochus has given up for now. He sits quietly on the white horse, his back straight and his short legs dangling halfway down the cloth. Harpinna has given up fighting too, and walks with her head low. All the man-colt says during the return journey is, 'Not tell Uncle Alexander I try escape, please?'

Charm and Tydeos glance at each other. Charm sighs. 'Don't worry, Ochus, it'll be our secret. We'll say you just wanted to see the battle, if anyone asks.'

Ochus gives her a little smile and strokes Zoroaster's withers. 'Thank you, Charmeia.'

She looks startled that he knows her name. But then she smiles, too.

One good thing came of that day. When Hoplite smelt his mother coming back and neighed to her from the horse lines, Harpinna was too tired to answer. She had obviously decided our colt was old enough to survive without her, so she was back in my herd again!

No longer an island

The Macedonians had six months of anger to work out that day, and Alexander did nothing to keep them under control. The city of Tyre, that had taken us so long to join to the shore, was ours by sunset.

Tyrian dead: 7,000
Tyrian soldiers crucified as a warning to others: 2,000
Tyrians sold as slaves: 30,000
Macedonian dead: 400
Horses dead: none (HURRAH!)
People spared: ambassadors from Carthage. Alexander was angry, but not stupid – Carthage is on the other side of Egypt, and we are going that way.

We didn't get to rename the city. But we did rename their god. When Alexander finally made his sacrifice in the temple of Tyre, he made it to 'Apollo Philalexander'.

WHAT A CHEEK!

I was the one who brought his man-colt hostage and Zoroaster back to camp, with Harpinna's help. What did Apollo do to deserve a god named after him? Nothing, except limp about the camp, complaining of the battle wound he got at Issus.

Sometimes, life is just not fair.

FIFTEENTH HOOFPRINT
GAZA, 332 BC

An unexpected arrow

After the example Alexander made of Tyre, no one dared so much as squeal at us the rest of the way down the coast. General Parmenio rejoined us, so we were a huge, strong herd when we reached the Phoenician border. It looked as though we might ride straight into the Egyptian world with no more fighting.

But at the last moment, a place called Gaza closed its gates to us.

Alexander laughed and said its boss must not yet have heard about Tyre. He ordered the army to make camp on the beach, and we led the Guard inland through the sand dunes to see if we could make Gaza change its mind.

I had some trouble in the desert. Size is not necessarily a good thing on soft sand. Also, I was thirsty and too hot from the march, so I was not quite as alert as usual. When

Alexander halted me at the top of a dune to take a look at the city, a herd of strange horses with silly dished faces and ridiculously high tail carriages came galloping over the top, and a curtain of arrows hissed out of my blind side towards us. I leapt in panic. But my hooves sank in the sand, and Alexander gasped as his weight jerked on my back. I'd carried riders in enough battles to know this was a bad sign, and felt a stab of shame.

Hephaestion whipped out his sword and yelled, 'After them, then!' He urged Petasios after the strange horses. But of the Guard, only Hades and Aura could really handle the sand. The others were soon left behind as the enemy fled into the city, waving their bows over their heads and whooping. The loose horses followed their friends through the gates, which slammed shut behind them.

They left me alone on top of the dune. I wanted to gallop after my herd, but knew I must stay with my rider. Alexander had fallen off me and lay in the sand near my hooves. Blood was spurting from his shoulder, where the arrow had found its way through a joint of his armour. I sniffed him to check he was not dead, then settled to my knees beside him. The dry desert wind lifted my mane and fluttered the black feathers of the arrow.

Alexander struggled up on his good elbow, flopped back and shut his eyes with a groan. He whispered, 'Bucephalas, my faithful horse . . . don't leave me. This isn't meant to happen. I can't die! Zeus is supposed to be looking after me . . . oh horse, it's all going dark . . .'

'*Alex!*' cried an anguished voice as Petasios stopped in a spray of sand beside us.

I whinnied in relief to my red friend. Hephaestion leapt off him, knelt beside Alexander and put a hand on the king's forehead. He closed a fist about the arrow sticking out of his shoulder, shook his head, and with a grimace removed his hand.

'Get up, you great lump!' he said to me, sticking his elbow into my shoulder. 'The king's too sick to ride you back to camp. We'll have to get a stretcher. Alex, hold on, do you hear? We won't let you die. It's only a scratch. You'll be fine.' But his voice faltered, which meant this was probably a lie.

The others returned, out of breath, and stared at the king in horror. Hephaestion yelled at them to get moving, couldn't they see the king needed a doctor, and what were they playing at, letting the Arabs get so close to him? He squealed like a stallion who knew he had just done the wrong thing by leading them after the enemy, and was trying to remind everyone he was still boss.

But it was my fault. All mine. I was so deeply ashamed, I let Iolaus lead me back to the horse lines without making a fuss. Hades had done better than me, so when he gave me flat ears I didn't even nip him.

My riderless state scared Charm. She rushed up to take my rein from Iolaus, her face as pale as Alexander's had been lying on the dune. 'What happened?' she gasped. 'Where's the king? Oh, Zeus, he's not—?'

Iolaus pulled a face. 'Dead? No, not yet. But I'm not sure how much longer we'll be able to keep him alive if he keeps on taking risks like this. Why do we have to beat down the walls of every city that closes its gates to us? Why can't we just go after King Darius and finish this stupid war? The longer we stay here, the more time the Persians will have to raise another army. Father might like being Regent of

Macedonia, but he won't keep the throne for long without us to defend it for him.'

Realising a circle of curious grooms had gathered, he muttered, 'Yes, well . . . the king's wounded, but he'll live. He'll have plenty of time to recover, anyway. Would you believe, General Parmenio wants us to build a mound around the city, the same height as Gaza's hill? I didn't join the army to build bridges across the sea and mountains in the desert! I'm a cavalryman, not a common labourer! I've got to go. The king needs me.'

Iolaus hurried off, still grumbling.

Charm stared at Zoroaster. 'It was the curse,' she whispered.

Tydeos made a face. 'It was those Arabs! King Alexander wasn't careful enough. He seems to think he's immortal, or something, since he cut the Gordian Knot. It's like when he jumped into that river at Tarsus, when he couldn't even swim! Maybe now he'll stop doing such stupid things.'

Charm put her arms around my neck and squeezed tightly. 'Oh, Bucephalas,' she whispered. 'At least *you're* all right. I suppose if Alexander's wounded, he can't do to Gaza what he did to Thebes and Tyre. That'll be a good thing, won't it?'

Alexander copies Achilles

Charm ought to have known Alexander better than that. Both his body and his pride had been hurt. He swore to knock down Gaza's walls and teach its boss a lesson he would never forget.

But our siege engines soon got stuck in the soft sand. When even the mules couldn't move them, the old mulemaster waved the sticks he had tied to his arms and yelled at his muleteers to get the mules out of range before the Gazians started shooting from the walls.

Meanwhile the Arab mercenaries who had wounded Alexander galloped out, picked off some of our men, and fled back in again.

On hearing the reports, Alexander threw things around his tent and shouted at his doctors and his Guard, who were all trying to keep him in bed. They didn't have a hope. When the mound around the city was finished, Alexander insisted on leading the attack himself, even though his shoulder was only half healed. He was too dizzy to ride me, and went off to Gaza in a chariot driven by Hephaestion. So once again, I had nothing to do.

I had to stay in the camp with the nervous grooms, until the men began to trail back with their wounded. That was when we learnt that a rock from one of Gaza's anti-siege catapults had cracked Alexander's leg as he'd led the charge over the battlements.

Charm clutched my mane and whispered, 'I don't care what Tydeos says! It's the Persian god's curse, I know it is. We should never have backed Zoroaster. Oh, Bucephalas, I think Alexander's going to get himself killed in this horrible place . . .'

But Alexander did not die in Gaza.

When we finally smell the king's sherbet sweetness in the horse lines, it is so drenched with other smells from the battle that I hardly recognize him. He is in a foul mood: limping with his cracked leg, a hand pressed to the bloody bandage on his shoulder, filthy, sweating, and red in the face. Leonnatus and Philotas follow, hauling between them an enormously fat man with brown skin. The prisoner's arms have been bound behind him, blood trickles from the corner of his mouth, and one of his eyes is swollen shut. The rest of the Guard hurry after them, all as sweaty and dirty as their king. The grooms stop what they are doing to stare.

'Charmides!' Alexander calls. 'Harness Bucephalas to a chariot! Put him with that big golden horse, Xanthus.'

'Wait, Alexander!' calls General Parmenio, frowning at his son Philotas as he hurries past. His hairy legs are bleeding and crusted with sand. 'This man ruled Gaza for the Persians. He deserves better treatment.'

'He deserves to be treated like the animal he is,' Alexander mutters through clenched teeth. 'This ugly creature is no more a man than Zoroaster is a stallion! He heard what happened to Tyre, yet he still dared to challenge me. Those Arabs of his nearly killed me in the desert with that arrow. He has condemned his city by refusing to acknowledge me as king, and even dares to suggest I'm the son of a commoner! He won't admit it, but he can only have heard that rumour from my father's interfering old horsemaster. He probably knows who was behind my father's assassination, too. Gaza is the gateway to Egypt. *Someone* must have told him to stop me from reaching the Siwa oracle.' He scowls at the prisoner. 'This is your last chance! Either tell me the truth, or die!'

The dark man's bruised mouth laughs at the king. 'You wouldn't see the truth, Alexander, if it hit you in the eye. If you carry on like you are, you'll come to the same bad end as that tyrant Philip you claim sired you.'

'Shut him *up*!' Alexander yells. 'Gag him.'

Leonnatus and Philotas glance at each other. Philotas coughs and says, 'But I thought you wanted him to talk?'

Alexander turns on them with a furious expression. 'I've

heard enough of his lies. *Do it!'*

Philotas glances at his father for confirmation. But Leonnatus tightens his lips, knots one of our bandages, puts it in the dark man's mouth and ties it behind his head. The boss of Gaza grins around the gag, his one open eye fixed defiantly on Alexander.

Charm puts a trembling hand on my neck and lifts her chin. 'I don't think Bucephalas has pulled a chariot before, Sir,' she whispers. 'I don't know about Xanthus, but warhorses aren't usually trained to pull chariots.'

Alexander clenches a fist. Charm shrinks closer to me, but he doesn't hit her. He presses his knuckles to his forehead and snaps, 'Put two of those Persian horses in a chariot, then. It'll make no difference to this ugly creature. *Move!'*

Charm and Tydeos run off to prepare the chariot, so they don't see what Alexander orders to be done to the boss of Gaza. This is probably just as well. Few humans have the stomach for such things. Even our grooms go pale. One youngster faints.

When Charm and Tydeos return, leading the Persian horses yoked to the chariot, Alexander's Guard is looking almost as sick as our grooms. General Parmenio shakes his head, mutters something about needing a bath, and strides off to his tent, ordering his son to follow him. Philotas casts an apologetic look at Alexander, and hurries after his father.

A lead rein has been attached to the prisoner's ankles, and Leonnatus fastens it to the back of the chariot. Alexander snatches up a whip and looks down at the former governor of Gaza, who is now quiet.

Alexander's breathing slows slightly as he crouches beside him. 'I am the reborn Achilles. This is what Achilles did to his enemy Prince Hector outside the walls of Troy, so I am treating you a lot better than you deserve. I want you to know that before you die.'

He climbs stiffly into the chariot and gathers up the reins in his good hand. He shouts at Charm and Tydeos to let go of the horses, grunts with the pain of raising his wounded arm, and lashes them with the whip. The horses take off immediately, as they've been trained to do. The prisoner's body jerks as the rein attached to his ankles tightens, and he bounces along behind the chariot in the dust and flying sand. The grooms run after it.

That is the last I see of the governor of Gaza, although a little later his ghost screams past the horse lines, lifting our manes and making us all shiver.

Tydeos puts his arm around Charm and whispers, 'Don't watch. The king is angry because he got wounded. He'll calm down soon. This is war. That man was our enemy. At least he'll die quicker than those poor men King Alexander had crucified at Tyre.'

Charm shudders and stares after the cloud of dust. 'No one deserves that,' she says in a fierce little voice. 'No one.'

An uneasy hush falls over the horse lines. Alexander's friends look at one another. I hear some of them whisper that this isn't what they came for, that if he's going to keep doing things like this they'd rather go home than follow him any further.

As for what made everyone so sick and faint: if you're squeamish you'd better skip to the next chapter now. If not . . .

Alexander, who read the *Iliad* every night, had merely copied what his hero Achilles did to his enemy. He pierced the dark man's ankles with a spear and threaded the rein through the holes so it would not come loose when he dragged the body along behind his chariot. The only difference being that when Achilles did it in the *Iliad*, his enemy was already dead.

Sixteenth Hoofprint
EGYPT, 332–331 BC

Alexander becomes Pharaoh

The world of Egypt is strange. It is fertile and beautiful on the wide banks of its river, where big lilies the scientists call 'lotus' grow. But not far back on either side lies desert. Close to the sea, the river spreads out into marshland, which is full of birds. The reeds are taller than Hoplite's head, and hide monsters that make horrible noises at night. We can hear them from our camp outside the dazzling white walls of their main city of Memphis.

Soon after we arrived, the Egyptian priests met us with a crown – but not a flimsy one like those Alexander had been given in Phoenicia, oh no! The Egyptian crown had a golden snake's head with emerald eyes curling out of the front. There must have been some kind of magic in it, because when the priests placed it on Alexander's head, thunder rolled around the huge columns of their temple. The Amazons looked

236

round, hoping the hole in the world might open again. But there were no angry Egyptian ghosts waiting to go through it, so it stayed shut.

I had to wait outside with the other horses, which meant I didn't see the ceremony. But we could hear the cheering as far away as the riverbank. 'ALEX-AN-DER! ALEX-AN-DER! LONG LIVE PHARAOH ALEXANDER! KING OF MACEDONIA, LORD OF ANATOLIA, LIBERATOR OF EGYPT!' (This time it might actually be true, since the Egyptians welcomed us as friends, and we didn't have to dominate anyone.)

'Did you expect that?' Hephaestion whispered as he and Alexander emerged, blinking, into the sunlight and mounted me and Petasios so we could parade through the streets. 'Pharaoh of all Egypt?'

Alexander laughed. 'No, but if it's their custom, why argue? Zeus must have been testing me back in Phoenicia. I have a good feeling about this oracle, my friend! And I'm thinking we should go after Darius, once we've finished here. I want to make sure the Persians don't simply recapture Anatolia and Egypt once my back is turned. Removing Darius will show them I mean business.'

Hephaestion looked unsure. 'You're holding his family hostage. He won't make trouble while he knows you're looking after them. If we go further east, he'll fight to defend his land.'

'So?' Alexander chuckled and slapped his friend on the thigh. 'We've defeated his army once. We can do it again.'

'Zeus might not want us to invade Persia,' Hephaestion said in a low tone, glancing round to check no one had heard.

'Then I'll ask the oracle what he wants me to do!' Alexander grinned as he brushed lotus petals out of my mane. 'Will that satisfy you, my friend?'

As soon as the parties were over, Alexander set off for Siwa. By this time he had recovered from the wound he'd received at Gaza, and was very cheerful when he came to the horse lines to say goodbye to me. He fed me some Egyptian pastries, which were not quite as tasty as Queen Ada's honey cakes, but still good. While I ate them greedily, he pulled my ears and whispered, 'Charm and General Parmenio will look after you, Bucephalas. I wish I could take you with me, but it's a month's trek across desert, and I'm going to need your strength when I get back. You have a good holiday and stay sound for when we go after King Darius.'

Then he mounted Xanthus and cantered off with his Guard, the cavalry, and the Amazons, while Charm and I had to stay behind in the camp with General Parmenio's veterans and the baggage train. Since Tydeos had gone with the other grooms, we were a bit lonely at first. But Charm did mutual grooming on my withers and talked to me in her soft voice until I settled. She said I needn't worry, because Alexander wasn't going to fight any more battles. She promised that once he had found out from the oracle who his father was, we'd go home – which seems unlikely, considering what he told me before he left.

The scientists rushed off upriver to see the pyramids and examine the strange way the Egyptians keep their dead, alive but not alive. Our grooms say that instead of burning a body, they take out its innards and keep them in a jar so they won't rot, then wrap the body in bandages. They do the same with their bulls and cats. If they try it on any of my herd, watch out!

The men took the dogs hunting in the marshes and came back laden with geese and fish. The officers organized games

to keep everyone occupied while they were waiting for
Alexander to return, and the weather stayed warm even
though it was winter. There was a good rolling place on the
riverbank, and I spent a lot of my time covered in black mud.

It was great . . . until Prince Ochus turned up.

Charm makes another mistake

With Alexander away, Prince Ochus often sneaks down to the
horse lines to groom Zoroaster. Since being dominated by us
at Tyre, he hasn't tried to run away again. But one day he
blurts out, 'Charmeia, will Uncle Alexander do Achilles chariot thing to my father?'

'No!' Charm says firmly, putting an arm around the man-
colt. 'Of course not. That bad man at Gaza wasn't a king like
your father, and King Alexander was sick from his wounds so
he wasn't thinking properly. He's not like that normally.
Anyway, after he gets back from the oracle we're going home.'

Ochus bites his lip. 'Aunty Barsine say Uncle Alexander
not go home yet.'

Charm gives the prince a sharp look. 'How does she know?'

'She go to his pavilion at night. She say he like to fight too
much. I want to see my father again before Uncle Alexander
kill him,' he adds in a little voice.

Charm's face twists. She goes very quiet, like she did at
Tarsus before she went to visit the Amazons. Then she grips
the man-colt's hand and whispers, 'I know you do, Ochus.
Don't give up hope. I'll see what I can do.'

What Charm does is very strange. A few days later she
bridles both me and Zoroaster, sneaks a look around and
climbs on to my back. Then she unties Zoroaster so she can
lead him beside me.

We trot along the riverbank until we're past the sentries. They wave to her. It's not unusual to see a groom exercising two horses at once, so they don't realize Charm NEVER exercises me with another horse. If the other horse weren't Zoroaster, there would have been trouble by now. But Zoroaster is far too meek to fight me. I give him a nip on the nose to warn him not to try anything, and prance sideways, itching to go faster. I hope we don't have to go at his slow pace the whole way.

Charm holds me firmly to a trot, scanning the reeds. She stiffens as a canoe noses into the bank. Ochus climbs out of it. He has a bundle, which she helps him tie across Zoroaster's withers. Then she boosts him up and, with a bit of struggle, vaults back on to me.

This is better. Now I haven't got stupid Zoroaster's head by my flank we can go faster. And we do! We gallop across the fields through the sprouting corn until we reach the edge of the desert. Charm is breathing very fast, and keeps looking back over her shoulder. This is a real problem for you humans. If you look behind, you can't keep an eye on the danger ahead.

As we go over the first dune a line of monsters appears. They're twice as big as a horse, and have necks that look as if they've been put on backwards. Men in long robes are perched on their humped backs. Zoroaster does not seem too bothered, but I squeal a challenge and go up on my hind legs in alarm. The monsters turn their funny heads towards us, and one of them makes a sound like a mule in pain.

I come down to earth and make myself huge, ready for battle. But Charm, who (amazingly) is still on my back, shouts, 'Stop it, Bucephalas! They're only camels. Haven't you seen camels before? They won't hurt you, silly!'

One of these 'camels' comes closer, and I give it flat ears. The man sitting on its back grins down at Charm with very white teeth. He looks at Ochus, who is sitting stiffly on Zoroaster, and says in a thick accent, 'This is King Darius' son? He is younger than I expected.'

Charm nods. 'Just keep him safe, please.' She urges me closer to Zoroaster and whispers to Ochus, 'These men will take you across the desert to Persia. I can't come with you – I have to take the king's horse back to camp. Tell your father I'll do my best to persuade King Alexander to free your grand-mother, mother and sisters. I'll make sure he doesn't hurt them, don't worry.'

The man on the camel grins some more and looks round. Another camel comes out from behind the dune, and I snort in alarm. Camels smell strong, and the second rider's face is wrapped in a cloth, but I'd know his smell anywhere. It is my enemy the old horsemaster.

'You're going to be in a lot of trouble for this, slave,' he says with an evil chuckle.

Charm stares at him, unsure. But when he pulls his scarf aside to reveal his face, she goes rigid with fear.

She quickly recovers her wits and pulls out her dagger. 'Get out of here, Ochus!' she yells, tugging me round so abruptly I lose my hind legs in the sand. 'Get back to the camp! It's a trick!'

But it is too late. Men armed with long pikes rise up from the dunes all around us. I recognize Macedonians from General Parmenio's command.

Ochus freezes. The leader of the camel men shakes his head at Charm. 'I am sorry,' he says. 'But what else could I do? I have to make a living. If I helped King Alexander's prize hostage to escape, my caravan would be finished for ever.'

Charm glares at the horsemaster. 'You—' she whispers. 'You've been spying on me!'

The horsemaster sits casually on his camel and smiles. 'Told you I'd follow you to the ends of the earth, didn't I? I must say, I underestimated your cunning, but did you really think it would be so easy to help the little Persian prince escape? What's the matter, slave? Can't you control that old nag of Alexander's yet?'

I am acting wild, worried by the pikes and strange animals surrounding me. But the camels don't seem very impressed by my flat ears and squealing. This is probably because they are bigger than me. When I feel Charm start to slip, I remember she is not Alexander. I calm down so she doesn't fall off, but lash out at anyone who gets too close.

The Macedonians keep a wary distance. They signal that Charm should throw down her weapon. She clutches the dagger tightly and grips my reins in a determined way, as if she means us to fight. Then she looks at Ochus and shakes her head.

She drops her dagger in the sand. A soldier picks it up, quickly scuttling out of range of my teeth. One of the Macedonians takes Zoroaster's bridle and leads him back towards the camp. The others indicate with their pikes that Charm should follow, on me, which she does with tears in her eyes. The horsemaster rides his camel close behind. I lash my tail at the camel and go sideways so I can keep my good eye on it. The horsemaster watches Charm, smiling in his dark way.

'General Parmenio will arrest you if you come back to our camp!' Charm says in a brave voice.

'Really?' the horsemaster says. 'And why is that?'

'You tried to kidnap Bucephalas at Thebes! And you attacked me in Halicarnassus. King Alexander wants you caught and punished.'

'You're the one who's in trouble, slave, not me. General Parmenio and I go back a long way. He'll be more than grateful for my bringing Prince Ochus back.'

I feel the hairs of Charm's legs prickle against my sides. 'I'm the king's personal groom,' she whispers. 'If you touch me, he'll kill you. You know what he did to the governor of Gaza, don't you?'

'Yes, I heard about that. Seems his temper has grown as bad as his horse's. But our fierce young Alexander is on the other side of Egypt, talking to the gods. By the time he gets back here, I'll be long gone.'

Charm shudders and grips my mane tighter. Ochus turns to look at her, his lip trembling. 'Charmeia, the general won't hurt my mother because I tried to run away, will he?'

Charm flings the horsemaster a look that is the human equivalent of flat ears. 'It was my idea, Ochus, not yours,' she says. 'I'm the one who'll be punished.'

Behind us, the horsemaster's smile widens. I lash my tail at his camel's nose, and the animal shies, making him grab its hump.

The horsemaster won't get near Charm while she is on my back. Camels might be big, but they are obviously stupid. I'm still the boss around here.

Betrayal

General Parmenio is waiting for us at the horse lines. He sends Ochus back to Lady Barsine's tent with two of his men, while a third man leads Zoroaster away. He grabs my reins himself and orders Charm to dismount. She slides off me, and her legs buckle. A soldier takes her arm to steady her. I squeal and shake my head at him, warning him to leave her alone, but the general gives my reins a hard jerk. 'Stop that, Bucephalas!' he snaps. 'I've had about enough of your temper.'

The horsemaster's camel lurches to its knees with a grunt so he can get off. Afterwards, it stays sitting down, chewing on a piece of hay. Stupid, as I said. Even a mule wouldn't sit in the dirt for very long by choice.

The general shakes his head at Charm. 'You're more dangerous to this army than all of King Darius' Persians put together,' he says. 'What did you think you were trying to do?'

She stares at her feet. 'Please don't punish Prince Ochus, Sir,' she whispers. 'It was my idea.'

'I know it was. An eight-year-old boy would never dream up anything so stupid.'

He frowns at her bowed head, and presses his lips together. Then he nods at the soldier to let her go. 'Here, do your job. Settle this horse back in the lines, and put his muzzle on. Use two tethers so he won't get loose!'

Charm eyes the horsemaster, who is leaning against his camel with his ruined leg stuck out to one side, smiling darkly.

'Bucephalas needs a roll, Sir,' she stammers. 'So does Zoroaster.'

'Do what I told you!' The general barks. 'The horses can have their roll later.'

Charm bites her lip and obeys. Her hands tremble as she fastens my muzzle and doubles my tether as ordered, the Macedonians watching her every move. She keeps glancing up at the general and the horsemaster, who are speaking in low voices as if they are members of the same herd who know each other well. Which they are, because for many years they both served under the one-eyed king.

A soldier brings me a bucket of water. I am thirsty after my fright with the camels in the desert, so I suck it up through my muzzle. The water tastes strange. I expect it's dirty, because they are not grooms and know no better. Charm holds on to my mane as I drink. 'Can I groom Bucephalas now?' she asks the men.

They shake their heads. One tugs my tether to make sure it is securely tied. Another takes Charm's elbow and steers her back to the general. The other men stand to attention, keeping people away from our part of the horse lines.

Charm takes a deep breath. 'I'm very sorry for what I did, Sir,' she whispers. 'I only wanted to get Prince Ochus safely back to his father. Please don't tell King Alexander.'

The general waves her to be quiet. He is looking at something the horsemaster has handed him. It is a piece of flattened grass with marks on it. He rolls it up, hands it back to him, and gives Charm a thoughtful look.

'This isn't the first time you've betrayed the king, is it, Charmeia? I know what you did at the Syrian Gates. If it weren't for young Alexander's amazing energy and luck, none of us would have got this far. Our bones would be rotting on the battlefield back at Issus, and you would be serving sherbet to the Great King's guests in a Persian palace.'

She trembles and looks at her feet.

'This scroll is very interesting. It's a list of all the garrison slaves at Methone. I always thought there was something suspicious about a girl who does a lad's job. I should have looked into your background before, especially as Alexander seems to think such a lot of you. The king's got no idea who you are, has he? But you are far too close to him, so I'm afraid I have to get rid of you. As it happens, the horsemaster has solved the problem for me quite neatly.'

He eyes me. I am feeling sleepy, and my legs feel like temple columns. It is hard to concentrate on what's happening to Charm, but she is so white I think she might faint.

'All right,' the general says to the horsemaster. 'You can take her. I don't care what you do with her. Just make sure she doesn't come near this army again. Alexander will be upset, but it can't be helped. There's one other groom who can manage the horse, and he'll be back soon enough.'

Charm stares at the general in terror as she realizes how he intends to punish her. She starts to run, but she doesn't get far. The Macedonians catch her and bind her wrists. She kicks and struggles as they easily lift her between them and carry her over to the horsemaster's camel. They push her against the animal's flank, pinch her nose and make her drink something from a leather flask. She splutters and tries to spit it out. 'Help!' she screams, twisting her head. '*Bucephalas!*'

I lift my head, which has drooped almost to the ground. But I am securely tied, and I feel very strange. I lose my balance and fall on my knees. It's too much effort to get up.

Charm stares at me in horror. 'What have you done to Bucephalas?' she cries. 'Let me go! He needs me. *Bucephalas!*'

'We put something in his water to calm him down. You'll feel the same way shortly. It's not harmful, just easier this way,' says General Parmenio, frowning at her.

Charm is still screaming and sobbing. But after a moment her struggles cease, and she sags against the camel. The horsemaster looks triumphant as the Macedonians tie her across its hump. He climbs up behind her and hits the camel with a stick, and the animal lurches to its feet.

'Thank you for remembering our old friendship, General,' he says. 'I'm glad there's at least one sensible officer left in the Macedonian army—' He breaks off as someone approaches on my blind side, and mutters a curse. 'Oh, Zeus, is that crazy muleteer still alive?'

There's a struggle going on behind me. I smell the old mulemaster, the one who lost his hands at Issus. He's using the sticks he has lashed to his wrists like weapons.

'Let the girl go!' he growls, shoving General Parmenio's men aside. He glares at the general. 'If you let that man take Bucephalas' groom, King Alexander's goin' to hear of it! He gave orders for him to be arrested if he ever turned up again.'

General Parmenio frowns.

'That's the man who broke my knee back in Pella and ruined my career!' the horsemaster hisses, glaring at the mule-master. 'Don't look like his career's going too well, either. What happened, Mulemaster? Someone chop off your hands because they were so dirty?'

'Yeah, and you've been trying to get *your* dirty hands on King Alexander's groom for years, haven't you?' growls the mulemaster, raising his sticks again. 'Let her go!'

General Parmenio sighs, and his sword flashes out.

The mulemaster grunts in surprise as blood spurts from his neck. Before his body hits the ground, his ghost whirls past me. I am so drowsy I hardly flinch. But the sky rumbles, and the men look round.

They do not know that the mulemaster defied the Persian curse by backing Zoroaster, the Persian sacred horse. Nor do they know about the horse bond. If they did, they might have thought twice about separating me and Charm.

'The man was no use to anyone crippled like that, anyway,' the general mutters, wiping his blade. 'No one's going to mourn him.'

The horsemaster looks at the dead mulemaster, and his smile widens.

'What are you waiting for?' the general snaps. 'Get that girl out of here fast, before any of the king's friends see you. These men are loyal to me. They won't talk. But you'd better stay away from this army in the future. Officially, Charmeia is only a groom, but I can't guarantee what King Alexander will do if he finds out you've taken her. I'll think of something so he won't come after you.'

The horsemaster nods, eyes me, and turns his camel.

As the camel lopes away, I try a whinny. It comes out like Hoplite's used to when he was a tiny foal. Charm makes no sound. Her red curls hang down as if she is dead, although her ghost is still inside her body.

To make things worse, the camel left an ENORMOUS pile of dung steaming in the horse lines, and there were no grooms to take it away. The smell of it drove me crazy. But the magic General Parmenio's men had put in my water had stolen my strength, so I couldn't even dominate it.

An outright lie

I don't know who looked after me during the next few days. My water was brought in a bucket, always with more magic in it. But even in my sleepy state, no one dared try to ride me, and I'm sure I bit several of the general's men when they removed my muzzle so I could eat my hay.

Then one morning my water tastes clean, and the clouds in my head begin to lift. By the time I hear the familiar whinnies of the other horses I am feeling more myself. I whinny in joy, greeting them one by one:

Petasios!
Borealis!
Xanthus!
Harpinna!
Apollo!
Arion!
Hades!
Electra!
AURA!

There is a lot of whinnying and rushing about as the horses who went with Alexander are taken for their rolls and settled in the lines. Their grooms gossip nonstop about their journey to the oracle. They are dirty, sunburnt and excited.

Seeing me in the horse lines, Tydeos calls out, 'Charm? Charm! You'll never guess what happened on the way back from Siwa! The king found a wonderful piece of land between the river and the sea. He's planning to build a huge city there, with great harbours so people can travel into Egypt more easily. He laid it all out with chalk and flour. It'll be the biggest city you've ever seen – with twelve villages inside it, and there'll be canals, and temples to all the gods, and . . .' He laughs. 'Charm, come out! Where are you hiding? *Charm?*'

He ties Petasios and Borealis in their usual places, one on each side of me, still looking about for Charm. 'What have you done with your groom, Bucephalas? She must have heard us come back. We made enough noise.'

I am so pleased to smell someone familiar, I nicker to him softly. He gives me a startled look. 'What's up with you, you great brute? Glad to see me, or something?' He rubs my nose, and frowns when his fingers come away covered in dirt. 'You're filthy! What have you two been up to while we've been away?'

This time he sounds worried.

I nudge him again and snort. He runs his hands down my legs, stands back and looks at me, puzzled. 'You're definitely not yourself. You're not ill, are you, Bucephalas? I suppose I'll just have to look after you till Charm gets back.'

With me and Zoroaster to settle as well, it takes Tydeos longer than the other grooms to finish his work. As he is giving us our hay, shouts come from the end of the horse line, and I smell Alexander's sherbet sweetness.

The king, smiling and suntanned like the grooms, strides easily towards us, all trace of his limp gone. He calls for Charm. Of course, she doesn't appear.

When questioned, Tydeos shakes his head and says, 'I don't know, Your Majesty. I haven't seen her since we got back. Maybe she went to get some medicine for Bucephalas? He doesn't look quite himself.'

Alexander gives me an appraising look as he feeds me a pastry. I lick his palm. He runs a hand down my neck, looks at the dust on it, and frowns like Tydeos did earlier.

'Find me Charmides!' he shouts.

Some of the grooms hurry off to obey. Tydeos stammers, 'I'm sure she must have a good reason for not being here, Your Majesty.'

That is when General Parmenio appears, carrying something in his hand. It smells faintly of Charm, and for a moment I think she is back. I swing round on my tether and nicker hopefully. But it is only her purple scarf, the one Alexander gave her at Issus. It's torn and covered in blood.

Alexander stares at it. His fists clench, and some of the light goes out of his eyes. But he raises his gaze to General Parmenio and tilts his chin. 'What's this? Why is my horse unattended and dirty?'

'I'm sorry, Alexander, but my men found this scarf down by the river. They think your groom must have been attacked by a crocodile. I organized a search party, of course, but we didn't find her body. That's the trouble with a girl doing a boy's job. She must have got careless when she was washing. This Egyptian river is dangerous for those who don't know it. My men have done their best with Bucephalas, but he's a difficult horse to manage.'

As you know, this is an OUTRIGHT LIE.

I lash my tail and give the general flat ears. He eyes me warily, but keeps his attention on Alexander. He makes himself huge as if he expects a battle, and holds out the bloodied scarf. 'I'm sorry, but I'm sure you understand I can't be everywhere at once looking out for grooms. I hope the oracle gave you good news?'

Alexander takes the scarf and frowns. He looks hard at the general and says in a level tone, 'Thank you for your efforts, General. That's the trouble with leaving my camp in the care of an old man. This wouldn't have happened if I had been here, but not even a son of Zeus-Ammon can be everywhere at once.'

General Parmenio flushes. He says in a low tone, 'It was your idea to go gallivanting off to Siwa, when you should have been here negotiating a peace treaty with King Darius! His last offer was very generous. All the lands west of the Euphrates, his daughter's hand in marriage, and his son as a permanent hostage. You are already Captain of the Hellenic League, Lord of Anatolia, and now Pharaoh of Egypt. No Macedonian king has ever ruled so great an empire. If I were you, Alexander, I'd accept. We've finished what we came to do. We've thrown the Persians out of Anatolia, and liberated Egypt into the bargain. The men are ready to go home.'

Alexander's face flushes, too. He snaps at the open-mouthed grooms to find themselves something useful to do, and they melt away. But, being grooms, they hover behind the baggage carts to listen. Tydeos stares at Charm's bloody scarf, his face white.

Alexander rests a hand on my quarters and takes a deep breath. He is standing on my good side, so I can see him. He makes himself huge without seeming to try. Even in his dusty tunic with his head bare, he looks more of a boss than the general ever does.

'I'd accept Darius' offer, too, if I were you, General Parmenio,' Alexander says quietly. 'You're an old man, so it's understandable you should have an old man's fears. The Siwa oracle told me I'm the son of Zeus-Ammon, who changed himself into a snake to visit my mother the night she conceived me. King Philip is my mortal father, and his old horse-master is a liar and a traitor, as everyone knew all along. I'm not afraid of the Persians, or their curses. Did King Darius conquer the Gordian Knot? No! I did. We've already beaten their army once, so we can beat it again. I could marry Darius' daughter right now if I so wished. I already have the lands Darius is offering me. Prince Ochus will soon learn to love me as a father. I'm the son of a god! What do I need with the ransom Darius is offering for the rest of his family? I don't want more gold. I don't want a frightened Persian wife back in Macedonia. The oracle told me the only way to avoid King Philip's fate is to claim all the lands as far as the eastern ocean in the name of my holy father Zeus. I will be rewarded with immortality, and so will every man brave enough to follow me!' He looks at Charm's bloodied scarf, and a shadow crosses his face. 'Tell the men to break camp, General. There'll be no more talk of going home. We're starting after Darius tomorrow.'

General Parmenio stares at Alexander as if he is seeing him properly for the first time.

Alexander glares back. 'Well?' he says softly. 'Why are you still here? The gods spoke to me at Siwa. Do you dare question their authority?'

The general shudders slightly and hurries away.

Son of Zeus

After Alexander had gone, Tydeos stood frozen to the spot. The other grooms ventured out from their hiding places and glanced at one another. I nudged Tydeos, and he gave a great shuddering gasp and turned to me with tears in his eyes. 'No,' he whispered. 'She *can't* be dead. Eaten by a crocodile! It can't be true, it *can't!*'

I wanted to tell him she was alive. But he didn't understand horse talk, so I nickered and nudged him again. When he finally took a comb and started to groom the dirt out of my coat, it was such a relief that I acted as gentle as Aura and did not nip him even once.

Groom-gossip was subdued that night, because of what they thought had happened to Charm. But they had so much to talk about, they couldn't keep quiet for long. While Tydeos went off to be alone, they argued about what the oracle had *really* told Alexander. The main theories are:

He is the son of Zeus, like he told everyone, and he is taking us all to the edge of the world.

He is the son of the old horsemaster, and he has made up the story about being the son of Zeus as an excuse to go after King Darius.

He is the mortal son of King Philip, and is afraid to take us home in case someone assassinates him too.

Oh, and guess what he's calling his fine new Egyptian city? Alexandria!

You'd think he might have named it after poor Charm.

Seventeenth Hoofprint
MESOPOTAMIA, SUMMER 331 BC

Missing Charm

When we left Egypt, we took plenty of food with us in the mule carts. The men were in high spirits after Alexander told them what the oracle had said, and our nosebags were full every evening. But I was missing Charm and left most of my barley. It was worse than when she went away after Thebes, because then at least her smell had lingered in my stall. This time we were moving on every day, and I couldn't find her spring grass scent anywhere as we retraced our hoofprints up the coast to Tyre, nor as we set out east across the plain to look for King Darius.

As soon as we left the coast behind, it grew seriously HOT. There were no trees to shade us from the sun, only endless dust that made us cough. When we camped, Tydeos tried his best to groom the sweat off me. But he didn't have water to bathe me because we needed every drop we carried to drink, so he had to use his mitten, and I HATE my belly being cleaned that way. After I'd nipped him a few times he gave up, only to get shouted at by Alexander for not looking after me properly.

Poor Tydeos. I think he was missing Charm, too.

Alexander kept her blood-stained scarf twisted around his belt. He fingered it thoughtfully as Petasios and I walked side by side at the front of our huge herd. 'Do you think my groom was really eaten by a crocodile in Egypt?' he asked Hephaestion.

His friend gave him a sharp look. 'Alex! I do believe you're pining for Charmides as much as your horse is!'

'Don't be ridiculous. She was only a groom.'

'So why do you keep looking behind you? Persia's that way!' Hephaestion pointed at the shimmering horizon ahead of us.

Alexander sighed and took a swig from his water-skin. 'She's not dead, my friend, I *feel* it. Maybe she ran away again, though I never thought she'd leave Bucephalas – Oh, stop looking at me like that! I only want her back so my horse will start eating again. Look at him, he's wasting away in this heat. At this rate, I'll be riding a skeleton by the time we get to Persia.'

Hephaestion laughed, making Petasios toss his head. 'You've got King Darius' wife, who is supposed to be the most beautiful woman in all Persia, and her two marriageable daughters captive in your baggage train, yet you're worrying about a slip of a groom?' He gave Alexander an amused look. 'I should have guessed. She's defied you every step of the way, yet you've never really punished her, have you? Not even after that business with the passes at Issus. It's a good thing she's gone, if you ask me. Imagine the scandal! The great King Alexander, brought to his knees by a slave-girl who dresses like a boy!'

'You of all people know it's not like that!' Alexander snapped. He paused and looked over his shoulder again. 'How far do you think I can trust General Parmenio?'

Hephaestion sobered at once. 'Are you worried the men won't follow you across the Euphrates? Old Parmenio won't try the same trick he did at the Granicus, Alex, don't worry. He knows if he does, the phalanx will follow *you* this time, and he'll be the one left on the riverbank with a handful of men to face the enemy. Somehow, I doubt he'll come out of it as well as you did.'

Alexander sat a bit straighter on my back and smiled. 'You're right there. After all, General Parmenio isn't the son of a god.'

We walked on a bit, with just the thudding of our hooves and the creak of the men's armour breaking the silence. Hephaestion gave Alexander a sideways look. 'Did the Siwa oracle *really* say you're the son of Zeus?'

Alexander's eyes glinted. 'Do you think I'd make up something like that?'

Hephaestion looked unsure. 'And is it true the oracle promised you'd defeat Darius, reach the edge of the world, and become immortal?'

Alexander rested a sweaty hand on my crest and squinted at the horizon. 'Yes.'

If you ask me, that was a stupid question. What did Hephaestion expect Alexander to say? No?

'What about your father's assassination?'

Alexander stiffened. 'I need to speak to my mother about

that. It was unclear.'

'But you asked the oracle if all King Philip's murderers had been punished, didn't you?' Hephaestion pressed. 'You still haven't told me what it said to that.'

'It doesn't matter what the oracle said!' Alexander smiled to take the sting out of his words. 'Don't worry, my friend. I'm not going to let anyone slip a knife between *my* ribs. I'm the reborn Achilles and the son of Zeus, remember. When I've won the Persian crown and reached the edge of the world, I'll be a god as well as a king. Then I won't have to worry about my father's murderers, Persian curses, General Parmenio, or anyone else for that matter.'

He gathered up my reins determinedly.

'According to the Greek maps, we're getting close to the Euphrates. Take some men on ahead and find some boats to bridge the river. I don't want any delay crossing it. We need to find some shade before the men melt. Macedonians are not made for these temperatures!'

The land between two rivers

Hephaestion's bridge of boats shifted under our hooves, upsetting Electra and the other youngsters, so there was a lot of snorting and shouting as we crossed the Euphrates. On the other side we caught some enemy spies, who had come north from their city of Babylon to see what we were up to.

They were a small herd, easily dominated, and the ones we didn't catch ran away. But Alexander was suspicious and didn't chase them. Threatened by my flat ears and the king's sword, the captured spies soon told us that King Darius' entire army was waiting downriver to trap us in a place where the Persians had once dominated the Greeks. The boss of Babylon had orders to retreat before us and burn all the crops so our men would be tired and hungry by the time we got there.

Ha! How stupid do they think we are?

General Parmenio favoured making camp on the west bank. But Alexander sent an order to the Amazons, who rode at the back of our herd, to burn the bridge behind us so no one could retreat. Then he turned my head into the rising sun, and we continued northeast away from the river. General Parmenio squealed a bit, but ordered his men to follow us, because he didn't want to fight the Persians himself with only half a herd.

The Babylonian herd watched us go in dismay.

The land on the east side of the Euphrates was called Mesopotamia, which means 'the land between the rivers'. Mostly it was farmland, with canals criss-crossing the fields to water the crops. There was wheat to fill our nosebags, and trees to shade us from the fierce sun. Only small villages lay on our route. The people either ran away before we got there, or begged us not to hurt them and gave us their goats and sheep to feed the men. Since King Darius had not expected us to come this way, there were no soldiers to protect the vulnerable members of his herd from us. Alexander didn't bother dominating them. He treated the people of Mesopotamia like young foals, showing them he was boss without hurting them, because he knew they were no threat.

The next river, the Tigris, was shallow enough to cross without swimming. Although the baggage carts got a bit wet, and some of the shorter men had to be helped through the deepest parts by their friends, no one minded very much because it was lovely and cool in the water. We caught some more enemy spies, and discovered from them that King

Darius' army was now camped only about half a day's march away, having rushed across from the Euphrates to stop us marching further east into Persia. Alexander smiled grimly and ordered the men to dig a ditch around the camp and set spikes in it to stop the Persians attacking us in the night. Then he retired to his pavilion to talk tactics with General Parmenio.

Groom-gossip for the next three days was all about the coming battle. King Darius' herd is supposed to be bigger than ours. The grooms claim he has a million men and horses! I hope this is not true. We have only 40,000 men and 7,000 horses, and that's a lot less than a million.

The Amazons say that because of the horse bond, Charm's absence weakens Alexander. So if our grooms are right, we're in a HUGE amount of trouble.

When the moon went out

On the third night, I am in my normal spot in the horse lines between Petasios and Borealis. Tydeos has gone off with the other grooms. Ever since Charm disappeared in Egypt, he has been drinking so much magic it makes him sick in the mornings. We horses have had no work for the past three days, only lead-outs to stretch our legs, so I am feeling a bit fresh. When Aura nickers to me from the mares' lines, a shiver goes through me. She's coming into foal-season again, and her dappled summer coat glows beautifully under the full moon.

While I am remembering the last time I managed to run with a mare – Harpinna, back at Halicarnassus! – the light fades from Aura. Even Zoroaster is getting difficult to see. My coat prickles. The sentries light torches, and one of the men points to the sky and cries, 'Look! A monster is eating the moon!'

My coat stands on end. Petasios whinnies nervously, and

Borealis shifts his backside into me. The sentries stare at the sky and whisper uneasily. They say it is a bad omen before a battle.

None of them see a dark-skinned man run across from the hostages' pavilion and steal a bridle. The thief creeps behind the horse lines, bent double to keep out of sight. I whinny a warning, but he keeps well away from me. He eyes Zoroaster, but does not dare pass my lashing tail. Instead, he darts over to the mares' lines, where Aura nickers to him like the gentle mare she is. He smiles and puts the bridle on her.

The moon has now been fully eaten. It is very dark when the thief scrambles on to Aura's back and heads her out of the lines. He guides her between two stakes (easy, because they are pointing the other way to keep enemies out), twists his fingers in her mane and gallops her at the ditch.

'Hey!' shouts one of the sentries, finally realizing something is wrong. 'One of the Persian queen's slaves is escaping!'

A trumpet blares the alert call, but too late. Aura, being both well trained and brave, leaps the ditch and vanishes into the night with the thief. The sentry tosses his spear after her, but it falls short.

I whinny wildly after my mare and rear up to break my tether. But before I can gallop after her, Prince Ochus races out of the hostages' tent.

'Charmeia!' he sobs, his thin face streaked with tears. 'Where Charmeia?'

I haven't seen Ochus since Egypt, and his smell reminds me of what happened to Charm, which makes me forget Aura.

Tydeos grabs the man-colt and shakes him. 'Was that one of your slaves who just stole our mare? He was lucky not to get speared! What's your mother thinking of, letting him run off like that?'

The prince's face twists. He clenches his fists and bursts into tears. 'My mother's dead!' he sobs.

Tydeos stares at him in confusion. The moon is coming back now, but their faces are still in shadow. 'The Persian queen's dead?' Tydeos looks fearfully at the hostages' pavilion. 'Oh Zeus, Alexander didn't kill her, did he?'

Ochus shakes his head again. 'She get sick on journey. She die tonight. One of her slaves say he go to my father's camp with the news. I tell him to take Zoroaster, but he must get confused. Not hurt him, please. He only slave.' He looks pleadingly at the sentries, who have gathered round to make sure Ochus does not escape as well. They seem embarrassed by the prince's tears.

'He's probably in the Persian camp by now, you little eel,' grunts one of the sentries. 'Galloped off on the grey mare like all the devils were after him.'

Ochus sniffs. 'He get away?' Some of the tension runs out of him. 'Good! He will tell Father what happen. Then after the battle, Father will come and rescue me and my sisters and Granny Sisygambis and Aunty Barsine.'

One of the sentries takes the prince's arm to escort him back to his pavilion, but Tydeos stops him. 'No – wait!' He crouches down so he is level with the man-colt. 'Charmeia's gone, Ochus. We haven't seen her since Egypt. General Parmenio thinks she was eaten by a crocodile, but I ...' His voice cracks, and he continues in a harsher tone. 'You were in the camp when she disappeared. Did you see her go to the river?'

Ochus bites his lip, glances at me, then whispers something to Tydeos.

Tydeos' breath comes faster. He grips the man-colt's shoulders and says, 'What did General Parmenio do to her?'

But Ochus shakes his head. 'I not see. His soldiers take me back to Aunty Barsine. I get a spanking because running away not good behaviour for a prince. Then Mother get sick, and Aunty Barsine say it my fault because I make her worry so much. But Charmeia not get eaten by crocodile. She not that silly.'

'No,' Tydeos whispers, a little smile playing at the corners of his mouth. 'I *knew* it couldn't be true ... Charm's still alive!'

I smell Alexander's sherbet sweetness and nicker to him. Tydeos looks round wildly, but there is no time to hide because the king is already striding down the horse lines towards us. The sentries rush back to their posts. The grooms quickly straighten their tunics and swill out their mouths with some of our water. Tydeos doesn't get a chance, because Ochus is clinging to his arm.

Alexander obviously hasn't slept: there are dark circles under his eyes. Perita, now quite grown-up, trots at his heels. But when she smells Ochus, she bounds past the king to lick the man-colt's face. Ochus puts his arms around the dog's neck and stares defiantly at Alexander.

'I'm very sorry to hear about your mother, Ochus,' the king says quietly. 'I've sent a message to your father myself. There was no need for your slave to risk his neck stealing one of our horses. Go back to Lady Barsine now. You can take Perita with you.'

Alexander waits until the sentry has led the man-colt and the dog away. Then he glares at the men and grooms. 'How did this happen?' he snaps.

Tydeos stammers, 'We're very sorry, Your Majesty. But

we were asleep, and the moon—'

'*Drunk*, more like!' Alexander shouts. He strides up and down the line of frightened grooms, sniffing their breath and shaking his head in disgust. 'Don't any of you realize this is the battle we've been heading towards ever since we left Pella? All those cities we captured, all the men who have died . . . all that effort was so we could come *here*, to the very borders of Persia, and challenge King Darius on his home ground. He has every last fighting man in his empire camped half a day away. If we win this battle, the Persian army will never recover. Darius' crown will be mine, and all his lands. There will be no one left to stop me reaching the edge of the world!'

As the king speaks, his fists clench and unclench, and little shudders go through his body. The sentries fidget, uncomfortable. Tydeos looks at his feet and says nothing.

Alexander draws a final, shuddering breath and presses his knuckles to his forehead. The men and grooms tense. Tydeos closes his eyes. But the king sighs and lowers his fist. When he next speaks, it is in a quieter tone. 'You're only grooms. You can't be expected to understand. But you're lucky that slave took the mare. If he'd stolen Bucephalas, I'd have turned the lot of you out of this camp without your hands, like that old muleteer General Parmenio tells me killed himself in Egypt because he couldn't bear to live any longer as a cripple!'

He pauses to let this sink in, then orders everyone back to their posts with instructions to stay alert, because we are breaking camp tomorrow and going to meet Darius. 'There's to be no more drinking until after we've won this battle,' he continues, and his lips twitch up at one corner. 'Then we can *all* celebrate.'

Tydeos shivers at his lucky escape. He peers at the king and whispers, 'Are we really going to win, Sir? Everyone's saying King Darius' army is much bigger than ours, and the moon went out . . .'

The other grooms and sentries creep closer to hear the king's reply. Alexander flicks a hand at the moon and laughs. 'My seer tells me the eclipse was a sign that Macedonia will darken the light of Persia before this month is out. It's a bad omen for Darius, but a good one for us! As for these silly rumours about the size of King Darius' army, the prisoners we captured were probably exaggerating. Even if they weren't, one Macedonian is worth ten Persians. We'll get Demetrius' mare back again soon enough, don't you worry!'

A huge herd

Alexander might have told our grooms not to worry, but next morning, in the cool time before sunrise, when he vaulted on to me the shadows around his eyes were even deeper. He called the Guard, and we galloped into the hills to take a look at the Persian army.

I could tell there were strange horses ahead long before we saw them. We could hear them whinnying as their grooms gave them breakfast. I flared my nostrils to catch the smells: sweat, smoke, barley, oil, men, stallions, LOTS of mares. As we crested the ridge, my skin tightened with excitement.

I filled my lungs and let out a shuddering neigh. Some of the Persian horses looked round, but most were too far away to hear me. The sun rose huge and red out of the haze over the plain, bringing more and more of the enemy herd into view. Most seemed to be cavalry like us, but there were a few chariots, too. The sun flashed fire from their wheels as they drove up and down the lines and lines of horses, looking very tiny below us.

On my back, Alexander was silent. He raised a hand to shade his eyes against the sun. His other hand held my rein so tightly I had to toss my head to tell him he was hurting my mouth. He trembled slightly, moved his lips as if counting under his breath, and whispered, 'Oh, Zeus, Hephaestion . . . have I made a very big mistake?'

Fortunately, the rest of the Guard did not hear this. They, too, were staring at the army, and whispering uneasily among themselves. Iolaus looked as pale as snow. Electra had joined the Guard to carry Aura's rider Demetrius. My filly was behaving very well, considering she had the big Achilles shield resting on her withers, but I missed my special mare.

Hephaestion nudged Petasios forward until his knee touched Alexander's. He said in a professional voice, 'Nearly all cavalry, exactly as the Persian captives said. They have new weapons . . . longer spears . . . what looks like better armour . . . chariots, of course, with something on their wheels, I can't quite see . . . blades, I think.' He glanced at Alexander. 'We'll have to watch out for them, or they'll gash the horses' legs.'

Alexander gave his friend a grateful look, sat up straighter and took a deep breath. 'Yes, it's going to be a cavalry battle – the best sort! I don't see any foot-soldiers. Do you?'

'A few.' Hephaestion pointed to the middle of the herd. 'Not many. Probably only Darius' bodyguard.' He glanced back at our army, which was still marching into position through the hills. 'What do you think, Alex? The men are rested and eager to fight. Shall we attack before the Persians wake up?'

The Guard heard this and gathered up their reins, trying

to look as if they weren't scared. Their horses had already sensed their nerves and danced closer to me. I trembled with excitement. My rider wasn't scared, of course, but he felt a bit less confident than usual.

Alexander shook his head and narrowed his eyes. 'I'm going to have to think about this. They'll outflank us easily. Their cavalry outnumbers ours at least five to one. They've been camped here long enough to have set traps. You heard what those Persian spies we caught said about pits and hidden stakes. I want a closer look at the ground down there.'

Hephaestion looked worried. 'What about General Parmenio's idea of a night attack to target and kill Darius?'

Alexander shook his head and made himself huge. 'No, my friend! No more assassinations. This battle must be won properly, or not at all. I'd rather win tomorrow and have Darius escape again, than kill him and leave all those Persians down there to fight me another day under another leader.'

'But you have King Darius' only son and heir captive.'

Alexander smiled. 'Do you really think that matters to them? Since when has legitimacy had anything to do with power? How long do you think it'd take Antipater to seize the throne of Macedonia if I were to die here today? And General Parmenio's just waiting for someone to kill me, so his son Philotas can be king. Or maybe you fancy leading the army, Hephaestion? Or *you*, Iolaus?'

He turned and made a playful jab at Iolaus' ribs with the shaft of his spear. The Guard looked a bit alarmed.

'No one's going to kill you, Alex, don't be silly!' Demetrius said.

'They won't get close enough, and they wouldn't dare,' Ptolemy added. 'Everyone knows you're favoured by the gods.'

'You're the son of Zeus, aren't you?' said Perdiccas.

'And it's different for you, anyway. The Persians respect their king's family. You don't have an official heir yet—'

Craterus should have known better than to mention that. Alexander's fist tightened on my rein, and his cheeks flushed. 'Enough! We're wasting time. I need a cavalry escort. See to it, will you, Hephaestion. I'm going down there.'

I lashed my tail in Xanthus' face as we cantered down the slope. But Alexander felt determined again and had stopped trembling.

As we trotted around that plain under the burning sun, with half our cavalry as escort and the horses of the Guard close around me, Alexander grew more and more confident. We didn't find any pits with stakes – just a vast area of levelled ground with the stones removed, perfect for galloping over. I was impatient to try it out, but Alexander kept me on a tight rein and wouldn't let any of us out of a trot.

Meanwhile, a small herd of Persians trotted their horses up and down nearby and called out squealing threats.

'Where's your great army, King Iskander?'

'We only see a few boys not old enough to shave.'

'Our Great King Darius say if you go home, he send you some golden toys to keep you amused. He say you should leave war to men, or we teach you a hard lesson tomorrow!'

Alexander ignored them. He told the Guard to pretend we were planning a night attack on the Persian camp like General Parmenio had advised, then he carried on surveying the plain, making notes on a piece of flattened grass balanced on my withers. Since he was obviously too busy to squeal back, I squealed at their horses to put them in their place. And every time I found a pile of Persian dung, I made sure I dominated it.

When we got back to camp, Alexander disappeared into his pavilion with his notes. He turned away everyone who tried to join him, even Hephaestion. He worked through the hot afternoon and most of the night. Finally, his lamp flickered out, so I knew my rider slept at last.

Eighteenth Hoofprint
GAUGAMELA, AUTUMN 331 BC

Alexander's plan

After their telling-off the previous day, our grooms were up before dawn. They fed us our pre-battle breakfast of barley soaked in honey (of which I managed only two mouthfuls) and groomed us until we shone. Tydeos combed out my tail almost as carefully as Charm would have done, and checked my girth straps and bridle fastenings at least ten times. All this fuss put me on edge. I had to nip him on the arm to make him stop.

Every horse in the lines knew we were getting ready for battle. You could feel the tension rippling in the air. Off in the haze of smoke that hung over our camp, the men were putting on armour and checking their weapons. Trumpets sounded and officers shouted orders. Foot-soldiers jogged past to form neat squares on the edge of the plain. Cavalrymen came for their horses, and the lines emptied. By the time the sun rose, only we horses of the Guard remained.

The Amazons cantered past on their little horned horses painted with blue circles, and the Guard came down with arm- fuls of spears and javelins. They propped these against a cart and stood nearby, talking in excited voices and looking over their shoulders. The grooms untied their horses and walked them up and down, ready for them to mount. Only Alexander had not yet arrived, so no one did.

Tydeos put a hand on my nose and whispered, 'I'm sorry, old horse. I can't keep you out of this battle. If Charm were here, she'd find a way, but I'm not as brave as she is. I daren't defy the king. Just come back in one piece, in case Charm – just in case. Oh, where *is* the king? I can't stand this waiting!'

A man in battle-scarred armour strode towards us, and everyone stiffened. But it was only General Parmenio. He frowned at the Guard. 'No sign of him yet?'

They shook their heads.

'One of you go and fetch him, then! The men are ready. If we wait much longer, there won't be time to finish this battle before dark. Tell him we want to know what his plans are. Zeus, if Alexander doesn't come and lead us today, this is going to be a massacre!'

That could have meant one of two things:

We were going to massacre the Persians.
The Persians were going to massacre us.

The Guard glanced at one another. Hephaestion cleared his throat and said, 'Alex said we weren't to disturb him, Sir. He hasn't slept for four days. I think he's still in bed. He needs his rest.'

The general stared in disbelief at the king's pavilion.

'You're telling me he's overslept, today of all days? Looks like I'll have to go and wake him up myself, then!' He strode off, grumbling under his breath.

Finally, after the sun has climbed much higher in the sky, and even the Guard are beginning to get worried, I smell Alexander's sherbet sweetness. I let out a ringing neigh of welcome, and Tydeos clamps his hand over my nostrils in alarm. 'Shh, Bucephalas! He'll be here—'

Before Tydeos can finish speaking the king arrives, smiling. The circles have faded from around his eyes. He is wearing his reinforced Troy helmet with its white plumes, but has left the Achilles armour in the baggage train. He's chosen to wear his old snake-haired breastplate, which means this is going to be a serious battle. He runs straight up to me and offers me a pastry left over from his breakfast, which I am too excited to eat. I blow crumbs all over him. He laughs and springs on to my back in a great bound, like he used to do back in Macedonia.

I rear up high, catching his excitement, and Tydeos ducks.

'Don't just stand there, boy!' Alexander says. 'I've a battle to win. Hand me my javelins!'

Tydeos hurries to obey. But as he passes up the javelins, he takes a deep breath and whispers, 'Your Majesty, I've discovered something happened back at the camp while we were away visiting the Egyptian oracle. Charm might not have been eaten by a crocodile, after all. See, General Parmenio arrested her because she tried to help Prince Ochus escape, and—'

I am dancing about so much, Alexander doesn't hear properly. He frowns down at Tydeos. 'What's that? Don't bother me with it now, boy. King Darius awaits!'

He gathers up my reins, tucks his spear and javelins under

his arm, and trots me over to the Guard. 'Hurry up, gentle-men!' he calls. 'Mount up! Let's show these Persians what we Macedonians are made of.'

'Have you a plan then, Alex?' Hephaestion asks, trotting Petasios beside me.

Alexander grins. 'Yes, I've a plan. Even old Parmenio couldn't fault it. Stick close to me, and ride as you have never ridden before. This is going to be the greatest battle of our lives!'

It takes some time to get everyone in position to Alexander's satisfaction. We trot up and down the ranks, while he checks every division from several angles. He doesn't seem interested in what the Persians are doing, although out of the corner of my good eye I can see the Guard casting worried glances at the far side of the plain, where the enemy is lining up.

They have reason to be worried. The Persian herd stretches across the entire horizon, and we can hear their horses whin-nying in the distance. They might not have a million, but they have many thousands more men and horses than we do. As I've said before, this is NOT GOOD.

Finally, everyone is where Alexander wants him. I wonder if he's had too much sun. The phalanx is at the back, quite a long way behind everyone else. Most of our cavalry are on the wings, curving almost in a circle and facing the wrong way – sideways to, rather than facing the Persians. There is a line of foot-soldiers at the front with their long pikes, but not many. Some of the cavalry is with us, at the front where they should be, and the Amazons are hiding in the hills to pick off the enemy as they flee. But we're not nearly a big enough herd to dominate the Persians. We will have to be very fierce.

Nervous sweat gleams on our necks as I halt in front of the troops so Alexander can make a speech. We chew our bits and arch our necks. Alexander hands his javelins and shield to Hephaestion and rides me a few steps forward to face his men. I make myself huge. Behind me, the Guard line up knee-to-knee as if they are on parade:

Petasios – handsome, faithful, and my best friend – carrying Hephaestion.

Borealis – a bit slow but comfortingly solid – carrying Leonnatus.

Xanthus – trouble in the lines, excellent in battle – carrying Craterus.

Arion – quietly does his job – carrying Attalus.

Hades – small, but quick on his feet – carrying Iolaus.

Apollo – still a bit vain but has learnt how to fight – carrying Perdiccas.

Harpinna – an amazing fighter – carrying Ptolemy.

Electra – my beautiful filly, fighting her very first battle! – carrying Demetrius and the Achilles shield.

There is a hush. Even the Persians at the far side of the plain go quiet.

'We are going to win today!' Alexander begins, and there is a huge cheer from our herd. When it dies away, he says a lot of boring things about honour and glory, which make the men nod and look fierce. Then he prays to 'his father Zeus', and draws his sword to personally make the pre-battle sacrifice. I snort as goat's blood sprays across my nose.

The men give Alexander another great cheer as he retrieves his weapons from Hephaestion. When he whirls me round to take my place at the front of the army, all the men behind us ready their spears, and all the horses and foot-soldiers make themselves huge.

A whole army, all making itself huge at once!

I have never, in all my years of battle, seen that before.

Dominating the Persians

The excitement infects me. I begin to shiver, even though it is so hot, and every single one of my muscles goes tense. On my cloth, Alexander is tense, too. He holds me to a walk as we advance, but I am ready to gallop at the slightest shift of his weight. The Persian herd is getting slowly closer. We can hear their men squealing insults across the plain. None of our herd replies. We advance in silence and with strict discipline. It is like a big parade.

The Persian horses kick up dust, which makes their herd seem even bigger. I suppose we are making dust, too, because some of the men in the phalanx behind us cough. But our horses don't make so much of it.

'Come on, come on,' Alexander mutters as we get closer. 'Charge, you Persian cowards. Why don't they charge?'

'There's King Darius,' Hephaestion says, nodding towards the chariots in the centre of the Persian line, their wheel blades flashing. 'Hiding behind that lot.'

'Yes.' Alexander still does not shift his weight. 'We won't be able to see much once the charge starts. Remember where Darius is, gentlemen! Watch for my signal.'

There are a few tense nods. The other horses are as ready to gallop as I am, but disciplined enough to obey their riders. The excitement is getting to Electra, though, who goes sideways in her eagerness to pass me. Demetrius is having trouble holding both her and the big Achilles shield. I swing my head at the filly and give her a little squeal, which makes all the horses jump.

Still we walk. The Persians ahead of us are drifting sideways, trying to see how many troops we have behind us. Because our men are curved back in a circle, they can't see them properly. Maybe Alexander is cleverer than I thought.

'Your plan's working, Alex!' Hephaestion calls, excited. 'If they keep this up, they'll soon be in the rough ground at the edge, and their horses and chariots will be in trouble.'

The Persian herd is so close now, I can smell their horses. The enemy directly opposite us have spotted Alexander's helmet. They point at us and shout. Then one of their horses leaps forward, and a whole section of the herd at the end of their line breaks away and follows it. Trumpets blare in the distance.

A shudder goes through Alexander. He hisses, *'Yes!* They're falling for it, gentlemen. Be ready for my signal ...' A ripple of anticipation goes down our line. But Alexander's weight stays in the exact centre of my back. He raises his first javelin and signals to the officers behind him. The enemy, and their great cloud of dust, have already gone round to engage the troops behind us. Screams, shouts and panicky sword clashes suggest they've found our phalanx, and rather more men than they bargained for.

Still Alexander holds my rein tightly. He makes more signals, and the trumpets pass them on. Then Hephaestion shouts, 'The chariots, Alex! Look out!'

Racing towards us are pairs of crazy Persian horses, completely out of control, dragging chariots with blades flashing on their wheels. As the dust billows around them, they head for our front line of foot soldiers, who melt out of their path and let them through to meet a phalanx hiding in the dust behind with a hedge of pikes. There are yells of alarm from the Persian drivers, who can't pull up in time, crashes and thuds, and the screams of dying horses.

This is too much for Electra. She takes three huge leaps and breaks from the Guard into a wild gallop, her head in the air and the bit between her teeth. Demetrius drops his javelins, and almost loses the Achilles shield too.

Alexander curses, then shouts, 'Follow me!' At last, he eases my rein and leans slightly forward. It is what I have been waiting for. I leap into a gallop, chasing my runaway filly.

'ALALALALALAI!' Alexander yells, putting his heels into my sides and heading me at the Persian line.

Behind us, the Guard echo the war cry.

'ALALALALALAI! ALALALALAI! ALALALALAI!'

And there is a great thunder of hooves as everyone follows us.

Oh, this is WILD! I can barely see. Dust is everywhere. The noise of battle is incredible. Ghosts whirl around me as men and horses die. But the plain is beautifully level, I have Alexander on my back, and I gallop through it all fearlessly. I catch up with Electra and bite her on the neck. She puts her head down and feels the bit again. Demetrius' relieved face flashes past us as he gets her back under control and takes his place behind us with the Achilles shield.

We form a tight wedge as we've been trained to do, with me at the front and the cavalry behind, so closely packed that I can hear the men's shields knocking together and feel the hot breath of the other horses on my quarters. There's going to be a few sore heels after this, but no one dares tread on mine. Petasios is beside me, Hephaestion's elbow brushing

Alexander's as they sight on the Persian line and balance their javelins for the throw. Our riders exchange coltish grins. Then they launch their javelins through the dust in perfect unison and make two more Persian ghosts.

'*Now*, gentlemen!' Alexander yells, and does a strange thing. Instead of urging me on through the Persian line to trample and kill more of the enemy, he digs his right knee hard into my ribs and clamps his right leg against my cloth, dragging my rein hard left against my neck. I swerve at once, feeling the wrench along my tendons, and head off at an angle along the startled enemy line. Petasios comes with me, tossing his head in surprise. The others make the turn behind, still in our wedge. It is perfect – until one of the blade-wheeled chariots without a driver appears out of the dust right beside me.

The Persian horses, wild-eyed and flat out, are on a collision course.

Hephaestion yells a bad word and hauls Petasios off to the side to give me room to manoeuvre. Alexander's weight shifts a little, and his knees turn me just in time. The nearest horse brushes my flank, and the blade on the wheel hisses past my blind spot. I leap to avoid it and feel a fierce sting like a mosquito bite on the side of my hind leg. Then it's gone, and I forget the pain. But there's a frantic neigh behind me, and a grey horse tumbles head over heels in the dust with a horrible crunch of bone.

'Attalus is down!' Hephaestion yells.

Attalus rolls clear and springs to his feet, but Arion is still thrashing on the ground behind us. As we race on, the chariot – now on one wheel – barges past the others and somehow gets through without hitting anyone else, the Persian horses dragging it on its side.

'His horse broke a leg!' Demetrius yells, catching up with us on a foaming Electra. 'Attalus is on his feet . . . do we go back for him, Alex?'

Alexander does not look round. 'No. Stay with me. Close up! I'm going for Darius!'

He urges me even faster towards the dim shapes of the enemy chariots in the centre, where the Persian line is breaking up because of everyone going sideways earlier. 'Second javelins, gentlemen!' Alexander yells. 'Make them count!'

He jerks on my cloth, and his javelin flies into a Persian chest, knocking the rider backwards off his horse and releasing his ghost. I squeal in triumph. Now the Guard and the cavalry all throw their final javelins. There is a hissing like rain, and more Persians fall. Some of their horses get hit, too. But there is no time to be sad, because suddenly there are enemies all around us. Alexander is stabbing with his spear, Hephaestion and Petasios are fighting fiercely beside us, and I have to leap to avoid the long, curved Persian blades.

The gap Arion left has been filled by another horse. Its rider is Laomedon, who rode Electra before Demetrius needed her. He flashes Alexander a quick grin, and grimly stabs a Persian with his spear. I whinny at the little bay he is riding to get closer, and leap to carry Alexander out of range of another scimitar.

I collect a few cuts. None of them hurt. That's what it's like in a battle, as if a small man-colt is slapping you from all sides. Irritating, but not painful. At least, not at the time. I look after my rider so well, no enemy blade or spear touches Alexander.

I have to keep snorting to clear my nose. The sweat pours off my sides. There is white foam on my neck. I cannot see more than five horses around me, though the noise and screams tell me there are thousands close by. Then another chariot comes into view, and I break into a fresh sweat as I remember what happened to Arion. But this chariot still has a driver, and there is an important-looking Persian standing behind him, gripping the sides and shouting orders. He is tall with dark skin and curly black whiskers. His helmet is wrapped in blue and white cloth. Gold glitters at his wrists and from the sides of the chariot. I can smell him from here. He smells of fear.

When Alexander sees him, he hauls my head round, hurting my mouth. 'King Darius!' he yells in his shrill voice, drawing his sword.

The man in the chariot turns his head, and his dark eyes widen in alarm. He shouts a warning, and his driver hauls the horses round and whips them into a gallop. Horns sound in the Persian line, and gaps open up around us with shouts of confusion. More trumpets blare – this time they're ours. Fierce shouting comes from the direction of our lines, and I see our phalanx with lowered pikes, charging through the dust after a herd of fleeing Persian cavalry.

'The Persians are retreating, Alex!' Hephaestion shouts, turning Petasios so he can see better. 'You've done it. I think you've actually done it!'

The Guard cheers.

Alexander shakes his head impatiently. 'It's not over yet. Don't let Darius get away! Guard, follow me!' He urges me after the chariot.

I am tired, and so are the other horses. We try our best, but the Persians surrounding the chariot fight fiercely and keep getting in the way. Hephaestion gets left behind, and yells as an enemy spear pierces his shoulder.

Alexander's head snaps round. '*Hephaestion!*' We have galloped no more than a few strides after the fleeing chariot, yet he turns me back at once to help.

But it is not yet time for Hephaestion's ghost to leave him. He grits his teeth, pulls out the spear and keeps it, since he's already broken his own. 'You go on, Alex!' he shouts, clasping his wound. 'I'll be fine.'

Alexander casts an anguished glance after Darius' fleeing chariot, but stays to examine Hephaestion's shoulder. 'Can you still fight, my friend?'

Hephaestion nods, while I nip Petasios on the nose for letting his rider get wounded.

'Good, then stay here and help General Parmenio clean up the stragglers. The rest of you, come with me!'

But as Alexander wheels me round to resume the chase after King Darius, Perdiccas yells, 'Look out, gentlemen! Behind you!'

That's the trouble when the enemy is in retreat, and you have galloped so far through their lines. All those who charged past you during the battle then turn round and come back towards you, going the other way. We whirl as one to find ourselves facing a whole herd of Persians, their horses draped with bundles that spill golden coins and cups behind them in the dust.

One of them is leading a mule with a jewelled box strapped to its back. It is one of OUR mules – the cheek of it! Others have the Persian women we took captive at Issus sitting behind them on their horses, clinging to their waists. When they recognize Alexander, the Persians check their horses in dismay and stare round wildly. The women scream.

Alexander is already panting from the battle, but his breathing gets even faster. He casts a final frustrated look at Darius' vanishing chariot, gathers up my reins and shouts, 'Those men have been looting our camp! Don't let them get away! They've stolen my *Iliad*!'

The Guard, and those of the cavalry still with us, growl in their throats. Alexander grips his sword tighter and heads me straight for the Persian leading the mule. The thief pales, drops the mule's rein and turns his horse to flee, but I am too quick for it. I bite it on the neck to drive it back, and Alexander's sword flashes across the Persian's throat.

His ghost lurches from his body, while enemy blood sprays my ears and Alexander's cheek. The other Persians have recovered from the shock of coming face to face with the Macedonian king, and are fighting furiously. They have the stolen captives in the middle of their group, and I can smell Prince Ochus among them. One of the Persians has the man-colt perched on his horse's withers.

I don't think Alexander has noticed the man-colt yet. But Ochus stares in horror as my rider kills Persian after Persian with his sword, until the blade is red and both he and I are soaked in enemy blood. Dust sticks to it and turns us both brown.

Some of our herd also give up their ghosts, because the Persian thieves know that surrendering won't save their lives. Finally, though, they are beaten, and the few survivors huddle with the stolen captives, ringed by our cavalry. Gold litters the plain like flowers. My hooves chink on it as Alexander walks me forwards.

A dented cup rolls away as I kick it. He rides me right up to the Persian holding Ochus, wipes an arm across his face –

which just smudges the dust and blood, making it look worse – and stares at the prince. The man-colt is very brave and meets his gaze.

'Leaving me already, Ochus?' Alexander says in his quiet, dangerous tone. 'What's the matter? Don't I treat you well enough?'

'Not hurt our prince, please,' says the Persian holding him. 'We think Great King Darius win the battle. We take his children back to him, that is all.'

'The "Great King" *did* win the battle,' Alexander snaps. 'You're looking at him.'

He gives the two sobbing princesses, who are still clinging to their rescuers' waists, a disgusted look. Then he turns his attention to Ochus. 'Where are your grandmother and Lady Barsine?'

'Granny Sisygambis not come,' Ochus says, sitting up very straight. 'She say she too old for galloping about battlefields. She say she wait for Father to escort her back himself. Aunty Barsine stay to look after her.'

Alexander shakes his head. 'Is an old woman the only one with any sense around here?' he shouts. 'You could all have been killed! Hephaestion, you take Prince Ochus back to camp. See him and the princesses safely back to their pavilion and double the guard – and someone catch that stupid mule before it trots off into the hills with my *Iliad*!'

One of the cavalrymen goes after the mule. Hephaestion takes Ochus up on to Petasios with him but hesitates, watching Alexander uneasily. The others put the Macedonian dead across the backs of the spare horses. They leave the Persian bodies where they lie, because there are so many of them. A few loose horses are rounded up before they can get lost in the dust. Alexander shakes his head at the three Persian thieves left alive. They've been dragged off their horses and forced to their knees in front of me.

'Please, King Iskander,' says the man who was caught with Ochus. 'Spare us! We only do what we think best for our Great King's family. He very upset when his wife die. He worry about them.'

Alexander scowls, and rides me so close to the prisoners that my hooves stamp near their knees. They put their arms over their heads and cower away from my flat ears and snapping teeth. 'You were stupid, and you've delayed me. If Darius gets away, it'll be your fault. You don't deserve to live. But since you've begged for your lives, and I am a greater king than Darius, I'll return the favour he showed my wounded at Issus. Then, if we don't catch King Darius tonight, maybe you can find your way back to him and give him a message from me.'

The Persians go a funny colour as they realize what he means. The Macedonians seize them and stretch their arms out on the ground. Alexander backs me up to give them space. Then he gives a sharp nod. A sword flashes down, twice for each man. The Persian women cry out in protest. Ochus makes a small sound in his throat and buries his face in Hephaestion's shoulder. His sisters scream at Alexander in Persian. I don't know what they're saying, but it sounds to me like mares squealing.

The prisoners stare at their severed hands lying in the dust among the spilled gold, as if they can't believe what Alexander has just had done to them. Blood pours from their wrists. Even the Macedonians grimace as they tie rags around the bloody stumps to stop the mutilated men from bleeding to death before they reach their camp.

Alexander speaks to the three prisoners as if nothing has happened. 'Tell Darius that I am the Great King of Persia now. Tell him that so far I have treated his family as my family, and his son as my son. But if he tries to raise another army against me, then I will give his daughters to my men to use as slaves, and kill the boy. If Darius wants to live, he must surrender himself to me. Otherwise, I will hunt him to the ends of the earth. *Go!*'

The handless Persians stagger through the gap our cavalry make for them and stumble off into the dust. Ochus stares in disbelief at Alexander, blinks rapidly, and is sick down Petasios' shoulder.

Chasing King Darius

As the sun sank into the dust and turned everything around us red, I began to look forward to my roll. But Alexander turned my head to the east, pulled my ear and whispered, 'Come on, Bucephalas. I need your speed now.' He put his bloody sword back into its scabbard, called the Guard to follow, and dug his heels into my sides.

We chased King Darius well into that night, overtaking some of his fleeing herd and passing his abandoned chariot. Alexander did not even pause to draw his sword, so it was just as well the frightened Persians took off across the fields when they saw us coming. I found my second wind and forgot my wounds as we galloped through the littered bodies of men and horses. I was determined to do better than Xanthus did after Issus. My hind leg was stiff where the chariot blade had cut me, and the other three felt as if they had boulders tied to them, but I did not slacken my pace. There were piles of dung smelling of Aura in the road, and every time I found one, a fresh surge of energy kept me galloping onwards.

Eventually, though, my breath stopped coming so easily, and bubbles of something hot and bitter kept blocking my throat. If Alexander had asked me for more speed, I would have found it for him, but he finally noticed I was bleeding from the nose and pulled me back to a trot. There were some big, round-roofed huts near the river, and he turned me towards them. As soon as we stopped, my knees gave way, and Alexander had to pretend that he had told me to settle down.

He slipped off me, held on to my head while I drew shuddering breaths past the blood in my nose, and whispered, 'Oh, Bucephalas ... don't you dare die on me, horse! Even Darius isn't worth that.'

Meanwhile, the other horses stood around me with drooping heads, heaving rib cages and flaring nostrils. The men dismounted in relief, as wobbly-kneed as we were. Some of them went to investigate the huts, while the others led us to the river for a drink and found us some hay. Alexander tended me himself. He wiped the blood from my nose with his tunic and led me up and down until the stiffness went from my legs. Then he took the Guard into one of the huts, while the rest of the men curled up on the ground nearby.

Scenting another of Aura's dung piles nearby, I sent one last weary whinny into the night. But she did not reply.

How Aura led the Persian herd

It is still dark when Alexander mounts me again. We trot along the river road by moonlight, following Aura's trail. The blood has stopped coming out of my nose, though my hind leg is now very stiff, so I am lame behind.

As the sun rises, we reach a town. Its garrison is deserted, so when Alexander and I lead our weary herd through the gates of Arbela, there is no one left for us to fight. This is just as well, because we are only a small herd now. We have not only fought a fierce battle, but have galloped through most of the night and must look a real sight. The humans who live in this town are still scared of us, though. They run into their houses and slam their doors. Alexander stares wearily after them and trots me to the palace.

It is deserted. Our hooves echo in the marble courtyard. A fountain splashes into a pink marble bowl, the smell of water making me thirsty. Doors bang in the wind. A few goats and dogs wander loose in the yard. Some women and old men creep out of the dark doorways and lie down in the dirt before me and Alexander, pressing their foreheads to the ground.

'Where's King Darius?' Alexander asks. But they don't seem to understand, so he calls Laomedon forward to translate.

'They say the Great King's gone, Alex,' Laomedon says, after questioning the slaves. 'He and the remains of his army headed into the mountains last night. Four, maybe five thousand men. We won't catch them now.'

Alexander does not seem surprised. He sighs and rides me round the courtyard. My hooves echo in the silence and my stride is broken by lameness – clop, clop, clop-clop, clop, clop, clop-clop. I am so tired I can barely hold my head up. But as we pass the stables, I catch a familiar scent inside. AURA! I summon the last of my strength and send her a ringing whinny.

A few of the cavalry horses who came with us on the chase

whinny back. I fidget, wanting to sniff the dung piles I can see lying over by the entrance, but Alexander won't let me. Then I hear Aura whinny back, very faint. All the horses of the Guard flicker their ears. I whinny again and dance sideways, grabbing my bit in my teeth.

Alexander smooths my mane and frowns at the stables. He tells Iolaus, 'Go and check inside.' Iolaus hands Hades' reins to Demetrius and stamps past us, grumbling that he's not a groom. All the Guard are tired and grumpy, so Alexander ignores this.

We wait. The slaves stay quiet, with their faces still pressed to the ground. I manage to get my nose into the fountain bowl and gulp a few mouthfuls. The water is warm.

Then Iolaus comes back out of the stables leading Aura. Her head hangs low, her lovely dappled coat crusted in dried sweat. Her flanks and sides are covered in whip marks, raw and bleeding. She is limping too, with little snorts of pain each time she puts her bad leg down. She looks twice my age, and that's a lot of years. If it weren't for her smell and her familiar whinny, I would not have recognized her.

'I think it's the mare the Persian queen's slave stole, Alex.' But Iolaus sounds doubtful, and looks to Demetrius for confirmation.

Demetrius leaps off Electra, abandoning my filly in the middle of the yard, and rushes across to take Aura's head. 'Oh, my poor brave little mare . . .' he says, stroking her nose and running his hand down her swollen leg. 'What have those horrid Persians *done* to you?'

I nicker to Aura, who raises her head a little and manages a small nicker back.

One of the kneeling slaves says something, and Laomedon

translates. 'This man says King Darius was riding the grey mare when he arrived. He must have abandoned his chariot at his camp, and changed horses again here. How about that, Alex? One of our own mares helped the Persian king get away!'

'Not without a fight, by the looks of it,' Alexander mutters. 'Bucephalas knew she was in there, didn't you, old horse? Was that why you nearly killed yourself last night, chasing after Darius, you silly horse? I should have guessed you were after a mare rather than the Persian king!'

He looks round the yard and sighs. 'Laomedon, tell those Persian slaves to get up and make themselves useful. These horses need someone to look after them until our grooms get here, and I could do with a bath!'

The battle at Gaugamela was the dustiest I have ever been in, and the first time our herd has ever won against a much bigger herd. But many of our horses had their manes shaved in mourning for their lost riders, and Attalus – who had survived the battle on foot – cut off a lock of his mane in mourning for Arion, who never got up again.

Groom-gossip said the plain at Gaugamela stank of rotting Persian dead for days, because so many of them had died that there was no one left from the enemy herd to collect up the bodies for their god. Even crows get full eventually.

This is how we dominated the Persians at Gaugamela:

Persian prisoners: none, except slaves found in their baggage train.
Persian dead: 50,000, including Ochus' mother the night the moon went out.
Macedonian dead: 1,500.

Horses dead: 1,000, including Arion, who had to be put down after his leg was broken by the runaway chariot. (VERY SAD.)

Prisoners spared or rescued: Aura, the three Persians who had their hands chopped off, and Prince Ochus.

But considering what Tydeos tried to tell Alexander before the battle, I think Prince Ochus could soon be in very big trouble.

NINETEENTH HOOFPRINT
ARBELA, WINTER 331 BC

Wounded

Even small battles are exhausting. Our last one was like being struck by a thousand thunderbolts, and that was before our midnight chase after King Darius.

The next day I was so stiff I could barely stand. My hind leg where the chariot clipped me had swelled to twice its normal size, and many smaller cuts I hadn't noticed during the fighting now began to HURT. I couldn't bear to be touched, so I kicked the wall whenever the Persian grooms came near; this meant I didn't get fresh water or barley, though they threw some hay into my stall to keep me quiet. Aura was in the next stall, but I couldn't bear even her soft nose questing through the bars. I nipped her (very gently, because she's still my favourite mare) until she left me alone.

When Tydeos finally arrived with the rest of the army, the Persian grooms pointed to my stall and tried to tell him how wild I was. Since they didn't speak Greek they mimed flat ears, just like Alexander had done to warn Ochus about me after the battle of Issus. One of them made a pathetic attempt at a squeal and kicked the wall, pretending to be me.

Tydeos straightened his tunic and pushed past them with a smile. 'You got to watch that horse,' he told them. 'Bucephalas has been trained to kill Persians. Let me through. I know how to handle him.' When he saw me tied to the manger where Alexander had left me the night before, he drew a shocked breath. 'Zeus, you poor old horse! You're a walking skeleton. What has King Alexander *done* to you?' Then he looked over the wall, saw the state of Aura, and whistled. 'You two aren't going anywhere for a while, that's for sure.'

Tydeos was right. Aura and I had to stay behind in Arbela with General Parmenio's veterans to recover, while Alexander took the Amazons and the rest of the army south to 'liberate' Babylon from the Persians. At least, that's what he told General Parmenio he was going to do – though it sounds more like dominating to me.

It was good to be with my favourite mare, but I missed Charm's fingers mutual grooming my withers. Every time I heard footsteps approach my stall, I flared my nostrils in the hope that it was her or Alexander.

But when I did finally smell someone familiar, it was neither of my favourite humans.

Horse thief

We have been in Arbela about a month when news comes of a raid by the Persian resistance on one of our new garrisons. General Parmenio's men gallop off at once to deal with it. Tydeos is out exercising Aura, and the Persian grooms have gone with him to exercise the spare horses. Although it is humiliating to be left behind, I am secretly relieved to be in my stall away from the flies, where I can lie down to rest my bad leg.

I am not expecting Aura back so soon, so the scrape in the next stall makes me jump. It's not her, of course. Even dozing, I would notice my favourite mare coming back in. But the smell coming over the partition is almost as familiar. It brings memories of Charm lying helpless across a camel's back. I scramble to my feet, snorting in alarm, and toss my head against the chain that fastens me to the manger.

The old horsemaster limps into my stall and chuckles at my wild eye and flat ears. He is wearing Persian-style trousers that cover his twisted leg, and has grown his whiskers long. A dagger is thrust through his sash; I can smell fresh blood on the blade. He is carrying my bridle, my muzzle and a long whip.

'Still up to your old tricks, I see,' he mutters. 'Don't expect any help this time, Bucephalas. The sentries have already felt my dagger between their ribs. General Parmenio's men are off dealing with a little diversion my Persian friends arranged, and you'll never see your girl-groom again.' He chuckles nastily.

I lunge for him, but his whip slices across my nose. I rear back against my tether, startled by the pain. He takes advantage of this to limp close to my shoulder where I can't reach him with my teeth. His hand darts up on my blind side. Before I know what he intends, he grabs my ear. He twists hard until I lower my head, then he jams the bit between my snapping teeth.

'You don't scare me, horse,' he says as he secures the straps and fastens my muzzle over the top. 'I've had more experience of bad-tempered stallions than you've had hot mashes, and I heard you were half dead after the battle at Gaugamela. Give up the fight and make it easy on yourself.'

He unchains me and tries to lead me out of the stall. I rear up and try to get him with my hooves, but he ducks. When I come down he gives me another slice on the nose with the whip. It hurts so much I barge out of the stall backwards, dragging him at the end of my reins. He doesn't try to stop me, just leans back and lets me pull his weight out of the stable into the courtyard.

After being inside, the Mesopotamian sunlight dazzles me. I instantly feel the heat burning my black coat. The horsemaster drives me up against the fountain with his whip, and twists my ear again to force my head round to my girth. He kicks me behind the fetlocks, trying to make me settle down for him to mount. I fight him with all my strength. But my hooves slip, and I crash on to my side.

It hurts. As I lie there, bruised, he climbs stiffly on to my back.

'Fight all you like, Bucephalas,' he hisses, still holding my head at that unnatural angle so I can't get up. 'Wear yourself out. Then we'll go for a good long gallop across the plain, see how long an old horse like you can keep fighting in this heat.'

I squeal in rage and snap at him inside my muzzle. The horsemaster just laughs. Then I hear Aura's whinny in the distance. I whinny back as loudly as I can. The horsemaster frowns at the gates. While he is distracted, I make a supreme effort and struggle to my feet.

I am really mad now and act wild. He wraps his legs around me, but the one that was crippled by the mulemaster doesn't grip as well as when he tried to ride me in Pella. By the time Aura's hooves clatter into the yard, and Tydeos yells, 'Oi! You! What do you think you're doing with the king's horse?' the horsemaster's whip has gone and his weight is shifting.

I put my head between my forelegs and give a final buck that sends my enemy sprawling at Aura's feet. She shies, and Tydeos falls off over her shoulder. With an agile twist, he lands on his feet and finds himself face to face with his old boss.

'What are *you* doing here?' he demands, finally recognizing the horsemaster. 'What were you doing with Bucephalas?'

The horsemaster eyes me acting wild around the fountain, and takes Aura's reins. 'Nice mare, this,' he says, changing the subject. 'I remember her from Pella. Are those whip scars on her flanks? Alexander lose his temper with her, did he?'

'Never mind the mare,' Tydeos says. 'Bucephalas has whip marks, too, and I just saw you give them to him! You're supposed to be put under arrest if you come near our horses. Everyone knows how you tried to kidnap the king's horse at Thebes. Stay where you are!'

He shouts for the sentries, but no one comes.

The horsemaster sighs, whips out his dagger and points it at Tydeos. 'Shut your mouth,' he says. 'Or it won't just be the sentries I kill.' He scrambles awkwardly on to Aura's back and heads her for the gate, where the Persian grooms are returning with the other horses.

'Stop him!' Tydeos calls. 'He's stealing that mare!' But the Persian grooms don't understand his Greek words. As they hesitate, the old horsemaster barges through them and urges Aura into a gallop.

My enemy is disappearing into the dust with my favourite

mare, and they are just standing there! Tydeos tries in vain to catch me, but I swerve around him and gallop after Aura's white tail, my lameness forgotten, whinnying at the top of my lungs.

The horsemaster looks round in surprise, and a slow smile spreads across his face. 'So all I needed was a mare in season? I wish I'd thought of that in the first place. It would have saved us both a lot of trouble.' He looks back at Tydeos, giving chase on one of the other horses, and laughs out loud. 'I think your stupid groom's going to be in a lot of trouble when Alexander finds out he let me take you *and* the mare. Come on, then, old horse! Catch us if you can!' And he urges Aura off the road and across the plain.

There are some fresh Persian dung piles nearby, but I don't have time to stop and dominate them. We gallop into the rising dust, Tydeos' shouts fading behind us.

Ghosts on the outside

By the time I catch up with Aura, I can hardly get my breath. I've lost a lot of fitness, and my hind leg is hurting. I still can't bite because of the muzzle, but I lean on Aura's neck to pull her up. She lowers her head and snorts dust from her nose. The horsemaster, chuckling at my heaving sides and the white foam on my flanks, leans down and takes my rein.

'Good,' he says. 'We're just in time to meet my friends, the ones who caused that little diversion in the Macedonian garrison. The Persians appreciate a man of my talents, unlike that young hothead Alexander. He's going to regret dismissing me back in Pella.'

Aura pricks her ears, and I lift my head. A whole herd of horses is galloping towards us. They're raising a great deal of dust, so we can't yet see them, but I can smell the horses and recognize the Amazon herd. I neigh a welcome, while the horsemaster sits confidently on Aura's back, smiling. He can't recognize their smell like I can, and still thinks they are his friends.

Ha, is he in for a shock!

The Amazons surround us in a whooping circle. By the time the horsemaster realizes they are not the Persian herd he was expecting, it is too late. He tries to make Aura flee, but I dance backwards, almost dragging him off her back.

Queen Penthesilea rests her axe on her knee and bares her teeth at the old horsemaster. 'Where are you going with the king's horse?' she demands.

The horsemaster stares in disbelief at the little horned horses with their blue circles. Then he raises his gaze to the Amazon queen, taking in her braided hair, her axe and bow, and her leather clothes. Seeing the others in her herd are all women, too, he relaxes slightly. 'Out of my way, woman!' he says. 'I'm exercising these horses.'

'Oh, yes? Then why is King Alexander's groom racing after you, shouting that you are a thief?'

The horsemaster's eyes narrow. He rests his hand on his dagger. While he is concentrating on the Amazons, I swing my head and knock him off Aura's back.

Queen Penthesilea laughs. She rides her horse close to him. 'Bucephalas also seems to think you are a thief,' she says. 'What shall we do with him, sisters? Kill him? Or truss him up and deliver him to King Alexander?'

The horsemaster moves fast, despite his twisted leg. He grabs the Amazon queen's elbow and plunges his long Persian dagger up to the hilt into her body. The other Amazons hiss angrily.

A normal human would be dead from such a blow. But, as you already know, Queen Penthesilea's ghost is on the outside. My coat stands on end as her ghost whirls and thickens about the blade. There is no blood. The Amazon queen straightens up with a look of amusement, pulls out the dagger and points it at the horsemaster's throat. The blade is cleaner than when it went in.

The horsemaster stares at it in confusion. His confidence is gone now, and he smells scared. 'Who *are* you?' he whispers.

'Do you not know your legends, horse thief? How we fought at Troy and gained our immortality? I am Queen Penthesilea of the warrior women you call Amazons. King Alexander cut the Gordian Knot, which opened a hole in the world and summoned us. We must serve him until the hole opens again to let us go home. He sent us north to report on the successful surrender of Babylon. Fortunately, we arrived just in time to help General Parmenio put down your little Persian uprising.'

'That's ridiculous! Amazons don't exist.'

'Really? I wonder if my axe exists? Shall I test it on your neck, horse thief?'

Tydeos finally catches up with us. He looks relieved when he sees I am unharmed. 'Thank Zeus you caught the thief!' he says to the queen. 'Can you take him back to Arbela? General Parmenio will know what to do with him.'

Queen Penthesilea shakes her head. 'He just tried to kill me, so I think I will kill him.'

The horsemaster pales. He is trapped in the centre of the Amazon herd. But he speaks to Tydeos rather than to the women, his voice sly. 'If you let these unnatural women kill me, boy, you'll never know what I did with your girlfriend.'

Tydeos stiffens. He jumps off his horse, leaving its reins dangling, and pushes past the Amazon queen. 'What do you know about Charm?' he demands. '*Where is she?*'

The Amazons glance at one another. Tydeos is breathing very fast.

Queen Penthesilea grabs the horsemaster's whiskers in her callused fist and says, 'What did you do with Charmeia? Speak, thief, or you will feel the edge of my axe! If you tell us the truth, maybe I will let you live a little longer.'

The horsemaster gives her a wary look. 'Is that a promise?'

'On my horse's horn and the honour of my people. But I will know if you lie. There will be no second chances for you.'

The horsemaster glances at Tydeos and chuckles. 'What do you think I did with her? Alexander has hostages, so it's only fair the Persians should have one too. Since Alexander hasn't got an heir yet, and his mother is safe at home in Pella, his groom was the closest thing to family I could find. I needed something to trade for my freedom, so I gave her to King Darius for his harem.'

There is a shocked silence.

The Amazons growl like dogs. Queen Penthesilea narrows her eyes and tightens her fist on her axe. Tydeos flushes with anger and launches himself at the horsemaster.

'You sneaky son of a *snake*! If the Persian king so much as *touches* Charm, I'll . . . I'll . . .'

I don't hear what Tydeos wants to do to the horsemaster, because at that moment Aura lifts her tail and squirts at me. Her smell is glorious. The horsemaster spoke the truth about one thing: though it is rather late in the year, Aura is definitely in foal-season! The heat must have confused her. When I nip her hindquarters to drive her away from the Amazon herd, she nickers at me, pleased.

Tydeos and the Amazons do not notice us. They are too busy arguing about what to do with their prisoner. They have two choices:

Take him to Babylon and hand him over to Alexander.
Take him back to Arbela and hand him over to General Parmenio.

I could have told them what they should not do, but I was with my mare. While the humans argued, Aura and I trotted into the shade of some trees beside a nearby canal and quietly made our first foal together. Ha!

Twentieth Hoofprint
Susa, Winter 331 BC

Our huge herd

The Amazons and Tydeos took their prisoner to General Parmenio. How were they to know? Back in Egypt, they were at Siwa with Alexander when the general gave Charm to the horsemaster and killed the mulemaster for trying to save her.

I'm sure you don't need me to tell you what happened next. My enemy mysteriously 'escaped' and fled into the mountains. (Ha! If you believe that, you'll believe anything. Prisoners don't escape from the Macedonian army that easily, not unless someone leaves their door open accidentally-on-purpose.) General Parmenio said the man wasn't worth chasing, no harm had been done, and both he and Alexander had more important things to worry about than a horse thief.

I was a bit nervous in my stall after that, but Tydeos never again made the mistake of leaving me alone. As soon as I was sound again, we marched south with General Parmenio along the fertile bank of the Tigris to meet Alexander and the rest of the army on the road from Babylon.

The wind blew rain in our faces as we approached the crossroads, bringing smells from Alexander's camp long before we saw the tents and banners. I caught the familiar odours of horse dung, sweat, oil, leather, smoke from the campfires, fresh bread and olives, mixed with stranger ones of damp camel, spices, and musky lions. It smelt and sounded like a much bigger herd than the one Alexander took with him to liberate Babylon. After my long convalescence, it was VERY exciting. I arched my neck and danced impatiently at Aura's side, picking up my knees as high as a colt, and tossing my mane.

Tydeos, who was riding Aura and leading me, cursed as my lead rein slipped through his fingers. 'Steady, Bucephalas,' he muttered. 'Don't be stupid now, or you'll hurt your leg again. Then I'll be in even more trouble than I am already for letting that horsemaster nearly get you in Arbela – *Zeus*! Where did all those new men come from?'

As we reached the ford our riders saw what we horses had smelt long ago. The camp was HUGE. Tents spread across the entire plain, swamping the canals and fields. Alexander's white pavilion glowed like a sun in the middle, and King Darius' captured one sparkled beside it. On a mound beyond the camp, the polished brick walls of a large city gleamed in the rain. Water glittered everywhere.

General Parmenio pulled up his horse and scowled at all the fluttering banners. 'What does he think he's playing at now?' he muttered. 'Those aren't just the reinforcements from Pella he told me about! I see Greek banners . . . Anatolian mercenaries . . . more horses . . . Babylonians . . . Egyptians . . . *camels*, for Zeus' sake! We've defeated the Persian army. We don't need all these men to capture a couple of undefended palaces.'

He spun his horse round so roughly, the poor thing reared. He glared at Tydeos as if the size of Alexander's herd were his fault. 'You, boy! Take Bucephalas to the king's lines before he gets loose again. I'm going to sort out this nonsense right now.' He galloped off with his guard, kicking up lumps of earth, and leaving us with the Amazons.

As we made our way through the camp, the rain stopped and the sun came out. We glimpsed gold glittering under many of the tent flaps, even those of ordinary soldiers. The Macedonians wore new cloaks, and the officers' helmets had new plumes. We spotted many Greek-style helmets with noseguards, and everywhere men were training for battle. A herd of cavalry trotted past us on strange horses, and one left a pile of steaming dung right under my nose. I paused to dominate it, and almost pulled Tydeos over Aura's tail.

'What are you going to tell the king?' Queen Penthesilea asked, riding her little horned horse with its faded blue circles beside Aura.

'I don't know!' Tydeos grimaced and gave my lead rein a jerk, because I was dancing around him to protect my mare from the lions in the cages we were passing.

Queen Penthesilea laughed as she reined her horse out of the way. 'At least Bucephalas looks well! I think that is a good sign for Charmeia.'

Tydeos gave her a sharp look. 'What do you mean?'

'I mean the horse bond that links the three of them – Charmeia, Bucephalas and Alexander. Bucephalas was injured and unhappy in Arbela, so one of those bonded to him must also have been injured and unhappy. But Alexander was flushed with victory after winning his battle against the Persians, so it must have been poor Charmeia suffering. But now the horse is recovered, I think Charmeia is also well. Do not worry, Tydeos. I am sure we will find her very soon.'

Tydeos stopped Aura so he could sort out our reins. He stared at the Amazon queen. 'You *knew* she wasn't dead?'

Queen Penthesilea nodded. 'I suspected. So did King Alexander. He feels the bond, too.'

'Why didn't you tell me? I thought she'd been attacked by a crocodile, until Prince Ochus told me about General Parmenio arresting her! Even then, I wasn't sure. Not until that wicked old horsemaster told us what he'd done with her.'

'Would you have believed me?' Queen Penthesilea said gently. 'You were drowning your sorrows in beer a lot of the time, and I did not wish to raise your hopes. You care for her, I can tell. It is good. But you should know she is a very mixed-up young woman. I am not sure she knows herself how much of her love for Alexander is due to the horse bond, and how much is due to her own heart.'

Tydeos made a face and let us walk on. 'Where do you think King Darius is keeping her?'

'I suppose it depends how important he thinks she is to King Alexander. But whether or not Alexander cares for Charmeia, both he and Bucephalas depend on her for their power. So, I agree we must find her, and quickly, before the Persians decide she's no use as a hostage and get rid of her.'

'I'll help find her!' Tydeos gripped my lead rein more firmly and gave the Amazon queen a determined look. 'Are we going now?'

Queen Penthesilea chuckled. 'Patience, Tydeos. You cannot leave Bucephalas untended to chase the length of Persia after King Darius. His army might have been defeated at Gaugamela, but he still has more men with him than we Amazons could handle alone, despite our being unable to die. Let us see what King Alexander says first, shall we? We might find Charmeia in Susa. I actually doubt King Darius believes Alexander would care so much for a common groom. He probably left her behind in his palace with his other unimportant slaves.'

'Or he might have taken her with him because he's so desperate now he's lost his army, he's willing to try anything.' I could feel Tydeos' anxiety vibrating along my lead rein.

Queen Penthesilea nodded gravely. 'It is possible.'

'What do you think the old horsemaster meant about her being the "closest thing to family" Alexander had?'

The Amazon queen frowned. 'I do not know. Maybe you should ask Charmeia when we find her? She might tell you what she will not tell anyone else. Speaking of which, you have not yet answered my question.'

She gazed at Tydeos, waiting.

'I'll tell the king everything,' he mumbled. 'Even though I'll be in trouble for leaving Bucephalas alone in the stables, when he'd warned me not to. One of the other grooms could easily have exercised Aura for me that day, only I needed to do something to take my mind off Charm ...' He shook his head. 'I'll tell him when the time's right.'

'Good.' The Amazon queen nodded again. 'But be careful how much you say about Prince Ochus' part in it. It might be easier for the boy if the king does not realize Charmeia got kidnapped while helping him escape.'

305

'Too late for that,' Tydeos mumbled, obviously remembering what he'd said to Alexander before Gaugamela. But the queen didn't hear, because just then Aura and I smelt our friends.

I filled my lungs and let out a ringing neigh to announce my presence. Aura whinnied, too, almost as loudly. Petasios whinnied back at once. Then Electra's shrill neigh rang out. Xanthus answered Aura. (He didn't know about our foal.) Harpinna whinnied to me. Then Borealis, Apollo and Hades neighed to us both, competing with Hoplite's high little whinny. Zoroaster whinnied last of all, after a pause, as if he had politely waited for the others to finish.

Arion's whinny was missing, of course. But the others were all fine. And I was so happy to be back in the lines with my friends around me, I ate up every last grain of my barley, for the first time since leaving Egypt.

Squealing on the Royal Road

Alexander brings me a whole bag of honey cakes the next morning while I am dozing after breakfast. As soon as I smell him coming, I stop resting my hind leg and neigh a welcome.

His mane has grown lighter in the sun of this hot world. A golden collar gleams at his neck, and he is wearing a fancy new tunic that shows off his suntan and his muscles, dented by sword cuts. Soon he'll have as many battle scars as me. Perita trots at his heels, also wearing a new collar that glitters in the sun.

Alexander's gaze darts along the horse lines, checking things. His hand flicks out, pointing to nosebags left in the dirt, unfolded cloths, overturned buckets . . . and the grooms leap to put things right. His stride is long and firm, like a stallion who knows he is the boss and does not expect a challenge.

Tydeos jumps to his feet, tugs his tunic straight and wets his lips. But Alexander has eyes only for me. After looking closely at my hind leg which was injured at Gaugamela, he comes to my head and holds my nose hard against his tunic.

'Bucephalas,' he murmurs, rubbing the white patch between my eyes. 'My faithful old horse! I'm sorry you missed Babylon. They threw rose petals over me, enough to fill your entire stable in Pella! There were so many people, it took two days for everyone to hear that I had arrived. I didn't ride Xanthus into the city, though. I entered Babylon in a chariot, so you needn't be jealous.'

I nudge him, because I can smell the honey cakes in his pocket. He laughs and feeds me a handful. 'There, you greedy thing! You're not pleased to see me at all, are you? You're just thinking of your belly, as usual.'

This isn't true, because I'm also thinking of Aura and our unborn foal. But it is a long time since I've tasted honey cakes, so I make the most of them.

Out of the corner of my good eye, I see Tydeos creeping closer. He clears his throat. 'Your Majesty, there's something I have to tell you—'

But before he can tell Alexander about the horsemaster, General Parmenio strides down to the horse lines, calling for the king. He sounds angry. The grooms point to me and make themselves scarce. Tydeos melts away behind a pile of our cloths. Perita growls low in her throat, and Alexander looks round with a grimace. 'Never any peace,' he mutters. 'What do I have to do to get some time alone with my horse?'

He gives me a pat and steps out of the lines. He stands on my good side where I can see him and rests one hand on my quarters, daring General Parmenio to come any closer. Perita sits at his heel and fixes her yellow eyes on the general.

'I've just seen your plans for the army, Alexander!' the general says abruptly. 'I don't agree with some of your promotions. Why have you split up the cavalry? And what's all this about youngsters getting promoted over the older officers who served under you and your father for years? The men won't like that at all.'

Alexander smiles slightly. 'As you pointed out to me yesterday, General, my army is bigger now than it has ever been. I have reorganized things to make it more efficient. The old ways were fine when the army was small and old men were in charge. But now *I'm* commander . . .' He pauses to make sure the general doesn't miss this. 'I have decided some new ideas are in order. It makes a lot more sense to promote young men for fighting well than it does to promote old men for getting grumpy and slow.'

The general's face flushes. 'And what are you planning to do with this great army of yours, Alexander? Your reinforcements arrived rather late for the battle, but no doubt they'll all have their greedy eyes on a share of the Persian treasure. How do you plan to share it out?'

'I plan to make them earn it,' Alexander says smoothly. 'There might be some fighting at Susa. And then we need to secure Persepolis, with all its treasure houses and fire altars. We can hardly go home without giving the men their full reward.'

'Yes, there might be fighting in the Persian cities – but it'll just be old men and women throwing stones! We both know King Darius' army was finished at Gaugamela. Even if you're planning to hunt down the remainder and finish off Darius, you won't need seventy thousand men to do it! If you want my advice, you'd best turn your attention to affairs back in Macedonia, rather than push any further east.'

'I don't want your advice, General.'

Tension crackles between them, prickling my coat like the air before a thunderstorm. I lash my tail. Beside me, Petasios and Borealis fidget and snort.

Alexander steps closer to the general and makes himself huge so he can look him in the eye. Perita follows him, growling softly, her hackles raised.

'You have served me well, General,' Alexander says softly. 'I know I wouldn't have made it this far without you. But you are near the end of your life, and I am only at the start of mine. There are wonders out there none of us has ever seen! Babylon was just a taste. The scientists are still there, measuring the walls and trying to work out how the hanging garden is planted, arguing over which is the greatest wonder so they can add it to their list. I'd rather take seventy thousand men with me into Persia and finish this war quickly, than head east with half the number and spend years fighting skirmishes in the mountains against the local tribes. Wouldn't you agree?'

His voice is still quiet, but you know as well as I do how dangerous that can be. The general glares a moment longer at Alexander, who stays huge before him, shining with energy and health.

Finally, this is too much for General Parmenio. He lowers his gaze, and grunts. 'I agree, it would be best to finish Darius as quickly as possible, grab his treasure from Persepolis, and head home rich and covered in glory. If you promise we'll go straight back to Macedonia once the Persian crown is yours, I'll do my best to explain your new policies to the men.'

Alexander grins and slaps him on the shoulder. 'I knew you'd approve, General! Tell the men to break camp. Let's show this fine army of ours the Royal Road to Susa!'

I should probably explain here about the Persian cities. King Darius is such a big boss, he doesn't just have one palace. He has two:

Susa for the winter.
Persepolis for the summer.

But Alexander already has four:

Pella in Macedonia.
Halicarnassus (when Queen Ada dies) in Anatolia.
Memphis in Egypt.
Babylon in Mesopotamia.

Soon he'll have Susa and Persepolis, too. This will make him the biggest boss there ever was.

Dominating Susa

Can you imagine how it feels to lead a herd of seventy thousand men, nearly ten thousand horses, and a baggage train almost as long as our column of fighting men marching with their long pikes? Even without King Alexander sitting on my cloth, it would have been enough to make my head spin and my blood throb. With the king's hand firm on my rein, and him shining with energy and confidence, I was so proud that I arched my neck and pranced all the way along the Royal Road.

After the battle at Gaugamela and Alexander's shake-up of the army, we lost two from the Guard. Craterus got command of a cavalry division (probably because he made that remark about Alexander not having an heir), so Xanthus had to go to the back of the army with him. Ha! And Attalus got command of the archers and a scruffy pony to ride, because he had let Arion fall and break a leg in the battle. So my special herd was now down to seven:

Petasios, carrying Hephaestion.
Borealis, carrying Leonnatus.
Apollo, carrying Perdiccas.
Hades, carrying Iolaus.
Electra, carrying Laomedon.
Aura, carrying Demetrius.
Harpinna, carrying Ptolemy.

As soon as the boss of Susa saw our army approaching, he hurried out to surrender, bringing mule carts laden with treasure and a string of camels draped in Persian rugs. Alexander accepted the gifts graciously, and we entered the city through a massive blue and gold gateway guarded by stone monsters twice the height of a horse. I made myself huge. Demetrius carried the big shield of Achilles beside us, and the white plumes of Alexander's helmet fluttered against the wide Persian sky.

At first, the Persian women clasped their children close, and old men with sun-darkened skin stared at us with hostile eyes. But Alexander rode me up the steps of King Darius' winter palace, ordered a herald to blow a trumpet, and announced that his army would not be allowed to loot or plunder the city because he was now their Great King and everything in it belonged to him.

A ripple of relief ran through the assembled people, and there was no trouble. No one threw flowers or cheered the king, but it didn't matter because their herd had already run away, so they were well and truly dominated.

The royal stables were very grand. They had walls of blue brick with gold and white patterns. The mangers were great blocks of blue marble licked smooth by hundreds of tongues. Zoroaster was excited to be back, and kept sniffing things. He snorted when he recognized his old stall. But since it was the biggest one, surrounded by wooden columns with pearl decoration at the top, Tydeos led me into it and I passed water to make it mine.

Our grooms said we'd be home by next winter, rich as kings.

As I said before, you should never believe groom-gossip.

Demon king

It is a few days before we see Alexander again. He comes into the stables with Hephaestion, the two of them laughing like man-colts. Perita bounds ahead of them and runs into all the corners sniffing at the interesting smells. Alexander is wearing a new helmet. It has two curly horns, like a ram's. When he reaches my fancy stall, he pulls a horrible face and says, 'Grrr, Bucephalas! See, they're calling me a demon-king now!'

His voice echoes in the huge stable. When I give the horns flat ears, he laughs and pulls off the helmet. 'Silly old horse! It's me. See?' He runs his hand over one of the patterns on the wall and stares up at the columns. 'Look at this, Hephaestion!' he says. 'Even King Darius' stables are full of treasure! But no treasure beats my Bucephalas. Don't you think he looks great? You wouldn't think he was twenty-five years old, would you? When we reach the edge of the world, he's going to live forever, just like me!'

'He's got dried sweat under his belly,' Hephaestion points out, and Alexander frowns.

He runs his hand over my matted hair and mutters a curse. 'Where's that good-for-nothing groom? *Tydeos!*'

Tydeos creeps out of Aura's stall. 'I'm sorry, Your Majesty. I'll wash him at once! Only . . .' He looks round to check none of the other grooms are near, and glances at Hephaestion. 'I need to talk to you alone, Your Majesty. It's very important.'

Alexander fingers the horns of his demon-helmet. 'What is it? Something about Bucephalas? Hephaestion knows every-thing I do. Speak.'

Tydeos swallows and lowers his voice. 'Sir, please don't be angry with me, but it's about Charmeia . . . I mean, Charmides.'

There is a heartbeat of silence. Hephaestion gives Tydeos a sharp look.

'What about her?' Alexander says in a rough voice. 'She ran away in Egypt and Parmenio thinks a crocodile got her, the idiot girl.'

'She didn't run away, Sir! And she's not dead! Back in Arbela, we – that is, the Amazons and I – caught the man who kidnapped her from the camp in Egypt. He told us he'd sold her to King Darius for his harem. I'm really sorry. See, I made the mistake of leaving Bucephalas alone in the stables, and ...' Tydeos' confession tumbles out, jumbled up with his worries about Charm.

Alexander's breath quickens. He silences Tydeos with an impatient hand. 'Where is he?'

'King Darius, Sir? I thought no one knew—'

'No, you fool! The man you caught in Arbela. The one

who took Charmides!'

Tydeos swallows. 'Er . . . he fled into the hills, Your Majesty, after he escaped from our prison in Arbela. The general said it wasn't worth chasing him.'

A frown flickers across Alexander's face. He glances at Hephaestion and says softly, 'And did you recognize the horse thief, Tydeos?'

Tydeos looks at his feet and mumbles, 'It was the old horsemaster, Sir. The one you dismissed from Pella.'

Alexander throws his horned helmet out into the passage, making me and all the horses in the nearby stalls jump. Perita darts away with her tail between her legs. The king strides around my stall, one fist pressed to his forehead and his face turning red. Hephaestion watches him a moment, then pushes Tydeos out of the door. 'Make yourself scarce,' he advises.

But Alexander darts out an arm to stop Tydeos leaving. Breathing hard, he says between clenched teeth, 'Before the battle at Gaugamela, you tried to tell me something about Prince Ochus. Was that also to do with Charmides?'

Tydeos bites his lip and whispers, 'In a way.'

'Well, out with it! And make sure it's the truth this time! I'm sick of people whispering and plotting behind my back.'

'I—' Tydeos looks as if he wishes he hadn't said anything, but he dares not lie to the king. He whispers, 'Charm was trying to help the prince escape in Egypt, Sir. That's how the horsemaster got hold of her. I know I should have told you before, but there never seemed to be a good time, and I thought Charm was dead until Ochus told me what happened.'

'Get out of my sight!' Alexander pushes Tydeos out of my door so hard that he stumbles. He closes his eyes and whispers, 'Am I so terrible, Hephaestion, that Prince Ochus wants to run away so badly? Haven't I let him play with my dog and treated him like my own son?'

Hephaestion grimaces. 'The boy's nearly nine and he speaks Greek well now. He knows why you're looking after him, Alex.'

'But *Charmides!* How could she betray me like that? I trusted her!'

'I'm sure she was only doing what she thought was best for the boy. At least you know she's still alive.'

'Alive, and in Darius' power! You've seen how he treats my people. What possible use would a groom be without hands?'

Alexander beats his forehead against the blue wall. Hephaestion looks alarmed and rushes across to pull him away. There is blood on the king's face when he turns, and a big smear of it on the bricks.

'Alex, for Zeus' sake!' Hephaestion dabs at the blood with a corner of his cloak. 'She's only a groom. I don't expect Darius has harmed her. We might even find her in Persepolis when we go there in the spring.' He smiles, trying to sound optimistic.

Alexander pushes his friend's hands away, breathing hard. 'I want this palace searched! Turn it upside down. Question all the slaves. Ask if anyone's seen a girl answering Charmides' description. We're not spending the rest of the winter kicking our heels here! We'll set out for Persepolis in the morning.'

Hephaestion frowns. 'Through the mountains, Alex, in the snow? Is that wise? There are reports of a resistance force occupying the pass—'

Alexander punches his friend on the shoulder, making him

wince and go a funny colour. 'Since when have mountains and snow stopped us?' he says with a sharp laugh. 'You're growing soft on Persian luxury, my friend, and you're not the only one. It's about time we had a good fight in the cold to wake us all up!' He gives Hephaestion an impatient look. 'Oh, stop moaning! What's wrong? I didn't hit you that hard.'

Hephaestion is clasping his shoulder, still pale. 'Gaugamela . . .' he whispers, and Alexander's face crumples in remorse.

'Oh, Zeus, your wound? I'm sorry, I forgot. But I bet it doesn't hurt half as much as my head does when people make me angry like that fool of a groom did just now. At least we know the truth at last. I'll have to think what to do about General Parmenio – he's getting careless in his old age. Come on, we've work to do.'

Hephaestion manages a smile. Alexander pats me, retrieves his demon helmet, and whistles to Perita. I snort in relief as they leave.

By the time Tydeos creeps back into my stall with a wet sponge to deal with the sweat on my belly, I am licking Alexander's blood off the wall. It tastes sweet, like it usually does, so I don't think he is a demon quite yet.

Twenty-first Hoofprint
Zagros Mountains,
Winter 331 BC

Enemies in the pass

We left Ochus' grandmother and sisters in the palace in Susa, along with most of the presents Alexander had been given by the cities we'd dominated so far. But before we set out, Ochus was marched out of the palace by two grave-faced Macedonians and lifted into one of the cages that used to contain lions. Lady Barsine flung a look at Alexander that was the equivalent of flat ears, hitched up her skirts, and ran to comfort the prince.

All the way across the plain to the mountains, the Guard whispered among themselves, afraid to raise their voices. Hephaestion kept looking over his shoulder and shaking his head. Alexander stared stonily between my ears and kept me to a brisk trot. He did not speak until we reached the foothills, where he halted me to let the others catch up.

'Well?' he said, his voice echoing in the steep rocks. 'What's wrong, gentlemen? Let's have this out now, before we go any further and I have to rely on you to watch my back.'

The Guard glanced at one another. No one spoke.

'It's not the boy's fault, Alex,' Hephaestion said at last. 'You'd try to run away, too, if you were in the hands of your father's enemy, and your father was still alive. You should have left Prince Ochus with his grandmother and sisters in the palace. What's the point of dragging him along with us?'

Alexander sighed. 'If I had left him in Susa, how long do you think it would be before some ambitious Persian satrap tried to use the boy to raise another army against me? It won't hurt him to travel in a cage for a while. I want to give him something to think about. It might make him appreciate how well I treat him, when I decide to let him out.'

'Either that, or he'll hate you for it.'

'He's my hostage. He has to learn to respect me one way or another. The Greeks learnt the hard way. If necessary, Prince Ochus will learn the hard way, too.'

Iolaus nudged Hades closer to me, frowning. 'But Alex, the boy's only nine! He's still too small to—'

We never find out what Iolaus was going to say, because just then a whole herd of tribesmen come sliding down the cliffs and block the road in front of us. They are wearing tatty robes over their trousers, but are armed with bright spears. They grin cheekily at Alexander.

The Guard immediately forget their quarrel with the king and draw their swords.

'Watch those cliffs!' Perdiccas shouts. 'Someone ride back and warn General Parmenio there's trouble up here! Demetrius, bring that shield here and guard the king's back!'

Alexander squints at the men on the cliffs, then eyes the ones in the road. He holds up his hand. 'Wait, gentlemen. They're not Darius' men.'

'Who are you?' he demands.

Their boss swaggers forward and makes a deep, mocking bow. In heavily accented Greek, he says, 'We are Uxian people. This is our road. All travellers who pass this way must pay toll.'

I give him flat ears, and he backs up a step. The Guard are still nervous, but Alexander smiles.

'Do you know who I am?'

'Yes, Your Majesty. You are King Iskander, the Macedonian demon with wild hair who flies through the air. But your men not fly. If you want to bring them through our pass, you have to pay toll. Great King Darius pays.'

Alexander raises an eyebrow at Hephaestion. He is still smiling, but his eyes are like chips of stone. 'And how much is this toll?'

The Uxian looks back down the road, sizing up our army. 'One horse and five mules for every thousand men.'

The Guard frown as they try to work this out.

'That's a lot of horses,' Alexander says, still smiling. 'I can't spare that many. And we're going to need all our mules for carrying the treasure away from Persepolis. Do you know how big my army is?'

His voice is quiet. The silly Uxian does not know how dangerous this is.

'It must be very large army if you defeat Great King Darius. Maybe hundred thousand men? That make one hundred horses and five hundred mules.' He eyes me, puts his head on one side and grins at Alexander. 'Or perhaps we just

319

take your big black horse and five hundred mules? People say you are Great King now, so you afford to pay. It only way you ever be as great as King Darius.'

THAT was a mistake.

Alexander's hand tightens on my rein. He breathes faster. Hephaestion winces, draws his sword and rides Petasios closer to me. Petasios' red ears flatten and he gives a little squeal, arching his neck ready to fight.

But Alexander has grown a lot more confident since Tyre, and controls his temper. He narrows his eyes at the Uxian boss. 'Your guess is close, but I'll have to make a head count of my baggage train to make it fair. I lose count of my camp followers. Go and wait for me up in the pass, and I'll come to you with my horse. Then, I give you my word as a great king and son of Zeus, you'll receive the payment you deserve, from my own hand.'

The Uxian grins and bows again, then he and his men vanish back up the cliffs.

'You're not really going to give him Bucephalas?' Hephaestion says, horrified.

'Did you hear me say I would give him my horse?' Alexander runs a hand down my neck, while I dance and snort indignantly. 'I'll certainly ride Bucephalas up there, but my hand will have a sword in it when I do. So will yours. It won't be my army that pays this toll. The Uxians will pay it – with their blood.'

The Guard grin at one another and sit up straighter. But Hephaestion is less happy. 'They might be able to hold the pass against us, Alex. We don't know how narrow it is yet. We'll force our way through eventually, of course, but they could kill a lot of our men first.'

Alexander laughs, his eyes glittering with mischief. 'That's why we're not going to *use* the pass, gentlemen! Go find me someone who knows these mountains, and get Craterus up here. It's time for him to prove he can lead those men I gave him.'

I shiver all over, sensing that there will be a battle soon. The cheek of it, expecting Alexander to give ME to them for passing through their mountains!

Obviously, Alexander refused to pay the Uxian toll because he would never give me away. Five hundred mules would have been no great loss.

Dominating the Uxians

That night, Craterus' men climb up and hide on the heights above the pass, while we follow our guide round to the other side along a steep, stony track. It is cold at the top, and the cliffs fall away beneath us. But we have trained in the mountains of Macedonia, and not one of us puts a foot wrong. Behind us, we have Attalus' archers, the Maedi javelin throwers, the Amazons, and the pick of the cavalry.

As the sky pales, we gallop down through the sleepy Uxian villages. Alexander's sword cuts down tents, while I leap ropes and scatter their flocks of sheep with my teeth and heels. Their old men stagger out into the mist, wiping sleep from their eyes. Their women and children scream and flee. We don't bother chasing them.

We continue down to the far side of the pass, where we pause to regroup. The Uxian warriors who squealed at us yesterday are just visible in the mist. Most of them are still rolled up in their cloaks, asleep. The rest sit on rocks with their spears across their knees, looking the wrong way. Alexander smiles, puts a finger to his lips and sends Attalus with his archers up the cliffs to cover us. Then he walks me slowly forward.

When we are close enough, Alexander glances round at the Guard and grins. He raises his sword over his head, digs his heels into my ribs, and yells 'ALALALALAI!' as if he has the entire army behind him.

The sleeping Uxians spring up in alarm and grab their spears. Those who are already awake shout in horror as we gallop out of the mist. They take one look at me, charging towards them with Alexander on my back, and run in all directions. Our arrows bring down a few. Some of them scramble up the rocks, where Craterus' men are hiding, and there is a confusion of screams and whirling ghosts as they run into the Macedonian javelins. The Uxian boss and the rest of his herd flee back down the pass.

Laughing in delight at the way his trick has worked, Alexander puts his heels in my sides and urges me after them. Hephaestion shouts for him to wait, but Alexander is glowing with the excitement of battle, and my blood is up. We catch up with the Uxian boss, and I knock him down with my shoulder as I gallop past.

Alexander leans down from my cloth and slices the boss's right arm with his sword. 'That's for blocking my road!' he shouts. Then he wheels me round and slices the boss's left arm. 'And that's for suggesting I am not as great a king as Darius!' He raises his sword a third time. 'And *this* is for daring to demand that I give you my horse Bucephalas!'

The Uxian boss closes his eyes. 'Please, King Iskander!' he shrieks. 'Not kill me! I know where Persians hide in mountains to attack your army. I help you.'

Alexander pauses. As the Guard pull up around us, panting, he lowers his sword and gives the prisoner a thoughtful look. 'How many Persians?' he snaps.

The Uxian peers up at Alexander and says slyly, 'We collect twenty-five horses and one hundred and twenty-five mules from one of the Great King's satraps, seven days ago.'

Alexander's eyes narrow. He frowns at the cliffs. 'There are twenty-five thousand Persians in these mountains? Are you lying to me?'

'No, Your Majesty! Why would I? They go into high mountains and not come out. They take old trade route through the Persian Gates to Persepolis. Let me live, and I show you secret paths, short cut. Get you through mountains a lot quicker.' The Uxian manages a grin through his pain. 'Good trick with pass, King Iskander. Maybe you use same trick on Persians?'

Alexander puts his sword away, and orders Leonnatus to take the Uxian boss up on to Borealis. As he stretches the kinks out of his shoulders, he eyes the snow-capped mountains with a challenging smile.

'You're not really thinking of taking the army up through the Persian Gates, Alex?' Hephaestion whispers. 'Twenty-five thousand men could hold that pass against us till next winter!'

'We can't leave twenty-five thousand Persians at our backs, my friend. Besides, if they learn we've taken the long way round, they'll simply head on through the pass and evacuate Persepolis before we get there. If Charmides *is* in their hateful city, I'm not going to let them keep her.'

'It'll take forever to get the baggage train through in this weather, Alex,' says Ptolemy, frowning at the white peaks.

'Then we won't take the baggage train.'

'But—'

'But, but, but!' Alexander laughs and gives Ptolemy a playful slap on the arm. 'Where's your sense of adventure gone, gentlemen? Remember what fun we had with the Thracians and the Illyrians back in Macedonia? Yet now you're scared to follow me into these tame mountains to deal with a few frightened Persians. You'll soon be advising me to turn round and go home, like General Parmenio always is!'

'We're not scared, Alex,' Hephaestion says quietly. 'You know we'd follow you to the ends of the earth. We're just looking out for you. It only takes one stray javelin or a lucky arrow. Remember what happened at Gaza. It'd be much safer to keep the army together, take the long route, and deal with the Persians when we get to Persepolis.'

'That's why I command this army, and not you!' Alexander is still flushed from dominating the Uxians. 'The son of Zeus fears no earthly weapon. I have nearly eighty thousand men. I hardly need them all to assault a pass. We'll take the young men who still have an appetite for adventure, and General Parmenio can take the rest round the slow way with the baggage train.'

Hephaestion sighs. 'At least let poor Prince Ochus out of that cage first. I'm sure he's learnt his lesson by now.'

But Alexander shakes his head as he gathers up my reins. 'With General Parmenio's record of letting prisoners escape? No, my friend. The boy stays safely locked up until we get to Persepolis – which won't be long now, gentlemen! The Persian crown is within our grasp.'

Dominating the Persians

Surprisingly, General Parmenio hardly squealed at all when Alexander told him of his plans to divide the army so he could dominate the Persians in the mountains. But he glanced at the Uxian prisoners being sent back to Susa and said Ochus' grandmother would be upset because she had a soft spot for the tribe. Alexander said that was why he hadn't killed their boss, and was instead paying him to guide them into the mountains.

This was, as you know, a lie. The Uxian boss didn't get any payment that I saw, unless you count a few extra days of life.

We marched over those icy mountain tracks for five days, leading a herd of twenty thousand men. Philotas, given the choice of coming with us or going with his father, wavered a bit, but then came galloping after us on Zephyr with his little herd at his heels.

Alexander smiled grimly and patted my neck. 'See, Bucephalas? Even Philo knows old Parmenio's days are numbered.'

The road was narrow and stony, twisting up over steep ridges. It grew colder as we climbed. We trotted through patches of snow and splashed across icy fords, snorting particles of ice into the air. Above us, the peaks were white.

On the fifth day, we made camp at the mouth of the pass they call the Persian Gates. Since we didn't have our grooms, Alexander settled me himself and gave me my nosebag. It grew bitterly cold. We huddled up close in the horse lines, mares and stallions together, while flurries of snow drove down the pass and melted on our backs. There was no squealing, because we were all far too miserable to make trouble.

When it grew dark, the Guard came back with some little leather bags, clumsily sewn. Working by torchlight, Alexander picked up my feet, one by one, and tied a bag around each hoof. Then he bridled me and put on my cloth. Our riders extinguished their torches, and we set off up a steep, narrow path, following our Uxian guide. My legs ached from stepping high through snow drifts, but the leather bags kept ice from balling in our hooves, so none of us slipped. We were a shadowy ghost herd, creeping though the starlit mountains, leaving bands of our warriors on the way:

The Amazons at the campsite, with instructions to burn enough fires for all of us.

Attalus and 3,000 archers at the top, above the sleeping Persians.

Philotas and 7,000 cavalry at the far side with orders to take the road to Persepolis and secure the bridges.

By the time the sky paled, the rest of us were on the other side of the pass behind the Persian camp. We were tired, but we'd got round them in the night without them seeing us. Ha!

You can probably guess what comes next. It is the same trick Alexander played on the Uxians, and it works just as well on the Persians. They fight more fiercely than the Uxians did. But trapped between our three strong herds, they don't stand a chance. Eventually, the survivors flee, and Alexander gallops me along the road to Persepolis. The Guard follow, still grinning at the way we dominated them.

We find Philotas' herd waiting for us at the river. In the distance, the city of Persepolis shimmers white and gold on the Persian plain. Alexander, who had let me ease back to a trot to catch my wind, gathers up my reins again and heads me straight for the bridge. But Zephyr is standing on it, blocking our way. Some of Philotas' men stand behind her. The rest of his herd form up on the bank, nervous but alert.

326

As we approach, Philotas takes a deep breath and says, 'Alex, I'm very sorry, but the Persians you chased out of the mountains have forded the river further north. Persepolis is their holy city. They're not going to give it up without a fight. I think we'd better wait for Father.'

I nicker to Zephyr, pleased to see her. But Alexander scowls at her rider. 'What are you playing at, Philo? I told you to secure the bridges so the Persians couldn't get across, not hold them against me! If we don't hurry, that troublesome satrap will have time to flee with Persepolis' treasure before we get there. Get out of my way!'

Philotas shakes his head. 'We've just trekked through the Zagros Mountains in deep snow, negotiated an impossible mountain trail in the dark, and fought two battles. The men and horses are exhausted. I think we should camp here and wait for the rest of the army before we tackle Persepolis.'

'When I want your advice, I'll ask for it,' Alexander says in a dangerous tone, narrowing his eyes at Philotas. 'Did your father put you up to this? I'm sure I don't need to remind you that I'm in command of this army, not General Parmenio. Move your men off that bridge at once, before Bucephalas tramples them. I'll deal with you later.'

Philotas pales, but holds Zephyr on a tight rein. The Guard stiffen. The men behind Philotas glance at one another and whisper uneasily. My legs feel too wobbly to trample anyone, but I make myself as huge as I can. On my cloth, Alexander tightens his lips and drops his hand to his sword.

'No, Alex!' Hephaestion hisses, squeezing Petasios beside me on the narrow bridge. He grips the king's arm and whispers, 'Philo's an idiot to try to hold the bridge against us, but he's right. The men are tired, and poor Bucephalas looks spent. If there's going to be a battle for Persepolis, it makes sense to rest first. I don't mean we should wait for Parmenio and the baggage train. But it wouldn't hurt to let the horses graze, and send a party out hunting so we can give the men a hot meal—'

Alexander might have listened, but just then our Uxian prisoner jeers that the Macedonian army has run out of people to fight so it is fighting against itself, and makes a run for the bridge. I expect he thought Philotas would hold the bridge long enough for him to escape. But Alexander's legs clamp against my sides, and his sword catches the Uxian across the neck before he reaches the first span.

Alexander wheels me off the bridge and jumps me up on a flat rock so he can address the men. He pulls off his helmet so his wild mane blows in the sunlight. As he sweeps his blood-drenched sword towards the city on the other side of the river, he shines with the same power as when he cut the Gordian Knot.

'Over there is Persepolis, the most hateful city in the whole world!' he shouts in his shrill voice. 'That is where the Persians worship demons on their fire altars. That is where the Persian kings make the world bring them treasure and force Greeks to scrape their foreheads on the floor before their proud feet! That city, gentlemen, is the heart of your enemy's power. Destroy it! Burn it to the ground! Seize all the slaves you want. Go take your reward, my friends, and wreak your revenge!'

A ripple goes through the men. They mutter at first, then shout and bang their shields.

'Revenge! Revenge for our people!'

Even the Macedonians seem to have forgotten they once

fought against Greeks, and join in the cry.

Philotas knows when he has been dominated. He rides Zephyr out of the way, shaking his head. 'Father's not going to like this when he gets here,' he warns, as the cavalry mount up and take off across the bridge with a wild thudding of hooves. Foot-soldiers seize their pikes and follow at a run. I plunge against my bit, impatient to follow my herd now I have my second wind.

Hephaestion shouts, 'Not the palaces, Alex! Remember Charm might be in one of them!'

Alexander flings Philotas a contemptuous look as he urges me after the others. 'Don't touch the palaces!' he yells as we catch up. 'They're *mine!*'

Twenty-Second Hoofprint
PERSEPOLIS, SPRING 330 BC

Squealing at Persepolis

The Persians who had fled from the pass made a final brave stand outside Persepolis. But they had very few men left, and after Alexander's speech our herd was WILD. We soon sent their ghosts whirling across the plain, and the city, which had no high walls to keep us out, was ours.

Alexander led the Guard straight to King Darius' summer palace, which was even bigger than the one at Susa. We trotted up the steps and through a forest of huge, glittering columns. Leaning over my neck to pass through the doorways, Alexander tore down curtains with his sword and rode me across the marble floors and soft Persian carpets. Everywhere, statues of monsters glared at us, and strange creatures stared from the hangings on the walls. Slaves screamed and fled. I flared my nostrils, looking for Charm. But none of the women in their filmy dresses and tinkling jewellery smelt like spring grass.

Finally, we came to a huge room containing a plain white bowl of flickering fire, where Alexander let me clop to a halt. He sat panting on my cloth, his sword drooping from his hand, and stared at the fire. The flames reflected in his eyes. His mane stuck to his forehead with sweat, and he had smears of blood on his face.

Two priests ran out of the shadows and cursed him. They said he had defiled their holy city with his barbarian filth. It's true we were dirty, but we *had* marched all the way from Susa, and fought two battles in the mountains on the way. Perdiccas and Leonnatus dismounted, seized the priests and dragged them away from the king. Apollo and Borealis wandered off among the columns, nosing around for hay. They didn't find any, though. The fire-room belonged to the Persian god, and gods don't eat hay.

Alexander sighed and dropped his sword with a clang that echoed through the halls. He pressed his knuckles to his forehead. 'So tired, Hephaestion,' he whispered. 'So tired. Why does my head hurt so much?'

Hephaestion slid off Petasios, picked up the king's sword and returned it to his scabbard. 'You just need a rest, Alex,' he said softly. 'You did it. Persia is ours.'

Alexander shrugged. 'I suppose it is.' He sighed again. 'But I never expected to feel like this, my friend.'

'Like what?' Hephaestion obviously did not understand. He grinned at the king and slapped him on the thigh. 'Come on, you'll feel much better after a bath and something to eat. Let's go and inspect King Darius' treasure houses before old Parmenio gets here, huh?'

This made Alexander sit a bit straighter on my cloth. 'Yes, and Bucephalas can inspect the stables. I'm going to see if I can persuade those priests to crown me Great King of Persia before we go any further.'

'Further?' Hephaestion said, frowning a little.

'We have to find Darius, my friend. And Bucephalas wants his groom back. She's obviously not here, or she'd have come running by now.'

To please the Persian god, the crowning ceremony was supposed to take place at the Persian New Year festival, so we stayed in Persepolis until the weather got warmer and crops started to grow on the river plain. The mules were kept busy carrying loads of treasure back to Susa, while we horses got a well-deserved rest in King Darius' huge stables.

'There's only Ecbatana left for the Persians to hide in,' Tydeos told me as he combed my mane. 'Everyone says we'll be heading up there, just as soon as King Alexander's been crowned Great King. Then we'll find Charm.'

But the New Year came and went, and still we didn't leave Persepolis. There was no festival that I noticed, and none of the people cheered or threw flowers. Alexander strode about the stables, finding fault with everything. All the unbroken three-year-olds learnt to carry a rider, including my colt Hoplite, and the men grumbled that at this rate King Darius would have time to raise another army against us. Our grooms even claimed, with nudges and winks, that the king had found a beautiful princess in the palace and wanted to spend more time with her – which proves how stupid they are. Alexander talked to me quite a bit that summer, and the only female on his mind was Charm.

Meanwhile, the little Amazon horses galloped north to Ecbatana and back again, carrying rolls of flattened grass. No one knew what they contained, though they were probably more squeals.

If you ask me, it was obvious why we were waiting. If members of a dominated herd refuse to obey you, like the Persian priests when they refused to crown Alexander, then you need to show them who is boss before they cause trouble. Alexander had to think of the best way to do this. He couldn't just kill them, because he still wanted to be crowned Great King.

Grudge me not this small piece of earth

One morning, very early before our grooms are awake, I catch a familiar scent. I scramble to my feet, disturbed by the memories it brings. It is Prince Ochus. I've not seen him since before the battle at the Persian Gates, when Alexander had him locked in a lion cage.

He has grown a bit taller, but his face is thinner and he has deeper shadows under his eyes. He walks tensely, surrounded by the Guard. The men are all wearing their armour. Alexander looks grim, and has a dagger thrust through his belt. Perita trots at his heels. I whinny a welcome, confused by the armour. Ochus isn't old enough to fight. It would be like taking three-year-old Hoplite into battle.

Ochus has no weapon, though. He is dressed in a Macedonian tunic that is too big for him, and waits silently as Alexander tells Tydeos to help the prince bridle Zoroaster. Alexander puts on my bridle and cloth himself, and the Guard do the same for their horses. Tydeos is sent to load a mule with packs of food. They seem anxious to get going, because they leave the rest of the grooms sleeping and lead us out themselves into the early morning haze over the plain.

Aura is not yet too big with foal to be left behind, so we

333

are the same herd that climbed round the Persian Gates, though this time our road is much easier. We trot through the quiet streets, past the smashed remains of Persian statues and bloodstained bricks, snorting at the lingering ghosts. Tydeos stares after us in confusion. He dare not ask where we are going.

As we head out across the plain, Lady Barsine races out of the palace, her mane flying loose. 'No, Alexander!' she cries, stumbling to her knees. 'Please! He's only a child! Don't do this, *please!*'

Alexander tightens his lips. Ochus casts an anguished look over his shoulder at his nurse. But Zoroaster's reins are in Leonnatus' hands, so Ochus has no control over the big white horse. When Alexander urges me into a canter, the Guard follow, dragging Zoroaster with them. Lady Barsine's sobs are soon left behind.

We collect Craterus' cavalry and some empty carts from the main camp and ride north for two days. Perita runs ahead of us, panting and wagging her tail. The Guard chat among themselves, as usual, and seem to be treating the outing like a sightseeing trip. But Alexander barely speaks to anyone, and I can feel his tension rippling along my reins. It upsets me, so I toss my head and lash my tail at the other horses. Ochus doesn't speak at all. He sits straight-backed on Zoroaster, gazing out across the plain. Sometimes a tear glitters in his eye, and I see him quickly wipe it away before anyone notices.

We haven't brought Alexander's pavilion, so at night the Guard have to make do with sharing small tents. And we don't have our grooms, so they have to settle us in the lines themselves. I don't mind, because at least Alexander is not afraid to clean the sweat off my belly. I'd rather have Charm, though.

I can't think what there is to see out here. It is just a dusty plain with a distant line of mountains, and it's getting very hot now that summer is here. But on the evening of the second day, we come to another Persian city called Pasargadae, crossed by copper-coloured shadows. Alexander leaves Craterus and his cavalry there with the mule carts, ordering him to collect all the treasure from Pasargadae and be ready for his signal. He says he's taking the prince to see the tomb of his ancestor, and we Guard ride on into the sunset with Zoroaster and Ochus between us, Perita bounding ahead.

A shadowy building rises from the plain. It has steps up all four sides and a little house on top. Torches planted around it flare in the dusk, making the winged monsters carved on its walls ripple, and their golden scales glitter. My coat prickles. Inside the ring of torches I can see an ancient human ghost, so strong that it has lingered an unusual number of years in this place.

Alexander tenses as we get nearer to the tomb. He halts me and squints into the shadows as if he, too, can see the ghost. All the Guard fall silent. Ochus clutches Zoroaster's mane with tight fingers and stares at the torches.

Hephaestion rides Petasios up beside me and whispers, 'The boy's terrified, Alex. Don't you think you should tell him why you brought him here?'

Alexander gives his friend a distracted look. 'The less he knows, the better.'

'It's not fair on him. What's he supposed to think? Secrecy was fine while you were negotiating, but now we're here—'

Alexander jerks my rein, making me snort in protest. 'All right!' he says. 'I'll talk to the boy. Though I'm going to look pretty stupid if they don't come.'

He trots me over to Zoroaster's side and frowns down at the man-colt. The white horse nickers to me, while the prince stares at Alexander with frightened eyes.

'Ochus, why do you think I brought you here?'

The man-colt bites his lip and whispers, 'You're going to kill me, aren't you?'

Alexander stares at him in surprise. 'Kill you? Why on earth would you think that?' His face flickers. 'Just because I locked you in a lion cage for a few days doesn't mean you're no longer my adopted son. Did Lady Barsine tell you I was going to kill you? I'll have words with her when I get back.'

'You said you would, if my father tried to raise another army against you.' The prince's whisper is even fainter than before.

'You did, Alex,' Hephaestion reminds him gently. 'After Gaugamela, remember?'

Alexander waves an impatient hand. 'I was angry. They stole my *Iliad*! You don't want to take too much notice of what I say when I'm angry, Ochus. Besides, King Darius isn't raising another army against me. These pockets of resistance are nothing to do with him, I know that. They're merely ambitious satraps, provincial governors trying to seize power for themselves now that Darius' army has been defeated. I'll soon deal with them as the traitors they are. I didn't just bring you here to see the tomb, Ochus. I brought you out here to send you back to your father.'

Ochus trembles even more, staring at the tomb and its lurking ghost.

Hephaestion smiles. 'The poor boy still thinks you're going to kill him, Alex. He obviously thinks you've already killed King Darius.' He ruffles Ochus' mane. 'Your father isn't dead, you silly thing. King Alexander has been writing to him secretly for months, and the Amazons have been galloping back and forth with messages. It'll be all right, you'll see. Your father has someone in his camp who the king wants back just as much as King Darius wants you, so we're going to trade you for her. That's only fair, isn't it? Cheer up! Your people will be here any moment.'

The Guard glance at one another. They obviously didn't know all the details, either. But they smile fondly at Ochus, and the man-colt looks across the dark plain in sudden hope.

'My father is coming for me?' he says with a catch in his voice. 'Truly?'

'He's sending someone,' Alexander says with a little smile. 'One of his officers. Seems I couldn't persuade King Darius to come himself.'

Ochus' face falls a bit, but his eyes have renewed hope in them. 'Thank you, Uncle Alexander,' he says gravely in careful Greek. 'I shall not forget this when I am Great King of Persia.'

Alexander frowns and says in a sterner tone. 'You realize *I'll* still be Great King of Persia, don't you? Darius has promised to surrender his crown to me once he gets you back safe. Remember, I still have your sisters and grandmother under Macedonian guard in Susa.'

Ochus' forehead creases. 'But you cannot be the true Great King, Uncle Alexander. Our priests say you cannot. Only one of royal Persian blood can make the bond with the god through the sacred white horse and slay the fire demon.' He strokes Zoroaster's neck. 'When I am old enough, I will take the spirit of a white colt so I may bond with the god like my father did. But I will not make war against you, because you are my adopted uncle now,' he adds quickly.

Hephaestion nods at this sensible remark.

But Alexander's hand tightens on my rein. 'Your priests are fools!' he snaps. 'They'll see sense soon enough. If they don't, I'll give them something to think about. Enough of this talk of royal blood, Ochus, or you'll make me angry again. Tell me what it says up there above the door of the tomb.'

Ochus smiles. 'It says, *Know, traveller, that I am Cyrus the Great who founded the Empire of the Persians. Grudge me not this small piece of earth that covers my body.*'

'Is the boy right, Laomedon? He didn't even look.'

'Yes, Alex . . . I think so. It's quite archaic, isn't it?'

'Father brought me out here before the war started,' Ochus explains. 'He told me always to remember what the words on the tomb said, because no matter how great a king I become, my body will one day end up in a place like this. That is why I think you bring me here to kill me. I am ashamed.' He hangs his head.

Alexander gives the writing above the tomb a funny, squinty look. I feel a shiver go through him. Then he looks round at the dusty plain and chuckles. 'Your ancestor Cyrus is welcome to this patch of earth. It's not much use for anything else.'

Bessus

It grows darker, and the stars come out in a silver fizz that makes the sky seem huge. The members of the Guard sit on the steps of the tomb, holding the reins of their horses and talking in hushed voices. The ghost has hidden itself inside, so I am a bit calmer. But Alexander paces up and down, dragging me after him.

Suddenly, he stops and squints across the dark plain. 'At

last,' he whispers, as a dust cloud, kicked up by horses' hooves, comes out of the night.

I whinny, and one of the horses whinnies back. Alexander vaults on to me and reaches for the dagger in his belt. 'How many do you see?' he says. 'Have they kept to the terms? Get the trumpet ready. As soon as Charmides is safe, send the signal.'

'Looks like there's only a handful of them,' Hephaestion says, springing off the bottom step on to Petasios' back. 'They have someone riding double on the second horse. It's a girl, Alex! Can't see her very well, but it looks like she has red hair.'

'Good!' Alexander sits up straighter and smiles. 'Everyone stay alert. If one of those Persians so much as looks at his weapon, take Prince Ochus back to the city and wait for me there. Laomedon, you come with me.'

He takes a deep breath and trots me between the flaring torches. Electra follows me, shying at the flames and the dark door of the tomb where the ghost went. The Persian herd stops on the other side, eyeing us warily.

Into the shadows walks a black Persian stallion. When I squeal at him, he has the cheek to squeal back. His rider has a curly beard and holds himself like a boss. He watches Alexander carefully from eyes set very close together, and glances at Laomedon. He says something in Persian, which Laomedon translates.

'He says he's Bessus, the Great King's satrap in Bactria. He says it's good to meet the demon-king Iskander at last, but you were supposed to come to this meeting alone.' Laomedon doesn't use the Persian's tone, which sounded like squealing to me.

'This is my interpreter,' Alexander snaps. 'Where's my groom? I want to see her.'

Laomedon translates this, and the Persian smiles. 'She is ready to return to you. But first I bring my interpreter, also, in case of tricks.'

He lifts a hand, and a small brown mare trots across from the Persian herd to join us. Her rider sits awkwardly on her cloth with one leg stuck out to the side. His smell makes me rear up and snap my teeth in fury. It is my enemy.

Laomedon stares at the newcomer. 'Alex, isn't that—?'

Alexander goes for his dagger. But the horsemaster is careful to keep his mare behind Bessus, and we cannot reach him without first doing battle with the Persian boss. Alexander grinds his teeth in frustration. 'Traitor!' he hisses. 'You're going to pay for what you've done.'

'Alexander,' the horsemaster says, baring his teeth in return. 'You'd do well to remember you're a long way from home, and I doubt that brute of a horse you insist on riding will last the journey back to Macedonia. How old is he now? Twenty-five? Twenty-six? You once dismissed me for obeying your father's orders. Do you blame me for finding alternative employment?'

Bessus watches this exchange, his little eyes sly.

'You've done more than enough to make up for it! You made a mistake coming here. You won't escape this time.' Alexander's hand tightens on his dagger.

'Alex,' Laomedon whispers, his voice tense. 'I think there are more Persians out there. We're too exposed in this place. Let's make it quick, huh?'

Alexander squints at the dark plain. 'Let's get this over with,' he says to Bessus in a rough tone.

Laomedon translates, and Bessus says, 'First you send King Darius' son across to my men.'

'Both together,' Alexander snaps. 'No tricks. They pass within sight of us, one each side.'

The Persian inclines his head and makes a signal with his hand. Alexander does the same, and Ochus rides Zoroaster slowly through the torches towards the Persian herd. His face is set, and he looks very tense. He keeps looking uneasily at Bessus. On my blind side – so I can't see her very well – the girl with the red hair slides off the Persian horse and walks towards us. She is about the same size as Charm, and in her long, dusty cloak she looks the same in the dark. But she doesn't smell anything like my favourite groom. She smells of burnt bread, and seems very frightened.

I stamp my foot, squeal at the horsemaster, and give the black stallion a nip on the nose. He nips me back. Our riders haul on our reins to separate us. Alexander squints at the girl in the cloak, his heart beating hard and fast. Bessus smiles through his thick beard at Ochus. Laomedon whispers, 'She looks unharmed, Alex, though it's difficult to tell for sure under that cloak. Do you want me to check?'

'No,' Alexander says. 'Secure the traitor first!' With a flick of his hand, he signals the Guard to arrest the horsemaster.

The horsemaster draws a long knife from under his robe and flings it at Alexander. At the same time, Bessus wheels his black stallion and seizes Zoroaster's reins. Ochus gives a little gasp and screams, 'Uncle Alexander! This man not take me back to Father! He bad man! Help!' Bessus growls something at the prince in Persian, and both horses break into a gallop. On the other side of the tomb, the girl runs for cover. I leap from a standstill, carrying Alexander out of the knife's path. It pierces my cloth and grazes my flank on its way to the ground.

With a furious yell, Alexander whips out his dagger and urges me after my enemy. Bessus is almost back with his Persian herd, dragging Zoroaster and Ochus after him. The horsemaster seizes a spear from the nearest man and aims it at the king. But before he can throw it, a dark streak launches itself off the steps of the tomb and fastens its teeth in the horsemaster's elbow. Brave Perita!

The horsemaster growls and thumps the dog between the eyes until she lets go and rolls under the mare's feet. He stabs downwards with the spear, and Perita lets out a horrible howl. The mare kicks in panic, and there is a high-pitched yelp as Perita's body flies through the air and hits the steps of the tomb. Her ghost leaves her broken body in a long thin thread and blows away across the plain.

Alexander yells, 'The signal! After them, you idiots!'

Our trumpet blares into the night. The Persians have split into two groups, one following the horsemaster, the other surrounding Bessus and the prince. The Guard don't seem to know which group to chase.

For a moment it looks as if we are going to lose both Ochus and the horsemaster. But then Ochus sees the motionless Perita, and hauls on Zoroaster's reins.

'No! I not go with you!' he yells. 'Uncle Alexander, Bessus want Persian crown for himself!'

Bessus slaps the prince's face and tries to pull him on to his black horse.

Alexander, furious and armed with only his jewelled dagger, gallops me straight at the struggling pair.

'No, Alex!' Hephaestion cries. 'There's too many of them! Wait for Craterus!'

The Persians surround us, armed with scimitars they had hidden under their robes. Bessus laughs at Alexander's little dagger, then his eyes widen at the tomb behind us and he goes white. I feel something brush my tail and think it is one of the Guard catching up, but the wind that whirls past me is not a mortal wind. I shiver as the ancient ghost of Cyrus the Great blows through the Persian herd, making their horses rear and neigh in terror. The Persians back away from Alexander, take one look at our cavalry streaming out of Pasargadae, and flee.

'Don't let them get away, you fools!' Alexander shouts at Craterus. 'Catch that treacherous horsemaster, and get me some prisoners! I need up-to-date information. Someone take this boy and keep him safe. Where's my groom Charmides? I want to talk to her. *Now!*'

Xanthus and the rest of the cavalry gallop past us, kicking up dust. I want to be at the front of the herd, where I belong, but Alexander won't let me go after them. He holds me on a tight rein and examines the graze the horsemaster's knife left on my flank, while yells and screams come out of the night as our cavalry catch some of the Persian stragglers.

I nip Zoroaster's nose to drive him back to our herd, and we horses of the Guard snort and dance around the shadowy tomb. Most of the torches went out when Cyrus' ghost rushed past, so it is quite spooky. Zoroaster looks thoroughly ashamed of himself. Ochus slides off his back and kneels beside poor Perita, stroking her motionless body and sniffing.

Alexander satisfies himself that my wound is just a scratch and stares down at the prince. 'Oh, stop that,' he says impatiently. 'She's only a dog. She died doing her job, protecting me. What's all this about Bessus wanting the Persian crown? Does your father know? He must have trusted him if he sent him here to collect you.'

Ochus gives Perita's body a final sad stroke. 'He is bad man, but he has royal blood. I think he wait a long time, until my father is weak. Sometimes Mother—' he hesitates slightly '—and I heard him plotting in the palace, back at our New Year Festival when I am very young. He not think I understand, but I remember.' Ochus gives Alexander a tight smile. 'Bessus think I am still a child, but I am not stupid. I hate Bessus. He say many bad things about my father. I rather stay with you – and Charmeia.'

He looks at the tomb, where the girl took refuge.

Ptolemy appears at the door, gripping her arm tightly. Her hood is down, and the one remaining torch lights up her terrified face. She is quite a bit older than Charm. Only the light skin and the red hair are the same. Ptolemy shakes his head. 'I'm sorry, Alex . . .'

Alexander finally realizes the full extent of the horsemaster's trick. As he stares at the woman, his breathing quickens and his face flushes. His fist clenches against my withers. With a furious yell, he throws his dagger at the steps.

Ptolemy jumps back in alarm as it clatters at his feet, and drags the woman with him to safety. 'Alex, it's not the poor girl's fault! What shall I do with her?'

Ochus has stopped crying. He stares at the tomb. 'It not Charmeia,' he says sadly.

'No, it's not.' Alexander's voice is icy. 'That was a mistake. I don't care if King Darius sent Bessus to play that trick on me, or if it was the horsemaster's idea. I'm going to show all these treacherous satraps with their eyes on the Persian crown who's in charge around here. We're going back to Persepolis, gentlemen, and we're going to finish this, once and for all. If those proud Persian priests love their holy fire so much, then they'll get holy fire. I'm the son of Zeus. I have no reason to be afraid of their curses.'

The Guard glance at one another. Hephaestion whispers, 'You can't mean to burn down the temples and palaces, Alex? You know what General Parmenio said. It's never a good idea to mess with the gods. Remember how you thought the Persian god cursed you, back in Phoenicia?'

Alexander glares at his friend. 'Those palaces and temples are *mine* now, not General Parmenio's, or the Persian god's! I can do what I like with them! Are you with me, or not? Because anyone who isn't can go join that traitor of a horse-master and his Persian friends, and be hunted down as I will hunt them all down, once I have my faithful army at my back again. When I catch that satrap Bessus, I'm going to make an example of him. Will that please you, Ochus? Will it make me as great a king as your father? Do you think your god would approve of me *then*?'

Ochus does not answer. He is a very sensible man-colt.

Ptolemy puts his arm around the woman. 'You're safe now,' he says. 'Do you understand? We'll take you back to Persepolis. It belongs to King Alexander now.'

The woman breaks free, runs down the steps and falls to her knees before Alexander in a mess of hair and filthy cloak.

'I'm sorry, King Alexander! They said I had to do it, or they'd kill me. I didn't know why, I swear! I'll tell you all I know. We hear things in the harems. Maybe I can help you find your girl?' She looks up, her eyes fierce. 'I only ask that you let me be there when you burn the palace. I want to pay the Persians back for everything they've done to me. I was a little girl when they captured me. Now I am nothing. Their god's curse can't do anything worse to me than they have already done.'

Alexander frowns down at her. Some of the fury trickles out of him. 'What's your name?' he asks.

'Thais, Your Majesty. From Athens.'

Alexander wheels me in a circle. 'See, gentlemen?' he shouts. 'This Greek woman has more guts than you do! She can ride back with the prince on Zoroaster, and I want no more talk of curses. Let's leave this tomb before all our bones rest here with those of Cyrus the Great!'

While the Guard boost the woman and Ochus up on to Zoroaster's back, Alexander lifts Perita and lays her over my withers. I turn my head to snort at her, but her smell is fading fast, and she will never nip my heels again.

Alexander rests his hand on her bloodstained coat and stares across the dark plain. 'Oh, Perita, am I going to lose all those I love out here in Persia?' he whispers, so quietly that only I can hear.

I nudge him with my nose to remind him I am wounded and need my groom. A dead dog is sad, but not as sad as a dead horse.

Dominating Persepolis

When we got back to Persepolis, Alexander left us in the camp outside the city and ordered that all the other horses from the royal stables, down to the smallest foals, be brought out to join us. Then he held a big party in his pavilion with plenty of magic for the men to drink.

Tydeos bathed my wound with a tight expression, muttering under his breath about Alexander taking too many risks. He didn't know about the failed attempt to get Charm back, which was probably just as well.

Towards midnight, a procession of men and women wove their way through the camp to the city, wearing flowers around their necks and carrying torches. The women played flutes, and the men sang in their rough soldiers' voices. They disappeared through the palace gates, taking their noise and fire with them, and for a while it was quiet in the camp. I rested my leg and mutual groomed with Petasios.

Then we smelt smoke, and saw flames leap above the walls. Soon, a fierce orange glow lit up the plain halfway to the mountains. Even in the horse lines we could feel its heat warm against our backsides. In the hottest part of the fire, where it crackled against the sky, an enormous monster with wings of flame flew up with a furious howl into the Persian night.

All the horses in the camp threw up their heads and plunged against their tethers, including placid Zoroaster. The men left behind in the camp snatched buckets, yelled at our grooms to help, and raced to collect water from the river. But they soon realized it was a waste of effort, and stood watching silently as Persepolis burned.

In my experience, there are three reasons why you humans drink magic:

You want to forget something, like Tydeos when he thought Charm had been eaten by a crocodile.

You are celebrating.

You are terrified of something and need courage.

Since the Guard had nothing to celebrate that night, I was a bit anxious for Alexander. But in the morning, he strode down to the horse lines in his armour, smelling of smoke and snapping out orders to break camp. He vaulted on to me, turned my head to the north and put his heels into my sides. The Guard had to gallop to catch up.

Hephaestion called for him to be careful in case Bessus' men were still around, but Alexander laughed at his friend's worry. 'So much for your Persian curses!' he shouted to the ash-heavy sky, spreading his arms and letting me gallop even faster. 'See, proud Persian god, I am still alive! You might have killed my dog, but you can't touch me! I am the reborn Achilles and the son of Zeus-Ammon. I am *invincible!*'

Twenty-third Hoofprint
CASPIAN GATES, SUMMER 330 BC

Squealing at Ecbatana

We marched slowly north for many days, going from oasis to oasis, our baggage train huge with Persian treasure, and the mountains a shimmering line to our left. Each time we camped, more deserters from King Darius' army joined us, and were hauled off at once to Alexander's pavilion so he could interrogate them. Groom-gossip said we were chasing King Darius, whose baggage train and harem had been sent east to a place called the Caspian Gates, which would take him out of Persia.

Tydeos bit his lip when he heard this, and forgot he was supposed to be grooming me. 'If King Darius has got his harem with him, that means he may still have Charm! Oh, I wish King Alexander would hurry. We're going so *slowly*.'

This was just as well for us horses, since it was very hot and Aura's foal was growing big inside her. Every time I

349

looked out of the corner of my eye, I saw a flicker in the sky. It wasn't a ghost, though. The fire demon from Persepolis was following us, just waiting for an excuse to strike.

Eventually, we reach another city, the one called Ecbatana which Tydeos said was the last place the Persians had to hide. The gates open as soon as they see us coming. Alexander smiles and calls for his Troy armour. But before he can ride me into the city to accept its surrender, we hear hoofbeats drumming behind us, and I smell General Parmenio's horse.

The Guard look round, and Alexander sighs. 'Here it comes,' he mutters.

General Parmenio scowls at Alexander. His horse dances on the spot, agitated by the general's angry grip on the reins.

'What's all this I hear about you trying to exchange Prince Ochus for your missing groom, Alexander?' he snaps. 'That woman you brought back from the tomb at Pasargadae was at a party given by my son Philotas last night, and she told him what happened at the tomb of Cyrus the Great. Are you completely mad, exposing yourself to the enemy like that? Were you going to endanger our entire campaign for the sake of a single *slave?*'

'Philo, you traitor!' Hephaestion whispers, as if Philotas is still in the Guard with us – which he hasn't been since Alexander threw him out of our special herd back in Anatolia and gave him a herd of his own to keep him out of mischief. Ptolemy, who took Thais to the party, flushes.

Alexander's fist tightens on my rein. His voice is icy. 'You seem to be forgetting I am the son of Zeus, and he watches over me. Part of the deal was that King Darius would surrender his crown to me in return for his son. As for Charmides, she is my groom and I want her back. You were wrong about her being eaten by a crocodile in Egypt. What's more, I've discovered that my father's old horsemaster, who has already insulted my mother and tried to discredit me with his treacherous lies, sneaked in and took Charmides from the camp *while you were in charge*, General.'

This is definitely squealing, although not very loud.

The general's cheeks flush. He opens his mouth and closes it again. He looks carefully at Alexander and says, 'So the girl's alive and King Darius has her? So what? I expect she's having an easier time of it in his harem than she ever had looking after your horse. If you want my advice, we should secure Ecbatana and wait. By all reports, Darius is little more than a fugitive in his own country, while his satraps are quarrelling among themselves. It sounds as if this man Bessus was trying to get his hands on Prince Ochus to further his own ambitions, and has taken most of the Persian forces with him. Darius is probably on his way back here right now to beg our protection. I know if I were the Great King, I'd swallow my pride and turn my attention to what really matters in this world – my son and heir. But it's not something you would understand, Alexander. You don't seem to have time between burning cities to take a wife, let alone sire an heir.'

Alexander's breathing quickens. The Guard cringe.

Alexander says in a tough tone, 'First, General, you are not the Great King. I am. Second, I don't need an heir because I don't plan to die. And believe me, the *last* thing I'd do is crawl to my enemy for protection from my own men. If my enemy held a son of mine captive, I would go after him with all my strength. And if I couldn't kill him, I'd die fighting! That's why I'm going after Darius to get my groom back. Then I'm going after Bessus and that traitor of a horsemaster to teach them both a lesson. If you don't like it, you can stay here. I don't need old men like you grumbling and moaning behind my back all the time. As from today, I'm disbanding the Hellenic League. Any man who wishes, can go home. From this day on, I want only men I can trust in my army.'

He looks pointedly at the Guard, and their horses fidget nervously, which is a sure indication of how their riders are feeling. Some of them can't meet Alexander's gaze. But Hephaestion brings Petasios close to me and rests a hand on the king's arm. 'We're all with you, Alex, whatever you decide to do. You know that.'

The general presses his lips together, and his sunburnt face hardens. He says quietly, 'Alexander, I have served you as faithfully as I served your father King Philip. Everything I have done is for the good of Macedonia, this army and the campaign. You wouldn't have got this far without me, despite what you say about being the son of Zeus, and you know it. Yet now you insult me by suggesting you can't trust me?'

Alexander meets his glare, chin tilted, and says smoothly, 'You've proven yourself more than trustworthy since the Granicus, General.' He leaves a little pause to make quite sure the general remembers what he did there. 'But I am in command of this army, and I've made my decision. Go tell your men they can go home if they wish. I'll pay them each a bonus above their normal pay. Every man who leaves will receive one talent as a reward for his services so far. But any who want to stay with me can re-enlist, and I'll pay them a mercenary's wage from now on plus two talents—' He smiles. 'No, make that three talents each, as danger money for their courage. I can afford to be generous these days, thanks to King Darius' treasure.'

The general's jaw drops. The Guard draw a collective breath. That's three times the price of Petasios for every man in the army who stays, which is a *lot* of gold.

Alexander narrows his eyes at the general. 'From here onwards, we're going to be riding fast after King Darius. I need someone to stay behind in Ecbatana, to organise transport of the treasure back to Pella, keep an eye on the local tribes and supervise the pay-offs. That would be a good job for you, General, not too arduous for your old bones. And if King Darius does turn up here, as you seem to think he will, I'll need someone I can trust to deal with him. I'll pick you up on the way back and we can ride home together in triumph and glory.'

'I might be old, but I can still ride fast—'

Alexander raises an eyebrow. 'You want to come with us? Why?'

'No reason,' the general mutters, avoiding the king's gaze. 'So you're going after Bessus and the horsemaster after you've found King Darius?'

Alexander laughs. 'I'm going to catch both the traitors *and* get my groom back. It's a task for young men. That's why I'm ordering you to stay here. Any more objections, General?'

What could General Parmenio say?

As to why he was so desperate to be there when we caught up with King Darius and his harem, I expect you've already guessed. I think General Parmenio's going to be in BIG trouble when Alexander finds out what really happened in Egypt.

Battles that are a long time coming are always the worst.

Kissing the *Iliad*

That evening, after we'd eaten and dozed through the hottest part of the day, Alexander ordered the Guard to form up. He mounted me, and I stood on a flat-topped rock as Hephaestion placed the box containing the king's copy of the *Iliad* in the

353

dust below us. Then all the men filed past, choosing whether to stay or to leave the army. It worked like this:

Stay – kiss the *Iliad* to show you are faithful to Alexander, and take your three talent bonus from a smiling Hephaestion. Cheers from everyone, plus you're rich beyond your wildest dreams.

Leave – walk past the box and take your one talent pay-off from General Parmenio. Boos and hisses from Alexander's friends, and you're not as rich as you would have been if you'd stayed.

Alexander wore his Troy helmet, its plumes lifting on the evening breeze, and I made myself huge for the occasion. My rider felt tense at first, but slowly relaxed as man after man kissed the box. Some of the Macedonians went so far as to throw themselves on their knees before us and begged to be allowed to stay and fight even without payment.

Alexander watched the entire process with a stony expression. But as the last man kissed the box, he smiled slightly and lifted his sword into the cooling air. Energy shone around him, fiercer and brighter than ever before.

'Onward!' he cried in his shrill voice, jumping me off the highest side of the rock. 'We ride after King Darius!'

The cheers must have been loud enough to hear back in Persepolis.

Well, what would *you* have done? Three talents is more than a soldier earns in twenty-four years on normal army pay. But that was not the only reason the men stayed. They'd have been almost as rich if they left. They stayed because they did not want to be parted from Alexander.

Crows

Even though the older men stayed with General Parmenio, we were still a big herd when we set out east after King Darius. Ochus came with us, riding Zoroaster with our baggage train, though Alexander left Lady Barsine behind in Ecbatana, saying the prince wasn't a baby any more and didn't need her to nursemaid him.

It was like the mountains back in Illyria all over again, only hotter. We marched through the nights and mornings while it was cool, and camped in the afternoons. Our riders gave us mouthfuls of water from their own flasks. On our right shimmered a white seabed that smelt of salt but had no water in it, and behind us flickered the fire demon. I think some of the men wished they'd chosen to go home, despite being rich beyond their wildest dreams. They, too, sensed the demon.

Hoplite, whom Alexander had told Tydeos to ride to give him some experience, soon stopped frisking about and plodded along as sensibly as an old horse. At least this spared Tydeos more bruises. During our march north from Persepolis, he'd fallen off every time Hoplite threw a coltish bucking fit, much to the amusement of the other grooms.

My eyes watered with the glare, and I kept stumbling over stones. Only Alexander's firm hand, holding up my head, kept me from falling. All the horses of the Guard were having a bad time, but Aura suffered most of all. I nickered to her whenever she staggered, to remind her she was carrying my foal and must not give in. We swished the flies from one another's faces with our tails as we struggled on, but some of the cavalry horses were not so strong. They collapsed under their riders, and had to be given water. Some struggled up again after drinking. Others, who were too far gone, stretched out on their sides with a sigh, and their ghosts rippled past us on breaths of shivery wind. We left their bodies for the crows. There are always crows in horrible places like this, waiting for horses to die.

Eventually, after eleven horrible days of thirst and heat, we come to a narrow gorge between high cliffs. It looks very dark in there after the glare of the morning sun, but it seems quiet enough. Alexander holds up his hand and lets me stagger to a halt. 'What do you think, Hephaestion? Are the Persians in there, waiting to ambush us?'

Hephaestion looks back at the line of drooping men and horses behind us. 'The men are in no condition to fight even if the Persians are in there, Alex. We need water and food. The horses are half dead. That poor mare Aura is carrying a foal, for Zeus's sake! We should have left her in Ecbatana.'

Alexander sighs. 'We have to get through the Caspian Gates and find the next oasis. If we stop here, we'll all be dead by morning. Loosen your swords, gentlemen, and stay alert. Tell Attalus to take his archers up the cliffs to cover me. I'm going in.'

He walks me a few paces forward into the pass. It is eerie, and my hooves echo. I keep a good lookout for the fire demon. But nothing attacks us, except crows with their droppings. At least it is cooler between the cliffs. Something white trickles down the cliff-face. I stretch out my nose to lick it. It is salt and very good.

Alexander leans over my neck to scrape the salt from the cliff with his finger so he can lick some as well. 'What do you think, Bucephalas? Do we trust those villagers who told us King Darius has already passed through the Gates?'

The crows are very bold here. They circle overhead, cawing and diving at one another. My hairs rise, and I prick my ears and stare at the crows. Alexander stares up at them too.

He pats my neck. 'Clever horse! Something dead or dying up ahead. Let's go and see, shall we?'

The Guard whisper and stare round nervously as we walk deeper into the pass. My nose is so clogged up with dust, and the salt so strong, at first I cannot smell anything else. When we see a crumpled heap of cloak and red mane lying on the track ahead of us, I am as surprised as Alexander.

I shoot up my head and prick my ears, trying to focus on the small human and smell her at the same time. My heart beats faster as I catch a whiff of spring grass, bringing a surge of memory: gentle hands, comfort, relief from pain ... I think it is . . . I KNOW it is—

'Alex!' Hephaestion whispers. 'That looks like—'

'Silence!' Alexander says roughly, staring up the cliffs, where our archers kneel with arrows on their bowstrings. 'It might be a trick. Watch yourselves, gentlemen.'

He sits rigidly on my cloth, staring from the crumpled form to the cliffs and the circling crows. One dives at the huddle of cloak. Charm – I KNOW IT IS HER! – stirs and moans. I let out a ringing neigh, paw the rock and snatch at my bit impatiently.

'Stop that, Bucephalas!' Alexander hisses, still squinting at the cliffs. 'If the Persians are here, you've just announced our presence.'

I neigh again, the sound echoing round the cliffs.

Hephaestion looks at me and smiles. 'Bucephalas recognizes her, too, Alex. If the Persians were here, they'd have attacked by now. Shall I go and check?'

'No, I'll go! She's my groom. Stay close to me, gentlemen.

Be prepared for anything.'

Finally, Alexander lets me walk forward. When we are nearly there, I drag the reins from his hand and lower my head to sniff Charm. She is not dead. Under the cloak, she is wearing a long red dress with a ragged hem, and sandals with little jewels on them. She blinks at me, and reaches out a trembling hand to touch my nose.

'Bucephalas?' she says in a cracked voice. 'Clever horse . . . you found me!'

I snort at her and settle to my knees with a contented sigh.

Alexander slips off me. He kneels beside Charm and unstops his flask. Taking her head in his arm, he strokes the tangled curls out of her eyes and pours the last of his own water into her mouth. She swallows, still staring at me, her eyes full of joyful tears. I don't think she realizes it is the king holding her. Then she stiffens and focuses on his face.

'Your Majesty! I'm sorry—'

'Just answer my questions,' Alexander says gruffly. 'Are the Persians hiding up here?'

'No, Your Majesty. I haven't seen any soldiers since I left King Darius' camp.'

'You're safe now, Charmides. But I want to know everything. What happened in Egypt, what you saw in Darius' camp, how you escaped. Everything.'

'Of course, Your Majesty,' Charm whispers, stiffening again. 'I'm sorry—'

'And don't keep saying "sorry"! It's my fault this happened. General Parmenio's right about one thing. Sometimes I forget other people care about different things, and that's a mistake for a king. Can you walk?'

'I don't think so, Your Majesty.'

Alexander grunts. 'We haven't any spare horses, but I'm not leaving you here to wait for the baggage train. Bucephalas is strong. You can ride with me.'

'But you're the king!'

Charm's protests do no good. He lifts her on to my withers and jumps on behind her. Then he clamps his legs to my sides and says, 'Up, Bucephalas! Let's go!'

Hephaestion and the Guard glance at one another with raised eyebrows. But Alexander doesn't notice. His arms are around Charm to stop her falling off my back, and we are leading the herd again. It is the first time I have carried Charm on my cloth with Alexander, so it feels a bit strange. But she isn't heavy, and I am carrying my two favourite humans!

I am so proud and happy, I forget my thirst, lift my hooves and arch my neck. Behind us, the Guard follow, still exchanging wondering smiles.

This is as it should be. The three of us, together.

Charm's story

Alexander took Charm off to his pavilion as soon as we had made camp, so Tydeos and the other grooms didn't realize she was back. They were busy in the horse lines, watering us and giving us salt in our barley to replace what we'd sweated during the march. After her nosebag, Aura lay down with a sigh of relief, and she wasn't the only horse to do so. Mares in foal should never be made to go on marches like that.

I lay down, too. Just for a bit. After all, I had been carrying a double load.

Tydeos is sponging Aura with water to cool her down, when I smell Charm again. I scramble to my feet and whinny.

She is still wearing her red dress and fancy sandals, though she has washed her face and looks much better. Alexander obviously fed and watered her while they were talking. The sun going down behind her gives her a red halo.

Tydeos stares at her, rigid. Maybe he thinks she is a ghost.

Charm hesitates. Then she sees Aura, stumbles to the mare's dappled side and runs a hand over her distended belly. 'How long has this mare been in foal?' she asks. 'She looks half dead. What have you been doing with these poor horses while I've been away? Is that big speckled horse Bucephalas' colt? Have you backed him yet? And how did Bucephalas get that nasty scar on his hind leg? Looks like it went deep—'

'Hey, slow down!' Tydeos grins from ear to ear. He touches her hand, as if to check it is real. 'Charm, stop it! You come back after a whole *year*, and already you're bossing us all around like nothing's happened! Never mind the horses. However did you get here? Does King Alexander know you're back?' He glances at the king's pavilion, stained pink by the sunset, its sheets fluttering in the hot wind.

Charm smiles tensely. 'Where do you think I've been all day? He wanted to know everything, too.'

Tydeos' grin fades slightly. He starts to ask something about Alexander, but the other grooms have noticed Charm. They crowd round, staring at her dress and sandals.

'About time you came back, Charmides!' they call.

'We've had to look after your horses as well as ours!'

'Bucephalas has been pining for you. He went right off his food, didn't start eatin' again till after the big battle at Gaugamela.'

'And you should've seen the trouble poor Tydeos had backin' Hoplite without your help—'

360

'Leave her alone, you dolts!' Tydeos shoos them away with a laugh, and moves round Aura so he can hug Charm. She stiffens a bit at first, then relaxes and gives him a little kiss on the lips. All the grooms whistle and cheer.

Finally, Charm and Tydeos come to see me.

Charm examines the scar the chariot made on my hind leg at Gaugamela, while Tydeos holds my head and watches her as if she might vanish again the moment he takes his eyes off her. 'Don't panic, it's healed fine,' he says. 'He was lame for ages, but the king let me stay with him in Arbela. Actually, I'm glad Bucephalas got injured, 'cause that's where we caught the horsemaster and learnt what he'd done with you.'

'You caught the horsemaster?' Charm looks up sharply. 'Alexander didn't tell me that.'

'But he escaped,' Tydeos says. 'General Parmenio let him go.'

Charm sighs. 'Yes ... he would, wouldn't he . . . they're old friends, aren't they? I could hardly believe it when he gave me to the horsemaster in Egypt.'

Now it is Tydeos' turn to stare. 'What do you mean, General Parmenio *gave* you to the horsemaster? We all assumed the horsemaster kidnapped you from the camp – Oh, Zeus, does the king know?'

'He does now,' Charm says, resting her arm over my neck and mutual grooming my withers. 'It's probably a good job you left the general behind in Ecbatana. Alexander's absolutely furious with him, but he's not planning on going back there until after he's caught up with King Darius and got Bessus and the horsemaster in chains. Maybe by the time we get back, he'll have calmed down a bit.' She sighs. 'It was horrible, what General Parmenio did to me, but I don't think he deserves what Alexander is planning to do to him.'

'Never mind General Parmenio! You still haven't told me how you got away. Did King Darius touch you? Because if he did . . .'

Charm smiles and took his hand. 'No, Tydeos, he didn't touch me. He didn't touch any of us, the whole time I was in his harem. He had a few other things on his mind – Alexander, mostly.' She smiles again. 'King Darius isn't the barbarian everyone says he is, you know. He cares deeply about his family, his country and his god. He wept when he heard Alexander had burnt Persepolis. I feel quite sorry for him. But at least he'll get to see Ochus again soon.'

They sit on a pile of our cloths near my head, exchanging their news in low voices. This is how Charm got away:

King Darius' officers asked him to give the Persian crown to Bessus.
King Darius refused, not very politely.
The Persian herd started fighting among themselves, and the harem guards went to help their king.
Charm escaped in the confusion.

'You ran all the way up here on your own?' Tydeos interrupts. 'You might have been killed! How did you know we'd even be here?'

'I had a dream, of course.' Charm smiles at me, then glances at Aura, who is sleeping on her side with her huge belly sticking up. 'Now Alexander knows where Bessus and King Darius are, I think we're going to rest here for a few days before going after them. He's sent some men off to find supplies.'

Tydeos gives her a strange look. 'You're nuts, Charm, you

know that? Is it that horse bond thing the Amazon queen's always going on about? Because if it is, the sooner you break it, the better. Alexander doesn't really care about any of us. He loves his horse more than any human being, and despite that he's going to get Bucephalas killed in battle one day – *now* what's wrong?'

Charm stares at Alexander's pavilion and says in a tiny voice, 'Nothing.'

'Oh, I see. You still worship him, don't you, even after all the horrid things he's done? Well, let me tell you the rest. Since Egypt, he's had the hands cut off some poor Persians for trying to steal his *Iliad*, killed about ten thousand others, and burnt their holy city to the ground. I don't know what he did in Babylon, but he kept poor Prince Ochus locked in a lion cage all the way from Susa to Persepolis. And that's just what I know about. There's rumours of awful things happening to prisoners, like pouring oil-from-the-ground over them and setting them alight to see if they burn.'

Charm stays silent, biting her lip.

'You know it could never work anyway, don't you?' Tydeos says gently, putting his arm round her again. 'Alexander's a king and the son of Zeus. He's also Pharaoh of Egypt and Lord of Anatolia, and soon he'll be Great King of Persia, too. One day he'll marry a princess. If he shows you any attention, it's only as much as King Darius would show one of his harem slaves.'

Charm gives him a startled look and laughs. 'Is *that* what you're so upset about? That's not why we're so close. You are an idiot sometimes, Tydeos!'

Tydeos frowns. 'What do you mean?'

Charm stares a bit longer at Alexander's pavilion. She says

in a tight little voice, 'Because it wasn't just any old Macedonian soldier who raped my mother after the battle at Methone, that's why!'

Before she can explain further, the dogs start barking and the sentries yell as two strange horses gallop out of the night through our boundary torches. Their riders' robes billow against the flames, revealing scimitars thrust through wide sashes. They get halfway to Alexander's pavilion before the sentries manage to disarm them.

'Those men!' Charm cries, jumping to her feet. 'They were fighting for King Darius when Bessus tried to take over! Something awful must have happened.'

A flap of the pavilion is thrown back, and Alexander hurries out. His mane is untidy and he is barefoot, but he has a dagger in his fist.

As soon as the Persians see him, they prostrate themselves at his feet. 'King Iskander, we need your help! The demon Bessus has declared himself Great King! He's taking our rightful king as his prisoner back to Bactria, where he plans to raise another army against you. We beg you to help us free King Darius before it is too late!'

The shouting wakes the men in the nearest tents, and the news travels fast through the camp. Some of the Macedonians mutter that Alexander is the demon, and that it is already too late for the Persians. Others hiss at them to shut up.

Nine people wanted us to set out after Bessus and his prisoner immediately:

Alexander, Hephaestion, Ptolemy, Perdiccas, Leonnatus, Laomedon, the two Persians and Prince Ochus.

About twenty thousand people said we should wait for our

supplies and let the horses recover first:

Charm, Tydeos, and the rest of our grooms.
Demetrius (thinking of Aura).
Iolaus (thinking of his father Antipater back in Macedonia).
Philotas.
The cavalry, especially those who had lost horses to the fire demon on our march from Ecbatana.
The foot-soldiers, who had also lost many of their herd on the march.

The Amazons did not vote, but stroked their blue-painted horses and waited to see what would happen.

It was no contest. Alexander got his way, as usual.

Hoplite leads the herd

While Alexander questioned the Persians about a short cut that would get them ahead of Bessus, trumpets alerted the camp and the men were ordered to assemble for parade. Alexander chose five hundred of the fittest foot-soldiers and dismissed the rest. Then he and his Guard strode down the horse lines, picking out the fittest horses and ordering our grooms to get them ready.

Charm put her arms protectively about my neck and refused to let anyone near me with a bridle. But when Alexander reached us, he shook his head impatiently and said, 'I'm not stupid, Charmides. Bucephalas stays here. Tydeos, go and put my battle-cloth on that colt you've been training. He's young and looks like he's got plenty of spirit. I'll ride him instead.'

Aura stayed behind with me. So did all the horses who were lying down at the time, which made the choosing easy because that was most of them. This left only Petasios, Electra, Borealis, Apollo, Hades and Harpinna for the Guard. So Zoroaster, who had carried only a light load so far, got the job of carrying Demetrius.

When Zoroaster was led out, Ochus ran across and tried to scramble up on to him, but Alexander chuckled and plucked the man-colt off by the ankle. 'No, Ochus. You can't come with me this time. Wait here with Charmides.'

It was a strange feeling to stand in the horse lines and watch Alexander trot Hoplite to the front of the column. My colt made himself huge, arched his neck and gave a little squeal. When Alexander set his heels in his sides, he took off at such a fast gallop across the desert that even Petasios had a hard job keeping up with him. As the Guard gave chase, the five hundred mounted horses followed in excitement – which was just as well, because some of the foot soldiers Alexander had chosen to ride them obviously didn't know much about horsemanship. The Amazons galloped after them, and the fire demon followed.

When they had gone, the camp was very quiet. Charm put an arm around Ochus and said, 'It'll be all right, Ochus. Alexander's going to catch the bad men and rescue your father. They'll be back in a few days with King Darius, you'll see.'

My groom was correct about one thing. Three days later, Alexander did come back with King Darius. But things were far from 'all right'.

The Great King

After three days in Charm's care, I am feeling almost my old self again. As soon as I hear Petasios' weary whinny, I shoot up my head and neigh a welcome to my friends. Their whin-nies come back one by one: Electra, Hoplite, Borealis, Harpinna, Apollo, Hades . . . I am relieved to hear them. Our grooms, too, run up the road more eagerly than usual to meet the returning horses.

Then I see Alexander leading Hoplite at the front. My colt is limping badly and his head hangs low. He looks twice as old as me. I can see only six of the Guard. Directly behind them rumbles a covered wagon, driven by Demetrius and drawn by two oxen. A large dog follows with its tail drooping. Demetrius throws back the flaps as he stops. Stretched out on the floor is a man's body, covered by Alexander's cloak.

'This doesn't look good,' Charm breathes, looking round for Ochus. 'Best keep the prince away.'

Ochus gives a little cry, struggles away from a Macedonian sentry who tries to hold him back, and races to the wagon. None of the Guard stops him. The dog looks up and whines as Ochus drags off the cloak and throws himself on to the body.

'Father!' he wails. *'Father!'*

It is the tall, dark-bearded king I saw in the chariot at Gaugamela. His eyes are closed. Someone has washed his face, oiled his mane, and crossed his hands on his chest. A blue and white band encircles his head. He looks as if he is sleeping. But underneath the scent of oil and flowers, he smells like men who have been left lying on the battlefield too long. His ghost hovers above the wagon, but Ochus cannot see it.

The men shake their heads and silently hand their horses over to the grooms, who lead them away to the lines, looking back over their shoulders. Alexander tosses Hoplite's reins to Tydeos and mutters, 'Look after him. He's a brave colt. He carried me well.' Then he tilts his chin, puts a hand on the dog's collar and says to Ochus, 'I want you to know I didn't kill your father. We found him dying. He wouldn't cooperate with the Persian traitors, so that coward Bessus murdered him before he fled.'

Ochus is crying. Charm doesn't seem to know whether to go and help Tydeos with Hoplite, or stay to comfort the prince. More Macedonians emerge from their tents to stare at the dead king and his son.

'Hoplite's very lame,' Tydeos mutters sadly, stroking my colt's speckled nose. 'Poor colt. It's the baggage train for you, my lad.'

Charm gives my colt a distracted look. 'Where's Zoroaster?' she says suddenly, frowning at the returning horses. 'I don't see him.'

I had almost forgotten Zoroaster. I didn't hear his whinny with the others. As I neigh to find out where he is, there is a rush of flame in the sky and a horrible groan from the mares' lines as the fire demon we saw rise from the ashes at Persepolis strikes in all its terrible glory. The grooms shout for help and rush over that way. It's my Aura! She's on the ground, and I can smell blood.

I whinny desperately to her, pulling at my tether to save her from the demon. Charm races over and pushes through the grooms, ordering them to fetch warm water and cloths. But I know it is no good. Mares do not have their foals in the daytime by choice, especially not when there's so much else going on. The foal has come too early. My poor Aura!

It's over quite quickly. The fire demon takes the foal's ghost and flies away. I calm down a bit. Charm gets Aura on her feet and leads her out of the lines, while the grooms wrap the foal's body in an old cloth and carry it away from the disturbed mares. As they pass me, I see one of its long legs dangling out from the cloth. Beneath the blood, our foal is pure white.

Charm is stroking Aura and rubbing her ears, telling her she'll live to have another colt, and that albinos are often not very strong so it's no surprise she lost this one.

Tydeos is stroking Hoplite's neck and telling him his legs will get better soon.

Alexander is stroking Ochus' mane and promising him he'll avenge his father's death.

None of them has seen King Darius' ghost, which ripples closer to the wagon.

I let out a ringing neigh to warn them, and they look round. Ochus shrugs off Alexander's hand and wipes his tears on his sleeve. He kisses his father's folded hands and forehead, and pats the whining dog. Then he eases the blue and white band from his father's head, stands on the seat of the wagon, and makes himself huge.

'My father is dead!' he says in Greek, holding up the crown. 'I am Ochus of the royal bloodline, heir to the Persian Empire! Today, the crown of Persia is mine. But I surrender it to Uncle Alexander, for him to wear until I am old enough to take the white colt's spirit and become king myself. Bessus is an evil man and a traitor. You must go after him and punish him.'

There is a respectful silence as the prince climbs down from the cart and hands the blue and white band to Alexander. This done, the hugeness goes out of Ochus, and he kneels to hug the dog. It obviously knows his smell, because it licks his face and wags its tail a little. The men, who were loading up their tents ready for the return march to Ecbatana, look a bit ashamed.

Alexander smiles slightly.

'You heard the boy!' he shouts in his shrill voice. 'Bessus has fled to Bactria. He's scared of us now, but if we turn round and go home as General Parmenio wants us to do, it'll be no time at all before the traitor Bessus raises an army and crosses the Hellespont to take his revenge on Macedonia and Greece. Only a few days more, and we'll finish him. So, who's with me? We have only to avenge King Darius' death by punishing the traitor, and Persia with all its riches is ours!'

As he puts on the crown, there is a flash in the sky above the mountains. Thunder rumbles as the barrier between our world and the world of ghosts tears, like it did back in Anatolia when Alexander cut the Gordian Knot.

The men shout and cheer.

'HURRAH FOR GREAT KING ALEXANDER! ALEX-AN-DER! ALEX-AN-DER! GREAT KING OF PERSIA!'

King Darius' ghost whirls away through the hole, along with the fire demon that took Aura's foal. The Amazons look up, their eyes alight with joy because the hole in the world is open again and they can go home. We horses flicker our ears and dance nervously.

Alexander ruffles Ochus' hair. 'Well done,' he says. 'You can keep the dog. It was watching over your father's body. Dogs are more faithful than men.'

Then, AT LAST, he comes to the lines to give me an apple.

I press my teeth against his palm, impatient for more, and he pulls my ear. His hands are trembling.

'Ah, Bucephalas,' he sighs. 'At least *you're* feeling better. Listen to the fools cheering me! At the next sign of hardship, they'll be moaning again about going home, you'll see. I'm not going to finish my life like Darius, left to die alone in an old wagon, murdered by my own men. If it can happen to a great king like him, it can happen to me. So before we go any further, I'm going to have to deal with a few things I should have dealt with long ago.' He glances round to check no one is listening. 'This isn't going to be easy, though. I just don't know who to trust any more, horse! If General Parmenio can betray me like he did back in Egypt when he gave my groom to the horsemaster, how many of my officers might be ready to betray me by running a spear through my back? Oh, this isn't what it was meant to be like! I'm Great King of Persia, and my head still hurts.'

I don't really know what he means by this. But I expect his head hurts because King Darius' crown is too small. Alexander's head, as you've probably realized by now, is almost as big as mine.

That was how we dominated the Persians at the Caspian Gates. It was a very strange battle – against a demon, rather than spears and arrows. But we still won.

Persian dead: one (King Darius).
Macedonian dead: 30 killed by the Persian fire demon.
Horses dead: 100, including Zoroaster and Aura's foal. (VERY sad!)
People spared: Charm and the 365 women in King Darius' harem.

The grooms say that is one mare for every day of the year, which is silly because it would mean King Darius could have made 365 new foals every year. So far, I have seen only Ochus and his two sisters, which is three.

It's just as well Prince Ochus doesn't know Aura's stillborn foal was a white colt. Had it lived, it would have been the next sacred horse of the sun, after Zoroaster. Alexander is Great King of Persia now, so I think the white colt's death is a very bad omen for the Persian royal bloodline.

Twenty-fourth Hoofprint
ZADRACARTA, LATE SUMMER
330 BC

The sea again

Some places in the world are good for horses, and Zadracarta on the southern shore of the Caspian Sea is one of them.

When we came out of the mountains where so many horses had died and saw the water glittering ahead of us, hardly anyone could believe it was real. The men whooped like man-colts, threw down their weapons, and plunged in to scrub the caked battle-grime from their bodies and manes. We horses did the same, pawing at the water and splashing our riders. Electra and several other youngsters got down to roll, making their riders yell and laugh as they got ducked.

I would have loved a roll, too, but I was carrying King Alexander, the reborn Achilles, son of Zeus, Lord of Anatolia, Pharaoh of Egypt, and Great King of Persia. So I just dipped my muzzle up to my eyes and snorted spray all over Petasios, who pushed his nose through the waves and did the same to me. The water was rather salty, but sweeter than the sea back home. The breeze from the sea was cool, and the earth green as far as we could see.

Everyone praised Alexander for bringing us here.

With food and rest, we horses soon recovered our strength. Although there were wolf and bear smells in the forest, they didn't bother us because we knew our grooms would not let them near us. Meanwhile, our herd swelled with officers and mercenaries from the Persian army, who hurried to join us once they heard about King Darius' death. It began to get difficult (at least for you humans, who can't smell the difference) to tell who was Persian and who was Macedonian, since Alexander and his friends took to striding around the camp in billowing Persian robes. Alexander even gave orders that we horses of the Guard were to wear Persian tassels on our bridles and cloths – which was pretty silly, if you ask me, because we are already beautiful. Then he took the cavalry on a raid in the hills to find more horses to replace those who had died. He took Tydeos and most of the other grooms with him. The Amazons went, too, so they could look for the hole in the world before it closed.

This meant the horse lines were almost deserted. But I didn't mind being left behind, because my favourite groom stayed to look after me and my favourite mare was tethered nearby. All three of us needed time to recover.

Me – from battle injuries and the chase after King Darius.
Charm – from her kidnapping ordeal.
Aura – from losing her white foal.

But the men were getting nervous about Alexander's plans, and none of us got quite as much rest as the king intended.

A plot against the king

One morning, when Charm rides me back from my gentle exercise on the beach, I smell Demetrius in the horse lines. Since the Achilles shield was not needed on the raid, Alexander left him in charge of the camp. But Demetrius is not wearing his Persian cloak today, just his old Macedonian tunic, and he is alone. He strokes Aura's nose while Charm settles me. When she picks up my bridle and sits on a pile of cloths to finish sewing on the blue and white tassels that match the crown Alexander took from King Darius, he wanders over.

Charm scrambles to her feet, flustered. 'I'm sorry, Sir, I didn't see you there!'

'No, don't get up.' Demetrius keeps a wary distance from my heels and crouches beside her. He glances round to check that the other grooms Alexander left in the camp are busy elsewhere. 'I wanted to talk to you while the king isn't here.'

Charm frowns. 'What about, Sir?'

'These tassels . . .' Demetrius says, touching her work. 'What do you grooms think of them?'

Charm smiles and runs the blue silk threads through her fingers. 'I think they're pretty. Bucephalas will probably eat them, though – he's not used to wearing Persian harness!'

'Nor are Macedonians,' Demetrius says with a sigh. 'Did you know Alex has given us permission to marry our captive Persian women and bring them along with the army? So far, the men have been allowed home on leave between campaigns to visit their families. Now Alex says it's getting too far for them to keep going back to Macedonia for holidays, and the women will help take their minds off their wives. Says it's only fair now he has King Darius' harem.' Demetrius doesn't notice Charm's sudden stillness. He makes a face. 'Not that he's touched a single one of them, of course! Seems our Great King cares more for his groom than any Persian princess.'

Charm flushes and puts down my bridle. 'Please don't make fun of me, Sir.'

'I'm not,' Demetrius says, watching her carefully. 'You don't know how upset he was when he heard you might have been eaten by that crocodile. Once he found out you were alive and in Darius' hands, he was even willing to exchange Prince Ochus for you. Then, when that went wrong, he brought the army out here after you.'

'After King Darius, you mean. He wanted the Persian crown!'

'Maybe. But he wanted you back just as much.'

Charm looks angry. She starts to scramble to her feet again. But Demetrius puts a hand on her wrist. 'No, please stay. I'm not making fun of you. I'm just telling you how it is. I don't even know if the king realizes how much he cares for you. It's hard to tell what he's thinking sometimes. Obviously, your dreams are useful to him, and you're the only other person who can ride Bucephalas. But we saw him give you his own water and take you up on Bucephalas at the Caspian Gates.' He glances round again and lowers his voice to a whisper. 'Some of us believe that, wherever you and the horse go, Alexander will follow. Even if it means turning back and heading home.'

Now Charm is listening, her eyes wary.

'Most of the men have had enough,' Demetrius continues.

'We've done what we came to do. The Persian Empire will never have the same power again. If this man Bessus does ever raise another army and come across the Hellespont after us, we can fight him then. But we think it unlikely he'll dare venture past the Euphrates. However, back home, the Greeks, Thracians, and Illyrians are all chewing at our borders, and we're stuck out here unable to get back in a hurry if we need to defend our families. I know you don't like all the killing, and if Alexander turns back, Bucephalas won't have to fight in any more battles. We'd like you to help us.'

It goes so quiet I can hear the other horses tearing grass with their teeth. I stop grazing so I can hear what Charm says.

She stares at my bridle lying in her lap. 'If I told Alexander what you just said, he'd execute you as a traitor,' she whispers.

'I know that, but I'm willing to take the risk. Philotas said we should force you to come with us, but I'd like you to help us of your own accord. It'll make things much easier for all of us.'

Charm gives him another wary look. She eyes her dagger, which is tucked into her bedroll, out of reach.

'Don't be alarmed,' Demetrius says, following her gaze. 'I know you don't want Bucephalas to get hurt, which is why you've defied Alexander so often. We're simply offering you a chance to get the old horse to safety. The local Mardian tribe is going to help us. They live to the west of here, and they're real horsemen who know these mountains well. They've promised to take you and the horse back to their village by a secret route through the forests, where they'll look after you for as long as it takes us to persuade Alexander to turn round and take us home. We'll tell him the Mardians kidnapped you, which should keep him from pressing any further east until General Parmenio—'

Charm's face, which has started to look interested, closes at the mention of the general's name. 'No!'

Demetrius puts a finger on her lips. 'Shh, Charmeia! Listen to me a moment. Philotas told me what General Parmenio did to you in Egypt. It was horrible for you, I know. But you have to understand he was doing what he believed best for the army at the time. He thought you had too much influence over Alexander, and were sabotaging our campaign by lying to the king about your dreams and trying to help Prince Ochus escape. He thought getting you out of the way was a good idea. The horsemaster was just convenient, that's all. General Parmenio had no idea back then how much Alexander cared for you, or I doubt he'd have risked you falling into Persian hands. The horsemaster has nothing to do with this. We don't even know where he's got to. If he fled east with Bessus, like Alex thinks, then I doubt he'll trouble any of us again. But we need Parmenio because he has the veterans on his side. You'll be well out of the way by the time he gets here.'

'Who else is in this plot?' Charm demands, her face tight.

'Philotas, of course. General Parmenio. Me—' He hesitates. 'Others who think the same way. It's best if you don't know their names, in case something goes wrong.' He gazes across the sea. 'Alexander doesn't intend to stop when he catches Bessus, you know. He plans to take us on and on, until he finds the eastern edge of the world. Have you any idea how many more battles that'll mean? How long do you think it'll be before Bucephalas stops a spear like that poor mare Alex was riding at the Granicus?'

Charm is still shaking her head. But her face twists like

378

Ochus' did when he saw the body of his father.

'Charmeia,' Demetrius says gently, lifting her chin so he can see her eyes. 'I won't lie to you. What we're doing is very dangerous. Alex will be furious when he realizes we tricked him. Some of us might get killed. But if it stops him dragging us all with him to die in some Zeus-forsaken place on the other side of the world, it'll be worth it. I worship the king. We all do. We don't want to see him hurt, any more than you want to see Bucephalas hurt. But sometimes you have to be firm with someone you love, to keep them from harming themselves. Once we persuade him to turn back, we'll have won. Not even Alexander will be able to convince the men to come this far east again.'

Charm blinks and whispers, 'What are you going to do to Alexander?'

Demetrius smiles. 'We'll simply disarm him and take him home with us. Philotas will probably assume command until we get back to Pella. Once we're there, I'm sure we'll be able to persuade Alex to see sense and stay to look after his own kingdom. He'll still be King of Macedonia. Bucephalas will get the retirement he deserves, and Alex won't touch you because we'll say the Mardians kidnapped you against your will.'

I smell strange horses and neigh a challenge. Charm stiffens. A scruffy herd is trotting along the beach towards the camp, bows slung over their riders' shoulders. Demetrius glances up and smiles. 'Ah, good, here they are! Come on, quietly. Get Bucephalas ready.'

'Now?' Charm looks round, confused. 'But Tydeos—'

'I'm sorry, we can't wait for your friend to get back. I'll tell him you're safe. I can't come with you, I'm afraid. I have to be here when Alex returns. Quickly, before the sentries notice something's up. We've taken care of the ones watching this side of the camp, but there's not a moment to lose.'

Charm bows her head. She realizes she can't wait for Tydeos, because that would mean waiting for Alexander. But she refuses to put the bridle on me until Demetrius agrees to let her take Prince Ochus as well, to get him out of the way of Alexander's temper. While Demetrius runs to the camp to collect him, Charm rips the tassels off my and Aura's bridles, and gets us ready.

Demetrius returns with the prince and boosts him up on to Aura. As we trot down to the beach, I am so happy to have my favourite groom on my back and my favourite mare at my side, I can put up with King Darius' old dog trotting along quietly behind us.

Charm smiles tightly at the man-colt and says, 'Don't worry. I'll make sure you get safely back to your grandmother and sisters in Susa. I won't let Alexander hurt you.'

Ochus bites his lip and strokes Aura's neck. 'Uncle Alexander would never hurt me. He says I am his own son, now my father is dead. I wanted to stay and wait for him to come back, but Demetrius says there might be fighting.'

'There might be,' Charm whispers. 'Macedonians against Macedonians – oh, Ochus, I hope I'm doing the right thing! What if there's a fight and Alexander gets hurt? He gets so mad sometimes, he doesn't stop fighting even when he's wounded. They might not realize, and—' Her voice breaks. 'What if they kill King Alexander like Bessus' men killed King Darius?'

'No one will ever beat Uncle Alexander in a fight,' Ochus says confidently. 'He is much too strong.'

But Demetrius stays in the horse lines, watching us go. Out

of the corner of my eye, I see him grip one of the posts and tremble all over, like we horses do before a battle.

Aura finds what she had lost

I don't know if Charm had second thoughts, because her hands are never as firm on my reins as Alexander's, which means her emotions don't travel as clearly along them. But as we came within smelling distance of the Mardians, I felt her weight shift on my back, and her hand dropped towards her dagger.

By then it was too late, because the Mardians had surrounded us with their little horses. The ones on the outside of the circle pulled the bows off their shoulders and put arrows to the strings.

'Who the boy and the dog?' growled their dark-maned boss. 'Our friend say just you and black horse.'

'He's just a captive we picked up on the way,' Charm said quickly. 'I'm looking after him because he lost his mother and father. The dog's his. It'll make no trouble.'

The boss scowled at the big black-and-tan dog, which crouched on its belly in the sand and growled at him. Then he frowned and looked more closely at Ochus, who sat very straight on Aura's cloth. Wisely, the prince said nothing.

The Mardian boss shook his head and snapped an order to his men. One of them grabbed Aura's reins and dragged her into a gallop after his horse. But I bit the boss when he tried to grab mine.

'Leave him!' Charm said in a tight voice. 'Don't worry, I'm coming with you. I want the fighting to stop more than anyone else.'

The Mardian horses might have been small, but they had

a terribly high opinion of themselves. I had to nip one who tried to lean on me, and kick another on the nose, before they saw sense and left me a decent space. Their riders eyed me warily as we entered the forest and headed up into the mountains.

We followed the Mardian herd along paths that didn't look like paths until we were on them. Aura carried Ochus under the low branches easily enough, but Charm had to lie along my neck as the tracks got narrower and gloomier. She didn't say anything, though, and after climbing all day we came out of the trees on to a high plateau, where huts crouched between the wind and the clouds. A huge herd grazed nearby, including lots of mares with foals. The Mardian horses whinnied to their friends and wandered across to greet us, since they were not tethered to lines.

The boss-stallion, a tough-looking bay with a white streak down his nose, made himself huge and squealed a challenge at me. I squealed one back.

Charm gripped my rein tightly and said, 'No, Bucephalas! We'll be in enough trouble as it is, when King Alexander gets back.'

Aura stared at the mares and foals, her beautiful ears pricked and her brown eyes sad. Then she did a very strange thing. She gave a little nicker, took hold of her bit and trotted off to the village with Ochus hauling at her reins.

'Ochus!' Charm called, sounding worried. 'Keep her away from that stallion!'

But Aura had the bit between her teeth, which was most unusual for her. Worried, I sent a whinny after her. She took no notice! I snatched at my reins and danced sideways, impatient to go after her before the Mardian stallion got to her.

Charm held me back and said to the Mardian boss, 'I'm sorry, but our grey mare's a bit upset. She lost a foal recently.'

Then I realized what Aura was up to. By one of the huts at the edge of the village, a goat stood tethered to a stake. A small golden foal lay in the grass nearby. The Mardian women were trying to make the foal get up and suckle from the goat, but it kept flopping back down again to stare at the herd with eyes as sad as Aura's.

Ochus slid off Aura. He put his arms around the foal and lifted it to its feet. Aura nudged it with her nose until it staggered round to her flank and found her milk. Soon its small tail was flicking and Aura was grazing happily.

The bay stallion stared at them and snorted. Then he gave me flat ears and lowered his head. He kept a wary eye on me, though. I kept an eye on him, too. He hadn't submitted to me, but we were like General Parmenio and Alexander. For the moment we needed each other, so I didn't fight him for his herd.

The women smiled at Aura and the foal.

Even the Mardian boss smiled. 'Your mare lose foal? Our foal lose mother in fight against bear. Think they find each other, yes? That filly not like goat milk. We think she die of broken heart. Now your mare save her.'

Battle for a mare and foal

At dawn, a curl of smoke rises from the forest below us. Charm is rolled tightly in her cloak beside me, so doesn't notice it at first. She had a bad night, moaning and thrashing about in her sleep. I think she had another dream.

Ochus shakes her awake. 'Fire, Charmeia!' he hisses into her ear. 'You think Uncle Alexander comes after us?'

Charm leaps up and stares at the smoke, white-faced. The Mardian boss rushes out of his hut, bow in one hand, a quiver of arrows in the other. 'Mount up!' he calls to Charm and Ochus. 'We go. Now!'

Charm fumbles with my bridle. I throw up my head, disturbed by her panic, and she shouts at me, which is MOST unusual. Ochus starts to bridle Aura, but the Mardian boss drags over a small brown horse and tells him to mount that one instead. 'Your mare stay with our foal,' he reminds him, turning Aura loose and waving his arms to shoo her and the filly across to the bay stallion's herd.

I'm not letting the Mardian stallion have my special mare! I drag the bridle from Charm's hands and take off after Aura, making myself huge.

The bay stallion also makes himself huge when he sees me galloping towards his herd, and comes to meet me with bared teeth and flat ears. I am twice his size (good), twice his weight (good), and twice his age (not so good). Also, he is surprisingly quick. Neither of us manage to do any real damage to the other before the Mardians gallop up with their whips and separate us.

All my attention has been on the fight, so I don't realize we have been surrounded by another herd until Darius' dog barks a warning and a sentry yells, 'King Alexander's men!' But the new arrivals smell familiar, and I calm down a bit as I recognize the Amazon herd.

'It's Queen Penthesilea!' Charm sobs in relief, grabbing my mane and pulling me away from the bay stallion.

The Mardians have arrows on their bowstrings, ready to fly. The Amazons raise their half-moon shields and grip their axes. But Charm wriggles up on to my back and urges me between the two herds, guiding me with her knees and voice because my bridle broke when I trod on the flapping reins. 'No, don't fight!' she cries, raising her hands as if to catch the arrows. 'They're friends!'

Finally, the Mardians realize the newcomers are not Alexander's Macedonians. They stare at the Amazon herd in amazement, and lower their bows.

Charm sits tensely on my back as Queen Penthesilea gallops up to us. She eyes my bridleless state and says, 'Thank our horses' horns we found you in time! King Alexander is furious! Did you really think you could hide from him? The horse bond lights your trail like a torch before his eyes! He is bringing the entire army up here after you, burning villages on the way. He is in a mighty rage. You must take Bucephalas back to him at once.'

Charm closes her eyes. Some Mardians must have understood her words, for they turn pale and look to their families. The women and children cluster together, staring at us with accusing eyes.

The Mardian boss frowns at Queen Penthesilea. 'You promise if we help you, King Iskander take his army back to Ecbatana and lead his wild-haired Macedonians home. You not tell us he burn our forests and villages!'

'That kidnap plan was nothing to do with us! King Darius' death reopened the hole in the world, so we are on our way home. King Alexander has more power now than any man ever had. We shall not fight for him any more. He is becoming too dangerous to follow. I only came up here for Charmeia's sake. The army is less than half a day behind us, but it is not too late. I suggest you take his horse and the prince back to him and apologise. You could always say you kidnapped Bucephalas as a joke because he stole some of your horses on his raid. You might have to give him something valuable, though, to show you are sorry.' She eyes the bay stallion's herd. 'He still needs more cavalry mounts.'

The Mardian boss scowls at Ochus. 'I *know* that boy familiar! He grown a lot since I see him, but I recognize the dog from when the Great King's army pass this way. It belong to King Darius, it never leave his side.' He turns his scowl on Charm. 'You should not bring the Persian prince! You put our families in danger. I agree, we return him right away. But I not coward. We still take you and horse to next village, hide you there.' He grins, baring white teeth.

Charm bows her head. 'No,' she whispers. 'You don't understand. He wants me and Bucephalas back more than he wants Prince Ochus. That's how he followed us. It's the horse bond. We shouldn't have come. I've listened to the wrong people, and put you all in terrible danger. I'm sorry.'

Charm's choice

While the Mardians got ready for the journey, cutting horses out of their herd to take with them as a peace offering, the Amazon queen helped Charm sort out my bridle.

'You do not have to go back, Charmeia,' she said quietly. 'I promised I would ask if you wanted to come with us, when we went home.'

Charm looked up sharply. 'You're leaving *now*?'

'The hole in the world opened again when Alexander took the Persian crown. We must go before it closes. We shall ride north across the steppe back to our own country.' Queen Penthesilea hesitated. 'It will not be possible for you to bring Bucephalas. The horse bond is too strong. King Alexander will chase us to the ends of the earth if we take his horse. You will be free of Alexander in our country. But if you really want to come with us, you must first break the bond between you and Bucephalas.'

Charm's hand tightened on my rein. Her eyes searched the Amazon queen's. 'I didn't know it was possible to break the horse bond.'

'There is one way. Death.'

Charm stared at her in horror.

Queen Penthesilea smiled. 'Only one of you. The easiest thing would be to kill the horse. I know a quick, painless way that stops the heart. Bucephalas is old. King Alexander would not suspect if the Mardians told him he had died on his way up this mountain. Then you will be free to come with us, and King Alexander will be free to go his own way with those who are brave or stupid enough to follow him.'

'*No!*' Charm's arms went around my neck, and she hugged me tightly. 'No, *never!*'

The Amazon queen patted me, and looked sadly at her. 'I thought you would say that. But once the bond is broken, you might feel differently. You may even form another bond with a younger horse—'

'I won't!'

Queen Penthesilea sighed and lowered her voice. 'The only other way is to kill King Alexander. That will be harder. But if you want to be free of him, Philotas and General Parmenio are already considering it as a last resort.'

'No!' Charm looked utterly horrified. '*Kill King Alexander? No!*' Then she frowned. 'But they can't kill him, can they? He's the son of Zeus, and soon he'll reach the edge of the world. Then he'll be immortal, like the oracle said.'

The Amazon queen gave her a sad look. 'Do you really believe that, Charmeia?'

'The grooms say *you're* immortal!' Charm set her jaw. 'You don't die. You've not lost a single warrior since you joined us, have you?'

The queen sighed again and touched her scarred cheek. 'There was a time when I lost many warriors. This is not the edge of the world, Charmeia, and King Alexander is not immortal, believe me. There is a difference between legend and reality. Alexander might like to think he is his hero Achilles, but this is not the *Iliad*, and even Achilles was killed in the end. Think about it.'

This upset Charm again. 'But Demetrius said they wouldn't hurt the king – oh, I knew something like this would happen! I should never have agreed to come up here in the first place. Everything I try to do ends up going *wrong*.' She stared at the smoke in the valley, tears in her eyes.

'Again, it is the horse bond that makes you care for Alexander so much,' Queen Penthesilea said gently. 'After his death, I promise you will feel differently. You'll come to love another, or maybe to live with us as a warrior without men.'

Charm sobbed into my mane. 'Just go. I told you, I'm not a warrior like you. I don't care if it is the horse bond making me feel like this. I won't let you kill Bucephalas, and I won't let anyone hurt Alexander. If there's no other way to break the bond between us, then I don't want to break it! Also, there's Tydeos . . . you don't understand. You're not human, are you? You belong in legends like the *Iliad*. Go home through your hole in the world. I don't care. Just leave me alone. Please . . .'

Queen Penthesilea rested a callused hand on Charm's shoulder. 'Eventually, the bond will break of its own accord,

Charmeia. No one lives forever – king, groom, or horse. When it happens, maybe one of you will find your way to us. I hope it is you. Good luck, and remember – the edge of the world is always further than you think.'

The Amazon herd trotted off into the forest, and that was the last anyone saw of their horned horses in this world.

The wall across the world

Though we travelled as fast as possible, we had with us half the mares and foals and all the colts old enough to be broken from the bay stallion's herd, which meant we couldn't take the narrow paths. After the fuss I'd made earlier, Ochus rode Aura with the golden filly trotting at her heels. We went the long way round and met some of Alexander's men, fresh from burning villages en route.

Philotas was leading them. He pressed his lips together, exchanged a few whispered words with the Mardian boss, and brought Zephyr alongside me. While I nickered a greeting to the yellow mare, he frowned at Charm. 'The king mustn't know any of us were involved, Groom,' he said. 'Understand?'

She nodded, her fingers playing with my mane. My reins were knotted on my withers where I'd broken them before my battle with the Mardian stallion, but they were just for show. Up on the plateau, Charm had learnt how to transfer her wishes to me through fingertips and knees alone.

Philotas grunted. 'We're going to have to think of something else. Not a word to anyone!'

Charm took this very seriously. For the next few days, she hardly spoke at all – not even to Tydeos, who hugged her and said in his half-joking, half-sincere tone that it was about time she stopped getting herself kidnapped.

She wasn't the only one in the camp afraid to talk. Alexander was furious that the Amazons had left his army. He ordered his scouts to find their trail, and stormed about his tent, hurling things to the ground. The tension in the air made us horses prickly, and our grooms shouted at us for stepping on their toes and nipping them. Meanwhile, the Mardian boss disappeared into Alexander's pavilion, and everyone held their breath.

The Mardian boss must have been a very clever talker. By the time Alexander emerged, dressed in his Persian cloak and wearing his blue and white crown, he had calmed down. He kept the youngest Mardians as hostages to ensure their tribe behaved itself in future, and sent their boss back to his forests with dire warnings not to touch his property again. Then our grooms led the new horses to the vacant places in our lines, and there was a lot of squealing and kicking until we all settled.

The next day, the trumpets sounded the order to break camp. While our grooms rushed around packing, Charm polished me carefully and spent a lot of time making sure I looked Persian enough for King Alexander – arranging the strings of blue and white tassels so they fluttered annoyingly whenever I tossed my head, and fastening so many of them to my cloth that they hung down my tail like Zoroaster's silly bells used to.

She stiffened when Alexander came to the lines, but he just rested his hand briefly on her head and promised he would never leave her with people he couldn't trust again. Then he leapt on to my cloth and cantered me towards the rising sun, his Guard hurrying to catch up.

Demetrius was not with them.

We found Alexander's scouts waiting for us out on the steppe. But when we galloped across to them to see if they had found the Amazons' trail, they shook their heads and pointed to the ground. Alexander frowned at the hoofprints, which stopped in mid-stride as if the Amazon horses had taken off and flown away like birds.

While I sniffed the ground in confusion, Alexander stared at the sea of waving grass that stretched to the northern horizon. He rode me a short way ahead of the Guard until the grass tickled my knees. Clenching his fist on my withers, he muttered, 'All women are crazy, warriors or not! Do you know what their proud queen said to me, Bucephalas? She dared tell me that a king is only a king for as long as he remembers who made him one! I'll come back and deal with their little country after I've punished Bessus and that treacherous old horsemaster of my father's. She'll be sorry she left me like this!'

Then his shoulders slumped, and he clutched my mane like Charm does sometimes. 'Oh Bucephalas, what am I doing wrong? Why did the Amazons leave? Didn't I give them a fair share of the spoils? There are more wonders out here in the east than a man can dream of, and we have the strength and power to defeat any army in the world! I just don't understand why everyone wants to go *home*.'

But he let the Amazons go, because not even a horse could follow a trail which vanished so completely that even its smells had gone.

Before we marched east after Bessus and the horsemaster, Alexander sacrificed a goat to Zeus and ordered his men to build a strong wall to keep the wild northern tribes and their strange powers out of his empire.

So it seems the Amazon queen was right, and we are still looking for the edge of the world.

TWENTY-FIFTH HOOFPRINT
LAKE SEISTAN, AUTUMN 330 BC

What are fences for?

Acting on information from Persian deserters, we went south in search of Bessus and his herd. We reached a place called Lake Seistan, only to find that they had lied to us, and Bessus had taken the fastest route back to Bactria. This put Alexander in an even worse mood. The grooms said we'd be on the march again by morning, but Alexander did an unexpected thing. He told his officers to take the best houses in the nearby town, and ordered the men to build strong fences around the camp, as if we were going to stay all winter.

The camp remained on high alert for the rest of that month, and our grooms were not allowed to exercise us out of sight of the guards. Alexander said the increased security was because of the threat of an attack from Bessus' herd. But we horses know all about fences. As well as keeping your enemies out, fences keep you in.

One morning, when we returned from our exercise on the shores of the lake, we found the number of sentries at the gates of the camp had been doubled. Men were running back and forth between the camp and the town, and there was a lot of excited shouting.

Charm tensed on my back, and Tydeos urged Hoplite up beside me. My colt had come sound again during the march south, but of course he pretended he'd forgotten most of what Tydeos had taught him. Tydeos had fallen off three times that morning, and was in a grumpy mood.

'What's going on *now*?' he said.

'I don't know . . .'

'Do you think it's the Persian resistance?'

'Don't be stupid. They wouldn't dare attack our camp.' But as we rode back to the horse lines, Charm kept looking over her shoulder.

'What's wrong?' Tydeos said.

'Nothing.'

'Yes, there is! You've been acting like a scared foal ever since Zadracarta. Don't worry, Alexander's not about to let anyone kidnap you again.'

Charm shook her head. Her hands trembled as she swapped my bridle for my halter and muzzle so she could take me for my roll.

I was rubbing my mane in the sand when I smelt Demetrius. He had been down to the horse lines to see Aura and the golden filly several times since we arrived. Normally, he let the filly – now named Caspia after the sea where we'd rescued her – lick his hands. But today he pushed Caspia's nose aside and hurried straight up to Charm. 'You haven't said anything to the king about the Mardians, have you?' he whispered, glancing over his shoulder.

'Of course not, Sir! Why?'

'Because he's just arrested Philotas!'

'Oh, Zeus!' Charm's hands flew to her mouth. She let go of my lead rein and seemed to forget me completely. I took advantage of this to get down for another roll – bliss!

Demetrius dodged my waving hooves and took her elbow. 'I can't even get in to see him. Hephaestion and Craterus are interrogating poor Philo, and they're arresting people all over the place. Security's tight. No one can get into or out of the town or the camp without a pass. The king is in a terrible mood.'

'He's found out about the plot, hasn't he?' Charm whispered, trembling like a foal.

'He must have. It's the only explanation. I can't stay, there are too many people around. I think I'm being watched. If something happens to me, remember to say the Mardians kidnapped you and the horse against your will. Whatever Philo says, I'll back you up.' He cast a frightened look over his shoulder as some of Craterus' men pushed through the horse lines and marched our way. 'They're coming! I've got to go before they see us together. I'm really sorry I got you into this, Charmeia. May Zeus help us all!'

I rolled over one more time and grunted with pleasure. Charm gave me a distracted look. By the time she pulled me to my feet and looked for Demetrius again, he had gone.

Groom-gossip at the time was wild. They said a hundred of Alexander's closest officers and friends had been stoned to death after being named by Philotas under torture, and that Alexander had sent some men on racing camels to Ecbatana to arrest General Parmenio.

I don't know how much of this was true. Knowing our

grooms, they were probably exaggerating. But every day Demetrius failed to turn up to see Aura, Charm got more anxious. Alexander didn't ride me in all that time, or even come down to the horse lines, which was probably just as well, considering the state Charm was in.

Then, ten days after Philotas was arrested, the order came to shave off Zephyr's mane.

Charm buried her face in her hands as the yellow hair fell to the ground. There was no surer sign that Philotas was dead. Our grooms breathed a sigh of relief and said that would be the end of it, because Alexander had now punished everyone involved in the plot. But Charm and I knew he had not.

A present from Ecbatana

The next morning, we see Alexander again. He is wearing his demon-horned helmet and his Persian cloak, and he strides down to the horse lines as if he owns half the world – which he almost does, now. Hephaestion follows, dark shadows under his eyes. The rest of the Guard hurry behind, though there is still no sign of Demetrius. A new man called Peucestas carries the shield we took from Troy.

Alexander orders our grooms to get us ready for a parade. He taps his foot impatiently as Charm bridles me and puts on my cloth. His presence makes her hands shake, so it takes her twice as long as usual. She darts the king frightened glances as she adds the strings of silly tassels.

Alexander takes my rein from her without a word. He taps my shoulder until I settle on my knees for him. Then we lead the way to the parade ground. Out of the corner of my eye, I see Charm holding Tydeos' hand so tightly that her knuckles are white.

Some of the men are already assembled in their silent squares. Others hurry across to join them. It is a very big, impressive parade. Alexander rides me to my place at the front, and the Guard line up behind me. Petasios, Electra, Borealis, Apollo, Harpinna, Hades – only Aura is missing. Instead of my favourite mare, Hoplite stands at the end of the line with the new man Peucestas on his back, nervously carrying the big shield of Achilles. My colt is dancing in excitement, so I nip him on the nose to tell him to behave.

Alexander jerks my rein. 'Stop that, Bucephalas! Don't *you* let me down, as well.'

I don't know what he means. I would never let him down. I chew my tassels, expecting the men to begin their manoeuvres. But Alexander does not give the order, and the trumpets remain silent. The wind flutters the banners as everyone waits.

Finally, we see a puff of dust in the distance on the road from the west. Alexander grips my rein tighter and mutters, 'At last! *This* will teach them all to plot behind my back.'

I can smell the camel already. It comes galloping across the parade ground towards us, startling Hoplite into a rear. His young rider only just manages to keep hold of the Achilles shield. The camel's rider is carrying a round object wrapped in a cloak. Now we are closer, I see the material is stiff with blood. Flies buzz around it as he throws it down in front of us. It bounces once, and a man's head rolls out.

I snort at the head in surprise. It STINKS. I can't tell whose it is, because its life-smell has been replaced by the foul battlefield one. Its eyes are open, but its ghost has long gone. Alexander has been expecting my reaction, and holds me firmly between his legs and hands, while I paw the ground in agitation.

The other horses of the Guard snort at the head, too. The men in the front ranks stir uneasily. Whispers pass back through the squares, rippling to the edge of the ground, where our grooms are standing on the baggage carts to see.

Alexander waits until everyone is silent again. He draws his sword and points it at the head and its swarm of flies. No one dares say a word.

'That is how I deal with traitors!' he calls in a shrill voice. 'General Parmenio dared plot to assassinate me and put his son Philotas on the throne of Macedonia! I sent his death warrant to Ecbatana. Take a good look as you parade past, and satisfy yourselves this is really the general's head. Then go back to your tents and write letters to your families. We'll be pushing further east soon, so this is the last chance you'll get to write home for a while. You need not worry. Philotas named everyone involved in the plot, and I have rooted out and punished all the traitors. I know the rest of you are faithful to me, so I will reward you by not charging the normal fee to post your letters home. Every man who has left family or a loved one at home will, in addition, receive a one talent bonus for continuing with me in pursuit of Bessus. Those in the baggage train who write to their families will receive half a talent each.'

More uneasy whispers ripple through the assembled men, but they are too disciplined to break ranks or show more reaction than that. By the time Alexander backs me away from General Parmenio's head and takes the Guard to the side of the ground, the army is silent again.

The trumpets blare to start the parade.

Alexander twists my mane around his fingers and watches with a fixed expression as the men file past the general's head.

It is like when we watched them kiss the *Iliad*, back in Ecbatana. Alexander is tense at first, then relaxes as more and more of his herd troop past the head without stopping. Some of the men glance down at it and quickly away. A few go white and dart terrified glances at the king. One youngster trembles so much, he drops his pike. He picks it up, red-faced, and runs after his division. It is all very boring, and I chew off three of my tassels before they have finished.

Finally, Alexander rides me back to the horse lines and dismounts. As he hands my rein to Charm, he looks hard at her. 'I want you to write a letter as well, Charmides,' he says. 'I don't want Bucephalas' groom to miss out on the bonus.'

Charm bites her lip. She whispers, 'But I haven't got any family to write to, Sir.'

'That doesn't matter. There must be someone you can write to. The Amazon queen, perhaps? I know you two were close.'

Charm goes even paler, and her hands start to tremble again. 'But I don't know where the Amazons live! How will the letter get to her, Sir?'

Alexander gives her an impatient look. 'Someone else, then! That's an order, Charmides.'

'But Sir, I can't write . . .'

Alexander does not hear her faint protest. He waves her away and calls Hephaestion across. 'As from today, you're to take command of half Philotas' cavalry,' he says. 'I need someone I can trust in charge of them.'

Hephaestion looks no happier about this than Charm did about writing a letter. 'But I want to stay with you—'

'No arguments! I can easily find someone else keen to

watch my back in exchange for a place at the king's table.'
Seeing Hephaestion's stricken expression, he sighs and says in
a gentler tone. 'You've deserved this promotion for some time,
my friend. I've been selfish keeping you at my side so long.'

'But Alex, I *want* to be at your side! I don't care about
promotion.'

'Nonsense. Every man cares about promotion. Look at that
idiot Philo! I knew he had his greedy eyes on my throne, right
from the start. He got what he deserved.' Pressing a hand to
his forehead, he strides back to his pavilion, his cloak billowing in the breeze.

Hephaestion stares after him, tears in his eyes.

Embarrassed, Charm slowly takes the remaining tassels and
my cloth off me. She darts a glance at the new member of the
guard, who has propped the Achilles shield against a post so
he can talk to Hoplite and rub his ears. Hoplite seems relieved
someone loves him, and is making the most of the attention.
The other members of the Guard are also lingering with their
horses, reluctant to go after the king.

Charm sidles up to Hephaestion and whispers in a tight
voice, 'Sir? What happened to Demetrius?'

Hephaestion presses his lips together and strokes Petasios,
who is tethered next to me as usual. 'This is a bad business,
Charmeia, a very bad business,' he says softly. 'Demetrius
wasn't tortured, I saw to that. Philo was a different matter.
He plotted to kill the king! We had to find out who else was
involved. Craterus did most of the rough stuff, but I had to
be there because Alex said the son of Zeus-Ammon couldn't
get involved in such things, and he needed me to watch in his
place. I hope I never have to do anything like that again.'

He takes a deep breath, as if remembering something very

bad. Then he continues in a brighter tone. 'Now General Parmenio's gone, everything will be better, you'll see. Alex never liked sharing the command with him. You know how they were always arguing. Old Parmenio treated him like a little boy, and Alex never liked that, not even when we were small. Craterus is going to be his second-in-command now. This is a fresh start for us all, like when we were campaigning back on the Macedonian borders. That was a good time, wasn't it? You needn't be afraid, Charmeia. The bad stuff's over now. Just . . .' He glances at the king's pavilion. 'Just be careful what you write in your letter.'

Charm stiffens. Before she can say anything else, Hephaestion smiles at her, pats Petasios and hurries after Alexander.

I nudge Charm to remind her I haven't had my roll yet, and she clutches my mane and presses her face to my neck. 'Oh, Bucephalas! Alexander's *never* going to stop, is he? He's just going to go on and on fighting, until everyone is dead! Poor Demetrius! He'd never have got involved in a plot to kill the king! He only wanted to go home. And how could Alexander throw General Parmenio's head on to the ground like that, in front of the whole army? Why does he have to keep killing everyone? *Why?*'

She ought to know by now. She's been round horses long enough.

When two stallions challenge each other for leadership of the herd, it is natural for the stronger horse to dominate the weaker. This battle has been a long time coming. General Parmenio was a strong boss. He would never submit to Alexander, so the battle had to be to the death. And all the other members of the herd had to see the result, so that they would think twice about challenging Alexander.

Sometimes, there is just no other way.

Charm writes a letter

All the grooms are writing letters, even those who have no families and can't read. They all want their half-talent bonus, because if they save up enough money they'll be able to buy their freedom when they get back to Macedonia. Alexander knows most of them can't write, so he has sent one of the army scribes down to the horse lines to do it for them.

Charm and Tydeos sit on a pile of cloths near my head, where it is quieter. They have their pieces of flattened grass on their laps, but so far without marks because the scribe is busy.

'You could always write to Queen Ada back in Halicarnassus,' Tydeos says. 'She'd remember you. She might even send us some more of her honey cakes. That'd be good!'

Charm gives him a disgusted look. 'I don't want that old scribe to write my letter for me. I don't trust him. Hephaestion said . . . oh, never mind.'

'I'll do it for you,' Tydeos says.

She darts him a surprised look. '*You* can write?'

'I'm not as thick as I look!' Tydeos grins at her. 'We all had to learn at my last place. Our master thought it would make us better grooms. Takes me ages, though, and it makes my hand hurt. So keep it short.'

Charm looks a bit happier. 'Is that who you're going to write to? Your old master?'

Tydeos makes a face. 'No. I'm going to write to my mother back in Thessaly and tell her I'll be home soon with enough money to start my own horse farm! I'll buy a few cheap mares, sneak them in with someone else's stallion, and sell their foals to buy more mares.' He looks sideways at Charm. 'A whole talent would be even better. We might afford a stallion, then, too.'

Charm's face closes. 'Just help me with my letter. I'll tell you what to put.'

Tydeos grins and picks up the stylus. 'All right, but go slow. It's been ages since I did this.'

This is what Charm told Tydeos to write:

Dear Queen Ada,

We are in Persia. Bucephalas is fine. He has a three-year-old colt called Hoplite and a five-year-old filly called Electra, who are both in the Guard. King Alexander is fine. General Parmenio is dead. I can't stop thinking like a slave yet, because the horse bond is too strong, but one day I will.

Love, Charmeia.

Tydeos gave her a funny look. But he kept making marks on the flattened grass until he had finished what she said. Then he frowned and added something else at the bottom. Charm did not notice, because she couldn't read.

I only know because of what happened afterwards.

Alexander reads seventy thousand letters

The letters were collected up and loaded into carts to start the long journey back through our string of garrisons to Anatolia, Greece and Macedonia. I don't think any of them contained squealing threats like the ones Alexander and King Darius used to send each other. They were probably nickers and whinnies, like the letter Charm wrote to Queen Ada. Writing them seemed to calm the men. When Alexander announced we wouldn't be spending the winter here, after all, but would be marching on after Bessus to finish the campaign, they began to ready their weapons and pack without complaint.

But the trumpets didn't sound the order to break our lake-side camp for many days. Alexander moved out of the town and shut himself alone in his pavilion, where the lamps burned day and night. When he finally emerged, he had dark rings around his eyes and squinted in the sunlight. He seemed much happier, though. He even smiled at some of the grooms as he brought a bag of apples down to the horse lines for us.

Alexander took my muzzle against his chest, and I inhaled his sweet sherbet smell. While I nudged him for apples, he said quietly without turning round, 'Charmides, tell me every-thing you know about this horse bond.'

Charm, who was standing tensely in the shadows nearby, started like a nervous filly. 'H-horse bond, Sir?'

'I read your letter.'

She shivered all over and fiddled with my mane. I blew at her, happy to be with my two favourite humans.

Charm spoke without looking at Alexander. 'It's a magic bond, Sir. The Amazon queen told me it was called a horse bond, but Queen Ada saw it first, back in Halicarnassus. They say it's between me and Bucephalas and . . . you, Sir. I'm sorry. I don't know how it happened.'

Alexander frowned at her red curls, which she had tied up with a twist of blue and white cord left over from my tassels. 'Magic? Are you sure?'

'I'm not sure of anything, Sir. But the Amazons said it hap-pens sometimes between a human and a horse. Queen Penthesilea said she'd never seen it work between a horse and two humans before, but she says it won't break until . . . one of us dies.' It was a whisper.

Alexander laughed. 'You don't want to take too much

notice of what the Amazon queen said, Charmides! It's obvious she ran off home because she was afraid I might put her immortality to the test.' He frowned, and his hand shot out and gripped her chin, forcing her to look at him. 'Is it true what Demetrius said, that the Mardians forced you to go with them back in Zadracarta?'

Charm started to say yes, it was true, then burst into tears.

Alexander sighed. 'Tell me the truth, Charmides,' he said. 'Don't you start lying to me, too.'

'I'm sorry!' she sniffed. 'I should never have gone with the Mardians. I shouldn't have let Demetrius talk me into it! Poor Demetrius, he was only upset about Aura losing her foal, he'd never have hurt you . . . it's all my fault he's dead. And Philotas, and General Parmenio, and all those others . . .'

Alexander shook his head and let her go. 'Philotas and General Parmenio were going to kill me and take my throne,' he said in a tough voice. 'They had to die. But Demetrius isn't dead, you silly girl. Do you really think I could give the order to have one of my closest friends stoned? He's merely under arrest. He's out of the Guard, of course. I can't trust him any more to carry my shield. But for now he's alive, and so are most of the other idiots Philotas named.'

She stared at him, her eyes still wet, but hope lighting up her face. 'Really?'

'Don't you believe the word of your king? I've created a new division in my army called the Disciplinary Company. They'll serve in that until they prove their loyalty to me, or die trying.'

Charm wet her lips and bowed her head. She said miserably, 'Then you'd better put me in the Disciplinary Company, too.'

Alexander narrowed his eyes. 'Don't be silly, Charmides.

You're my groom. You have to stay with me and Bucephalas. Besides, you came back of your own accord, didn't you? I forgive you.'

Her gaze flew to his face. 'I'll never try to leave you again, Alexander, Sir,' she whispered. 'I promise.'

Alexander nodded. He gave Charm another long look. Then his lips twisted up at one corner. 'Ah, Charmides! Aren't you even a little bit angry I read your letter?'

'I . . . you're the king, and the son of Zeus, Sir. You can do anything you like.'

He chuckled. 'Hmm. I think some of the men might disagree. But I've sent your letter on to Queen Ada now, so the honey cakes you asked for will no doubt arrive eventually. When they do, I'll send them down here for Bucephalas.'

It was Charm's turn to look surprised. 'Honey cakes, Sir? But I didn't ask for—' She broke off and looked at Tydeos, who was combing out Petasios' tail. He flushed.

Alexander frowned at Tydeos, and ordered him to move Petasios to the other end of the line so Hoplite could join the horses of the Guard. As I whinnied after my red friend, Alexander told Charm she should never trust a scribe, and promised he'd send Prince Ochus to teach her how to write her own letters, because the boy had more sense than all his men put together.

Obviously, Prince Ochus wrote only good things about Alexander in *his* letter to his grandmother and sisters in Susa.

The Disciplinary Company

When we left Lake Seistan, things had changed. By executing General Parmenio and Philotas and punishing the others involved in the plot, Alexander had dominated all immediate challenges for the herd. As he mounted me to lead the army onwards, his eyes gleamed with a new, cold power.

I was still the boss, of course. But with Hephaestion leading half of Philotas' old herd, Demetrius in the Disciplinary Company, and Aura still suckling Caspia, the Guard consisted of:

Electra, carrying Laomedon.

Borealis, carrying Leonnatus.

Apollo, carrying Perdiccas.

Hades, carrying Iolaus.

Harpinna, carrying Ptolemy.

Hoplite, carrying the new man Peucestas with the Achilles shield.

A pretty grey Persian mare carrying King Darius' brother Oxarthes, who had joined us at Zadracarta to help look for Bessus.

Alexander gave the other half of Philotas' cavalry to Cleitus, who, if you remember, saved Alexander's life at the Granicus. Cleitus mounted poor, short-maned Zephyr, who spent the whole of the first day searching the snow-covered rocks for Philotas' ghost. It is always sad to lose your rider, and worrying to carry a new one until you know you can trust them. Mares worry about this more than stallions.

The new Disciplinary Company marched in the middle, made up of the men Philotas had named and those Alexander did not trust any more after reading their letters. These men shuffled along on foot with their heads bowed in shame. Demetrius was among them, carrying a short spear and looking very small. One of the Persians who had joined us at Zadracarta had been promoted to be their boss. He rode a

406

Persian horse and carried a long whip.

'Feel free to beat any man who steps out of line,' Alexander told their Persian boss as we set out. 'I want these men in the front line at every battle, and those who refuse to fight will get garrison duty at the furthest outposts of my empire. They can grumble about me all they like among themselves. But if any one of them so much as looks at a man from another company, you will report him to me and give him ten lashes. Understand?'

The Persian nodded gravely. 'It will be exactly as you say, King Iskander.'

Alexander frowned at Demetrius and wheeled me back with an impatient jerk on my rein. 'And make sure you keep a careful record!' he added. 'Those who serve me faithfully and fight well can win transferral back to their old company. But they have to prove themselves worthy of my trust.'

The Persian smiled. 'You are truly a Great King, Iskander.'

Which, if you ask me, was a clever thing to say. It certainly made Alexander smile and sit straighter as I cantered past the long column of men and horses to take our place at the head of the army. He was wearing his Troy helmet again with the white plumes, and before we left he renamed the town on the shores of the lake where all the arrests had taken place.

For once, though, he didn't call it Alexandria.

From that day, the place where Alexander had got rid of all the challengers for his herd became known as Prophthasia – which, in case your Greek is a bit rusty, means 'anticipation' or 'hope'.

Different! But, anticipation of WHAT?

TWENTY-SIXTH HOOFPRINT
BACTRIA, 329 BC

Zeus hides the edge of the world

To reach Bactria, King Darius' brother said we had two choices:

Go back the way we had come until we met the road from Zadracarta, and then turn due east (the easy route, but also the one Bessus expected us to take).

Continue east through the mountains, turn north along the Kabul valley, and double back over the Caucasus range (supposed to be impossible in winter).

No prizes for guessing which way Alexander chose.

We climbed high, right into the clouds. There was not much snow if we were careful to stay on the road, but it was *cold*. Every time we camped, we had to paw through the frozen crust for thin yellow stalks to graze. On all sides snow-capped peaks pierced the sky, while the wind cut through our winter coats.

At night I did my best to shield young Hoplite from the weather. Our grooms folded our cloths over our backs, and we all squeezed up close for warmth. But poor Borealis on the end of the line shivered through the nights with his tail tucked between his legs, and his ribs stuck out even more than mine. Charm sneaked extra handfuls of barley into his nosebag, but it made little difference. Our riders were no happier, hunched in their cloaks with their bare legs shaking and their fingers too swollen to grip our reins. It was a good job we didn't have to fight any battles on that march, I can tell you, because I'm not sure any of us could have moved faster than a trot, and the men could barely grip their spears. Lots of ghosts, human and horse, shivered into the freezing air during that march.

Besides wanting to catch the traitor Bessus unprepared by attacking him from the rear, there was another reason Alexander took the hardest route. But we horses only found out what it was when we stopped in the shadow of the mountains to dig the foundations for yet another Macedonian garrison: Alexandria-under-the-Caucasus. Ha, there's a surprise.

Our riders fell silent as they considered the line of jagged peaks that barred our way. We chewed our bits, and poor Borealis' ears flicked back in misery. But Alexander stared up at the snow-bound mountains with the familiar light in his eyes that meant trouble.

He rode me forward a few paces and whispered, 'Look, Bucephalas! The Caucasus Mountains! Aristotle says you can see the edge of the world from the highest pass! That's where Zeus chained immortal Prometheus to a rock as punishment for giving men the gift of fire, and sent a vulture to peck out his liver every day for a thousand years. Prometheus grew a new liver overnight, so the torture could begin afresh. Maybe

I'd better make the proper sacrifices before I go up there, eh?'

He pulled my ear, like he used to do back in Macedonia. Then his face took on the stony expression he'd worn most days since we left Lake Seistan, and he wheeled me back to join the Guard, shouting for someone to fetch Charm. The others all looked at Iolaus, who trotted off on Hades grumbling under his breath that he wasn't a messenger boy.

Perdiccas cleared his throat. 'Alex, are we stopping here before we—?'

Alexander cut him off. 'If I were Bessus, I'd set an ambush in one of these passes. We've seven routes to choose from. Which one would you take the army through, if you were commander?'

Perdiccas stared up at the snowy peaks and stroked Apollo's winter-furred neck. 'I'd choose the lowest, Alex, with the easiest climb and the least snow. I know it'll be thawing soon, but the men are half starved and the horses are no better. They can't go on much longer without grazing.'

Alexander nodded. 'That's what I thought you'd say. If Bessus has heard we're coming this way he'll assume the same, so the lowest pass is out. But does he still have that treacherous horsemaster with him, whispering in his ear about me?'

'We could take one of the middle passes to confuse him,' Laomedon ventured.

'Or split the army up, send the baggage train through the lowest pass and take the cavalry over one of the others?' Ptolemy suggested.

Alexander gave him a scathing look. 'Don't be stupid! That's hostile territory over there. The last thing we want to do now is divide our men, when Bessus might be waiting on the other side to pick us off. Have you learnt nothing?

Where's Iolaus got to – ah, at last!'

Hades trotted up, with Charm perched awkwardly on his withers in front of Iolaus. My groom gave me an anxious look. After satisfying herself that I was all right, she slithered off Hades and bowed her head to Alexander.

He frowned down at her. 'Any dreams about these mountains, Charmides?'

She gazed up at the snowy peaks and shivered. 'No, Sir, no dreams. I'm sorry.'

Alexander smiled. 'Good! Then we'll take the highest pass. It's the most direct, and Darius' brother tells me the land on the other side of this range is fertile. The crops should be growing by the time we get down, so we'll be able to rest and eat before we fight. Someone bring me a sheep! I need to make a sacrifice to my father Zeus.' He glared at the Guard, who were all looking at Iolaus again. 'Why is everyone so slow to obey me lately? *Move!*'

The cooks used what little food remained to give the army a hot meal before tackling the pass, and we horses had double rations in our nosebags that night. In the morning, we set out on the long climb over the Caucasus Mountains. No one complained that we were taking the highest pass. In fact, those of the Guard who had been in the Aristotle school with Alexander seemed almost as excited about seeing the edge of the world as he was.

It was a long, slow, leg-trembling climb. The road from Lake Seistan had been bad enough for horses, but this was much steeper. Halfway up, our riders tied little leather bags over our hooves like they did back at the Persian Gates, and we struggled on through knee-deep snow to the crest of the pass. We were so high up, and the air was so thin and cold, we could barely breathe. Poor Borealis staggered from one side of the path to the other, his flanks heaving and blood dripping from his nose.

Alexander urged me on with his strong legs every time I tried to slow down, so we reached the top ahead of everyone else. While I gulped the thin air and tried to turn my tail to the wind, Alexander shaded his eyes and squinted eastwards for a long while, his heart beating very fast. The army was strung out below us like a snake, winding all the way back down to the newest Alexandria. Clouds filled the valleys behind us. I could not see anything under them.

As the Guard caught up, Alexander turned, frustrated. 'Do you see it, gentlemen? Can anyone see the ocean at the edge of the world?'

'I just see clouds,' Perdiccas said.

'I see water . . . I think,' Ptolemy said.

'Maybe Zeus is hiding the edge of the world from us because he doesn't want us to go there?' Leonnatus suggested, stroking Borealis' sweaty neck. The brown stallion's legs were still trembling from the climb. 'Alex, I don't think my horse is going to make it much further without a rest—'

Alexander scowled. 'We haven't time to rest! Zeus is hiding the ocean, precisely because he *wants* us to go there and see it with our own eyes!'

Then Iolaus, who had been sulking at the back on Hades, looked the other way and groaned. 'Forget the ocean . . . look what Bessus has done!'

Alexander rode me to the other side of the pass and uttered a curse. The rest of the Guard joined us and stared silently.

It was bad. Below us, in a shimmering haze, lay the valleys of Bactria, and the fertile fields Darius' brother had promised.

But instead of the crops that should have been growing in them, we could see only black earth and deserted villages. Through the haze of smoke, a river glimmered in the distance. Bessus had used the same trick the Persians had tried at Tarsus – he'd burnt all the available food.

'Zeus help us all,' Leonnatus whispered in dismay.

Alexander turned on him with a scowl. 'Pull yourselves together, gentlemen! This isn't the first time we've been hungry. We'll just have to press on. At least it doesn't look as if he plans to fight us here. The plains on the banks of the Oxus will be much better for our phalanx and the cavalry. We'll soon finish him off when we get there.'

The Guard stared at the distant river with hopeless eyes. They knew that what seems close from the top of a pass is a lot further away than it looks. It was all too much for Borealis, who gave a horrible groan and crumpled into the snow. Even as Leonnatus leapt off him, Borealis' ghost rose slowly from his body and limped over to the rocks at the side of the trail.

I shivered all over.

My friend! My solid brown friend! DEAD!

I raised my head and let out a wild neigh that was answered back down the trail by Petasios and several other horses.

Alexander jerked my rein and shouted at the Guard to stop being so defeatist. He said they'd soon find more horses once they got out of the mountains, and Bessus was obviously scared of us or he wouldn't have burnt all the crops and fled.

Poor Borealis didn't even get the next city named after him, because Alexander was in such a hurry to catch Bessus and the horsemaster that none of us stopped there. The most important city in Bactria kept its silly name of Balkh.

Deserters

Our enemy's trail led to the river we'd seen from the top of the pass, but first we had to cross a horrible desert, which was the last thing we needed after tackling snow-bound mountains in winter. Alexander, however, made the men march day and night, and kept pushing me into a trot when I would rather have walked. By the time we reached the River Oxus, and discovered Bessus had burnt all the bridges to stop us following him across, only Hephaestion's cavalry was still with us.

Alexander scowled at the smoking remains of a bridge and cursed under his breath. 'This Bessus is getting seriously annoying,' he muttered.

Hephaestion smiled. 'You've got him on the run, Alex. We'll catch him. We've just crossed the Caucasus Mountains in winter with nothing to eat but our mules, and marched across a desert with nothing to drink but wine. Nothing stops us. The men worship you, Alex. They'll do anything you tell them, because they know you'll always get them through the tough times, and you'll always be the first into battle. They might fear you sometimes but they will always love you. I never realized before you gave me my command, but you're like a god to them.'

Alexander cheered up a bit at this. 'That's not surprising. The oracle did say I'm the son of Zeus, after all.'

He ordered the Guard to light fires as a guide for the rest of our herd, then rode me slowly beside Petasios while he and Hephaestion made plans to cross the river. As flames crackled to life along the riverbank, he squinted into the darkness and demanded, 'Where's the rest of my army? They're so slow!'

'They'll be here, Alex,' Hephaestion said. 'They haven't got old Parmenio to lead them home now, have they?'

Alexander smiled grimly. 'Only his ghost.'

Men and horses appeared out of the night in a straggling line, exhausted, and finally the baggage train trailed in with our grooms. But not all our herd had followed us across the desert. The Thessalian cavalry had discovered there was a direct road west from Bessus' captured city, and gone that way instead.

Alexander's hand trembled on my rein as Commander Cleitus brought him the bad news. Apparently, the Thessalians had requested that their final pay and bonuses be sent to Ecbatana so they could pick them up on their way back to Greece. While I stretched out my nose and nickered to Zephyr, pleased to see she had made it across the mountains and the desert, Alexander said to Cleitus in a dangerously quiet tone, 'And you just let them go?'

'What else could I do?' The old cavalryman met his gaze. 'They were volunteers, remember? General Parmenio's execution upset them. They'd had enough.'

'And what about you, Cleitus?' Alexander said, still quietly. 'You served under General Parmenio. Have *you* had enough?'

'My cavalry will follow you until we've finished what we came to do,' Cleitus said carefully.

'And mine!' Hephaestion said. Putting a hand on Alexander's arm, he whispered, 'Commander Cleitus saved your life at the Granicus, Alex. You don't have to worry about his loyalty. Your army has followed you through snowbound mountains and across deserts to get here. We've lost a few thousand Greeks who didn't want to fight in the first place, that's all. Half their mounts were exhausted, anyway. We've plenty of men left to deal with Bessus.'

Alexander closed his eyes and gripped my mane. He controlled his breathing and nodded to Cleitus, his face stony. 'Thank you for the message. Hephaestion, go and arrange the necessary funds for the Thessalians. Tell your men to start making rafts with their tent covers. Use your horses' hay to stuff them so they'll float. We'll start the crossing tonight.'

Cleitus gave him a sharp look. 'Tonight, Alexander?'

'Yes, tonight! I've got to catch Bessus and that traitor of a horsemaster before the rest of my army decides to leave me.'

He acted tough until Cleitus left. But when we were alone in the night with the black water of the Oxus sliding past us, the hugeness went out of him and he gripped my mane in confusion.

'I don't understand, Bucephalas! Why are they all so scared of following me these days? First the Amazons, then General Parmenio and that idiot Philo, and my shield-bearer Demetrius. And now the Thessalians. Who's going to be next? I can't stop now, when we're within sight of the edge of the world and immortality! Even if the oracle was wrong about that, how can I possibly go home to Pella and hunt lions, after having all of Persia kneel at my feet?'

I nudged him to remind him I wanted my supper before someone stitched it into a raft, and he sighed. 'Ah, my faithful horse! At least *you'll* never leave me. Come on, let's see if we can find your groom.'

Harpinna leads the herd

It took us five days to cross that river. We horses swam across with lines of rafts tied to our tails, then swam back again to collect more rafts, and back across again, until we had crossed the Oxus seven times. We saw some of Bessus' scouts on the other side when we resumed our march. They took one look at us and fled across the plain. I don't think they were expecting to see us so soon – ha! Alexander let them go so they could take the bad news to their boss.

A few days afterwards, a messenger arrived from the Persian resistance and told Alexander that they now had a new leader called Spitamenes, who would hand the traitor Bessus over to us so we could finish things here and take our men home. All Alexander had to do was send a Macedonian officer with a small escort to collect the prisoner.

'It's bound to be another trick!' Alexander muttered. 'Look what happened last time I agreed to meet Bessus, back at the tomb of Cyrus the Great.'

'But the message is from this new man, Spitamenes,' Leonnatus pointed out. 'If he's telling the truth, Bessus is a prisoner.'

Since he'd lost Borealis, Leonnatus was now riding Aura, who kept neighing for the golden Mardian filly. I gave her a special nicker, because I knew what a sad time this was for her. It was even harder for Aura than normal, because of having lost her own foal.

Oxarthes looked a bit confused at the mention of Cyrus the Great's tomb. But he nodded and said, 'I know Spitamenes. He is an excellent fighter who once fought in my brother Darius' army. He comes from this area, and he follows our prophet Zoroaster and worships the sacred flame. I believe he'll hand the traitor over as he promised.'

Alexander gave King Darius' brother a narrow-eyed look. 'Maybe. And maybe the message came from Bessus himself, in the hope of luring me to a remote place where he can kill me. I want a volunteer to take five thousand men and go to meet this Spitamenes to arrange the transfer of the prisoner. Once there, you'll leave most of the men in hiding and go on with a small escort as requested, but take a trumpeter with you in case there's trouble. The rest of us will make camp here. When you're satisfied it's not a trick, send a message to me.' His eyes glinted, like they used to back in Greece whenever he dared his friends to volunteer for a special mission. 'It's dangerous. Whoever goes will be a hero.'

The Guard glanced at one another. No one looked very keen. Iolaus fiddled with Hades' mane, obviously hoping he wouldn't get the job.

Oxarthes said, 'I'd happily do it, King Alexander. But they asked for a Macedonian, and if I go Spitamenes will probably kill me. He does not understand your vision of Persians, Macedonians and Greeks forming one nation.'

'Nor, it seems, do most of my Macedonians,' Alexander muttered. But if anyone heard, they kept quiet.

'I'll go,' Ptolemy said.

The others breathed again, and Harpinna was soon trotting off proudly at the head of a herd of five thousand men and horses. As Ptolemy urged her into a canter, she made herself huge and arched her speckled neck.

Over the next few days, I was lonely in the horse lines without Petasios or Borealis. Charm took pity on me and tethered Apollo next to me instead. He was not as solid as Borealis, nor as familiar as Petasios, and he wasn't my own colt like Hoplite. But I'd known him a long time, and he had not complained once going over the mountains or across the desert. After giving him flat ears to warn him not to steal any of my hay, I put my teeth gently on his withers and we began to mutual groom. BLISS!

By the time Charm came back from settling Aura, who was still prone to fits of frantic neighing for Caspia, we had reached each other's rumps. She smiled at our half-shut eyes and scratching teeth. 'There, Bucephalas,' she said, patting my neck. 'That's better, isn't it? Don't worry, Harpinna will be back soon. King Alexander's had a message from Ptolemy. It doesn't seem to be a trick, and I haven't had any bad dreams about it. We're going to collect Bessus tomorrow.'

Groom-gossip was all about Bessus that night. They said Alexander had told Spitamenes to chain the traitor naked to a post at the side of the road with a slave collar around his neck. They said he was going to drag him to death behind his chariot, the same way he had killed the boss of Gaza. This was clearly stupid, because we didn't bring any of our chariots over the Oxus with us.

Also, the grooms didn't know about the trick at the tomb of Cyrus the Great when Bessus was supposed to have returned Charm in exchange for Prince Ochus, but brought the horsemaster and his knife instead. If they had, they might have known Alexander wanted the traitor to have a much slower death.

The punishment for traitors

In the morning, Alexander orders Tydeos to get Aura ready for Prince Ochus, and tells Charm to put all my tassels and my best parade cloth on me. Then we lead the army up the road to find Bessus, Ochus riding proudly on Aura beside his Uncle Oxarthes.

The two grey mares make a good pair, but Aura's dapples are darkest and most beautiful. She neighed a few times to Caspia as we left the lines, but being up front with the Guard puts her out of hearing distance of the filly, and she soon pricks her ears and relaxes her mouth to Ochus' gentle hands.

When we come to the chained Bessus, Alexander halts me and stares down at him with a funny expression. You humans always look strange without your clothes on, because we horses don't often see you undressed. Bessus' muscular body is covered in black curly hair and lots of bruises. The heavy collar around his neck is made of wood and chained to a post at hock height, so he is on his knees. A deep cut across his forehead trickles blood down the side of his face where it forms a crust in his whiskers. Flies are feasting on it. His hands are bound tightly behind him, and he hasn't got a tail to flick the flies away.

His black eyes glitter with hatred as he stares up at Alexander. He bares his teeth at Oxarthes and Ochus and says, 'I see Iskander has been forced to adopt King Darius' family, because he is too young and irresponsible to have any of his own.'

Alexander's eyes narrow. King Darius' brother rides his grey mare closer to the post and spits on the prisoner. 'Silence! You'll speak only when you're spoken to.'

But Bessus keeps grinning up at Alexander. 'What are you waiting for, Macedonian midget? Kill me! I know you want to. Your precious little groom's dead, you know. She ran off back in the Caspian Gates. By now, her bones will have been pecked clean by the crows.'

Alexander's fist clenches, but he keeps his hand away from his sword. Bessus obviously has no idea Charm found us.

Oxarthes snaps something in Persian, and an angry stream of squeals passes between them. Ochus listens silently, his face grave and his fist resting on the jewelled dagger in his belt.

Alexander motions Oxarthes back, and rides me up to the post so I am nearly stepping on the prisoner's legs. He frowns down at Bessus and asks, 'Why did you betray and kill your own king?'

Bessus bares his teeth. 'To please you, Iskander! You wanted Darius dead. I saved you the trouble. You should reward me and set me free.'

'I am Great King of Persia now, and you are a traitor! You'll die a traitor's death.'

'You'll never be Great King of Persia,' Bessus growls. 'The priests wouldn't bless you, would they? Only those of the royal blood can rule Persia. You're a barbarian invader, nothing more. Kill me, and have done with it.'

Alexander's breathing quickens. This time his hand does go to his sword, and Bessus' gaze follows it. His eyes glitter.

But Oxarthes touches the king's elbow and says, 'King Iskander, he killed my brother, who was the rightful Great King, and took the upright crown for himself. He must stand trial before a Persian court and be publicly executed in a painful manner. But first he must have his nose and ears cut off to show he is a traitor, in the way of our people.'

Bessus tugs at his bonds and squeals something in Persian, which Oxarthes ignores, although it makes Ochus bite his lip.

Alexander narrows his eyes. He draws his sword and lowers it to Bessus' right ear. Bessus cringes, and his sweat sharpens. 'I can do this quickly or slowly,' Alexander says. 'Tell me the truth! Where is my father's horsemaster?'

Bessus looks confused.

'You must remember! The Macedonian who was with you at the tomb of Cyrus the Great and tried to kill me. The one who killed my dog! He fled with you from the Caspian Gates.

Where did he go? Is he with Spitamenes?'

The prisoner bursts out laughing. 'How would I know? King Iskander conquers a hundred cities and defeats King Darius' immortal army, and he is worried about a lame barbarian from his own country who can hardly walk without his horse? Maybe you ought to look for him among the Scythians?' He laughs so much, he coughs up blood.

Alexander stares down at him in disgust. He puts his sword away and backs me further from the post. He looks thoughtfully at Prince Ochus and says, 'This man killed your father. It's about time you bloodied that dagger I gave you. Cut off his ears and nose for me. Don't be afraid. He can't hurt you now.'

Ochus swallows. He looks down at Bessus and shakes his head slightly.

'Let me have the honour, King Iskander,' Oxarthes says quickly, drawing his own dagger.

But Alexander rides me between the grey mare and the post so Oxarthes can't reach the prisoner. 'No,' he says. 'I want Prince Ochus to do it.'

'The prince is only ten.'

'When I was ten, I killed my first lion. When I was twelve, I tamed Bucephalas. When I was sixteen, I led an army into my first battle and killed a man for the first time! I'm not asking the boy to kill him, merely to take off a couple of ears and a nose. It doesn't matter if he makes a mess of it, because Bessus doesn't deserve to be treated any better. It'll be good training for when the boy is older and ready to fight at my side. Take out your dagger, Ochus, get down off that mare and do it. Come on. You're no coward, I know that.'

Slowly, Ochus slips off Aura's back and draws his dagger.

Bessus bares his teeth at him and rattles his chains. The prince hesitates. Bessus laughs and says something in Persian. Ochus' fist tightens on the dagger.

Alexander smiles coldly. 'Go on!'

But Ochus cannot do it. He sets the dagger to Bessus' ear, makes a line of blood and snatches his hand back. There are tears in his eyes when he turns to face us. 'Please, Uncle Alexander . . . let Uncle Oxarthes do it.'

Bessus laughs out loud. 'You'd better hurry up and sire yourself a son who can stomach the sight of blood, King Iskander! This pretty pup of Darius' will never be strong enough to sit on your throne after you've got yourself killed.'

Alexander leaps down off my back, seizes Ochus' hand and forces the blade against the prisoner's ear. '*Do it!*' he shouts. 'If you don't, I'll have you whipped for disobeying me in front of my men!'

Ochus shakes his head. 'No, I cannot . . .'

'You can, and you will!' Alexander hisses. He drags his hand down, and Bessus' ear half comes off, messily. Bessus screams. Ochus struggles free, drops the dagger, grabs Aura's reins and vaults on to her. He gallops back the way we came, past the long column of horses and men towards the tail of our army. I throw up my head and stare after them. No one is holding my rein, but I don't move. The bond with my rider is too strong.

Alexander is furious. All the men nearby are staring at him. His face flushes and his breathing quickens. He glares after Ochus and yells in a shrill voice, 'Since no one else seems willing to do it, I'll teach this traitor a lesson myself!'

He strides down the road, pushing startled men aside until he finds one of the carts handing out water to the troops. He grabs a stick from the surprised muleteer and comes back with it at a run. In my blind spot, the stick turns into a long Macedonian pike, and suddenly I am surrounded by ghosts.

Sweat bathes me. I am already disturbed by Bessus' smell, but Alexander's shouting upsets me even more. The king rains a flurry of blows on Bessus' back, grunting, '*That*'ll teach you to call me a barbarian midget! *That*'ll teach you to murder your rightful king! *That*'ll teach you to give sanctuary to my father's horsemaster!' The bond between us loosens. I whirl round and gallop after Aura.

Alexander stops, his stick raised for another blow. '*Bucephalas!*' he shouts, a note of terrible fear in his voice.

Out of the corner of my good eye, I see him frown at the stick in his hand as if he doesn't remember how it got there. He drops it and backs away from the prisoner, clutching his wild mane with blood-spattered hands.

The Guard stares at him in embarrassment and concern. No one says a word.

I hesitate, ashamed of my panic. But the blood is not Alexander's, and the only enemy in sight is chained to a post with a yoke around his neck. My rider does not need me. My favourite mare does.

I catch up with Aura at the baggage train, where we find Charm leading Caspia. Aura neighs to her adopted filly, but Caspia likes being with humans because the Mardians gave her goat's milk in the first few days of her life.

Charm stares at my empty cloth in horror. 'What happened to the king? Oh Zeus, Bessus didn't—?'

Ochus shakes his head. 'Not to worry, Charmeia. Uncle Alexander is fine. Bucephalas got loose while he was dealing with the prisoner, that is all.'

She gives the prince's face a closer look. I think she can tell he has been crying, but she doesn't mention it. 'Bucephalas wouldn't just run off! What happened, Ochus? Did Alexander send you back?'

Ochus sits very straight and smiles. He hides his sore hand from her. 'Everything is fine. Uncle Alexander and Uncle Oxarthes have Bessus prisoner now, and they are going to punish him for killing my father.'

Tydeos hurries up and takes Caspia from Charm so she can check me over for injury. Satisfied I am not hurt, she strokes my nose. 'Hear that, Tydeos? Alexander's caught Bessus! Maybe now he'll take us home.'

Some of the muleteers and grooms riding in the carts over-hear, and the news passes through the baggage train like one of Alexander's city fires. Men start to cheer. 'We're going home! It's nearly over! We've caught Bessus, and we're going home!'

Which only goes to show how little grooms and muleteers know about dominating. Bessus was merely a beaten stallion turned out of his own herd. The herd was still at large with a new, stronger stallion, and our enemy the horsemaster had escaped to create more trouble. Alexander still needed to show Spitamenes, the new leader of the Persian resistance, that he was boss.

Two kinds of prisoners

Before Alexander took the army north in search of Spitamenes, he sent Hephaestion's herd back to Balkh with the prisoner Bessus and instructions to collect the men we'd left at the River Oxus on the way. He sent Ochus, Charm and me with them. He also sent Peucestas and the shield of Achilles, because he wanted to ride Hoplite himself. He told the Guard that since he was the son of a god and nearly immortal, he didn't need a shield-bearer any more.

He told the men that my running off while he was interrogating the prisoner proved I needed a rest. He said the hard march had upset me and I was, after all, twenty-seven years old. Ha! My age had nothing to do with it, as you know. Besides, Alexander used the same excuse for Prince Ochus, saying the boy was over-tired, when he was only ten!

I don't know what he told Ochus in private. But when Alexander said goodbye to me in the lines, he stroked my nose, apologised for frightening me with the mule stick, and promised it would never happen again.

'Hephaestion will look after you and Charmides, Bucephalas,' he whispered, pulling my ear. 'It's time Hoplite saw some action, and this campaign is just the thing for him to cut his teeth on. Spitamenes is obviously scared, or he wouldn't have given me Bessus. It won't take me long to find my father's old horsemaster, then we can head back over the Caucasus and look for the edge of the world – only don't tell anyone, will you? I've still got to think of an excuse to persuade the army to follow me further east.'

Hoplite must have grown without my noticing. When Alexander vaulted on to him and my colt made himself huge, he looked like my reflection. We both had white hairs in our coats, though Hoplite's came from his mother, and mine were where my coat had grown over battle scars. He gave a cheeky little squeal and a buck, and Alexander laughed.

As I watched my proud colt trot off at the head of the army carrying the king, a shiver went through me. Abandoning Alexander on the roadside with Bessus was the first time I had ever left my rider of my own will. I hung my head as Tydeos boosted Charm on to my back, and even her fingers mutual grooming my withers did not make me feel better.

On Alexander's orders, Bessus was forced to run all the way back to Balkh behind a mule cart, naked but for his wooden yoke. His back bled from the beating Alexander had given him, and maggots seethed in the wounds where his nose and ears used to be. By the time we got back to Balkh, the traitor who had murdered his king was well and truly dominated.

This was just as well, because it was the most dominating our herd would do for a while.

Twenty-seventh Hoofprint
BALKH, 329–327 BC

Defeat

The stables in Balkh were cool and airy, built around courtyards filled with fountains and trees. They had the same smell as all other stables: horse sweat, dung, hay and barley. But the shame of leaving Alexander at the roadside upset me so much that I could not settle, and went off my feed. Despite Charm's care, my coat became dull, and my ribs stuck out like Borealis' had before he collapsed.

Charm spent ages trying to make my coat shine again with the wooden comb and olive oil, walked me by the river like she used to do in Pella, and added different treats to my manger to tempt me into eating:

Herbs – boring, boring, boring.
Apples – sweet and crunchy, but boring.
Dates – sticky, ugh.

Pomegranates – suspicious, so I left that whole feed without touching it.

Camel's milk – for foals!

But nothing could replace Alexander's hands on my reins, his voice in my ear, and his strong legs trembling with excitement against my sides. I thought I would die if he never rode me again.

Prince Ochus missed Alexander too. He wore a bandage around the two smallest fingers of his right hand, because Alexander had broken them when he tried to make him cut off Bessus' ear. But he kept asking Charm when the king would be back, until she lost her temper and shouted that she didn't know and she didn't care. She said if Alexander was stupid enough to keep fighting he deserved to get himself killed, but at least he couldn't get me hurt under him this time.

This was a lie, because she told me she missed Alexander as much as I did.

One night when I was lying in my stall I felt a sharp pain in my leg, and the air around me sparkled, like when my eye got damaged in battle. I scrambled to my feet and neighed in terror. Charm woke up at once and sprang to my side. 'What's wrong, Bucephalas?' she cried. 'You're covered in sweat, you silly horse . . .' She put a hand on her heart, stared at the door and whispered, 'It's Alexander, isn't it? Oh, Zeus, what trouble has he got himself into *now*?'

We found out a few days later, when Hephaestion came to the stables shouting for the grooms to get the horses ready for his men.

'A messenger got through from Soghdiana,' he explained to Charm as he strapped a battle-cloth on Petasios. 'There's been heavy fighting against Spitamenes and his resistance force. Don't spread it around, but I think we were defeated at Maracanda. Then the Scythians attacked the hill forts on the northern frontier, and Alex had to go up there and drive them back. He's been injured. The messenger says he was hit on the head by a large rock and went blind for a while. Seems a sniper shot an arrow through his leg as well, and then he drank some infected water. He's apparently very sick and can hardly speak or walk . . . I don't know how much to believe, but I'm to take him more siege engines and his chariot. I knew I should never have let him go north without me.'

Charm's hands flew to her mouth. She ran to fetch my bridle.

'No, Charmeia!' Hephaestion ordered. 'You're to stay here with Prince Ochus.'

'But, Sir! Alexander needs Bucephalas if there's going to be more fighting. Hoplite doesn't know enough about battle yet. That's obviously why the king got hurt.'

Hephaestion sighed, put a hand on her shoulder and said, 'If Alex can't walk or see straight, Charmeia, he certainly can't ride. That's why I'm taking him a chariot. He didn't ask for you. Try not to worry. If he's really as sick as the reports say, I'll bring him back with me. And if he isn't, I'll help him finish off this Spitamenes, *then* I'll bring him back. If you're bored, you can always start training that Mardian filly.'

That winter in Balkh was a lonely, tense time. Except for my stall and Caspia's, the stables stayed empty. Frost formed on the statues, and Charm had to break the ice on the water troughs so we could drink. With all the other grooms away in Soghdiana with the army, there was no gossip. The Macedonian garrison which had been left to look after us stared anxiously from the walls, blew on their hands, and gripped their spears tightly. If there was news from the north, we didn't hear it.

Huddled in Petasios' empty stall, Prince Ochus taught Charm more letters. When they got bored with that and the prince's fingers had healed, they taught Caspia how to settle on her knees for when she grew old enough to carry a rider. Caspia became so good at this that they taught the filly more tricks. Soon Caspia would stand on her hind legs on command, or lie flat on her side and play dead.

If you ask me, it was all pretty silly. But I suppose there wasn't much else for them to do.

A present from Soghdiana

The spring rains have made the desert bloom with flowers before we finally see a Macedonian column marching towards the city. Charm catches her breath and shades her eyes. I throw up my head and whinny in excitement to find out which horses are with them.

Only one whinny I recognize comes back – the grey Persian mare who carries Darius' brother. There are lots of strange whinnies, though, very cheeky and full of themselves. In the middle of the column is a herd of big, strong-looking horses. Some are being ridden bareback by man-colts, laughing and chattering to one another in their own tongue. Part of the phalanx marches behind them.

Charm trots me out to meet them, and the man-colts stare at her curiously. Her face falls when she sees it is only Darius' brother Oxarthes leading the herd. But she wets her lips and calls, 'Sir, how is King Alexander?'

Oxarthes gives her a sharp frown. 'Take that horse away,

Groom! It looks sick. I don't want ours catching something from it.'

'Bucephalas isn't ill, Sir. He's just off his food.'

'That's the *king's* horse?' Oxarthes blinks, and takes a closer look at me. 'I wouldn't have known it was the same animal! What on earth have you been doing to him?' He shakes his head. 'Never mind, I'm glad you're here. I've a message for you. You'll be pleased to know King Iskander is back on his feet. He sent these horses and boys on ahead for training.'

'Training for what?' It is Charm's turn to blink.

'For his army, naturally.'

'But they're only boys—'

'Soghdian boys, yes. And these horses are Soghdian-bred. They'll make excellent cavalry when they're old enough, and there will be more recruits for the phalanx soon. Officially, they are hostages to ensure their fathers' good conduct. But I think they do not mind so much.' He looks over his shoulder at a boy who is standing up on his horse's back with the reins in his teeth, and sighs. 'I am supposed to teach them Greek. I just hope my Soghdian is up to it. King Iskander does not realize even we Persians sometimes cannot understand these people. Prince Ochus is to train with them. It'll do my nephew good to have something to occupy his body as well as his mind, perhaps help toughen him up a bit. These Soghdian boys are a fierce lot.'

'Is the fighting in the north over, then?' Charm glances at the men. 'Is the king coming back?'

'Not yet.' Oxarthes frowns a little. 'As I explained to King Iskander, the Soghdians will fight over every handful of dust. Just conquering their cities is not enough. First, he has to build more fortresses. Then he has to hunt Spitamenes down and finish him. But he sent you a gift to cheer you up – it's back in the baggage train. Come and see.'

Charm looks puzzled. But she turns me to follow the Persian mare.

We trot back down the column past the Soghdian man-colts (who are all attempting the standing-up trick now) and past the men with their long pikes, until we reach the mule carts.

I smell Alexander's gift at once and stop dead, nearly throwing Charm over my shoulder. Sweat breaks out all over me, and I tremble with bad memories. Charm grabs my mane in alarm. 'Bucephalas, what's wrong?' Then she sees our gift, too, and pales.

It is our enemy, the horsemaster.

He smells twice as strong as usual, because he is filthy. He is tied behind the cart like Bessus was on our march back to Balkh, naked with a wooden yoke around his neck, his wrists bound. His lame leg looks as if it has been dragged along the ground most of the way. Both his knees are bruised. There are whip marks on his back. He looks like a broken-down horse, slumped over the tail of the cart, so relieved to have been allowed to stop that he does not look up.

Charm bites her lip and stares at the prisoner in silence.

Oxarthes watches her curiously. 'King Iskander said to tell you this man will never hurt you again. He said, if you want, I am to allow you to help me torture him.'

Charm shakes her head, looking sick.

'Well, I did not think it right for a girl.'

'How did you catch him?' Charm whispers.

The horsemaster raises his head at the sound of her voice. His eyes are half shut with bruises, and crusted with blood and flies. But they flicker open in recognition. He hisses, 'You'd better watch out, slave! My Scythian friends know where you and that old nag are hiding—'

'Silence!' Oxarthes says, kicking him in the mouth.

Charm sucks in her breath. 'Please don't!'

Oxarthes gives her a strange look. 'King Iskander has ordered that his last days be made as uncomfortable as possible. Not only has he betrayed us to the enemy, but he shot the arrow that pierced the king's leg, and roused the Scythian tribes against us. We chased them into the steppe, which they didn't expect, and managed to capture him there. He is to share Bessus' fate, but not until King Iskander gets back.'

Charm makes a choked sound, drags my head round with uncharacteristic savageness and kicks her heels into my sides.

Relieved to be away from my enemy's smell, I break into a gallop. We thunder flat out past the Soghdian herd, Charm crouched over my mane with tears in her eyes. The Soghdian horses plunge and buck in excitement, and there is sudden laughter as the man-colt who was standing up with his reins in his teeth loses his balance and falls off.

A present from Anatolia

The Soghdian horses filled the stables with excited squealing and neighing. I had to teach them who was boss, which wore me out. Charm was tired, too, because she had the job of teaching the Soghdian man-colts proper stable routine, and no colt likes being bossed about by a filly. Meanwhile, Ochus trained with them on the horse ground. The Macedonian officers were trying to teach them proper parades, so there was much shouting and laughter. The prince collected a lot of bruises from their blunt javelins, until Charm had the bright idea of training Caspia to carry him. The golden filly had not yet turned three, but the mountain roads had made her tough. She was so clever and quick that Ochus soon got his revenge, impressing the Soghdian man-colts with the silly tricks he'd taught her.

Soon after this, Charm brought a bulging bag into my stall. 'That's Prince Ochus and the orphaned filly sorted out,' she told me with a smile. 'Now there's just you. This came from Queen Ada. I think you're going to eat today!' As she spoke, she emptied out my stale mash, replaced it with fresh barley, and added something from the bag.

I could hardly believe my luck. HONEY CAKES!

I gave a little nicker of joy, plunged in my nose, and ate up properly for the first time since abandoning Alexander.

More of the army trickled back that winter, bringing with them more captives and treasure, and also the news that Spitamenes was dead. After our herd chased them on to the steppe, the scared Scythians cut off his head and sent it to Alexander as a peace offering.

Zephyr came back with them, her head low and her mane shaved off *again*. Charm led the poor mare into Petasios' empty stall, patted her, and shook her head sadly. 'Commander Cleitus,' she said.

I nickered to Zephyr in sympathy. It is hard to lose a second rider so soon after the first.

Tydeos was still with Alexander, but we finally got to hear groom-gossip again. It seemed I had not missed a big battle, after all, but lots of little ones. Alexander had divided his army into five columns, which had split up and played a game to see who could dominate the most Soghdians and Scythians. Afterwards, they all met up in Maracanda and had a big party, at which Alexander had to dominate some of his own herd because they made themselves too huge. That was when Commander Cleitus died – at the end of Alexander's spear. The grooms whispered that the king had been in an extremely bad mood because of the way the Soghdians kept attacking his men and then vanishing into their deserts and hills.

The results of the dominating game were:

Apollo and Perdiccas: 3,000 Soghdians.
Harpinna and Ptolemy: 7,000 Soghdians.
Xanthus and Craterus: 15,000 Soghdians and 800 Scythians.
Petasios and Hephaestion: 20,000 Soghdians.
Hoplite and Alexander: 65,000 Soghdians and 2,000 Scythians.

As you can see, Alexander is still way ahead of everyone else, even though he almost died.

Charm went quiet when she heard how Alexander had killed Cleitus. Then she stroked my nose and whispered that she would look after me, and I wasn't to worry because the killing was nearly over. The grooms said the king had gone to finish off a few fortresses where the remaining Soghdian resistance had holed up, and that he would be back before spring.

But first, Alexander had one more surprise for us.

Princess Roxanne

One morning, when Caspia and I return to the stables after a race along the riverbank carrying our riders (which I won), there is a strange smell in my stall. I stop dead. Charm's cheeks are flushed from our gallop, and our breath steams in the cold air. The sun is so bright I can't see inside. For a moment I am convinced there is a ghost in the corner, and tremble all over.

Charm stiffens. 'What's wrong, Bucephalas?'

Ochus stiffens, too. This makes Caspia stop and snort. Then she gives the soft nicker she reserves for greeting humans, and the panic leaves me.

It is only a girl-filly, crouched in the corner of my stall with her arms wrapped tightly around her knees. A long, black mane falls over her frightened eyes. She is wearing a patterned dress with a stain on the skirt where she has been sitting in my dung. I don't know her smell, though, which is sharp with fear. So I am still wary.

'I think it's one of the Soghdian captives, Ochus,' Charm says, her voice softening. 'You'd better get her out of there before I take Bucephalas in. I'll hold Caspia.'

'No need.' Ochus takes the reins over the filly's head and puts the ends in her teeth. 'Stay, Caspia,' he says, and goes into my stall.

He tries speaking to the girl-filly, first in Persian, then in Greek. But she presses back against the wall and stares at him with frightened eyes. He pulls a face at Charm, and says something in stumbling Soghdian. The girl-filly takes a shuddering breath and gabbles something back. Ochus gently lifts her mane out of her eyes, and his hand freezes. I see a shimmer in the air between them, like the light that surrounds Alexander when he is excited and happy.

Charm whispers, 'Oh! She's beautiful!'

Ochus and the girl-filly are still gazing at each other. The girl raises her slender fingers to touch Ochus' hand. He smiles and rests his palm against her cheek, and she closes her eyes as the tension runs out of her.

I nudge Charm to remind her I want my hay.

'Bring her out, Ochus!' she calls. 'Bucephalas is getting impatient.'

Ochus takes the girl-filly's hand and leads her out into the sunlight. Her dress is thick wool in many shades of red. She and Ochus are about the same height, and they are in danger of getting soppy, so I stamp my foot and shake my head. The girl-filly eyes me warily. Then she sees Caspia holding her reins in her teeth and giggles.

While Charm settles me, Ochus and the girl-filly settle Caspia together, communicating with hand signals and glances. Finally, Ochus leaves her stroking Caspia and comes into my stall. He whispers in Greek, 'She says she is a princess. Her name is Roxanne, and she says Alexander is going to marry her.'

Charm's comb stops halfway through my tail. 'That can't be right! She's too young.'

'She's my age,' Ochus says. 'Eleven and a half. She's old enough.'

'But Alexander can't *marry* her! He wouldn't come all this way to marry a Soghdian girl!' Charm stops pretending to comb my tail and rushes over to the partition to get a better look at Roxanne. She shakes her head. 'You must have misunderstood, Ochus. Your Uncle Oxarthes told me not even Persians understand Soghdian.'

'I picked up some words from the other boys when we were training, so I think I am right. That is why she is so frightened. She says King Alexander is a demon-sorcerer who gave his soldiers magic wings so they could fly up the cliffs to capture her father's fortress. Her father was so terrified when he saw them all standing up on the rock above him, he gave Roxanne to Alexander so he would not kill all the people like he did in the other Soghdian towns.'

Charm smiles. 'Then you must have got it wrong!

Alexander's not a demon or a sorcerer. And our men can't fly, that's just silly!'

Ochus looks grave. 'I do not think I am wrong, Charmeia. I think Roxanne is as beautiful as my mother was, and a great king like Alexander should have a beautiful wife.' He stares at the girl-filly with a bleak expression.

Roxanne is still stroking and kissing Caspia, who enjoys such attention. Charm and Ochus have been whispering, so I don't think she can hear them. She wouldn't understand their Greek words, anyway. But when Ochus clenches a fist and says in a fierce tone, 'I *hate* Uncle Alexander!' she must recognize Alexander's name, for her frightened look returns and she stares out into the yard.

'It's all right, Roxanne. King Alexander's not here.' Charm shakes her head. 'The poor girl's terrified. Tell her, Ochus. Tell her Alexander isn't back yet, and we'll look after her. I'll think of something. The king can't possibly mean to marry her. There must be something we can do.'

Ochus nods and unclenches his fist. He goes back to Caspia's stall and whispers something in Roxanne's ear. Her face lights up like a dark sun.

'I've told her I will look after her,' Ochus says, straightening his shoulders and resting a hand on his jewelled dagger. 'I can fight now. I will ask Uncle Alexander to let Roxanne go free. Then, when I am old enough to be king, I will visit her father and ask him to let her marry *me*.'

Charm stares at Ochus in growing horror as she realizes what he means. As you've probably guessed, Charm was thinking only of her own feelings for Alexander, not Ochus' feelings for Roxanne, which were blindingly obvious to me and Caspia.

'Oh, Ochus . . .' she whispers. 'Be careful!'

'I will be very careful.' Ochus smiles at Roxanne again. 'We will wait until Uncle Alexander is in a good mood.'

You humans make everything so complicated! To me, it is very simple:

Ochus loves Roxanne.
Roxanne loves Ochus.
Alexander doesn't love any woman, except maybe his mother.

So WHY is Alexander going to marry Roxanne?

A fine parade

When the king finally returned, I barely recognized the big, battle-scarred young stallion who barged, stamping and snorting, into the stall next to mine. Hoplite had a scar across his chest and another scar down his left shoulder. His mouth was cracked at the corners, and there were whip marks on his backside. When I gave him a little squeal over the partition to tell him to behave himself, he reared and came at me with bared teeth.

Tydeos threw him some hay and leant against the wall in relief. 'He's even worse than Bucephalas used to be!' he muttered. 'It's all King Alexander's fault. He rode him too hard and cut his poor mouth to bits. After he got injured, he swore he'd teach him how to be a proper warhorse. But Hoplite kept bucking, and King Alexander didn't like that one bit. Don't tell nobody, but he even threw the king off once!' Tydeos glanced round to check no one was listening, and grinned. 'It was pretty funny, really, and King Alexander's own fault for trying to ride before he was properly better. He was so dizzy he could hardly stand up, let alone keep his balance on a bucking horse. Except he was in such a rotten mood, no one dared tell him so.'

His expression turned grave again. 'Oh Charm! You've no idea how bad it's been! The king kept flying into terrible rages – you know how he gets when his head hurts? But now he has them a lot more often than before. Even his friends in the Guard are scared of him. I once forgot to put all of Hoplite's tassels on, and he had me thrashed for it. I've still got the scars – look.'

He tugged up his tunic to show Charm his back, and she put a hand over her mouth. 'Oh, Tydeos . . . I'm sorry. Where is he now? He usually comes straight to see Bucephalas.'

Tydeos shrugged. 'I told you. He's changed.'

It is five whole days before Alexander comes to see me. There is a shout at the stable gate, and all the Soghdian boys and grooms run out into the yard, lie down in the dirt and press their foreheads to the ground.

I snort in surprise. This is *very* strange behaviour!

Charm is combing out my tail, and Tydeos is in the next stall putting olive oil on the corners of Hoplite's sore mouth, so they don't see what is happening at first. Then Tydeos looks out and gasps, 'It's the king! Quick, Charm . . . we have to kneel before him too, now.'

Charm peers out into the yard at the Soghdian boys and gives a nervous laugh. 'That's a Persian thing. I'm sure he doesn't mean us.' She starts to use my comb on her own mane.

'He *does*!' Tydeos finishes with Hoplite and looks anxiously out into the yard. 'Please, Charm! You don't understand how angry he gets. It takes the littlest thing these days.'

Charm is still fiddling with her mane and smoothing down

her tunic. Her cheeks and neck flush red. I can smell
Alexander's sherbet sweetness now, and push my head over
the door in excitement. The smell stirs my blood and reminds
me of battle. My heart thuds against my ribs.

The king is wearing a blue-bordered Persian cloak. The
blue and white crown he took from King Darius holds his
mane in place, and the Achilles breastplate glitters over the
top of a new tunic. The Guard hurry behind him, all wearing
their Persian cloaks too. King Darius' brother Oxarthes is with
them. Alexander ignores the kneeling man-colts and makes
straight for my stall.

I neigh a joyful welcome.

'Charm!' Tydeos says in a strangled tone and hurries outside to lie face down before the king.

Alexander ignores him too, and stops at my stall to give me
a long look. 'Bucephalas,' he says with a sigh, putting his hand
on my nose.

I neigh again and search his pocket for honey cakes. He
gives a quick laugh and pushes my nose away. 'No, not now.
Where's your groom got to?'

Charm ventures out, wiping her sweaty hands on her tunic,
and bows her head to Alexander. The Guard glance at one
another.

Hephaestion clears his throat. 'Charmeia,' he says softly.
'You should do proskynesis before the king now. Like the others, see? Kneel and press your forehead to the ground, then
put your fingers to your lips and blow him a kiss . . .'

But Alexander waves Hephaestion back with an impatient
hand. He gives Charm a long, hard look. 'Is Bucephalas fit?'
he asks.

Charm darts him a quick glance from under her fringe.

'Yes, Sir. He's well, but he's missed you.'

Alexander smiles. 'Good. Because I'm fed up with riding that colt. Get Bucephalas ready for a parade. Use his best cloth with all the tassels. And get that grey mare Aura ready for Princess Roxanne, tassels and best cloth as well. We're getting married today, so we must look good.'

Charm sucks in her breath. 'But, Sir—'

Tydeos mouths something at her, shaking his head. Alexander, who was saying something to his Guard, swings back. His eyes narrow. 'What is it, Charmides?'

'Princess Roxanne can't—' Charm loses her nerve and bows her head.

'Did you have a dream?' Alexander marches back and seizes her chin in his hand, forcing her to look at him. 'Well? If you've had a prophetic dream about our marriage, Charmides, I want to hear it!'

There are tears in Charm's eyes. She has backed up so far, her mane is close enough for me to touch it with my nose. I blow into it, and she jumps. 'I-I haven't had any dreams about your marriage, Sir . . . I'm sorry.' It is barely a whisper.

Alexander frowns, shakes his head and releases her. 'Good. It's a beautiful day! The sun is shining. The fighting's over. Anahita, goddess of the Oxus, is waiting to marry me to my beautiful young bride! But first, I want my young Successors to show me what they can do. Get them mounted, and someone go and find Prince Ochus. I want him to show me what he's learnt, too. Let's leave these people with a spectacle they won't forget!'

Oh, that was a fine parade!

I carried Alexander proudly on my cloth, surrounded by a shimmering halo of white and blue. Aura carried Princess

Roxanne, sitting sideways on her cloth, with a careful stride. Roxanne wore a long red dress encrusted with gold, and a golden crown on her dark mane. Her eyes were lined in black, and her lips painted red. Tydeos had washed Aura's tail so that it floated like a white cloud in the sunlight. She was in foal-season again, so she looked even more beautiful than usual.

The statue of the local goddess, Anahita, was carried out of the city and placed on a platform in the middle of the parade ground. Her crown of stars glittered, and a robe of dead otters and strings of fresh flowers draped her body. Several sacrifices died in front of her: a white ox, a pale camel, and several lambs. Their ghosts whirled away reluctantly, because it was too soon for them. But nothing could scare me when I had Alexander on my back and my favourite mare beside me.

There were trumpet blasts and music, then the Soghdian boys demonstrated how well they had learnt to be Macedonians by doing their parade. Alexander watched them with a stony expression, nodding when they performed their battle manoeuvres well, and scowling when they got it wrong. He picked out five boys who had made bad mistakes and ordered them to be taken away and beaten. Princess Roxanne sat very straight in her beautiful dress and crown, her eyes dry and her face expressionless. But she kept twisting her fingers in Aura's mane as she watched the manoeuvres, and she smelt very afraid.

When it was Prince Ochus' turn, he and Caspia did so well that not even Alexander could find fault. He beamed at Ochus and told him to bring Caspia up with the Guard. Roxanne's eyes strayed sideways. She and Ochus exchanged a quick, desperate glance as he took his place. Neither of them dared say a word.

Finally, a loaf of bread was carried out and set at Anahita's feet. Alexander slipped off me and helped Roxanne down from Aura's back. Roxanne's legs gave way, so he had to catch her in his arms. Some of the men smiled, thinking this romantic. But out of the corner of my eye, I saw Caspia dance sideways as Ochus clenched his fist on her reins.

Alexander led Roxanne to the statue, where he let her sink to her knees. He drew his sword, took Roxanne's limp hand and put it on the hilt. Then he covered her slender fingers with his own, raised the blade and sliced through the loaf with as much force as he might have used to slice off an enemy's head.

The sky above Anahita's crown crackled with sudden lightning. Every horse on the parade ground shot up its head. Caspia reared, Aura whinnied in fear, and my coat stood on end as all the ghosts Alexander had made in Soghdiana streamed past us with a furious howl.

Iolaus had been given the job of holding us. I ripped my reins out of his hand and nipped Aura until she did the same. I had only one thought – to drive my favourite mare away from the danger. With the lightning crackling above and the ghosts at our heels, we galloped from the parade ground, scattering men and onlookers before us.

But the ghosts soon vanished, the sky turned blue, and everyone whispered that Anahita had blessed the king's marriage. By the time Charm and Tydeos came running to catch us, Aura and I were grazing side by side, having made another foal together. Ha!

Alexander's wedding night

That night Charm cannot sleep. Alexander's pavilion is wreathed in orange flowers, and glows with lamps. She cannot take her eyes off it. Eventually, she crawls out of my hay, whispers an apology to me and goes to find Tydeos. All the other grooms have gone to one of the parties to celebrate the king's wedding night, so the stables are quiet when a lone figure staggers into the yard.

I whinny in delight, because it is Alexander.

He lets himself into my stall. He has been drinking magic, so his movements are rough and jerky. But I do not mind, because when he grips my mane and rests his arm over my neck, it feels very nice. I nibble his tunic, looking for honey cakes.

'Bucephalas,' he whispers. 'Oh, horse! Why do they make me so *angry*? That idiot historian of mine has been writing all sorts of terrible things about me. I pay him to make me into a hero, and he's turning me into a demon! I don't even remember doing half the things he claims I did in Soghdiana. And then he had the cheek to quote the *Iliad* at me, telling me Hephaestion would make a better king than me! And on my own wedding night!'

He groans and clutches my mane. 'I can't go back to the party, and I can't go to my pavilion. That girl's there. Roxanne. Every time I see her, I remember why I had to marry her. If I hadn't done something, my men would still be dying out there in the deserts and hills. I've never lost a battle in my life, but these crazy Soghdians really will fight to the death over a handful of dust! It was all I could think of to get her father on my side and stop the fighting . . . no one seems to understand it's much harder for me than it is for them. Things just keep getting more and more complicated, horse! And Demetrius . . . do you know what the crazy fool did? He ran to cover me with his own shield when I got hit by that rock in the fighting. Even though I had punished him by putting him in the Disciplinary Company, he still risked his own neck to save my life. Why did he *do* that, horse? Why? Was I wrong about him? What if I was wrong about the others, too? Philo, General Parmenio, all the rest – oh, my head hurts! I thought I was going blind, up in the north. I saw things . . . horrible things . . .' His voice lowers, frightened. 'Do you ever see ghosts, Bucephalas?'

Of course I see ghosts. I want to tell him it is normal, but I don't know how.

Alexander presses his knuckles to his forehead and slides down my shoulder into my hay. I am worried and sniff at him. But he is not dying. He keeps muttering to me. More stuff about the fighting in Soghdiana, the edge of the world, his stupid historian, the *Iliad*, how many people want to kill him, and how much his head hurts.

I get bored and blow into his mane.

Eventually, he stops muttering and staggers to his feet to throw up the magic drink in a corner of my stall. While he is doing this, the five Soghdian boys he ordered to be beaten earlier creep into the yard and start whispering over by the fountain. I have no idea what they are up to – in my experience, man-colts are always up to something – but one has a knife, and they run off towards the camp.

Alexander watches them from the shadows of my stall, and his eyes narrow. 'I knew it!' he hisses. 'See, Bucephalas? I can't trust anyone. Those boys are obviously plotting to kill me while they think I'm distracted by my little bride! Looks like I'm going to have to teach them a lesson, too. Oh, this is so tiresome. Why won't anyone just let me get *on* with things?'

Brushing the hay off his cloak, he gives me a quick pat and staggers off into the night, calling for his Guard.

A better man than Alexander?

Before we set off for India, the five Soghdian man-colts who were whispering in the night were tied to posts and stoned to death on the parade ground for plotting to kill the king. The other Successors watched the execution with frightened eyes and cast terrified glances at Alexander. It's going to be a while before any of them dare plot anything again.

Then the royal historian Alexander had been complaining about was dragged out. Two of the Guard tied him to a post and beat him, trying to make him admit it had all been his idea. Alexander sat astride me nearby, watching with narrowed eyes.

The historian would not admit anything of the sort. But he hissed at Alexander, 'If you don't like what I write about you, King Alexander, you shouldn't do such things in the first place. It's no good saying you're the reborn Achilles. Even Achilles didn't massacre as many innocent people as you have done.'

Alexander's fist tightened on my rein. His breathing quickened, and he gave the order for the poor historian to be stoned to death too. But Hephaestion trotted Petasios out of formation, put a hand on the king's arm and whispered, 'Alex, please! Who's going to write the rest of your story if you kill your historian? It won't make any sense if you get someone else to finish it.'

Alexander's face went bright red. He shook his friend off and yelled at him to get back in his place. But as he raised his arm to give the signal for the stoning to start, the historian shouted, 'A better man than you by far is Hephaestion!'

Alexander leant down from my back, grabbed a stone from the pile and threw it himself. The stone hit the historian on the mouth. Alexander's aim is excellent, even when his head is hurting.

The historian spat out a bloody tooth and shouted louder, 'A better man than you by far is Hephaestion, yet death will not spare him!'

A hail of stones hit him, thrown by Macedonians anxious to stop him making the king's mood even worse.

'A better man than you by far is Hephaestion, yet death—' yelled the prisoner one more time, before a stone finally hit him on the head and knocked him out.

Hephaestion closed his eyes and clutched Petasios' mane. But Alexander's fury shuddered out of him when the prisoner stopped shouting. He pressed a fist to his forehead, and ordered the Macedonians to lock the historian in one of the empty lion-cages with his writing materials. 'He'll finish my story whether he likes it or not,' he said. 'And from now on, he'll write exactly what I tell him to write.'

Before we left the parade ground, Alexander trotted me forward a few paces and held up his hand for silence. A hush fell over the assembled men as the king announced:

'Today, I ride back over the Caucasus Mountains to find the edge of the world. Anyone who is too afraid to come with me can leave their weapons here and go back to Ecbatana with Oxarthes, who is taking the traitor Bessus there for execution before a Persian court. I will pick you up on our way back. But be warned, I will consider you under arrest for desertion, and I won't hesitate to act if you plot against me. Don't make the mistake of thinking I won't know what you're up to. I'm sure none of you has forgotten what happened to General Parmenio.'

He paused to let this sink in.

The men glanced uneasily at one another and shuffled their feet.

Alexander's smile was like the sun breaking through clouds as he continued. 'If, however, you choose to follow me, I promise you treasure and wonders beyond your wildest dreams. In addition, I will give each man who comes with me a bonus of five talents. Grooms, scientists and engineers will get another half talent each. Today is a new beginning. It is my wish that from now on, Macedonians, Greeks, and Persians will live together under one ruler and be known as Alexandrians. I have shown you the way by taking a Soghdian wife and training these Soghdian boys in my army. But war is only the first stage. When the fighting is over, there will be a thousand years of peace in my empire. Those who follow me to the edge of the world will be rewarded for their courage many times over. Just one small land called India lies between us and immortality. Let us go there, gentlemen, and show these Indians the glory of our new Alexandria!'

Thunderous cheers greeted these words. Alexander punched the air and laughed. His white and blue cloak dazzled in the sunshine. He was wearing his Troy helmet with the white plumes and shining with his old energy again. I felt the power rippling through him and made myself huge.

We retraced our hoofprints to the mountains, accompanied by the familiar sound of jangling bits, thudding hooves, creaking carts, snorts and whinnies, braying mules, barking dogs, and the marching feet of eighty thousand men. The Soghdian Successors stayed behind to complete their training, but we were still a huge herd. And somewhere back in the baggage train, my enemy was locked in a cage, awaiting his execution. Ha!

That was how we dominated the Soghdians, who fight over every handful of dust:

Soghdian dead: 110,000, including Spitamenes (murdered by the frightened Scythians) and five man-colts (stoned to death by Alexander).
Scythian dead: 2,800.
Macedonian dead: 24,500, including Cleitus.
Horses dead: 200, including Borealis on the way over the Caucasus Mountains (VERY, VERY, VERY SAD).
Prisoners and hostages: Bessus, the old horsemaster, 30,000 Soghdian Successors, 10,000 Soghdian horses, Alexander's historian, and Princess Roxanne.

We're getting close to the end of our journey, so I probably ought to tell you before we go any further why Alexander got so worked up on the parade ground, and why Hephaestion was so upset. The lines the historian quoted were stolen from the *Iliad*. They referred to Achilles' best friend, who was killed in the fighting at Troy, after which Achilles (who, if you remember, was supposed to be invincible) went mad with grief and got himself killed, too.

Hephaestion is Alexander's best friend. If he dies before we reach the edge of the world, I don't know what Alexander will do.

Twenty-eighth Hoofprint
Charsadda, 327 bc

Fighting Alexander

Alexander sent messengers on ahead with squealing threats for the Indians, ordering their bosses to meet him in the Kabul valley to surrender their lands. Then he sent Hephaestion with the main army and baggage train through one of the lower passes of the Caucasus Mountains, while we led the Guard and half of the cavalry back over the highest pass which we'd used before.

No one dared question the king. He claimed he needed to go to the top to make sacrifices to his father Zeus-Ammon for a successful campaign in India, but you can probably guess the real reason. The weather was a lot better than the last time we'd crossed the mountains, and Alexander wanted another look at the edge of the world.

It is only the second time we have retraced our route since setting out from Pella. We keep coming across our herd's old dung piles, smashed wine jars, and bits of broken armour our men threw away on the march out. The climb is not as difficult this time, because most of the snow has melted. But the air is thin, and I am not yet fully fit after Balkh, so I jog up the slope, which is easier for horses than walking uphill.

This soon makes Alexander impatient. 'Walk properly, can't you, Bucephalas?' he mutters, jerking my rein, which hurts my mouth. 'You're worse than that colt of yours!'

This is not true. Behind me, Hoplite's dark coat is covered in foam, because he has been jogging nearly all the way from Balkh. Peucestas gave up trying to make him walk ages ago.

At the top of the pass, Alexander leans forward, eager for a glimpse of the edge of the world. But I stop dead and blow through my nostrils. At the side of the track is the skeleton of a large horse, its bones picked clean and bleached by the sun. And in the shadows under the crags, Borealis' ghost is waiting.

My whole body goes rigid with fear. I tremble and sweat. Alexander, who is still looking for the edge of the world and not paying attention to his riding, loses his balance and nearly falls over my head. He pushes himself back on to my cloth and digs his heels angrily into my sides. 'Get on with you, horse! What's wrong with you today?'

Behind me, the other horses of the Guard have stopped and are blowing through their nostrils, too. I am not sure they can see Borealis' ghost like I can, but they know I would not make such a fuss unless I had seen something dangerous.

Ptolemy draws his sword, glancing warily at the crags. 'What's happening, Alex? Is it an ambush?'

Alexander scowls. 'There's nothing there! It's this stupid horse of mine. He's been playing me up ever since we left

453

Balkh! I don't know what my groom's been doing to him. Get on with you, Bucephalas!' He jerks my reins from side to side to make me unbrace my forelegs, and brings his spear down across my quarters.

It hurts.

I give a small buck to warn him to stop hitting me, and he yells in rage. The spear is suddenly whirling on my blind side, and blows rain down on me out of the dark, bringing panicky memories. Alexander's heels dig into my sides, his legs clamp against my cloth, and his hands jerk at my sore mouth. It is as bad as when the horsemaster tried to 'tame' me back in Pella.

I forget it is Alexander on my back, and rear so high I am in danger of toppling over backwards. He has to throw his arms around my neck to stay on. When I come down again, I whip round on my hocks and throw three huge bucks. Anyone else would have been off at the first. But Alexander barely shifts on my cloth. He grits his teeth, hauls up my head and whacks me again. No matter what I do, I cannot dislodge him.

This is the first time I have ever fought Alexander, and it is HORRIBLE.

'Alex!' Leonnatus calls. He steadies Aura, who is trying to whip round and bolt back down the trail because I am upsetting her. 'For Zeus' sake! That's Bucephalas you're riding, not some half-trained colt! If he's not going forward, you can be sure there's a good reason for it.'

The other horses of the Guard are giving half rears, upset as well. Hoplite snorts at me in sympathy. If this is what happened to him in Soghdiana, then no wonder he was so bad-tempered when he came back.

I don't know how our battle would have ended, because both of us would rather die than be dominated. But Leonnatus' voice gets through to Alexander. He stops hitting me, closes his eyes and gives a little shudder. I calm down a bit and stop acting wild.

'I think it's that skeleton,' Leonnatus says, softer. 'This is where Borealis died, remember? Maybe the horses remember, too?'

Alexander squints at the crags. He pales and trembles all over, like I did earlier. He throws down his spear and presses a hand against my sweaty neck, chirruping to soothe me. 'Whoa, Bucephalas, steady now . . . I'm sorry, horse . . . it's over.'

I stand still, also trembling. Borealis' ghost is watching us with pricked ears. Alexander squints at it again, shudders, and slips off me.

'All right,' he whispers, retrieving his spear. 'I know what's wrong now. I can see him, too. But we have to go past. If you don't go past, none of the other horses will. Come on, my brave Bucephalas. I'll go first, see?' He takes my reins gently over my head and walks forward, keeping the spear low so as not to startle me.

I trust him, so I follow.

Borealis' ghost stays where it is, watching us silently. My coat prickles as we pass it, but it doesn't attack us. The Guard follows, the other horses pricking their ears at the shadows. Alexander vaults on to me again and pats my damp neck. He looks back at the crags, laughs, and shakes his head.

'Horses!' he mutters to his Guard, and they smile in relief.

He made his sacrifice further on, where the pass started its descent. We horses grazed at the side of the road with Iolaus and Leonnatus to watch us, while Alexander climbed the crags with the two sheep we'd driven up with us. I don't know if Zeus let him see the edge of the world this time, because he didn't say anything when he came down. But from where we were standing, it was hidden in a blue haze.

By the time we set off again, Alexander seemed to be back to his old self. He rode me in his familiar, firm way, running an apologetic hand down my neck whenever he thought no one was watching. This made me calmer, too. But all the way down to Alexandria-under-the-Caucasus, he kept glancing over his shoulder, and I knew he could see what I saw.

Borealis' ghost was following us, lurking in the shadows of my damaged eye.

A dream of monsters

When we met up again in the Kabul valley, Charm went quiet as she ran her hand over the weals on my flanks. She rubbed ointment into the cuts at the corner of my mouth and groomed me very gently, whispering, 'Poor old horse, what has he been doing to you?'

Tydeos whistled when he saw the state of me. 'Alexander's getting worse, isn't he? If he can do that to his favourite horse, kill his friends, and stone young boys to death, what'll he do to *us* if we annoy him? Things are going bad, Charm. We've got money now. I'm getting out as soon as I can. I don't want to be dragged off to India as spoils when the men decide they've had enough and abandon us all out here. If you've any sense, you'll come with me.'

Charm gave him an exasperated look. 'The men aren't going to abandon Alexander! You heard them cheering him back in Balkh. They still worship him, whatever he does. And you know I can't leave Bucephalas, especially not now. If you want to go, I'll cover for you as long as I can. But Alexander doesn't like losing his grooms any more than he likes losing his battles, so you'd best be careful he doesn't catch you.'

'You could bring Bucephalas.'

'After what happened last time? Don't be silly.'

Tydeos sighed. 'I'm not going nowhere without you.'

'Then you're stuck, aren't you?' Charm pretended to treat my wounds. But her hands trembled, and she soon gave up pretending and hugged my nose. 'I had another dream last night,' she whispered.

Tydeos looked up from fixing Hoplite's tether. 'What did you dream this time?'

She pressed her hand against my neck with a sigh. 'Alexander and Bucephalas were fighting a battle against huge grey monsters. I saw Bucephalas fall in the mud with javelins sticking out of him, and . . . oh Tydeos, he didn't get up again!'

Tydeos frowned. 'Have you told anyone?'

'No, not yet. I have to be sure.'

Tydeos shook his head. 'I wouldn't tell the king, if I were you. He probably wouldn't believe you, anyway, not after what you did at Issus.'

'But what if it's *true*?'

'I'm sure it isn't, Charm.'

'I've been right before.'

Tydeos chewed his lip. 'What did these monsters look like?'

Charm sighed. 'I didn't see them clearly, but they were as big as houses, with feet like tree trunks. They made a terrible noise, and they had enormous curved teeth growing out of their faces. Each one had a long tentacle that could wrap itself around a horse, pick it right up off the ground and crush it to death—' She gave a little laugh. 'Oh, forget it! It sounds ridiculous now.'

Tydeos grinned, too. 'You've been listening to too much camp gossip! It's enough to give anyone nightmares. I'm sure there aren't any monsters like that in the world. And if there are, King Alexander will soon deal with them like he deals with everything else.'

Charm smiled, too, because groom-gossip at that time was wild. Here are just a few of the things our grooms claimed we'd find in India:

Giant ants that dig up gold.

People who have a tail and the head of a dog.

Horned horses. (You know where they got THAT idea from!)

The water of life.

Wise men who wear no clothes and know the answer to every question.

But I was a bit worried, because Charm's dreams have come true before.

Elephants

A few days later, the first of the Indian tribes arrived, bringing gifts for Alexander from their boss Prince Ambhi. In the distance, advancing slowly through the smoke haze from our campfires, we saw a column of large grey animals with flapping ears and long noses, their backs and heads glittering with jewels. The wind was blowing the wrong way, so I could not smell them. But Charm's hands flew to her mouth, and she raced off with Tydeos at her heels. The other grooms hurried after them.

We horses were left unattended in the lines. I shifted my weight uneasily from one hind leg to the other. Beside me, Hoplite munched his hay, calmer now he was being ridden by Peucestas rather than Alexander. On my other side, Apollo sniffed my mane and tried to mutual groom, but I was not in the mood. Borealis' ghost had trotted off when we made camp, but I kept expecting it to reappear, which made me more nervous than usual.

When Charm came back, she was very pale. 'They're exactly like my dream, Bucephalas!' she whispered. 'They have little huts on their backs that the Indians ride in, and they're *huge!* Oh, horse, what should I do? Alexander's talking to the Indians. They've brought him gifts and treasure, but if my dream's true they'll fight us . . . yet how can it be true if they're surrendering? And now that the elephants have come to the camp and everyone's seen them, Alexander will say I made up my dream to protect you! I should have told him before they came. I'm such an idiot, listening to Tydeos. What does he know about India and the edge of the world? Not even Alexander knows what's out there!'

When the Indians left, the elephants stayed. We horses could smell them faintly when the wind changed. Their strong odour made us uneasy because we had never come across anything like it before. If one of them snorted through its long nose while we were dozing, it made us jump. Charm spent a lot of time in the lines, soothing us all. When the grooms took us out for exercise, they rode us in the opposite direction so we wouldn't have to pass the place where the elephants were tethered. Worse, Alexander spent more time with them than he did with us, training his men how to fight the grey monsters. Every day when we returned from our exercise, we saw the phalanx out on the plain beneath the mountains with an elephant stamping and whirling in their midst, making its horrible noise as our men attacked it with javelins and spears.

Charm tried several times to tell Alexander about her dream. But when he eventually came to the horse lines to see me, he told her not to bother him. His gaze slid sideways looking for Borealis' ghost. Then he snapped at the grooms to get us ready, because he wanted us to train against the elephants, too. He armed our riders with the phalanx's long pikes so they would be able reach the enemy in the little huts on the backs of the monsters.

This was a disaster from the start. The cavalrymen were not used to carrying the heavy pikes, and kept dropping them. Every time the elephant made its horrible noise or stamped a foot and made the ground shake, a horse whipped round and someone fell off. Not me or Alexander, of course – elephants might be frightening, but you can't dominate an enemy if you run away.

Eventually, Alexander lost his temper. Ignoring Hephaestion's warning shout, he headed me straight for the elephant and gave me the order to leap as if we were on parade. While we were in the air, he lifted his pike like an enormous javelin and launched it into the little hut on the monster's back, exploding the hay-stuffed sacks we were using as targets.

'Is Bucephalas the only one in my army who's not afraid of the Indians' secret weapon?' he cried as we landed. '*That*'s how to deal with these war-elephants! I want five elephants with their tusks sawn off like this one for training, and the rest left intact so you can practise against the real thing. Prince Ambhi has offered us his city of Taxila to use as our military base across the Indus if we'll help him see off his troublesome neighbour, Prince Porus. Before we leave this valley, gentlemen, I want every man and every horse ready to face the worst the Indians can throw at us!'

The men muttered uneasily, and the horses snorted, sensing their riders' nerves. I could have shown them how to be brave, but that was the end of my elephant-dominating. The monster had swung its trunk at us when we attacked it, causing me to land awkwardly from my high leap. By the time I got back to the horse lines, the tendon I'd injured at Halicarnassus had started to swell.

Charm patted me and promised she would stop Alexander taking me into battle against the elephants if it was the last thing she did. This was brave of her, but rather stupid. If it comes to a battle between Charm and Alexander, who do *you* think will win?

Another plot against the king

For the journey through the mountains to India, the army split into two. Alexander wanted to dominate all the local tribes that had refused to surrender, and said the baggage train would only slow him down. So he sent Hephaestion and Perdiccas through the easiest pass with the main force to look after the wounded and anyone else who couldn't fight, while he mounted Electra and took the rest of the army, the Disciplinary Company (with Demetrius on probation after saving the king's life in Soghdiana), and the siege equipment into the hills.

This meant I got to stay with Aura, who was too big with

foal to fight, and Prince Ochus got to stay with Roxanne.
Charm was the only one of us who was unhappy, since
Tydeos had to go with the horses of the Guard. Also, before
he left, Alexander had told her to decide how she wanted him
to punish the old horsemaster who, like the king's reluctant
historian, was still trailing along in a cage at the back of the
baggage train.

Only one city on our route had not sent Alexander any
gifts, and we had orders to dominate it on our way. But the
boss of Charsadda would not send out his army to meet us,
and neither Hephaestion nor Perdiccas dared take the sort of
risks Alexander would have done to force their way in, so it
turned into a siege. This gave Prince Ochus time to make
more trouble.

One cold bright morning, the prince turns up in the horse
lines with Roxanne just as Charm is about to take me for my
walk. She seems glad of the company, and lets them lead
Caspia and Aura behind me. When we reach the river, they
take off our muzzles and let us graze the yellow winter grass.
It is rather tasteless, but makes a change from hay. Ochus gets
Caspia to do her play-dead trick, which makes Roxanne laugh.

The filly gets to her feet, shakes herself, and settles down
to graze next to me. Roxanne watches Charm carefully, then
wets her lips and says in her broken Greek, 'Ochus tell me
Alexander talk much to you. You have special relationship
with him, maybe?'

Charm grips my withers tightly. 'Sometimes he talks to me.
Not very much, though.'

'Do he tell you things about me?' Roxanne watches her
closely.

Charm shakes her head. 'No, I'm sorry. We mostly talk

about Bucephalas.'

Roxanne sighs. 'Ochus think—' She frowns and starts again. 'Ochus say Alexander not love any woman. He not come to me on our wedding night. I would kill him that night, if he did. I ask the Successors to bring me a knife. But Alexander not come, so I not have to use it. He not come to me since, either. He say Ochus teach me talk Greek first, then when I grow up we can be properly married. But I think he not really love me.'

Charm frowns as Roxanne speaks. 'Oh, Zeus!' she whispers. 'You mean those poor boys in Balkh were stoned to death because of *you*?'

Roxanne raises her chin. 'They know the risk when they bring me knife. They good Soghdian boys. Alexander kill very many of our people! I swear to kill him in revenge. But now Ochus think of a better way. He say I must wait until I old enough to have baby. Then we tell everyone my baby is King Alexander's. I am Alexander's queen, so when I have avenged my people's deaths I will be able to marry Ochus, and he will be king until our son grow up.'

This is typical complicated human stuff.

While Charm is distracted, I take the opportunity to nibble Aura's lips. She nickers to me and snorts frost into the air. She has grown a furry white coat for the winter, and she looks very beautiful with her big foal-belly.

Charm pales as she works out what Roxanne has said. 'No! Ochus, tell her! Alexander will be furious if he finds out you're plotting against him. You know what he does to people who anger him – oh, Zeus, why are you telling me this?' She glances nervously at the sentries, but they are too far away to hear.

The prince regards Charm with his dark eyes. 'You helped me before, when I was a hostage. If Uncle Alexander dies in battle, we won't have to kill him. We know about your dreams. He listens to you. You must continue to keep him alive until Roxanne is pregnant. Then we simply need you to stop warning him when you dream he will die.'

Charm closes her eyes. 'You silly things! I don't have dreams about Alexander – I have dreams about his horse! And it's no good, anyway, because the king doesn't listen to me any more.'

They frown at each other, and Roxanne whispers something in Soghdian. Ochus whispers back.

'Please, Charmeia?' he says. 'Help us.'

'I can't help you. And you're crazy if you think you can get away with plotting to kill Alexander! You know what he did to Philotas and General Parmenio – do you imagine he'll think twice before doing the same to you?'

Her voice has risen, making the sentries look round. She drops my reins and grips Roxanne's arm.

'Listen to me!' she hisses. 'I was about your age when I went to the palace in Pella to kill King Philip. I had poison in a mule's hoof. I was going to put it in the king's food. Bucephalas saved me. He saved me from doing something very stupid. I understand what you're feeling. I wanted to kill King Philip because he had attacked my home and ruined my mother's life. But later, I was glad I hadn't done it. Even if I'd got away with it, do you think I'd have been able to live with myself? Do you think I'd have been able to look Alexander in the eye, knowing I'd killed his father? Do you understand what I'm saying, Roxanne? Do you? Ochus, tell her!'

Roxanne looks angry, then frightened. She snatches her arm free and raises her chin. 'I not scared of King Alexander.'

'That's a lie. I saw you hiding like a frightened rabbit in Bucephalas' stable in Balkh.'

'That was when he first capture me. I not scared of him any more,' Roxanne sniffs.

'Then you should be! You should be more scared than anyone else! How long do you think his generals and friends will let you and Prince Ochus live, if they find out what you are planning?'

'They won't find out, Charmeia,' Ochus says, glancing at the sentries. 'We'll be very careful.'

'Ha!' Charm shakes her head. 'As careful as telling me? I'm not just Alexander's groom, you know. When the Macedonians invaded Methone and made my mother pregnant with me, it wasn't just any soldier who raped her that night . . . it was King Philip himself, half-blinded by an arrow and crazy with the pain! He was my father as much as Alexander's, which makes me Alexander's half-sister. *Now* do you understand?'

They stare at her in amazement. Ochus' mouth is slightly open. Roxanne goes pale. Suddenly, they both look very scared.

'Is that why Alexander talk to you?' Roxanne whispers.

Charm shakes her head, still angry. 'No, don't be stupid! I haven't told him I know who raped my mother. How do you think he'd react? He's Great King of Persia, and I'm a groom! He talks to me because of Bucephalas . . . the horse bond . . . oh, you wouldn't understand.'

Roxanne frowns.

'You won't tell Uncle Alexander what we said, will you?'

Ochus says. 'Please, Charmeia, don't! I not bear it if he hurt Roxanne.'

Charm snatches up the end of my reins and takes a shuddering breath. 'Of course I won't tell him! Do you think I want to see any more people tortured and killed? It's bad enough I have to decide about the horsemaster! Just don't tell me any more. I can't help you. I can't even help Bucephalas.'

Ochus whispers something to Roxanne. The young queen smiles, pushes her hair behind her ears and says, 'But King Philip die, anyway, Charmeia. His own Guard assassinate him.'

Wearing elephant skin

When we got back to the horse lines, we found Hephaestion waiting for us. He frowned at Ochus and Roxanne and sent them back to the camp, then nodded at a pile of wrinkled grey skins that the grooms were unloading from a nearby mule cart. The mule's long ears were flat with distaste, and we horses flared our nostrils in unease. But they were only like the dead lion-skins Alexander wears after hunting. The ghosts of the elephants had fled back in the Kabul valley.

'We're going to try something,' Hephaestion said to Charm. 'Put these skins on the horses instead of their cloths at night. Start with Bucephalas, then Petasios and Apollo . . . that filly Caspia seems sensible enough, so you can try her too. Best keep them away from Aura, though. I don't want her getting upset and losing her foal a second time. If this works, then at least we might have some horses that can bear the smell of elephants by the time we meet up with the king again.'

'Is there definitely going to be a battle against the Indians then, Sir?' Charm asked, biting her lip.

Hephaestion smiled. 'Not if we can help it. Alex is going to try for a peaceful settlement with Prince Porus. He's more worried about meeting war-elephants in battle than he lets on.'

The elephant skins were heavy, made us sweat, and smelt foul. I bucked mine off several times. So did Petasios. Charm got fed up with replacing them and strapped them on to us with lead reins.

Caspia didn't buck. She simply lay down on her side and played dead, until Charm got so worried she took the skin off her. Then the filly scrambled to her feet again, raised her head and curled her upper lip. Fillies and mares do this when they smell something peculiar, like stale elephant. All the grooms laughed at her, and she didn't have to wear the skin again.

Indus

After about a month, the men finally broke through the walls of Charsadda with their catapults and killed its boss. We left a Macedonian garrison to look after the city, and we didn't bother renaming it. What would we have called it? Hephaestionia? Perdiccasia? Ha! I can think of better names for a city. But I had to stand in the horse lines wearing my elephant skin all through the battle, so I suppose it wouldn't have been fair to name it after me.

We reached the River Indus first, and waited for Alexander. By this time, the weather was warm enough for the mares to foal. Aura hung stubbornly on to ours for several nights. Then, when Charm dozed off, she whinnied softly, lay down in the lines and quietly gave birth to a colt as black as the Indus at night.

I nickered anxiously to my mare, remembering what had

happened to our white foal at the Caspian Gates. But no tiny ghost rose from the black colt, and when Aura licked it clean, I could smell its new-foal scent.

By the time Charm stirred and rubbed her eyes, the colt was on his feet and suckling strongly with his black tail wagging. She laughed and stroked Aura's nose, calling her clever and feeding her handfuls of barley. The other grooms gathered round to admire the colt.

'Is it Bucephalas' foal?' one of them asked.

Charm gave him an amused look. 'Of course! Look how big and strong he is already! I'm going to call him Indus, because he was born here at the edge of the world.'

Aura had her foal just in time, because the next day there was much whinnying and excitement as the horses who had gone dominating with Alexander returned to the lines, footsore and weary. My filly Electra had suffered the most. Alexander was dragging her by one rein, which he's always telling our grooms not to do, walking very fast with a hand pressed to his upper arm. Electra jogged behind him, throwing up her head every time he jerked her mouth. There was foam on her neck, blood on her bit, and a deep scratch down her left shoulder.

'I hope Bucephalas is sound now!' he called. 'Because I'm sick of riding young horses who don't know enough about battle to watch out for arrows.'

Charm took Electra's reins and tried again to tell Alexander about her elephant dream. But, sensing Borealis' ghost (which had followed us through the pass), Electra whirled and trod on her toe. Alexander squinted at the ghost, shivered, and hurried off to his pavilion, calling for Iolaus to bring him wine.

Later, Tydeos told us Electra had let the king get wounded

twice – once with an arrow in the shoulder, and once on the ankle with a stone. That's why my filly was in disgrace. Even so, Alexander had dominated far more Indians than we had on our way through the mountains. He had massacred an entire town after saying they could go free if they opened their gates, dominated a fortress even the legendary hero Hercules had failed to dominate, and nearly killed himself by drinking too much magic to take away the pain of his wounds. Here are the scores.

Alexander:

Indian dead: 25,000.

Macedonian dead: 250.

Horses dead: 5.

Prisoners: none. (Alexander massacred them all.)

Hephaestion and Perdiccas:

Indian dead: 1,500.

Macedonian dead: 50.

Horses dead: none (unless you count Caspia pretending).

Prisoners: none. (Hephaestion and Perdiccas left the survivors at Charsadda to rebuild their homes.)

As you can see, Alexander is still way ahead of everyone in the dominating game. If we were finished, he would be the biggest boss ever.

But I am not sure the River Indus is the edge of the world, like Charm thinks. I can see grass on the other side.

Twenty-ninth Hoofprint
TAXILA, SPRING 326 BC

Squealing at Taxila

When Alexander has made all the proper sacrifices, we cross the bridge of boats Hephaestion's men built while we were waiting. Then we march towards Prince Ambhi's city, which he has promised to surrender to us for our military base. But as we approach, the gates open and a whole herd of war-elephants stamps out to meet us.

Each elephant has a hut swaying on its back, with yellow and orange flags fluttering overhead. Indians in glittering armour walk between them, blowing on long trumpets that make the whole plain vibrate. I flicker my ears uncertainly. Behind the elephants and the trumpeters, we can see yet more Indians advancing in a line across the plain, carrying spears that glint in the sunshine. The elephants are a long way off still, but they are noisy and very, very frightening.

As soon as he sees them, Alexander halts me and flings up

a hand. 'A trap, Bucephalas!' he hisses, his eyes gleaming with the challenge. 'That treacherous Ambhi has led us into a trap with all his fine words and promises! I *knew* he was plotting something. Ha, so now he's going to find out what we Macedonians are made of!' His excitement at the prospect of battle makes me excited, too.

He shouts for our trumpeters to blow the battle call. The horses of the Guard flare their nostrils and dance on the spot as their riders tighten their reins. Everyone except Alexander looks rather pale. But we are a very well trained herd. Behind us I hear shouts, the creak of armour, the rattle of weapons, and the pounding of feet as the phalanx fans out into position. Horses gallop everywhere as the cavalry hastily arm them-selves with shields and javelins. Alexander jams on his Troy helmet and calls for someone to bring him a long pike.

As a man runs up with one, there is a tiny whinny behind us, and the thud of small hooves. My colt, Indus, bursts through the men, bucking and shaking his head, making some of them laugh and others curse. Aura is close behind, carry-ing a wild-eyed Charm, and Prince Ochus is giving chase on Caspia.

'Get that mare and foal back to the baggage train, girl!' Leonnatus yells, trying to catch her reins as she rides past. 'Didn't you hear the trumpets? There's going to be a battle!'

Obedient as ever to her rider's wishes, Aura swerves around Zephyr and gallops straight up to me. I nicker to my favourite mare, while Alexander gives Charm a distracted look.

'What in Zeus' name do you think you're doing, Charmides?' he snaps. 'We're making battle formation! Get back where you belong, and take Prince Ochus with you. This is no place for grooms and children!'

'Please, Sir, Alexander!' Charm gasps. 'You have to listen to me! I've been trying to tell you for ages . . . I had a dream about this battle! You can't ride Bucephalas against those elephants, Sir. If you do, he'll die!'

Alexander presses his knuckles to his forehead and shuts his eyes, maybe remembering that he once ordered her to tell him about her dreams. But that was a long time ago. His whole body is so tense that I tremble as well. Does he want me to charge the elephants from all the way back here?

I get ready to attack, but he holds me back. A shudder goes through him. He eyes the advancing Indian line, waves back the Guard, who are at a loss to know what to do about Charm, and grips her wrist.

He takes a deep breath. 'All right, Charmides! Tell me what you dreamt. And make it fast.'

Charm trembles even more. But she whispers, 'Bucephalas fell, Sir, fighting an elephant! He had javelins sticking out of him, and he was covered in mud. He didn't get up again. I didn't see – I'm sorry, Sir, but I didn't see what happened to you.'

Her wrist is still imprisoned in Alexander's fingers, and her spring-grass smell is sharp with fear. Indus stops playing and trots across to nudge Aura's hind leg, looking for milk.

Alexander stares at Charm with narrow eyes. He says very softly, 'And is this a true dream, Charmides?'

'Yes! I swear it on the name of Zeus, your father!'

He nods and lets her go. 'Mud . . .' he says thoughtfully, looking down at the dusty plain. He looks a bit happier. 'Then this is not the battle you dreamt of, Charmides! Take that mare and foal back to the baggage train, and don't interrupt me again at such a crucial moment, not even if you dream the sky falls on our heads. I've made allowances for you because you can handle Bucephalas. But if you show me up before my men again, I'll be forced to punish you as I would any one of my slaves who disobeys me.'

Charm rubs her wrist and stays silent.

Leonnatus raises an eyebrow. 'Do you want someone to escort her back to the baggage train, Alex?'

Alexander shakes his head. 'The girl will go.' He glares at Charm until she turns Aura and rides back through the phalanx, her shoulders trembling. Indus gives me a cheeky little squeal and follows his mother.

Alexander stares after them. Then he sees Caspia, who lay down when she got close enough to smell the elephants, and frowns at Ochus, who is trying to make her get up. 'What's wrong with that filly?'

The Guard laughs nervously. 'Look! The Mardian filly's doing proskynesis before the king!'

Hephaestion winces. 'She kept doing that when we put the elephant skin on her, Alex. I think we've trained her to play dead when she smells elephants. I'm sorry, I thought it would help. Prince Ochus is too young for battle, anyway, and at least Bucephalas and Petasios have learnt not to fear them.'

'And Apollo!' Perdiccas says, stroking the palomino's neck. 'He's being really brave, Alex, see?'

Alexander gives them an exasperated look. 'We can't win a battle with just three horses! We'd all better hope Charmides' dream *isn't* true.' He strokes my neck and squints at the advancing elephants. He seems worried, even though there is no mud. The members of the Guard glance uneasily at one another. Then a small band breaks away from the enemy herd and trots towards us, leaving the elephants behind.

Alexander relaxes slightly. 'Is that a messenger coming to talk?' he asks, and the Guard all shade their eyes.

'I think it's Prince Ambhi himself, Alex!' Leonnatus says in relief. 'Just his personal guard. No elephants!'

Alexander nods and waves away the man with the pike. He wipes the sweat off his brow and leans across my neck to untangle my tassels. He straightens with a grim smile. 'All right, gentlemen. Keep your swords loose and come with me.'

He clamps his legs against my cloth and trots me to meet the Indian boss, his chin tilted and a tough expression on his face. I make myself huge. The Indian horses are wearing bright cloths, and their tassels glitter with gold threads. But as soon as they see me, they arch their necks and clap their lips in submission.

Prince Ambhi bows his head to Alexander and offers him a fancy sword, hilt first. 'My city of Taxila is yours, King Alexander,' he says through his interpreter. 'These elephants and the treasure they carry are also yours, since I heard the last ones I gave you met with unfortunate 'accidents'. I hope you weren't alarmed by the size of my army. I apologise for any misunderstanding. I wished merely to welcome you to my city in the proper style, as befits such a great king as yourself.'

Alexander accepts the fancy sword. But he narrows his eyes at Ambhi and snaps, 'You were stupid to bring your entire army out to meet us like that! We could have slaughtered you.'

Prince Ambhi smiles. 'I will send extra gifts to make up for scaring you, King Alexander. Please accept my humblest apologies.'

I don't know if the interpreter got the word 'scaring' right. If so, he was a bit stupid to translate it so accurately. Alexander's hand tightens a little on my rein. But he is no longer the hot-blooded man-colt who threw the gold crown back at the Tyrians in Phoenicia and started a six-month siege. He passes the fancy sword to Hephaestion, controls his rage, and says, 'Go back to your army and open your gates to receive me. I'll enter your city in person to receive your gifts. The son of Zeus-Ammon fears no man.'

'As you wish, King Alexander.' Ambhi bows and leads the other Indians back to his herd at a gallop.

Alexander watches him go with narrowed eyes. 'Keep battle formation until we're sure it's not a trap,' he orders. 'And when Ambhi sends his gifts, double their value from my treasure chests and send them straight back again. I'll show this proud Indian ruler that the son of Zeus and emperor of the known world doesn't need his gold!'

'Do you want us to kill him for insulting you like that, Alex?' Ptolemy says, dropping his hand to his sword. 'We can easily take his city *and* his gold.'

But Alexander shakes his head and runs a hand down my neck, staring thoughtfully after Prince Ambhi. 'No, we need him until we've dealt with this troublesome Porus and the other Indian rebels in the east. I want to avoid doing battle with elephants until I'm confident we're absolutely ready to face them.'

The Guard look relieved, and so do all the men behind us, when the news ripples back that there isn't going to be a battle, after all.

If you ask me, Prince Ambhi had it about right when he claimed to have scared us.

The wise man

We camped on the plain outside the walls of Taxila, while Alexander and his friends went into the city to meet Prince Ambhi and the other Indian bosses who had accepted Alexander's invitation to come and surrender. Needless to say, Prince Porus was not among them. After a few curious stares at our army, everyone else in the city got on with what they had been doing before we came.

I had never seen such a busy place! Thousands of humans thronged the streets, barefoot, with dirty cloths wrapped around their heads. The bosses rode on elephants decked out with tassels, and had funny-coloured whiskers – red, blue, snowy white. They wore jewelled feathers in their head-cloths. The air smelt of dung and unfamiliar spices, and the noise was *awful*. All day, we heard the cries of humans, sheep, oxen, and the horrid sound elephants make with their long noses. And at night, millions of mosquitoes took over.

Although the cavalry trained with special long javelins, lighter and easier to carry than the pikes, their horses still would not go near the elephants. I couldn't show my herd how to be brave, because Alexander stayed in the city talking to the Indians. Charm got quieter and quieter as she and Tydeos watched the chaos on the parade ground. Then one evening, when the sun was sinking into red fire over the mountains, she brought a wrinkled little Indian man to the horse lines.

He wore a white rag tied around his waist, and his skin was nearly as dark as Hades' coat. He smelt strange. I gave him flat ears to warn him to stay away from my herd. But he stood very still and quiet, watching me with his black eyes.

'This is the horse,' Charm said, stroking me. 'Bucephalas, behave yourself. This is a very wise man. His tribe knows the

476

answer to every question. He's going to tell us more about the horse bond.'

The little man's eyes crinkled. He walked right up to me, put his hand on my tether, then waved his other hand on my blind side.

My heart thumped. But before his hand could turn into a pike, he rubbed it behind my ear, whispering in his own language. His voice was soothing, and although Borealis' ghost came closer, I lowered my head and rested it on his shoulder.

Charm stared, amazed. 'Bucephalas never lets strangers touch him like that! How did you know about his blind spot?'

'The horse told me.'

I did?

Charm smiled. 'He seems to like you.'

'I think this horse sees things men do not,' said the wise man, still watching me. 'Why do you want to break the bond that links your lives?'

Charm's face tightened. 'So I can take Bucephalas somewhere safe, and King Alexander won't come after us. I've been a slave all my life. Now I want to be free!'

The wise man gently let go of my head. It drooped to the ground, I felt so sleepy and warm. It was a very nice feeling. I didn't even mind when Borealis rested his ghostly teeth on my withers.

'Ah,' said the wise man. 'Freedom – that is a much bigger thing.'

'If the bond is broken, I'll be able to buy my freedom with the bonuses King Alexander has given us. As it is, I can't leave the king. Neither of us can.'

'There is no bond, except that which is in your own heart.'

Charm looked worried. 'But the Amazon queen said there

was! She said only death could break it. But there must be some other way, surely? Please tell me how.'

'Hmm, death. I am not sure the Amazons understand death. Some say that in their country, the dead ride with the living. I do not know if that is true. Here in our world, the dead outnumber the living. But since we cannot see them, only the living matter. I think this horse bond you talk of, my child, is just another name for love.'

Charm glanced at the city, where Alexander was staying, and said, 'That's not true!' But she flushed as she spoke.

The wise man smiled. 'Do not be ashamed. I've seen how your King Alexander makes people love him. Even those who fear him, also love him so much they will die for him. It is hard for you, because he is a king and you are just a groom. But when we are dead, it will not matter what we were in life. Every one of us is the same – we will have just the small piece of earth where our bones rest. You, me, the horse, King Alexander. Where our ghosts go I cannot say, but I know they do not make war on other ghosts, because they all have the same amount of earth and do not need more. But until then we must make our choices and feel the love and pain that arises from them. That is the joy and the curse of life.'

Borealis' ghost stared over my withers at the wise man, ears pricked. As the Indian peered closer at the place where he stood, I felt a big drop of rain fall on my back.

Not noticing it, Charm shook her head. 'What about the edge of the world, then? Is it close to here, like Alexander says? Will it make him immortal?'

The wise man held out his hand to catch a raindrop and sighed. 'I think it is a different place for everyone. Your king says the oracle promised him immortality when he reaches it,

478

so maybe it is close for him. Certainly, no one will forget Alexander's name after the things he has done. Maybe you, too, will find your freedom at the edge of the world. It is said to be a place where all dreams come true.'

Charm stared through the camp fires into the darkness of the east, and whispered, 'That's what I'm afraid of! I dreamt Bucephalas would die there . . . in the mud.' The next raindrop fell in her mane, and she looked up with a terrified expression.

'Then you will be free of your horse bond, won't you?' the wise man said gently. 'I think the time is coming when you will have to choose between the horse and your freedom. You cannot have it both ways, my child.'

Thirtieth Hoofprint
River Jhelum, Summer 326 BC

A miserable march

In the morning, the trumpets sounded for us to break camp. The rain had stopped. But the air smelt moist, and it was hotter than ever.

Alexander was in a hurry. He urged me into a trot as soon as he was mounted. I instantly broke into a sweat. Behind me, the other horses of the Guard were sweating, too. Their riders wiped their foreheads and frowned at the sky. Prince Ambhi, the boss of Taxila, rode with us on his brown Indian horse, accompanied by his interpreter on a mule. I squealed at it as we set out.

Things are getting bad, if we have mules in the Guard.

'We have to get there before the river swells,' Alexander muttered. 'Porus has been playing games with me, sending all those messages pretending he wanted to reach a peaceful settlement and promising to come to Taxila. He was just delaying us until the rains came and he had a chance to march his army here. Faster!'

Alexander kept everyone moving as fast as they could. But by the time we reached the ford, the rain was falling in sheets, and the dust had turned to the mud Charm had dreamt about. My hooves squelched and slipped. I tucked in my tail and flattened my ears to stop the water getting in them. The men pulled their cloaks over their helmets to stop them going rusty, and stared miserably at the fast-flowing brown water.

The Guard stopped around Alexander, silent. I nickered in sympathy to my steaming friends, who were all trying to turn their tails against the rain. Worse still, on the far bank a line of elephants awaited us, with Indian spearmen and archers sheltering under their massive legs. When they saw us, they shouted excitedly. The enemy soldiers ran to the edge of the trees and bent their long bows. Arrows flew towards our bank, but fell short and were whirled away in the flood.

Alexander snapped at Ambhi, 'Are you sure this is the only way across?'

'This is the ford we normally use,' Ambhi said through his interpreter. 'It's the only safe crossing during the monsoon. That's why Prince Porus has brought his army here to stop you. Are we going to charge him straight away? He is not so confident. He doesn't have as many men as we do. Once we get across the river, you should be able to beat him.'

Normally, this would be true. As I've explained before, the herd with the most men and horses usually wins. But this enemy has elephants. Also, this river reminded me of the Granicus. I shivered as I remembered how I lost my rider there and nearly drowned.

Alexander frowned at the stamping elephants, which were

barely visible through the rain, and looked down at the rushing water. I felt him shiver, too. 'I'm not taking my horses across that, not with those elephants waiting for us! Tell the men to make camp. I'm going to ride along the bank and find somewhere else for us to cross.'

We left the Indian boss to pass on the order, and squelched along the riverbank. Electra, Apollo, Hades, Harpinna, Hoplite and Zephyr followed me in a miserable line, trying to tuck their heads under each other's tails. On the far bank the elephants made their horrible noises among the trees, and kept pace with us.

'How many do you see?' Alexander said.

'Looks like quite a few, Alex,' Laomedon said, bringing Electra up next to me. 'They're watching all the places where the river narrows.'

'How many?' Alexander snapped. 'You can count, can't you?'

'About fifty?' Laomedon ventured.

'Even I can see more of the beasts than that!'

'At least a hundred,' Perdiccas said. 'And there are probably more of them back at Porus' camp.'

Alexander closed his eyes. 'Right, that's what I feared. I'm going to have to think about this. Attacking across that ford would be suicide, so we'll have to wait for my boats to come over from the Indus. Meanwhile, I want you to keep the men occupied. Patrol in both directions and make a note of all possible crossing points. I want to know exactly where Porus has stationed his troops, and how many men and elephants he has at each.'

As he spoke, his fingers played with my mane, faster and faster. His voice became shriller as the old excitement shone in his eyes.

'I want a parade every day on the riverbank in full sight of Porus' men, horses as well as the phalanx. Keep all weapons polished, and whip any man who complains. Ptolemy, you'll do the same at night. Work out a rota so the men and horses all get their share of rest. I want Porus so nervous by the time we're ready to attack, he won't know which direction we're coming from! If he thinks I'm going to sit on this riverbank and wait two months for the rains to stop, he can think again. We'll show this proud Indian prince we're not afraid of his elephants!'

We shifted our hooves in the mud, and our riders looked at the monsters on the far bank. No one spoke.

Alexander turned on the Guard with a scowl. 'What's the matter? We're going to win this battle, like we've won all our other battles. Fear is a disease, and I don't want it infecting my army. You must set a good example to the men. Understand, gentlemen?'

The others nodded, as miserable as their horses. On the way back, I let Electra put her head under my tail.

Our grooms rigged up a tent cover between baggage carts in an attempt to keep our hay and cloths dry, but it didn't work for long. The rain got everywhere. Our barley was soggy. Our bits tasted of rust. Our cloths clung to our backs. Our bridles smelt of mildew. Everyone – humans and horses – splashed through the mud with their heads low. Even rolling in it was no fun after the first few times, because it stayed wet on our coats so our grooms couldn't get us clean.

Alexander was the only one who didn't let the rain dampen his excitement. He rode me every day, and insisted Charm put on all my tassels and my parade cloth. He wore his Troy helmet with its soggy plumes, the Achilles armour, and his blue and white Persian cloak. The coming battle took his mind off Borealis' ghost, and he stopped looking over his shoulder so often. When he mounted me, we looked so good my heart lifted. But by the time we got back, my bit was rusty again, my cloth spattered with mud, and my legs tired from cantering up and down the bank so Alexander could talk to the men and give speeches. Don't ask me what he said. It was boring stuff about glory and honour and immortality and the edge of the world. But his words made the men cheer and work harder, so I suppose he knew what he was doing.

It didn't stop raining, though. Not even Alexander could control the weather.

Charm pleads with Alexander

Charm grimaces as she picks up my feet to scrape out the mud. My hooves have not been dry since we got here, and I'm not the only one. She prods a sensitive spot, and I flinch. 'Half the horses will be lame soon,' she mutters. 'Bucephalas' feet are rotting away!'

'Then King Alexander won't be able to ride him in the battle, will he?' Tydeos says, doing the same for Apollo's. 'Isn't he going to take him out today? He's usually down here before now.'

Charm looks at the sagging, dripping tents. The men are busy further along the bank, calling instructions to one another. I see part of Alexander's white pavilion being carried towards the river's edge.

Charm sees it too, and stiffens. 'Something's going on. They're moving the king's tent.'

Tydeos puts Apollo's hoof down. 'Not only the king's tent . . . the men are arming for battle, look!'

The grooms have all noticed the unusual activity in the camp, and their tension infects us. All down the line, horses throw up their heads and whinny. The rain is easing slightly. Men in full armour are picking up their weapons and running to form up in columns out of sight of the river. Unlike other days, when they shouted continually as they paraded and galloped their horses up and down, they are being as quiet as possible.

Hephaestion comes to the lines, his helmet dripping, and calls softly, 'Battle-cloths, everyone. Rough bits. No tassels. And when the king comes, no proskynesis. We don't want Porus' men to see where he is.'

Charm sucks in her breath. She runs to me, picks up my hoof with the sensitive spot and pulls out her dagger. I don't know what she is going to do, but I trust her, so I nibble her damp mane.

'I'm sorry, horse,' she whispers. 'This will hurt a bit, but I can't let him ride you in this battle.' She presses the point against my hoof, pauses, then gulps and sets my leg down, shaking her head in horror at what she nearly did. She blinks up at Hephaestion. 'Sir, Bucephalas has a touch of foot-rot from all this mud. Can't you persuade the king to ride another horse? Xanthus, maybe?'

Hephaestion makes a face. 'I'm afraid not, Charmeia. Craterus needs Xanthus, and you know as well as I do that Bucephalas is the only horse here who will face elephants. Alex needs him for this battle more than in any before. Come on, quickly now, get his cloth on him. We've had news of another Indian prince coming south to join forces with Porus. If that happens, we'll be outnumbered, never mind the elephants. We have to get across this river tonight.'

Charm shakes her head and grips my mane. Everything is wet, but I think there are tears on her cheeks.

Hephaestion sees them, too, and lowers his voice. 'Try not to worry. The king has a clever plan. We're going upstream to meet our boats. There's an island in the middle of the river there, so the channels are narrow. Porus' troops don't know we've explored that far. By the time he finds out what we're up to, we'll be on the far bank behind his army. Craterus is staying here with half the men, and he'll cross the ford as soon as Porus is distracted. Porus hasn't enough men to send against us both, and his elephants move slowly. We'll trap them between us. Alex won't take any unnecessary risks with the horses.'

'But my dream!'

Hephaestion frowns. 'In school, Aristotle told us that if we're not careful we make our dreams come true, the bad ones as well as the good—'

Before he can say any more, I smell Alexander.

The grooms do not notice him immediately. He is wearing a plain Macedonian helmet, so at first glance he looks like a normal cavalryman. But his chin is tilted up, his eyes are gleaming, and he strides through the mud with energy shining around him as if he owns the world. Even if they can't smell him, I don't understand how they could not know Alexander.

Then one groom gasps and drops on his face in the mud, and the others quickly follow. Alexander waves an impatient hand at them. 'Get up out of that muck and get the horses ready! Hephaestion, didn't you tell them I'm supposed to be in disguise? Where's Bucephalas? Why isn't he ready? Charmides! Get *moving*.'

Charm stands protectively in front of me, her arms spread. 'No,' she says in a brave voice. 'I won't let you ride him today.'

Alexander glares at her.

Tydeos' eyes widen. 'Charm!' he hisses. 'What are you *doing*?'

Hephaestion's eyes widen, too. He says quickly, 'I'm sorry, Alex, the girl obviously doesn't know what she's saying. It's this weather. No one's used to it . . . maybe she's got a fever?'

'Charmides!' Alexander snaps. 'If you don't get my horse ready this instant, I'll have you put under arrest.'

Charm falls to her knees in the mud at Alexander's feet. 'Please, Sir,' she whispers. 'Please don't ride Bucephalas in this battle! I told you about my dream. It's muddy today.'

Alexander starts to breathe faster. Hephaestion grabs hold of Charm's arm and shakes her. 'Don't be stupid!' he hisses. 'Get up and obey the king!'

Alexander looks as if he is about to say something to Charm, then shakes his head and mutters, 'Oh, I haven't time for this! You, Tydeos! Get my horse ready at once.'

'Don't you dare, Tydeos!' Charm shouts.

She struggles against Hephaestion's grip and tries to reach her dagger. Hephaestion takes it from her and tightens his lips. 'Be sensible, Charmeia!' he says. 'What's got into you today?'

Tydeos casts a stricken look at Charm and avoids her eyes. He puts my battle-cloth on me. I shiver as he fumbles with the straps of my bridle. Although Alexander has ridden me every day we've been here, I know very well that this is not going to be another trot by the river. I toss my head, impatient to get on with it.

'*No*, Tydeos!' Charm yells, still struggling. 'Don't! Bucephalas is going to die in this battle! I dreamt it!'

I dance anxiously as Tydeos leads me out. When Alexander taps my shoulder, I am far too upset to settle to my knees for him. He makes an impatient sound and leaps on to my back. He gathers up my reins and glares down at Charm.

'When I return, I expect you to have come to your senses,' he says in an icy tone. 'All right, Hephaestion. Let the girl go, and get on your horse.'

Hephaestion relaxes his grip, but Charm has not given up. She stumbles after me, flings herself at my rein and hangs on, making me throw up my head. Sobbing and pleading, she clutches Alexander's ankle.

This is VERY upsetting. Has my favourite groom gone mad?

The king fends her off with his foot and shouts for his men. Two Macedonians come running, seize Charm and drag her away from me. They force her to her knees in the mud and hold a sword at her throat, looking questioningly at the king. Charm stares up at Alexander with terrified eyes. Her sobs stop, and her spring-grass smell sharpens with fear.

Tydeos and Hephaestion both take a step towards her, but hesitate when Alexander raises his hand. The other grooms watch in horror.

'Lock her in one of the empty cages,' Alexander orders, giving Charm a peculiar look. 'Make sure she stays there until after the battle. I'll deal with her when I get back.'

The Macedonians haul Charm to her feet. Again, she begs Alexander not to ride me, and struggles fiercely. But Hephaestion has taken her dagger, and she is not as big or as strong as the men.

'Bucephalas!' she cries, as they drag her away. *'Bucephalas!'*

Upset, I plant my forelegs and whinny to her. Alexander loses his temper and swears at me. He grabs a spear from one of the men and brings it down on my quarters with a sharp whack. I squeal and give a small buck. But before it can turn into a battle like the one we had in the high pass over the Caucasus Mountains, Charm stops struggling and calls, 'No, Bucephalas! Don't fight him. They haven't hurt me. See?'

She gives me a final anguished look, then bows her head to Alexander.

Since she is no longer fighting, I calm down. Alexander mutters something under his breath about crazy females, and trots me over to his pavilion. The last I see of Charm is her tear-streaked face as the soldiers march her away through the mud.

Roxanne pleads with Alexander

At the king's pavilion, Iolaus is waiting for us dressed in Alexander's blue and white cloak and the Troy helmet, which is too big for him. This is very strange, but Alexander doesn't seem to mind.

He puts his hand on Iolaus' shoulder and says, 'Make sure Porus' men can see you clearly. Craterus is briefing all the men and the grooms. They'll know they're supposed to do proskynesis before you. Don't stand for any nonsense, now! And keep that helmet on whenever you're outside. Our plan won't work unless Porus believes you're me.'

'Just as long as he doesn't try to stick an arrow in me,' Iolaus says, fingering the cloak nervously.

Alexander laughs. 'Believe me, Porus is going to be far too busy coping with us to bother shooting at you!'

Iolaus still doesn't look happy. He mutters something

under his breath about getting all the rotten jobs. But Alexander doesn't hear, because just then Caspia trots up with Prince Ochus sitting very straight on her back.

I whinny a greeting to the filly, and she nickers to me. She is wearing a battle-cloth. Ochus has a long Persian sword thrust through his sash, and a spiked helmet glitters beneath his yellow turban. He looks grave and determined.

Alexander frowns at the sword. 'Ochus, what do you think you're doing? I told you, no training today.'

'I'm coming with you,' Ochus says, raising his chin. 'I'm not a child any more, and I'm good with my sword now. I can help watch your back.'

Alexander's eyes flicker with surprise. He leans across, puts his hand on the man-colt's shoulder, and says more gently, 'That's very brave, Ochus. But I didn't fight my first battle until I was sixteen, and believe me this battle isn't going to be suitable for a thirteen-year-old boy who has never killed a man. Go back and look after Roxanne for me.'

Ochus bites his lip and glances back at the camp. He whispers, 'Please, Uncle Alexander. I know about Charmeia's dream, and you must not die in this battle. You're short of Guard members. Please take me with you. I am your heir, so I should learn what battle is like. When you asked me to cut off Bessus the traitor's ear, I was afraid and ran away. I am afraid today, too, but I will never run away again.'

Alexander gives him a closer look, admiration replacing the surprise. 'Seems you've grown up faster than I thought. But you can't come. It's too dangerous. And don't you go spreading any rumours in the camp that I'm going to die in this battle, or I'll have you whipped, prince or not! I haven't worked so hard, and come this far, to have my men spooked by a silly groom's dream. The girl probably made it up, anyway. She's done that before.'

He wheels me round to join the others. Ochus bites his lip, checks his sword and tightens his chin-strap. With a stubborn expression, he turns Caspia to follow us. But Roxanne runs across his path, the hem of her red dress dragging in the mud. She flings herself at Caspia's reins, just like Charm did at mine, and speaks very fast in Soghdian. Ochus leans down and whispers something to her. Roxanne shakes her head, tears in her eyes.

Alexander gives the girl-filly a look of frustration. 'I told you to keep my wife away from the riverbank!' he snaps at her two guards, who arrive panting from the chase. 'Take her back to her pavilion at once, and make sure she stays there! What's wrong with everyone today? If we don't get going soon, we'll never even make it out of camp before Porus realizes something's up.'

Roxanne glares at the men, who had moved closer to take hold of her arms. She catches her breath and pushes her long mane behind her ears. 'Please, my husband,' she begs. 'Please not take Prince Ochus into this battle!'

Alexander frowns at her, then at Ochus. Something changes in him, like a cloud covering the sun.

'Oh, I see!' he says, narrowing his eyes. 'I let the prince teach you Greek, and the next thing I know you two are exchanging kisses behind my back!' He laughs and gives Ochus a twisted smile. 'So, my brave prince, do you still want to see what a real battle is like?'

Ochus nods nervously.

'Good! Then you can join my Guard and get a close-up view. But I can't be looking out for you once the fighting starts. If you get into trouble, you're on your own.'

'*No!*' Roxanne wails.

But Ochus straightens his shoulders and trots Caspia after us, his expression hovering between pride and fear.

Out of the corner of my eye, I see Roxanne standing between her guards, staring after Alexander and the prince. She looks more terrified than when I found her hiding in my stall back at Balkh.

Omens

We marched upstream as fast as we could. When it grew dark, Alexander passed an order back that no one was to speak, in case Porus' lookouts heard us. Only the squelch of our hooves, the creak of damp leather, and the heavy breathing of the foot-soldiers could be heard above the whine of the mosquitoes. The rain stopped, and steam rose from the leaves. The air made our coats prickle.

Suddenly, the sky cracked with a white flash. Several horses bolted past me, Caspia among them. I reared up in shock. But Alexander held me on a firm rein until the others pulled up and trotted back, shame-faced. The storm crashed above us and lightning forked into the ground on all sides, leaving smoking holes. Back in our column, men shrieked. We horses smelt burnt flesh and flickered our ears uneasily.

'Zeus is warning us not to fight today,' Peucestas whispered, staring over his shoulder. 'He's aiming at the pikes! It's a bad omen.'

Alexander laughed, in a better mood now we were finally on the move. 'It's a *good* omen, gentlemen, not a bad one! Remember how the moon went out before the battle against the Persians at Gaugamela? My father Zeus-Ammon is helping us. With all this racket going on, Porus' lookouts won't hear a thing. Take off your helmets, if you're worried about Zeus striking you.'

He urged me into a canter. The Guard tugged off their metal helmets and followed. There was no more talk of omens, good or bad, because at our faster pace they had to concentrate on avoiding the trees.

Past midnight, when the lightning had given way to more torrential rain, we boarded the waiting boats by torchlight. It was not easy, and took some time because every horse had to be coaxed on board. On our boat, we found a very soggy and miserable Zephyr. Demetrius, wrapped in his cloak, was crouched at her head. Alexander patted him on the shoulder and thanked him for saving his life in Soghdiana. It was good to see Demetrius back with a horse – but considering Zephyr's record of losing her riders, I hoped he would be very careful.

We doused the torches and used the current to take us along the shore of the island. We were so quiet, no one spotted us until the first ten boats had cleared the headland and were heading for the far bank. Then an Indian horse appeared on the other side of the river, stared at us, and galloped off downstream with its rider yelling a warning. Somewhere in the darkness, Indian trumpets blared.

Alexander gave the order to land, and our boats made for the bank in a hiss of dark water. We jumped out, thankful to have solid ground under our hooves again, even if it was mostly mud. Our riders mounted, our herds formed up, and we set off at a smart trot to find the Indians.

Before I'd gone ten strides, the ground crumbled under my hooves. I scrabbled back in terror. Alexander jerked forwards on my cloth and slammed his hand against my withers. He sucked in his breath as I came to a snorting stop at the brink of a black torrent. 'Zeus!' he cursed, shaking his fist at the sky. 'I thought we were across. Where did that come from?'

The Guard stared in horror. 'We're cut off, Alex!' Leonnatus cried, looking up and down the bank. 'We'll have to get the boats again.'

Alexander glared at the flood, gripped my mane tightly and dug his heels into my sides. 'No time! It can't be that deep. Follow me!'

First blood

I jump, because I trust him. But it IS deep. For a moment I think there is no bottom, and panic. It is like the Granicus all over again. Ghosts whirl around me. Then I feel mud under my hooves, and I struggle up on to higher ground. Alexander is still on my cloth. He looks pale. But it is all right, because I am strong.

Caspia is among the first to follow me. The little filly's head disappears. Then she works out how to swim, and reaches the higher ground beside me with Ochus clinging to her mane. Caspia's eyes have white rings around them, but Ochus grips her reins firmly and urges her after me. After seeing us disappear, the phalanx find a shallower place further upstream, and the men wade across chest-deep, their pikes held over their heads.

We scramble up the far bank and hurry inland before any more channels can open up. Alexander whirls me on the spot with his sword in the air, urging them on, and the men cheer when they see how confident he is.

Then we are galloping!

Behind me, I hear the splashing of twenty thousand hooves. The Macedonian battle cry echoes from fifteen thousand throats. My blood throbs. Caspia is right behind me, ing flat out. The rain glitters on Ochus' long eyelashes, and part of his turban has come unwound. His teeth are bared in excitement. My head whirls with excitement, too. I forget the mud and the rain.

Some enemy chariots and cavalry gallop out of the trees towards us. But they don't have as many horses as we do, and their boss is a very young Indian, not much older than Ochus. They hesitate when they see us.

Alexander grins and draws his sword.

We charge them without even stopping to form a line. Alexander heads me straight for the leading chariot, and his blade flashes down. The man-colt inside ducks, but his driver falls out and the first Indian ghost shimmers into the rain. As the chariot lurches past us, the man-colt drops to one knee and bends his long bow. The arrow flies at Alexander. It is a good aim, and I have to leap to avoid it. My hooves slip in the mud, and my old injury from Chaeronea gives a wrench of pain. The arrow misses Alexander, but as I land it pierces the soft skin behind my elbow just in front of my girth.

It goes in deep. Pain shoots through me, and the ghosts fleeing from the battlefield take on a strange solidity.

Then an Indian horse careers into me, and the feathered shaft of the arrow snaps off. The man-colt in the chariot abandons his bow and grabs the reins. He is heading straight for Caspia and Ochus. Alexander leans down, pulls a javelin out of the mud and throws it at the enemy cavalryman, then he whirls me round, his sword ready to kill the next. I don't think he realizes I am wounded. There is too much mud on me.

The enemy chariots are in trouble on the riverbank. Their wheels get stuck in the mud. Their drivers fall easily to our javelins and swords, until the bank is littered with enemy dead. Some horses are in the river, struggling in the current. Their ghosts shimmer in the rain before disappearing.

Out of the corner of my good eye, I see Ochus fighting the man-colt who leads the Indian herd. Both of them look terrified, but determined. Caspia lays back her little ears and bares her teeth at the Indian horses. Ochus' long Persian sword flashes, and the man-colt's ghost ripples away as his body plops face down in the mud, pooling blood. As Ochus stares down at it, another Indian gallops up behind the prince and raises his sword. Hephaestion yells a warning and gets the Indian in the neck with one of his javelins, while Ochus gallops Caspia back to us. Seing this, the rest of the enemy flee.

Alexander claps the prince on the shoulder. 'Well done,' he says. 'I think that was one of Porus' sons.'

Ochus stares at all the dead bodies, leans over Caspia's shoulder and is sick in the mud.

Alexander grins, his eyes still glittering with the excitement of battle. 'Don't say I didn't warn you! I was sick after my first battle, too. It gets easier. Stay close to Peucestas, he'll look after you. Everyone else, form up. That was just a taster – we haven't met the elephants yet.'

As the others gather around me, stamping and snorting, I whinny to check they are all right. The familiar whinnies come back: Caspia, Electra, Petasios, Apollo, Zephyr, Harpinna, Hoplite, Borealis . . .

BOREALIS?

My arrow wound sends a shooting pain through me, and I shiver in the rain. That is the first time I have EVER heard a ghost whinny.

Our last battle

It was nearly midday before we found the rest of the enemy. We caught the smell of the elephants long before we saw them. Every horse in our herd flickered its ears nervously. I forgot the pain of the arrowhead buried behind my elbow and broke into a trembling sweat.

Alexander smiled grimly and tightened my rein. 'Don't let me down now, old horse,' he whispered. 'One last effort, and you'll be back with your groom before evening.'

He seemed to have forgotten he'd ordered that Charm be put in a cage.

I shivered all over as we came out of the trees, and I wasn't the only one. The men fell silent. Facing us in an unbroken line across the plain was Prince Porus' army. Foot-soldiers in the middle with their long bows and javelins, cavalry and chariots on the wings . . . and, spaced along the line of men like towers in a battlement wall, elephants carrying huts stuffed with Indians on their backs. As Perdiccas had said earlier, a lot more than a hundred of the monsters.

While we waited for our phalanx to catch up, Alexander dismounted and examined the land, exactly like he'd done back at Gaugamela. His Guard followed him tensely, eyeing the elephants. But Prince Porus made no move to attack us. He sat in his hut on the biggest elephant at the centre of his line, and waited patiently for the rest of our herd to come out of the trees. He'd obviously heard how we had dominated his son earlier, and he wasn't going to let us do the same to him.

My wound hurt, but the arrowhead was hidden in the fold of skin behind my elbow under a crust of blood and mud, and Alexander was too preoccupied and excited to notice I was lame. He muttered to himself and eyed the enemy line over little rises in the land. Finally, he was satisfied. He vaulted on to me and called his officers across.

'I'm dividing the cavalry into three,' he announced. 'Demetrius, you hide your men behind this hill. The phalanx can hide behind that one. Perdiccas, stay in the trees over on the right. Hephaestion, you bring your men with me. We'll attack their left wing first. Hopefully, Porus will think I'm too scared to bring many of my horses against his elephants, and will think that's all we have. When he sends his cavalry and chariots across to finish us off, Perdiccas can join us from the trees. That'll force Porus to bring the rest of them across from the right, so Demetrius can go round the back and attack them from behind. As soon as we've put their cavalry out of action, the phalanx can attack the centre. You all know the best techniques for killing elephants now. Take as many of them out as you can, then we'll help you with those archers. But wait for my signal. I don't want you going in with enemy cavalry on your heels. Ochus, you ride for the ford and find Craterus. Tell him where we are, and tell him to hurry. Peucestas, you go with the prince.' His eyes sparkled. 'It isn't going to be easy, gentlemen. But we're going to win this battle!'

Thunderous cheers greeted this speech. I made myself huge and forgot the pain of my wound. Ochus tightened his reins and whispered something in Caspia's ear. Peucestas gripped the big shield of Achilles and stared anxiously after Alexander.

Alexander drew his sword and looked round at the Guard with a man-coltish grin. His eyes shone with excitement, as they used to back in Macedonia. His legs trembled, hard and tight against my cloth. His breathing quickened. 'Right, everyone ready? Keep your formation, gentlemen . . . *Charge!*'

Oh, it is wild! It is exciting! It is slippery!

Petasios and I gallop side by side, our riders knee-to-knee. Most of the horses are wary of the elephant at the end of the line, so our charge isn't as straight as usual. But the Indian horses don't like the elephants any more than we do, so they are waiting for us well out of reach of the monsters. They hold their formation until an Indian trumpet blows. Then they charge us in a ragged, whooping herd.

Our javelins hiss through the rain, and several horses and riders roll over in the mud and give up their ghosts beneath my hooves. I leap to avoid them, and Alexander's sword flashes as he dispatches more ghosts. The Indian riders grin at him. They think they're going to win, because they believe they have more men than us. They haven't seen the Macedonians hiding in the trees.

More enemy chariots stream towards us from the other side of the plain. Alexander waits until the last moment, winks at Hephaestion and waves to our trumpeter. The blast sounds a bit damp, but it is loud enough, because a great answering cry sounds from the trees.

'ALALALALALALALAI!'

Brave Apollo appears at full gallop followed by his herd, with his pale tail streaming through the storm and Perdiccas yelling on his back.

The Indians whirl in alarm to face this new threat, and Alexander cuts down another enemy from behind, making another ghost. He waves his arm again as the chariots from the Indian right wing race across to help their struggling herd, and another damp trumpet blast brings Demetrius on Zephyr, with the rest of our herd splattering behind them, their faces covered in mud but grinning because the king's plan is working perfectly.

But Zephyr is scared of the elephants, and the charge goes wide as the others follow the silly mare. The Indians realize they've been tricked, and reform their line to bring the elephants into the battle.

'Where's Craterus got to?' Alexander yells, cutting down another of the enemy. 'Watch those elephants! They're breaking out of the trap!'

One of the biggest elephants is lumbering straight towards me, followed by several desperate enemy foot-soldiers who have broken away from our phalanx.

'Porus!' Alexander hisses. He leans down and plucks a javelin out of one of the dead Indians. 'Come on, Bucephalas, this is our chance to finish it!'

He digs his heels into my sides, and we charge the elephant.

I am not afraid. The tall Indian boss in the elephant's hut looks down at us with astonished eyes and grabs his spear. I leap as high as I can, though it tears my wound. At the top of my leap Alexander hurls his javelin.

It pierces Prince Porus through the shoulder, and the enemy boss cries out in pain. Several javelins fly down at Alexander from the guards in Porus' hut. This never happened in training, so I am caught unawares. I twist to avoid them, but catch two on my quarters and one in my shoulder. It feels like being thumped by a bad-tempered groom. They don't really hurt, but my legs wobble as I land.

'*Alex!*' Demetrius cries, fighting to get Zephyr closer to us so he can protect the king with his little shield. The trees around me blur, and I can barely feel Alexander on my cloth. I am aware of my friends leading a wild, brave charge against the elephants. Then Zephyr bumps into me as an Indian arrow hisses into Demetrius' thigh, knocking me off balance.

Just when it looks like we are in real trouble, a trumpet sounds in the woods behind us, and Craterus comes galloping out of the trees on Xanthus, leading his herd. Our phalanx advances on the elephants with shields locked and pikes lowered. Yelling battle cries, our men slash the long noses of the monsters, stab their legs, and do all the other things they've trained for. One of the elephants falls with a crash that shakes the ground, and its huge ghost whistles past me, making me shiver all over.

The sky grows darker.

'Porus is getting away, Alex!' Demetrius shouts, pressing a hand to his wounded leg and pointing after the biggest elephant, which is lumbering off into the trees on its own.

Alexander plucks out the javelin stuck in my shoulder, grips it in a determined fist, and puts his heels into my sides. I make a huge effort, but my legs are getting wobblier with each stride, and every breath hurts. I can't even see Porus' elephant through all the ghosts, so we soon get left behind.

At last, Alexander realizes something is wrong. The battle-fever leaves him, and he pulls me up. He strokes my trembling neck. 'What is it, Bucephalas?' he whispers. 'What's wrong, old horse?'

I can't tell him. But at that moment my knees give way. Darkness closes around me. I see only ghosts, ghosts, ghosts.

Alexander jerks my head up in alarm and digs his heels into my sides. 'No! I won't let you die! I *won't*. You're my immortal horse. Those little Indian spears didn't go in very deep. You've had worse wounds. You need a rest, that's all. You'll be fine when we get back to camp . . .'

Hephaestion rides up to report the capture of Prince Porus, but Alexander waves him away impatiently. 'Take the prisoner back to camp. Give him something to eat and treat him with respect. I'll discuss the surrender of his lands later. I've got to see to Bucephalas.'

He slips off me and takes my reins over my head. I stagger after him through the piles of bodies and the mud, past the dead elephant and back downriver to the ford. It is still raining. We are followed by a trail of weary, mud-spattered horses and men. On the way, we meet more of Craterus' herd finishing off the Indians and elephants that fled the battlefield. Alexander does not stop. One of his hands holds my bit in a tight grip, and the other holds my mane, keeping my nose off the ground so I don't trip over it. When I am not sure I can take a step further, he whispers in my ear and I do.

When we reach the ford, Alexander clutches my withers as if *he* needs the support, not me. A small golden horse is lying on its side in the mud. Caspia! Hoplite stands beside her, head down and flanks heaving. Peucestas kneels nearby, covering something with the big shield of Achilles. I can see a strip of muddy yellow cloth coming out from under the rim. I can hardly raise my head far enough to check, but it looks like Prince Ochus under the shield.

Peucestas leaps up when he sees the king. 'Alexander, I'm sorry! There was an elephant! The filly lay down, and the prince's leg got trapped beneath her. One of the Indians put an arrow in him . . . he died bravely, poor boy. But I can't get the filly off him. I think she's dead, too.'

Some of the men rush across and try to move Caspia, but she is heavy even though she is small. I summon the last of my strength and nicker to tell her the elephants have gone. She opens her eyes and scrambles to her feet at once. Under the shield, Ochus lies motionless.

Alexander stares at the dead man-colt with a peculiar expression. 'Don't just stand there!' he snaps. 'Take the prince's body back to camp, and someone let my groom out of her cage. Bucephalas needs her.'

The men lift Ochus on to the Achilles shield, and we follow them. I try my best to make myself huge for Alexander. But the ford finishes me. Long before we reach the horse lines, my legs give way and I lie down in the mud. It is strange, but there is no pain any more. Dark clouds fold around me, and I see Borealis standing before me, solid as a real horse, with his brown ears pricked.

Alexander takes off my bridle and cloth. I hear him shouting for the horse doctor, but my eyes are dark. When feet splash towards me, and a warm human lies across my neck and strokes my face, I know from her smell it is Charm.

'Bucephalas . . .' she whispers. 'Bucephalas, don't die, oh please don't die!'

I nicker softly as her tears fall into my mane.

More feet run towards us, and I hear Roxanne's voice screaming at Alexander.

'You've killed my Ochus! I *hate* you! I'll hate you forever! . . . Oh, Ochus, wake up, please wake up . . .'

But Prince Ochus' ghost is gone.

Alexander must be all right, because back at the camp the men are chanting his name and cheering. I think that means we dominated the Indians.

But Charm is crying so much, I hear nothing else for a long while.

THIRTY-FIRST HOOFPRINT
BUCEPHALA, 326–324 BC

Victory?

I do not like the horse doctor. Every time he comes to see me, he does something to me that hurts. I want to tell him to go away. But my legs won't work, and I can barely make flat ears. He's still scared of me, though. He makes Charm put my muzzle on me, and sit on my head while he's treating me. Also, he's useless, because he hasn't found the arrowhead buried behind my elbow. It's trapped beneath me, and it hurts all the time.

I think I am lying on a flattened tent. There is another tent stretched over poles and tied down at the corners to form a makeshift stall around me. The rain splatters noisily overhead, and drips fall on my legs. I can hear my friends whinnying in the distance, but I do not have the strength to whinny back.

I can still smell the river, though I am no longer by the ford where I collapsed. I can remember sliding through the mud behind two mules, who complained at my weight but dragged me behind them all the way up the hill. Before they were led away, they lowered their noses and blew at me in sympathy.

Mules aren't so bad, after all.

Charm has not left my side since Alexander brought me back to camp. Tydeos brings her food and my medicine, while she strokes my nose and whispers to me. She keeps it up all day and night, which is a bit annoying because I am very tired.

Charm says this is how we dominated the Indians at the River Jhelum:

Indian dead: 23,000, including Porus' son.
Macedonian dead: 14,000, including Prince Ochus.
Horses dead: 3,000, almost including ME!
Elephants dead: 120.
Prisoners: Prince Porus, and 10,000 Indian slaves for building work.

I do not care. I'd like to leave my body and mutual groom with Borealis, who is waiting patiently beside me. But every time I start to drift through the dark clouds towards his ghost, Charm's voice tugs me back.

'As soon as the men have recovered from the battle, Alexander's taking them to find the edge of the world,' she tells me. 'It's not far from here. Then he'll bring back some magic water from the eastern ocean to make you better. He's building a city here to celebrate our victory over the Indians, and Demetrius is going to be left in command of the garrison, so we'll be all right . . .'

Did she say city? It *must* be my city this time!

'. . . and Craterus is building a fleet to take us all home when Alexander gets back. The scientists think the River Jhelum might take us back to Egypt, because they've found some Egyptian reeds growing on the bank. So even if you can't walk by then, we can put you on a boat and sail you to the big Alexandria in Egypt, and from there across the sea to Pella. We'll be home before you know it, Bucephalas, and Alexander's promised you can retire in the mare pasture . . .'

I am too tired to think about mares. What's my city *called*?

'So many men died here, Bucephalas! Everyone's sick of the fighting. Roxanne says Alexander took Prince Ochus into the battle on purpose to get him killed. I don't know if that's true—'

A corner of my shelter blows loose in a sudden gust, and Charm breaks off to stare at it. Borealis is standing out there in the night, looking in.

I manage a small nicker, and Charm jumps up at once. She brings me herb-smelling water, and holds the bucket under my nose so I can drink.

'Are you thirsty, Bucephalas? Are you hungry? You must eat!' She takes away the bucket and brings me a handful of barley mash soaked in honey, which I lick from her palm to please her.

She gulps down a sob and strokes my cheek.

'Oh, I know Prince Porus is Alexander's prisoner, and the new city's going to be called Nike, which means Victory, but it feels like we lost! None of the men are partying. They're just drinking to forget the battle. I think those elephants frightened them almost as much as they frightened you poor horses. And Caspia got poor Ochus killed! It's my fault. It was a mistake to teach her those silly tricks. Even Alexander's Guard has had

506

enough. They're going to try to talk Alexander into going home. But I hope he finds the edge of the world first, otherwise you won't get your magic water to make you better . . .'

I hear no more. My eyes have closed and my head is back on the ground, surrounded by dark clouds.

Alexander called his new city Nike!

What do I have to do to get a city named after ME?

My own worst enemy

The next time the clouds clear from my head, everything is much quieter and Charm is not with me.

I am still lying under my shelter, although the sides have been tied back. It has stopped raining. The sun steams in a golden haze. I can see barefoot Indians piling up mud-bricks to dry. Boats ferry them across the river to build the foundations of the new city.

Borealis is grazing nearby. When he sees I am awake, he whinnies and trots over. He sniffs my nose. As he does this, something black charges out of my blind spot and I hear Indus' cheeky little squeal. The colt rears and strikes out at Borealis with his small hooves. His ghost vanishes. Indus comes back to earth and paws my shoulder. I raise my head and flatten my ears to tell him to leave me alone, and pain shoots through me. In the distance, Aura whinnies anxiously.

Indus will not give up. He nudges me with his nose and keeps pawing the ground, shaking his mane. Charm comes running back. 'Shoo!' she says, waving her arms at Indus. 'Go back to your mother, you silly colt! Bucephalas is sick. He doesn't want you bothering him.'

Indus keeps trying to get his nose under my elbow, where the arrowhead is buried. It has been swelling for some time now, and it feels hard and tight. I move, and a shooting pain goes through me as the wound explodes, splattering my colt's nose with pus. He leaps back with a squeal, raises his head and curls his upper lip. Charm stares at him in amazement. Then she lies down and pushes her hand under me. She brings it out smeared in pus and blood.

'Oh, Zeus . . .' she whispers. 'Oh, Bucephalas! You're wounded, and it's infected. That horse doctor's useless! I'm going to get help. Wait here!'

I'm not going anywhere, believe me.

She races off, and I drift back into the dark clouds, because moving took all the strength from me. Men come back with Charm and tie lead reins around my fetlocks. She takes my tail and pulls. Between them, they roll me over. More pain shoots through me, and I neigh in terror. Borealis is watching me again, his ears pricked. But at least Indus has gone back to his mother. There is a horrible smell. I think it is me.

When the clouds clear once more, Charm is sponging my arrow wound, and I hear Demetrius' voice.

'Looks like it's gone deep. It could have hit his lung, which would explain why he's having trouble breathing. This climate's bad for wounds.' He pauses and says gently, 'The horse is thirty years old, Charmeia. That's like one of us being ninety. It'd be kinder to put him down.'

'No!' Charm spreads her arms across me. 'Alexander will be back soon with the magic water from the edge of the world. Bucephalas will get better then. He *will*.'

Demetrius sighs. 'Charmeia . . . you must know this immortality thing is just a story? Alex is extremely unlikely to find the water of life in India, even if such an elixir exists. It's just something he told the men, to make them follow him further east.'

'The Amazons were supposed to be a story too, weren't they?' Charm says stubbornly, her eyes glittering with tears. Her hand drops to her dagger. 'I won't let you kill Bucephalas!'

Demetrius shakes his head. 'Maybe if we'd seen his wound earlier . . . sometimes this horse is his own worst enemy. The horse doctor was obviously too scared to examine him properly. I don't know who you're going to find to remove the arrowhead. I've just had one like it dug out of my thigh, so I know how much it hurts. But it'll have to come out, or he hasn't a chance of surviving until Alex gets back – if he comes back. I've a feeling the edge of the world is a lot further than he's told everyone it is.'

I can't see their faces. But when Charm speaks again, her whisper sounds scared. 'He's *got* to come back. He promised! He'll come back for Bucephalas. We can't let him die so far from home . . . we *can't*.'

Demetrius says softly, 'I'll help you, if you're determined to try. You'll need something to sew up the wound afterwards. These Indian arrows are barbed like a spiny leaf, so you have to cut deep, you can't just pull . . . I'll show you the one that came out of my leg, so you know. Bucephalas isn't going to like it much. He's still got a spark of life in him, the brave old horse!'

'He'll let me do it,' Charm whispers, stroking my nose. 'He's got to.'

It hurt more than you can imagine. More than being branded. More than a spiked bit. More than a whip. More, I imagine, than the Scythian thing the Persians did to poor Zoroaster – no, maybe not more than that.

But Charm whispered to me all the time, and Demetrius sat on my head to keep me still. The arrowhead came out with lots of pus and infected flesh. Then Charm sewed up the wound and put herb-paste on it. As she cleaned her dagger, Borealis' ghost breathed down her neck. Charm frowned and looked round. I tried to warn Borealis to keep away from her. But the effort was too much, and the dark clouds smothered me once more.

Demetrius ordered the slaves to build a stable for me on this side of the river. At some stage, I assume the mules must have dragged me into it. I don't remember that bit. But I know I am out of the heat and lying in a deep bed of straw when I smell Alexander's sherbet-sweetness again.

The edge of the world

I flare my nostrils, which is about all I can manage now. Aura and Indus are munching hay in the next stall. Caspia is next to them, thrown out of the army in disgrace, her mane shaved off in mourning for Prince Ochus. Borealis stands in the empty stall on my other side. He doesn't need hay, because he's a ghost. Charm is curled up in her cloak next to me, sound asleep. She has been awake all night talking to me, and she is exhausted.

Outside, men shout and laugh, trumpets blare, and horses whinny to their friends – all the familiar noises of our huge herd making camp. It sounds as if they have won another battle. But when Alexander walks into the stable, there is no light of victory shining around him. His mane is stuck to his head where his helmet has squashed it. His white cloak is grubby. His eyes shift nervously from side to side as if he's looking for Borealis' ghost. He peers over my door, pauses a moment, then lets himself in.

'Bucephalas,' he sighs, stroking my cheek. 'So it's true –
you waited for me. Oh, old horse! Where did it all go wrong?'

Charm starts awake. Seeing Alexander, she scrambles to
her feet and bursts out, 'Did you find it?' Then she blushes
and kneels in the straw to kiss the king's dirty toes.

Alexander gives her the same sort of look he gave me. 'Get
up, Charmides,' he says in a weary tone. 'There's no one to
see you do proskynesis here, except the horses, and who are
they going to tell? The edge of the world is further than I
thought. My men are cowards! We found another river as
wide as the Jhelum, and they got scared they'd find more
Indians and war-elephants on the other side. They refused to
follow me across. I'd have gone on alone, if they didn't need
me so much. I am their god and their king, and kings and gods
are not free to do things like that. You don't know how lucky
you are, just being a groom.'

'Sir?' she says, staring at him wide-eyed.

'I'm telling you I didn't find it!' Alexander snaps. 'Don't
you understand? There is no magic water. There is no immortality. The oracle in Siwa lied to me. My army wants to go
home. I've shown them the wonders of the world, and all they
want to do is crawl back to their pathetic little farms and families! Their ambitions are so small, Charmides, so small . . .
One of Parmenio's old officers led the revolt. He dared tell me
that the sign of a great man is knowing when to stop! I should
have got rid of all the old guard when I got rid of General
Parmenio. Now it's too late. I can hardly execute my entire
army, can I?'

He presses his knuckles to his forehead. 'I'm not taking
them back to Macedonia, if that's what they think. I'm going

to make another court out here in the east, perhaps at Susa or Babylon. Somewhere I can keep a careful eye on my empire. And I'm going to replace Antipater back in Macedonia. I know he's been plotting behind my back for years. I'll just have to rethink things a bit . . .' Energy glimmers around him again as he starts planning his new empire, but Charm is not listening.

'No magic water?' she whispers, looking at me. 'But Bucephalas—'

Alexander takes a deep breath. 'I know. The old horse is dying. I'm surprised he held on this long, after what the horse doctor told me. An arrow in his lung. He didn't dare take it out. Said it would kill him for sure, at his age. The Amazons might have helped him, but they've gone home.' He mutters something about the edge of the world, then says, 'Did you know there's a Queen Penthesilea in the *Iliad*, too? In the very last line, she comes to help Troy and does battle with Achilles, who is supposed to have killed her. I've been wondering about their country, and whether the tales about them being immortal can be true. But I expect Amazons pass the same names down through generations just like we do, and the reason no one can find their land is because it's so small and insignificant.' He shakes his head at me and says more gently, 'I'll mount an expedition when we get back as far as the Caspian Sea. But even if the Amazons do know the secret of immortality, it's too late for Bucephalas now.'

'I took the arrow out,' Charm says, so quietly the king doesn't take it in at first.

Alexander keeps muttering about the *Iliad*, and the edge of the world perhaps being in a different place than he'd thought. But Charm's words finally get his attention. 'You took it out?'

Charm bites her lip. 'Me and Commander Demetrius.

Bucephalas is no better, though.' She pauses and asks in small voice, 'Will you let me go and find the Amazons, Sir? If Tydeos stays here to look after Bucephalas, I could maybe take Aura and some of your men . . .?'

Alexander's face softens. He fingers Charm's mane. 'Ah, Charmides . . . Charmeia. You're so faithful. I know you'd go to the ends of the earth to save the old horse, if you could. You've more loyalty in these few hairs than most of my men have in their entire bodies.' He lets the curl fall against her flushed neck. 'But it's out of the question. I need all my men, and I need Tydeos to look after the other horses.'

Charm's face twists. 'What about me?'

Alexander sighs. 'I'm not going to make you leave Bucephalas, don't worry. The old horse deserves a friend at his side when he dies. But he obviously can't travel in that state, and we're leaving as soon as the fleet is ready. We won't be back this way, so I release you. You're free. I'll give you three talents to help you start your new life, and papers to say you are a free citizen of the empire, under my protection. When the old horse is gone and you want to go home, show them at any Macedonian garrison, and they'll give you food and shelter for as long as you need, and an escort when you're ready to move on.'

Charm stares at him. 'You're freeing me?'

The king smiles. 'Can't have my half-sister remain a slave all her life, can I?'

Charm sucks in her breath. All the blood drains from her face. Then, although Alexander has told her not to, she does proskynesis before him.

'Forgive me, Your Majesty! I didn't know how to tell you! I wanted to, but there never was a right time. I thought you'd be angry with me and make me leave Bucephalas . . . oh, please forgive me!'

She's face down on the ground beside me, so she doesn't see Alexander's expression, which is a cross between puzzlement and sorrow. He gives Borealis' ghost a quick look. 'Get up, Charmeia,' he says in his weary tone. 'It's hardly your fault my mortal father raped your mother after the battle at Methone, is it? I've known who you are ever since I captured the horsemaster in Soghdiana. General Parmenio knew as well, apparently, but he kept it from me. I was right to have him executed. If I was going to punish you for lying to me, I'd have done so long before now.'

'It's worse than that, Sir,' Charm breathes, trembling as she peers up at him. 'You still don't know why I went to Pella. I hated King Philip for what he'd done to my mother! I had poison in a mule's hoof—'

'Enough,' Alexander says, cutting her off with an impatient hand. 'I know all about that, too. Queen Ada told me in her last letter – I think she was worried what I might do if I found out from someone else. Demetrius has asked to stay on here, so he'll look after you. I'm also going to leave the old horsemaster with you, since you've been so reluctant to let me kill him. That's how I know you weren't involved in my mortal father's murder. You can't bear to see anyone suffer, can you, not even your worst enemy? But I'm sure you'll decide a suitable fate for him eventually, even if it's just leaving him to rot in his cage. Tell Demetrius, when you do decide, and he'll carry out your orders as if they were my own. Before we leave, I'm going to give Bucephalas a funeral grander than any horse has ever had. This stable looks good here, so I'll build a new city around it in his memory. Call it Bucephala, so no one will forget how brave he was.'

Charm's eyes fill with tears. Borealis looks questioningly at me over the partition. I find a sudden surge of strength and give him flat ears.

BUCEPHALA!

My city. Mine!

Borealis is going to have to wait a bit longer for me to join him. I want to see what my city looks like when it's finished.

Healing

I didn't see my funeral, although the smell of burning flesh got everywhere, even into my stall. Charm said they used the pyre to burn the bodies of all the horses and men who had died from their wounds while Alexander was off looking for the edge of the world, so no one noticed that mine wasn't among them. There were guards around my stable to keep everyone away, and the men were too excited about going home to take much notice of the building works. Tydeos had not forgotten us, though. The day the fleet set sail, he came into my stall and stroked my cheek.

'He's no better, is he?' he said. 'Are you sure you want to stay behind, Charm? You can still travel home with us, even though King Alexander has freed you. I wouldn't want to stay here. It rains too much.'

'You dolt! That's only a couple of months a year. It's sunny now, isn't it?'

Tydeos made a face. 'I'll write to you with all the gossip. You'd best wait till we get somewhere more friendly before you write back, though, or your scrolls might never reach me. Can you remember the letters Prince Ochus taught you?'

Charm smiled. 'I'll practise. I won't have much else to do.'

She gazed at him, and he gazed back. 'Tydeos . . .'

'No soppy stuff!' Tydeos stood up with a grin. 'This isn't goodbye. You can come after us as soon as Bucephalas – when it's over. And if you don't, I'm coming back here to find you just as soon as I've saved up enough money to buy my freedom and some mares to start my horse farm. King Alexander might've let you go, but you can't escape from *me* that easy!'

Charm started to laugh, caught her breath, and rummaged in her bedroll. 'You can have the gold Alexander gave me. I don't need it.'

'Nor do I.' He fended her off, still grinning. 'The king's still giving out bonuses. I'll be rich soon. You keep it till you've got enough to buy a decent stallion, and we'll start our horse farm together!'

Then, finally, it was peaceful again. At least, as peaceful as it could be with a city being built around us.

When Alexander had gone, Charm tried everything she could think of to make me better. She brought a procession of local wise men to my stable, and they gave her foul-smelling pastes to put on my wound, and weird things to put in my food. None of these cures worked, mainly because I would not touch my feed if it smelt suspicious. I grew weaker because I wouldn't eat. Eventually, in desperation, Charm went to the only knowledgeable person in Bucephala she had not so far asked for advice.

By this time I am too far gone to realize what she is doing, and am lying on my side with my eyes closed. But when the old horsemaster limps into my stall and his smell reaches me, my body does a strange thing. It breaks into a sweat and twitches, and one of my hind legs kicks out. I haven't done that for a long time. It hurts.

'Now, don't worry, Bucephalas,' Charm murmurs, coming to kneel at my head. 'The horsemaster's here to help you. I've promised him his freedom in exchange for making you better. He knows a lot about horses. Be sensible and let him examine you.'

Charm has brought my enemy into my stall!

My hind leg twitches again. In my heart, I am rearing and kicking to keep him away from Charm. But my body remains lying in the straw.

I roll my eye at him. The horsemaster leans on his crutch and stares down at me. He is dirty and thin, and his whiskers have grown even longer than before. He wears a good cloak, though, over his ragged tunic.

'Well?' Charm whispers, looking up at him. 'Can you cure him?'

'What if I can't?' growls my enemy, sending more sweat washing over me. He glances at the two guards in the passage. 'Are you going to order me locked back in that cage and tortured to death as punishment?'

'No,' Charm says quietly. 'I told you. Alexander said it's my decision, so you'll go free, whatever happens. Even if Bucephalas dies. But you've got to try. Look at him! He's fought this long, and he's so brave. I have to try everything I can to save him.'

The horsemaster looks at me with narrowed eyes, making me tremble with bad memories. He prods me with his crutch and grunts. 'This horse is suffering. You should have put him down months ago.'

'You haven't even examined him!'

'I don't need to. Anyone can see he's dying. He's thirty years old, for Zeus' sake! You're crazy, keeping him alive so

517

long. The king's already led his funeral procession. He's a lost cause. I'll do it for you, if you can't stomach the deed yourself, which you obviously can't. That's the trouble with letting a girl do a man's job.'

Tears spring to Charm's eyes. 'Are you sure he's suffering?' she whispers. 'Is there *nothing* we can do?'

The horsemaster makes a face. 'Nothing, except a sword through the heart.'

Charm bows her head and strokes my sweaty neck. 'Then I'll see to it,' she whispers. 'You can go.'

The horsemaster shakes his head as his guards escort him to the door. He keeps looking back at Charm and me, as if afraid it is a trick. I relax slightly as his smell fades.

But just as my enemy reaches the door, there is excited shouting outside. A Macedonian sentry races past, shouting, 'The king's dying! A messenger just arrived from one of the rebel fortresses downriver! King Alexander led a charge over the wall, and only three men followed him. The scaling ladders broke. An arrow pierced his lung! Peucestas covered him with the Achilles shield, but the king's dying. King Alexander's dying!'

The horsemaster blinks at his guards, and a slow smile spreads across his face. They look at each other, wide-eyed, and hurry off after the sentry. Charm stares after them in dismay, while I look round nervously for Alexander's ghost. I don't see it, though.

Charm takes a trembly breath and continues to stroke me. 'No,' she whispers. 'It can't be true. We'd know if the horse bond broke.'

The horsemaster limps back to my stall and looks down at Charm. 'Hear that, girl-groom? Alexander's finally gone and got himself killed! When this news spreads, there's going to be no safe place this side of the Hellespont. I'm getting out of here, but I'm going to need a horse and someone to look after me. My health's not improved any in that cage the king kept me in, so you're coming with me.'

Before Charm realizes what he intends, he seizes her wrist and wraps the lead rein around it.

She gasps. 'Stop it! What are you doing? I'm a free citizen now! King Alexander's not dead! When he hears of this, he'll come back here and kill you—'

'I doubt it,' the horsemaster growls, lashing her wrists together. 'And you're not free any more. That document the king gave you isn't worth the papyrus it's written on if he's dead. You owe me for wrecking my career back in Pella. Who's going to care what happens to a common groom, when the world's falling apart around them?'

'No!' Charm cries, struggling, frightened now. 'I know I made you lose your job, but I made up for it. I stopped Alexander executing you, and I've set you free! You promised to help Bucephalas . . . you *promised*! Help! Guard!'

But the guards have gone to spread the awful news, and do not hear her cries. The horsemaster tears a strip off his ragged tunic and stuffs it into Charm's mouth.

Charm tries to reach her dagger with her bound hands, but the horsemaster snatches it away from her and holds the point at her cheek. 'Shut up and stop struggling, slave!' he hisses. 'Or I'll mark this pretty cheek of yours with a permanent scar. Now, Bucephalas obviously isn't going to be much use to us. So we'll take that grey mare. Nice colt. It can run behind us.' He drags Charm to her feet and marches her out into the passage, where he loops her leash around a hook. Then he seizes

Aura's bridle and opens her stall.

There is so much noise outside now, no one can hear what's happening in the stables. The horsemaster is trying to get the bridle on Aura, who thinks he has come to threaten her colt and gives him flat ears in the fierce way of a mare protecting her foal. Indus squeals and rears bravely. The horsemaster growls and hits him with his crutch. Indus squeals again, this time in pain, and races back behind his mother. Charm makes a muffled sound of protest and tries to get her gag off.

My colt and my favourite groom, hurt! My favourite mare about to be stolen!

Something stirs inside me. Making a huge effort, I roll over, put my forelegs under me and sit up. Borealis' ghost stares at me in surprise and fades a little. With a massive heave, I am on my feet. My legs tremble. But I am much thinner than I was, so they just about support me.

I stagger out the open door of my stall, make myself huge and squeal in rage.

The horsemaster looks round. His eyes go wide.

'Impossible!' he breathes.

That is the last word he ever says.

Aura, furious because he hit her colt, rears up and hits him on the back of the head with her hoof. He stumbles out into the passage, dazed, and I take a chunk out of his neck with my teeth. He tastes HORRID. The effort of making myself huge finally catches up with me, and I crash down on him with my full weight. Bones crunch. He thrashes a little. Then his ghost shimmers away from under me, and he lies still.

I am puffing as much as if I had carried Alexander into a battle. Charm finally gets her leash free of the hook and tears off her gag. 'Stay there, Bucephalas!' she cries, stumbling out into the night. 'I'll fetch help!'

Aura calms down. She whinnies, first to her colt, and then to me. Indus whinnies back. Caspia neighs to me, and I manage a tiny nicker to tell them I am all right. Aura's door is still open. She walks round and sniffs me to check I am not dead. I can see her more clearly now. Indus sniffs me, too. I raise my head and reach for a mouthful of hay.

It is good. I am hungry again!

That is how Charm finds us when she comes back with the guards. They look at the horsemaster's broken body and shake their heads. Then they look at me and shake their heads again.

'I'd never have believed it,' says one. 'The old horse has come alive again!'

'I don't reckon King Alexander's really dead, neither,' says the other. 'I reckon we should wait till we have proof. You know how he always looks like he'll never recover, then comes out of his pavilion laughing at us all for being so worried about him. Zeus only knows what he'd do to us, if he heard we'd abandoned our posts.'

Charm is not listening. She kneels beside me with her arm over my neck, pushing Indus' curious nose away and patting me so hard I am afraid she'll knock me over again.

'The horsemaster *did* heal you!' she says, laughing and crying at the same time. 'He really did! You hated him so much, you came back to life to save me! Oh, Bucephalas! Oh, old horse! Don't you ever, *ever* scare me like that again!'

Gossip from Tydeos

My city, I have to admit, proved disappointing. It was brown and crowded, with small mud-brick houses and narrow streets and the usual noise and smells. But on the riverbank the men had built a big statue of me with Alexander on my cloth, rearing into the Indian sky. Ha! They won't forget us in a hurry.

The rumours of Alexander's death proved false, as the horse bond had already told us. Over the next year, Charm received regular letters from Tydeos and read them to me while I was recovering. Most of them were soppy nickers and whinnies. But he wrote some groom-gossip, too:

> Alexander recovered from his arrow wound and dominated all the Indian fortresses on his way downriver, to teach them he was still the boss.

> The river didn't lead to Egypt, like the scientists said it would, but to a horrible desert where 60,000 people and 3,000 horses died (including poor Xanthus), and the men had to eat *mules* because they ran out of supplies. They must have been desperate, that's all I can say.

> When the army eventually reached Susa, the Macedonians took Persian wives in a mass marriage ceremony. King Alexander married one of Ochus' sisters, which made Roxanne hate him even more.

> Tydeos got promoted to horsemaster.

Charm gripped this last letter tightly, a big smile on her face. 'Hear that, Bucephalas? Tydeos has been made royal horsemaster! He says the army's on its way back to Ecbatana. You're strong enough to travel now. We can meet him there!'

Tydeos? Royal horsemaster? It's a good thing we are going back, because I am getting seriously worried about Alexander's sanity.

THIRTY-SECOND HOOFPRINT
BABYLON, 323 BC

A mule's hoof

We left my city in the spring, before the rains came. Aura led the herd carrying Demetrius, and Charm rode Caspia so she could lead Indus, who was not yet old enough to be backed. She let me run free behind, since I was still a bit weak after nearly dying in India. She knows now that the horse bond links us too strongly for me to run off and leave her. Borealis' ghost followed us, hiding in the shadows of my damaged eye.

Alexander had already dominated all the cities and lands we marched through, so there was no fighting. We went slowly with plenty of rests, which was just as well, since my legs were wobbly at the end of every day. We used the easy pass to get out of India, then took the lowest pass over the Caucasus Mountains, so Borealis did not have to see his skeleton, then took the direct road back from Balkh. As we marched further west, we heard more news of Alexander – disturbing reports of massacres, that made Charm go quiet and the men frown. At the Caspian Gates, Zoroaster's ghost shimmered out of the shadows and trotted up to Borealis' ghost. They greeted each other joyfully and began to mutual groom.

By the time we arrive in Ecbatana, it is spring again. We have spent a whole year travelling back from India, which is better than the four years it took to fight our way out there. But outside the walls, we find only patches of yellow grass, blackened earth, smoking funeral pyres, and hoofprints in the mud. Alexander and his army have gone.

Charm drags us straight to the stables. 'Tydeos!' she calls. 'Tydeos!'

Even though I am exhausted after our long march, I can sense something is wrong. I flare my nostrils, disturbed. Hay blows everywhere. Leather buckets, left in the passage with water in them, have gone mouldy. Most of the stalls are empty and smell of stale dung. But out of the shadows at the far end comes a desperate, lonely whinny. Aura and Caspia prick their ears. Indus gives a little squeal and shakes his head. I neigh in joy and trot down the passage.

Petasios! My faithful red friend!

Charm catches up with me and sucks in her breath as she looks over the door of Petasios' stall. His mane has been hacked off (which, as you know, is a bad sign for his rider), and his tail cut too short for him to flick away flies. His coat is dusty and his ribs stick out. His water is dirty, and he's wearing his muzzle, so he won't have been able to eat his hay.

I stretch my head over the door and nicker to him in sympathy.

Charm whispers, 'Oh, you poor horse. How did Hephaestion die? Was there another battle? Why are you wearing your muzzle in your stall? Where's Tydeos?'

But if Tydeos were here, he would never have let Petasios get so thin and dirty. His smell lingers on the rake, but it is faint.

Charm shoves Indus into the stall across the passage, puts Aura next door to him and Caspia on the other side, and lets me into the stall next to Petasios. The red horse immediately pushes his nose over the partition and tries to mutual groom with me. Charm takes his muzzle off, pats him and whispers, 'You'll be all right now. I'll look after you.'

Hearing our whinnies, a groom finally appears. He sees Charm in Petasios' stall and hurries across, eyes wide. 'Watch that horse!' he says. 'He's mad.'

Charm shakes her head. 'Don't be silly. Petasios is one of the nicest stallions you'll ever know. I'll do him – he knows me. You go and see to that grey mare. *She* won't bite you. What happened to Hephaestion?'

The groom pulls a face. 'Caught a fever at a party, didn't he? Died a few days later. The king went crazy! He crucified the doctor, then led his cavalry off into the hills and killed everyone he could lay his hands on.'

Charm goes pale and whispers, 'I thought all the killing had stopped.'

'You've no idea!' the groom says. 'King Alexander ordered us to cut off the chestnut stallion's mane and tail in mournin' for Commander Hephaestion, and said he never wanted to see nobody else ridin' that horse, not ever. We didn't dare take him out of his stall while the king was still in the city. And then when the king went off to Babylon, the horse got so mad we couldn't handle him, not even on a lead rein.'

'I'm not surprised,' Charm says. 'He's a warhorse, not a mule! He needs proper exercise and care.' She collects the dung from Petasios' stall in a bucket, and comes to take the stale dung out of mine. I nibble her mane as she works, but she pushes my nose out of the way.

'Where's Tydeos . . . the king's new horsemaster?'

'Said he had somethin' important to do.' The groom frowns. 'He went off to Babylon with King Alexander. They're goin' to give Commander Hephaestion a big funeral there. They took all the best horses and most of the grooms with them. That's why this place is so dirty. Can't be expected to do it all myself, can I? I've still got all the garrison horses to see to, and the commander here is one of General Parmenio's old grumps. Always complaining about somethin' or another . . .'

The groom grumbles on, but Charm is no longer listening. She has been watching me nose around my stall and lift my tail to dominate the stale smells. In the corner of my stall, under some mouldy hay, is something particularly foul – a mule's hoof. It has been hollowed out and fitted with a metal lid, and has an interesting sweet smell. I push my tongue inside to explore.

Charm freezes. She stares at the hoof and goes very pale. 'Poison,' she whispers. 'Hephaestion was poisoned!'

The groom stares at the mule hoof in confusion. Charm drops it in her bucket with a tight look, and orders him to help her clean out the stalls.

Over the next few days, the stables were a whirlwind of scrubbing and sweeping and polishing. Charm put a bridle and cloth on Petasios and took him out to exercise, much to the garrison groom's admiration. After that, he still grumbled, but he worked harder when she was around. Charm made him help her back Indus, and begged Demetrius to take us to Babylon. But Demetrius said the king had not sent for him, the heat would be bad in the south at this time of year, and we should wait until Alexander came back from the funeral. He promised to send a message saying that we were waiting for him in Ecbatana, so Charm had to be content with that.

She chewed her lip and exercised us every morning along the road to Babylon, staring hopefully across the plain. But still the army did not come, and she turned us back to the stables with a sigh. 'At least the king's still alive, Bucephalas,' she said, patting me. 'I can feel it. He'll be back for you soon, don't worry. Then Tydeos will come, too, and maybe we'll find out what's been going on.'

We did find out. But not in quite the way Charm hoped.

Ghosts

One night, when I am lying in my stall dozing, I feel a sharp pain behind my elbow where the Indian arrow wounded me. It is like the arrowhead piercing my lung all over again, and my heart gives three rapid thuds and stops. Sweat bathes me. I neigh in terror. All the horses scramble to their feet and neigh in alarm. Borealis and Zoroaster shimmer out of the shadows and whinny to me in joy.

Charm is curled up in her cloak in a corner of my stall, exhausted after a battle with young Indus on the training ground. But our frantic neighs wake her. She sits up with a start and stares at me. 'Oh, horse, I was having such a dream! Alexander drank some poison at a party and collapsed like Hephaestion did, and then – *oh!*' She puts her hand over her heart and goes very pale. '*It's going!* I can hardly feel it any more!' She grabs my head and hugs it hard to her chest, trembling all over like a horse before battle. 'It's just like the Amazon queen said. I think the horse bond's breaking! Stay with me, Bucephalas, don't you leave me too . . .'

She begins to cry like she will never stop. It is all very puzzling, because my heart has started beating again, so the bond isn't broken yet. When the pain fades, I am warm all over. Even the stiffness from my battle scars has gone. I still have a lump on my forehead where the Macedonian pike hit me back before everything started, but my eye seems better. I nicker softly and nudge Charm to tell her I'm hungry and want my breakfast.

She gets up, looks at me for a long moment, then shivers and wipes her eyes. 'Oh, old horse, I have to go to Babylon! You understand, don't you? I think something very bad has happened to Alexander.'

Charm runs to tell Demetrius about her dream. In the morning, she puts on Indus' bridle with trembling hands and leads him out into the yard, where the men are already mounted. She leaves my door open so I can follow them, as I did on the way back from India. Borealis and Zoroaster come, too.

Demetrius trots Aura to the front of the herd and gives Charm a steady look as she scrambles up on Indus. 'This had better be a true dream, Charmeia,' he says. 'Because if it isn't, we're going to be in a lot of trouble.'

We take the road to Babylon. We go faster than we travelled back from India, but I feel fitter than I have done in years. After we've been several days on the road, a herd of Macedonian soldiers gallop past us in the opposite direction. Recognizing Demetrius, their boss pulls up his sweaty mare and shouts, 'You'd best be quick if you're hoping to talk to the king! He's got a terrible fever. The doctor thinks it's his old arrow wound from India, gone bad inside, but rumours are already going round about poison. Everyone says he's going to die this time for sure! Can't stop – got to get the news to Ecbatana!' They gallop off in a cloud of dust.

Charm puts a hand to her mouth and closes her eyes. Demetrius glances at her, gathers up his reins and shouts to his men, 'Charmeia's dream is coming true! Hurry! We have to hurry.'

Arion's ghost is waiting for us at the ford across the Tigris, grey ears pricked. When he sees me, he trots up to blow a greeting. His breath is warm and his lips feel like lily petals. Borealis and Zoroaster whinny to him in delight. Several caravans are waiting to use the ford, but none of their mules and camels will go near it because of the three ghosts, so we get to cross first. It is fun to gallop through a river without a rider, and I make the most of it, splashing Aura until my favourite mare squeals and gives me flat ears.

We canter across the recently harvested fields and along the lush banks of the Euphrates. Finally, the huge blue and gold gate of Babylon shimmers in front of us. There are bulls and monsters on the walls, glittering in the sunset. But the gate is shut. A crowd of angry people are shouting at the Macedonian guards, and several caravans have given up trying to get in, and have set up camp outside. We trot through them all. Aura throws up her head and pricks her ears at the archers on the high wall.

'Halt!' a guard calls down from the battlements. 'No nearer, or we'll shoot. Identify yourselves!'

'Open up, you idiots!' Demetrius calls. 'I have to see the king.'

The Macedonian guards peer closer at him. 'Commander Demetrius!' one says. 'I'm sorry, Sir, we didn't recognize you. We've strict orders not to let anyone through tonight. The gate will open tomorrow at sunrise for official business only.'

Demetrius shakes his head. 'Open this gate at once! I've brought King Alexander's groom with me. He left her to nurse his horse, and he'll want to see her before he dies.'

The Macedonians look uncertainly at one another. 'You mean that girl he freed back in India?'

'Yes, Bucephalas' groom! The king will be furious if he discovers you kept her out of the city.'

'If the king's dying, it won't matter who we keep out,' mutters one of the men.

Charm rides Indus to the front of the herd, and I follow her. Aura nickers to me. The guards fall silent and take a wary step back.

'That's *him!*' one says in an awed whisper. 'That's the king's horse, back from the dead!'

'Don't be stupid! It's one of his colts, that's all. The old horse never looked so good, even when he first came to Pella.'

I give flat ears to the guard who said that. He jumps as my teeth snap near his ear. Their boss squints at me and shivers. 'Open the gate,' he says.

'Sir?'

'Open it! I'll take responsibility. If we can't trust Commander Demetrius and the king's own groom, who can we trust? Move!'

'But General Perdiccas said while the king's sick we should trust *nobody—*'

I lift a hind leg and swish my tail in the guard's face. This time he goes pale and shuts up. The others run to unbar the gate for us.

We trot through an echoing passage under the wall and emerge in a wide avenue of blue walls decorated with more monsters. At every junction, we find a roadblock of overturned carts guarded by grim Macedonians. Demetrius has to repeat his story at each one, and I have to give them flat ears to make them let us through. A half-built pyramid of steps looms against the stars, covered in scaffolding.

'The ziggurat,' Demetrius says. 'I heard Alex was rebuilding it. At least he still respects the gods.'

It is dark by the time we reach the palace. The guards at the bridge make Demetrius leave his sword with them. 'Turn left for the stables, then go straight across and join the queue,' they tell him. 'You'll see where. Half the world's in there, waiting to see the king before he dies.'

The stable walls are blue in the dusk. As Demetrius hurries off, another ghost ripples out of the shadows to greet us. It is Xanthus with his scarred head. He must have followed the army back from the desert. I nicker to him, and he trots joyfully across to join us. Grooms hurry back and forth, carrying armfuls of hay and slopping buckets of water. Torches burn in the passages. Hundreds of horses neigh and bang their doors, impatient for their feed.

Charm looks round desperately. 'Where is he?' she whispers. 'I'll never find him among this lot.'

For a moment, I think she means Alexander. Then there is a choked cry behind us, and Tydeos races out of the dusk. With a look of intense joy, he throws his arms around Charm. They hold each other tightly, ignoring us horses.

'King Alexander's dying,' Tydeos whispers to her.

Charm bites her lip. 'I know. I dreamt it, and when I woke

up the bond was breaking, and Bucephalas . . .' Her voice falters, and she takes a deep breath. 'How did it happen?'

'Bucephalas looks well,' Tydeos says, changing the subject and eyeing Indus in admiration. 'I knew you wouldn't let him die.'

There is a heartbeat of silence.

Then Charm gives a little laugh. 'You dolt! This is Indus. I've backed him. Don't you even know the difference between an old warhorse and a newly-broken colt yet? What sort of horsemaster are you?'

I whinny, but Tydeos does not hear me. He gives Indus a closer look. 'Really? He's the image of his sire! Like Bucephalas must have looked when he was younger, anyway.' Then he realizes she is blinking back tears, and sobers. 'Oh Charm . . . I'm sorry. Did the old horse suffer much?'

Charm shakes her head and wipes a hand across her eyes. 'Never mind that! Just tell me what's been going on, and how I'm going to get in to see Alexander. They even made Demetrius join the back of the queue.'

Tydeos lowers his voice to a whisper. 'Iolaus gave the king poisoned wine at a party. I don't know how many people were involved, but the plan was to blame it all on Antipater if anyone got suspicious – say he wanted to keep the Macedonian throne for himself, and panicked when King Alexander came back from India. Roxanne never forgave Alexander for getting poor Prince Ochus killed in that horrid battle at the Jhelum, so she helped us. She's pregnant now, you know? She slept with the king after he married Ochus' sister, but her baby isn't born yet, so no one knows if it's a boy. We tried the poison out on Hephaestion first to see how much we'd need, and started with just a small amount so it would look like the king died of fever. The doctor had more poison to put in his medicine. We never thought he'd last this long, but Alexander always was stronger than other men, wasn't he?'

'What do you mean, "we"?' Charm breathes.

Tydeos makes a face and puts his arms around her again. He says very quietly, 'You must have found the mule's hoof? I left it in the stable under the muck where the garrison groom would never see it. You're the only one who ever mucks out properly under all the mangers.'

Charm stares at him in horror. 'Oh, Tydeos! You can't mean you were part of a plot to kill Alexander? And poor Hephaestion! What did he do wrong?'

Tydeos puts a finger to her lips. I have to prick my ears to hear his whisper. 'Hephaestion did his share of torturing and killing, you know that. And they needed someone to get hold of the mule hooves.' He gives her a pleading look. 'I did it for you, Charm. Soon it'll be over. The bond will break for good, and you'll be free. Indus will make an excellent stallion to start our horse farm, and—'

As he speaks, a gust of wind lifts my mane, and I catch a whiff of Alexander's sherbet sweetness. It is very faint and nearly smothered by sickness, but I would know his smell anywhere! My groom is paying no attention to me. Something tugs at my heart. The four ghost horses prick their ears at the palace and whinny. They are impatient to leave the world.

Aura neighs sadly as I whirl away from her and gallop into the night, and Charm looks round with a shiver. Her eyes go wide. '*Bucephalas?*' she whispers, and starts after me. I almost go back to her. But she's got Tydeos now, she doesn't need me any more. My rider does.

Babylon's gardens are the size of pastures. I jump a wall

and gallop through trees hung with lanterns, where herds of humans are sitting around the fountains talking in hushed voices. Someone calls, 'Hey, isn't that the king's horse?' But the others laugh at him and tell him he's seeing ghosts. Borealis, Zoroaster, Xanthus and Arion are galloping after me, so maybe he is.

At the far side of the garden, an archway guarded by two Macedonians with crossed pikes leads into the palace. A line of people is slowly filing through. I give them flat ears, and push my chest against the crossed pikes. The guards' eyes widen. For a moment, they struggle to hold me back. Then the barrier gives way, and I am through. Before they can recover, several people from the queue follow me.

'Hey!' the guards shout. 'Come back here!'

But the whole mass of people surges forward, and the guards have to draw their swords to keep them out. I leave their shouts and screams behind me as I trot down the blue and yellow corridors, following Alexander's smell.

I have never seen Alexander looking so small and weak. He lies on a couch in a darkened room hung with cloths of glittering Persian monsters. His tangled mane lies on a blue and white cushion. He's dripping with sweat. The Guard stands around him, tense as spears. Hephaestion is missing, of course. So is Iolaus.

Perdiccas kneels at the king's side, holding the royal seal. A nervous doctor is mixing medicine in a golden cup. Roxanne sits on a little stool at Alexander's feet, her black mane loose around her shoulders and her belly swollen under her robe, clearly in foal. She is staring intently at her husband's face and doesn't notice me.

Darius' brother kneels on the other side of the couch, kissing the king's hand. Alexander's eyes are closed and his skin glistens with sweat. He doesn't answer when Oxarthes speaks to him. His ghost hovers just above the couch, holding on to the edge with white knuckles. It looks scared and angry.

I whinny and settle to my knees. A wind lifts the cloths, and everyone in the room glances round.

Alexander's ghost stares at me. A look of puzzlement crosses its face, followed by relief. A fierce joy lights its eyes. It lets go of the couch and drifts towards me.

'*Alexander!*'

Charm has caught up at last. She darts past me to the couch and throws herself across the king's body. 'Please don't die! I've trained Bucephalas' colt for you to ride in your next battle, and everyone's ready to follow you again. They were scared in India, but now you're back it'll be just like it was in the old days . . .'

Alexander's ghost smiles at Charm, though she doesn't see this because she is crying over his body. With an effort, it climbs on my back and clutches my mane with ghostly hands. It is very light. I rise gently to my feet, afraid it might float off.

Perdiccas grips Charm's arm and pulls her away. 'Leave him, Charmeia,' he says gently. 'The king's gone.'

A deep hush fills the room as everyone stares in disbelief at the couch. The torches darken, and thunder cracks over the palace as the hole in the world opens one last time. The Guard look up in alarm. Roxanne lets out a terrible wail and throws herself across the king's feet, and all the people in the room – slaves and soldiers alike – begin to wail and tear at their clothes in despair.

Their misery fills me. I have lost Alexander! Now my mane

will be cut, and I will have to find a new rider.

But Alexander's hand runs down my neck and pulls my ear. 'Come on, Bucephalas,' he whispers. 'Let's get away from these idiots, shall we?' And with a shiver of joy, I realize his ghost is still sitting on my back.

I make myself huge and carry him back through the corridors and out into the garden. No one tries to stop us. Everyone is too busy running, wailing and shouting, while lightning crackles around them and thunder rolls around Babylon's walls.

'The king is dead!' they cry. 'King Alexander's dead!'

The news travels faster than we do. By the time we reach the garden, all the people waiting to see the king are sobbing, too. Torches and lamps all over the city have been blown out by an unnatural wind. People stumble out of their houses with bundles of belongings and make a run for the gates. Others raise their arms to the half-completed pyramid and call on their god to help them. In the space of a heartbeat, the streets are filled with darkness, disbelief and panic.

Still on my back, Alexander gives them a bewildered look. 'It's all falling apart, horse, falling apart so quickly. Am I dreaming? I can barely feel you under me. It's like riding a horse made of air. It must be the potion that doctor's giving me. It's poisoned my brain! I wanted to die after Hephaestion left me, but it's about time I got up. I've so much still to do . . .'

I don't think he realizes he's dead yet. It's a good job he's got me to look after him.

To escape the confusion in the streets, we turn into another garden. This one is deserted and rises up into the stars. A wind rustles the leaves of the trees as I trot through the shadows. We find another river, though I don't think it is the

Euphrates. I'm not sure where it came from, but it flows across our path, reflecting the stars, wide and dark and fierce.

Alexander stares at it. 'More water,' he whispers. 'It looks like the river that Achilles fought in the *Iliad*. You'll have to jump it, Bucephalas. One last time, horse, for me?'

He trots me back a few strides and turns me to face the river. He tightens his knees and leans forward. A golden glow of energy surrounds him, like it used to back in Pella when he was a man-colt. He shouts the Macedonian war cry for courage:

'ALALALAI! ALALALALAI!'

It still has the power to stir my blood. I spring into a gallop and fix my good eye on the far bank to judge the distance. It is the biggest leap I have ever made. But I'm not just any horse. I have Alexander on my back, and I trust him. If he thinks we can do it, then we can.

As I take off, lightning flashes across the sky. It reflects from the water beneath us, and I catch a glimpse of little Psylla, who died at the Granicus, on the far bank waiting for us with the other dead horses from my herd. Alexander must be able to see all the humans he killed waiting there, too, because he gasps, 'Oh Zeus, Bucephalas, so many! I never knew there would be so many ghosts . . .'

The wind goes silent in my ears. Together, we fly.

THE FINAL HOOFPRINT

The hole in the world opened by Alexander's death is fast sealing itself around us, and when it closes this time, we will be on the other side with the ghosts. So I must tell you the rest very quickly.

Since the Guard no longer needed its horses for battles, Charm and Tydeos took all the surviving members of my herd back to Anatolia to start their horse farm. They saved:

Aura, my special mare, now white with age.

Petasios, my faithful red friend.

Caspia, who still does silly tricks.

Hades, not as quick as he used to be.

Harpinna, battle-scarred and stiff in the joints.

Apollo, still a bit vain.

Electra, my huge filly, now a beautiful black mare.

Hoplite, my tough colt, who will always be rather bad-tempered.

Zephyr, who kept losing her riders.

Indus, who is the image of me.

As for their riders . . . poor Iolaus, who got all the rotten jobs, was executed for poisoning the king, and Charm cut Hades' mane in mourning. Ptolemy took the king's body back to Egypt and placed it in a fancy tomb in the centre of his big Alexandria so everyone could see it lying there. Perdiccas tried his best to keep the empire together, but it wasn't long before everyone started fighting again. Roxanne gave birth to a healthy man-colt and called him Alexander, though he never lived up to the name, and when he was thirteen someone assassinated him and his mother.

It is time for you to slip off my back now and return to your own world, where I understand warhorses are no longer needed because men have other ways of dominating one another. It must be a very strange place.

Go on! Don't argue, or I'll buck you off! I feel great, though I am older than any horse has ever been. I think I must be immortal, for I am growing a horn like the horses in Queen Penthesilea's herd. I will know soon enough, because Alexander says we are going to find the Amazons so we can dominate them.

I am Bucephalas.

I have a city named after me, and Alexander's ghost rides on my back.

No one will ever forget us, for we have journeyed to the edge of the world and dominated death.

HA!

AUTHOR'S NOTE

Most of what we know about Alexander the Great was propaganda written by his royal historian, or by his friends and admirers several years after his death. Being a horse lover, I wondered what his warhorse Bucephalas, who carried Alexander for thousands of miles from Macedonia to India, would have thought of it all. And being a fantasy writer, I wanted to write Alexander's story in the magical spirit of the *Iliad*, which was the king's bedtime reading when he was on campaign. This book is the result.

Many of the characters you meet in it were real people, though I have allowed the Persian Prince Ochus a bigger part than the historians traditionally give him. I have also added the following fictional characters (naturally, I like to think they *might* have been real):

Bucephalas' groom, Charmeia, and her friend Tydeos.
The evil horsemaster.
Demetrius the Guardsman.
The Amazons.

The horses Alexander's men rode would have been real enough, but we know nothing about them except for Bucephalas himself, so I have invented their names and characters. As for research: I am too young to have served in Alexander's army, but I have been a racehorse groom, so I know what it is like to send a horse into danger (be it a race or a battle), desperately hoping – like Charmeia – that my charge will return unhurt.

I would like to take this opportunity to thank Barry

Cunningham, self-confessed 'old warhorse' of children's publishing, for having the vision to take on such an ambitious work, my editors Helen Wire and Imogen Cooper for asking all the right questions, and the whole Chicken House team for their enthusiasm and support.

Sometimes a book comes along that an author feels they were always meant to write. Such was this one for me, and I hope you enjoy Bucephalas' version of history as much as I enjoyed helping him tell it!

Katherine Roberts, Stroud, February 2006

SELECT BIBLIOGRAPHY
of some of the books I used for research

Budiansky, Stephen, *The Nature of Horses*, Weidenfeld and Nicolson, 1997.

Clayton, Peter A, and Price, Martin J, (editors), *The Seven Wonders of the Ancient World*, Routledge, 1988.

Church, Alfred J, *A Young Macedonian in the Army of Alexander the Great*, Seeley and Co, 1890.

Fox, Robin Lane, *Alexander the Great*, Penguin, 1986.

Green, Peter, *Alexander of Macedon 356–323 BC – a Historical Biography*, University of California Press, 1991.

Homer, *The Iliad*, translated by Robert Fagles, Penguin Classics, 1990.

Humble, Richard, *Warfare in the Ancient World*, Guild Publishing, 1980.

Nemet-Nejat, Karen Rhea, *Daily Life in Ancient Mesopotamia*, Greenwood Press, 1998.

Roberts, Monty, *The Man Who Listens to Horses*, Arrow, 1997.

Stoneman, Richard (translator), *The Greek Alexander Romance*, Penguin Classics, 1991.

Wood, Michael, *In the Footsteps of Alexander the Great*, BBC Books, 1997.

Xenophon, *The Art of Horsemanship*, translated by Morgan, M H, J A Allen and Co., 1962.

OTHER BOOKS BY KATHERINE ROBERTS

Spellfall

The Echorium Sequence
Song Quest
Crystal Mask
Dark Quetzal

The Seven Fabulous Wonders
The Great Pyramid Robbery
The Babylon Game
The Amazon Temple Quest
The Mausoleum Murder
The Olympic Conspiracy
The Colossus Crisis
The Cleopatra Curse

Tracy Borman's *Crown & Sceptre* is hugely impressive. A breath-taking amount of research has been packed painlessly into this compelling and engaging ... of Britain's kings and queens. Lively, pacy and marvello... ...cise and informative, it grips the reader from ... ...page. A stunning tour de force and a remarkable achie...

Alison Weir

Tracy Borman's *Crown & Sceptre* is a crisp, delightfully clear, and perfectly weighted compendium – it brims with need-to-know fac..., laced with intriguing, revealing, detail. She cleverly tells the tale of Britain, through the prism of monarchy. This is Our Island Story for the modern age.

Charles Spencer

Not just a brilliant compendium of biographies, but the biography of an institution: a marvellous read.

Tom Holland

Quite simply dazzling – in its scope, its drama, its unexpected detail. Every aspect of modern monarchy – from the rites of the coronation to ritual humiliation in the court of public opinion – is placed in the context of almost a thousand years of history; and the institution at the heart of British life stands out all the more clearly for it. Whether or not they knew it, this is the book the royal family has been waiting for.

Sarah Gristwood

Enlightening, gripping and skilfully composed, Tracy Borman navigates the twists and turns of the British monarchy with an expert hand. A pacy narrative that's simply bursting with colour and intrigue, *Crown & Sceptre* is both powerful and compulsively readable. A masterpiece.

Nicola Tallis

Tracy Borman is joint Chief Curator of Historic Royal Palaces and Chief Executive of the Heritage Education Trust. She studied and taught history at the University of Hull and was awarded a PhD in 1997.

Tracy is the author of a number of highly acclaimed books including *The Private Lives of the Tudors: Uncovering the Secrets of Britain's Greatest Dynasty*, *Thomas Cromwell: The Untold Story of Henry VIII's Most Faithful Servant*, *Matilda: Wife of the Conqueror, First Queen of England*, *Elizabeth's Women: The Hidden Story of the Virgin Queen* and *Witches: A Tale of Sorcery, Scandal and Seduction*. Tracy is also a regular broadcaster and public speaker, giving talks on her books across the UK and abroad.

CROWN & SCEPTRE

1000 Years of Kings and Queens

TRACY BORMAN

HODDER

First published in Great Britain in 2021 by Hodder & Stoughton
An Hachette UK company

This paperback edition published in 2022

I

Copyright © Tracy Borman 2021

A CIP catalogue record for this title is available from the British Library

Paperback ISBN 9781529339536
eBook ISBN 9781529339512

Typeset in Dante MT Std by Palimpsest Book Production Limited,
Falkirk, Stirlingshire

Printed and bound in Great Britain by Clays Ltd, Elcograf S.p.A.

Hodder & Stoughton policy is to use papers that are natural, renewable
and recyclable products and made from wood grown in sustainable forests.
The logging and manufacturing processes are expected to conform to the
environmental regulations of the country of origin.

Hodder & Stoughton Ltd
Carmelite House
50 Victoria Embankment
London EC4Y 0DZ

www.hodder.co.uk

Also by Tracy Borman

Henry VIII and the Men Who Made Him
The Private Lives of the Tudors: Uncovering the Secrets of
Britain's Greatest Dynasty
Thomas Cromwell: The Untold Story of Henry VIII's
Most Faithful Servant
Witches: A Tale of Sorcery, Scandal and Seduction
Matilda: Wife of the Conqueror, First Queen of England
Elizabeth's Women: The Hidden Story of the Virgin Queen
Henrietta Howard: King's Mistress, Queen's Servant
The Story of the Tower of London
The Story of Kensington Palace

Fiction
The King's Witch
The Devil's Slave
The Fallen Angel

To Honor, with heartfelt thanks for all the inspiration

And in loving memory of my cousin, Andrew Picksley

ACKNOWLEDGEMENTS

Fittingly enough, I first discussed the idea for this book with my editor, Rupert Lancaster, at the Tower of London, that bastion of royal history. I was both excited and daunted at the prospect of taking on such a vast subject, but Rupert's encouragement and good humour sustained me throughout. I also owe a huge debt of gratitude to my American editor, George Gibson, whose exceptional eye for detail and insightful comments helped to shape the book from the outset. My agent, Julian Alexander, has, as ever, played the indispensable role of advisor, editor and champion – both of the book itself and of me as an author – and I couldn't be more grateful. I would also like to thank Ben Clark and Isabella Wilson at The Soho Agency for always being so positive and helpful.

I feel very fortunate to have been supported by the wider team at Hodder once more. I am particularly indebted to Juliet Brightmore for gathering such an inspired collection of images, which really bring the characters and themes I have written about to life. Rebecca Mundy and Caitriona Horne have provided fantastic publicity and marketing support, and Cameron Myers and Ciara Mongey have been unfailingly efficient and helpful. Nick Fawcett did an absolutely wonderful job on the copy edit and saved me many blushes, and I am grateful to Virginia Williams for her excellent proof-reading. Geraldine Beare's work on the index was as painstaking as ever.

My research was greatly assisted by the works of other historians of the monarchy, most notably Alison Weir, whose exceptional book *Britain's Royal Families: The Complete Genealogy* was an invaluable source of reference. I also drew on works by Sir David Cannadine, whose insights into British royal history are as shrewd as they are enlightening. I am deeply grateful to Michael Wood for sharing his research on Æthelstan, widely regarded as England's first king and the subject of Michael's forthcoming book. The military historian Julian Humphrys provided invaluable advice on the battles that feature in the book and on the English Civil War, as well some of the early medieval monarchs. Canon Roland Riem was kind enough to give me a tour of the excellent *Kings & Scribes* exhibition at Winchester Cathedral, and I am very grateful to Catherine Hodgson for arranging this. I would also like to thank Hector MacLeod for sharing some fascinating material on Mary, Queen of Scots and her son, James VI and I. One of the most extraordinary moments in my research was when Paul Fitzsimmons, Sandi Vasoli and James Peacock brought my attention to the exquisitely decorated 'Anne Boleyn falcon' that once adorned the Great Hall at Hampton Court and was taken down at her fall. It is a remarkable survivor and I will be forever in their debt for so generously sharing its story with me.

My sincere thanks go to Rupert Gavin, Chair of Historic Royal Palaces, for the interest he has shown in the book in general and the Anglo-Saxons in particular. Kate Harris, my curatorial colleague at Historic Royal Palaces, unearthed some gems relating to royal fashion and a whole suite of anecdotes on everything from Edward VIII and Wallis Simpson to Queen Elizabeth II's childhood. Another colleague, Charles Farris, Public Historian for the History of the Monarchy, has been equally generous with his time and knowledge, as has my fellow curator and Tudor enthusiast Alden Gregory, an expert on the Field of Cloth of Gold. I am also grateful to Research Manager Laura Tompkins for her advice on medieval sources.

Most of *Crown & Sceptre* was written during lockdown, which made the support of family and friends even more important than usual. I would like to express my warmest thanks to Honor Gay for her endless enthusiasm and wisdom, and for keeping me going by requesting a 'Fact of the day' throughout my research. The Reverend Stephen Kuhrt read the first (and considerably longer) draft in two days' flat and I am so grateful for his advice on the religious history, as well as for his unceasing encouragement. Huge thanks are also due to my parents, John and Joan Borman, and to my sister, Jayne Ellis, and her family, for always being there for me. Finally, to my husband Tom and to Eleanor, Lucy and Lottie, for putting up with my early starts and late finishes, and for ensuring that I never ran out of cake.

Contents

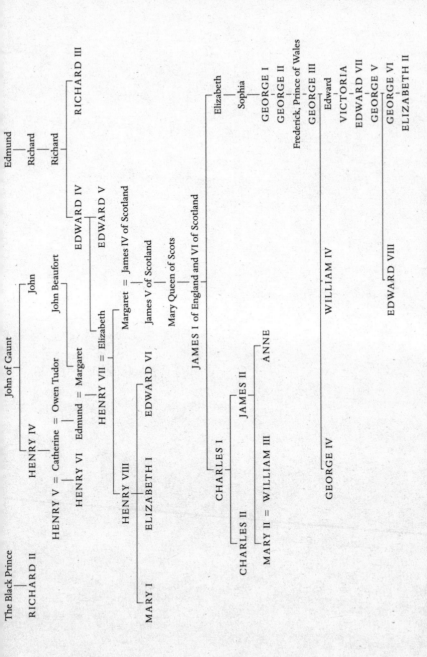

PREFACE

'The mass of people expect a King or Queen to look and play the part. They want to see a Crown and Sceptre and all that sort of thing. They want the gilding for their money.'

The politician Viscount Halifax's views on the role of the monarchy were expressed to Queen Victoria's secretary during her protracted mourning for her beloved husband Albert. Although his remarks had a very specific purpose – namely, to persuade the queen out of her self-imposed retirement – they neatly encapsulate the value that his fellow Victorians placed on the crown. Arguably, it is a value that has changed little in the one hundred and fifty or so years since.

By the time Victoria ascended the throne in 1837, the sovereign no longer ruled; they reigned. Since the Glorious Revolution of 1688, real power had been vested in the government, not the crown. Thus, Victoria was able to give up her public duties for more than a decade after Albert's death in 1861, safe in the knowledge that it would be business as usual for her ministers. The same scenario would have been inconceivable during the centuries of personal rule that had preceded 1688, when the likes of William the Conqueror, Edward I and Henry VIII had wielded authority over every aspect of their subjects' lives.

And yet, as Lord Halifax was at pains to point out, the sovereign's absence still had far-reaching consequences. Victoria's people missed the reassuring (if empty) symbol of national leadership that she provided. They also missed the pomp and pageantry, the royal visits, processions and ceremony that had been a feature of life for more than a millennium. What mattered to the vast majority of her subjects was 'not the constitutional but the theatrical side of monarchy', as one contemporary reflected.

The same is true of today's monarchy. Politically, Queen Elizabeth II has less power than her subjects, for they can vote a new government in, while she can only acknowledge its arrival. Yet for as long as the monarch retains the three traditional functions cited by the Victorian essayist Walter Bagehot – to be consulted, to encourage and to warn – she can bring the value of a perspective drawn from longer and wider experience. The fact that the British monarchy is hereditary, rather than being reliant upon the popularity contest fought out between the leaders of the main political parties, enables it to stay focused upon the wellbeing of the nation as a whole and not be distracted by what is likely to win the most votes.

The monarch's constitutional role might serve a useful purpose, but on its own it is hardly enough to ensure the survival of this ancient institution. This is where the 'gilding' that Lord Halifax referred to comes in. The real power of the crown comes from the almost magical aura with which it is surrounded. 'Perhaps the most profound satisfaction that Royalty provides is that it gives us a Paradise to inhabit', remarked the writer Virginia Woolf on the eve of the Second World War. In a culture obsessed with celebrities, the royal family has star quality in abundance. To critics, the 'froth and saccharine' and 'goggling adulation' of committed monarchists is 'mindless'.[1] But recent political history has proved how potent such emotional responses can be – witness the Brexit campaign of 2016.

Elizabeth II is already Britain's longest-reigning monarch, having overtaken her great-great-grandmother Queen Victoria on 9 September 2015, and the longest-reigning female head of state in the world. In 2024 she is set to take the world record from Louis XIV, the so-called 'Sun King' of France, who reigned for seventy-two years and one hundred and ten days. As the queen approaches the seventieth anniversary of her accession in February 2022, debates about the role of the monarchy are bound to be reignited. The focus of these will no doubt be on its future, yet the key to this lies in its past.

In light of this, there has never been a more apposite moment to consider the history of the British monarchy. It is one of the most iconic and enduring institutions in the world. The English law courts are around eight hundred and fifty years old; Parliament is seven hundred and fifty years old; but the monarchy, as a political institution, is 1,150 years old. Elizabeth II can trace her descent to Egbert, the ninth-century King of Wessex, which means that (with the exception of the Interregnum from 1649 to 1660) the crown boasts a dynastic continuity distinct from other monarchies in the world. The ceremony followed at the queen's coronation was largely the same as that used for the Anglo-Saxon kings 1,080 years earlier.

Despite the almost unimaginable change that has taken place during the twelve centuries of its existence, the monarchy has survived, weathering the storms of rebellion, revolution and war that brought many of Europe's royal families to an abrupt and bloody end. It has been described as 'an institution which, even at its weakest moments, had shown surprisingly rock-like characteristics', but also 'a fragile thing . . . the most delicate flower of its sceptered isle'.[2] The monarchy's unique survival owes much to the fact that, for all its ancient traditions and protocol, the royal family has been made to evolve and adapt in response to the needs and opinions of the people.

This book will explore the history of the monarchy from 1066 to the present day. At the heart of it are the extraordinary characters of the monarchs themselves. Some were revered; others reviled. As Walter Bagehot observed: 'The benefits of a good monarch are almost invaluable, but the evils of a bad monarch are almost irreparable.'[3] For as long as monarchs ruled, rather than merely reigned, the reliance on personality was both the greatest strength and the greatest weakness of the crown. Alongside the shining examples of royal power and majesty is a colourful cast of weak, lazy or evil monarchs, usurpers, bastards, pretenders, rebels, domineering consorts and disloyal subjects.

It was not until 1603 that the British monarchy became a single, united entity. Prior to that, the sovereigns of England and Scotland were separate, rival dynasties. The Scottish monarchy is said to have been founded by the ninth-century king, Alpin, whose house was succeeded by those of Dunkeld, Balliol, Bruce and finally Stuart. Its history is beyond the scope of this study, except for when Scotland's fortunes were intertwined with England's. In the same way, the history of Wales before it became subject to English monarchical rule in 1283, and of the Gaelic kingdoms of Ireland prior to their wholesale conquest by the Normans in 1175, will be considered only in the context of England's kings and queens.

That said, in the 1,250 years since Alfred the Great's accession in 871, when England emerged as a coherent political entity, there have been only a few years when the throne has been unambiguously English. Its incumbents have included the French Normans, the Welsh-born Tudors, the Scottish Stuarts, the Hanoverians and their German successors whose lineage endures to the present day.

In telling the story of Britain's monarchy, *Crown & Sceptre* will include some of the most notable events in the country's history, but only when these either influenced or were influenced by the sovereign. In the latter stages of the monarchy's history, such overlap becomes less frequent – an interesting fact in itself, as it illustrates the declining role of the sovereign in the nation's affairs.

The starting point is 1066, when William the Conqueror defeated the Anglo-Saxon king Harold at the Battle of Hastings and established the Norman dynasty in England. It was only after Hastings that a single, undisputed monarch held the crown of England. But the foundations for this decisive moment were laid centuries before.

INTRODUCTION
The Early Kings of England

The origins of England's monarchy can be traced to the second century BC, when Celtic and Belgae tribesmen, emigrating from continental Europe, settled in England. They established a number of tribal kingdoms, stretching as far north as Yorkshire, over each of which ruled a king or occasionally a queen. They minted coins, maintained a lively trade with the Continent, and were prosperous enough to attract the attention of the Roman Emperor, Julius Caesar, who launched expeditions to England in 55 and 54 BC. Emperor Claudius had greater success a decade later, and the Roman Conquest was largely completed by AD 34.

Thereafter, Rome became what one historian has described as 'perhaps the purest, the most absolute monarchy the world has ever seen'.[1] At its zenith during the early second century AD, this vast empire extended from the Bay of Biscay in the west to the River Euphrates in the east, and from Scotland in the north to the Sahara in the south. 'Caledonia' was the name given to the territories that roughly comprised modern-day Scotland and it was inhabited by the Picts, while 'Britannia' lay to the south and encompassed England and Wales. Rome never annexed Ireland (or 'Hibernia'), although it did exert some influence over the native Celts, notably in religion and trade.

The Roman occupation of England set a precedent that would be repeated numerous times over the next eight hundred years: its conquest and annexation to a larger, or at least a more dominant territory by an overseas invader. After the collapse of Roman rule in the early fifth century, the Barbarian invasions in Europe prompted a number of Germanic peoples to flee to England.

From the mid-fifth century, an estimated 200,000 Anglo-Saxons arrived in Britannia – a substantial number, given that the native population was less than two million. According to legend, a native Briton named Arthur Pendragon led the defence against the Saxon invaders – a story that was embellished over the centuries to include his wife Guinevere and companion Lancelot, a Knight of the Round Table, along with the wizard Merlin and the sword Excalibur. There is no contemporary evidence for the legend, but it proved so enduring that a thousand years later one of England's kings would commission a genealogical chart showing his descent from Arthur.

As the Anglo-Saxons put down roots, so their blood, laws, politics, customs and traditions began to infiltrate and, ultimately, supplant those of the Britons. The impact of their language – Old English – was particularly prominent, with new words, place names and eventually a new name for their conquered island: the land of the Angles, or *Ængla Land*. Although the Anglo-Saxons initially clung to their pagan beliefs, Christianity gradually spread across their newly conquered land from the late sixth century. In 597 England became part of the Roman Catholic Church and remained so for almost a thousand years, until Henry VIII ejected papal authority and made himself head of a new Church of England.

Once the Anglo-Saxons had become established, the institution of monarchy gradually began to take shape, along with seven kingdoms – or a 'Heptarchy'. In the early ninth century, Wessex emerged as the dominant kingdom, thanks largely to the efforts of its leader, Egbert (or Ecgbehrt), who is often cited as England's first true king. By the time of his accession in 802, the Heptarchy faced a grave new threat from overseas. Originating from Denmark and Norway, the Vikings had become the most feared pirates in Europe. They had first raided Northumbria's shores in the late eighth century, destroying the monastic church of Lindisfarne. From 835 the raids became more frequent; then, in 865, the hit-and-run approach was replaced by a full-scale invasion of England. Within the space of ten years, they had conquered Northumbria, East Anglia and most of Mercia.

The only Anglo-Saxon kingdom to survive was Wessex, but it seemed a matter of time before this, too, was wiped out. Its salvation – and that of the entire Anglo-Saxon people – was largely down to its king, Alfred, who inherited the throne in 871. As well as vanquishing the Viking threat in Wessex, he united a formerly disparate and warring set of kingdoms and became the first leader to be styled 'king of the Anglo-Saxons'. He was also the first king to fully realise the potency of royal magnificence. 'What shall I say of the treasures incomparably fashioned in gold and silver at his instigation?' enthused his contemporary biographer, Asser. 'And what of the royal halls and chambers marvellously constructed in stone and wood at his command?'[2] Alfred was admired for his formidable intellect, too, and left behind the greatest written legacy of any English king. In short, he was an inspiring model of kingship and deserved his sobriquet, 'the Great'.

Alfred died in October 899 at around the age of fifty. He bequeathed to his successors a kingdom substantially larger than the one he had inherited, together with the continuing challenge of defending it from the Vikings. His son, Edward the Elder, was acknowledged as overlord in northern Britain and was the first of several Anglo-Saxon kings to be crowned at Kingston-upon-Thames, south-west of London. Edward further strengthened his inheritance by siring no fewer than eighteen children.

Edward's eldest son and successor, Æthelstan, is often viewed as the founder of the English monarchy. Much of this is based on his own PR. One of the earliest paragons of royal propaganda, he was often described as 'king of the English' on his coins and in his charters, and even on occasion as *rex totius Bryttanniæ* ('King of all Britain').[3] Shortly after his accession, a poem was composed to celebrate the fact that England was now 'made whole' (*Perfecta Saxonia*).[4] Æthelstan was also the first king to be depicted wearing a crown, and it became his custom to move in state across his kingdom, presiding over assemblies where he promulgated laws and issued charters.

Another early king who bolstered the royal image was Æthelstan's nephew, Edgar, who ascended the throne in 959. His coronation, which did not take place until 973, is the first in England for which a detailed description survives. It would serve as a model for all future coronations up to the present day, including that of Elizabeth II at Westminster Abbey on 2 June 1953.[5] To begin, the new monarch was presented to the congregation by the presiding cleric (who from 1154 was almost always the Archbishop of Canterbury). Next came the threefold oath, by which Edgar swore to uphold the Church of God and his Christian people in peace; to combat selfishness, greed and iniquity among his subjects; and to be a just and merciful king.[6] The most sacred part of the ceremony followed when the new king was anointed with holy oil to confirm his semi-divine status. He was then invested with the royal insignia: the ring, sword, crown, sceptre and rod. Finally, the newly crowned monarch received the homage of his leading subjects.

During the proceedings, the anthem 'Zadok the Priest and Nathan the Prophet' was sung for the first time and has been at every subsequent coronation, with Handel's arrangement for George II's coronation in 1727 being the best known.[7] A lavish coronation banquet followed, during which the king's champion rode into the hall and challenged any rival claimant to the throne. The banquet continued in more or less the same form until 1831, when it was abandoned by William IV in the interests of economy.

Although Edgar had contributed a great deal to royal ceremony and tradition, there was not yet an agreed set of rules for the succession. The Salic law established in France in around AD 500, whereby women were excluded from inheriting the throne, was generally accepted, but the principle of primogeniture less so. In general, the monarch was selected by a council known as the Witan, a precursor of Parliament, from among the members of the royal family. In contrast to later years, when a sovereign inherited the throne by dint of their birth alone, this meant that a weak incumbent could quite easily be replaced with another.

This is precisely what happened during the reign of Edgar's third son, Æthelred, who earned the nickname 'the Unready' or 'the Redeless' ('without counsel' – a pun on his name Æthelred, meaning 'noble counsel'). In 1013 he lost his throne to the Viking leader and King of Denmark, Sweyn Forkbeard, who arrived with a huge invasion force and rapidly conquered large swathes of the kingdom. Æthelred fled with his wife Emma and their two sons to her native Normandy. Sweyn died a few months later and the invaders chose his son Cnut as the new king. But the native English invited Æthelred to take back his throne, on condition that he redress certain grievances and accept new limits to his power.

Æthelred died shortly afterwards and was briefly succeeded by his short-lived son, then Cnut ascended the throne virtually unopposed and proceeded to marry the dowager queen Emma to strengthen his claim. The following year she was crowned Queen of England for a second time. The rites used for her consecration stressed that she was to share in Cnut's power and rule, not just be a passive, silent partner according to the traditional model for consorts.

In around 1018 Emma bore Cnut a son, Harthacnut, and it was agreed that he would take precedence in the English succession over the children from their previous marriages. This agreement led to years of bitter fighting between rival blood claimants, which were finally ended by the accession of Edward (later known as the Confessor), Emma's eldest son by Æthelred, in 1042. He was crowned 'with great honour' in the cathedral at Winchester, the ancient capital of Wessex, on Easter Day 1043.[8] The symbolism was clear: his accession was a rebirth for England's monarchy. The throne had returned to the House of Wessex.

Edward was nearing forty years of age at the time of his coronation. He had spent more than half of his life as an exile in Normandy and identified far more with the people there than with his new English subjects. The powerful lord Godwin, whom King Cnut had made Earl of Wessex, was waiting in the wings to contest his crown. Increasingly aware of the need to secure the succession, in 1045 Edward married Godwin's daughter, Edith. The *Vita Ædwardis* describes her as 'more like a daughter than a wife', which has led to speculation about Edward's sexuality.[9] When the queen showed no signs of pregnancy after several years of marriage, the rivalry between the potential successors to the throne intensified.

The person with the best hereditary claim was Edward the Exile, son of the king's late half-brother Edmund Ironside. But a far more powerful contender was Harold Godwinson, Earl of Wessex, eldest surviving son and heir of Earl Godwin, who had died in 1053. His hereditary right to the throne was tenuous, but he enjoyed immense support among the English people. The great warrior kings of Scandinavia also laid claim to England because, although the Vikings had been driven out in the mid-tenth century, there were still extensive Scandinavian settlements, particularly in the north of the country. King Sweyn Estrithson of Denmark, a nephew of King Cnut, and King Harald III Hardrada of Norway, who had no real hereditary right, both coveted the English crown and had the military might to pose a serious threat.

One of the overseas candidates had the edge over his rivals, however – even if, on the face of it, he should not have stood a chance. William 'the Bastard', as he was commonly known, was the illegitimate son of Duke Robert of Normandy and may have been as young as six when, in the absence of legitimate heirs, he succeeded his father in 1035. A turbulent childhood spent on the run from rapacious relatives and would-be assassins had chiselled him into one of the most fearsome warriors of the age. The *Anglo-Saxon Chronicles* describe him as 'stern beyond all measure to those who opposed his will'.[10] William's tenuous blood claim to the English throne derived from his great-aunt Emma's marriages to Æthelred the Unready and Cnut. It was bolstered by that of his wife, Matilda of Flanders, a direct descendant of Alfred the Great – not to mention most of the royal families of Europe. Duke William claimed that he had been promised the throne by Edward the Confessor, whose Norman bias was well known, although this is contested by English sources.

With the duke and his rivals poised to stake their claim to England, the scene was set for a year that would shape the entire future of its monarchy.

Part 1

The Normans (1066–1154)

The fierce and crafty race of the Normans

The Norman Conquest of 1066 remains one of the most famous dates in English history. By the end of it, the crown had changed hands three times, ushering in not just a new ruling elite, but an entirely new nation, with new laws, customs and even a new language. Had the Battle of Hastings been decided in Harold Godwinson's favour, instead of Duke William's, England would probably have become part of the northern Scandinavian world, rather than opening it up to the culture, religion and traditions of Western Europe. By the time of William's death in 1087, less than one hundredth of the population was Norman, yet an entire social revolution had taken place. During a period of brutal suppression, the Anglo-Saxon aristocracy were either killed or displaced and the new Norman landowners introduced the feudal system, whereby the native population only held land in return for military obligations. But while much was lost to the conquerors, the Norman dynasty put an end to centuries of Viking raids, abolished the burgeoning slave trade of pre-Conquest England, developed the economy, and created an impressive architectural legacy of fine stone castles, cathedrals and churches. It also created a strong monarchy that would gradually complete the unification of England and break up the divisions between Normans and Saxons so that only Englishmen remained.

William the Conqueror (1066–87)

'With God's help I will conquer'

B Y THE MIDDLE of the eleventh century, England had emerged
as a kingdom worth fighting for. It was one of the most prosperous realms in Western Europe, and its Anglo-Saxon kings had
amassed a rich treasury. Its geographical location was a blessing as
well as a curse. Although it was vulnerable to invaders, it was also
well placed for trade with Scandinavia and the Continent. Within
England, there were a number of impressive urban areas, notably
London, York and Winchester, many of which were burgeoning centres
of trade. The twelfth-century chronicler, Henry of Huntingdon,
described the kingdom as 'an island of the utmost fertility', abundant
in all manner of flora and fauna, with rich veins of iron, tin, lead and
other minerals.[1]

Whoever succeeded Edward the Confessor could also take advantage of a sophisticated system of governmental administration. The
king could levy taxes across a population of between one and a half
and two million when he needed to generate funds; he could also
raise a national army and navy. He had a central secretariat to issue
documents in his name, and there was a single, national silver
currency. A similarly efficient organisational structure existed at a
local level, with defined communities and courts within shires and
their sub-divisions, known as hundreds. The religious life of the
kingdom was also increasingly ordered, and the English Church was
an effective unitary body. It comprised the two archbishoprics of
Canterbury and York, numerous bishoprics and monasteries, and a
huge number of village churches.

All of this lay within tantalising reach of the rival claimants
'panting for the spoils of England' in 1066.[2] Edward the Confessor,
whose health had been declining since the previous autumn, was

unable to attend the dedication of his magnificent new abbey at Westminster on 28 December 1065. A little over a week later, he was dead. He had not settled the vexed question of the succession before he breathed his last. Of all the contenders, it was Harold Godwinson who was quickest off the mark. It is possible that, as he claimed, the king had bequeathed the crown to him on his deathbed. He certainly had the most support among the Witan and the population at large, and was crowned on 6 January, most likely in Westminster Abbey. But there was enough doubt surrounding his right to the throne to prompt his rivals into action.

Foremost among them was William of Normandy, who was 'deeply incensed' upon hearing of Harold's accession and immediately began making 'warlike preparations'. He also appealed to Pope Alexander II 'to urge the justice of his campaign'.[3] It was a shrewd move, and one that none of his rival claimants had thought to make. Alexander gave his blessing for the enterprise and issued an edict to the English clergy advising them to submit to William's authority. The bastard Duke of Normandy now had God on his side.

Meanwhile, in England, there was a growing sense of unease. In April 1066, just three months after Harold's accession, 'a sign such as men never saw before was seen in the heavens. Some men declared that it was the star comet, which some men called the "haired" star'. This 'star' was Halley's Comet, and contemporary chroniclers (some with the wisdom of hindsight) claimed that 'it portended, as many said, a change in some kingdom'.[4]

Not all of the omens went Duke William's way. For weeks, unfavourable winds confined his forces to Normandy's shores. Then, when they were finally able to set sail and landed on the coast of Sussex, William stumbled upon the beach as soon as he disembarked. His troops looked on aghast at such an ominous sign, but their quick-thinking duke loudly proclaimed: 'My lords, by the splendour of God! I have taken possession of the land in my two hands.'[5]

In early autumn, Harold's attention was suddenly drawn to the north, where his exiled brother Tostig had joined forces with Harald Hardrada of Norway and invaded. On 20 September, in the first of the three great battles of 1066, they defeated Edwin and Morcar at Fulford and captured York, the most important city in the north.

Mustering his forces, Harold marched north and crushed Hardrada and Tostig's forces in a ferocious attack at Stamford Bridge. But he and his men soon had to turn tail and embark upon the long march south because news had arrived of Duke William's landing in Sussex.

By 13 October, Harold and his army had arrived at Senlac, close to the present-day town of Battle in East Sussex. The duke's forces were quartered about five miles away, around Hastings. The battle that took place on 14 October was finely balanced and lasted for most of the day, with 'great slaughter on either side'.[6] Duke William fought ferociously in the thick of the action. When a rumour that he had been killed spread panic among his men, he was said to have taken off his helmet and ridden alongside them crying: 'Look at me. I am alive, and with God's help I will conquer.'[7] The decisive moment came late in the day when the English king was slain. Legend has it that Harold was killed by an arrow in the eye, but other sources suggest he was cut down by a group of knights, possibly after having been wounded by the arrow.[8] Their leader, the 'Bastard' of Normandy, would henceforth be known as William the Conqueror, King of England.

As decisive as it was, Hastings marked the start, not the end, of William's campaign to conquer England. It would take nearly five years of bitter fighting before he was finally able to wrest full control over his new kingdom. His first challenge was to take the capital, London, which was so far from accepting the Norman duke as its ruler that it had elected the fifteen-year-old Edgar the Ætheling (meaning 'throneworthy'), great-nephew of Edward the Confessor, as king instead. William rapidly assembled his forces after Hastings and advanced towards the city. He also ordered a detachment of his army to Winchester in order to secure its surrender and that of Queen Edith, Edward the Confessor's widow and Harold's sister, who had become a figurehead for the beleaguered English.

'In the year of our Lord 1066, the Lord, who ruleth all things, accomplished what He had long designed with respect to the English nation; giving them up to destruction by the fierce and crafty race of the Normans', bemoaned the chronicler Henry of Huntingdon some sixty years after the event.[9] In a tactic that would be repeated many times in the years to come, William's troops brought terror wherever they went, forcing the new king's subjects into submission with brutality and bloodshed. Entire villages and towns were razed to the ground, their citizens raped or murdered. The *Anglo-Saxon Chronicles* paint a stark picture of the cruelty and violence of the Norman regime, which would see thousands of native Englishmen butchered and vast swathes of land laid to waste. Anyone who dared to defy the new king was either mutilated or put to death.

Within a few short weeks, both London and Winchester had capitulated. Then in early December, William marched to Berkhamsted, some thirty miles north-west of London, where Edgar the Ætheling had taken refuge. Upon the Conqueror's arrival on 10 December, Edgar immediately relinquished the crown, and William was declared King of England.

Distrustful of the 'evil inhabitants' of London, William ordered two massive strongholds to be built at its western and eastern reaches, thus enabling him to hold the city in a vice-like grip. This same tactic was applied to other key towns and cities, and before long the whole kingdom was covered with hastily constructed wooden castles. These were soon replaced by stone ones, which fulfilled the dual function of defensive fortresses and places of residence for the new Norman magnates. They also served as a powerful – and permanent – symbol of William's dynasty.

In London, the new king commissioned a huge new tower to be built in the heart of his new eastern fortification. In around 1075–79, work began on the gigantic keep or 'great tower' (later called the White Tower), which formed the heart of what from the twelfth century became known as the Tower of London. It was the most imposing emblem of monarchy that the country had ever seen, dwarfing all other buildings for miles around. The message was clear: the Normans were here to stay.

Although William eschewed many of the trappings of royalty established by his Anglo-Saxon predecessors, he appreciated the need to reinforce his authority as king. He therefore ordered preparations to be made for his coronation. With reports of fresh threats to his authority arriving on an almost daily basis, the ceremony was arranged with great haste and took place on Christmas Day 1066. It was heavily symbolic: a new king being crowned on the anniversary of the heavenly king's birth. In order to further bolster his legitimacy and present the new regime not as a conquest but as the restoration of Edward the Confessor's rightful successor, William chose Westminster Abbey as the location, where Edward lay buried. He also decreed that the service should follow that used for previous English kings. But he did commission a magnificent new crown in the style of Solomon (the ancient King of Israel, renowned for his wisdom), 'fashioned out of gold and precious stones', including a sapphire, an emerald, and a large ruby at its centre.[10]

Far from being a cause for celebration, William's coronation was a tense, sombre affair. The crowds who had gathered outside the abbey were silent and subdued and the only cheering came from the Conqueror's own men. During the ceremony, when one of William's Norman bishops sought the assent of those present for their new king, the answering shouts were so loud that they alarmed the guards keeping watch outside the abbey. Fearing an uprising, they went on the rampage and torched a series of houses in the neighbouring city of London. The congregation took flight and the ceremony had to be hastily concluded by the handful of 'terrified' clergymen who had stayed behind. The episode tested the nerves of England's newly crowned king, who according to one hostile chronicler was 'trembling from head to foot'.[11]

William attempted to erase the memory of this fiasco with another show of royal pageantry. It was during his reign that the custom of 'crown-wearings' became firmly established. Usually held at the religious festivals of Christmas, Easter and Whitsun, these magnificent occasions were attended by all of the leading dignitaries and clerics of the kingdom, and were designed to remind his people that he was their crowned and anointed king. Such occasions did not come naturally to William. As Duke of Normandy, he had never allowed the formalities of state business to interrupt his military campaigns. Even on his wedding day, he had insisted on wearing a helmet to walk down the aisle.

The Norman court was given a much-needed injection of glamour by the arrival in 1068 of the new king's wife, Matilda. She received a cold reception from the native Saxons, who referred to her as 'the strange woman'. They were suspicious of the fact that she was spoken of as 'la Royne' by the Normans, which implied that she was a female sovereign in her own right. But Matilda soon became the acceptable face of the Norman monarchy, compensating for her husband's brutality with her charm and grace. She was also quick to exert a positive influence on the royal court. Even the Anglo-Saxon chroniclers could not help but be impressed by the magnificent spectacle that William and Matilda presented, clad from head to toe in gold-encrusted robes and eating their meals from gold and silver platters.

Matilda was crowned amid a 'very rich festival' on Whit Sunday (11 May), one of the most important dates in the Christian calendar.[12] Thenceforth, she became the first royal consort of England to be formally styled 'Regina'. Matilda was pregnant at the time of her coronation and, shortly before the child was due, she set out for Yorkshire in the hope that giving birth there would help secure the loyalty of one of the most troublesome parts of her husband's new kingdom. She made it as far as Selby, fourteen miles south of York, where she was safely delivered of her tenth and last child, Henry. At a stroke, Matilda had achieved more towards Anglo-Norman integration than her husband had during two years of bitter campaigning. Many Saxons regarded the new Norman prince as the only legitimate heir to the throne, taking precedence over his elder brothers Robert, Richard and William.

But the challenges of governing two separate realms on either side of the Channel led to fresh trouble. No sooner had William and Matilda set sail to spend Christmas 1068 in Normandy than Edgar the Ætheling headed south to Northumbria and led a huge uprising. His intention was to seize the throne from William and re-establish the Anglo-Saxon monarchy. His cause attracted swathes of men hostile to the Norman regime, and in February 1069 the rebels won a major victory by taking the city of York.

In alarm, William embarked for England once more. By April 1069, he had reclaimed York and proceeded to exact a terrible revenge. Throughout the rest of that year and well into the next, he launched a series of attacks on a vast swathe of territory stretching from the

Humber to the Tees. During this 'Harrying of the North', his forces burnt villages to the ground, destroyed crops and livestock, and slaughtered thousands of men and women. Thousands more died of starvation after their food stores were laid to waste.

It would take many more years of uprisings until England's first Norman king finally subdued his subjects and vanquished the threats from overseas. He did not do so by bloodshed alone. The notion of feudalism had been around since at least the ninth century, but William reinforced it with much greater vigour than before. The idea was based on the conception of the state as a pyramid, with each layer of society obtaining protection from the layer above in return for obligations such as military service. At the apex of the pyramid was the king, to whom all other layers ultimately owed loyalty. He was in theory the only landowner in the kingdom, the others being only landholders at his discretion.

This system was vital to William's monarchy because, as ruler of two separate territories divided by the Channel, he was obliged to delegate much of his authority to his nobles. They acted as his representatives in the local areas over which they held sway, ensuring that royal authority was disseminated throughout the kingdom. The system worked well under a strong king such as William, who ensured that none of his nobles obtained too much land – and therefore power – in a particular area. But under weak or unpopular kings, it could rapidly break down, as subsequent reigns would show.

William was so confident in his overlordship that in August 1086 he summoned all free tenants to a huge assembly in Salisbury and made them swear an oath of loyalty directly to himself, rather than to their immediate superiors. At the time, a huge survey of the kingdom was underway. Henry of Huntingdon records:

> The king being now all powerful, he sent justiciaries through every shire, that is, every county of England, and caused them to inquire on oath how many hides, that is, acres sufficient for one plough for a year, there were in every vill, and how many cattle; he made them also inquire how much each city, castle,

village, vill, river, marsh, and wood was worth in yearly rent. All these particulars having been written on parchment, the record was brought to the king, and deposited in the treasury, where it is preserved to this day.[13]

This staggeringly detailed survey would become one of the most famous documents in English history and was known as Domesday Book.[14] The name was coined by the native English, who put it on a par with the Last Judgement. As well as telling the king how much his domain was worth, it also provided a stark illustration of the destruction wrought by the Norman Conquest. Most of the native population had lost their land to the conquerors, and the value of that land had decreased as a result of the ensuing conflict. William was acutely aware of this, and he also suspected that some of his Norman followers had evaded the liabilities of their Anglo-Saxon predecessors. Domesday Book gave him the information he needed to take back control and the power to reassert the rights of the crown. He was determined that it would act as a definitive reference point for any future disputes over land – and in particular, crown – ownership.

Henry of Huntingdon, who was otherwise critical of William's monarchy, acknowledged that he was 'the most powerful of all the kings of England, more renowned than any of his predecessors'.[15] In the space of just two decades, he had undermined, and sometimes destroyed, the liberties, laws, customs and even the language of his new kingdom. The image of the civilising conquerors abolishing the barbarous practices of the native people is grossly misleading and owes much to Norman propaganda. William himself recognised that the English system of government was more sophisticated than that of his native duchy. His advisory council, or *curia regis*, was to all intents and purposes the Witan that had advised the Anglo-Saxon kings for centuries. Conscious of his illegitimacy, he had also been careful to uphold royal tradition.

In religion, too, William was in accord with his new subjects. If anything, the Normans were even more devout Christians than the Anglo-Saxons. Great Romanesque churches sprang up across the country, becoming as much a symbol of Norman pre-eminence as the imposing castles from which William and his men had stamped their authority. 'You may see everywhere churches in villages, in towns and cities monasteries rising in a new style of architecture; and with new devotion our country flourishes', the foremost twelfth-century historian William of Malmesbury recorded.[16]

To the untrained eye, the apparatus of the Norman monarchy was therefore much as it had been in the time of Edward the Confessor. But there was one crucial difference: William was king by conquest, not conciliation, and his regime was supported by formidable military power. This may have been enough to subdue his English subjects, but a new threat was bubbling under the surface that would catch William completely unawares.

A theme that recurs time and again in the history of the English monarchy is the difficult, often treacherous, relationships between the sovereign and their heir. The tradition began with William and his eldest son, Robert, nicknamed 'Curthose' because of his small stature. Robert was a feckless and arrogant young man whose impatience for power was matched by his father's reluctance to give him any. In 1077, he rebelled against William and attempted to seize the key Norman stronghold of Rouen. When that failed, he fled into exile in Flanders, where he prepared to launch another attack. Father and son fought each other in open combat when their forces clashed at Gerberoi in southern Normandy two years later. Robert gained the upper hand but flinched from delivering the killer blow, either due to an attack of conscience or, as some chroniclers have it, because he only recognised William at the eleventh hour. In the aftermath, he escaped to exile once more and never posed a threat to his father again.

William was dismayed to discover that his wife Matilda had secretly supported their son's rebellion. He never forgave either of them. On his deathbed in September 1087, he bequeathed England to his third son William, his second son Richard having died in a hunting accident some years before. It took the earnest persuasions of his advisers to prevent him from disinheriting his eldest son altogether. At length, the dying king agreed that Robert should inherit the Duchy of Normandy.

William's final bequest destabilised the fragile Anglo-Norman dynasty that he had fought so hard to establish. Within weeks of his death, Normandy was on the brink of civil war and his sons were engaged in a fierce battle for superiority that would dominate European politics for years to come.

William II (1087–1100)

'He was always harassing this nation'

ENGLAND'S NEW KING was about twenty-seven years old when he ascended the throne. Nicknamed 'Rufus', due either to his bright blond hair or to his ruddy complexion, he took great care over his appearance and dressed in the latest fashions. His new subjects looked askance at his long, pointed shoes, which curled like scorpions' tails at the ends. There were rumours of homosexuality, fuelled by the fact that he never married or had children. Malmesbury was responsible for much of the gossip. He claimed that it became common at the royal court for young men to 'rival women in delicacy of person, to mince their gait, to walk with loose gestures and half naked'. Other chroniclers condemned the new king's 'obscene fornications' and 'unspeakable debauchery'.[1]

Whatever his personal tastes, Rufus understood the need to put on a good show. Henry of Huntingdon opined: 'Kings are like gods to their subjects. So great is the majesty of this earth's highest that people never weary of looking at them.' The new king continued his father's practice of celebrating the major festivals of the Christian year with 'sumptuous and magnificent banquets', which all the great nobles of the kingdom were commanded to attend, as well as overseas visitors who would carry back tales of the English king's dazzling court.[2]

Rufus had the same ferocious temper as his father, too, and Archbishop Anselm compared him to a wild bull when provoked. Less intelligent than his brothers, he nevertheless won praise for his common sense and wit. Malmesbury claimed that the new king concealed his true nature in order to intimidate his courtiers: 'In public and in assemblies his bearing was haughty and stiff. He would stare at people with a menacing look in his eyes . . . and intimidate those he was speaking to by adopting a harsh tone and a studied severity. In private and in the chamber with his friends he was easygoing and relied a great deal on joking.'[3]

William II was also greedy for glory and riches. 'His energy of mind was such that no kingdom was beyond the reach of his ambition', observed Malmesbury.[4] Knowing that his accession had contravened the rightful order, Rufus was quick to claim his new kingdom, setting sail for England before his father had died. He made straight for the ancient Wessex capital of Winchester to secure the royal treasure and was crowned king by Archbishop Lanfranc within a fortnight.

Having spent a great deal of time with his father, Rufus was a seasoned warrior and commander but had little experience of England. He attempted to win over his resentful new subjects by distributing his father's treasure among the churches and counties. His only mistake was in allowing his half-uncle Odo, Bishop of Bayeux (who had been imprisoned by the Conqueror), to recover all his English fiefs and the earldom of Kent. Odo soon set about organising a rebellion against the king and recruited a number of high-ranking Normans, as well as Rufus's brothers, Robert and Henry. He also had the support of Edgar the Ætheling, who had spent most of his time in exile since the Conquest. In the spring of 1088, the conspirators launched their attack. The king, based in London, was quick to mobilise his forces and soon crushed the threat. Wisely, after banishing Odo, Rufus showed mercy to most of the nobles who had supported him.

As far as his brother Robert was concerned, though, the king was intent upon revenge. The 1090s were dominated by the shifting hostilities and alliances between Robert and William, with their wily younger brother Henry flitting between the two, always with an eye to his own advantage. It took the pope to intervene before a truce was finally concluded in February 1096. Robert agreed to surrender Normandy to Rufus for 10,000 marks of silver. Although this was supposed to be for just three years, Robert abandoned his duchy a few months later to go crusading. Rufus was now Duke of Normandy as well as King of England – a far greater inheritance than he could have hoped for as merely the younger son of a duke.

* * *

Greatly though he revelled in his titles, Rufus soon experienced the same challenges of ruling a cross-Channel empire that his father had battled with. After taking charge of Normandy, he spent more than half of his time on the Continent. The institution of monarchy was itinerant once more, but the king's absences did not present such a risk to his authority in England as it had during his father's reign because, by now, the Norman nobility was deeply entrenched. Any threat that these nobles themselves might have posed was offset by the strong bonds of homage and fealty that the king had established. When he was in England, Rufus made his kingly presence fully felt by all. His progresses around the country were likened to the ravages of an invading army, and he levied heavy taxes to pay for his overseas campaigns. Little wonder that, as a contemporary monk reported: 'When it became known that the king was coming everyone fled to the woods.'[5] William intensified the resentment among his English subjects by pushing his own rights hard – for example by enlarging the royal hunting preserves. 'He was always harassing this nation with military service and excessive taxes, for in his days all justice was in abeyance', lamented one contemporary.[6]

In 1097 the king embarked upon two major building projects, both aimed at strengthening his monarchical image and authority. The first was at his main residence, Westminster, where he commissioned a magnificent new hall. Measuring 240 by 67 feet, it was by far the largest hall in England – probably in Europe too. Even so, when the king first came to inspect it and one of his attendants remarked that it was much bigger than necessary, he retorted that it was not half large enough and was a mere bedchamber compared to what he had in mind. At the Tower of London, meanwhile, more mindful of defence than of image, Rufus continued work on his father's huge central keep or 'Great Tower' and reinforced the bailey surrounding it.

According to the *Anglo-Saxon Chronicles*, by now, the 'wicked' and 'terrible' king was 'hated by well-nigh all his nation' for his tyranny, greed and brutality.[7] William of Malmesbury concurred: 'The king was arrogant beyond measure and often did things for no good reason but simply because he possessed immense power.'[8] Although there had been glimpses of a beneficent monarch who founded new abbeys and enabled religious orders such as the Benedictines to flourish, there were many more of a grasping and merciless king who quarrelled with his archbishop of Canterbury and plundered the resources of his people.

When out hunting on 2 August 1100 in the New Forest, one of the royal hunting preserves that he had seized, Rufus was shot in the heart by an arrow. Who fired it and whether it was an accident or murder has been debated ever since. It is commonly thought to have been one of the king's own men – possibly Walter Tirel, Count of Poix, a renowned soldier. William's elder brother Richard had also been killed in a hunting accident there, which must have made the surviving brother Henry nervous because their mother Matilda had once been told of a prophecy that three of her sons would die in the New Forest.

Henry had been among Rufus's hunting party and was quick to take the initiative – so quick, in fact, that some historians believe he had a hand in his brother's death. He stole a march on the powerful barons who supported his elder brother Robert by hastening to Winchester to seize control of the royal treasure. In the face of opposition from Robert's supporters, he argued that, unlike his older sibling, he had been born to a reigning king and queen, which made his the stronger claim.[9] Eventually, the barons conceded and elected him king. Henry arranged a hasty coronation at Westminster Abbey on 5 August, just three days after Rufus's death.

Henry I (1100–1135)

'He would rather contend by counsel than the sword'

THERE WAS A whiff of the usurper about England's new king, who had claimed the throne ahead of his elder brother Robert. But the tradition of primogeniture in the English royal succession had not yet taken hold as it had in Normandy, and there were various precedents for younger sons inheriting the crown, not least Henry's immediate predecessor. An even more useful example to Henry, given that he claimed the throne in Winchester, was that of Alfred the Great, who had leapfrogged his elder brother's sons to become king.

The new king was so anxious to confirm his status that his coronation was hastily arranged and officiated over by the Bishop of London. Henry was quick to apologise to Archbishop Anselm, assuring him: 'I beg you not to be displeased that I have accepted the royal title without your blessing . . . But the need was urgent because enemies would have risen up against me and the people I have to govern, and in consequence my barons and people were unwilling to delay the ceremony longer.'[1]

Amid this whirlwind of events, nobody had given much thought to the dead king, least of all his successor. Rufus's body was brought to Winchester and laid to rest without ceremony in the Old Minster. Henry was too busy to attend, and instead made the most of his late brother's unpopularity in order to boost his own. In the hurriedly drafted coronation charter, he pledged to reform the 'unrighteous acts that took place in his brother's time' and to restore 'the law of King Edward [the Confessor] together with such emendations to it as my father made with the counsel of his barons'.[2] Determined to maximise the public relations benefits of the charter, Henry ordered that it be sent out to shire courts and bishoprics. For Henry, the charter had been merely one of several expedients to bolster his precarious hold on the throne and he went on to break a number of the promises within it. Yet it still represented a significant moment in England's constitutional history. The just and liberal vision of kingship that it provided served as a precedent for Magna Carta more than a century later.

From the beginning of his reign, Henry set out to prove that he was different from his predecessor. Some of the contrasts between the two brothers needed no explanation. First, and most obvious, was their sexuality. The new king was addicted to women and had as many as twenty-four bastards by his numerous mistresses – more than any other English king. Henry was willing to acknowledge all of them, partly to prove his virility, but also to put them to good use. His sons were enlisted to support him, both militarily and politically, while his daughters were married off to neighbouring princes in order to secure alliances.

Another facet of Henry's kingship in which he differed from Rufus was his caution. 'He would rather contend by counsel than the sword; he conquered without bloodshed if he could, and if not, with as little as possible.'[3] William of Malmesbury's assessment was an accurate one. Henry's preference for diplomacy over battles is something that characterised not only his kingship, but that of virtually all of England's longest-reigning, most stable and, ultimately, successful monarchs. Military glory was a tantalising prospect and one that few other kings of the period could resist, but those who did were often richly rewarded.

Rather than seek to extend his territories, Henry was content to defend them – but only once he had recovered all of his father's lands and privileges. The first six years of his reign were the most turbulent as he set out to reunite England and Normandy while trying to secure his newly won throne.

Upon his return from crusade in the autumn of 1100, Robert Curthose resumed his lordship over Normandy and once more began planning a campaign to conquer England. He found considerable support among the English nobility and launched an invasion in the summer of 1101. If Robert had had the foresight of his younger brother, upon landing on England's shores he would have made straight for Winchester and seized the royal treasury. Instead, he prevaricated, giving Henry the chance to rally his troops.

The two armies met at Alton in Hampshire. Bloodshed was narrowly avoided when the barons on both sides mediated a peace between the brothers. Duke Robert agreed to relinquish his claim to the English throne in return for custody of all Henry's holdings in Normandy except Domfront, as well as an annuity of 3,000 marks. But it was an uneasy truce. During the years that followed, Henry embarked upon a charm offensive towards the Anglo-Norman barons, gradually winning the majority of them over to his cause through patronage and marriage to his bastard daughters.

Henry maintained peace throughout England for the remaining thirty-three years of his reign – an achievement that was both considerable and unmatched by any other medieval monarch. He did so through both force and reward, meting out severe punishments to any wrongdoers and rewarding loyal followers with lands, titles and other patronage. Bolstered by his growing body of supporters, in 1106 Henry took more aggressive action by crossing to Normandy and challenging his elder brother to a battle at Tinchebrai in the south-western corner of the duchy. Among Robert's supporters was Edward the Confessor's nephew, Edgar the Ætheling, who had joined the duke on crusade and lent his campaign legitimacy. But Henry's victory was decisive. Robert was captured and remained his younger brother's prisoner until his death twenty-eight years later.

Although the king's harsh treatment of his brother sparked widespread criticism, it was typical of Henry's pragmatic approach to kingship. If he had shown greater mercy and set Robert free, it would have been only a matter of time before Curthose made fresh trouble. As it was, the Anglo-Norman territory that had been so hard won by their father was now firmly under Henry's control.

England's king consolidated his monarchy in other ways. In November 1100, he married Edith, daughter of King Malcolm III of Scotland. This was a shrewd move. Edith (who adopted the Norman name Matilda upon her marriage) had the blood of the West Saxons, as well as the Scottish kings, flowing through her veins. She was therefore pleasing to the population both north and south of the border. The marriage also gave Henry's claim to the throne a welcome boost. The two children it produced, Matilda and William, had a direct hereditary link to the old English royal line.

Thanks to the queen consort's influence, the royal court became a vibrant cultural centre, attracting writers, poets and musicians from far and wide. Henry's influence on the court was no less profound. It was during his long reign that its structure became more clearly defined. At the heart of his court was the domestic household, or *domus*. This was divided into several parts, including the chapel, which looked after the royal documents, and the chamber, which managed the royal finances, while the master-marshal was responsible for travel and accommodation – an important role given the itinerant nature of the court at this time.

Beyond the *domus* was the wider circle of servants, confidantes and other close associates known as the *familia regis*. This included the king's mounted household troops – in effect, a standing army up to several hundred strong – which could be deployed across England and Normandy as required. Formal gatherings of court were known as *curia*. For the first part of his reign, Henry continued the tradition established by his father of holding regular crown-wearing ceremonies at such gatherings, but these became less frequent as the years went by and his hold on the throne was strengthened.

There was no shortage of other dazzling court displays, though. The twelfth-century writer, cleric and courtier Walter Map recorded: 'This king's court was in the forenoon a school of virtues and wisdom, and in the afternoon one of hilarity and decent mirth.'[4] Henry invested huge sums in constructing lavish new palaces and other royal buildings, including a private menagerie of exotic animals at Woodstock Palace in Oxfordshire. At the same time, he made sure that life at his court was subject to stringent rules and etiquette – certainly far stricter than had been imposed by any of his predecessors. For example, members of his court were prohibited from pillaging neighbouring villages, as had become common during the reign of his brother Rufus. As well as sending out a message that the king was in absolute control of all he surveyed, his new rules were designed to win favour with his humbler subjects.

At the centre of all this carefully controlled splendour was Henry himself. His contemporary, William of Malmesbury, described him as sociable and witty, informal in speech, and temperate in eating and drinking. Given the reputation he gained in his youth as a scholar (earning him the nickname 'Beauclerc'), it is perhaps not surprising that Henry became a great patron of learning. 'He was inferior in wisdom to no king in modern times, and . . . clearly surpassed all his predecessors in England,' enthused one admiring contemporary.[5] His reign boasted more notable writers and historians than any that had gone before, with the likes of Malmesbury, Orderic Vitalis, Henry of Huntingdon and Eadmer of Canterbury all leaving a rich legacy of chronicles and other works.

The encouragement of learning and literacy also had a profound effect on government. Henry I was the first of England's kings to put royal administration on a more formal and regulated footing. The records from his reign are unprecedented in their abundance and detail. They include 1,500 charters – more than three times as many as those produced during the combined reigns of his father the Conqueror and brother Rufus. The king's sweeping reforms encompassed every aspect of government, from law and order to the minting of coins. Royal justice became much more visible as a result, and Henry won praise by outlawing the long-cherished court practice of pillaging the localities through which the king and his entourage passed. Local goods were now requisitioned at fixed, fair prices, and household officials were given allowances for subsistence. The reforms of the royal household were encapsulated in the *Constitutio domus regis*, a detailed document that provided guidance for his immediate successor but would influence court administration for generations to come.

The king's overhaul of governmental administration also resulted in the establishment of the exchequer to control royal finances. This produced a kingdom-wide financial survey each year in the form of the pipe roll. Instituted in 1130, these accounts would continue to be taken for the next seven hundred years, and the pipe rolls form the oldest continuous series of records kept by the English government. Taken together, Henry I's reforms transformed medieval government from an itinerant and often poorly organised household into a highly sophisticated administrative kingship based on permanent, static departments.

Henry's personal involvement in this rigorous new system of government was considerable. According to Oderic Vitalis: 'He inquired into everything, and retained all he heard in his tenacious memory. He wished to know all the business of officials and dignitaries; and, since he was an assiduous ruler, he kept an eye on all the happenings in England and Normandy.'[6] Such was Henry's contribution to the rise of administrative kingship in England that he was lauded by some nineteenth-century historians as the first constitutional monarch.[7]

While the king was bringing greater order to the administration of his realm, his relations with France were proving increasingly troublesome. The accession of an assertive new king, Louis VI, in 1108 posed a threat to Normandy's borders, as did that of the young Count of Anjou, Fulk V, who became Count of Maine in 1110. The two men soon allied with Count Robert II of Flanders in an attempt to oust Henry from Normandy and make his nephew, William Clito – the only legitimate son of the captive Robert Curthose – its duke. In characteristic style, Henry favoured diplomacy over warfare and concluded a favourable peace settlement in 1113, pledging his son and heir William to Fulk's daughter Matilda of Anjou. Louis joined the pact shortly afterwards.

But this uneasy truce did not last for long, and the next few years were dominated by bitterly fought campaigns. A low point came for Henry at Christmas 1118 when his forces suffered a heavy defeat and his life was threatened by an assassin within his own household. This seemingly relaxed and affable king would never enjoy a peaceful night's sleep again and took a sword and shield to his bed every night.

Things moved in his favour the following year with the collapse of Fulk's earlier pact with Louis and the death of the Count of Flanders. Henry's newfound accord with Fulk V was cemented when his son William at last married Matilda of Anjou, and the King of France finally acknowledged Henry's right to Normandy. On 25 November 1120, having concluded a definitive peace on all sides,

Henry set sail for England. But his triumph soon turned to disaster when the *White Ship*, which carried his son William and two of his illegitimate children, sank soon after leaving the harbour at Barfleur.[8] All but one of the three hundred or so people who had been on board the *White Ship* were drowned, Prince William included.

'No ship was ever productive of so much misery to England', Malmesbury lamented.[9] The disaster had a profound effect on the stability of Henry's regime. The peace agreements with Anjou and France that he had worked so hard to achieve were now null and void, since they had both depended on his son William's marriage to Matilda of Anjou and homage to Louis VI. Worst of all, the loss of Henry's only legitimate son had thrown the royal succession into doubt. Suddenly it looked like the mighty Anglo-Norman dynasty his father the Conqueror had worked so hard to establish would unravel in Henry's own lifetime. Little wonder it was said that, after hearing of the catastrophe, the king never smiled again.

Desperate to secure his throne, Henry almost immediately married again, his first wife Matilda having died two years earlier. His new bride Adeliza (or Alice), daughter of the Duke of Lorraine, was crowned in January 1121, a day after the wedding. Although the new queen was young, beautiful and, as her later history proved, fertile, she was unable to give Henry the children he so desperately needed.[10] Malmesbury recounted how the king – 'In grief that the woman did not conceive . . . and in fear that she would always be barren' – was forced to look elsewhere for a successor.

Henry still had one legitimate child living, his daughter Matilda. However, although Salic law might not have been officially adopted in England, the prospect of a female sovereign was both unprecedented and abhorrent to most of his subjects. The king was getting desperate, though. Matilda's marriage to the Holy Roman Emperor, Heinrich V, had not produced any children, and when he died in 1125, Henry summoned his daughter to join him in Normandy. Given that he had not seen her since she had left to marry Heinrich at the age of eight, he needed to find out whether she was the stuff that monarchs were made of. He also discussed the matter with his advisers, but there was fierce disagreement between them. In the end, those in favour of Matilda's succession prevailed, and on New

Year's Day 1127 Henry ordered his court to pledge their support to his daughter as heir to England and Normandy. Among those present was the king's nephew, Stephen, the younger son of his sister Adela, Countess of Blois, and a major Anglo-Norman landholder.

Although the succession had been agreed, the fact that a woman was due to inherit the throne and that many of Henry's subjects on both sides of the Channel were opposed to the idea enabled his international rivals to take advantage. Louis VI once more threw his support behind William Clito's rival claim to Normandy. Henry responded by arranging a marriage between his daughter and Geoffrey 'Plantagenet', son of Fulk V, Count of Anjou and Maine. Geoffrey's sobriquet may have been inspired by the fact that he wore a sprig of the yellow broom flower (planta genista) in his helmet. The name would become a very familiar one in the history of the English monarchy.

As well as trying to strengthen his position against France, the wily Henry was, as ever, hedging his bets. Although he had publicly declared his support for his daughter Matilda as the future queen, he was hoping that she might still give him a grandson who could succeed to the throne in her place. The marriage took place in June 1128. Matilda was then a widow of twenty-five, while her bridegroom was just fourteen. Six weeks later, William Clito was killed in battle. Now everything rested upon the fruit of Matilda's marriage. Although it proved a turbulent one and the couple separated for a while, in March 1133 Henry was overjoyed when news arrived that his daughter had given birth to a son, named in his honour. The following year, she had another, Geoffrey. Henry spent time with both of his grandsons and took great delight in them, not least because they seemed to represent a secure future for his Anglo-Norman dynasty.

Relations between Henry and his daughter and son-in-law became increasingly strained, however. Suspecting that they lacked support in England, Matilda and Geoffrey made increasingly aggressive demands, such as urging the English king to give them custody of the royal castles in Normandy. He refused, no doubt fearing Geoffrey would try to seize control of the duchy.

By now, the king was in his mid-sixties and his health was no longer as robust as it had been throughout his long reign. In late

November 1135, while enjoying his favourite pastime of hunting at Lyons-la-Forêt in Normandy, he suddenly fell ill. Henry of Huntingdon claims the culprit was 'a surfeit of lampreys' that the king had devoured, against his physician's advice. His condition deteriorated over the course of a week and he died on 1 December.

Most historians who have judged Henry as ruthless, cunning and cruel have viewed him with modern eyes. When measured against the standards of his day, he appears both impressive and successful. Orderic Vitalis, who did not flinch from criticising his contemporary rulers, declared him 'the greatest of kings'. During his thirty-five-year reign, Henry had achieved greater stability than England had enjoyed since 1066 and had transformed the apparatus of monarchy, placing it on a firmer administrative footing than ever before. 'God grant him peace, for peace he loved,' intoned Hugh of Amiens, Abbot of Reading and Archbishop of Rouen, at Henry's deathbed. It was a fitting epitaph.

Matilda and Stephen (1135–54)

'The abominable madness of the traitors'

THE ACCESSION OF Matilda was an important moment in the history of the monarchy. Never before had England been ruled by a woman. Viewed through modern eyes, this was a positive step: after all, some of England's most successful monarchs have been female. But in an age when women were viewed as the weaker sex in every single respect, it was regarded as little short of a catastrophe. There was no sense that Matilda's reign might set some useful precedents for future queens regnant; rather, the mood was that in future such a scenario must be avoided at all costs.

It was not only Matilda's gender that made her unacceptable to her English subjects. She was a virtual stranger. After leaving England at the age of eight in 1110, Matilda had spent only a fleeting amount of time there. The most notable occasion, in 1130, was hardly to her credit. She had rowed with her second husband, Geoffrey Plantagenet, whom she considered far beneath her in status, and had returned to her native kingdom in high dudgeon. The new queen, who was still known as 'Empress' by dint of her first marriage, also had cause to regret her poor relationship with her father towards the end of his life. If they had resolved their differences and she had been at his side at the end, he could have confirmed her as his heir, witnessed by all of the powerful nobles who had clustered around his deathbed. But the fact that Henry died with their conflict unresolved threw the Anglo-Norman succession into doubt and allowed others to take advantage.

Principal among them was Matilda's cousin, Stephen of Blois. Not everyone was taken in by his genial nature. He was variously described as a 'fool' and 'a man of less judgement than energy', while Malmesbury 'doubted the truth of his words and the reliability of what he promised'.[1] When Stephen heard of his uncle's death, he was in his wife's county of Boulogne and therefore within easier reach of England than Matilda, who was still living in Anjou. Spying his chance, he immediately crossed the Channel, hurried to London and laid claim to the English throne.

Although this was contrary to the late king's wishes, Henry had shown favour towards his nephew during his lifetime and may even have considered naming him as his successor. The fact that Stephen was William the Conqueror's grandson also bolstered his position, as did his marriage to Matilda, daughter and heir of Eustace III, Count of Boulogne, in 1125. He had also spent a good deal more time in England than his cousin Matilda and had been present at the major gatherings of court. 'He had by his good nature and the way he jested, sat and ate in the company even of the humblest, earned an affection that can hardly be imagined', observed Malmesbury.[2]

Upon arriving in London to claim the throne, Stephen immediately went on a charm offensive, making promises to both the church and laity. Instrumental to his success was his brother Henry, Bishop of Winchester, who secured the support of the head of the English administration, Roger of Salisbury, and of the royal treasurer, William de Pont de l'Arche. By no means all of the late king's English subjects were in favour of this new candidate, but with Matilda still on the other side of the Channel there seemed to be no viable alternative. On 22 December 1135, Stephen was duly crowned king by Archbishop William of Canterbury.

His succession to the Norman domains was initially less certain. Upon Henry I's death, the barons there had elected Stephen's brother, Thibaud of Blois, as their ruler. But as soon as news of Stephen's coronation in England reached Normandy, they accepted him as their duke instead. The united Anglo-Norman regime had therefore been restored – for now at least. Stephen's accession was further strengthened when the pope gave it his formal blessing.

But trouble was already brewing on both sides of the Channel. In 1138, Matilda's half-brother Robert, Earl of Gloucester, renounced his allegiance to Stephen and asserted the justice of his half-sister's cause. He was soon joined by other defectors. 'After Easter the abominable madness of the traitors flared up', reported Henry of

Huntingdon.[3] A series of uprisings threatened the king's authority in the west of England. These were swiftly – and brutally – put down by Stephen and his men. He also came to terms with King David I of Scotland, who had taken advantage of the turbulence in England by launching a series of raids across the border.

The uneasy peace would not last. In early 1139, the Empress appealed to Pope Innocent II that her inheritance in both England and Normandy should be restored. Her cousin Stephen also sent a delegation to Rome. Even though Pope Innocent had confirmed his kingship, he now refused to either give sentence or adjourn the case. His successors were no more willing to pass judgement, preferring to await the outcome of events.

Frustrated by the lack of papal support, Matilda took more decisive action. In September 1139, she and her half-brother Earl Robert set sail for England. Having landed in Sussex, they made their way to the west of the country, where Stephen's rule was weakest. It was not long before a number of prominent magnates joined her cause and Matilda was in a strong enough position to force her cousin to negotiate. But their attempts to reach a peaceful settlement came to nothing and as the months wore on, military action began to appear inevitable. Early in 1141, Robert of Gloucester and his son-in-law Ranulf, Earl of Chester, led an army against Stephen. The two sides met at Lincoln on 2 February and the king was defeated. He was taken prisoner and held at Bristol. Meanwhile, Matilda's husband Geoffrey made successful incursions into Norman territory. As a result, many prominent Anglo-Normans changed their allegiance to the Empress.

In March, Henry, Bishop of Winchester, received Matilda ceremoniously in his cathedral, along with six other bishops and a number of abbots. The symbolism was clear: he was conferring his own – and God's – blessing upon her as the rightful ruler. The following month, a legatine council formally accepted her as 'lady of England and Normandy' (a variation of 'lord of the English' given to a king before he was crowned) and plans were made for her coronation at Westminster Abbey.

Matilda's triumph was short-lived. Although he was her captive, Stephen refused to renounce his claim to the throne, which prompted uncertainty and division among the Empress's supporters. According to hostile sources such as the *Gesta Stephani*, Matilda's obstinate and haughty behaviour drove many to abandon her in favour of her more personable cousin. It describes her 'grim look, her forehead wrinkled into a frown, every trace of a woman's gentleness removed from her face', and how she often 'blazed into unbearable fury'.[4] Another contemporary agreed that she was 'a woman who had nothing of the woman in her'.[5] It is true that Matilda had inherited the notorious Plantagenet temper and always insisted upon being accorded the honour and state to which she had grown accustomed in Germany. But her years as Empress had also given her valuable experience of politics and diplomacy, and much of the criticism levelled against this 'unwomanly' ruler was rooted in the misogyny of contemporary chroniclers.

Ironically, even though she was battling for her place in the male-dominated world of twelfth-century politics, it would be a woman who would prove to be Matilda's undoing. In the summer of 1141, she made her way to Westminster to be crowned queen. But encamped on the opposite bank of the Thames was another Matilda, wife of the ousted King Stephen. She had drawn upon the considerable manpower of her native Boulogne, together with support from William of Ypres and members of the English nobility, to amass a formidable army. Seeing this, the citizens of London swiftly changed allegiance and attacked the Empress as she arrived for her coronation. Having beaten a hasty retreat to Oxford, she surrounded herself with those magnates still loyal to her and planned her next move.

At the end of July 1141, Matilda and her army marched on Winchester, but were outnumbered by the forces of her namesake. Her half-brother Robert of Gloucester was captured and once again the Empress made her escape. She rode at breakneck speed westwards to Devizes, straddling her horse like a man, it was disapprovingly noted. Exhausted, she eventually dismounted and was carried on a litter between two horses, which gave rise to the legend that she had escaped hidden in a coffin.

In November 1141, Earl Robert negotiated his release in return for that of Stephen. He also secured the castles of Devizes and Oxford for his half-sister, and it was in the latter that Matilda set up court with her dwindling body of supporters. Early in December, a church council restored Stephen to power and excommunicated his opponents, 'excepting only the lady of the Angevins herself'.[6] The newly restored king spent Christmas at Canterbury and made sure to uphold the customary crown-wearing on the feast day, conscious of what it symbolised.

But if he had won back England, Stephen was soon to lose all hope of regaining Normandy. The Empress's husband and his Angevin forces had been able to make more decisive gains after news had reached Normandy of Matilda's victory at Lincoln in 1141. Over the next three years, Geoffrey won a series of campaigns, bringing more and more territories under his control, until finally being invested as Duke of Normandy at Rouen in January 1154.

Stephen could not have contested Geoffrey's victory even if he had wished to: he had enough to do in England, where his hold on the throne remained precarious. The south-east alone was firmly under his control, which meant it was only here that he could raise taxes. A monarch was only as mighty as the wealth he commanded, so this seriously limited his power. Meanwhile, support for his cousin remained strong in the west of England and in Wales. Throughout the kingdom, even those local barons who were nominally faithful to the king defied royal discipline. They struck their own coinage, imposed their own justice, levied fines and taxes, and built more than a thousand baronial castles across the country.

From her base in Oxford, Matilda sent word to her husband in Normandy, pleading with him for military assistance. Geoffrey replied that he would only deal through Earl Robert, so his wife had little choice but to dispatch her most loyal supporter across the Channel. During his absence, Stephen's army laid siege to Oxford and in December 1142 Matilda made the most dramatic escape of her life. Accompanied by only a handful of knights, she slipped unseen from the castle and crossed the frozen Thames, wearing a white cloak as camouflage against the snow. Upon reaching Wallingford, she was escorted by her supporter, Brian fitz Count, to Devizes. She would remain there, holed up in the almost impregnable castle, for the next six years.

* * *

Although Stephen was nominally king, his realm was still engaged in civil war. Decisive leadership was called for, but this was something that Stephen was incapable of providing. 'It was the king's custom to start many endeavours with vigour,' noted the contemporary chronicler Gervase of Canterbury, 'but to bring few to a praiseworthy end.'[7] The only spark of hope for the future lay in the person of Matilda's eldest son. Henry, then aged nine, had crossed to England with Robert of Gloucester in late 1142 and proceeded to divide his time between his mother's court and that of his uncle, Stephen. For all her supposed obstinacy, Matilda was enough of a realist to recognise that only her son's accession would achieve peace in the kingdom. From the time of his arrival, she seems to have abandoned her personal ambitions in favour of championing her son's inheritance.

But this, too, was far from straightforward. Stephen had sons of his own: Eustace, who was two or three years older than Henry, and William, who was his brother's junior by about ten years. To bolster his position, Eustace was made Count of Boulogne in 1146–7. Meanwhile, the death of her principal supporter, Robert of Gloucester, in 1147, prompted the Empress to leave England for good. The focus of her ambitions, and those of her cousin Stephen, was now firmly on their respective sons. Eager to prevent Eustace from gaining the upper hand in Normandy, Henry spent the next few years flitting from one side of the Channel to the other. In 1150, when he was approaching his seventeenth birthday, he was invested by his father as Duke of Normandy. At the same time, Stephen sought to adopt Capetian custom by having his son Eustace crowned in his own lifetime. For this, he needed the support of the church, which was a major obstacle because relations between them had quickly soured. The king had promised reform but instead had abused his position by securing key church offices for his family and supporters.

In 1151, Matilda's son Henry was formally recognised as Duke of Normandy by Louis VII, King of France. He immediately set about planning an invasion of England, but was delayed by the annulment of Louis' marriage. As Duchess of Aquitaine, his estranged wife Eleanor was one of the wealthiest and most powerful women in Western Europe. Her union with the French king had been annulled on the basis that they were close kin, but the real reason was that it had produced no male heirs and the couple were at loggerheads. In her thirtieth year and eleven years' Henry's senior, Eleanor still presented an irresistible prospect for the young duke. Her famed beauty and vivaciousness may have been part of the attraction, but her considerable landed inheritance was a good deal more so. Upon their marriage in May 1152, just eight weeks after the annulment of Eleanor's first, Henry inherited a greater portion of French lands than the King of France himself.

Drawing on his vast new empire, Henry invaded England in the summer of 1153 and forced Stephen to come to terms. The beleaguered king had little choice but to acknowledge him as his heir in the Treaty of Wallingford. His eldest son, Eustace, 'greatly vexed and angry', withdrew from court and died a short while later, it was said, of a broken heart.[8] Stephen's younger son William was also passed over in the new agreement, an indication of how wearied Stephen was by the protracted struggle to secure his throne.

Henry made an immediate impression upon his future subjects. 'All the people loved him', reported the *Anglo-Saxon Chronicles*, 'for he did good justice, and made peace.' This 'new light' offered hope after the bitter years of civil war and offered the decisive leadership that Stephen so woefully lacked, as the same chronicle recorded: 'No man durst do other than good for the great fear of him.'[9] Having achieved his purpose, Henry returned to Normandy at Easter 1154. Despite his humiliating capitulation, Stephen tried to keep up appearances by going on progress to the north of his kingdom, 'encircling the bounds of England with regal pomp, and showing himself off as if he were a king'.[10] But he had always been painfully aware of the limits of his kingship. According to William of Malmesbury, during a particularly troublesome period of his reign Stephen had lamented: 'When they have chosen me king, why do they abandon me? By the birth of God, I will never be called a king without a throne!'[11] Now, more than ever, he was a king with only the trappings, not the substance, of royal power.

The loss of his eldest son and of everything for which he had fought for almost nineteen years seemed to weaken Stephen's already failing health. On 25 October 1154 the king, then aged about sixty-two, was staying at Dover Priory when he was 'suddenly seized with a violent pain in his gut, accompanied by a flow of blood' and died shortly afterwards.[12]

'Never did the country endure greater misery' than during Stephen's reign, observed the *Anglo-Saxon Chronicles*. Violence had been the keynote of a dynasty that had won the throne by conquest, and this had overshadowed the positive and more peaceable reforms that the Normans had made to the exercise of royal authority. And, in the end, the Norman monarchy had torn itself apart. But the crown itself had proved more resilient, enabling it to survive intact and welcome not just a new incumbent but a new dynasty. Now it seemed that, at last, the long years of civil strife, when 'Christ and his saints were asleep', were over.[13]

Part 2

The Plantagenets (1154–1399)

'From the Devil they came and to the Devil they will return'

The name Plantagenet applies to the three related ruling dynasties of Anjou, Lancaster and York: fourteen monarchs in total, their reigns spanning more than three hundred years.[1] The most dynamic and energetic dynasty in British royal history, they fostered the legend that they were descended from Melusine, the daughter of Satan, who married an early Count of Anjou, then vanished in a puff of smoke when he forced her to attend Mass. The yellow broom flower that inspired their sobriquet was later embodied in the family arms. Henry II was the first and is generally agreed to be the greatest of the Plantagenet kings. His vast empire stretched from the Scottish border almost to the Mediterranean, and from the Somme in the north of France to the Pyrenees in the south. For much of the period, England waged costly wars with France and Scotland, with mighty warrior kings such as Edward I and III and Henry V achieving celebrated victories. Among the greatest contributions of the Plantagenets was the development of English law and their magnificent architectural legacy. The monarchy also evolved to become much more closely aligned with the interests of the people, while the rise of Parliament prescribed new limits on royal power.

Henry II (1154–89)

'A human chariot dragging all after him'

WITH THE PEACEFUL accession of Henry II to the English throne in October 1154, the dynastic ambitions of his grandfather and namesake were not merely realised, but spectacularly superseded. England's new king reunited Henry I's Anglo-Norman inheritance, but also brought the lands and riches of Anjou and Aquitaine with him. He was compared to 'a cornerstone joining the two peoples' and, rather less accurately, as 'a king of the English race'.[1]

Like his great-grandfather, William the Conqueror, Henry II had already been chiselled into a fearsome warrior by the time he took the throne. Years of campaigning to protect his Duchy of Normandy had given him vital skills of diplomacy, too. Above all, he had youth on his side. He was twenty-one years old when he became King of England, and his restless energy and exuberance seemed boundless. The twelfth-century scholar Herbert of Bosham compared him to a 'human chariot dragging all after him'.[2]

When the new king was at court, he preferred to stand rather than to sit, much to the discomfort of those present, who were obliged to follow suit. Contemporaries marvelled at the speed with which he moved from one part of his vast domain to another: 'He must fly rather than travel by horse or ship.'[3] Travel would be a dominant theme of his reign. It has been calculated that he spent 37 per cent of his time in England and 40 per cent in Normandy, with the remaining time divided between Anjou, Aquitaine and other parts of France.

Henry listened patiently to those who sought his assistance and was generous to any of his subjects who experienced misfortune. But if crossed, his temper could be ferocious. When someone once praised his rival the King of Scots, he flew into such a rage that he 'fell out of bed screaming, tore up his coverlet, and threshed around the floor, cramming his mouth with the stuffing of his mattress'.[4] His distinctive blue-grey eyes, which were 'dove-like when he [was] at peace', would gleam 'like fire when his temper [was] aroused', and flash 'like lightning' when he was in a passion.[5] He loved and hated with equal ferocity, and was as liberal with his family as he was unforgiving to his enemies.

The new king had a strong, athletic physique, although his legs were slightly bowed from the countless days spent riding through his domains. He had reddish hair, which he kept closely shaved, as is depicted on his effigy at Fontevrault. It is no surprise that his leisure hours were spent in energetic pursuits such as hunting, and whenever he sought solace from the tumults of court he would flee to his beloved forests. But Henry's mind was as sharp as his physique. He was later described as 'very well up in letters' and Walter Map, a close associate, claimed that he knew 'all tongues spoken from the coasts of France to the river Jordan, but making use only of Latin and French'.[6] As well as spending many hours reading, he also enjoyed intellectual debates with his advisers and clerics. 'There is no one more subtle, and no one more magnificent to be found', enthused the French diplomat, Peter of Blois.[7]

Almost immediately after ascending the English throne, Henry was beset by troubles across the Channel. In December 1155, his brother Geoffrey raised a revolt, demanding that Henry hand over Anjou, the Touraine and Maine, as he claimed their father had willed it. For once, Henry resorted to diplomacy rather than war and held a family conference that included his mother, Empress Matilda. Increasingly isolated, Geoffrey was eventually forced to relinquish his claims, and from 1158 his elder brother had all of their father's domains, along with England and Aquitaine, firmly under his control.

Henry was now the most powerful ruler in Western Christendom. 'In all parts of his realm the king won the renown of a monarch who ruled over a wider empire than all who had hitherto reigned in England,' recounted a contemporary, 'for it extended from the far border of Scotland to the Pyrenees.'[8] By 1175, it included Ireland, which made Henry the first English king to claim authority there.

'The whole world was too small a prize for a single courageous and powerful ruler,' he once declared.[9]

Henry later boasted that in these early years of his reign he had attained the authority of his grandfather, Henry I, who 'was king in his own land, papal legate, patriarch, emperor, and everything he wished'.[10] Not all of his subjects were as impressed as he expected them to be. At a picnic one day, seeing the king mending a leather bandage on his finger with a needle and thread, the Bishop of Lincoln quipped: 'How like your cousins of Falaise you do look.' This was a sly reference to the bastardy of Henry's great-grandfather William the Conqueror, whose mother had been the daughter of a humble tanner from Falaise. It should have earned the bishop a sharp reprimand – or worse, but luckily for him, the king appreciated the joke.[11]

Formidable a character he may have been, but Henry's boast about his powers in England was not entirely accurate. By the time of his accession, the extent of the crown's authority had been well established. It was neatly summarised by the contemporary scholar John of Salisbury. He described the state as a body, the head of which was the king and the soul the church. Since the king was God's representative on earth, it was right that anyone who committed treachery against him should be put to death. But just as his subjects owed fealty to him, so the king owed fealty to the church. If he acted against it in any way, Salisbury argued, then his subjects were duty-bound to oppose or even assassinate him. Likewise, any monarch who was too weak to uphold the rights and interests of the church could no longer command the loyalty of his subjects. In short, kings were subservient not just to God but to Rome.[12] This balance of power between king and church was well understood by Henry's subjects, but it was less readily accepted by the king himself.

The prospect of wielding power over such a vast domain motivated Henry to resume the administrative advances that his grandfather had begun. He selected some of Henry I's advisers, along with his mother and youngest brother, William FitzEmpress, and a number of trusted nobles from either side of the Channel. The post of chancellor was awarded to a relative outsider, Thomas Becket, Archdeacon of Canterbury. There are echoes of a later chancellor, Thomas Wolsey, in Becket's background and capabilities. The son of a Norman farmer who had moved to London after the Conquest and set up in trade, Becket had the ambition and vision to transform the chancellorship from a second-rank position into one of enormous influence. Soon, he had won the king's absolute confidence and his power exceeded all others. Like Wolsey, Becket delighted in the trappings of his office and lavished huge sums on surrounding himself with ostentation. The new king would have done well to heed his mother's advice. Perhaps mindful of her own experience, the Empress Matilda had warned him to trust no one, his nobles in particular, and urged 'that he should spin out all the affairs of everyone, hold long in his own hand all posts that fell in, take the revenues of them, and keep the aspirants to them hanging on hope'.[13]

Henry had shown better judgement in ignoring his mother's counsel 'to be much in his chamber and little in public'.[14] From the very beginning of his rule, the new king was determined to overawe his subjects and rivals with displays of royal magnificence. Aware that Stephen's rule had been fatally weakened by a lack of control over the localities, Henry made his presence felt throughout the realm, either in person, through representatives, or in bricks and mortar. The Treaty of Wallingford had ordered the overmighty barons to demolish any unlicensed castles or surrender them to the crown. At the same time, Henry set about creating an impressive number of his own. Even the most humble of his building commissions carried the message that here was a ruler to be respected, admired and feared. A leper house he commissioned in Caen in 1161 left the contemporary historian Robert de Torigni unable to express anything but 'astonishment'. A rash of other building projects followed throughout Henry's domains, all varying in scale but never magnificence. Within a few years, Normandy, Anjou, Maine, the Touraine, Aquitaine and England were all littered with new castles, palaces, hunting lodges and manor houses.

Foremost among Henry's building projects in England was the imposing square keep at Dover Castle, set on the white cliffs so that it could be seen for miles around. As a potent symbol of royal power, it was second only to William the Conqueror's 'Great Tower' in London and would have been seen by the numerous pilgrims who made their way to Canterbury later in the reign. Similarly impressive castles were constructed at Nottingham, Scarborough and Newcastle. In a more romantic vein, Henry also commissioned Everswell in Woodstock for his mistress Rosamund Clifford. This immense architectural legacy on both sides of the Channel enabled Henry not only to project his authority but also to create a common style throughout his sprawling empire.

The scale of Henry II's achievement must not obscure the darker side of his reign. The imposition of hefty fines and taxes afflicted the lower classes of society in particular, with the landed elite largely being spared them. The church also suffered from these financial burdens, and the fact that episcopal offices were often left vacant for an unduly long time added to a growing resentment against the monarchy. This would find ultimate expression the following century in the reign of Henry's notorious youngest son, John. But many believed that his father was just as guilty of driving the monarchy towards excess.

In 1162, as a sign of his esteem, Henry promoted Thomas Becket to the archbishopric of Canterbury. This made him supreme in both church and state. To Henry's annoyance, immediately after being installed as archbishop, Becket resigned the chancellorship. It soon became clear that he was intent upon asserting the church's privileges over the crown. Matters came to a head in January 1164, when Henry summoned a council at Clarendon and forced Becket to recognise the 'ancient customs' that restricted the church's jurisdiction over crimes committed by the clergy. The ensuing Constitutions of Clarendon made it clear that the church was subordinate to the crown in all except matters of belief. Under intense pressure, Becket swore to the Constitutions, but subsequently revoked his submission and all the bishops followed his lead.

Becket also meddled in more personal matters, thwarting the king's plans to marry his brother William FitzEmpress to Isabella, the widow of King Stephen's son William of Blois, on the grounds of consanguinity. When William FitzEmpress died in 1164 with the issue still unresolved, Henry was distraught and held Becket directly responsible. Later that year, the king summoned Becket to

Northampton to answer a series of accusations, including hints of corruption. Rather than humbly submit himself to Henry's mercy, the archbishop defiantly brandished his cross and strode out of the hall. He subsequently fled to Flanders, eventually finding refuge at a Cistercian abbey, where he lived under the protection of the French king for the next five years.

Distance worked little positive effect on relations between king and primate. Henry's fury was stoked whenever he heard the latest report of how Becket was drawing more supporters to his cause and delighting in the self-importance and intrigue that his exile afforded. Eventually, to resolve what was rapidly becoming a diplomatic crisis involving not just the French king but the Holy Roman Emperor and the papacy, an uneasy truce was concluded. In 1170, Henry permitted Becket to return to England and regain his archbishopric.

But it was obvious to all that Becket was not forgiven. The king failed to return all of the lands and revenues that he had promised, and – tellingly – he stayed in Normandy rather than accompanying the archbishop to England, as he had promised. If Becket had shown himself to be repentant, things may have turned out very differently. But he arrived like an avenging angel, excommunicating all those who had opposed him. When he heard of this, Henry was incandescent with rage. 'What miserable drones and traitors have I nourished and promoted in my household, who let their lord be treated with such shameful contempt by a low-born clerk!' he ranted.[15] Oral tradition later refined his words to: 'Who will rid me of this turbulent priest?'[16]

Upon hearing them, four of the king's knights set off at once for England. On the afternoon of 29 December 1170, they confronted Becket in Canterbury Cathedral. A visiting monk described the horror that followed as one of the 'wicked' knights 'leapt upon him [Becket] suddenly and with his sword struck him on the head, cutting off the top of the crown'.[17] Further blows followed, of such severity that the sword carried by one of the knights was shattered on the stone of the abbey floor.

Becket's murder prompted outrage among the clergy across Europe. Pope Alexander III was so appalled that he refused to speak to any Englishmen for a week. When King Henry heard the news, he went into seclusion for three days – apparently from shock. Fearing excommunication, he was quick to come to terms with the pope and later made an elaborate show of penance, kneeling at the door of Avranches Cathedral in Normandy.

As the Becket scandal began to recede, another was gathering ground. Thus far, Henry's marriage to Eleanor of Aquitaine had proved a resounding success, politically as well as dynastically. A highly able woman with energy to match her husband's, Eleanor had played an active part in the government and administration of the English kingdom, despite her numerous pregnancies. During Henry's prolonged absences, Eleanor had fulfilled the vital role of keeping the monarchical flame alive, presiding over great ceremonial courts and making sure to be as visible as possible to her subjects.

Henry's queen had also fulfilled the more traditional consort role of providing heirs. They had seven surviving children – four boys and three girls. Most were betrothed to European potentates, notably the eldest son and heir, Henry, who was espoused to Louis VII's daughter Margaret, while his brother Richard was betrothed to Margaret's sister Alice. In 1170, the fifteen-year-old Prince Henry was anointed as co-King of England, and in August 1172 he was re-crowned at Winchester with Margaret as his queen. Shortly before, Prince Richard had been formally installed as Duke of Aquitaine.

But appearances were deceptive. While the English king was content to see the inheritance of his children thus confirmed, he had no intention of ceding authority to them in his lifetime. Realising this, in 1173, when he was just shy of his eighteenth birthday, Prince Henry furiously demanded that his father hand over either England, Normandy or Anjou. He was supported by his younger brother Richard, who was no less aggrieved at their father's unwillingness to share his power. The king's refusal plunged his realm into a bitter civil war as he fought to control his own flesh and blood. To make matters worse, his sons' rebellion was encouraged not just by the French king and other foreign rivals eager to take advantage, but by their mother, Eleanor. The sense of isolation Henry II felt, having been betrayed by his close family, was increased by the knowledge that he could no longer call on the support and advice of his indomitable mother, Matilda, who had died in 1167.[18]

But Henry's energy and resourcefulness never wavered, even though he was fighting a rebellion on numerous different fronts. As ever, he seemed to travel with greater speed than his adversaries. His wife Eleanor was captured as she tried to join her sons in Paris and was quickly imprisoned so that she could play no further part in her sons' rebellion. The fact that Henry had built upon his grandfather's administrative reforms meant that he could draw on a sophisticated network of trusted subordinates not just to carry out his orders, but to judge for themselves the best means and moment to act. As a result, within two years the rebellion had been crushed. Henry never forgave his wife's betrayal and, having failed to have the marriage annulled, he kept Eleanor a prisoner for the rest of his life.

In 1183, Prince Henry died after contracting dysentery during another campaign against his father in France. Far from settling matters, this prompted a succession crisis among the younger brothers, Richard, Geoffrey and John. Ironically, given that so much of England's monarchical history is dominated by the quest for a male heir, many of Henry II's problems stemmed from the fact that he had too many of them. The rivalry between his sons grew ever more intense as each vied for a portion of their father's sizeable inheritance. Henry could not settle the matter by bequeathing everything to his eldest surviving son Richard, because the prospect of permanently uniting Aquitaine with England, Normandy and Anjou would have posed too great a threat for the French king to ignore.

In August 1186, a fatal accident at a joust in Paris removed Henry's third son Geoffrey from this tangled mess of filial rivalries and disputed inheritance. But Louis VII's son and heir Philip II, who had become King of France in 1180 at the age of just fifteen, had the energy and swiftness of action to match his English rival. He was quick to claim the wardship of Geoffrey's two daughters, but Henry was not about to relinquish the Angevin lordship of Brittany, especially as he knew that his son's widow was pregnant (she gave birth to a son, Arthur, in March 1187). Soon, the two kings were on the brink of a full-scale war.

Although Henry rallied the support of his two surviving sons, Richard and John, he was 'stupefied' to discover that the elder of them had been secretly negotiating with the French king.[19] In a shocking move, in November 1187 Richard knelt before Philip and gave him homage for Normandy, Anjou and Aquitaine. In return, the French king agreed to support Richard's planned rebellion against his father. Everything that Henry had striven to protect for more than thirty years looked set to crumble into dust as soon as he was dead.

Open aggression between Philip and Richard against the English king soon followed. In the summer of 1189, after a series of military encounters on the Maine-Blois border, Henry was caught unawares and fled to Chinon in Anjou. His energy sapped by exhaustion and the summer heat, the ill health that he had been suffering for several months became more pronounced. Those who witnessed his peace talks with Richard and Philip on 4 July noticed that the fifty-six-year-old king looked ill. There was one last flash of his Angevin spirit, though. With little choice but to accede to the unfavourable terms that were pressed upon him, he whispered in his son's ear: 'God grant that I may not die until I have my revenge on you.'[20]

But God was not listening. Two days later, Henry died, broken by the discovery that his youngest son John had also turned against him. According to the chronicler Ralph of Diceto, when Henry's elder son Richard came to pay his respects to his late father, 'blood at once began to flow from the dead king's nostrils as if his spirit was moved with indignation'.[21] Henry was laid to rest at the abbey of Fontevrault in Anjou. His remarkably lifelike effigy gives the sense that this warrior king, a force of nature whose restless energy had enabled him to wield power over a vast empire for almost thirty-five years, might rise and take up arms again as soon as he has caught his breath.

Richard I (1189–99)

'Courage carried to excess'

DESPITE THE TURBULENCE that had preceded Henry II's death, his dominions passed intact to his eldest son. In fact, Richard inherited a position of power that was perhaps even greater than that of his father. Being born on English soil may have given Richard an advantage over his predecessor. But he had little good to say about the country and once complained that it was 'cold and always raining'.[1] His actions soon made it clear that he regarded England as a minor part of his vast Angevin empire and that its primary purpose was to fund his foreign ventures.

After paying his respects to his late father at Fontevrault, Richard made his way to Normandy, where he was formally installed as duke on 20 July 1187. Courting popularity among his new subjects, he promised to restore the estates of all those whom his father had disinherited. The prospect of his extending the same pledge to England meant that he was greeted with widespread rejoicing when he landed at Portsmouth on 13 August. Three weeks later, he was crowned at Westminster. But a series of anti-Jewish riots in Westminster and London marred the celebrations. Although Richard managed to restore order, further riots broke out as soon as he left England, culminating in 1190 with the massacre of the entire Jewish population of York, who had taken refuge in the royal castle.[2]

Richard may have regretted this terrible episode, but from the outset of his reign it was obvious that his attentions were focused elsewhere. Upon the fall of Jerusalem to Saladin, Sultan of Egypt and Syria, in October 1187, Richard had pledged to join Philip of France on a crusade to the Holy Land. He now prepared to make good his promise. The new king's crusading zeal would define his reign and shape his monarchy, earning him the sobriquet 'Lionheart'.

But it would leave England utterly depleted. It would also give truth to a remark made shortly before Richard's accession, that 'the abundance of resources, or the lack of them, exalts or humbles the power of princes'.[3]

In order to finance the crusade, in 1189 Richard embarked upon a reorganisation of government, appointing new justiciars, replacing or rearranging sheriffs, and confirming old and making new grants. But the new offices and privileges were sold rather than conferred. The contemporary chronicler Roger of Howden shrewdly observed that the new king had 'put everything up for sale'.[4] Such a tactic was not new, but the speed and scale with which it was enforced certainly was. Even though he had inherited a sizeable treasury from his father, Richard was not satisfied until he had plundered all of the resources at his disposal. He apparently even quipped that he would have sold London if he could have found a buyer.

While the new king's fundraising efforts soon bore fruit, the governance of his kingdom proved a thornier problem. His brother John had no intention of joining him on crusade; neither was he satisfied with the lordship of Ireland that Richard had bestowed upon him. The king therefore made a placatory gesture by endowing him with a number of great estates, although he made sure to bestow real power – and castles – upon trusted ministers such as William de Longchamp and Walter de Coutances.

If Richard could not entirely trust his younger brother, there was another family member upon whom he could rely utterly: his mother, Eleanor of Aquitaine. One of his first acts as king was to order her release. Aged about sixty-seven at her son's accession, Eleanor's energy and enthusiasm were undiminished by her prolonged imprisonment: if anything, she seemed more buoyant than ever. Now that her son Richard was king, she would enjoy greater power and influence than she had as queen consort. Ruling England in Richard's name, she went from 'city to city and castle to castle', holding 'queenly courts', releasing prisoners and exacting oaths of loyalty to her son.[5] She defended the crown as fiercely as if it had been her own and once signed a letter to Pope Celestine III: 'Eleanor, by the wrath of God, Queen of England'.[6]

Satisfied that his realm was in safe hands, Richard crossed the

Channel in December 1189 and met Philip to confirm that their joint crusade would be launched from Vézelay on 1 April 1190. In the event, their departure was delayed until June and the two kings' armies soon became separated. Family concerns drew Richard to Sicily, where his sister Joanna was being kept a virtual prisoner following the death of her husband the previous year. Having secured her release, Richard spent the winter months of 1190–1 bolstering his resources. In April 1191, having amassed a huge fleet of two hundred ships and as many as 17,000 men, he set sail from Messina.

In a little over a month, Richard had conquered Cyprus and taken a wife. For some time, his mother had promoted the Spanish princess, Berengaria of Navarre, as a bride for her son. Eleanor was so determined to bring the marriage to pass that she personally accompanied Berengaria to Messina so that the wedding could take place while Richard was on crusade. In May 1192, after another year of bitter campaigning against Saladin, word reached Richard that his brother John had been making the most of his long absence by plotting treason with the French king. It is an indication of how little store Richard set by his English responsibilities that he decided to stay and fight. An account of one of the bloodiest days of the conflict at Jaffa provides a glimpse of the king's reckless bravery as he surged into the heart of the battle like a 'ferocious lion', mowing down the enemy 'as if he were harvesting them with a sickle'. He eventually emerged from the fray, 'his body completely covered with arrows, which stuck out like the spines of a hedgehog.'[7]

Meanwhile in England, it was only thanks to Richard's indomitable mother that John was kept in check – for now. By September 1192, battle-weary and in poor health, Richard agreed a three-year truce with Saladin. He had failed to take Jerusalem, but the entire coast from Tyre in the north down to Jaffa, forty or so miles north-west of Jerusalem, was now in Christian hands. The crusade had therefore been a dazzling success, and, thanks to the French king's early retreat, the triumph was Richard's alone.

But it was short-lived. On his way back, Richard was captured by Leopold of Austria and held prisoner at the castle of Dürnstein. The wily Austrian ruler realised the value of the captive king and for several months the potentates of Europe haggled over his ransom.

In February 1193, the Holy Roman Emperor, Heinrich VI, made Leopold an offer he could not refuse and Richard was transferred to his custody. In the meantime, Richard's position had been further eroded when his treacherous brother John once more pledged his allegiance to King Philip of France, who promised to mount a full-scale invasion of England and put John on the throne. In the event, this support did not materialise. Undaunted, John sailed to England, loudly proclaiming that his brother was dead and asserting his own claim. Although he won some followers, most Englishmen remained loyal to Richard, whose cause their mother Queen Eleanor continued to champion tirelessly.

Finally, in June 1193, once more thanks to Eleanor, who had travelled to Germany to counsel her son and had also appealed to the pope, the Emperor agreed to release Richard in return for a crippling ransom. 'The devil is loosed', Philip of France wrote to Richard's brother John after hearing the news.[8] His alarm was precipitate. It was not until February 1194 that Richard was able to pay enough of the ransom to secure his release.

Upon the king's return to England on 13 March, support for his treacherous brother soon collapsed. The last of John's garrisons to hold out was at Nottingham, but after some vicious fighting the castle fell to the king and his forces on 28 March. Contrary to legend, whilst in Nottingham, Richard encountered neither Robin Hood nor John's evil sheriff. This story only arose in the sixteenth century and was embellished by the works of later authors such as Sir Walter Scott. In fact, if Robin Hood existed at all then modern scholarship has proved that the earliest he could have been active was twenty years after Richard's death. The crusading king did, though, visit Sherwood Forest, which 'pleased him greatly'.[9] Three weeks later, conscious of the need to project his monarchical authority, Richard was re-crowned at the ancient seat of royal power, Winchester. He subsequently made an uneasy peace with John and named him heir if his marriage to Berengaria produced no children.

'No age can remember or history tell of any king who demanded and took so much money from his kingdom as this king extorted and amassed within the five years after his return from his captivity', remarked the chronicler Ralph of Coggeshall.[10] Financing the king's crusades had been expensive enough, but the crippling fine with which he secured his liberty had also fallen upon his domains. Only the fact that it had all been in an honourable cause helped safeguard Richard's reputation as king.

Richard propagated his image as a great crusading king through his self-congratulatory letters and statements. He also appreciated the importance of regal display and dignity. The magnificence of his dress was widely commented upon, and he was the first King of England to employ the royal 'we' on his charters. He always couched his military campaigns – the crusades in particular – in religious terms. This was more than propaganda: he was deeply committed to fulfilling what he believed to be God's will.

If Richard had remained in England, things might have turned out differently. But, thanks to the various deals that John had struck with Philip, Normandy was in a perilous state and a great deal of territory had been lost to the French king. On 12 May 1193, Richard set sail across the Channel, never to return. His mother took the reins of power once more. Although she had effected the reconciliation between her sons, Eleanor was fully alive to the threat that John still posed. She had already strengthened England's coastal defences after hearing of his alliance with the French king, and in April 1193 she had taken custody of the royal castles of Windsor, Wallingford and the Peak.

Her son Richard spent the next few years battling to regain and defend his territories in Normandy and parts of his Angevin inheritance. Thanks to his skill in tactics and his bravery in battle, by 1198 he had won back most of his lands. That year, he focused his efforts on the Vexin, the border between his Angevin lands and those of Capetian France, and won a resounding victory at Gisors. Philip only narrowly escaped with his life and had to be dragged out of the River Ethe. Following the encounter, the French king was left with little but Gisors itself. The battle would prove decisive in another respect, for it was here that Richard adopted the motto *Dieu et mon Droit* ('God and my Right'), which is still used by the British monarchy today.

Having regained his lands, Richard planned to return to the Holy

Land once more in response to Pope Innocent III's call for a new crusade. But first he was obliged to journey south to Aquitaine in order to suppress a rebellion encouraged by the French king. On 26 March 1199, he was shot in the shoulder with a crossbow bolt while reconnoitring Châlus-Chabrol, a small castle in the Limousin. On its own, the wound was not serious, but it seems to have been mistreated by a surgeon and soon turned gangrenous. Realising that he was dying, Richard had no choice but to confirm John as his heir. Before he breathed his last on 6 April, the forty-one-year-old king forgave the man who had shot him.

There was a tradition for a monarch's remains to be laid to rest in several places, particularly when he or she had ruled over a dispersed territory. In his will, Richard directed that his brains, his blood and his entrails should be buried at Chalûs, where he sustained the fatal blow, his heart at Rouen and his body at Fontevraud, at the feet of his father, Henry II.[11] The grisly Chalûs bequest was quietly ignored.

'O death! Do you realise whom you snatched from us', lamented one chronicler, 'the lord of warriors, the glory of kings'.[12] Richard had spent less time in England than any other king (just six months in ten years), yet from the moment of his death and ever since he has been hailed as one of its greatest monarchs, the epitome of chivalry and valour. There is no denying what one contemporary described as his 'courage carried to excess'.[13] Frequently, he had put himself in danger while on campaign, such as when he went against the advice of his deputies to rescue a contingent of his men in difficulties, declaring: 'I sent those men there. If they die without me, may I never again be called a king.'[14] Such actions had secured the devotion of his troops, who 'would wade in blood to the Pillars of Hercules if he so desired'.[15] They also ensured that even in his lifetime he was already known as *Cœur de Lion*.

Fairly or not, Richard would be the standard against which future kings of England would be measured. The overwhelmingly positive record of his achievement left behind by contemporary chroniclers was repeated by other historians in the centuries after his death. The sixteenth-century chronicler Ralph Holinshed called him 'a notable example to all princes'.[16] His glamorous reputation was propounded by Walter Scott's *Ivanhoe*, and by his fictitious association with the legendary Robin Hood, when the crusading king returns home just in time to prevent his wicked brother John from usurping the throne.

More recent scholars have criticised Richard for wasting English men and money on the crusades and other overseas campaigns aimed more at personal than national glory. It is true that when judged as a King of England, his long absences abroad and the crippling costs of his military exploits overshadow – or at least, take the shine off – his other achievements. But it is only when viewed as the head of a dynasty with far wider responsibilities than English ones alone that Richard's reign can be properly assessed. The fact that his achievement was generally lauded by his contemporaries on both sides of the Channel should perhaps carry more weight than the criticism levelled against him many centuries later.

Perhaps, though, what really cemented Richard's reputation as England's chivalrous hero is that his reign tends to be compared with that of his immediate successor.

John (1199–1216)
'A very bad man'

HENRY II'S SONS have been assigned the collective name of 'the Devil's Brood'. None deserved that dubious sobriquet more than John. England's most notorious king grew up under a cloud of resentment. As the youngest of five sons, he had little hope of ever enjoying any real power, let alone the crown itself. When he was a teenager, his father Henry II had given him the nickname 'Lackland', but in fact John had been his favourite and he had been anxious to provide for him. Henry's efforts on behalf of his youngest son had encouraged his greed and ambition, not to mention his treachery against his elder brothers.

None of John's schemes had amounted to anything, but he soon forgot his disappointment when, at the age of thirty-two, he at last inherited the throne of England. The treacherous actions that had defined him for the past two decades were not so easily overlooked by his new subjects. Here was not a king to respect and admire. Far more appealing in some men's eyes was John's twelve-year-old nephew, Arthur of Brittany, son of his late brother Geoffrey. Richard I had so favoured Arthur that he had named him heir to the English throne upon embarking on crusade in 1190. Even though he had subsequently chosen John, Arthur's temporary elevation made him a potent threat to the new king – one who would become ever more alluring as the ranks of John's opponents grew.

From the moment he succeeded his elder brother, John was beset with troubles in France. His erstwhile ally Philip proved a false friend when he immediately invaded Normandy and occupied the county of Évreux. Meanwhile, the barons of Anjou, Maine and Touraine declared for Arthur of Brittany, and in Aquitaine the Count of

Angoulême and the Vicomte of Limoges (both allies of the French king) resisted John's authority. The new king left Aquitaine in the capable hands of his mother and focused his efforts on Anjou. Eleanor did not have a high opinion of her youngest son, but he was the only one left to her and she defended his authority with as much ferocity as she had his elder brother's. On the very day of her son Richard's funeral, she was busy restoring lands to members of the aristocracy in an attempt to win favour for their new duke. Directing affairs in her homeland would occupy this formidable woman until the end of her long life.

In January 1200, John concluded a treaty with the French king. Although Philip recognised John as the rightful heir to Richard with regard to his French possessions, thereby dismissing Arthur of Brittany's claim, John accepted Philip's right as the legitimate feudal overlord of his lands in France – something that Richard had never done. The agreement earned him the nickname 'John Softsword' among English chroniclers.

The unfavourable peace only lasted two years. With the resumption of hostilities, John decided to remove one threat to his authority. Arthur of Brittany was captured by the king's barons in July 1202 and imprisoned at the Castle of Falaise, birthplace of William the Conqueror. According to the annals of Margam Abbey in Wales, one night after dinner, 'drunk and possessed by the devil', John murdered Arthur 'with his own hand, and tying a heavy stone to the body cast it into the Seine'. Although it was never proven, Arthur's disappearance several months into his captivity gave credence to the theory that the young man had been put to death by John's hand or at least at his orders, which further eroded his support in the region. Philip was quick to take advantage. By the end of 1204, he had taken possession of almost all John's continental empire. Until now, Aquitaine had remained loyal thanks to the efforts of John's mother, but her death that year dangerously weakened the English crown's authority there.

Undeterred, John turned to England for help in recovering his territories. But his subjects felt little loyalty towards a king they had hardly seen, and whose previous conduct had done nothing to recommend him. The expedition was cancelled, but John remained in England and spent the next few years trying to raise funds for a continental campaign – as well as hoarding some for himself. Soon, the kingdom was beset by crippling taxes, which sparked widespread resentment and led to a crisis in the king's relations with his powerful barons. Before long he was confiscating clerical posts and property to sell at a vastly inflated rate. When Pope Innocent III excommunicated him in November 1209, he cared little: profit mattered more to him than piety.[1]

John also alienated the outlying principalities of his domain. Thanks to his father creating him Lord of Ireland, he had a greater stake there than any previous King of England. But he continued the policy that he had begun during Richard's reign of encouraging the advance of English conquerors at the expense of the native population, which sowed the seeds of dissent. In Wales, meanwhile, he eventually abandoned the traditional overlordship of the English kings over the local rulers and Marcher lords in favour of a more aggressive policy. But aggression was not matched by skill, and by the end of his reign the English crown was weaker there than it had been since his father first brought it under the authority of the English monarchy. John was no less combative towards Scotland, launching a surprise invasion attempt in the summer of 1209 and forcing King William to buy his 'goodwill' with a heavy fine and the custody of his two daughters.

The English king's supremacy over the British Isles was both fleeting and unstable. But it was enough to fool the author of the thirteenth-century *Barnwell Chronicle* that there was 'no one in Ireland, Scotland and Wales who did not obey his nod—something which, as is well-known, none of his predecessors had achieved'.[2] In 1211, as John was preparing another continental campaign, news arrived that the Welsh had risen against him. He responded with characteristic brutality, hanging twenty-eight Welsh hostages at Nottingham. While there, he learned of a plot against his life involving some of his most powerful magnates and officials. When the popular preacher, Peter of Wakefield, prophesied the imminent end of the reign, John had him and his son hanged. But the events had left him badly shaken. From that time forward he went everywhere with an armed bodyguard.

* * *

In 1214, John embarked upon what would be his final campaign to win back the lands he had lost in France. Although he enjoyed some early success, it ended in ignominious failure, due at least in part to his English magnates refusing to support it. The king returned to England humiliated and, thanks to a weighty fine imposed by Philip as part of their truce, virtually penniless. His lack of money was significant: never again would he be able to browbeat his English subjects into submission.

Within a few months of John's return, a group of powerful barons in the north and east were preparing to oppose his rule. In January 1215, they arrived in London, armed, to meet their king. John made conciliatory noises, promising to heed their demands for reform and the confirmation of Henry I's coronation charter. But he was buying time so that he could enlist the pope's support and recruit mercenaries from across the Channel. The two sides pledged to meet again in April, at Northampton, but John failed to attend. On 5 May his opponents formally renounced their fealty and appointed Robert Fitzwalter, Constable of Baynard's Castle, as their leader.

This self-proclaimed 'army of God' quickly gathered huge support, and on 17 May the city of London opened its gates to them. The rebels also took the key strategic cities of Lincoln and Exeter, forcing King John to accept their terms. On 15 June, he met the barons at Runnymede, close to Windsor, to discuss their demands. These were articulated in the Magna Carta ('Great Charter'), a document as radical as it was lengthy.

The purpose of Magna Carta was to win support for the barons' cause, so they made sure to include something for everyone. Its sixty-three clauses included vague promises such as: 'To no one will we sell, to no one will we deny or delay right or justice', as well as specific ones like the promise to remove fish weirs from England's rivers. Above all, though, it was both a commentary on, and a condemnation of, John's style of kingship: his oppression, corruption and extortion.

Magna Carta included proposals for political reform, an overhaul of the justice system and the protection of church rights. The most radical clauses called for the restoration of lands and liberties that had been wrongfully taken by the crown, and the sanctioning of 'lawful rebellion' against the king. These amounted to the total destruction of King John's sovereignty and that of his successors. More than any other detail, they reveal the depths of distrust in which the king was held. Their inclusion in the charter made the renewal of hostilities inevitable.[3] But for now, John was impatient to bring the whole sorry episode to a close, so he agreed to the charter and peace was declared four days later.

Granted 'to all the freemen of the realm and their heirs forever', the ramifications of Magna Carta would echo down the centuries and can still be felt today. Never again would a sovereign be able to ride roughshod over the rights of his subjects – at least, not unless they were prepared to face the consequences. It was the origin of what would later be described as a constitutional monarchy.

Within the space of a month, John had written to Innocent III asking him to annul the charter. When the pope's excommunication of the rebels arrived in September, this gave the king the justification he needed to declare war on the barons. Within a few short weeks, both England and Wales were engaged in a bitter civil war between the barons and their supporters and those who remained loyal to the crown. Although John achieved some military success, he failed to win over any of the rebel leaders. Then, in April 1216, he was diverted by a French invasion off the Kentish coast. The barons had offered the crown to Philip's son Louis, who had just enough English royal blood in his veins to justify a claim. Louis and a body of French troops landed, unopposed, on the Isle of Thanet and marched to London with little resistance. He was proclaimed King Louis I of England at St Paul's Cathedral, amid great pomp and ceremony. Although he was not crowned, many nobles flocked to pay him homage, as did King Alexander II of Scotland. By mid-June, Louis had captured Winchester and was soon in control of over half the kingdom.

Ironically, Louis was only prevented from claiming the entire kingdom by the death of his rival. In October 1216, the forty-eight-year-old King John fell ill with dysentery.[4] He struggled on as far as Newark, losing part of his baggage train in the Wash estuary (although probably not, as one chronicler claimed, the crown jewels) and died at Newark on 19 October. According to his wishes, he was buried at Worcester Cathedral wearing the cowl-like coif of unction he had worn at his coronation. The celebrated chronicler Matthew Paris repeated the belief voiced by many that 'Foul as it is, Hell itself is made fouler by the presence of John.'[5]

Few mourned the passing of one of the worst kings ever to occupy the throne of England. The judgement of an author in the entourage of Robert de Béthune, one of John's leading commanders in the civil war, that the king 'was a very bad man, cruel and lecherous', is typical of most contemporary accounts.[6] His cruelty had been proven on numerous occasions, and the charge of lechery was also justified. He had at least seven illegitimate children by his mistresses, and a number of his barons – Robert Fitzwalter in particular – complained that he had subjected their wives and daughters to sexual harassment. Little wonder that, as the English monk, Walter of Coventry, remarked: 'Before his end his people deserted him, and at his end few mourned for him.'[7] He had been the first King John of England and, mercifully, he would be the last.

Henry III (1216–72)

The shadow of a name

BORN IN WINCHESTER on 1 October 1207, Henry III was the eldest of King John's five children by his second wife Isabella of Angoulême and was named after his illustrious grandfather. He had succeeded his father amid the most turbulent of circumstances, with half of the country in revolt and a foreign prince occupying the throne of England. To make matters worse, Henry had only just turned nine, so even if he managed to wrest back the crown, his kingdom would face the uncertainty of a minority rule. And yet, with the odds stacked against him, Henry would become England's longest-reigning monarch, a record that stood for more than five hundred years.

When he was still a child, Henry had been warned not to follow the example of his 'criminal ancestor' (his father, King John) or else God would deny him a long life. It was a lesson he heeded. It was obvious from his earliest days that Henry was of a very different mettle to his father, whom he had seen little of during his childhood. The chronicler Matthew Paris claimed that by the time Henry succeeded to the throne, he spoke with unusual 'gravity and dignity'.[1] Certainly, he was more cerebral than physical. While he largely failed in his knightly training, he showed a passion for art and a veneration for Anglo-Saxon saints that would endure a lifetime. The turbulence of his early years also left a lasting impression, particularly the civil war that followed his father's repudiation of Magna Carta and his mother's desertion of her children nine months after King John's death, when she returned to France and remarried. Of a naturally reserved and timorous nature, Henry was easily moved to tears and had inherited none of the notorious Angevin temper.

★ ★ ★

The young king was crowned on 28 October at Gloucester Abbey by those clergy still loyal to the crown. The event was an important moment in the history of the monarchy because it established the precedent that the succession automatically passed to the king's eldest son, regardless of age. As such, it put an end to the damaging dynastic disputes that had beset the Norman and Angevin kings. As soon as the ceremony had been concluded, William Marshal, Earl of Pembroke, assumed the regency. But the rebel forces, led by the French king's son, remained strong, and the stalemate was only broken by a decisive victory by Marshal's forces at Lincoln on 20 May 1217. The French prince soon lost heart and was bribed to leave. Without their leader, the rebels quickly dispersed. The regent wisely showed them leniency, and at a great council held at Winchester in October and November, Magna Carta was modified and reissued. The Scottish king agreed to a peace, but the Welsh leader Llewelyn the Great kept most of his recent conquests.

In May 1220, Henry was crowned for a second time, with far greater pomp, at Westminster Abbey. He had spent most of his reign in his schoolroom, so his ministers were anxious to display him to his subjects, lest they should think of rebelling again. Three years later, the young king was taken to Wales, decked in his first suit of armour decorated with the royal coat of arms, to receive Llewelyn's submission. Finally, on 8 January 1227, the eighteen-year-old king held a council at Oxford and 'by common counsel' declared himself of full age, thereby formally ending more than ten years of minority rule.

For the next few years, Henry continued to be dominated by the powerful ministers who had been governing the country until he came of age, notably Hubert de Burgh, an English nobleman who had served King John as chief justiciar and continued in that post, and Henry's tutor, the Frenchman Peter des Roches, Bishop of Winchester. Although he deferred to them in most matters, there was one ambition that Henry was determined to fulfil: the recovery of the lands in France that his father had lost. The sudden death of Louis VIII in November 1226 after just three years on the throne presented an opportunity that Henry was keen to exploit. However, one of the legacies of his father's disastrous reign was that the crown was no longer able to raise funds on a whim. It would take more than three years before Henry was in a position to launch a campaign.

On 3 May 1230 Henry, decked out in full regalia with crown, sceptre and a white silk mantle, landed at St Malo with a substantial force. Despite being invited to invade by those opposed to French rule in Normandy and Poitou, Henry and his brother Richard were soon hamstrung by illness, fatigue and shortage of money. By the end of October, they were on their way home, having failed to make any gains. The Anglo-Norman empire established by William the Conqueror would never be revived, although it would be many years before the kings of England finally accepted that fact.

It had been a salutary lesson for the young king: the scale of his warlike ambitions was not matched by the resources of the royal treasury. Only prolonged periods of peace could produce the savings necessary for Henry to live off his own means, without sinking the crown into further debt. Inadequate finance remained a fatal weakness of his rule, and one that would hamper his successors.

The power struggles that began during Henry's minority had a long tail. By the early 1230s, England was once more on the brink of civil war. Up until then, the king had been little more than a bystander in the growing turmoil, but in 1234 he took full control of his government. The king selected advisers and courtiers who had not been part of the old factions and was careful not to show too much favour to any of them. It was a shrewd move: over-reliance on favourites became a trademark of weak monarchs. His decisive action ushered in a period of political stability that would endure for fifteen years. No longer beset by the threat of renewed civil war, Henry was able to focus on other matters, notably the strengthening of his dynasty.

On 20 January 1236, Henry married Eleanor, daughter of the Count of Provence, who, then aged about twelve or thirteen, was at least fifteen years younger than him. The marriage brought Henry valuable connections, notably his bride's brother-in-law, Louis IX, King of France. On a personal level, too, Henry found his new wife appealing. Beautiful and clever, Eleanor proved a wise and trusted confidante, one who favoured moderation and reconciliation. She was crowned at the same ceremony as her wedding in Westminster

Abbey. Her aesthetically minded husband ensured that the occasion set new standards of ostentation. He also established a new tradition: that the monarch would spend a night before their coronation at that most potent symbol of royal power, the Tower of London – a custom that would endure for more than four hundred years.[2]

Royal image was something to which Henry would dedicate an increasing amount of attention and expense during the years that followed. His belief in the dignity and ritual of kingship had a profound impact upon the public perception of the monarchy. In his view, the status of the crown had declined during the reigns of his predecessors and he was determined to correct that. It is telling that in seeking inspiration, he passed over the Angevin and Norman kings and sought instead to emulate the Anglo-Saxon king, Edward the Confessor, whom he adopted as his patron saint. Henry admired how Edward had brought peace to England and reunited his people – achievements that were particularly pertinent to a king whose life and reign had been blighted by civil war. Encouraged by his peace-loving new wife, Henry embarked upon a policy of leniency and appeasement, accepting the limitations of royal power in order to safeguard it.

Henry's kingship was further strengthened in June 1239 by the birth of his son at Westminster. Widespread rejoicing was tempered when the king made it known that he expected gifts from his people. 'God gave us this child, but the king is selling him to us,' muttered one resentful subject.[3] Three days later, the tiny prince was christened at the abbey with the name Edward, in honour of the king's patron saint. Giving her husband a son and heir elevated Eleanor to a status enjoyed by few queens consort before her. From henceforth, she became the king's principal adviser.

On the surface, monarchical power seemed to be enhanced during Henry's reign, but this owed more to image-making than reality. The king and his consort had certainly brought much-needed peace and stability to his realm, but this had only been achieved by adhering to the limits of royal power imposed by the rebellious barons during his father's reign. In fact, Henry's authority – and that of virtually all his successors – was circumscribed by the terms of Magna Carta and its later iterations, which limited the crown's activities in almost every sphere of England's political, social, economic and judicial life. Although there was no means of enforcing these if the monarch chose to ignore them, Henry knew that the price of doing so was a return to the turmoil of civil war that had plagued his childhood.

As Henry's long reign wore on, he became increasingly lax and careless in the exercise of royal authority, which resulted in the provinces and even the court itself enjoying greater autonomy. It was during the 1230s and 1240s that the term 'Parliament' was first used to describe large gatherings of the royal court. The 'parleys' between the king and his subjects about affairs of state increasingly included the issue of taxes to support the king's ordinary revenues or for particular projects, such as overseas campaigns. During Henry's reign, the membership of these parliaments broadened beyond major barons to representatives from across the localities. What appeared a purely administrative expediency would in the years to come evolve into one of the greatest threats that the monarchy had faced throughout its long history.

In contrast to his predecessors, Henry travelled little, preferring a more sedate and tranquil life. Because he spent more time in the royal palaces than they had, he invested greater sums in their upkeep and enhancement. Here, his lifelong passion for art and architecture found full expression. Early in his reign, the king had begun a massive programme of building at the Tower of London. As well as strengthening the castle's defences, he made it into a more comfortable royal residence, adding sumptuous private apartments for himself and his wife. He also commissioned an expert ditch-digger from Flanders to improve the moat, resulting in its successfully flooding for the first time in its history. Among his more aesthetic alterations was an order to have William the Conqueror's Great Tower 'whitened both inside and out' so that it could be seen for miles around – thus inspiring the name by which it is still known today.

It was during Henry's reign that the royal menagerie begun by his father at the Tower was fully established. It was soon filled with a host of exotic beasts from across the globe, including lions, a 'pale' (polar) bear and, most extraordinary of all, an elephant. Sadly, the latter only survived for two years, but the king so revered it that he had its bones sent to Westminster Abbey, where they were carved into reliquaries and caskets to house saints' relics. The king spent the rest of his reign making improvements to the Tower. By the time of his death, he had laid out £9,000 (equivalent to around £6.5 million today) on shaping it into the magnificent residence and fortress that is recognised by modern-day visitors.

But this expense was dwarfed by the money Henry lavished on the royal complex at Westminster. Inspired by his fascination with Edward the Confessor, he rebuilt the palace and abbey at a cost of almost £55,000 (around £40 million), creating the ultimate symbol of kingly magnificence. With the extensive use of statuary, stained glass and Italian marble, Henry was deliberately imitating the style favoured by his rivals King Louis IX and Emperor Frederick II: if he could not defeat them on the battlefield, then he might at least outshine them in bricks and mortar. The abbey was custom-built for crowning the kings of England, which would remain its primary function for the next eight hundred years.

Meanwhile, Henry's new palace complex at Westminster became the focus for a court life dominated by ceremony, piety and pageantry. Visitors were dazzled by brightly painted walls filled with images of favoured saints such as Edward the Confessor, as well as beautifully intricate stained-glass windows and embroidery shot with gold thread. Other building projects took place at Dover, Lincoln and the royal castle of Windsor, where a sumptuous new palace inspired many others across the kingdom. By the end of his reign, Henry had transformed more than three-quarters of the royal residences of England – some of which would remain iconic symbols of monarchy right up to the present day.

The king had a passion for other trappings of royalty too. He was an avid collector of regalia, jewels and clothes fashioned from the finest and most expensive materials. Some of these were for his own personal use, and the rest were distributed as gifts to favoured attendants and subjects. It is interesting to speculate whether the richness and splendour with which Henry surrounded himself inspired him to seek greater authority than he was permitted under the terms of Magna Carta and its successors. Certainly, he guarded his royal prerogatives ever more jealously as the reign progressed, and from the 1240s onwards he repeatedly rejected proposals that infringed upon them. Although he had learned enough from his father's example to keep his kingship within the bounds of the law, he was not always consistent in accepting the limits of his authority, which led to political tensions.

Henry's dazzling architectural legacy and priceless collections had only been made possible by the prolonged period of peace, during which the royal coffers had swelled considerably. But all of that changed in what would be the most turbulent decade of his reign. The problems had begun with complaints in English-held Aquitaine about the overweening authority of its lieutenant, Simon de Montfort, Henry's brother-in-law. Rather than defending Montfort, the king ordered a formal investigation. Although this cleared his brother-in-law of oppression, it left Montfort deeply resentful of the king and also involved crippling expense, plunging the crown back into debt. Disagreement over the king's policies and his frequent requests for subsidies created divisions within his court. By the end of the 1250s, it was as riven by faction as it had been during Henry's minority.

There were problems elsewhere, too. Wales was in rebellion, the king's relations with the church had deteriorated, and the country was beset by harvest failure and famine. Confidence in the monarchy was at the lowest point of the entire reign, and few members of the court believed that Henry would be able to lead his kingdom out of the crisis. The chronicler Matthew Paris, who knew Henry personally, could not but condemn his style of kingship: 'The king was reproached with advancing and enriching the interests of all foreigners, and with despising and pillaging his own natural subjects, to the ruin of the whole kingdom.'[4]

The situation erupted at a Parliament summoned by the king in April 1258, when seven of the most powerful barons in the kingdom – including Simon de Montfort and probably secretly supported by Queen Eleanor – formed a pact to expel their rivals from government. They stormed the palace of Westminster and presented the king with an ultimatum: he must abandon his personal rule and govern through a council of twenty-four barons and churchmen. Fearing imprisonment, Henry soon capitulated. The 'Provisions of Oxford' effectively made the king subject to Parliament – the first clash in what would be the most turbulent, at times explosive, relationship in the history of the monarchy.

The new regime lasted three years. Although the king was kept in honour and comfort in his newly restored palaces, his power was systematically eroded. Anxious not to overreach his authority and plunge the country back into civil war, he was also personally afraid of Simon de Montfort and sought solace in religious, rather than political, activities. Henry's weakness was such that when presented with several opportunities to exploit the growing divisions within the baronial regime, he remained a passive observer of the turmoil into which his kingdom had been thrown. Even when his eldest son and heir, Edward, formed a pact with Montfort and tried to push through radical new legislation, the king refused to act.

Approaching his twentieth birthday, the prince was made from an entirely different mould to the king. At six foot two inches (earning him the nickname 'Longshanks'), Edward's 'great stature, towering head and shoulders above the average', overawed contemporaries.[5] Here was a prince in the mould of his great-grandfather, Henry II; one who already inspired greater confidence among the English people than his father ever had.

It needed a strong ruler to reunite the kingdom, and Henry fell woefully short. Although he was briefly returned to power in 1260, he failed to reconcile Montfort, who launched a fresh rebellion three years later. In panic, Henry sought refuge at the Tower. He took Eleanor with him, but even she had lost faith in the king, and she attempted to leave the fortress so that she might join their son Edward. When Montfort's rebel force entered the city, Henry had little choice but to accept their terms. Although Montfort pretended to rule on his behalf, he and his supporters quickly replaced the royal government and household with their own men. Soon, he was king in all but name.

But still the old divisions had not been healed, and this time the king decided to take advantage of his enemy's weakness, even though it meant launching a war that he had spent most of his reign trying desperately to avoid. Mustering an army of royalists (including his son Edward, who had switched his allegiance), Henry confronted Montfort at Lewes in May 1264. As a military leader, the king was no match for his opponent and, despite commanding the larger force, he was swiftly defeated. After nearly fifty years, all Henry retained was 'the shadow of a name', as one contemporary chronicler put it.⁶ His power had been entirely eclipsed by a mere subject.

As he had so often in times of crisis, the captive king retreated into himself, forgetting the cares of state by repeatedly hearing the Mass of his idol, Edward the Confessor. Any hope of restoring royal authority now rested upon his wife Eleanor, who had fled to France to rally an invasion force, and his son Edward, who had formed a new army and was pursuing Montfort's forces through the Welsh Marches. In the ensuing Battle of Evesham, fought on 4 August 1265, the rebel leader was killed. Edward's father, who had been forced by Montfort to accompany his army, was almost killed too, but his son's troops recognised him in the nick of time and escorted him to safety. The leaderless rebels fought on for another two years before finally submitting to Henry's authority.

The king's personal rule endured for the remainder of his reign, more thanks to the efforts of his family and the general exhaustion of his subjects than to any positive actions on his part. In October 1269, Henry conjured up one last, glorious illusion of royal power when the body of St Edward was at last transferred to the shrine in Westminster Abbey that he had been constructing for so many years. Now heavily in debt, he had been unable to finish the works and had had to pawn most of the jewels adorning the shrine. But, increasingly conscious of his mortality, Henry was determined to enjoy this moment of triumph before it was too late. Together with his sons Edward and Edmund and his brother Richard, he bore the Confessor's relics to the shrine. It is telling that despite the general magnificence of the occasion, Henry and his queen had judged it expedient not to wear their coronation crowns as planned.

Henry hardly stirred from his beloved Westminster for the rest of his life. With the onset of a new decade, his health began to seriously falter. After a final pilgrimage to Walsingham and Ely in September 1272, he returned to Westminster in time for the feast of

St Edward. The following month, he suffered a total collapse and died on 16 November, aged sixty-five. At his request, he was buried in Westminster Abbey in front of the church's high altar, in the former resting place of Edward the Confessor.[7] His body was dressed in full royal regalia. To the end, he had clung to the belief that luxury was vital to kingship.

Henry III had reigned – if not ruled – for fifty-six years and twenty days. Arguably, it was an achievement to have held on to his throne for longer than any of his predecessors, although his example was proof that longevity did not always equate to either stability or success. He had been a merciful king, peace-loving and, above all, pious. That he largely failed as a ruler was due to his fearful nature and unworldliness, which rendered him incapable of managing his court, his barons and his subjects at large. His reign had witnessed important legal, social and institutional developments, but Henry could claim little credit for any of them. Among them was the rise of Parliament, which in time would become a more dangerous threat to monarchical authority than war, rebellion or succession crises. Henry's kingship had been one of the most lustrous in history and had left behind a magnificent legacy in architecture and art. But it would be the task of his successor to make real the illusion of power that he had created.

Edward I (1272–1307)

'Towering head and shoulders above the average'

THANKS TO HIS father's inability to rule effectively and his will-ingness to cede authority to those who could, Edward I came to the throne rich in experience from his thirty-three years on earth. He had learned that the only way to unite and control a kingdom still in turmoil after almost sixty years of recurrent civil war was with an iron fist. He was as brutal and uncompromising as his predecessor had been merciful and irresolute. There were occasional glimpses of humour, but many more of temper. The royal accounts include a payment for the repair of his daughter's coronet after he had thrown it into a fire.

When news reached Edward that he was now King of England, he was in southern Italy, on his way back from the Holy Land. Surprisingly, perhaps, he seemed in no hurry to claim his throne. Instead, he made a leisurely journey through Italy, took part in a tournament in Savoy, then did homage for his French lands to Philip III, acknowledging the French king's status as feudal lord, and journeyed to Aquitaine, where there was news of rebellion. It was not until August 1274, almost two years after his father's death, that the new king finally set foot in England.

Seventeen days after his arrival, on 19 August, Edward was crowned amid spectacular pomp and ceremony. But while his father would have viewed this show of monarchical splendour as an end in itself, for Edward it was merely a prelude to the serious business of governing his new realm. According to one account, the new king removed his crown during the ceremony and swore that he would never wear it again until he had won back everything his father had lost.

After appointing his key officials, the king ordered an immense survey into the state of his kingdom – the largest since Domesday

Book – and instructed his commissioners to inquire into all manner of business. The primary purpose, though, was to find out what rights and lands had been lost by the crown during his father's long reign, as well as to investigate official corruption. It was an impressive undertaking and the scale of the returns was so vast that the government struggled to make use of it. Its symbolic value was no less considerable: Edward had shown himself to be a champion of his ordinary subjects; a just and fair king who would put right past wrongs.

Edward became more actively involved in legislation than any monarch before him. The numerous statutes issued during his reign constitute one of his greatest achievements. The first of these, issued at Westminster in 1275, was one of the most ambitious. Comprising fifty-one clauses, it dealt primarily with law and order, as well as the contentious issue of land tenure, and did much to clarify relations between lords and tenants. It also sought to protect the rights of rich and poor alike, echoing some of the wording of Magna Carta. The statute had such a profound impact on English law that elements of it are still in force today.

The king was personally and actively involved in this and a number of subsequent statutes. His experience of the baronial regime of the late 1250s and early 1260s made him determined to improve the way in which the law operated. Much of Edward's legislation was very much in the spirit of Magna Carta, but this time the king was dictating it, rather than simply reacting to it.

Having begun to set his kingdom in order, Edward soon turned to its neighbours. Wales had shaken off English rule during the turbulence of the 1260s and was now under the authority of Llywelyn ap Gruffudd. In 1276, faced with the superior forces of the English king's army, Llywelyn came to terms. But he and his supporters resented the subjugation of Wales to English jurisdiction and four years later the country was in open revolt once more. Edward's response was characteristically swift and brutal. He took another sizeable army across the border and crushed the Welsh rebels. Llywelyn was killed in battle and in April 1283 the last Welsh stronghold surrendered. The victory was followed by a full-scale English settlement. The Statute of Wales, passed in 1284, made the principality almost entirely subject to English administration, government and law, and would remain in force for nearly three hundred years. The king later created his son, Edward, Prince of Wales to strengthen royal authority there. The title would continue to be conveyed upon the heir to the English throne all the way up to the present day, although it is now largely symbolic.

Llywelyn's dynasty was destroyed and most of the Welsh aristocracy were disinherited in favour of Edward's followers. The most visible demonstration of the conquest was in the imposing new castles that Edward built at Conwy, Caernarfon, Harlech – and, after a later uprising, at Beaumaris in Anglesey. In contrast to his father's architectural commissions, these were built for practical rather than aesthetic purposes. They still stand as a symbol of English domination.

Edward's warlike approach to kingship was as expensive as it was effective. Raising funds for his campaigns became a dominant theme throughout his reign, particularly as he had inherited an empty treasury and a whole raft of debts from his father. For all his bullish approach to kingship, he was alive to the dangers of levying substantial taxes upon a people so newly reconciled to royal authority. Initially, he relied heavily upon loans from Italian bankers, together with the occasional modest subsidy from Parliament. His debts continued to escalate and by the end of his reign they amounted to around £200,000 (in the region of £122 million today).

Although they had come at a cost, Edward's achievements during the first two decades of his kingship were considerable. He had brought his rebellious subjects to heel in England and Wales and re-established royal government after the turmoil of the 1260s. He is sometimes called the 'Father of Parliament', but while he summoned more parliaments than any of his predecessors, this was because he needed money to fund his campaigns, rather than because he was keen to increase the rights of his people. Nevertheless, during his reign Parliament evolved into an institution through which the crown could achieve its aims, as well as a forum where petitions could be heard and wrongs corrected. Among his continental peers, meanwhile, the king presented himself as a peacemaker and ruled Aquitaine far more effectively than his predecessors. As a result, he won greater respect for the English monarchy than had existed for almost one hundred years.

But all of this looked set to crumble in the 1290s. The opening of the new decade was marked by a series of catastrophes. First among them was the collapse of Edward's plans to marry his six-year-old son and heir, Edward of Caernarfon, to Margaret, queen-designate of Scotland. An agreement was reached in 1290, but Margaret's death that autumn left the English king's hopes in tatters. Then, on 28 November, his beloved queen, Eleanor of Castile, died. Eleanor had been the very model of a queen consort. Aged thirteen at the time of her wedding, she had spent most of her married life pregnant, giving birth to at least fourteen children. Of the five sons, only the youngest, Edward, survived into adulthood. But Eleanor's achievement should not be measured by her fertility alone. Better educated than most medieval queens, she had been an active patron of the arts and had encouraged the use of her native Spanish style in the tapestries, carpets and tableware that adorned the royal palaces. She had also been a shrewd businesswoman and had acquired a considerable amount of land and manors during her tenure.

Most royal marriages were made for politics rather than love, but Eleanor and her husband had been devoted to each other. They had rarely been apart, and the queen had often accompanied Edward on his military campaigns – including those in Wales in 1284, when she had given birth to their son Edward at Caernarfon Castle. Her husband is not known to have strayed from the marital bed or to have fathered children out of wedlock, something that very few medieval English kings could claim. His reaction to Eleanor's death provides a rare glimpse of a more tender side to his nature. 'In life I loved her dearly,' he wrote, 'nor can I cease to love her in death.'¹ The king ordered that her embalmed body be carried in great state from Lincoln to Westminster Abbey. He accompanied the procession for most of its long journey and directed that memorial crosses be built at the site of each overnight stop. These 'Eleanor Crosses', as they became known, were based upon those that had marked King Louis IX's funeral procession in France. They served as an image of Edward's kingship, as well as a testament to his grief, and some still survive today.² He later remarried, to Margaret of France (forty years his junior), and named their only daughter in Eleanor's honour.

With only one surviving son, Edward I's dynasty suddenly seemed precarious. Although each of the prince's childhood illnesses were a cause of great concern, the king was too preoccupied with waging war and controlling his dominions to spend more than the most fleeting of time with his infant son – a fact that would have serious consequences for the younger Edward's ability to rule. His influence can be felt, though, in the purchase of a toy castle for the prince, together with a treatise on warfare. Prince Edward showed little interest in such pursuits. Certainly, there is no record of his ever taking part in a tournament, although this may have been out of concern for his safety. Instead, he enjoyed activities such as swimming, rowing and digging, all of which were considered inappropriate for a future king. The young prince's other interests were of a more pious nature. From at least the age of six, Edward had Dominican friars in his household, marking the beginning of a close spiritual and personal relationship with the Order. There were flashes of his father's temper, though, as well as a streak of cruelty, which, in adulthood, would occasionally manifest itself in fierce vindictiveness.

The death of the queen-designate of Scotland sparked a dispute over the right to the Scottish throne between Robert Bruce and John Balliol, followed by eleven other claimants. Edward assumed the role of adjudicator between the various candidates and chose Balliol. But he proceeded to treat him as a vassal, interfering in legal cases and demanding control of Balliol's foreign policy. When Balliol tried to assert his independence by concluding the 'Auld Alliance' with France, Edward resorted to force. In 1296, he crossed the border with an army, and in the space of just twenty-one weeks he had conquered the entire kingdom, ousting Balliol from the throne and earning himself the sobriquet *Malleus Scotorum* ('Hammer of the Scots'). In a highly symbolic move designed to prove that Scotland was no longer a kingdom but a mere province of England, Edward ordered the removal of the ancient Stone of Scone, upon which the kings of Scotland were crowned, to Westminster, where it resided until the late twentieth century.[3] It was later fitted into King Edward's chair, upon which all English and British sovereigns have been crowned since the end of the fourteenth century.

The English king's triumph was tempered by the war with France that had begun in 1294 and continued for four long and cripplingly expensive years. Little was achieved, and the conflict laid the foundations for the Hundred Years' War forty years later. The demands of fighting a war on two fronts sparked a political crisis at home. In 1295, the so-called Model Parliament forced Edward to concede that no further taxation could be raised without the 'good will and assent' of Parliament. This was a pivotal moment in the history of the crown's relationship with Parliament, enabling the latter to effectively hold the monarch to ransom. It also guaranteed that Parliament would need to meet regularly, particularly during the reign of a warlike king such as Edward, who was perpetually in need of funds.

Meanwhile, opposition to Edward's attempts to press his subjects into military service, requisition foodstuffs to feed his army, and impose heavy taxes, had grown sharply. As a result, by the time the king set sail for Flanders in August 1297, England was once more on the brink of civil war. During his absence, the council agreed to demands that Edward's strictures be abolished and that the king must be persuaded to abandon the 'rancour and indignation' that characterised his relationship with his leading nobles.[4] Edward would hardly have approved such measures himself, but matters had gone so far while he was away that he had little choice but to confirm them.

The Scots also made the most of the English king's absence. Following his triumph there in 1296, Edward had left the government in the hands of trusted English officials. But the following year, the Scots revolted. Robert Bruce, grandson of the earlier claimant of the same name, was one of the leaders, although the most effective figurehead was the charismatic Scottish knight William Wallace, who fought alongside another prominent rebel, Andrew Moray. In September, they achieved a major victory when they routed the English forces at Stirling Bridge. The English king was swift to retaliate, leading a 30,000-strong force to Falkirk, where he dealt a crushing blow to the rebels. But he was only able to establish limited control.

Trouble was brewing closer to home, too, thanks to the increasing waywardness of the Prince of Wales. During his teenage years, Prince Edward developed a taste for close male favourites. 'Princes . . . raise some persons to be, as it were, companions and almost equals to themselves, which many times sorteth to inconvenience', remarked the courtier and philosopher, Francis Bacon, three centuries later.[5] Over-reliance on favourites is a theme that runs throughout some of the most disastrous reigns in British royal history and Prince Edward's would be a prime example. In 1300, a new attendant joined his household. Piers Gaveston was the son of a Gascon knight and had served in Edward I's army in Flanders. He had evidently distinguished himself, because he had subsequently been appointed a yeoman in the royal household. The fourteenth-century chronicler Geoffrey Baker described Gaveston as 'graceful and agile in body, sharp witted, refined in manners . . . [and] well versed in military matters'.[6] Little wonder that the king judged him a suitable role model for his son.

'Upon looking on him the son of the king immediately felt such love for him that he entered into a covenant of constancy, and bound himself with him before all other mortals with a bond of indissoluble love, firmly drawn up and fastened with a knot.'[7] This description of their first meeting is corroborated by other chroniclers, who, with some unease, referred to the sixteen-year-old prince's love for Gaveston as 'immoderate', 'excessive' and 'beyond measure'.[8] It is easy to see why both contemporaries and later historians assumed that the relationship between the two men was sexual. But while it was certainly close, the evidence for the future king's homosexuality is largely derived from later, hostile sources. Both men would marry and have children, including illegitimate ones. Whatever the true nature of their relationship, the power and influence that Gaveston came to exert over Edward is incontrovertible.

Determined to mould his son into a warrior king, Edward I, in the same year as Gaveston's appointment, commanded the prince to attend the siege of Caerlaverock in Scotland. The king used his son to strengthen England's position with her continental neighbours, too. In May 1303 Prince Edward was betrothed to Philip IV's daughter, Isabella. The public demonstrations of dynastic harmony contrasted sharply with an increasingly fractious relationship between father and son. In 1305, they quarrelled over a relatively minor matter and the king banned Gaveston from his son's presence.

Edward might have been a fearsome warrior king, but he did not appreciate the need to win the support of those he wished to dominate. In 1304, he had attempted to crush the Scottish threat once and for all when he captured Stirling Castle and forced the surrender of those who had continued to rebel against his authority. William Wallace was arrested, tried and executed the following year. But in 1306, Robert Bruce staked a fresh claim to the throne and proceeded to win a number of decisive victories over the English. Edward was so enraged that in May 1307 he set out for Scotland himself. By then, his health was faltering badly and he was in no fit state to travel. He made it as far as Burgh by Sands near Carlisle, then collapsed with dysentery. When his servants tried to lift him from his bed at noon on 7 July so that he could eat, he died in their arms.

The king's corpse was brought south for burial, but it was not until the end of October that he was finally laid to rest in Westminster Abbey. On the side of his tomb, which was unusually plain because of the depleted royal treasury, the inscription can still be seen: *Edwardus Primus Scottorum Malleus . . . Pactum Serva* ('Here is Edward I, Hammer of the Scots . . . Keep the Vow'). Even in death, Edward refused to admit defeat.

Edward II (1307–27)

'Passionately attached to one particular person'

E DWARD I HAD bequeathed his son a dubious inheritance. The crown was in great debt, the war with Scotland was all but lost, and the English nobles were growing resentful thanks to the late king's failure to carry out the reforms he had promised. Even for the most able of rulers, these would have been considerable challenges. Edward II's contemporary biographer confidently declared that God had endowed the new king with so many gifts that he was 'equal to or indeed more excellent than other kings'.[1] Few others thought the same.

One of Edward II's first acts as king was to recall Piers Gaveston, whom his father had banished abroad. In August 1307, he created his favourite Earl of Cornwall, and two months later he arranged for him to marry his niece, Margaret de Clare. It was immediately obvious just how much influence the royal favourite would enjoy. The new king's contemporary, Ranulf Higden, remarked that he was 'passionately attached to one particular person, whom he cherished above all'. No one was in any doubt who that person was. Much to the resentment of his leading nobles and churchmen, when Edward set out for his own wedding to Isabella, daughter of Philip IV of France, the following January, he left Gaveston as regent of England.

The king could not be parted from his favourite for long, and within little over a fortnight he had returned with his twelve-year-old bride in tow. On 25 February 1308, he was crowned at Westminster amid one of the most dazzling events in English royal history. The coronation had become increasingly elaborate since its first recorded iteration in 959 and was now the most ostentatious of all royal ceremonies. The proceedings took an entire day and were followed by several more of tilts, tourneys and feasting, the latter requiring the construction of forty new ovens.

The event was heavy with symbolism. As had become customary, when Edward II processed to Westminster Abbey, he was bare-headed and devoid of his robes of state so that the contrast when he emerged after the ceremony in all his glittering regalia would be truly awe-inspiring: a symbol of his transformation from an ordinary mortal into God's anointed. But Edward's coronation oath included a new clause to uphold 'the laws and rightful customs which the community of the realm shall have chosen'.[2] This ensured that neither the new king nor his successors would be able to ignore such rights as his father had done. Edward also swore to uphold the laws of Edward the Confessor, whose place in royal ideology had been firmly established in the reign of his grandfather, Henry III.

The splendour of the occasion did not quite disguise the rumblings of discontent among the nobles present about the prominence given to the new king's favourite. Gaveston had sent shockwaves through the abbey by immediately preceding the king in the procession and carrying the crown of St Edward the Confessor in his 'filthy hands'.[3] He also took the sword after it had been used during the ceremony and fastened the spur on his royal master's left foot. Dressed in rich clothes of purple velvet embroidered with pearls that almost outshone the king's own regalia, Gaveston's arrogant behaviour at the banquet that followed horrified the new queen's half-uncles, Charles de Valois and Louis d'Évreux, who left in disgust.

The author of the contemporary *Vita Edwardi Secondi* shrewdly observed that if Gaveston 'had from the outset borne himself prudently and humbly towards the magnates of the land, none of them would have opposed him'.[4] But the royal favourite was incapable of such moderate behaviour. His arrogant, showy nature soon made a host of dangerous enemies for both himself and the king. Gaveston provided a convenient focus for all the complaints against the monarchy that had been gathering since the flouting of Magna Carta by King John and his successors. When calls for a reform of royal government began to be voiced, they centred around the favourite, rather than the king, thus neatly avoiding any hint of disloyalty. A similar tactic would be used in later reigns, notably in

1536 when the participants in the Pilgrimage of Grace claimed that they were rebelling against the actions of Thomas Cromwell, not his royal master Henry VIII.

When it became clear that Edward II had no intention of abandoning Gaveston, his magnates went further still. On 28 April 1308, a delegation led by his late father's confidant, Henry de Lacy, Earl of Lincoln, declared that their allegiance was to the crown, rather than the person of the king. Until now, crown and monarch had been inextricably bound, their union emphasised by the anointing, upon which the 'person' transcended their human state to become God's representative on earth. Separating the king from his crown made Edward dangerously akin to the mere mortals over whom he ruled – and, therefore, dispensable.

The magnates also demanded that Gaveston be stripped of his earldom and sent into exile. To their surprise, Edward agreed. He sent his favourite to Ireland as lieutenant. But he subsequently appealed to the pope to annul Gaveston's exile, and by the following summer Piers was back in England and reinstated as Earl of Cornwall. The favourite's arrogance was undiminished by his brief spell abroad. Rather than employing diplomacy in his dealings with the powerful earls who had opposed him, he gave them slanderous nicknames, such as 'Burst-belly' for the Earl of Lincoln.

The earls' resentment against the royal favourite boiled over into open hostility in October 1309 when they refused to attend a council meeting because Gaveston would be present. The king became so alarmed that he sent his favourite away for his protection. Pressing home their advantage, the earls threatened to withdraw their allegiance from Edward unless he agreed to the appointment of twenty-one 'ordainers' to draft detailed proposals for reform. The king had little choice but to agree.

The resulting document was almost as lengthy – and revolutionary – as Magna Carta a century before. Its forty-one clauses dealt with a whole range of grievances and proposed a series of restrictions to the monarch's authority. The king was forbidden to go to war or leave the kingdom without his barons' consent. Neither could he make any gifts of land or appoint key officials unless the barons in Parliament had sanctioned it. Gaveston was named 'as the evident enemy of the king and his people', and the ordinances demanded that he 'be completely exiled . . . forever without ever returning'.⁵

This last demand was likely the main reason why Edward initially rejected the ordinances on the basis that they infringed his sovereignty. But eventually, faced with intense pressure from Parliament, he gave way. The ordinances were published throughout the kingdom on 11 October 1311, but the very next day Edward began proceedings to have them annulled by the pope. Thus began a battle between the king and his barons that would last for the next eleven years, plunging the country into one of the worst crises since Magna Carta.

When it became clear that the king would not give up his favourite, the Archbishop of Canterbury excommunicated Gaveston in accordance with the ordinances. This gave Edward's nobles the justification they needed to hunt him down. Gaveston was seized at Scarborough Castle, which the king had granted to him for his protection, and in June 1312 he was beheaded without ceremony.⁶ Edward II's grief and fury deepened the chasm between him and his magnates. The king's greatest ire was directed towards his cousin, Thomas of Lancaster, who had been instrumental in Gaveston's death and continued to oppose Edward at every turn.

The king's position was strengthened in November 1312 when Queen Isabella gave birth to their first child, a son, Edward. The following month, an uneasy treaty was agreed, whereby the king would pardon the nobles for his favourite's death if they submitted to his authority. But relations between Edward and his magnates remained fraught with mutual suspicion and resentment. This was intensified by the rise of a new group of royal favourites, in particular Hugh Despenser and his father of the same name, a bitter opponent of Lancaster. As the years wore on and the king drew other enemies of his cousin around him, it seemed inevitable that their hostility would boil over into all-out war.

In early 1314, the king was distracted by events north of the border. The two English strongholds of Roxburgh and Edinburgh castles had fallen to the Scots, and the constable of Stirling had agreed to surrender that castle if the English did not come to his relief. Edward immediately saw this as an opportunity to prove that he was as mighty a warrior as his father had been and began mustering his forces. Although his army was numerically superior to the Scots, it was plagued by disagreements between its commanders, which Edward lacked the experience to resolve. As a result, he suffered a crushing defeat at Bannockburn near Stirling on 24 June. The shameful episode would haunt Edward for the rest of his reign.

The uneasy peace that had been established between the king and his nobles was shattered in 1321 when Lancaster and his supporters attacked the Despenser lands in Wales. Upon hearing of this, the king immediately began rallying troops to defend his favourite. For more than a year, England was plunged into a bitter civil war. By March 1322, Edward had his cousin on the run and the decisive moment came when the royal forces crushed the remnants of Lancaster's army at Boroughbridge in Yorkshire. Lancaster was captured and tried before the king at Pontefract on 22 March. The verdict was swiftly delivered: the earl was found guilty of treason and beheaded outside his castle on the same day. It had taken almost ten years, but Edward had finally avenged Gaveston's death.

The king's victory proved hollow. The systematic confiscations of land from Lancaster's supporters that followed sparked fierce resentment against the crown. Even more ominously, Edward had created a dangerous precedent by having such a high-ranking nobleman as Lancaster executed on the grounds of treason, particularly as he was so closely related to the king. Undaunted, Edward embarked upon a rule of tyranny. 'The harshness of the king has today increased so much that no one however great and wise dares to cross his will', recorded his contemporary biographer. 'Thus parliaments, colloquies, and councils decide nothing these days. For the nobles of the realm, terrified by threats and the penalties inflicted on others, let the king's will have free play. Thus today will conquers reason. For whatever pleases the king, though lacking in reason, has the force of law.'[7]

In Edward's eyes, he had at last become a king of whom his father would have been proud. To mark this fact, in 1324 he commissioned a series of frescoes in Westminster Palace to depict the life of Edward I. The king should perhaps have focused on the living, not the dead. Relations between him and his wife had been strained for some time thanks to his preference for the younger Despenser's company. Whether or not Edward's relationship with his favourite was sexual, it was deeply resented by Isabella. When her husband dispatched her and their son Edward to France to resolve a developing conflict with her brother Charles IV in 1324, she refused to return until Despenser had been removed from court. Soon afterwards, she began a sexual liaison with Roger Mortimer, a powerful Marcher lord who had fought for Lancaster during the civil war. Following the Battle of Boroughbridge, he had been captured and sentenced to death. This had been commuted to life imprisonment and he had been taken to the Tower of London, but he escaped to France in August 1323.

When news of his wife's infidelity was brought to the English king, his fury against her was abiding and absolute. A year later, the Bishop of Hereford attested that the king 'carried a knife in his hose to kill queen Isabella, and had said that if he had no other weapon he would crush her with his teeth'.[8] For her part, Isabella, who became known as the 'She-Wolf of France', began making preparations to depose her husband with an invading force. To bolster her cause, in the summer of 1326 she arranged the betrothal of her thirteen-year-old son Edward to Philippa, daughter of the powerful Count of Hainault. Her husband responded with a letter to his son, echoing the furious exchanges he had had with his own father. He expressly forbade the young Edward to go ahead with the marriage and warned that if he disobeyed: 'He will ordain in such wise that Edward shall feel it all the days of his life, and that all other sons shall take example thereby of disobeying their lords and fathers.'[9]

The king's righteous indignation against his wife and son made him blind to the fundamental weakness of his own position. As a result, he failed to make the necessary preparations to defend against an invasion, and on 24 September 1326 his wife and her supporters landed, unopposed, at Orwell in Suffolk. To Edward's dismay, many of his followers deserted him and he was forced to flee London with the younger Despenser. They made for South Wales, hoping to garner support from the favourite's lands.

Meanwhile, in order to avoid any accusations of treachery, on 15 October Queen Isabella and her son proclaimed that they had come to save the kingdom from the tyrannies of the Despensers and others. Eleven days later, Prince Edward was proclaimed guardian of the realm at Bristol, and the following day the elder Despenser, who had been swiftly captured by Isabella and Mortimer, was executed in the same city. Events were now moving rapidly beyond the king's control. On 16 November, he and his young favourite were seized at Llantrisant, near Caerphilly. Edward was taken to Monmouth Castle, where he was stripped of the great seal, and from there to Kenilworth in the custody of the Earl of Leicester. To his great distress, before he reached Warwickshire, he learned that the younger Despenser had been executed.

On 7 January 1327, the Parliament that Isabella and Mortimer had summoned in the king's name met at Westminster. Edward II refused to attend, and in his absence a set of six articles outlining his defects as king was presented to the assembly. They read as a manual of how not to rule a kingdom. The king, it said, had 'done all that he could to ruin his realm and his people, and what is worse, by his cruelty and lack of character he has shown himself incorrigible without hope of amendment'.[10] Prominent among Edward II's many failings was that he had allowed himself to be influenced and governed by evil councillors, who had prompted him to disregard his coronation oath and plunge his kingdom into ruin. Perhaps most tellingly of all, Edward was accused of devoting himself to 'unsuitable' pastimes. The inference was clear. Parliament concluded there was no means of repairing Edward's kingship, only of ending it.

On 20 January, a delegation of officials arrived at Kenilworth to present the charges to Edward himself. They demanded that he resign his throne in favour of his son. Struggling to control his emotions, Edward bowed to pressure. In a symbolic gesture, his steward of the household, Sir Thomas Blount, broke his staff of office. Five days later, the deposed king's fourteen-year-old son acceded to the throne and was crowned Edward III at Westminster Abbey on 1 February 1327.

The queen's triumph was complete, but her ousted husband was not without support. Within a few weeks, one of his Dominican followers led a plot to free him. This prompted his son to have him transferred to Berkeley Castle in Gloucestershire at the beginning of April. Shortly after another plot was discovered, Parliament was informed that Edward had died at Berkeley on 21 September. To remove any doubt that he was really dead, his body was removed to Gloucester for public display on 22 October. Two months later, he was buried in the city's abbey, his son Edward III and widow Isabella in attendance.[11]

The official line was that Edward had died of natural causes. It is possible that he had a pre-existing condition or that the shock of his deposition had caused his demise. But he was only forty-one at the time of his death and the contemporary sources paint a picture of a man in the same robust health that he had enjoyed for most of his life. More likely is that the plots to free him had prompted Isabella or her lover Mortimer to have him quietly murdered. Rumours soon began to circulate about how this was achieved, the most notorious of which is that his bowels had been burnt out with a red-hot spit or poker inserted into his anus. Although the latter probably owes more to the moralising views of Edward's critics, it has proved the most enduring of all the theories about his death.

Edward II had proved more starkly than any other ruler in British royal history the dangers that could ensue from giving too much power to favourites. He had ignored the wishes of magnates and ordinary subjects alike, and stubbornly upheld what he viewed as his royal prerogative. But England was no longer a kingdom that could be ruled by sheer force of will. The restrictions to royal authority enshrined in Magna Carta and reinforced by the 'ordainers' of 1309 had been severely tested but had endured. All future monarchs would disregard them at their peril.

Edward III (1327–77)

'Glorious, graceful, merciful and magnificent'

E DWARD III HAD ascended the throne amid the most challenging of circumstances, deposing an unpopular and largely incompetent father, and inheriting a legacy of unresolved domestic strife and hostile relations with both France and Scotland. To say the odds were stacked against him would be an understatement. The same had been true of his father when he became king twenty years earlier. Unlike Edward II, though, his son was universally praised. One chronicler described him as having a 'face more like an angel's than a man's, for there was such a miraculous light of grace in it'.[1] In common with celebrated monarchs such as Elizabeth I and Queen Victoria, Edward III personified the values of his age. And those values were deeply rooted in the culture of chivalry, with knights and castles, pageantry and tournaments, and, above all, a heroic king to lead the kingdom to victory.

Given the new king's tender age, it was natural that a council of leading nobles and clerics be appointed to guide him. But its power was soon contested by his mother Isabella and her lover Mortimer. They quickly wrested control from the council and rendered the boy king virtually incapable of independent action. Although he was only fourteen at the time of his accession, Edward displayed a wisdom and shrewdness beyond his years. Rather than allowing himself to be manipulated into taking precipitate action, he watched and waited for events to unfold. He soon had ample proof that the regime of his mother and Mortimer was alienating some of the most powerful men in the kingdom. When Mortimer was given the title Earl of March at the Parliament of October 1328, it sparked a rebellion led by the Earl of Lancaster. This was swiftly put down, but the hostility towards Mortimer simmered on and it was not long before Edward began to share it.

In October 1330, Mortimer, who had heard Edward was plotting against him, summoned him and his followers to Nottingham, where they were interrogated by a great council. Under cover of night, the king and some of his most trusted men stole into Nottingham Castle through an underground passage. Taken by surprise, Mortimer was arrested and forced to hand over the keys to the castle – and, in effect, the kingdom. The following day, 20 October, just short of his eighteenth birthday, the king issued a proclamation announcing that the government of the realm now rested in his hands.

In deposing the man who most of his subjects viewed as a treacherous usurper, Edward had immediately resolved many of the divisions within his new kingdom. He proceeded to make a series of conciliatory measures aimed at strengthening his magnates' trust in the new monarchy. He also led a number of campaigns to Scotland in order to stabilise the situation there and protect English interests. Then, in 1337, his attention was drawn across the Channel.

On 24 May, Philip VI formally confiscated the English-held Duchy of Aquitaine and the county of Ponthieu on dubious grounds. Edward was already contemplating laying claim to the French throne. In the March Parliament he had created six new earls in order to garner military support from among his most powerful subjects. In imitation of the French monarchy, he also introduced the title of duke into England by creating his six-year-old son, Edward, Duke of Cornwall. At around the same time, he quartered the fleur-de-lis on the royal arms to signal his intentions.

As the kings of England and France made warlike preparations, neither could have predicted the length or scale of the ensuing conflict that would become known as the Hundred Years' War.[2] It was Edward III who drew first blood. In the spring of 1346, he sailed across the Channel with a huge fleet and landed off the coast of Normandy. Whether this was planned or the English had been blown off course, their sudden arrival sparked panic among the French camp. After taking Caen on 27 July, Edward and his army headed for Paris, sacking many towns along the way before diverting north, hoping to connect with an allied Flemish army that had invaded from Flanders. By the time Edward heard that the Flemish had turned back, it was too late to change course, because Philip VI and his far larger army were in hot pursuit. The two sides met just outside the village of Crécy-en-Ponthieu and a fierce battle took place on 26 August. The superior tactics of Edward's army gave the English a decisive victory – one that would still be celebrated (somewhat wistfully) by his successors centuries later. It was also at Crécy that the king's son, now Prince of Wales, who had led the vanguard, inherited the motto *Ich Dien* ('I serve') from the King of Bohemia, who was killed in the battle. This has remained the motto of all subsequent princes of Wales.

On his way back to England, Edward laid siege to the town of Calais. His battle-weary army was plagued with dysentery and many deserted, but Crécy had taken a much heavier toll on the French and they struggled to relieve the town. When, in October, news arrived that a Scottish invasion of England had been successfully repelled, resulting in the capture of David II, it gave Edward and his men heart. They maintained the siege and, after eleven months, Calais finally fell. In many respects, this was an even greater triumph than Crécy because it would give the English monarchy a strategically important foothold in northern France for more than two hundred years.

Edward III returned home triumphant, having already secured his place as one of the greatest monarchs in English history. His chivalrous reputation was further enhanced during the celebrations that followed. At one of the many tournaments the king hosted, he conceived the idea of founding a new order of knighthood dedicated to the Virgin Mary and St George. Its name was derived from the emblem of a garter and its headquarters were at Windsor Castle, where Edward had already begun building a round table. The twenty-six knights who were admitted to this prestigious new order met for the first time at Windsor on the feast of St George (23 April) 1349. The symbolism of the order, with its blue robes, rather than English royal red, and the choice of the French motto *Honi soit qui mal y pense* ('Shame upon him who thinks ill of it') suggests that it was intended to mark the triumphs at Crécy and Calais, but also to promote Edward's claim to the French throne.[3] The Order of the

Garter remains the most senior order of knighthood in the British honours system today.

The king's determination to make Windsor the focus of a new royal cult of the legendary King Arthur led to his commissioning major building works there during the 1350s and 1360s. The fact that it was the place of his birth strengthened the allusions to Edward's role as the new Arthur. The increasing confidence of his kingship also found expression in works at the royal palaces of Westminster, Eltham, Sheen, Kings Langley, Woodstock, and Leeds Castle. For all Edward's reputation as a fearsome warrior king, these building projects reveal a penchant for modern conveniences. His baths at Windsor, Westminster and Kings Langley were supplied by a sophisticated new system of hot-water pipes. Other innovations appeared in the royal palaces during his reign, including mechanical clocks.

Edward strengthened the image and institution of monarchy in other ways. More than any king before him, he made use of a whole suite of media to convey his authority and magnificence: art and architecture, clothing, religious ceremony, sermons and proclamations. These served the practical purpose of disseminating his word throughout every level of society and commanding his subjects' respect. It was during Edward's reign that the 'Englishness' of the monarchy became more established. Even though, like his predecessors, Edward ruled a territory that spanned both sides of the Channel, the establishment of Middle English as the spoken and written language of the elite helped strengthen a new national identity. Culturally speaking, it also led to Edward being viewed as the first truly English king since 1066.

Edward's ambitions to launch another French campaign were hampered by economic and political factors. But the decisive blow was dealt by an unprecedented catastrophe that began in the autumn of 1348 and held England in its grip for the next eighteen months. A terrifying disease arrived in the summer of 1348 and rapidly spread across the kingdom. The bubonic plague – or Black Death, as it became known – was the most devastating epidemic that the world had ever seen. In the space of just over a year it had wiped out at least 30 per cent of England's six-million-strong population, although recent research suggests the death toll may have been closer to 60 per cent. The disease was indiscriminate in the damage it wreaked, claiming the lives of rich and poor alike. Edward's thirteen-year-old daughter Joan perished at the start of the outbreak, and within a matter of weeks his infant sons Thomas and William had followed their sister to the grave.

A measure of a ruler's greatness is how they respond to crises. Although the king and his family had suffered a devastating loss, his energy and resolve never wavered. He took care to avoid London during the peak of the epidemic but made sure that there was minimum interruption to state business. Only large gatherings such as Parliament and certain law courts had to be abandoned until the plague had abated. In response to the acute shortage of manual labour that the catastrophe had caused, in June 1349 the king and council issued the ordinance of labourers, the precursor of the Statute of Labourers in 1351. Edward was also the only leader in Europe to put in place a comprehensive mechanism for enforcing it, creating a judicial structure from which the justices of the peace would later emerge. A suite of other financial and legal reforms followed and, as a result of all this, England's economy recovered more quickly than that of any of its continental neighbours. The extent to which this success can be laid directly at Edward's door is debatable. Perhaps his greatest achievement was in selecting able and loyal ministers, but, in contrast to his father, not showing too great a favour towards any of them. The turmoil of Edward II's reign now seemed a distant memory as king and government worked in harmony, to great effect.

With the government of the realm settled, during the 1350s the king was again able to focus upon the war with France and Scotland. He was assisted in this by his eldest son and heir, Edward. After distinguishing himself at the Battle of Crécy, the prince went on to become one of the most successful English commanders during the Hundred Years' War. Although he was known as 'the comfort of England', a model of chivalry and one of the greatest knights of his age, the young Edward's brutality is well documented in the French sources and may have inspired the sobriquet 'Black Prince'. One of the prince's most notable successes was at the Battle of Poitiers in

1356, when he captured the French king, John II. The fact that David II of Scotland was still being held captive in England put Edward III in a strong negotiating position.

The English king now faced the appealing dilemma of negotiating large ransoms for his prisoners' release or launching campaigns to seize their thrones for himself. He began with the former. A draft treaty with France was drawn up in 1358, which set the price on John's release at £666,666 (almost £332 million). When the two sides failed to reach an agreement, Edward began preparing for another military campaign. In late 1359, he and his three eldest sons set sail for Calais and proceeded to lay siege to Rheims. The city was where the kings of France were traditionally crowned, and Edward was so confident of success that he had brought a crown with him. But Rheims was well defended, and after five weeks the English king was forced to abandon the siege. He had little more success in the rest of the campaign and eventually returned to London to reopen talks.

A treaty was finally ratified by Parliament in January 1361 and celebrated with great pomp by the king and his family at Westminster Abbey. They had good cause for jubilation: the agreement not only promised Edward a ransom of £500,000 (almost £249 million), but secured English sovereignty over Calais, Ponthieu and an enlarged Duchy of Aquitaine. A settlement had also been agreed with Scotland, which brought England a further £66,666 (around £33 million) and gave its king suzerainty over the Scottish monarchy.

By the time Edward celebrated his fiftieth birthday at the 1362 Parliament, he had established a stronger monarchy in England than had existed for almost two hundred years. As well as achieving peace within his realm, he had made it one of the most powerful players on the international stage. His victories against France and Scotland had been consolidated by the dynastic marriages he negotiated for his brood of at least twelve children. Every subsequent monarch of England up to the present day can claim their descent from Edward III. In contrast to earlier reigns, a remarkable spirit of amity and unity characterised his large family. Perhaps the failings of Edward's own parents made him determined not to repeat them.

Death, rather than treachery, would break up this domestic harmony during the 1260s. In the winter of 1260–1, two of Edward's daughters died within months of each other, possibly from another outbreak of plague. Then in 1269 he lost his beloved queen, Philippa. She had been Edward's loyal and steadfast companion for more than forty years, bearing him numerous children, often travelling with him on campaign and acting as regent. Theirs had been one of the most successful and, it seems, happy marriages in royal history, and Edward mourned her loss deeply. He did not have the heart to continue with the French campaign he had planned and delegated this instead to his son, the Black Prince.

In fact, Edward would never set foot on French soil again. In 1372, the king, now in his sixtieth year, led a huge expedition to protect his lands in Aquitaine. But his fleet was plagued by bad weather and eventually returned home without reaching its destination. It was hardly a fitting end to Edward's campaigning days. By 1376, the crown was desperately short of money. In April that year, the so-called 'Good Parliament' refused to grant the king the taxes that he so desperately needed. Edward was too ill to attend and the Black Prince, who had returned to England upon the loss of Aquitaine in 1371, led an attack on the abuses of the king's younger son John of Gaunt's administration. But by then, the prince was morbidly ill with dysentery and he died before the session had ended, his father at his side.

The king's own health had been faltering for a number of years, and although there is no direct evidence of dementia, his mental capacity seems to have declined during the early 1370s, perhaps because of a series of strokes. Presiding over Parliament in place of his ailing grandfather was the nine-year-old Richard of Bordeaux, the only surviving legitimate child of the Black Prince. By this time, primogeniture was well established in the English monarchy, so the king had already taken steps to secure the succession in Richard's favour. Aware of the rumours circulating that his own son, John of Gaunt, had designs on the throne, Edward had made sure that Richard was brought before Parliament so that they 'might see and honour [him] as the true heir apparent'.[4] In November, the Black Prince's titles of Prince of Wales, Duke of Cornwall and Earl of Chester were conferred on the boy.

On 23 April, the king was at Windsor to see Richard and another grandson, John of Gaunt's son Henry (known as 'Bolingbroke' after his place of birth), admitted to the Order of the Garter. It was a proud moment, but one that might have given the king cause for disquiet, for he knew he was close to death and that his kingdom faced a period of prolonged minority rule under his grandson. Edward was now so weak that he was taken back to Sheen straight after the ceremony and died there two months later. The twisted face of his wooden funeral effigy, which was probably carved from a death mask, suggests he had died of a stroke.

Within a few years of Edward III's death, chroniclers and poets were already harking back to the middle years of the fourteenth century as the golden age of a golden king. The chronicler Thomas Walsingham declared that the late king 'among all other kings and princes of the world had been glorious, graceful, merciful and magnificent'.[5] Such praise was mostly due to the spectacular military success that Edward had accomplished in both France and Scotland in his heyday. But his achievements extended well beyond that. Having ascended the throne during one of the most turbulent periods in the history of England's monarchy, Edward had quickly won the loyalty of his subjects and established a harmonious and effective government. His reign marks one of the most prolonged periods of domestic peace enjoyed by England throughout the entire Middle Ages.

Richard II (1377–99)

'The Crown was cracked'

T HE NEW KING had big shoes to fill with his ten-year-old feet. The cult of his chivalrous grandfather was already taking shape when Richard inherited his throne. But then, the boy king was used to living in the shadow of a mighty ruler. His father, the Black Prince, had achieved dazzling military conquests and held Aquitaine in thrall as its duke. Young though he was, Richard must have been painfully aware that he was a poor imitation of both men. A contemporary chronicler scathingly described him as being 'of the common stature, his hair yellowish, his face fair, round and feminine, sometimes flushed; abrupt and stammering in his speech, capricious in his manners'.[1]

The sense that Richard had not been destined for the throne was heightened by the fact that he was the younger of his father's two sons (the elder had died six years earlier), as well as by the overbearing presence of his uncle, John of Gaunt, whose lust for power was all too obvious. The fact that the new king had been born on French, not English, soil also set him at a disadvantage. Richard had spent the first four years of his life in Bordeaux and had travelled to England after the death of his elder brother in 1371.

Nevertheless, the measures that Edward III had put in place ensured that his grandson succeeded to the throne uncontested. The record of his coronation on 16 July 1377 is the earliest detailed account of an English coronation ritual to survive. One of the eyewitnesses described the dazzling spectacle: 'They rode towards Westminster through the crowded streets of the city of London, which were so bedecked with cloth of gold and silver, with other conceits to entertain the onlookers, that you might suppose you were seeing a triumph of Caesar or ancient Rome in all its splendour.'[2] With a healthy dose of hindsight, a later chronicler recorded how various misfortunes had befallen Richard at his coronation, most ominously when, at the banquet, 'a sudden gust of wind carried away the crown from his head'.[3]

The last minority rule had been that of Henry III in the early thirteenth century. Then, a regent had been appointed to manage affairs until the king reached maturity, but there was no hint of such a plan now. Instead, from the moment of his accession, Richard II nominally exercised all the powers of kingship. This presented an opportunity for those around him to take advantage of the king's youth and inexperience. Rapacious officials such as Aubrey de Vere were able to seize effective control of royal patronage, while the king's uncles, John of Gaunt and Thomas of Woodstock, enjoyed a considerable level of influence. It was not long before there were mutterings in the Commons against these power-hungry officials. In October 1378, the House demanded to know 'who would be the king's councillors and governors of his person', and complained about the excesses of the royal household, which Richard had been unable to rein in.[4]

What sparked even greater resentment were the heavy taxes levied to sustain England's military commitments, notably in Calais and on the Scottish border, and to fund various ill-fated expeditions to France. The situation was made worse by the population decline resulting from the persistent outbreaks of plague. The unrest came to a head in November 1380 when Parliament granted a new poll tax requiring everyone over the age of fourteen, whether rich or poor, to pay one shilling to the crown. This constituted a week's wages for a master craftsman and a month's wages for an agricultural labourer. Instrumental in bringing about the new tax was Simon Sudbury, Archbishop of Canterbury and Lord Chancellor, who became a focus for popular resentment.

When the tax collectors returned with only two-thirds of the money, the council sent them back again in the spring of 1381. This prompted widespread resistance, known as the Peasants' Revolt, under the leadership of the charismatic Walter (or Wat) Tyler. He quickly amassed a huge body of supporters, and in June 1381 he marched on London with 20,000 men.

The fourteen-year-old king was hastily moved to the Tower for his safety, along with his mother Joan, the 'Fair Maid of Kent', and they were guarded by a garrison of a thousand men. Upon reaching London, the rebels headed straight for the Tower and quickly surrounded it. The king agreed to meet them, but as soon as the gates were opened to let him out, four hundred rebels rushed in. Ransacking their way to the innermost parts of the fortress, they reached the king's bedchamber. The renowned author Jean Froissart describes how the rebels 'arrogantly lay and sat and joked on the king's bed, whilst several asked the king's mother . . . to kiss them'.[5] Joan escaped with only a loss of dignity, but it had been a deeply shocking episode, illustrating the extent of the rebels' disdain for monarchical power.

Steeled into more decisive action, Richard rode out to meet the rebels at Mile End, offering them charters of freedom and a pardon for their rebellion. It was a dangerous tactic – even his personal bodyguard had lost their nerve and stayed behind at the Tower. But the young king's courage paid off. The rebels professed their loyalty to him and insisted that their opposition was only directed towards the royal officials and landowning nobility. Richard wisely showed clemency, granting them charters of freedom if they agreed to return peacefully to their homes.

But while the king was at Mile End, a group of rebels had found the despised Lord Chancellor leading prayers in the Tower's chapel. Without hesitation, they dragged Sudbury and a number of his companions up to nearby Tower Hill and beheaded them. The archbishop's severed head was then set upon a pole on London Bridge, as was the fate for executed traitors.[6]

The king and his entourage took refuge in the great wardrobe, near Blackfriars, where the royal clothes and accoutrements were stored. But the following day, 15 June, Richard had it proclaimed that all rebels who remained in London should appear before him at Smithfield. This time, Wat Tyler was present. He arrogantly addressed the king as 'Frer' ('Brother'), which so antagonised Richard's followers that one of them set upon the rebel leader and killed him. The situation could have quickly turned ugly, but the young king showed extraordinary presence of mind by riding towards the rebels calling: 'I am your leader: follow me.'[7] This distracted many of the rebels from the fracas surrounding the dead Tyler, allowing time for the London militia to arrive and disperse them.

It soon became clear that the king had little intention of keeping his promises. Within two weeks of the meeting at Smithfield, he rode out to Essex to witness the execution of some of the rebels, and on 2 July he formally revoked the charters of pardon that he had pledged. The episode had left a lasting impression on the young king, convincing him that disobedience, no matter how justified, constituted a threat to order and stability within his realm and must not be tolerated. During the years that followed, this idea took firm root in Richard's mind, shaping his idea of kingship – with disastrous results.

The role that Richard had played in quelling the Peasants' Revolt proved that he had reached maturity. The question of his marriage soon followed. A number of potential brides had already been proposed. Of these, the government favoured Anne of Bohemia, daughter of the late Emperor Charles IV and sister of the Emperor-elect and King of Bohemia, Wenceslas IV. Aged fifteen, she was just a few months older than Richard, and the match offered the tantalising prospect of an Anglo-Imperial alliance directed against the French. Negotiations duly proceeded and the marriage took place on 20 January 1382.

But the king's new bride proved an unpopular choice with many of his subjects. The behaviour of her Bohemian retinue aroused resentment, as did the financial burden that the marriage entailed, Richard having promised to lend his new brother-in-law more than £16,000 (almost £10 million today). Worse still, the hoped-for Anglo-Imperial alliance never bore fruit. Neither did the marriage produce any heirs. There are no hints in the contemporary sources that Anne ever fell pregnant. Yet she and Richard did grow genuinely fond of each other, and the young king's status was certainly enhanced by having the daughter of an emperor as his bride.

As he approached adulthood, Richard began to surround himself with courtiers and advisers of his own choosing. They included Michael de la Pole, a former follower of his father, who had been appointed by Parliament to 'advise and govern' the king after the Peasants' Revolt. He rapidly superseded the powers that Parliament had envisaged for him, and in 1383 the king appointed him chancellor. Even greater favour was shown towards Robert de Vere, Earl of Oxford, who was closer in age to the king and soon enjoyed more influence than any other member of the court. In 1385, de Vere was made Earl of Suffolk and the following year the king created him Duke of Ireland, which meant that de Vere now enjoyed the same rank as the king's three uncles. This served to intensify the mounting resentment against a young man already despised for his arrogance and greed. One of those who resented him most was the king's uncle, John of Gaunt, Duke of Lancaster, who saw de Vere as a threat to his own authority.

Richard should have heeded the parallels that were being drawn between his favourite and Piers Gaveston. Instead, by continuing to lavish riches upon de Vere and others at a time when the crown was still heavily in debt, he aroused further hostility within his government. The king's standing was not helped by worsening relations with France and Scotland, and by his apparent reluctance to take up arms as his grandfather had done. When he turned eighteen in January 1385, the pressure to prove his manhood by going to war could no longer be ignored. In July, he led an expedition to Scotland. As this was the king's first campaign, the occasion was laden with symbolism. Upon his army's entry into Scotland, Richard created new knights and bestowed the titles Duke of York and Duke of Gloucester upon his uncles Edmund Langley and Thomas of Woodstock.

But the expedition heightened the tension with another of his uncles, John of Gaunt. Richard ignored his advice to press further into Scotland after the success of his troops' initial raids and instead declared that he would lead them home. Relations between them continued to worsen, and in July 1386 Gaunt left court for an expedition to Spain, intent upon pursuing his claim to the Castilian throne, which he derived from his marriage to Constance of Castile. In his absence, Richard's other uncles, York and Gloucester, took over the leadership of those who sought to destroy the influence of de Vere and de la Pole.

Things came to a head in the so-called 'Wonderful Parliament' of October 1386. In response to a threat of invasion from France, de la Pole called for an enormous subsidy to bolster England's defences. The Commons, probably at the behest of Richard's uncle, the Duke of Gloucester, demanded the removal of de la Pole before they would continue with business. The king, who had refused to meet Parliament, inflamed the situation further by sending a message that he would not dismiss so much as a scullion from his kitchen at their request.

But neither the king nor his favourites were a match for Gloucester and his followers. On 20 December, the duke crushed de Vere in a pitched battle close to Oxford. According to a number of chroniclers, Richard was deposed for three days and was only restored to the throne because his uncle's faction could not agree on a successor. An anonymous poem described how the king's enemies had 'privily plucked the royal power away' until 'the Crown was cracked'.[8] Woefully lacking support, military or otherwise, Richard had little choice but to agree to summon a Parliament in which his favourites were put on trial for treason. The 'Merciless Parliament', as it was named, condemned all of the king's inner circle to death. The two most hated, de Vere and de la Pole, had fled overseas, but the sentence was passed in their absence. The others were condemned and executed.

The absence of those men who had sparked such resentment during the past ten years significantly reduced the opposition to the king himself. By May 1389, Richard had taken full control of his government. Now aged twenty-one, he successfully argued that it was his right. He made no apology for past wrongs, pointing out that these had been committed while others were in charge, but vowed that from that time forward, he would apply all his energies towards the wellbeing of his people.

Things began well. Richard made no move to recall his favourites from exile; nor did he replace them with others. Rather, he seemed content to rule through and with his government. The political situation was made even more stable by his reconciliation with his uncles, the Duke of Gloucester and John of Gaunt, the latter returning to England in November 1389. Gaunt commanded a great deal of respect throughout the court and kingdom, and his steadying influence helped to rebuild confidence in his nephew's authority.

Feeling more secure on his throne, Richard spent the early part of the 1390s enhancing the ceremonial aspects of his monarchy. 'He was prodigal in his gifts, extravagantly splendid in his entertainments and dress', remarked a contemporary with a mixture of admiration and disapproval.[9] The Tudor chronicler, Ralph Holinshed, may have been exaggerating when he claimed: 'there reported daily to his court above ten thousand persons', but he was in a good position to judge that Richard 'maintained the most plentiful house that ever any king in England did either before his time or since'.[10]

Richard introduced a more elaborate form of address at court, replacing 'highness' with 'royal majesty' or 'high majesty'. One eyewitness described how it became the king's custom to sit enthroned in his chamber after dinner, requiring anyone upon whom his gaze alighted to bow down to him. Many of these ideas were inspired by the French court. The same was true of Richard's adoption of the broom-cod (*planta genista*) as one of his personal emblems. Although this has been mistakenly seen as a nod to his Plantagenet ancestors, it referred to the French Order of the Broom-cod.

Richard's cultural tastes were also influenced by France. In 1395, Jean Froissart arrived at court and presented the king with a manuscript of his poems. The king patronised home-grown talent, too, and his court became a centre for some of the brightest literary and artistic stars of the age. Included among them were the poets John Gower and Sir John Montagu, and most notable of all, Geoffrey Chaucer, who has come to be regarded as 'the father of English literature'. His most celebrated work was *The Canterbury Tales*, a collection of twenty-four stories told by a group of pilgrims as they travelled together from London to Canterbury to visit the shrine of Saint Thomas Becket. Although the characters were fictional, Chaucer used them, and the tales they exchanged, to paint a satirical and at times highly critical portrait of English society at the time. He was particularly damning of the church and showed most of the characters as being more concerned with worldly than spiritual matters.

An architectural expression of Richard's kingship was begun in 1393, with the rebuilding of Westminster Hall. The king donated £1,685 towards the cost (equivalent to around £1.1 million today) and considered it money well spent as a means of conveying his magnificence. The finished hall was decorated throughout with Richard's favourite heraldic badge – a white hart in chains – and the new hammerbeam roof was the largest of its kind in England. The hall is the oldest part of the original palace still standing today and provides a breathtaking glimpse of the young king's vision for his monarchy.

The fact that many of Richard's ideas about royal ceremony and image-making were borrowed from France suggests that he never embraced the traditional enmity between the two countries. Rather, he began to advocate the idea of a truce. The sticking point was Aquitaine. A draft treaty drawn up in 1393 proposed that England's share of this territory should be significantly enlarged, but – crucially – that Richard would hold the Duchy of the King of France by *liege homage*, whereby one sovereign pledged fealty to another. This was deeply unpopular with Parliament, particularly those members who could recall the glory days of his grandfather's campaigns against the French king. But neither side had the will or resources to renew hostilities, so in 1396 a twenty-eight-year truce was agreed.

As part of this, Richard pledged to marry Charles VI's seven-year-old daughter Isabella, his beloved first wife, Anne of Bohemia, having died at Sheen Palace two years earlier.[11] Richard's new wife was not a popular choice with his subjects, who rightly judged that it would be a long time before she would give him any heirs. They also distrusted their king's friendship with France, fearing that it would end in his returning Calais to the French king. One of the most prominent opponents to the Anglo-French truce was the king's uncle, Gloucester, and his supporters, the earls of Arundel and Warwick. Without warning, Richard had all three men arrested in July 1397, which pushed the simmering political tensions into open hostility.

When Parliament met at Westminster two months later, the king ordered two hundred of his Cheshire archers to surround the building. His chancellor, Edmund Stafford, proceeded to preach a sermon declaring that power rested solely with the king, and that any who attempted to usurp it should be punished with the full force of the law. John of Gaunt presided over the ensuing trial of his brother Gloucester and the earls of Arundel and Warwick. All three were found guilty of treason and sentenced to death. Arundel was executed immediately, but Warwick's life was spared and he was sent into exile. No action could be taken against Gloucester because he was already dead. He had been sent to Calais after his arrest and kept prisoner there, and it is likely that Richard had sent illicit instructions that his uncle should be quietly murdered.

Unrepentant, the king confiscated the disgraced men's estates and redistributed them among his supporters. Then, in a highly symbolic ceremony, he made the Lords and Commons swear an oath on St Edward the Confessor's shrine at Westminster to uphold the decisions of Parliament or suffer the penalties of treason. Given that the king now effectively controlled Parliament, this was a declaration of his absolute authority.

Richard's subsequent actions smack of insecurity, as well as tyranny. He made full use of the treason law as a means of oppressing anyone who dared to flout his royal power or prerogative. Any subject heard to slander the king would be hauled before the court of chivalry. This was a clear violation of the original Magna Carta, which promised that offenders would be dealt with 'according to the lawful judgement of his equals and the law of the land', and it aroused opposition among his people.[12]

What they needed was an alternative candidate for the throne. The king had no children, so all eyes turned to his other kin. The one with the strongest claim was John of Gaunt, eldest surviving son of Edward III, whose position was bolstered by the fact he had a healthy adult son and heir, Henry Bolingbroke (who had sons of his own), to succeed him. His rival was Edmund Mortimer, fifth Earl of March, the great-grandson of Edward III's second surviving son, Lionel, Duke of Clarence (John of Gaunt was the third son). In Bolingbroke's favour was the fact that he was descended from a direct male line, whereas Edmund's descent was through his grandmother, Philippa of Clarence. Moreover, Edmund was only seven years old, whereas Bolingbroke was a grown man and a proven soldier. But Bolingbroke was insecure enough to fall prey to malicious gossip in late 1397 that the king's advisers were plotting to exclude him and his father from the succession. His furious reaction was enough to have him exiled to France.

The question of the succession was brought back to the fore in February 1399 when John of Gaunt died. Bolingbroke, who had taken up residence in Paris, now attempted to claim his father's inheritance, which was due to him by law. The king was keenly aware of the threat that an exiled but wealthy Duke of Lancaster would pose to his security. In a pretence at upholding the law, he set up a parliamentary committee to repeal Bolingbroke's right to claim his inheritance and, at the same time, to extend his exile from ten years to life.

Believing he had settled the matter, Richard embarked upon an expedition to Ireland in June that year, aimed at bolstering his waning authority there. But his cousin had succeeded in gathering a sizeable body of supporters in France and at the beginning of July he landed with an invasion force at Ravenspur in Yorkshire. Within days, the north of England was under Bolingbroke's control, and as he marched south, more supporters flocked to his standard. Richard had taken most of his followers with him to Ireland, and there were few left in England willing to defend his crown.

When Richard heard the news of his cousin's invasion, he sent the Earl of Salisbury to rally troops on his behalf. The king himself finally set sail in August and landed off the coast of south-west Wales. But, seeing that the kingdom was slipping from his grasp, most of his army defected to Bolingbroke. Richard was persuaded to travel north-east to Flint so that he could meet his cousin and discuss terms. It was a trap. As soon as he arrived, Henry took him to Chester and from there to London, where he was lodged in the Tower on 2 September 1399.

Bolingbroke immediately set up a parliamentary committee to inquire how Richard was to be set aside. It swiftly concluded that deposing the king was entirely justified on account of his 'perjuries, sacrileges, sodomitical acts, dispossession of his subjects, reduction of his people to servitude, lack of reason, and incapacity to rule'.[13]

Satisfied that he could now legally depose his cousin and claim the throne for himself, Bolingbroke visited Richard in the Tower to deliver the news. According to the official account of the meeting, the ousted king accepted his fate with 'a cheerful countenance', giving his cousin a signet ring as a token of his goodwill. This is contradicted by every other source. The chronicler Adam Usk, who had been a member of the committee that deposed Richard, visited him in the Tower shortly afterwards. He found him utterly distraught and ranting against a kingdom that had 'exiled, slain, destroyed, and ruined so many kings, so many rulers, so many great men'.[14]

On 30 September, Richard's deposition was confirmed by an assembly of Lords and Commons in his newly rebuilt hall at Westminster. No fewer than thirty-nine accusations against the king were read out, at the heart of which was that he had disregarded 'the rightful laws and customs of the realm', preferring to act 'according to his own arbitrary will and do whatever he wished'.[15] Great emphasis was placed upon the fact that he had broken the oath taken at his coronation and had thus betrayed his people. The outcome was assured.

By now, Richard's spirit was utterly broken. When told that the assembly had confirmed his deposition, he replied that 'he looked not hereafter, but hoped that his cousin would be a good lord to him'.[16] They were the words of a defeated man – and, perhaps, a remorseful one. Now that he had been stripped of all hope, Richard might have reflected on the part he had played in his downfall. His stubborn belief in the sacredness of royal authority and prerogative had blinded him to the realities of kingship – and, ultimately, brought him to destruction.

Whereas Edward II had been deposed in favour of his legitimate son and heir, Richard's throne had passed to a man whose claim was arguably superseded, or at least matched, by others. Disrupting the royal succession in this way created a dangerous precedent and made the crown fundamentally unstable. Henry IV and his Lancastrian successors were no longer viewed as unimpeachable, God-appointed beings, but as claimants who might be supplanted by a more appealing alternative if the need arose.

This new element of uncertainty and potential instability introduced into the monarchy was the most abiding legacy of Richard II's reign. Its tendrils would reach beyond his immediate successors and undermine even seemingly potent royal dynasties such as the Tudors. But for now, it acted as the prelude for one of the most turbulent centuries in the entire history of the English monarchy.

Part 3

Lancaster and York (1399–1485)

'Round the throne the thunder rolls'

The deposition of Richard II ushered in not just a new ruling family, the Lancastrians, but one of the bloodiest periods in the crown's long history. The Wars of the Roses, as they were later styled, were actually a series of conflicts with different causes. They dominated the fifteenth century and saw the throne change hands no fewer than seven times. The seeds of dissent had been sown during the reign of Edward III, who died leaving three sons and a daughter, some of whom had married into powerful noble families, bolstering their claim even further. The conflict centred around the houses of York and Lancaster, the former descended from Edward III's second and fourth sons, Lionel of Clarence and Edmund, Duke of York, and the latter from his third son, John of Gaunt, Duke of Lancaster. By the end of the struggle, one of the only Lancastrian claimants remaining was Henry of Richmond (the future Henry VII), a descendant of John of Gaunt by his then-mistress, Katherine Swynford.

Henry IV (1399–1413)

'Indirect crooked ways'

U PON CLAIMING THE throne, Henry Bolingbroke, England's first Lancastrian king, was quick to justify his deposition of Richard II. He insisted that 'the realm was on the point of being undone for default of governance and undoing of the good laws'.[1] Parliament was careful to uphold the fiction that he had inherited the throne 'through the right God had given him by conquest'.[2] Few of his new subjects would have argued against the justice of getting rid of Richard. But many more were dubious about whether Bolingbroke was his rightful successor.

Bolingbroke was crowned Henry IV just two weeks after his cousin's deposition. His insecurity was revealed by a number of refinements to the ceremony. He dispensed with the tradition that the senior churchmen and nobles should meet at Westminster 'to consider about the consecration and election of the new king'.[3] For obvious reasons, Henry was anxious to avoid any hint of election and worked from the premise that the crown was his by right – something that his successors would emulate. Eager to curry favour with the most powerful men of the realm, the new king marked his coronation by creating what became known as Knights of the Bath, a tradition that was continued at every subsequent coronation. The name was derived from the long-established tradition of knights-to-be taking a bath prior to receiving their honour, which may have symbolised spiritual purification. Henry IV was also the first English king to be anointed with a sacred oil reputedly given by the Virgin Mary to Thomas Becket, as well as the first to be enthroned on the 'Stone of Scone' which Edward I had taken from Scotland in 1296. But none of this was enough to dispel his insecurity. During the traditional banquet that followed, when the king's champion rode into the hall and defied all present to gainsay Henry's title, the new king declared that, if necessary, he would defend the crown himself.

Two days later, the king had his eldest son, Henry (then aged thirteen), invested in Parliament as Prince of Wales. It was a first step towards securing the throne for his descendants, which in turn bolstered his own position. To emphasise the continuity of the succession, Henry repeatedly stressed that he would rule as his predecessors had done, with no infringement of the prerogatives he had inherited from them. But to win the throne in the first place, he had made a number of promises, the keeping of which severely hampered his freedom of action. Of greatest import was his pledge to reduce taxation, knowing how unpopular this had made Richard II.

This promise was borne of inexperience, rather than deceit. For all John of Gaunt's ambitions for himself and his heirs, he had involved Henry in very few public affairs during Richard II's reign. Instead, he had focused upon his son's military training, taking him on numerous campaigns and encouraging his participation in tournaments. As a result, Henry had developed a strong competitive instinct that spurred him on to take the throne, but now that he had it, he lacked the ability to exercise his authority effectively.

From the outset, the new king continued to treat his Lancastrian lands and those of his late wife, Mary de Bohun, as his own personal property, to be administered separately from crown lands. He used their revenues to fund huge retaining fees, and also bought his new subjects' loyalty with lavish grants of land. As a result, royal household expenditure soared to £53,000 (more than £32 million in today's money) in the first year of Henry's reign alone. To make matters worse, he was unable to persuade Parliament to overlook his earlier promise and grant new taxes.

As Henry struggled to establish his authority, the shadow of Richard II loomed ever larger. At the end of 1399, the ousted king had been taken to Pontefract Castle, seat of the Duchy of Lancaster, and placed under close guard. He might have lived out his days there in quiet retirement had it not been for a plot by a group of lords, including John Montagu, third earl of Salisbury and Thomas le Despenser, a descendant of Edward II's favourites, to assassinate

Henry and his sons and restore Richard to the throne. The main plotters of the so-called Epiphany Rising were rounded up and killed in January 1400. In early February, the council issued an ominous order that if Richard still lived, he should be securely guarded, but 'if he has departed this life, then he should be shown openly to the people'.[4] The implication was clear: if the ousted king was alive, then he would not be so for long. Sure enough, by mid-February, Richard was dead. When his skeleton was examined in the nineteenth century, it showed no sign of violence. It is more likely that he had been starved to death. Only Henry would have had the authority to command such a deed.

To remove any doubt that Richard was dead, the king ordered that his body be brought to London with the face exposed. He also attended the funeral service at St Paul's, after which the late king's remains were taken for burial not at Westminster Abbey, the traditional resting place of monarchs, but at the Dominican Friary at Kings Langley. This was probably a deliberate attempt by Henry to draw parallels between Richard and another deposed king, Edward II, whose favourite Piers Gaveston was laid to rest there.

The King of Scots, Robert III, was quick to take advantage of his English rival's instability and from the outset refused to acknowledge him as king. Henry took the bait and waged war on Scotland, but as one contemporary scathingly noted: 'nothing worthy of remembrance was done'.[5] He was soon distracted by another of England's neighbours. On his journey back to London, he received the alarming news that a Welsh esquire named Owain Glyn Dŵr had proclaimed himself Prince of Wales and raided English-held towns in north Wales and Shropshire. The king immediately diverted to Shrewsbury and gathered forces for a counter-attack. But while he successfully quelled the threat to England's borders, he made no impact upon Glyn Dŵr's growing body of support within the principality. By June the following year, much of northern and central Wales was under his control. Among the powerful Welsh nobles who joined the revolt were the brothers Rhys and Gwilym ap Tudur, forefathers of Henry VII, founder of the royal Tudor dynasty.

In response, the English king appointed the powerful nobleman Henry 'Hotspur' Percy to suppress the rebels. During the next few years, a series of fierce battles was fought between Glyn Dŵr's followers and the English forces, none of which proved decisive. The king's failure to offer the concessions required to end the conflict would be one of the greatest mistakes of his reign. As the rebellion dragged on, so the costs mounted. With no prospect of being able to raise sufficient taxes, and having lost a huge amount of his own lands to the Welsh rebels, the king's debts were mounting.

Henry was also under increasing pressure from the Percy family to reward their service and had no other recourse but to grant them a host of senior offices and titles. Aware of the danger of concentrating so much power in one family, he took steps to reduce it. Hotspur responded by mustering troops in Cheshire and Wales and, knowing the abiding loyalty there towards Richard II, putting out word that the former king was still alive, even though his body had been publicly displayed prior to burial. Matters came to a head in July 1403, when the royal forces clashed with those of the Percys near Shrewsbury. The king's eldest son and heir Henry fought alongside his father and almost died when an arrow struck him in the face. Hotspur was killed in the battle, which won the day for the English king.

Still Henry IV could not sit comfortably on his throne. In 1403 and 1404, the French launched a series of naval attacks on the south coast of England. In 1405, some 2,500 French troops arrived in Wales to reinforce Glyn Dŵr. The renewal of conflict with France was something that the king neither wanted nor could afford. He was hard-pressed even to defend the English-held territories in Aquitaine, which left his treasury more depleted than ever. But he soon had to deal with yet another threat within his own borders. In May 1405, news reached him of an uprising in York led by the Earl of Northumberland and others, and with the apparent support of Richard Scrope, Archbishop of York. Henry's response was as brutal as it was swift. Having promised to listen to their grievances, he had Scrope and his associates condemned for treason on 8 June and beheaded outside York the same day.

The execution of a prelate sent shockwaves across the kingdom. It also revealed the strain under which the king was labouring. Shortly afterwards, his health completely broke down and he was forced to retire from his royal duties for a time. The same thing happened during the 'Long Parliament' of 1406, which was dominated by the crown's dire financial situation. The nature of the king's illness is not certain, but it was serious enough for him to nominate a council of seventeen men to assist him in the task of government. This was later streamlined to a smaller executive body under the leadership of the king's eldest son and heir, Prince Henry. Among its members were Edward, Duke of York (a grandson of Edward III) and the king's illegitimate half-brother, John Beaufort, Earl of Somerset, both of whom would go on to play a prominent role in the history of the monarchy.

Henry's ill health persisted for the remainder of his reign, limiting his participation both in government and in military campaigns. He was careful to retain the appearance of control, as is demonstrated by the numerous letters under the great seal that were still certified *per ipsum regem* ('by the king himself'). He also attended important ceremonial occasions, such as the Garter service at Windsor on St George's Day. Increasingly, though, royal authority was devolved to his eldest son. Although Prince Henry proved a competent and popular leader, this led to tensions with his father, who was painfully aware that many of his leading nobles were now looking to the younger Henry for leadership and advancement.

The rising tensions soon spilled over into the country as a whole, thanks to the impatience of the prince's followers to see him assume full power. The Beauforts were particularly forceful in this respect. In the autumn of 1411, Henry Beaufort, one of John of Gaunt's illegitimate children by his mistress Katherine Swynford, called for the king to resign his throne in favour of Prince Henry. The king's response was decisive. At the Parliament held shortly afterwards, he declared that he wished for no sort of 'novelty' in proceedings.[6] He proceeded to dismiss a number of his son's followers from office, replacing them with his own loyal retainers.

By the beginning of 1413, the king's health had deteriorated so sharply that it was obvious the prince would not have to wait much longer. The will that Henry IV had drawn up during another bout of sickness at the beginning of 1409 suggests that he was plagued with guilt for usurping Richard's throne. He refers to himself as 'sinful wretch' and laments the 'life I have misspent'.[7] But such sentiments were typical of devout men, as Henry was known to be, and may simply reflect a pious fear of death and judgement. It would be left to later commentators, notably Shakespeare, to attribute an overbearing remorse to a king who rarely, if ever, expressed it. The second play that bears his name ends with the famous lines:

> By what by-paths and indirect crooked ways
> I met this crown, and I myself know well
> How troublesome it sat upon my head.[8]

On 10 February 1413, the king appeared in Parliament for the last time and requested a grant of taxation so that he could lead a crusade to the Holy Land. Few present could have believed him capable of following this through. He did, though, make it to a Jerusalem of sorts: the chamber in Westminster Abbey named after that city. It was there that the king collapsed on 20 March and was taken to the abbot's house nearby. According to a French chronicler, as he lay dying, the king sent for his son and told him: 'What right have you to it [the throne]? For well you know I had none.'[9] As he had wished, Henry was buried in Thomas Becket's chapel in Canterbury Cathedral. Despite his repeated protestations about the justice of Richard II's deposition, at the end, even he shrank from the thought of being interred in Westminster Abbey, where the kings whose line of succession he had broken lay buried.

Henry V (1413–22)

'The mighty and puissant conqueror'

ENGLAND'S NEW KING was twenty-six years old when he inherited the throne from his father. The famous portrait, originally painted soon after his accession, shows him in profile so as to conceal the wound sustained at Shrewsbury. His thick brown hair is shaved so short around his skull that it gives him the appearance of a monk, which was perhaps deliberate, given the intense piety that Henry V displayed from the time of his accession. His features are striking rather than handsome: a long, straight nose, oval-shaped eyes and prominent lips. Although the portrait only shows his head and shoulders, he appears lean and of above-average height. Later descriptions concur that he was tall and graceful, but that he could outrun all others, and that when angry, his sparkling eyes could instil as much fear as those of a lion.

Henry V was not born to be king, but had learned his craft from the age of thirteen, when his father had ousted Richard II from the throne. Having gained valuable experience in government during Henry IV's incapacity, he was more than ready to assume full control upon his father's death. The French chronicler Enguerrand de Monstrelet tells a story of how the prince had once taken his father's crown from his bedside to see how it fitted. Bursting with ideas and energy, and with a wealth of military experience to draw upon, the younger Henry presented an appealing alternative to a king who had never quite shaken off the stain of usurpation.

On Passion Sunday (9 April) 1413, three weeks after his father's death, Henry V was crowned at Westminster Abbey. Outside, the crowds who had gathered to see their new king shivered as the snow fell. Some took it as an ominous sign that austerity lay ahead, while others believed it signalled the arrival of better days. Aware of the uncertainty among his subjects, the king immediately set out to prove that his reign marked a new beginning and the chance to heal old wounds. One of his earliest acts was to order the removal of Richard II's body from Kings Langley so that it might be reburied with all due ceremony at Westminster Abbey, next to his beloved first wife, Anne of Bohemia. As well as demonstrating Henry's respect for the king whom his father had usurped, this also put an end to conspiracy theories that Richard was still alive and sheltering in Scotland, ready to take back his throne. The new king also restored titles to those men whom his father had disinherited after the Epiphany Rising of 1400 and offered pardons (at a price) to others. Even the Percys were encouraged to seek the restoration of their favour and estates.

Such concessions went a long way towards smoothing over the disputes of the past. Henry also made his desire for peace and stability felt further down the social scale. He was particularly concerned to ensure that justice, public order and financial probity were upheld. The way in which he settled a dispute between two north-country gentlemen was typical of his no-nonsense approach. The king summoned them to his presence when he was about to go to dinner and told them that if they were not reconciled 'by the time that he had eaten his oysters, they should both be hanged before ever he supped'. The two men meekly obeyed to settle their differences and, as the chronicler recorded: 'After that, there durst no lord make no party nor strife; and thus he began to keep his laws and justice, and therefore he was beloved.'[1]

But a conspiracy that broke out just a few months after Henry's accession proved he could not yet rest easy on his throne. It was led by his close friend Sir John Oldcastle (the inspiration for Shakespeare's Falstaff), who had been imprisoned in the Tower because of his adherence to Lollardy, a new religious movement that was critical of the Roman Catholic Church and called for reform. Oldcastle managed to escape the Tower and proceeded to organise a revolt, which included an attempt to kidnap the king. When it failed, he fled to Wales but was later arrested and executed. The controversy gave Henry the chance to flex his muscles and prove that, for all his conciliatory stance, he would show no mercy towards those who opposed him.

The king's resolve was tested again in July 1415, when a conspiracy was uncovered that aimed to put an unwitting Edmund Mortimer, fifth Earl of March, on the throne in Henry's stead. Mortimer was the great-grandson of Lionel, Duke of Clarence, second son of Edward III, which made his claim superior to that of the king, who was descended from Edward's third son, John of Gaunt. The ringleaders were rounded up and beheaded. Mortimer escaped reprisals because it was he who had informed Henry of the plot as soon as he had heard of it.

To prove his loyalty, Mortimer took part in the expedition to France that the king launched a few days later. The French king, Charles VI, had long suffered from a mental disorder that was frequently debilitating. As a result, real power rested with his sons, but their bitter rivalries were tearing the country apart. This presented an opportunity that Henry was quick to take advantage of. It was clear that he had ambitions for the French throne itself, but his first move was more cautious. In the spring of 1414, he dispatched envoys to the French king to assert his claim to the territories that had been granted to England by the terms of Edward III's Treaty of Brétigny in 1360. He also instructed his envoys to demand the hand in marriage of Charles VI's youngest daughter, Catherine of Valois, along with a substantial dowry.

When the envoys returned empty-handed, Henry's thoughts immediately turned to war. He declared his intention in the November Parliament and began making preparations shortly afterwards. His resolve was strengthened by the arrival of some French ambassadors with an insulting gift from the dauphin of some tennis balls 'because he [Henry] should have somewhat to play withal, for him and his lords'.[2] Neither was Henry daunted by a plot to assassinate him that was almost certainly funded by the French.

As Henry's plans for war with France took shape, they stirred memories of his illustrious great-grandfather. Accounts of Edward III's French campaigns, and those of his son the Black Prince, began to circulate in great numbers, whipping up the country into a jingoistic fervour. Now was the chance for England to erase the humiliations of the past few decades and seize victory over its old rival once more.

On 14 August 1415, Henry and an army of up to 12,000 men (larger than Edward III's force in 1359) landed close to the town of Harfleur in Normandy. Returning the dauphin's insult, the English king's forces proceeded to batter the town with 'hard and great gun stones [cannon balls], for the Dauphin to play withal'.[3] Harfleur surrendered on 22 September. Having fortified it, Henry proceeded with a substantially reduced body of men to Calais.

On 24 October, the weary English force, which had been constantly harassed by the enemy on the long march north-east, finally encountered the French head-on, close to the village of Agincourt. The ensuing battle was heavily weighted against them. The French army was superior in size and had far greater energy. But in the English troops' favour was the inspirational courage and leadership of their king. They also had luck on their side. On the night before the battle, it rained heavily, making the ground underfoot very soft.

Early in the morning of 25 October, Henry rallied his men, reminding them of the justice of their cause and that the whole of England was praying for their victory. He then lured the enemy into battle. It quickly became apparent that the size of the French army was working against itself, as it lacked cohesion, self-discipline and a single, decisive command. Its movements were also hampered by the sodden ground underfoot, making it vulnerable to the disciplined and relentless volleys of arrows shot from the English longbows. Panic rapidly spread among the French ranks as they tried to turn on their heels but were bogged down in the mire. They became easy prey for Henry's archers, who joined in the hand-to-hand fighting once their arrows had run out.

Within a matter of hours, Henry V and his men had won one of the most celebrated victories in English history. Around six thousand French soldiers were killed, ten times the number of English casualties. The unexpected victory boosted morale and prestige among Henry V's army and started a new period of English dominance in the war against France. It also made the king's subjects more willing to fund future expeditions and, crucially, bolstered his fledgling Lancastrian dynasty.

The triumphant king and his men returned home shortly afterwards and received a heroes' welcome in London on 23 November. Here was a king who knew how to appeal to popular opinion. The city had provided a major financial contribution to his French campaign, so he made sure that it was fully involved in the victory celebrations. Even Parliament was swept up in the mood of rejoicing and awarded Henry duties on wine imports for life, together with a number of other taxes. He had only been king for just over two and a half years, but already it was clear that England was his to command.

The king made the most of the time that he spent in his native kingdom. As well as working hard to maintain peace and dispense justice throughout England, he also established his court as a centre of learning and culture. Henry himself had benefited from a sound education and was fluent in both French and Latin. More significantly, though, he followed Edward III's example by encouraging the establishment of English as the language of court – and, in time, the kingdom. 'Our mother tongue, to wit, the English tongue, hath in modern days begun to be honourably enlarged and adorned', noted the London Company of Brewers with obvious approval.[4] The general acceptance of a 'King's English' during his reign would be one of Henry V's most enduring legacies.

Almost exactly a year after Agincourt, King Henry was granted a double subsidy by Parliament to launch a fresh campaign against France. Attempts to persuade Charles and his sons to grant him the lands to which he laid claim had failed, so Henry resolved upon taking them by force. In August 1417, he landed with an army of 10,500 men close to the town of Harfleur, which was still in English hands after its conquest two years earlier. But in the intervening period, other coastal towns had built walls to defend themselves in case Henry should return. Among them was Caen, the second-largest town in Normandy, where Henry's ancestor William the Conqueror lay buried. The English king advanced there at once and it fell to his siege on 4 September, giving him another vital foothold in the duchy. The king then made good use of the winter months by dispatching his able commanders to take other towns nearby.

In July 1418, Henry resumed the leadership of his army and captured Rouen, the capital of Normandy, which became his base for the remainder of the campaign. It would be the largest city taken by siege throughout the entire Hundred Years War, and following its surrender the rest of upper Normandy submitted to the English king's authority. But an even greater prize lay within his grasp. The following year, he dispatched troops towards Paris. They succeeded in capturing Pontoise, a strategically important town that lay on the road from Rouen to Paris. A few days later, Thomas, Duke of Clarence, the eldest of the king's brothers, went to reconnoitre the gates of Paris itself. Events moved even more decisively in Henry's favour on 10 September 1419, when, probably on the orders of the dauphin Charles, John the Fearless, Duke of Burgundy, was struck in the face with an axe, killing him instantly. A century later, a Carthusian monk showed the French king, Francis I, the skull and quipped: 'This is the hole through which the English entered France.'[5]

Whereas Duke John had tended to play the English and French kings off against each other, his successor, Philip the Good, openly favoured Henry, who was quick to take advantage. In December 1419, Philip declared himself ready to accept a truce between England and France, whereby Henry would be recognised as heir to the French throne after Charles VI's death. Several months of negotiations followed until, on 21 May 1420, the Treaty of Troyes was formally sealed. By its terms, Henry was to marry Catherine of Valois and be recognised as heir to the French throne, followed by 'his heirs forever'.[6] In the meantime, Henry would act as regent for the ailing Charles, aided by a council of French officials. His marriage to the French king's daughter was solemnised on 2 June.

But while the King of France had agreed to the treaty, the dauphin had not. The fact that he had considerable support motivated Henry to crush any resistance before it could take hold. Just two days after his wedding, he set out with his ally the Duke of Burgundy to capture a number of well-fortified towns on the upper reaches of the Seine that were under the dauphin's control. He arrived back in Paris on 1 December amid great popular rejoicing. The terms of the Troyes agreement were ratified a week later. This time, Henry made sure of his inheritance by having the dauphin's claim to the French throne invalidated because of the part he had played in the late Duke of Burgundy's murder.

Henry proved as active a monarch in France as he was in England, and his influence on its government was profound. He held councils, made appointments to the church and the military, and issued royal letters in his name as heir. After celebrating Christmas 1420 in Paris with the eyes of his prospective new kingdom upon him, Henry embarked for England with his wife Catherine, leaving his brother Thomas, Duke of Clarence, to manage affairs in France. It had been three and a half years since he had last set foot on English soil, but thanks to the effective government he had established there – not to mention his heroic status as the conqueror of France – he returned to a settled and loyal domain. The new queen was greeted with no less adulation, and she was crowned at Westminster in late February 1421. Shortly afterwards, the royal couple embarked upon tours of the kingdom and were greeted with rejoicing wherever they went.

The English Parliament had acknowledged that their king would 'sometimes be on this side of the sea and sometimes on the other.'[7] While Henry's English subjects gloried in his dominance over France, there was some disquiet about the amount of time he spent there. The machinery of government was effective enough to allow for an absentee king, but Henry insisted that all matters were referred to him for approval, which caused frustrating delays and resentment – as did the fact that even during his brief sojourns in England, he tended to be preoccupied with French affairs.

Not long after returning to London, grave news arrived from France. Henry's brother Thomas had been killed in an attack by a Franco-Scottish force. It was a stark reminder of how much England's success in France depended upon the king's presence. In June 1421, he set sail across the Channel once more. After rendezvousing with his army in Calais, he journeyed south to Paris, then toured parts of the Loire, in part to show himself to his future subjects, but also to look out for any threats to his authority. Determined to root out any remaining support for the dauphin, in October he laid siege to the fortified town of Meaux, thirty miles east of the capital. After seven long and gruelling months for the English forces, Meaux finally capitulated.

It had been a hard-won victory. The appalling conditions had taken their toll on Henry's army, which was weakened by sickness and declining morale. The long siege had also depleted the English king's financial resources, making him all too well aware of the huge cost involved in upholding the Treaty of Troyes. The arrival of his queen in May 1422 brought him a measure of comfort. She had given birth to a son, Henry, the previous December, but had left the baby in England for his safety. Her husband would never meet him.

By the time of Catherine's arrival, the king was already showing signs of illness. He may have been suffering from dysentery or fluid loss. By 26 August, his symptoms were so severe that he added a codicil to his will. He left the guardianship of his infant son to his brother Humphrey, Duke of Gloucester, who was also to take charge of the kingdom as a whole, although the vague definition of his powers would lead to trouble. The personal care of Prince Henry was assigned to the king's illegitimate uncle, Thomas Beaufort, Duke of Exeter. Meanwhile, Philip of Burgundy was given first refusal to manage Henry's French inheritance until his son came of age, and if he declined this he was to be assigned to Henry's brother John, Duke of Bedford.

'If death had come to Henry V armed in the manner of a soldier, I believe Henry would have been the victor', opined a contemporary Augustinian canon.[8] On 31 August, a little over two weeks before his thirty-sixth birthday, Henry breathed his last in the royal castle at Vincennes, near Paris. His widow Catherine accompanied his body on its long journey back to London, where he was buried 'with great solemnity' at Westminster Abbey on 7 November.[9]

The king was greatly mourned by people at all levels of society and on both sides of the Channel his subjects were 'unspeakably distressed', as Thomas Walsingham observed. They admired and respected his integrity and decisiveness, his love of order and justice, and his refusal to show favouritism towards anyone. The fact that there had been very little change of personnel among his closest advisers and courtiers speaks volumes: he had been a man who aroused great loyalty. Even his enemies had admired his honour and chivalry, and his ability to stay calm at times of crisis. He had been one of England's busiest kings – 'magnificent in action', as Walsingham put it – and had been as assiduous in the business of government as he had the pursuit of military glory.[10] His clarity of vision and his strong, capable leadership had inspired courtiers, armies and kingdoms to follow him.

In short, Henry V had encapsulated all of the qualities that made both a great man and a great monarch. Shakespeare's portrayal of an archetypal hero, immortalised in the 1940s by Laurence Olivier and, later, Kenneth Branagh, has rarely been contradicted. His fifteenth-century biographer hailed him as 'the mighty and puissant conqueror', and even modern historians agree that Henry V was 'the greatest man that ever ruled England'.[11] But his example also highlighted a recurrent theme in the history of the British monarchy: strong kings might create strong kingdoms, but they could not guarantee their survival.

Henry VI (1422–61 and 1470–1)

'Utterly devoid of wit or spirit'

Henry V would have been a hard act to follow for any man, no matter how well versed in the art of kingship. For an eight-month-old baby, it was impossible. Moreover, upon the death of the father he had never known, the infant Henry became king not only of England, but also of France. It was an inheritance that his father had spent most of his reign fighting for, but that his son would prove entirely incapable of fulfilling.

Henry VI was the youngest monarch ever to ascend the English throne and the prospect of a long minority was an ominous one. Previous examples from England's royal history hardly instilled confidence among the new king's subjects. But it is a testament to the loyalty and unity his father had inspired that the Lancastrian dynasty was strong enough to weather the storm. It also helped that Henry V had made detailed provisions for the governance of his realm.

At least initially, the new king's mother, Catherine of Valois, played an active part in affairs and stayed close to her infant son, who lived with her throughout the first decade of his life. There is a touching description of her holding Henry in her arms when he attended his first Parliament in 1423. For much of his childhood, the young king was surrounded by members of Henry V's former establishment, all of whom sought to instil the same qualities in him that had been so admired in his father. He received an excellent education in 'good manners, letters and languages', and every quality expected of a virtuous Christian prince.[1] The contemporary sources give no hint that he was anything other than a contented, healthy child who would one day grow into a king of whom his father would have been proud.

But in the year 1429, this cosseted existence came to an abrupt end. Although Henry VI's uncle, Bedford, had achieved a number of victories in France, the heroic actions of a young French woman known as Joan of Arc had inspired the French forces and sparked a revival in the fortunes of the young king, Charles VII. Joan, a farmer's daughter from Domrémy in Lorraine, claimed to have seen heavenly visions instructing her to support Charles VII and recover France from English domination. In late 1429, when she was only about seventeen years old, she took part in the siege of Orléans. This resulted in the first major victory for France since the humiliation of Agincourt and earned Joan the nickname 'Maid of Orléans'.

Charles VII's coronation at Rheims on 29 July 1429 flouted the Treaty of Troyes and could not be ignored. Plans began at once for the English king to make his first visit there so that he could be crowned in Charles's stead. But first, he had to be crowned in England. This was arranged with some haste at Westminster on 5 November, when Henry was just shy of his eighth birthday. To push home the point that he was king of two realms, much of the French coronation service was incorporated into the English. It was more than just a symbolic moment: the king was vested with the powers of kingship that had been exercised in his name since his father's death seven years before. Even though others would continue to rule for him, this marked the formal end of his protectorate.

Young though he was, Henry seems to have understood the significance of the occasion. He reportedly looked around 'sadly and wisely' as the crown was placed on his head – a crown that would weigh no less heavily upon him as he grew to maturity.[2] His mother was seated close by, for reassurance, but her stabilising influence, upon which he had come to rely, was soon to be withdrawn. At around the same time as her son's coronation, Catherine began a relationship with a Welsh squire named Owen Tudor, who was far beneath her in status. This was in spite of a recent statute governing the future marriage of a queen dowager, which had been introduced after Catherine's liaison with Edmund Beaufort, Count of Mortain. By 1430, the king had moved to a separate residence from his mother and her influence waned considerably thereafter.

Plans for Henry VI's coronation in France now began in earnest. In April 1430, he crossed the Channel with an impressive entourage of courtiers and soldiers. The predominance of French forces in the

Seine Valley made his progress to Rouen much slower than anticipated, and it was late July by the time he finally took up residence
in that city. Meanwhile, the Duke of Bedford had used his nephew's
coronation at Westminster, and the dual monarchy that it had emphasised, to reassert his position in France. He launched a campaign
aimed at blackening Joan of Arc's character. She had been captured
during an attack on the forces of England's ally, Burgundy, close to
the town of Compiègne in northern France. She was subsequently
handed over to the English commanders, Bedford among them, and
put on trial for the dubious charges of heresy and cross-dressing –
the latter thanks to her having donned soldier's clothing when
fighting for France. The legality of the trial has since been called
into question, but Joan was found guilty and condemned to death
by burning. The horrific sentence was carried out at Rouen on 30
May 1431.

At the end of that year, Bedford's ten-year-old nephew, Henry VI,
made the journey to Paris and was crowned in Nôtre-Dame Cathedral
on 16 December. The occasion was marred when a group of Parisians
invaded the coronation banquet. The failure of the young king 'Henri
II' to distribute the expected largesse worsened the already tense
atmosphere. With undignified but necessary haste, Henry and his
entourage returned to Rouen and set sail for England in February
1432. It had been his first and last visit to France.

In the same year that Henry VI succeeded to his French inheritance,
his tutor and governor Richard Beauchamp, Earl of Warwick, noted
that he was 'grown in years, in stature, of his person and also in
conceit and knowledge of his high and royal authority and estate'.[3]
This hints that the young king was beginning to assert his independence and was less easily directed by those around him, which did
not go down well with the officials who had grown used to
controlling him. In November 1434, Henry's councillors told him
that despite 'great understanding and feeling, as ever they saw or
knew in any Prince, or other person of his age', he was still too
inexperienced to rule without them. They also urged him not to
appoint any officials of his own choosing or to change the direction
of policy without consulting them.[4]

Even though Henry VI was now approaching the age when, according to royal tradition in both England and France, kings began to shoulder their full responsibilities, the glimpses we have of him in the contemporary sources suggest that he was in many respects still hopelessly naïve. When his powerful uncles, Bedford and Gloucester, quarrelled over how to assert England's position in France, the young king begged them to settle their differences and be friends. Likewise, when in the summer of 1435 news arrived that England's vital ally, the Duke of Burgundy, had defected to Charles VII, destroying all hopes of reclaiming English sovereignty in France, the thirteen-year-old Henry burst into tears.

Subsequent events caused the young king to feel increasingly isolated. The Duke of Bedford died in September 1435, and the following May, the Earl of Warwick resigned as his guardian. The king's mother had been a distant figure ever since her marriage to Owen Tudor, by whom she had four children, but her death in January 1437 heightened Henry's sense of loneliness.[5] The vacuum was soon filled by his domineering uncle, Humphrey, Duke of Gloucester, and his great-uncle, Cardinal Beaufort, who sought to control the king in public and private. Henry was little more than a bone being fought over by two vicious dogs, which intensified his naturally fearful nature. Pope Pius II, who was kept closely informed of affairs in England, later remarked that Henry was 'more timorous than a woman, utterly devoid of wit or spirit'.[6]

But Henry did have some positive qualities. Contemporaries in both England and France described him as personable, dignified and well mannered. They also praised his intellect, which was advanced for his age. As his earlier flash of independence showed, he was not entirely content to rely upon others. His minority ended in around 1435, when he was fourteen years old – younger than any other King of England since 1066. In October that year, he attended his first council meeting, and during the following year he made a number of appointments and grants in his own name. When he reached the age of sixteen, Henry began to play a more consistently active role in government, as evidenced by his personal authorisation of warrants.

In November 1437, the king took part in a crown-wearing ceremony. These ceremonies more than doubled during his reign, as his hold on the throne grew more precarious. He also embraced the practice of touching for the 'King's Evil'. This special ceremony had been devised by the eleventh-century king Edward the Confessor. The monarch would sit enthroned while a procession of his scrofulous subjects knelt before him to receive the royal touch on the diseased area. Henry performed each ceremony with great aplomb. 'Those who witness these deeds are strengthened in their loyalty to the king', remarked one eyewitness, 'and this monarch's undoubted title to the throne is thus confirmed by divine approval.'[7]

In 1440, Henry began planning another expression of his royal authority, as well as of his passion for learning: the building of Eton College in Windsor and King's College in Cambridge. Eton was to provide free education for seventy poor boys, who would then go on to King's College. Henry's boast that Eton was 'the lady mother and mistress of all other grammar schools' was justified: no other King of England had endowed a public grammar school of such a size.[8]

Eton's foundation charter of 11 October 1440 suggests that Henry saw this as a means of making his mark as king and of expressing his already intense piety. Prudery as well as piety incited the king to make strenuous efforts to shield the pupils of Eton from the corrupting influence of courtiers in the nearby Windsor Castle. When one of his nobles brought some scantily clad ladies to dance before the king at his Christmas court, Henry averted his eyes before storming out of the chamber. He could not abide bad language and 'restrained many . . . from hard swearing either by mild abomination or harsh reproof'.[9]

While Henry enjoyed the trappings of kingship, he showed little interest in its practical application. In matters of government and politics, he continued to rely heavily upon others for advice – Gloucester and Beaufort in particular. The latter's influence had been steadily increasing during the previous few years, thanks in no small part to his rival's absences across the Channel, where he succeeded in defending Calais. The Cardinal had long been in favour of peace with France, and his great-nephew came to share that view. It seems to have been the king's own decision in 1440 to release from the

Tower Charles, Duke d'Orléans, the highest-ranking prisoner captured by his father at Agincourt. This sparked the fury of his uncle Gloucester, who stormed out of Westminster Abbey when Orléans took an oath promising to adhere to the terms of his release.

Allowing his father's prisoner to walk free may have been a placatory measure, but at the time Henry had no intention of surrendering his English lands or of relinquishing his title of King of France, even though it held little meaning. He soon came to realise, though, that he lacked the resources to consolidate his rule in northern France and Gascony. He therefore resorted to the more pragmatic step of marrying a princess of French royal blood in order to cement a more lasting peace between the two countries. In 1444, he was betrothed to Margaret, daughter of the Duke of Anjou and niece of the French queen.

Henry's representative on that occasion was William de la Pole, Duke of Suffolk. Suffolk had a distinguished record of military service under Henry V, but his ambitions lay in the political sphere. Following his appointment as steward of the king's household, his influence over the young king grew rapidly. By the mid-1440s, he was Henry's most intimate and favoured adviser, with authority that stretched beyond the royal household into a host of government departments. In June 1444, Suffolk secured the wardship and marriage of Margaret Beaufort, the richest heiress in the kingdom. She was also of royal blood, being the great-granddaughter of John of Gaunt by his mistress Katherine Swynford.

The deaths of Henry's powerful uncle, Gloucester, and his greatuncle, Cardinal Beaufort, in 1447, left Suffolk with no effective rival at court. It was not long before the duke began to abuse his position, conveying titles and offices on his circle of associates, all of whom became subject to as much resentment as Suffolk himself. Yet the king himself seemed blind to his failings. Over-reliance upon favourites was a mistake that several of his predecessors had made, with disastrous results. But it was one that Henry seemed destined to repeat.

Thanks in no small part to Suffolk's abuses, the size and cost of the royal household rose sharply during the 1440s. As well as accommodating his close friends and their associates, Henry also extended his largesse towards his two half-brothers, Edmund and Jasper Tudor, the sons of his mother's second marriage, in whose welfare he had begun to take a particular interest. By 1445, it was deemed necessary to limit the number of attendants to four hundred and twenty for fear that there would not be enough left in the royal coffers for the new queen's establishment. Repairs were subsequently undertaken at the king's favourite palaces of Westminster and Windsor, along with some Thames-side manor houses he liked to stay in, so that they would be fit for his new wife. But all of this came at considerable expense.

In the spring of 1445, Margaret of Anjou arrived in England. She and Henry were married at Titchfield Abbey in Hampshire on 22 April. The following month, she made her ceremonial entry into London and was crowned at Westminster Abbey. The symbolism was carefully designed to convey the diplomatic advantages of the marriage: the new queen was portrayed as the dove of concord in the accompanying pageants. But while Henry V's marriage to a French princess had sealed England's victory over France, his son's was a different matter entirely. There was widespread suspicion about the concessions that Henry VI's agents had made in order to secure the match, with many believing that much of England's French territory would soon be surrendered to Charles VII.

On a personal level, the marriage appeared more of a success. Henry referred to Margaret as his 'amiable wife', and they spent a great deal of time in each other's company.[10] Margaret, described by others as 'a great and strong laboured woman', also took an active interest in her husband's affairs.[11] She founded a Cambridge college close to his, appropriately named Queens'.[12] Many of her attendants were the same as those who served in the king's household, which made it easy for the queen to become closely acquainted with her husband's business. Her obvious energy and enthusiasm for state affairs contrasted with the king's *laissez-faire* approach.

Henry's lack of interest in his kingly responsibilities was most painfully evident in military matters. In stark contrast to his illustrious father, he was the first English king never to command an army against an external enemy. Not having set foot on French soil after his coronation there in 1432, he made half-hearted plans to visit in the mid-1440s for peace talks with Charles VII, but they came to nothing. He never went on campaign to Scotland or visited Ireland, and his only recorded journey to Wales as king was in 1452, when he ventured just over the English border to Monmouth. Only in the trappings of the military life did Henry show an interest and he regularly attended the Garter festivities at Windsor on St George's Day.

In May 1449, hostilities with France resumed. Within a few months, the English garrison at Rouen had been crushed and Henry's Norman inheritance lost. Meanwhile, the French took advantage of Henry's woefully inadequate naval resources by raiding a series of English coastal towns. To make matters worse, the Duke of Burgundy acted against England's cloth trade with the Low Countries, cutting off a vital supply of income for Henry.

Events now spiralled rapidly out of control. In January 1450 Parliament issued orders for Suffolk to be sent to the Tower on suspicion of exploiting his favour with the king to impoverish the crown and plot Henry's death. Anxious to protect his favourite, the king banished him from the kingdom before any trial could take place, but Suffolk was captured while boarding a ship and executed on 2 May.

Opposition within government soon spilled out into the kingdom as a whole and Henry's subjects gave vent to the frustrations they had been harbouring for many years. In the summer of 1450, an Irishman named John (or Jack) Cade led a rebellion in Kent. The proclaimed grievances made clear how little respect the king had left. 'We say our sovereign lord . . . has lost his law, his merchandise is lost, his common people is destroyed, the sea is lost, France is lost, the king himself is so set that he may not pay for his meat nor drink, and he owes more than ever any King of England ought.'[13] Significantly, Cade took the name John Mortimer in order to identify himself with the family of the king's rival, Richard, Duke of York. By the time Cade reached London, he had amassed a considerable army of support. It would be the largest popular uprising of the century.

Henry's mishandling of the crisis betrayed the extent of his naivety, as well as his lack of judgement. Rather than listening to the rebels' petitions and offering terms, he immediately responded with force.

But many of his troops sympathised with the rebels and began to mutiny. Then, at the worst possible moment, the king's defeated soldiers returned from Normandy, reminding both the rebels and the royal forces of Henry's ineptitude. Realising that he was failing to bring the situation under control, the king retreated to the Midlands, which allowed the rebels to take over the capital. Total disaster was only averted thanks to the actions of the queen, who offered a general pardon to the rebels if they agreed to disperse. Jack Cade was subsequently captured and executed, and the king – still intent upon brutality – embarked upon a tour of the most disaffected areas, gathering 'a harvest of heads'.[14]

The situation was inflamed again in September by the return of Richard, Duke of York, from service in France. The duke was regarded by some as Henry's rightful successor. His grandfather, Edmund, was the fourth surviving son of Edward III and the founder of the York dynasty, while his three-times great-grandfather on his mother's side was Lionel, second surviving son of Edward III. Richard had inherited vast estates and had served the crown in both Ireland and France. But in the wake of Cade's revolt, his political ambitions centred upon England, where he saw the chance to capitalise upon the king's weakness.

Henry was not inclined to acknowledge York as his heir, preferring John of Gaunt's grandson Edmund Beaufort, second Duke of Somerset (formerly his late mother's lover), whose family he had long favoured. This pushed York even further into opposition. Following his return to England, he took the stance of a reformer who sought better government and the punishment of the 'traitors' who had lost Normandy. In so doing, he garnered considerable support and presented an increasingly appealing alternative to a king who was rapidly losing the love – and loyalty – of his subjects.

Relations between the king and York reached a nadir in early 1452 when the duke led a body of men to London with the aim of forcing Henry to recognise him as heir. But he arrived to find the gates barred against him on the king's orders and had no choice but to agree never to rebel against his sovereign again. Meanwhile, the king bolstered his dynastic position by conferring earldoms upon his two half-brothers, Edmund and Jasper Tudor, and giving them the wardship of Margaret Beaufort. This signified his hope that the Beaufort line would be intertwined with his own, thus strengthening the Duke of Somerset's position as successor-in-waiting.

But shortly afterwards, a dramatic and wholly unexpected event turned the tide in York's favour again. In August 1453, the king suffered a complete mental and physical collapse. This may have been prompted by news of England's defeat at the Battle of Castillon, which resulted in the loss of almost all its holding in France, notably Aquitaine, which had been held by the English crown for three centuries. The battle is traditionally seen as the end of the Hundred Years' War. It was a bitter blow to a king who was already feeling embattled on all sides. Henry's attendants were alarmed by the severity of his symptoms, observing that it seemed as if he had 'no natural sense nor reasoning power'.[15] He completely withdrew into himself and neither recognised nor responded to anyone. The king's illness has been variously ascribed to catatonic schizophrenia and a depressive stupor. Whatever the cause, no English monarch since 1066 had suffered such a debilitating breakdown. For almost a year and a half, Henry remained in seclusion at Windsor, attended day and night by a team of servants who fed and clothed him, and helped move him from room to room.

The king's collapse threw his dynasty into uncertainty. He had not formally named his heir and had no children of his own. The only glimmer of hope was that his wife Margaret was pregnant. Two months after her husband's breakdown, she gave birth to a son, Edward. When the child was presented to the king at the beginning of the following year, he showed no sign of joy or understanding. One eyewitness described how 'once he looked on the Prince and cast down his eyes again, without any more'.[16]

Although the dynastic crisis had been averted, more pressing was the need to decide who should rule in the king's absence. Somerset and York were engaged in a bitter struggle for power when another candidate staked her claim: Queen Margaret. Parliament met to decide the issue and it was York who emerged triumphant. He was appointed protector and defender of the king and realm for as long as Henry remained incapacitated. He wasted no time in having his rival, Somerset, imprisoned without charge.

Bitterly resentful at having been passed over, and deeply distrustful of York, the queen kept a close eye on his activities during the next few months. The rivalry between them would grow ever more intense during the years ahead, their struggle for the crown tearing England apart. But for now, the situation was resolved by the recovery of the king at Christmas 1454 – as sudden and unexpected as whatever had caused his illness. His suffering had evidently courted a great deal of sympathy because there was widespread rejoicing. 'Blessed be God, the King is well amended', reported a correspondent of John Paston on 9 January 1455.[17] This time, Henry was full of joy when his wife presented their infant son to him.

The king's return left York out in the cold and made him vulnerable to the machinations of his enemies at court. But now that the duke had tasted power, he wanted more. Gathering his supporters around him – prominent among whom were the powerful Neville family – he resolved to take the crown by force. On 22 May 1455, his army clashed with the royal forces at St Albans. The ensuing battle traditionally marks the beginning of what later became known as the Wars of the Roses, a prolonged and bloody tussle for the throne between the houses of Lancaster and York, symbolised by a red and white rose respectively. It resulted in a resounding defeat for the king, who was left undefended beneath his banner and wounded in the neck. The Duke of York's chief rival Somerset was killed, along with other Lancastrians such as the Earl of Northumberland, a member of the king's own household.

Still maintaining a pretence at loyalty, York and his Neville allies presented themselves before the king on bended knee. The duke's objective was to assume the role of chief councillor to Henry, but after everything that had passed, this did not make for a comfortable situation. Nevertheless, the two men did their best to disguise their mutual hostility. They entered London together shortly after the battle and York formally made his peace with the king. The crown-wearing held at St Paul's Cathedral on 25 May was heavy with symbolism as Henry received the crown from the duke's hands.

If the king was prepared to accept the duke's supremacy, his wife and her supporters were not. During the six months that York held the reins of power, Margaret schemed to undermine him.[18] She made sure that her husband acknowledged their son Edward as his uncontested heir and garnered support from several influential nobles whom York had alienated. By February 1456, the duke's position had become untenable and he resigned the protectorship. But with the king's health still uncertain and his dynasty dependent upon a one-year-old child, his rival's departure did little to stabilise the situation.

To compound matters, during the second half of the 1450s, Henry and his family spent an increasing amount of time away from London, in the Midlands. Judging from the rarity of his signature on warrants and other official documents during this time, he played only the most passive role in governmental affairs. When he did raise his head above the parapet, it was for ceremonial matters, such as attending tournaments, visiting his foundations at Eton and King's, and going to Westminster Abbey to discuss designs for his tomb. On these rare public appearances, eyewitnesses noted that he was so docile and disengaged that he seemed simple. If Henry was not interested in exercising power, his wife Margaret was determined to do it for him. She dictated most of his actions and it was even rumoured that she urged him to abdicate in favour of their son Edward.

In 1459 York and his followers gathered at Ludlow, where they faced the royal army. But most of the Yorkist nobles were reluctant to bear arms against Henry: he may have been incompetent, but he was the anointed king. When part of the Yorkist army defected to the king's side, its leaders deserted their troops and fled overseas. By now, the queen was deeply embittered against York and his supporters. Rather than make conciliatory moves to bring them back on side, she pursued them relentlessly, insisting that they face charges for disloyalty. At the Parliament of November 1459, she had her wish when the Yorkist leaders were attainted.

Capturing them was another matter. York had established a base in Ireland, and a body of his closest allies, including his son Edward, Earl of March, and Richard Neville, Earl of Warwick, had fled to Calais. In the summer of 1460, these allies returned with an army and confronted the royal forces at Northampton. In the ensuing battle, the king was captured and many of his troops either deserted or were killed. Although the Yorkist victors stopped short of deposing Henry, they took him to London and installed him in the bishop's palace. It was obvious to everyone that he was their prisoner. The shock was too much for Henry's fragile mental state and he suffered another collapse.

At the October Parliament, the Duke of York claimed the throne and ordered that the customary crown-wearing on St Edward's Day (13 October) be cancelled. But there was still reluctance among its members to depose an anointed king, so at the end of the month, Henry was finally brought out in public and made to acknowledge York as his heir, disinheriting his own son Edward. York declared that after Richard II's death the crown should have belonged to Edmund Mortimer (his own uncle), and therefore all three Lancastrian kings had reigned unlawfully. He concluded that Henry IV had 'usurped and intruded upon the royal power'.[19] It is significant that from this time, York began to style himself Richard Plantagenet, emphasising his descent from the true royal line, rather than the usurping Lancastrians.

York did not enjoy his pre-eminence for long. Queen Margaret began rallying support in Wales and Scotland, accompanied by her seven-year-old son to emphasise that he, not the Yorkists, was the rightful heir to the throne. On 30 December 1460, her Lancastrian forces, led by York's fiercest enemy, Henry Beaufort, third Duke of Somerset, son of the second duke who had been killed at St Albans five years before, crushed the Yorkists at Wakefield in Yorkshire. York was slain in the battle and his second son, Edmund, was captured and executed.

It was a decisive victory, giving Margaret the chance to march on London and recover possession of her husband. But when she and her army reached St Alban's, the Earl of Warwick and his Yorkist troops barred their way. He had brought Henry VI with him, and the captive king allegedly spent the ensuing battle sheltering under a tree a mile or so away. When the queen's forces triumphed once more, her husband was so overjoyed that he knighted their son on the spot.

But the Yorkist cause was far from over. Following the defeat at Wakefield, York's eighteen-year-old son and heir, Edward, Earl of

March, had routed a Lancastrian army led by the king's half-brother, Jasper Tudor, and his father Owen, at Mortimer's Cross, close to the Welsh border. Edward was an exceptional warrior, having been trained in warfare from a young age, and was already a force to be reckoned with.

Meanwhile, Margaret and her army had failed to enter the capital. Their reputation for pillage had caused the Londoners to bar the gates, so the queen and her husband had been obliged to retreat north to Dunstable with a rapidly dwindling force. London proved much more welcoming to Edward, Earl of March, when he arrived fresh from his victory at Mortimer's Cross. He promptly declared Henry VI unfit to rule and had himself crowned Edward IV on 4 March 1461.

Edward IV (1461–70 and 1471–83)

'For his pleasure and magnificence'

THE CROWN HAD changed hands so swiftly over the preceding few months that Edward IV knew he had to do more than just go through the ceremonial aspects of kingship. Within a matter of days, he had mobilised his forces once more and marched north to confront the Lancastrian army at York, where the ousted King Henry VI, Margaret and their son Edward were waiting. On 29 March, the two sides met near the village of Towton, fourteen miles south-west of York. A large and bloody battle ensued. Some sources claim that as many as 50,000 soldiers were engaged in the long and exhausting hand-to-hand combat, the snow swirling around them as they fought to the death. The majority were Lancastrians, but thanks to Edward's leadership and the timely arrival of additional forces, it was the Yorkists who won the day. The fact that the battle had taken place on Palm Sunday, one of the most important dates in the religious calendar, seemed to indicate God's blessing upon England's new king.

In the wake of the battle, the defeated king and his family fled to Scotland, where the queen regent, Mary of Guelders, pledged her support. Henry himself seems to have accompanied some Lancastrian raids in northern England during the next two years. But an Anglo-Scottish truce signed in December 1463 deprived the fallen king of his allies. Eighteen months later, he was captured in Lancashire by the Yorkists and taken to the Tower, where he remained for the next five years. Meanwhile, Edward IV consolidated his victory by stripping the Lancastrians of their lands, titles and wealth. In the years following Towton, no fewer than one hundred and thirteen Acts of Attainder were passed against those who had opposed the king.

* * *

Even though he was the principal beneficiary of the Lancastrian spoils, the 'kingmaker' Earl of Warwick, a cousin of the king on his mother's side, soon began to cause trouble. The source of his grievance was the king's new wife, the beautiful widow Elizabeth Grey (née Woodville), whom Edward married in May 1464. The story goes that the young king, who 'thought upon nothing but women and that more than reason would', had been infatuated upon first setting eyes on Elizabeth as she had waited by the roadside to petition him for the return of her late husband's lands.[1] Elizabeth refused to be his mistress, so he took her as his wife.

Aware that his ambassadors were trying to secure him a French bride as part of an alliance with Louis XI, Edward initially kept the marriage a secret. When he finally broke the news to his council in September, it created both a scandal and a serious division between the king and his most powerful ally, the Earl of Warwick. Warwick's hostility towards the new queen was deepened by Edward's enthusiasm for marrying her large family into the royal circle. Within the space of two years, he found aristocratic husbands for five of Elizabeth's sisters. He also proved generous with titles and offices for the men in her family. Such was the Woodvilles' power that rumours began to spread that Edward had been bewitched by his wife's mother, Jacquetta de Luxembourg.

Gradually, Warwick began to build up his power base. This included an alliance with the king's own brother, George, Duke of Clarence, who also resented the influence of the queen and her family. To seal their pact, Clarence married Warwick's daughter, Isabel. In May 1470, both men set sail for France, where Margaret of Anjou and her son had taken refuge at the court of Louis XI, who had pledged to support her in restoring her husband to the throne. That autumn, Warwick led an invasion force that succeeded in overthrowing Edward, who fled abroad, and releasing Henry VI from captivity.

Now in his fiftieth year, the restored King Henry VI presented a pitiful figure. When he appeared in public, eyewitnesses were shocked that he was 'not worshipfully arrayed as a prince, and not so cleanly kept as should seem such a prince'.[2] When it came to monarchy, such things mattered. At around the same time as Henry's restoration, the influential lawyer, Sir John Fortescue, penned the political treatise, *The Governance of England*, in which he set out the principles of kingship. One of the most important was that a monarch should not stint upon fine clothes and furnishings: 'It shall need that the king have such treasure, as he may make new buildings when he will, for his pleasure and magnificence; and as he may buy him rich clothes, rich furs . . . convenient to his estate royal.'[3]

During the nine years that he had occupied the throne, Edward IV had fully embraced the concept that magnificence was synonymous with power. A visitor to his court in 1466 remarked that the English king had 'the most splendid Court that could be found in all Christendom'.[4] By contrast, after his release Henry VI lived 'in great poverty' as if he was still a prisoner, and refused to maintain a lavish household.[5] In other ways, too, Henry fell short of what was expected of a king. His subjects knew that it was his wife Margaret and Warwick who wielded power on his behalf, which hardly inspired either respect or loyalty.

Realising that support for the restored Lancastrian king was at a low ebb, in March 1471 Edward of York returned from exile in Flanders. His brother Clarence, having broken with Warwick, was by his side and together they advanced towards London. Edward had always enjoyed popular support in the capital, and it was with apparent ease that he took possession of the king and returned him to the Tower. Two days later, he forced Henry to accompany him to Barnet, north of the city, where a Lancastrian army had gathered. In the ensuing battle, the Earl of Warwick was killed, robbing the Lancastrians of their most powerful supporter.

Still, Edward could not sit securely on his throne. He might have had the Lancastrian king under lock and key, but Henry's wife and son remained at large. On the very same day that Edward defeated Warwick at Barnet, Margaret and her son had landed at Weymouth and headed towards Wales, gathering a large force as they went. Edward's army intercepted them at Tewkesbury on 4 May, when the indomitable Margaret led her Lancastrian troops in battle. Her son Edward, then seventeen, was killed either during the encounter or shortly afterwards. For years, the queen had fought relentlessly, often ruthlessly, to safeguard her husband's throne, but the death of their only child broke her spirit. She was taken captive after the battle and joined her husband in the Tower.

With Warwick dead and the former king and queen his prisoners, Edward IV appeared to have vanquished his Lancastrian rivals once and for all. But by now he had come to the conclusion that no matter how enfeebled Henry was, for as long as he drew breath there was always the danger that his supporters would try to restore him to the throne once more. On 21 May, just hours after Edward's return from Tewkesbury, Henry died in the Tower. Although the Yorkists claimed that the former king had expired from 'pure displeasure and melancholy', few believed them.[6] There can be little doubt that Henry had been murdered at Edward's orders. It is significant that he had been in the close keeping of the king's brother, Richard, Duke of Gloucester.

To erase all doubt that Henry was dead, the following evening his body was taken to St Paul's and displayed 'open visage, that he might be known'.[7] The manner of Henry's death ensured that he was vener-ated as a martyr and miracles were soon associated with his name. In an attempt to suppress these, Edward IV had the late king's statue removed from the rood screen of York Minster. But his veneration continued and would reach new heights during the reign of his half-nephew, the first Tudor King of England.

Even Henry VI's illustrious Tudor successors would not have pretended that he should be remembered for his kingship, though. His thirty-nine-year reign was the third longest since the Norman Conquest, but it had also been one of the most turbulent. The lustre of his father's glorious military monarchy had quickly faded and by the time of Henry VI's death, almost all of the English territories across the Channel had been lost. Worse still, England itself had suffered sixteen years of bloody civil war. The crown had been so dangerously destabilised as a result that even the advent of a strong king like Edward IV was not enough to secure its future.

After reclaiming his throne in 1471, the Yorkist king seemed intent upon settling old differences by diplomacy rather than the sword. Although he deprived many Lancastrian nobles of their lands and riches, he made them welcome at court and offered them positions of influence. Dominic Mancini, an Italian visitor to Edward IV's court, described the king's charismatic appeal:

> I have many times seen our neighbours here when they were summoned before the King. When they went, they looked as though they were going to the gallows. When they returned they were in high spirits . . . he had welcomed them as though he had always known them and had spoken so many kind words . . . he plucked the feathers from the magpies without making them cry out.[8]

On the whole, Edward's strategy worked. With the old king and his son both dead, the fire had gone out of the Lancastrian cause – as had most of their bloodline. 'And so no-one from that stock remained among the living who could now claim the crown', one contemporary observed upon Henry VI's demise.[9] This was not quite accurate, but it did reflect the general sense of hopelessness among the beleaguered Lancastrian supporters, most of whom proved willing to be reconciled to their new king. The few notable exceptions included the late king's half-brother Jasper Tudor and his nephew Henry, who fled to Brittany with some Lancastrian supporters upon Edward's restoration.

The fact that, on a personal level, Edward IV inspired much greater confidence than his predecessor helped to calm the troubled waters of the previous two decades. An able and far-sighted ruler, he had the natural qualities of leadership that Henry VI had so painfully lacked. His consciousness of the power he wielded made him overbearing at times, and there were also flashes of a formidable temper. But this was tempered by his amiable nature, which made him approachable to all, rather than a few cherished favourites. 'He was so genial in his greeting', Mancini observed, 'that if he saw a newcomer bewildered at his appearance and royal magnificence, he would give him courage to speak by laying a kindly hand on his shoulder.'[10]

In appearance, too, Edward cut an impressive figure. Proud of his tall, athletic stature, 'he was wont to show himself to those who

wished to watch him', Mancini remarked, 'and he seized any opportunity that the occasion offered of revealing his fine stature more
protractedly and more evidently to onlookers'.[11] The king's attrac-
tiveness was enhanced by his charisma and self-confidence. Highly
sexed, he had already had a string of mistresses by the time he took
the throne, and he would have no fewer than ten children (seven
girls and three boys) by his wife Elizabeth. During Edward's exile in
1470, Elizabeth had given birth to their first son, Edward, who was
heir to the throne.

The magnificence of Edward's person and court inspired a wealth
of enthusiastic accounts by contemporary observers. The *Crowland
Chronicle* described the splendour of one Christmas when Edward
made his entrance, dressed in the latest fashions 'like a new and
incomparable spectacle set before the onlookers'. It concluded that
his court was 'such as befitted a mighty kingdom'.[12] This is exactly
what Edward intended and he did not stint on the expense. His
magnificent new great hall at Eltham Palace displayed the confidence
and power of the Yorkist monarchy, while major works at Windsor
Castle included the enlargement of St George's Chapel. He was also
an active patron of the arts and financed one of the first books to
be printed in English by William Caxton in 1477.[13]

Edward was the first monarch to fully appreciate the importance
of establishing the 'other-worldliness' of the crown by enhancing
the privacy, as well as the public magnificence, of the royal family.
The creation of a private suite of chambers for the king or queen
can be traced to as early as the twelfth century. But Edward took
this to another level by providing himself and his family with
luxurious private lodgings. The first of the ceremonial rooms *en
route* to the king was the 'great' or 'guard' chamber, staffed by his
personal bodyguard. Next came the presence chamber (or throne
room), where the king dined in state, received important visitors
and met his council. Beyond that lay the privy chamber, which was
both the king's bedroom and private lodgings, and the name of
the organisation that populated and governed these inner rooms.
All of this was subject to a great deal of formal ceremony, designed
to emphasise the divine nature of the sovereign. Separating the
king from his subjects in this way enhanced the mystique of

monarchy and elevated those who were fortunate enough to be admitted to the royal presence.

The first half of the 1470s saw a gradual settling of old rivalries and resentments as Edward's authority became more fully embedded across the kingdom. The strengthening of his dynasty was greatly assisted by his growing brood of children. Soon after the king's return to power, his infant son Edward was created Prince of Wales and Earl of Chester, and the leading dignitaries of the kingdom swore an oath of allegiance to the tiny prince, recognising him as heir to the throne. When Prince Edward was four years old, he was made a knight of the Garter. Shortly afterwards, the king named him keeper of the realm during his visit to France in June 1475. The following year, Prince Edward was transferred to Ludlow so that he could exercise his authority as Prince of Wales. A second son, Richard, had been born in 1473, making the Yorkist succession seem secure well into the future.

But alongside this growing sense of unity within the realm as a whole, a dangerous division was opening up between the king and his brother George, Duke of Clarence. Although they had been reconciled upon Edward's return from exile in 1471, the trust between them had never been fully restored and Clarence was bitterly resentful of what he perceived as a gradual erosion of his power. In 1477, he was accused of conspiring against the crown and sent to the Tower. His guilt is not certain, but Parliament was convinced enough to have him attainted for 'unnatural, loathly treasons' and sentenced to death.[14]

Contemporaries were in no doubt that it was Edward alone who had destroyed his brother. For all his appeasement towards others who had opposed him, treachery within his own family was something that he could not tolerate. It was the king who had brought pressure to bear upon Parliament to reach a guilty verdict, despite none of its members speaking out against the duke. He also made sure that the sentence was carried out. Clarence was privately executed at the Tower on 18 February 1478. According to Mancini, as a final concession, the duke was allowed to choose the manner of his death and opted to be 'plunged into a jar of sweet wine'.[15]

Clarence's death also proved the extent to which Edward was master of his domain. His was a very active model of kingship and, in stark contrast to his predecessor, he took a keen interest in every aspect of government. One of his greatest achievements was one that had eluded many monarchs before him: financial stability. Forasmuch as he gained the reputation for magnificence, Edward only invested royal funds when he judged it would strengthen the crown. During his reign, a much more rigorous system of financial administration was introduced, and the king was more circumspect in the distribution of patronage. He also maximised his income from wardships, ecclesiastical vacancies and other royal rights, as well as significantly increasing the volume of lands owned by the crown. To administer these, he developed the royal chamber – a new financial department, distinct from the exchequer.

Other aspects of Edward's kingship were less impressive. Disappointingly, given his reputation as a strong and authoritative monarch, he was not particularly active in the administration of justice, unless the case involved his own interests. While he was swift to act against any lawlessness that threatened the political stability, there was increasing criticism of the king's failure to tackle other breaches of the law. The House of Commons complained about certain 'persons' who appeared exempt from justice 'as either been of great might, or else favoured under persons of great power'.[16]

Of even greater disappointment were Edward's military campaigns. After several short-lived truces, he led an English army across the Channel in July 1475. Expectations were high, given his prowess in the field of combat. But there was no significant military action, and the following month the English and French kings concluded a seven-year truce. As part of this, Edward's eldest daughter Elizabeth was pledged in marriage to the dauphin Charles, and Louis agreed to pay Edward a substantial pension. Although this meant that Edward had no need to raise taxes until 1482, the perception among his subjects was that he had been bought off by his French rival.

Edward's relations with Scotland excited even more criticism. In 1481, he commenced plans to lead a major campaign north of the border. But in the event, he decided to delegate the command to his youngest brother Richard, Duke of Gloucester. The English army entered Edinburgh unopposed but withdrew after Gloucester came to terms with James III. England's only gain was the border town of Berwick, which Richard had captured, but this was rightly viewed as a meagre reward for a campaign that had promised much more.

The failings of Edward's foreign policy have been interpreted as a sign that he was losing his grip on affairs, and that this in turn was due to his faltering health. But this owes more to hindsight than any contemporary evidence. It is true that by the mid-1470s, the king no longer cut such an athletic figure as in his youth. His tendency to overindulge in feasting as well as women had resulted in considerable weight gain. The *Crowland Chronicle* described him as 'a gross man . . . addicted to conviviality, vanity, drunkenness, extravagance and passion' but admitted that his mind was as sharp as ever.[17]

Edward's sudden illness at Eastertide 1483 took everyone by surprise – not least the king himself. The cause remains uncertain. Inevitably, given the speed of his demise, there were rumours of poison. French chroniclers blamed the king's overindulgent lifestyle. Perhaps more reliable is Mancini, who claimed that the king had caught a chill while boating on the river. Edward's symptoms worsened so rapidly that he hastily ordered his affairs. He added codicils to his will and set out his wishes for the governance of his realm, urging his warring family and nobles: 'From this time forward, all griefs forgotten, each of you love the other.'[18] With his eldest son and heir Edward only twelve years old, the dying king knew that the country stood on the brink of another minority, with all the potential catastrophe that entailed.

On 9 April, ten days after first taking to his bed at the palace of Westminster, Edward IV died, just shy of his forty-first birthday. He was buried at his new chapel of St George's, Windsor, later that month.

For all his vices, Edward had formed a dramatic but welcome contrast to his predecessor. His reign has been viewed as the beginning of a 'modern' or 'Renaissance' monarchy. But while Edward had made some reforms, notably to the crown's financial administration, he should not be credited with creating a new model of kingship. Rather, he had restored the form and traditions of medieval monarchy, which had been undermined during the turbulence of Henry VI's reign. Edward's readiness to exercise power through trusted officials and associates was entirely typical of other medieval kings. Its success, like theirs, rested largely upon the force of his personality.

But therein, too, lay the essential vulnerability of Edward's regime. His sudden death robbed him of the chance to further stabilise his kingdom and resolve the lingering divisions once and for all. Now that the king had been cut off in his prime, it left his Yorkist regime in some disarray and gave fresh hope to the Lancastrian rivals who were waiting in the wings.

Edward V (1483)

'Those two Princes who were foully murdered'

O N HIS DEATHBED, Edward IV had made provision for his son to be crowned immediately and had fixed the date of 4 May 1483. But the more pressing issue was who would take control during the new king's minority. Although Edward had named his brother Richard, Duke of Gloucester, as Lord Protector of the Realm, there were fears that the dowager queen and her ambitious family would try to seize power. Elizabeth's brother Anthony, Earl Rivers, had been appointed governor of the prince upon his transfer to Ludlow in 1476 and his influence on the boy was profound.

As the only surviving brother of the late king, whose loyalty had been proven many times during his fifteen years of service, Richard of Gloucester was the natural choice to lead the realm and enjoyed far greater popularity than the grasping Woodvilles. He and his supporters resolved, as a first step, to wrest the young king from the custody of his uncle, Lord Rivers. At the dowager queen's request, her brother escorted her son to London with an armed escort of 2,000 men. But when the party reached Stony Stratford, sixty miles north-west of the capital, it was intercepted by Richard and a large entourage. He took possession of his nephew and arrested Rivers, along with other leading members of the new king's household. Ostensibly, this was for Edward V's protection, but the queen and her family rightly understood it as a declaration of war. As soon as the news reached her, she fled to sanctuary at Westminster with her daughters and younger son, Richard, Duke of York.[1]

Edward V entered London with his uncle Gloucester on the day that should have been his coronation and was housed in the royal lodgings in the Tower. Shortly afterwards, the duke was formally named Lord Protector. The situation appeared settled and Richard began making plans for his nephew's coronation, which had been postponed to 22 June. But there were soon signs that all was far from well. On 10 June, Gloucester appealed to the city of York, asking for military help against the Woodvilles, who he claimed 'have intended and daily doth intend to murder and utterly destroy us'.[2] The extent to which they posed a genuine threat is doubtful. Elizabeth was in sanctuary at Westminster and her foremost supporter, her brother Anthony, was Richard's prisoner. It has been conjectured that Richard was using their hostility to justify bolstering his power – and, ultimately, taking the throne.

The summary execution of Edward IV's chamberlain and friend, William, Lord Hastings, three days later was also justified on the basis that he was a threat to the stability of the realm. Hastings had just attended a stormy council meeting at which he and Lord Stanley, John Morton, Bishop of Ely and Thomas Rotherham, Archbishop of York, had been accused of conspiring against Richard. All four men were associated with the Woodvilles and it is likely that they had objected to Richard's plans to seize the crown.

Events now moved with terrifying speed. Gloucester had the young king in his keeping, but he knew that he needed his other nephew, Richard, in order to prevent the queen from using the boy against him. On 16 June, the Archbishop of Canterbury, Cardinal Bourchier, persuaded Elizabeth to hand over her second son so that he might attend his brother's coronation six days later. But as soon as Prince Richard had joined Edward in the Tower, their uncle postponed the coronation to 9 November. This was an ominous sign for the queen and her family – not least her two sons, who were now entirely subject to their uncle Gloucester's will.

On the day that Edward V should have been crowned, the theologian Dr Ralph Shaw preached a sermon at Paul's Cross aimed at promoting Richard's claim. 'A certain parchment roll' was issued, which made it clear that 'no certain and uncorrupt blood of the lineage of Richard, duke of York [father of Edward IV and Richard], was to be found except in the person of the said Richard, duke of Gloucester'.[3] According to Mancini, Richard initially asserted that Edward IV had been illegitimate. If this is true, he soon changed tack and argued instead that his late brother's sons were bastards, a claim that was repeated in Shaw's sermon. It was alleged that Edward IV had contracted a secret marriage with a lady named Eleanor Butler before his marriage to Elizabeth Woodville. This was supported by Robert Stillington, Bishop of Bath and Wells, who had been briefly imprisoned and fined for speaking out against Edward IV in 1478.

On 25 June, Elizabeth Woodville's brother Anthony was taken from his prison in Pontefract Castle and beheaded. The following day, Richard 'obtruded himself into the marble chair' in the Great Hall at Westminster during a ceremony modelled on that of his brother when he had taken power from Henry VI in 1461. He had taken the precaution of summoning 'fearful and unheard-of numbers' of armed men, primarily from the north, in order to bolster his position.[4] His coronation on 6 July set the seal on his triumph. The Woodvilles had been all but annihilated, and the new king appeared to have no rivals to his throne.

Even before the crown had been placed on Richard's head, fears for the safety of his nephews in the Tower were expressed. Mancini talked of how men burst into tears at the very mention of the boys. Edward himself was reported to be filled with foreboding. His physician John Argentine recorded how the boy prepared for his death every day by making a confession and penance. Later in July, the new king learned of a conspiracy to rescue the princes from the Tower. The men who were tried had no standing or influence, but it is likely that there had been others behind it.

The last recorded sighting of Edward and his brother was on 16 June. The *Great Chronicle* noted that 'the children of King Edward' were 'seen shooting [arrows] and playing in the garden of the Tower sundry times'. According to Mancini, soon afterwards the boys were 'withdrawn to the inner apartments of the Tower proper, and day by day began to be seen more rarely behind the bars and windows'. This suggests that Richard had moved them from the Garden Tower (later renamed the Bloody Tower) to the White Tower, where royal captives tended to be held. Other chroniclers concur that the boys were 'holden more straight' from that time onwards.[5]

What happened next forms one of the darkest chapters in the history of the English monarchy. It is now widely accepted that some time during late summer or early autumn 1483, the two princes were quietly murdered. The fact that by September Richard III's opponents were seeking to put Henry Tudor on the throne suggests that the princes were believed to be dead by then. At whose hands will probably never be known. Richard III has long been the prime suspect, but there were others with a vested interest in getting them out of the way – not least Henry Tudor. He and his Lancastrian supporters had only to wait in the wings for the House of York to tear itself apart, just as their own dynasty had when it was in power. Framing Richard for the murder of his nephews would be a swift way of achieving this.

In 1674, King Charles II ordered the demolition of what remained of the royal palace to the south of the White Tower. Beneath the foundations of the privy staircase that led into the Norman chapel inside the White Tower, workmen uncovered a wooden chest containing two skeletons. They were clearly the bones of children, and their height coincided with the age of the two princes when they disappeared. An eyewitness described 'pieces of rag and velvet' which adhered to the bones – the latter material being worn only by royalty and nobility. The same witness was in no doubt about their identity: 'This day I . . . saw working men dig out of a stairway in the White Tower the bones of those two Princes who were foully murdered by Richard III.'[6]

The skeletons became something of a tourist attraction and remained on display for the next four years, until Charles II arranged for their reburial in Westminster Abbey. They have lain there ever since, with a brief interruption in 1933 when a re-examination confirmed that the skeletons were those of children aged about twelve and nine years.

But there was another twist to the tale. In 1789, during repairs in St George's Chapel, Windsor, the workmen accidentally broke into the vault of Edward IV and Elizabeth Woodville. They discovered what appeared to be a small adjoining vault, which contained the coffins of two unidentified children. The tomb was resealed before any examination could be carried out and was inscribed with the names of two of the couple's children who had predeceased them:

George, first Duke of Bedford, and Mary of York. However, two lead coffins labelled with each of their names were subsequently discovered elsewhere in the chapel.

In 2012, the discovery of Richard III's skeleton during an archaeological dig in Leicester revived interest in the fate of the two princes. There were calls to have the skeletons at Westminster and Windsor re-examined. To exhume any deceased royal requires the permission of the reigning sovereign. Elizabeth II declined to grant it, preferring to let the remains of the children – whatever their identity – rest in peace.

Richard III (1483–5)
'Close and secret'

A T TURNS REVILED and revered, Richard III divides opinion more than any other monarch in English history and his brief reign has been the subject of intense debate for more than five hundred years. He began his life at Fotheringhay Castle in Northamptonshire on 2 October 1452, the youngest surviving child of Richard, Duke of York, and Cecily Neville, a forthright and ambitious woman who claimed descent from John of Gaunt and his third wife Katherine Swynford. Seeking to blacken his reputation, later detractors claimed that Richard was 'retained within his mother's womb for two years . . . emerging with teeth and hair to the shoulders'.[1]

Little is known of Richard's childhood, but he soon became embroiled in the turbulence of his father's rivalry with the House of Lancaster. He was just eight years old when his father and elder brother Edmund were killed at the Battle of Wakefield, and he was soon afterwards sent to safety in Burgundy with his brother George. They had only been there for just over a month when news arrived of their eldest brother Edward's victory at Towton and they returned to England for his coronation in June 1461.

As he reached maturity, Richard, who was created Duke of Gloucester soon after Edward's accession, became active in his elder brother's service. The contemporary historian John Rous praised Richard as a 'noble knight' who always bore himself with honour.[2] Raised in a strongly military household, he proved a vital support to Edward in his clashes with the Lancastrian forces. His military prowess was admirable, given the physical challenges that he battled against. The discovery of his skeleton revealed that as well as being of a small, slight stature, he suffered from severe scoliosis, or curvature of the spine. This confirmed the posthumous description of him as a 'crook back', which famously inspired Shakespeare's villainous portrayal.[3]

Richard was rewarded handsomely for the efforts that he had taken on Edward's behalf, becoming Constable of England and later admiral. He was also granted considerable estates, including those belonging to the fallen Earl of Warwick. Before long, Richard had established a great northern power base, centred upon Middleham Castle in north Yorkshire. His marriage to Warwick's younger daughter, Anne Neville, widow of Henry VI's son Edward, brought him yet further lands. The north would always remain loyal to Richard, despite the turbulence that followed elsewhere in the kingdom. A century later, Francis Bacon reflected: 'The memory of King Richard was so strong [in the north] that it lay like lees in the bottom of men's hearts, and if the vessel was but stirred it would come up.'[4]

It was to Yorkshire that Richard embarked on progress soon after becoming king in July 1483. He had only just departed from London when he received news of a plot to rescue his nephews from the Tower. The fact that the main perpetrators were never discovered heightened Richard's insecurity. Although he had neutralised the threat posed by the late king's wife and her family, he knew that the last surviving Lancastrian claimant, Margaret Beaufort's son Henry Tudor, was waiting in the wings – or, more precisely, in Brittany.

Whatever dark deeds were committed in the Tower of London during his absence, Richard continued northwards on his progress and entered York to great rejoicing on 29 August. He remained in his northern power base for several weeks, the obvious support for him there perhaps lulling him into a false sense of security. But not long after embarking upon the long journey south, he heard that a rebellion had broken out in Henry Tudor's name. The Lancastrian heir had assembled a fleet and reached the shores of Plymouth, where he awaited the signal to advance. The uprising quickly spread across the southern counties of England and involved many of the king's closest officials. Most shocking of all was the treachery of the then-Constable of England, Henry Stafford, Duke of Buckingham, in whom Richard had vested great trust and authority. It was

Buckingham's failure to win wider support for the rebellion that led to its collapse and Tudor's retreat to Brittany. The duke was put to death on 2 November 1483.

Buckingham might have become a mere footnote of history were it not for the theory that he had murdered the princes in the Tower. This was first put forward in a contemporary Portuguese document, which stated that upon embarking on his progress in July 1483, Richard had entrusted the care of his nephews to Buckingham, 'under whose custody the said Princes were starved to death'. It was repeated in a document of English origin written two or three decades later.[5] The theory is that the duke had acted on his own initiative, either because he believed it was in Richard's interests or because, as a descendant of Edward III, he had ambitions for the throne himself. But if Buckingham had conspired to murder the princes without Richard's knowledge or sanction, the king would have had him publicly blamed for it, not least to deflect the growing suspicion against himself.

As it was, Richard's primary concern in the wake of Buckingham's execution was to bring the southern counties more firmly under his control. He distributed the lands and offices forfeited by the rebels among trusted servants, most of whom were from his northern heartland. Rather than asserting royal authority, however, this created even greater resentment towards the 'usurper' king.

The toll that all of this was taking on Richard can be glimpsed in contemporary accounts and portraits. The youngest of the York sons, he did not seem to have inherited the ebullient self-confidence of his brothers (Edward IV in particular), but was of a more nervous disposition. Portraits show him with a careworn face, tight-lipped and fiddling with the rings on his fingers. Polydore Vergil later described how the king was often seen biting his lip and 'ever with his right hand pulling out of the sheath to the middle, and putting in again, the dagger which he did always wear'.[6] His agitation is often ascribed to the guilt and paranoia he felt after usurping the throne. But his nervousness and insecurity seemed more inherent and may have had its roots in the turbulence of his childhood.

A further indication of Richard's inner turmoil is revealed by his private devotions. He had always been a pious man, but there was a growing desperation to his religious observances after he assumed the throne. Inside his book of hours is a prayer copied in his hand that relates to unjustly persecuted heroes and heroines of the Old Testament. The king also became prone to public outbursts of distress, such as when he met Nikolaus von Poppelau, a German visitor to court in 1484. The stranger was surprised by Richard's candour when he blurted out: 'With my own people alone and without the help of other princes I should like to drive away not only the Turks, but all my foes.' Poppelau subsequently praised the king's 'great heart', and even the critical Vergil testified to his 'courage . . . high and fierce'.[7] Later, more hostile commentators describe Richard as 'close and secret . . . arrogant of heart, outwardly companiable where he inwardly hated'. But such claims are corroborated by few of the contemporary sources. 'I never liked the conditions of any prince so well as his,' remarked the Bishop of St David's after meeting the king during his royal progress, 'God hath sent him to us for the weal of us all.'[8]

At the beginning of 1484, Richard took measures to strengthen his control at the heart of government. In January, Parliament confirmed his kingship by a statute entitled *Titulus Regius*. This was followed by a few months of apparent peace within the realm. But ill fortune was soon snapping at the king's heels again. In April that year, his only son and heir, Edward, died suddenly at Middleham Castle, aged just ten. Richard and his wife Anne were plunged into 'a state almost bordering on madness, by reason of their sudden grief'.[9] The *Crowland Chronicle* was quick to interpret this as a sign of God's displeasure with the usurper Richard, especially as it had occurred almost exactly a year after his brother Edward's death.

The loss of his son made Richard's position even more unstable. In July 1484 there were murmurings of further dissent. Seditious rhymes and ballads were pinned to the doors of St Paul's Cathedral, including the famous verse:

The Cat, the Rat and Lovell our Dog
Rule all England under a Hog.

This referred to three members of Richard's inner circle: William Catesby, Richard Ratcliffe and Francis, Viscount Lovell, while the 'hog' was the white boar of the king's emblem. Although there were other men close to Richard, the rhyme neatly encapsulates the increasingly narrow clique that he drew about him as his paranoia deepened. He was right to be suspicious. At the same time that the rhyme appeared, the king heard of 'great treasons' in the south-west and appointed a commission to investigate.[10] Further unrest broke out in Essex and Hertfordshire in the winter of 1484-5 and involved members of Richard's own household.

The more plots that were discovered, the more threads were traced to the Lancastrian heir in Brittany. Henry Tudor had been steadily enhancing his position ever since Richard took the throne. In order to win vital support among the House of York, at Christmas 1483 he had pledged to marry Edward IV's eldest daughter, Elizabeth, if he won the throne. Always, he seemed to be one step ahead of his rival, thanks in no small part to the machinations of his mother, Margaret Beaufort, and the dowager queen, Elizabeth Woodville, who had secretly planned this betrothal. When Richard III had almost secured Brittany's agreement to surrender their Lancastrian exile, Henry escaped to France and won the backing of King Charles VIII. Now that he had a far more powerful ally, Tudor attracted many more men to his cause.

With his own supporter base rapidly dwindling, Richard began cultivating an unlikely ally: the Woodvilles. At the beginning of March 1484, Elizabeth and her daughters had left sanctuary after the king had promised that they would not be harmed in any way – and, more specifically, that they would not be taken to the Tower. The death of his wife Anne later that month sparked rumours that Richard would marry his niece Elizabeth himself. These were fuelled during the Christmas celebrations that year, when the king made a show of paying the princess particular attention. If his intention was to win support from the Woodville fraternity, it worked. Soon, a number of formerly hostile nobles had bound themselves to him. But his flirtation with Princess Elizabeth may also have been a ploy to ruin her reputation and thereby end Henry's Tudor's plans to marry her. When his Lancastrian rival heard, it 'pinched him by the very stomach'.[11]

In the event, Richard's dalliance with his niece came to nothing. His close advisers, Catesby and Ratcliffe, argued strongly against it on the grounds that the church was unlikely to grant dispensation for a marriage of such close kin. They also pointed out that Richard's northern allies would look askance at such an alliance and would suspect that he had murdered Anne Neville in order to marry Elizabeth. Richard eventually put an end to the rumours by making a public denial that he had ever considered marrying his niece.

By the summer of 1485, the Lancastrian heir judged that the time was ripe to push his claim. With assistance from the French and Scots, as well as his Woodville allies, he assembled an invasion fleet. In public, Richard exalted at the news because he was confident of victory and hoped it would be taken as a sign that God smiled upon his regime. After he had crushed Tudor's force and rid himself of his main challenger, he would 'comfort his subjects with the blessings of unchallenged peace'.[12]

On 7 August, Henry Tudor landed with a small army off the Pembrokeshire coast. Together with his uncle Jasper and another staunch Lancastrian, John de Vere, Earl of Oxford, he marched towards England, gathering supporters along the way. By the time he reached the Midlands, he had amassed an army of about five thousand men – still around three thousand short of the royal force.

The two armies met near Dadlington in Leicestershire on 22 August. According to the *Crowland Chronicle*, the king had spent a restless night, tormented by dreams of 'a multitude of demons'.[13] The battle (named after the nearby town of Market Bosworth) went against him from the beginning, when his vanguard was defeated by de Vere and his rearguard (under the Earl of Northumberland's command) failed to join the fighting at all. But at a crucial moment, Richard noticed that Henry Tudor and his bodyguard had been separated from the main Lancastrian force and decided to risk everything in a bid to reach and kill his rival. William Stanley, whose brother Thomas was married to Tudor's mother Margaret Beaufort, now ordered his troops to join the Lancastrian side. Outnumbered, the king and his entourage were driven back towards the edge of a marsh, into which Richard's horse fell. The king got to his feet and fought on. To his last breath he was seen 'fighting manfully in the thickset press of his enemies'.[14] Recent analysis of his skeleton revealed eleven wounds, mostly to the skull – two of which would have been fatal. Richard's body was stripped and carried to Leicester tied to a horse. It was probably displayed as proof of his death before being laid to rest at Greyfriars Church.

According to legend, the crown that Richard had worn over his helmet was found in a hawthorn bush and handed to the Lancastrian victor. It was a symbolic moment. The crown had passed not just to a new king, but a new dynasty. The Yorkist king had not been the first claimant to usurp the English throne from the rightful heir, but he had paid a heavier price for it than any other, destroying himself and all but a remnant of his House. His death marked the close of one of the most violent periods in the history of the monarchy.

Part 4

The Tudors (1485-1603)

'Kings' games are played on scaffolds'

The advent of the Tudors has traditionally marked England's transition from a medieval to an early modern kingdom. They withstood rival claimants and overseas foes to become one of the greatest dynasties in English royal history. In stark contrast to the period that went before, none of the Tudor monarchs were either murdered or deposed, and they wielded far greater power than their Plantagenet predecessors. The era saw the strengthening of England's national identity, thanks in no small part to Henry VIII's sweeping religious and political reforms and his break with Rome, and to the country's colonial expansion. There was significant economic growth, too, and the flowering of the English Renaissance in the arts and architecture. The sheer drama of the Tudor period, with a king who married six times, a Virgin Queen and a royal court that eclipsed all others in magnificence, has made it one of the most enduringly popular in English history.

Henry VII (1485–1509)

'Suspicious of everything'

Eᴺɢʟᴀɴᴅ's ꜰɪʀꜱᴛ Tᴜᴅᴏʀ monarch was born at Pembroke Castle in Wales on 28 January 1457 to the thirteen-year-old Lady Margaret Beaufort. She had been a widow for almost three months, her husband Edmund Tudor having died of a sudden illness. Intensely pious and formidably ambitious, Lady Margaret doted upon her son from the beginning and saw him as the chief hope of the beleaguered Lancastrian dynasty.

To say that Henry Tudor's path to the throne had been a tortuous one would be an understatement. Having fled Wales when Edward IV seized back the crown in 1471, he had spent most of the next fourteen years as an outcast in Brittany under threat of arrest and execution. Upon finally returning to Wales in a bid to wrest the throne from Richard III in August 1485, his ragtag army of mercenaries had been far outnumbered by those of the king. And yet, as his indomitable mother had confidently predicted, God had smiled upon his endeavours and he was now King Henry VII of England. For how long was anyone's guess.

During the previous two years, the crown had changed hands three times, so it seemed only a matter of time before a rival claimant would oust this latest incumbent, particularly as Henry's bloodline did not bear close scrutiny. His mother was descended from Edward III, but in an illegitimate line. Although the Beauforts had subsequently been legitimised, in 1407 Henry IV had declared that they should not be allowed to inherit the crown. This, and the stain of bastardy, made Henry's right to the throne more tenuous than any King of England since William the Conqueror. At the time of his accession, there were no fewer than eighteen claimants with a superior right to the throne to his – including his prospective wife, Elizabeth of York.[1]

The new Tudor king was not without merit, though. Polydore Vergil described him as 'extremely attractive in appearance', with a 'slim, but well-built and strong' figure, above the average height, and a 'cheerful', animated face. More importantly, Henry had the shrewdness and political guile to succeed. John Fisher, Bishop of Rochester, who knew the king well, had nothing but praise for him: 'His wisdom in governance, was singular, his wit always quick and ready . . . his person goodly and amiable . . . his dealings in time of perils and dangers was cold and sober with great hardiness.'[2]

Two months after his triumph at Bosworth, Henry VII was crowned at Westminster Abbey. Anxious to bolster his legitimacy, he used the occasion to emphasise the continuity of the succession. The ceremony was based upon Edward IV's, and Henry also commissioned Edward's Parisian tailor, George Lovekyn, to make his coronation robes. Henry retained Lovekyn as his tailor thereafter and always took care to dress in Plantagenet fashions, rather than those of the Breton or French court. He lavished huge expense on his wardrobe during the early years of his reign, and visitors to court were impressed by his 'splendidly generous' hospitality.[3] For a king who later became notorious as a miser, it was worth the expense. The credibility of Henry's kingship rested upon such external shows.

Shortly after his coronation, Henry's first Parliament was convened. Conscious of the need to strengthen the new king's regime, it formally invited him to take Elizabeth of York as his bride. According to Vergil, Elizabeth declared herself an 'unhappy creature' at being 'united with a man who is the enemy of my family'.[4] But her royal upbringing had taught her that duty came ahead of personal desire and the marriage was celebrated on 18 January 1486. The houses of Lancaster and York were united at last. Just eight months later, the union was strengthened by the birth of a prince, Arthur. The choice of name was significant: Henry VII had commissioned a family tree showing his descent from the legendary King Arthur.

The ending of the Wars of the Roses that Henry's marriage symbolised was expressed in other ways. Although he appointed a close circle of Lancastrian advisers and servants, such as Sir Reynold Bray and Richard Fox, he also retained a significant number of officials from Edward IV's time. They included John Morton, formerly Bishop of Ely, who was promoted to the hallowed position of Archbishop of Canterbury and Lord Chancellor. Even some nobles who had fought on Richard's side at Bosworth were gradually allowed back into favour. The Tudor propaganda machine also got to work. Throughout the palaces, the emblem of entwined red and white roses was scattered. It was also on prominent display in court pageantry and featured in the poetry that was published during the new reign. The Tudor rose is still one of the most instantly recognisable symbols of monarchy today.

Henry VII soon learned that the divisions of the past were not so easily healed. It is telling that when embarking upon the first progress of his reign, he appointed an armed bodyguard to accompany him. While he turned a smiling face to the pageants that lined his processional route through the Midlands and south-west, he was inwardly disturbed by news of risings in Yorkshire, Warwickshire and Worcestershire. Without a figurehead, these rebellions were quickly suppressed.

But in early 1487, Henry faced a more serious threat. In Ireland, a young man claiming to be Edward, Earl of Warwick, son of Edward IV's brother George, Duke of Clarence, had won so much support that he had been proclaimed king. Henry VII had taken the precaution of placing Warwick in the Tower at the beginning of his reign. But the supporters of the 'pretender' (whose real name was Lambert Simnel) claimed that he had escaped. The plot quickly attracted members of the powerful Yorkist fraternity. The queen's own mother, Elizabeth Woodville, was suspected of involvement. Meanwhile, John de la Pole, Earl of Lincoln, nephew of Edward IV and Richard III, fled to the Netherlands to join his aunt Margaret of York, dowager Duchess of Burgundy. With Margaret's help, he began gathering men and arms to launch an invasion in Warwick's name.

Pole landed in Ireland with 2,000 mercenaries supplied by his aunt and saw the pretender crowned Edward VI in Dublin on 24 May. Thousands of Irish troops now fled to his cause, and two weeks later Simnel's army landed off the Cumbrian coast. He marched through the northern counties, amassing more support from Ricardians hostile to the new Tudor regime. Although the pretender's army was impressive, the king had assembled one twice as large and far better equipped. When the two sides met at East Stoke, near Newark, on 16 June, Simnel's troops were defeated. Among the casualties was John de la Pole, which removed another rival claimant from Henry's path. It had been an easy victory and the king was merciful to those who had taken part. He even pardoned Simnel himself and set him to work in the royal kitchens as a spit-turner. But the whole episode had left the new king with a profound sense of unease.

Resolved to strengthen his hold on the crown, in November 1487 Henry arranged the coronation of his queen. Just a month later, another conspiracy was uncovered – this time within his own household. Realising that the new King of England sat unsteadily on his throne, his international rivals began circling like vultures. Among them was the newly crowned King of Scots, James IV, who soon began dabbling in Yorkist conspiracies.

Desperate for allies, in February 1489, Henry agreed a treaty with the Duchess of Brittany, promising military assistance against the King of France in return for support for any attempts he might make to reassert English rights across the Channel. The same month, Henry concluded an alliance with the Archduke of Austria, Maximilian I, and in March he signed the Treaty of Medina del Campo with the joint monarchs of Spain, Ferdinand and Isabella. The latter included the promise of a marriage between their daughter, Catherine of Aragon, and Prince Arthur. All of this constituted an impressive diplomatic achievement, one that greatly strengthened Henry's kingship.

Towards the end of 1489, the Tudor dynasty was strengthened by the birth of Henry and Elizabeth's second child, Princess Margaret. Her elder brother Arthur was created Prince of Wales the following day amid great ceremony. Less than a year later, the queen was pregnant again. But as Elizabeth began her confinement at Greenwich, her husband was preoccupied with the threat from another pretender to his throne.

Perkin Warbeck was a young man, possibly of Flemish descent, who claimed to be Richard, Duke of York, the younger of the princes in the Tower. Like Simnel, he won the support of Margaret of Burgundy, who formally recognised him as her nephew, and he had strong backing in Ireland. More worrying for Henry was that there were many in England willing to pledge their allegiance to him. Vergil observed: 'The rumour of Richard, the resuscitated Duke of York, had divided nearly all England into factions, filling the minds of men with hope or fear.'[5] Despite all the king's efforts to secure his realm, the old antipathies between York and Lancaster that had torn the country apart for so many years looked set to be revived.

On 28 June 1491, the king received the welcome news that his wife had been delivered of a son, who was named after his father. But there were soon far gloomier tidings of Warbeck's growing support. He had been honourably received by a host of continental rulers, including Charles VIII, King of France and Philip of Habsburg, Duke of Burgundy. Even Henry's erstwhile ally, Maximilian, showed him favour by inviting him to the funeral of his father, Emperor Frederick III, and recognising him as King Richard IV of England.

The pretender was quietly winning support closer to home, too. From early 1493, some of Henry's most senior courtiers were drawn into the plot, including Sir William Stanley, who had secured victory for him at Bosworth. As yet, the king did not know the identity of Warbeck's supporters at court, but he was alarmed enough to over-haul the staffing and structure of his privy chamber, reducing its members to just six and ensuring that it was closely guarded at all times. Henry's first biographer, Francis Bacon, describes how the king was intent upon 'keeping of distance . . . not admitting any near or full approach, either to his power or to his secrets'.[6] As well as making the monarch less accessible, this new 'institutionalised distance' established greater rigour and ritual around his appearances in public.[7] As a result, his courtiers fought more fiercely for the king's attention than they had been obliged to before.

At the same time that he was setting his private affairs in order, Henry devised a number of public displays to project the magnifi-cence of his dynasty. Until now, he had paid little heed to his younger son Henry's upbringing, focusing his attention on that of his heir,

Prince Arthur. But in September 1494, he organised a lavish ceremony to create the three-year-old prince a Knight of the Bath. The following month, he bestowed the title Duke of York upon him. The choice of title was significant because it signalled that the previous holder, Edward IV's younger son Richard, was dead, and that Warbeck was nothing more than a fraud.

This public expression of Tudor legitimacy was followed by a series of arrests of leading suspects in the Warbeck conspiracy, culminating in the trial and execution of Sir William Stanley in February 1495. The king was no longer inclined to mercy, even for one who had won him the throne. On 3 July, a contingent of Warbeck's forces landed at Deal in Kent, but were swiftly killed or captured. Meanwhile, the pretender was obliged to leave Ireland after failing to defeat the royal authorities there. He found a more willing accomplice in the form of James IV and spent the next two years as an honoured guest at the Scottish court.

Previous English kings had rushed headlong into war on their northern neighbour for far less provocation. But Henry's style of monarchy once again proved both more cautious and diplomatic. Wars involved uncertain outcomes, as well as considerable expense. The latter could only be met by taxation, if Parliament proved willing to grant it, and Henry was anxious not to antagonise his new subjects, painfully aware of how tenuous his hold on the throne was. In order to deprive the pretender of his Scottish ally, he therefore proposed his daughter Margaret as a bride for James. Unfortunately, the King of Scots was not of the same mind. He rejected the offer and proceeded to launch an invasion. This was soon repelled by Henry's forces, and he was obliged to ask Parliament for a hefty subsidy to fund a counter-attack. The tax was granted and Henry's forces triumphed, but as he had feared the heavy burden that this imposed upon his subjects sparked rebellion.

In May 1497, a 15,000-strong army of Cornish rebels marched towards London, gathering support along the way, and encountered the royal forces at Blackheath. The rebels were swiftly put down, but resentment rumbled on in the south-west and Warbeck was invited to lead them. The pretender gladly accepted. In September, he landed in Cornwall and was declared 'Richard IV' on Bodmin

The ancient Coronation Stone in Kingston-upon-Thames, Surrey. The stone is believed to have been used for the crowning of seven Anglo-Saxon kings, the first being Edward the Elder in 900.

Egbert, King of Wessex from 802 to 839, is often cited as being England's first king. The current queen, Elizabeth II, can trace her descent from him.

One of the most famous documents in English history, Domesday Book was a vast survey commissioned by William the Conqueror in 1085 to find out the value of his newly conquered lands.

The coinage was one of the most effective ways of making the monarch visible to their people. William the Conqueror probably ordered pennies such as this to be struck towards the end of 1066.

Henry I's nightmares, as illustrated in John of Worcester's chronicle, c.1140. Among the problems of kingship that are disturbing Henry's sleep is the loss of his only legitimate son and heir on the White Ship.

Henry I bequeathed the throne to his daughter, Matilda, who is widely recognised as England's first queen regnant. Her claim was disputed by her cousin Stephen, plunging the kingdom into civil war.

King John's seal on the Magna Carta. He soon broke the terms of the charter but it marked a pivotal moment in the relationship between crown and people.

Edward III (shown here in his Garter robes) established the Order of the Garter in 1349. It remains the most senior order of knighthood in Britain today.

The Wilton Diptych, in which Richard II, flanked by saints, is presented to the Virgin and child. The painting encapsulates the image of sacred majesty that Richard strove to create.

At his coronation, Henry IV became the first English king to be anointed with a sacred oil reputedly given by the Virgin Mary to Thomas Becket, as well as the first to be enthroned on the 'Stone of Scone'.

Henry V's posthumous portrait shows the hero of Agincourt in profile, possibly to disguise a scar from an arrow wound that he sustained in his youth.

Richard III was reported to be of a nervous disposition. This portrait shows him, brow furrowed, fiddling with the rings on his fingers.

The most famous painter of the Tudor age, Holbein the Younger had a profound influence on Henry VIII's public image. In this painting, the king is shown in typically magisterial pose.

The Field of Cloth of Gold was a spectacular meeting between Henry VIII and his greatest rival, Francis I, King of France, in 1520. This painting was probably commissioned towards the end of Henry's reign, as he sought to recapture the glories of his youth.

Henry VIII's coronation oath, altered in his own hand during the Reformation to reflect his newly won supremacy over the church.

Valor Ecclesiasticus (or 'Value of the Church'), commissioned in 1535, was the most detailed survey since Domesday Book. It told Henry VIII how much wealth the Church had in England and Wales – and how much he could get his hands on.

Henry VIII was a more prolific palace builder than any other monarch. One of the most spectacular survivors of his architectural legacy is the Great Hall at Hampton Court Palace.

Henry VIII liked to decorate his palaces to honour his wives – and remove all trace of them when they fell from grace. This exquisite carved falcon, Anne Boleyn's emblem, probably once adorned the Tudor apartments at Hampton Court.

Edward the Confessor established a ceremony in which the monarch would touch – and reputedly cure – sufferers of the scrofula (known as the 'King's Evil'). Here, Mary Tudor performs the task.

The defeat of the Spanish Armada in 1588 catapulted Elizabeth I to iconic status and led to England's emergence as a world power. This painting was part of a dazzling PR campaign to mark her navy's victory.

England's first Stuart king, James I, commissioned this magnificent tomb for his Tudor predecessor, Elizabeth I, as well as another (larger) one for his mother, Mary, Queen of Scots, whose execution Elizabeth had ordered in 1587.

The Coronation Chair in Westminster Abbey has been the centrepiece of coronations for more than 700 years.

The ceiling of St Mary's Church in Beverley, East Yorkshire, is decorated with the portraits of forty kings of England.

St George's Chapel, Windsor, home of the Order of the Garter, is where almost every monarch since George III is buried.

First built by William the Conqueror, the Tower of London has remained a potent symbol of royal authority ever since.

Moor. He then marched to Exeter with a band of around eight thousand followers, but they were far outnumbered by Henry's troops and quickly disbanded. Warbeck himself fled to sanctuary, but agreed to meet Henry at Taunton, where the king promised to spare his life. Henry was true to his word – initially, at least. After forcing Warbeck to publicly admit that he was an imposter, he even welcomed him to court.

Having vanquished his most potent enemy, Henry proceeded to undertake some very public displays of kingship. Formal crown-wearings became a regular feature of court life, as did ceremonies to touch for the 'King's Evil'. Another practice that had begun with Edward the Confessor and was revived by Henry VII involved the giving of 'cramp-rings'. These rings were believed to cure a number of ills, including rheumatism and epilepsy, and were given out by the monarch on certain feast days. Their healing properties came from the fact that they had been touched by the sovereign.

Meanwhile, the use of Henry's dynastic badges on buildings, charters and the liveries of his servants became widespread, proclaiming his inherited right to rule. The king also attempted to have Henry VI canonised in order to sanctify his Lancastrian heritage. Henry created symbols of his fledgling dynasty in bricks and mortar, too. Following the destruction by fire of Sheen Palace at Christmas 1497, he ordered the building of a new royal residence at nearby Richmond. When completed, it was a fairy-tale palace with clusters of domed towers and turrets behind a high curtain wall. It soon became Henry's favourite residence.

'He well knew how to maintain his royal dignity', Vergil concluded, 'and everything belonging to his kingship, at all times and places.'[8] But there was something forced about Henry's displays of majesty. Having spent most of his life as an exile from the royal court, he was unfamiliar with the apparatus of monarchy and no amount of money could disguise the fact. He also lacked the charisma of his former rival, Edward IV, and his natural reserve often made him appear awkward at court gatherings. A Spanish envoy named Pedro de Ayala who visited the English court observed: 'He [the king] likes to be much spoken of, and to be highly appreciated by the whole world. He fails in this because he is not a great man. He spends the time he is not in public or in his council, in writing the accounts of his expenses with his own hand . . . He is much influenced by his mother.' De Ayala concluded that the king was 'disliked' by most of his subjects.[9]

Two Italian visitors to Henry's court in October 1497 noted his spare physique and prominent cheekbones, as well as the greying hair around his temples. One of them reported that the king was 'suspicious of everything . . . he has no one he can trust, except his paid men at arms'.[10] His paranoia was justified. News of Yorkist conspiracies seemed to arrive on a daily basis. In August 1499, the king received word that Perkin Warbeck, who had been imprisoned in the Tower since fleeing the court in June 1498, was conspiring with his fellow prisoner, Warwick. They had a body of supporters who planned to free both men and place one of them on the throne. Henry could no longer afford to be merciful. Warwick and Warbeck were convicted and executed in November 1499.

'England has never before been so tranquil and obedient as at present', reported the Spanish ambassador in January 1500.[11] But Henry was not allowed to enjoy his newfound security for long. In August 1501, Edmund de la Pole, Earl of Suffolk, nephew of Edward IV, left the country in search of allies on the Continent and assumed the Yorkist title of 'White Rose'. He soon drew a number of powerful Yorkist sympathisers to his cause, including Lord William Courtenay and Sir James Tyrell, one of Richard III's most trusted servants. Thanks to the sophisticated network of spies and informants that he had built up during his reign, the English king swiftly rounded up most of the conspirators, although Suffolk himself evaded capture.

Thomas More later claimed that during Tyrell's interrogation, he confessed to the murders of Edward V and his brother Richard. Although this does not appear in any of the contemporary accounts of his confession, it is intriguing that Queen Elizabeth chose to visit the Tower while he was being held prisoner there. Commenting on Tyrell's execution in May 1502, Vergil observed: 'He paid by his own death the appropriate penalty for his previous crimes.' More explicitly, the king later 'gave out' that while in the Tower, Tyrell was 'examined and confessed' to murdering the princes. If this was by proclamation, then it has not survived, which adds to the mystery that still surrounds the fate of the two young boys.[12]

Not long after bringing the Suffolk conspiracy to light, Henry was able to turn his mind to more positive matters. On 14 November 1501, his son Arthur, then fifteen, married Catherine of Aragon at St Paul's Cathedral. It was the most spectacular royal wedding there had ever been. Thousands of people lined the streets, craning to catch a glimpse of the Spanish princess, who was decked out in 'costly apparel both of goldsmith's work and embroidery, [with] rich jewels'.[13] The bride was led into the church by her soon-to-be brother-in-law, the ten-year-old Prince Henry. The younger Tudor prince stole the show with his gallantry and charisma, outdancing most of the other guests at the celebrations that followed. His energetic presence formed a stark contrast to the groom, who appeared gaunt and ill. Catherine's physician observed that he had 'never seen a man whose legs and other bits of his body were so thin' and later claimed that the prince was too weak to consummate the marriage – something that Catherine herself corroborated.[14]

A seemingly endless round of entertainments followed at the king's new palace of Richmond. The guests were also treated to a host of allegorical pageants celebrating the union of the English and Spanish crowns, and the might of the Tudor dynasty. One of these even went so far as to identify King Henry with God the Father and Arthur with Christ his Son. When the celebrations had finally drawn to a close, Arthur and his bride took up residence at Ludlow. Early the following year, Henry sealed another dynastic marriage when the King of Scots finally consented to take Princess Margaret as his bride as part of the Treaty of Perpetual Peace.

But the greatest catastrophe of Henry VII's reign was just around the corner. On 2 April 1502, Prince Arthur died. Although his death has been ascribed to the sweating sickness, one of the most virulent diseases of the age, there is little evidence for this. More likely is that the prince had been suffering from a lingering illness, as suggested by his gaunt appearance when he married Catherine.

In their grief, the king and queen clung to each other, weeping.

Elizabeth comforted her husband with the assurance that they were still young, and that she might give him another child. But Arthur's death had dealt Henry's dynasty a severe blow and left the Anglo-Spanish alliance in tatters. Hope flared when the queen fell pregnant a month or so later. But this, too, ended in tragedy. The child – a girl – was born on 2 February 1503 and lived for only a few days. The queen followed her to the grave nine days after the birth, on her thirty-seventh birthday.

In his grief, Henry retreated into his privy apartments at Richmond for so many weeks that his councillors began to fear that there would be an uprising. To their consternation, they soon learned that he had fallen prey to what may have been the onset of tuberculosis. If news of the king's sickness had leaked out to the wider court and country, it could have spelt disaster for the dynasty. Coming so soon after the deaths of Queen Elizabeth and Prince Arthur, this latest crisis might also be taken as a sign that God had entirely forsaken the Tudor monarchy.

Henry survived the illness, but when he finally re-emerged into public life, the toll it had taken upon him was all too obvious. Looking much older than his forty-six years, his hair had turned white and his face was heavily lined. Grief had robbed the king of his more laudable virtues and left behind only bitterness, introversion and an all-consuming paranoia. 'He was a prince, sad, serious, full of thoughts, and secret observations: and full of notes and memorials of his own hand . . . keeping (as it were) a journal of his thoughts', observed Bacon.[15]

Despite his obvious frailty, the king soon turned his mind to business. One of the most pressing issues was how to salvage his alliance with Spain. His daughter-in-law Catherine was still in England and Henry was determined to keep her there. Ferdinand was also keen and had proposed that she marry the king's younger son, Henry. But the English king had other ideas. To the great consternation of both courts, he suggested that he marry Catherine himself. Queen Isabella wrote at once to upbraid him for proposing 'a very evil thing . . . which offends the ears'.[16] It may have been gamesmanship on Henry's part, aimed at making the Spanish monarchs even more determined that their daughter should marry his younger son. Not long afterwards, negotiations to secure a papal dispensation for Catherine and Prince Henry's marriage began.

At the same time, the king sealed a prestigious marriage agreement with the Duke of Burgundy, in which he pledged his younger daughter Mary to the duke's son, Charles of Ghent, grandson of Ferdinand and Isabella. Upon the death of his father, Charles stood to inherit a sprawling empire that included Castile and Aragon, the Netherlands and, potentially, the position of Holy Roman Emperor.[17] By placing diplomacy rather than war at the heart of his foreign policy, Henry VII arguably achieved more for England's security and prosperity than any of his Plantagenet predecessors. Having won the throne by conquest, the king was not averse to waging war when it was expedient, but he did not fall prey to the same vanity that had inspired centuries of English kings to pursue personal glory at the expense of their country's resources. His approach marked the beginning of a more peaceable, modern monarchy.

In these later years of his reign, Henry became ever more obsessed with filling the royal treasury and overhauling the administration of the crown's finances. The deaths of some of his long-standing officials left the way open for new men of the same mind as the king to take control. Two of the most despised were Richard Empson and Edmund Dudley. Both were astute lawyers, but Vergil claimed that they had been promoted by the king 'not so much to administer justice as to strip the population of its wealth, without respite and by every means fair or foul'.[18] With their assistance, the king introduced new and increasingly burdensome taxes upon the clergy, the merchant class and the population at large. He also ruthlessly exploited his feudal rights over those who held land directly from the crown and imposed heavy fines upon those who were found to be evading their liabilities. Royal commissioners toured the shires more frequently than ever before in order to identify new sources of income. All of this was in line with the law, but the king also embraced more corrupt practices, such as selling offices or even his favour in lawsuits.

By the end of his reign, Henry had transformed the royal finances and amassed greater wealth than had been enjoyed by any king for generations. Arguably, this was vital to strengthening the new Tudor monarchy – many times, history had proved that impoverishment made the crown dangerously vulnerable. But there was a fine dividing line between prosperity and greed. The Venetian ambassador referred to Henry VII as 'a very great miser', but was grudgingly impressed that he had 'accumulated so much gold that he is supposed to have more than well nigh all the other Kings of Christendom'.[19] Vergil observed that Henry's subjects 'considered they were suffering not on account of their own sins but on account of the greed of their monarch'.[20] The king's growing rapaciousness had done more to challenge their loyalty than any of the pretenders to his throne.

Henry's parsimonious and increasingly distrustful nature made him less inclined to enrich or empower those who served him than many of his predecessors had been. Rather than bestowing key positions on favourites, regardless of whether they were capable of fulfilling them effectively, he appointed lawyers, clerics and household men to manage the work of government. He also expanded the jurisdiction of the courts, which severely limited the nobility's freedom of action. All of this made him a far more effective king than many who had gone before, albeit one who was more feared than loved.

Henry's thoughts also turned to his legacy. Shortly after his wife's death, work had begun on a spectacular new chapel at Westminster Abbey. With its breathtaking fan-vaulted ceiling and sumptuous carvings and decorations, the Lady Chapel was rightly described by the sixteenth-century historian John Leland as 'the wonder of the world'. Its bronze gates displayed a host of Tudor royal emblems: the Beaufort portcullis, the lions of England, the fleurs-de-lis of France, and the crown and thornbush, which may symbolise Henry's triumph over Richard III at Bosworth. The chapel would become the burial place of fifteen kings and queens (Henry VII and his wife Elizabeth included) and remains one of the most awe-inspiring expressions of monarchy ever created.

The king's health had never fully recovered from the prolonged bout of sickness he had suffered in 1503. Four years later, when he was in his fiftieth year, he was so incapacitated that his ministers began to speculate on the succession. By the beginning of 1509, it was obvious that Henry would not live much longer. In February, he moved to Richmond. There, he lingered on for almost two months, but died 'in an agony of pain and penitence' at around 11 p.m. on 21 April, surrounded by his most trusted attendants.[21]

Anxious to ensure a smooth succession, his close officials and servants kept his death secret for two full days while they made arrangements. Even the king's son and heir, Henry, was apparently kept in ignorance. But rumours of the king's demise were already circulating in the city the following day. Fearing unrest, those who were privy to the secret began to quietly stock the royal armoury. They need not have worried. Henry VIII would be the first monarch since 1421 to accede to the throne peacefully as a crowned king, rather than by usurpation or conquest.

Most of the late king's requests for his commemoration were carried out, notably the magnificent tomb at Westminster by Pietro Torrigiano, with its extraordinary lifelike effigies of Henry and his queen. But Henry had also left provision for a gold-plated statue of himself, kneeling in full armour, holding the crown as he had received it at Bosworth: at the hands of God. This was to be placed atop the shrine of Edward the Confessor, the most hallowed of all English monarchs. For the new king, though, this was evidently a bequest too far. The statue would remain a figment of his late father's imagination.

Henry VIII (1509–47)

'One supreme head and king'

T HERE HAD BEEN other examples in the history of the English monarchy of a king marking the beginning of his reign by distancing himself from the one before. Sometimes, this was to justify the deposition of his predecessor or to establish a new dynasty. Neither was true of Henry VIII, yet he went to greater lengths than any other monarch before him to prove how different he was from his father.

Some differences the new king did not have to prove. Physically, Henry VIII appeared the very opposite of his predecessor, whose slight frame had become increasingly emaciated in his later years. Now aged seventeen, Henry had matured into an impressive young man: strikingly handsome and with an athletic physique that had been honed by the many hours spent hunting and at the tiltyard. At six foot two inches, he towered over most other men at court. 'In this eighth Henry, God combined such corporal and mental beauty, as not merely to surprise but to astound all men', the Venetian ambassador enthused.[1] Another foreign envoy agreed that his 'acquirements and qualities are so many and excellent that I consider him to excel all who ever wore a crown'.[2]

With his auburn hair, fair complexion and broad-shouldered physique, the new king closely resembled his Yorkist grandfather, Edward IV. Like him, he was extrovert, affable and open-handed, and could dominate, as well as charm, any gathering. Less positively, he had inherited his grandfather's vanity, gluttony and licentiousness. But for now, everyone focused on the laudable characteristics they shared. 'For just as Edward [IV] was the most warmly thought of by the English people among all the English kings, so this successor of his, Henry, was very like him in general appearance, in greatness of mind and generosity and for that reason was the more acclaimed and approved of by all', observed Vergil.[3]

One of the new king's first acts was to issue a proclamation inviting anyone who had 'sustained injury, or loss of goods' during his father's reign to present their case to him. His treatment of Henry VII's despised officials, Empson and Dudley, provides the first flash of a brutality that would become ever more terrifying as his reign progressed. The king sent both men to the Tower and declared that 'the loss of many an honest man's goods . . . should now be recompensed with the loss of their heads'.[4] Even though Parliament did not confirm the attainder, Henry pushed ahead with it and the two men went to their deaths in August 1510.

Another marked change in royal policy was the new king's attitude towards his nobles. While his father had 'kept a straight hand on his nobility', Henry VIII released many of them from the bonds that had been imposed upon them.[5] He also invited them to take part in court revels, jousts and other entertainments, and gave them some of the most sought-after positions in the royal household. By the end of his reign, over half of the noble families in England owed their titles to him.

The new king soon turned his mind to more personal matters. On 11 June 1509, shortly before his eighteenth birthday, he finally married his late brother's widow, Catherine of Aragon, putting an end to years of diplomatic wrangling between England and Spain. They were crowned a little under two weeks later. Thanks to the full treasury that his father had bequeathed him, Henry was able to stage a ceremony so magnificent that it eclipsed any in living memory. Even Edward Hall, whose chronicle is filled with detailed descriptions of court ceremonies and pageants, was almost at a loss for words. 'For a surety more rich nor more strange nor curious works hath not been seen than were prepared against this coronation', he concluded.[6]

It was immediately obvious that Henry VIII's approach to his royal duties would be very different to his father's, too. Henry VII had been involved in the minutiae of government, poring over account books, statutes, court papers and the like, often adding notes and corrections in his own hand. It was a highly personal monarchy that brought every aspect of government under the king's direct control. But while this meant that he had bequeathed an efficient and tightly run structure to his son, its continued success depended upon the new king showing the same level of interest and commitment.

Henry VIII had come to the throne as the archetypal spare heir: pleasure-loving, gregarious and carefree. Until his elder brother Arthur's death in 1502, he had enjoyed almost untrammelled freedom to indulge his love of jousting, gambling and other pleasurable diversions. When he became heir to the throne, his father had tried to curb his wayward tendencies, with little success. Although he gloried in his newfound status as king, with all of the privileges and unfettered authority that it carried, Henry had little patience for the more routine affairs of state and found writing 'somewhat tedious and painful'. Instead, he spent most of his days out hunting and lived 'in continual festival', as his new wife put it.[7]

Perhaps not surprisingly for a king who set pleasure ahead of politics, Henry loved to be surrounded by his high-spirited companions at all times. The number of Henry's privy chamber staff rose dramatically during the early part of his reign: from the handful of servants whom his father had retained to as many as fifty attendants. Some privy chamber officials, such as Henry's childhood companion Charles Brandon, Duke of Suffolk, also served on the council, blurring the lines between the monarch's public and private worlds.

If the king mixed business with pleasure, then for the first few years of his reign it was the latter that predominated. 'Although always intelligent and judicious, he nevertheless allowed himself to be so allured by his pleasures, that, accustomed to ease, he for many years left the administration of the government to his ministers', recalled an Italian envoy.[8] This presented an opportunity that one minister in particular was quick to grasp.

Thomas Wolsey was the son of a butcher, but his 'very active and assiduous mind in matters of business' had propelled him into court circles during Henry VII's reign.[9] Realising that the new king was bent on recreation, Wolsey made an immediate impression by assuring him 'that he shall not need to spare any time of his pleasure for any business that should necessary happen in the council'.[10] In

June 1509, Henry VIII appointed Wolsey royal almoner, which involved distributing largesse on the king's behalf and enabled the holder to deal in all manner of legal, financial and ecclesiastical matters. Wolsey proved so able and efficient that before long he had become Henry's deputy and mouthpiece. The young king was 'wonderfully pleased' with this state of affairs. 'It came to such a pass', observed a contemporary, 'that the King intervened in nothing, and this Cardinal [Wolsey] did everything.'[11]

With his able servant managing the bulk of government business, the new king's domestic life also appeared to be thriving. On New Year's Day 1511, Queen Catherine gave birth to their first living child, a son. The boy was named after his father, and the news of his arrival was proclaimed across London, prompting days of public rejoicing. Henry and his wife attended the magnificent jousts and pageants that were held the following month at Westminster to celebrate the birth. But a few days later, disaster struck. The seemingly healthy child suddenly sickened. His death on 22 February plunged the nation into mourning. But, as yet, there was no reason to doubt that many more children would follow.

The king was soon distracted by plans for his first major military campaign since ascending the throne. The focus was England's traditional enemy, France. Like his predecessors, Henry had inherited the title King of France, but he took it more seriously than most. Having learned nothing from his father's impressive diplomacy, he cherished ambitions to revive the Hundred Years' War and win back the lands once held by the English monarchy. In 1513 he led an army into the Low Countries and succeeded in capturing Thérouanne and Tournai from the French king, Louis XII. This victory, which would become known as the Battle of the Spurs, would be celebrated by Henry for the rest of his reign. In his absence, England had won a more significant one against the Scots at Flodden. Henry's queen, whom he had left as regent, famously sent him a piece of the bloodied coat of James IV, who died in the battle, so that he might use it as a banner at the siege of Tournai.

Henry returned home victorious, but his campaign in France had come at a high price: around £1,000,000 (around £663,000,000 today)

– approximately ten times Henry's normal revenue. In a worryingly short space of time, he had all but exhausted the considerable resources that his father had bequeathed him. During the years that followed, it became increasingly obvious that the only element of his forebears' campaigning that Henry would experience was the crippling expense.

Within a year of his victory in France, the diplomatic situation shifted, depriving Henry of his allies, notably the Holy Roman Emperor, Maximilian I. Under pressure from the pope, in the summer of 1514, the English king made peace with France and agreed to marry his eighteen-year-old sister Mary to the elderly Louis XII. A little under three months after their wedding that October, the French king was dead. His cousin and successor, the twenty-year-old Francis I, swiftly became the English king's fiercest international rival. Like Henry, the new French king saw himself as a true Renaissance prince: cultured, well educated and a great patron of the arts. His athletic physique rivalled Henry's, he excelled in all manner of sports and was just as 'given to pleasure'.[12] Renowned for his sexual prowess, Francis fathered numerous children by his mistresses, as well as seven children by his wife Claude – a source of envy to his English rival, who still had no child to show for more than five years of marriage.

Boasting considerable wealth, Francis set about creating an impressive building legacy, including the magnificent Château de Chambord. Not to be outdone, the English king embarked upon a series of ambitious building projects of his own, earning him a place in English history as the most prolific royal builder of all time. During the course of Henry's reign, the stock of palaces rose from twelve to about fifty-five. One of the most spectacular was Nonsuch in Surrey. Designed as a celebration of the power of the Tudor dynasty, its name was a boast that there was no other palace like it in the world – a deliberate sideswipe at his French rival.

Henry sought to enhance his reputation as a Renaissance prince through his patronage of the arts. Most famous among the numerous foreign artists he engaged was the brilliant painter, Hans Holbein, whose startlingly lifelike portraits provide a window into the Tudor court. Both Erasmus and Thomas More praised the new king as a patron of good letters. He was the first English monarch since King

Alfred to write and publish a book – an impressive achievement, given his professed dislike for writing. Published in 1519 and entitled *Defence of the Seven Sacraments*, it was a theological treatise defending Catholicism against the teachings of Martin Luther, a radical German priest who had published an attack on the Roman Catholic Church two years earlier. The pope rewarded Henry with the title *Fidei Defensor* (Defender of the Faith). The English king's greatest cultural achievement, though, was in music. He excelled at the lute, virginals and recorder, and could also play the organ, then a notoriously difficult instrument. A keen singer and composer, he often performed with his courtiers. By the time of his death, he possessed over three hundred instruments.

In June 1520, Henry VIII's attention was once more drawn across the Channel when he came face to face with his French rival at a spectacular two-week event known as the Field of Cloth of Gold. Held on neutral territory close to Guînes in northern France, it was intended as an expression of the mutual accord between the two kings, whose intense rivalry threatened to upset the delicate balance of power in Europe. In reality, though, it presented an opportunity for each to outshine the other in magnificence and accomplishments. The man behind it was Thomas Wolsey, now a cardinal, who had long advocated peace between England and France, and who set about creating a showpiece such as the world had never seen.

After their carefully stage-managed greeting, 'these two noble kings went together into the rich tent of cloth of gold . . . arm in arm'.[13] But the intense rivalry between the two monarchs soon showed through the dazzling splendour. Henry might have bested his French rival in magnificence, but when he was beaten in a wrestling match that he challenged Francis to on a whim, things rapidly turned sour. After taking leave of the French king at the end of the event, Henry made his way to nearby Gravelines and concluded an alliance with Charles V, who promptly declared war on France.

Not long after the king had returned to England, he faced the first serious challenge to his regime. His policy of appeasement towards the English nobility appeared to have worked well, and during the first decade of his reign Henry was troubled by few of the threats that had plagued his father. But this harmony was disrupted by one of the most powerful Yorkist claimants. Edward Stafford, Duke of Buckingham, was the son of Katherine Woodville, a sister of Edward IV's queen. Like the Tudors, he could trace his descent from Edward III's son John of Gaunt, through the Beaufort family. So strong was his claim that when Henry VII had fallen seriously ill in 1503, many had whispered that Buckingham would succeed to the throne if the king died, rather than the king's own son, Henry.

Fiercely ambitious and dangerously volatile, the duke resented the influence of the 'boys' with whom Henry was surrounded.[14] But his greatest loathing was reserved for the king's low-born deputy, Wolsey, whose power was by now so unfettered that he was referred to as the *alter rex* ('other king'). Disappointed with high office, Buckingham boasted of his royal blood to anyone who would listen and even began talking of rebellion. The king had already instructed Wolsey to 'make good watch' on him, and by April 1521 the Cardinal had gathered enough evidence to have the duke arrested on suspicion of treason.[15] The following month, Buckingham was found guilty of having 'divers times . . . imagined and compassed traitorously and unnaturally the destruction of the most royal person of our said sovereign lord the king'.[16] He was executed the next day.

This marked a turning point in Henry's relations with his nobles. The open-handedness of his early reign had been replaced by the same paranoia that had characterised his late father's dealings with the nobility. At its root was the fact that after twelve years as king, he still had no male heir. His marriage to Catherine of Aragon had produced only one surviving child, the Princess Mary (born in 1516), and the thirty-five-year-old queen had shown no sign of pregnancy for two years. For the first time since the twelfth century, England faced the prospect of a female sovereign. As the daughter of Europe's great warrior queen, Isabella of Castile, Catherine did not see this as a disaster. But to her husband and his subjects, it was little short of a catastrophe.

Henry might have been more inclined to cling to the hope of another child by Catherine or to reconcile himself to leaving the throne to his daughter Mary if it had not been for his growing interest in a lady who first appeared at court in 1522. Anne Boleyn was the second of three surviving children born to the ambitious courtier, Thomas Boleyn, and his wife Elizabeth, daughter of Thomas Howard, second Duke of Norfolk. A combination of shrewd political acumen and advantageous marriages had transformed the Boleyn family from relatively obscure tenant farmers into titled gentry with a presence at court.

Anne was in her early twenties when her father secured her a place in Queen Catherine's household. Like her sister Mary, who had been Henry VIII's mistress for a while, she had spent time at the French court in service to Queen Claude, wife of Francis I. Anne's French manners and dress set her apart from the other ladies of Catherine's household. Although she was not considered beautiful – her skin was far too 'swarthy' and her bosom was 'not much raised' – she had an irresistible self-confidence and sense of style that drew men to her.[17]

It took Henry four years to notice Anne, but he made up for lost time. His interest rapidly turned into an all-consuming obsession. By 1526, there was no longer any hope of Queen Catherine bearing another child, whereas Anne was much younger and from fertile stock. What stoked Henry's ardour even more was the fact that she refused to become his mistress. Having seen how quickly her sister Mary had been discarded, Anne seemed determined to hold out for a greater prize.

In May 1527 the king took the first, secret steps towards having his marriage annulled, with the assistance of his trusted servant, Wolsey. To secure this, he required a dispensation from Rome. At the heart of his case was a passage in the Bible that stated if a man had sexual relations with his brother's wife, they would be childless.[18] But it was far from straightforward. Catherine insisted that her marriage to Arthur had not been consummated, and Pope Clement VII was dominated by her nephew, Emperor Charles V, so was reluctant to do anything against his wishes. The more Clement prevaricated, the more insistent Henry became that his marriage had offended God and must be dissolved. According to one contemporary, the king was so adamant that 'an angel descending from Heaven would be unable to persuade him otherwise'.[19]

Driven by his obsession for Anne Boleyn and the urgent need for a male heir, the king applied pressure on the pope to allow the case to be heard in England. After almost two more years of delays, in June 1529 a legatine court opened at Blackfriars in London with Lorenzo Campeggio as the papal representative. The most dramatic event of the hearing occurred on 21 June, when Queen Catherine appealed directly to Henry to admit that she was a virgin when she married him. He refused to reply, either because his conscience would not allow it or because he wished to bring the confrontation to a swift end. The proceedings dragged on until the end of July, at which point Campeggio adjourned the court until October.

By then, Wolsey was clinging on to power by his fingertips. Throughout the tortuous negotiations of the previous two years, his enemies at court (the Boleyn faction in particular) had been making the most of his failure to resolve the king's 'Great Matter'. In late October 1529, Henry had Wolsey charged in the Court of King's Bench with the offence of *praemunire* – breaching the statute made during Richard II's reign to prevent the assertion of papal jurisdiction against the supremacy of the monarch. Wolsey was dismissed from office and eventually made his way to York, where he was still archbishop. He was perhaps saved from a worse fate when, on his way back to London to face further charges a year later, his already fragile health gave way and he died on 29 November 1530.

The Cardinal's demise left a gaping hole at the centre of royal government. The man who filled it was not one of his many enemies, but a former protégé. Thomas Cromwell was the son of a Putney blacksmith and brewer who from an early age had sought to better himself. As a young man, he had travelled around France, Italy and the Netherlands, making a name for himself as a merchant and picking up the radical religious ideas that were spreading from Germany. Upon his return to England early in Henry VIII's reign, he established himself as a successful lawyer and man of business, and by the 1520s he was working for Wolsey.

Cromwell's unorthodox and cosmopolitan career gave him an edge over the other men of Henry VIII's court when he first appeared there in the wake of Wolsey's fall. Within an impressively short space of time, he was being referred to as 'the man who enjoys most credit with the king'.[20] For all his faults, the king was astute in his selection of advisers and recognised that here was a man of exceptional ability, just like his predecessor. Surrounded as he was by sycophants and flatters, Henry also appreciated Cromwell's no-nonsense, straight-talking approach.

Although Cromwell was a convenient replacement for the Cardinal, there was a significant difference in his relationship with the king. In the early years of his reign, Henry had been content to leave the majority of state business to Wolsey, but it was clear that he now intended to exercise a much tighter control. Partly this was because Henry no longer spent the majority of his time hunting and pursuing the other pleasurable pastimes of his youth, but it was also because the annulment was a matter in which he had a close vested interest. 'I do not choose any one to have it in his power to command me, nor will I ever suffer it', he told the Venetian ambassador.[21] It was a decisive moment in Henry's reign; a transition from carefree kingship to active monarchy.

Cromwell was quick to realise that his authority would be more prescribed than his late patron's had been. As he ruefully remarked to the imperial ambassador, Eustace Chapuys: 'The king, my master, is a great king, but very fond of having things his own way.'[22] The trouble was, Henry was far from consistent and his actions did not always, or even often, derive from a clear political strategy. He was secretive, too. 'If I thought that my cap knew my counsel, I would cast it into the fire and burn it,' he once declared.[23] His capricious nature would become ever more prominent in the years to come, which made the task of anticipating the royal will fraught with danger.

In the latter part of 1530, the Great Matter underwent a dramatic shift. Henry instructed his agents in Rome to deny the pope's right to consider Catherine's appeal because: 'In [our kingdom] we are supreme and so rule that we recognise no superior.'[24] In other words, if the pope failed to grant the annulment, Henry would simply bypass or, better still, break from Rome. At the suggestion of the new Archbishop of Canterbury, Thomas Cranmer, the king now shifted his campaign to the universities of Europe. The opinions of various leading theologians were canvassed about the justification of setting the king's power above the pope's. Building on this, Cranmer and his team of researchers proceeded to draft a theological justification for the annulment and a break with the papacy. In the process, he absorbed many of the evangelical ideas that were sweeping across Europe, which would come to be known as Protestantism. By questioning the practices of the Roman Catholic Church, these helped to justify the annulment – and spark a sweeping reformation of England's religious life.

Even before his desire for an annulment pushed the issue to the fore, Henry had guarded his God-given monarchical power jealously and was particularly sensitive to any encroachments by the church. As early as 1515, he had declared: 'By the ordinance of God we are King of England, and kings of England in time past have never had any superior but God only.' Five years later, he referred to his 'absolute power', which he claimed was 'above the laws'. To counter any criticism that he had thereby contravened his coronation oath, Henry later altered this in his own hand so that he swore to protect the 'lawful' rights of the church only when these were 'not prejudicial to his jurisdiction and dignity royal'.[25]

But while the king fully embraced the notion of supremacy over his own church, he was at heart a religious conservative and therefore uneasy about many of the reformist principles that underpinned the annulment. He was determined that England would remain a Catholic country; just not a Roman Catholic one. There was the international situation to consider, too. Catherine's nephew, Charles V, was the most powerful sovereign in Europe and Henry was desperate to keep him as an ally. The other great potentate, Francis I, was unlikely to risk his own favour with the papacy on behalf of his English rival. Worse still, Henry was aware of opposition within his own kingdom. There was widespread sympathy and support among the people for the 'true queen', Catherine, and they despised Anne Boleyn as the 'Great Whore'. Hostile placards began to appear in London, and both the court and council became polarised between religious reformists and conservatives.

In February 1531, convocation, the parliament of the English Church, was ordered by Henry to recognise the king as 'sole protector and also supreme head of the church in England'. After weeks of haggling, it eventually agreed, on condition that the words: 'as far as the law of Christ would allow' be added. In the spring of 1532, Parliament passed the Act in Conditional Restraint of Annates. This was an attempt to put pressure on the pope by ending the payments (or annates) made to Rome by senior English clerics and diverting them to Henry's treasury. It was a decisive step forward in the break with Rome by bringing the clergy more directly under the king's authority. But, as Cromwell was at pains to point out to his sovereign, it also swelled the royal coffers. Within two years it had raised an estimated £30,000 (equivalent to around £9.6 million), which prompted Chapuys to observe: 'These are devices of Cromwell, who boasts that he will make his master more wealthy than all the other princes of Christendom.'[26]

By the beginning of 1533, Henry was so confident of securing an annulment that he married Anne Boleyn in a private ceremony at Whitehall. There was an added incentive to contract the marriage in haste. Having been assured that the crown was within her grasp, Anne had finally consented to a full sexual relationship with Henry and had quickly fallen pregnant. It was vital that their child be born in wedlock for it to be accepted as a legitimate heir to the throne.

Cromwell and Cranmer set to work with renewed impetus. In April 1533, Parliament passed the Act in Restraint of Appeals, which required all ecclesiastical cases to be heard in England, rather than Rome. The triumphant preface made it clear how profound a moment this was in the history of the English monarchy: 'Where by divers sundry old authentic histories and chronicles it is manifestly declared and expressed that this realm of England is an empire, and so hath been accepted in the world, governed by one supreme head and king.'[27] From thenceforth, none of Henry's subjects were permitted to appeal to the 'Bishop of Rome', as the pope was now referred to, but must submit themselves to the king's authority alone. The Act empowered Cranmer to hear the case for the annulment. On 23 May he formally pronounced Henry's marriage to Catherine null and void, and his marriage to Anne valid. As well as reducing Catherine to the status of dowager Princess of Wales, this rendered her daughter Mary illegitimate. The seventeen-year-old princess (now simply 'Lady Mary') had been supplanted by the child that the new queen carried in her womb.

Pope Clement responded by ordering the English king to take Catherine back and condemning his marriage to Anne. This was the first test of Henry's authority and he responded with force: the English Church was under his jurisdiction now, not Rome's. His new wife, visibly pregnant, was crowned on 1 June amid spectacular pomp and ceremony, including a flotilla of fifty barges, gloriously arrayed pageants and even a fire-breathing dragon. The queen gave birth on 7 September, not to the hoped-for son and heir, but to a daughter, Elizabeth. It was a humiliating setback for Henry and seemed to make a mockery of everything he had gone through to secure the marriage. But, as he rather tactlessly remarked to Anne, she was still young and boys would soon follow.

In 1534, Parliament confirmed the Submission of the Clergy, which acknowledged that the law of the church would in future depend upon the consent of the king, in the same way as secular laws required his approval in Parliament. Henry angrily stamped down initial resistance from the bishops and crowed that they were now 'lower than shoemakers'.[28] It was a triumph for Cromwell and his reformist allies, but anathema to the religious conservatives at court. Principal among these was the Lord Chancellor, Thomas More. Henry had been only eight years old when first introduced to this leading light of Renaissance Humanism. More's sharp intellect and affable manner had made a lasting impression on the young prince, and as king, Henry had shown him great preferment. But More's seemingly inexorable rise was halted by the gathering religious storm. Shortly after the Submission of the Clergy, he tendered his resignation.

As well as pushing through Henry's religious reforms, Parliament passed a suite of legislation that tightened the crown's grip on would-be offenders. The treason statute he had inherited from Edward III, condemning any overt attempt to kill or dethrone the prince, did not go far enough. Between 1531 and 1544, a series of new offences were classified as high treason. By the terms of an Act of 1534, even speaking against the king was treason. Neither were his subjects permitted to criticise Henry's marriages, forge his privy seal, signet or sign manual, or refuse to swear the oath renouncing papal authority.

Other legislation now came thick and fast. In March 1534, the Act of Succession recognised Henry and Anne's children as lawful successors to the throne and required all the king's subjects, if commanded, to take an oath recognising its validity. Even though he was no longer a member of the government, Thomas More was among the first to be called upon. He had quickly become one of the main figureheads for opposition to the king's new marriage, so Henry was determined to make him openly conform. The difficulty was that the preamble to the Act included a refutation of papal authority. 'This is like a sword with two edges', More lamented, 'for if a man answer one way it will destroy the soul, and if he answer another it will destroy the body.' After procrastinating for as long as possible, he refused to take the oath. Furious at More's 'obstinacy', Henry sent him to the Tower on 17 April 1534, shortly followed by his fellow conservative, Bishop John Fisher, who had also rejected the oath.[29]

Their fate was sealed by the Act of Supremacy, which was passed in November 1534, and recognised the king as 'the only Supreme Head on earth of the Church of England'.[30] For the first time in England's history, its people were required not only to act as the king directed, but to believe as he did. What emerged during the years following the break with the papacy was a unique form of Christianity, distinct from both Rome and Lutheranism, and shaped at least in part by the king himself.

In separating his kingdom from Rome and making himself head of the English Church, Henry had not merely fallen out with the pope, as various monarchs had before him. He had redefined kingship. Supremacy over the church was now integral to the identity of the monarch. Like the Old Testament King David, Henry was answerable to God alone. From thenceforth, the highest-ranking members of the clergy held office only during the king's pleasure and were styled 'by royal authority'.

The new legislation claimed its first high-profile victims in the summer of 1535, when More and Fisher were beheaded on Tower Hill. Both men rapidly attained the status of martyrs and proved more dangerous to the king in death than they had been in life. More's reported last words that 'he died the King's good servant but God's first' became a slogan for the religious conservatives.[31] The king now risked a backlash from the Catholic potentates of Europe, foremost among whom was Emperor Charles V. But for now, he held his nerve and sanctioned a number of other reforming measures, notably the publication of the first complete modern English translation of the Bible by William Tyndale. The frontispiece was a masterful piece of Henrician propaganda. Designed by Hans Holbein, it shows Henry VIII enthroned directly beneath God as he distributes the Bible to the bishops in the presence of the laity.

For all his public bluff and bluster, in private the king was increasingly troubled. His new queen had not delivered either the promised marital bliss or, more crucially, the male heir that he so desperately needed. The fiery nature that had so attracted Henry before their marriage was wearisome in a wife, and the ever-vigilant Chapuys noted that in private he 'shrank from her'.[32] Anne had miscarried twice after Elizabeth's birth, but towards the end of 1535 she fell pregnant again. With her husband harbouring grave doubts about their marriage, it felt like the last throw of the dice.

January 1536 was marked by three events, each of which would have far-reaching consequences. The first was the death of Catherine of Aragon, who had been suffering from a prolonged illness (possibly cancer) for much of her exile from the court. Henry and Anne appeared at court decked out in yellow to celebrate the passing of the woman whom most of the king's subjects had persisted in regarding as the true queen. But the king's buoyant mood was brought to an abrupt end two weeks later when he suffered a heavy fall from his horse while jousting at Greenwich. Although the report that he was knocked unconscious for two hours can be discredited, the accident left him with a serious wound to his leg. It also served as a salutary reminder to the forty-four-year-old Henry and his subjects of his mortality, intensifying his need to secure the succession with a son.

Just five days after Henry's accident, on 29 January, the third – and arguably most catastrophic – event occurred. As Catherine's body was being laid to rest in Peterborough Cathedral, Queen Anne miscarried. 'The Concubine had an abortion which seemed to be a male child which she had not borne three and a half months, and on which the King has shown great distress', Chapuys reported with barely concealed triumph.[33] This time, Henry gave full vent to his anger and frustration. He had taken Catherine's death as a sign that heaven smiled upon his marriage to Anne, but now he ranted that 'God did not wish to give him male children'.[34] The woman for whom he had overturned the entire religion and government of his kingdom had become utterly abhorrent to him. Less than four months later, Anne was beheaded after being found guilty of adultery with five men, including her brother George. The charges, which were almost certainly false, were devised by Cromwell, now an implacable enemy of the queen. Even though Anne had few friends at court and was widely despised as the 'Concubine', the courage with which she defended herself at her trial and, four days later, met her death won the admiration of many. Even Henry was heard to remark: 'She hath a stout heart!'[35] Although he ordered all traces of Anne to be removed from his palaces, a few can still be seen today. One of the most extraordinary is a richly decorated falcon (Anne's heraldic badge) that probably once adorned the Tudor apartments at Hampton Court and was recently acquired at auction (see figure 3, p. 6).

While the king's marriage was unravelling, his religious reforms were surging ahead. The so-called 'Reformation Parliament' that had first met in November 1529 and had reconvened regularly to push through legislation breaking England from Rome, met again in February 1536. A suite of new measures was passed, including the stripping away of traditional Catholic images, relics, miracles and pilgrimages. Shrines were subsequently destroyed – most notably that of St Thomas Becket at Canterbury, which sent shockwaves through the more conservative sectors of the population.

The greatest destruction of all, though, was reserved for England's monastic life. For more than a century, there had been calls to reform the kingdom's monasteries. There were numerous examples of abbots steeped in sin, their religious houses feeding off the fat of the land and leaving the people in the surrounding communities to starve. Cromwell had been busily gathering evidence, quietly ignoring the genuine piety and good works that many monasteries still embodied, in order to justify their piecemeal destruction. He was also careful to make the king fully conversant with the extent of their wealth. Henry was easily persuaded. The French ambassador, Charles de Marillac, described the king as 'so covetous that all the riches in the world would not satisfy him'.[36] Now that he was head of the church, the wealth of the monasteries was his for the plundering.

The Dissolution of the Monasteries, which began in the spring of 1536, brought the crown incalculable riches. The suppression of the smaller houses alone generated in excess of £70,000 (around £30 million) during the first two and a half years – incentive enough for the king to sanction the dissolution of the larger houses during the years that followed. It was all done with bewildering speed. Across the country, teams of workmen appointed by royal officials stripped each monastery of its treasures – even the lead from the roof was taken off and either sold or reused by the crown. The total amount raised from the sale of the jewels, plate, lead and other valuables was estimated at £100,000 (more than £42 million today). The annual incomes of the houses, meanwhile, brought the crown a further £32,000 (£13.5 million).

The destruction of the monasteries was a brutal symbol of Henry's reformation and of his monarchy, and was widely condemned across Roman Catholic Europe. The French ambassador, Marillac, was outraged that the English king had 'perverted the rights of religion, marriage, faith and promise, as softened wax can be altered to any form'.[37] The vast majority of Henry's own subjects viewed it as a shocking act of vandalism. It was not long before anguish turned to opposition.

On 1 October 1536, Thomas Kendall, vicar of Louth in Lincolnshire, used his weekly sermon to speak out against the king's agents, who were expected in the town the following day. It was rumoured that these men were planning to raid all of the local churches, as well as the monasteries. The rumours spread like wildfire, and within days almost all of north Lincolnshire was up in arms. Revolts soon broke out in the northern counties, which, at the greatest distance from the court in London, had often proved the most challenging for the crown to control. Before long, members of the northern nobility had joined the uprisings, which became known collectively as the Pilgrimage of Grace.

This was the greatest threat to the king's authority that he had faced during his twenty-seven years on the throne. Although Henry sent sizeable forces to suppress the uprisings, they were outnumbered by those of the rebels. His commanders had little choice but to negotiate a truce, promising that the king would listen to the rebels' grievances. But as soon as the royal troops had brought the situation under control, this promise was broken. Henry ordered the execution of more than two hundred rebels and had the leaders brought to London for interrogation. Rather than heeding their grievances, he upbraided them as 'brute and beastly' commoners who had dared to 'find fault with your prince'.[38]

What now began was little short of a reign of terror. Henry boasts the dubious achievement of putting to death more English notables than any other monarch before or since. His victims included wives, members of the peerage, high-ranking clergymen, ministers, intimate friends and attendants. Nobody was safe. As the courtier-poet Thomas Wyatt shrewdly observed: 'circa Regna tonat' ('round the throne the thunder rolls').[39] Far from being cowed by opposition, the king's belief in the justice of his actions was strengthened. Henry had an innate ability to believe his own publicity. His version of events was always the right one, even if it flew in the face of reality.

One of the king's most outspoken critics was the cleric Reginald Pole, grandson of Edward IV's brother, George, Duke of Clarence. In 1536, from the safety of Italy, he sent the king this stinging rebuke: 'You have squandered a huge treasure; you have made a laughing-stock of the nobility; you have never loved the people; you have pestered and robbed the clergy in every possible way; and lately you have destroyed the best men in your kingdom [Fisher and More], not like a human being, but like a wild beast.'[40]

Henry responded with all of the brutality for which he was now notorious. Pole might be beyond his grasp, but he took his revenge against those closest to him. His brother Geoffrey was forced to provide evidence against another brother, Henry, as well as the king's own cousin, Henry Courtenay, Marquess of Exeter. Both were put to death. Most horrific of all was the punishment meted out to Reginald's aged mother, Margaret. She was imprisoned in the Tower for two and a half years before being beheaded in a horrifically blundered execution at the age of sixty-eight.[41] The so-called 'White Rose' faction had been all but obliterated.

At the same time as bringing his English subjects to heel, Henry took decisive measures to exert his authority over the outlying parts of his domain. In 1536, Bills were presented in Parliament aimed at integrating Wales and England, imposing English law and institutions into the principality, dividing it into counties on the English model and banning the Welsh language for all official business. The government of Calais was more thoroughly dealt with than ever before, including granting it two seats in Parliament like any English borough. Taken together, this legislation can be viewed as a deliberate move towards a sovereign unitary state and another potent expression of Henry's supreme monarchical authority. The previous five hundred years had been marked by costly overseas wars and bloody rebellions, during which the crown had been at turns won, lost, threatened and stabilised. But now the law had proved mightier than the sword. English royal power had reached its zenith through the statute book.

The king's stridently self-confident public image disguised a growing paranoia. 'He dares not trust a single man', claimed ambassador Marillac.[42] His ongoing failure to father a son heightened Henry's vulnerability as the only surviving male scion of the Tudor dynasty. But in October 1537, all of that changed. Jane Seymour, whom Henry had married a few days after Anne Boleyn's execution, gave birth to a healthy boy, Edward. Henry's joy was dampened by Jane's death from an infection twelve days later. Paradoxically, now that he at last had the male heir he had hankered after for almost thirty years, it seemed to intensify his insecurity. In an age of high infant mortality, the succession rested upon the fragile life of a tiny baby.

Henry's paranoia was further stoked by a growing sense of his own mortality. In the years following the jousting accident of January

1536, he had been unable to exercise as he once had and had gained a colossal amount of weight. 'The King was now overgrown with corpulence and fatness, so that he became more and more unwieldy', observed the chronicler Edward Hall. Henry also suffered acute pain from a chronic leg ulcer that regularly produced dangerous attacks of fever. Determined to betray no hint of frailty in public, he insisted on walking unaided (albeit leaning heavily on a staff), but in private he was lifted between the floors of his privy lodgings in a Tudor-style stairlift, and 'carried to and fro in his galleries and chambers' on richly decorated chairs.[43]

Thanks in no small part to Cromwell, throughout these years of the king's declining health, there was no interruption to the progress of his reforms. The last twelve parliamentary sessions of Henry's reign produced more than five hundred Bills. But in contrast to previous reigns during which Parliament had been particularly active, this enhanced, rather than challenged, the position of the monarchy. Parliament neither questioned nor opposed Henry's supremacy, but strengthened it by statute. It was with some justification that in 1542 he declared: 'We, at no time stand so highly in our estate royal as in the time of Parliament, wherein we as head and you as members are conjoined and knit together into one body politic.'[44]

The extent to which the king himself, rather than his most able minister Cromwell, was directing this legislation is difficult to gauge. Certainly, Henry was much more actively engaged in the government of his realm than he had been in the early years of his reign. But Cromwell's hand can be seen more clearly than his sovereign's in the majority of the new legislation. It is likely that the king mostly sanctioned measures that his minister had initiated. 'Cromwell rules all', observed Reginald Pole at the height of the Reformation.[45] But Henry was not a man to be ruled by anyone – at least, not knowingly. A natural bully, he even resorted to violence on occasion, hitting his minister 'well about the pate . . . as it were a dog'.[46]

To curry favour, Cromwell headed the search for a new bride for his master. Jane Seymour might have given Henry a male heir, but every king needed at least one spare. He also had an incentive to seek his next wife abroad. England's security in Europe rested largely upon the traditional enmity between Charles V and Francis I. But the prospect of a rapprochement between the two potentates was becoming ever more real, which left Henry in desperate need of new allies. This strengthened the case for Cromwell's preferred candidate: Anne, the younger daughter of Johann, Duke of Cleves, who, like Henry, had expelled papal authority from his domain. Having seen Holbein's portrait of Anne, Henry gave his assent to the match and she made her way to England at the end of 1539.

Their first meeting could not have gone worse. 'I like her not! I like her not!' the king shouted at the hapless Cromwell, complaining that his betrothed was 'nothing so well as she was spoken of'.[47] It was more than just Anne's appearance that Henry found repellent: she did not possess the courtly refinements that he had come to expect in a wife. But the marriage had been contracted and Henry had no choice than to go ahead with it in January 1540. He drew the line at consummating it, though, and instructed Cromwell to arrange an annulment with all due haste.

Cromwell's enemies confidently predicted that the Anne of Cleves fiasco would be his downfall. In fact, he weathered that storm but had no defence against a conspiracy led by the Duke of Norfolk, who convinced Henry that his chief minister was plotting treason. They pointed to the fact that Cromwell kept a large number of servants and retainers and claimed that he had been overheard to remark: 'I hope to be a king myself one day.'[48] They also made much of the minister's friendly overtures towards Henry's elder daughter Mary, hinting that he planned to marry her in order to bolster his claim to the throne. It was all utterly groundless: Cromwell might be powerful, but he was still just the son of a blacksmith and was far too shrewd a man to cherish such overblown ambitions. But it took little to ignite the suspicions of a king who was by now as deeply paranoid about threats to his crown as his father had been. Cromwell was arrested on 10 June 1540 and sent to the Tower. After being condemned of a string of trumped-up charges, he was beheaded on 28 July.

On the same day, Henry married the Duke of Norfolk's niece, Katherine Howard, having secured an annulment of his marriage to Anne of Cleves with Cromwell's help. The apparent ease with which he was able to instantly move on from someone he had been close to – whether minister, wife or confidant – bordered on the pathological. His new bride was still a teenager and more than thirty years his junior. Although young, Katherine was no innocent. She was probably only about twelve years old when she had her first sexual liaison, with her music teacher, and at least one other had followed. All of this had been carefully concealed from the king.

Soon realising that there was no viable replacement for Cromwell, Henry began to rule through the council, which gradually became a permanent 'privy council' of nobles and officials. But without the leadership of a chief minister, Henry's policies lacked focus and his religious reforms foundered. Increasingly, he sought a middle ground between the radicals and conservatives at his court. He signalled this in typically brutal fashion two days after Cromwell's execution by ordering the burning at the stake of three evangelicals and three conservatives known to be loyal to Rome.

The 1540s were not kind to Henry. In October 1541, his son Edward fell dangerously ill with a quartan fever, a form of malaria. Panic-stricken, the king immediately summoned 'all the doctors in the country', including William Butts, his own personal physician.[49] To his enormous relief, Edward recovered, but it had been a salutary reminder of the fragility of the succession.

The prospect of begetting a spare heir was slim. By the time he married Katherine Howard, Henry had been suffering from impotence for a number of years. When he discovered that his young wife had been seeking sexual gratification away from the marriage bed, he was devastated – particularly as her lover was Thomas Culpepper, a close attendant of the king. Katherine's scandalous past was also uncovered, which left Henry humiliated as well as heart-broken. The men involved were executed in December 1541, and Katherine was put to death the following February.

'Since he heard of his late wife's conduct he has not been the same man', reported Chapuys.[50] It would be the beginning of a steady decline for the king, both mentally and physically. Culpeper's betrayal made him even more watchful and suspicious of the other men who served him. From now on, Henry increasingly ruled by fear, abandoning the desire for unity that he had expressed in the wake of Cromwell's execution.

The king's sixth and final marriage, to the twice-widowed Katherine Parr, brought him a degree of comfort and companionship. She distracted the king from his cares with lively conversation and a steady, calming presence. The new queen was popular with her stepchildren, too, and it was thanks to her that the king's neglected daughters, Mary and Elizabeth, were restored to the royal succession. Unusually well educated for a woman in this age, Katherine was of strong reformist opinions, some of which were expressed in her book, *The Lamentation of a Sinner*. Her radical ideas landed her in trouble when a plot led by the conservatives at court resulted in the king issuing a warrant for her arrest. It was only thanks to Katherine's being able to assure Henry in person of her compliance that she avoided the fate of her predecessors.

In 1544, Henry appointed his wife regent while he embarked on one last quest to recapture the French inheritance of his medieval ancestors. In alliance with Emperor Charles V, he sent a huge invasion force of almost forty thousand men across the Channel. Despite being morbidly obese and in crippling pain, Henry personally took command of his forces at Boulogne in July and was triumphant when the French surrendered two months later. But shortly after arriving back in England, he received news that Charles V had concluded a peace with Francis I, leaving Henry's men to face the French alone. Worse still, in July 1545 the French launched a counter-attack. From Portsmouth, Henry witnessed the Battle of the Solent and watched in horror as his flagship, the *Mary Rose*, was sunk. By the following June, a lack of funds compelled him to make peace with his French rival. Although England would retain Boulogne for eight years, the town was hardly sufficient recompense for the huge expense involved. In his last-gasp attempt at playing the warrior king, Henry had gone out with a whimper, not a bang.

On Christmas Eve 1545, the king, now aged fifty-four, delivered the closing speech in Parliament. Many of its members shed a tear to see their once invincible sovereign leaning heavily on a staff, visibly pained by his ulcerated leg. Acutely aware that his government was riven with factions, Henry exhorted those present to 'study and take pains to amend one thing which is surely amiss and far out of order, to the which I most heartily require you, which is that charity and concord is not amongst you, but discord and dissensions beareth rule in every place'.[51]

With Henry's health failing and his only son still in his infancy, the prospect of a minority rule seemed ever more certain. Although Prince Edward would ascend the throne uncontested, certain changes that his father had made to the legislation surrounding the royal succession before his birth would have far-reaching repercussions. The 1536 Act of Succession stated that in the absence of legitimate children of his own, the king had the right to nominate his heir.[52] Henry's intention had been to bypass the children of his two sisters, Margaret and Mary, whose descendants were, respectively, the Stuarts of Scotland and the Grey family. But by making the royal succession more a matter of choice than inheritance, Henry had bequeathed a dangerous legacy to his heirs, one that would plague every Tudor monarch until the end of the dynasty.

On 30 December 1546, Henry revised his last will and testament. He confirmed Edward as his heir, followed by Mary and Elizabeth. As Prince Edward was only nine years old, the will also made provision for the government of the country during his minority. The king nominated sixteen executors to function as his son's privy council under the leadership of Edward Seymour, Earl of Hertford, brother of the late Queen Jane. In making Seymour merely the first among equals and obliging him to secure the consent of the rest of Edward's council before taking any action, the king was clearly trying to prevent an abuse of royal authority.

By the beginning of 1547, Henry's life was ebbing rapidly away and he remained in strict seclusion at Whitehall Palace while rumours of his death abounded. Although his body was failing, his mind was not. More alive to threats against his throne than ever, on 19 January he sent his last victim to the block. Henry Howard, Earl of Surrey, had been foolish enough to boast of his royal blood by displaying the royal arms and insignia in his own heraldry. For good measure, on 27 January the king also ordered the execution of his father, the Duke of Norfolk. But the duke had a lucky escape. Early the following morning, the king breathed his last.

* * *

Henry VIII might be best remembered for his six wives, but his legacy is far more profound than that. He rejected papal authority, wielded absolute spiritual sovereignty over his subjects and established an independent Church of England, which still exists today. In so doing, he ushered in sweeping reforms to both the religious and political life of his people, filling the royal treasury with plundered church wealth and significantly enhancing the importance of Parliament. Among the huge number of statutes and reforms that were introduced during his reign, one of the most significant for the future of the monarchy was the requirement, for the first time, that subjects' beliefs must align with those of their sovereign. Thereafter, ideological conformity and non-conformity became dominant features of English life.

In the centuries following his death, Henry has often been judged a tyrant, driven by selfish desires and greed. In part this is justified: the king that he became was in all essential respects the same as the indulged and petulant child who had dominated the royal nursery at Eltham Palace. But, thanks largely to his highly effective use of propaganda, this was never how he was viewed by his loyal subjects. The accounts left behind by his courtiers, officials and ambassadors, as well as the popular ballads of the time, suggest that he was everything a king should be: magnificent, chivalrous, militaristic and awe-inspiring. Above all, the sheer force of his personality had enabled him to fully realise the power of the English crown. As he reminded the Earl of Surrey in the later years of his reign, as 'sovereign lord and prince . . . of our absolute power we be above the laws'.[53]

Henry's reign had witnessed the apogee of personal monarchy in England. Thereafter, partly because of what he had set in train, government would become progressively larger and more bureaucratic, royal authority diminishing in directly inverse proportion. And the Protestant faith, which his reforms had paved the way for, would challenge and ultimately destroy the English monarchy a century later.

Edward VI (1547–53)

'A youth who most assuredly was destined for rule'

H ENRY VIII'S DEATH was concealed from his subjects for two full days, just as his own father's had been. His son and successor was informed of it by his uncle, Edward Seymour, who was quick to take control. He persuaded the council to make him Governor of the King's Person and Protector of the Realm, as well as Duke of Somerset.

On 31 January, a proclamation announced Edward VI's accession. The wording hinted at radical changes to come. As Henry VIII's son had come to the throne 'fully invested . . . in the crown imperial of this realm', appointed by God not man, nothing was needed to confirm his authority.[1] The theme was taken up at the new king's coronation on 20 February 1547. Whereas previously, the monarch had made certain promises to the church and people, the new oath reinforced the royal supremacy over every aspect of England's religious, political, social and economic life. As such, it provided ardent reformers such as Archbishop Cranmer with the legal grounding they needed to usher in even more radical reforms than had been seen in Henry VIII's day.

In order to dispel any lingering thoughts that the monarchy's power would be eroded now that a boy king occupied the throne, Cranmer broke with centuries of royal tradition by giving a coronation speech. Addressing Edward, he declared: 'Your Majesty is God's Vicegerent, and Christ's Vicar within your own Dominions.'[2] The anti-papal sentiment continued in the celebrations and masques that followed. Edward took great delight in all of them.

Although England faced years of minority rule, confidence in the young king's potential was high. The martyrologist John Foxe praised Edward 'for his sage and mature ripeness in wit and all princely ornaments . . . I see but few to whom he may not be equal.'[3] Polydore Vergil described Edward as: 'A youth who most assuredly was destined for rule, for virtue and for wisdom. He is endowed with the highest talents and has aroused the greatest expectations among all men.'[4]

The new king was certainly an accomplished young man who had been educated for his future role from infancy. His religious training was every bit as rigorous as the rest of his extensive curriculum, which justifies the claim that he was England's best-educated king. He had received close guidance from Archbishop Cranmer, who had inspired him with a passion for the Protestant faith. For all his radical reforms, Henry VIII had remained a Catholic at heart, as had his church. But his son was determined to change that.

Edward's court mirrored that of his late father in splendour and refinement and, like Henry VIII, the young king invested enormous sums in what has been termed the 'theatre' of Tudor majesty, including an extensive wardrobe and some of the most expensive jewels on the European market.[5] Edward was like his father in other ways, too. Indulged from birth as Henry's 'precious jewel', he was just as fond of having his own way and when crossed his temper could be equally savage. The full-length portrait painted in the year of his accession shows him striking a deliberately similar pose to his father: hands on hips, legs astride and wearing heavily padded clothing to make his youthful physique more imposing.

Soon after Edward's coronation, Cranmer wrote to the young king, urging him 'to finish and bring to pass that your father did most godly begin'.[6] Edward needed no persuasion. He made no secret of his vehement hatred of Catholicism and once wrote an essay in which he declared that the pope was 'the true son of the devil, a bad man, an Antichrist'.[7] Every day, Edward listened with rapt attention as ten chapters of the Bible were read to him, and in 1550 he began his own independent study of it, highlighting passages for special enquiry.

From the beginning of the reign, a suite of radical religious reforms was introduced that led to the stripping away of every remnant of medieval Christianity: the richly decorated church interiors, the mystery plays, maypoles, holy day pageants, pilgrimages and other cherished traditions that had long been a part of everyday life. Flying in the face of growing popular disquiet, in January 1549 Parliament passed the Act of Uniformity, which established Archbishop Cranmer's Book of Common Prayer as the only legal form of worship in England. From thenceforth, the Catholic Latin Mass, which had been celebrated throughout the kingdom for centuries, was banned. England was now a Protestant country.

Although Edward was just eleven years old when the new prayer book was introduced, he had a firm grasp of the complex theology that underpinned it. He was rapidly maturing into a serious, priggish young man for whom religion was all-consuming. 'In the court there is no bishop, and no man of learning so ready to argue in support of the new doctrine as the king', reported the imperial ambassador.[8] Edward gave his full support to Cranmer in implementing uniformity of worship for all. The Book of Common Prayer was followed by an even more radical version three years later. This provided a model for worship within the Church of England for the next four centuries.

While these religious reforms were being implemented, a storm was gathering at the heart of government. The king's uncle, Somerset, had courted the resentment of his fellow councillors by breaching the already considerable authority he enjoyed as Lord Protector. He seemed determined to make himself 'the king of the king', as one contemporary observed, and 'had no one here superior to him in any degree of honour'.[9] The councillor who resented this most was Somerset's own brother, Thomas Seymour, Baron Sudeley. Every bit as ambitious as his elder brother, but lacking his subtlety, Sudeley began scheming to oust him from power. Rather than fight his brother in the political arena, he used his considerable charisma to ingratiate himself with members of the royal family.

In April or May 1547, Sudeley secretly married the late king's widow, Katherine Parr. They had known each other for some time and Katherine would probably have married him sooner, had she not caught Henry VIII's eye. The unseemly haste with which the dowager queen married her former suitor caused a scandal at court and the young king noted that his uncle Somerset was 'much offended'.[10] One of the few people who seemed to approve of the match was Henry VIII's younger daughter, Elizabeth. She was extremely close to Katherine and had lived with her at Chelsea since her father's death. Rather than disassociating herself from her former stepmother, as her half-sister Mary urged, she chose to remain at Chelsea after Sudeley had moved in – with disastrous results. It was not long before Sudeley began making inappropriate advances towards the thirteen-year-old princess. On one occasion, he burst into her bedchamber before she was up and dressed, and proceeded to 'strike her upon the back or on the buttocks familiarly'.[11]

There was another young woman of royal blood in Katherine's household who became the focus of her new husband's attentions. Lady Jane Grey was the daughter of the king's cousin, Frances, Duchess of Suffolk, who in turn was the daughter of Henry VIII's younger sister Mary. Born in October 1537, Jane was very close in age to Edward and, like him, of 'godly learning' and intensely pious. Little is known of her early years, but there is evidence to suggest an unhappy childhood at her parents' estate at Bradgate Park in Leicestershire.

According to the terms of Henry VIII's will, Jane was fourth in line to the throne, which prompted Sudeley to secure her wardship and move her to live with him and Katherine at Chelsea. He promised her father, Henry Grey, Marquess of Dorset, that he would find her a husband 'much to her father's comfort' and, when pressed, vowed that this would be none other than the king.[12] At Chelsea, Lady Jane was educated alongside Princess Elizabeth under the tutelage of evangelical scholars appointed by Katherine. Jane won praise for her intense piety and 'towardness' and, like Elizabeth, became deeply attached to the dowager queen.

This domestic harmony was destroyed when Katherine, who was pregnant with Sudeley's child, discovered him in a clinch with Elizabeth and furiously ordered the princess to leave her house at once.[13] But when the dowager queen died soon after giving birth to a short-lived daughter in September 1548, Sudeley renewed his attentions towards the princess. By Christmas that year, the court was alive with rumours that he was on the verge of taking Elizabeth as his wife.

All the while, Sudeley had been secretly cultivating his nephew the king. Aware that his elder brother Somerset strictly controlled access to the boy, he had bribed some of the privy chamber servants into facilitating his nightly visits. Edward had entered into the subterfuge with a child's delight. But in January 1549, Sudeley's schemes were discovered and he arrived to find the chamber door locked. When the king's dog began barking, Sudeley shot it dead. To be caught outside the king's bedchamber with a loaded pistol was a serious offence, and his brother was quick to interpret it in the worst possible terms. Sudeley was arrested on suspicion of high treason and imprisoned in the Tower.

A key part of the evidence against Sudeley was that he had conspired to marry the king's sister without the council's permission – an offence punishable by death. Two of Elizabeth's closest attendants were taken to the Tower for interrogation and the princess herself was subjected to intense questioning at her residence in Hatfield. Although the king's officials found no evidence of wrongdoing on Elizabeth's part, Sudeley was convicted of thirty-three charges of treason – most of them fabricated. Somerset did not flinch from sending his younger brother to the block on 20 March 1549.

The Lord Protector's casual dispatching of his own flesh and blood did little to bolster his waning popularity. The first serious resistance to his regime arose in Devon and Cornwall in June 1549, followed by numerous other uprisings elsewhere. Opposition to the religious reforms combined with discontent at the increasingly prevalent practice of enclosure – the fencing of common land by landlords for their own use, which deprived peasants of a place to graze their animals. To make matters worse, some tenants were forced off their farms so that the landlords could convert arable land to pasture for sheep, which had become more profitable with the increasing demand for wool. Together with inflation, rising rents, declining wages and high levels of unemployment, this created a climate ripe for rebellion. In July, some 16,000 malcontents led by the charismatic yeoman Robert Kett stormed the city of Norwich and defeated a royal army sent to crush it. Order was eventually restored, but only after expending almost all of the young king's reserves.

Undaunted, Edward was determined that all of his subjects, regardless of rank or status, must conform. His elder half-sister Mary earned a sharp reprimand in January 1551 for refusing to give up the Mass. This worked little effect upon her, as the young king noted in his journal two months later: 'She answered that her soul was God's and her faith she would not change.'[14] They remained at loggerheads for the rest of the reign. By contrast, the younger of Edward's sisters, Elizabeth, who had been educated with him for a time, shared his reformist views and was openly conformist. As a result, Edward grew closer to her, while Mary was left out in the cold.

The young king weathered the storm of 1549, but his uncle and Lord Protector did not. Somerset's flagrant disregard for the authority of Edward's council eventually alienated his erstwhile ally, John Dudley, Earl of Warwick, a leading member of the council. When Somerset realised that Dudley was conspiring to deprive him of power, he pursued him 'with the most unrelenting hatred'.[15] But Dudley's support was greater and, in October 1549, he led a successful coup to oust the Lord Protector from office. Edward himself was persuaded to order his uncle's arrest. Although Somerset was subsequently released and readmitted to the privy council, he was deprived of any real power from that day forward.

Dudley was now the dominant force and took care to surround the young king with men of his own choosing. Nobody could gain access to Edward without his sanction, and he made sure to visit his royal master regularly in order to influence his views. But in contrast to his predecessor, Dudley treated Edward as a king whose opinions he sought and respected, not a boy who could be moulded to his will. He realised that Edward's precociousness was matched by his sovereign will and a determination to uphold the royal supremacy for which his father had fought so hard. When the Bishop of Gloucester was confirmed in July 1550, Edward went through the order of service himself and angrily deleted any references to saints from the oath of supremacy. The following year, his Lord Chancellor earned the sharp reprimand: 'The number of councillors does not make our authority'

– or, in other words, royal authority was vested in the king himself, not his council.[16]

But in other respects, Dudley had failed to learn from the example of his predecessor. With power came greed, and he soon began to hanker after even greater advancement. In October 1551 he was raised to the dukedom of Northumberland, a move that fuelled the growing resentment against him. The same month, he discovered that Somerset was conspiring against him and wasted no time in having him sent to the Tower on trumped-up charges of treason. He was put to death the following January. With customary brevity, the young king recorded in his journal: 'The Duke of Somerset had his head cut off upon Tower Hill between eight and nine o'clock in the morning.'[17]

In April 1552, Edward noted that he was 'sick of the measles and smallpox'.[18] Although the young King recovered, declaring: 'we have shaken that quite away', his constitution seems to have been fatally weakened. Measles is known to suppress immunity to tuberculosis, the symptoms of which Edward began to display that Christmas. In March the following year the Venetian envoy reported that the king was dying.

It was probably around this time that Edward drafted his 'Devise' for the succession.[19] The king's natural successors were his two half-sisters, Mary and Elizabeth. But his father's Succession Act of 1536 had given him the legal basis to make his own choice. He was apparently motivated to disinherit them because of the risk that they might marry a foreigner who would undermine both 'the laws of this realm' and 'his proceedings in religion'.[20] According to Sir Edward Montague, chief justice of the common pleas, the king also believed his sisters bore the 'shame' of illegitimacy. An extraordinarily convoluted alternative was proposed. The crown would pass in succession to Protestant males or, in their absence, to one of their would-be mothers who would rule not as queen but as 'governess' supported by a council of advisers. Edward nominated as governess first his cousin Frances Brandon, then her daughters, Jane, Katherine and Mary Grey, and after that Margaret Clifford, the daughter of Frances's younger sister.

The 'Devise' was drafted in Edward's own hand and it is likely to have been a true reflection of his wishes. But a significant amendment was subsequently made, almost certainly at Dudley's behest. As the king's health deteriorated, the wording was altered to favour his cousin, Lady Jane Grey: 'Jane's heirs male' became 'Jane *and* her heirs male'. It is no coincidence that Jane was about to become Dudley's daughter-in-law.

Jane had remained with Katherine Parr until her death and had been the chief mourner at her funeral. Following Sudeley's fall, she had returned to her childhood home of Bradgate Park. Her parents still wished to make a good marriage for her, though, and from October 1551 they made frequent visits to court with their eldest daughter. Jane proved more interested in her studies than in finding a husband and displayed a very uncourtier-like refusal to bend her views to suit those of her superiors. When Princess Mary presented her with a rich gown of gold and velvet, she refused to wear it, declaring: 'It were a shame to follow my Lady Mary against God's word and leave my Lady Elizabeth which followeth God's word.'[21]

When it became obvious that the young king did not have long to live, Jane's parents shifted their ambitions for her marriage to the next best candidate: Guildford Dudley, son of the man who had ruled England since ousting Protector Somerset. Jane tried to resist but 'by the urgency of her mother and the violence of her father, who compelled her to accede to his commands by blows', she went ahead with the ceremony, which was conducted at the Dudleys' London residence on 21 May 1553.[22]

Dudley may have prompted the amendment to the Devise, but Edward also strongly favoured Lady Jane Grey as his successor. Jane's reputation as an intensely devout evangelical convinced him that, even more than his half-sister Elizabeth, she could be trusted to further his Reformation. Edward therefore made it clear that the reworded Devise had his blessing. When one of his lawyers questioned its legality, the dying king 'with sharp words and angry countenance' commanded him and all others to accept it.[23]

When Edward died on 6 July, aged just fifteen, it was with this prayer on his lips: 'O Lord God, save thy chosen people of England! O my Lord God, defend this realm from papistry, and maintain thy true religion.'[24] They were fitting words for England's first Protestant monarch. He had overseen sweeping religious change during his brief reign and, had he lived longer, would have striven to eradicate all traces of Catholicism from the kingdom.

With the death of Henry VIII's 'precious jewel', the male Tudor line was extinguished. It was now left to the female members of the dynasty to make their mark.

Lady Jane Grey (July 1553)

The crown was not a plaything

O N 10 JULY, four days after Edward VI's death, the sixteen-year-old Lady Jane Grey was proclaimed queen. The Bishop of London preached a sermon at Paul's Cross declaring her right to the throne and denouncing the princesses Mary and Elizabeth as bastards. Shortly afterwards, Jane and her husband Guildford entered the Tower of London amid great ceremony. Eyewitnesses noted that she was 'very short and thin, but prettily shaped and graceful', while her new husband was 'a tall strong boy with light hair'.[1] Both were bedecked in the Tudor colours of white and green.

But it would take a good deal more than such displays to convince the people of England that Jane was the rightful heir. Even though she had been proclaimed queen in London and across the kingdom – even as far away as the Channel Islands – there was a notable lack of rejoicing among her new subjects. England was not used to queens; neither did it welcome one who had disrupted the firmly established hereditary succession. Jane herself harboured grave doubts about the justice of her accession. Upon hearing that she was queen, she was 'stupefied and troubled', and fell to the ground weeping and declaring her 'insufficiency'. Ever willing to sacrifice her desires to a higher purpose, though, she prayed that if the crown was 'rightfully and lawfully hers', God would grant her grace to govern the realm to his glory and service.[2]

Although she had been thrust upon the throne by her father-in-law, the young queen soon made it clear that she would not simply act as his puppet. She refused to make his son Guildford king, reputedly saying that 'the crown was not a plaything for boys and girls'.[3] This prompted a furious row with her husband's family. 'Thus in truth was I deceived by the duke [of Northumberland] and the council and ill-treated by my husband and his mother,' she lamented, after realising the extent to which she had been manipulated by them.[4]

Dudley's propaganda had tried to whip up fears that if Mary Tudor seized the throne, she would subject England to popery and bring swathes of foreigners into the country. This fear was real enough, but it did not obscure the fact that she was Henry VIII's daughter, a princess of the blood. Even many religious reformers viewed her as the rightful successor. Upon hearing that her half-brother was close to death, Mary Tudor had fled to East Anglia before Dudley and his supporters could act against her. Setting up camp at Framlingham Castle, the ancient fortress of the Dukes of Norfolk, she attracted ever greater numbers to her cause, most of whom were staunchly traditional men opposed both to the religious reforms of Edward's reign and the attempts to overthrow the rightful Tudor succession. Convinced of the justice of her cause, Mary also wrote to the council, demanding that she be recognised as queen.

Alarmed by rumours of the forces that were gathering in ever greater numbers to support Mary Tudor, on 19 July the council capitulated and abandoned Jane. Dudley, who had ridden over to Norfolk to take possession of Mary, was captured, sent to the Tower and executed the following month. His daughter-in-law now resided there not as queen, but as a prisoner.

Upon her accession just nine days before, Lady Jane Grey had possessed all the resolve and commitment to further her late cousin's religious reforms. As it was, the only dubious accolade she would enjoy was that of being England's shortest-reigning monarch.

Mary I (1553–8)

'A queen and by the same title a king'

LADY JANE GREY aside, Mary Tudor was England's first queen regnant for more than four hundred years. The last incumbent, the Empress Matilda, had held on to power for only a few months and had plunged the country into civil war. It was hardly an inspiring example of female sovereignty. 'A woman is never feared or respected as a man is, whatever her rank,' explained Mary, Queen Dowager of Hungary to Charles V, when resigning her regency. Little wonder that Henry VIII had been so desperate to sire a legitimate male heir. When his son Edward had lain dying and his councillors had tried to justify preventing his half-sister Mary from inheriting the throne, they had protested 'the inferiority of the female sex', even though they had subsequently named another woman as heir.[1]

The accession of a queen regnant presented practical as well as political problems. Traditionally, officials in a monarch's private household, the privy chamber, and their public executive body, the privy council, had been of equal importance, and in some cases interchangeable. But it was imperative that a queen be attended by female servants, so this well-established arrangement could no longer continue. The political influence of the privy chamber declined markedly as a result.

Mary's sex also presented challenges for her coronation as there was no precedent for the anointing of a woman as ruler in her own right, the Empress Matilda never having been crowned during her brief tenure. In the event, it was decided to proceed with all of the usual protocol for crowning a king. Even this was problematic, though, because the last incumbent had been a staunch Protestant. The new queen therefore made sure that the ceremony would do nothing to compromise her Catholic beliefs and even went to the trouble of secretly obtaining holy oil from the Continent so that she would not be tainted by that used to consecrate her 'heretic' half-brother. She also refused to sit in the same coronation chair as Edward. The wording of the oath was carefully examined to ensure that in swearing to uphold England's laws, she was not committing herself to upholding the religious reforms of the previous two decades.

The magnificence of Mary's coronation strengthened her image as queen, but the practical issues of female sovereignty soon resurfaced. All of the monarchical powers were based upon a male ruler and it was not clear whether they could or should apply to a woman. Such uncertainty could not continue, so in April 1554 Parliament passed 'An Act for declaring that the Regal power of this realm is in the Queen's Majesty as fully and absolutely as ever it was in any of her most noble progenitors kings of this Realm'.[2] Put simply, the Act determined that there would be no distinction between men and women with regard to the powers of the crown. This would potentially benefit not just Mary, but every subsequent queen regnant.

Even though Mary shared her contemporaries' prejudice against women – an opinion reinforced by her traditional education – she had what one eyewitness described as 'a terrible and obstinate nature' and was determined to assert her authority.[3] Aware that she lacked ex-perience in the political arena, she spent long hours poring over state papers and considering governmental appointments. 'Respecting the government and public business, she is compelled (being of a sex which cannot becomingly take more than a moderate part in them), according to the custom of other sovereigns, to refer many matters to her councillors and ministers,' the Venetian ambassador condes-cendingly observed.[4] When an issue affected her closely, however, she could be just as single-minded and dogmatic as her father.

This was expressed most forcefully through Mary's unbending resolve to return England to the Roman Catholic fold. From her earliest days, she had been taught to revere the 'true faith'. Her maternal grandparents, Ferdinand and Isabella, had been the most powerful Catholic figureheads in Christendom, and her mother, Catherine of Aragon, had always cherished the rituals and traditions of Catholicism. The turmoil of her father's break with Rome and the annulment of his marriage to her mother had made Mary cling even more fiercely to her beliefs. She had incurred Henry's rancour by refusing to accept his supremacy over the church or to recognise Anne Boleyn as the new queen. Although she had eventually submitted in public, in her heart she had stayed faithful to Rome. Her more open non-conformity during her half-brother Edward's reign had made it clear that if she ever came to the throne, she would seek to overhaul his reforms.

A month after her accession, Mary sent shockwaves across the court by declaring her intention to give the late king a Catholic burial. It was only after her council urged that this would inflame religious tensions that she finally accepted a compromise. The public ceremony followed Protestant lines, but a private Mass was also held. Mary had shown just enough of the sensitivity to popular sentiment that was key to the success of the Tudor monarchs. The motto that she adopted – 'Truth, the daughter of time' – sent a clear message about the impending restoration of Catholicism, though. She and her fellow religious conservatives had weathered the storm of the Reformation and would soon find their reward.

Mary's first Parliament reinforced the 1543 Act of Succession by declaring Henry VIII's marriage to Catherine of Aragon valid. This meant that plans for the abolition of the royal supremacy and the restoration of papal authority in England would not be bound up with the issue of Mary's legitimacy. The same Parliament also discussed the issue of the new queen's marriage. If the kingdom was to avoid a succession crisis, then it was vital the thirty-seven-year-old queen take a husband as soon as possible. Mary was in full agreement. Within weeks of her accession, she privately admitted to the imperial ambassador that she 'knew not how to make herself safe and arrange her affairs' without a husband.[5]

The queen already had a candidate in mind. Because of her late mother, she felt a natural affinity for Spain and as a child had been betrothed to its king, the Holy Roman Emperor Charles V. Although Charles had broken their betrothal by marrying his cousin, Isabella of Portugal, his twenty-six-year-old son Philip was still unmarried. As a Catholic prince from her mother's homeland, he was ideal in

Mary's eyes. Her council did not agree. After all, fears that England would become a mere satellite of a foreign power if either of Edward's sisters came to the throne had helped to justify Lady Jane Grey's accession. On 16 November 1553, a parliamentary delegation formally petitioned the queen to choose an English husband. But Mary would brook no opposition.

Realising that it was futile to dissuade the queen from her choice, her council resolved to carve out a marriage settlement that would significantly restrict her husband's powers. Although it was agreed that Philip 'should have and enjoy jointly together with the said most noble Queen his wife the style, honour and kingly name of the Realm', his role was confined to simply 'aiding' Mary, rather than ruling over her, as would be the expected prerogative of any husband at that time. An Act of Parliament confirmed that Mary 'as a sole queen' would continue to 'enjoy the Crown and Sovereignty' of her kingdom exactly as she had before her marriage.[6] The marriage settlement was agreed in January 1554.

But Mary had failed to appreciate the strength of feeling among her xenophobic people. 'The English . . . are most hostile by their nature to foreigners,' remarked the Venetian ambassador.[7] Stark proof of this came with a popular uprising early in 1554, led by Thomas Wyatt and involving a group of influential noblemen that included Lady Jane Grey's father. Although there was a strong Protestant undertone to the rebellion, the participants claimed that their primary motive was to 'stir against the coming in of strangers and Spaniards'.[8]

Wyatt drew a considerable body of supporters to his cause, and in January 1554 they marched towards London. On 1 February, Mary dispatched the Duke of Norfolk to crush the rebels before they reached the capital. But his troops deserted, leaving the queen and her council virtually undefended. This was the first serious test of Mary's queenship and she rose to the challenge. Rallying the loyal troops who had gathered at the Guildhall in the heart of London, she gave an impassioned speech, assuring them: 'If a prince and governor may as naturally and earnestly love her subjects, as the mother doth the child, then assure yourselves, that I being your lady and mistress, do as earnestly and tenderly love and favour you.'[9] For this one, fleeting occasion, Mary seemed entirely at ease as a female sovereign, assuming a maternal role over her subjects. It was a theme that would be taken up often – and to even more dazzling effect – by her half-sister Elizabeth.

Mary's address was a decisive factor in defeating the rebels, although they had already fallen into some disarray. But the uprising had seriously destabilised a regime in its infancy, and those closest to the new queen urged that she rid herself of any rival claimants. First and foremost was the woman she had ousted from the throne. Lady Jane Grey and her husband Guildford had been condemned for treason in November 1553. Mary knew that they had been little more than innocent bystanders in the plot to put Jane on the throne, so she had been inclined to mercy. They had remained her prisoners in the Tower but with no prospect of any action being taken against them. All of that changed when Henry Grey threw in his lot with Wyatt. He had effectively signed their death warrants, as well as his own. On 12 February 1554, Jane watched from her lodgings as the headless body of her husband was brought back from the execution site on Tower Hill before going to her own, more private, death.

But there was another, even more dangerous rival still living. Mary's half-sister Elizabeth had been implicated in the plot, thanks to Wyatt claiming that he had written to tell her of his plans. Even though she was almost certainly innocent of any involvement, Mary knew that many of the rebels had hoped to put her younger sister on the throne in her stead. Elizabeth was brought to London for questioning. With great presence of mind, she stoutly insisted on her innocence, assuring her sister in the famous 'tide letter': 'I protest before God I never practised, counselled or consented to anything prejudicial to you or dangerous to the state.'[10] Under pressure from her council, Mary sent Elizabeth to the Tower, where she remained a prisoner for more than two months. The queen refused to sign her execution warrant, however, knowing that there was insufficient evidence and that the people would protest against it. Her sister was released on 19 May (the anniversary of her mother's execution) but kept under close surveillance thereafter.

Although Mary had successfully dealt with Wyatt's rebellion and its aftermath, her image had been permanently damaged by the experience. It did not help that she lacked the personal charisma and authority of the other Tudor monarchs, most notably her father. Popular ballads celebrated Henry VIII's fame, and in political circles his name had become synonymous with an all-powerful king. Even Mary herself, when faced with the tendency of her masculine court-iers to treat her orders more lightly than they would have done those of a king, declared: 'She only wished [her father] might come to life again for a month.'[11]

Nevertheless, the queen could look forward to happier times. On 25 July 1554 she married Philip of Spain at the ancient Wessex capital of Winchester. During the ceremony, Mary stood on Philip's right in the opposite of the traditional arrangements for royal weddings, which was intended to emphasise her superiority. She adopted the same position whenever she and her husband appeared in public, and also occupied the king's apartments in her palaces, while Philip resided in the queen's. Mary soon made it clear, though, that she intended to give her new husband more authority than the marriage settlement had prescribed. She told the Lord Privy Seal 'to obey his [Philip's] commandment in all things'.[12] To confirm what she saw as their joint sovereignty, she ordered a new coin to be struck in honour of their marriage. This showed the couple facing each other, and above their heads was a crown, equally placed between them.

On a personal level, Mary was ecstatic with her new husband and appeared to have fallen passionately in love from the moment she laid eyes on him. Philip was a good deal less enamoured of his wife, who was eleven years his senior. One of his attendants scathingly remarked: 'It will take a great God to drink this cup.'[13] Philip knew his dynastic duty, though, and within weeks of the wedding the queen was displaying signs of pregnancy. Her stomach began to swell and she often felt nauseous. The sad reality is that Mary's symptoms probably resulted from long-standing menstrual problems. But by November, she was so certain of her condition that she publicly celebrated it with a procession to St Paul's Cathedral, where the *Te Deum* was sung. Only months later, when her symptoms had receded, did the queen admit she had been mistaken.

Although the marriage would fail to produce an heir, it bolstered Mary's campaign to return England to the Roman Catholic fold. Thus far, she had not found it as easy as she had predicted to turn the clock back. A major stumbling block had been the issue of the church lands that had been seized by her father during the dissolution and distributed among his councillors and favourites. Even the religious conservatives among them objected to the idea of relinquishing their recently won prizes.

To help her overcome such obstacles, Mary enlisted the help of Cardinal Reginald Pole. An outspoken and often vociferous opponent of the Reformation, he had been a thorn in Henry VIII's side throughout his years in exile on the Continent. But Mary revered him as a champion of the true faith and in November 1554 she arranged for his return to England, as papal legate. At the end of that month, he delivered a speech to Parliament calling for the revocation of all ecclesiastical legislation since 1529, with the notable exception of laws pertaining to church lands.

Thereafter, work began in earnest to restore every element of the Roman Catholic religion other than the monasteries. Pole and Mary appointed known religious conservatives to key bishoprics. They also made full use of the printing press as a religious propaganda tool, distributing scores of Catholic treatises, sermons and catechisms across the kingdom. Many of the trappings of the old faith were also reintroduced, including church decorations such as rood screens, and the revival of liturgical music in the royal chapels. In recognition of his efforts, Pole was made Archbishop of Canterbury in March 1556.

While some of Mary's subjects welcomed the return of the faith to which they had clung throughout the turbulence of Henry VIII and Edward VI's Reformation, others were fiercely opposed to it. Even the papacy was not as conformable as Mary had expected. Far from welcoming England back with open arms, Pope Paul IV, a hard-line traditionalist appointed in the summer of 1555, revoked Pole's legatine authority and demanded his return to Rome to answer charges of heresy. He also delayed the confirmation of the new bishops.

There was little Mary and Pole could do about Rome, but they were determined to tackle intransigence within England. Their unflinching pursuit of heretics overshadowed every other aspect of the reign, earning the queen the sobriquet 'Bloody Mary'. Her mistaken belief was that those of her subjects who refused to conform had been manipulated by a small group of leaders. If these were removed, then her subjects would realise the error of their ways and return to the Catholic fold. The reinstatement of the fourteenth-century heresy laws in 1555 gave Mary and Pole *carte blanche* to hunt down those whom they believed responsible and condemn them to be burnt at the stake. The first victim of this new regime was the clergyman-preacher, John Rogers, who was consigned to the flames in February 1555. Other high-profile reformers soon followed, notably Hugh Latimer and Nicholas Ridley in October that year, and – most shocking of all – in March 1556 Thomas Cranmer, Henry VIII's Archbishop of Canterbury and leader of his Reformation.

Eliminating the Protestant leaders worked the opposite effect to the one Mary intended. The horrific manner of their deaths had excited sympathy even among religious conservatives and had strengthened the resolve of the reformists, who were of a greater number than the queen had judged. Undeterred, she expanded her pursuit of heretics, condemning ever more to be burned at the stake. By the summer of 1558, about two hundred and ninety people, mostly from the lower classes, had been put to death. The ranks of sympathisers had grown with each burning so that by the end of Mary's reign Protestantism had taken a firmer hold than when she had ascended the throne.

The queen's growing unpopularity was exacerbated by a disastrous event in early 1558. Aware that England lacked the financial resources to support an aggressive foreign policy, Mary and her government had resisted any involvement in continental hostilities. But in 1557 the revival of the Italian Wars, in which the main combatants were France and Spain, forced Mary's hand. Her husband Philip, who had departed England to deal with imperial matters in 1555, returned to plead with the queen for her assistance. Overjoyed to see her husband, Mary acceded to his request and persuaded her government to follow suit. But in order to avoid the intervention of an English expeditionary force, King Henry II of France arranged a surprise attack on Calais in January 1558. The English garrison was completely overwhelmed, and within a matter of days Thomas Wentworth, deputy of Calais, was obliged to hand over the keys of the town to the French.

The loss of Calais was a devastating blow. It was the last English outpost in France, a reminder of former military glories, and for almost two hundred years it had given English monarchs the right to style themselves ruler of France. Legend has it that Mary was so distraught when she heard the news that she declared the name 'Calais' would be found engraved on her heart. She was soon comforted, though, by a growing conviction that she was pregnant. Overlooking her previous experience, she wrote at once to her husband, telling him their child would be born the following March, and made a will, 'thinking myself to be with child in lawful marriage'.[14]

Few people shared Mary's confidence. 'She the more distresses herself, perceiving daily that no one believes in the possibility of her having progeny, so that day by day she sees her authority and the respect induced by it diminish,' remarked one observer at court.[15] Undeterred, in February 1558, Mary entered her confinement. As the weeks dragged on with no sign of any labour pains, she became increasingly despondent. It is possible that the swelling in her stomach was due not to pregnancy, but to cancer. Even during her first confinement, it had been rumoured that 'she was deceived by a Tympanie [tumour] or some other like disease, to think herself with child'.[16]

By April 1558, the queen had given up hope of a child and re-emerged into public life. The fact that she invited her half-sister to Richmond that month and entertained her with great ceremony was taken by many as an indication that she would name Elizabeth her heir. 'Madam Elizabeth already sees herself as the next Queen', her husband's envoy, the Count of Feria, disapprovingly noted.[17] Still Mary prevaricated. Although Elizabeth had been discreet in her observance of the Protestant faith and had attended Mass in the Chapels Royal, she had made it clear that she would not continue her half-sister's campaign to bring England back to Roman Catholicism.

With her health now rapidly deteriorating, Mary could not avoid the issue for much longer. On 28 October, she added a codicil to her will, acknowledging that there would be no 'fruit of her body' and confirming that the crown would go to the next heir by law. But she failed to say who that heir would be. Only when faced with intense pressure from her council did Mary finally relent. On 8 November, she sent word to Elizabeth at Hatfield confirming her as successor. Shortly afterwards, Mary dispatched her most trusted servant, Jane Dormer, to relay her final wishes to her half-sister. These were to uphold the Roman Catholic faith 'as the Queen has restored it', to be good to her servants, and to pay her debts.[18] Elizabeth's response was noncommittal.

On 17 November, between four and five o'clock in the morning, Mary slipped from a life that had been marked by tragedy and heartache. Her husband, who had refused to return to his dying wife's side, expressed 'reasonable regret' when told of her passing, but almost immediately began making overtures for Elizabeth's hand in marriage. Neither did her subjects express any real sorrow. The one person who would have mourned the late queen most, her faithful archbishop and confidant, Reginald Pole, died the same day.

Mary had been just forty-two years old at the time of her death and, as with her half-brother Edward, there was a sense of unfinished business. Her programme of religious reform – or, rather, restoration – had not had time to take full effect, her Spanish marriage had produced a great deal of resentment but no heir, and the country was suffering from two years of poor harvests, famine and a flu epidemic. Although she had been a hard-working and conscientious ruler, Mary had lacked the natural authority and presence to inspire confidence and respect. It is hardly surprising that most of her former subjects rejoiced at the change of regime, clinging to the hope of better times that it represented.

Even though she tends to be unfavourably compared with her half-sister, Mary deserves credit as the first woman to successfully claim the throne of England, overcoming competing claims and determined opposition. Carving out a position as queen regnant had been a considerable challenge. By the end of her reign, a number of important precedents had been set, most notably the 1554 Act confirming that a 'sole queen should rule as absolutely as a king'. In the address given at Mary's funeral service, John White, Bishop of Winchester, declared that she had been 'a queen and by the same title a king also' and that thanks to her, Elizabeth was now 'both king and queen . . . of the realm'.[19]

Elizabeth I (1558–1603)

The heart and stomach of a King

MORE THAN ANY other monarch, Elizabeth I had learned from the mistakes of her predecessors, her half-sister in particular. First and foremost, the new queen had been given a stark lesson in the disaster that could ensue from taking a husband, particularly if he was a foreigner. She had also witnessed the dangers inherent in pursuing a highly dogmatic and uncompromising policy, no matter how close to her heart it might be. The reigns of both her siblings had pulled England first one way, then another, leaving a kingdom that was even more deeply divided than it had been during their father's Reformation. Committed Protestant though she was, Elizabeth appreciated the need for compromise.

The new queen was quick to appoint her key advisers. Principal among them was William Cecil, who had served her for a number of years and whom she trusted above all others. He would occupy this position for the next forty years, working so closely with Elizabeth that it is often difficult to separate his decisions from hers. She made her privy council much leaner than it had been in Mary's day, excluding overt Catholics and others with close links to her late sister. She also dismissed all of its clerical members, which meant that her new council was entirely secular. At the same time, she reordered the royal household, showing favour to those who had served her loyally as princess and to her Boleyn relatives.

The most significant of all the new appointments, though, was Elizabeth's new Master of the Horse, an extremely prestigious role that was awarded to Robert Dudley, son of the executed traitor John Dudley, Duke of Northumberland, and for a while Elizabeth's fellow prisoner in the Tower. They had first met at the age of eight and their shared traumas had strengthened the bond between them. By the time Elizabeth came to the throne, they were so close that it sparked rumours of a sexual liaison, although Dudley was already married. Their turbulent relationship would become one of the dominant features of Elizabeth's reign.

Attractive, charismatic and vivacious, the new queen inspired much greater confidence than her late sister and there was widespread rejoicing upon her accession. But there were misgivings, too. Mary might have laid the foundations for female sovereignty, but she had not made it any more appealing. Published in the same year that Elizabeth came to the throne, John Knox's *Monstrous Regiment of Women*, which took Mary as an example, declared: 'To promote a woman to bear rule . . . is repugnant to nature' because their 'imbecility' rendered them utterly incapable of wielding power effectively.[1]

In confronting such prejudice, the new queen's first step was to make sure that her subjects appreciated how different she was to her predecessor. From the very beginning, Elizabeth I proved highly adept at propaganda, surrounding herself with poets, playwrights and chroniclers who conjured up potent imagery to reinforce both the legitimacy and strengths of her rule. She was the 'clear and lovely sunshine' that dispersed the 'stormy, tempestuous and blustering windy weather of Queen Mary'.[2] At times of crisis, the queen would remind her subjects that no matter what they faced, it was as nothing to the sufferings inflicted upon them by her dogmatic, pro-Spanish predecessor.

Elizabeth has often been hailed as a feminist icon. In fact, she shared the general belief in the inferiority of women and saw herself as a shining exception. She also played on the supposed weaknesses of her sex to great effect in order to manipulate her male-dominated court. When pressured by Parliament to take a husband, she pleaded that 'the weight and greatness of this matter' was too much for her feminine understanding. Time and again, she drove her advisers to distraction with her procrastination and 'answers, answerless'. She was also unpredictable. 'It is very troublesome to negotiate with this woman, as she is naturally changeable,' complained the Count of Feria.[3] Few of her male contemporaries seemed to realise that this was a deliberate ploy. But when the occasion demanded, Elizabeth made much of her 'princely' qualities. 'I have the heart of a man, not of a woman, and I am not afraid of anything,' she once declared. Whenever she needed to stamp her authority upon overbearing councillors or ambassadors, she would compare herself to Henry VIII. In one of her speeches to Parliament, she asserted: 'And though I be a woman, yet I have as good a courage, answerable to my place, as ever my father had.'[4]

A master of showmanship, Elizabeth immediately set about planning a series of carefully crafted public relations exercises. The first and most lavish was her coronation, which took place at Westminster Abbey on 15 January 1559. In selecting the date, Elizabeth had consulted her astrologer, Dr John Dee, to whom she often turned for guidance. The spectacular showpiece cost £16,000 (£3.7 million) and included a series of lavish pageants depicting the new queen as an earthly Virgin Mary, chosen by God as the mother of his people in England.

Elizabeth took up the same theme in the first Parliament of her reign, which was held shortly afterwards, averring: 'In the end, this shall be for me sufficient, that a marble stone shall declare that a queen, having reigned such a time, lived and died a virgin.'[5] Few present believed her. It was inconceivable that the queen would not wish to marry. Elizabeth herself admitted: 'There is a strong idea in the world that a woman cannot live unless she is married, or at all events that if she refrains from marriage she does so for some bad reason.'[6] As a self-confessed 'weak and feeble woman', she surely needed the guidance of a husband, as her half-sister Mary had. Even more crucially, she needed an heir. The throne had changed hands three times in eleven years and Elizabeth was the last of Henry VIII's children, so if she died childless it might prompt a succession crisis. Disregarding the new queen's expressed intent to remain single, her councillors proceeded to cast about for a suitable candidate from among the princes of Europe. Elizabeth made a show of giving careful, even enthusiastic, thought to each proposal, aware of the diplomatic advantage of keeping the suitors in play.

A similar vagueness applied to Elizabeth's religious stance. The product of Henry VIII's break with Rome and his marriage to Anne Boleyn, she had been raised a Protestant and her motto *Semper eadem*

('Always the same') has been taken to mean that she would never change her beliefs. But the new queen had learned from her half-sister's example and had no intention of forcing these beliefs upon her new subjects. The famous declaration that she 'would not open windows into men's souls' was made by Francis Bacon, rather than Elizabeth, but it neatly summed up her approach. Under her direction, Parliament agreed a new Act of Supremacy, whereby the queen's title was changed from supreme head to supreme governor of the Church of England – as it has remained ever since. This satisfied the objections expressed by both Protestants and Catholics that only Christ could be head of the church. An Act of Uniformity was also introduced, which imposed a new Book of Common Prayer. This was based upon Edward VI's second book of 1552, but with significant amendments to those elements that had sparked most criticism. The new Act was passed with the narrowest of margins, and all of Elizabeth's bishops voted against it. It was obvious that the religious divisions still ran deep.

Elizabeth was painfully aware that the majority of her Catholic subjects viewed her more as an illegitimate usurper than as their rightful queen. The fact that her parents' marriage had been annulled shortly before her mother's execution had rendered her a bastard. Even though Henry VIII had later restored her to the order of succession and Parliament had passed a statute confirming her legal right to the throne, the stain of bastardy still hung over her. This gave strength to rival claimants. Ironically, given the prejudices against female rule, all of the leading contenders were women. Descended from Henry VIII's sisters, they were also cousins of the new queen.

Among them was Mary Stuart, daughter of Mary of Guise and James V of Scotland, who was the son of Henry VIII's elder sister, Margaret Tudor. The threat from Mary had been made more potent by her marriage to François, dauphin of France, in April 1558. The very day after Elizabeth's accession, Mary and her new husband began to style themselves King and Queen of England and included the English royal arms in Mary's shield. In July 1559, the French king, Henry II, died in a jousting accident and his son inherited the throne.

Becoming Queen of France undoubtedly enhanced Mary's position, but she was still technically barred from inheriting the English throne because Henry VIII had excluded the Scottish branch of his family. Instead, it was the descendants of his younger sister Mary who at first seemed to pose the greater threat. The Spanish ambassador reported that Elizabeth 'could not abide the sight' of Lady Katherine Grey, sister of the nine days' queen.[7] Both Katherine and her sister Mary had been treated with honour during the previous reign, but were now demoted to lesser positions within the royal household.[8] This made Katherine resentful towards the new queen, as well as a target for the schemes of those who wished to see Elizabeth ousted from the throne. In November 1560, she strengthened her claim by secretly marrying Edward Seymour, eldest son of the former Lord Protector and nephew of the late Jane Seymour.

But at first the court gossips were too distracted by another scandal to notice. Two months earlier, Amy Dudley (née Robsart), wife of the queen's favourite, had been found dead at the bottom of a short flight of stairs at their home in Oxfordshire. Further investigation suggested foul play, and both the queen and Robert Dudley were suspected of having ordered Amy's death so that they might marry. Elizabeth was almost certainly innocent of any involvement. She might have loved Dudley, but there is no indication that she ever seriously entertained the idea of marrying him. As she made clear: 'I will have but one mistress here, and no master!'[9] More likely is that if Amy had been murdered, it was at the hands of one of Dudley's rivals, who rightly judged that the resulting scandal would wreck any hopes he cherished of one day marrying the queen.

In August 1561, the scandal of Katherine Grey's illicit marriage finally broke. By then, Katherine was seven months pregnant but had concealed her condition and remained in service to the queen. Elizabeth wasted no time in throwing her and Seymour into the Tower. Katherine gave birth to a son shortly afterwards, which made her even more of a threat, particularly as there was as yet no prospect of Elizabeth having a child of her own.

A little over a year later, the question of the succession became more pressing when the queen fell ill with smallpox while staying at Hampton Court. Few of her councillors expected her to survive, and as she lay in feverish delirium they called an urgent meeting to discuss whether Katherine Grey or Mary Stuart should succeed her. Against the odds, Elizabeth recovered, and when she heard that her councillors had been busy debating her successor, she 'wept with rage'. Her mood was hardly improved by news that arrived from the Tower the following February. Against the queen's orders, the gaolers had taken pity on Katherine and her husband and allowed them to visit each other in secret. The result was that Katherine had given birth to another son. When Elizabeth heard of this, she turned 'the colour of a corpse'.[10]

Determined to prevent any more mishaps, Elizabeth ordered that the couple be removed from the Tower and taken to separate safe houses, many miles apart. Katherine never saw her husband or eldest son again. She sank into a deep depression and went on virtual hunger strike, which hastened her death in January 1568 at the age of about twenty-seven. Lady Mary Grey suffered a similarly miserable fate. Failing to learn from her sister Katherine's example, she too married in secret. Even though her husband, Thomas Keyes, was only a low-ranking member of the court, Elizabeth's suspicion of the Greys was so deeply ingrained that she had the couple imprisoned far from each other and they were never reunited.

With the Grey sisters out of the picture, Mary Stuart excluded from the succession by the terms of Henry VIII's will, and Elizabeth showing no more inclination to marry than when she had ascended the throne, the stability of her regime rested entirely upon the safety and well-being of the queen herself. Considering neither of her siblings had been long-lived, this seemed a very precarious position indeed. A speaker in the House of Commons expressed the misgivings felt by many: 'If God should take her Majesty, the succession being not established, I know not what shall become of myself, my wife, my children, lands, goods, friends or country.'[11]

Even though Mary Stuart was in theory barred from inheriting the English throne, her rivalry with Elizabeth dominated the 1560s. In December 1560, Mary's young husband died suddenly only eighteen months after becoming King of France and she returned to her native Scotland as queen. She did not receive the warmest of welcomes. The Queen of Scots' Catholicism was at odds with her largely Protestant kingdom and she faced the same prejudice against female rulers as Elizabeth. Her response was entirely different. From the outset, she made it clear that she would marry again. Elizabeth had revelled in her position as the most desirable bride in Europe, but now she had a rival. Worse still, Mary was eight years younger and her beauty was widely praised.

The intensely personal nature of the rivalry between the two queens was made obvious when Mary sent her envoy, Sir James Melville, to Elizabeth's court in 1564. Pushing aside the political matters that Melville wished to discuss, Elizabeth quizzed him on every aspect of the Scottish queen's personal appearance and accomplishments – from what colour her hair was to how well she played the lute. 'She was earnest with me to declare which of them I judged fairest', he recalled. 'I said, She was the fairest Queen in England, and mine the fairest Queen in Scotland. Yet she appeared earnest. I answered, They were both the fairest ladies in their countries; that her Majesty was whiter, but my Queen was very lovely.' Still Elizabeth persisted, asking next who was the tallest. When the beleaguered Sir James admitted that the Scottish queen was the tallest, Elizabeth snapped: 'Then . . . she is too high; for I myself am neither too high nor too low.'[12]

The Queen of Scots' choice of husband was crucial to England's security. Elizabeth was so anxious that Mary might marry into another powerful continental dynasty that she even advocated her favourite, Robert Dudley, as a potential suitor. But Mary made her own choice in July 1565, when she married her cousin Henry, Lord Darnley, the grandson of Henry VIII's sister, Margaret Tudor. The veneer of charm and good looks that had first attracted Mary soon wore thin and it became clear that this arrogant, vain and dangerously unstable man was a singularly unsuitable choice as consort. Within months of the wedding, Elizabeth's ambassador in Scotland reported: 'I know now for certain that this Queen repenteth her marriage, that she hateth Darnley and all his kin.'[13] But by then, she was already pregnant with his child.

Events spiralled rapidly out of control. In a fit of jealous rage, in March 1566, Darnley had his wife's Italian secretary and confidant,

David Rizzio, brutally murdered while she looked on in horror. The birth of their son, James, three months later did nothing to reconcile the warring couple. On the night of 9 February 1567, there was a huge explosion at the house of Kirk o'Field in Edinburgh, where Darnley was staying. His body and that of a servant were discovered in the grounds, but it was clear that they had not died as a result of the blast. Neither was there any sign that they had been shot, strangled or beaten. The likelihood is both men had been suffocated, but the exact nature of their deaths and who was responsible remains a mystery. In a shocking move, Mary then fled from Edinburgh with the chief suspect, James Hepburn, Earl of Bothwell. She married him in May, possibly under duress.

All of this spelt disaster for Mary's rule in Scotland. The powerful Scottish lords who controlled government raised an army and confronted the queen and her new husband at Carberry Hill on 15 June. There was no battle because by then Mary's forces had dwindled away. Bothwell fled into exile and the Queen of Scots was taken to Edinburgh, where she was publicly denounced as an adulteress and murderer. She was then taken prisoner in Loch Leven Castle and on 24 July, a few days after miscarrying Bothwell's twins, she was forced to abdicate in favour of her infant son, James. The Earl of Moray, James V's illegitimate son, was appointed regent.

When she heard of this, Elizabeth abandoned all her former pretence of 'sisterly' affection towards her fellow queen and wrote a furious letter of admonishment. 'How could a worse choice be made for your honour than in such haste to marry such a subject, who besides other and notorious lacks, public fame hath charged with the murder of your late husband,' she demanded.[14] There was more than a touch of smugness here. Mary had ruled with her heart and paid a terrible price for it. Elizabeth had ruled with her head, sacrificing personal passions for statecraft. Now, at last, she was reaping the rewards.

For almost a year, matters appeared more settled. Then in May 1568, the Queen of Scots escaped from Loch Leven and raised an army of 6,000 men. They were routed by Moray's forces at the Battle of Langside on 13 May and Mary fled south with a greatly diminished band of men. Realising that to turn back would almost certainly mean death, the beleaguered queen made the fateful decision to throw herself on the mercy of her cousin.

At first, it seemed the right decision. Mary was honourably lodged at Carlisle Castle and Elizabeth wrote to congratulate her on her escape. The Queen of Scots confidently expected that she would soon be on her way northwards again, an English army in tow. For Elizabeth, it was not that simple. If she helped restore Mary to her throne, the Scottish queen would pose as great a threat as she had before she had been deposed. Likewise, if she gave Mary safe conduct to France, she might raise an army with which to invade not just Scotland but England too. Keeping the ousted Queen of Scots on English soil would mean that she was within tantalising reach of the many English Catholics who wished to see her crowned in Elizabeth's place. It was with good reason that Cecil warned: 'The Queen of Scots is, and always shall be, a dangerous person to your estate.'[15]

In January 1569, Mary was moved to Tutbury Castle in Staffordshire and placed in the custody of the Earl of Shrewsbury and his wife, Elizabeth (better known as Bess of Hardwick). Although she was kept in considerable luxury, any pretence that she was Elizabeth's honoured guest was soon abandoned: it was obvious to everyone – not least Mary herself – that she was her prisoner. It was not long before plots began to swarm around the captive queen. A few months after Mary's move to Tutbury, Thomas Howard, fourth Duke of Norfolk, schemed to marry her and restore her to the Scottish throne. His expectation was that in time, they or their heirs would succeed the English queen. No sooner had Elizabeth consigned Norfolk to the Tower than news broke of a rebellion in the north of England led by a group of Catholic lords who planned to depose Elizabeth and replace her with Mary.

The following year brought more ill tidings. The assassination of the Scottish regent, Moray, on 21 January 1570 was an indication of a growing pro-Marian reaction. Shortly afterwards, Pope Pius V issued a bull of excommunication against Elizabeth, releasing her Catholic subjects from their allegiance to her. The following year, William Cecil and Francis Walsingham, Elizabeth's spymaster, uncovered a plot led by the Florentine banker Roberto Ridolfi, which yet again aimed to put Mary on the English throne. Among those implicated were the Duke of Norfolk, the Spanish ambassador and even the pope. Parliament demanded the heads of both Mary and Norfolk, but Elizabeth contented herself with the latter. By now, she felt as trapped by the situation as Mary. 'I am not free, but a captive,' she lamented, and told a visiting ambassador: 'I am just as anxious to see Mary Stuart out of England as she can be to go!'[16]

As she battled to protect her throne in England, Elizabeth's adventurers were helping to realise her imperial ambitions overseas. From the 1570s, English seafarers sought to establish alternative routes to the lucrative markets of China and the East Indies, which were then dominated by Spain and Portugal. Although these were mostly private ventures, the queen was quick to grasp the potential for profit. The East India Company was founded in 1600 to trade in the Indian Ocean region and during the following two centuries would rise to account for half of the world's trade, making England a world power rather than just a small island to be tussled over by France and Spain. Elizabeth also directly sponsored a number of her adventurers' voyages and tacitly encouraged the privateering exploits of men such as Sir Francis Drake, Sir John Hawkins and Sir Walter Raleigh, who made successful careers out of plundering Spanish treasure ships. All three men undertook voyages to the Americas and established a settlement on Roanoke Island (dubbed 'Virginia'), while Hawkins was one of the first promoters of the transatlantic slave trade. Drake's pre-eminence was established in 1580 when he became the first English sailor to complete a circumnavigation of the globe.

The exploits of these adventurers greatly enhanced Elizabeth's reputation, both at home and abroad, and accelerated her rise to almost iconic status. The 1570s saw the beginning of a golden age of court culture, with Elizabeth as its focus and inspiration. All of the entertainments, ceremonies and intrigues centred around her as the Virgin Queen, at once both aloof and alluring. As one of her most ardent admirers, Sir Christopher Hatton, observed: 'The Queen did fish for men's souls, and had so sweet a bait that no-one could escape her network.'[17]

To the untrained eye, most of the Elizabethan court entertainments appear decadent, even hedonistic. But, ever watchful of her reputation as an unmarried queen, Elizabeth quickly established a strict etiquette and ceremony from which no courtier was allowed to stray. Thus a contemporary was able to recall: 'The court of Queen Elizabeth was at once gay, decent, and superb.'[18] Although the vast majority of Elizabeth's flirtations were nothing more than play-acting on both sides, she demanded absolute fidelity, both emotional and political, from her male courtiers and would brook no rival for their affections. Politics and personal relations were more closely intertwined than ever before. Even sober advisers such as William Cecil, Lord Burghley, were treated with the same playfulness. He was Elizabeth's 'Spirit', while Robert Dudley was her 'Eyes' and Hatton her 'Lids'. Foreign suitors were drawn into the game, too. Francis, Duke of Anjou and Alençon, was given the affectionate nickname 'Frog' by Elizabeth during their highly elaborate courtship in the late 1570s.

Sir Robert Naunton, who had had first-hand experience of life at Elizabeth's court, revealed the political stratagem that lay at the heart of all this: 'She was absolute and sovereign mistress . . . those to whom she distributed her favours were never more than tenants at will and stood on no better ground than her princely pleasure and their own good behaviour.'[19] The queen's notoriously unpredictable temper was another device by which she exerted control. 'When she smiled, it was a pure sun-shine, that everyone did choose to bask in, if they could', wrote her godson, Sir John Harington, 'but anon came a storm from a sudden gathering of clouds, and the thunder fell in wondrous manner on all alike.'[20]

This demonstrated Elizabeth's growing confidence in her gender. During the early part of her reign, she had drawn more attention to her masculine attributes than her feminine ones. As it progressed, she gave full expression to both. She was the beguiling but forbidden fruit to her courtiers, an infuriatingly indecisive and parsimonious woman to her councillors, a mother to her people, and the Virgin Queen to all. But when it suited her, she would suddenly invoke her 'kingly' majesty in order to show courage in the face of rebellion, assert her opinions in council and Parliament, and upbraid her officials if they refused to do her will.

Elizabeth's confidence as a female monarch rested upon her appearance, as well as her behaviour. As age began to overtake her, the rituals involved in preserving the so-called 'mask of youth' became ever more elaborate – and costly. She shared the natural parsimony of her grandfather, Henry VII, but when it came to keeping up appearances, no expense was spared. Foreign ambassadors were dazzled by her gorgeous costumes, fashioned from cloth of gold and silver, and dripping with priceless jewels. One of them claimed she had in excess of six thousand dresses in her wardrobe.[21] The queen also owned more than eighty wigs and a plethora of different cosmetics to conceal the deepening lines on her face and maintain her famously white complexion.

As well as displaying her magnificence to the court, Elizabeth made sure to be visible to her subjects. That she did so while enhancing the mystique of monarchy was a masterstroke. Her progresses are the stuff of legend. They provided the only opportunity for those living outside of London to see their sovereign. Although the queen never ventured further west than Bristol or further north than Stafford, she took care to be seen by as many of her people as possible on the way, as well as on her return to the capital.

Those who hosted the queen on progress bore a heavy financial burden. Some of the great prodigy houses of the age were built or extended for the sole purpose of receiving her. Nobody lavished more expense than Elizabeth's favourite, Robert Dudley, whose 'princely entertainments' at Kenilworth Castle in 1575 ran up a staggering bill of £60,000 (around £12 million) in building works alone. It was his last but futile throw of the dice in attempting to persuade the queen to marry him. Not long afterwards, he took Lettice Knollys, one of her Boleyn relatives, as his bride. When Elizabeth found out, she was so furious that she boxed Lettice's ears and banished her from court.

During her reign, Elizabeth also firmly established a series of set-pieces with her poorer subjects. The most notable of these was Maundy Thursday, when she washed the feet of as many poor women as the years of her age, gave them purses containing the same number of silver pennies, and distributed clothing, claret, loaves and fishes. Occasions such as this greatly enhanced Elizabeth's popularity and reinforced her image as a Virgin Mary figure on earth.

But there remained a significant number of committed Catholics who still hoped to see her ousted from the throne. Even though the number of plots and assassination attempts discovered by

Walsingham's spy networks showed no sign of abating, Elizabeth resisted most of Parliament's attempts to introduce stricter legislation against her Catholic subjects. Neither did she have any patience with the extremists of her own religion (the so-called 'hot Protestants'), but continued to strive for a middle way in religion.

The active role that Elizabeth played in moderating Parliament's religious legislation was mirrored in other areas of her government. Even the most senior of her officials could not act without her sanction. Perhaps thinking that military matters were beyond a woman's understanding, in 1580 the privy council decided to dispatch a thousand troops to the Scottish borders. When their royal mistress heard of this, 'she would none of it' and cut the force by half before cancelling it altogether.[22] The queen made it clear that her councillors were there by her choice alone, and that if their services were 'no longer to be used in that public function then it shall please her Majesty to dispose of the same'.[23]

The greatest challenge to Elizabeth's sovereignty over her council concerned the vexed issue of what to do with the captive Queen of Scots. In November 1582, fourteen years after her flight to England, Mary wrote a long and embittered letter to her cousin, listing everything that she had suffered at her hands and demanding 'satisfaction before I die, so that all differences between us being settled, my disembodied soul may not be compelled to utter its complaints before God'.[24] Each year seemed to bring a fresh plot to place Mary on the English throne. In November 1583, Elizabeth's agents uncovered a conspiracy led by Sir Francis Throckmorton, the cousin of Elizabeth's lady-in-waiting, Bess Throckmorton; he had been promised assistance by both France and Spain. By now, Elizabeth was 'utterly distrustful' of this 'bosom serpent', while her Commons condemned Mary as 'the most notorious whore in all the world'.[25]

In January 1585, Mary was transferred to the custody of Sir Amyas Paulet, an austere man with little sympathy for the fallen queen. This heightened her desperation. The following summer, she heard of a conspiracy in her name led by Anthony Babington, a Catholic gentleman known to Mary, and threw caution to the wind. Word soon reached Walsingham's ears and he set a trap for the Scottish queen, intercepting her correspondence with the plotters. It was not long before Mary incriminated herself by mentioning Elizabeth's assassination. When her letter was delivered into Walsingham's hands, he inscribed it with a hangman's noose.

After nineteen years of plots and conspiracies, Elizabeth finally had the proof she needed to put Mary to death. But while she publicly railed against the 'treacherous dealings' of this 'wicked murderess', in private she recoiled from the idea of judging and executing an anointed sovereign, keenly aware of how dangerous a precedent this would set. She also feared a backlash from Catholic Europe if Mary was executed. Only after intense pressure from Cecil and Walsingham did the queen agree that her cousin should be put on trial. This took place at Fotheringhay Castle, Northamptonshire, in October 1586. Although Mary defended herself with skill and dignity, the guilty verdict was assured.

On 4 December, Parliament proclaimed the sentence: Mary would be put to death. But this could only be carried out when Elizabeth had signed the execution warrant. For weeks she agonised, retreating to her favourite palace of Richmond in the hope of escaping her councillors. When a delegation came to press the case once more, she rounded on them: 'If it had pleased God to have made us both milkmaids with pails on our arms, so that the matter should have rested between us two; and that I knew she did and would seek my destruction still, yet could I not consent to her death.'[26]

Shortly afterwards, Elizabeth received a long and impassioned letter from the 'daughter of debate' herself, forcing her cousin to confront the terrible reality of having an anointed queen executed. 'When my enemies have slaked their black thirst for my innocent blood, you will permit my poor desolated servants altogether to carry away my corpse, to bury it in holy ground, with the other Queens of France, my predecessors, especially near the late queen, my mother', she wrote. She also reminded Elizabeth of their kinship by making reference to Henry VII – 'your grandfather and mine'. Robert Dudley reported that the letter had 'wrought tears' from his royal mistress, who pleaded that the 'timorousnes of her [own] sex and nature' made it impossible for her to act.[27] The same ploy had worked in the past, but this matter could no longer be delayed.

On 1 February 1587, Elizabeth's secretary, William Davison, brought a pile of documents for her to authorise, including Mary's death warrant. He later insisted that the queen had been fully aware of what she was signing and that she had ordered him to have the warrant sealed before giving it to the Lord Chancellor, who should 'use it as secretly as might be'.[28] Having waited so long for their royal mistress to act, Elizabeth's councillors were quick to see her orders carried out. Just a week after it had been signed, the former Queen of Scots mounted the scaffold in the great hall of Fotheringhay Castle. She was barely recognisable from the beautiful woman who had so entranced the world. An eyewitness described her as: 'round shouldered, of face fat and broad, double chinned . . . borrowed hair'.[29] When her ladies took off her outer gown, it revealed an under-dress of scarlet, the colour of martyrs. As soon as her head had been struck off, that is exactly what she became.

Upon being told that her cousin had been executed, Elizabeth appeared stupefied. 'Her words failed her . . . she was in a manner astonished', claimed her earliest biographer, William Camden.[30] But the next morning, the queen flew into such 'heat and passion' that she screamed out against the execution 'as a thing she never commanded or intended'. She then set about 'casting the burden generally upon them all', but, as Davison ruefully admitted, 'chiefly upon my shoulders'.[31] Determined to make her hapless secretary a scapegoat, Elizabeth sent him to the Tower and subjected him to a full interrogation by the Star Chamber. He was subsequently fined £10,000, a sum far beyond his means, and ordered to stay in prison for as long as Her Majesty pleased.[32] The queen then 'gave herself over to grief, putting herself into mourning weeds, and shedding abundance of tears'.[33] She also wrote to Mary's son, James VI of Scotland, bewailing 'that miserable accident which (far contrary to my meaning) hath befallen'.[34] James was quick to excuse her of all blame. The Scottish envoy, Sir James Melville, scornfully remarked that 'the blood was already fallen from his Majesty's heart'.[35]

Not all of Elizabeth's foreign rivals were so easily appeased. Chief among them was Philip II of Spain. 'It is very fine for the Queen of England now to give out that it was done without her wish', he declared, 'the contrary being so clearly the case.'[36] Mary herself had written to Philip upon hearing of her sentence, urging him to avenge her death by invading England and taking the crown. He soon began preparing to do just that. In truth, though, he was no more sincere than Elizabeth herself. Relations between their two countries had been hostile for a number of years, thanks to the activities of Elizabeth's privateers. The English queen's support for the Dutch rebellion against Spanish rule, confirmed by the Treaty of Nonsuch of 1585, had fuelled Philip's desire for revenge.

On 30 May 1588, 130 ships carrying over 18,000 men set sail from Lisbon. This 'invincible' Armada was to be merely an escort for the main invasion force, the Duke of Parma's army, which was stationed in the Netherlands. It was the greatest threat that Elizabeth had faced in her reign and that England had faced since the Norman invasion more than five hundred years before. When messengers brought news that the Spanish fleet had been spied in the Channel, Elizabeth was spurred into action. On 8 August, she travelled to Tilbury, where her land forces had gathered to repel the expected invasion. Ever conscious of the power of image, she instructed her ladies to dress her in a military-inspired outfit with a plumed helmet and steel breastplate over a white velvet gown. The speech that she gave to her assembled troops has gone down in history as the most brilliant of all her public addresses; the epitome of the dazzlingly effective PR that she had employed throughout her reign. She famously assured them that although she had 'the body of a weak and feeble woman', she had 'the heart and stomach of a King, and a King of England too' and vowed to fight alongside them if Parma's troops reached her shores.

In fact, by the time she delivered this famous speech, the Spanish had been all but vanquished. The Armada had failed to rendezvous with Parma's forces, which had given the English fleet (under the able command of Charles Howard, who was assisted by Drake, Hawkins and Martin Frobisher) the chance to seize the initiative. With the use of eight fireships, and greatly helped by the weather, they won a small but decisive victory. The Spanish fleet was driven northwards and a number of ships were lost in the Atlantic and on Irish coasts. Less than half of the original fleet made it home to Spain, and only 3,000 men.

Elizabeth was quick to make the most of the victory. 'God breathed and they were scattered', declared the medal that was struck soon afterwards. The famous Armada portrait shows the queen trium- phant, her hand resting on a globe while in the background her navy destroys the Spanish fleet. Even her most implacable adversaries were forced to acknowledge the greatness that she had attained. 'She is only a woman, only the mistress of half an island, and yet she makes herself feared by Spain, by France, by Empire, by all!' exclaimed a dumbfounded Pope Sixtus V.[37] Elizabeth had apparently conquered not just Philip II's Armada, but the widely held prejudices against female sovereignty.

The Armada was a pivotal moment in Elizabeth's monarchy, trans- forming her image into one of invincible majesty that became ever more idealised as her long reign progressed. She had attained myth- ical status, but in her own lifetime. It was in finally resolving the complex question of what to do with the Queen of Scots, and in dealing with the dramatic repercussions that followed, that Elizabeth was able to mature into the Gloriana of legend. Her confidence was matched by that of her kingdom: England had faced down the might of Spain and had begun to establish itself as a world power.

But for Elizabeth, the year 1588 brought private sorrow, as well as public triumph. Just a few short weeks after the victory, her closest favourite, Robert Dudley, Earl of Leicester, died suddenly, possibly of a malarial infection. He had served her loyally to the end, walking beside her horse as she had delivered her speech at Tilbury. The brief note that he wrote her a few days before his death, thanking her for the medicine she had sent him and enquiring after her own health, became her most treasured possession. She inscribed it 'his last letter' and kept it in a locked casket by her bed for the rest of her life.[38]

In July 1589, Henry III of France, the last of the Valois kings, was assassinated. His successor was the Bourbon king of Navarre, Henry IV. As a Protestant, he was a natural ally for England, but his claim was contested by the Duke of Parma and a league of Catholics within France. Henry was eventually obliged to convert to Catholicism in order to secure his throne, which was hardly welcome news for

Elizabeth. But it was ongoing hostility with Spain that dominated the 1590s. The ominous presence of the Duke of Parma and his huge army just across the North Sea was hard to ignore, and Philip II was intent upon making up for the humiliation of the Armada.

Although she preferred diplomacy over aggression, Elizabeth's privateers continued to plunder Spanish treasure ships from the New World, and she sanctioned a number of naval campaigns against Spain, notably to Cadiz in 1596 and the 'Islands Voyage' to the Azores in 1597. The same year, Philip launched a third Armada against England, the second having been battered back by storms in 1595. He had assembled almost as large a fleet as for the 1588 enterprise, but yet again it was dogged by bad weather when it reached the English Channel, and those ships that were neither wrecked nor captured eventually retreated back to Spain. It would be Philip's last attempt to invade England and he died a little under a year later.

From 1598, what little resources Elizabeth had left in the royal treasury were spent on maintaining her support of the Dutch and in trying to bring Ireland under her control. As nominal queen, Elizabeth had continued the policy of her predecessors by appointing viceroys to exercise her authority there, but with limited success. As well as resisting English rule, the Irish had also rejected her religious reforms. The fact that the country remained Catholic made it a tantalising prospect for Elizabeth's continental enemies, Spain in particular. In 1597, the French wryly observed that the queen 'would wish Ireland drowned in the sea'.[39]

The situation reached crisis point with an uprising led by the charismatic Hugh O'Neill, second Earl of Tyrone. He achieved a crushing victory over English forces at the Battle of Yellow Ford in August 1598, which plunged most of Ireland into open rebellion. Elizabeth responded by dispatching 17,000 troops – the largest army ever sent to Ireland by the Tudors. She entrusted the command to her new favourite, Robert Devereux, Earl of Essex, who was appointed lord lieutenant of Ireland. But Essex, a vain and arrogant young man more intent upon personal than national glory, was not the stuff that great commanders were made of. Having failed to subdue Tyrone, he flouted Elizabeth's orders by concluding a treaty with him and then returned home without permission. In his absence, Tyrone proclaimed a virtually independent nation, governed by Irishmen under the authority of the pope, with only nominal English sovereignty. The damage that Essex had done was repaired by his successor, Charles Blount, a much more able commander. By early 1603, he had subjugated Ireland to English rule once more, although Elizabeth did not live to see the honourable truce that he concluded with Tyrone, bringing to an end the Nine Years' War.

These later years of Elizabeth's reign were blighted by troubles at home, too. There is a tendency to see post-Armada England as a 'Golden Age', with 'Good Queen Bess' presiding over a time of peace and prosperity. Certainly, there was a flowering of culture and literature, with the likes of William Shakespeare and Edmund Spenser penning prose glorifying the queen and her court, while adventurers such as Sir Walter Raleigh extended England's fledgling empire. But the late 1590s were also marked by war-weariness, inflation, high taxation, poor harvests and recurrent plague. There was a corresponding rise in social unrest, with crime and vagrancy becoming commonplace.

The moderation that had characterised so much of Elizabeth's reign seemed to have given way to unqualified royal sovereignty. The judges presiding over a trial in 1591 involving religious dissent declared that the realm of England was 'an absolute empire and monarchy'.[40] But this image distorts the truth of a more complex situation, in which power increasingly centred upon the privy council. The notion of absolute royal power was more propaganda than reality, evoked to bend people to the will of the Elizabethan regime.

Although Elizabeth had been mentally and physically robust for the majority of her reign, by the late 1590s, her grip on affairs appeared to be loosening. 'The court was very much neglected,' observed one of its members, 'and in effect the people were generally weary of an old woman's government.'[41] The fact that Elizabeth made no new appointments either to her privy council or to the nobility made the competition for places ever more fierce. In turn, this fuelled the vicious rivalry that dominated the politics of her later years, which inspired the famous observation by Sir Robert Naunton: 'The principal note of her reign will be that she ruled much by faction and parties, which she herself both made, upheld, and weakened as her own great judgement advised.'[42] But this factionalism resulted more from a lack of royal control than from the assertion of it.

The gulf between the queen's carefully constructed public face and the private one that lay beneath the layers of makeup, heavy wigs and ostentatious gowns grew ever wider as the 1590s drew to a close. Despite all her efforts, there was nothing Elizabeth could do to disguise her increasing age and infirmity. In November 1597, Henry IV of France dispatched his ambassador, Andre Hurault-Sieur de Maisse, to secure Elizabeth's military assistance. His description of the sixty-five-year-old queen is brutal but perhaps more accurate than the flattering accounts of a beauty that time had not touched. Her long, thin face 'appears very aged', he reported, 'and her teeth are very yellow and unequal . . . Many of them are missing so that one cannot understand her easily when she speaks quickly.' But the same restless energy that had kept Elizabeth's figure slight and her mind sharp throughout her long reign was still in evidence. De Maisse could not but admire: 'how lively she is in body and mind and nimble in everything she does'.[43]

Elizabeth was not the only member of her court to have aged. Although she had outlived the majority of those who had served her since her early years as queen, her most trusted official was still in post when the French ambassador paid another visit in 1598. William Cecil, Lord Burghley, had remained by his royal mistress's side throughout the forty, often turbulent, years that she had occupied the throne. Now approaching his seventy-eighth birthday, he was extremely frail – De Maisse described him as 'very old and white' – and he died shortly afterwards.[44] Elizabeth repaid his loyal service by tenderly nursing him during his final illness, sitting on his bed and feeding him with a spoon.

Burghley's death left the door open for other ambitious men to take his place. In part, this was filled by his son, Robert Cecil, who became secretary of state, a position that he had informally exercised for almost a decade. A highly able administrator, Robert had learned his craft under his father's careful eye. But while she appreciated his efficiency, Elizabeth never trusted the son as she had the father and called him her 'pygmy', on account of his diminutive stature.

Cecil's main rival was another Robert, the Earl of Essex. The queen's 'Sweet Robin' was the son of her despised rival, Lettice Knollys. Although he was more than thirty years her junior, he acted the part of a lover whenever he was in her presence, then poked fun at her in private as a 'crooked' old woman.[45] Elizabeth seemed to return his devotion, which stoked his already overbearing arrogance. After defying her orders in Ireland, Essex assumed that he would be instantly forgiven, but returned to find himself deep in disgrace. Desperate to win back favour, he resolved upon a reckless scheme that ended with a futile, almost farcical rebellion on 8 February 1601. Although he protested that he had rebelled against members of the government rather than the queen herself, this rang hollow. His supporters had financed the staging of Shakespeare's *Richard II*, and the theme of usurpation had not been lost on Elizabeth. 'I am Richard II, know ye not that?' she had asked indignantly.[46] Much as she had revelled in the young earl's attentions, she knew his life could not be spared. He was at least afforded the privilege of a private execution inside the Tower on 25 February.

'These troubles waste her much', reported Sir John Harington. 'She walks much in her privy chamber, and stamps with her feet at ill news, and thrusts her rusty sword at times into the arras in great rage . . . the dangers are over, and yet she always keeps a sword by her table.' The queen was plagued, too, by talk of the succession, which 'every day rudely sounded' in her ears.[47] In 1600, the government official and keeper of records, Thomas Wilson, observed: 'This crown is not like to fall to the ground for want of heads that claim to wear it.'[48] He proceeded to give an account of at least twelve people with some kind of claim to the English throne.

For several years now, the attention of officials and subjects had been increasingly drawn north of the border to the leading candidate, James VI. Henry VIII had barred his Scottish relatives from inheriting the English throne, but as the great-great-grandson of Henry VII, James's bloodline was stronger than any other candidate. 'They adored him as the Sun rising, and neglected her as now ready to set', Camden neatly observed.[49] James's nearest competitor was his cousin, Arbella Stuart, the great-granddaughter of Henry VIII's sister,

Margaret Tudor and James IV of Scotland. Although her bloodline was weaker than the King of Scots, many considered her claim stronger because she was born on English soil. But in temperament, Arbella was entirely unsuitable as a future queen. Elizabeth thought her 'haughty' when she was first presented at court in 1588, aged thirteen, and her blind arrogance only increased in the years to come, encouraged by her ambitious grandmother, Bess of Hardwick. She was dangerously unstable, too, and by 1603 she was described as 'half mad' by a Venetian envoy.[50]

Setting aside the question of her succession, in October 1601 the queen appeared before the last Parliament of her reign. The atmosphere was strained, thanks to a controversy over monopolies, but by the time Elizabeth had finished her speech, there was hardly a dry eye in the house. 'To be a king and wear a crown is a thing more glorious to them that see it than it is pleasant to them that bear it', she reflected. 'For myself, I was never so much enticed with the potent name of a king, or royal authority of a queen, as delighted that God hath made me his instrument to maintain his truth and glory and this kingdom from dishonour, damage, tyranny and oppression . . . And though you have had, and may have, many mightier and wiser princes sitting in this seat, yet you never had nor shall have any that will love you better.'[51] With these words, she neatly encapsulated the challenges of monarchy, as she saw them. It would be Elizabeth's final public appearance of note, and she had saved the best until last.

In January 1603, the queen left the court in Whitehall and moved to her favourite palace of Richmond, to which she could 'best trust her sickly old age'. She lingered on until March, when she rose from her bed and would not return to it for three days and nights, refusing food or rest, 'and was greatly emaciated by her long watching and fasting'. As one contemporary observed: 'It seems she might have lived if she would have used means, but she would not be persuaded, and princes must not be forced.'

Finally, in the early hours of 24 March, the last of the Tudor monarchs 'departed this life, mildly, like a lamb, easily like a ripe apple from the tree'.[52] Although Elizabeth's wishes for the succession had remained uncertain to the end, her ring was conveyed at once to James

VI, signalling that he was now King of England. On 28 April, the late queen was laid to rest next to her half-sister Mary in Westminster Abbey. The new king ordered a magnificent tomb for her and, later, the same for his mother, Mary, Queen of Scots.

At the end of her reign, Robert Cecil reflected that the queen had been 'more than a man, and, in truth, sometimes less than a woman'.[53] She had certainly confounded the stereotypes of female rule. Her first biographer, William Camden, claimed that she 'surprised her sex'.[54] This implies that Elizabeth had triumphed in spite of being a woman, whereas in fact she had made a glorious virtue of her gender. Her feminine traits had enabled her to stand out in a world dominated by men – and to dominate these men in turn. But she had also promoted her masculine characteristics when she had judged it expedient, such as when reproving her councillors: 'Had I been born crested, not cloven, you would not speak thus to me!'[55]

Even so, the eagerness with which the late queen's subjects scrambled to pay homage to the new king suggests an element of relief that after fifty years of female sovereignty, the natural order of things had been restored. But it would not be long before the people of England would hark back to the 'golden age' of the Tudors, and of Elizabeth in particular. A popular seventeenth-century polemic declared:

A Tudor! A Tudor! We've had Stuarts enough,
None ever reign'd like old Bess in her ruff.[56]

Part 5

The Stuarts (1603–1714)

'Kings are justly called gods'

The accession of James VI of Scotland to the English throne in 1603 united the two kingdoms for the first time. His persecution of Catholics and witches led to turbulence and bloodshed, and his dynasty was almost wiped out by the most notorious terror plot in history. By contrast, his son and successor, Charles I, antagonised Parliament by tolerating Catholics (and marrying one) and by insisting upon his royal prerogatives at the expense of its authority. The struggle between king and Parliament eventually led to civil war and Charles's execution. Although the monarchy was restored in 1660, the Great Plague of 1665 and the Great Fire the following year plunged the kingdom into fresh catastrophe. The Stuarts' obsession with the Divine Right of Kings led to the so-called Glorious Revolution of 1688 and the 1701 Act of Settlement, which ushered in a new, constitutional monarchy and permanently eradicated the prospect of a Catholic incumbent.

James I (1603–25)

A little God

B Y THE TIME James VI and I succeeded Elizabeth I in March 1603, he had ruled his native kingdom for thirty-five years. He had been just thirteen months old when his mother, Mary, Queen of Scots, had been forced to abdicate – a 'cradle king', as he called himself.[1] The prospect of having a king on the throne at last, and an experienced one at that, was welcomed across England. 'Many have been the mad caps rejoicing at our new King's coming', reported the late queen's godson, Sir John Harington.[2]

All the talk was of the new king's virtues. Referred to as 'the bright star of the North', James was renowned for his intellect. He had received an exceptional (if harsh) education at the hands of Scotland's leading scholars. James later remarked that they had taught him to speak Latin "ere I could speak Scottish'.[3] He was a product of the strict Scottish Reformation, too, and grew up with a strong aversion to Catholicism. By the age of seventeen, he already had an extensive library, which included classics, history, theology, political theory, geography and mathematics, as well as books on hunting and other sports. Even by royal standards, James was an intellectual phenomenon. His passion for learning provides the first glimpse of an obsessive nature that would find other, more destructive outlets in adulthood.

James's body was not as strong as his mind. For the first six or seven years of his life, he had been unable to stand up or walk without assistance. As a young man, he had to be tied onto his horse due to the weakness of his legs, and throughout his life he tended to walk while leaning on the shoulder of an attendant. He suffered in silence, though, thanks to the lack of nurturing influences, most notably his mother. The regent, James Stewart, first Earl of Moray, had ensured that the young prince was surrounded by men hostile to the erstwhile Queen of Scots.

James's distrust of his mother deepened into a more general antipathy towards women that found expression in witch-hunting. In 1597, he became the only monarch in history to publish a treatise on the subject. *Daemonologie* was a global bestseller of its day, republished several times and later translated into Latin, French and Dutch. The book lamented 'the fearful abounding at this time, in this country, of these detestable slaves of the Devil', and sparked a surge in the number of witchcraft cases brought before the Scottish courts. Half of those arrested (the vast majority of them women) were put to the flames.

The Scottish king penned other influential works, notably on the nature of monarchy. His two most famous tracts were written in 1598–9: *Basilikon Doron* and *The Trew Law of Free Monarchies*. At the heart of James's thesis was an unshakeable belief in the divine nature of kingship. In *Basilikon Doron*, which he intended as a practical manual on kingship for his eldest son and heir, Henry, he declared that God 'made you a little God to sit on his throne, and rule over other men'. The 'glistering worldly glory of Kings' was bestowed on them so that they might become 'bright lamps of godliness and virtue', lighting their subjects' way towards similar good behaviour.[4] His thesis would define not only his own monarchy but that of almost all his Stuart successors.

The two books also throw light upon the Scottish king's derisory attitude towards his prospective kingdom. He described England as 'reft by conquest from one to another', its laws subverted by William the Conqueror and his Norman regime.[5] By contrast, his native Scotland was a purer state, its independence a source of pride. James also poked fun at England in 1600 when he observed that Scotland was adopting Pope Gregory XIII's new calendar (meaning that the beginning of the year was now 1 January rather than 25 March), as all other civilised countries were doing. England, which was no longer subject to papal authority, upheld the old Julian calendar instead.

There was a hint of disdain, too, in James's reaction to the news that Elizabeth I had died and he was now King of England. As form dictated, he thanked the late queen's councillors on her behalf for their loyal service and asked that they praise God for giving them their new king. But while Robert Cecil and the rest of the privy council were anxious for the king to embark for his new kingdom, James told them that he could not simply leave Edinburgh at a moment's notice. He therefore instructed them to keep England ordered and peaceful until his arrival, which sparked panic among his new councillors because he had not given them the specific authorisation they needed to act. The new king was therefore obliged to send two further letters with the correct form of words, but he could not resist adding that he hoped they might now do as he had asked.[6] This early exchange highlighted the clash of cultures between the two kingdoms and would prove an ominous indication of what lay ahead.

In April 1603, the king finally embarked upon the long journey south. Crowds flocked to meet him as he made his ponderously slow progress to London. He used the journey to show off both his largesse and his brutality. With one hand, he doled out knighthoods and with the other he ordered the summary hanging of a thief without due process of law. He and his huge cavalcade were greeted with wild rejoicing at every stop. Even the plague that swept through London shortly before James's arrival did not dampen the celebratory mood, although it wiped out nearly a quarter of the capital's population. The new king's state entry had to be postponed, though, and attendance at his coronation in Westminster Abbey on 25 July was curtailed due to the ongoing risk of infection.

Praise echoed in the new king's ears. Roger Wilbraham, a London lawyer, enthused: 'The King is of the sharpest wit and invention, ready and pithy speech, an exceeding good memory; of the sweetest, pleasantest and best nature that ever I knew.' Not everyone was so impressed. The waspish Venetian ambassador, Scaramelli, marvelled at how the new king's councillors stood about him 'almost in an attitude of adoration', even though 'from his dress he would have been taken for the meanest of courtiers'. Others agreed that, in sharp contrast to the late queen, James lacked 'great majesty' and 'solemnities'. 'His walk was ever circular, his fingers ever in that walk fiddling about his codpiece', a scornful courtier noted. Although 'crafty and cunning in petty things', the new king was slow to grasp 'weighty affairs', which led one contemporary to coin the famous description of him as 'the wisest fool in Christendom'.[7]

Neither did James's court impress his new English subjects. The clash of cultures was evident in the king's love of garish and riotous masques. Elizabeth I's godson was appalled to see high-born ladies and gentlemen 'wallow in beastly delights' during these 'strange pageantries', with the players themselves being too drunk to perform. The absence of a firm controlling hand such as Elizabeth's soon led to a sharp decline in standards across the court. Lady Anne Clifford, whose aunt had been one of the late queen's closest companions, was appalled at 'how all the ladies about the Court had gotten such ill names that it was grown a scandalous place'. Harington agreed: 'I never did see such lack of good order, discretion, and sobriety, as I have now done.'[8] There was a shocking rise in the number of pimps and prostitutes at court, and even official employees such as laundresses were known to supplement their income by selling sexual favours.

Most shocking of all, though, was James's own private life. 'Our virtuous King makes our hopes to swell,' declared Thomas Wilson, a protégé of Robert Cecil, at the beginning of the reign.[9] In outward appearances, James was indeed a model of conventionality: not for him the single life that his predecessor had so stubbornly pursued, to the detriment of the succession. He had been married to Anne of Denmark for thirteen years by the time he became King of England and the couple had three surviving children. But he had long preferred the company of his male favourites and rumours of his homosexuality abounded. Sodomy was at that time a capital felony punishable by death, but the new king was said to have personally intervened to save a Frenchman who had been arrested for the crime. The contrast with the celebrated Virgin Queen seemed to grow sharper with each passing day.

In common with his Tudor predecessor, Henry VIII, James neglected state business in the pursuit of pleasure. He told his council that hunting was 'the only means to maintain his health' and so 'desires them to take the charge and burden of affairs, and foresee that he be not interrupted or troubled with too much business'.[10] Before long, the Venetian envoy reported that the new king had 'sunk into a lethargy of pleasures, and will not take heed of matters of state . . . He seems to have forgotten that he is a King, except in his kingly pursuit of stags, to which he is quite foolishly devoted.'[11]

There was yet another cause for grievance among the English people. Even though James was known to be a staunch Protestant, the fact that he was also the son of a celebrated Catholic martyr gave those of the 'old faith' cause to hope that he would grant them greater freedom of worship than they had enjoyed under Elizabeth. Before becoming King of England, he had offered reassurance that he would not persecute any Catholics who were 'quiet and . . . obedient'. He soon went against his word. While the late queen had turned a blind eye to private Catholic practices, James insisted upon a much stricter observance of the reformed faith, declaring: 'Who can't pray with me, can't love me.' Early in his reign, he and his councillors began drafting new legislation for the persecution of Catholics. The Jesuit priest, John Gerard, encapsulated the bitter disappointment that spread among the Catholic community. 'A flash of lightning, giving for the time a pale light unto those that sit in darkness, doth afterwards leave them in more desolation.'[12]

Within a worryingly short space of time, England's new king had courted widespread resentment. By the summer of 1603, this already ran so deep that there were those willing to stake their lives on ridding the kingdom of their new monarch. The Bye Plot involved a group of Catholics who planned to kidnap the king in order to secure a number of concessions for the practice of their religion. But it lacked powerful supporters and soon collapsed in disarray. More serious was the Main Plot, which aimed to oust James from the throne and replace him with his cousin, Arbella Stuart. Its ring-leaders, who had sought funding from Spain, were men of much greater influence – none more so than the late queen's favourite adventurer, Sir Walter Raleigh. When the conspiracy was uncovered, Raleigh and his fellow plotters were arrested and condemned. Although the leader, Henry Brooke, Lord Cobham, was subsequently released, Raleigh would spend the next thirteen years in the Tower of London, becoming one of its longest-serving prisoners. He was eventually released in 1616 to lead an expedition to Venezuela in search of the fabled El Dorado, City of Gold. Its failure led to Raleigh's execution soon after his return, in October 1618.

In attempting to settle the most contentious issue of the day, James faced a greater challenge than his Tudor predecessors. He belonged to one church in England and another in Scotland, and somehow had to reconcile the two, as well as the sizeable number of subjects who fervently disagreed with both. Elizabeth's religious settlement had been a pragmatic compromise, but one that left a number of important issues unresolved. The new king was not fazed by the challenge. The Scots had a much stronger tradition of debate than the English, and James had spent years countering the forcefully expressed opinions of his detractors, one of whom once called him 'God's silly vassal'.

James decided that the differing opinions should be aired at a major conference held at Hampton Court in January 1604. Although the hard-line Puritans and Catholics left disappointed, the king did achieve a broader consensus than his predecessor. The conference also resulted in the commissioning of a new Bible in the English vernacular, which became known as the King James Bible. A few months later, James held another conference, at Somerset House, its purpose to end the twenty-year war with Spain. The negotiations were successful and the ensuing treaty established peace between the two countries. Not all James's subjects shared his satisfaction in allying Protestant England with the most potent Catholic power in Europe.

The new king soon had other matters to attend to. Two days after Elizabeth I's death, the antiquarian and Member of Parliament, Sir Robert Cotton, had written a treatise extolling the name of Britain. This highlighted examples from history of smaller kingdoms uniting to form a more impressive whole and made it seem the simplest of tasks for the British Isles to do the same. In reality, it was fraught with difficulty. The underlying problem was that the English thought that Scotland should be incorporated into England (as a number of their kings had tried to achieve in the past), while the Scots believed that the two kingdoms should be equal partners. They were hardly encouraged by England's attempts to subjugate Wales and Ireland, which had led to a great deal of bloodshed over the centuries.

Despite the difficulties, James was determined to bring about a full union of his two crowns. In his mind, Scotland was the superior kingdom and he brought his Scottish experience to bear on his English rule. He was the first – and last – King of England to do so. His successors, born or at least raised in England, increasingly saw themselves as English and approached the issue of the unification from that perspective.

The issue dominated the first Parliament of the reign, which met in March 1604. In his opening speech, James urged that England and Scotland should not just be united by one king, but by one law and one people.[13] This was both simple and hopelessly naïve, the triumph of theory over practicality that characterised James's approach to kingship. Neither was there much support for the proposal that James adopt the title of King of Great Britain. There were fears that giving up the 'sceptred isle' of Shakespeare would lead to the loss of England's identity, both at home and abroad.

Having lost patience with Parliament, on 20 October 1604 James issued a proclamation confirming his title of King of Great Britain. The rhetoric painted a picture of two mighty nations united not just by their monarch but by language, religion and coastline, as God had always intended. To strengthen this new 'united kingdom', the following month the king announced that a shared currency would be issued: a twenty-shilling piece known as the 'unite'.

Any further debate on the issue was cut short by one of the most dramatic events in the history of the monarchy. The simmering resentment among England's Catholics found an outlet in a plot to blow James and his Parliament to the heavens with a huge cache of gunpowder hidden underneath the House of Lords. It was masterminded by a group of thirteen gentlemen fanatics led by the charismatic Robert Catesby and his cousin Thomas Wintour. The blowing up of Parliament when it reconvened on 5 November 1605 would be a prelude to a popular revolt in the Midlands, where most of the plotters were from. Although there was a strong anti-Scottish theme to the plot, it was not intended to destroy the Stuart monarchy altogether. Rather, it would place James's nine-year-old daughter Elizabeth on the throne, bypassing her brothers Henry and Charles. This was not some sentimental desire to return England to female monarchy. Elizabeth would be a puppet queen whom the plotters would marry to a good Catholic prince and thus restore the kingdom to the 'true' religion.

Thanks to an anonymous tip-off, the House of Lords was searched at around midnight on 4 November, just hours before the plot was due to be executed. Guy Fawkes was discovered with thirty-six barrels of gunpowder – more than enough to reduce the House of Lords and all of the surrounding buildings within a mile radius to rubble. Under interrogation, a number of the plotters hinted that there had been some 'great patron' behind their scheme. Speculation as to who this might have been has been rife ever since. One of the most popular theories is that the king's own chief minister, Robert Cecil, had sponsored the plot as a means of whipping up fear and hatred of England's Catholics – ensuring, of course, that it would be discovered in time.

Whoever was behind it, this was certainly the result. The Gunpowder plotters suffered the horrors of a traitor's death and were hangéd, drawn and quartered in front of huge crowds in January 1606. The thwarting of their plot became a cause of national celebration, as prescribed by the Observance of the Fifth of November Act that Parliament passed the same month. James was determined to ensure that his English subjects would never forget how he had vanquished his enemies. Every year, special sermons were preached, church bells rung and bonfires lit. The anniversary has proved one of the most enduring in England's history, even though the Act itself was repealed in 1859. When rumours began to circulate that the plot had been a devilish conspiracy, it inspired James to introduce much harsher legislation against suspected witches, prompting a resurgence of the so-called 'witchcraze' that had long since abated south of the Scottish border.

The Gunpowder Plot was only a temporary distraction from James's campaign to secure a union between his two kingdoms. Sidestepping Parliament, he issued a proclamation announcing a new British flag: the 'Union Jack' (for Jacobus, or James). Its design sparked bitter rows between the English and Scottish heralds as each tried to make their own cross more conspicuous. James tried to calm the troubled waters during the third session of Parliament in November 1606, when he gave an impassioned speech imploring his English subjects to recognise that Scotland was a civilised nation – although he could not resist adding that it was more governable than England. He reassured Parliament that his new kingdom enjoyed greater prominence within the British Isles, whereas Scotland was 'seldom seen and saluted by their King'.[14] He spoke the truth: during the remainder of his reign, he only visited Scotland once, in 1617, although his keen interest in Scottish affairs never wavered.

James's rhetoric fell upon deaf ears. Parliament voted overwhelmingly against the union and the king had little choice but to abandon the idea. Undaunted, in the 1610 Parliament he gave a rousing speech on the nature of kingship. 'The state of monarchy is the supremist thing upon earth,' he told the assembled dignitaries. 'Kings are justly called gods, for that they exercise a manner of resemblance of divine power upon earth . . . They make and unmake their subjects, they have power of raising and casting down, of life and death, judges over all their subjects and in all causes and yet accountable to none but God only.'[15] It was the clearest expression yet of the Stuarts' inherent belief in their divine right to rule – a belief that would shape their monarchy and set them on a collision course with Parliament.

Frustrated with his intractable English government, James spent an increasing amount of time hunting and in the company of his favourites. For most of his early reign, his closest companion was a young Scotsman named Robert Carr, whom he created Earl of Somerset. But in 1614, Carr was supplanted by the man who would come to dominate King James and his entire court for the rest of the reign. The second son of a sheep farmer and his beautiful but penniless wife Mary, George Villiers enjoyed a meteoric rise to fortune after first meeting the king at Apethorpe Hall in Northamptonshire during his summer visit. Aged twenty-two, he was described as: 'the handsomest-bodied man in all of England; his limbs so well compacted, and his conversation so pleasing, and of so sweet a disposition'.[16]

King James, twenty-six years his senior, was instantly captivated. Soon after their first meeting, he appointed Villiers his cupbearer, which gave the new favourite frequent access to the royal presence. Further promotions followed in rapid succession, culminating in the dukedom of Buckingham in 1623.

The two men grew so close that they frequently shared a bed and James declared he wanted Buckingham to become his 'wife'. They also had pet names for each other: 'dear Dad' and 'sow' for the king, and 'Steenie' for the duke, after St Stephen, who was said to have the face of an angel. Buckingham's angelic appearance disguised the heart of a devil. Ruthlessly ambitious, he destroyed any rivals who threatened his hold over James. When the king took a fancy to a new young courtier named Arthur Brett, Buckingham had him sent into exile. He also instigated the impeachment of Brett's brother-in-law Lionel Cranfield, the Lord Treasurer.

Ever with an eye to the future, Buckingham took care to cultivate the king's younger son, Charles. The elder, Henry, had been struck down by typhoid fever in 1612 when he was eighteen years old. His death had been widely regarded as a tragedy for the kingdom because Henry had been accomplished and popular – far more so than his father the king. By contrast, his younger brother Charles, who was just shy of his twelfth birthday when he became the heir to the throne, had been largely overlooked. A weak and sickly child, he had been slow to develop and was painfully shy. Although he overcame most of his physical infirmities when he reached adulthood, he retained a stammer for the rest of his life.

James immediately began to instruct his younger son in every aspect of monarchy. Francis Bacon enthused that he was 'the best tutor in Europe'.[7] Charles gained practical experience, too, accompanying his father on state visits and progresses, and from 1617 playing an active role in government. In contrast to other heirs in waiting, he remained intensely loyal to the king. He was also greatly influenced by the Duke of Buckingham, who, with characteristic condescension, called him 'Baby Charles'.[8]

The king's carefully maintained policy of peace with his continental neighbours was threatened in 1619 when his daughter Elizabeth and her husband Frederick, the Elector Palatine, rashly accepted the offer of the Bohemian crown. A league of Catholic forces, including those supplied by King Philip III of Spain, was soon ranged against them. This put James under pressure from hard-line Protestants to take up arms on behalf of the Elector. Family loyalty also demanded that he do so. But the king rightly viewed his son-in-law's actions as foolhardy and had no desire to make an enemy of Spain or disrupt the fragile stability of Europe. He therefore pursued a more conciliatory policy aimed at restoring Frederick to his rightful Palatinate territories.

There was a darker side to James's foreign policy. Like his predecessor, Elizabeth I, he actively pursued the establishment of colonies in America. In 1616, Jamestown was founded as the capital of Virginia and three years later '20 and odd Negroes' were landed there.[19] This is commonly viewed as the beginning of African slavery in North America, a trade that would be exploited ever more aggressively by James's successors until its abolition almost two hundred years later. From the crown's perspective, slavery was a necessary and entirely acceptable expedient in developing Britain's trade and empire. But it would be widely condemned by later generations and remains one of the most shameful chapters in the long history of the monarchy.

By the 1620s, James appeared increasingly careworn. The dedicatory epistle to a tract he published in 1620 reflects a king 'being grown in years . . . weary of controversies', and laments that 'the crown of thorns went never out of my mind, remembering the thorny cares, which a King . . . must be subject unto'.[20] For years, James had suffered from kidney problems and arthritis, and both became more acute in later life. In his weakened state, in March 1625 the fifty-seven-year-old king fell prey to a fever, stroke and severe dysentery. There is no small irony in the fact that, having hunted witches for most of his life, at the end James called for the services of a wise woman.

The first King of Britain was buried in Westminster Abbey on 5 May, close to the tombs of his mother Mary and predecessor Elizabeth. He was widely mourned on both sides of the border, his reputation as a king of scholarship, wit and peace rapidly taking root. But it was his Scottish subjects who felt the loss most keenly as they now faced for the first time an absentee monarchy under a king they had only seen in infancy.

Although James had not achieved the unity between his kingdoms that he had hoped for, he had established Britain as a viable political entity and done enough to ensure its survival long into the future.

Charles I (1625–49)

'An incorruptible crown'

O N HIS DEATHBED, James urged his successor to defend the church, protect his sister Elizabeth and remain loyal to the Duke of Buckingham. Charles swore to honour his wishes and regarded this promise as sacrosanct. Now that he was king, he idolised his late father. He commissioned an array of artwork in James's honour – notably Peter Paul Rubens' magnificent ceiling in the new Banqueting House at Whitehall, which showed his father ascending to heaven surrounded by angels – and lambasted anyone who even hinted at criticism of the late king.

One of Charles's first acts was to marry Henrietta Maria, the fifteen-year-old sister of Louis XIII of France. This brought the new king a powerful ally, but it was not without complications. His bride was a Roman Catholic, which made her an unpopular choice in England and prevented her from being crowned. She was escorted to her new kingdom by the Duke of Buckingham and arrived, timorous and still sick from the voyage, in June 1625. Eyewitnesses noted that she was 'for her age somewhat little'.[1] Her welcome in the capital was marred by torrential rain and the worst outbreak of plague in living memory. Aware that there was opposition to his marriage among members of the forthcoming Parliament, Charles made sure to consummate it before the session opened in June 1625. It was the first instance of what would become a dangerous habit of sidestepping Parliament in order to have his way.

In preparation for Parliament, the new king summoned the antiquarian Sir Robert Cotton to prove that 'the kings of England have used to be present in the time of the debates and examples of causes and questions in Parliament as well as at other time'.[2] Robert Phelips, one of Charles's most outspoken opponents, grumbled: 'We are the last monarchy in Christendom that yet retain our ancient rights and privileges.' Charles's supporters, meanwhile, pointed out that all of his continental peers had overthrown their 'turbulent' parliaments.[3] Even now, their perspectives were so radically opposed that there seemed little hope of compromise. The fact that Charles's own view of Parliament was coloured by his belief in the Divine Right of Kings did not help matters. In his opinion, its primary function was not to debate matters of policy but to vote him money.

Fears that the new king would allow greater freedoms for England's Catholic community were expressed in the House of Commons. Charles offered firm assurances that he would do nothing to undermine the Church of England, but he had already pledged to ease restrictions against Catholics in a secret treaty with his new brother-in-law, Louis XIII. The same treaty had promised naval support to suppress the Protestant Huguenots in France.

The bad-tempered atmosphere of Charles's first Parliament was intensified by a disagreement over the new king's plans for war against Spain. Charles had appointed Buckingham to command it as Lord Admiral, but there were objections on account of his youth and inexperience. Parliament granted a subsidy that was far short of Charles's expectations and the ensuing expedition was an ignominious failure.

Charles was crowned in February 1626. Preparations for the event had proved troublesome. His ceremonial entry into the city of London had to be postponed because of the plague, but he was averse to the idea anyway and eventually cancelled it altogether. At the rehearsal for his crowning, the king noticed that one of the dove's wings on top of the sceptre was missing and demanded that it be repaired. When the royal goldsmith replied that it could not be done in time, Charles flew into a fury and the hapless man was obliged to manufacture an entirely new dove. The ceremony itself proceeded without incident 'amidst an incredible concourse of people'. The text chosen for the sermon was later viewed as prophetic. 'Be faithful unto death', declared the Bishop of Carlisle, 'and I will give you the crown of life.'[4]

When Parliament met again in March 1626, it denounced Buckingham as the source of all the kingdom's evils and began proceedings to have him impeached. Charles immediately leapt to his favourite's defence. 'Remember that parliaments are altogether in my power for the calling, sitting, and continuance of them', he told the Commons.[5] When its members continued to urge the king to dismiss Buckingham, he dismissed them instead: Parliament was abruptly dissolved in June.

The king's show of power cost him dear. Not only had he exacerbated the rising tensions within his government, he had also forfeited the subsidy that he so desperately needed. His solution to the latter was to impose a forced loan upon his subjects. This was a financial success, raising more than £250,000 (around £30 million today), but it was disastrous for Charles's relations with his subjects. In November 1627, a test case heard in the King's Bench found that the king had a prerogative right to imprison without trial any subject who refused to pay the loan. Parliament responded by adopting a Petition of Right, which called upon the king to acknowledge that he could not levy taxes without its consent, nor impose martial law on civilians or imprison them without due process. There was more than an echo of Magna Carta in all of this and Charles's response evoked memories of King John. Although he assented to the petition on 7 June 1628, by the end of the month he had prorogued Parliament and reasserted his right to collect customs duties without parliamentary consent.

The gulf between the king and his people was widened by the assassination of Buckingham in August 1628, following his disastrous naval expedition in defence of the French Huguenots at La Rochelle. The action was a direct contravention of the terms of Charles's secret alliance with Louis XIII and was at least partly prompted by the king's stormy relations with his young wife. Disputes over Henrietta Maria's jointure, appointments to her household and her lack of discretion in the practice of her religion had soured the early months of their marriage. Buckingham's failure in France led to renewed calls for his impeachment. When Charles continued to stand by his favourite, an aggrieved army officer named John Felton, who had served under the duke, took matters into his own hands and stabbed Buckingham to death.

The duke's assassination marked a turning point in Charles's reign. He would never allow any member of his government to become so close to him or to dominate his private and public lives as Buckingham had done. Instead, the king sought solace in the company of his wife, with whom relations dramatically improved. Less positively, the loss of Buckingham made Charles an ever more distant figure as ruler – from ministers and subjects alike.

This was demonstrated by the first Parliament to meet after the duke's death. When the Commons launched an attack on Charles's religious policy, he brought the session to an immediate close. He subsequently declared that he would call no future parliaments 'until our people shall see more clearly our intents and actions . . . [and] shall come to a better understanding of us and themselves'.[6] Charles's uncompromising stance posed a grave threat to the relationship between monarch and Parliament that had developed over the past four centuries. Even Henry VIII, who as supreme head of the church had wielded greater power than any of his predecessors, had understood that kings must rule through Parliament, not bypass it. Anzolo Correr, the Venetian ambassador at court, remarked with perspicacity: 'As he [Charles] has given up governing by Parliament, as his predecessors did, it remains to be seen if he will go on and if he will be able to do by the royal authority what former kings did by the authority of the realm . . . [He] will be very fortunate if he does not fall into some great upheaval.'[7]

The king was at least enough of a realist to know that without Parliament, he could no longer afford to wage wars. In April 1629 and November 1630, he concluded peace treaties with France and Spain respectively, which ushered in a period of greater stability and prosperity than his kingdom had enjoyed since the beginning of the reign. Charles's personal life also became more settled. The new closeness between him and his consort was cemented by the birth of two male heirs: Charles in 1630 and James in 1633. In securing the succession, he had fulfilled his primary obligation as monarch, which gave his popularity a much-needed boost.

Feeling more secure on his throne, Charles established a new structure and ceremony at court. 'The face of the court was much changed in the reign of the king,' remarked one of its members, 'for King Charles was temperate and chaste and serious; so that the fools and bawds, mimics and catamites of the former court grew out of fashion.' Among the king's innovations was a suite of arcane rituals to emphasise his semi-divine status, which every servant, regardless of rank, was required to uphold. Access to the monarch's private chambers was strictly limited, while the function of the public rooms was more closely defined than ever before and the 'bawdry and prophane' occupants were replaced with 'men of learning and ingenuity in all arts'. Like his father, Charles was fond of masques, but under his watchful eye they were impeccably stage-managed. Britain's foremost architect, Inigo Jones, designed the staging, costumes and special effects, creating such dazzling spectacles that the court had never seen the like. Queen Henrietta Maria herself sometimes played a starring role. The only criticism of Charles's new-look court was that it was 'replenished with papists', thanks to his wife's connections.[8]

The shaping of Charles's court had been heavily influenced by his six-month sojourn in Madrid in 1623, when Prince of Wales. He had been greatly impressed by the refinement and formality of Philip IV's court, and even more so by the Spanish king's art collection, which was then the greatest in Europe. While there, he had been sketched by Velázquez and had purchased a set of Raphael cartoons. It had marked the beginning of a lifelong passion for collecting. As king, Charles would do more than any other monarch in British history to shape and embellish what became known as the Royal Collection, which today comprises more than a million objects from the fine and decorative arts. He patronised a wide range of artists, notably Peter Paul Rubens and Sir Anthony van Dyck, and was admired as 'a most excellent judge and a great lover of paintings, carvings, engravings'.[9] His own collection was so vast that a new privy gallery had to be constructed at Whitehall. Keen to project his royal lineage, Charles purchased an extensive suite of portraits of English kings from Edward III onwards, and of their many European royal relatives.

For the same reason, the king showed a keen interest in the Order of the Garter and always wore his George medal with pride.[10] He created an elaborate new ceremony for St George's Day, including competitions, feasts and a procession from London to Windsor. In contrast to some of his predecessors who had invested heavily in public displays of monarchy, Charles was just as interested in its practical application. He was assiduous in every aspect of government, from regular attendance of council meetings to reading and correcting draft reports and diplomatic correspondence, answering every petition and approving appointments. The absence of a chief minister after Buckingham's assassination gave rise to a more balanced system of government, with officials carefully selected by the king to represent a range of interests.

During these years of peace, Charles did not neglect his kingdom's military reserves. In response to an increase in French and Spanish shipbuilding, he commissioned several new vessels, including the *Sovereign of the Seas*, the largest ship that had ever been built in England. Charles funded these new ships from his own income, but there were insufficient funds to support their activities at sea. The privy council therefore revived the practice of ship money, whereby merchant ships were converted for use in war. This had been employed in the past, but only in times of emergency. When the levy was extended to the entire nation, it prompted widespread outrage. The first legal challenge to it came in 1637, led by John Hampden in Buckinghamshire, which, along with other land-locked counties, felt particularly aggrieved at paying the tax. Even though Hampden lost the case, his stand made him a national hero and fanned the flames of discontent.

The king's religious stance deepened the growing crisis. In his view, religious conformity was essential to the maintenance of royal power. He advised his eldest son: 'Take it as an infallible maxim from me, that, as the church can never flourish without the protection of the Crown, so the dependency of the crown upon the church is the chiefest support of regal authority.'[11] In reality, though, his subjects were still deeply divided between those who adhered to the Church of England and those whose beliefs were either too traditionally Roman Catholic or too radically Protestant to conform. Charles persecuted both with equal rigour, but the fact that his wife remained a Roman Catholic and her chapel became a refuge for others of that faith incited suspicions that he, too, had Catholic sympathies. These were heightened by his support for William Laud, Archbishop of Canterbury, who advocated reforms that had a distinctly Catholic flavour, notably an increased focus on ritual and ceremony.

There were even more grumblings against the king north of the border. Although he had been born in Scotland, Charles had shown little interest in it since moving to the English court in his infancy. He had retained his father's Scottish advisers, but they had been in England for so long that they were out of touch with affairs in Edinburgh. It was not until 1633 that he finally travelled to Scotland for his coronation. By then, he was widely resented as an absentee king, and any policies or reforms he tried to introduce were viewed with mistrust.

Matters came to a head when Charles attempted to establish a new prayer book. Although it had been drafted by Scottish bishops, it was seen as an English imposition and sparked immediate resistance when it was introduced in 1637. This began with rioting in the streets and attacks on senior clerics and politicians, and before long Scotland had been whipped up into a full-scale rebellion led by the Presbyterians (or 'Covenanters'). Any attempts Charles made to restore order served only to inflame the situation.

Eventually, having failed to reason with his Scottish subjects, the king raised an army and led it north. It was the first time since Edward II's tumultuous reign that a monarch had gone to war without calling a Parliament in advance. The Scottish rebels were quick to react. They gathered 30,000 troops and secured all of the key strategic footholds in the lowlands to impede the king's advance. Faced with such strong resistance, Charles lost his nerve. Having reached Berwick-upon-Tweed on the Scottish border, he concluded a truce. Both sides regarded this as only temporary, and the king immediately began to seek additional resources to strengthen his army.

Charles could not hope to muster the necessary forces alone, so in the spring of 1640 he called a Parliament in England, confident that its members would be motivated by the traditional antipathy towards the Scots and grant him a generous subsidy. But the so-called Short Parliament was dominated by complaints against the king's past infringements of his subjects' rights, notably the imposition of the despised ship money. It quickly became obvious that if Charles was to secure the subsidy he desperately needed to counter the Scottish rebellion, he would have to make substantial concessions to his English subjects. The deal that was eventually proposed was the very definition of short-term gain for long-term pain. Parliament would grant twelve subsidies amounting to around £600,000, but in return Charles must agree to permanently surrender ship money, which was worth more than £150,000 a year.

Before any agreement was reached, though, the king summarily dissolved Parliament. He had heard rumours of collusion between the parliamentary leaders (whom he called 'some few cunning and some ill-affected men') and the Scottish rebels.[12] Charles now faced a decision: accept his defeat in Scotland or fight on without the necessary funds. In choosing the latter, he made one of the gravest mistakes of his reign.

As the king desperately tried to muster new troops, the leaders of the Scottish rebellion took matters into their own hands. Charles's joy at the birth of his third son Henry in July 1640 was cut short by news that the rebellious Covenanters had defeated his poorly equipped army at the Battle of Newburn Ford and occupied nearby Newcastle. Hostilities were brought to an end by the Treaty of Ripon, whereby the Scots agreed to withdraw their troops only when the king had paid a generous settlement. In the meantime, he was to fund the soldiers' expenses at a rate of £850 per day. Lacking the money to honour the agreement, Charles had no choice but to call another Parliament.

The so-called 'Long Parliament' was convened in November 1640. From the outset, it made the most of the fact that it held a financial gun to the king's head and set about putting right what it considered the abuses of the past eleven years. It also ensured that Charles would never again be able to rule without it. In February 1641, it passed a Bill that took away the king's right to dissolve Parliament without its own consent. It stipulated, too, that Charles and his successors must assemble Parliament every three years at least.

The king's most powerful officials also came under fire. Most were driven from office, but Sir Thomas Wentworth (later Earl of Strafford) and William Laud were sent to the Tower on charges of treason. The beleaguered Charles could do little more than watch as his government collapsed around him. When Wentworth was condemned to death, he vowed: 'on the word of a King, you shall not suffer in life, honour or fortune'.[13] He did everything he could to make good his promise, even plotting with a group of army officers to free his former minister from the Tower. But with large crowds of angry protestors threatening to overrun the palace of Whitehall, Charles reluctantly put his signature to the execution warrant, lamenting: 'My Lord Strafford's condition is happier than mine.' Wentworth's fellow prisoner, Laud, reflected that the king's actions had proved him to be 'a mild and gracious prince, that knows not how to be, or be made, great'.[14]

Charles never forgave himself for Wentworth's death. He believed the horrors that followed were a punishment from God for his weakness as king, rather than the result of his having breached his monarchical authority. It was a fatal misconception, one that would hinder any prospect of a rapprochement with his opposers. But Charles had always considered himself above such complaints. 'Princes are not bound to give account of their actions', he observed, 'but to God alone.'[15]

In August 1641, Charles left behind his troubles in England for a fifteen-week visit to Scotland. While there, he ratified a treaty that in theory settled matters between himself and the Covenanters but in practice deprived him of any real authority. The king had barely recovered from this humiliation when news arrived of widespread rebellions in Ireland. The bloodiest of these was in Ulster, where hundreds of Protestant settlers were massacred. Worse still, the rebel leader claimed to be acting on Charles's orders. Even though this was a brazen lie, it was hugely damaging to the reputation of a king whom many believed to be a closet papist. Charles realised that to restore order in Ireland and protect his crown, he must dispel any ambiguity about his faith. From thenceforth, he transformed himself into a champion of the Protestant church bequeathed to him by his father, untainted by popery.

When the king returned to London in November, he immediately set about promoting his new image as the defender of Protestantism.

This won him enthusiastic support among the crowds who turned out to see him. They had also been reassured by his agreement with Parliament that he would not exceed his prerogative powers. But the situation remained extremely tense, particularly after the House of Commons passed the 'Grand Remonstrance', a long list of grievances against actions committed by Charles's ministers since the beginning of the reign. When the king asked Parliament for funds to quell the Irish rebellion, many members suspected that he intended to use the army against them. Meanwhile, Charles heard rumours that Parliament was planning to impeach his wife for colluding with the Irish rebels. This provoked him into decisive – and ultimately disastrous – action.

On 3 January 1642, Charles ordered Parliament to surrender five members of the Commons on the grounds of high treason. They included John Pym, his chief opponent, and John Hampden, the hero of the ship money debacle. When Parliament refused, the king ordered their arrest by force. But the men got wind of this and fled. The following day, Charles entered the House of Commons flanked by a large armed guard. It was the first time that an English monarch had done so and it constituted a grave breach of parliamentary privilege. Undaunted, he demanded to know where the five men had gone. The Speaker, William Lenthall, famously replied: 'May it please your Majesty, I have neither eyes to see nor tongue to speak in this place but as the House is pleased to direct me, whose servant I am here.'[16] His words marked a turning point: Parliament's authority now exceeded the king's.

Charles's rash actions had cost him the newly won trust of his people, too. Everywhere he went, he was jeered by angry crowds. In vain, he protested that he had only been acting against the men he deemed 'traitors', not Parliament itself. Fearing for his safety and that of his family, on 10 January he withdrew first to Hampton Court and then to Windsor.

In the king's absence, Parliament was quick to seize control of the capital. Events now moved apace. In February 1642, Charles sent his wife and eldest daughter abroad – ostensibly so that Mary could join her future husband, William of Orange, but nobody was fooled that it was for anything other than to remove them from the gathering storm. He then resorted to that trusted public relations tactic: a royal progress. Having taken a leisurely journey through East Anglia, he travelled northwards to York. On the way, he took every opportunity to explain to his subjects that he wished only to fulfil his coronation oath and defend the civil and religious liberties of his people. This message was reinforced by a flurry of printed pamphlets, proclamations and the like – a staggering 464 in the course of 1642, more than the previous seventeen years of his reign combined.

But if Charles had faced down his opponents with rhetoric, he would find it much harder to overcome them with force. On 23 April 1642, he was refused entry to Hull by the city's parliamentary governor, Sir John Hotham – an event that is traditionally viewed as the beginning of the Civil War. By early June, the king had privately decided that the only way to take back control of his kingdom was through armed aggression. He waited until the harvest had been gathered before publicly declaring war on his parliamentary enemies in Nottingham on 22 August. The initial response was heartening. Within a month, 20,000 men had flocked to his standard, including troops and munitions sent over by Queen Henrietta Maria.

The conflict that followed tends to be referred to as the English Civil War. In fact, it comprised three separate but concurrent civil wars in England, Scotland and Ireland. But for Charles, the priority was to seize victory in England, and he remained there throughout the hostilities. Initially, his forces (given the derogatory name 'Cavaliers' by the parliamentarians) controlled most of the northern and western counties, the Midlands and Wales, while Parliament's troops (or 'Roundheads', as the royalists called them) dominated London, the south-east and East Anglia, and also had control of the navy.

The first major battle was fought at Edgehill in Warwickshire on 23 October 1642. The king was ably assisted by his nephews, Princes Rupert and Maurice of the Rhine. Rupert proved a highly skilled commander and would go on to achieve some notable victories. But this first encounter was inconclusive. Thereafter, Charles set up his headquarters at Oxford and established a court in miniature, insisting on the same order and ceremony that he had established before the troubles began. Anxious for a degree of certainty in an increasingly uncertain world, he took refuge in routine, as one contemporary diarist described: 'He kept his hours most exactly . . . You might know where he would be at any hour from his rising, which was very early, to his walk he took in the garden, and so to chapel and dinner.'[17]

Throughout this time, Charles made vigorous attempts to bring his enemies to terms and showed himself to be far more inclined to peace than they, even though his army was not yet on the back foot. He was just as active in the various clashes of arms between the two sides, being present at eight of the fifteen major battles during the first four years of the war.

On 3 June 1643, Parliament voted again on a motion that they had rejected the day before. This time, it was agreed by just a single vote. The Dean and Chapter of Westminster was subsequently ordered to surrender the keys to the treasury where the royal regalia were kept so that an inventory of the contents could be taken. Anticipating resistance from the royalist staff at the abbey, the motion decreed that if necessary, the locks might be broken open.

The task was entrusted to Sir Henry Mildmay, Master of the Jewel House, and Henry Marten, Member of Parliament for Berkshire, both staunch parliamentarians. A contemporary account described how Marten

> made himself Master of the Spoil. And having forced open a great Iron Chest, took out the Crowns, the Robes, the Swords and Sceptre, belonging anciently to King Edward the Confessor and used by all our Kings at their inaugurations. With a scorn greater than his Lusts, and the rest of his Vices, he openly declares, That there would be no further use for these Toys and Trifles.[18]

Through this inventory, Parliament was doing far more than just making a record of how much royal wealth was contained within that treasury. It was calling into question the entire institution of monarchy, symbolised by these ancient regalia. Reporting on the inventory, the contemporary royalist newspaper, *Mercurius Aulicus*, scornfully observed: 'I doubt the king himself will be taken shortly to be some superstitious monument of decayed divinity and so thought fit to be removed.'[19] The words were prophetic.

The year 1645 marked a turning point in the conflict, thanks largely to Parliament's reorganisation of its forces, which saw the uniting of its three principal armies into a New Model Army. This was placed under the strong and experienced command of Sir Thomas Fairfax, with the able general and fiercely loyal parliamentarian Oliver Cromwell as his deputy. In June 1645, the new parliamentary army won a crushing victory over the royalists at Naseby and followed this up with what amounted to a series of death blows to the king's war effort. By the time Charles retreated to Oxford in October, he knew the war was lost unless succour arrived from overseas. It is a sign of how beleaguered he felt that he sent his son and heir, Prince Charles, into exile on the Continent for his protection.

The king made overtures for peace, but his parliamentary opponents would settle for nothing less than his complete surrender. After months of stalemate, Charles put himself in the hands of the Scottish Presbyterian army that was besieging Newark, in the hope of winning their support for his cause. The Scots took him to Newcastle, where he remained their prisoner for nine months, until they made a lucrative deal with the English Parliament and surrendered him into their hands in February 1647. For the next few months, Charles was moved from one safe house to the next, his surroundings ranging from the great houses of East Anglia and Hertfordshire to his own palace of Hampton Court.

Throughout this time, the king was treated with lenience, even luxury, and lived more 'as a guarded and attended prince than as a conquered and purchased captive'.[20] He was allowed to go hunting, play bowls and read books from the royal library. Surrounded by his servants, political advisers and visitors, he lacked neither company nor news. Although the parliamentarians had drafted a settlement – *The Heads of Proposals* – Charles refused to take it seriously. He had been informed of the divisions within the New Model Army and of the unpopularity of the taxes imposed by Parliament, both of which gave him hope that his English supporter base was growing.

He knew, too, that the hard-line Covenanters had lost control of the Scottish Parliament and that the situation in Ireland was also turning in his favour.

Then, in November 1647, Charles received news that incited him to take drastic action. There had been calls among the council for him to be put on trial, while others had proposed that he be made to either abdicate or accept a limited role which they would define. With no prospect of regaining his throne under anything like the circumstances he desired or expected, the king decided to escape. He managed to steal out of Hampton Court via an unguarded door and down to the river, where a boat was waiting to convey him to freedom. But his accomplices argued over where he should be taken. They eventually agreed on the Isle of Wight, where he could be protected by a disaffected parliamentarian colonel named Robert Hammond. It was a fateful choice. As soon as they arrived on the island, Hammond took the king prisoner at Carisbrooke Castle. Charles would remain there for the next thirteen months, during which time negotiations were reopened with his opponents.

A month after his arrival on the island, Charles struck a secret deal with the Scottish Covenanters, promising to establish Presbyterianism in England if the Scots helped him regain his throne. The Scots duly invaded England in the summer of 1648, plunging the country into a second civil war. A number of royalist risings broke out in support, most of which were put down by parliamentarian forces. In August, Cromwell's New Model Army defeated the Scots at the Battle of Preston, bringing this second phase of the conflict between king and Parliament to an end.

The net result had been more than just defeat for the royalist forces. Attitudes towards the captive king had hardened, particularly among the parliamentarian army. Although they accepted that he had been honour-bound to fight for his crown in the first civil war, they believed that he should have accepted its outcome rather than waging a second. Cromwell and his supporters argued that Charles was a tyrant who should be put on trial. They dismissed Hammond from his post and put the king in the custody of the army, then purged Parliament of any members who opposed the idea of a trial and still clung to the hope of an agreement. The remaining members formed the Rump Parliament after what had effectively been a military coup.

Even now, Cromwell and his supporters were not intent upon regicide, but wished to establish an elective form of monarchy in which the king would be chosen by Parliament. Their plan was to force Charles to abdicate in favour of his third son, Henry, Duke of Gloucester, who was in the hands of the parliamentarians. They made it clear to the captive king that the alternative was trial and execution, and the exclusion of his family from the throne. But he refused to submit to their demands, confident that there was enough division within their ranks to work in his favour. He was also keenly aware that there was no precedent for putting a King of England on trial.

Undeterred, the Rump Commons passed a Bill creating a new court for Charles's trial (the High Court of Justice), without the need for royal assent. A total of 135 commissioners were appointed, but half refused to attend. Those who remained were all staunch parliamentarians. Just before the trial took place, Parliament ordered that in future the monarch should be served his meals without ceremony. It might seem a trivial detail when Charles was about to fight for his life, but it struck at the heart of his royal dignity. As his predecessors had for centuries, Charles had always dined with the utmost ceremony, his dishes carried in to a fanfare of trumpets, an army of servers presenting them to him on bended knee. The king refused to accept the directive and from thenceforth took his meals in private, to avoid humiliation.

The trial began on 20 January 1649 in Westminster Hall. The king was charged with 'wicked designs, wars, and evil practices . . . for the advancement and upholding of a personal interest . . . against the public interest, common right, liberty, justice, and peace of the people of this nation'.[21] Charles's response was to utterly deny the authority of the court: 'No earthly power can justly call me (who am your King) in question as a delinquent . . . the authority of obedience unto Kings is clearly warranted, and strictly commanded in both the Old and New Testament.' Warming to his theme, Charles asserted: 'No learned lawyer will affirm that an impeachment can lie against the King, they all going in his name: and one of their maxims is, that the King can do no wrong.'[22]

In response, the prosecution insisted that 'the King of England was not a person, but an office whose every occupant was entrusted with a limited power to govern by and according to the laws of the land and not otherwise'.[23] The exchange went to the heart of the conflict and of Charles's monarchy, the king blindly insisting on his divine right to rule and his opponents asserting that this right was both defined and prescribed by Parliament. Whichever side emerged victorious would decide the future not just of Charles's reign but of the entire institution of monarchy.

The king held firm and for three days he scorned the court, refusing to enter a plea. The proceedings carried on regardless, prompting some of the commissioners to abandon the courtroom, determined to have no part in what had become merely a show trial. By the time the verdict was delivered on 26 January, barely a third of those originally called to attend were present. The following day, Charles was invited back to court to hear that he had been found guilty and was sentenced to death.

Parliament could risk no delay in carrying out the sentence. On the morning of 30 January, the king was escorted from St James's Palace to Whitehall. There, he had an agonising wait because a Bill was being rushed through Parliament, preventing anyone being declared monarch after Charles's death. It was after one o'clock in the afternoon when he was finally led out of the Banqueting House in Whitehall. One of his last sights on earth was the painted ceiling he had commissioned from Rubens, glorifying the Divine Right of the Stuart monarchy.

It was a bitterly cold afternoon when the fallen king emerged onto the scaffold that had been erected outside the palace. At his request, he wore two shirts so that he would not shiver and be thought fearful.[24] Defiant to the end, he declared that he had desired the liberty and freedom of the people as much as any monarch, but that they could only achieve this by being governed, rather than assuming any authority themselves, since: 'A subject and a sovereign are clean different things.' Having delivered his final words – 'I shall go from a corruptible to an incorruptible Crown, where no disturbance can be' – he gave the signal to the executioner, who severed his head with a single strike.[25]

According to one eyewitness, as soon as the king's head had fallen onto the scaffold, a moan 'as I never heard before and desire I may never hear again' rose from the crowd.[26] Some dipped their handkerchiefs into the pooling blood and kept them as a memento. In his scaffold speech, Charles had referred to himself as 'the martyr of the people' and a cult rapidly began to develop around his memory.[27] Anxious to dampen down such sentiment, the parliamentarians arranged a private burial in St George's Chapel, Windsor, rather than Westminster Abbey. They also gave orders for the late king's head to be sewn back onto his body before he was interred.

But the tide of royalist sympathy could not be checked. Ten days after the execution, a memoir purported to be written by the king was published. The *Eikon Basilike* (Greek for 'Royal Portrait') became a global bestseller, running to almost ninety editions in six different languages. Although the authorship is in doubt, it proved an enormously influential piece of royalist propaganda, inflicting more damage on the late king's adversaries than he had been able to in life. Charles's actions might have led to the monarchy's destruction, but the manner of his death, with the quiet dignity of a true Christian martyr, lit the path to its restoration.

The Interregnum (1649–60)

A man set above all others

S HORTLY AFTER CHARLES I's execution, an extraordinary delivery
arrived at the Royal Mint inside the Tower of London. On the
orders of Parliament, the crown jewels had been taken from their
home at Westminster Abbey to be melted down into coin. With the
king dead, the original purpose of these 'toys and trifles' of monarchy
was no longer required.[1] Into the flames went centuries of coronation
regalia: the state crowns of Alfred the Great, Henry VIII and, most
valuable of all, Edward the Confessor, along with numerous sceptres,
swords, coronets, rings and garments – all as priceless in historical
as in monetary value. Other items were sold off, while a handful
were later returned and remain as part of the collection today.

Meanwhile, in Westminster Abbey, 'Edward [the Confessor]'s staff
is broken, chair overturned, clothes rent . . . our present age
esteeming them the relics of superstition', as Thomas Fuller
lamented.[2] In July 1649, Parliament passed an Act 'for the sale of the
goods and personal estate of the late King', and during the years
that followed, Charles I's vast art collection was sold off, mostly to
monarchs overseas. To many, it was an act of robbery and vandalism;
to others, one of pragmatism. Above all, it was symbolic. The
monarchy had been extinguished. Britain was now a Commonwealth.

Charles I's death warrant had been signed by all fifty-nine of the
commissioners who saw his trial through to the end. Third on the
list was the man who had risen to become the most powerful in
England: Oliver Cromwell. Although Sir Thomas Fairfax was still
commander-in-chief, he had taken a back seat during the previous
few weeks, appalled at the prospect of regicide but lacking the resolve
to assert his authority as head of the army and stop the king's trial.

He resigned his command sixteen months later, by which time Cromwell was *de facto* leader. It was a role that he had neither sought nor expected. 'A man never rises so high as when he does not know where he is going,' he once remarked.[3]

Cromwell was already a household name by that time, thanks to his prominence in the numerous parliamentarian pamphlets and broadsheets circulated during the previous five years. He was an unlikely figurehead. Born in 1599 into a family of middling gentry whose only claim to fame was their descent from the sister of Henry VIII's chief minister, Thomas Cromwell, Oliver had begun his working life as a farmer. The outbreak of the Civil War had thrust him into the military arena, and by principle he was firmly on the side of the parliamentarians. Despite his lack of military experience, he displayed a natural aptitude for strategy and command and rose rapidly through the ranks. An intensely pious man, he had converted to Puritanism during the 1630s and firmly believed that God had guided his victories. The inextricability of warfare and politics during the conflict obliged Cromwell to play an active role in Parliament, and he made a name for himself in the Long Parliament of 1640.

Although he is often portrayed as a political and religious idealist, Cromwell was enough of a pragmatist to appreciate the precarious position that his regime faced after Charles's execution. Aware that the royalists had shifted their allegiance to the late king's son, Charles, the House of Commons proposed an Act on 7 February 1649 formally abolishing the office of king, which it stated was: 'unnecessary, burdensome, and dangerous to the liberty, safety and public interest of the people of this nation'.[4] It was passed the following month. But with the threat looming of foreign intervention on behalf of the royalists, as well as from Scotland and Ireland, and the urgent need to collect taxes in order to bolster the military resources, thereafter Cromwell pursued a policy of conciliation. He began by inviting back those who had left the Rump Parliament. In characteristically direct fashion, he told them to work for the programme of legal, religious and social reform that had long been planned, rather than waste their time regretting the king's death.

In the absence of the monarchy, executive power was vested in Parliament, together with a council of state, which was appointed to direct domestic and foreign policy. The council was dominated by army officials and, for the first few weeks, presided over by Cromwell. But by March 1649, the situation in Ireland had become so threatening that, having been appointed lord lieutenant, he was obliged to lead an army there to thwart any attempts at invasion on behalf of the royalists. This marked the third phase of the civil war. Although Cromwell avoided bloodshed wherever possible, his campaign has gone down as one of the most brutal episodes in Ireland's history. This was largely due to the massacre of more than five thousand troops and civilians during the sack of Drogheda and Wexford. It would be another three years before Ireland was finally brought under Commonwealth control.

Cromwell did not remain to enjoy this triumph. In May 1650, he set sail for England in order to organise another campaign – this time to Scotland, where the late king's eldest son and heir had been proclaimed Charles II. The campaign began badly, thanks to inadequate supplies, compounded by a series of strategic errors on Cromwell's part. But against considerable odds, his army won a crushing victory over the Scots at Dunbar on 3 September and proceeded to take control of Edinburgh. Cromwell was so elated at what he interpreted as the clearest sign yet of God's favour that he laughed uncontrollably. He declared the victory 'one of the most signal mercies God hath done for England and His people'.[5]

But the following year, while Cromwell was still engaged in Scotland, a contingent of Scottish royalists invaded England with 'Charles II'. Their intention was to capture London, but Cromwell and his army caught up with them at Worcester on 3 September – exactly a year after his triumph in Scotland. The invaders were routed and Charles only narrowly escaped capture in Shropshire (according to tradition, hiding in an oak tree) and fled to exile – first in France, then the Netherlands. This brought the third civil war to a close, and the scenes that accompanied Cromwell's triumphant return to London on 12 September echoed those of Roman emperors. 'He is a man set above all others', observed one member of the administration, 'and in effect, our king.'[6] As ever, though, Cromwell humbly assigned the victory to God and refused to fall prey to the sin of 'pride and wantonness'.[7]

* * *

Cromwell returned to find the Rump Parliament beset by divisions and disagreements and tried in vain to galvanise its members into more coherent action. It became painfully obvious that strong leadership was needed. There is even evidence to suggest that Cromwell considered the restitution of some form of monarchy. The idea of restoring the House of Stuart through Henry, Duke of Gloucester, had been mooted even before Charles I's execution. The fact that the prince was still in the hands of the regime and, at only ten years old, could be moulded to their designs lent him considerable appeal.

It has also been suggested that Cromwell had ambitions to become king himself – or as close to it as the new Commonwealth would allow. This partly rests on a reported conversation between Cromwell and Bulstrode Whitelocke, Lord Keeper of the Great Seal, in November 1652. Whitelocke recalled that his companion complained of the pride, sloth and self-seeking of the Rump Parliament, then exclaimed: 'What if a man should take upon him to be king?'[8] The remark was more likely born of frustration than of serious intention. During the years that followed, Cromwell actively tried to avoid taking a leading role. But his ill-judged aside has been used to blacken his reputation as a self-seeking and ruthless schemer who had plotted for the throne all along.

Eighteen months after returning to London, Cromwell was driven to desperate measures by the Rump's continuing delays and divisions. On 20 April 1653, he arrived in the Commons with forty musketeers and dissolved Parliament by force. That night a spoof notice was put up outside the palace of Westminster: 'This House is to be let: now unfurnished.'[9] Power was temporarily vested in a small council before another Parliament was called. This proved no more effective than the one that had preceded it, however, and after its dissolution in December 1653, Cromwell was invited to accept the *de facto* leadership of the kingdom as Lord Protector.

The position, which was bestowed upon Cromwell for life, gave him 'the chief magistracy and the administration of the government'.[10] Although his powers were limited by the council of state and, for the making of laws, by Parliament, he had some freedom to act on his own. He could prorogue and dissolve parliaments and had considerable influence over the army. In the eyes of Lord

Clarendon, who had been one of Charles I's leading advisers, Cromwell was 'without the name of king, but with a greater power and authority than had been ever exercised or claimed by any king'.[11]

Anxious to avoid any hint that he was a replacement for Charles I, when he was formally sworn in on 16 December 1653 Cromwell wore simple black clothing. But from that time onwards, he signed his name 'Oliver P' – 'P' being for 'Protector' – just as monarchs used an R after their name to mean 'Rex' or 'Regina'. He also tended to be addressed as 'Your Highness' and his daughters were styled 'princess'.[12] Early the following year, he moved into the royal palaces of Whitehall and Hampton Court. He was at pains to downplay his role, comparing himself to a good constable, set to keep the peace of the parish.

As soon as he had been conferred with the protectorship, Cromwell set about 'healing and settling' the nation after the turbulence of the civil wars and Charles I's execution. But throughout his time in office, he battled fierce opposition from those who urged more radical reforms in politics and religion. As the wranglings in Parliament and the divisions within the kingdom as a whole threatened to doom the Commonwealth to failure, there were increasing calls to re-establish a form of monarchy. In February 1657, Parliament offered Cromwell the crown as part of a revised constitutional settlement. As well as inheriting the powers formerly exercised by Charles I, he was to have an additional one: the freedom to nominate his own successor.

The proposal threw Cromwell into an agonising dilemma. He had been instrumental in eradicating the monarchy, so to accept the offer would be an unforgivable hypocrisy. Yet he was enough of a pragmatist to realise that the protectorate as originally conceived was untenable. Eventually, he agreed to accept everything but the title itself. Parliament insisted that it was all or nothing, but Cromwell held firm, declaring: 'I would not seek to set up that which Providence hath destroyed and laid in the dust, and I would not build Jericho again.'[13]

Parliament conceded the point. Cromwell would be king in all but name. He was reinstalled as Lord Protector on 26 June 1657 in a ceremony that bore all the marks of a coronation. King Edward's Chair was moved from Westminster Abbey to Westminster Hall for the occasion, and many of the same symbols and regalia were used, including a purple ermine-lined robe, a sword of justice and a sceptre – not, though, a crown. Cromwell's powers were set out in a legislative instrument, the *Humble Petition and Advice*. The new constitution bore a striking similarity to the old, notably the establishment of a house of life peers – essentially, a new House of Lords. This signalled a tacit acknowledgement that there had been little wrong with the ancient constitution by which monarchs had ruled for centuries; only with its last incumbent.

During the time that he enjoyed his hallowed new position, Cromwell took on more of the trappings of monarchy, such as the creation of peerages. But it was not destined to last. The Lord Protector had been plagued by malarial fevers for a number of years, and in the final months of his life he was devastated by the terrible suffering of his daughter Elizabeth, who was dying from cancer. She predeceased him by less than a month. The king without a crown died aged fifty-nine on 3 September 1658, the anniversary of his two greatest military triumphs.

Cromwell and his daughter were accorded the privilege denied to Charles I: a burial in Westminster Abbey. Prior to this, a wooden effigy of the Lord Protector with a wax mask lay in state at Somerset House in place of his actual remains, which had putrefied thanks to a bungled embalming. The effigy was vested with his robe of estate, a sceptre and orb placed in his hands and an imperial crown laid on a velvet cushion a little above his head. The ceremony was modelled on the lying-in-state of James I, as if to emphasise the continuity of monarchy. Cromwell would hardly have approved.

Even though the protectorate was not hereditary, Cromwell was succeeded by his son, Richard. Surprisingly, he had left no written evidence of his wishes, but recent scholarship suggests that he had nominated his son in his final hours, in the presence of witnesses. Just shy of his thirty-second birthday, Richard was the fourth of Cromwell's nine children. He was woefully ill prepared for his ominous inheritance, having been brought up as a simple country gentleman with little experience in either the military or political arena. The same had been true of the older Cromwell, but Richard lacked his father's natural ability, not to mention his strength of character and principles. Contemporaries sneeringly referred to him as 'Tumbledown Dick' and 'Queen Dick'.

Richard Cromwell was fully aware of his shortcomings. When, a few hours after his father's death, a delegation of councillors told him that he was the new Lord Protector, he replied with a regretful acknowledgement of his inexperience and the onerous task ahead. His accession was proclaimed in London the following day and was greeted with popular acclaim. All of his late father's powers were his for the taking. But it soon became painfully obvious that he was incapable of grasping them. He failed to win the trust and obedience of the army, and many questioned his commitment to the parliamentary and godly cause that his father had so strongly espoused. Troubles abroad and a growing financial crisis added to Richard's woes.

By April 1659, Richard was clinging to power by his fingertips. He had lost control of both Parliament and the army and, holed up at Whitehall Palace, he was under a form of house arrest. 'My confidence is in God and to Him will I put my cause', he wrote to his brother Henry. 'I know not whether a liberty or a prison [awaits me]'.[14] On 14 May, the newly recalled Rump Parliament had Richard's protectoral seal smashed as a symbol that his short-lived rule was at an end. A few days later, he signed the formal letter of resignation that had been drafted for him.

This brief, second protectorship was followed by a period of intense uncertainty as the various factions within government jostled for power. Eventually, it was the seasoned politician and military commander George Monck who seized the initiative. He had been in secret correspondence with Charles I's eldest son for a number of years and, having secured Scotland, he marched south to London with a sizeable army. Entering the capital on 3 February 1660, he restored the Long Parliament. 'Everybody now drinks the King's health without any fear, whereas before it was very private that a man dare do it', Samuel Pepys noted in his diary on 6 March.[15] Such confidence was well placed. On 1 May, a new Parliament formally invited Charles I's son to return from exile and be crowned king.

After eighteen of the most turbulent years in its history, the monarchy had been restored. But this had been prompted at least as much by Parliament's failure to create a viable alternative than by any deep-seated loyalty to the crown – a fact that future sovereigns would ignore at their peril.

Charles II (1660–85)

A little irregular pleasure

O N 23 May, Charles II set sail to claim the kingdom that had been restored to him and his Stuart heirs. He entered London six days later – his thirtieth birthday – amid wild rejoicing. At six foot two inches tall, he towered over most of his subjects, and his 'hair thick and black, in ample curls' was one of his most distinctive features.[1] So immense were the crowds thronging the streets that this striking new king and his entourage 'were seven hours in passing the City', while the river was crammed with so many boats and barges carrying spectators that 'you could have walked across', as the diarist John Evelyn recorded.[2] The restored king was fully aware, though, that the celebrations did not run very deep. This was far from an unconditional return to monarchy, all thoughts of republicanism having been abandoned.

A month earlier, Charles had struck a deal with Parliament from his exile in the Netherlands. He had agreed that there would be freedom of conscience rather than the imposition of a strict official church doctrine. He had also pledged pardons for almost all of the opponents to the former Stuart regime, with the exception of those who had been instrumental in his father's execution. Above all, he would rule in partnership with Parliament, rather than trying to impose the royal will upon it or simply disregard it altogether, as his father had done.

Even with this agreement in place, Charles faced an ominous task. He was aware of the threat posed by the radical religious and political minorities who would not be persuaded to conform to the new regime. Having fought in the civil wars, he was also alive to the deep divisions that they had left in each of the three countries. Initially, therefore, he adopted a conciliatory approach, retaining various prominent parliamentarians in office and refusing to demand the restoration of royalist land that had been seized during the Interregnum. But this angered his royalist supporters, who viewed it as gross ingratitude for everything they had done to further his restoration.

Neither Charles nor his government appeared to have a clear notion of whether or how to re-establish the powers lost by the monarchy at the opening of the Long Parliament twenty years before. Privately, while in exile the new king had expressed disapproval of a constitution in which the monarch's power was so restricted: 'A king who might be checked, or have his ministers called to account by a parliament was but a king in name.'[3] He was enough of a realist, though, to accept that conciliation was the order of the day.

The same could not be said of his brother, James, Duke of York, whom the king had appointed lord high admiral. He was deeply embittered towards those members of the new government whom he saw as obstructing the full restoration of royal power. James did, though, approve of his brother's treatment of the regicides. A total of fifty-nine commissioners had signed Charles I's execution warrant, and a further forty-five were deemed to have played a part in his death. The new king hunted them all down without mercy, even those who had fled to the Continent and America. Some of those who were captured were hanged, drawn and quartered. On 20 October 1660, the diarist Samuel Pepys recorded: 'I saw the limbs of some of our new traitors set upon Aldersgate, which was a sad sight to see; and a bloody week this and the last have been.'[4] Neither did the regicides who had died before the restoration escape Charles II's wrath: their remains were subjected to a posthumous execution.

On 30 January 1661, the twelfth anniversary of his father's execution, the king ordered that Oliver Cromwell's remains should suffer the same fate. There is some doubt as to whether the body that was hanged in its cerecloth from the gallows for several hours really was Cromwell's, given that it had decayed badly in the days after his death. Afterwards, it was put into a lime-pit below the gallows and the head, impaled on a spike, was exposed at the south end of Westminster Hall for nearly two decades.

On 23 April 1661, the new king was crowned amid one of the most sumptuous ceremonies in royal history. He had commissioned a dazzling new set of coronation regalia for the occasion, the centre-piece of which was the St Edward's Crown, fashioned from solid gold and studded with hundreds of precious stones. The same regalia are still in use today, although they have been refashioned a number of times since Charles's coronation.[5] Pepys, who was among the guests at Westminster Abbey, devoted several pages of his diary to the occasion and seemed genuinely overawed: 'So glorious was the show with gold and silver that we were not able to look at it, our eyes at last being so much overcome with it . . . no age hath seen the like in this, or any other kingdom.'[6]

The magnificence of the coronation suggests that Charles had heeded the 'Advice' from his childhood attendant, William Cavendish, Duke of Newcastle, which he had been sent shortly before his rest-oration:

> Ceremony though it is nothing in itself, yet it doth everything – for what is a king, more than a subject, but for ceremony and order? When that fails him, he is ruined. Therefore, your Majesty will be pleased to keep it up strictly, in your own person and court . . . when you appear, to show yourself gloriously to your people, like a God.[7]

Following the coronation, Charles revived other royal ceremonies and institutions in order to re-establish the mysticism and magic that had surrounded the monarchy before its destruction. The importance of such ceremonies had been impressed upon the new king in child-hood by the Duke of Newcastle. 'You cannot put upon you too much king', he told the eight-year-old Charles, and described the trappings of royalty as 'the mist [that] is cast before' all subjects.[8] As king, Charles embraced traditions such as touching for the King's Evil and royal dining in public, as well as re-establishing the Chapels Royal and their musical tradition.[9] The Order of the Garter ceremony was revived, too, and took place a few days before the coronation. The fact that Charles had chosen to be crowned on St George's Day (as did his successor) further strengthened the bond between the Order and the newly restored monarchy.

A new set of crown jewels was not the only royal accessory that

Charles was obliged to commission. Many of the ancient royal palaces had been sold or destroyed during the Commonwealth and most of those that survived were beyond salvage. The once lavish royal apartments at the Tower of London had fallen into a dire state of repair, as had Greenwich Palace, which the new king tried and failed to restore to its former splendour. Only Henry VIII's vast, sprawling palace of Whitehall remained habitable for the king and his court. Charles therefore reinstated this as the principal royal residence in London and established his brother (and successor) James at nearby St James's Palace. By an Act passed in May 1660, he was also able to demand the return of 'any of the King's goods, jewels, or pictures' that had been sold off after his father's execution. A large part of Charles I's extensive art collection was returned within a surprisingly short amount of time, and the new king added numerous acquisitions of his own.

Charles II has gone down in history as the 'merry monarch' – or to his courtiers, 'Old Rowley', after one of his favourite stallions.[10] This charismatic, attractive, pleasure-loving king had star quality in abundance. After a private audience with the king in the mid 1670s, a Parisian doctor named Charles Patin praised this 'truly rare' sovereign and enthused: 'the merits of his person give out more light than the splendour of majesty which surrounds them.'[11] Charles II seemed just what the country needed after almost twenty years of bloody civil wars and puritanical rule and once remarked that he did not believe 'God would damn a man for a little irregular pleasure'.[12] Life at the newly restored royal court was one long party, steeped in revelry, feasting and lovemaking. Although most of Charles's subjects adored him for it, others were shocked by the licentiousness. A visiting Italian diplomat disapprovingly noted: 'In the courtesies of a lover, he [Charles] forgets the decorum of a king.'[13]

The royal court was filled with some of the most beautiful women in the kingdom, many of whom attained the coveted position of royal mistress. Charles's love of women began early. At the age of eighteen, he took his first mistress, Lucy Walter, by whom he had a son, James (later Duke of Monmouth). A succession of others followed during his years in exile and he saw no reason to change his womanising habits after being restored to the throne in 1660. By then, he had already begun an affair with the most notorious of all his women: 'the exquisite whore', Barbara Villiers, with whom he had a long and increasingly tempestuous relationship. Widely considered to be the most beautiful woman of her day, she was also voraciously ambitious for power and riches. Her influence grew so great that she has been referred to as the 'uncrowned queen'. Charles was generous to his other mistresses, too. Louise de Kéroualle, Duchess of Portsmouth, had apartments at court 'ten times the richness and glory' of the queen's, according to John Evelyn.[14]

The new king's pursuit of pleasure found other outlets, too. During the Interregnum, theatres had been condemned as sinful and many had been closed down. But Charles ordered that they be reopened and, shockingly, issued a royal patent that in future all female roles should be played by women, rather than young men as had been the tradition for centuries. Bawdy 'Restoration comedy' became a popular new genre, and Charles was a regular visitor to Drury Lane and Lincoln's Inn Fields. It was at the latter that he first met the most famous of his mistresses, the celebrated actress Nell Gwyn.

The same bawdy atmosphere pervaded the flood of Restoration literature by the likes of John Dryden, John Wilmot, second Earl of Rochester, and Aphra Behn, one of the first women to earn her living through writing. As well as celebrating and at times parodying the royal court, they also focused their wit on the king himself. Rochester is credited with the following verse:

> We have a pretty, witty king,
> Whose word no man relies on,
> He never said a foolish thing,
> And never did a wise one.[15]

Far from being offended, Charles delighted in such ribaldry. Ambitious courtiers such as Sir Charles Berkeley and George Villiers, second Duke of Buckingham, soon realised it was one of the surest means of winning the king's attention. As Pepys shrewdly observed, Charles 'doth mind nothing but pleasures and hates the very sight or thoughts of business'.[16]

The new king had more respectable pastimes, too. He was an enthusiastic patron of the sciences and founded both the Royal Society and Royal Observatory, Greenwich. The French physician Samuel Sorbière was impressed by Charles's personal laboratory at Whitehall, and it was noted that he could converse intelligently with the elite of the science world. He was particularly interested in navigation, of which he was said to have 'a marvellous understanding'.[17] Charles also enjoyed horse-racing at Newmarket, which became a biannual excursion for the court. Like Henry VIII, he was obsessed with vigorous exercise – tennis in particular – but his other sporting interests (walking, fishing and swimming) were considered beneath his princely dignity. For all his love of royal ceremony, he was as informal and accessible as his father had been distant and aloof. 'The King was so much pleased in the country, and so great a lover of the diversions which that place did afford, that he let himself down from Majesty to the very degree of a country gentlemen', remarked the politician and diarist Sir John Reresby. 'He mixed himself amongst the crowd, allowed every man to speak to him that pleased, went a-hawking in mornings, to cock matches in afternoons (if there were no horse races), and to plays in the evenings.' Pepys agreed that Charles 'seemed a very ordinary man to one that had not known him.'[18]

Charles's lack of formality was likely the result of his many years in exile and endeared him to his ordinary subjects. But to others, 'lessening the distance fit to be kept to him' dangerously undermined his kingly authority.[19] They also criticised his laziness, claiming that he was 'given up to sloth and lewdness, to such a degree that he hated business, and could not bear the engaging in anything that gave him much trouble, or put him under any constraint'.[20] Arguably, though, after the turbulence of the Civil War and the strict Puritan regime that followed, this was precisely what his people needed. George Savile, first Marquis of Halifax, one of the leading politicians of the age, observed that while the king 'loved too much to lie upon his own Down-bed of Ease, his subjects had the Pleasure, during his Reign, of lolling and stretching upon theirs'.[21]

The decadence and display of Charles's court came at a price. Upon his accession, the so-called 'Cavalier Parliament' had voted Charles an ordinary revenue that it estimated would be sufficient for his needs and those of his government. But he soon exceeded it, prompting the introduction of a new 'hearth tax' in 1662. This yielded significantly less than anticipated and was also deeply unpopular with the new king's subjects, who began to mutter about the extravagance and corruption of his court.

The pressure on funds prevented Charles from pursuing as active a foreign policy as he desired. Launching aggressive and cripplingly expensive campaigns had challenged even the most secure of monarchies; for the newly restored Stuarts, it might spell disaster. Peace was thus the order of the day. Charles received overtures from both France and Spain, and felt a natural affinity with the former thanks to his mother, Henrietta Maria. He greatly admired his cousin, the 'Sun King' Louis XIV, and sought to emulate the splendour of his court, if not his absolute authority. It was with Louis' encouragement that Charles concluded a marriage alliance with Portugal early in June 1661. His bride, the twenty-three-year-old Catherine of Braganza, arrived in England the following May.

The alliance was a prestigious one for Portugal, but Charles's reputation as a womaniser gave Catherine's family some concern. After the wedding, he was at pains to assure his new mother-in-law: 'I wish to say of my wife that I cannot sufficiently either look at her or talk to her.'[22] But Catherine's unusual hairstyle prompted him to remark in private that he thought her more like a bat than a queen. While the couple were honeymooning at Hampton Court, Charles's mistress, Barbara Villiers, gave birth there to her second child by the king. Catherine was so shocked upon being introduced to her husband's mistress that she fainted, then had to suffer the humiliation of accepting Barbara as a lady of her bedchamber.

The king signed his first letter to Catherine: 'The very faithful husband of Your Majesty'.[23] Although he would prove anything but, he did develop a genuine affection towards his wife who, of all his many women, was the one who loved him most. Tragically, she was also the only one who did not bear him a child (he had fourteen by his mistresses). It is a testament to the esteem in which the king held his queen that he withstood pressure to end the marriage on the basis of her childlessness.

The conciliatory approach that Charles had adopted both at home and abroad during the early years of his reign had rendered the newly restored monarchy more stable. But the mid-1660s ushered in a series of crises that threatened to bring the crown to its knees. The first was the renewal of hostilities with the Dutch Republic, which had first begun during the Commonwealth, thanks to clashes over trade and overseas colonies. The king launched the second Anglo-Dutch War in March 1665. It began well, with a spectacular victory by his brother James at the Battle of Lowestoft in June. But the outbreak of plague the same month seriously impacted upon the war effort. The contagion had arrived the previous winter in a rat-infested consignment from Holland – it seemed that Britain was destined to be, literally, plagued by its Dutch rival. By the summer of 1665, the epidemic was raging across London, claiming as many as 100,000 lives, almost a quarter of the capital's population. The superstitiously minded among Charles's subjects attributed it to the appearance of Halley's Comet a few months earlier.

More catastrophe was to come. As early as 1597, King Charles II's grandfather, James VI and I, had gloomily predicted that 1666 would see the beginning of an apocalypse because of its link to the biblical Number of the Beast (666). Events seemed to prove him right. Shortly after midnight on 2 September 1666, a fire broke out in a baker's shop on Pudding Lane in the heart of the capital. Within hours, it had spread across the city at an alarming speed thanks to the prevalence of wooden buildings and a prolonged spell of dry weather. Samuel Pepys, who lived close to the outbreak, hastened to Whitehall to tell the king and his brother of the disaster. 'They seemed much troubled', he reported.[24] Charles immediately sent a message to Sir Thomas Bludworth, the Lord Mayor, ordering him to pull down houses in order to create firebreaks. But the mayor proved fatally indecisive, allowing the fire to continue its destructive march across London.

The city was in chaos as people raced to protect themselves and their valuables before fleeing their homes. The general air of panic was heightened by rumours that the fire had been started by Dutch immigrants, many of whom fell victim to vigilante justice. On the third day of the fire, St Paul's Cathedral was destroyed and the strong easterly wind fanned the flames dangerously close to Whitehall. Having climbed to the top of the bell tower in All Hallows' Church next to the Tower of London, Pepys described 'the saddest sight of desolation that I ever saw. Everywhere great fires.'[25] Another eyewitness lamented: 'You would have thought for five days together, for so long the fire lasted, it had been Domesday and that the heavens themselves had been on fire, and the fearful cries and howlings of undone people did much increase the resemblance.'[26]

Towards the end of 1666, a contemporary tract proclaimed: 'War, fire and plague against us all conspire.' But the narrative concluded on a hopeful note, with London – and indeed England – rising Phoenix-like from the flames. In the aftermath, King Charles, whose sinful life was blamed by some for the 'heavy calamity', commissioned a new city whose 'Beauty and Praise . . . shall fill the whole Earth'. Thanks to the brilliant plans that Sir Christopher Wren hastily drew up, a magnificent new city began to rise from the ashes. Many of the most iconic buildings of modern-day London were born in the wake of 1666, notably Wren's masterpiece, the new St Paul's Cathedral.

Charles and his people may have been glad to see the back of 1666, but the following year was not without its troubles. In June 1667, the Dutch launched a surprise attack on England, sailing up the River Thames and destroying a substantial part of the English fleet anchored off Chatham Dockyard and Gillingham. The king's own flagship, the *Royal Charles*, was taken back to the Netherlands as booty. In desperate need of money and allies, Charles made overtures towards France and in 1670 signed the Treaty of Dover. In return for a sizeable grant from Louis XIV, Charles promised to supply him with troops and to announce his conversion to Catholicism 'as soon as the welfare of his kingdom will permit'.[27]

This latter clause excited a great deal of opposition in Parliament, which had long been suspicious of the king's religious stance, particularly as he, like his father, had taken a Catholic bride. Its suspicions deepened when, two years later, Charles issued the Royal Declaration of Indulgence, pledging to suspend all penal laws against Catholics and other religious dissenters. It was at least in part to calm public fears that Charles agreed his brother's daughter Mary should marry their late sister's son, William of Orange, a staunch Protestant. Beautiful, tall and vivacious, the fifteen-year-old Mary reputedly wept for a day and a half when hearing of her intended union with the dour, diminutive and asthmatic Dutch prince, whom she married in November 1677. But against the odds, they became a devoted couple.

At the same time that his kingdom was engaged in the third Anglo-Dutch War, Charles established the Royal African Company. Its aim was to carve out a greater portion of the highly profitable transatlantic slave trade, at the expense of the Netherlands and France. Between its establishment in 1672 and the early 1720s, the company launched more than five hundred expeditions to Africa and transported around 150,000 African men, women and children – more than any other institution in the history of the Atlantic slave trade. The English share of the lucrative and increasingly brutal trade rose from 33 per cent to 74 per cent.[28] History might remember Charles as the merry monarch, but his active promotion of the slave trade is a permanent stain on his reputation and that of the British monarchy. The profits that he made from the trade inspired his successors to follow suit: slavery would remain a key source of income for the crown until its abolition in the early nineteenth century.

In 1678, Titus Oates, who had been both an Anglican and Jesuit priest, whipped up anti-Catholic hysteria once more by spreading rumours of a 'Popish Plot' to assassinate the king and even accused the queen of complicity. Relations between king and Parliament remained hostile, and there was growing opposition to the prospect of Charles's brother James inheriting the throne because of his conversion to Roman Catholicism in 1668. In 1679, the Commons introduced the Exclusion Bill, which sought to prevent the Duke of York from becoming king. Some members even supported the idea that Charles II's bastard son, the Duke of Monmouth, should inherit the throne instead. The controversy spawned two opposing political groups that still exist today. The 'Abhorrers', who fiercely objected to the Exclusion Bill, were named Tories (later Conservatives) – a term used for dispossessed Irish Catholic bandits; while the 'Petitioners', or supporters of the Bill, were called Whigs after the rebellious Scottish Presbyterians.

In an attempt to calm the situation, in March 1679, the king sent his brother into exile in Brussels. Upon his return a few months later, he appointed James high commissioner in Edinburgh to get him out of the way again. He had already sent his bastard son Monmouth to Scotland in June 1679 in order to quell an uprising. Monmouth did so with ease, which further enhanced his popularity on both sides of the border and led many to believe that his father would soon name him heir. But his supporters' hopes were dashed in July when Charles dissolved Parliament to prevent it from passing the Exclusion Bill. Monmouth continued to court popular opinion, though, and took care to present himself as a true Protestant. His uncle James also won support in Scotland during his three-year stay, to the extent that the Parliament there passed an Act making it high treason to alter the succession of the crown.

There was another possible successor to the throne, though. In October 1680, a group of influential members of Parliament drew up a scheme for the exclusion of the Duke of York in favour of William of Orange. In response, the king dissolved Parliament and dismissed the supporters of the scheme from office. Anxious to avoid the backlash that his father had suffered after employing a similar tactic, Charles issued a public declaration, appealing to all his subjects 'who cannot but remember that religion, liberty and property were all lost and gone when the monarchy was shaken off'.[29] He subsequently invited his brother back to court and banished Monmouth from it in an effort to prevent him from whipping up further support.

But the king's bastard son refused to relinquish his claim. In the spring of 1683, he attempted to take the throne by force. The so-called Rye House Plot was soon discovered and its leaders rounded up. Monmouth fled to the Continent and, ironically, found refuge in the court of William of Orange. In the aftermath, Charles aligned himself ever more closely with the Tory faction in government. He had apparently given up his earlier attempts to reunite the nation after the civil wars and firmly identified himself with the royalist fraternity. A number of Tory ministers now succeeded to power, all of whom were close to the king's brother. It became increasingly clear that James was his preferred successor.

Buoyed by this, and his success in Scotland, the king-in-waiting was in no mood to compromise. He viewed the Exclusion Bill as an attack not merely on himself as a Catholic but on the entire institution of monarchy, led by those who sought a return of the republic. 'Matters were come to such a head that the monarchy must be either more absolute or quite abolished,' he told his brother the king.[30] For the remainder of Charles's reign, James all but seized control. 'He directed all our counsels with so absolute an authority that the King seemed to have left the government wholly in his hands', reported the Scottish philosopher and historian, Bishop Gilbert Burnet.[31]

On 2 February 1685, the fifty-four-year-old king fell suddenly and seriously ill at Whitehall Palace with what may have been either a stroke or chronic kidney disease. Rumours quickly circulated that he had been poisoned by James or his Catholic supporters, eager to secure his accession. The Duke of York hastened to his brother's side. Knowing that James would succeed him, Charles famously implored him to look after his mistresses and 'let not poor Nelly starve'.[32] It may have been at his brother's urging that, on 5 February, the enfeebled king converted to Roman Catholicism. He died the next morning and was buried without ceremony in Henry VII's chapel at Westminster Abbey. 'The expense of it was not equal to what an ordinary nobleman's funeral will rise to', grumbled one contemporary.[33]

Charles II has secured his place in the popular imagination as a lovable rogue, a playboy prince who put the smile back on his subjects' faces after almost two decades of bitter civil war. For the next two centuries, his daring escape from Worcester in 1651 was publicly celebrated on 'Oak Apple day' as a symbol of royal resilience. John Evelyn summed up the indulgent view of the late king's admirers when he reflected that Charles had been 'a prince of many virtues and many great imperfections, debonair, easy of access, not bloody or cruel . . . an excellent prince doubtless had he been less addicted to women.'[34] By contrast, the king's Whig adversaries condemned him as dissolute, lazy and sinful – 'the most criminal of all English Princes' and 'a disgrace to the history of our country'.[35]

Beneath his 'merry' exterior, it is difficult to discern Charles's true nature and beliefs. Bishop Burnet opined that the king had 'the greatest art of concealing himself of any man alive', while another contemporary claimed that he was 'full of dissimulation'.[36] His actions in the later years of his reign suggest he shared both the Catholicism and the autocratic instincts of his brother James, but lacked the energy and resolve to follow them. Ambivalence and ambiguity were the keynotes of his reign. In part this was due to pragmatism: he rightly judged that the newly restored monarchy was too fragile to court further opposition. But it was also due to his deep disillusionment about human nature, sparked by the experience of his father's reign and demise. Burnet shrewdly observed that Charles II had: 'A very ill opinion both of men and women . . . He thought that nobody served him out of love: and so he was quits with all the world, and loved others as little as he thought they loved him.'[37]

James II (1685–8)

'A great king fell all at once'

A T FIFTY-ONE, JAMES II was one of the oldest monarchs to ascend the throne of England. He was also one of the least popular. Firmly and unapologetically committed to the Roman Catholic faith, he was openly autocratic and from the outset was determined to restore full monarchical power, unfettered by Parliament. It was not that James lacked awareness of the dangers that such an attitude could bring. Like his late brother, he had served with their father during the civil wars before fleeing to exile on the Continent. But his response to this experience was entirely different.

In his younger days, James had seemed very similar in character to his elder brother. 'The prince applies himself but little to the affairs of the country and attends to nothing but his pleasures', reported a Venetian visitor to court in 1661.[1] Like Charles, James had a reputation for lechery and Samuel Pepys once complained that he 'did eye my wife mightily'.[2] Shortly after the Restoration, he caused a scandal by marrying a commoner, Anne Hyde, who was already heavily pregnant with his child. He would have two daughters by her: Mary (who married William of Orange) and her younger sister Anne. After his first wife's death in 1671, James courted scandal of a different kind when he married the devout Roman Catholic, Mary of Modena, with the pope's blessing.

Despite the hostility that James's actions had whipped up during his brother's reign, his accession in February 1685 was remarkably peaceful. In large part, this was due to the new king's pretence at conciliation. 'He has made a speech to the Council that did charm everybody,' observed the Earl of Peterborough. 'Never king was proclaimed with more applause . . . I doubt not but to see a happy reign.'[3] But James soon went against his promise to uphold 'Church and State as it is by law established' and made it clear that he wished to put Catholicism on an equal footing with the Church of England (or Anglicanism).[4] This went beyond freedom of conscience and worship. Catholics were to be given positions of authority in government, which directly contravened the terms of Charles II's agreement with Parliament upon the restoration.

The new king was well aware of the opposition he was courting. It was with some haste that he was crowned on 23 April, before the English Parliament had a chance to meet. The event was 'all that art, ornament and expense could do to the making of the spectacle dazzling and stupendous', according to one eyewitness.[5] The celebrations culminated in a spectacular firework display centred on a blazing sun (the emblem of the absolutist French king, Louis XIV) and the great crowned figure of *Monarchia*.

But the dazzle did not quite blind those present to the fact that this unashamedly Catholic king was undergoing a Protestant ceremony. James was fully aware of this, too, and had ordered a number of modifications. Although the liturgy used at his brother's coronation was followed, the communion was omitted. The new king also decided against the traditional procession from the Tower to Westminster Abbey, uncertain of how he would be greeted by the crowds. The ceremony proceeded peacefully enough, but when the crown slipped from the new king's head it was taken as an ominous sign.

James had arranged for the Scottish Parliament to meet on the same day as his coronation. As he hoped, it set an example to its English counterpart by passing all the acts that the new king had scheduled, along with a very generous grant. By contrast, when the Parliament finally opened in London, the mood was instantly hostile. Aware of rumours that it intended to keep the new king short of funds so that he would remain dependent upon it, James warned: 'This would be a very improper method to take with me' and ordered those present to 'use me well'.[6] Although the Commons voted him the same revenue for life as his late brother had enjoyed, the new king's attitude had invoked deep resentment. Not long afterwards, Oliver Cromwell's decaying head was removed from its display in Westminster Hall.

* * *

Within days, James faced serious challenges to his rule, both in England and Scotland. In early May, Archibald Campbell, ninth Earl of Argyll, a leading Scottish politician and Presbyterian sympathiser, landed in Scotland from his exile in Holland, where he had become acquainted with the Duke of Monmouth. Argyll promptly declared James an unlawful sovereign, 'Having taken off his mask, and having abandoned and invaded our Religion and Liberties.'[7] Thanks to James's popularity in Scotland, the rebellion was easily suppressed. But a month later, what had been intended as a parallel rebellion was led by Monmouth, who landed with a small army at Lyme Regis in Dorset and issued a declaration: 'For the defence and vindication of the protestant religion and of the laws, rights and privileges of England . . . and for delivering the Kingdom from the usurpation and tyranny of us by the name of James, Duke of York.'[8] He, too, failed to raise the expected support, however, and was routed by the royal forces at Sedgemoor. James did not flinch from ordering his nephew's execution on 15 July 1685.

The king took these easy victories as a sign that both God and his subjects smiled on the new reign. In the latter at least he was mistaken. The rebellions were just the beginning of more widespread unrest in each of his realms. When James enlarged his standing army and placed various commands in the hands of Roman Catholics, it sparked great alarm. The English Parliament immediately objected and the king had it prorogued, never to meet again during his reign. Further opposition was whipped up in January 1686 when James published two papers found in his late brother's strongbox. Written in Charles's own hand, they argued the case for Catholicism over Protestantism.

The king's attitude towards Britain's colonies in America sparked fears that he would take the same approach closer to home. He ruled the colony of New York as an absolute monarch, which led William Penn, who founded Pennsylvania as a refuge for religious minorities in Europe, to claim that James intended to use it as a model for his kingship in England. James clearly had expansionist plans in America. The year after his accession, he merged the colonies of Connecticut, Massachusetts, New Hampshire and Rhode

Island under one jurisdiction: New England. Two years later, he brought New York and New Jersey into the same dominion. This vast new crown colony covered the whole area from Maine to the Delaware River, and there is evidence that James planned to extend it even further.

James's rule in America may have been absolutist, but there – as in Britain – he believed in religious toleration and introduced new laws banning the Puritans from trying to convert those of other religions, notably the Quakers. Even though the king made no secret of his Catholic sympathies, he was content to uphold Anglicanism and to tolerate other religious groups. His only issue was with the more radical sects who sought to stamp out all other beliefs except their own. These, he shrewdly observed, made religion 'only the pretence, and that the real contest was about power and dominion'.[9]

James expressed the same toleration towards people of different races. 'Suppose . . . there should be a law made that all black men should be imprisoned', he argued in one speech, 'it would be unreasonable and we had as little reason to quarrel with other men for being of different opinions as for being of different complexions.'[10] James's enlightened approach should not be overstated, however. Like his brother Charles II, he was alive to the potential profitability of the slave trade and fully supported the activities of the Royal African Company, which continued to transport huge numbers of African slaves to the Americas throughout his reign.

In February 1687, the king took the first step towards establishing religious freedom in Britain. He issued a Declaration of Indulgence in Scotland, allowing 'Moderate Presbyterians' to meet in their private houses and Quakers to convene in any place appointed for their worship. The declaration also suspended 'all laws, or Acts of Parliament . . . against any of our Roman Catholic subjects'. James made it clear he was acting on 'our sovereign authority, prerogative royal and absolute power, which all our subjects are to obey without reserve'.[11]

When this was received favourably in Scotland, it gave James the confidence to issue similar declarations in England and Wales and to suspend the Test Act, which barred Roman Catholics from high office. He began packing Parliament with his supporters and purged all the local government officers under the crown whom he knew to be opposed to his plan. However, in July 1687 James suddenly dissolved Parliament before it had even assembled. He had discovered that his nephew and son-in-law, William of Orange, had been lobbying its members to resist the repeal of the penal laws. Still lacking a son, James was aware that his opposers increasingly looked to the staunchly Protestant Prince of Orange as a more appealing alternative.

That summer James made a tour of the western counties of England in an attempt to increase support for his policy of toleration. He was warmly received in every place that he visited. But a disastrous encounter with the fellows of Magdalen College, Oxford, in September 1687 undermined much of the goodwill he had fostered. Earlier that year, the king had tried to meddle in the appointment of their president, but they had rejected his candidates. He now summoned them to a meeting at Christ Church and warned: 'Know I am your King. I will be obeyed . . . Let them that refuse it look to it. They shall feel the weight of their sovereign's displeasure.'[12] When this worked no effect, James had them stripped of their fellowships.

The king's treatment of the Magdalen fellows reveals the dangerously arrogant streak that would prove his undoing. Rather than learning from the lessons of the past, he firmly believed that if his father and brother had not bowed to their opponents, they would have achieved all of their ambitions. Monarchical strength, not compromise, was the order of the day. When his second wife fell pregnant in October 1687 after fourteen years of marriage, he was convinced she carried the male heir he so desired and took it as a sign that God smiled on his actions. Flying in the face of increasingly hostile public opinion, he stepped up his plans to establish Catholicism in England. He persuaded the pope to appoint four vicars-apostolic (akin to Roman Catholic missionaries) as bishops, one of whom he forced upon Magdalen College. In April 1688, James reissued the Declaration of Indulgence and ordered all Anglican clergy to read it to their congregations.

Amid the growing crisis, on 10 June 1688 Mary of Modena gave birth to a son, James Francis Edward. Until now, the heir presumptive had been James's eldest daughter Mary, a staunch Protestant. The prospect of a Catholic dynasty stretching far into the future was too much for some of his subjects to bear, and a group of influential Protestants (known as the 'Immortal Seven') began a rumour that the child was an imposter who had been smuggled into the queen's bedchamber in a warming pan to replace a stillborn child. They proceeded to make covert overtures to William of Orange, inviting him to invade in the name of the Protestant faith.

In late September, the king heard that his nephew and son-in-law were gathering an invasion fleet. In desperation, he made a series of brisk reversals, including the removal of Catholics from key posts and the reinstatement of their Anglican predecessors. He immediately ceased consulting his Catholic advisers and instead invited nine bishops (including four of his fiercest critics) to consult with him about the best means to restore the constitution in church and state. Their recommendations amounted to a complete – and humiliating – reversal of the king's religious policy, including the reinstatement of the Magdalen College fellows. Sensing that he was clinging to power by his fingertips, James agreed to them all.

But the suddenness of the king's reversal made his subjects suspicious and he failed to garner the hoped-for support. In public, James expressed outrage that his own daughter and son-in-law should think to oust him from the throne, but in private he made arrangements to convey his wife and infant son to safety in France, where he would join them if things went against him. In the middle of October, the king received the welcome news that William's fleet had been battered by a violent storm and forced to retreat to Holland. Rejoicing in the same divine providence that Elizabeth I had laid claim to a hundred years earlier, he declared: 'I see God Almighty continues his Protection to me by bringing the wind westerly again.'[13] But God proved frustratingly equitable when the 'Protestant wind' blew William's fleet to a safe landing at Torbay in Devon on 5 November, a propitious date in the Protestant calendar as it marked the thwarting of the Gunpowder Plot.

Expecting his son-in-law to advance towards London, James waited there for several days. But William had chosen to remain in the West Country so that his troops could recover from the voyage and he could attract more followers to his cause. The king therefore travelled west to rally his own forces and arrived in Salisbury on 19 November. This time, human frailty rather than divine providence intervened. A series of ill-timed and severe nosebleeds rendered James unable to deliver any rousing speeches to his troops and four days later he retreated to London. This prompted the defection of several key supporters to the Prince of Orange, notably Lord John Churchill, the future Duke of Marlborough. The king's morale was dealt a further blow when his younger daughter Anne, encouraged by Churchill's wife Sarah, defected to William's side.

On 11 December 1688, James fled from the capital, throwing the Great Seal of the Realm in the Thames in order to stall the forthcoming general election. He only made it as far as Kent, where he was captured and taken back to London. Although he was welcomed by cheering crowds, it soon became apparent that William of Orange was in control. He commanded his father-in-law to leave the capital before he made his own triumphant entry. The beleaguered king asked if he might journey to Kent. Suspecting that he planned to escape and not wishing to make a martyr of him, William agreed. On 23 December, James fled across the Channel, arriving in France on Christmas Day. Thus 'a great king . . . fell all at once', as Gilbert Burnet reflected. 'His whole strength, like a spider's web, was so irrecoverably broken with a touch that he was never able to retrieve, what for want both of judgement and heart, he threw up in a day.'[14]

History has not been kind to James II. He has been condemned as an absolutist monarch who rode roughshod over the rights and beliefs of his subjects in order to re-establish Catholicism in the three kingdoms. But this owes more to Protestant propaganda than to reality. In order to depose him, it was necessary to present William of Orange as the saviour of the British people: their liberty, faith and prosperity. In fact, the events of 1688 were neither glorious nor revolutionary but the replacing of one king by another in the interests of a relatively small minority. James had been an enlightened monarch driven by a genuine desire for religious toleration. But the way in which he had sought to achieve this had proved his downfall. An unbending belief in the absolute power of the crown was at odds with a country that still bore the scars of civil war, as his successors soon had ample proof.

William III and Mary II (1688–1702)

'My heart is not made for a kingdom'

WILLIAM AND MARY'S reception in their new kingdom was mixed. Mary's Stuart blood made her more acceptable to the British people, but the fact that she had betrayed her father attracted fierce criticism, even though she had done so because she shared their distaste for his Catholicism. Upon witnessing her and William's ceremonial entry into London, Evelyn noted with disapproval that far from showing any 'reluctancy . . . of assuming her Father's Crown . . . she came into Whitehall as to a Wedding'. Mary later reflected that she had been

fain to force myself to more mirth than became me at that time, and was by many interpreted as ill nature, pride, and the great delight I had to be queen. But alas, they did little know me . . . I have had more trouble to bring myself to bear this so envied estate than I should have had to have been reduced to the lowest condition in the world.[1]

There had been calls in Parliament for Mary to rule as sole monarch, but she had no desire to do so. As well as believing that women should defer to their husbands, she explained to her new subjects: 'My heart is not made for a kingdom and my inclination leads me to a retired quiet life.' William was equally opposed to the idea and protested that he would not be 'his wife's lackey'.[2]

Britain was ill prepared for a joint monarchy. The only near-precedent, Mary Tudor and Philip of Spain, hardly inspired confidence. Eventually, an agreement was struck whereby William would take the title of king only during his wife's lifetime. James II and the children from his second marriage were excluded from the succession, as were all

Catholics, since: 'It hath been found by experience that it is inconsistent with the safety and welfare of this Protestant kingdom to be governed by a papist prince.' This was particularly important, given that William and Mary were still childless after eleven years of marriage. The executive power of the crown was bestowed upon William alone, although it was subject to a number of restrictions. These were articulated by Parliament in the Declaration of Right, which was read out to the new monarchs in a ceremony at the Guildhall on 13 February 1689. It took statutory effect at the end of the year as the Bill of Rights.

The Bill marked a major turning point in the history of the British monarchy. Thenceforth, royal power would be severely restricted by Parliament. The monarch could no longer make war, raise or maintain a standing army, levy taxes, obstruct legislation or wield authority over the House of Commons. To further limit their independence of action, the monarch's expenses (later known as the Civil List) were to be controlled by Parliament and separated from those of the state. In short, the sovereign was transformed from a semi-divine being with wide-ranging powers into little more than a puppet. For the first time in its history (setting aside the short-lived attempt by the Dudleys and Seymours to set Lady Jane Grey on the throne), the monarchy had become a product, fashioned by those at the centre of political power.

Although the new king and queen still carried magnificent titles such as supreme governor of the Church of England and commander of the armed forces, they had been stripped of any ability to make their own decisions. The substance of royal prerogatives now rested with Parliament; only the style was retained by the crown. Just how radical – and permanent – a change this was has been obscured by the description it was assigned. 'Constitutional monarchy' was a euphemism for emasculation.

It was a watered-down version of monarchy that William and Mary's French counterpart, Louis XIV, would have scorned. 'Kings are appointed by God,' he once declared. 'They may do as they please.'[3] But here Britain was ahead of its European rivals. The age of absolutist monarchs was drawing to an end. Subsuming the crown to the will of Parliament might not have been very palatable to the new incumbents, but it safeguarded its future. A century later, absolute monarchy and the Divine Right of Kings would be wiped out in Europe, while the British monarchy continued to thrive. Its constitutional nature was key to this survival. Now that authority for almost all political, military, social and economic activity lay with the government rather than the sovereign, it would be blamed when things went wrong. A nineteenth-century American commentator neatly summed up how this shift had strengthened the crown, which 'touches the imagination whereas assemblies excite . . . criticism'.[4]

William and Mary's power was further regulated by the revised coronation oath that they took in a hastily arranged ceremony at Westminster on 11 April 1689. For the first time, this included a promise to obey 'the Statutes in Parliament agreed on'.[5] The rest of the ceremony confirmed the traditional royal prerogatives of supremacy over the church and control of the armies, foreign policy and the appointment of ministers. They were empty words, but provided just enough substance for the divinely inspired propaganda that had surrounded the new monarchs ever since William's invasion. The new king was less impressed than his subjects with 'the comedy of the coronation', which he grumbled was full of 'foolish old Popish ceremonies'.[6] The fact that the Archbishop of Canterbury, William Sancroft, had refused to perform the service because he believed James II to be the rightful king was an ominous sign.

On the same day that William and Mary were crowned in England, the Scottish Parliament declared that James II was no longer their sovereign. The 'revolution' might not have been glorious, but it was at least peaceful. It also marked a profound change in the image of monarchy. The decadence and display of the Restoration era were at an end. Staunchly Protestant, the new king's style was altogether more austere. As a native of the Netherlands, a republic that had consciously rejected regal splendour, he was eager to emphasise his difference from the ousted king, as well as from his ostentatious rival, Louis XIV. Socially awkward and rather aloof, he was obviously uncomfortable among his new people and preferred the company of a few close male favourites to the bustling life of court. He rejected the magnificence of the state bedchamber, with all its accompanying ceremonies and attendants, in favour of simple, private sleeping quarters. Only one man apart from the king had a key: William's Dutch groom of the bedchamber, Arnold Joost van Keppel. Keppel's own room was next door. This fuelled rumours of the king's homosexuality, even though he had an acknowledged mistress, Elizabeth Villiers, cousin of Charles II's notorious concubine, Barbara.

Queen Mary made more of an effort with her new subjects. Sarah Churchill's acerbic remark that the new queen 'wanted bowels' (or in other words, lacked gravitas) was prompted by the fact that Mary had a habit of talking too much and was rather flighty.[7] She did, though, make strenuous attempts to impose higher moral standards than the courtiers had been used to in recent times, judging this as vital to the monarchy's survival after the debauchery and excess of her uncle and father. 'The Court, that is usually the centre of vanity and voluptuousness, became virtuous by the impression of her example', observed one contemporary.[8] Virtue was admirable but hardly glamorous, and the post-1688 court lacked the glitter of former times.

Neither did the new monarchs set much store by those royal ceremonies intended to emphasise the divine nature of their positions, such as the practice of touching for scrofula. 'God give you better health and more sense!' William scornfully admonished the afflicted, who left disappointed when the practice was swiftly abandoned.[9] Far from presenting themselves as other-worldly beings, the joint monarchs were careful to stress their service to the nation in the speeches they gave and in their dealings with Parliament. In all of this, the couple were acting in a thoroughly modern and constitutional manner that was welcomed by some of the more forward-thinking members of government. But many of their subjects missed the theatre of majesty that Charles II had so effortlessly created. They even grew nostalgic about his brother. James II might have overreached his authority, but he was still a divinely appointed king and the ranks of his supporters ('Jacobites') increased in the wake of his deposition.

Upon his arrival in France, James had been received by his cousin, Louis XIV, who provided him with a château and a pension. But it came at a price. Eager to see his cousin back on the English throne, the French king was soon urging James to travel to Ireland, where support for him was strongest. On 12 March 1689, James landed at Kinsale with a French army. The Irish Parliament pledged their allegiance to him as king, and during the following year he steadily built up his military resources. By the summer of 1690 the former king posed a threat that his son-in-law could no longer ignore. Having already dispatched royal forces across the Irish Sea, to little effect, William now personally led an army to Ireland. The two sides clashed at the River Boyne, close to the town of Drogheda, and James was defeated. The battle turned the tide in William's favour and signalled an end to any real hopes James harboured of regaining his crown. He fled back to France, never to return to any of his former kingdoms.[10]

Having secured his throne, William became an absentee monarch as he led campaigns on behalf of his native Netherlands against their traditional enemy, France. While her husband was away, Mary acted as sole sovereign. It was not a task that she performed with any relish, lamenting that she felt 'deprived of all that was dear to me in the person of my husband, left among those that were perfect strangers to me: my sister of a humour so reserved that I could have little comfort from her'. The latter remark was sparked by a quarrel with Anne over money. The relationship between the two sisters was further soured by Sarah Churchill, whose influence over Anne was becoming ever more pronounced. Anne got on little better with her brother-in-law, William, whom she referred to as 'that Dutch monster'.[11] Within a short space of time, Mary was left complaining: 'I found myself here very much neglected, little respected, censured by all, commended by none.' But she had a tendency towards melodrama, and the truth was that her charisma and Stuart blood won her widespread popularity. Soon, Bishop Burnet was able to report that she had become 'so universally beloved that nothing could stand against her in the affections of the nation.'[12]

There was one aspect of monarchy that Mary enthusiastically embraced. Neither she nor her husband were content with the London palaces that they had inherited. St James's was too closely associated with the king they had ousted, and Whitehall was prone to flooding and damp, which aggravated William's chronic asthma. Just nine days into their reign, the king and queen visited Henry VIII's magnificent Thames-side palace in Surrey. William 'found the air of Hampton Court agreed so well with him that he resolved to live the greatest part of the year there'.[13] But the palace was hopelessly outdated so they immediately set about an ambitious programme of remodelling, with Mary at the helm. It was not quite as ambitious as the architect Sir Christopher Wren had hoped. The king had been at pains to point out that taxpayers' money was used for the nation's defence, not for the creation of 'sumptuous palaces'.[14] The finished result was still impressive, though: by 1698, Hampton Court had been transformed into a sumptuous Baroque masterpiece.

For all its splendour and modern comforts, the palace lay several hours' distance from the heart of government, which made it impractical as a year-round residence for the king and queen. One of their most influential ministers, the Marquess of Halifax, complained: 'The King's inaccessibleness and living so at Hampton Court . . . ruined all business.'[15] The couple found the perfect solution in Kensington, then a small village to the west of London with easy access to the capital and much cleaner air. They purchased a house on the edge of Henry VIII's old hunting ground, Hyde Park, and remodelled it as an elegant but modest royal palace: a symbol of their modern, constitutional monarchy. As at Hampton Court, Mary's influence could be seen throughout the interior, which was stuffed full of the porcelain that she adored, and for which she started a fashion in polite society. When she and William moved to Kensington on Christmas Eve 1689, it marked the beginning of four centuries of continuous royal occupation at Kensington – something that few other palaces can boast.

Although Queen Mary had been physically fit throughout her life, regularly walking between her palaces at Whitehall and Kensington, in late 1694 she contracted smallpox and died on 28 December, aged just thirty-two. Her death plunged the kingdom into mourning and left her husband utterly distraught. 'From being the happiest, I am now the most miserablest creature upon earth', he wailed. 'I have never known a single fault in her!' Even Mary's opponents voiced their admiration for 'the best woman in the world'.[16] Her funeral was held at Westminster Abbey on 5 March with all the pomp and ceremony that she and William had eschewed during their brief joint reign. The procession was the largest ever seen and the mourners entered the abbey to the strains of Henry Purcell's *Music for the Funeral of Queen Mary*.

The Jacobites' reaction jarred with this general air of sadness and respect. They insisted that Mary had been 'too bad a daughter and too good a wife', and that her premature death was a divine punishment for betraying 'the kindest of princes':

> Well here let her lie, for by this time she knows,
> What it is such a father and king to depose.[17]

As sole sovereign, William faced an unenviable task. He had never been fully accepted by his English subjects, who nicknamed him 'Rotten Orange' and 'Hook Nose'. They also resented his ongoing preoccupation with waging a cripplingly expensive war against Louis XIV. Ironically, though, this helped safeguard his throne by making him more conciliatory towards Parliament so that it would vote him the necessary funds. Otherwise, William might have given voice to his growing frustration at being little more than a puppet king. In private, he expressed outrage that Parliament 'used him like a dog' and snapped: 'Truly, a King of England . . . is the worst figure in Christendom.'[18] But his experience in the Netherlands had taught him the art of pragmatism in dealing with powerful representative bodies.

During the 1690s, the king ceded ever greater authority to Parliament, which in turn resulted in a more profound shift in the constitution than the revolution of 1688 had achieved. By the end of his reign, traditional royal prerogatives such as control of expenditure, the size of the army and the right to call and dissolve Parliament had been handed over to that institution. The king's desperation for military resources made him willing to work with whichever ministers – Whig or Tory – would help secure them. This led to the gradual replacement of the faction-dominated government by the working party system that is still in place today and paved the way for a politically neutral monarchy. It had taken a foreign king whose priorities were outside the realm to lay the foundations of the modern English government.

What had been welcomed by the English Parliament as freedom to act independently was taken as neglect by its counterparts in Edinburgh and Dublin. The Scots were particularly critical of the new king, perhaps naturally so given their lingering allegiance to the House of Stuart, which had ruled Scotland for more than three hundred years. Their lukewarm attitude to the crown would endure well beyond William and Mary's reign. As late as 1970, one royal commentator noted: 'The Queen's relationship to God changes as she moves over the Scottish border. She becomes less important.'[19]

In July 1700, a tragic event in the royal family prompted one of the most important pieces of legislation in the history of the British monarchy. Upon accepting the throne, William had agreed that the children of his sister-in-law Anne would take precedence over any offspring he had by a second wife. Despite being pregnant seventeen times, Anne had just one living child, William, Duke of Gloucester, by her husband George, Prince of Denmark. At a party held at Kensington to celebrate his eleventh birthday on 24 July, the boy complained of a sudden fatigue. He became feverish and died six days later, plunging his mother into a deep depression from which she never fully recovered. Upon hearing the news, William, who had been genuinely fond of his young nephew, lamented: 'It is so great a loss to me as well as to all England, that it pierces my heart.'[20]

The prospect of Anne's producing a healthy heir seemed distant, given her blighted obstetrical history and faltering health. This gave heart to the Jacobites, who had long desired the restoration of James II. Upon his death on 16 September 1701, they transferred their support to his twenty-two-year-old son and namesake, who became known as the 'Old Pretender'. Anxious to avoid the return of the old Stuart dynasty, Parliament passed the Act of Settlement. For the first time in its history, succession to the British throne was not solely hereditary but could be regulated by Parliament.

As well as reiterating the ban on Roman Catholics inheriting the throne, the Act confirmed the balance of power between monarch and Parliament that had been reached during William's reign so that no subsequent monarch could disrupt it. It also placed limits on the role of foreigners in government, which was important because after Anne there were no British candidates who qualified for the throne. The most senior Protestant Stuart was the Electress Sophia of Hanover, a granddaughter of James I. She was named heir in the event that Anne died childless, and the throne would then pass to her non-Roman Catholic heirs. The anti-Catholic sentiment that inspired the Act is demonstrated by the fact that there were no fewer than fifty Catholic heirs with a stronger blood claim than Sophia's.

The Act of Settlement was accepted in both England and Ireland, but the Scottish Parliament proved reluctant to formally abandon the House of Stuart. An agreement had still not been reached when William's reign came to an abrupt end a few months later. On 21 February 1702, the fifty-one-year-old king was thrown from his horse while hunting at Hampton Court and suffered a broken collarbone. According to the Jacobites, the horse had stumbled on a molehill and they lovingly referred to 'the little gentleman in black velvet' who had rid them of their unwanted monarch. In fact, William was recovering from the fall when he contracted a pulmonary infection, something to which he had long been prone because of his severe asthma, and he died on 8 March.

The king was buried privately at Westminster on the night of 12 April. Plans for a public monument to him were soon abandoned and he slipped into obscurity, where he has largely remained ever since. While he deserves credit for his religious toleration and for giving rise to the modern political system, as his erstwhile friend Gilbert Burnet reflected, William III 'took little pains to gain the affections of the nation'.[21] There was a sense of embarrassment, too, that the people of Britain had been obliged to summon a foreigner to rescue them from the disaster of a Catholic monarchy. All things considered, his reign was best forgotten.

But William deserves more credit than history has given him. The fact that he had been the only British monarch not to take for granted the rights and privileges due to him as a result of his royal birth shaped his entire outlook and approach. He had made great strides towards establishing religious toleration in England and Wales and had created a much more peaceful political system. His prolonged war with France had established an experienced army and a more robust system of financing it, laying the foundations for Britain to become a world power. Above all, the last Stuart king had put an end to the bitter conflict between crown and Parliament that had been waged since the accession of the first Stuart king a century earlier. Arguably, this had been achieved at the monarchy's expense, but it had created a system of government that was at once more stable and more permanent than any that had preceded it. In ceding authority to Parliament, William had not sold out the monarchy: he had safeguarded it for generations to come.

Anne (1702–14)

'I know my own heart to be entirely English'

THERE HAD BEEN little love lost between the new queen and her immediate predecessors, and she was quick to emphasise her most obvious advantage over them. Anne opened the first Parliament of her reign by declaring proudly: 'I know my own heart to be entirely English.'[1] It was exactly what her subjects wanted to hear after being ruled by a Dutchman for eight years. The queen also made clear her unswerving commitment to the Church of England. Eradicating all doubts that she might privately share her father's Catholic leanings, she insisted: 'I abhor the principles of the Church of Rome as much as it is possible for anyone to do.'[2] From the outset, she was more assiduous in her attendance of Parliament and the meetings of the new cabinet, a body of leading ministers in whom legislative and executive power was vested, than any monarch before or after. This won her respect even among those ministers who were hostile towards the crown.

Although Queen Anne displayed a firm commitment to the newly modernised monarchy, with all the limits to her authority it entailed, she exploited one power that Parliament could never touch: the almost supernatural aura that had long surrounded the crown. She revived the tradition of touching for the King's Evil and performed it with great aplomb. The celebrated writer and lexicographer Dr Samuel Johnson took part in the ceremony as a boy and cherished the memory for the rest of his life.

Anne was only thirty-seven at the time of her accession but she was not in the best of health. In her late twenties, she had begun to suffer from rheumatism and by the age of thirty-five she was a virtual invalid, unable to walk far without assistance. Her numerous pregnancies had taken their toll on her weight, exacerbating the problem. She had to be carried in a sedan chair to her coronation on St George's Day, 23 April 1702. 'Nature seems inverted when a poor infirm woman becomes one of the rulers of the world', observed an unsympathetic Scottish MP.[3]

Losing her mother at the age of six and being separated from her father because of his conversion to Catholicism had made Anne reserved and lonely. Jonathan Swift recalled an awkward reception at Windsor: 'The queen looked at us with her fan in her mouth, and once in a minute said about three words to some that were nearest to her; and then she was told dinner was ready, and went out.'[4] Uncomfortable in large gatherings, Anne preferred to spend her time with a few favoured companions.

By far the most influential of these was Sarah Churchill, Duchess of Marlborough, who upon first meeting Anne years before her accession realised: 'A friend was what she most coveted.'[5] They soon became utterly inseparable, sparking rumours of a sexual relationship. 'I can not live without you', Anne told Sarah. 'If ever you should forsake me, I would have nothing more to do with the world but make another abdication, for what is a crown when the support of it is gone?'[6] The two women referred to each other as 'Mrs Morley' and 'Mrs Freeman' so that the closeness of their friendship would not be disrupted by Anne's accession. One of Anne's first acts as queen was to make Sarah groom of the stole, mistress of the robes and keeper of the privy purse, giving her pre-eminence in the queen's private world. Sarah's husband John was appointed captain-general of the army, master-general of the ordnance and a knight of the Garter.

Even though Anne made a show of distancing herself from her late brother-in-law, she expressed her intention to uphold his domestic and international policies. The latter included ongoing hostility with France. Two months after her accession, England became embroiled in the War of the Spanish Succession, allying with the Dutch Republic and Austria in their fight against France and the new Bourbon dynasty in Spain. Queen Anne gave command of her forces, as well as of the Dutch and hired German troops, to the Duke of Marlborough. Although he was less experienced than the generals over whom he had authority, he dealt a crushing blow to the French at Blenheim in August 1704 – hailed as the greatest English victory since Agincourt three centuries earlier. The following year, the duke began building a magnificent new home in Oxfordshire that would carry the name of his most famous victory.

But cracks were already beginning to appear in the queen's relationship with Marlborough's wife. Sarah's constant warnings that most of the Tory members of government were secret Jacobites jarred with Anne's natural sense of moderation and she refused to act against them. The duchess had also begun to abuse her position in order to further her own interests and those of her family, and as keeper of the privy purse she kept the queen hopelessly short of money. When the favourite started to treat her royal mistress with open contempt, Anne reached the limits of her forbearance. In August 1708, the two women had a very public spat and the duchess told her royal mistress to 'Be quiet' as she stepped out of the royal coach. Anne never forgave this insult to her majesty and declared that 'she desired nothing but that she [Sarah] would leave off teasing and tormenting' her.[7]

The end came in a dramatic scene in April 1710 when the duchess, who by now had been supplanted by another favourite, Abigail Masham (with whom Sarah strongly hinted Anne was having a lesbian affair), pursued the queen to Kensington, where she received a sharp rebuttal. They never saw each other again. The following year, Anne dismissed Sarah and her husband from all their offices. The duchess was not a popular figure, but the ousting of the hero of Blenheim excited some criticism. 'I do not love to see personal resentment mix with public affairs,' remarked Jonathan Swift.[8]

From the outset of her reign, the queen had declared it 'very necessary' to unite England and Scotland.[9] This had first been mooted by James I a century earlier and Anne soon encountered the same obstacles that had defeated him. The talks that began in October 1702 broke down after a few months. In 1703, the Scottish Parliament passed the Act of Security, which decreed that the next monarch of Scotland need not be the same person as the successor to the English throne. England's Parliament retaliated with the Aliens Act, which banned all of the major Scottish export trades south of the border. Threatened by the loss of their lucrative trade, the Scots conceded. On 1 May 1707, the Act of Union was passed, whereby England and Scotland were 'for ever United into one kingdom by the name of Great Britain'. There would be one Parliament (in London) and Scotland agreed to acknowledge the House of Hanover as the rightful heirs to the British throne.

In celebration, Queen Anne attended a thanksgiving service at St Paul's Cathedral. 'Nobody on this occasion appeared more sincerely devout and thankful than the Queen herself,' observed the Scot Sir John Clerk.[10] The same year, work began on a magnificent royal propaganda piece for the ceiling of the Royal Naval Hospital in Greenwich. The 40,000-square-foot painting by James Thornhill was intended to celebrate the triumph of the Protestant monarchy, embodied by William and Mary and their successors. It was one of the most spectacular Baroque masterpieces in Europe and became known as 'Britain's Sistine Chapel'.

In January 1712, a general peace conference opened in Utrecht and the following spring a treaty was concluded between Britain, France, Spain and the Dutch Republic. This marked Britain's emergence as a world power. Despite the heavy losses that it had suffered, the country was more commercially effective than the Netherlands and its military might was superior to that of France. Moreover, Louis XIV now formally recognised Queen Anne's title and that of her Hanoverian successors, and expelled the 'Old Pretender', James Francis Edward Stuart, from France to Lorraine. Another service of thanksgiving was held at St Paul's to mark this victory for British diplomacy.

It would be the last great ceremonial event of Anne's reign, but to her genuine sorrow she was not well enough to attend. On Christmas Eve 1713, her health declined sharply and the royal physicians quietly advised that she was close to death. This sparked a flurry of activity among her ministers. Her chief adviser, Robert Harley, first Earl of Oxford, wrote to James Stuart, urging him to change his religion so that he might inherit the throne. Although it was rumoured that Anne herself wished her half-brother to succeed, to have recognised his claim would effectively have been to concede that she herself had usurped the throne. Whatever Anne's personal feelings about her distant relations in Germany, she remained committed to the Act of Settlement.

By February, the queen had rallied enough to resume some of her official duties. But the question of the succession was pushed to the fore again in June when news arrived that her immediate heir, Electress Sophia of Hanover, had died, succeeded by her son, George Louis. Acutely conscious that political and religious divisions threatened the peace of her kingdom, to her last breath Queen Anne tried to reassure the new Elector of her loyalty to the Hanoverian succession. She repeated the same at the cabinet meetings that she faithfully attended despite her faltering health.

On 30 July 1714, the queen awoke in her bedchamber at Kensington Palace and 'finding herself pretty well, rose from bed and got her head combed'.[11] But shortly afterwards, she suffered a violent stroke. Two days later, the forty-nine-year-old queen was dead. 'I believe sleep was never more welcome to a weary traveller than death was to her,' remarked her doctor.[12] That afternoon, a proclamation was issued from St James's Palace that the Elector of Hanover was now King George I.

Although the Stuart period would be remembered as one of great turbulence, Queen Anne's reign had proved a watershed between the civil wars and violence of the seventeenth century and the dawn of the more peaceful, civilised monarchy of the eighteenth. The portrayal of Anne as a weak and irresolute woman, 'born for friendship, not for government', as Samuel Johnson remarked, was heavily influenced by the memoirs of her embittered favourite, Sarah Churchill. Far from being 'very ignorant, very fearful, with very little judgement', Anne had shown a sensitivity to the changed nature of her position.[13] She understood that she had stepped into a role that required a delicate balance to be struck between the traditional powers of the monarch and the new limitations imposed by Parliament.

Like her ancestor, Elizabeth I, Anne had made a virtue of her sex. The more strident royal authority that had existed before the Glorious Revolution was defined by the generically masculine attributes of active leadership and command. It was with Anne that the feminine attributes of constitutional monarchy were first appreciated: 'the womanly virtues of hearth and home, nurturing and nourishing, morality and monogamy'.[14] Her progressive views on monarchy had eroded the centuries-old belief in divine hereditary right and advocated the benefits of a more conciliatory approach. It is no coincidence that some of the most successful monarchs since Anne have been matriarchs rather than men – Victoria and Elizabeth II foremost among them.

Part 6

The Hanoverians (1714–1910)

'Pimps, whelps and reptiles'

The death of Queen Anne with no direct heirs and the imperative to replace her with a Protestant monarch, rather than the heirs of her late father, the Stuart king James II, led to a German descendant sitting on the British throne. George I was the first of the Hanoverian kings and would be followed by three more rulers of the same name before the crown passed to William IV, then to his young niece Victoria. To begin with, the Hanoverians seemed to have little apart from their Protestantism to recommend them. Their unpopularity bolstered the supporters of James II's son and grandson, and the threat of a Jacobite invasion plagued George I and his successors for thirty years. Thereafter, the Hanoverian monarchy became more fully established and was able to weather the crises of George III's 'madness', his son's profligacy, and Queen Victoria's abandonment of her public duties for more than a decade. The two centuries of Hanoverian rule witnessed a revolution in industry and technology, the loss of America and the establishment of an empire 'on which the sun never set'. It also saw the continued erosion of the monarchy's power, but, conversely, a resurgence of its popularity.

George I (1714–27)

An honest, dull, German gentleman

WHEN THE HANOVERIANS had been confirmed as heirs to the British throne in 1701, it had had a dramatic effect upon the prestige of this relatively minor dynasty. The electorate of Hanover lay in what is today north-west Germany. For most of the year, its court resided at the palace of Herrenhausen, which became a magnet for scores of ambitious English courtiers during the later years of Queen Anne's reign. Some were decidedly unimpressed by what they found. Lady Mary Wortley Montagu, one of the greatest socialites of the age, dismissed the electoral palace as 'neither large nor handsome', and the Earl of Chesterfield described its chief incumbent, George Louis, as 'an honest, dull, German gentleman'.[1] After the death of his mother, the Electress Sophia, the social life at Herrenhausen had declined sharply. 'The elector is so cold that he turns everything into ice', complained the Duchess of Orleans.[2]

Reports of the future king's shortcomings bolstered Jacobite hopes that the Old Pretender, James Stuart, might inherit the British throne after all. But when George I was proclaimed king upon Queen Anne's death, 'not a mouse stirred against him in England, in Ireland or in Scotland'.[3] He might only have been the ruler of a distant German principality who had never set foot on English soil and had no command of the language, but he was Protestant and that was all that mattered – to Parliament, at least. On 6 August, it declared its loyalty to the new king in his 'undoubted right to the imperial crown of this realm, against the Pretender, and all other persons whatsoever'.[4] It also granted George the same revenue that the late queen had enjoyed.

The new king was in no hurry to take up his crown, preferring to stay in the familiar confines of Hanover. Aged fifty-four, George I was the oldest monarch to succeed to the English crown and was exceeded in Scotland only by the fourteenth-century king Robert II. Having spent all of his life in Hanover, he was so used to its ways that he found it hard to adapt to a different style of rule. 'His views and affections were singly confined to the narrow compass of his Electorate', sneered Lord Chesterfield, 'England was too big for him.'[5] Certainly in terms of size alone, George I's new kingdom dwarfed his native lands and its population was about ten times as large.

There were more fundamental differences between the two domains. In Hanover, the Elector reigned supreme over subjects accustomed to obedience and discipline. All government expenditure over £13 had to receive his personal sanction, and the army was regarded as his private property. By contrast, Britain was a constitution in which the power of the monarch was significantly limited by Parliament. George I was all too well aware that when two of the Stuart monarchs had challenged this, one had been executed and the other overthrown. 'I wish our Elector could have another kingdom, and our King of England his own,' confided the Duchess of Orleans, 'for I confess that I don't trust the English one iota, and fear that our Elector, who is now King, will meet with disaster . . . there are altogether too many examples of the unfair way in which the English treat their kings.'[6]

When George I finally set foot on English soil on 18 September 1714, he showed little enthusiasm for the task ahead. Ignoring the crowds who had turned out to greet him, he headed straight for Greenwich Palace, where his barge had docked, and went to bed without ceremony. Undeterred, his new subjects came out in their thousands to witness their king's ceremonial entry into London. They were astonished by the sight of George's Turkish grooms, Mahomet and Mustapha, and even more so by his mistresses. As the carriage passed by bearing the corpulent mass of Madame Kielmansegg (nicknamed 'the Elephant'), who was squeezed up against the emaciated frame of Madame Schulenburg ('the Maypole'), it prompted gasps of dismay and peals of laughter. Chesterfield described them as 'two considerable samples of his [George I's] bad taste and good stomach'. Criticism of the king's German entourage soon began to appear in pamphlets and newspapers. One decried them all as 'pimps, whelps and reptiles', and the unpopularity of these 'hungry Hanoverians' began to spread among the people at large.[7]

Things improved little once the Hanoverian court had settled into St James's Palace. The fact that George spoke no English made him awkward and aloof in social gatherings. Neither did he make much effort to embrace British royal traditions: the recently revived practice of touching for the King's Evil was quickly abandoned. His hatred of public spectacle meant that his court lacked glamour, particularly as he brought no queen with him. He had imprisoned his wife, Sophia Dorothea, at Ahlden House in Hanover many years before after discovering her infidelity. It was rumoured that he had ordered the murder of her lover, whose remains were discovered under the floorboards of Leineschloss Castle. George I's son, George Augustus, now Prince of Wales, had been devastated by the loss of his doting mother, for whom his cold and distant father was a poor substitute. It was said that when he was a young boy he had escaped to Ahlden, and swum across the moat in a desperate attempt to reach her. He grew to loathe the father who despised him in return, thus beginning a long tradition of hostility between fathers and sons in the Hanoverian line.

The new king was not entirely to blame for the decline of the royal court as the centre of the nation's political and social being. This had begun with the Glorious Revolution of 1689 and by the time George I ascended the throne, the hub of fashionable society had shifted from the royal palaces to London's great aristocratic houses, its clubs and coffee shops. It was there that gossip was exchanged, politics was debated, and intrigue and advancement were plotted. The new king's preference for private domesticity over public ceremony relegated his court to little more than a sideshow. The monarch's life was now more akin to that of a country gentleman.

The crown had not lost its lustre altogether, though. On 20 October 1714, the people of London turned out in huge numbers for George I's coronation. On the surface, everything appeared as it should be. George donned the traditional robes and observed the same ceremony that had sanctified the Stuart monarchs before him. But owing to the new king's lack of English, the proceedings had to be explained to him by the officials standing nearby. As they could speak neither German nor French, they had to resort to Latin as the only common language between them. George's foreignness was even more obvious when it came to the part of the service at which he was required to repeat the anti-Catholic declaration. His accent was so strong that none of the bystanders could understand him.

As the newly crowned king emerged from Westminster Abbey, shouts of 'Damn King George!' could be heard amid the cheers. During the coronation banquet in Westminster Hall, the king's champion rode into the hall and, as tradition dictated, challenged any person who did not acknowledge George as King of England. A woman promptly threw down her glove and cried out that his majesty, King James III, was the only lawful owner of the crown and that the Elector of Hanover was a mere usurper. She was hastily ushered from the hall.

There were even more worrying signs elsewhere in George's new kingdom. Jacobite riots broke out in Bristol, Norwich and Birmingham, followed by several months of unrest. The rebels had expressed their fear that the new king, as a Lutheran, would seek to overturn the Anglican Church, and they were also uneasy about his uncompromising stance on government. George had made it clear that he intended to play an active role in the forthcoming general election on behalf of the Whigs, who had paved the way for the Hanoverian succession. This deepened the Tories' natural aversion towards the new Protestant regime and strengthened their links with the growing number of Jacobite supporters.

The election was decided in favour of the Whigs, who proceeded to push through a series of strong measures in Parliament aimed at securing the king's position. These included the arrest and impeachment of his most outspoken critics, the strengthening of the army, and a new Riot Act. The measures were soon tested. The Jacobites began to gather their forces and had the full support of James Stuart, who planned to sail with an invasion force to the south-west of England and lead a march to London. At the same time, Jacobite forces in the Scottish borders and Highlands were mobilised. With hostility towards the new king building, James's supporters saw this as their best chance since the Glorious Revolution to restore the Stuart monarchy. A flurry of Jacobite pamphlets and ballads appeared, denouncing the Hanoverian regime and urging people to rise up in support of their rightful king.

For all the hype and expectation, the invasion was over almost before it began. Poor leadership and indecision among the Jacobite ranks, coupled with effective government intelligence, nipped the south-west rebellion in the bud. On the Scottish borders, the Jacobite forces advanced as far as Cumbria and captured Preston, but were then outnumbered and obliged to surrender. The rising in Scotland was initially successful, with both Perth and Aberdeen captured. But the same lack of leadership prevented the rebels from pushing home their advantage.

The Jacobite threat had been suppressed for now, but it would remain a thorn in the side of the Hanoverian monarchy for years to come. Even though (or perhaps because) James Stuart was untested as a king, he presented an appealing alternative to George I, particularly when the latter did anything to upset his subjects. The 1715 uprising did seem to prompt a change in the new king's attitude, though. While his supporters called for public celebrations to mark the crushing of the Jacobites, George responded that he did not consider it fitting that he should render thanks for having vanquished his own subjects.[8] His newfound sensitivity was also evident in his attitude towards the Anglican Church. The king was assiduous in his devotions while at court, listening patiently to long sermons in a language he did not understand. Whenever he visited Hanover, he made sure to be accompanied by an Anglican chaplain.

But for all his efforts, George's natural introversion and his preference for privacy over court ceremony made him seem both remote and reclusive. The fact that he spent more on the upkeep of his horses than on court display hardly endeared him to his subjects. The language barrier soon proved too great for him to play an active role in government and he ceased to preside over cabinet meetings, which paved the way for ambitious politicians, such as the influential Whig MP Sir Robert Walpole, to dominate. From the summer of 1716, the king began to make regular and increasingly prolonged visits to Hanover, and he would spend a quarter of his reign away from Britain.

The Prince of Wales and his wife Caroline took advantage of the king's absences by making themselves as affable and visible as possible. Prince George declared that his father's new subjects were 'the best, handsomest, the best-shaped, best-natured and lovingest people in the world, and that if anybody would make their court to him, it must be by telling him that he was like an Englishman'. His wife claimed that she would 'as soon live on a dunghill as return to Hanover'.[9]

What really swung the tide of popular opinion in the couple's favour, though, was that they threw themselves headlong into the full round of engagements offered by fashionable society, determined to add much-needed glamour and vitality to the Hanoverian court. 'The pageantry and splendour, the badges and trappings of royalty, were as pleasing to the son as they were irksome to the father,' observed the waspish courtier Lord Hervey.[10] The Wales's charm offensive worked so well that one contemporary diarist noted: 'I find all backward in speaking to the king, but ready enough to speak to the prince.'[11]

The growing tensions between the king and the Prince of Wales erupted in 1717 when a row over the christening of the latter's son resulted in the king throwing George and Caroline out of St James's Palace. They subsequently established a separate household at Leicester House (on the site of the modern-day Leicester Square in London), which soon began to eclipse that of the king and provided a focus for opponents to his regime, including Sir Robert Walpole, who had resigned from the cabinet earlier that year.

George I's public image was dealt a further blow by his increasing fixation with waging war on behalf of Hanover. Like other monarchs before him, he viewed foreign policy as a strictly royal prerogative, and William III had set a useful precedent for subordinating British interests to those of his native land. In October 1715, he declared war on Sweden and ordered the British navy to the Baltic in defence of Hanover. The fact that this also served to protect Britain's trade with Russia and prevent the Swedish king from offering support to James Stuart helped smooth the way with Parliament.

The king's preoccupation with his homeland was accentuated by his continuing failure to learn the language of his adopted one. Every time he gave a speech in Parliament, he began with a brief sentence in English before passing the text over to the Lord Chancellor to read on his behalf. This served as a regular reminder of his foreignness and provoked increasingly vociferous criticism. When William Shippen, a Member of Parliament and Jacobite sympathiser, complained that the king was 'unacquainted with our language and our constitution', it earned him a spell in the Tower.[12]

In the summer of 1717, the king's ministers persuaded him to embark on a public relations exercise that was as onerous to him personally as it was necessary to his public image, and he presided over a round of lively social gatherings during his residence at Hampton Court. The king was not entirely devoid of cultural refinement. His passion for the opera had inspired an active patronage of musicians such as the celebrated German composer George Frideric Handel and, later, the founding of the Royal Academy of Music. He also commissioned William Kent to decorate the state rooms at Kensington, which added some lustre to the Georgian court. But it still required a considerable effort for him to live in a much more 'public manner'.[13]

The king began by progressing to chapel every Sunday in full state, watched by crowds of people. Despite his hatred of the custom, he also dined in public once a week and held balls, assemblies and other elaborate entertainments almost every day. It was a valiant attempt to reassert his sovereignty, but it did not last. By the end of his stay at the palace, George had reverted to his accustomed ways, shunning society for the company of his mistresses. 'No lone house in Wales . . . is more contemplative than Hampton Court', scoffed Lady Mary Wortley Montagu. 'I walked there the other day by the moon, and met no creature of any quality but the king, who was giving audience all alone to the birds under the garden wall.'[14]

George I and his son were eventually reconciled – in public at least – in April 1720. Walpole was readmitted to the cabinet and proceeded to play a more active role than ever, steering the country through the so-called 'South Sea Bubble' crisis. The South Sea Company had been established in 1711 to trade with South America, but also as an alternative source of government funds to the Whig-dominated Bank of

England and East India Company. Eight years later, it was proposed that it should take over part of the government debt. Even though the company had no trade, this immediately prompted wild speculation. Many people gambled their entire fortune on what they regarded as a sure prospect and the king himself ventured a considerable sum. By August 1720, the price of stock had risen almost tenfold.

The inevitable crash, when it came, wreaked widespread havoc and thousands were rendered destitute overnight. Those who had enjoyed a brief glimpse of high society were thrown into the gutter, and many aristocratic families were ruined. Dismay and devastation were rapidly followed by anger and revolt, most of which centred – rather unfairly – on the king as the figurehead of the nation, rather than on his government, which was more directly responsible. All of the anti-German feeling that had been bubbling under the surface now burst out in a torrent of protests, propaganda and violence. There were even calls for the entire royal family to resign and return to Hanover.

With the government in crisis, Walpole spied his chance for glory. Under his guidance, Parliament used the estates of the directors of the South Sea Company to help the victims of the crash and divided the stock of the company between the Bank of England and East India Company. Walpole also defended the king in a number of skilfully crafted speeches, helping to restore George's credibility. His handling of the catastrophe so impressed the king that he declared his minister could 'convert even stones into gold'.[15] Walpole subsequently accrued so much power that he became known as the first, or 'prime' minister – a post that he was to retain for the next twenty years. For this reason, he is generally regarded as the first prime minister of Great Britain, even though the title was used to describe the pre-eminent position he had gained, rather than being an office that had been formally created.

During the years that followed, George entrusted British affairs to Walpole while he made ever more prolonged visits to his homeland. In June 1727, the king embarked for his electorate once more. He had reached the Netherlands when he complained of stomach pains. Dismissing them as indigestion, he insisted that the entourage press on to Hanover. By the time he reached the castle of Osnabrück, the place of his birth, on 10 June, his condition had deteriorated sharply. He died there the following day, probably as a result of a stroke, at the age of sixty-seven.

George I was deeply mourned in his native electorate, but few people in Britain regretted the passing of their first Hanoverian king. Although he had not lacked wit or affection, these qualities had largely been confined to his private acquaintances. In public, he had always appeared awkward and withdrawn, and his obvious preference for his native country had alienated many of his British subjects. They could hardly respect or admire a monarch who had spent considerably more on the upkeep of his horses than he did on courtly display.

Yet George I's achievement in securing the Hanoverian succession in the face of hostility both within and outside his new kingdom should not be underestimated. If the Jacobite threat had not been entirely vanquished, it had at least been held at bay. Moreover, in adhering to the British constitution, he had strengthened the precarious agreement between monarch and Parliament encapsulated in the Act of Settlement of 1701. The fact that his son and heir succeeded to the throne uncontested owes at least something to this achievement, although the suddenness of his death had also played a part, wrong-footing the Jacobites and leaving them unprepared to take decisive action.

'Dunce the second reigns like Dunce the first'

'DAT IS VON big lie!' Those were the words with which George II greeted the news that his father was dead and he was now King of Britain. Admittedly, he was somewhat bewildered after being awoken from his customary afternoon nap, and he quickly gathered his thoughts. He and his wife, who had been staying at Richmond, immediately made their way to London, where they were greeted with 'huzzas and acclamations' from the crowds who had already gathered 'to kiss their hands and to make the earliest and warmest professions of zeal for their service'.[1]

George II was crowned at Westminster Abbey on 11 October 1727. 'No words (at least that I can command), can describe the magnificence my eyes beheld', enthused one eyewitness who had managed to squeeze themselves 'as flat as a pancake' by the doors of Westminster Hall. Queen Caroline attracted the most admiration in her jewel-encrusted gown, which 'threw out a surprising radiance'.[2] At the end of the procession came the king himself. Drawing his squat frame up to its full height, he strutted out in the magnificent robes of state. But it was an unseasonably warm day and he soon became uncomfortable in the heavy velvet and ermine. To make matters worse, his crimson velvet cap, which was also lined with ermine, was too large for his head and kept falling over his bulbous eyes. By the time the procession finally reached the abbey, the king's face was as puce with rage as from the heat.

The coronation would be the first demonstration of the vaguely ridiculous, often farcical nature of George II's public appearances. The charm and conviviality that he had been so eager to convey as Prince of Wales were quickly abandoned. His true colours were less appealing. Although he would have hated the comparison, in some respects George's personality was remarkably similar to his father's. He was boorish, unrefined, obstinate and avaricious, with an intense hatred of intellectual pursuits. 'Dunce the second reigns like Dunce the first', sneered Alexander Pope in a poem published soon after the coronation.[3] The new king was also prone to 'sudden passions' and his temper could flare up at the slightest provocation. His eldest daughter Anne confided: 'When he is in his worst humours, and the devil to everybody that comes near him, it is always because one of his pages has powdered his periwig ill, or a housemaid set a chair where it does not use to stand, or something of that kind.'[4]

The turbulence of his upbringing had left George with a deep insecurity. He found refuge in an obsession with facts and figures and developed a keen interest in royal genealogy and military regiments. One courtier lamented his 'insisting upon people's conversation who were to entertain him being always new, and his own being always the same thing over and over again'.[5] Little wonder that his accomplished consort encouraged him to spend time with his English mistress, Henrietta Howard. The new king's obsession with detail also materialised in a love of order and routine. He even instructed his private attendants to number his underwear according to the days of the week. His days – and, therefore, those of his courtiers – moved with clockwork regularity. 'No mill-horses ever went in a more constant, true or a more unchanging circle', complained Lord Hervey.[6]

Even George II's long-standing affair with Mrs Howard was governed by the clock. The court gossips noted that he would enter her apartment at precisely seven o'clock every evening 'with such dull punctuality, that he frequently walked about his chamber for ten minutes with his watch in his hand, if the stated minute was not arrived'.[7] It was an affair of convenience rather than passion. George adored his wife but was anxious to uphold what he saw as the British royal tradition of taking a mistress, while Henrietta sought his protection from her violent husband. To keep up appearances, the king would spend three or four hours alone with her on each visit. Their relationship endured for almost twenty years, making it one of the longest in royal history, which perhaps owed something to the fact that Henrietta, a clever and witty woman who was friends with some of the greatest poets and playwrights of the age, was hard of hearing.

George II's subjects soon began to resent the sizeable allowance that Parliament had granted him and the heavy burden of taxation that had come with it. There were mutterings that all he cared about was 'money and Hanover', and that he was unwittingly dominated by his wife. A popular verse ran:

You may strut, dapper George, but 'twill all be in vain:
We know 'tis Queen Caroline, not you, that reign.

There was some truth to this. As Princess of Wales, Caroline had cultivated a mutually beneficial relationship with Robert Walpole, and she had become adept at subtly persuading her husband to promote the ideas and policies that she and Walpole had cooked up together. George appeared blissfully unaware that he was being manipulated. On one occasion, he boasted that he enjoyed far greater power than his predecessors. Charles I had been governed by his wife, Charles II by his mistresses, James II by his priests, William III by his male courtiers, and his father George I by 'anyone who could get at him'. He then turned to the assembled company and triumphantly demanded: 'And who do they say governs now?' He interpreted their embarrassed silence as assent.[8]

The fact that most of George II's papers have not survived has enabled the views of critics such as Hervey to dominate and – to an extent – obscure the influence that he exerted. Although Queen Caroline was certainly more politically active than most consorts and was entrusted with the regency whenever her husband returned to Hanover, George was more competent in governmental affairs than he has been given credit for. Perhaps not surprisingly, his main interest was in foreign affairs and he regarded military matters as his personal domain.

There were moments of confrontation between king and Parliament, which the contemporary commentator Sir John Perceval, first Earl of Egmont, attributed to the contradictions within the Bill of Rights and Act of Settlement: ''Tis a solecism in our constitution to leave the same powers in the Crown which it had when more absolute, now that the subject has grown more powerful.'[9] However, George was mostly content to let Walpole manage the day-to-day business of government as *de facto* prime minister, and it was during his reign that the decline of the monarchy's power over the House of Commons accelerated.

Family troubles arose early in the reign. 'The Hanoverians', it was said, 'like pigs, trample their young.'[10] The new king's relationship with Frederick, his eldest son and heir, was even more fractious than that with his own father had been. He once described the prince as 'a monster and the greatest villain ever born . . . the greatest ass and the greatest liar . . . and the greatest beast in the whole world', adding: 'I heartily wish he was out of it!'[11] Frederick had been left behind in Hanover upon George I's accession, a fact that he bitterly resented, and it was not until December 1728 that he finally arrived in England. History repeated itself as Frederick appeared as affable and cultured as his father was dour and boorish, and he soon became a focus for opponents of the king and Walpole. 'Whenever the Prince was in a room with the King, it put one in mind of stories one has heard of ghosts that appear to part of the company and are invisible to the rest', observed Lord Hervey.[12] Unable to bear his son's presence, George expelled him from St James's, just as his own father had done to him. Frederick duly set up court at Leicester House, which became known as 'the pouting place of princes'.[13]

In April 1736 the Prince of Wales married Augusta of Saxe-Gotha, a German princess. His new wife quickly fell pregnant and in July 1737 she gave birth to a daughter. The queen, who shared her husband's repugnance for their eldest son and cherished hopes that their younger son William, Duke of Cumberland, might inherit the throne, expressed satisfaction that Augusta had given birth to a 'poor, ugly little she-mouse' rather than a 'large, fat, healthy boy'.[14]

Caroline's triumph was short-lived. In November that year, she suddenly collapsed with violent stomach pains. She had developed an umbilical hernia during the birth of her eighth and final child in 1724 and her subsequent weight gain had aggravated the problem. Her doting husband kept a constant vigil by her bedside at St James's

Palace and her death on 20 November plunged him into deep mourning. When he opened Parliament two months later, its members watched in sympathy as he struggled to compose himself, and during his speech 'he often put his hand to his forehead, and as they thought had tears in his eyes'. At a reception later that day, one courtier noted that he talked only of the queen, and 'cried the whole time'.[15]

The prime minister also had cause to mourn Caroline's passing. She had been the mainstay of his power for more than twenty years and without her the king was susceptible to the persuasions of Walpole's rivals. But George's faith in him remained undiminished for the next four years and would no doubt have continued had it not been for the outbreak of war with Spain, something that Walpole had studiously tried to avoid. This fatally undermined his position and after losing his majorities in the 1741 election, he tendered his resignation in February 1742. In gratitude for his long service, George II elevated him to the peerage and continued to seek his advice in private until Walpole's death three years later.

The king's involvement in government declined further after Walpole's resignation, but he remained passionately committed to military affairs. On 27 June 1743 he became the last British monarch to lead his troops into battle when he took part in a conflict at Dettingen, part of the War of the Austrian Succession. The victory was not celebrated by all George II's subjects. The ambitious and highly skilled politician, William Pitt 'the Elder', a rising star in government, gave an impassioned speech in Parliament against embroiling Britain in wars that were favourable to Hanover. 'It is now too apparent that this great, this powerful, this formidable kingdom is considered only a province to a despicable electorate,' he declared, before sniping at the frequency of George II's visits to his native country.[16] The king was not known for his forgiving nature and cherished an abiding hatred of Pitt ever after.

With a large part of the British army engaged on the Continent, the Jacobites seized their opportunity to try once more to win the British throne for James Stuart. In August 1745, his son Charles ('Bonnie Prince Charlie') launched a rebellion in the Scottish Highlands, capturing Edinburgh and winning the Battle of Prestonpans in September. Emboldened by the victory, a Jacobite army marched across the border to England and reached as far south as Derby in December before turning back when the promised support did not materialise. It was not the first time that the Jacobites had confused indifference to the Hanoverians with enthusiasm for the Stuarts. Undeterred, Charles fought on, but his forces were routed at the Battle of Culloden in April 1746. George II's younger son, William, Duke of Cumberland, led the royal army and earned the moniker 'Butcher Cumberland' for his brutality towards the Highlanders.

Culloden would be the last throw of the dice for the supporters of the Stuart descendants. Many Scots were disillusioned with Charles's leadership, while in both England and Ireland Jacobitism became more a romantic notion than a serious intent to displace the Hanoverians. Pope Clement XIII had formally recognised James Stuart as King of England, Scotland and Ireland, but upon James's death in 1766 he did not extend the same courtesy to his son Charles. The latter spent most of his remaining years in exile, seeking solace in alcohol and women. When Charles died in 1788, his younger brother Henry became the last direct male descendant of James II. Altogether more peaceable than his late brother, he preferred to follow a career in the church than to mount a challenge for the British throne. He had no issue and the Stuart claim died with him in 1807.

The events of 1745–6 prompted a wave of patriotic fervour across England. A tune called 'God Save the King' began to be played in London theatres, having its first airing at the Theatre Royal, Drury Lane, on 28 September 1745, a week after the Battle of Prestonpans. It was sung to an arrangement by Thomas Arne, the composer of 'Rule Britannia', and proved so popular that members of the public burst into spontaneous renditions of it whenever the king appeared. In October that year, *The Gentleman's Magazine* published the lyrics, which increased its popularity even further. The National Anthem, as it became known, has been played at all major British events – from sporting competitions to military parades, and of course royal ceremonies – ever since.

The sudden loss of an eldest son and heir had been catastrophic for British monarchs in the past, but when George II experienced such a tragedy it proved the opposite. Frederick, Prince of Wales, had continued to be a thorn in his side after Queen Caroline's death, drawing opponents to his father's regime in ever greater numbers, including William Pitt. The prince made his impatience to become king all too obvious, and by 1751, with his father in his late sixties, he confidently expected that glorious day would soon come. But it was his own death that proved imminent. After a short illness, caused either by a blow from a cricket ball or a pulmonary embolism, Frederick died at Leicester House, aged just forty-four. He was the last Prince of Wales not to succeed to the throne. According to the laws of succession, Frederick's eldest son George now became heir apparent. At twelve years old, he hardly presented the same threat to the king that his father had done.

George II's final years were dominated by the Seven Years' War (also known as the French and Indian War), which was fought on multiple continents, with Britain battling for supremacy over France. Domestic affairs were also turbulent and there was bitter in-fighting between the king's ministers, over whom he had little control. Following the death of Henry Pelham, in 1754, who had served as prime minister for more than ten years, that office changed hands three times in as many years. As his father had before him, George increasingly sought solace by spending long sojourns in Hanover with his new mistress, Amelia Sophia de Walmoden. When the government urged him to return to London in 1755, George responded: 'There are kings enough in England . . . [I] should only go to be plagued and teased.'¹⁷

More positively, George II's later years were also a time of significant economic and social progress, with new levels of production in industries such as coal, shipbuilding and agriculture. While the foreign policy of most continental powers was primarily motivated by territorial gains and the protection of their dynasties, Britain's overseas ventures were driven by a desire to build a worldwide trading network for its merchants, manufacturers, shipbuilders and financiers. The English trader, spy and writer, Daniel Defoe, best known for his novel *Robinson Crusoe*, boasted that his country was the most 'diligent nation in the world. Vast trade, rich manufactures, mighty wealth, universal correspondence, and happy success have been constant companions of England, and given us the title of an industrious people.'[18] If George II can claim little credit for this success, he had at least been content to allow his ministers and financiers the freedom they needed to establish Britain's growing pre-eminence.

On the morning of 25 October 1760, the king rose from his bed at Kensington Palace at six o'clock as usual. He called for his hot chocolate, then retreated into the water-closet, methodical as ever in his habits. Waiting patiently outside, his *valet de chambre* was surprised by 'a noise louder than the royal wind', followed by a thud 'like the falling of a billet of wood from the fire'. He rushed in and found his royal master lying on the floor. There was a gash on his right temple caused by a heavy fall against the corner of a bureau, and his hand was stretched towards the bell that he had tried to ring for assistance. He whispered 'Call Amelia', then spoke no more.[19] Misunderstanding his request, the king's flustered servants scurried off to find not his mistress, as George had intended, but his daughter of the same name. By the time they returned, it was too late.

Robert Walpole's son Horace, one of the most celebrated social commentators of the age, scornfully remarked that there had been a 'diminution of majesty' during George II's reign. Within a month of the king's death, another contemporary reflected that he 'seems already to be almost forgotten'.[20] But George's lack of popular appeal should not obscure the successes of his thirty-three-year reign, even if most of these had been achieved by others. The Jacobite threat had finally been extinguished, enabling the Hanoverian succession to become more securely established. At the same time, the long ministries of the likes of Robert Walpole and Henry Pelham had stabilised the political regime. The foundations of the Industrial Revolution had been laid, the expansion of overseas trade had brought considerable prosperity to the nation and there had been a rapid rise in population. Thanks to these developments, and some notable military successes, by the end of George II's reign Britain was on the brink of becoming a great world power.

George III (1760–1820)

'An ulcer'd mind'

T HE ACCESSION OF the third George to occupy the thrones of
Great Britain and Ireland was greeted with more enthusiasm
than that of either of his predecessors. He was the first Hanoverian
monarch to be born in England and showed so little interest in 'the
horrid Electorate' that he never once visited it throughout his reign.[1]
He had apparently heeded his late father's advice to 'convince the
nation that you are not only an Englishman born and bred, but that
you are also this by inclination'.[2]

The new king also had youth on his side (he was twenty-two at
his accession) and was more physically appealing than either of his
predecessors. The Duchess of Northumberland's description
reflected the admiration of many others: 'He was in his person tall
and robust, more graceful than genteel . . . with an unparalleled
air of majestic dignity. There was a noble openness in his countenance, blended with a cheerful good-natured affability.'[3] A more
measured – and, time would prove, accurate – assessment was
provided by an American envoy to Britain: 'That he is a great and
wise king, I have not heard. I have heard him described as being
a great man in little things, and as being generally well-intentioned,
pertinacious and persevering.'[4]

George II's funeral was swiftly arranged at Westminster Abbey (he
was the last monarch to be buried there), but all eyes were trained
on the future. Determined to make a clean break with the past, his
grandson swept away the tedious customs and dreary entertainments
of the old court, along with most of its officials. Although the new
king was no great intellectual, from the beginning of his reign he
exerted a positive influence on the nation's cultural life. An avid

reader, he was determined to expand the library that George II had given to the British Museum. With the advice of such notables as Samuel Johnson, he steadily assembled 'one of the finest libraries ever created by one man' – the genesis of the modern-day British Library in London.[5] George III was an enthusiastic collector of art, too. As well as acquiring a large collection of paintings from Venice, he patronised the likes of Thomas Gainsborough and was active in the foundation of the Royal Academy. His greatest passion, though, was science, and his impressive collection of scientific and mathematical instruments still survives.

The new king was the first unmarried monarch to ascend the throne since Charles II in 1660, but he was no playboy prince and had higher morals than his predecessors. He wasted no time in throwing his late grandfather's mistress out of court and finding a wife for himself. After a long search, he settled on Charlotte of Mecklenburg-Strelitz, a small north German duchy in the Holy Roman Empire. They met for the first time on their wedding day, 8 September 1761, and were crowned a fortnight later. 'What is the finest sight in the world? A coronation. What is delightful to have passed? A coronation', remarked the waspish Horace Walpole with heavy sarcasm, before going on to pillory the 'wretched banquet' and 'foolish puppet show'.[6] The event was indeed shambolic, thanks to the abysmal lack of organisation – something that had characterised other coronations in recent times. One eyewitness scornfully remarked that the Dean of Westminster 'would have dropped the Crown, if it had not been pinned to the Cushion'.[7]

The same year, George III purchased Buckingham House and transformed it into a royal palace fit to be the monarch's main residence in London, as it has remained ever since. Having put his domestic affairs in order, he turned to the business of government. In this, too, he was determined to prove himself of a different mettle to his grandfather, whom he believed had been entirely subservient to his ministers.

But thanks to the king's ill-informed meddling, the first decade of his reign was one of political turmoil, with a rapid succession of prime ministers. The first incumbent, Thomas Pelham, Duke of Newcastle, worked closely with William Pitt, whom the king despised. He once described Pitt as 'a true snake in the grass' and claimed that he had 'the blackest of hearts'.[8] It was thanks to George III's influence that the prolonged period of Whig dominance was ended by the appointment of his former tutor, John Stuart, third Earl of Bute, as Britain's first Tory prime minister in May 1762. But the latter proved unequal to the task and his leadership collapsed within a year. The king made it clear to the new incumbent, George Greville, that there must be no rapprochement with Newcastle and Pitt, declaring: 'I would rather quit my Crown.'[9] But Greville's ministry proved just as turbulent as his predecessor's, thanks once more to George's interference in the minutiae of government.

The incessant bickering between the sovereign and his ministers had the opposite effect to the one that George intended. Rather than asserting his royal authority, he whipped up resentment within government, not least on the part of Prime Minister Greville. The premiership changed hands a further three times – including, to the king's horror, William Pitt's incumbency in 1766 – before the appointment of Frederick North, second Earl of Guildford, in 1770 ushered in some long overdue stability. He remained in post for the next twelve years.

Involving himself so closely in the numerous political spats of the 1760s had caused the king a great deal of stress and his health soon began to suffer. In the early months of 1765, he fell so ill from what he called his 'ulcer'd mind' that plans were made for a regency.[10] By the time North assumed power, the king had lost his earlier confidence and idealism and had become much more reserved, finding it hard to place his trust in anyone other than his closest family and attendants. His marriage to Charlotte brought him the comfort and stability he craved – as well as a brimming nursery. Their first son, another George, was born just eleven months into their marriage. A further eight sons and six daughters followed, the last born in 1783. As they reached maturity, many of these offspring – the sons in particular – would bring shame upon the royal family, earning their description as 'the most unloved royal generation in English history'.[11]

The Royal Marriages Act of 1772 was at least partly responsible for the exploits of the king's sons. It was inspired by the scandalous private lives of George III's siblings, whose marital (and extra-marital) exploits formed a sharp contrast to his own high morals. The king's brother Edward led a reckless, self-indulgent life and was soon 'in great disgrace at court', according to Horace Walpole.[12] Even more shocking was the scandal of his youngest sister Caroline, Queen of Denmark, who was arrested for adultery in 1772 and her lover executed. Meanwhile, the king's third brother, Henry, was sued for damages over his relationship with a married lady at court and proceeded to marry a widow who was considered far beneath him in status.

Anxious to avoid such scandals in future, George was instrumental in pushing through the new Act, which forbade the marriage of any member of the royal family under the age of twenty-five without the monarch's approval. Far from inspiring stricter morals within the royal family, as Queen Victoria's prime minister and confidant Lord Melbourne later remarked, the Act sent George III's sons, her uncles, 'like so many wild beasts into society, making love everywhere they went, and then saying that they were very sorry they couldn't marry them'.[13] Its repercussions would reverberate down the centuries.

As the 1770s wore on, the king was beset by more serious concerns than the embarrassing antics of his family. Although British rule was thriving in some parts of its growing empire, notably India, where the East India Company established a capital in Calcutta in 1773 and appointed its first Governor-General, there was growing unrest in Britain's American colonies. This had been sparked by attempts to impose heavy customs duties there to pay for the Seven Years' War. At the beginning of his ministry, Lord North tried to calm the situation by withdrawing all duties except a small tax on tea. His tactic might have worked had it not coincided with the massacre by British troops of rioters in the colony of Boston, Massachusetts, on the same day. By the time the Tea Act was introduced in May 1773, the situation had reached boiling point. In December that year, the tea ships moored in Boston harbour were ransacked by the inhabitants of the town, who threw the cargo overboard. The protest, which became known as the Boston Tea Party, turned violent when a customs officer was tarred and feathered.

News of the dissent was greeted with outrage in Britain. Even members of the government who had sympathised with America called for harsh reprisals. With the support of Parliament, Lord North ordered that the port of Boston be closed down and the charter of Massachusetts altered so that the crown had more direct control over its government. The colonists condemned these 'Intolerable Acts' and focused their vitriol on George III, whom they presented as a 'royal brute' and tyrant.[14]

During the summer of 1774, the Americans coordinated their resistance and an all-out war of independence began the following April, under the leadership of George Washington, commander-in-chief of the American army. Blame for the protracted American Revolution has been traditionally – and for the most part unfairly – placed at George III's door. The Declaration of Independence, issued on 4 July 1776, listed in detail his 'repeated injuries and usurpations' of the American people's rights and liberties and claimed that he had long planned to enslave them.

In fact, until the outbreak of hostilities, the king had shown little interest in America. Neither is there much evidence to support the belief that had he been less obstinate, America's independence would have been settled without so much bloodshed and expense. Throughout the crisis, the king acted only as a constitutional monarch supporting the policies of his government, and the majority of his subjects heartily approved of his uncompromising stance. No other eighteenth-century ruler would have willingly surrendered such a large part of their empire, and for most of the war the two sides were evenly matched, with an American victory far from assured.

Once Britain's commitment to the war had been confirmed, though, George III stuck resolutely to his course. He played an active role in raising and reviewing troops and bolstering the navy. He also encouraged his ministers to hold firm and headed off their parliamentary opponents. His prime minister, Lord North, was less resolute, particularly after the decisive American victory at Saratoga in 1777. North claimed that the defeat had weakened his mental capacity and asked to be released from office, recommending his opponent John Pitt, second Earl of Chatham and son of William Pitt the Elder, as his successor. In response, the king declared: 'I would rather lose the crown I now wear than bear the ignominy of possessing it under their shackles.'[15] To George's satisfaction, North capitulated and agreed to continue in office.

The American War of Independence dragged on for eight long years and escalated when Britain's continental rivals, France, Spain and the Dutch Republic, joined on the side of the rebels. As the costs rose, so too did opposition to the conflict in Britain. Late in 1781, news reached London that British troops had capitulated at the Siege of Yorktown in Virginia. Few members of Parliament had the stomach to continue the war and Lord North resigned the following March.

'America is lost!' the king lamented in a private memorandum that still survives in the Royal Archives.[16] He was so devastated that he drafted an abdication speech in which he expressed regret that he 'finds he can be of no further utility to his native country' and declared his intention to retire to Hanover.[17] The speech was never delivered, and on 3 September 1783 the Treaty of Paris was signed, bringing the war with America to a close and recognising its independence from Britain.

By the time John Adams was appointed American Minister to London in 1785, the king had become reconciled to the loss of his former colonies. 'I was the last to consent to the separation,' he admitted to Adams, 'but the separation having been made and having become inevitable, I have always said, as I say now, that I would be the first to meet the friendship of the United States as an independent power.'[18] Ironically, the collapse of George's rule in America sparked an enduring fascination there with the British royal family, one that is still very much in evidence today. 'It's the fairy stories that keep it going', remarked one historian. 'Whoever heard of a girl kissing a frog and it turning into a handsome senator?'[19]

In December 1783, William Pitt 'the Younger', son of 'the Elder', was appointed prime minister. His ministry began with an ominous motion carried in the House of Commons that to report the monarch's opinion in order to influence voting was a 'high crime and misdemeanour'.[20] Three years earlier, the outspoken Member of Parliament, John Dunning, had warned that the crown's influence in government was increasing and 'ought to be diminished'.[21] There followed a systematic erosion of what little political authority George III had enjoyed. A lesser – or lazier – monarch might have been content to hand over the reins of power altogether, but the king at least ensured that he was always well informed by his ministers. He also occasionally frustrated, or at least delayed, their schemes when they directly contradicted his own objectives – and the wishes of his people. For example, when the Commons passed a Bill for nationalising the East India Company in 1783, the king informed the House of Lords that he would regard any peer who voted for it as his enemy. The Bill was defeated shortly afterwards.

This served to boost George III's already buoyant popularity. It speaks volumes for his personal appeal that despite the loss of America and the endemic political turbulence, the people of Britain liked and respected him. In welcome contrast to his two predecessors, he had put Hanover's interests firmly behind those of Britain. He also won widespread acclaim for the courage with which he had faced down a number of assassination attempts. In May 1800, he was attacked twice on the same day: first when he was shot at while reviewing troops in Hyde Park, then, that evening, when a member of the audience at the Theatre Royal, Drury Lane, fired a pistol at him in the royal box. Both were very near misses, but according to eyewitnesses the king appeared entirely unperturbed.

The king's charitable work further bolstered his popularity. He was the first British monarch to seriously embrace good works and gave £14,000 (around £1.2 million) a year to charitable causes. He allowed his name to be associated with numerous philanthropic ventures, notably London's hospitals, and encouraged his sons to do the same. Not only did this make him 'the most bountiful sovereign that this nation has ever known', it also established what would become an increasingly prominent part of the monarchy's role.[22] A contemporary noted that at a time when 'all the thrones of Europe were thrown down with their monarchs', the king and his family had been spared by God so that they might continue their charity and 'benevolence'.[23]

Above all, George III's subjects admired his unimpeachable morals. In stark contrast to most of his predecessors, he had remained faithful to his wife and was a doting (if strict) father to their many children. This domestic harmony did not extend to relations between the king and his eldest son and heir, though. Prince George (known as 'Prinny') was as profligate and licentious as his father was frugal and restrained: 'a libertine over head and ears in debt and disgrace', as one contemporary observed. *The Times* condemned him as a thoroughly immoral man who 'at all times would prefer a girl and a bottle to politics and a sermon'. The prince himself admitted to being 'rather too fond of wine and women'.

In 1779, the seventeen-year-old prince had begun an affair with the actress Perdita Robinson. Spying an opportunity for enrichment, when the affair turned sour she threatened to print his love letters. Her silence was eventually secured by the king at a cost of £5,000 (£430,000 today). The prince's extravagant lifestyle soon ran up huge debts and his close affiliation with the king's political opponents, notably Charles James Fox, further antagonised his father. 'The king is excessively cross and ill-tempered, and uncommonly grumpy,' the petulant prince complained to his brother in 1781.[24]

A ceasefire of sorts was declared in 1783, when the king agreed to pay off £23,000 of his son's debts and give him the use of Carlton House in London in return for the prince's immediate reformation. Prinny did not stay true to his word. He immediately ordered lavish alterations to his new residence and within the space of just one year had amassed a staggering £100,000 (£8.6 million) in debts. It was apparently to escape them that he declared his intention to go and live abroad.

But in this, Prince George was at least equally motivated by a desire to elope with his new mistress, the widowed Maria Fitzherbert, a Roman Catholic, whom the prince described as 'the wife of my heart and soul'. His furious father complained bitterly about the 'unruly passions' of the Prince of Wales and grimly predicted that 'every absurdity and impropriety may be expected'.[25] In order to prevent the calamity of his son taking such an unsuitable bride and thereby forfeiting his succession to the throne under the terms of the Act of Settlement, which barred royal heirs from marrying a Roman Catholic, he sent orders to the prince in Brighton that he must not leave the country. Prince George was so distraught at being denied the woman he adored that he stabbed himself in a fit of passion – although not deeply enough to do any real damage.

Setting love firmly ahead of duty, in December 1785 the prince married his adored mistress. In order to keep the marriage under wraps, the following year he began building a new home for himself and his wife in Brighton, purchasing a farmhouse that he would transform into the ridiculously ostentatious Royal Pavilion. 'More the pomp and magnificence of a Persian satrap seated in all splendour of oriental state than the sober dignity of a British prince,' sneered one disapproving Member of Parliament.[26]

Prince George's antics provided endless material for the burgeoning press, which was rapidly becoming the most influential factor in the shaping of popular opinion about the monarchy. Throughout the previous seven hundred years of the crown's existence, the king or queen had been able to wield considerable control over their public image. The most skilled, such as Elizabeth I, had exploited this to dazzling effect, winning the hearts and minds of their people through a series of carefully thought-out public appearances, portraits, proclamations and the like. Members of the court and government had ensured that in turn these filtered down to the lower ranks of society. Now, though, control had shifted to the rash of newspapers and magazines that were being printed and circulated in ever greater numbers, placing the power to praise, criticise or condemn the crown and its incumbents in the hands of editors and journalists. It was the beginning of an inexorable rise in the influence of the popular press that would continue up to the present day. In time, it would prove a greater threat to the monarchy than rebellion, invasion or Parliament.

The Prince of Wales's extravagant lifestyle was completely at odds with the example set by his father. George III's court was a model of restraint and formality. 'If you find a cough tickling your throat, you must arrest it from making any sound,' complained the novelist, diarist and playwright Fanny Burney in 1785. 'You must not sneeze. If you have a vehement cold, you must take no notice of it.'[27] Although he maintained traditions such as the levée (or ceremony of dressing, established by Charles II) and held regular audiences, the king's shyness made these formal gatherings an ordeal and he famously filled any awkward silences with: 'What? What?'[28]

George III eschewed the traditional royal residences of St James's, Kensington and Hampton Court in favour of the quiet domesticity offered by Buckingham House and Kew Palace. Family dinners took precedence over more lavish entertaining, and the fare on offer was so frugal that it provided fodder for caricaturists such as George Cruikshank. The king's affectionate nickname 'Farmer George' was inspired by his interest in horticulture and his modest habits, which were more akin to a country gentleman than a sovereign of one of the most powerful kingdoms in the world. He never ventured beyond England's borders: indeed, he neglected most of this country too, rarely travelling further than his beloved Weymouth for sea bathing.

It may have been the disruption to his cherished routines caused by the Prince of Wales's antics that contributed towards the king's mental collapse towards the end of 1788. There had been earlier hints of mental instability, notably in 1765 when the then prime minister Lord Bute reported 'the king's countenance and manner a good deal estranged'.[29] On other occasions, he had appeared greatly agitated and babbled incessantly. The same was true of this latest episode. Fanny Burney related an encounter with the king, during which he spoke 'with a manner so uncommon . . . a rapidity, a hoarseness of voice, a volubility, an earnestness – a vehemence, rather – it startled me inexpressibly'. George's other symptoms included stomach pains, insomnia and even violence. The fact that he was 'very sensible of the great change there is in himself' must have made it a frightening experience for him, too.[30]

The contemporary diagnosis was a 'humour' in George's legs caused by a failure to change his wet stockings, which had then spread to his bowels.[31] Various other theories – ranging from lunacy to sexual repression – have since been propounded. The idea that the king was suffering from porphyria, a hereditary liver disease, gained a great deal of currency in the early twenty-first century, but recent studies suggest that mania was more likely the cause. Whatever was behind the king's malady, eighteenth-century medicine was ill-equipped to deal with it. Among the physicians who battled to bring his symptoms under control was Francis Willis, a Lincolnshire clergyman. His brutal methods included a strait-jacket and restraining chair – referred to by the beleaguered king as his 'coronation chair'.

With the ominous prospect of a regency looming, George began to show signs of recovery. On 17 February 1789, three days before the Regency Bill was to take effect, bestowing power upon the Prince of Wales, news of the king's convalescence was announced, to widespread rejoicing. The king's illness had excited a great deal of sympathy in the press. Newspapers devoted an increasing number of column inches to the 'Father of his people', all of which fanned the flames of public support. While this was partly prompted by pity, there was a palpable sense of relief at having avoided the regency of the profligate prince.

George's mental collapse left him physically exhausted, too, and he told Pitt that during what life was left to him he would 'only keep that superintending eye which can be effected without labour or fatigue'.[32] Although the king and his family subsequently spent more time in Weymouth, he was far from neglectful of state matters. Events across the Channel also made him acutely aware of the vital importance of providing a strong monarchical figurehead. In 1789, a bloody revolution in France resulted in the monarchy being overthrown and scores of aristocrats wiped out by the guillotine.

In January 1793 came the shocking news that King Louis XVI had been executed. His queen, Marie-Antoinette, followed him to the guillotine that October. The revolutionaries then declared war on Great Britain. These developments sparked a great deal of nervousness among the British landowning classes, as well as at court. Alive to the danger that they posed to his own throne, George III was quick to condemn the executions as the work of savages and welcomed war against 'that unprincipled country whose aim at present is to destroy the foundations of every civilised state'.[33]

The crippling expense of this new war was compounded by the unrelenting extravagance of the Prince of Wales. By 1795, his debts had spiralled to £630,000 (£48 million). It was at least partly with the prince in mind that in the same year the government introduced a new tax on hair powder, of which Prinny and his foppish friends were inordinately fond. Even though he was no friend to the prince, Pitt proposed that his income be more than doubled to £121,000 and a sinking fund established to repay it, but this was rejected by Parliament. Prince George himself admitted that there was nothing else for it but to break with his secret wife, Mrs Fitzherbert, and marry a wealthy princess. The unfortunate candidate was his cousin, Caroline of Brunswick. They hated each other on sight but were married in April 1795 and conceived a child on their wedding night – possibly their only conjugal encounter. A daughter, Charlotte, was born the following January and her parents separated two months later.

The king was soon beset by other matters than his eldest son's marital troubles. From the mid-1790s, the simmering discontent among Catholics in Ireland threatened to boil over into open rebellion. This was a matter for serious concern among the British government, given the weakness of Ireland's allegiance to the crown and the potential that it might collaborate with France. These fears were realised when a large-scale rebellion broke out in Dublin in May 1798 and rapidly spread through the surrounding areas. The main organising force was the Society of United Irishmen, a republican group that was influenced by the ideas of the American and French revolutions. Support soon arrived from revolutionary France.

Although the British forces swiftly brought the situation under control, Pitt was anxious to avoid a resurgence of trouble. He therefore advocated a scheme that he had been considering for some time: a union between Britain and Ireland. He argued that it would resolve the contentious issue of Catholic representation in Parliament because this Parliament would now be in Westminster, where the Catholics would constitute a small minority. The king saw the wisdom of this and the wheels were set in motion. In 1800, the British and Irish parliaments passed an Act of Union, which came into effect on 1 January 1801. George III was proclaimed King of the United Kingdom of Great Britain and Ireland, a title that he preferred to the proposed alternative: 'Emperor of the British Isles'.[34] At the same time, he finally abandoned the empty title 'King of France', which had been held by English and British monarchs since the reign of Edward III.

While the king was content to allow Catholic emancipation in Ireland, he had no intention of extending the privilege to Britain and claimed that this would breach his coronation oath. When he discovered that Pitt and his cabinet had been laying plans for just such a scheme, it prompted another sharp decline in his mental health. On 21 February, he confided to the son and assistant of his doctor, Francis Willis: 'I have prayed to God all night, that I might die, or that he would spare my reason.'[35] By the following morning, he was gripped by the same mania as before, talking incessantly and in a highly agitated state. Yet again, plans for a regency were drawn up, but the king recovered before they were put into effect.

This latest illness had taken its toll on the sixty-two-year-old king. He was weak, emaciated and poor-sighted. It had also wreaked havoc upon his once happy marriage. Queen Charlotte had been upset by her husband's violent behaviour and obscene language, and urged the ongoing attentions of Willis and his son, despite the king's abhorrence for them. Relations between the royal couple deteriorated so far that the queen locked her bedroom door against the king and took out her temper on their daughters. Lord Hobart, Secretary of State for War and the Colonies, lamented: 'It is a melancholy circumstance to see a family that had lived so well together, for such a number of years, completely broken up.'[36]

George's reign was plunged into further crisis by the revival of war with France in May 1803. The rise to prominence of the French statesman and military commander, Napoleon Bonaparte, gave the revolutionary army much greater cohesion. Following his election as Emperor of the French in May 1804, Napoleon led a series of major campaigns that established France's domination of Europe for more than a decade. With a Napoleonic invasion of Britain seemingly imminent, King George bravely declared: 'Should his troops effect a landing, I shall certainly put myself at the head of mine . . . to repel them.'[37] As if to prove the point, in October 1803 he personally reviewed thousands of army volunteers in London's Hyde Park, watched by a million spectators. *The Times* reported: 'The enthusiasm of the multitude was beyond all expression', and a member of court claimed: 'The King is really prepared to take the field in case of attack, his beds are ready and he can move at half an hour's warning.'[38] In reality, George was far from capable of taking command, either of his troops or of his mind. Although his recovery had been announced, he remained in a fragile state, easily upset and increasingly unpredictable.

Admiral Nelson's celebrated victory over Napoleon's fleet at Trafalgar in October 1805 ended the threat of invasion, but the war with France raged on. Two years later, Parliament achieved a victory of a different kind when it passed An Act for the Abolition of the Slave Trade. Although it did not abolish the practice of slavery altogether, the new Act prohibited it within the British Empire and encouraged other nations to follow suit. The king could claim no honour from this landmark event: he had long been an opponent of the abolitionist movement, headed by the Yorkshire politician and philanthropist, William Wilberforce.

The twenty-fifth of October 1809 marked the beginning of George III's fiftieth year on the throne. Only three other British monarchs had achieved this milestone (Edward III, Henry III and James VI and I), but the celebrations staged across the kingdom were marred by upheavals within the royal family. It was for good reason that the Duke of Wellington described the king's sons as 'the damndest millstones about the neck of any government that can be imagined'.[39] Further scandals between the warring Waleses had been reported in the press, such as the rumour that Princess Caroline had borne an illegitimate son. This was temporarily overshadowed by the shocking revelation in May 1810 that another of the king's sons, Ernest, Duke of Cumberland, had been found covered in blood, his valet dead in a nearby room. Although he was cleared of murder, the scandal was slow to recede.

On 25 October 1810, the king appeared in public for the last time at a reception to mark the fiftieth anniversary of his accession. It was obvious to all those present that the 'madness' had returned. Early the following year, Parliament passed The Regency Act, conferring George III's authority upon his eldest son and heir. This time, it did take effect and the regency formally began on 7 February 1811. Although the king showed signs of recovery three months later, his condition soon deteriorated. His mental state was exacerbated by the onset of dementia, and he also became completely blind, increasingly deaf and, at the end, unable to walk.

For a more dutiful and committed heir to the throne, the regency might have acted as a valuable training ground. As it was, what the forty-eight-year-old Prince George termed 'playing at King' was not at all to his taste.[40] Before long, he was seeking solace in the accustomed way. 'I much doubt . . . whether all the alcohol in the world will be able to brace his nerves up to the mark of facing the difficulties he will soon have to encounter', remarked one acquaintance.[41]

The prince regent's growing unpopularity contrasted with the public adoration for his gregarious daughter, Princess Charlotte. She was first in line to the throne after her father and there was little possibility of her parents producing an heir to supplant her. Her profile was further raised when she married Prince Leopold of Saxe-Coburg-Saalfeld in May 1816 and fell pregnant shortly afterwards. But joy turned to tragedy when in November 1817 she died after being delivered of a stillborn son. The outpouring of public grief was on a scale never seen before, surpassed only by that for the death of another Princess of Wales 180 years later. The people mourned the passing not just of a popular princess, but of the only legitimate grandchild of George III, which meant the succession was now thrown into doubt.

Grief turned to retribution. The prince regent was accused of showing inadequate sorrow at the loss of his daughter and was even held responsible for her death. His popularity plummeted further as a result of the outbreaks of popular violence and threats to the established order in the wake of the Duke of Wellington's victory over Napoleon at Waterloo in 1815, which had brought to a victorious end Britain's long-running war with France. The aftershocks of the wars sparked an economic depression, particularly in textile manufacture, with industrialists slashing wages in response to market forces. In the same year as Waterloo, the British government passed the first of the Corn Laws, which imposed a tariff on foreign grain in order to protect English grain producers. This led to an increase in the cost of food as people were forced to buy the more expensive and lower-quality British grain. Periods of famine and chronic unemployment ensued, which made the climate ripe for political radicalism to thrive. There were increasing calls for a thoroughgoing reform of the electoral system, which was rife with corruption and allocated insufficient representation to large urban centres.

By the summer of 1819, the government had grown so nervous about further riots that its response to a large but mostly peaceful demonstration at St Peter's Field in Manchester was to order the local magistrates to break it up with force. Cavalry charged into the 60,000-strong crowd with sabres drawn, killing several people, including a young child who was knocked to the ground. In the climate of bitter recrimination that followed, the prince regent became a figure of hate, thanks to his having authorised the use of force. Shortly after the catastrophe, he was 'hissed by an immense mob' outside the door of Carlton House.

Closeted away at Windsor, the king was no more sensible of the catastrophe than he had been of the death of Queen Charlotte, his wife of fifty-eight years, a few months before. 'He appears to be living in another world', remarked George III's last physician, Dr Heberden, 'and has lost almost all his interest in the concerns of this.'[42] The king's disordered mind deprived him of sleep and sparked endless chatter: at Christmas 1819, he spoke nonsense for fifty-eight hours together. A little over a month later, on 29 January 1820, death brought an end to the eighty-one-year-old king's troubles.

George III's reign had witnessed the final retreat of the crown as a political force, but it had created a new role in its place. The monarchy had emerged as the symbol of the nation, a bastion of duty, charity and respectability. 'I do not pretend to any superior abilities,' he once declared, 'but will give place to no one in meaning to preserve the freedom, happiness and glory of my dominions and all their inhabitants, and to fulfil the duty to my God.' In his seminal work on the British constitution, the nineteenth-century journalist Walter Bagehot described the sovereign as 'the head of our morality'.[43] It was a role that would be fully embraced in later reigns, particularly those of George III's granddaughter Victoria and four times great-granddaughter Elizabeth II. But it depended very much on the personality of the monarch and their ability to influence the popular press, which, as had become clear, was rapidly becoming the dominant force in British society and politics.

George IV (1820–30)

'Playing at King'

T HE IRISH STATESMAN and philosopher Edmund Burke opined
that if George III's eldest son and namesake should ever give up
a life in which he found 'little more than disgust', he might 'become
a great king'.[1] This was not entirely unrealistic. As a youth, George had
shown considerable promise and a sharp intellect. One of his mother's
German attendants had enthused about his 'elegant person', 'engaging
and distinguished manners' and 'affectionate disposition'.[2] He grew up
to be an excellent wit and raconteur, with a talent for impressions that
even impressed the Duke of Wellington. His Whig allies lauded him
as 'a true genius' and 'the first young man in Great Britain'.[3]

Promise was one thing; performance another entirely. Both as
regent and king, George proved to be the ultimate playboy prince,
steeped in 'gluttony, drunkenness and gambling', 'a spoiled, selfish,
odious beast'.[4] In short, one of the worst monarchs that Britain has
ever produced.

By the time the fifty-seven-year-old prince regent became king, the
British public had already grown tired of his profligacy and licentiousness, and the popularity of the crown had sunk to an all-time low.
'Pageantry and show, the parade of crowns and coronets, of gold keys
and sticks, white wands and black rods, of ermine and lawn, maces
and wigs, are ridiculous when men become enlightened, when they
have learned that the real object of government is to confer the greatest
happiness on the people at the least expense', declared John Wade in
The Black Book, a radical critique of the English establishment.[5] The
new king was hardly equipped to turn the situation around.

To make matters worse, George IV's estranged wife Caroline,
who had been living abroad, announced her intention to return and

claim her rights as queen. Caroline had courted scandal during her years in Italy, thanks to her affair with one of her servants, Bartolomeo Bergami. Even though he was hardly a shining example of marital fidelity himself, the king resolved to start legal proceedings against his wife – not just to secure a divorce but to have her tried for high treason. The latter was not possible, given that Caroline's affair had not taken place on British soil and her lover was not subject to its laws. But only after protracted wrangling with Parliament did George let the matter drop.

The whole controversy had whipped up further ill feeling against the new king. Public sympathy was firmly with Caroline and huge crowds gathered in the streets to voice their anger at her husband. There was alarm when soldiers began to 'skirmish in their barracks', and the influential Whig minister Lord Grey feared 'a Jacobin Revolution more bloody than that of France'.[6] Pushing home her advantage, the queen declared that she would blow her husband off the throne. The king was heard to petulantly remark that he would retire to Hanover and leave the British throne to his brother Frederick, Duke of York.

George IV's reign could not have got off to a worse start. Determined to assert his sovereignty and win over his subjects, he planned the most extravagant coronation in the entire history of the British monarchy. Even by his standards, the expense was eye-watering: £243,000 (around £14 million today), which dwarfed the budget of all those that had gone before. Guests inside Westminster Abbey on 19 July 1821 caught their breath as the king made his entry, 'buried in satin, feathers and diamonds . . . like some gorgeous bird of the East'.[7] George's estranged wife, whom he had banned from the occasion, suffered the humiliation of being turned away, which dented her husband's brief surge of popularity. She fell ill the same day and died three weeks later. The speed of Caroline's demise led to rumours of poison, although her physicians thought she had an intestinal obstruction and it has since been mooted that she had been suffering from cancer.

Soon after the coronation, the king embarked upon a tour of his dominions. He became the first British monarch since Richard II to

Painted to celebrate the glory of the Stuart dynasty and the union of the crowns of England and Scotland, Peter Paul Rubens' ceiling in the Banqueting House, Whitehall, was one of the last things Charles I saw before his execution in 1649.

The English Civil War leader Oliver Cromwell insisted on being depicted 'warts and all' when Sir Peter Lely painted this portrait in 1654.

This painting, probably based on eye-witness accounts and contemporary engravings, tells the story of Charles I's execution on 30 January 1649.

Upon the Restoration, Charles II commissioned a dazzling new set of coronation regalia to replace those that had been melted down during the Commonwealth. The same regalia are still in use today.

Medal struck to mark the accession of Britain's first joint monarchs, William III and Mary II, after the so-called 'Glorious Revolution' of 1688–9.

Caricature by the satirist James Gillray poking fun at George III and Queen Charlotte's frugal habits.

George III was so devastated by the loss of Britain's American colonies in 1783, after eight years of revolutionary war, that he drafted an abdication speech.

In 1822, George IV journeyed to Scotland for 'one and twenty daft days'. To court popularity north of the border, he revived the tradition of wearing Scottish tartan dress.

Queen Victoria strikes a melodramatic pose of mourning next to a bust of her beloved late husband, Albert, while her daughter Alice looks on.

The celebrations for Victoria's Diamond Jubilee in June 1897 included a carriage procession through the streets of London, which were thronged with well-wishers.

Victoria's eldest son and successor, the *bon viveur* Edward VII, helped to popularise the motor car, a relatively new invention at the time of his accession in 1901.

To counter rising criticism of the royal family during the First World War, George V replaced his family's German surname of Saxe-Coburg-Gotha with the quintessentially English 'Windsor'.

As Prince of Wales, the future Edward VIII's film star good looks and debonair charm made him the darling of high society.

The Instrument of Abdication, whereby Edward VIII renounced the throne for himself and his heirs in December 1936, after just ten months as king.

George VI and his family ('We four', as he called them) won popular sympathy and respect when his elder brother abdicated and he was duty-bound to take the throne.

Elizabeth II's coronation portrait by Cecil Beaton, June 1953. Aged twenty-five at the time of her accession, she would go on to become the longest-reigning monarch in British history.

The Queen's Silver Jubilee in 1977 was parodied by the punk band the Sex Pistols, whose single 'God Save the Queen' served as a protest against the 'fascist regime'.

Charles and Diana, Prince and Princess of Wales, established the tradition of the Buckingham Palace balcony kiss at their wedding on 29 July 1981. The event was not quite the fairy tale it seemed.

The tragic death of Princess Diana on 31 August 1997 prompted an enormous outpouring of public grief and a 'sea of flowers' was laid outside her Kensington Palace home.

Elizabeth II and her husband Prince Philip process through the huge crowds at the Golden Jubilee celebrations in 2002.

Royal wedding fever swept the nation when Prince Harry married Hollywood actress Meghan Markle in May 2018. Less than two years later, they caused a scandal by stepping back from official royal duties.

Queen Elizabeth II and her heirs (in age order): Princes Charles, William and George. The lack of male heirs has not beset the Windsors as it did other royal dynasties, notably the Tudors.

pay a state visit to Ireland, and the first since James II to venture north of the border. In 1822 he journeyed to Edinburgh and stayed for 'one and twenty daft days'.[8] It was well worth the effort: the Scots were naturally averse to the Hanoverian dynasty for ousting their native Stuarts, but George IV's charm offensive won them over. It was also thanks to this visit that the wearing of traditional Scottish tartan dress was revived, as the king had taken care to be seen in it as much as possible.

More than any of his Hanoverian predecessors, George appreciated the importance of royal pomp and ceremony, and during his reign the court regained some of its former glamour. The new king was a passionate patron of architecture and set about transforming his father's modest home, Buckingham House, into a far more lavish palace with the help of the celebrated architect John Nash. He had also encouraged Nash in his development of London's Regent Street and Regent's Park, both of which were named after him as prince regent.

George IV's attention was absorbed, too, by an ambitious programme of modernisation works at Windsor Castle, one of the oldest royal residences in England. These included raising the height of the Round Tower and remodelling the State Apartments. The works, which were still unfinished by the time of his death, cost in excess of £1 million (around £60 million today). The king had become so obsessed with these and other building projects that his last prime minister, the Duke of Wellington, complained he appeared 'not to be the least interested in public affairs'.[9] Perhaps, though, George had his priorities right. The monarchy had lost its political power, but thanks to his efforts its physical trappings had been considerably enhanced.

George IV was just as passionate about the arts and patronised a host of leading writers, poets and painters. Walter Scott was among his friends, he encouraged the novels of Jane Austen, acquired paintings by the likes of Rembrandt and Rubens, and commissioned new ones from an array of British artists, including Gainsborough, Reynolds, Stubbs and Constable. To his credit, he opened up this vast collection for public view, rather than accumulating for his 'own pleasure alone' as other monarchs had done before him.[10] He was also instrumental in the founding of the National Gallery in London in 1824. Even Wellington admitted that the nation would always be indebted to 'a most magnificent patron of the arts in this country, and in the world'.[11]

George's involvement in political affairs was a good deal less productive. He was staunchly opposed to Catholic emancipation, which called for the remaining restrictions on Roman Catholics imposed by measures such as the Test Act of 1672 to be removed. His views chimed with those of his first prime minister, Lord Liverpool. But by the time of Liverpool's resignation in 1827, the king had managed to alienate almost all of his colleagues, thanks to his laziness, indiscretion and brilliantly accurate but humiliating mimicry of their mannerisms. George Canning, his choice of successor to Liverpool, was so unpopular that what little sway the king held in government was destroyed. For the first time in history, the monarch lacked the support of both the Tories and Whigs.

Canning's administration was cut short by his death in August 1827, just four months after taking office. He was succeeded, briefly, by Lord Goderich before the Duke of Wellington was appointed. From the start, relations between the king and the hero of Waterloo were strained. Wellington found George's flighty, dissolute behaviour exasperating and was deeply irritated by his pretence that he had fought at the Battle of Waterloo disguised as a German general.

The king was no match for his formidable prime minister. By now, Wellington was a staunch advocate of Catholic emancipation and when he tried to force the issue with his sovereign, George veered between sobbing uncontrollably and rambling continuously – on one occasion for almost six hours without pausing to draw breath, echoing his father's bouts of insanity. At other times he threatened to abandon Britain to a Catholic king, by whom he meant his brother William, now heir to the throne after the death of Frederick, Duke of York, in 1827. When the Catholic Relief Act was passed in April 1829, allowing members of the Catholic Church to sit in Parliament, the king was in such a 'deplorable state' that he threw himself on the nearest sofa to recover.[12]

Having utterly failed to exert any influence over his government, George retired to Brighton, where he lived out his days steeped in alcohol, laudanum and women. Morbidly obese, his gargantuan appetite knew no limits. In April 1830 Wellington was scandalised to report that for one breakfast alone, the king had been served 'a pigeon and beef steak pie of which he ate two pigeons and three beef-steaks, three parts of a bottle of Mozelle, a glass of champagne, two glasses of port and a glass of brandy'.[13] As early as 1822, the Scottish artist David Wilkie, who painted a portrait of George IV to commemorate his visit to Edinburgh that year, described his royal subject as being 'like a great sausage stuffed into the covering'.[14]

It was obvious from the king's 'ghastly' appearance that he could not live much longer. In his final months, it was said that he was overcome with regret for his sinful, indulgent life and turned to God. He breathed his last at Windsor on 26 June 1830, crying: 'This is death!'[15]

'There never was an individual less regretted by his fellow-creatures than this deceased King', declared *The Times* after the announcement of George IV's death. Only his debtors and caricaturists had cause to mourn his passing. Although Wellington praised the late king's accomplishments in the eulogy he delivered to the House of Lords, in private he described him as 'the worst man he ever fell in with his whole life, the most selfish, the most false, the most ill-natured, the most entirely without one redeeming quality'.[16] Even those closest to George struggled to mourn him. One of his private aides noted in his diary: 'A more contemptible, cowardly, selfish, unfeeling dog does not exist. There have been good and wise kings but not many of them . . . and this I believe to be one of the worst.'[17]

If there was a palpable sense of relief at the passing of this profligate prince, in time his former subjects were able to reflect upon his personal virtues, as well as his vices. Wellington's final assessment is perhaps the fairest: 'He was . . . the most extraordinary compound of talent, wit, buffoonery, obstinacy and good feeling' that the duke had ever seen in his life.[18]

William IV (1830–7)

A plain-hearted and generous-spirited sailor

'H<small>E IS AN</small> immense improvement on the last unforgiving animal, who died growling sulkily in his den at Windsor,' remarked the writer Emily Eden upon William IV's accession. 'This man at least *wishes* to make everybody happy, and everything he has done has been benevolent.'[1] At sixty-four years old, William beat his predecessor's record as the oldest king to ascend the throne. He was the third son of George III and had spent all but the previous three years of his life with little expectation of ever being king.

In a sense, William had a much easier job of it than his predecessor: George IV was the very antithesis of a hard act to follow. Also in William's favour was his distinguished naval career, which included service in New York during the American War of Independence. This made him the first member of the royal family to visit America and also placed him in some danger when George Washington approved a plot to kidnap him. William's naval service won the praise of Admiral Nelson and earned him the nickname 'Sailor King'.

Of course, William was not perfect. Like his brothers, he had a strong sexual appetite and a string of mistresses, including the actress Dorothy Bland (known as Mrs Dorothy Jordan), his partner of twenty years. She bore him ten children and they lived in domestic harmony in Bushy House, south-west of London. But the death of his niece, Princess Charlotte, in 1817 had brought William a step closer to the throne and the following year he had married Princess Adelaide of Saxe-Meiningen at Kew Palace.

William's new wife proved a good influence, tempering his wilder instincts and encouraging a more frugal lifestyle. The couple were devoted to each other and only their childlessness marred an otherwise happy marriage.[2] As queen, Adelaide set the tone of court life.

Ladies of dubious virtue or those wearing revealing dresses were forbidden entry to the royal palaces. Although this earned the queen a reputation for prudishness in some quarters, most people welcomed it after the licentiousness and excess of George IV's court.

Adelaide's modest lifestyle chimed with that of her husband. An American visitor to court described the new king as 'a plain-hearted and generous-spirited sailor'.[3] William won further popularity by replacing his late brother's French chefs and German band with British ones, giving much of George IV's art collection to the nation and donating 150 of his birds and animals to the Zoological Society.

William's style of monarchy was much more informal than his predecessor's. He continued to live at Clarence House, his elegant but modest London residence, and suggested converting Buckingham Palace into barracks. At Windsor, he ordered the east terrace and the private drives through the park to be opened to the public, gave a banquet to three thousand of the town's poorer inhabitants on his birthday, and when staying in Brighton invited anyone he knew to dinner, urging them not to 'bother about clothes'.[4] 'The King . . . talks and shows himself too much,' Harriet Arbuthnot, a renowned diarist and close friend of the Duke of Wellington, scornfully remarked. 'I hope he will soon go out of town and be quiet.'[5] But William's accessibility made him popular with the less conservative of his subjects.

'Look at that idiot,' George IV once remarked about his brother and successor, 'they will remember me if ever he is in my place.'[6] In common with most of his Hanoverian predecessors, there was an air of the ridiculous about Britain's new king. The nineteenth-century historian Lytton Strachey claimed that William's 'sudden elevation to the throne after fifty-six years of utter insignificance had almost sent him crazy'.[7] Upon hearing that he was king, William drove about London in his carriage for hours, doffing his cap and offering lifts to startled passers-by. When he opened his first privy council meeting, he declared: 'Who is Silly Billy now?'[8] He chattered 'loudly and incessantly' throughout his brother's funeral service, and his fondness for giving speeches far exceeded his skill.[9] The unusual shape of his head, which bore a striking resemblance to a pineapple, also attracted ridicule. On the whole, though, William IV was a far more acceptable monarch than his predecessor. 'Altogether he seems a kind-hearted, well-meaning, not stupid, burlesque, bustling old fellow,' remarked the diarist Charles Greville, 'and if he doesn't go mad may make a very decent King, but he exhibits oddities.'[10]

The new king had inherited a considerable burden from his late brother, who had left the monarchy in such a perilous state thanks to his profligacy and incompetence that Sir Robert Peel, who became prime minister in 1834, declared that only a miracle could save it. William IV might not have been the stuff that great monarchs are made of, but he was at least more conscientious than his late brother. Prime Minister Wellington reported that he had done more business with the new king in ten minutes than he had with George IV in as many days. William was also more straightforward than his predecessor and had little interest in involving himself in political intrigues. His lack of sophistication bordered on naivety, though, and he was no match for the seasoned ministers of his government.

By the time of William's accession, the death of a monarch was followed by a general election. Wellington and the Tories secured the most votes but lost substantial ground to the Whigs. In November 1830 the duke was defeated in the Commons and replaced as prime minister by his Whig rival, Lord Grey. Grey's manifesto promised to reform the electoral system, which had changed little since the fifteenth century and was now deeply inequitable. Large towns such as Manchester and Birmingham were not permitted to elect any members of Parliament, whereas small boroughs such as Old Sarum, which had just seven voters, elected two members each. These 'rotten' or 'pocket' boroughs, as they were known, were often controlled by the landed gentry, whose tenants were obliged to vote according to their landlord's wishes, there being no secret ballot. Some particularly disreputable landowners even sold seats to prospective candidates.

Lord Grey's reforms met with powerful opposition and the First Reform Bill was defeated in the House of Commons in 1831. The prime minister urged his sovereign to dissolve Parliament in order to prompt another general election. William was reluctant, given that the country was already in a state of turmoil. But he eventually acceded and, amid dramatic scenes and noisy protests from Grey's opponents, called Parliament to a close. In the resulting elections to the Commons, the reformers were triumphant. However, the House of Lords remained bitterly opposed to the Bill.

In the midst of the controversy, William IV was crowned at Westminster on 8 September 1831. He had been reluctant to go ahead with the ceremony, arguing that his wearing a crown to dissolve Parliament dispensed with the need to formalise his reign in this way. He was persuaded by the traditionalists at court, but only on condition that the minimum expense was incurred: less than £30,000 (around £2 million today), a mere fraction of the amount lavished on his elder brother's coronation a decade earlier. When his Tory opponents threatened to boycott what they mockingly termed the 'Half Crown-nation', the king quipped that there would be 'great convenience of room and less heat'. The ceremonials were stripped back as far as possible, and for the first time in its history there was no coronation banquet. Throughout the proceedings it was painfully obvious that the new king held them in scant regard, acting as if he was 'a character in a comic opera'. By contrast, his consort Adelaide won praise for her 'dignity, repose and characteristic grace'. But when it came to the crowning itself, the enormity of the occasion finally dawned on William. 'It was a great moment when I actually felt the crown descending upon me and touching my temples', he reflected. 'I could not restrain a thrill, but not of joy . . . of awe, at the responsibilities Almighty God had been pleased to put upon me'.[11]

Despite widespread popular support for the king and the Reform Bill with which he was strongly identified, it was rejected again by the House of Lords in October 1831. This prompted unrest across the country, with many demonstrations quickly turning violent. Aware that parliamentary rules prohibited a Bill from being introduced twice in the same session, Lord Grey persuaded William to prorogue Parliament. He also urged the king to create enough new peerages 'to secure the success of the Bill' when it was put before the Lords again.[12] The king was anxious about permanently expanding the peerage, however, and the matter came to a head with Lord Grey's resignation. William attempted to restore Wellington to office, but the duke lacked support. The king's own popularity plummeted as a result of his ineffectual meddling. When he appeared in public, mud was slung at his carriage and he was hissed at. He eventually agreed to reappoint Grey and his ministry and to create the necessary peers, but this proved unnecessary and the Reform Act was finally passed in June 1832.

As well as creating a fairer, more representative election system, the Act proved a decisive moment in the development of a fully constitutional monarchy. In the past, the monarch had held some sway over the appointment of prime ministers, but this was now in the hands of the electorate. If a government was supported by a majority in the Commons, the monarch was obliged to accept it. This is precisely what happened in July 1834, when Lord Grey was replaced as prime minister by Lord Melbourne, whom the king disliked. His inability to do anything about it served as a stark reminder of how far the monarchy's power over government had diminished. William's father George III had been able to dismiss one ministry, appoint another and dissolve Parliament, confident that the electorate would vote in favour of the new administration. Already that seemed a distant memory.

With the king now approaching seventy and growing increasingly short-tempered due to faltering health, his relations with his government became ever more strained. When one of his illegitimate sons asked whether he would be entertaining during Ascot week, his father retorted: 'I cannot give any dinners without inviting the ministers, and I would rather see the devil than any one of them in my house.'[13] Aware that he could not rid himself of his cabinet, William resorted to frequent jibes. 'To be fretted by opposition upon every little matter is intolerable,' grumbled Prime Minister Melbourne.[14] After one particularly cantankerous meeting in July 1835, Greville regretfully noted: 'This . . . does more to degrade the monarchy than anything which has ever occurred: to exhibit the King publicly . . . as an unsuccessful competitor in a political squabble, is to take from the crown all . . . dignity.'[15]

Towards the end of his life, the king grew more philosophical about the demise of the crown's political authority. 'I have my view of things, and I tell them to my ministers,' he remarked. 'If they do not adopt them, I cannot help it. I have done my duty.'[16] His consort had already shown that the future of the monarchy lay not in government, but in philanthropy. As queen, Adelaide donated a significant portion of her household income to charitable causes, which won her praise and affection throughout Britain and overseas. In 1836, the capital city of the state of South Australia was named in her honour, as were numerous other places throughout the empire.

Adelaide also had an eye to the future in the kindness she showed towards her husband's niece, Princess Victoria, the daughter of William's younger brother Edward, Duke of Kent, who had died a few months after her birth in 1819. In the absence of any other legitimate male offspring, Victoria looked increasingly certain to inherit the throne. William was also fond of the young girl, but despised her ambitious mother. The Duchess of Kent had thrust her daughter into the limelight by arranging royal 'progresses' around the kingdom and had appropriated some of the state rooms at Kensington Palace for her use, against the king's express orders.

The animosity between them reached boiling point at a banquet held for William's seventy-first birthday in August 1836. When he spied the duchess and her seventeen-year-old daughter, he burst out: 'I trust to God that my life may be spared for nine months longer . . . I should then have the satisfaction of leaving the exercise of the Royal authority to the personal authority of that young lady, heiress presumptive to the Crown, and not in the hands of a person now near me' – by whom he meant the duchess, who was poised to become regent if her daughter succeeded as a minor.[17] The shocked silence that followed was broken only by Princess Victoria's sobbing.

William would have his wish. His niece reached her eighteenth birthday on 24 May 1837, by which time the king was dying 'like an old lion', as the Tory MP Benjamin Disraeli remarked. 'Poor old man!' Princess Victoria wrote in her diary, 'I feel sorry for him; he was always personally kind to me.'[18] William's devoted wife Adelaide remained by his side at Windsor, refusing to go to bed for ten days so that she might attend him. He died on 20 June and was buried in St George's Chapel after a funeral that Grenville described as a 'wretched mockery'.[19]

'He was not a man of talent or of much refinement', reflected *The Times*. 'But he had a warm heart, and it was an English heart.'[20] William IV had preferred modest to kingly habits, but these were exactly what were required after the vanity and excess of his predecessor and had helped to stabilise the crown. His reign had witnessed the retreat of the monarchy as a political force, but William might have enjoyed the fact that among the descendants of his many illegitimate offspring was the future British prime minister, David Cameron.

Victoria (1837–1901)

'I will be good'

IN MARCH 1830, the ten-year-old Princess Victoria was at her lessons when her governess, Baroness Lehzen, showed her a book containing a royal family tree. Until that moment, Victoria had been kept in ignorance of her proximity to the throne, but with her uncle, King George IV, close to death, it was decided to let her know about the awesome responsibility that lay ahead. As she studied the genealogy and her own place within it, realisation dawned. 'I see I am nearer the throne than I thought,' she observed, then vowed: 'I will be good.'[1]

By the time she became queen a little over seven years later, Victoria had spent almost all of her life at Kensington Palace. She was born there on 24 May 1819 – a 'pocket Hercules' according to her doting father, Edward, Duke of Kent, and 'a pretty little princess, plump as a partridge'.[2] Exactly one month later she was christened at the palace, with her uncle George, then prince regent, in attendance. His relations with the Kents were difficult and he vetoed their suggested names of Elizabeth, Charlotte and Augusta as being too 'royal', insisting that the child be named Alexandrina as a compliment to the Russian Emperor, Alexander I. Her middle name was Victoria, after her mother, and it was by this that she came to be known.

Victoria liked to perpetuate the myth that she suffered a miserable childhood at the hands of her controlling mother and her late father's equerry, Sir John Conroy, whom she referred to as a 'monster and demon incarnate'.[3] While it is true that as she edged closer to the throne the pair introduced stringent measures – known as the 'Kensington System' – to protect her safety (and their influence), for most of her early years, the future queen was a happy and indulged child, surrounded by adoring servants, toys and pets, and enjoying regular holidays by the sea. She grew so used to having her own way that she was prone to fearsome temper tantrums. In a vain attempt to check them, her governess introduced a 'Behaviour Book' for the princess to record her daily conduct. After one particularly stormy scene, Victoria admitted that she had been 'VERY VERY VERY VERY HORRIBLY NAUGHTY!!!!!', underlining each word four times.[4]

As she grew to maturity, Victoria found her mother and Conroy's control ever more suffocating. She was never allowed to be alone or to receive visitors without a chaperone. Even as a teenager, she was not permitted to walk down the stairs without holding an adult's hand. By the time she became queen, she was desperate to escape. At six o'clock in the morning of 20 June 1837, Victoria was awoken by her mother with the news that the Archbishop of Canterbury and the Lord Chamberlain had come to see her. 'I got out of bed and went into my sitting-room (only in my dressing-gown), and *alone*, and saw them', she recorded. 'Lord Conyngham then acquainted me that my poor Uncle, the King, was no more . . . and consequently that I am *Queen*.'[5]

Victoria carried out her first public duties without her mother or Conroy. After a conference with her prime minister, Lord Melbourne, she presided over a meeting of the privy council. The Duke of Wellington was impressed by the way she conducted herself with 'ease and . . . self-possession . . . as if she had been performing the part for years. She not merely filled her chair, she filled the room.' He concluded: 'I think that the Race of nervous young Ladies will soon be out of fashion.'[6] That night the new queen reflected on the first day of her reign.

> Since it has pleased Providence to place me in this station, I shall do my utmost to fulfil my duty towards my country; I am very young and perhaps in many, though not all things, inexperienced, but I am sure, that very few have more real good will and more real desire to do what is fit and right than I have.[7]

For the first time in almost a hundred years, Britain had both a young monarch and a lively court. Thousands of people thronged the streets for Victoria's public appearances and were full of admiration for 'the little queen'. Her charming, graceful and cheerful manner were widely praised, her every move was recorded and discussed in the press, and there were many references to her 'lovely' appearance. In fact, with her prominent eyes and small mouth Victoria bore a strong resemblance to her Hanoverian predecessors. She had inherited their stoutness, too, but at 4 feet 11 inches tall was a good deal shorter.

In the early days of her reign, Victoria relied heavily upon her prime minister, whom she described as 'a very straightforward, honest, clever and good man'.[8] They forged such a close relationship that it earned Victoria the nickname 'Mrs Melbourne', although in truth he was more of a father figure than a romantic attachment. The new queen also benefited from the guidance of her uncle Leopold, King of the Belgians, widow of George IV's daughter Charlotte. In the years before her accession, he had counselled: 'You are destined to fill a most eminent station: to fill it *well* must now become your study.'[9] His advice was both regular and sound. He urged his niece to make the most of court gatherings by listening to the conversation of learned people, to always be prudent, discreet and conservative, and to support the church.

The extent to which Victoria followed his advice in the social whirl of her early reign is questionable. The endless round of balls, dancing, dinners, theatre and opera was a source of evident delight to a queen who had spent much of her young life in seclusion, and she threw herself into them with relish, confounding the enduring image of a dour, prudish monarch who was rarely 'amused'. 'It is no exaggeration to say that the accession of Princess Victoria reinstated the English monarchy in the affections of the people', enthused *The Times*. 'George IV had made the Throne unpopular; William IV had restored its popularity, but not its dignity.'[10]

This 'dignity' would become central to Victoria's monarchy. She may have inherited a crown whose power had been dramatically eroded, but she would re-imagine it as something to be venerated, even adored. The monarchy was transformed into the living embodiment of the nation's history – an image that it still projects today. Much of the royal ceremonial that is assumed to be part of ancient royal tradition would in fact be invented, or at least amplified, during Victoria's reign.[11] For the first time since Elizabeth I, the sovereign was the mother of her people, a trusted figure who could nurture and guide them. Echoing a later royal princess, Victoria declared: 'My first desire is to live in the hearts of my people.'[12] The new queen's unblemished morals formed a welcome contrast to those of her two predecessors (the 'wicked uncles') and were soon lauded as a model for her subjects to emulate. A sermon delivered on the day of Victoria's coronation declared: 'The moral influence of a Queen, in a nation where the female character is revered, and the royal looked up to, must necessarily be vast.'[13]

The coronation, held on 28 June 1838, was – literally – the crowning glory of what had been the most auspicious beginning to a reign since the Hanoverians came to power. 'Be assured as a pageant it was unsurpassed in all history,' enthused one eyewitness. This was impressive, given the economy with which the so-called 'Penny Crowning' was staged.[14] Some members of the government had been opposed to the idea of it going ahead at all. 'Coronations were fit only for barbarous, or semi-barbarous ages', grumbled Earl Fitzwilliam, 'for periods when crowns were worn and lost by unruly violence and ferocious contests.'[15] It did not proceed without incident, but the various mishaps during the ceremony – including one of the dignitaries falling down the stairs while paying homage to the new queen – were forgotten in the joyous celebrations. Victoria was deeply touched by the enthusiasm of the 400,000-strong crowd who had turned out for the occasion. 'Their good-humour and excessive loyalty was beyond everything, and I really cannot say *how* proud I feel to be the Queen of *such* a Nation.'[16]

Victoria's youthful naivety had captured the hearts of her people, but it made her dangerously vulnerable to court politics. In February 1839, she was embroiled in a scandal that destroyed much of the goodwill generated by her accession. It involved her mother's lady-in-waiting, Lady Flora Hastings, a member of a prominent Tory family. In January 1839, Flora began to complain of pain and swelling in her lower abdomen. The queen's physician attended her and suspected she was pregnant, but her refusal to be examined prevented a firm diagnosis. As she was unmarried, the matter was hushed up, but Baroness Lehzen heard of it and spread a rumour that Lady

Flora was with child. When it reached Victoria's ears, she jumped to the conclusion that the despised Conroy was the father. In order to defend her virtue, Flora finally consented to a full medical examination, which found that the swelling was caused by advanced liver cancer and she had only a few weeks to live. Victoria was filled with remorse and for years after she would be plagued by nightmares at what she had made the dying woman suffer.

In the midst of the Flora Hastings controversy, Victoria was plunged into an 'agony of grief and despair' when her beloved Melbourne resigned after his Whig majority was depleted.[17] 'All, ALL my happiness gone', Victoria lamented in her journal. 'That happy peaceful life destroyed, that dearest kind Lord Melbourne no more my minister.'[18] The new incumbent, Sir Robert Peel, was far less charming. He soon petitioned the queen to change the composition of her household, in which ladies of Whig families predominated. Encouraged by Melbourne, she stoutly refused, and a stalemate was reached when Peel refused to form a government unless the queen complied. Melbourne called an urgent meeting of the cabinet, which supported Victoria's stance. To her immense joy and relief, 'Lord M' resumed his ministry shortly afterwards.

Although the crisis soon receded, it was taken by many of the new queen's ministers as an ominous sign that she planned to reverse almost two centuries of decline in the monarch's political authority. In fact, it had more to do with Victoria's determination to keep Melbourne in office than any deep-seated desire to challenge the constitution. But even this limited objective would prove hard to achieve. Ill feeling against Melbourne continued to simmer and the view that he was manipulating the young queen for his own gain became increasingly widespread. Victoria soon realised that she would need to find someone with whom could share the burdens of monarchy on a more permanent basis.

'She'll be a fool if she marries,' pronounced an American attorney after hearing of Victoria's accession. 'Let her think of Elizabeth.' Although she has since been defined by her marriage, Victoria seemed to agree with this sentiment. 'I dreaded the thought of marrying,' she later admitted. 'I was so accustomed to having my own way that

I thought it was 10 to 1 that I shouldn't agree with anybody.'[19] Like her Tudor ancestor, she was concerned that a husband might wish to curtail her powers. But added to her growing desire for advice and companionship was the need to secure the succession. This was particularly urgent, given that her uncle Ernest, who had become King of Hanover upon William IV's death (Salic law preventing Victoria from inheriting that throne), was waiting in the wings to replace her.

Once Victoria had accepted the necessity of marriage, her choice of husband was straightforward. From her earliest infancy, her uncle Leopold had cherished hopes that she would marry his nephew, Prince Albert of Saxe-Coburg and Gotha. Born just months apart and delivered by the same midwife, the two cousins had met at Victoria's seventeenth birthday celebrations in May 1836 and had struck up an instant rapport. As well as admiring the prince's 'extremely handsome' looks, Victoria had enthused that he was 'full of goodness & sweetness, & very clever & intelligent'.[20]

But it was only when the pair met again three years later that this initial attraction deepened into something stronger. 'Albert's *beauty is most striking*', Victoria recorded in her journal. 'He is so amiable and unaffected – in short, very fascinating; he is excessively admired here.' On 14 October 1839, just four days after Albert had arrived in England, Victoria wrote to Melbourne, telling him that she had changed her mind about marrying. Her prime minister agreed that Albert was 'a very agreeable young man', and the next day Victoria asked him to marry her. 'Oh! How I adore and love him, I cannot say!!' she wrote upon receiving his acceptance.[21] They were married on 10 February 1840 in the Chapel Royal at St James's Palace. The Archbishop of Canterbury had asked the queen whether he should omit the promise 'to obey', but she had replied that she wished 'to be married as a woman, not as a Queen'.[22] She was passionately attached to her new husband and within days of the wedding, she was pregnant.

From the outset, the royal couple made it their business to be seen in public as often as possible. This boosted their already burgeoning popularity but was not without risk. Four months after their wedding, they left Buckingham Palace in an open carriage for their customary ride around Hyde Park when a man named Edward Oxford fired at the queen with his pistol. Despite being only six paces away, he missed and the pregnant Victoria ducked out of the way before he fired again. Two years later, another would-be assassin made two attempts on the queen's life on consecutive days as she and her husband rode in their carriage. It is to the couple's credit that they refused to be cowed by such terrifying episodes, which won them even greater acclaim among the people. The perpetrators acted alone and were mentally unstable. Certainly, they did not represent any general discontent with the monarchy, whose popularity was greater than ever.

Victoria had been determined that her future husband would not encroach upon her queenly authority and had placed a number of restrictions on Albert's influence. Once they were married, though, she rapidly changed her stance. A census return for March 1851 lists Victoria's profession as 'The Queen' but cites Albert as head of the household.[23] At heart, Victoria was deeply conventional and adhered to the contemporary model of a devoted wife who was entirely dependent upon her husband. As well as deferring to Albert in the domestic sphere, she also ceded him ever more authority in the public one. Court life declined as a result, the more naturally reserved prince preferring the quiet of Windsor to the perpetual round of social engagements that his wife had so delighted in.

From the outset, Albert was determined to be the master in their relationship. He became his wife's private secretary, a position that he exploited so effectively that it became the most powerful in the entire royal household – and still is today. Over the years that followed, Victoria grew ever more submissive to his will. For a fiery-tempered woman used to having her own way, the occasional clash was inevitable. Whenever that happened, Albert treated her like a wayward child whose spirit must be broken, and rewarded her compliance by calling her his 'Dear Good, Little One'. Having been deprived of a father since her earliest infancy, Victoria responded with alacrity, desperate to please him. Albert's dominance became so complete that she herself acknowledged she had 'leant on him for all and everything—without whom I did nothing, moved not a finger, arranged not a print or photograph, didn't put on a gown or bonnet if he didn't approve it'.[24]

The queen's diminishing role in relation to her husband had another, more practical cause. From the birth of their first child Victoria (Vicky) in November 1840 until the ninth and last, Beatrice, in April 1857, the queen had little respite from pregnancy. With an ever-expanding nursery of heirs and spares, it is no surprise that she would become the first of England's queens regnant to be succeeded by her own child. When she gave birth to her eighth child, Leopold, in 1853, her doctors administered the new anaesthetic, chloroform, which made Victoria an advocate for this medical advance, encouraging other women to follow suit.

Although the queen was physically robust and her pregnancies were trouble-free, ever since the death of Princess Charlotte in childbirth convention had dictated that the expectant royal mother be treated as an invalid from the moment her condition was confirmed. To make matters worse, Victoria hated being pregnant and suffered from severe post-natal depression after several of the births, although it was not diagnosed as such at the time. With the queen incapacitated for such prolonged periods, her husband took over many of her duties. 'Oh! if only I could make him king,' she once lamented.[25] As it was, Albert had to settle for the title of prince consort.

For Victoria, the 1840s and 1850s were decades of domestic felicity, with regular and prolonged visits to the royal family's new homes of Balmoral Castle in Scotland and Osborne House on the Isle of Wight. There, with Albert directing everything from the children's play to the household staff, she could enjoy life as a normal Victorian housewife and almost forget her queenly duties altogether. Both she and her husband took a particular interest in the education of their eldest son and heir, Albert Edward ('Bertie'), Prince of Wales. His arrival in 1841 had been the cause of celebration since he was the first heir apparent born to a reigning monarch in almost eighty years. It was also the last royal birth with privy councillors in attendance to attest his identity.[26]

Victoria and Albert were determined that their eldest son and heir should grow up to be as unlike his profligate Hanoverian great-uncles as possible. As is often the case, however, their intentions had the exact opposite effect. Bertie was not a natural scholar, and the brutal treatment that his tutors meted out at his father's orders, including regular whippings, instilled fear rather than knowledge. His parents made no secret of the fact that they favoured his elder sister Vicky – something that Bertie was well aware of. 'Vicky will be Mama's successor,' he pronounced when just eight years old, 'you see Vicky will be Victoria the second.' While the queen and her consort lavished praise on their eldest daughter, they had nothing but criticism for Bertie. 'His nose and mouth are too enormous and he . . . wears his clothes frightfully—he really is anything but good looking,' scorned his mother.[27] Albert was no less scathing: 'I never in my life met with such a thorough and cunning lazybones.'[28] The close interest they took in Bertie's upbringing soon became suffocating, and just as the future Henry VIII had rebelled against his controlling father by indulging in a life of carefree pleasure, so Bertie later became the very model of a profligate prince.

For now, though, all was domestic bliss. 'Really, when one is so happy and blessed in one's home life, as I am, politics (provided my country is safe) must take only a second place,' Victoria reflected.[29] Developments at the heart of government during this time had made her even less inclined to interfere. Melbourne was defeated in the 1841 general election and Sir Robert Peel again took office. Victoria's opinion of him was hardly improved when he finally succeeded in having the most stoutly Whig ladies of her household replaced. Unwilling to let go of her precious 'Lord M', she kept up a secret correspondence with him and he continued to offer her advice. This was a clear breach of the constitution. If the queen's letters had been leaked, they would have amounted to a public declaration of her lack of confidence in her government. Baron Stockmar, whom Victoria's uncle Leopold had sent to advise her, urged her to stop the correspondence immediately. But it was only when Melbourne's health deteriorated sharply after he suffered a stroke in October 1842 that the queen finally accepted she must move on.

Stockmar went some way towards supplying Melbourne's place. Some of his advice was sound and moderate, notably that: 'The proper duty of the Sovereigns of this country is not to take the lead in change, but to act as a balance wheel on the movement of the social body.'[30] He was particularly outspoken on the constitution, which he argued gave 'the Sovereign in his functions a deliberative part'.[31] In other words, Victoria should consider the policies and practices of her ministers and offer her opinion as to whether they were in the national interest. If they listened to and acted upon this, she would give her public support to their decisions.

The fact that Stockmar referred to the sovereign in the masculine gender was significant because Victoria found it difficult to apply his guidance to herself. The monarch could only receive advice from the party in power, not the opposition, so was obliged to consult courtiers and friends in order to attain a more balanced view. This was far easier for a king than a queen, since his household attendants traditionally held positions in government too. The same dual role did not exist for female attendants – and besides, Victoria had been compelled to appoint ladies who were strictly impartial. Because of her isolated upbringing, she also lacked friends who could advise her. Little wonder that she came to rely upon Albert so completely.

The prince consort was quick to realise the potential of the monarchy's role in representing the national interest. 'Is the sovereign not the natural guardian of the honour of his country, is he not *necessarily* a politician?' he pointed out, employing the same male gender as Stockmar had.[32] Albert made no secret of his frustration with the limited powers of the crown, demanding: 'Why are princes alone to be denied the credit of having political opinions based upon an anxiety for the national interests and honour of their country and the welfare of mankind?'[33] Stockmar agreed that there was a danger the monarch would become 'nothing but a mandarin figure which has to nod its head in assent, or shake it in denial, as his Minister pleases'.[34]

If the political situation had not been in a state of flux throughout the 1840s, then such strident views might have led to a clash between crown and government. As it was, there were so many changes in ministers and parties that it gave the sovereign considerable room for manoeuvre in the political arena. 'The Crown's hand has not been played so well for a long time as it has been of late years,' remarked a German diplomat.[35] Albert in particular proved so effective that by 1850 he was able to proudly list his various powers to

Wellington as: 'The natural head of her family, superintendent of her household, manager of her private affairs, sole *confidential* adviser in politics, and only assistant in her communications with the officers of the Government . . . the private secretary of the sovereign and her permanent minister.'[36] It was in effect a dual monarchy, with Victoria providing the public face and Albert the private authority.

In 1845, Ireland was badly afflicted by a potato blight. During the Great Famine that followed, more than a million people died and another million emigrated. In a country that had traditionally felt less allegiance to the British monarchy than other parts of the realm, it was not surprising that Victoria became the subject of resentment, particularly given the financial burden that her growing family and frequent holidays was placing on the people. In response, the queen personally donated £2,000 (around £120,000 today) to the British Relief Association and supported a number of fundraising events. It was not enough to quell the rising hostility towards the 'Famine Queen', as the Irish radicals called her, and when they turned to violent protests she rapidly lost sympathy with their plight.

The following decade got off to a much more positive start with the opening of the Great Exhibition in 1851. Staged in the magnificent Crystal Palace in Hyde Park, it showcased the cream of nineteenth-century industry and culture. Prince Albert had been instrumental in its organisation, thanks to his active presidency of the Society of Arts. The Society had staged its first annual exhibition of manufacture in 1847, modelled on French and German precedents. Two years later, the idea to make this an international exhibition was proposed and Albert agreed to take the lead. Victoria was in raptures over the opening, describing it as 'the *greatest* day in our history, the *most beautiful* and *imposing* and *touching* spectacle ever seen'.[37] She was particularly gratified that it resulted in a boost to her husband's popularity.

The Great Exhibition epitomised the self-confidence of the Victorian era, which, in turn, was epitomised by the queen. Just as Elizabeth I symbolised the glories of her age, so Victoria became synonymous with the huge advances in technology, industry, science and the arts that were achieved during her long reign. By the time of Victoria's accession, the revolution in industry that had begun during George II's reign more than one hundred years earlier was in full swing, and pioneers such as Isambard Kingdom Brunel, Charles Darwin and Ada Lovelace put Britain at the forefront of engineering, science and technology. The same vibrancy characterised the arts, with Charles Dickens, the Brontë sisters and the Pre-Raphaelite Brotherhood winning international renown.

For all the burgeoning self-confidence of Victoria's domain, the years immediately following the Great Exhibition were overshadowed by overseas war and revolt. In 1853, Britain joined the allied forces of France, the Ottoman Empire and Sardinia in the Crimean War against Russia, which was attempting to gain territory and power in the Holy Land. From the outbreak of hostilities, Victoria played an active role – far more so than she had in the domestic affairs of her kingdom – and was an even firmer advocate for the war than her prime minister, Lord Palmerston. She became an inspiring figurehead for her troops, introducing the Victoria Cross 'For Valour' and visiting countless wounded British soldiers upon their return home. She also took a keen interest in the work of Florence Nightingale, whose activities in the war secured her reputation as the founder of modern nursing.

Peace was concluded in March 1856, but barely a year later news arrived of a violent mutiny by sepoys serving in the East India Company's army. This posed a considerable threat to British rule in India and led to terrible bloodshed on both sides, among civilians as well as the military. 'Altogether, the whole is so much more distressing than the Crimea, where there was *glory* and honourable warfare, and where the poor women and children were safe', Victoria lamented upon hearing of the massacres.[38] When the rebellion was finally suppressed, she supported her Governor-General Lord Canning's policy of clemency towards those Indians who had not been directly involved in the mutiny.

In January 1858, Victoria's eldest daughter and namesake was married to Prince Frederick of Prussia, grandson of Frederick III, King of Prussia and Emperor of Germany. It was the first in a succession of matches that would ally her children with continental royal families and result in Victoria becoming known as the 'Grandmother of Europe'. In time, her direct descendants would occupy no fewer than ten European thrones.

It was during this time that the concept of a royal family, rather than just the monarch, as a focus of public interest began to gather ground, thanks in no small part to the sheer size of Victoria's brood. 'A family on the throne is an interesting idea,' opined a disapproving Walter Bagehot. 'It brings down the pride of sovereignty to the level of petty life.'[39] At its best, the 'petty life' that the queen and her consort espoused provided a model of domestic harmony for her people to emulate.

The advent of photography in 1839 proved hugely influential in perpetuating the image of domestic bliss. Whereas in the past, people had relied upon seeing painted and widely copied portraits of the royals, or at the very least their faces on the nation's coinage, now carefully curated photographs became 'the stock-in-trade of the monarchy-mongering business'.[40] The danger of shining a spotlight on the royal family through such media lay in if and when the apparent domestic harmony was disrupted by troublesome offspring. Then the family who had surrounded the sovereign like a glimmering halo might instead tarnish its reputation.

This was demonstrated by the exploits of the Prince of Wales. Years before, Victoria had confided that she dreaded 'when he will be of age and [I] can't hold him except by moral power. I try to shut my eyes to that terrible moment.'[41] By the time Bertie reached his twentieth birthday in 1861, he had gained the reputation of a playboy and kept company with a string of actresses and other women of ill repute. In some quarters, though, his genial manner and good humour were seen as a welcome contrast to his strait-laced and didactic parents. As well as making him a popular guest at high-society gatherings in both London and Paris, the prince's personable nature won favour on diplomatic visits, such as those he made to Canada and the USA in 1860. Once he had completed his studies at Oxford and Cambridge, the prince established himself more firmly in the fashionable social scene. Like his mother, his annual routine was dictated by the seasons – but with rather different results.

Whereas Victoria chose Balmoral or Osborne for her yearly retreats, her eldest son headed for the French Riviera. Here, as in London, he led a bohemian lifestyle that included regular trips to the opera, theatre and gambling halls in the company of his mistresses.

The glittering society that surrounded the Prince of Wales made his parents' court appear even more staid and dull. Most evenings, the entertainments on offer were confined to polite conversation and embroidery. The tone of court life was further dampened by Victoria's rigorous – and frequent – application of mourning etiquette. The death of a close relative of the king or queen obliged all courtiers to wear black and the royal couple would go into virtual seclusion for three months. Even distant connections required black to be worn and normal court activities to be suspended.

All of this was a mere prelude to what the year 1861 would usher in. It began with the death of the King of Prussia, which meant that Victoria's daughter and her husband were now Crown Prince and Princess of Prussia. Then, in March, the queen's mother, to whom she had grown closer since her marriage to Albert, died. Victoria was so grief-stricken that she suffered a complete nervous breakdown and retired from public life for several months. At the end of October, after reluctantly resuming her duties, Victoria took up residence at Windsor with her husband. Soon after, news broke that the Prince of Wales, who was just shy of his twentieth birthday, had been conducting a closet affair with an actress, Nellie Clifden. His dismayed parents feared that the carefully laid plans for Bertie's marriage to Princess Alexandra of Denmark now lay in tatters.

When Albert fell ill shortly afterwards, it was attributed to shock. In truth, his health had been deteriorating for some time and recent research suggests that he might have been suffering from stomach or bowel cancer. At first, Victoria found his illness 'tiresome' and was irritated to be deprived of his guidance at such a time.[42] But the seriousness of his condition struck her like a blow when, on 9 December, his doctors diagnosed typhoid fever. Five days later, the forty-two-year-old prince consort was dead.

The queen's grief spiralled to irreversible depths. 'All, all was over', she wrote in her diary on the day of her husband's death.[43] Having been utterly dependent upon him for more than twenty years,

Victoria refused to relinquish his hold over her. 'His wishes – his plans – about everything, his views about everything are to be my law!' she wrote. 'And no human power will make me swerve from what he decided and wished.'[44] The queen proceeded to immerse herself in a state of mourning the like of which the royal court had never seen. She wore black for the rest of her life, and her courtiers were obliged to follow suit for a prolonged period of official mourning, during which the palaces were swathed in black crepe. The grieving widow withdrew from all public and social appearances; only family and close attendants were admitted to her presence. She surrounded herself with images of her late husband and hung a photograph that had been taken of him on his deathbed over his pillow in every bed she slept in. The queen's journal and letters were filled with descriptions of her unfathomable misery. The latter were written on paper edged so deeply in black that there was barely room for her handwriting.

At first, the public were sympathetic. But when their queen showed no signs of resuming her duties after the conventional year of mourning, preferring the solitude of Windsor and only emerging into public to unveil one of the numerous memorials to her late husband, they grew uneasy. The semi-affectionate nickname 'widow of Windsor' soon gave way to more vociferous criticism. In 1864, a protestor pinned a notice onto the railings of Buckingham Palace that announced: 'These commanding premises to be let or sold in consequence of the late occupant's declining business.'[45] The same year, Victoria's absence from the opening of Parliament sparked widespread criticism in the press. Even The Times insisted: 'It is impossible for a recluse to occupy the British throne without a gradual weakening of that authority which the sovereign has been accustomed to exert.'[46]

With the popularity of the monarchy at its lowest ebb since Victoria's accession, a republican movement gathered momentum. In vain, the queen's ministers pleaded that she resume her full royal duties. But she refused to receive them in person, and when privy council meetings were held she sat in one room and they in another, with a secretary acting as go-between. Her behaviour became so extreme that there were whispers she had inherited the strain of madness that ran through the Hanoverian line. Fearful of upsetting their royal mistress's fragile mental state, her attendants pandered to her every whim, which only exacerbated the situation. Without Albert's controlling presence, the excessively indulged, obstinate and petulant child she had been found full expression. In private, her exasperated family and attendants complained of 'the extreme difficulty there was in managing her or in the slightest degree contradicting her'.[47]

But Victoria soon found a man to, if not replace Albert, then at least provide the dominating influence that she craved. John Brown had been a ghillie (outdoor servant) to the queen and her husband during their visits to Balmoral and became a close friend to her when she returned to the castle for prolonged periods after Albert's death. His brusque manner with the queen shocked contemporaries: none of her courtiers or ministers would have dared refer to her as 'woman' or admonish her so frankly as he did. But Victoria loved it. Brown was accustomed to 'speaking the truth fearlessly and telling me what he thought and considered to be "just and right," without flattery', she later reflected.[48] His domineering nature was tempered by an utter dedication to the queen's service. 'He had *no* thought but for me, my welfare, my comfort, my safety, my happiness.'[49]

John Brown became the queen's constant companion whenever she was at Balmoral, and the pair became so close that there were rumours of an affair or even a secret marriage – the queen was widely referred to as 'Mrs Brown'. The nature of their relationship will probably never be known for certain, particularly as Victoria's own account of it was later destroyed. When Brown died in March 1883, she gave herself over to intense mourning. 'The comfort of my daily life is gone,' she bewailed, 'the void is terrible – the loss is irreparable!'[50] The queen commissioned a life-sized statue of her faithful companion for the grounds of Balmoral and wrote a memoir of him. The latter was not intended for public circulation, but the queen's private secretary judged it scandalous enough to have it quietly destroyed.

Victoria's relationship with Brown had stoked the growing republican sentiment to 'fever-heat'. A letter written by Viscount Morley to one of his fellow radicals reveals the depth of resentment against 'the great dull Coburg at Balmoral . . . a pampered woman . . . whose sorrows are sentimental, selfish, undignified, gross. She is an anachronism . . . like a sorrowful poodle with indigestion, in cotton wool and silks when the mass of men and women have to toil through pressing misery, squalor, horror, with their aching hearts and without a word of sympathy.' A rally held in London's Trafalgar Square demanded her removal, and in 1871 a pamphlet entitled 'What does she do with it?' laid the queen's finances open to scrutiny. One political activist protested that there should be no more 'grants to princely paupers', while another won loud applause when he declared that a republic was only a matter of education and time.[51]

In stark contrast to his mother's sombre and cloistered existence, the Prince of Wales was busy indulging in all the pleasures that aristocratic society had to offer. His marriage to Alexandra of Denmark had done little to curb his sexual exploits, and in 1870 he was embroiled in a scandalous divorce case involving the wife of a Member of Parliament. 'To speak in rude and general terms', observed the Liberal prime minister William Gladstone, 'the Queen is invisible and the Prince of Wales is not respected.' What he termed 'this great crisis of Royalty' spelt grave danger for the crown.[52] A towering figure of Victorian politics, Gladstone had begun his first term of office in 1868 and would go on to serve a further three, more than any other British prime minister. His popularity among the working classes earned him the sobriquet 'The People's William' and he had a better grasp of public opinion than his sovereign. But Victoria harboured a strong dislike of him, which made her less inclined to heed his advice, no matter how sound.

While republicanism had become a more cohesive movement than at any time since the English Civil War, most of the public resentment against Victoria was prompted by seeing too little of her, rather than any deep-seated desire to abolish the institution of monarchy. As the Whig politician Lord Halifax pointed out to Victoria's private secretary: 'The mass of people expect a King or Queen to look and play the part. They want to see a Crown and Sceptre and all that sort of thing. They want the gilding for their money.'[53] Interestingly, it mattered little to Victoria's subjects that throughout her seclusion she had continued to fulfil her constitutional duties, working assiduously through all of the papers sent to her by government. The ceremonial and symbolic role of the monarch was much more important to them. Thus, as Bagehot shrewdly observed: 'The Queen has done almost as much to injure the popularity of the monarchy by her long retirement from public life as the most unworthy of her predecessors did by his profligacy and frivolity.'[54]

Time and again, Prime Minister Gladstone pressed upon his sovereign the 'vast importance' of the 'social and visible functions of the monarchy' for both 'the social well-being of the country' and the 'stability of the throne'. Even Victoria's daughter, Princess Alice, became exasperated with her refusal to grasp the seriousness of the situation. 'She thinks the monarchy will last her time . . . and we must sit quietly and let the approaching calamity crush us without an effort.'[55]

It took a near-catastrophe to salvage the situation. In November 1871, almost exactly ten years since his father's death from typhoid, the Prince of Wales fell ill with the same disease. For several weeks, the nation held its breath as the life of their future king hung in the balance. When Bertie recovered, there was widespread rejoicing, sounding the death knell of the republican movement. Gladstone was quick to take advantage by organising a service of thanksgiving at St Paul's Cathedral. On 27 February 1872, Victoria drove in state through London for the first time since Albert's death and was rewarded by 'wonderful enthusiasm and astounding affectionate loyalty'.[56]

The thanksgiving celebration proved a turning point for the monarchy. Not only did it quash any remaining republican sentiment, it also established a precedent for the large-scale ceremonial occasions that would become the hallmark of the British royal family in the following century. In the past, such ceremonies had been arranged as courtly pageants in which the majority of the nation played no part, but the rise of the popular press made them accessible to everyone, no matter how far removed from the scene. The queen's withdrawal has been compared to a 'chrysalis . . . from which emerged a transformed monarchy more mysterious and more popular than ever before'.[57]

The increasing prominence of royal ceremony had a profound effect on Victoria herself, too. Seeing the adoration of the crowds both surprised and comforted her, breaking down the barriers she had erected around herself over the past two decades. Gradually, she let go of some of the misery in which she had been steeped since Albert's death. Even though she still eschewed certain high-profile duties such as the state opening of Parliament and insisted on spending prolonged periods at Balmoral and Osborne, her popularity continued to soar for the remainder of her long reign.

Victoria's court was reinvigorated by the revival of receptions and dinners for visiting dignitaries, such as the Shah of Persia's state visit in 1873. But it was hardly the glittering social centre that it had been for much of the monarchy's history. The queen's limited education meant that she lacked the ability to converse with people whose interests and backgrounds differed from her own. 'I personally never heard her say anything at dinner which I remembered next morning,' Lord Ribblesdale complained. 'She ate fast and seldom laughed.'[58] Given that plates were cleared as soon as the sovereign had finished eating, newcomers were quietly advised to prioritise their meal over polite conversation. A visit to court was uncomfortable in other ways. The queen fervently believed that overheated rooms were bad for one's health, so visitors and staff were forced to shiver in silence.

Having re-emerged into public life, Victoria played a more active role in government than ever before. By 1874, she had seen eight different prime ministers come and go, and the general election held in February that year resulted in the Conservative leader Benjamin Disraeli taking office for the second time. Disraeli did more to shape the modern Conservative Party than any other politician, and his administration is often identified with the golden age of the British Empire. His battles with the Liberal Party leader William Gladstone dominated the 1870s. A charming and erudite man, Disraeli had quickly won favour with the queen thanks to his deferential manner and judicious use of flattery – something that she had not found in a prime minister since her beloved 'Lord M'. He once advised that when addressing the queen, 'You should lay it on with a trowel.'[59] Their flirtatious relationship called to mind the days of Elizabeth I and her courtiers: Disraeli even referred to Victoria as 'Faerie Queen', borrowing from Edmund Spenser's famous poem.

Encouraged by Disraeli, and freed from Albert's domineering influence, Victoria finally felt able to make a meaningful contribution to the political life of her country. The innate strong will that had not been seen for many years gradually began to re-emerge. Her long-suffering private secretary, Sir Henry Ponsonby, recorded: 'When she insists that 2 and 2 make 5, I say that I cannot help thinking they make 4. She replies there may be some truth in what I say, but she knows they make 5. Thereupon I drop the discussion.'[60] Her obstinate opinions were often well grounded, though, and her longevity commanded respect in the ever-changing political arena, as did her exceptional powers of memory.

The queen soon grew so self-assured that members of Disraeli's government feared she might disrupt the fine balance of power between monarch and constitution. Lord Derby cautioned his prime minister against 'encouraging her in too large ideas of her personal power, and too great indifference to what the public expects'. The fact that Victoria never sought to overstep her authority owes much to Disraeli's careful handling of her. 'I never deny; I never contradict; I sometimes forget', he once confided.[61] But it was also thanks to the queen's understanding that her influence could more effectively be used in a neutral and detached way, rather than her becoming 'one combatant among many' in the political arena. Gladstone described this as a 'subtle and silent, yet an almost entire transformation' of the monarch's role.[62] It provided a blueprint for all future monarchs up to the present day.

The partnership between queen and prime minister was for the most part harmonious and fruitful. But Disraeli had a harder time of it whenever issues close to Victoria's heart arose. Religion was one of these. The queen described herself as 'Protestant to the very *heart's core*' and it was thanks to the pressure she applied that Disraeli pushed through the Public Worship Regulation Act in 1874. This aimed to restrict the growth of Catholic practices, which had been steadily developing within sections of the Church of England since the early 1830s.[63] Two years later, Victoria was instrumental in the passing of the Royal Titles Act, whereby she was created Empress of India. This was almost certainly prompted by her desire to assert her status as the most senior monarch in Europe, setting her above the emperors of Russia and the newly unified Germany.

Now that she was an empress as well as a queen, Victoria began to take a much closer interest in her colonial territories. Although her empire was the largest in the world, the expansionist designs of her European peers led to conflict and there was not a single year of her long reign in which the British army was not engaged in defending her territories. In Victoria's favour was the fact that many of her children had married into Europe's royal dynasties. Most had proved as fertile as their mother. Victoria became a grandmother at the age of thirty-nine and a great-grandmother at the age of sixty. She greeted the news of each new offspring with the same lack of enthusiasm that she had shown towards her own children. 'When they come at the rate of three a year it becomes a cause of mere anxiety for my own children and of no great interest', she wrote to her eldest daughter Vicky upon the birth of the latter's eighth child.[64] The arrival of her great-grandson Edward (the future Edward VIII) in June 1894 prompted greater pride. 'It seems that it has never happened in this country that there should be three direct heirs as well as the sovereign alive,' she reflected.[65] For much of the monarchy's history, the shortage of heirs had been a source of instability; now there was almost an excess of them.

In 1880, Disraeli was defeated and Gladstone became prime minister for the second time. The queen was utterly dismayed. She had made no secret of her intense hatred of 'that madman Gladstone', and the five years of his ministry eroded the harmonious collaboration between crown and Parliament that Disraeli had fostered.[66] Victoria's mood was hardly improved by the fall that she suffered in March 1883, which left her plagued with rheumatism and painfully aware of her advancing years. Even now, after reigning for forty-five years, she did not feel secure on her throne. Republicanism might have declined, but the assassination attempt she had suffered during her visit to Eton the previous year (the last of eight during the course of her reign) had taken its toll on her confidence. The death of her fourth son, Leopold, in 1884 was another cruel blow. He suffered from haemophilia, a genetic disorder that afflicted a number of the queen's descendants.[67]

It was with some difficulty that Victoria's ministers persuaded her to go through with the celebrations for her Golden Jubilee in 1887. She refused to wear her crown and robes of state for the service of thanksgiving at Westminster Abbey, substituting them for a bonnet laced with diamonds and a simple landau coach. This was in order to emphasise the public role that she had sought to play in recent years. She had supported housing reform, public works schemes for the unemployed and the Sunday opening of museums. In so doing, she had proved more in tune with the mood of her subjects than some of her ministers, and she rightly judged that the simple style adopted for her jubilee elevated her above the opulent trappings of royalty.

Victoria's popular touch extended to other parts of her vast realm. She did not share her British subjects' natural xenophobia but expressed a 'very strong feeling (and she has few stronger) that the natives and coloured races should be treated with every kindness and affection, as brothers, not – as alas! Englishmen too often do – as totally different beings to ourselves, fit only to be crushed and shot down'.[68] Following her Golden Jubilee, the queen welcomed the first of many Indian servants into her household. Abdul Karim soon filled the place in her affections left vacant since the death of John Brown. He taught her Hindustani, introduced her to curry and fed her growing interest in Indian culture – as testified by the extraordinarily opulent Durbar Room that she installed at Osborne, which resembled more a wedding cake than a traditional royal reception room.

Victoria might have been progressive in her attitude towards different races, but when it came to the campaign for Women's Rights, she was deeply conservative. 'It was dangerous, unchristian and unnatural' to give women the vote, she said – a 'mad, wicked folly'. Neither was she in favour of greater democracy, as espoused by such legislation as the second Reform Act of 1867. Addressing herself in the third person, she wrote to the Liberal politician William

Forster: 'She cannot and will not be the Queen of a democratic monarchy', warning that those radicals who had agitated for reform 'must look for *another monarch*; and she doubts they will find one'.[69]

What she lacked in modernity, Victoria made up for in longevity. On 23 September 1896, the seventy-seven-year-old queen beat her grandfather George III's record and became Britain's longest-reigning monarch. It was with some pride that she recorded in her journal: 'Today is the day on which I have reigned longer, by a day, than any English sovereign.'[70] Resisting calls to mark this momentous achievement with a public ceremony, Victoria declared that she would celebrate her sixtieth year on the throne instead. The accession day (20 June) was commemorated by a service of thanksgiving at St George's Chapel, Windsor. A more public celebration took place two days later, on 22 June 1897, when the queen rode in a carriage on a six-mile procession through London, witnessed by vast crowds of well-wishers and troops from all over the empire. An open-air service was held outside St Paul's so that Victoria could take part from within her carriage rather than climb the steps to the cathedral.

At the suggestion of her colonial secretary, the Diamond Jubilee was made a Festival of Empire. Among the gifts that Victoria sent across the empire to commemorate the occasion was a white silk shawl to the American abolitionist and former slave Harriet Tubman. The significance of the colour was lost on neither woman: white was synonymous with freedom and power.[71]

But it was charity, rather than empire, that would prove increasingly important in safeguarding the future of the monarchy. Victoria shared her late husband's view that the purpose of royalty was to be the 'headship of philanthropy'. It has been estimated that during the course of her reign she donated around £650,000 (£40 million) to charitable causes.[72] From her Diamond Jubilee to the present day, all major royal celebratory events have had a fundraising element.

By now, Victoria's health was fading rapidly. Lame from rheumatism and confined to a wheelchair, she was losing both her sight and her memory. Many expected she would appoint her eldest son as regent. Bertie's marriage to Princess Alexandra in 1863 had lent him at least a semblance of respectability, not to mention a rapidly expanding brood of children. Attractive and amiable, his wife devoted herself to their upbringing and was apparently content for her husband to seek diversion in his round of unrelenting social engagements. She turned a blind eye to his mistresses, too, who included the actress Lillie Langtry and the clever and vivacious society hostess Alice Keppel, whose affair with Bertie would dominate his later life.

Aware of her heir's scandalous exploits, Victoria kept going by sheer force of will. She had other motivations, too. Worsening relations between Britain and Kaiser Wilhelm II of Germany, Victoria's grandson, were the source of intense anxiety for the ageing queen, as was the onset of the second Boer War in South Africa. Determination to help counter both of these threats to her realm drove her on. 'After the Prince Consort's death I wished to die,' she confided to a correspondent, 'but *now* I wish to live and do what I can for my country and those I love.'[73] The queen's contribution to the morale of her army was considerable. She inspected troops from her wheelchair, visited those who returned sick or injured, and sent a tin of chocolate to each soldier serving in the field at Christmas.

In 1900, Victoria spent her own Christmas at Osborne, according to the tradition she had started with Prince Albert. It had been a gloomy year, punctuated by the deaths of her beloved second son Alfred ('poor darling Affie') and of her Danish grandson Prince Christian. Her eldest child, Vicky, was dying of spinal cancer and the queen was painfully aware that her own death was imminent. 'It is a horrible year,' she reflected, 'nothing but sadness & horrors of one kind & another.'[74] No longer able to write her journal, she dictated it to her granddaughter, Princess Helena, but even this proved too much in the end. The last entry in the diary that she had kept for almost seventy years was dated 13 January 1901.[75] Nine days later, surrounded by her family, Britain's longest-reigning monarch breathed her last.

It is perhaps no surprise that the woman who had transformed mourning into an art form had prepared detailed instructions for her burial. As well as the arrangements for her lying-in-state and funeral (which was to be bedecked with white and gold rather than black, ironically), she had also left secret orders to her dressers about the items that were to be buried with her. Mementos of Albert predominated, of course, and a photograph of the dead queen shows her swathed in her wedding veil. When her body was placed in the coffin, it rested on Albert's dressing-gown and cloak, a plaster cast of his hand by her side. Only when the late queen's family had left the room were her other, more secret, instructions carried out. A picture of John Brown and a lock of his hair were placed in her left hand, hidden from view by a bunch of flowers. His mother's wedding ring, which he had given her shortly before his death, was placed on one of her fingers.

Once the coffin had been sealed, it was conveyed across the Solent between two rows of battleships and cruisers for the funeral at Windsor on 2 February. It was then interred next to Albert's in the royal mausoleum at Frogmore in Windsor Great Park.

There had been a palpable sense of disbelief among the silent crowds who had lined the processional route from Victoria Station to Paddington, from where the queen's body had been taken to Windsor for burial. Just prior to her death, Lytton Strachey had summed up the public mood:

> It appeared as if some monstrous reversal of the course of nature was about to take place. The vast majority of her subjects had never known a time when Queen Victoria had not been reigning over them. She had become an indissoluble part of their whole scheme of things, and that they were about to lose her appeared a scarcely possible thought.[76]

Victoria had been the mainstay of British life for more than sixty-three years, one of the few constants in a rapidly changing, often turbulent world. She had symbolised one of the most self-confident ages in British history: an age when it led the world in industry, engineering and transport, and boasted 'an empire upon which the sun never set'. 'In her the public saw the British Empire', the *Chicago Tribune* reported at the Diamond Jubilee celebrations of 1897. 'She was a symbol, an allegory of England's grandeur, and the might of the British nation.'[77] Likewise, Victoria's style of monarchy, with its strong emphasis on morality and family, had inspired the values of the age. The crown had also become more closely aligned with the views of its people. Victoria's last prime minister, Lord Salisbury, remarked: 'I have always felt that when I knew what the Queen thought I knew pretty certainly what view her subjects would take.'[78]

Victoria's main contribution to the evolution – and survival – of the monarchy, though, had been to make it a focus for pomp and pageantry on a scale never seen before. At the beginning of her reign, one minister had gloomily remarked: 'Some nations have a gift for ceremonial . . . In England the case is exactly the reverse . . . some malignant spell broods over all our most solemn ceremonials, and inserts into them some feature which makes them all ridiculous.'[79] By its end, Britain's royal ceremonial occasions were the envy of the world. The late queen had provided a glittering example of how spectacle could not only bolster the monarchy but reinforce the self-esteem of the nation. Monarchy and pageantry had become inseparable and have remained so ever since.

The popularity of the monarchy had been waning in 1837; by 1901 it had been spectacularly restored. Not since Elizabeth I had a monarch achieved such mythic status. Most towns in Britain have a statue of Victoria, or a park, hospital, street, public house or theatre named after her. Even though the British empire has long since fragmented, there are still memorials to her throughout the former colonies. She even inspired widespread devotion in America, which had long since rejected British royal authority. 'Had Victoria been on the throne, instead of George III, or if we had postponed our rebellion until Queen Victoria resigned, it would not have been necessary,' remarked the American secretary of state, William M. Evarts, in 1878.[80]

The only drawback to the late queen's success was that it made her a hard act to follow. As the novelist Henry James remarked: 'We all feel a bit motherless today: mysterious little Victoria is dead and fat vulgar Edward is king.'[81]

Edward VII (1901–10)

'A thorough and cunning lazybones'

THE FIRST MONARCH of the House of Saxe-Coburg and Gotha, Albert Edward – 'Bertie', as he was commonly known – had waited longer for the throne than any other heir apparent in British history.[1] Yet throughout the forty years of his maturity, he had been deprived of the opportunity to familiarise himself with anything other than ceremonial duties. His mother had refused Prime Minister Gladstone's suggestion that the Prince of Wales should see copies of the cabinet papers that were sent to her. As a result, by the time his mother died in January 1901, the fifty-nine-year-old prince had grown so used to his indulgent lifestyle that becoming king held little appeal.

Even so, he was quick to make a break with the past and informed the privy council that he would reign as Edward VII because the name Albert would forever be associated with his late father. The new king's reputation as a playboy soon spawned the nickname 'Edward the Caresser', and his court was instantly transformed into the vibrant nexus of society that royal courts had been for centuries. 'There was nothing dowdy about our King Edward,' observed the contemporary novelist Rose Macaulay. 'He set the stakes high, and all who could afford it played.'[2] His love of glamorous social gatherings and entertainments enhanced, rather than tainted, his royal majesty. 'He was every inch The King of England and every inch The First Gentleman in Europe,' declared one admiring aristocrat.[3]

The new court was the subject of intense scrutiny and endless gossip at all levels of society. 'What, at each successive meal, forms the daily courses of the royal table. How much is paid for the tea, coffee, tobacco and snuff at Buckingham Palace. The exact work allotted to each of His Majesty's dressers . . . Such are the problems that exercise the speculation of innumerable well-paid writers, or are discussed . . . by thousands of firesides', complained one *Times* correspondent.[4] Fashionable society was quick to imitate the style of the new king and his circle. An oyster satin dress worn by his mistress Alice Keppel was copied by other court ladies before filtering down to the wider public, while her royal lover popularised such sartorial innovations as side creases in trousers and leaving the lowest button of a waistcoat unfastened.

Edward VII breathed new life into Buckingham Palace and Windsor Castle, which he said resembled 'Scottish funeral parlours' rather than seats of majesty, and lavished huge sums on their refurbishment.[5] He also superintended the redesign of the royal parks surrounding Buckingham Palace, widening the Mall and commissioning a magnificent memorial statue to his mother in a new public space directly in front of the palace.

A generous subsidy from Parliament of £470,000 (equivalent to around £37 million today) per annum, along with some astute personal investments and the rents from the Duchy of Cornwall, made all of this possible – and made Edward the highest-paid monarch in British history. He did not fritter it all away on social diversions. One of his first acts was to launch a 'Coronation Appeal' in aid of London hospitals, which raised a colossal £600,000 (equivalent to around £47 million today).[6]

A reminder of the new king's advancing age was provided when the coronation itself had to be postponed because of his ill health. After undergoing an operation to treat appendicitis and peritonitis, Edward VII was finally crowned in a shortened ceremony held in August 1902. He clearly gloried in the pageantry of the event, as he did in other major royal occasions. His ancestor Henry VIII would have approved of Edward's state portrait by Sir Luke Fildes, which shows the king bedecked in his coronation robes striking a pose very reminiscent of the larger-than-life Tudor sovereign. Decades of indulgent living meant that he shared his ancestor's corpulence, too – members of his close acquaintance nicknamed him 'Tum Tum'.[7]

The new king's Scottish subjects refused to accept him as Edward VII, given that he was the first Edward to hold the crown there, and it was even omitted in loyal addresses given by the Church of Scotland. To curry favour, the new king and his consort embarked upon a tour soon after the coronation, visiting the west coast of Scotland, the Isle of Man and Wales. In 1903, they travelled to Ireland, where the initially frosty reception was thawed by Edward's naturally genial manner. He toured various parts of the country by motor car, a relatively new invention that he helped to popularise, and won further acclaim by attending a number of horse-racing events, a passion shared with his Irish subjects.

Edward VII was the first monarch to be proclaimed Emperor of India and ruler 'of the British Dominions beyond the seas'. Arthur Balfour, leader of the House of Commons, had reminded him of this upon his accession: 'All the patriotic sentiment which makes such an Empire possible centres in him . . . and everything which emphasises his personality to our kinsmen across the seas must be a gain to the Monarchy and the Empire.'⁸ The new king took a keen interest in overseas affairs, something for which he was better equipped than for many of his other duties. By the time he came to the throne, he had travelled more widely than any other British monarch and, thanks to his favourite annual retreats, could speak fluent French and German. He was also closely related to the rulers of Denmark, Germany, Greece, Portugal, Russia and Spain, justifying his nickname as the 'Uncle of Europe'. Like his mother, he was free of racial prejudice and condemned it in others.

Despite Britain's blood ties with Germany (Kaiser Wilhelm II was Edward's nephew), relations between the two countries had been deteriorating for a number of years. In 1902, Edward reluctantly agreed to host a visit by the Kaiser at Sandringham, the Norfolk estate that he had acquired forty years earlier when Prince of Wales. The king's celebrated charm worked no effect upon his nephew, however, and when the latter returned to Germany Edward was heard to exclaim: 'Thank God, he's gone.'⁹

The king subsequently arranged an ambitious overseas tour for the spring of 1903 – the first state visit abroad by a British monarch since Victoria's to France in 1855. The ambitious itinerary had been planned by Edward himself and was not without controversy. To the horror of his cabinet, not to mention the Church of England, he insisted upon visiting the pope in Rome – the first time a British or English sovereign had done so. In his more familiar stomping ground, Paris, the king met with an unusually frosty reception, thanks to the British government's failure to mark the centenary of the French Revolution fourteen years earlier. But Edward's affability and charm won the day, and the tour was declared a triumph.

Edward VII was not the only member of the royal family to be regularly seen abroad. Shortly after his accession, he had sent his son and heir, George, on the most extensive imperial tour yet made by a future monarch. The itinerary included Australia, New Zealand, Ceylon, Singapore, Mauritius, South Africa and Canada. Representing the British crown across the empire in this way set a model for what would become a principal duty of the monarchy for the next hundred years and more.

The king and his son bucked the tradition of hostility between a monarch and his heir that had dominated the previous two centuries. Determined not to repeat his mother's mistakes, Edward VII made sure to involve Prince George, who had become heir apparent upon the death of his elder brother Albert in 1891, in the business of government. With George having spent most of his young life in the navy, this was something for which the prince was wholly unprepared. But he had always been the more confident of Edward's two sons and was quick to learn. Shortly after his grandmother Queen Victoria's death, George had inherited her private secretary, Lord Stamfordham, and had so benefited from his wisdom and experience that he later remarked: 'He taught me to be a King.'[10]

Rather than feeling threatened by the prince's often forcefully expressed opinions, his father encouraged them. These opinions sometimes chimed with the public mood, such as when George declared upon his return from the imperial tour that many of the people he had met thought 'the old country must wake up'.[11] In a similar vein, after his tour of India in 1905–6, George was disturbed by the sense of superiority he had encountered among many white civil servants and called for 'wider sympathy' among the British ruling elite there.

Although his father had once called him a 'thorough and cunning lazybones', King Edward played as active a role in government as his royal prerogative allowed. The Treasury minister Sir Edward Hamilton confidently reported that the king was 'more constitutionally minded than was the Queen', but Edward found the limitations of his role deeply frustrating at times, particularly as he had suffered forty powerless years as king-in-waiting. 'The position of a British monarch is one of great influence but little direct power, at any rate in matters of importance', reflected a member of the Privy Council in 1904.[12] The king was enough of a realist to accept this and made the most of what little authority he had. He took back control of a number of offices that his mother had delegated to others, such as the supervision of the royal parks. He also revived the tradition of opening Parliament, something that had lapsed during Victoria's long reign. But the area that most interested the new king was foreign policy. He took his role as nominal head of the armed forces extremely seriously and threw himself headlong into the controversial issue of army and naval reform.

In April 1908, Henry Campbell-Bannerman resigned as prime minister on the grounds of ill health and was replaced by his fellow Liberal, Herbert Asquith. The king received the news while staying in Biarritz and signalled his disapproval by refusing to return home, which meant that Asquith was obliged to make the long journey to the south of France to receive his formal appointment. Asquith's relations with the king improved little during his administration. Although they were both opposed to giving votes to women, they differed on almost every other aspect of policy.

The following year was dominated by a constitutional crisis when the Tory majority in the House of Lords rejected Asquith's 'People's Budget', which among other measures included high taxation for landowners. The state opening of Parliament had been a more tense affair than usual and was described as a 'beastly humbug' by a young Australian journalist called Keith Murdoch (father of Rupert). At the heart of the conflict was a class war, which so depressed the king that he introduced his son and heir George to the Secretary of State for War as 'the last king of England'.[13]

On 21 February 1910, the king and queen opened Parliament. It would be Edward's last state appearance. A heavy smoker, he suffered from increasing bouts of bronchitis and collapsed during his customary visit to Biarritz the following month. While controversy continued to rage in Parliament, the king, whose condition was kept secret, attracted criticism for remaining in France. He was deemed fit enough to travel home in late April, but upon his arrival at Buckingham Palace it was clear that he was still very sick. His wife Alexandra was called back from a visit to Greece and upon her arrival was shocked to find her husband frail and confused. He even failed to recognise his long-standing mistress, Alice Keppel. When on 6 May the Prince of Wales told Edward that his horse, Witch of Air, had won at Kempton Park races, it sparked a moment of lucidity. 'Yes, I have heard of it,' he replied. 'I am very glad.' They were the last coherent words he spoke; he died that night.

'His lighter side . . . obscured the fact that he had both insight and influence,' observed the late king's grandson, Edward VIII.[14] *The Times* agreed that Edward VII's authority was 'not the same as that exercised by Queen Victoria but in some respects it was almost the stronger of the two'.[15] Despite his initial reluctance, it was obvious that Edward had enjoyed being king. The epoch that bore his name epitomised his energy, charm and brashness, and above all the freedom from the strictures of Victorianism. 'If the Victorian era was the era of respectability, the Edwardian will probably be known as the epoch of that frisky futility known as smartness', sneered one commentator a year before the king's death.[16]

Thirteen years later, Rose Macaulay provided a more reflective – and, arguably, accurate – assessment:

Those brief ten years we call Edwardian now seem like a short spring day. They were a gay and yet an earnest time. A time of social reform on the one hand, and social brilliance on the other . . . The onrush of motor-cars and the decline of bicycles and the horse; extravagant country house parties at which royalty consented to be entertained, with royal bonhomie and royal exactions of etiquette.[17]

It was a legacy that won Edward VII the abiding affection of his people, even if it was not one that his mother would have approved of.

Part 7

The Windsors (1910 onwards)

'The Merry Wives of Saxe-Coburg-Gotha'

The House of Windsor was created by a change of name rather than bloodline. During the First World War, George V judged it expedient to rid his family of their German surname of Saxe-Coburg-Gotha and replace it with the quintessentially English 'Windsor'. Although the Windsor monarchs weathered the storms of two world wars, affairs of the heart posed an arguably greater threat to their crown. The abdication of Edward VIII so that he could marry the American divorcee Wallis Simpson was followed nineteen years later by Elizabeth II's sister almost giving up her royal status for love. In more recent times, the queen's grandson, Prince Harry, resigned from his royal duties for the sake of his wife, another American divorcee. The marital crises of the 1990s and the death of Princess Diana shook the monarchy to its core, but Elizabeth II's extraordinary longevity saved it from the brink of abyss.

George V (1910–36)

'Grandpa England'

THERE WAS MORE than an echo of Henry VIII about Britain's new king, George V. Born a spare heir, he had not expected to inherit the throne until the sudden death of his elder brother. But he had always been the more popular of the two princes. His grandmother's prime minister, Gladstone, described him as 'not only likeable but perhaps loveable'.[1] Like his Tudor predecessor, George was prone to fierce and often terrifying bouts of temper, particularly towards his offspring. Soon after becoming heir to the throne, he had been encouraged to take as his wife his dead brother's fiancée and second cousin once removed: Princess Mary of Teck, a great-granddaughter of George III. She would not be the first of six wives, though, for the marriage was a resounding success and she quickly produced the required heirs. Their firstborn was a son, Edward, known to the family by his seventh name, David.

George V was devasted by the death of his father. 'I have lost my best friend and the best of fathers', he lamented. 'I never had a [cross] word with him in my life. I am heart-broken and overwhelmed with grief.'[2] Unlike his late grandmother, he did not allow grief to stand in the way of his official duties, but began his reign in decisive manner. In preparation for his opening of Parliament in February 1911, the Accession Declaration Act was passed because George objected to the anti-Catholic wording of his speech. From thenceforth, British monarchs were simply required to declare their Protestant faith and their promise to uphold the Protestant succession.

George V and Queen Mary's joint coronation took place in June that year. The new king found the long and tiring ceremony 'a terrible ordeal'. No fewer than 60,000 troops lined the route from Buckingham

Palace to Westminster Abbey, and the ceremony was followed by a Festival of Empire at The Crystal Palace, built for the Great Exhibition in 1851.[3] The king and queen then embarked upon a visit to Ireland and Scotland before travelling to India for their official instalment as Emperor and Empress. The ceremony was the most spectacular in British imperial history. A new Imperial Crown of India was made for the occasion and is still part of the crown jewels, although it has not been worn since. As part of the proceedings, George declared the shifting of the Indian capital from Calcutta to Delhi.

The new king soon had matters to attend to back home. The controversy over Asquith's budget rumbled on. Even though the House of Lords had finally approved it in April 1910, the government was determined to prevent a repeat of its earlier obstructiveness. The proposed Parliament Bill aimed to restrict the Lords' powers for the first time in its history. But it needed the king's assent and he was extremely reluctant to give it. Only after intense pressure from the cabinet did he give way, grumbling: 'I disliked having to do this very much.'[4] The controversy was still raging when George became embroiled in another, of an altogether more personal nature. A republican journalist claimed the king was a secret bigamist. The story had little basis and George made light of it at first. But he could not let such a slur pass and won a libel action against the publication – the first such action taken by the royal family.

Once the Parliament Bill had been passed, the prime minister wasted no time in putting it into effect over the contentious issue of Home Rule in Ireland. The king had strong opinions of his own, but Asquith cautioned him not to become embroiled in the matter. The prime minister's remarks provide one of the most vivid illustrations of how far relations between crown and government had changed over the centuries. 'We now have a well-established tradition of two hundred years that, in the last resort, the occupant of the Throne accepts and acts upon the advice of his ministers,' Asquith told him. 'The sovereign may have lost something of his personal power and authority, but the Crown has been thereby removed from the storms and vicissitudes of party politics . . . the Crown would [otherwise] become the football of contending factions.'[5]

* * *

On 4 August 1914, the king sat down to write his diary. After taking note of the weather, he recorded: 'I held a Council at 10.45 to declare War on Germany, it is a terrible catastrophe but it is not our fault . . . Please God it may soon be over.'[6] His prayer would not be answered. Far from being 'over by Christmas', as many believed it would be, the First World War (or Great War, as it was known) dragged on for four long and arduous years. It was the largest and most devastating conflict in history. More than 70 million military personnel were mobilised, around 9 million of whom were killed, along with 10 million civilians.

Its origins belied the hugely destructive war that it would become. On 28 June 1914, Archduke Franz Ferdinand, heir to the Austro-Hungarian Empire, was assassinated by a Bosnian Serb Yugoslav nationalist. Austria-Hungary declared war on Serbia the following month and, thanks to a network of interlocking alliances, the great powers of Europe were quickly drawn into the conflict. By the end of July, it had escalated from a local war to a global one. On 1 August, Germany declared war on Russia in support of Austria-Hungary and the following day France entered the conflict on the side of Russia. The same day, Kaiser Wilhelm demanded passage through Belgium so that his army might attack France. When this was refused, he invaded Belgium on 3 August and declared war on France.

George V preferred stamp-collecting to state affairs and had a strong aversion to war. 'We shall try all we can to keep out of this and shall remain neutral,' he had apparently told his first cousin, Prince Henry of Prussia, upon his visit to Buckingham Palace on 26 July 1914.[7] The prince reported this to his brother, Kaiser Wilhelm II, who exaggerated it and claimed that his uncle the British king had broken his word. The web of kinship so carefully spun across Europe's rulers by Queen Victoria had exacerbated rather than resolved the rising tensions.

King George was acutely aware that his desire for Britain to remain neutral chimed with the wishes of his people. But with France under threat of German occupation, the conflict was edging perilously close. Ten years earlier, Britain had signed the *entente cordiale* with France, putting an end to the centuries-old rivalry between the two countries and providing security for both in the face of growing

German aggression. Now, that alliance was being put to the test. 'At this moment public opinion here is dead against our joining in the War,' the king wrote in his journal, 'but I think it will be impossible to keep out of it as we cannot allow France to be smashed.'[8]

It is to George V's credit that once Britain had entered the war, he threw himself behind it. Recognising the symbolic importance of his role, he wore uniform throughout the conflict and resided at Buckingham Palace, eschewing his favoured retreat of Sandringham so that he could be at the centre of the war effort. The king had inherited none of his father's extravagance, but, in sympathy with the hardships his people were enduring, he now adopted an even more frugal lifestyle than usual – including, from April 1915, teetotalism.

The years that George had spent in the navy equipped him well for the 450 visits he made to Britain's troops, some of which took him to the heart of the conflict. In December 1914 he travelled to the western front and, during the course of the visit, was thrown from his horse, fracturing his pelvis. The soldiers whom the king met appreciated his lack of pretension and his understanding of military affairs. The fact that his eldest son was in the Grenadier Guards and his younger son, Prince Albert ('Bertie'), was a serving officer in the navy also won him credit. As well as meeting British troops in the field, the king made no fewer than three hundred visits to hospitals, munitions factories and shipyards, and boosted morale further by awarding 50,000 medals for gallantry.

For all George's efforts, as the war progressed criticism of the monarchy increased. This had nothing to do with the king's actions, but related to his heritage. Even though he was the first British monarch since 1830 to speak English with no trace of a German accent, both he and his wife were of German descent and bore German titles, as did various other members of the royal family. Every single British monarch from George I to Queen Victoria had married a German. Early in the war, George V had been obliged to accept the replacement of his first cousin by marriage, Prince Louis of Battenberg, as first sea lord. He had also come under intense pressure to dismiss eight knights of the Garter who were from enemy nations. Still the ill feeling persisted. When the celebrated writer H.G. Wells referred to Britain's 'alien and uninspiring court', the king retorted: 'I may be uninspiring, but I'll be damned if I'm alien!'[9]

Unjustified though such criticism was, George was enough of a pragmatist to recognise that action must be taken. On 17 July 1917, he announced by royal proclamation that all descendants of Queen Victoria would henceforth bear the name of Windsor. He also renounced the use of the titles of princes of Saxe-Coburg and Gotha for himself and his heirs, although retained the succession to those duchies. The surnames of other senior royals were also anglicised: the Prince and Princess of Teck became the Cambridges and the Battenbergs became the Mountbattens. By the same proclamation, he restricted the use of the titles 'Royal Highness' and 'Prince or Princess of Great Britain and Ireland', and informed the privy council that he and his wife would encourage their children to take English, rather than German, spouses. Upon hearing the news, his first cousin, Kaiser Wilhelm II, sneeringly remarked that he looked forward to seeing a production of 'The Merry Wives of Saxe-Coburg-Gotha'.[10]

The same year, George faced an even greater test of his family loyalty when his first cousin, Tsar Nicholas II of Russia (whom he closely resembled), was overthrown in the Russian Revolution. At first, the British government offered political asylum to Nicholas and his family, but fears that this might ignite a revolution in Britain prompted the king to oppose the idea. The offer was subsequently withdrawn – with fatal consequences. On 17 July 1918, Tsar Nicholas and his immediate family were assassinated by the Bolsheviks. 'It was a foul murder', George lamented. 'I was devoted to Nicky, who was the kindest of men and a thorough gentleman: loved his country and people.'[11] The king never expressed regret about his part in the tragedy and it has been mooted that he had encouraged plans for the British Secret Service to undertake a rescue mission.

On 7 August 1918, the king visited the western front for the second time that year. It was well timed: the same day, the British army secured victory when it at last broke through the German line. An armistice was signed on 11 November. 'Today has indeed been a wonderful day,' George reflected, 'the greatest in the history of the

Country.'[12] Wild celebrations were staged across the kingdom. The king and queen appeared on the balcony of Buckingham Palace and the noise from the crowds was too great for George to deliver the speech he had prepared. On the following five days, the royal couple drove through the streets of London and attended ceremonies of thanksgiving at Westminster and St Paul's. The conclusion of a peace treaty in June 1919 prompted further celebrations. In November that year, a national act of remembrance was established and the king supported the idea of a two minutes' silence at 11 a.m. on 11 November. On the same date in 1920, he unveiled the cenotaph memorial in Whitehall, which has been the focus of Remembrance Day commemorations ever since.

After the euphoria of victory had died down, Britain was left to reflect on the devastation. Around 886,000 British soldiers had been killed, including 57,470 casualties on a single day (1 July 1916) during the Battle of the Somme. The economic cost was catastrophically high, too. For George V, the personal toll was all too obvious. The fifty-three-year-old king had aged more in the previous four years than he had since reaching maturity. He was keenly aware of being almost the only monarch in Europe to retain his throne: those of Austria, Germany, Greece, Russia and Spain had all fallen to revolution and war. Being a monarch who reigned, rather than ruled, had been key to this survival. He had borne far less responsibility for the outbreak of war than the Russian Tsar or the German Kaiser, and had instead acted as a symbol of the national effort without having to lead it in any meaningful way. The same was not true of the numerous British ministers and generals whose careers were brought to an abrupt end by the war – indeed, the king was the only person in the British political sphere who held the same position at the end of the war as at its start.

The post-war years were troublesome for George and his government. Even before the conclusion of hostilities, there were calls for the monarchy to be overhauled, dispensing with 'the ancient trappings of throne and sceptre', as H.G. Wells put it in a letter to *The Times*.[13] The king's relations with the prime minister, David Lloyd George, who had been sworn in at the end of 1916, were more acrimonious in peacetime than they had been during the war. Lloyd George failed to consult the king about his plans for the trial of his cousin, Kaiser Wilhelm II, and they also clashed over the growing crisis in Ireland.

The Irish War of Independence had broken out in 1919, with the Irish Republican Army ranged against the forces of the crown. The increasingly bloody three-year conflict led to the end of British rule in most of Ireland. The king helped to calm the troubled waters by attending the opening session of the newly established Parliament in Northern Ireland in June 1921, at which he gave a speech calling for conciliation. It was largely thanks to his efforts that the Irish Free State established a few weeks later remained part of the British Empire. 'Now after seven centuries there may be peace in Ireland,' George reflected with satisfaction.[14] In fact, the treaty led to a civil war that would rage for many years to come.

The rise of socialism and the Labour movement during the 1920s was a source of concern for the king, who mistakenly associated both with republicanism. He came to realise, though, that the socialists were willing to come to terms with the monarchy if he took the first step. At the beginning of his reign, the celebrated novelist Hall Caine, who knew the royal family well, had urged the new king that his best chance of stabilising the monarchy was 'by bringing the throne and the people into line'.[15] Although naturally conservative, George was enough of a realist to see when times were changing and to move with them. In adopting a more inclusive and democratic approach, he proved that – just occasionally – an old dog could be taught new tricks. He made friendly overtures towards moderate Labour Party politicians and trade union officials and tried to bring the monarchy closer to the working classes by creating a new ethos of public service and duty. In so doing, he set the blueprint for a modern monarchy, more in touch with its subjects at all levels of society. This resulted in a surge of popularity at a time when economic crises could have fanned the flames of republican sentiment.

The king's new attitude towards the Labour Party was tested when the general election of 1923 brought no clear majority for any of the three parties. On 24 January 1924, he invited Ramsay

MacDonald to become Britain's first Labour prime minister. 'Today 23 years ago dear Grandmama died', he reflected in his diary that day. 'I wonder what she would have thought of a Labour Government.'[16] Even though its first administration lasted less than a year, George's positive, common-sense approach had helped to ensure that it would be accepted as one of the three major political parties.

The contemporary writer Compton Mackenzie declared that George 'had all the talents but none of the genius of monarchy'. But if by 'genius' he meant active and decisive statesmanship, then in an age when the monarch's role was to advise, agree and mediate, this would have been a disaster. It was precisely his sense of moderation and restraint that made George V the ideal monarch to oversee such a turbulent period in British history.

Worsening conditions and diminishing wages for coal miners sparked a General Strike in 1926. The king again proved to be in touch with the working classes when he advised the Tory prime minister, Stanley Baldwin, not to take inflammatory action against the strikers. 'Try living on their wages before you judge them,' he told him.[17] George's modernising drive continued that year when he hosted the Imperial Conference. Although he valued the empire, he recognised that it could not continue in the same form, particularly after the seismic changes brought about by the Great War. The conference agreed that Britain's overseas dominions would become 'autonomous communities within the British Empire, equal in status, in no way subordinate one to another'. Their independence was formalised by the Statute of Westminster in 1931, which described the monarch as 'the symbol of the free association of the members of the British Commonwealth of Nations'.

Although the question of empire had been largely settled, George grew increasingly concerned by developments in Germany, where Adolf Hitler and his National Socialist German Workers (Nazi) Party capitalised upon the severe economic depression to seize power in 1933. Soon, the Nazis controlled every aspect of German life and ousted all other political parties. The following year, George warned the German ambassador that there would be a war within ten years if the Nazis were not stopped. 'I will not have another war. *I will not*', he told Lloyd George in 1935.[18]

There were troubles closer to home, too. The king's relationship with the Prince of Wales had never been easy. As a child, David had been described by his mother as 'very sensitive'. The strict upbringing that he and his siblings experienced hindered his development. He was bullied by his nanny and was often the focus of his father's violent rages.[19] Like him, David and his younger brother Bertie were enrolled in naval college, but here too the elder prince was subjected to bullying and was nicknamed 'Sardine' by his fellow students.

Only when he grew to maturity did David find his natural milieu. His striking good looks, debonair charm and unmarried status made him the darling of the press and high society. He became the most photographed celebrity of the day and something of a fashion icon. 'The average young man in America is more interested in the clothes of the Prince of Wales than in any other individual on earth', reported *Men's Wear* magazine during David's visit to the United States in 1924.[20] Adopting a more informal style than most other royals, the prince was the first to use a handshake when making official visits and held out the promise of a more modern approach when he became king. 'The job . . . as I tried to interpret it, was, first, to carry on associations with worthy causes outside politics and clothe them with the prestige of the Prince's high position,' he later remarked, 'and, second, to bring the Monarchy, in response to new conditions, ever nearer the people.'[21]

The prince's easy charm and grace masked a streak of cruelty and arrogance. Upon hearing of the death of his thirteen-year-old brother John in January 1919, he callously remarked that it was 'little more than a regrettable nuisance' and wrote such an insensitive letter to his mother that he later apologised.[22] The extensive travels that he undertook on the king's behalf had given him little appreciation for other cultures. Rather, he believed that whites were inherently superior and made a number of derogatory comments about the Empire's subjects, describing indigenous Australians as 'the most revolting form of living creatures I've ever seen!!'[23] He was neglectful of his royal duties, too. Although he was active in charity work, he was prone to cancel or delay visits when the mood took him.

The Prince of Wales's profligate lifestyle was at odds with his father's modest habits of stamp-collecting and shooting. George made no secret of the fact that his second son was his favourite. In April 1923, Bertie married Lady Elizabeth Bowes-Lyon in Westminster Abbey, the first time a royal prince had been married there since Richard II in 1382. Lady Elizabeth was a far more suitable choice than the various women whom the elder prince had courted and George V wrote to offer his hearty congratulations, adding: 'I feel that we have always got on very well together (very different to dear David).' He doted on Bertie's eldest daughter, Elizabeth, whom he nicknamed 'Lilibet' in imitation of her early attempts to pronounce her name, while she called him 'Grandpa England'.[24]

By contrast, David's private life was a source of growing concern for the king and queen. Like his grandfather Edward VII, the Prince of Wales had a weakness for married women and kept a string of mistresses. It was one of them, Lady Thelma Furness, who in January 1931 introduced the thirty-six-year-old prince to her fellow American, Wallis Simpson, who was two years his junior. 'She is flat and angular, and could have been designed for a medieval playing card,' was the verdict of one observer. On the surface, there was nothing remarkable about Mrs Simpson. She was neither well educated nor accomplished (her first conversation with the prince was about central heating) and could boast few achievements beyond making the most of her second husband's connections. None of this mattered to David. 'To him, she was the perfect woman,' a close friend recalled.[25] The prince found her forthright manner and blatant irreverence irresistible. But the true secret of her appeal may have been in the fact that she resisted his advances. According to David's own testimony, Wallis was never his mistress. Like Anne Boleyn before her, she made her royal beau 'slavishly dependent' on her by keeping him at arm's length.[26]

Wallis may have mixed in the highest circles on both sides of the Atlantic, but as a future consort she was entirely unsuitable. She had divorced her first husband, a US naval officer, in 1927, after having at least two affairs, and the following year she had married Ernest

Simpson, an American-born British shipbroker who lived and worked in London. Although the prince strenuously denied their affair, his infatuation with Wallis was obvious to everyone who saw them. In 1935, he caused shockwaves by introducing her to his mother at a party at Buckingham Palace. Divorcees were generally excluded from court and the king was furious when he heard of it. But, fatally, neither he nor the queen seems to have discussed the matter with their son directly. The same year, David holidayed twice with Mrs Simpson and continued to shower her with money and jewels. 'I love you more & more & more each & every minute & miss you so terribly here', he wrote during a brief separation at Easter 1935, adding anxiously: 'You do too don't you my sweetheart?'[27]

As the 1930s wore on, the king found refuge in regularity. In common with his Hanoverian ancestors, he was a creature of habit, 'his occupations being predictable to the day, indeed almost to the hour', according to the royal librarian Sir Owen Morshead.[28] The king did, though, embrace a range of new spectator sports and established the tradition of royal attendance at the football cup final at Wembley, international rugby matches at Twickenham, test matches at Lord's, tennis at Wimbledon, and race meetings at Ascot, Epsom and Goodwood. It was his horse that suffragette Emily Davison threw herself under at the Derby at Epsom on 4 June 1913. She died of her injuries four days later and was rapidly hailed as a martyr by the women's suffrage movement.

In 1932, George made himself accessible to an even greater number of his people by establishing another royal tradition: the Royal Christmas speech. Such an innovation had originally been suggested by John Reith, the first Director General of the British Broadcasting Corporation (BBC), in 1923. The king had been reluctant to agree, grumbling that it would ruin his Christmas, but he was eventually persuaded that it was what his people wanted. His first Christmas speech was written for him by Rudyard Kipling and delivered from Sandringham. It proved so popular that it became an annual fixture, later broadcast through television.

A willingness to respond to his people's wishes had made George a popular king and there was an outpouring of affection for him at his Silver Jubilee in May 1935. After attending a service at St Paul's Cathedral, the king recorded his astonishment at: 'The greatest number of people in the streets that I have ever seen in my life . . . The enthusiasm was indeed most touching.'[29] Ramsay MacDonald, who began his second term as prime minister in 1929, was quite overcome:

> We all went away feeling that we had taken part in something very much like a Holy Communion . . . This Jubilee is having a miraculous effect on the public mind and on the King himself. He is finding confidence and is showing the Prince of Wales's aptitude for saying the right popular thing and feeling the popular mind. But with it all he retains the demeanour and the status of a King and does not step down to get on a lower level.[30]

This marked an important moment in the evolution of the crown. As one historian put it: 'Monarchy was no longer simply in alliance with religion; it had become a religion.'[31]

To the king's great sadness, a month later MacDonald resigned as prime minister. 'I hoped you might have seen me through,' George told him. 'You have been the Prime Minister I have liked best.'[32] MacDonald would only have needed to serve another few months for the king to get his wish. Although abstemious in his habits, George had been a heavy smoker from a young age and, like his late father, had suffered from chronic bronchitis for years. In his final diary entry, dated 17 January 1936 at Sandringham, the seventy-year-old king admitted to feeling 'rotten'.[33] Three days later, members of his privy council gathered around his bedside as he attempted to discuss political events. According to an unsubstantiated account, when one of his doctors tried to cheer him by suggesting he would soon be convalescing at Bognor Regis, a favourite seaside retreat, he retorted: 'Bugger Bognor'.[34] He died that evening.

The senior royal doctor, Viscount Dawson, later admitted that he had hastened the king's end with two lethal injections so that his suffering would not be prolonged. He was likely also motivated by a desire that George should die before midnight so that his passing would be announced in the morning edition of *The Times*, rather than in 'less appropriate . . . evening journals'.[35] The news was also relayed by radio, Prime Minister Baldwin giving a speech that had been altered by John Reith so that it reflected what he called 'the moral authority, honour and dignity of the throne'. It sparked 'that individual but widespread sense of loss which a monarch, personally unknown in any direct way to most of his subjects, can provoke'.[36]

George V had been neither the most charismatic nor, bluntly, the most interesting of Britain's monarchs. But he had won widespread admiration for his devotion to service. Even if he had been so inclined, he could not have neglected his duties, thanks to the sheer scale of them. His reign witnessed more demands upon the crown than any other in the nineteenth or twentieth century: the Parliament Bill, Home Rule in Ireland, the incorporation of the Labour Party into the constitution, and, of course, the onset of global war. His sense of moderation and restraint had made George the ideal monarch to oversee such a turbulent period in British history. He had brought a new style to the monarchy, too: less pretentious and more accessible, though still upholding its separateness, and with an emphasis on duty and service. In so doing, he had set the tone for his successors – with one notable exception.

Edward VIII (1936)

'I know there is nothing kingly about me'

GEORGE V'S DEATH at Sandringham in January 1936 ushered in the second 'Year of Three Kings' in the history of the monarchy. Upon hearing of his father's demise, David – now King Edward VIII – flew to London and kept vigil with his brothers over the late king's body at Westminster Hall. 'My heart goes out to the Prince of Wales tonight', observed the American-born British politician and diarist Sir Henry 'Chips' Channon, 'as he will mind so terribly being King. His loneliness, his seclusion, his isolation will be almost more than his highly strung and imaginative nature can bear.'[1] Years before, George V had gloomily predicted: 'After I am dead, the boy will ruin himself within 12 months.'[2]

From the very start of his reign, Edward broke with protocol. When the new coinage was struck, tradition dictated that the monarch should face in the opposite direction to that of their predecessor. But the new king insisted that he face left as his father had done so that the parting in his hair could be seen. His informal style of monarchy might have chimed with the modernity of his younger subjects, but it exasperated his officials and flouted the constitution in a dangerous way. The new king's ministers soon realised that he had none of George V's diligence in reading voluminous state papers. More worryingly, Edward made little secret of his sympathy for Nazism, which was in direct conflict with Prime Minister Stanley Baldwin's position.

There are photographs of the new king looking obviously bored as he carried out his public duties. 'Being a Monarch . . . can surely be one of the most confining, the most frustrating, and over the duller stretches, the least stimulating jobs open to an educated, independent-minded person,' he later remarked. 'Even a saint would on occasion find himself driven to exasperation by the taboos which invisibly and silently envelop a constitutional monarchy.'[3] It soon became obvious that Edward was not being disingenuous when he confided to his prime minister: 'I know there is nothing kingly about me.'[4]

As they had been when he was Prince of Wales, Edward's energies were primarily channelled into his social life. He soon established a second court at Fort Belvedere, a folly on the border of Windsor Great Park that had been refurbished for his use before he came to the throne. This afforded greater privacy than Buckingham Palace, which meant that he was able to live openly with Wallis Simpson. It is remarkable that the British press, who knew all about the relationship, remained silent, which meant that the general public knew nothing about the affair.

Extra-marital relationships were nothing new in the history of the monarchy, but the fact that Edward showed no inclination either to give up Mrs Simpson or to settle the succession by marrying was a source of grave concern within the royal household, the government and the church. As supreme governor of the Church of England, the king could hardly ignore its interdict on marriage to a divorcee. The Archbishop of Canterbury, Cosmo Gordon Lang, privately warned the king about his behaviour. 'That encounter was my first intimation that I might be approaching an irreconcilable conflict', Edward recalled.[5]

On 27 October, Mrs Simpson secured a decree nisi – ironically, on the basis that her husband had been unfaithful. The king's private secretary Alex Hardinge grasped the enormity of this new development more swiftly than the prime minister, who seemed to think that Edward would eventually tire of his mistress. The very next day, Hardinge urged the king's younger brother Bertie to prepare himself for an abdication. To the outside world, everything appeared as it should be. On 3 November, Edward opened Parliament and plans were soon underway for his coronation. Significantly, though, this was scheduled for 12 May 1937 – before Mrs Simpson's divorce would be finalised and she would be free to marry again.

On 16 November the king informed Baldwin that he intended to marry Wallis Simpson. His private secretary had once remarked that

Edward 'appeared to be entirely ignorant of the powers of a constitutional monarch'.[6] The truth of that was proved as Edward went
on to ask his prime minister's advice as to the best means of marrying
Wallis and retaining his crown. When Baldwin pointed out the
impossibility of what he proposed, Edward threatened to abdicate.
That evening, he told his mother and sister that he would give up
the throne for Mrs Simpson if necessary and repeated the same to
his brothers the next day. Upon hearing what lay ahead, Bertie 'broke
down and sobbed like a child'.[7]

Still clinging to the belief that a solution was possible, on
25 November the king proposed to Baldwin the idea of a morganatic
marriage, whereby he would remain king but Mrs Simpson would
not become queen consort. But the Statute of Westminster (1931)
stipulated that 'any alteration in the law touching the Succession to
the Throne or the Royal Style and Titles' required not just the consent
of the English Parliament but its counterparts throughout the
Commonwealth. The king's typically flippant response was that there
were 'not many people in Australia' and their opinion did not matter,
but even he appreciated that opening the monarchy up to such
widespread scrutiny was best avoided.[8]

By early December, all attempts at reaching an agreement had
failed. When the press finally broke their silence on 3 December,
Wallis Simpson left for Cannes, declaring: 'I feel like an animal in
a trap.'[9] Increasingly isolated, Edward was given a fleeting glimmer
of hope when senior politician Winston Churchill showed sympathy
for his plight. Churchill understood what his fellow ministers did
not: that Mrs Simpson was 'as necessary to his [Edward's] happiness
as the air he breathed'.[10] Although he voiced his support for a
morganatic marriage, the weight of the cabinet was against the
king and on 5 December Edward told the prime minister that he
would abdicate.

On the morning of 10 December, witnessed by his three brothers,
the king signed the instrument of abdication, which stated: 'I . . .
do hereby declare my irrevocable determination to renounce the
Throne for Myself and for My descendants . . . immediately.'[11]
Edward then turned to his brother Bertie and said: 'God bless you,
Sir. I hope you will be happier than your predecessor.'[12] Bertie gave

his own account of the 'dreadful moment': 'When D and I said good-bye we kissed . . . and he bowed to me as his King.'[13]

'We woke in the reign of Edward VIII and went to bed in that of George VI,' remarked Chips Channon's wife, Honor.[14] Edward had made history, but not in a way that he or his successors would wish to remember. His 327-day reign was the shortest of any since Lady Jane Grey, and he was the first monarch to give up their throne since James II almost two hundred and fifty years before.

The following night, 'His royal highness Prince Edward' delivered a worldwide broadcast, in which he famously explained: 'I have found it impossible to carry the heavy burden of responsibility and to discharge my duties as King . . . without the help and support of the woman I love.' Perhaps in an attempt to deflect any criticism from Wallis, he added that the decision 'was mine and mine alone'.[15] 'The hushed abdication broadcast from Windsor Castle has replaced the crunch of the axe on Tower Green,' remarked one royal observer.[16] While listeners wept, the now former king appeared 'quite unmoved', recalled his brother's secretary. 'His last act prior to broadcasting his message and then leaving the country was to sit in his bedroom with a whisky and soda having his toe-nails seen to.' Having delivered the speech, Edward turned to his adviser Walter Monckton and said: 'It is a far better thing I go to.'[17]

The abdication might have saved Britain from an unsuitable king, but as the Labour MP George Hardie remarked, it had done 'more for republicanism than fifty years of propaganda'.[18] It had also introduced a destabilising element to the monarchy. It was generally understood that a king or queen inherited the throne because it was their birthright and that their subjects' duty was to obey them. Edward had broken that understanding and made the succession more a matter of personal choice – which could, of course, work both ways.

George VI (1936–52)

A rocking throne

'I PRAY TO God my eldest son will never marry and have children, and that nothing will come between Bertie and Lilibet and the throne,' George V had remarked shortly before his death.[1] His prayers had now been answered. Four days after his accession, England's new king celebrated his forty-first birthday. It was also the anniversary of his great-grandfather Prince Albert's death – at Queen Victoria's suggestion, he had been named after him.

Although he had always been his father's favourite, Bertie, now George VI, had grown up shy and reserved, and his public appearances had been hampered by the stammer he had developed in childhood. Sport provided a much-needed outlet and he became such an accomplished tennis player that he made it to the first round of the men's doubles at Wimbledon in 1926. By far the greatest source of happiness, though, came from his marriage to Elizabeth Bowes-Lyon, whom he described as 'the most marvellous person in the World in my eyes'.[2] Four years after Princess Elizabeth's arrival, the couple had another daughter, Margaret Rose. 'We four', as George affectionately referred to his family, lived in a private house, 145 Piccadilly, London, rather than in one of the royal palaces. They would have been content to remain ensconced in this comparatively modest domesticity if George's brother had not had other ideas.

The realisation of the enormous change that had taken place within their family soon dawned on the new king's daughters. Fittingly, the ten-year-old Princess Elizabeth was in the middle of a history lesson when her uncle signed the instrument of abdication. A few days later, she saw a letter in the hall of their house in Piccadilly addressed to 'Her Majesty the Queen'. 'That's Mummy now, isn't it?' she remarked to her sister. 'Does that mean that you will have to be the next queen?' Margaret asked. When her sister replied that she would, Margaret said simply: 'Poor you.'[3] Elizabeth was now heir presumptive – while there was still the prospect of her parents having a son, she could not be heir apparent. She was keenly aware of this fact and, according to her maternal grandmother Lady Strathmore, began 'ardently praying for a brother'.[4]

Many times in its history, the crown has been best served by those incumbents who were not supposed to inherit. The same pattern looked set to be repeated now. Even though Britain's reluctant new king privately admitted to feeling 'quite unprepared' for the enormous burden that his elder brother had placed on his shoulders, he acted with greater wisdom and decisiveness in the days following the abdication than Edward had done throughout the ten months that preceded it. Painfully aware of what he called 'the inevitable mess' in which his brother had left the crown, he assumed the regnal name George VI to emphasise continuity with his father's reign and restore confidence in the monarchy.[5] From the outset, he made it clear that he had taken the mantle of power unwillingly but from a strong sense of duty, which provided a welcome contrast to Edward's selfish actions.

These were still perilous times for the monarchy, though. George himself confided to his father's old doctor that he feared 'the whole fabric' of the crown might 'crumble under the shock and strain of it all'.[6] The leader of the left-wing Independent Labour Party firmly believed that it would. 'All the King's horses and all the King's men, could not put Humpty-Dumpty back again,' he pronounced in the House of Commons.[7] It was not the first time in the history of the English monarchy that disaster had been presaged with a sudden or dramatic change of monarch – notably the bloody advent of the Tudors, the Glorious Revolution and the replacement of the Stuarts with the Hanoverians. None of these predictions had come true, and neither did the monarchy 'crumble' now. In fact, as one contemporary commentator remarked, to the 'amazed admiration' of the 'entire world', George VI ascended the throne 'without a ripple'.[8]

The new king was conscious of the need to resolve the status of his predecessor. At his suggestion, Edward was given the title 'his royal highness the Duke of Windsor'.[9] From thenceforth,

George made it clear that he wanted nothing further to do with his elder brother or the woman for whom he had given up the throne. To the new Duke of Windsor's fury, George refused to grant the title 'her royal highness' to Wallis after she and Edward married in June 1937, and forbade any member of the royal family to attend the ceremony. The duke was omitted from the Civil List, which made him solely reliant upon the new king for his income. George was evidently generous because his elder brother lived out his days with Wallis in luxury and at leisure, residing mostly near the Bois de Boulogne in Paris and in New York, as well as serving for a brief spell as Governor of the Bahamas. Frustrated, embittered and increasingly bored, Edward sought distraction in high-society gatherings and, together with his wife, assumed celebrity status. His resentment towards the royal family was all too evident when, many years later, he made a brief visit to his dying mother, Queen Mary. 'Ice in the place of blood in the veins must be a fine preservative', he wrote to Wallis.[10]

George VI was quick to learn his new duties. He was assiduous in reading the dispatches from his government and had a greater grasp of his constitutional duties than his elder brother ever had. His quiet, unassuming personality was also perfectly suited to the role. In the aftershock of the abdication, the very last thing the monarchy needed was another brash incumbent like Edward VIII, or even one as forthright as his father George V. Instead, for the monarchy to survive, tact and diplomacy were required, and above all a steady dedication to duty – something that both George VI and his eldest daughter Elizabeth fully understood. The new king also benefited from a wife who was at once a comfort and a confidante, more so than any queen consort in recent history. The obvious domestic harmony he enjoyed put the monarchy back at the moral heart of Britain, as it had been in Victoria and Albert's time. It also provided an important new bond between the crown and the people.

The new king was crowned on the same day that his elder brother should have been: 12 May 1937. This expediency meant that George VI's coronation was the only one since George III's in 1761 that was held less than a year after the monarch's accession. The king was awoken before dawn by the noise of preparations outside Buckingham Palace and privately admitted that he had 'a sinking feeling' when he realised what day it was.[11] In accordance with his wishes, the procession was broadcast to a worldwide audience, although the service itself remained the private religious ceremony that this intensely pious monarch believed it should be. That evening, he delivered a broadcast with greater confidence (and barely a stammer) than many had predicted. An article in the special coronation edition of the *Evening Standard* reflected: 'The position of the King has changed since the reign of the old Queen. The monarchy has been completely nationalised . . . Queen Victoria became a symbol, almost an idol. But her present successor is more completely symbolic of his office.'[12]

George VI's early reign was dominated by the growing certainty of another global war. Aware of his constitutional duties, he gave his support to the new prime minister, Neville Chamberlain, in his policy of appeasement towards Adolf Hitler. When Chamberlain returned from negotiating the Munich Agreement in September 1938, the king took the unprecedented step of inviting him to appear with the royal family on the balcony of Buckingham Palace. This was described by the historian John Grigg (later Lord Altrincham), an outspoken critic of the monarchy, as 'the most unconstitutional act by a British sovereign in the present century'.[13]

The king and queen's tour of Canada and the United States the following year provided a welcome distraction from the worsening international situation. It was the first visit to North America by a reigning monarch and served an important political purpose – namely, to secure support for the coming war. George VI was painfully aware that he faced unfavourable comparisons to his elder brother, who was something of a celebrity across the Atlantic, but he and his consort won widespread admiration. Their meeting with American President Franklin D. Roosevelt was a resounding success and established a bond of friendship that would bring significant advantages to Britain in the years ahead.

Two months after the king and queen's return, on 3 September 1939, Britain declared war on Nazi Germany because it had pledged military support to Poland in the event of a German invasion. Thanks to the advances in communications technology since the First World War, George VI was able to play an even more prominent public role in the global conflict than his father had done. He and his wife Elizabeth took the near-fatal decision to remain in London throughout the conflict. They were staying at Buckingham Palace on the night of 9 September 1940 when the palace was bombed on the first of nine separate occasions, one of the devices exploding perilously close to the king's study. The queen famously declared: 'I am glad we have been bombed. It makes me feel we can look the East End in the face.'[14] Thereafter the royal couple spent their nights at Windsor but returned to London each day. Their solidarity with their people was enhanced by the fact that they endured the same rationing restrictions. When the American First Lady Eleanor Roosevelt came to stay at Buckingham Palace, she noted the limited food and bathwater, as well as the lack of heating.

The royal family's greatest sacrifice, though, came in August 1942 when the king's younger brother George, Duke of Kent, was killed on active service. Undeterred, the king continued his morale-boosting efforts, both at home and abroad. In June 1943, he visited military forces in North Africa and Malta, followed by Normandy, southern Italy and the Low Countries in October 1944. He also (reluctantly) revived his father's tradition of the Christmas broadcast, in the first of which (at his daughter Elizabeth's suggestion) he quoted lines from a poem that struck an instant chord with his people:

I said to the man who stood at the Gate of the Year,
'Give me a light that I may tread safely into the unknown.'[15]

The king's unrelenting energy contrasted sharply with his ageing and infirm prime minister. In May 1940, Chamberlain resigned and, to George's initial dismay, was replaced by Winston Churchill, once a close ally of his elder brother Edward. Churchill had all of the energy, vision and gift for public speaking that his predecessor lacked and rapidly supplanted the king as leader of the national war effort. Despite George's reservations, he and Churchill developed a close, collaborative relationship. On 10 September – the day after

Buckingham Palace was bombed – they started meeting for lunch there once a week, with no advisers or secretaries present. This became their custom throughout the remainder of Churchill's administration – a total of more than two hundred lunches.

With Churchill in the ascendancy, George played a largely symbolic, if still important, role and was particularly vital to the country's morale. During the Blitz, he and his wife visited numerous bombed areas across England, often at short notice in order to avoid the usual disruptions of a royal visit. 'I feel that this kind of visit does do good at such a moment', the king recorded in his diary, 'and it is one of my main jobs in life to help others when I can be useful to them.'[16] Having witnessed the often-heroic civilian work following the air raids, the king created and designed the George Cross and George Medal to recognise civilian bravery, although many of the awards went to servicemen. Throughout the war, his popularity was at an all-time high, with the result that whenever he appeared in newsreels shown in cinemas, it sparked spontaneous applause.

The fact that George rose so ably to the challenge of leading his country through the war was mostly due to his keen sense of duty and his appreciation of the needs of the people. But it was probably also at least partly due to his desire to repair the damage that his errant elder brother had wreaked by his association with the Nazi cause. The Duke and Duchess of Windsor had made a well-publicised visit to Hitler's Germany in October 1937, during which they had met Hitler and the duke had given a full Nazi salute. Even more worrying were reports received by the British government during the war that the former king was privately colluding with Hitler. Top-secret papers recently released from The National Archives in London include a British intelligence report of 7 July 1940 that claimed the Germans had been 'negotiating with the Duchess of Windsor who desired at any price to become Queen'. It went on to say that the Germans believed 'King George will abdicate during the bombing of London', and that 'having first changed public opinion by propaganda', they would instal a new government 'under Duke of Windsor'.[17] Although the duke denied such reports, his links with Hitler and the Nazis remain the subject of intense debate.

* * *

Although a member of government had suggested that the king's daughters be evacuated to Canada for their safety, this met with a firm rebuttal from the queen: 'The children won't go without me. I won't leave without the King. And the King will never leave.' The princesses spent most of the war at Windsor Castle where, despite everything, their parents managed to maintain a semblance of the domestic harmony that had characterised their early childhood. One of Elizabeth and Margaret's childhood friends recalled with some envy: 'In that castle, with its gilded rooms and red corridors, there is an atmosphere of happy family life that I myself have never known.'[18] But duty was never far away. It was from Windsor that in October 1940 the fourteen-year-old Princess Elizabeth delivered her first radio broadcast, as part of the BBC's *Children's Hour*, offering the assurance: 'We know, every one of us, that in the end all will be well.' Eighty years later, with her country in the grip of a global pandemic, she would offer a similar assurance.

In April 1944, the princess celebrated her eighteenth birthday. The present that delighted her most was a corgi named Susan. The puppy would be the progenitor of the many corgis that Elizabeth owned until the death of the last of the line, Willow, in 2018, seventy-four years and fourteen dog generations later. In the midst of the birthday celebrations, plans were underway for Operation Overlord, better known as D-Day. King George was fully supportive of this huge seaborne invasion of German-occupied France – the largest ever launched by Britain. He even proposed to accompany it in person, as did Churchill. Both men were talked out of it and the king contented himself with delivering a rousing speech on 5 June 1944, the eve of the operation. Almost 160,000 Allied troops crossed the English Channel the following day, and by the end of June a total of 875,000 had disembarked on Normandy's beaches. There had been a heavy loss of life on both sides, but the operation had laid the foundations for an Allied victory in Western Europe.

On 8 May 1945, the king made another broadcast to the nation, giving thanks for Victory in Europe. He and his family were prominent in the wild rejoicing that followed, responding to chants from the crowds of 'We want the king!' by appearing several times on the balcony of Buckingham Palace, driving in state through the streets of London and attending services of thanksgiving. Princesses Elizabeth and Margaret took the unprecedented step of mingling anonymously with the celebrating crowds in the streets of London. In a rare interview, the elder princess later recalled being 'swept along by tides of happiness and relief'.[19]

The personal toll that the war had taken on their father the king, as it had on millions of his subjects, was evident when he gave a speech to Parliament in Westminster Hall, his voice faltering as he mentioned the death of his brother. As soon as George had finished speaking, Churchill waved his top hat and called for three cheers. However, despite his becoming an iconic war leader, characterised by his decisive actions and rousing speeches, in the election that followed the end of the war Churchill and his Tory Party were heavily defeated by the Labour leader Clement Attlee. On 26 July 1945, the king reluctantly accepted his prime minister's resignation. 'We said goodbye and I thanked him for all his help to me during the 5 War Years', George noted in characteristically understated style.[20]

During the post-war years, the disintegration of the British Empire gathered pace. In August 1947, British India became the two independent dominions of India and Pakistan, so George VI relinquished his title of emperor. The empire was now a commonwealth – and a dwindling one at that. Nevertheless, the king took his duties as its leader seriously and, together with his wife and daughters, embarked on a tour of South Africa in the winter of 1947. During the trip, George's eldest daughter Elizabeth gave a broadcast on her twenty-first birthday in which she dedicated herself to the service of the Commonwealth.

Later that year, the dutiful princess courted rare controversy by announcing her engagement to Prince Philip of Greece and Denmark, nephew of George VI's cousin, Lord Mountbatten.[21] They had first met as children, then again just before the outbreak of the war, when Elizabeth was thirteen years old. Her father 'found it difficult to believe that his elder daughter had really fallen in love with the first young man she had met'.[22] According to one courtier, both he and his wife had reservations about their prospective son-in-law, whom they felt was 'rough, ill-tempered, uneducated and would probably not be faithful'.[23] Although he was a British subject and had served in the Royal Navy during the war, Philip had been born in Greece and his sisters had married German noblemen with Nazi links. It was reported that Elizabeth's mother referred to him as 'The Hun', and that some of the king's advisers thought Philip – 'a prince without a home or kingdom' – was well beneath his fiancée in status.[24]

To deflect some of this criticism, Philip renounced his Greek and Danish titles, converted from Greek Orthodoxy to Anglicanism and took the surname of his mother's British family, Mountbatten. Just before the wedding, on 20 November 1947, King George VI created his prospective son-in-law a royal highness (but not a prince) and Duke of Edinburgh. Although there was great public interest in the occasion, staging a wedding of full royal splendour would have been out of kilter with the economic hardship of post-war Britain. It was therefore kept comparatively simple and the princess used ration coupons to buy the material for her wedding dress. The couple's first child, Charles, was born almost exactly a year later, followed by Anne in 1950. As she grew to adulthood, Princess Anne became as outspoken as her father, prompting one newspaper to call her: 'The Royal Family's own little gift to Republicanism'.[25]

Increasingly, Princess Elizabeth took on those royal duties for which her ailing father had grown too weak. In May 1951, the king was well enough to open the Festival of Britain, held on the centenary of the Great Exhibition and with the same aims of promoting British industry, arts and science. But it was obvious to all who saw him that his health had declined sharply. Three months later, he had his entire left lung removed after a malignant growth was discovered, the result of being a lifelong smoker. He was unable to deliver his customary speech at the State Opening of Parliament in November, and his Christmas broadcast that year had to be recorded in sections, rather than delivered live. He assured the nation that he had come through his recent illness.

On 31 January 1952, against the advice of his doctors, the king went to London Airport (Heathrow) to wave his daughter and her husband off on a flight to east Africa, the first stage of a tour that would encompass Australia and New Zealand. George then journeyed to Sandringham to enjoy some shooting. Six days later, when his valet went to wake him, he found the king dead in his bed. He had died from a coronary thrombosis, aged fifty-six. News was conveyed at once to his daughter Elizabeth, who flew back from Kenya as Queen Elizabeth II.

As George VI himself had admitted after his brother's abdication, he had inherited 'a rocking throne' and had tried 'to make it steady again'.[26] He had succeeded to a remarkable degree, despite facing the considerable challenges of global warfare and the erosion of empire. He had not made history: history had happened to him. But if his had not been the most flamboyant monarchy, it was the straightforward, down-to-earth style that had lain at the heart of its success. By presenting himself as a dutiful, family-orientated sovereign, head of 'The Family Firm', as he termed it, George had provided a model for his eldest daughter to emulate.

Elizabeth II (1952–)

'Fundamentally sensible and well-behaved'

'I DECLARE BEFORE you all that my whole life whether it be long or short shall be devoted to your service.' The pledge that Britain's new queen made on her twenty-first birthday, four years before she inherited the throne from her father, has been much quoted since. Other monarchs had made similar declarations – the promise to serve their country, their church and their people is implicit within the coronation oath – but few have fulfilled them with greater consistency and none for as long as Elizabeth II.

Upon meeting the two-year-old Princess Elizabeth, Winston Churchill had been impressed by the 'air of authority and reflectiveness astonishing in an infant'.[1] Her cousin Margaret Rhodes described her as 'fundamentally sensible and well-behaved', while a childhood companion recalled that she was 'placid and unemotional, she never desires what doesn't come her way'.[2] Her younger sister Margaret could not have been more different. High-spirited and mischievous, she 'always wants what I have', Elizabeth once complained to their nanny, Marion Crawford ('Crawfie').[3]

Even though Elizabeth II was Britain's eighth queen regnant, almost immediately there were issues relating to her gender. First, there was the question of names. Philip suggested that the new royal house should be called the House of Edinburgh, while his uncle advocated Mountbatten. However, Elizabeth eventually chose the option favoured by Winston Churchill, who had been re-elected prime minister a few months before her accession, that she should retain the name Windsor. 'I'm just a bloody amoeba,' her husband complained. 'I am the only man in the country not allowed to give his name to his own children.'[4] The issue of the new queen's regnal name was more easily solved. When asked by what name she wished to be known, Elizabeth replied: 'My own, of course. What else?'[5]

The day after her return to London, the new queen made her Declaration of Accession at St James's Palace, with the privy council in attendance. 'My heart is too full for me to say more to you today than that I shall always work, as my father did throughout his reign, to uphold constitutional government and to advance the happiness and prosperity of my peoples, spread as they are the world over.'[6]

It is ironic that the less powerful the monarchy has become, the heavier the workload each incumbent has inherited. Elizabeth had been made all too well aware of this during her father's reign, and her own commitment to hard work was immediately apparent. 'She loves her duty and means to be a Queen,' observed Harold Macmillan, a future prime minister.[7] He was right. The queen has pored over state papers, held meetings with ministers, performed the state opening of Parliament every year of her reign except 1959 and 1963, when she was pregnant with Princes Andrew and Edward respectively, undertaken countless visits across the country and abroad, and performed the myriad other ceremonial and constitutional duties required of her position. But there have been maternal duties, too. Her first prime minister, Winston Churchill, agreed to alter the time of his regular Tuesday evening audience with the monarch so that the queen could make her accustomed visit to her children's nursery.

Duty rather than reform was Elizabeth's watchword from the outset of her reign, and any small changes to the pattern of monarchy were mostly prompted by her husband. 'No one wants to end up like the brontosaurus, who couldn't adapt himself, and who ended up stuffed in a museum,' he once remarked.[8] It was Prince Philip's suggestion that their children be sent to school rather than receiving the traditional education at home – something that no previous monarch had countenanced. Although the intention was laudable, the results were patchy. Prince Charles famously loathed his time at Gordonstoun, the draconian school in Scotland that his father had attended.

By the time of Elizabeth II's accession, Buckingham Palace had become firmly established as the monarch's principal London residence.

It was also the main headquarters of her household, which justified Prince Philip's wry remark that he and his wife were 'living over the shop'.[9] For all its stately grandeur, previous monarchs had complained about the palace's lack of creature comforts. Edward VIII found the 'dank, musty smell' abhorrent, while his brother George VI described the palace as an 'icebox'.[10] During Elizabeth's reign, these drawbacks have been rectified by the installation of such modern conveniences as central heating and even a swimming pool, and the royal family live primarily in about a dozen rooms in the north wing of the palace, which afford greater privacy and homeliness. The state rooms, which are now opened to the public every summer, are mainly in the west wing.

Elizabeth II's coronation was staged in Westminster Abbey on an unseasonably cold, wet June day in 1953. Extensive preparations had been underway for months. The Duke of Norfolk, who as earl marshal was responsible for the proceedings, had drawn up no fewer than ninety-four diagrams, 'each depicting different parts of the ceremony in which every minute was worked out, and every move-ment within each minute prescribed', as an attendant of the queen recalled.[11] By the time the day dawned, one of the ladies-in-waiting was so overwrought that she almost fainted. By contrast, the queen was the very image of calm. 'You must be feeling nervous, Ma'am,' an attendant observed. 'Of course I am, but I really do think Aureole will win,' she replied, a wry reference to her horse's forthcoming race at the Derby.[12]

All of the preparation was worth it. The event has been described by a leading authority as 'the most impressive ever staged in the Coronation's thousand and more years history'.[13] We have ample evidence of this, thanks to the fact that it was also the first British coronation to be televised. A staggering 8,251 invited guests were crammed into the abbey and the two-and-a-half-hour ceremony was broadcast to 20 million people. Prince Philip had advocated televising the ceremony, an idea that had met with considerable opposition within the royal household. But the queen supported her husband and, as the *New York Times* recorded, the event marked 'the birth of international television'.[14] Only for the most sacred part of the ceremony – the anointing and communion – were the cameras turned off.

A *New Statesman* journalist described the scene:

> I had a sudden feeling, craning at my glimpse of the bare-headed Queen at her anointing, sitting motionless with lowered eyes under her gold canopy, a sensation that was like something spoken aloud: 'There is a secret here' . . . What that secret was, I could not say. No doubt it was the primitive and magical feeling which ancient and beautiful ceremonials still evoke, in no matter how rational a breast.

The seasoned politician Chips Channon was no less overawed. 'What a day for England and the traditional forces of the world. Shall we ever see the like again?'[15]

The coronation had been a triumph, eliciting huge popular acclaim in England and making the British monarchy the envy of the world. 'However much we valued our republic and celebrated our independence from Britain, Queen Elizabeth represented splendour, tradition, and majesty that our republic did not have and somehow envied – and still does', recalled an American scholar half a century later.[16] A German journalist who attended wrote of the 'immeasurable prestige and grip on the national imagination' that the event had inspired, and declared: 'It is doubtful whether at any time in the last thousand years the British Monarchy has occupied such an enormous place in the thoughts and emotions of British citizens as at the present moment.' The prime minister, Winston Churchill, concluded with satisfaction that the coronation had strengthened the link between the crown and the nation's identity.

Elizabeth II's coronation had also sparked an obsessive interest in the royal family on a scale never seen before. 'As every editor of every popular newspaper or magazine knows, there is an insatiable demand for every scrap of information regarding the functioning of the Monarchy and the life of the Royal family', reflected one commentator. 'In the everyday conversation of British families, Royalty nowadays occurs with a frequency probably shared only by their most intimate relations and friends.' Thanks to the advent of television, the British monarchy was now the subject of global fascination, too. The *New Statesman* warned: 'For this reason, it cannot afford to make mistakes.'[17]

There was talk of a new Elizabethan Age, but this optimism faded with the lustre of the coronation. As the new queen herself admitted in her second Christmas broadcast: 'Frankly, I do not myself feel at all like my great Tudor forebear, who was blessed with neither husband nor children, who ruled as a despot and was never able to leave her native shores.' Neither was the second Elizabeth's kingdom the global power that the first's had been; rather it was a nation battling with the aftermath of war and the fall of empire. Elizabeth II's coronation in Scotland more accurately reflected this. The coronation robes were dispensed with and the queen carried a handbag over her arm. This hardly smoothed the ruffled feathers caused by the royal household having ignored the Scottish proposal that she ought correctly to be proclaimed Elizabeth II and I north of the border.

Greater tact was shown towards the Commonwealth. The new queen had asked that her coronation gown be embroidered with the floral emblems not just of the United Kingdom but of her wider domains. The concept of empire was formally abandoned at last and the queen was given the new title: 'Head of the Commonwealth'. Together with her native land, this gave her dominion (in title, if not in practice) over a realm spanning more than ten million square miles and occupied by almost one billion people. The queen's commitment to the Commonwealth was demonstrated by the seven-month tour that she and her husband undertook in the same year as her coronation. They visited thirteen countries and covered a total of 40,000 miles. It would be the first of many overseas visits, making Elizabeth II the most widely travelled head of state in the world.[18]

If the new queen and her family were the subject of 'everyday conversation', there was no shortage of subject matter. Elizabeth's younger sister Margaret was twenty-one years old at the time of the accession and had grown into a celebrated beauty. Her vivacious personality made her the darling of high society and her name was linked with more than thirty eligible bachelors. However, the man with whom she formed a passionate attachment was Peter Townsend, her late father's equerry. Margaret and Townsend had often been seen in public together, but he was fifteen years her senior and married, so there was no reason to suppose theirs was anything more than a professional relationship. But when he divorced his wife in 1952, rumours began to fly.

In April the following year, Townsend proposed to Margaret and she accepted. She informed her sister the queen, whose consent was required by the terms of the Royal Marriages Act of 1772. The Church of England's position on senior royals marrying divorcees had already been made clear during the abdication crisis sixteen years earlier. As head of the church – and as a devout Christian – Elizabeth faced a conflict between royal and family loyalties. Her Archbishop of Canterbury, Geoffrey Fisher, was strongly opposed, and members of the government argued that the marriage would constitute as great a threat to the monarchy as Edward VIII's had. Churchill advised the queen that if her sister chose to relinquish her royal title, it would reinforce the message that an heir to the throne could easily leave the line of succession and be replaced by another.

Aware that, according to the 1772 Act, when Margaret reached her twenty-fifth birthday in 1955, she would no longer need her sister's permission to marry, the queen was minded to wait. Her prime minister agreed and arranged a posting for Townsend in Brussels. It was well judged. Although the couple kept in touch regularly, Margaret's feelings cooled over the two years that they were apart. Oblivious to this, press speculation that she and Townsend would soon set a date to marry reached fever pitch. 'Nothing much else than Princess Margaret's affairs is being talked of in this country', reported the *Guardian* after Townsend's return. Finally, on 31 October 1955, Margaret issued a statement: 'I have decided not to marry Group Captain Peter Townsend . . . Mindful of the Church's teachings that Christian marriage is indissoluble, and conscious of my duty to the Commonwealth, I have resolved to put these considerations before others.'[19] Ever since, she has been portrayed as the heartbroken princess deprived of her true love by the coldly indifferent royal establishment, when in fact she had simply moved on.

As the scandal of her sister's love life began to fade, Elizabeth's style of monarchy emerged into the spotlight. It was far less glamorous, but it offered the stability and constancy that was needed to safeguard the crown. 'The Sovereign has, under a constitutional monarchy such as ours, three rights – the right to be consulted, the right to encourage, the right to warn', asserted the nineteenth-century author Walter Bagehot in his essay on the constitution.[20] It was still an accurate appraisal a century later and one that influenced the queen, who read his work – as did her father, grandfather and, later, her son Charles. Bagehot's definition of royal power would have had Henry VIII spinning in his grave, but the withdrawal of the crown from active participation in government had led to a closer bond between the monarch and her people.

The queen was not immune from criticism, though. 'Is the New Elizabethan Age going to be a flop?' asked the *Daily Mail* in September 1956, and claimed the so-called popular monarchy was 'as toffee-nosed as it has ever been'.[21] Despairing at the scenes of popular rejoicing that seemed to accompany Elizabeth II's every appearance, the playwright and actor John Osborne compared the 'circus' of monarchy to 'a gold filling in a mouth full of decay . . . It distresses me that there should be so many empty minds, so many empty lives in Britain to sustain this famous industry; that no one should have the wit to laugh it out of existence or the honesty to resist it.'[22]

A famously acerbic playwright was one thing; a titled Tory MP quite another. In August 1957, Lord Altrincham caused a storm by publishing an article criticising the monarchy as a whole and Elizabeth in particular, 'a priggish schoolgirl' who was 'unable to string even a few sentences together without a written text'. A rash of articles appeared in the press defending the queen, and Altrincham was given police protection after he was attacked when leaving a television studio. He later defended his views, but also qualified them, insisting that he was a strong supporter of constitutional monarchy. He urged that Elizabeth should be allowed to be 'her own natural self' rather than a 'synthetic creature'. 'The perfect modern Queen is no haughty paragon, but a normal affectionate human being, sublimated through the breadth . . . of her experience and the indestructible magic of her office.'[23]

Though incendiary, Altrincham's comments were perceptive and far-sighted. It would be another four decades before the queen and her family were shocked into reviewing their traditionally formal and distant approach. But she did take some of his suggestions on board in the shorter term. Altrincham was invited to meet with her assistant private secretary, Martin Charteris, after which Elizabeth was given help to improve her diction for her speech at Christmas 1957. Further changes were subsequently introduced to make the palace and its occupants more accessible, such as increasing the number of invitations to the garden parties at Buckingham Palace and Holyrood House to 40,000 per year, and the advent of that staple of any royal visit: the walkabout.

Charteris later told Altrincham that he had done 'a great service to the monarchy'.[24] Decades later, Altrincham himself reiterated that he had acted to protect, rather than to damage the crown: 'I was rather worried by the general tone of comment, or the absence of comment really, in regards to the monarchy . . . the monarchy was not so much loved as it should be and cherished, but worshipped in a kind of quasi-religious way.'[25] The point was well made. As has been proven on numerous occasions in its long history, unquestioning acceptance of the monarchy renders it more, not less, vulnerable. Only by adapting and modernising – even to a limited degree – can it remain relevant and in touch with its people.

The queen's inherent vulnerability was starkly demonstrated by a tragic event that occurred on 21 October 1966. The Welsh village of Aberfan lay at the foot of a mountain slope on which a large mining colliery spoil tip had been created. A period of heavy rain led to a dangerous build-up of water within the tip, which caused it to suddenly slide downhill as a slurry, engulfing the village's junior school and killing one hundred and sixteen children and twenty-eight adults. It was the worst mining disaster in British history. Amid the grief and anguish, people cast about for a scapegoat. Although most of the fury centred upon the National Coal Board, the queen was severely criticised for failing to visit the scene of the catastrophe. At first, she sent her husband Philip, and only after eight days did she finally go to Wales herself. Her reasoning was sound: she had no wish to disrupt the rescue effort with the usual fuss that surrounded the sovereign's visits. But she later admitted that her failure to visit sooner was the 'biggest regret' of her reign.

It may have been a wish to repair some of the damage that prompted the queen to take an unprecedented step three years later when, with some misgivings, she allowed the public a glimpse of 'real life' at Buckingham Palace. As one critic noted, *The Royal Family* documentary was 'devoted to the proposition that the Queen is a human being'.[26] Seventy-five days of filming in 172 locations resulted in a 110-minute film aired by the BBC on 21 June 1969. It showed the queen, her husband and children as they had never been seen before – 'off duty' at home, cooking, chatting and eating together.

It was an unmitigated disaster. Viewers watched a family doing their best to appear relaxed and casual while achieving the exact opposite. Worse still, instead of dissipating the endless speculation and gossip in the media that had prompted the queen to agree to the documentary in the first place, it made the royal family open season for press intrusion on an unprecedented scale. David Attenborough was reported as predicting that trouble might ensue because 'once the tribesfolk had seen inside the headman's hut the mystery was gone, and they would tire of seeing it repeated'.[27] The damage could not be undone, although the queen did mitigate it by ordering the film to be withdrawn from view. From thenceforth, she guarded her accustomed privacy and discretion even more fiercely than before.

A few days later, the queen and her family returned to the more familiar territory of pomp and pageantry at the investiture of her eldest son Charles as Prince of Wales. The event, held at Caernarfon Castle, was well received by the crowds who attended, thanks in part to the fact that the eighteen-year-old prince had spent time in Wales and delivered part of his speech in Welsh. Almost all of the major royal occasions during Elizabeth II's reign have been attended by large crowds, their cheers seeming to make a lie of – or at least to drown out – the republican sentiment voiced in the press and elsewhere.

In October 1969, the queen and her family were in the spotlight again when she welcomed the astronauts from the Apollo 11 mission to Buckingham Palace. Three months earlier, 600 million television viewers worldwide had watched breathlessly as Neil Armstrong and Buzz Aldrin became the first men to walk on the moon. After the return of their triumphant mission, Armstrong, Aldrin and fellow astronaut Michael Collins embarked upon a tour of twenty-four countries in thirty-eight days. The crew were presented to Elizabeth II, her husband Philip and children, Princess Anne, Prince Andrew and Prince Edward on 14 October 1969. What should have been a public relations triumph for the palace proved the opposite and the meeting was famously awkward. Armstrong, who was suffering from a heavy cold, inadvertently coughed in the queen's face repeatedly, prompting her to raise her hands in mock surrender.

The queen has never given any hint that her lack of political power has been a source of frustration, but has appeared willing to subsume her personal opinions to those of her government. In a speech made during a visit to Philadelphia in 1976, she defined statesmanship as being: 'To know the right time, and the manner of yielding what is impossible to keep.'[28] The following year, she turned a blind eye to the mockery of the Canadian prime minister, Pierre Trudeau, during his visit to Buckingham Palace. An outspoken republican, he flaunted his disapproval by sliding down banisters and pirouetting behind the queen's back. Elizabeth's refusal to be provoked won him over: he later reflected on 'the grace she displayed in public' and 'the wisdom she showed in private'.[29] Trudeau's reaction is typical of many others. While they are vociferous in their criticism of the monarchy as an institution, even the most hardened republicans have expressed admiration for the queen's unflinching sense of duty and her adherence to the constitution.

While the queen herself continued to command respect, the 1970s brought further embarrassment for her family – 'The Firm', as Prince Philip allegedly called them. In February 1976, tabloid photos were published showing her sister Margaret swimming off the coast of the private island of Mustique with her lover Roddy Llewellyn. Aged twenty-eight, he was seventeen years her junior and the press lambasted the princess for wasting the public's money on holidays with her 'toy boy'. The scandal put an end to Margaret's marriage to Antony Armstrong-Jones, Earl of Snowdon. For a time, they had been one the most glamorous couples in the world, hosting glittering parties for Hollywood stars and rock bands at their Kensington Palace home. But their relationship had always been tempestuous, riven by scandal and infidelity on both sides. Their acrimonious split would be the first of a series of high-profile marital breakdowns that would shake the monarchy to its core.

With the monarchy's public image at one of the lowest ebbs of Elizabeth II's reign, there were fears within the palace that the celebrations to mark her Silver Jubilee in 1977 would fall flat. The event was parodied by the punk band the Sex Pistols, who released the single 'God Save the Queen' as a protest against the 'fascist regime'. The record sleeve featured a defaced version of the queen's official Silver Jubilee portrait, in which the sovereign was blinded and gagged by the track title and band name. The single went to the top of the UK charts. 'Does Britain need a Queen?' was one of the questions asked in a major national poll conducted at this time, to which 16.4 per cent answered 'No' – 5 per cent higher than in previous polls.[30] But the result meant that there was still an overwhelming majority of people in favour of the monarchy, and they were in full evidence during the jubilee celebrations. Events were held throughout the United Kingdom and Commonwealth, attracting crowds in their thousands.

On 29 July 1981, the world watched as the queen's eldest son, Charles, Prince of Wales, married Lady Diana Spencer in a dazzling ceremony at St Paul's Cathedral. From the very beginning, their courtship had been played out in the glare of the media. The question of who the heir to the throne would marry had been on everyone's lips for some time, intensifying after Charles turned thirty in November 1978. The prince's name had been linked to a string of different women, including his long-term companion Camilla Parker Bowles (née Shand), a direct descendant of Edward VII's long-term mistress, Alice Keppel.[31]

Charles's great-uncle, Lord Mountbatten, who had been assassinated by the Irish Republican Army in 1979, had counselled Charles to 'sow his wild oats' while he was single, 'but for a wife he should choose a suitable, attractive, and sweet-charactered girl before she has met anyone else she might fall for'.[32] The virginal Diana Spencer appeared to fit the bill perfectly. The Spencers were one of the most distinguished noble families in the country – 'more royal than the royals', as one source remarked.[33] Charles remembered Diana as a 'splendid sixteen-year-old' when they first met in 1977. Although not academically gifted, she had a talent for music and dance and a natural aptitude with children – a skill she put to use as a nursery assistant and nanny after moving to London in 1978. Nicknamed 'Shy Di' by the press, Diana rapidly became a figure of intense public interest. Before long, she was hounded by photographers and journalists wherever she went. Public fascination with the monarchy was nothing new, but this was the beginning of media intrusion on a scale never seen before.

'This is the stuff of which fairy tales are made,' pronounced the Archbishop of Canterbury, Robert Runcie, in his wedding address.[34] To the outside world, Charles and Diana appeared blissfully happy as they exchanged their vows, watched by the 2,600 guests and an estimated global audience of 750 million. At least one million people had flocked to London to catch a glimpse of the procession and the balcony appearance at Buckingham Palace, with the now-traditional kiss. The *New York Times* hailed the occasion as a potent symbol of 'the continuity of the monarchy in the UK' – an observation that would prove deeply ironic.[35]

The reality was very different to the fairy tale. The couple barely knew each other – Diana later claimed that they had only met thirteen times before the engagement (fewer than the number of dress fittings she had prior to the wedding) and had little in common. Cracks soon began to appear in their relationship, although only those within Charles and Diana's most intimate circles knew that there was any cause for concern.

Their incompatibility aside, the main source of trouble was the fact that the prince was in love with his former girlfriend, Camilla Parker Bowles, whom he had first met in the early 1970s. The royal family had considered Camilla unsuitable as a bride for the future king because she was a commoner with a public dating past. She subsequently married one of her former partners, Andrew Parker Bowles, who had dated Charles's sister Anne for a time. Charles seems to have renewed his relationship with Camilla by the early 1980s, despite the fact that they were both married. It was later revealed that Diana discovered evidence of their relationship shortly before her wedding. She considered calling it off but her sisters told her: 'Bad luck . . . your face is on the tea-towels so you're too late to chicken out.' Diana recalled that on the eve of the wedding: 'I felt I was a lamb to the slaughter.'[36] But the Duke of Edinburgh had urged his eldest son to 'do the right thing' and the wedding had gone ahead.[37] The birth of their first child, Prince William, less than a year later, followed by Prince Harry in 1984, seemed to set the seal on the couple's happiness.

There was a discernible shift in public attitudes towards the monarchy during the 1980s. The media frenzy did not abate after Charles and Diana's wedding, but shifted to the opinions and private lives of the royal family as a whole. Editors of the major British newspapers realised that nothing guaranteed sales more than a headline about the royals. In September 1986, an editor at the *Observer* remarked: 'The royal soap opera has now reached such a pitch of public interest that the boundary between fact and fiction has been lost sight of . . . it is not just that some papers don't check their facts or accept denials: they don't care if the stories are true or not.'[38]

The editor may have had in mind the storm that had been whipped up about the queen's relationship with Margaret Thatcher, who was elected Britain's first female prime minister in 1979. 'The weekly meetings between the Queen and Mrs Thatcher . . . are dreaded by at least one of them', an insider revealed, claiming that the prime minister behaved more like a queen than Elizabeth herself.[39] During the ten-week Falklands conflict in 1982, Margaret Thatcher temporarily replaced the queen as the most potent symbol of national identity. 'No wonder they stand on ceremony,' she reputedly remarked of the Windsors, 'what else have they got?'[40] She later denied the reports of a rift between Downing Street and the palace, and the queen awarded Thatcher with two honours after her retirement from office, as if to prove the rumours false.

Still the media frenzy showed no sign of abating, particularly as it was supplied with ample fodder as the 1980s wore on. In July 1982, the world was scandalised by a report that an intruder had broken into Buckingham Palace. Michael Fagan was an unemployed thirty-three-year-old London man under the occasional delusion that his father was Rudolf Hess. With remarkable ease, he twice broke into the palace and on the second occasion made it into the queen's bedroom. The queen, who was awoken when he pulled back one of the curtains, showed considerable sang-froid by keeping him talking while she tried in vain to call for help. The palace police eventually arrived a full eight minutes after she had first raised the alarm. Fagan was arrested and sent to a psychiatric hospital, from which he was released three months later.

Although the incident prompted widespread admiration for the queen's bravery, as well as outrage at the shortcomings of the palace security, not all the royal press stories were so positive. In 1987, Elizabeth's youngest son, Prince Edward, made the royal family the subject of ridicule by staging the charity game show *It's a Royal Knockout*. Contestants included four senior royals: Princess Anne, Prince Andrew and his wife Sarah Ferguson, and Prince Edward himself. Although the intentions behind it were admirable, namely to raise money for charity and present a more informal side to the royal family, it was a deeply embarrassing spectacle and has gone down as one of the worst public relations disasters in the history of the monarchy.

The royal stories and scandals that dominated the headlines during the 1980s were as nothing to those of the following decade. On 24 November 1992, the queen marked the fortieth anniversary of her accession with a speech in which she famously called it her *annus horribilis*. In March, her second (and it is said, favourite) son, Prince Andrew, had separated from his wife, Sarah Ferguson. The following month her daughter Anne divorced Captain Mark Phillips, and in November a devastating fire at Windsor Castle destroyed some of the most precious parts of that ancient royal residence. The total cost of the repairs was in excess of £36 million and the queen agreed that Buckingham Palace should be opened to the public in order to help pay for the restoration. The prime minister, John Major, also announced reforms to the royal finances, including the queen's paying income tax and a reduction in the Civil List. This was prompted in part by the huge cost of the Windsor repairs, but also by growing criticism about the amount of public money spent on the crown.

But this 'horrible year' was not quite at an end. In December, the Prince and Princess of Wales announced their separation. By now, Diana had become the most photographed woman in the world – the closest thing to a global superstar that the royal family has ever produced. 'With Princess Diana, royalty met Hollywood head on', as one American author remarked.[41] She and Charles had been hailed by *Time* magazine as 'the most glamorous couple on earth', but Diana's popularity far exceeded that of her husband.[42] She eclipsed him on the numerous public engagements that they undertook during their marriage. Compassionate, accessible and tactile, the princess had the common touch that her husband so obviously lacked. But there were other, graver, sources of tension in the marriage, not least the twelve-year age gap and their wildly differing characters and interests. Most damaging of all, there had been infidelity on both sides.

The unravelling of the Wales's marriage was played out on a very public stage. Every detail that the press could glean about the cause of the split was dissected and debated at length. Their formal separation in December 1992 was by no means the end of the story. While Buckingham Palace tried to play down the scandal, Diana courted the publicity. Far from being the docile and dutiful wife whom Lord Mountbatten had recommended to his great-nephew, 'the virgin bride became the mouse that roared'.[43] More than a decade spent as a senior royal had strengthened Diana's character and opinions, and she had also grown highly skilled at using the media to her advantage. She secretly cooperated with Andrew Morton, whose book, *Diana: Her True Story*, was published in 1992 and uncovered a host of shocking details about her marriage. The book made Prince Charles so unpopular that there were calls for him to relinquish his right to the throne.

The Prince of Wales retaliated by cooperating with a publication of his own. But while Jonathan Dimbleby's biography (published in 1994) tried to present Charles's side of the story and convince readers of his virtues, it merely served to draw attention to his shortcomings. In June the same year, the prince gave a television interview during which he admitted to having an affair with Camilla Parker Bowles, but only after his marriage to Diana had irretrievably broken down. This was almost completely eclipsed by the now-infamous interview that Diana gave with *Panorama* journalist Martin Bashir in November 1995. In this broadcast, which was watched by millions worldwide, she claimed that her marriage had been 'a bit crowded' because of her husband's longstanding affair with Mrs Parker Bowles, but also admitted to infidelity herself with James Hewitt, a former cavalry officer.

Until now, the queen had kept her counsel on her eldest son's marital troubles. But the full force of the damage that this acrimonious battle was inflicting upon the royal family hit her when the interview was broadcast. The very next day she urged Charles and Diana to seek 'an early divorce'.[44] The decree absolute was issued in 1996. Towards the end of that year, as thoughts began to turn to the queen's forty-fifth year on the throne, when she would exceed the reign of the first Elizabeth, the press ruminated on the state of the monarchy. The failure of three out of four of her children's marriages prompted the *Guardian* to declare that they had 'swapped majesty for the status of international soap stars'. *The Times* was more measured but reported a 'strong mood' that only the queen's person sustained the monarchy and that without her there would be a republic.[45] At the same time, a general election was looming and Tony Blair's New Labour embodied the growing sense of 'out with the old, in with the new'.

Now at a safe distance from 'The Firm', Diana thrived in her newfound freedom, acting as an advocate for causes close to her heart and becoming the 'queen of people's hearts' that she had told *Panorama* she wished to be. She also continued to be close to her sons, Princes William and Harry, whose upbringing she had ensured was less formal than was typical for royal offspring and included a much wider range of everyday experiences, such as visits to theme parks and fast-food restaurants. Her ability to relate to people, no matter their background or experience, was vividly demonstrated when she visited hospitals, hugging victims of AIDS and leprosy, or walked along a path strewn with landmines in war-torn Angola. Hers was the royal touch of earlier centuries, bringing comfort and relief to sufferers across the world. This philanthropic role, particularly with humanitarian causes, shone a beacon to her future, promising greater happiness and fulfilment than she had ever found within the royal family.

But it was not to last. On 31 August 1997, exactly one year after her divorce had been finalised, the princess was killed in a car crash in Paris with her new partner, Dodi Fayed. Few events in British history have prompted the scale of national dismay and bewilderment that followed. An estimated 1.3 million floral tributes were placed outside the gates of Buckingham Palace and Kensington Palace, and within days they were waist high, stretching as far as the eye could see. Weeping crowds queued for up to twelve hours to sign the books of condolence at St James's Palace. The news dominated every television and radio channel for weeks on end.

Grief turned to outrage as the queen remained at Balmoral, where she and her family – including Charles and Diana's sons, William and Harry (then aged fifteen and twelve), had been on holiday when the news arrived. Meanwhile, the press ignited the increasing public anger towards the royal family by calling for the flag above Buckingham Palace to be flown at half-mast, despite the fact that the queen was not in residence. The senior churchman Wesley Carr later recalled: 'At one point it felt to me that I might even be the last Royal Dean of Westminster, and that the next one would inherit a republic.'[46]

Eventually, the palace responded to the dangerously high level of public hostility, thanks in no small part to the new prime minister. Tony Blair deftly captured the public mood when he gave a speech shortly after Diana's death praising her as 'the people's princess'. At his prompting, the queen and her family returned to London, and she and Prince Philip mingled with the crowds outside Buckingham Palace. The queen also made a television broadcast in which she expressed admiration for her former daughter-in-law and spoke of her feelings 'as a grandmother' to Diana's sons. When the flag was finally flown at half-mast, it prompted cheers among the crowds gathered outside the palace. Throughout her reign, the queen had been strictly governed by royal protocol and had refused to be swayed by either public opinion or political pressure. This was the first major exception to that in forty-five years and it paid dividends. The vitriol of the press and public dissolved almost overnight.

Diana's funeral eclipsed her wedding in the level of public interest that it generated. A state funeral in all but name, it was held in Westminster Abbey and attended by around two thousand guests, most of whom were personal friends of the late princess or representatives of the charities she supported. Over a million people lined the four-mile route from Kensington Palace to Westminster Abbey, while an estimated 2.5 billion people watched the ceremony on television. Diana's younger brother Charles, Earl Spencer, gave the funeral address, which slammed the press for hounding his sister to her death. There was also implied criticism of the royal family. The sound of applause from the sprawling crowds watching the broadcast on large screens outside filled the abbey as the earl returned to his seat.

In the years since Diana's death, there has been a tendency to view the extraordinary level of public grief – even hysteria – that it sparked as a strange phenomenon, a momentary loss of reason by a people known for their 'stiff upper lip'. Yet a similar outpouring of grief had been witnessed upon the death of Princess Charlotte of Wales in 1817 and, more recently, that of Elizabeth II's father, George VI. The German author and journalist Sebastian Haffner wrote of the latter in 1952: 'Can one really say that the mood of the hundreds of thousands who waited their turn in the February sleet of 1952 to pass by the bier of George VI was frivolous? . . . He would be a poor psychologist who failed to notice the deeply, solemnly, helplessly serious core of feeling in the British monarchist revival.'[47]

By the time of Diana's death, the monarchist revival of the 1950s had abated, so the public reaction perhaps had more to do with the personal connection they felt with the princess, rather than with the crown. Her glamour, charm and informality had shone an unflattering light on the Windsors, who appeared stiffly formal and staid by comparison. She had made their accustomed reserve seem more arrogant than dignified; their procedures and protocol 'unacceptably Victorian'.[48] Although the queen had been admired for her years of unflinching duty, that seemed inadequate to fill the gaping void left by her former daughter-in-law's death. There was a much more significant backlash against Prince Charles, whom many believed was now too compromised a figure to inherit the throne and that it should pass instead to his son William. Such was the opposition to the idea that he would one day marry Camilla Parker Bowles that he was obliged to issue a public statement that he had no intention of remarrying.

'I for one believe that there are lessons to be drawn from her life and from the extraordinary and moving reaction to her death,' the queen had declared during her broadcast on 5 September 1997.[49] In the weeks and months that followed, experts speculated endlessly about the impact that Diana's death would have upon the monarchy. Although there was some effort on the part of Elizabeth II and her family to mirror her example – a walkabout outside McDonald's, tea in a Glasgow housing association bungalow, and Prince Charles addressing the queen as 'Mummy' at her ninetieth birthday celebrations in 2018 – it was far from the seismic shift that some had predicted. Besides, as the queen herself irritably remarked when reading of this 'new informality' in the press: 'Don't they realise I've done it before?'[50]

Instead, Diana might be compared to other estranged royals who had shaken the monarchy to its core during their lifetime, but whose long-term effect on the institution was minimal. George IV's rejected wife Caroline was just as much the 'people's princess' as Diana, but had been largely forgotten a generation later. Edward VIII had equalled the Princess of Wales's glamour and celebrity, and, like her, had offered the promise of a more modern and approachable monarchy, but had quickly become a pathetic and directionless outcast. But Diana's legacy differs from theirs in one crucial respect: she left behind progeny, one of whom will inherit the throne. Prince William's physical resemblance to his mother, as well as his informal and approachable style, mean that, as one commentator put it: 'Diana has not finished with the British monarchy yet.'[51]

The year 1997 had been the worst of Elizabeth's long reign. It closed with the decommissioning of the royal yacht *Britannia*, the ceremony for which saw the queen shed a tear. Significantly, Tony Blair's government did not propose a replacement.

The twenty-first century was ushered in amid an atmosphere of anti-royalism, with ever more questions being raised about royal finances. Although the queen herself continued to attract consistently high approval ratings, the criticism was directed at her wider family and, perhaps more worryingly, at the institution of monarchy itself. The ill feeling engendered by the marital crises and scandals of the 1990s was such that as Elizabeth approached her fiftieth year on the throne in 2002, there were fears that any Golden Jubilee celebrations would be poorly attended.

For the queen, it would be a year marked by sadness as well as celebration. Her sister Margaret died in February and their 101-year-old mother the following month. This prompted widespread sympathy for the queen and gave fresh impetus to the street parties and other commemorative events that were staged across the country that summer. During the course of the year, Elizabeth II and her husband undertook extensive tours of the United Kingdom and Commonwealth.

By now, the Duke of Edinburgh had had ample time to become accustomed to his role as consort. Despite courting controversy with a number of ill-judged remarks, he had proved a source of enduring support for the queen and their marriage was hailed as one of the most successful partnerships in royal history. It was certainly the longest: in November 2007, Elizabeth II became the first British monarch to celebrate a diamond wedding anniversary. Then aged eighty-one, her energy appeared undiminished – as did the scale of her commitments.

The new century brought more positive publicity for the royal family, too. In March 2005, the queen gave her formal consent to the marriage of her eldest son Charles to Camilla Parker Bowles. It is an indication of how much had changed since Edward VIII's abdication in 1936 and Princess Margaret's ill-fated engagement to Peter Townsend in 1953 that a divorced heir to the throne could be granted permission to marry another divorcee. Even an institution grounded in centuries of seemingly unbreakable tradition could learn from past mistakes.

The marriage was not without complications, though. The difficulty of securing a licence for the ceremony to be held at Windsor

Castle meant that it was transferred to the nearby Guildhall. This was the first time that a member of the royal family had been married in a civil ceremony in England, which in itself was the source of some controversy. As head of the Church of England, it was not appropriate for the queen to attend a civil ceremony, but she was present at the blessing held afterwards in St George's Chapel. She also attended the reception in the castle and, in a speech littered with references to her beloved horse-racing, she declared her satisfaction that: 'My son is home and dry with the woman he loves.'[52]

The general acceptance of Prince Charles's new marriage was a testament to the carefully planned public relations campaign by his office to restore both his and Camilla's reputation in the wake of Diana's death. But the tenuous nature of this was demonstrated when the television series *The Crown* cast the prince and his second wife in an unflattering light, reviving much of the criticism levelled at them by the late princess and her global army of supporters.

The Prince of Wales's relationship with the press has never been easy. He has variously been presented as an ill-informed meddler and a hopeless idealist, although his long-standing concern for environmental issues is no longer the subject of derision that it has been in the past. Royal historians have been critical, too, drawing attention to his 'vanity, petulance, arrogance and self-centredness', and claiming that he is less Prince Charming and more 'the whinger of Windsor'.[53]

By contrast, Prince Charles's sons have enjoyed almost unbroken adulation from the public and press alike. This was stoked by the marriage of the eldest, Prince William, to Catherine (Kate) Middleton in April 2011. The couple met at St Andrew's University in 2001 and had one of the longest courtships in royal history. Painfully aware of his mother's unpreparedness for her role as a royal consort, Prince William was apparently determined to ensure that any partner he chose would be fully cognisant of what lay ahead. Their wedding, which was staged at Westminster Abbey, attracted greater public interest than any since that of William's parents thirty years earlier. As well as the estimated 2 billion people in 180 countries who tuned into the television broadcasts, there were 72 million live streams on YouTube.

'The marriage of Prince William of Wales and Catherine Middleton . . . appears to have secured the future of the British throne for, at the least, half a century to come', predicted one royal expert.[54] The celebrations to mark the queen's Diamond Jubilee the following year seemed to support that. Huge crowds braved the unseasonably cold, wet June weather to watch the splendid river pageant, the fly-past by Second World War aircraft, and the obligatory balcony appearance at Buckingham Palace. A pop concert featuring acts from the previous six decades of the queen's reign was held on 4 June, which had been made a national holiday. The only false note was sounded by a small republican demonstration outside City Hall, at which one of the activists gave a speech comparing the end of the monarchy to the abolition of slavery, women securing the vote and equality for homosexuals. It was drowned out by chants of 'Long live the Queen!' Elizabeth II's popularity was given a further boost the following month when the Olympic Games opened in London and she played a brief but starring role in a James Bond sketch with actor Daniel Craig, delivering the iconic line: 'Good evening, Mr Bond.'[55]

The popularity of the newly created Duke and Duchess of Cambridge and the generation of young royals they represented was enhanced by the marriage of William's younger brother Harry to Meghan Markle in 2018. Once more, there was proof of how much had changed since Edward VIII's abdication because, like his great-great-uncle, Harry's choice of bride was an American divorcee. Meghan Markle's career as an actress lent their courtship the lustre of celebrity, and the wedding, celebrated at St George's Chapel in Windsor on 19 May, was attended by a host of Hollywood stars. To mark the occasion, the queen granted her grandson and his wife the titles Duke and Duchess of Sussex. With their informality, multiculturism (the duchess is of African-American descent) and passion for humanitarian causes, they made a thoroughly modern royal couple.

But any hopes that the queen might have cherished about the future role that her younger grandson and his wife might play were dashed when, in January 2020, the Duke and Duchess of Sussex announced that they were stepping back as senior royals and moving to America with their young son Archie. Although there had been rumours of a rift between the couple and other members of the royal family, as well as an increasingly fractious relationship with the media, the announcement sent shockwaves across the world – not to mention within Buckingham Palace itself. The queen was said to be greatly saddened by her grandson's decision and held talks with him, his brother William and their father Charles, in an attempt to reach a solution. These did not change Harry's decision, and while he and his wife were deprived of their Royal Highness titles, the queen made it clear that he would be welcomed back into the family if ever he changed his mind.

Prince Harry's departure from the royal family had temporarily obscured another, altogether more serious threat to the crown's public face. It was reported that the queen's second son, Prince Andrew, had become embroiled in a scandal thanks to his friendship with the American financier Jeffrey Epstein, a convicted sex offender. Allegations of a liaison between the prince and an underaged girl who had been trafficked for sex by Epstein filled the headlines of newspapers across the globe. Against advice, in November 2019 Prince Andrew gave an interview for BBC's *Newsnight* in which he strenuously denied the allegations.[56] The interview was panned by the media as a 'car crash', 'nuclear explosion level bad' and the worst public relations crisis for the royal family since the death of Diana. A few days later, a statement from Buckingham Palace announced that the prince was suspending his public duties 'for the foreseeable future'.

While the press might cheerfully predict the 'end of the House of Windsor' with each fresh scandal, abolishing the monarchy is hardly a straightforward task. A whole suite of parliamentary legislation would need to be drafted, agreed and passed, which, even assuming there was the will, would be a tortuous exercise. Another option would be for republicans to organise an attack on Buckingham Palace and capture its occupants. But even in the days after Princess Diana's death, when hostility towards the royals seemed to reach fever pitch, there was never any hint of coordinated action against them.

Neither is there any prospect of the royals themselves declaring that they have had enough. A family governed by a sense of duty and tradition to the extent that the current queen shows no inclination to retire even though she is well into her nineties is hardly likely to collectively agree to throw in the towel. 'If . . . people feel it has no further part to play', Prince Philip once remarked with charac-teristic frankness, 'then for goodness' sake let's end the thing on amicable terms without having a row about it.'[57] He knew how big that 'if' was. The final possibility would be to hold a public referendum on the future of the monarchy when there is a change of reign. But, as the British government and its citizens are painfully aware following the Brexit referendum, such a course can lead to years of political, social and economic turmoil.

Britain has at least arrived at a version of monarchy that is for the most part inoffensive. A 'Crowned Republic', in the words of Alfred, Lord Tennyson, it retains the trappings and charisma of royalty without obstructing the democracy with which it is now surrounded. The semi-divine nature of monarchy that still existed at the beginning of Elizabeth II's reign, with 35 per cent of the population believing that she had been chosen by God, has all but receded. The queen's personal faith might be strong, but she no longer exercises the same authority over the religious life of her people. The 'supreme head of the church of England' established in Henry VIII's day has been watered down to a 'supreme governor of this realm as well in all spiritual or ecclesiastical causes as temporal'. Prince Charles has indicated that when at last he becomes king, he wishes to be 'Defender of Faith' rather than 'Defender of *the* Faith', as every monarch has been since the pope conferred the title on Henry VIII in 1521.

Another way in which the queen has made the monarchy more in tune with the times is to lessen its burden on the public purse. The number of royals who are entitled to direct government funding has been significantly reduced. At the same time, major royal events such as the Diamond Jubilee are now more dependent upon private donations and sponsorship. As a result, the cost of the crown today is around £41 million per year, which equates to 51 pence per tax payer. Monarchists point to the fact that the royals bring more tour-ists to Britain than any other attraction and that events such as royal weddings provide a major boost to the economy.[58] If most people would agree that the long-serving queen represents value for money, however, the same does not extend to all members of her family, particularly those who have been embroiled in embarrassing scandals.

The sang-froid that Elizabeth II displayed in public during each one of these is typical of the approach she has taken throughout her reign. Whatever she may feel in private, in public she appears unchanged. To some this is admirably dignified; to others, unfeeling and remote. Her instinct to uphold royal privacy and tradition in an age obsessed with overnight celebrities and reality television might appear out of touch. But given that some aspects of the 'establishment' and its members would not bear close scrutiny, it is also expedient. Many times, history has proved the wisdom of Bagehot's remark that 'royal mystique' is essential to the survival of the monarchy.[59]

The year 2021 would bring both scandal and sorrow for the queen. Early in the year, the Duke and Duchess of Sussex recorded an interview with the American talk-show host and television producer Oprah Winfrey in which they explained the reasons for their sudden departure from royal life. Broadcast on 7 March, it contained shocking allegations against the royal family, the most damaging of which was racism. As with other royal scandals, it fuelled republican sentiment in Britain and the Commonwealth. 'The royal family has always been presented as the Rock of Gibraltar for all constitutional monarchies', the chairman of the Australian Republican Movement wrote in the *Sydney Morning Herald*. 'What we in fact see is extreme dysfunction and possible racism.' Reporting on the story, the American news network CNN considered the likelihood that the controversy would lead to an abolition of the monarchy, and concluded: 'If history teaches us anything, it's never to underestimate the power of Elizabeth.'[60]

A month later, the pendulum of sympathy swung back towards the queen when the death of her husband of seventy-three years was announced. Prince Philip had only recently returned to Windsor Castle after a prolonged spell in hospital, during which he had been treated for a pre-existing heart condition. He died on the morning of 9 April, two months shy of his hundredth birthday. The queen reportedly described her husband's death as 'having left a huge void in her life'. More than 13 million viewers in the United Kingdom watched the television coverage of his funeral at St George's Chapel, Windsor, eight days later, which was attended by just thirty members of the royal family because of COVID-19 restrictions. The duke had planned every detail, including the design of a specially adapted Land Rover hearse.

Funerals are traditionally a time for looking back, but the death of the longest-serving royal consort in history prompted thoughts of the future. Most people in Britain do not remember a time when Elizabeth II was not on the throne. '*Semper Eadem*' ('Always the same') was the motto of her Tudor namesake, but it neatly describes her own style of monarchy, with its quiet steadfastness and unwavering dedication to duty. Such constancy has led to a tendency to take the queen and her reign for granted. But there was a new air of fragility to the grieving widow of almost ninety-five as she sat alone in the quire of St George's Chapel, deprived of her 'strength and stay' for the first time in eight decades. It served as a salutary reminder that even this extraordinarily resilient, dependable monarch cannot go on for ever.

Early in the reign of Elizabeth II's father, *The Times* predicted that a monarch's success would depend not on their 'intellectual brilliance or superlative talent of any kind, but upon the moral qualities of steadiness, staying power and self-sacrifice'. During a reign that has witnessed an almost unimaginable scale of change, the queen has acted as 'an anchor for our age', in the words of General Ban Ki-moon, Secretary General of the United Nations General Assembly.[61] Along the way, she has broken all sorts of records: longest-reigning monarch in British history and longest-reigning female head of state in the world (since 9 September 2015), the first British monarch to reach their Sapphire Jubilee (6 February 2017), and the oldest living monarch (since 23 April 2019), to name but a few. She currently shares with George III the record of being served by the most prime ministers (fourteen), although the odds are that by the end of her reign she will have broken that, too. In a speech given on the day when the queen broke the first of these records, the then prime minister David Cameron aptly referred to her as 'a golden thread running through three post-war generations'.[62]

Although the queen is viewed as a stalwart of tradition, the monarchy has undergone a significant degree of modernisation during her long reign. Some of the more anachronistic customs of court life, such as the presentation of debutantes and the protocols concerning divorcees, have been abolished. The palace is no longer staffed by 'tweedy aristocrats' but by specialists in administration, the arts and social media.[63] Royal finances have become more stream-lined. Elizabeth II has also introduced new legislation giving equal pre-eminence to female heirs in the British line of succession for the first time in history – a subtle but revolutionary change.

When asked in 1992 which of her many duties she considered most important, the queen replied unhesitatingly: 'investitures'. Each year, about twenty-five ceremonies are held at which she recognises the distinguished service of three thousand or more military and police personnel, civilians and voluntary workers with medals and, occasionally, knighthoods. While it is these personal interactions that the queen enjoys most, she has shown no less commitment to the myriad other royal occasions, such as Trooping the Colour, all of which still attract considerable interest across the world.

The royal heritage and tradition that Elizabeth II upholds is an essential part of Britain's DNA; the reason why millions of visitors flock to its palaces each year, devour stories about the royal family in the press and watch countless royal documentaries. Many aspects of national life still bear the stamp of the monarch: the government is 'Her Majesty's', the crown brings cases for trial into the law courts, and numerous companies trade under the proud banner of a royal charter. Meaningless titles, perhaps, but they speak to the enduring image and tradition of monarchy in Britain.

The queen's dedication to duty shows no sign of abating. She continued to fulfil her constitutional role during the global pandemic of 2020–21 (mostly via video calls), and in stark contrast to her great-great-grandmother Victoria, she returned to her official duties just four days after her husband's death. Alongside these duties, Elizabeth II is patron of more than six hundred charities and organisations. Despite reaching her ninety-fifth birthday in April 2021, she does not intend to abdicate, although she is expected to cede more of her public duties to Prince Charles in future. Her Platinum Jubilee in February 2022 may provide an opportunity to renew her pledge to the nation, as she did at her Diamond Jubilee ten years earlier: 'I . . . give thanks for the great advances that have been made since 1952 and . . . look forward to the future with a clear head and warm heart.'[64]

'The heart of Kings is unknowable', declares the biblical book of Proverbs.[65] It is no small irony that in this age of mass communication, we have fewer of Elizabeth II's personal opinions and feelings on record than those of her predecessors. We know that she likes horse-racing and corgis, spends her summers at Balmoral and her Christmases at Sandringham. But her spoken words are almost entirely the work of others. The speeches she gives at the opening of Parliament are drafted by the prime minister and their advisers, and she must read them out, word for word, even if she disagrees with any of the content. Every royal visit, dinner and walkabout is informed by a thorough briefing from her aides, with suggestions of what to say to whom. Only occasionally has the queen found ways of expressing her views in public. When she opened Parliament in 2017, she wore a blue hat decorated with yellow flowers, a tacit message of her support for the European Union in the wake of Brexit.

What we do have in ample evidence, though, is the queen's unwavering sense of duty and the stabilising presence she has given to the monarchy during the past six decades. Those qualities might not grab the history headlines in the same way as the king who married six times, the queen who 'lived and died a virgin', or the monarchs who ruled by conquest. But the very lack of personal drama has arguably been the secret of Elizabeth II's success.

Epilogue

'We must not let in daylight upon magic'

'The history of the monarchy in this country is a one-way street of humiliation, sacrifices and concessions in order to survive. First the barons came for us, then the merchants, now the journalists. Small wonder we make such a fuss about curtsies, protocol and precedents. It's all we have left. The last scraps of armour as we go from reign to reign to being nothing at all. Marionettes.'

(*The Crown*, Season 2)

B Y THE END of Queen Victoria's reign in 1901, there were eighteen European monarchies and three republics. Now only twelve monarchies remain, of which ten are hereditary and two (the Vatican City and Andorra) are elective.[1] Most modern monarchs, Elizabeth II included, enjoy only symbolic power and bear little resemblance to their medieval and early modern ancestors. Only the pope in Rome exercises absolute authority.

While there is no immediate prospect of the British monarchy ending, recent research has revealed a great deal of uncertainty about its longer-term future. A 2006 MORI poll conducted on behalf of the *Sun* newspaper looking at the British public's attitudes towards the monarchy showed that a significant number of people were not convinced it would still exist in fifty years' time, and a substantial majority believed that it would be abolished by the end of the twenty-first century. Interestingly, 30 per cent of participants were in favour of discontinuing the monarchy after Elizabeth II's death – far more than objected to the concept of monarchy itself.

A change of reign is bound to spark debate about the purpose and role of the monarchy. Elizabeth II has gone some way towards modernising the institution, but there are likely to be calls for it to be further streamlined. Reducing the cost of the crown to the public or making it entirely self-sufficient is one way in which its future might be safeguarded. Another is to reverse the shift of focus from sovereign to royal family that occurred during Victoria's reign. The current queen has succeeded in spite of 'The Firm', not because of it.

If and when he becomes king, Prince Charles will be the oldest person to ascend the throne in British history. Examples from the past thousand years have proved that, on the whole, the longer an heir to the throne waits to inherit, the less successful an incumbent they will be – witness George IV and Edward VII, among others. Indeed, some of our most successful sovereigns have been those who never expected to inherit the throne at all, such as Elizabeth I, George VI and Elizabeth II. Rather than preparing potential monarchs for the role that lies ahead, a long time spent as heir to the throne often leads to frustration, disillusion and even ridicule.

In Charles's favour, though, is the fact that he has put his time in waiting to good use, especially in recent years, when he has taken on more roles for the queen. Perhaps more than any other member of the royal family since his late wife, he has also embraced the monarchy's philanthropic role. Through the various Princes Trusts he has established, he has sought to help the unemployed, ethnic minorities, those with physical or mental disabilities and other disadvantaged groups. The emergence of a 'Welfare Monarchy' was hailed by the *Times Literary Supplement* in 1993 as 'the most important development in the history of the monarchy over the past 200 years'. A leading academic concurred: 'The monarchy is only likely to be in real danger when the begging letters cease to arrive at Buckingham Palace.'[2]

As Prince Charles prepares for his future role, he would be well advised to reflect upon the past millennia of royal history and draw lessons from it. Of course, seeking to emulate the traits of Britain's most successful monarchs is fraught with difficulty because each was very much of their time. The decisive leadership of William I, Edward III and Henry V was perfectly suited to an era when England's kings ruled by conquest. Elizabeth I and Queen Victoria embodied the self-confident, imperialistic values of their age and won widespread adulation as 'weak and feeble' women in a male-dominated world. In more recent times, George V and George VI overcame the increasing irrelevance of the monarchy in the political arena by providing a national figurehead for the war effort. But there are certain lessons that stand the test of time.

As has been shown time and again in the history of the British crown, the most successful sovereigns have been those who have proved adept at managing their public image. This has involved a delicate balancing act. As James I observed: 'A King is as one set on a stage, whose smallest actions and gestures, all the people gazingly do behold.' But the temptation to feed the insatiable appetite for royal stories, photographs, film footage and the like with anything other than carefully curated access should be firmly resisted. As one journalist put it: 'The further one goes down the corridors of the Palace . . . the more threadbare the carpets become.' During Queen Victoria's reign, Walter Bagehot urged: 'Our royalty is to be reverenced, and if you begin to poke about it you cannot reverence it . . . We must not let in daylight upon magic.'[3]

Mystique does not necessarily mean remoteness. As Princess Diana once observed: 'It's vital that the monarchy keeps in touch with the people.'[4] Some of the most popular monarchs in British history are those who have led a riotous, even notorious private life, or whose lack of formality has endeared them to their people. Those ultimate royal rakes, Charles II and Edward VII, kept a bevy of mistresses, sired numerous illegitimate children between them, and were the life and soul of every party. Yet they never forgot their royal dignity. Thus, in 1681, at the height of the Exclusion Crisis, the same Charles II who had excited disapproval for his 'profaneness and dissolution' asserted his majesty by appearing in full royal regalia.[5] Likewise, when Edward VII's beloved mistress Lillie Langtry poured a handful of ice down his back as a joke during a costume ball, the king was so furious that he spurned her for a long time afterwards.

Monarchs such as Charles II and Edward VII were forgiven their lapses in morality because they upheld and asserted their royal dignity when it mattered. They also fulfilled their royal duty. This is something that even the most charismatic and popular monarch must never neglect. Edward VIII's playboy lifestyle was irresistible to admirers all over the world. But that changed abruptly when he chose to relinquish his duty for the woman he loved. Thereafter, he was presented as a profligate wastrel, selfish and vain, his life lacking all meaning. A similar shift in public attitudes towards Prince Charles's younger son Harry took place after he gave up his official royal duties and started a new life in America with his wife Meghan Markle.

Perhaps the most vital ingredient for success is one that is difficult to emulate: character. The crown has survived numerous incumbents ill suited to the position over the past thousand years, but now that the role is almost entirely symbolic, personality is of paramount importance. The last six decades have proved that the decidedly unglamorous qualities of duty and dignity are highly prized, as even the queen's fiercest critics have admitted. 'No breath of scandal has ever touched her', observed Lord Altrincham. 'She behaves decently because she *is* decent.'[6]

Any future monarchs who are not blessed with such a character would be well advised to take refuge in the trappings of monarchy that have long been beloved of people not just in Britain but across the globe. The sumptuous palaces and glorious pageantry, the glittering regalia and centuries-old ceremonies. These 'toys and trifles' of monarchy, so disdained by Oliver Cromwell's supporters during the English Civil War, may be the key to its continuity, its longevity and, ultimately, its survival.

'Always changing, and always the same.'[7] This description of an ideal monarchy is as accurate as it is contradictory. As well as striving for relevance, the crown should retain those traditions that have defined it for centuries. Royal ceremony and spectacle, we are reminded, still hold 'cathartic and consoling power'. The thread of continuity that the monarchy symbolises can offer a vital sense of certainty in a rapidly changing world, even if it lacks any real power to influence that change.[8]

The continuity that lies at the heart of the British monarchy was neatly encapsulated by Lord Lyndhurst, who served as Lord High Chancellor during the reigns of three nineteenth-century monarchs. 'The sovereign always exists,' he declared, 'the person only is changed.'

When quoting from original sources, I have modernised the spelling and punctuation for ease of reference.

NOTES ON SOURCES

PREFACE

1. Strong, R., *Coronation: A History of Kingship and the British Monarchy* (London, 2005), p. 424; Bogdanor, V., *The Monarchy and the Constitution* (Oxford, 1995), p. 30; Nicolson, H., *Monarchy* (London, 1962), pp. 168, 301.
2. Nairn, T., *The Enchanted Glass: Britain and its Monarchy* (London, 1988), p. 20; Luce, H., 'Monarchy: The Vital Strand', in Murray-Brown, J. (ed.), *The Monarchy and its Future* (London, 1969), p. 132.
3. Taylor, M. (ed.), Bagehot, W., *The English Constitution* (Oxford, 2009), p. 72.

INTRODUCTION

1. Starkey, D., *Crown & Country – The Kings & Queens of England: A History* (London, 2010), p. 5.
2. Cannon, J. and Griffiths, R., *The Oxford Illustrated History of the British Monarchy* (Oxford, 1988), p. 278.
3. In 1626 the antiquarian Sir Robert Cotton took a copy of Æthelstan's coronation book to present to Charles I in the hope that it would form part of his own crowning ceremony. Charles spurned Cotton's offer by having the royal barge rowed past its mooring point, where the antiquarian was waiting. (BL Cotton Tiberius A II – Coronation Gospels of Æthelstan, first quarter of the eleventh century.)
4. BL Cotton MS Augustus II 23; *Carta Dirige Gressus*.
5. The seminal work on English coronations is Strong, *Coronation*.
6. The same pledge by the king that it was his sacred duty to maintain peace, good order and the rule of law among his Christian people was repeated at subsequent coronations in the tenth and eleventh centuries. (BL Additional MS 57337 ff. 60v–61r.).
7. The Bible tells of how Zadok and Nathan anointed King Solomon in c. 970 BC: 1 Kings 1:38.
8. *Anglo-Saxon Chronicles*, p. 162.

9. Barlow, F. (ed. and trans.), *The Life of King Edward Who Rests at Westminster* [*Vita Ædwardis*] (Oxford, 1992), p. 24.

10. *Anglo-Saxon Chronicles*, p. 219.

PART 1: THE NORMANS (1066–1154)

WILLIAM THE CONQUEROR (1066–87)

1. Forester, T. (ed. and trans.), *The Chronicle of Henry of Huntingdon* (Felinfach, 1991), pp. 1–2.

2. Chibnall, M. (ed. and trans.), *The Ecclesiastical History of Orderic Vitalis*, 6 vols (1968–78), Vol. II, p. 145.

3. Mynors, R.A.B., Thomson, R.M. and Winterbottom, M. (eds. and trans.), *William of Malmesbury, Gesta Regum Anglorum: The History of the English Kings*, Vols. I and II (Oxford, 1998–9), Vol. I, p. 447; Malmesbury, *Gesta Regum Anglorum*, Vol. I, p. 449.

4. *Gesta Normannorum Ducum*, Vol. II, pp. 162n, 163. The Bayeux Tapestry represents it as coinciding with Harold's coronation, which was a case of dramatic licence for it could only have been seen in England between 24 and 30 April. For other contemporary records of the phenomenon, see: *Anglo-Saxon Chronicles*, p. 194; *Orderic Vitalis*, Vol. II, p. 135; *Ingulphus's Chronicle*, pp. 137–8; *The Chronicle of John of Worcester*, Vol. II, p. 601.

5. Burgess, G.S. and Holden, A. (ed. and trans.), *Wace, The Roman de Rou* (Jersey, 2002), p. 241. His account is corroborated by *The Chronicle of Battle Abbey*, p. 35. Malmesbury provides a slightly different account, crediting one of William's knights with this flash of inspiration: 'You have England in your hand, duke, and you shall be king!' *Gesta Regum Anglorum*, Vol. I, p. 451.

6. *Anglo-Saxon Chronicles*, pp. 199–200. See also: OV II, p. 173.

7. Davis, R.H.C. and Chibnall, M. (eds.), *The 'Gesta Willelmi' of William of Poitiers* (Oxford, 1998), p. 131. For a similar account, see: *Orderic Vitalis*, Vol. II, p. 175.

8. Wace claims that Harold continued fighting after his eye was 'put out' by an arrow and was subsequently felled by a blow to the thigh, whereupon 'there was such a throng . . . that I cannot say who killed him' (*Roman de Rou*, p. 287). A grisly account of his slaughter is provided by Guy Bishop of Amiens (Barlow, *The Carmen de Hastingae Proelio of Guy Bishop of Amiens*, p. 33).

9. *The Chronicle of Henry of Huntingdon*, p. 208.

10. Barlow, *The Carmen de Hastingae Proelio*, p. 45.

11. *Orderic Vitalis*, Vol. II, p. 185. For another account of the incident, see: *Gesta Willelmi*, p. 151.

12. Wright, T. (ed.), *The Chronicle of Pierre de Langtoft, in French Verse, from the earliest period to the death of King Edward I*, 2 vols. (London, 1866–8), Vol. I, p. 413.

13. *The Chronicle of Henry of Huntingdon*, pp. 215–16.

14. Domesday Book still survives – remarkably intact – in the collections of The National Archives, E 31/2 and E 31/1.

15. *The Chronicle of Henry of Huntingdon*, p. 217.

16. Malmesbury, *Gesta Regum Anglorum*, Vol. I, p. 461.

WILLIAM II (1087–1100)

1. Williamson, D., *The Kings and Queens of England* (London, 2002), p. 38; *Ordericus Vitalis*, Vol. V, p. 203; *The Chronicle of Henry of Huntingdon*, p. 449.

2. *The Chronicle of Henry of Huntingdon*, p. 605; Malmesbury, *Gesta Regum Anglorum*, Vol. I, p. 509.

3. Malmesbury, *Gesta Regum Anglorum*, Vol. I, p. 567.

4. Malmesbury, *Gesta Regum Anglorum*, Vol. I, p. 577.

5. Cussans, *Kings & Queens of the British Isles* (London, 2017), p. 75.

6. *Oxford Illustrated History of the British Monarchy*, p. 120.

7. *Anglo-Saxon Chronicles*, p. 235.

8. Winterbottom, M. (ed.), William of Malmesbury, *Gesta Pontificum Anglorum*, Vol. I (Oxford, 2007), p. 543.

9. This was known as porphyrogeniture, also referred to as 'born to the purple': a system of political succession that favours the rights of sons born after their father has become king, over older siblings born before their father's ascent to the throne.

HENRY I (1100–35)

1. *Oxford Illustrated History of the British Monarchy*, p. 114.

2. Douglas, D.C. and Greenaway, W. (eds.), *English Historical Documents*, Vol. II (London, 1953), p. 434.

3. Malmesbury, *Gesta Regum Anglorum*, Vol. II, p. 488.

4. *Oxford Illustrated History of the British Monarchy*, p. 162.

5. *Oxford Illustrated History of the British Monarchy*, p. 131; *Oxford Book of Royal Anecdotes*, p. 61.

6. *Ordericus Vitalis*, Vol. VI, p. 100.

7. For example, William Stubbs and Edward Freeman.

8. The two illegitimate children were Richard of Lincoln and Matilda of Perche. There is some confusion over whether Richard was Henry I's legitimate son of the same name, by his first wife Matilda. Two contemporary sources claim he was, while others claim that the legitimate Richard died in infancy. See: Weir, *Britain's Royal Families*, p. 47. A detailed account of the tragedy is provided by Spencer, C., *The White Ship: Conquest, Anarchy and the Wrecking of Henry I's Dream* (London, 2020).

9. Starkey, *Crown & Country*, p. 148.

10. After Henry's death Adeliza married William d'Aubigny, son of a royal butler, and bore several children.

MATILDA AND STEPHEN (1135–54)

1. *Plantagenet Chronicles*, p. 69; *Oxford Illustrated History of the British Monarchy*, p. 138.

2. Malmesbury, *Gesta Regum Anglorum*, Vol. II, p. 18.

3. *The Chronicle of Henry of Huntingdon*, pp. 712–13.

4. *Oxford Illustrated History of the British Monarchy*, p. 138.

5. Starkey, *Crown & Country*, p. 160.

6. Malmesbury, *Gesta Regum Anglorum*, Vol. II, p. 63.

7. Gervase of Canterbury, *The Chronicle*, cited in Cussans, *Kings & Queens*, p. 56.

8. Potter, K.R. (ed. and trans.), *Gesta Stephani* (Oxford, 1976).

9. Starkey, *Crown & Country*, p. 172.

10. Howlett, R. (ed.), William of Newburgh, *Historia rerum Anglicarum*, Rolls series (London, 1884), p. 94.

11. Malmesbury, *Gesta Regum Anglorum*, Vol. II, p. 22.

12. Stubbs, W. (ed.), *The historical works of Gervase of Canterbury*, 2 vols., Rolls series, 73 (London, 1879–80), Vol. I, p. 159.

13. *Anglo-Saxon Chronicles*, p. 268.

PART 2: THE PLANTAGENETS (1154–1399)

1. Plantagenet has been attributed as a surname to all the kings of England descended from Henry II until the death of Richard III in 1485. But Henry II and his successors were usually identified by reference either to their parentage or their places of birth, and it was not until the fifteenth century when Richard, Duke of York, styled himself Plantagenet that it came into common usage. It was also borne by the illegitimate sons of his successors, Edward IV and Richard III. The name was cited in Shakespeare's

King John (Act V, scene vi, line 12) and was commonly used by historians from the late seventeenth century.

HENRY II (1154–89)

1. *Oxford Illustrated History of the British Monarchy*, p. 140.
2. *Patrologia Latina*, Vol. CCXC, p. 1322.
3. Stubbs, W. (ed.), Ralph de Diceto, 'Ymagines historiarum', *Radulfi de Diceto . . . opera historica*, 2 vols., Rolls series, 68 (1876), Vol. I, p. 351.
4. Robertson, J.C. and Sheppard, J.B. (eds.), *Materials for the history of Thomas Becket, archbishop of Canterbury*, 7 vols., Rolls series, 67 (1875–85), Vol. VI, pp. 71–2.
5. *Patrologia Latina*, Vol. XXVII, pp. 48–9; see also Gerald of Wales, *The Conquest of Ireland*, cited in *Oxford Illustrated History of the British Monarchy*, p. 151.
6. *Oxford Illustrated History of the British Monarchy*, p. 137.
7. Cussans, *Kings & Queens*, p. 71.
8. William of Newburgh, *History of England*, cited in *Oxford Illustrated History of the British Monarchy*, pp. 82–3.
9. *English Historical Documents*, Vol. II, p. 410.
10. Butler, H.E. and Millor, W.J. (eds. and trans.) and Brooke, C.N.L. (revised), *The letters of John of Salisbury*, 2 vols. (Oxford, 1979–86), Vol. II, p. 581.
11. Bates, D., *William the Conqueror* (Stroud, 2004), p. 58.
12. Nicolson, *Monarchy*, p. 154.
13. *Oxford Illustrated History of the British Monarchy*, p. 137.
14. Ibid.
15. Robertson and Sheppard, Vol. I, pp. 121–3; Vol. II, p. 429; Vol. III, pp. 127–9, 487.
16. Lyttelton, G., *The history of the life of King Henry the Second*, 2nd edn., 4 vols. (1767–71), Vol. IV, p. 353.
17. Robertson and Sheppard, Vol. III, p. 142; Ralph Lewis, B., *Monarchy: The History of an Idea* (Stroud, 2003), p. 54.
18. In accordance with her wishes, Matilda had been buried before the high altar in the abbey of Bec. The translation of her proud epitaph reads: 'Great by birth, greater by marriage, greatest in her offspring, here lies the daughter, wife, and mother of Henry.'
19. The chronicler Roger of Howden hinted at a homosexual relationship between the French king and his English rival's son: 'Philip honoured Richard so highly that every day they ate at the same table and shared the same dishes; at night the bed did not separate them. The king of France loved him as his own soul and their mutual love was so great that

the lord king of England was stupefied by its vehemence.' Stubbs, W. (ed.), *Gesta regis Henrici secundi Benedicti abbatis: the chronicle of the reigns of Henry II and Richard I, ad 1169–1192*, 2 vols., Rolls series, 49 (London, 1867), Vol. II, p. 7.

20. Keefe, T.K., 'Henry II', *Oxford Dictionary of National Biography* (Oxford, 2004).

21. *Oxford Illustrated History of the British Monarchy*, p. 167.

RICHARD I (1189–99)

1. Wilson, D., *The Plantagenets: The Kings That Made Britain* (London, 2014), p. 48.

2. An uneasy peace was established thereafter, but the Jews continued to be subject to persecution and abuse, and exactly one hundred years after the York massacre Edward I expelled them from England.

3. *Oxford Illustrated History of the British Monarchy*, p. 158.

4. Howden, *Gesta . . . Benedicti*, Vol. II, p. 90.

5. Stubbs, W. (ed.), *Chronica magistri Rogeri de Hovedene*, 4 vols., Rolls series, 51 (London, 1868–71), Vol. III, p. 4.

6. Cockerill, *Eleanor of Aquitaine: Queen of France and England, Mother of Empires* (Stroud, 2019), p. 346.

7. Ailes, M. and Barber, M. (eds. and trans.), *The crusade of Richard Lionheart by Ambroise*, (New York, 2003), Vol. II, p. 620; Asbridge, T., *Richard I: The Crusader King* (London, 2019), p. 4

8. *Chronica magistri Rogeri de Hovedene*, Vol. III, pp. 216–17.

9. Howden, *Gesta . . . Benedicti*, Vol. III, p. 24

10. Stevenson, J. (ed.), *Radulphi de Coggeshall chronicon Anglicanum*, Rolls series, 66 (London, 1875), p. 93.

11. Nichols, J. (ed.), *A Collection of all the Wills, now known to be extant, of the Kings and Queens of England . . . From the reign of William the Conqueror, to that of Henry the Seventh* (London, 1780), p. 11.

12. Asbridge, *Richard I*, p. 91

13. Ailes and Barber, *Crusade of Richard Lionheart*, Vol. I, pp. 12, 152.

14. Ibid., Vol. II, pp. 7345–8.

15. Appleby, J.T. (ed. and trans.), *Cronicon Richardi Divisensis tempore regis Richardi primi* (London, 1963), p. 21.

16. Holinshed, R., *Chronicles of England, Scotlande and Irelande* (London, 1578), Vol. II, p. 266.

JOHN (1199–1216)

1. The quarrel between King John and the pope led to the closure of all churches in England between 1208 and 1214. The only other time in England's history when this happened was during the 2020–1 pandemic.

2. Stubbs, W. (ed.), *Memoriale fratris Walteri de Coventria / The historical collections of Walter of Coventry*, 2 vols., Rolls series, 58 (London, 1872–3), Vol. II, p. 203.

3. The best source for Magna Carta, including a full transcript, is: Holt, J.C., *Magna Carta*, 2nd edn. (Cambridge, 1992).

4. Coggeshall's claim that John had always been a slave to his appetite is backed up by the household accounts, which show that he regularly failed to observe the dietary restrictions of the church on Fridays and religious festivals.

5. Starkey, *Crown & Country*, p. 202.

6. Michel, F. (ed.), *Histoire des ducs de Normandie et des rois d'Angleterre* (Paris, 1840), p. 105.

7. *Memoriale fratris Walteri de Coventria*, Vol. II, p. 232.

HENRY III (1216–72)

1. Madden, F. (ed.), *Matthaei Parisiensis, monachi Sancti Albani, Historia Anglorum, sive . . . Historia minor*, 3 vols., Rolls series, 44 (London, 1886–9), Vol. II, p. 196.

2. The last monarch to stay at the Tower before their coronation was Charles II.

3. Prestwich, M., *Edward I* (London, 1988), p. 4.

4. Starkey, *Crown & Country*, p. 208.

5. *Oxford Illustrated History of the British Monarchy*, p. 207.

6. Luard, H.R. (ed.), *Flores historiarum*, 3 vols., Rolls series, 95 (London, 1890), Vol. II, p. 505.

7. When Henry's body was exhumed in 1290 for reburial in a grander tomb built by his son Edward, eyewitnesses noted that his body was in perfect condition and that his long beard remained well preserved – believed to be a sign of saintly purity. The following year, to honour his Angevin ancestors, his heart was removed and reburied at Fontevraud.

EDWARD I (1272–1307)

1. Fisher, *Monarchy and the Royal Family*, p. 134.

2. Of the twelve crosses, only three survive – none in its entirety. The best preserved is at Geddington in Northamptonshire. The monument known

as Charing ('Chère reine'/'dear queen') Cross, which stands in front of the railway station of that name in London, was built in 1865. The original London cross stood on the south side of Trafalgar Square, but was destroyed in the English Civil War.

3. On Christmas Day 1951, a group of enterprising Scottish students stole it from Westminster Abbey and returned it to Scotland, badly damaging it in the process. After some negotiation between the Scottish and English governments, it was brought back to London in time for the coronation of Queen Elizabeth II. But in 1996, amid growing support for Scottish devolution, the prime minister John Major announced that the stone would be kept in Scotland when not in use at coronations. The stone is now housed among the Honours of Scotland (the Scottish crown jewels) at Edinburgh Castle.

4. Prestwich, M., 'Edward I', *Oxford Dictionary of National Biography* (Oxford, 2004).

5. Bacon, F., 'Of Friendship', *Essays* (London, 1598).

6. Giles, J.A. (ed.), *Galfridi le Baker de Swinbroke chronicon Angliae temporibus Edwardi II et Edwardi III*, Caxton Society, 7 (London, 1847), p. 4.

7. Haskins, G.L., 'A Chronicle of the Civil Wars of Edward II', *Speculum*, Vol. XIV (Chicago, 1939), pp. 73–81.

8. Hamilton, J.S., 'Piers Gaveston', *New Oxford Dictionary of National Biography* (Oxford, 2004).

Edward II (1307–27)

1. Denholm-Young, N. (ed. and trans.), *Vita Edwardi Secundi* (London, 1957), p. ix.

2. Chrimes, S.B. and Brown, A.L. (eds.), *Select Documents of English Constitutional History* (London, 1964), p. 4.

3. Strong, *Coronation*, p. 104.

4. *Vita Edwardi Secundi*, p. 15.

5. Rothwell, H. (ed.), *English Historical Documents*, Vol. III (London, 1975), pp. 529–39.

6. Gaveston's body was removed by the king's beloved Dominican friars to Oxford, where it remained for over two years until Edward had it taken to his favourite palace, Kings Langley in Hertfordshire. An elaborate funeral was held in January 1315 at the royal chapel and Gaveston's remains were finally laid to rest in the Dominican house close by.

7. *Vita Edwardi Secundi*, p. 136.

8. Goodman, A.W. (ed.), *Chartulary of Winchester Cathedral* (Winchester, 1927), p. 105.

9. *Calendar of Close Rolls, 1323–1327*, p. 577.

10. Articles of Deposition, in *Select Documents of English Constitutional History*, pp. 147–77.

11. Rumours that the deposed king escaped from Berkeley persisted for many years. They were taken so seriously that in March 1330 Edward's half-brother, Edmund, Earl of Kent, was executed for plotting to restore the late king. Before her death in 1258, Isabella left instructions that she be buried with Edward's embalmed heart over her breast, more to prove that he really was dead than as a final act of wifely devotion.

EDWARD III (1327–77)

1. Thomas Walsingham, quoted in *Oxford Book of Royal Anecdotes*, p. 125.

2. In fact, it would last for more than 116 years, ending with the fall of Bordeaux to the French on 19 October 1453.

3. According to popular tradition, Edward found a garter on the ground that belonged to his queen or mistress. Upon returning it to her, some of his knights began to laugh, at which he upbraided them with the words that would become the Order's motto.

4. *Rotuli Parliamentorum*, 6 vols. (London, 1767–7), Vol. II, p. 330.

5. Cited in *Oxford Book of Royal Anecdotes*, p. 125.

RICHARD II (1377–99)

1. *Oxford Illustrated History of the British Monarchy*, p. 232.

2. Ralph Lewis, *Monarchy*, p. 44.

3. Chronicle of Adam Usk, cited in *Oxford Book of Royal Anecdotes*, p. 126.

4. *Rotuli Parliamentorum*, Vol. III, p. 35.

5. Borman, T., *The Story of the Tower of London* (London, 2015), p. 68.

6. Simon of Sudbury's remarkably preserved skull is now kept in the church of St Gregory in Sudbury, Suffolk.

7. Stow, G.B. (ed.), *Historia vitae et regni Ricardi Secundi* (Pennsylvania, 1977), p. 66.

8. *Mum and the Sothsegger*, cited in Nicolson, *Monarchy*, p. 200.

9. *Oxford Illustrated History of the British Monarchy*, p. 232.

10. Holinshed's Chronicles, cited in *Oxford Book of Royal Anecdotes*, p. 133.

11. The king had been so grief-stricken upon Anne's death that he had ordered the palace to be razed to the ground.

12. Magna Carta, 1215, clause 39. The same clause was included (at number 29) in the reissue of 1225.

13. Given-Wilson, C. (ed. and trans.), *The Chronicle of Adam Usk, 1377–1421* (Oxford, 1997), p. 63.

14. *Chronicle of Adam Usk*, p. 65; *Oxford Book of Royal Anecdotes*, pp. 134–6.

15. *Rotuli Parliamentorum*, Vol. III, p. 419.

16. Ibid., p. 424.

PART 3: LANCASTER AND YORK (1399–1485)

HENRY IV (1399–1413)

1. *Rotuli Parliamentorum*, Vol. III, p. 423.

2. Nicolson, *Monarchy*, p. 195.

3. Strong, *Coronation*, p. 131.

4. Nicolas, N.H. (ed.), *Proceedings and ordinances of the privy council of England*, 7 vols., Records Commission, 26 (London, 1834–7), Vol. I, pp. 111–12.

5. Watt, D.E.R. (et al.), Bower, W., *Scotichronicon*, 9 vols. (Aberdeen, 1987–98), Vol. VIII, pp. 36–7.

6. Given-Wilson, C. (ed.), *The Parliament Rolls of Medieval England, 1275–1504*, 16 vols. (Woodbridge, 2005), Vol. VIII, p. 517.

7. Nichols, *Collection of Wills*, pp. 203–5. Henry IV's will was the first royal will to be written in English, rather than Latin or French.

8. William Shakespeare, *Henry IV*, Part 2.

9. Cited in *Oxford Book of Royal Anecdotes*, p. 144.

HENRY V (1413–22)

1. Brie, F.W.D. (ed.), *The Brut, or, The chronicles of England*, 2 vols., Early English Text Society, 131, 136 (London, 1906–8), Vol. II, pp. 595–6.

2. *The Brut*, Vol. II, p. 374.

3. Ibid., p. 375.

4. Cussans, *Kings & Queens*, p. 103.

5. Curry, A., *Henry V, Playboy Prince to Warrior King* (London, 2018), p. 91

6. Curry, *Henry V*, p. 97

7. *Parliament Rolls*, Vol. IX, p. 251

8. Taylor, F., 'The chronicle of John Strecche for the reign of Henry V (1414-1422)', *Bulletin of the John Rylands Library*, Vol. XVI Part i (Manchester, 1932), pp. 137-87

9. After her death in 1437, Catherine was buried in the old Lady Chapel at Westminster Abbey. Her tomb was deliberately destroyed during extensions to the abbey in the reign of her grandson, Henry VII. The first Tudor king may have ordered her memorial to be removed so as to

distance himself from his illegitimate ancestry. In the course of the works, her coffin lid was accidentally lifted, revealing her corpse, which became a tourist attraction for many years. In 1669, the diarist Samuel Pepys celebrated his birthday by visiting the tomb: 'On Shrove Tuesday 1669, I to the Abbey went, and by favour did see the body of Queen Catherine of Valois, and had the upper part of the body in my hands, and I did kiss her mouth, reflecting upon it I did kiss a Queen: and this my birthday and I thirty-six years old and I did kiss a Queen.' Loveman, K. (ed.), *The Diary of Samuel Pepys* (New York, London and Toronto, 2018), p. 633. It was not until 1878 that Catherine's remains were properly re-interred, in the chantry chapel of Henry V.

10. Curry, *Henry V*, pp. 113, 117

11. Livio dei Frulovisi, T., *Vita Henrici quinti regis Angliae* (1437); McFarlane, K.B., *Lancastrian Kings and Lollard Knights* (Oxford, 1972), p. 133. See also: Stubbs, W., *The constitutional history of England in its origin and development*, 3rd edn., 3 vols. (Oxford, 1878).

HENRY VI (1422–61 AND 1470–1)

1. *Calendar of Patent Rolls, 1422–9*, pp. 491–2.

2. Gairdner, J. (ed.), 'William Gregory's chronicle of London', *The historical collections of a citizen of London in the fifteenth century*, Camden Society, new series, 17 (London, 1876), p. 165.

3. *Proceedings and ordinances of the privy council*, Vol. IV, p. 134.

4. Ibid., pp. 287–9.

5. There is some debate about whether Catherine and Owen Tudor actually married, thanks in part to the fact that no record of a ceremony survives. Mostly, though, this is based on propaganda put about by her grandson Henry Tudor's rival, Richard III.

6. Wolffe, B.P., *Henry VI* (London, 1981), p. 20.

7. Bloch, M., *The Royal Touch: Sacred Monarchy and Scrofula in England and France* (London, 1973), p. 65.

8. Myers, A.R. (ed.), *English Historical Documents*, Vol. IV (London, 1969), pp. 918–19.

9. *John Blacman's Memoir*, quoted in *Oxford Book of Royal Anecdotes*, pp. 156–7.

10. Nichols, *Collection of Wills*, p. 11.

11. *Oxford Illustrated History of the British Monarchy*, p. 238.

12. Margaret's successor as queen consort, Elizabeth Woodville, was also involved in the foundation, hence the title Queens' College, rather than Queen's.

13. Cussans, *Kings & Queens*, p. 105.
14. *Gregory's Chronicle*, p. 197.
15. Flenley, R. (ed.), *Six town chronicles of England* (Oxford, 1911), p. 140; Giles, J.A. (ed.), *Incerti scriptoris chronicon Angliae de regnis trium regum Lancastrensium*, Part IV (London, 1848), p. 44.
16. John Stodeley's newsletter, cited in *Oxford Illustrated History of the British Monarchy*, p. 238.
17. Gairdner, J. (ed.), *The Paston letters, A.D. 1422–1509*, 6 vols. (London, 1904), Vol. III, p. 13.
18. *Oxford Illustrated History of the British Monarchy*, p. 238.
19. *Rotuli Parliamentorum*, Vol. V, p. 463.

EDWARD IV (1461–70 AND 1471–83)

1. Cussans, *Kings & Queens*, p. 108.
2. Halliwell, J.O. (ed.), Warkworth, J., *A chronicle of the first thirteen years of the reign of King Edward the Fourth*, Camden Society, old series, Vol. X (London, 1839), p. 11.
3. Fortescue, J., *The Governance of England*, edited by Plummer, C. (Oxford, 1885), p. 125.
4. Letts, M. (ed.), 'The Travels of Leo of Rozmital', *Hakluyt Society*, 2nd series, CVIII (1957), p. 45.
5. Thomas, A.H. and Thornley, I.D., *The Great Chronicle of London* (London, 1938), p. 215; Fortescue, J., *The Governance of England*, edited by Plummer, C. (Oxford, 1885), pp. 352–3.
6. Bruce, J. (ed.), *Historie of the arrivall of Edward IV in England, and the finall recoverye of his kingdomes from Henry VI*, Camden Society, Vol. I (London, 1838), p. 38.
7. *Great Chronicle of London*, p. 220. Henry VI's body was then taken upriver to Chertsey Abbey for a modest burial. In 1484, Richard III transferred the body to a new shrine at St George's Chapel, Windsor, in a symbolic act of reconciliation.
8. Cussans, *Kings & Queens*, p. 109.
9. Kingsford, C.L., *English historical literature in the fifteenth century* (Oxford, 1913), p. 375.
10. Mancini, quoted in *Oxford Book of Royal Anecdotes*, p. 166.
11. Mancini, quoted in *Oxford Book of Royal Anecdotes*, pp. 165–6.
12. Pronay, N. and Cox, J. (eds.), *The Crowland Chronicle Continuations, 1459–1486* (London, 1986), p. 149.
13. *The Dictes and Sayenges of the Phylosophers* was originally an Arabic work

and was translated into English by the queen's brother, Anthony Woodville.

14. Hicks, M., 'George, duke of Clarence', *New Oxford Dictionary of National Biography* (Oxford, 2004).

15. Mancini, quoted in *Oxford Book of Royal Anecdotes*, p. 172.

16. *Rotuli Parliamentorum*, Vol. VI, p. 8.

17. *Oxford Illustrated History of the British Monarchy*, p. 290.

18. Thomas More's *History of King Richard III*, quoted in *Oxford Book of Royal Anecdotes*, p. 173.

EDWARD V (1483)

1. Elizabeth and Edward IV's youngest son, George, had died in 1479, aged two.

2. Attreed, L.C. (ed.), *The York House Books, 1461–1490*, 2 vols. (Stroud, 1991), Vol. II, p. 714.

3. *The Crowland Chronicle*, quoted in *Oxford Book of Royal Anecdotes*, p. 178.

4. *The Crowland Chronicle*, cited in Cussans, *Kings & Queens*, p. 111.

5. Borman, *Tower of London*, p. 82.

6. Borman, *Tower of London*, p. 83.

RICHARD III (1483–5)

1. *Oxford Book of Royal Anecdotes*, p. 186.

2. *Oxford Illustrated History of the British Monarchy*, p. 294.

3. The first known reference to Richard as a 'crook back' was in 1491 (see: Raine, A. (ed.), *York Civic Records*, Vol. II (Wakefield, 1941), pp. 71–3.

4. Lockyer, R. (ed.), Bacon, F., *The History of the Reign of King Henry the Seventh* (London, 1971), p. 94.

5. Lopes de Chaves, A., *Livro de Apontamentos (1438–1489)*. Alvaro Lopes de Chaves (1438–89) was private secretary to the Portuguese king, Alfonso V. The later document belonged to Christopher Barker (Suffolk Herald from 1514–22) and is now in the collection of the College of Arms in London, MS 2M6.

6. Ellis, H. (ed.), *Three books of Polydore Vergil's 'English history'*, CS, 29 (London, 1844), p. 227.

7. Armstrong, C.A.J. (ed. and trans.), *The Usurpation of Richard the Third: Dominicus Mancinus ad Angelum Catonem de occupatione regni Anglie per Ricardum tercium libellus*, 2nd edn. (Oxford, 1969), p. 137; *Polydore Vergil's 'English History'*, p. 227.

8. *Oxford Book of Royal Anecdotes*, pp. 187–8.
9. Horrox, R., 'Richard III', *New Oxford Dictionary of National Biography* (Oxford, 2004).
10. Ibid.
11. *Polydore Vergil's 'English History'*, p. 215.
12. *The Crowland Chronicle*, p. 176.
13. *Oxford Book of Royal Anecdotes*, p. 192.
14. *Polydore Vergil's 'English History'*, p. 224.

PART 4: THE TUDORS (1485–1603)

HENRY VII (1485–1509)

1. Weir, *Britain's Royal Families*, p. 146.
2. John Fisher's sermon at Henry VII's funeral, quoted in *Oxford Book of Royal Anecdotes*, pp. 206–7.
3. Hay, D. (ed. and trans.), *The Anglica Historia of Polydore Vergil, A.D. 1485–1537*, Camden series, Vol. LXXIV (London, 1950), p. 145.
4. Hay, *Polydore Vergil*, p. 3.
5. Hay, *Polydore Vergil*, p. 67.
6. Starkey, D., 'Intimacy and Innovation: The Rise of the Privy Chamber, 1485–1547', in Starkey, D., et al. (eds.), *The English Court from the Wars of the Roses to the Civil War* (London, 1987), p. 74.
7. Starkey, D., 'Representation through Intimacy: A Study in the Symbolism of Monarchy and Court Office in Early Modern England', in Lewis, I. (ed.), *Symbols and Sentiments, Cross-Cultural Studies in Symbolism* (London, 1977), p. 203.
8. Williams, C.H. (ed.), *English Historical Documents 1485–1558* (London, 1967), p. 387; *Polydore Vergil*, p. 151. See also: Stow, J, *The Annales, or Generall Chronicle of England* (London, 1615), p. 486.
9. *Calendar of State Papers, Spain* [*CSPS*], Vol. I, pp. 177–8.
10. *Calendar of State Papers, Venice* [*CSPV*], Vol. I, 1202–1509, pp. 263–4.
11. *CSPS*, 1485–1509, p. 213.
12. Alison Weir provides a thorough analysis of Tyrell's imprisonment and alleged confession in *Elizabeth of York: The First Tudor Queen* (London, 2013), pp. 380–4.
13. Licence, A., *In Bed with the Tudors: The Sex Lives of a Dynasty from Elizabeth of York to Elizabeth I* (Stroud, 2013), p. 52.
14. Weir, *Elizabeth of York*, p. 374.
15. Bacon, *King Henry the Seventh*, p. 165.

16. Borman, T., *The Private Lives of the Tudors* (London, 2016), p. 66.

17. The Duke of Burgundy's sudden death in 1506 threw this agreement into uncertainty and the betrothal was eventually abandoned.

18. Hay, *Polydore Vergil*, p. 129.

19. *CSPV*, Vol. I, p. 346. According to one estimate, by the time of his death Henry VII had accumulated around £300,000 (£145 million) in cash, bonds and jewellery.

20. Cussans, *Kings & Queens*, p. 123.

21. Gunn, S., 'Henry VII', *New Oxford Dictionary of National Biography* (Oxford, 2004).

Henry VIII (1509–47)

1. *CSPV*, Vol. IV, p. 293.

2. *CSPV*, Vol. II, p. 400.

3. Hay, *Polydore Vergil*, p. 151.

4. Grafton, R., *A Chronicle and Mere history* (1809), pp. 235–6.

5. Bacon, *King Henry the Seventh*, p. 166.

6. Hall, *Chronicle*, p. 502.

7. BL Additional MS 19398 fo. 44; *CSPS*, Vol. II, p. 71.

8. *CSPV*, Vol. IV, p. 293.

9. Brown, R. (ed. and trans.), *Four years at the court of Henry VIII: Selection of despatches written by the Venetian Ambassador, Sebastian Giustinian, and addressed to the Signory of Venice, January 12th 1515, to July 26th 1519*, 2 vols. (London, 1854), Vol. I, p. 128.

10. Sylvester, R.S. (ed.), Cavendish, G., *The Life and Death of Cardinal Wolsey*, Early English Text Society, original series, 243 (London and New York, 1959), pp. 11–12, 79.

11. Cavendish, *Cardinal Wolsey*, p. 12; Hume, M.A. (ed. and trans.), *Chronicle of King Henry VIII of England . . . written in Spanish by an unknown hand* (London, 1889), p. 1.

12. Bacon, *King Henry the Seventh*, p. 179.

13. Dillon, J., *Performance and Spectacle in Hall's Chronicle* (London, 2002), pp. 79–80.

14. Weir, A., *Henry VIII: King and Court* (London, 2001), p. 97.

15. Brewer, J.S., et al. (eds.), *Letters and Papers, Foreign and Domestic, of the Reign of Henry VIII, 1509–47*, 21 vols. and 2 vols. addenda (London, 1862–1932) [*LP Henry VIII*], Vol. III, Part i, no. 1.

16. Luders, A., et al. (eds.), *Statutes of the Realm* (1820–40), Vol. III, p. 246.

17. *CSPV*, IV, p. 365.

18. Leviticus 20:21.

19. *LP Henry VIII*, Vol. IV, Part ii, no. 4858.

20. *CSPS*, Vol. IV, Part II, p. 669.

21. *Four years at the court of Henry VIII*, Vol. I, p. 237.

22. *CSPS*, Vol. V, Part II, p. 257.

23. Sylvester, R.S. (ed.), Cavendish, *The Life and Death of Cardinal Wolsey*, p. 184.

24. Haynes, A., *Collection of State Papers Relating to Affairs in the Reigns of King Henry VIII, King Edward VI, Queen Mary and Queen Elizabeth, From the Year 1542 to 1570 . . . Left by William Cecil, Lord Burghley . . . at Hatfield House* (London, 1740), Vol. VII, p. 262.

25. Ogle, A., *The tragedy of the Lollards' Tower. The case of Richard Hunne, with its aftermath in II. the Reformation Parliament, 1529–3: a review of events from the downfall of Wolsey to the death of Elizabeth* (Oxford, 1959), p. 153; *State Papers, Henry VIII*, Vol. III, p. 53; BL Cotton MS Tiberius D viii f. 89.

26. Merriman, R.B. (ed.), *Life and letters of Thomas Cromwell*, 2 vols. (Oxford, 1902), Vol. I, p. 135; *LP Henry VIII*, Vol. VII, no. 1554.

27. Elton, G.R., *The Tudor Constitution: Documents and Commentary* (Cambridge, 1960), p. 344.

28. Ellis, H. (ed.), Hall, E., *The union of the two noble and illustre famelies of Lancastre & Yorke* (London, 1809), p. 788; *LP Henry VIII*, Vol. V, no. 1013.

29. Wriothesley, C., *A Chronicle of England During the Reigns of the Tudors, from AD 1485 to 1559*, edited by Hamilton, W.D., 2 vols., Camden Society, new series, 11, 20 (London, 1875–7), Vol. I, p. 29; Rogers, E.F. (ed.), *The Correspondence of Sir Thomas More* (Princeton, 1947), p. 250.

30. Bray, G. (ed.), *Documents of the English Reformation* (Cambridge, 1994), p. 114.

31. Hitchcock, N.V. (ed.), Harpsfield, N., *The life and death of Sr Thomas Moore, knight*, Early English Text Society, original series, 186 (London, 1932), p. 266.

32. Weir, A., *The Six Wives of Henry VIII* (London, 1991), p. 293.

33. Wriothesley, *Chronicle* Vol. I, p. 33; *LP Henry VIII*, Vol. X, p. 102.

34. *LP Henry VIII*, Vol. X, no. 351.

35. *LP Henry VIII*, Vol. X, p. 330.

36. *LP Henry VIII*, Vol. XV, no. 954.

37. *LP Henry VIII*, Vol. XV, no. 954.

38. *LP Henry VIII*, Vol. XI, no. 780(2).

39. Daadler, J. (ed.), Wyatt, T., *Collected Poems* (Oxford, 1975), 185.

40. Schenk, W.H., *Reginald Pole* (London, 1950), p. 71.

41. A horrified Chapuys reported on 'a wretched and blundering youth who literally hacked her head and shoulders to pieces in the most pitiful manner'. It was said to have taken eleven blows of the axe before Lady Margaret's head was finally severed.

42. *LP Henry VIII*, Vol. XV, no. 954.

43. Weir, *Henry VIII*, p. 493; Hayward, M. and Ward, P., *The Inventory of King Henry VIII: Textiles and Dress* (London, 2012), Vol. II, p. 105.

44. Elton, *Tudor Constitution*, p. 277.

45. Mayer, T. (ed.), *Correspondence of Reginald Pole, Volume 1: A Calendar, 1518–1546* (Aldershot, 2002), p. 98.

46. *State Papers of Henry VIII*, Vol. II, pp. 551–3n.

47. Merriman, *Life and letters*, Vol. II, pp. 268–76; *LP Henry VIII*, Vol. XV, nos. 823, 824.

48. Hume, *Chronicle of King Henry VIII*, pp. 96–7.

49. Chapman, H., *The Last Tudor King: A Study of Edward VI* (London, 1961), p. 52.

50. *LP Henry VIII*, Vol. XVII, Appendix B, no. 13.

51. Borman, T., *Henry VIII and the Men Who Made Him* (London, 2018), p. 403.

52. As this was before Edward had even been conceived, the king probably had in mind his illegitimate son, Henry Fitzroy, upon whom he had doted since his birth in 1519 but who died shortly after the Act came into effect.

53. *State Papers of Henry VIII*, Vol. III, p. 53.

EDWARD VI (1547–53)

1. Hoak, D., 'Edward VI', *New Oxford Dictionary of National Biography* (Oxford, 2014).

2. Strype, J., *Memorials of the most reverend father in God Thomas Cranmer* (London, 1672), Vol. II, pp. 144–5.

3. Williams, *English Historical Documents*, p. 394.

4. Hay, *Polydore Vergil*, p. 337.

5. Loades, D., *John Dudley: Duke of Northumberland, 1504–1553* (Oxford, 1996), p. 202.

6. Cox, J.E. (ed.), *The Works of Thomas Cranmer, Archbishop of Canterbury, Martyr, 1556* 2 vols. (Cambridge, 1844, 1846), Vol. II, pp. 418–19.

7. Starkey, *Crown & Country*, p. 303.

8. *CSPS 1550–1552*, p. 63.

9. Williams, *English Historical Documents*, p. 415.

10. Perry, M., *The Word of a Prince* (London, 1990), p. 45.

11. *State Papers of Henry VIII*, p. 99.

12. *State Papers of Henry VIII*, pp. 82–3.
13. *State Papers of Henry VIII*, p. 96.
14. Falkus, C., *The Private Lives of the Tudor Monarchs* (London, 1974), p. 54.
15. Williams, *English Historical Documents*, pp. 415–16.
16. The National Archives SP 10/13, no. 55.
17. Falkus, *Private Lives*, p. 57.
18. Falkus, *Private Lives*, p. 63.
19. This controversial document still survives today. Inner Temple, London, Petyt MS 538, Vol. 47, fo. 317.
20. Brewer, J.S. (ed.), Fuller, T., *The church history of Britain*, 6 vols. (London, 1845), Vol. IV, pp. 138–9.
21. Strype, J., *Ecclesiastical memorials*, Vol. II (London, 1822), pp. 195–6.
22. Strickland, A., *The Tudor Princesses* (London, 1868), p. 136.
23. Fuller, *The church history of Britain*, Vol. IV, pp. 138–40.
24. Skidmore, C., *Edward VI: The Lost King of England* (London, 2007), p. 260.

Lady Jane Grey (July 1553)

1. Davey, R., *The Nine Days' Queen: Lady Jane Grey and her times* (London, 1909), p. 253.
2. Stone, J.M., *The History of Mary I, Queen of England, as found in the Public Records, Despatches of Ambassadors, in original private letters, and other contemporary documents* (London, 1901), pp. 497–8.
3. Davey, *The Nine Days' Queen*, p. 260.
4. Stone, *The History of Mary I*, p. 499.

Mary I (1553–8)

1. *CSPS Mary I 1553–4*, XI, p. 50.
2. Richards, M., 'Mary Tudor as "Sole Quene"? Gendering Tudor Monarchy', *Historical Journal*, Vol. 40, no. 4 (Cambridge, December 1997), pp. 908–9.
3. *CSPV*, VII, p. 329.
4. *CSPV*, VI ii, p. 1056.
5. *CSPS Mary I 1553–4*, XI, p. 252.
6. Richards, 'Sole Quene', pp. 908–9.
7. *CSPV*, VII, p. 601.
8. Nichols, J.G. (ed.), *The Chronicle of Queen Jane, and of two years of Queen Mary*, Camden Society, old series, Vol. 48 (London, 1850), p. 69.

9. Cattley, S.R. (ed.), *The acts and monuments of John Foxe*, 8 vols. (London, 1837–41), Vol. VI, pp. 414–15.

10. PRO SP 11/4/2 f. 3–3v. The letter is so named because Elizabeth wrote it in order to delay her departure for the Tower. By the time she had finished it, her captors had missed the tide.

11. *CSP Spain, 1554*, p. 167.

12. BM Cotton MS Vespasian Fiii fo. 23.

13. *Oxford Illustrated History of the British Monarchy*, p. 333.

14. Loades, D., *Mary Tudor*, p. 189.

15. *CSPV*, VI, Part II, p. 1060.

16. Loades, *Mary Tudor*, p. 143, quoting John Foxe.

17. Adams, S. and Rodríguez-Salgado, M.J., 'The Count of Feria's Dispatch to Philip II of 14 November 1558', *Camden Miscellany*, Vol. XXVIII (London, 1984), p. 335.

18. *CSPS Mary I 1554–8*, XIII, p. 438.

19. BM Cotton MS Vespasian D XVIII fo. 104.

ELIZABETH I (1558–1603)

1. Knoxe, J., *First Blast of the Trumpet Against the Monstrous Regiment of Women*, 1558 (New York, 1972), pp. 9–10.

2. Holinshed's Chronicle, quoted in Plowden, A., *The Young Elizabeth: The First Twenty-five Years of Elizabeth I* (Stroud, 1999), p. 209.

3. Marcus, L.S., Mueller, J. and Rose, M.B., *Elizabeth I: Collected Works* (Chicago and London, 2002), p. 70; *CSPS Elizabeth 1558–67*, I, p. 63.

4. Haigh, C. (ed.), *Elizabeth I* (London and New York, 1988), pp. 21–2; *Collected Works*, p. 97; Weir, A., *The Life of Elizabeth* (New York, 1998), p. 222.

5. Haigh, *Elizabeth*, p. 20.

6. Somerset, A., *Elizabeth I* (London, 1991), p. 90; Plowden, A., *Tudor Women: Queens and Commoners* (Sutton, 2002), p. 154.

7. *CSPF Elizabeth 1558–9*, p. 443; *CSPS Elizabeth 1558–67*, I, p. 45.

8. *CSPS Elizabeth 1558–67*, I, p. 45.

9. Levin, C., *The Heart and Stomach of a King: Elizabeth I and the Politics of Sex and Power* (Philadelphia, 1994), p. 172.

10. Jenkins, E., *Elizabeth the Great* (London, 1965), pp. 141–2.

11. Hartley, T.E. (ed.), *Proceedings in the parliaments of Elizabeth I*, 3 vols. (Leicester, 1981–95), Vol. I, p. 138. For a similar statement made in 1572, see ibid., p. 376.

12. Francis Steuart, A. (ed.), *Sir James Melville: Memoirs of His Own Life, 1549–93* (London, 1929), pp. 95–7.

13. Schutte, K., *A Biography of Margaret Douglas, Countess of Lennox, 1515–1578, Niece of Henry VIII and Mother-in-law of Mary, Queen of Scots* (Lampeter, 2000), p. 199.

14. *Elizabeth I, Collected Works*, p. 118.

15. Weir, *Elizabeth*, p. 201.

16. Chamberlain, F., *The Sayings of Queen Elizabeth I* (New York, 1923), pp. 233, 246.

17. Haigh, *Elizabeth*, p. 87.

18. Boyle, J. (ed.), *Memoirs of the Life of Robert Carey . . . Written by Himself* (London, 1759), p. 73n.

19. Cerovski, J.S. (ed.), Sir Robert Naunton, *Fragmentia Regalia or Observations on Queen Elizabeth, Her Times and Favourites* (London and Toronto, 1985), pp. 41–2.

20. Harington, Sir J., *Nugae Antiquae: Being a Miscellaneous Collection of Original Papers in Prose and Verse: Written in the Reigns of Henry VIII, Queen Mary, Elizabeth, King James, etc* (London, 1779), p. 125.

21. An inventory at her death proved this to be an exaggeration, but the total listed (1,900) was still impressive.

22. Hunt. L., MSS HA 1214, 13067.

23. Lodge, E., *Illustrations of British history, biography and manners, in the reigns of Henry VIII, Edward VI, Mary, Elizabeth, & James I*, 3 vols. (London, 1838), Vol. II, pp. 276–7.

24. N. Williams, *Elizabeth I, Queen of England* (London, 1967), p. 256. See also: *CSPF Elizabeth 1581–82*, p. 589; *CSPS Elizabeth 1580–86*, III, p. 495.

25. *CSPF Elizabeth 1571–74*, p. 373; HMC *Salisbury* II, p. 428; *CSPF Elizabeth 1584–85*, pp. 166–7; Hartley, *Proceedings*, Vol. I, pp. 312, 438.

26. *Collected Works*, pp. 186–8, 199–202; Chamberlain, *Sayings*, pp. 240–3.

27. *Collected Works*, p. 134; Strickland, A., *The Life of Queen Elizabeth* (London, 1910), pp. 476–7.

28. BM Cotton MS Titus C VII ff. 48–53.

29. Ballard, G., *Memoirs of Several Ladies of Great Britain who have been celebrated for their writings or skill in the learned languages, arts and sciences* (Detroit, 1985), p. 175.

30. Camden, *Elizabeth*, p. 115.

31. BM Lansdowne MS 1236 fo. 32.

32. Davison was released the following year, thanks to the intercession of his friends at court, and probably never paid the fine. The queen refused to re-employ him.

33. Camden, *Elizabeth*, p. 115; See also: *CSPV*, VIII, p. 256.

34. Falkus, *Private Lives*, pp. 115–16.

35. HMC *Salisbury* III, p. 230; *CSPF Elizabeth 1586–8*, p. 276; Melville, *Memoirs*, p. 315.

36. Weir, *Elizabeth*, p. 381.

37. Haigh, *Elizabeth*, p. 173.

38. In the letter, Dudley referred to himself as Elizabeth's 'poor servant'. Above the word 'poor', he added the symbol that the queen used to denote his nickname of 'Eyes' – 'ōō'. The letter is now preserved in The National Archives. SP 12/215 f. 65.

39. Harrison, G.B. and Jones, R.A. (eds.), *De Maisse: A journal of all that was accomplished by Monsieur de Maisse, Ambassador in England from Henry IV to Queen Elizabeth, Anno Domini 1597* (London, 1931), p. 51.

40. Guy, J. (ed.), *The Reign of Elizabeth I: Court and Culture in the Last Decade* (Cambridge, 1995), p. 11.

41. Weir, *Elizabeth*, p. 470.

42. Naunton, *Fragmenta Regalia*, pp. 41–2.

43. De Maisse, *Journal*, pp. 25–6, 36–9, 55.

44. De Maisse, *Journal*, p. 27.

45. Camden, *Elizabeth*, p. 172.

46. Nichols, *Progresses*, Vol. III, pp. 52–3.

47. Harington, *Nugae Antiquae*, p. 90; Falkus, *Private Lives*, p. 124; *Calendar of State Papers, Domestic, Elizabeth, 1580–1625*, Addenda, p. 407.

48. Fisher, F.J. (ed.), Wilson, T., 'The state of England anno dom. 1600', *Camden miscellany*, Vol. XVI, Camden Society, 3rd series, Vol. 52 (London, 1936), p. 5.

49. Ibid.; Camden, p. 222.

50. *CSPV*, VII, p. 564; *CSPD Elizabeth 1601–03*, p. 302.

51. Hartley, *Proceedings*, Vol. III, pp. 296–7.

52. Bassnett, S., *Elizabeth I: A Feminist Perspective* (Oxford and New York, 1988), p. 258; Merton, C., 'The Women Who Served Queen Mary and Queen Elizabeth: Ladies, Gentlewomen and Maids of the Privy Chamber, 1553–1603' (Cambridge PhD thesis, 1992), p. 90; Birch, T., *Memoirs of the Reign of Queen Elizabeth from the year 1581 till her Death*, Vol. II (London, 1754), pp. 506–7; Boyle, J. (ed.), *Memoirs of the Life of Robert Carey . . . Written by Himself* (London, 1759), p. 140; Pasmore, S., *The Life and Times of Queen Elizabeth I at Richmond Palace* (Richmond, 2003), p. 65; Bruce, J. (ed.), *The Diary of John Manningham*, Camden Society (London, 1868), entry for 23 March 1603.

53. Haigh, *Elizabeth*, p. 22.

54. Camden, *Elizabeth*, quoted in Haigh, *Elizabeth*, p. 22.

55. Weir, *Elizabeth*, p. 221.

56. Miller, J., *Popery and Politics in England, 1660–1688* (Cambridge, 1973), p. 74.

PART 5: THE STUARTS (1603–1714)

JAMES I (1603–25)

1. Sommerville, J.P. (ed.), *King James VI and I: Political Writings* (Cambridge, 1994), p. 189.

2. Harington, *Nugae Antiquae*, Vol. I (London, 1804).

3. Nichols, The *Progresses, Processions, and Magnificent Festivities of King James the First*, Vol. I (London, 1828), p. 129; Gilson, J.P., *Catalogue of Western Manuscripts in the Old Royal and King's Collections* (London, 1921), p. xxviii.

4. Craigie, J. (ed.), *The Basilicon Doron of King James VI*, 2 vols., Scottish Text Society, 3rd series, vols. 16, 18 (Edinburgh, 1944–50), Vol. I, pp. 25, 175.

5. Craigie, J. (ed.), *Minor Prose Works of King James VI and I* (Edinburgh, 1982), p. 71.

6. Oxford, Bodleian Library, MS Ashmole 1729, fos. 51, 56.

7. Stewart, A., *The Cradle King: A Life of James VI & I* (London, 2003), pp. 171–2; Weldon, Sir A., *The Court and Character of King James* (London, 1650), pp. 179, 186.

8. Harington, *Nugae Antiquae*, Vol. I, pp. 348–522; Akrigg, G.P.V., *Jacobean Pageant or The Court of King James I* (London, 1962), p. 242.

9. Stewart, *Cradle King*, p. 175.

10. Nichols, The *Progresses, Processions, and Magnificent Festivities of King James the First*, Vol. I (London, 1828), p. 491.

11. Stewart, *Cradle King*, p. 175; *Oxford Illustrated History of the British Monarchy*, p. 361.

12. Wormald, J., 'James VI and I', *New Oxford Dictionary of National Biography* (Oxford, 2004).

13. Cussans, *Kings & Queens*, p. 138; Sommerville, *King James VI and I*, p. 162.

14. Somerville, *King James VI and I*, p. 164.

15. Ralph Lewis, *Monarchy*, p. 125.

16. Gregg, P., *King Charles I* (London, 1981), p. 49

17. Spedding, J., Ellis, R.L. and Heath, D.D. (eds.), *The works of Francis Bacon*, 14 vols. (London, 1857–74), Vol. XIII, p. 239.

18. Halliwell, J.O. (ed.), *Letters of the kings of England*, 2 vols. (London, 1846–8), Vol. II, pp. 123, 149; Yorke, P. (ed.), *Miscellaneous State Papers from 1501 to 1726*, 2 vols. (London, 1778), Vol. I, p. 410.

19. Olusoga, D., *Black and British: A Forgotten History* (London, 2017), p. 72.

20. Sommerville, *King James VI and I*, pp. 231–2.

CHARLES I (1625–49)

1. Historical Manuscripts Commission, *The manuscripts of Henry Duncan Skrine, esq. Salvetti correspondence*, Vol. XVI (London, 1887), p. 22.

2. Cotton, R., *Cottoni Posthuma: divers choice pieces of that renowned antiquary Sir Robert Cotton . . . preserved from the injury of time, and expos'd to public light, for the benefit of posterity* (London, 1651), pp. 41–57.

3. *Oxford Illustrated History of the British Monarchy*, p. 389.

4. Strong, *Coronation*, pp. 246, 250; Revelation 2:10.

5. Jansson, M. and Bidwell, W.B. (eds.), *Proceedings in Parliament, 1625* (London and New Haven, 1987), Vol. II, p. 395.

6. Larkin, J.F. (ed.), *Stuart Royal Proclamations: Proclamations of Charles I, 1625–1646* (Oxford, 1983), Vol. II, pp. 223, 228.

7. *Oxford Illustrated History of the British Monarchy*, p. 373.

8. Lucy Hutchinson's *Memoirs of the Life of Colonel Hutchinson*, quoted in *Oxford Book of Royal Anecdotes*, p. 255.

9. *Memoirs of Colonel Hutchinson*, quoted in *Oxford Book of Royal Anecdotes*, p. 255.

10. The medal was the only adornment he wore at his trial in January 1649.

11. Halliwell, *Letters of the kings of England*, Vol. II, p. 418.

12. Smith, D.L., *The Stuart Parliaments, 1603–1688* (London, 1998), p. 121.

13. Knowler, W. (ed.), Radcliffe, G., *The earl of Strafforde's letters and dispatches, with an essay towards his life*, 2 vols. (Dublin, 1739), Vol. II, p. 416.

14. Trevor-Roper, H., *Archbishop Laud 1573–1645* (New Haven, 2000), p. 409.

15. Gardiner, *Constitutional Documents*, p. 83.

16. Robertson, G., *The Tyrannicide Brief* (London, 2005), p. 62.

17. Parsons, D. (ed.), *The Diary of Sir Henry Slingsby* (London, 1836), p. 45.

18. Helylyn, P., *Aerius Redivivus: or The History of the Presbyterians* (London, 1670), pp. 461–2.

19. Strong, R., *Coronation: A History of Kingship and the British Monarchy* (London, 2005), p. 234.

20. Humphrys, J., *The Private Life of Palaces* (London, 2006), p. 35.

21. Gardiner, S.R. (ed.), *The Constitutional Documents of the Puritan Revolution* (Oxford, 1903), pp. 371–4.

22. Ibid., pp. 374–6.

23. Robertson, *Tyrannicide Brief*, p. 15.

24. A shirt purported to be one of those Charles I wore for his execution

was on display at the Banqueting House, Whitehall, for many years.

25. Lockyer, R. (ed.), *The Trial of Charles I: a contemporary account taken from the memoirs of the last years of the reign of King Charles by Sir Thomas Herbert and John Rushworth* (London, 1959); Carlton, C., *Charles I: The Personal Monarch* (London, 1995), pp. 353–4; Gregg, *King Charles I*, p. 444; Hibbert, C., *Charles I* (London, 1968), pp. 157, 279.

26. Hibbert, C., *Charles I* (London, 1968), p. 280.

27. Herbert, *Memoirs of Charles I*, pp. 129–30.

THE INTERREGNUM (1649–60)

1. Strong, *Coronation*, p. 234.

2. Ibid., p. 247.

3. Cannadine, D., *History in Our Time* (New Haven and London, 1998), p. 32.

4. Starkey, *Crown & Country*, p. 347.

5. Kenyon, J. and Ohlmeyer, Jane (eds.), *The Civil Wars: A Military History of England, Scotland, and Ireland 1638–1660* (Oxford, 2000), p. 66.

6. Miller, L. (ed.), *John Milton & the Oldenburg Safeguard* (New York, c. 1985), p. 49.

7. Carlyle, T. and Lomas, S.C. (eds.), *The letters and speeches of Oliver Cromwell*, 3 vols. (London, 1904), Vol. I, letter 183, 4 September 1651.

8. Spalding, R. (ed.), *The Diary of Bulstrode Whitelocke, 1605–1675* (Oxford, 1990), pp. 281–2.

9. *Oxford Illustrated History of the British Monarchy*, p. 394.

10. Gardiner, *Constitutional Documents*, p. 406.

11. *Oxford Illustrated History of the British Monarchy*, p. 393.

12. Gaunt, P., *Oliver Cromwell* (Oxford, 1996), p. 156.

13. *The letters and speeches of Oliver Cromwell with elucidations by Thomas Carlyle* (1845–), p. 137, 13 April 1657.

14. BL MS Lansdowne 823, fos. 371–2.

15. *Pepys Diary*, p. 25.

CHARLES II (1660–85)

1. Flecknoe, R., *Heroic Portraits: with other misellary [sic] pieces, made and dedicated to his Majesty* (London, 1660), sig. Bv

2. Ralph Lewis, *Monarchy*, p. 130.

3. Airy, O. (ed.), *Burnet's History of my own time*, 2 vols. (Oxford, 1897–1900), Vol. I, p. 167.

4. *Pepys Diary*, p. 63. Twenty-one others fled the country, but some were captured and imprisoned or murdered by royalist sympathisers. An account of their varying fates is provided by Spencer, C., *Killers of the King: The Men Who Dared to Execute Charles I* (London, 2015).

5. In 1671, 'Colonel' Thomas Blood, a mercenary who had fought in the Civil War, staged an audacious attempt to steal the star items of the Crown Jewels from the Tower of London. He almost got away with it but was apprehended with his accomplices as they fled from the fortress. To general astonishment, Charles II pardoned Blood and granted him lands in his native Ireland, as well as a pension of £500 a year.

6. *Pepys Diary*, pp. 85–8.

7. Slaughter, T.P., *Ideology and Politics on the Eve of the Restoration: Newcastle's Advice to Charles II* (Philadelphia, 1984), pp. 44–5.

8. Ellis, H., *Original Letters illustrative of English History*, First Series (London, 1969) Vol. III, p. 290.

9. It has been estimated that Charles touched more than 90,000 of his subjects for the King's Evil. Starkey, *Crown & Country*, p. 360.

10. The term 'merry monarch' was coined by John Wilmot, second Earl of Rochester, whose famous verse ran: 'Restless he rolls from whore to whore / A merry monarch, scandalous and poor'. Miller, J., *Charles II* (London, 1991), p. 95.

11. Jackson, C., *Charles II: The Star King* (London, 2018), p. 10.

12. Cussans, *Kings & Queens*, p. 147.

13. Jackson, *Charles II*, p. 76.

14. Cooper, T. (ed.), *Tudors to Windsors: British Royal Portraits* (London, 2018), p. 109.

15. Doble, C.E. (ed.), *Remarks and Collections of Thomas Hearne*, 11 vols. (Oxford, 1885), Vol. I, p. 308.

16. *Pepys Diary*, p. 193.

17. Sorbière, S., *Relation d'un Voyage en Angleterre* (Cologne, 1666), p. 65.

18. Browning, A. (ed.), *Memoirs of Sir John Reresby* (Glasgow, 1936), p. 259; Jackson, *Charles II*, p. 60.

19. Brown, M.N. (ed.), 'A character of Charles II', *The Works of George Savile, Marquis of Halifax*, 2 vols. (Oxford, 1989), Vol. II, p. 497.

20. Airy, *Burnet's History*, Vol. II, p. 468.

21. Brown, 'A character of Charles II', p. 504.

22. Porter, L., *Mistresses: Sex and Scandal at the Court of Charles II* (London, 2020), p. 98.

23. Porter, *Mistresses*, p. 102.

24. *Pepys Diary*, p. 421.
25. *Pepys Diary*, p. 427.
26. Borman, T., *The Story of Kensington Palace* (London, 2019), p. 19.
27. Fraser, A., *King Charles II* (London, 1979), p. 275.
28. Olusoga, *Black and British*, pp. 72–5.
29. Seaward, P., 'Charles II', *New Oxford Dictionary of National Biography* (Oxford, 2004).
30. Clarke, J.S. (ed.), *The life of James the Second, king of England*, 2 vols. (London, 1816), Vol. I, pp. 659–60.
31. Airy, *Burnet's History*, Vol. II, p. 5.
32. Fraser, *King Charles II*, p. 456.
33. Airy, *Burnet's History*, Vol. II, p. 463.
34. Miller, J., *Charles II* (London, 1991), pp. 382–3; Jackson, *Charles II*, p. 76.
35. Dalrymple, J., *Memoirs of Great Britain and Ireland*, 3 vols. (London, 1790), Vol. I, p. 63; Fox, C.J., *A History of the Early Part of the Reign of James the Second* (London, 1808), p. 23.
36. Foxcroft, H.C. (ed.), *A Supplement to Burnet's History of My Own Time*, (Oxford, 1902), p. 48; [Sheffield, J., Duke of Buckingham], *The Character of Charles II, King of England. With a short account of his being poisoned* (London, 1696), p. 9.
37. Airy, *Burnet's History*, Vol. I, p. 168. One of the best assessments of Charles II's character and reign is Hutton, R., *Charles II: King of England, Scotland and Ireland* (Oxford, 1989). See in particular: p. 446.

JAMES II (1685–8)

1. Turner, *James II*, p. 60.
2. Miller, J., *James II* (New Haven and London, 2000), p. 46.
3. Northamptonshire Record Office, Isham correspondence, 1379.
4. Clarke, *Life of James the Second*, Vol. II, p. 4.
5. Strong, *Coronation*, p. 309.
6. Clarke, *Life of James the Second*, Vol. II, p. 14.
7. Greaves, R.L., *Secrets of the Kingdom: British Radicals from the Popish Plot to the Revolution of 1688–89* (Stanford, 1992).
8. *The London Gazette*, 15 June 1685, p. 1.
9. Clarke, *Life of James the Second*, Vol. I, p. 594.
10. Sowerby, S., *Making Toleration: The Repealers and the Glorious Revolution* (Cambridge, MA, and London, 2013), p. 42.
11. Clarke, *Life of James the Second*, Vol. II, p. 107.

12. Fairfax, H., *An impartial relation of the whole proceedings against St Mary Magdalen College* (London, 1688).

13. Historical Manuscripts Commission, *The manuscripts of the earl of Dartmouth*, 3 vols. (London, 1887–96), Vol. I, p. 169.

14. *Oxford Illustrated History of the British Monarchy*, p. 426.

WILLIAM III AND MARY II (1688–1702)

1. Ibid., p. 435.

2. Doebner, R. (ed.), *Memoirs of Mary, Queen of England, 1689-1693, together with her letters and those of James II and William III to the Electress Sophia of Hanover* (Leipzig, 1886), p. 11.

3. Ralph Lewis, *Monarchy*, p. vii.

4. Prochaska, F., *The Eagle & the Crown: Americans and the British Monarchy* (New Haven and London, 2008), pp. 107–8.

5. *An Exact Account of the Ceremonial at the Coronation of their most Excellent Majesties King William and Queen Mary* (London, 1689).

6. Starkey, *Crown & Country*, p. 399.

7. Tinniswood, A., *Behind the Throne: A Domestic History of the British Royal Household* (New York, 2018), p. 123.

8. Bates, W., *A sermon preached upon the much lamented Death of . . . Queen Mary* (London, 1695), p. 25.

9. Starkey, *Crown & Country*, p. 400.

10. The Irish resented what they saw as James's desertion and nicknamed him *Séamus an Chaca* ('James the Shit').

11. Van der Kiste, *William and Mary*, p. 138; Cussans, *Kings & Queens*, p. 154.

12. Doebner, *Memoirs of Mary*, p. 14; Foxcroft, *Supplement to Burnet's History*, p. 373.

13. Borman, *Kensington Palace*, p. 23.

14. *Short reflections upon the present state of affairs in England* (London, 1691), p. 25.

15. Borman, *Kensington Palace*, p. 23.

16. Cobbett, W., *Parliamentary history of England: from the Norman Conquest in 1066 to the year 1803*, 12 vols. (London, 1812–20), Vol. V, p. 631; Airy, *Burnet's History*, Vol. IV, pp. 246-7; Keates, J., *William III & Mary II, 1688-1702* (London, 2018), p. 59.

17. Strickland, A., *Lives of the Queens of England*, 6 vols. (London, 1901–4), Vol. VI, p. 130.

18. Foxcroft, H.C. (ed.), *The life and letters of Sir George Savile . . . first marquis of Halifax*, Vol. II (London, 1898), p. 207; Starkey, *Crown & Country*, p. 401.

19. Nairn, *Enchanted Glass*, p. 74.
20. Chapman, H., *Queen Anne's Son: A Memoir of William Henry, Duke of Gloucester* (London, 1955), p. 142.
21. Airy, *Burnet's History*, Vol. II, p. 85.

ANNE (1702–14)

1. Claydon, T., 'William III and II', *New Oxford Dictionary of National Biography* (Oxford, 2004).
2. *Oxford Illustrated History of the British Monarchy*, p. 458.
3. Cussans, *Kings & Queens*, p. 155.
4. Dalrymple, J., *Memoirs of Great Britain and Ireland* (Dublin, 1773), Vol. II, p. 180.
5. Churchill, S., *Account of the Conduct of the Dowager Duchess of Marlborough from Her First Coming to Court, to the Year 1710* (London, 1742), p. 13.
6. *Oxford Illustrated History of the British Monarchy*, p. 452.
7. Borman, *Kensington Palace*, p. 44.
8. *Oxford Illustrated History of the British Monarchy*, p. 457.
9. Somerset, A., *Queen Anne: The Politics of Passion* (London, 2012), p. 212.
10. Ibid., pp. 316–17.
11. Gregg, E., 'Anne', *New Oxford Dictionary of National Biography* (Oxford, 2004).
12. Cussans, *Kings & Queens*, p. 155.
13. *Oxford Illustrated History of the British Monarchy*, pp. 457, 459; Green, D., *Queen Anne* (London, 1970), p. 330.
14. Cooper, *Tudors to Windsors*, p. 20.

PART 6: THE HANOVERIANS (1714–1910)

GEORGE I (1714–27)

1. Lord Mahon (ed.), *The Letters of Philip Dormer Stanhope, Earl of Chesterfield*, 5 vols. (London, 1845–53), Vol. II, p. 452; Lord Wharncliffe (ed.), *The Letters and Works of Lady Mary Wortley Montagu*, 2 vols. (London, 1887), Vol. I, p. 6.
2. Kroll, M. (ed.), *Letters from Liselotte, Elisabeth Charlotte, Princess Palatine and Duchess of Orleans, 'Madam', 1652–1722* (London, 1970), p. 167.
3. Fraser, A. (ed.), Clarke, J. and Ridley, J., *The Houses of Hanover and Saxe-Coburg-Gotha* (London, 2000), p. 12.
4. Gibbs, G.C., 'George I', *New Oxford Dictionary of National Biography* (Oxford, 2004).

5. Chesterfield, *Letters* II, 452.

6. Kroll, *Letters from Liselotte*, 167.

7. Chesterfield, *Letters* II, 458; Borman, T., *Henrietta Howard: King's Mistress, Queen's Servant* (London, 2007), p. 51.

8. Hatton, R.M., *George I: Elector and King* (London, 1978), p. 291.

9. Cowper, S. (ed.), *Diary of Mary Countess Cowper, Lady of the Bedchamber to the Princess of Wales, 1714–20* (Murray, 1865), p. 99; Wilkins, W.H., *Caroline the Illustrious, Queen-Consort of George II and sometime Queen-Regent* (London, 1904), p. 133.

10. Borman, *Henrietta Howard*, p. 66.

11. Matthews, W. (ed.), *The Diary of Dudley Ryder 1715–1716* (London, 1939), p. 310.

12. Torbuck, J., *A collection of the parliamentary debates in England (1668–1741)*, 21 vols. (1739–42), Vol. VII, p. 15.

13. Thurley, S., *Hampton Court: A Social and Architectural History* (New Haven and London, 2003), p. 254.

14. *Works of Lady Mary Wortley Montagu*, Vol. I, p. 311.

15. Wilkins, *Caroline the Illustrious*, p. 301.

George II (1727–60)

1. Hervey, *Memoirs*, Vol. I, p. 25.

2. Lady Llanover (ed.), *The Autobiography and Correspondence of Mary Granville, Mrs Delany*, 3 vols. (London, 1861), Vol. I, pp. 137–9.

3. Davis, H. (ed.), *Pope: Poetical Works* (Oxford and New York, 1990), 'The Dunciad', p. 725.

4. Chesterfield, *Letters*, Vol. II, pp. 453–4; Hervey, *Memoirs*, Vol. II, p. 320.

5. Hervey, *Memoirs*, Vol. II, p. 321.

6. Earl of Ilchester (ed.), *Lord Hervey and His Friends 1726–38: Based on letters from Holland House, Melbury and Ickworth* (London, 1950), p. 169.

7. Hervey, *Memoirs*, Vol. I, 41; Historical Manuscripts Commission, *The Manuscripts of the Earl of Egmont: Diary of Viscount Percival Afterwards First Earl of Egmont*, 3 vols. (London, 1920–3), p. 134; Walpole, H., *Reminiscences: written in 1788 for the amusement of Miss Mary and Miss Agnes* edited by Paget Jackson Toynbee (Oxford, 1924), p. 68.

8. Hervey, *Memoirs*, Vol. I, pp. 68–9.

9. Ralph Lewis, *Monarchy*, p. 146.

10. Starkey, *Crown & Country*, p. 421.

11. Ralph Lewis, *Monarchy*, p. 143.

12. Hervey, *Memoirs*, Vol. II, p. 371.

13. Borman, *Henrietta Howard*, p. 238.

14. Van der Kiste, J., *George II and Queen Caroline* (Stroud, 1997), p. 157.

15. Borman, *Henrietta Howard*, p. 239.

16. Starkey, *Crown & Country*, p. 430.

17. Williams, B., *The Whig Supremacy 1714–60* (Oxford, 1962), pp. 15–16.

18. Hoppit, J., *A Land of Liberty? England 1689–1727* (Oxford, 2000), p. 344.

19. Borman, *Henrietta Howard*, p. 267.

20. Black, J., *The Hanoverians: The History of a Dynasty* (London, 2004), p. 110.

GEORGE III (1760–1820)

1. Ralph Lewis, *Monarchy*, p. 146.

2. Young, G., *Poor Fred: The People's Prince* (London, 1937), p. 174.

3. Greig, J. (ed.), *The diaries of a duchess: extracts from the diaries of the first duchess of Northumberland, 1716–1776* (London, 1926), p. 35.

4. Prochaska, *The Eagle & the Crown*, p. 27.

5. Miller, E., *That Noble Cabinet: A History of the British Museum* (London and Ohio, 1974), p. 125. By the time of his death in 1820, the library comprised more than 65,000 volumes and 19,000 tracts and pamphlets, as well as the first substantial British collection of maps and charts.

6. Lewis, H.W.S. (ed.), *The Yale Edition of Horace Walpole's Correspondence*, 48 vols. (London, 1937–83), Vol. XXXVIII, Part II, pp. 126–7.

7. Strong, *Coronation*, p. 394.

8. Sedgwick, R. (ed.), *Letters from George III to Lord Bute, 1756–1766* (London, 1939), pp. 44, 47.

9. Ibid., p. 210.

10. Sedgwick, *Letters to Lord Bute*, p. 241.

11. Cannadine, D., 'The Context, Performance and Meaning of Ritual: The British Monarchy and the "Invention of Tradition", 1820–1977', in Hobsbawm, E. and Ranger, T. (eds.), *The Invention of Tradition* (Cambridge, 1992), p. 109.

12. Lewis, W.S. (ed.), *The Yale Edition of Horace Walpole's Correspondence*, 48 vols. (London, 1937–83), Vol. XXII, p. 524.

13. Aspinall, A. (ed.), *The Later Correspondence of George III*, 5 vols. (London, 1962–70), Vol. II, xxxviii.

14. Cannon, J., 'George III', *New Oxford Dictionary of National Biography* (Oxford, 2004).

15. Fortescue, J. (ed.), *The correspondence of King George the Third from 1760 to December 1783*, 6 vols. (London, 1927–8), Vol. IV, p. 59.

16. Royal Archives, George III, Add 32/2010/11.

17. Fortescue, *Correspondence of King George the Third*.

18. Adams, C.F. (ed.), *The works of John Adams, second president of the United States, 1735–1826*, 10 vols. (Boston, 1850–56), Vol. VIII, pp. 255–7.

19. *Oxford Book of Royal Anecdotes*, p. 515.

20. Cannon, 'George III'.

21. Ibid.

22. Cannadine, *History in Our Time*, p. 27.

23. Prochaska, F., *Royal Bounty: The Making of a Welfare Monarchy* (London and New Haven, 1995), p. 20.

24. Cussans, *Kings & Queens*, p. 169; Aspinall, A. (ed.), *The Correspondence of George, Prince of Wales, 1770–1812*, 8 vols. (London, 1963–71), Vol. I, p. 73, Vol. II, pp. 2–3; Aspinall, *Later Correspondence of George III*, Vol. V, p. 22.

25. Aspinall, *Later Correspondence of George III*, Vol. I, p. 85; Aspinall, *Correspondence of George, Prince of Wales*, Vol. III, p. 133.

26. *Oxford Illustrated History of the British Monarchy*, p. 543.

27. Ibid., p. 512.

28. Barrett, C.F. (ed.), *Diary and letters of Madame D'Arblay*, 7 vols (London, 1842–6), Vol. II, p. 375.

29. Smith, W.J. (ed.), *The Grenville papers: being the correspondence of Richard Grenville . . . and . . . George Grenville*, 4 vols. (London, 1852–3), Vol. III, p. 122.

30. *Diary and Letters of Madame d'Arblay* [Fanny Burney], quoted in *Oxford Book of Royal Anecdotes*, pp. 320–1.

31. Duke of Buckingham and Chandos [Grenville, R.], *Memoirs of the court and cabinets of George the Third*, 4 vols. (London, 1853–5), Vol. II, pp. 6–7.

32. Stanhope, *Life of William Pitt*, Vol. II, Appendix vii.

33. Aspinall, *Later Correspondence of George III*, Vol. II, p. xiv.

34. *Later Correspondence of George III*, Vol. III, p. 435n, no. 2274.

35. Brooke, J., *King George III* (London, 1972), p. 370.

36. Hogge, G. (ed.), *The journal and correspondence of William, Lord Auckland*, 4 vols. (London, 1861–2), Vol. IV, p. 214.

37. Jesse, J.H., *Memoirs of the life and reign of King George the Third*, 3 vols. (London, 1867), Vol. III, p. 330.

38. Brooke, *George III*, p. 597.

39. Ralph Lewis, *Monarchy*, p. 152.

40. Aspinall, *Correspondence of George, Prince of Wales*, Vol. VIII, p. 52.

41. Grieg, J. (ed.), *The Farington Diary*, 8 vols. (London, 1922–8), Vol. VII, p. 22.

42. Macalpine, I. and Hunter, R., *George III and the Mad-Business* (London, 1969), pp. 160–1.

43. Brooke, J., *George III*, new edition (London, 1985), frontispiece; St John-Stevas, N. (ed.), *The collected works of Walter Bagehot*, 7 vols. (London, 1965–74), Vol. V, p. 235.

George IV (1820–30)

1. *The Manuscripts and Correspondence of James, First Earl of Charlemont*, 2 vols., HMC (London, 1891–4), Vol. II, p. 98.
2. *Journals of Mrs Papendiek*, Vol. I, pp. 132–3, 144.
3. Derry, J., *The Regency Crisis and the Whigs, 1788–9* (Cambridge, 1963), pp. 34–6.
4. Aspinall, *Correspondence of George, Prince of Wales*, Vol. II, pp. 2–3; *Oxford Illustrated History of the British Monarchy*, p. 541.
5. Wade, J., *The Black Book* (London, 1820), cited in Cannadine, D., 'The Context, Performance and Meaning of Ritual: The British Monarchy and the "Invention of Tradition", 1820–1977', in Hobsbawm, E. and Ranger, T. (eds.), *The Invention of Tradition* (Cambridge, 1992), p. 101.
6. Lean, E.T., *The Napoleonists: A Study in Political Disaffection, 1760–1960* (London, 1970), p. 118.
7. Pope, W.B., *The Diary of Benjamin Robert Haydon* (Cambridge, MA, 1960), Vol. II, pp. 348–50.
8. Prebble, J., *The King's Jaunt: George IV in Scotland, 1822* (Edinburgh, 2000).
9. Bamford, F. and the Duke of Wellington (eds.), *The Journal of Mrs Arbuthnot, 1820–1832*, 2 vols. (London, 1950), Vol. I, p. 295.
10. Grenville, *Memoirs*, Vol. I, p. 277.
11. Hibbert, C., 'George IV', *New Oxford Dictionary of National Biography* (Oxford, 2004).
12. Lord Colchester (ed.), *A political diary, 1828–1830, by Edward Law, Lord Ellenborough*, 2 vols. (London, 1881), Vol. I, pp. 376–7, 384–5.
13. Wellesley, G. (ed.), *Wellington and His Friends* (London, 1965), p. 70.
14. Smith, E.A., *George IV* (London and New Haven, 1999), pp. 266–7.
15. Smith, *George IV*, p. 271.
16. Hibbert, C., *George IV: Regent and King, 1811–1830* (London, 1973), p. 310.
17. Baker, K., 'George IV: A Sketch', *History Today*, Vol. LV, issue 10 (October, 2005), pp. 30–6.
18. *A portion of the journal kept by Thomas Raikes, from 1831 to 1847*, 4 vols. (London, 1856–7), Vol. I, p. 92.

WILLIAM IV (1830–7)

1. Van der Kiste, J., *George III's Children* (Stroud, 1994), p. 178.
2. The couple had two short-lived daughters early in their marriage, and Adelaide also suffered two miscarriages.
3. Prochaska, *The Eagle & the Crown*, p. 15.
4. Somerset, A., *The Life and Times of William IV* (London, 1980), p. 119ff.
5. *Oxford Illustrated History of the British Monarchy*, p. 548.
6. Quennel, P. (ed.), *The Private Letters of Princess Lieven to Prince Metternich, 1820–1826* (London, 1937), p. 372.
7. Nairn, *Enchanted Glass*, p. 283.
8. Cussans, *Kings & Queens*, p. 172.
9. *Oxford Illustrated History of the British Monarchy*, p. 545.
10. Strachey, L. and Fulford, R. (eds.), *The Greville memoirs, 1814–1860*, 8 vols. (London, 1938), Vol. II, p. 6.
11. Ziegler, P., *King William IV* (London, 1971), pp. 193–4; Allen, W.G., *King William IV* (London, 1960), pp. 131–2; Gosling, L, *Royal Coronations* (Oxford, 2013), pp. 40-1.
12. Earl Grey, Henry (ed.), *The Reform Act, 1832: the correspondence of the late Earl Grey with His Majesty King William IV and with Sir Herbert Taylor*, 2 vols. (London, 1867), Vol. II, pp. 102, 113.
13. Somerset, A., *The Life and Times of William IV* (London, 1980), p. 200.
14. Walpole, S., *The Life of Lord John Russell*, 2 vols. (London, 1889), Vol. I, p. 269.
15. Strachey and Fulford, *Greville Memoirs*, Vol. III, p. 223.
16. Ziegler, *King William IV*, p. 276.
17. Strachey and Fulford, *Greville Memoirs*, Vol. III, p. 309.
18. Benson, A.C. and Viscount Esher (eds.), *The letters of Queen Victoria*, 3 vols. (London, 1907), Vol. I, p. 73.
19. Strachey and Fulford, *Greville Memoirs*, Vol. III, p. 382.
20. *The Times*, 20 June 1837.

VICTORIA (1837–1901)

1. Royal Archives Y203, Baroness Lehzen to Queen Victoria, 2 December 1867.
2. Royal Archives VIC/MAIN/M/3/3, 24 May 1819, The Duke of Kent to the Dowager Duchess of S-C; Baron E. von Stockmar and Müller, G.A., *Memoirs of Baron Stockmar*, Vol. I, 1872, p. 78.
3. Fulford, R. (ed.), *Dearest Child: Letters between Queen Victoria and the Princess Royal, 1858–1861* (London, 1964), pp. 111–12.

4. Royal Archives VIC/MAIN/Add/A7/23, Queen Victoria's Conduct Books.

5. Royal Archives, Queen Victoria's Journal, 20 June 1837, p. 64.

6. Duke of Wellington to the Duchess of Northumberland, 20 June 1837, Private Collection.

7. Royal Archives, Queen Victoria's Journal, p. 65.

8. Viscount Esher (ed.), *The Girlhood of Queen Victoria: A selection of Her Majesty's Diaries between the years 1832 and 1840*, 2 vols. (London, 1912), Vol. I, p. 197.

9. Murphy, D., *The Young Victoria* (New Haven and London, 2019), p. 119.

10. Benson and Esher, *Letters of Queen Victoria*, Vol. I, p. 26.

11. See Cannadine, 'The British Monarchy', pp. 101–64.

12. Lacey, *Royal*, p. 20.

13. Strong, *Coronation*, pp. 363–4.

14. Prochaska, *The Eagle & the Crown*, p. 45; Fisher, G. and H., *Monarchy and the Royal Family* (London, 1979), p. 36.

15. Strong, *Coronation*, p. 417.

16. Royal Archives, Queen Victoria's Journal, 28 June 1838.

17. Charlot, M., *Victoria: The Young Queen* (London, 1991), p. 141.

18. Ziegler, *King William IV*, p. 273.

19. Nevins, A. and Halsey Thomas, M. (eds.), *The Diary of George Templeton Strong: Young Man in New York 1835–1849* (New York, 1952), p. 71; Royal Archives, Queen Victoria's Journal, 18 April 1839.

20. Royal Archives, Queen Victoria's Journal, 18 May 1836, pp. 278–80.

21. Benson and Esher, *Letters of Queen Victoria*, Vol. I, p. 237; Woodham-Smith, C, *Queen Victoria: Her Life and Times*, Vol. I (London, 1972), p. 184.

22. *Oxford Book of Royal Anecdotes*, p. 369.

23. TNA, HO 107/1478, Census return for St George Hanover Square district, including Buckingham Palace.

24. Fulford, R. (ed.), *Dearest Mama: Letters between Queen Victoria and the Crown Princess of Prussia, 1861–1864* (London, 1968), p. 23.

25. Longford, *Victoria*, p. 179.

26. Thereafter, only the home secretary was present. The last royal birth this official attended was that of the current queen's cousin, Princess Alexandra, in 1936. The custom was ended ahead of Prince Charles's birth in 1948.

27. Davenport-Hines, R., *Edward VII* (London, 2018), p. 4; Fulford, *Dearest Child*, p. 245.

28. *Oxford Illustrated History of the British Monarchy*, p. 579.

29. Longford, E., *Queen Victoria: Born to Succeed* (London, 1964), p. 184.

30. Nairn, *Enchanted Glass*, p. 99.

31. Benson and Esher, *Letters of Queen Victoria*, Vol. I, pp. 352–3.

32. Connell, B. (ed.), *Regina v Palmerston: The Correspondence between Queen Victoria and her Foreign and Prime Minister, 1837–1865* (London, 1962), p. 142.

33. Connell, *Regina v Palmerston*, p. 142. See also: Bogdanor, V., *The Monarchy and the Constitution* (Oxford, 1995), p. 25.

34. Baron Stockmar to the Prince Consort, 1854, cited by Blake, R., 'The Crown and Politics in the Twentieth Century', in Murray-Brown (ed.), *The Monarchy and its Future*, p. 11.

35. Stuart, C.H., 'The Prince Consort and Ministerial Politics, 1856–9', in Trevor-Roper, H. (ed.), *Essays in English History* (London, 1964), p. 69.

36. Martin, T., *The Life of His Royal Highness The Prince Consort*, 5 vols. (London, 1875–80), Vol. II, p. 260.

37. Benson and Esher, *Letters of Queen Victoria*, Vol. II, p. 383.

38. Benson and Esher, *Letters of Queen Victoria*, Vol. III, p. 313.

39. *Oxford Illustrated History of the British Monarchy*, p. 625.

40. Schama, S., 'The Domestication of Majesty: Royal Family Portraiture, 1500–1850', *Journal of Interdisciplinary History*, Vol. XVII, no. 1 (Massachusetts, 1986).

41. Cussans, *Kings & Queens*, p. 181.

42. Benson and Esher, *Letters of Queen Victoria*, Vol. III, pp. 470–1.

43. Cussans, *Kings & Queens*, p. 176.

44. Benson and Esher, *Letters of Queen Victoria*, Vol. III, p. 606.

45. Hibbert, C., *Queen Victoria in her Letters and Journals* (London, 1984), p. 310; Longford, *Victoria*, p. 321.

46. *Oxford Illustrated History of the British Monarchy*, p. 563.

47. Kennedy, A.L., *My Dear Duchess: Social and Political Letters to the Duchess of Manchester, 1858–1869* (London, 1956), p. 189.

48. Baird, J., *Victoria the Queen: An Intimate Biography of a Woman* (New York, 2016), p. 406.

49. Ibid.

50. Ibid.

51. Bogdanor, *The Monarchy and the Constitution*, p. 29; Nairn, *Enchanted Glass*, pp. 327, 338; *Oxford Illustrated History of the British Monarchy*, p. 565.

52. *Oxford Illustrated History of the British Monarchy*, p. 565.

53. Ponsonby, A., *Henry Ponsonby, Queen Victoria's Private Secretary: His Life from his Letters* (London, 1943), p. 72.

54. Bagehot, *Collected Works*, Vol. V., p. 258.

55. Cannadine, 'The British Monarchy', p. 119; *Oxford Illustrated History of the British Monarchy*, p. 565.

56. Benson and Esher, *Letters of Queen Victoria*, Vol. II, p. 194.

57. Hayden, I., *Symbol and Privilege: The Ritual Context of British Royalty* (Arizona, 1987), p. 69.

58. *Oxford Illustrated History of the British Monarchy*, p. 574.

59. Longford, *Victoria*, p. 401.

60. Cussans, *Kings & Queens*, p. 174.

61. Blake, R., *Disraeli* (London, 1966), p. 548; Longford, *Victoria*, p. 403.

62. Gladstone, W.E., *Gleanings of Past Years* (London, 1879), Vol. II, p. 84; *British Monarchy Miscellany*, p. 388.

63. Benson and Esher, *Letters of Queen Victoria*, Vol. II, p. 302.

64. Fulford, R. (ed.), *Darling Child: Private Correspondence of Queen Victoria and the Crown Princess of Prussia, 1871–1878* (London, 1976), p. 40.

65. *Oxford Illustrated History of the British Monarchy*, p. 571.

66. Fulford, *Darling Child*, p. 251.

67. Six years earlier, Victoria had lost her second-eldest daughter Alice to diphtheria.

68. Benson and Esher, *Letters of Queen Victoria*, Vol. II, p. 361.

69. *Oxford Illustrated History of the British Monarchy*, p. 569.

70. Benson and Esher, *Letters of Queen Victoria*, Vol. III, p. 79.

71. The shawl is now preserved in the Smithsonian's new National Museum of African American History and Culture.

72. Prochaska, *Welfare Monarchy*, pp. 77, 80.

73. Mallet, V. (ed.), *Life with Queen Victoria: Marie Mallet's Letters from Court, 1887–1901* (London, 1968), p. 213.

74. Longford, *Victoria*, p. 558.

75. Victoria's diaries ran into 122 volumes. After her death, her youngest daughter Beatrice transcribed and (often savagely) edited the diaries covering her mother's accession onwards. It is a source of enduring regret to historians of the period that in the process she burned the originals.

76. Strachey, L., *Queen Victoria* (London, 1921), p. 309.

77. Prochaska, *The Eagle & the Crown*, p. 101.

78. Longford, *Victoria*, p. 567.

79. Cussans, *Kings & Queens*, p. 188.

80. Prochaska, *The Eagle & the Crown*, p. 82.

81. *Oxford Illustrated History of the British Monarchy*, p. 578.

Edward VII (1901–10)

1. His record has since been beaten by the current Prince of Wales. Charles became Britain's longest-serving heir apparent on 20 April 2011, and the longest-serving Prince of Wales on 9 September 2017.

2. Davenport-Hines, *Edward VII*, p. 50.

3. Davenport-Hines, *Edward VII*, p. 66.

4. Lo Hui-Min, *The Correspondence of G.E. Morrison*, Vol. I (Cambridge, 1976), pp. 165–6.

5. Davenport-Hines, *Edward VII*, p. 56.

6. Every subsequent coronation has been marked by a similar appeal.

7. Davenport-Hines, *Edward VII*, p. 23.

8. Bogdanor, *The Monarchy and the Constitution*, p. 39.

9. Magnus, P., *King Edward the Seventh* (London, 1964), p. 307.

10. Fisher, *Monarchy and the Royal Family*, p. 88.

11. Matthew, H.C.G., 'George V', *New Oxford Dictionary of National Biography* (Oxford, 2004).

12. Davenport-Hines, *Edward VII*, p. 105.

13. Lacey, *Royal*, p. 230; Heffer, S., *Power and Place: The Political Consequences of King Edward VII* (London, 1998), pp. 282–3.

14. Windsor, HRH, The Duke of, *A King's Story* (London, 1951), p. 69.

15. *The Times*, 7 May 1910.

16. Davenport-Hines, *Edward VII*, p. 49.

17. Davenport-Hines, *Edward VII*, p. 50.

Part 7: The Windsors (1910 onwards)

George V (1910–36)

1. Matthew, H.G.C. (ed.), *The Gladstone Diaries*, 14 vols. (Oxford, 1994), Vol. XIII 1892–1896, 16 February 1893.

2. Royal Archives, King George V's diary, 6 May 1910; Rose, K., *King George V* (London, 1984), p. 75.

3. Fisher, *Monarchy and the Royal Family*, p. 30.

4. Royal Archives, King George V's diary, 16 November 1910; cited in Rose, *George V*, p. 121.

5. *Oxford Illustrated History of the British Monarchy*, p. 590.

6. Nicolson, H., *King George the Fifth: His Life and Reign* (London, 1952), p. 247.

7. Ibid., pp. 245–6.

8. Royal Archives, King George V's diary, 2 August 1914; Rose, *George V*, p. 168.

9. Nicolson, *George the Fifth*, p. 308.

10. Cussans, *Kings & Queens*, p. 182.

11. Royal Archives, King George V's diary, 25 July 1917; Rose, *George V*, p. 216.

12. Royal Archives, King George V's diary, 11 November; Rose, *George V*, p. 222.

13. Prochaska, *Welfare Monarchy*, p. 182.

14. Nicolson, *George the Fifth*, p. 361.

15. Prochaska, *Welfare Monarchy*, p. 171.

16. Royal Archives, King George V's diary, 24 January 1924; Rose, *George V*, p. 326.

17. Rose, *George V*, p. 340; Sinclair, D., *Two Georges: The Making of the Modern Monarchy* (London, 1988).

18. Rose, *George V*, p. 387.

19. Brett, M.V. (ed.), *The Journals and Letters of Reginald, Viscount Esher*, 4 vols (London, 1934–8), Vol. II, p. 330.

20. Flusser, A.J., *Dressing the Man: Mastering the Art of Permanent Fashion* (New York, 2002), p. 8.

21. Windsor, *A King's Story*, pp. 215–16.

22. Ziegler, P., *King Edward VIII: The Official Biography* (London, 1990), p. 80.

23. Godfrey, R. (ed.) (1998), *Letters from a Prince: Edward, Prince of Wales, to Mrs. Freda Dudley Ward March 1918–January 1921* (London, 1998), letter dated 11 July 1920.

24. Wheeler-Bennett, J.W., *King George VI: His Life and Reign* (London, 1958); Pimlott, B., *The Queen: Elizabeth II and the Monarchy* (London, 2012), p. 15.

25. Lord Birkenhead, *Walter Monckton: The life of Viscount Monckton of Brenchley* (London, 1969), p. 125.

26. Bloch, M., *The Duchess of Windsor* (London, 1996), p. 50; Ziegler, P., 'Windsor (Bessie) Wallis, duchess of Windsor (1896–1986)', *New Dictionary of National Biography* (Oxford, 2004).

27. *Oxford Illustrated History of the British Monarchy*, p. 604.

28. Matthew, 'George V'.

29. Nicolson, *George the Fifth*, p. 524.

30. Marquand, D., *Ramsay MacDonald* (London, 1977), p. 775.

31. Starkey, *Crown & Country*, p. 482.

32. Marquand, *Ramsay MacDonald*, p. 777.

33. Royal Archives, King George V's diary, 17 January 1936. Cited in Nicolson, *George the Fifth*, p. 530.

34. Roberts, A., *The House of Windsor*, edited by Fraser, A. (London, 2000), p. 36.

35. Watson, Francis, 'The Death of George V', *History Today*, Vol. XXXVI (London, 1986), pp. 21–30.

36. Starkey, *Crown & Country*, p. 483; Matthew, 'George V'.

Edward VIII (1936)

1. *Oxford Book of Royal Anecdotes*, p. 452.
2. Ziegler, *Edward VIII*, p. 199.
3. *Oxford Book of Royal Anecdotes*, p. 467.
4. Paterson, M., *A Brief History of The House of Windsor: The Making of a Modern Monarchy* (London, 2013), p. 81.
5. Windsor, *A King's Story*, p. 274.
6. Cussans, *Kings & Queens*, p. 191.
7. Wheeler-Bennett, *George VI*, p. 286.
8. Bradford, S., *King George VI* (London, 1989), p. 188.
9. Windsor, Duchess of, *The Heart has its Reasons* (London, 1956), pp. 259–60.
10. *Oxford Book of Royal Anecdotes*, p. 459; Lacey, *Royal*, p. 92.
11. The National Archives PC 11/1 Instrument of Abdication, 10 December 1936.
12. *Oxford Book of Royal Anecdotes*, p. 459.
13. Wheeler-Bennett, *George VI*, p. 287.
14. *Oxford Book of Royal Anecdotes*, p. 459.
15. Donaldson, F., *Edward VIII* (London, 1974), p. 295.
16. *Oxford Book of Royal Anecdotes*, p. 517.
17. *Daily Telegraph*, 7 December 1986; *Oxford Book of Royal Anecdotes*, p. 460.
18. Rhodes, J.R., *A Spirit Undaunted: The Political Role of George VI* (London, 1998), p. 115.

George VI (1936–52)

1. Rose, *George V*, p. 392.
2. Royal Archives – Letter from George VI to his daughter princess Elizabeth shortly after her wedding. Released by the Royal Household to commemorate the Queen and the duke of Edinburgh's sixty-eighth wedding anniversary on 20 November 2015.
3. Paterson, *House of Windsor*, p. 157.
4. Lacey, *Royal*, p. 104.
5. *Oxford Book of Royal Anecdotes*, p. 473; Paterson, *House of Windsor*, p. 101.
6. Paterson, *House of Windsor*, p. 101.
7. Martin, K., *The Magic of Monarchy* (London, 1937), p. 101.
8. The economist and social reformer Beatrice Webb, cited in Pimlott, *The Queen*, p. 37.
9. The National Archives PREM 1/461: Approval of titles for Prince Edward, including 'His Royal Highness' and 'The Duke of Windsor'.

10. *Oxford Book of Royal Anecdotes*, p. 468.

11. 'The King's Memorandum of the Coronation', cited in Wheeler-Bennett, *George VI*, p. 312.

12. Complete Coronation Edition. *Evening Standard*, 12 May 1937.

13. Hitchens, C., 'Mourning will be brief', *Guardian*, 1 April 2002.

14. Judd, *George VI* (London, 2012), p. 184.

15. Haskins, M.L., *The Desert* (privately printed, 1908).

16. Wheeler-Bennett, *George VI*, p. 479.

17. Cadbury, D., *Princes at War: The British Royal Family's Private Battle in the Second World War* (London, 2015), p. 175.

18. Fitzalan Howard, A., *The Windsor Diaries: A Childhood with the Princesses* (London, 2020), p. 44.

19. Bond, J., *Elizabeth: Eighty Glorious Years* (London, 2006), p. 10; Pimlott, *The Queen*, p. 79.

20. Wheeler-Bennett, *George VI*, p. 636.

21. Mountbatten was the anglicised version of his family name, Battenburg.

22. Wheeler-Bennett, *George VI*, p. 751.

23. Bradford, *George VI*, p. 420.

24. Brandreth, G., *Philip and Elizabeth: Portrait of a Marriage* (London, 2004), p. 314; Crawford, M., *The Little Princesses* (New York, 1950), p. 180.

25. Fisher, *Monarchy and the Royal Family*, p. 202.

26. Letter from George VI to his brother the Duke of Windsor, quoted in Rhodes, *A Spirit Undaunted*, p. 127.

ELIZABETH II (1952–)

1. Brandreth, *Philip and Elizabeth*, p. 105; Lacey, R., *Royal: Her Majesty Queen Elizabeth II* (London, 2002), p. 81; Shawcross, W., *Queen and Country* (Toronto, 2002), pp. 21–2.

2. Brandreth, *Philip and Elizabeth*, pp. 105–6; Fitzalan Howard, *Windsor Diaries*, pp. 65, 100.

3. Lacey, *Royal*, p. 187.

4. Pimlott, *Elizabeth II and the Monarchy*, pp. 183–5; Lacey, *Royal*, p. 173.

5. Fisher, *Monarchy and the Royal Family*, p. 226.

6. Ibid., p. 227.

7. Macmillan, H., *Pointing the Way 1959–1961* (London, 1972), pp. 466–72.

8. Hamilton, W., 'The Crown, the Cash and the Future', in Murray-Brown (ed.), *The Monarchy and its Future*, p. 67.

9. Fisher, *Monarchy and the Royal Family*, p. 9.

10. Ibid., p. 11.

11. Glenconner, A., *Lady in Waiting: My Extraordinary Life in the Shadow of the Crown* (London, 2020), p. 60.
12. Gristwood, S., *Elizabeth: The Queen and the Crown* (London, 2017), p. 12.
13. Strong, *Coronation*, p. 494.
14. *New York Times*, 3 June 1953.
15. Nairn, *Enchanted Glass*, p. 17; Strong, *Coronation*, p. 490.
16. Prochaska, *The Eagle & the Crown*, p. 164.
17. Sebastian Haffner, quoted in Nairn, *Enchanted Glass*, p. 20; *New Statesman*, 1 June 1960.
18. To date, the Queen has visited 114 countries across the globe.
19. Warwick, C., *Princess Margaret: A Life of Contrasts* (London, 2002), p. 205. Margaret and Townsend's love letters are in the Royal Archives, but will not be released until a hundred years after the princess's birth (2030).
20. Bagehot, W., *The English Constitution*, cited in Fisher, *Monarchy and the Royal Family*, p. 153.
21. Lacey, *Royal*, p. 196.
22. Lacey, *Royal*, p. 182.
23. Grigg, J., 'The Monarchy Today', *National and English Review* (London, August 1957). Fisher, *Monarchy and the Royal Family*, p. 231.
24. *The Ultimate Family: the making of the royal house of Windsor* by John Pearson (London, 2012).
25. Pearson, *The Ultimate Family*.
26. Julian Critchley, *The Times*, 20 June 1969.
27. Nairn, *Enchanted Glass*, p. 36.
28. *New York Times*, 7 July 1976.
29. Trudeau, P.E., *Memoirs* (Toronto, 1993), p. 313.
30. Lacey, *Royal*, p. 245.
31. Weir, A., et al., *The Ring and the Crown: A History of Royal Weddings, 1066–2011* (London, 2011), p. 150.
32. Weir et al., *The Ring and the Crown*, p. 150.
33. Diana was descended from two of Charles II's illegitimate sons: the Dukes of Grafton and Richmond. This means that when her son William becomes king, he will be the first British monarch descended from Charles II.
34. Dimbleby, J., *The Prince of Wales: A Biography* (London, 1994), p. 290.
35. *New York Times*, 29 July 1981.
36. Morton, A, *Diana: Her True Story – In Her Own Words* (London, 2019), pp. 196–7
37. Prochaska, *The Eagle & the Crown*, p. 181; Weir et al., *The Ring and the Crown*, p. 153.

38. Donald Trelford, *Observer*, 21 September 1986.

39. *Oxford Book of Royal Anecdotes*, p. 506.

40. Cannadine, *History in Our Time*, p. 39.

41. Prochaska, Frank. *The Eagle and the Crown* (New Haven, 2008), p. 189

42. Prochaska, *The Eagle & the Crown*, p. 189; *Time*, 16 November 1985.

43. Cannadine, *History in Our Time*, p. 74.

44. Weir et al., *The Ring and the Crown*, p. 159.

45. Pimlott, *The Queen*, p. 585.

46. Cannadine, D. (ed.), *Westminster Abbey: A Church in History* (New Haven and London, 2019), p. 356.

47. Sebastian Haffner, quoted in Nairn, *Enchanted Glass*, pp. 20–1.

48. Cannadine, *History in Our Time*, p. 79.

49. Quoted in Lacey, *Royal*, p. 379.

50. Lacey, *Royal*, p. 380.

51. Cannadine, *History in Our Time*, p. 85.

52. Weir et al., *The Ring and the Crown*, p. 181.

53. Cannadine, *History in Our Time*, p. 72.

54. Paterson, *House of Windsor*, p. 27.

55. Kelly, A., *The Other Side of the Coin: The Queen, the Dresser and the Wardrobe* (London, 2019), p. 168.

56. Kevin Rawlinson, *Guardian*, 20 November 2019
    Camilla Tominey, *Telegraph*, 18 November 2019
    Léonie Chao-Fong, *Express*, 16 November 2019

57. *Oxford Book of Royal Anecdotes*, p. 513.

58. William Hamilton's essay, 'The Crown, the Cash and the Future' provides an interesting analysis of the cost of the monarchy to the public. See also: St John-Stevas, J., 'The Monarchy and the Present'. Both are in Murray-Brown (ed.), *The Monarchy and its Future*, pp. 59–70, 220–22.

59. Ralph Lewis, *Monarchy*, p. 175.

60. CNN online article, 2 April 2021.

61. BBC News, 7 July 2010.

62. Gristwood, *Elizabeth*, p. 147.

63. Pimlott, *The Queen*, p. 581.

64. The Queen's Diamond Jubilee message, Royal Household, 6 February 2012.

65. Proverbs 25:3.

Epilogue

1. Seven of the twelve monarchies are kingdoms: Denmark, Norway, Sweden, Spain, the Netherlands, Belgium and the United Kingdom; three are principalities: Andorra, Liechtenstein and Monaco; Luxembourg is a Grand Duchy and the Vatican City is a theocratic state.

2. Prochaska, F., 'But the Greatest of These – Civil Society and the "Welfare Monarchy"', *Times Literary Supplement*, 15 January 1993; Prochaska, *Welfare Monarchy*, p. 283.

3. Lacey, *Royal*, p. 139; Nairn, *Enchanted Glass*, p. 314; Murray-Brown, J., 'Lifting the Curtain', in Murray-Brown. (ed.), *The Monarchy and its Future*, p. 181; *British Monarchy Miscellany*, p. 388.

4. Paterson, *House of Windsor*, p. 225.

5. The diarist John Evelyn, quoted in Ralph Lewis, *Monarchy*, p. 176.

6. Lord Altrincham, *The Times*, 29 May 1977.

7. Pimlott, *The Queen*, p. 295

8. Pimlott, *The Queen*, p. 295; Prochaska, *The Eagle & the Crown*, p. 197; Nairn, *Enchanted Glass*, p. 354; Bogdanor, *The Monarchy and the Constitution*, p. 305.

BIBLIOGRAPHY

1. Archival sources

British Library

BL Cotton MS Augustus II 3 – The 'Ismere Charter' of Æthelbald, king of the Mercians, citing him as 'Rex Britanniae', 736

BL Cotton MS Augustus II 20 – The Council of Kingston, 838

BL Additional MS 57337 ff. 60v–61r – The Anglo-Saxon coronation order in the Anderson Pontifical

BL Cotton MS Cleopatra BXIII, ff. 55v–56r – The Old English coronation oath

BL Cotton MS Augustus II 23 – Charter of King Æthelstan to Eadwulf, citing Æthelstan as 'King of all Britain'

BL Cotton MS Augustus II 23 – poem celebrating Æthelstan's accession

BL Cotton MS Tiberius A II – Coronation Gospels of Æthelstan

BL Cotton MS Tiberius A III, ff. 2v–3r, *Regularis Concordia* ('The Monastic Agreement' of King Edgar

BL Cotton MS Tiberius B V/1 fo. 56v – World map made in Southern England, 1025–50

BL Additional MS 33241, ff. 1v–2r *Encomium Emmae reginae*

BL MS Cotton Nero D.x, fo. 110v – unpublished chronicle from Edward II's reign attributed to Nicholas Trivet

BL Additional MS fo. 262r – Henry IV orders a suit of clothes for one of his minstrels

BL Cotton MS Tiberius D viii f.89 – Henry VIII's coronation oath, altered in his own hand during the Reformation

BL MS Lansdowne 823, fos. 371–2 – Richard Cromwell's letter to his brother Henry, May 1659

517

The National Archives

E 31/2 and E 31/1 – Great and Little Domesday Book

SP 10/13, no. 55 – Edward VI's reprimand to the Lord Chancellor, 1551

SP 11/4/2 f. 3–3v – Princess Elizabeth's 'Tide Letter', 17 March 1554

SP 12/215 f. 65 – Robert Dudley's 'last letter' to Elizabeth I

SP 14/8 fo. 93 – James I's admonishment to the Commons, 1604

HO 107/1478, Census return for St George Hanover Square district, including Buckingham Palace, 30 March 1851

PC 11/1 Instrument of Abdication, 10 December 1936

The National Archives PREM 1/461: Approval of titles for Prince Edward, including 'His Royal Highness' and 'The Duke of Windsor', December 1936

PREM 11/1565, Princess Margaret's letter to Anthony Eden, August 1955

Royal Archives

George III Add 32/2010/11 – George III laments the loss of America (undated, but probably drafted in early 1783)

RA41774–41775 – The future George IV creating a scandal in the press

VIC/MAIN/Add/A7/23, Queen Victoria's Conduct Books

Y203 Baroness Lehzen to Queen Victoria, 2 December 1867

Queen Victoria's Journal

King George V's diary, 6 May 1910 – grief on the death of his father, Edward VII

King George V's diary, 16 November 1910 – the king reluctantly approves the Parliament Act, restricting the powers of the House of Lords

King George V's diary, 2 August 1914 – the king expresses his anxiety that war can no longer be avoided

King George V's diary, 4 August 1914 – the king records that war has been declared

King George V's diary, 25 July 1917 – the king reflects on the murder of his cousin, Tsar Nicholas II

King George V's diary, 11 November – the king's reaction to the signing of the armistice, ending the First World War

King George V's diary, 24 January 1924 – the king's reflection upon Ramsay MacDonald being appointed Britain's first Labour prime minister

King George V's diary, 17 January 1936 – the king's last entry

Oxford, Bodleian Library

Hatton MS 20, ff. ii v–1r – King Alfred's preface to his translation of the *Pastoral Care* by Gregory the Great

Ashmole MS 1729, fo. 9 – Thomas Seymour's criticism of his brother's treatment of their nephew, Edward VI, 1548

Ashmole MS 1729, fos. 51, 56 – James I's instructions to the privy council upon his accession in England, 1603

Cambridge, Corpus Christi College

MS 383, ff. 56v–57r – The treaty between King Alfred and King Guthrum, c. 880

Inner Temple Library, London

Petyt MS 538, Vol. 47, fo. 317 – Edward VI's 'Devise' for the succession, 1553

Lambeth Palace Library

MS 683 Elizabeth I's translation of Tacitus, *Annales*, c. 1590s

Northamptonshire Record Office

Isham correspondence, 1379 – The Earl of Peterborough's observations on James II's accession, 1685

2. *Printed Primary sources*

Ailes, M. and Barber, M. (eds. and trans.), *The Crusade of Richard Lionheart by Ambroise* (New York, 2003)

Airy, O. (ed.), *Burnet's History of my own time*, 2 vols. (Oxford, 1897–1900)

An Exact Account of the Ceremonial at the Coronation of their most Excellent Majesties King William and Queen Mary (London, 1689)

An order of the lords spiritual and temporal, and commons assembled at Westminster . . . for a publick thanksgiving (London, 1689)

Appleby, J.T. (ed. and trans.), *Cronicon Richardi Divisensis tempore regis Richardi primi* (London, 1963)

Armstrong, C.A.J. (ed. and trans.), *The Usurpation of Richard the Third: Dominicus Mancinus ad Angelum Catonem de occupatione regni Anglie per Ricardum tercium libellus* (Oxford, 1969)

Aspinall, A. (ed.), *The Correspondence of George, Prince of Wales, 1770–1812*, 8 vols. (London, 1963–71)

Aspinall, A. (ed.), *The Later Correspondence of George III*, 5 vols. (London, 1962–70)

Attreed, L.C. (ed.), *The York House Books, 1461–1490*, 2 vols. (Stroud, 1991)

Bamford, F. and the Duke of Wellington (eds.), *The Journal of Mrs Arbuthnot, 1820–1832*, 2 vols. (London, 1950)

Barlow, F. (ed. and trans.), *The Life of King Edward Who Rests at Westminster* (Oxford, 1992)

Benson, A.C. and Viscount Esher (eds.), *The letters of Queen Victoria*, 3 vols. (London, 1907)

Birch, T., *Memoirs of the Reign of Queen Elizabeth from the year 1581 till her Death* (London, 1754)

Bloch, M. (ed.), *Wallis & Edward: Letters 1931–1937* (London, 1986)

Boyle, J. (ed.), *Memoirs of the Life of Robert Carey . . . Written by Himself* (London, 1759)

Bray, G. (ed.), *Documents of the English Reformation* (Cambridge, 1994)

Brett, M.V. (ed.), *The Journals and Letters of Reginald, Viscount Esher* (London, 1934–8)

Brewer, J.S., et al., (eds.), *Letters and Papers, Foreign and Domestic, of the Reign of Henry VIII, 1509–47*, 21 vols. and 2 vols. addenda (London, 1862–1932)

Brewer, J.S. (ed.), Fuller, T., *The Church History of Britain*, 6 vols. (Oxford, 1845)

Brie, F.W.D. (ed.), *The Brut, or, The chronicles of England*, 2 vols., Early English Text Society, 131, 136 (London, 1906–8)

Broughton, V.D. (ed.), *Court and private life in the time of Queen Charlotte, being the journals of Mrs Papendiek*, 2 vols., (London, 1887)

Brown, M.N. (ed.), 'A character of Charles II', *The Works of George Savile, Marquis of Halifax*, 2 vols. (Oxford, 1989)

Brown, R. (ed.), *Calendar of State Papers and Manuscripts, Relating to English Affairs, Existing in the Archives and Collections of Venice*, Vols. I–V (London, 1864–73)

Brown, R. (ed.), *Four years at the court of Henry VIII: Selection of despatches written by the Venetian Ambassador, Sebastian Giustinian, and addressed to the Signory of Venice, January 12th 1515, to July 26th 1519*, 2 vols. (London, 1854)

Browning, A (ed. and trans.), *Memoirs of Sir John Reresby* (Glasgow, 1936)

Burgess, G.S. and Holden, A. (ed. and trans.), *Wace, The Roman de Rou* (Jersey, 2002)

Butler, H.E. and Millor, W.J. (eds. and trans.) and Brooke, C.N.L. (revised), *The letters of John of Salisbury*, 2 vols. (Oxford, 1979–86)

Calendar of the Close Rolls preserved in the Public Record Office: Henry VII 1485–1509 (London, 1955)

Calendar of Letters, Despatches, and State Papers, relating to the negotiations between England and Spain, preserved in the archives at Simancas and elsewhere (London, 1866–92)

Calendar of Patent Rolls, preserved in the Public Record Office, Henry VII: Vol. I 1485–1494 (London, 1914)

Calendar of State Papers, Milan

Camden, W., *The Historie of the Most Renowned and Victorious Princesse Elizabeth, late Queene of England* (London, 1630)

Campbell, A. (ed. and trans.), *Encomium Emmae*, Camden Society, 3rd series, LXXII (London, 1949)

Cattley, S.R. (ed.), *The acts and monuments of John Foxe*, 8 vols. (London, 1837–41)

Cerovski, J.S. (ed.), Sir Robert Naunton, *Fragmentia Regalia or Observations on Queen Elizabeth, Her Times and Favourites* (London and Toronto, 1985)

Chamberlain, F., *The Sayings of Queen Elizabeth I* (New York, 1923)

Chibnall, M. (ed. and trans.), *The Ecclesiastical History of Orderic Vitalis*, 6 vols. (Oxford, 1968–78)

Chrimes, S.B. and Brown, A.L. (eds), *Select Documents of English Constitutional History* (London, 1964)

Churchill, S., *Account of the Conduct of the Dowager Duchess of Marlborough from Her First Coming to Court, to the Year 1710* (London, 1742)

Clarke, J.S. (ed.), *The Life of James the Second, King of England*, 2 vols. (London, 1816)

Clifford, D.J.H. (ed.), *The Diaries of Lady Anne Clifford* (Stroud, 1992)

Connell, B. (ed.), *Regina v Palmerston: The Correspondence between Queen Victoria and her Foreign and Prime Minister, 1837–1865* (London, 1962)

Cotton, R., *Cottoni Posthuma: divers choice pieces of that renowned antiquary Sir Robert Cotton . . . preserved from the injury of time, and expos'd to public light, for the benefit of posterity* (London, 1651)

Craigie, J. (ed.), *Minor Prose Works of King James VI and I* (Edinburgh, 1982)

Dasent, J.R., *Acts of the Privy Council of England*, Vols. I and II (London, 1890)

Davis, R.H.C. and Chibnall, M. (eds.), *The 'Gesta Willelmi' of William of Poitiers* (Oxford, 1998)

Delaborde, H.F. (ed.), Œuvres de Rigord et de Guillaume le Breton, historiens de Philippe-Auguste, 2 vols. (Paris, 1882–5)

Denholm-Young, N. (ed. and trans.), Vita Edwardi Secundi (London, 1957)

Doebner, R. (ed.), Memoirs of Mary, Queen of England, 1689–1693, together with her letters and those of James II and William III to the Electress Sophia of Hanover (Leipzig, 1886)

Doran, S. (ed.), Henry VIII: Man and Monarch (London, 2009)

Doran, S., The Tudor Chronicles (London, 2011)

Douglas, D.C. et al., (eds.), English Historical Documents, 10 vols. (London, 1953–77)

Duke of Buckingham and Chandos [Grenville, R.], Memoirs of the court and cabinets of George the Third, 4 vols. (London, 1853–5)

Duke of Buckingham and Chandos [Grenville, R.], Memoirs of the court of George IV, 1820–30, 2 vols. (London, 1859)

Ellis, H., Original Letters Illustrative of English History, 1st series, Vols. I and II (London, 1969)

Ellis, H. (ed.), Hall, E., The union of the two noble and illustre famelies of Lancastre & Yorke (London, 1809)

Esher, Viscount (ed.), The Girlhood of Queen Victoria: A selection of Her Majesty's Diaries between the years 1832 and 1840, 2 vols. (London, 1912)

Falkus, C., The Private Lives of the Tudor Monarchs (London, 1974)

Fisher, F.J. (ed.), Wilson, T., 'The state of England anno dom. 1600', Camden Miscellany, Vol. XVI, Camden Society, 3rd series, Vol. 52 (London, 1936)

Forester, T. (ed. and trans.), The Chronicle of Henry of Huntingdon (Felinfach, 1991)

Fortescue, J. (ed.), The correspondence of King George the Third from 1760 to December 1783, 6 vols. (London, 1927–8)

Francis Steuart, A. (ed.), Sir James Melville: Memoirs of His Own Life, 1549–93 (London, 1929)

Fulford, R. (ed.), Darling Child: Private Correspondence of Queen Victoria and the Crown Princess of Prussia, 1871–1878 (London, 1976)

Fulford, R. (ed.), Dearest Child: Letters between Queen Victoria and the Princess Royal, 1858–1861 (London, 1964)

Fulford, R. (ed.), Dearest Mama: Letters between Queen Victoria and the Crown Princess of Prussia, 1861–1864 (London, 1968)

Gairdner, J. (ed.), Letters and Papers Illustrative of the Reigns of Richard III and Henry VII, 2 vols. (London, 1861–3)

Gairdner, J. (ed.), The Paston letters, A.D. 1422–1509, 6 vols. (London, 1904)

Gairdner, J. (ed.), 'William Gregory's chronicle of London', The historical *collections of a citizen of London in the fifteenth century*, Camden Society, new series, 17 (London, 1876)

Galbraith, V.H. (ed.), *The Anonimalle Chronicle, 1333 to 1381* (Manchester, 1927)

Gidley, L. (ed. and trans.), *Bede's Ecclesiastical History of the English Nation* (Oxford, 1870)

Giles, J.A. (ed.), *Galfridi le Baker de Swinbroke chronicon Angliae temporibus Edwardi II et Edwardi III*, Caxton Society, 7 (London, 1847)

Gilson, J.P., *Catalogue of Western Manuscripts in the Old Royal and King's Collections* (London, 1921)

Given-Wilson, C. (ed. and trans.), *The Chronicle of Adam Usk, 1377–1421* (Oxford, 1997)

Given-Wilson, C. (ed.), *The Parliament Rolls of Medieval England, 1275–1504*, 16 vols. (Woodbridge, 2005)

Godfrey, R. (ed.) (1998), *Letters from a Prince: Edward, Prince of Wales, to Mrs. Freda Dudley Ward March 1918–January 1921* (London, 1998)

Goodman, A.W. (ed.), *Chartulary of Winchester Cathedral* (Winchester, 1927)

Greig, J. (ed.), *The Diaries of a Duchess: Extracts from the Diaries of the First Duchess of Northumberland, 1716–1776* (London, 1926)

Earl Grey, Henry (ed.), *The Reform Act, 1832: the correspondence of the late Earl Grey with His Majesty King William IV and with Sir Herbert Taylor*, 2 vols. (London, 1867)

Hall, E., *A Chronicle; containing the history of England, during the reign of Henry the fourth and the succeeding monarchs, to the end of the reign of Henry the eighth* (London, 1809)

Hallam, E.M., *The Plantagenet Chronicles* (London, 1989)

Halliwell, J.O. (ed.), *Letters of the kings of England*, 2 vols. (London, 1846–8)

Halliwell, J.O. (ed.), Warkworth, J., *A chronicle of the first thirteen years of the reign of King Edward the Fourth*, Camden Society, old series, Vol. X (London, 1839)

Harington, Sir J., *Nugae Antiquae: Being a Miscellaneous Collection of Original Papers in Prose and Verse: Written in the Reigns of Henry VIII, Queen Mary, Elizabeth, King James, etc* (London, 1779)

Harrison, G.B. (ed.), *The Letters of Queen Elizabeth* (London, 1935)

Harrison, G.B. and Jones, R.A. (eds.), *De Maisse: A journal of all that was accomplished by Monsieur de Maisse, Ambassador in England from Henry IV to Queen Elizabeth, Anno Domini 1597* (London, 1931)

Hartley, T.E. (ed.), *Proceedings in the parliaments of Elizabeth I*, 3 vols. (Leicester, 1981–95)

Haskins, G.L., 'A Chronicle of the Civil Wars of Edward II', *Speculum*, Vol. XIV (Chicago, 1939)

Hay, D. (ed. and trans.), *The Anglica Historia of Polydore Vergil, A.D. 1485–1537*, Camden series, Vol. LXXIV (London, 1950)

Haynes, A., *Collection of State Papers Relating to Affairs in the Reigns of King Henry VIII, King Edward VI, Queen Mary and Queen Elizabeth, From the Year 1542 to 1570* (London, 1740)

Helylyn, P., *Aerius Redivivus: or The History of the Presbyterians* (London, 1670)

Historical Manuscripts Commission, *Calendar of the Manuscripts of the Most Honourable the Marquess of Bath, preserved at Longleat, Wiltshire, 1533–1659* Vol. V (London, 1968)

Historical Manuscripts Commission, *Calendar of the Manuscripts of the Marquis of Salisbury, Preserved at Hatfield House, Hertfordshire*, Vol. I (London, 1883)

Historical Manuscripts Commission, *The manuscripts of Henry Duncan Skrine, esq. Salvetti correspondence*, Vol. XVI (London, 1887)

Historical Manuscripts Commission, *The Manuscripts of His Grace the Duke of Rutland, preserved at Belvoir Castle*, Vol. I (London, 1888)

Historical Manuscripts Commission, *The manuscripts of the earl of Dartmouth*, 3 vols. (London, 1887–96)

Historical Manuscripts Commission, *The manuscripts of the Marquess of Abergavenny, Lord Braye*, Vol. XV (London, 1887)

Historical Manuscripts Commission, *Report on the manuscripts of Allan George Finch*, 5 vols. (London, 1913–2004)

Historical Manuscripts Commission, *Report on the Manuscripts of Lord De L'Isle & Dudley, preserved at Penshurst Place*, Vols. I and II (London, 1925)

Hitchcock, N.V. (ed.), Harpsfield, N., *The life and death of Sr Thomas Moore, knight*, Early English Text Society, original series, 186 (London, 1932)

Holinshed, R., *Chronicles of England, Scotlande and Irelande* (London, 1578)

Holt, J.C., *Magna Carta*, 2nd edn. (Cambridge, 1992)

Houts, E. van (ed.), *The Gesta Normannorum Ducum of William of Jumièges, Orderic Vitalis, and Robert of Torigni*, 2 vols. (Oxford, 1992–5)

Howlett, R. (ed.), *Chronicles of the reigns of Stephen, Henry II, and Richard I*, Rolls series, 82 (London, 1884)

Howlett, R. (ed.), William of Newburgh, *Historia rerum Anglicarum*, Rolls series, 82 (London, 1884), p. 94

Hume, M.A. (ed. and trans.), *Chronicle of King Henry VIII of England . . . written in Spanish by an unknown hand* (London, 1889)

James, M.R. (ed. and trans.), Blacman, J., 'Henry the Sixth': a reprint of John Blacman's memoir (Cambridge, 1919)

Jesse, J.H., Memoirs of the life and reign of King George the Third, 3 vols. (London, 1867)

Kaulek, J. (ed.), Correspondance politique de MM. de Castillon et de Marillac, ambassadeurs de France en Angleterre (1537–1542) (Paris, 1885)

Kennedy, A.L., My Dear Duchess: Social and Political Letters to the Duchess of Manchester, 1858–1869 (London, 1956)

Keynes, S. and Lapidge, M. (ed. and trans.), Alfred the Great: Asser's Life of King Alfred and other contemporary sources (Harmondsworth and New York, 2004)

Kroll, M. (ed.), Letters from Liselotte, Elisabeth Charlotte, Princess Palatine and Duchess of Orleans, 'Madam', 1652–1722 (London, 1970)

Larkin, J.F. (ed.), Stuart Royal Proclamations, 2 vols. (Oxford, 1973, 1983)

Legg, J.W. (ed.), English Coronation Records (London, 1901)

Lewis, W.S. (ed.), The Yale Edition of Horace Walpole's Correspondence, 48 vols. (London, 1937–83)

Lockyer, R. (ed.), Bacon, F., The History of the Reign of King Henry the Seventh (London, 1971)

Lockyer, R. (ed.), The Trial of Charles I: a contemporary account taken from the memoirs of the last years of the reign of King Charles by Sir Thomas Herbert and John Rushworth (London, 1959)

Lodge, E., Illustrations of British history, biography and manners, in the reigns of Henry VIII, Edward VI, Mary, Elizabeth, & James I, 3 vols. (London, 1838)

Loveman, K. (ed.), The Diary of Samuel Pepys (New York, London and Toronto, 2018)

Luard, H.R. (ed.), Flores historiarum, 3 vols., Rolls series, 95 (London, 1890)

Lyttelton, G., The history of the life of King Henry the Second, 2nd edn., 4 vols. (1767–71)

Madden, F. (ed.), Matthaei Parisiensis, monachi Sancti Albani, Historia Anglorum, sive . . . Historia minor, 3 vols., Rolls series, 44 (London, 1886–9)

Mahon, Lord (ed.), The Letters of Philip Dormer Stanhope, Earl of Chesterfield, 5 vols. (London, 1845–53)

Mallet, V. (ed.), Life with Queen Victoria: Marie Mallet's Letters from Court, 1887–1901 (London, 1968)

Marcus, L.S., Mueller, J. and Rose, M.B., Elizabeth I: Collected Works (Chicago and London, 2002)

Martin, T., The Life of His Royal Highness The Prince Consort, 5 vols. (London, 1875–80)

Matthew, H.G.C. (ed.), *The Gladstone Diaries*, 14 vols. (Oxford, 1994)

Merriman, R.B. (ed.), *Life and letters of Thomas Cromwell*, 2 vols. (Oxford, 1902)

Michel, F. (ed.), *Histoire des ducs de Normandie et des rois d'Angleterre* (Paris, 1840)

Mynors, R.A.B., Thomson, R.M. and Winterbottom, M. (eds. and trans.), William of Malmesbury, *Gesta Regum Anglorum: The History of the English Kings*, Vols. I and II (Oxford, 1998–9)

Nichols, J. (ed.), *A Collection of all the Wills, now known to be extant, of the Kings and Queens of England . . . From the reign of William the Conqueror, to that of Henry the Seventh* (London, 1780)

Nichols, J.G. (ed.), *The Chronicle of Queen Jane, and of two years of Queen Mary*, Camden Society, old series, Vol. 48 (London, 1850)

Nichols, J.G. (ed.), *Literary Remains of King Edward the Sixth*, 2 vols. (London, 1857)

Nichols, J.G. (ed.), *Narratives of the days of the Reformation*, Camden Society, old series, Vol. 77 (London, 1859)

Nicolas, N.H. (ed.), *Proceedings and ordinances of the privy council of England*, 7 vols., Records Commission, 26 (London, 1834–7)

Parsons, D. (ed.), *The Diary of Sir Henry Slingsby* (London, 1836)

Perry, M., *The Word of a Prince* (London, 1990)

Potter, K.R. (ed. and trans.), *Gesta Stephani* (Oxford, 1976)

The private life of King Edward VII, Prince of Wales, 1841–1901: By a member of the Royal Household (New York, 1901)

Pronay, N. and Cox, J. (eds.), *The Crowland Chronicle Continuations, 1459–1486* (London, 1986)

Quennel, P. (ed.), *The Private Letters of Princess Lieven to Prince Metternich, 1820–1826* (London, 1937)

Robertson, J.C. and Sheppard, J.B. (eds.), *Materials for the history of Thomas Becket, archbishop of Canterbury*, 7 vols., Rolls series, 67 (1875–85)

Robinson, H. (ed.), *Original Letters Relative to the English Reformation*, 2 vols. (Cambridge, 1846–7)

Rotuli Parliamentorum, 6 vols. (London, 1767–7)

Sedgwick, R. (ed.), *Letters from George III to Lord Bute, 1756–1766* (London, 1939)

Sedgwick, R. (ed.), *Some Materials Towards Memoirs of the Reign of King George II, By John, Lord Hervey*, 3 vols. (London, 1931)

Sewell, J.P.C. (ed.), *Personal letters of King Edward VII* (London, 1931)

Sommerville, J.P. (ed.), *King James VI and I: Political Writings* (Cambridge, 1994)

Spalding, R. (ed.), *The Diary of Bulstrode Whitelocke, 1605–1675* (Oxford, 1990)

Stevenson, J. (ed.), *Radulphi de Coggeshall chronicon Anglicanum*, Rolls series, 66 (London, 1875)

Stevenson, J. et al. (eds.), *Calendar of State Papers, Foreign Series, of the Reign of Elizabeth I, 1558–1591* (London, 1863–1969)

Stow, G.B. (ed.), *Historia vitae et regni Ricardi Secundi* (Pennsylvania, 1977)

Stow, J, *The Annales, or Generall Chronicle of England* (London, 1615)

Strachey, L. and Fulford, R. (eds.), *The Greville memoirs, 1814–1860*, 8 vols. (London, 1938)

Stubbs, W. (ed.), *Chronica magistri Rogeri de Hovedene*, 4 vols., Rolls series, 51 (1868–71)

Stubbs, W. (ed.), *Gesta regis Henrici secundi Benedicti abbatis: the chronicle of the reigns of Henry II and Richard I, AD 1169–1192*, 2 vols., Rolls series, 49 (London, 1867)

Stubbs, W. (ed.), *The historical works of Gervase of Canterbury*, 2 vols., Rolls series, 73 (London, 1879–80)

Stubbs, W. (ed.), *Memoriale fratris Walteri de Coventria / The historical collections of Walter of Coventry*, 2 vols., Rolls series, 58 (London, 1872–3)

Stubbs, W. (ed.), Ralph de Diceto, 'Ymagines historiarum', *Radulfi de Diceto . . . opera historica*, 2 vols., Rolls series, 68 (1876)

Swanton, M. (ed.), *The Anglo-Saxon Chronicles* (London, 2000)

Sylvester, R.S. (ed.), Cavendish, G., *The Life and Death of Cardinal Wolsey*, Early English Text Society, original series, 243 (London and New York, 1959)

Sylvester, R.S. (ed.), More, T., *The History of King Richard III* (London and New Haven, 1976)

Taylor, F. and Roskell, J.S. (eds. and trans.), *Gesta Henrici quinti / The Deeds of Henry the Fifth* (Oxford, 1975)

Thomas, A.H. and Thornley, I.D., *The Great Chronicle of London* (London, 1938)

Tillotson, J., *A sermon preached at Lincoln's Inn on 31th [STET] of January 1688[9]* (London, 1689)

Vincent, J. (ed.), *The Derby Diaries, 1869–1878: A Selection from the Diaries of Edward Henry Stanley, 15th Earl of Derby* (London, 1994)

Walpole, H., *Reminiscences: written in 1788 for the amusement of Miss Mary and Miss Agnes* edited by Paget Jackson Toynbee (Oxford, 1924)

Walter, H. (ed.), *Tyndale's works*, 3 vols., Parker Society (Edinburgh, 1848–50)

Wharncliffe, Lord (ed.), *The Letters and Works of Lady Mary Wortley Montagu*, 2 vols. (London, 1887)

Wellesley, G. (ed.), *Wellington and His Friends* (London, 1965)

Williams, C.H. (ed.), *English Historical Documents 1485–1558* (London, 1967)

Winterbottom, M. (ed. and trans.), *Gildas: The Ruin of Britain and Other Works* (London, 1978)

Wood, M.A.E., *Letters of Royal and Illustrious Ladies of Great Britain*, 3 vols. (1846)

Wriothesley, C., *A Chronicle of England During the Reigns of the Tudors, from AD 1485 to 1559*, edited by Hamilton, W.D., 2 vols., Camden Society, new series, 11, 20 (London, 1875–7)

Yorke, P. (ed.), *Miscellaneous State Papers from 1501 to 1726*, 2 vols. (London, 1778)

3. Secondary sources

Adams, S. and Rodríguez-Salgado, M.J., 'The Count of Feria's Dispatch to Philip II of 14 November 1558', *Camden Miscellany*, Vol. XXVIII (London, 1984)

Allen, W.G., *King William IV* (London, 1960)

Allison, R. and Riddell, S., *The Royal Encyclopedia* (London, 1991)

Anglo, S., *Spectacle, Pageantry and Early Tudor Policy* (Oxford, 1969)

Asbridge, T, *Richard I: The Crusader King* (London, 2019)

Baird, J., *Victoria the Queen: An Intimate Biography of a Woman* (New York, 2016)

Bates, D., *William the Conqueror* (Stroud, 2004)

Bentley, T. and Wilsdon, J. (eds.), *Monarchies: What are Kings and Queens For?* (London, 2002)

Bernard, G. and Williams, P. (eds.), Loach, J., *Edward VI* (New Haven and London, 1999)

Black, J., *The Hanoverians: The History of a Dynasty* (London, 2004)

Black, P., *The Mystique of Modern Monarchy* (London, 1953)

Bloch, M., *The Duchess of Windsor* (London, 1996)

Bloch, M., *The Royal Touch: Sacred Monarchy and Scrofula in England and France* (London, 1973)

Bogdanor, V., *The Monarchy and the Constitution* (Oxford, 1995)

Bond, J., *Elizabeth: Eighty Glorious Years* (London, 2006)

Bradford, S., *Diana* (London, 2006)

Bradford, S., *King George VI* (London, 1989)

Bradford, S., *Queen Elizabeth II: Her Life in Our Times* (London, 2011)

Brand, E., *Royal Weddings* (Oxford, 2011)

Brandreth, G., *Philip and Elizabeth: Portrait of a Marriage* (London, 2004)

Breay, C. and Story, J. (eds.), *Anglo-Saxon Kingdoms: Art, Word, War* (British Library, 2018)

Brewer, C., *The Death of Kings: A Medical History of the Kings and Queens of England* (London, 2004)

Brooke, C., *The Saxon and Norman Kings* (Glasgow, 1976)

Brooke, J., *King George III* (London, 1972)

Burgess, G., *Absolute Monarchy and the Stuart Constitution* (Yale, 1996)

Cadbury, D., *Princes at War: The British Royal Family's Private Battle in the Second World War* (London, 2015)

Cannadine, D., *History in Our Time* (New Haven and London, 1998)

Cannadine, D. (ed.), *Westminster Abbey: A Church in History* (New Haven and London, 2019)

Cannon, J. and Griffiths, R., *The Oxford Illustrated History of the British Monarchy* (Oxford, 1988)

Carlton, C., *Charles I: The Personal Monarch* (London, 1995)

Carpenter, D., *The Reign of Henry III* (London, 1996)

Chapman, H., *The Last Tudor King: A Study of Edward VI* (London, 1961)

Charlot, M., *Victoria: The Young Queen* (London, 1991)

Cobbett, W., *Parliamentary history of England: from the Norman Conquest in 1066 to the year 1803*, 12 vols. (London, 1812–20)

Cockerill, S., *Eleanor of Aquitaine: Queen of France and England, Mother of Empires* (Stroud, 2019)

Cooper, T., *Elizabeth I & Her People* (London, 2013)

Cooper, T. (ed.), *Tudors to Windsors: British Royal Portraits* (London, 2018)

Crawford, M., *The Little Princesses* (New York, 1950)

Curry, A., *Henry V: Playboy Prince to Warrior King* (London, 2018)

Cussans, T., *Kings & Queens of the British Isles* (London, 2017)

Davenport-Hines, R., *Edward VII* (London, 2018)

Davey, R., *The Nine Days' Queen: Lady Jane Grey and her times* (London, 1909)

David, A., *The British Monarchy Miscellany: A Collection of Royal Facts, Lists and Trivia* (London, 2019)

Davis, J.P., *The Gothic King: A Biography of Henry III* (London, 2013)

Delderfield, E.R., *Kings & Queens of England and Great Britain* (Newton Abbot, 1998)

Dillon, J., *Performance and Spectacle in Hall's Chronicle* (London, 2002)

Dimbleby, J., *The Prince of Wales: A Biography* (London, 1994)

Doran, S., *Elizabeth: The Exhibition at the National Maritime Museum* (London, 2003)

Elton, G.R., *The Tudor Constitution: Documents and Commentary* (Cambridge, 1960)

Fisher, G. and H., *Monarchy and the Royal Family* (London, 1979)

Fitzalan Howard, A., *The Windsor Diaries: A Childhood with the Princesses* (London, 2020)

Flanagan, M.T., *Irish Society, Anglo-Norman Settlers, Angevin Kingship: Interactions in Ireland in the Late Twelfth Century* (Oxford, 1989)

Fraser, A., *King Charles II* (London, 1979)

Fraser, A., *The Six Wives of Henry VIII* (London, 1993)

Fraser, A. (ed.), Clarke, J. and Ridley, J., *The Houses of Hanover and Saxe-Coburg-Gotha* (London, 2000)

Frye, S., *Elizabeth I: The Competition for Representation* (New York and Oxford University Press, 1993)

Fryman, O. (ed.), *Kensington Palace: Art, Architecture and Society* (New Haven and London, 2018)

Fulford, R., *Hanover to Windsor* (London, 1972)

Gaunt, P., *Oliver Cromwell* (Oxford, 1996)

Gillingham, J., *William II: The Red King* (London, 2019)

Glenconner, A., *Lady in Waiting: My Extraordinary Life in the Shadow of the Crown* (London, 2020)

Goff, M., Goldfinch, J., Limper-Herz, K. and Peden, H., *Georgians Revealed: Life, Style and the Making of Modern Britain* (London, 2013)

Gosling, L., *Royal Coronations* (Oxford, 2013)

Greaves, R.L., *Secrets of the Kingdom: British Radicals from the Popish Plot to the Revolution of 1688–89* (Stanford, 1992)

Green, D., *Queen Anne* (London, 1970)

Gregg, E., *Queen Anne* (London, 1980)

Gregg, P., *King Charles I* (London, 1981)

Gristwood, S., *Elizabeth: The Queen and the Crown* ((London, 2017)

Gristwood, S., *Game of Queens: The Women Who Made Sixteenth-Century Europe* (London, 2016)

Guy, J. (ed.), *The Reign of Elizabeth I: Court and Culture in the Last Decade* (Cambridge, 1995)

Haigh, C. (ed.), *Elizabeth I* (London and New York, 1988)

Hall, M., *Art, Passion & Power: The Story of the Royal Collection* (London, 2017)

Hall, P., *Royal Fortune: Tax, Money and the Monarchy* (London, 1992)

Hardie, F., *The Political Influence of the British Monarchy 1868–1952* (London, 1970)

Harrison, T., *Diana: The Making of a Saint – How the Death of a Princess Led to the Birth of a Cult* (London, 2006)

Harvey, J., *The Plantagenets* (Glasgow, 1972)

Hawksley, L., *Elizabeth Revealed: 500 Facts about The Queen and Her World* (London, 2018)

Hibbert, C., *Edward VII* (London, 1976)

Hibbert, C., *Charles I* (London, 1968)

Hibbert, C., *George IV: Regent and King, 1811–1830* (London, 1973)

Hibbert, C., *Queen Victoria in her Letters and Journals* (London, 1984)

Hilliam, C., *Crown, Orb and Sceptre* (Stroud, 2001)

Hilliam, D., *Kings, Queens, Bones and Bastards: Who's Who in the English Monarchy from Egbert to Elizabeth II* (Stroud, 2008)

Hilton, L., *Queens Consort: England's Medieval Queens* (London, 2009)

Hobsbawn, E. and Ranger, T. (eds.), *The Invention of Tradition* (Cambridge, 1992)

Hutton, R., *Charles II: King of England, Scotland and Ireland* (Oxford, 1989)

Jackson, C., *Charles II: The Star King* (London, 2018)

Judd, D., *George VI* (London, 2012)

Keates, J., *William III & Mary II: Partners in Revolution* (London, 2018)

Kelly, A., *The Other Side of the Coin: The Queen, the Dresser and the Wardrobe* (London, 2019)

Kenyon, J.P., *The Stuarts: A study in English Kingship* (Glasgow, 1972)

Kenyon, J.P. and Ohlmeyer, Jane (eds.), *The Civil Wars: A Military History of England, Scotland, and Ireland 1638–1660* (Oxford, 2000)

Keynes, S. and Smyth, A.P. (eds.), *Anglo-Saxons: Studies Presented to Cyril Roy Hart* (Portland, 2006)

Kingsford, C.L., *English historical literature in the fifteenth century* (Oxford, 1913)

Kozlowski, B., *Long Live the Queen! 23 Rules for Living from Britain's Longest-reigning Monarch* (Nashville, 2020)

Lacey, R., *Royal: Her Majesty Queen Elizabeth II* (London, 2002)

Lander, J.R., *The Limitations of English Monarchy in the Later Middle Ages* (Toronto, 1989)

Legg, L.W. (trans.), Schramm, P., *A history of the English coronation* (1937)

Lehmberg, S.E., *The Later Parliaments of Henry VIII* (Cambridge, 1977)

Licence, A., *In Bed with the Tudors: The Sex Lives of a Dynasty from Elizabeth of York to Elizabeth I* (Stroud, 2013)

Loades, D., *John Dudley: Duke of Northumberland, 1504–1553* (Oxford, 1996)

Loades, D., *Mary Tudor. The Tragical History of the first Queen of England* (Richmond, 2006)

Loades, D., *Princes of Wales: Royal Heirs in Waiting* (London, 2008)

Lofts, N., *Queens of Britain* (London, 1977)

Longford, E., *Elizabeth R* (London, 1983)

Longford, E., *Queen Victoria: Born to Succeed* (London, 1964)

Longford, E. (ed.), *The Oxford Book of Royal Anecdotes* (Oxford and New York, 1989)

Lynn, E., *Tudor Fashion: Dress at Court 1485–1603* (New Haven and London, 2017)

Macalpine, I. and Hunter, R., *George III and the Mad-Business* (London, 1969)

Magnus, P., *King Edward the Seventh* (London, 1964)

Marschner, J., *Enlightened Princesses: Caroline, Augusta, Charlotte, and the Shaping of the Modern World* (New Haven and London, 2017)

Martin, K., 'The Evolution of Popular Monarchy', *Political Quarterly*, vii (London, 1936)

Martin, K., *The Magic of Monarchy* (London, 1937)

McFarlane, K.B., *Lancastrian Kings and Lollard Knights* (Oxford, 1972)

Miller, H., *Henry VIII and the English Nobility* (Oxford, 1986)

Miller, J., *Charles II* (London, 1991)

Miller, J., *The Glorious Revolution* (London, 1983)

Miller, J., *James II* (New Haven and London, 2000)

Miller, J., *The Stuarts* (London, 2003)

Molloy, F., *The Sailor King: William the Fourth, His Court and His Subjects*, 2 vols. (London, 1903)

Monod, P.K., *The Power of Kings: Monarchy and Religion in Europe 1589–1715* (Yale, 1999)

Morris, C., *The Tudors* (London, 1987)

Mortimer, I., *Medieval Intrigue: Decoding Royal Conspiracies* (London, 2010)

Morton, A., *Diana: Her True Story* (London, 2019)

Murphy, D., *The Young Victoria* (New Haven and London, 2019)

Murray-Brown, J. (ed.), *The Monarchy and its Future* (London, 1969)

Nairn, T., *The Enchanted Glass: Britain and its Monarchy* (London, 1988)

Neale, J.E., *Elizabeth I and her Parliaments, 1559–1581* (London, 1953)

New Oxford Dictionary of National Biography (Oxford, 2004)

Nicolson, H., *King George the Fifth: His Life and Reign* (London, 1952)

Nicolson, H., *Monarchy* (London, 1962)

Ogle, A., *The tragedy of the Lollards' Tower. I. The case of Richard Hunne, with its aftermath in II. the Reformation Parliament, 1529–3: a review of events from the downfall of Wolsey to the death of Elizabeth* (Oxford, 1959)

Olusoga, D., *Black and British: A Forgotten History* (London, 2017)

Paterson, M., *A Brief History of The House of Windsor: The Making of a Modern Monarchy* (London, 2013)

Pearson, J., *The Ultimate Family: The Making of the Royal House of Windsor* (London, 2012)

Penn, T., *Winter King: Henry VII and the Dawn of Tudor England* (London, 2012)

Pimlott, B., *The Queen: Elizabeth II and the Monarchy* (London, 2012)

Plowden, A., *Two Queens in One Isle: The Deadly Relationship between Elizabeth I and Mary, Queen of Scots* (Sutton, 1999)

Plumb, J.H., *The First Four Georges* (London, 1956)

Ponsonby, A., *Henry Ponsonby, Queen Victoria's Private Secretary: His Life from his Letters* (London, 1943)

Poole, A.L., *From Domesday Book to Magna Carta, 1087–1216*, 2nd edn. (Oxford, 1955)

Porter, L., *Mistresses: Sex and Scandal at the Court of Charles II* (London, 2020)

Prestwich, M., *Edward I* (London, 1988)

Prochaska, F., *The Eagle & the Crown: Americans and the British Monarchy* (New Haven and London, 2008)

Prochaska, F., *The Republic of Britain, 1760–2000* (London, 2000)

Prochaska, F., *Royal Bounty: The Making of the Welfare Monarchy* (New Haven and London, 1995)

Ralph Lewis, B., *Kings & Queens of England: A Dark History* (London, 2019)

Ralph Lewis, B., *Monarchy: The History of an Idea* (Stroud, 2003)

Rappaport, H., *Magnificent Obsession: Victoria, Albert and the Death that Changed the British Monarchy* (London, 2011)

Redworth, G., 'Matters Impertinent to Women: Male and Female Monarchy under Philip and Mary', *English Historical Review*, Vol. XL, no. 4 (Oxford, December 1997)

Rhodes, J.R., *A Spirit Undaunted: The Political Role of George VI* (London, 1998)

Richards, M., 'Mary Tudor as "Sole Quene"? Gendering Tudor Monarchy', *Historical Journal*, Vol. XL, no. 4 (Cambridge, December 1997)

Richardson, G., *Renaissance Monarchy: The Reigns of Henry VIII, Francis I and Charles V* (Oxford, 2002)

Ridgeway, H., 'King Henry III and the "Aliens", 1236–1272', in Coss, P.R. and Lloyd, S.D. (eds.), *Thirteenth-Century England: Proceedings of the Newcastle upon Tyne Conference* (Woodbridge, 1987)

Ridley, *Bertie: A Life of Edward VII* (London, 2012)

Roberts, A., *The House of Windsor* (London, 2000)

Rose, K., *King George V* (London, 1983)

Royal Commission on Historical Monuments, England, *An inventory of the historical monuments in London*, Vol. I (London, 1924)

Schama, S., 'The Domestication of Majesty: Royal Family Portraiture, 1500–1850', *Journal of Interdisciplinary History*, Vol. XVII, no. 1 (Massachusetts, 1986)

Shawcross, W., *Queen and Country* (Toronto, 2002)

Shears, W.S., *The King: The Story and Splendour of the British Monarchy* (London, 1937)

Sinclair, D., *Two Georges: The Making of the Modern Monarchy* (London, 1988)

Skidmore, C., *Edward VI: The Lost King of England* (London, 2007)

Smith, E.A., *George IV* (London and New Haven, 1999)

Somerset, A., *Elizabeth I* (London, 1991)

Somerset, A., *The Life and Times of William IV* (London, 1980)

Somerset, A., *Queen Anne: The Politics of Passion* (London, 2012)

Somerset Fry, P., *Kings & Queens of England and Scotland* (London, 2018)

Souden, D., *The Royal Palaces of London* (London and New York, 2008)

Spencer, C., *Killers of the King: The Men Who Dared to Execute Charles I* (London, 2015)

Spencer, C., *The White Ship: Conquest, Anarchy and the Wrecking of Henry I's Dream* (London, 2020)

Starkey, D., *Crown & Country – The Kings & Queens of England: A History* (London, 2010)

Starkey, D., et al., (eds.), *The English Court from the Wars of the Roses to the Civil War* (London, 1987)

Stewart, A., *The Cradle King: A Life of James VI & I* (London, 2003)

Stone, J.M., *The History of Mary I, Queen of England, as found in the Public Records, Despatches of Ambassadors, in original private letters, and other contemporary documents* (London, 1901)

Strachey, L., *Queen Victoria* (London, 1921)

Strickland, A., *Lives of the Queens of England*, 6 vols. (London, 1901–4)

Strickland, A., *The Tudor Princesses* (London, 1868)

Strong, R., *Coronation: A History of Kingship and the British Monarchy* (London, 2005)

Strong, R., *Holbein and Henry VIII* (London, 1967)

Strong, R., *The Tudor and Stuart Monarchy* (Woodbridge, 1995)

Strype, J., *Ecclesiastical memorials*, 2 vols. (London, 1822)

Stubbs, W., *The constitutional history of England in its origin and development*, 3rd edn., 3 vols. (Oxford, 1878)

Tallis, N., *Crown of Blood* (London, 2016)

Tallis, N., *Uncrowned Queen: The Fateful Life of Margaret Beaufort, Tudor Matriarch* (London, 2019)

Taylor, M. (ed.), Bagehot, W., *The English Constitution* (Oxford, 2009)

Thompson, D., *Queen Victoria: Gender and Power* (London, 1990)

Thurley, S., *The Royal Palaces of Tudor England* (New Haven and London, 1993)

Tinniswood, A., *Behind the Throne: A Domestic History of the British Royal Household* (New York, 2018)

Trevor-Roper, H. (ed.), *Essays in English History* (London, 1964)

Trowles, T., *Treasures of Westminster Abbey* (London, 2008)

Turner, F.C., *James II* (London, 1948)

Uglow, J., *A Gambling Man: Charles II's Restoration Game* (London, 2009)

Van der Kiste, J., *William and Mary* (Stroud, 2003)

Warwick, C., *Her Majesty* (Köln, 2012)

Warwick, C., *Princess Margaret: A Life of Contrasts* (London, 2002)

Weir, A., *Britain's Royal Families: The Complete Genealogy* (London, 1996)

Weir, A., *Children of England: The Heirs of King Henry VIII* (London, 1997)

Weir, A., *Henry VIII: King and Court* (London, 2001)

Weir, A., *The Life of Elizabeth* (New York, 1998)

Weir, A., *Mary, Queen of Scots and the Murder of Lord Darnley* (London, 2003)

Weir, A., et al., *The Ring and the Crown: A History of Royal Weddings, 1066–2011* (London, 2011)

Western, J.R., *Monarchy and Revolution: The English State in the 1680s* (London, 1972)

Wheeler-Bennett, J.W., *King George VI: His Life and Reign* (London, 1958)

Wilkins, W.H., *Caroline the Illustrious, Queen-Consort of George II and sometime Queen-Regent* (London, 1904)

Williams, B., *The Whig Supremacy 1714–60* (Oxford, 1962)

Williamson, D., *The Kings and Queens of England* (London, 2002)

Wilson, D., *In the Lion's Court* (London, 2002)

Wilson, D., *The Plantagenets: The Kings That Made Britain* (London, 2011)

Windsor, Duchess of, *The Heart has its Reasons* (London, 1956)

Windsor, HRH, The Duke of, *A King's Story* (London, 1951)

Wolffe, B.P., *Henry VI* (London, 1981)

Woodham-Smith, C., *Queen Victoria: Her Life and Times*, Vol. I (London, 1972)

Young, G., *Poor Fred: The People's Prince* (London, 1937)

Ziegler, P., *Crown and People* (London, 1978)

Ziegler, P., *King Edward VIII: The Official Biography* (London, 1990)

Ziegler, P., *King William IV* (London, 1971)

INDEX

PICTURE ACKNOWLEDGEMENTS

Inset pages 1 – 16

Courtesy of the author: 1 above right. Alamy Stock Photos: 1 centre/ The Picture Art Collection, 2 below right/Album, 3 above right/Art Collection, 4 above/Album, 4 centre right/Niday Picture Library, 5 above left/Heritage Image Partnership, 5 centre/Photo 12, 5 below right/Album, 6 centre/Steve Vidler, 7 centre right/The Picture Art Collection, 7 below/Angelo Hornak, 8 above left/Norman Barrett, 8 above right/Jorge Tutor, 8 below right/Peter Lane, 9 below/The Picture Art Collection,10 above/Heritage Image Partnership, 11 above right/Granger Historical Picture Archive, 11 centre left/The Picture Art Collection, 11 below right/Niday Picture Library, 13 above left/ Art Collection 3, 13 above right/Chronicle, 14 above left/John Frost Newspapers, 14 below left/Michael Kemp, 15 above and below/PA Images, 16 above/Howard Sayer, 16 below left/Ink Drop. © Cecil Beaton/Victoria and Albert Museum, London: 14 centre right. Bridgeman Images: 2 centre, 3 below, 7 above left, 8 centre left, 10 below. © British Library Board. All Rights Reserved/Bridgeman Images: 3 above left. © The Cromwell Museum/Bridgeman Images: 9 above right. Paul Fitzsimmons/Marhamchurch Antiques: 6 below left. © Fitzwilliam Museum/Bridgeman Images: 2 above right. Photo © Historic Royal Palaces/Bridgeman Images: 9 above left, 12 below right. Look and Learn/Peter Jackson Collection/Bridgeman Images: 12 centre left. Photograph by Ranald Mackechnie/Camera Press London: 16 below right. © The National Archives:1 below, 6 above, 13 below left. © Royal Collection/Royal Collection Trust © Her Majesty Queen Elizabeth II 2021/Bridgeman Images: 4 below left. Royal Collection Trust/© Her Majesty Queen Elizabeth II 2021: 12 above right.